WELCOME TO MANY-ARROWS

... Toogwik Tuk said with a respectful bow. "The presence of Clan Karuck and its worthy leader makes us greater."

Grguch let his gaze drift slowly across the three visitors then around the gathering to Hakuun. "You will learn the truth of your hopeful claim," he said, his eyes turning back to Toogwik Tuk, "when I have the bones of dwarves and elves and ugly humans to crush beneath my boot."

Dnark couldn't suppress a grin as he looked to Ung-thol, who seemed similarly pleased. Despite their squeamishness at being so badly outnumbered among the fierce and unpredictable tribe, things were going quite well.

A KINGDOM OF ORCS THAT WILL CHANGE THE MAP OF FAERÛN FOREVER!

"R.A. Salvatore is the best descriptive writer ever for fantasy battle scenes. No one writes them better than he."
—Conan Tigard, *Reading Review*

"By the end of *The Orc King*, the possibilities are almost endless, and Salvatore's message is clear—(change) can be terrifying, painful, glorious, and heartrending, but it is also inevitable, and it is coming to Drizzt's corner of the FORGOTTEN REALMS® (world)."
—David Craddock, Fantasy Book Critic
(fantasybookcritic.blogspot.com)

"*The Orc King* finds Drizzt's whirling scimitar blades tackling both familiar foes and refreshingly ambiguous moral challenges ... The story line marks the continuation of Salvatore's maturation as a writer, introducing more complex themes into a frequently black-and-white fantasy landscape."
—*Kirkus*

R.A. SALVATORE

TRANSITIONS

The Orc King

The Pirate King
October 2008

The Ghost King
October 2009

THE LEGEND OF DRIZZT

Homeland

Exile

Sojourn

The Crystal Shard

Streams of Silver

The Halfling's Gem

The Legacy

Starless Night

Siege of Darkness

Passage to Dawn

The Silent Blade

The Spine of the World

Sea of Swords

THE HUNTER'S BLADES TRILOGY

The Thousand Orcs

The Lone Drow

The Two Swords

THE SELLSWORDS

Servant of the Shard

Promise of the Witch-King

Road of the Patriarch

THE CLERIC QUINTET

Canticle

In Sylvan Shadows

Night Masks

The Fallen Fortress

The Chaos Curse

R.A. SALVATORE

FORGOTTEN REALMS

THE ORC KING

TRANSITIONS I

THE ORC KING
Transitions, Book I

©2008 Wizards of the Coast, Inc.

All characters in this book are fictitious. Any resemblance to actual persons, living or dead, is purely coincidental.

This book is protected under the copyright laws of the United States of America. Any reproduction or unauthorized use of the material or artwork contained herein is prohibited without the express written permission of Wizards of the Coast, Inc.

Published by Wizards of the Coast, Inc. FORGOTTEN REALMS, WIZARDS OF THE COAST, and their respective logos are trademarks of Wizards of the Coast, Inc., in the U.S.A. and other countries.

Printed in the U.S.A.

The sale of this book without its cover has not been authorized by the publisher. If you purchased this book without a cover, you should be aware that neither the author nor the publisher has received payment for this "stripped book."

Cover art by Todd Lockwood
Map by Todd Gamble
Original Hardcover Edition First Printing: October 2007
First Paperback Printing: July 2008

9 8 7 6 5

ISBN: 978-0-7869-5046-1
620-21959740-001-EN

U.S., CANADA,
ASIA, PACIFIC, & LATIN AMERICA
Wizards of the Coast, Inc.
P.O. Box 707
Renton, WA 98057-0707
+1-800-324-6496

EUROPEAN HEADQUARTERS
Hasbro UK Ltd
Caswell Way
Newport, Gwent NP9 0YH
GREAT BRITAIN
Save this address for your records.

Visit our web site at www.wizards.com

PRELUDE

Drizzt Do'Urden crouched in a crevice between a pair of boulders on the side of a mountain, looking down at a curious gathering. A human, an elf, and a trio of dwarves—at least a trio—stood and sat around three flat-bedded wagons that were parked in a triangle around a small campfire. Sacks and kegs dotted the perimeter of the camp, along with a cluster of tents, reminding Drizzt that there was more to the company than the five in his view. He looked past the wagons to a small, grassy meadow, where several draft horses grazed. Just to the side of them, he saw again that which had brought him to the edge of the camp: a pair of stakes capped with the severed heads of orcs.

The band and their missing fellows, then, were indeed members of *Casin Cu Calas,* the "Triple C," an organization of vigilantes who took their name from the Elvish saying that meant "honor in battle."

Given the reputation of *Casin Cu Calas,* whose favorite tactic was to storm orc homesteads in the dark of night and decapitate any males found inside, Drizzt found the name more than a little ironic, and more than a little distasteful.

"Cowards, one and all," he whispered as he watched one man hold up a full-length black and red robe. The man flapped it clean of the night's dirt and reverently folded it, bringing it to his lips to kiss it before he replaced it in the back of one wagon. He reached down and picked up the second tell-tale garment, a black hood. He moved to put that, too, in the wagon but hesitated, then slipped the hood over his head, adjusting it so that he could see through the two eye-holes. That drew the attention of the other four.

The other *five*, Drizzt noted as the fourth dwarf walked back around a corner of the wagon to regard the hooded man.

"Casin Cu Calas!" the man proclaimed, and held up both his arms, fists clenched, in an exaggerated victory pose. "Suffer no orc to live!"

"Death to the orcs!" the others cried in reply.

The hooded fool issued a barrage of insults and threats against the porcine-featured humanoids. Up on the side of the hill, Drizzt Do'Urden shook his head and deliberately slid his bow, Taulmaril, off his shoulder. He put it up, notched an arrow, and drew back in one fluid motion.

"Suffer no orc to live," the hooded man said again—or started to, until a flash of lightning shot through the camp and drove into a keg of warm ale beside him. As the keg exploded, liquid flying, a sheet of dissipating electricity momentarily stole the darkness from the growing twilight.

All six of the companions fell back, shielding their eyes. When they regained their sight, one and all saw the lone figure of a lean dark elf standing atop one of their wagons.

"Drizzt Do'Urden," gasped one of the dwarves, a fat fellow with an orange beard and an enormous temple-to-temple eyebrow.

A couple of the others nodded and mouthed their agreement, for there was no mistaking the dark elf standing before them, with his two scimitars belted at his hips and Taulmaril, the Heartseeker, again slung over one shoulder. The drow's long, thick white hair blew in the late afternoon breeze, his cloak flapped out behind him, and even the dull light remaining could do little to diminish the shine of his silvery-white mithral-lined shirt.

Slowly pulling off his hood, the human glanced at the elf then back at Drizzt. "Your reputation precedes you, Master Do'Urden," he said. "To what do we owe the honor of your presence?"

" 'Honor' is a strange word," Drizzt replied. "Stranger still coming from the lips of one who would wear the black hood."

A dwarf to the side of the wagon bristled and even stepped forward, but was blocked by the arm of the orange-bearded fellow.

The human cleared his throat uncomfortably and tossed the hood into the wagon behind him. "That thing?" he asked. "Found along the road, of course. Do you assign it any significance?"

"No more so than the significance I assign the robe you so reverently folded and kissed."

That brought another glance at the elf, who, Drizzt noticed, was sliding a bit more to the side—notably behind a line etched in the dirt, one glittering with shiny dust. When Drizzt brought his attention more fully back to the human, he noted the change in the man's demeanor, a clear scowl replacing the feigned innocence.

"A robe you yourself should wear," the man said boldly. "To honor King Bruenor Battlehammer, whose deeds—"

"Speak not his name," Drizzt interrupted. "You know nothing of Bruenor, of his exploits and his judgments."

"I know that he was no friend of—"

"You know nothing," Drizzt said again, more forcefully.

"The tale of Shallows!" one of the dwarves roared.

"I was there," Drizzt reminded him, silencing the fool.

The human spat upon the ground. "Once a hero, now gone soft," he muttered. "On orcs, no less."

"Perhaps," Drizzt replied, and in the blink of an astonished eye, he brought his scimitars out in his black-skinned hands. "But I've not gone soft on highwaymen and murderers."

"Murderers?" the human retorted incredulously. "Murderers of orcs?"

Even as he finished speaking, the dwarf at the side of the wagon pushed through his orange-bearded companion's arm and thrust his hand forward, sending a hand-axe spinning at the drow.

Drizzt easily side-stepped the unsurprising move, but not content to let the missile harmlessly fly past, and seeing a second dwarf charging from over to the left, he snapped out his scimitar Icingdeath into the path of the axe. He drew the blade back as it contacted the missile, absorbing the impact. A twist of his wrist had the scimitar's blade firmly up under the axe's head. In a single fluid movement, Drizzt pivoted back the other way and whipped Icingdeath around, launching the axe at the charging dwarf.

The rumbling warrior brought his shield up high to block the awkwardly spinning axe, which clunked against the wooden buckler and bounced aside. But so too fell away that dwarf's determined growl when he again lowered the shield, to find his intended target nowhere in sight.

For Drizzt, his speed enhanced by a pair of magical anklets, had timed his break perfectly with the rise of the dwarf's shield. He had taken only a few steps, but enough, he knew, to confuse the determined dwarf. At the last moment, the dwarf noticed him and skidded to a stop, throwing out a weak, backhanded swipe with his warhammer.

But Drizzt was inside the arch of the hammer, and he smacked its handle with one blade, stealing the minimal momentum of the swing. He struck harder with his second blade, finding the crease between the dwarf's heavy gauntlet and his metal-banded bracer. The hammer went flying, and the dwarf howled and grabbed at his bleeding, broken wrist.

Drizzt leaped atop his shoulder, kicked him in the face for good measure, and sprang away, charging at the orange-bearded dwarf and the axe thrower, both of whom were coming on fast.

Behind them, the human urged them in their charge, but did not follow, reaffirming Drizzt's suspicions regarding his courage, or lack thereof.

Drizzt's sudden reversal and rush had the two dwarves on their heels, and the drow came in furiously, his scimitars rolling over each other and striking from many different angles. The axe-thrower, a second small axe in hand, also held a shield, and so fared better in blocking the blades, but the poor orange-bearded fellow could only bring his great mace out diagonally before him, altering its angle furiously to keep up with the stream of strikes. He got nicked and clipped half a dozen times, drawing howls and grunts, and only the presence of his companion, and those others all around demanding the attention of the drow, prevented him from being seriously wounded, or even slain on the spot. For Drizzt could not finish his attacks without opening himself up to counters from the dwarf's companions.

After the initial momentum played out, the drow fell back. With typical stubbornness, the two dwarves advanced. The one with the orange beard, his hands bleeding and one finger hanging by a thread of skin, attempted a straightforward overhead chop. His companion half turned to lead with his shield then pivoted to launch a horizontal swing meant to come within a hair's breadth of his companion and swipe across from Drizzt's left to right.

The impressive coordination of the attack demanded either a straight and swift retreat or a complex two-angled parry, and normally, Drizzt would have just used his superior speed to skip back out of range.

But he recognized the orange-bearded dwarf's tenuous grip, and he was a drow, after all, whose entire youth was spent in learning how to execute exactly those sorts of multi-angled defenses. He thrust his left scimitar out before him, rode his hand up high and turned the blade down to intercept the sidelong swing, and brought his right hand across up high over his left, blade horizontal, to block the downward strike.

As the hammer coming across connected with his blade, Drizzt punched his hand forward and turned his scimitar to divert the dwarf's weapon low, and in doing so, the drow was able to take half a step to his left, lining himself up more fully with the other's overhead strike. When he made contact with that weapon, he had his full balance, his feet squarely set beneath his shoulders.

He dropped into a crouch as the weapon came down, then pushed up hard with all his strength. The dwarf's badly-injured top hand could not hold, and the drow's move forced the diminutive warrior to go right up to his tip-toes to keep any grasp on his weapon at all.

Drizzt turned back to the right as he rose, and with a sudden and powerful move, he angled and drove the dwarf's weapon across to his right, putting it in the path of the other dwarf's returning backhand. As the pair tangled, Drizzt disengaged and executed a reverse spin on the ball of his left foot, coming all the way around to launch a circle kick into the back of the orange-bearded dwarf that shoved him into his companion. The great mace went flying, and so did the dwarf with the orange beard, as the other dwarf ducked a shoulder and angled his shield to guide him aside.

"Clear for a shot!" came a cry from the side, demanding Drizzt's attention, and the drow abruptly halted and turned to see the elf, who held a heavy crossbow leveled Drizzt's way.

Drizzt yelled and charged at the elf, diving into a forward roll and turning as he went so that he came up into a sidelong step. He closed rapidly.

Then he rammed into an invisible wall, as expected, for he understood that the crossbow had been only a ruse, and no missile could have crossed through to strike at him through the unseen magical barrier.

Drizzt rebounded back and fell to one knee, moving shakily. He started up, but seemed to stumble again, apparently dazed.

He heard the dwarves charging in at his back, and they believed beyond any doubt that there was no way he could recover in time to prevent their killing blows.

"And all for the sake of orcs, Drizzt Do'Urden," he heard the elf, a wizard by trade, remark, and he saw the lithe creature shaking his head in dismay as he dropped the crossbow aside. "Not so honorable an end for one of your reputation."

* * * * *

Taugmaelle lowered her gaze, stunned and fearful. Never could she have anticipated a visit from King Obould VI, Lord of Many-Arrows, particularly on this, the eve of her departure for the Glimmerwood, where she was to be wed.

"You are a beautiful bride," the young orc king remarked, and Taugmaelle dared glance up to see Obould nodding appreciatively. "This human—what is his name?"

"Handel Aviv," she said.

"Does he understand the good fortune that has shone upon him?"

As that question digested, Taugmaelle found courage. She looked up again at her king and did not avert her eyes, but rather met his gaze.

"I am the fortunate one," she said, but her smile went away almost immediately as Obould responded with a scowl.

"Because he is human?" Obould blustered, and the other orcs in the small house all stepped away from him fearfully. "A higher being? Because you, a mere orc, are being accepted by this Handel Aviv and his kin? Have you elevated yourself above your race with this joining, Taugmaelle of Clan Bignance?"

"No, my king!" Taugmaelle blurted, tears rushing from her eyes. "No. Of course, nothing of the sort . . ."

"Handel Aviv is the fortunate one!" Obould declared.

"I . . . I only meant that I love him, my king," Taugmaelle said, her voice barely above a whisper.

The sincerity of that statement was obvious, though, and had Taugmaelle not averted her gaze to the floor again, she would have seen the young orc king shift uncomfortably, his bluster melting away.

"Of course," he replied after a while. "You are both fortunate, then."

"Yes, my king."

"But do not ever view yourself as his lesser," Obould warned. "You are proud. You are orc. You are Many-Arrows orc. It is Handel Aviv who is marrying above his heritage. Do not ever forget that."

"Yes, my king."

Obould looked around the small room to the faces of his constituents, a couple standing slack-jawed as if they had no idea how to react to his unexpected appearance, and several others nodding dully.

"You are a beautiful bride," the king said again. "A sturdy representative of all that is good in the Kingdom of Many-Arrows. Go forth with my blessing."

"Thank you, my king," Taugmaelle replied, but Obould hardly heard her, for he had already turned on his heel and moved out the door. He felt a bit foolish for his overreaction, to be sure, but he reminded himself pointedly that his sentiments had not been without merit.

"This is good for our people," said Taska Toill, Obould's court advisor. "Each of these extra-racial joinings reinforces the message that is Obould. And that this union is to be sanctified in the former Moonwood is no small thing."

"The steps are slow," the king lamented.

"Not so many years ago, we were hunted and killed," Taska reminded. "Unending war. Conquest and defeat. It has been a century of progress."

Obould nodded, though he did remark, "We are still hunted," under his breath. Worse, he thought but did not say, were the quiet barbs, where even those who befriended the people of Many-Arrows did so with a sense of superiority, a deep-set inner voice that told them of their magnanimity in befriending, even championing the cause of such lesser creatures. The surrounding folk of the Silver Marches would often forgive an orc for behavior they would not accept among their own, and that wounded Obould as greatly as those elves, dwarves, and humans who outwardly and openly sneered at his people.

* * * * *

Drizzt looked up at the elf wizard's superior smile, but when the drow, too, grinned, and even offered a wink, the elf's face went blank.

A split second later, the elf shrieked and flew away, as Guenhwyvar, six hundred pounds of feline power, leaped against him, taking him far, and taking him down.

One of the dwarves charging at Drizzt let out a little cry in surprise, but despite the revelation of a panther companion, neither of the charging dwarves were remotely prepared when the supposedly stunned Drizzt spun up and around at them, fully aware and fully balanced. As he came around, a backhand from Twinkle, the scimitar in his left hand, took half the orange beard from one dwarf, who was charging with abandon, his heavy weapon up over his head. He still tried to strike at Drizzt, but swirled and staggered, lost within the burning pain and shock. He came forward with his strike, but the scimitar was already coming back the other way, catching him across the wrists.

His great mace went flying. The tough dwarf lowered his shoulder in an attempt to run over his enemy, but Drizzt was too agile, and he merely shifted to the side and trailed his left foot, over which the wounded dwarf tumbled, cracking his skull against the magical wall.

His companion fared no better. As Twinkle slashed across in the initial backhand, the dwarf shifted back on his heels, turning to bring his shield in line, and brought his weapon arm back to begin a heavy strike. Drizzt's second blade thrust in behind the backhand, however, the drow cleverly turning his wrist over so that the curving blade of the scimitar rolled over the edge of the shield and dived down to strike that retracted weapon arm right where the bicep met the shoulder. As the dwarf, too far into his move to halt it completely, came around and forward with the strike, his own momentum drove the scimitar deeper into his flesh.

He halted, he howled, he dropped his axe. He watched his companion go tumbling away. Then came a barrage as the deadly drow squared up against him. Left and right slashed the scimitars, always just ahead of the dwarf's pathetic attempts to get his shield in their way. He got nicked, he got slashed, he got shaved, as edges, points and flats of two blades made their way through his defenses. Every hit stung, but none of them were mortal.

But he couldn't regain his balance and any semblance of defense, nor did he hold anything with which to counter, except his shield. In desperation, the dwarf turned and lunged, butting his shield arm forward. The drow easily rolled around it, though, and as he pivoted to the dwarf's right he punched out behind him, driving the pommel of his right blade against the dwarf's temple. He followed with a heavy left hook as he completed his turn, and the dazed dwarf offered no defense at all as fist and hilt smashed him across the face.

He staggered two steps to the side, and crumbled into the dirt.

Drizzt didn't pause to confirm the effect, for back the other way, the first dwarf he had cut was back to his feet and staggering away. A few quick strides brought Drizzt up behind him, and the drow's scimitar slashed across the back of the dwarf's legs, drawing a howl and sending the battered creature whimpering to the ground.

Again, Drizzt looked past him even as he fell, for the remaining two members of the outlaw band were fast retreating. The drow put up Taulmaril and set an arrow retrieved from the enchanted quiver he wore on his back. He aimed center mass on the dwarf, but perhaps in deference to King Bruenor—or Thibbledorf, or Dagnabbit, or any of the other noble and fierce dwarves he had known those decades before, he lowered his angle and let fly. Like a bolt of lightning, the magical arrow slashed the air and drove through the fleshy part of the dwarf's thigh. The poor dwarf screamed and veered then fell down.

Drizzt notched another arrow and turned the bow until he had the human, whose longer legs had taken him even farther away, in his sight. He took aim and drew back steadily, but held his shot as he saw the man jerk suddenly then stagger.

He stood there for just a moment before falling over, and Drizzt knew by the way he tumbled that he was dead before he ever hit the ground.

The drow glanced back over his shoulder, to see the three wounded dwarves struggling, but defeated, and the elf wizard still pinned by the ferocious Guenhwyvar. Every time the poor elf moved, Guenhwyvar smothered his face under a huge paw.

By the time Drizzt looked back, the killers of the human were in view. A pair of elves moved to gather the arrow-shot dwarf, while another went to the dead man, and another pair approached Drizzt, one riding on a white-winged steed, the pegasus named Sunrise. Bells adorned the mount's harness, bridle, and saddle, tinkling sweetly—ironically so—as the riders trotted up to the drow.

"Lord Hralien," Drizzt greeted with a bow.

"Well met and well done, my friend," said the elf who ruled the ancient expanse of the Glimmerwood that the elves still called the Moonwood. He looked around, nodding with approval. "The Night Riders have been dealt yet one more serious blow," he said, using another of the names for the orc-killing vigilantes, as did all the elves, refusing to assign a title as honorable as *Casin Cu Calas* to a band they so abhorred.

"One of many we'll need, I fear, for their numbers do not seem diminished," said Drizzt.

"They are more visible of late," Hralien agreed, and dismounted to stand before his old friend. "The Night Riders are trying to take advantage of the unrest in Many-Arrows. They know that King Obould VI is in a tenuous position." The elf gave a sigh. "As he always seems to be, as his predecessors always seemed to be."

"He has allies as well as enemies," said Drizzt. "More allies than did the first of his line, surely."

"And more enemies, perhaps," Hralien replied.

Drizzt could not disagree. Many times over the last century, the Kingdom of Many-Arrows had known inner turmoil, most often, as was still the case, brewing from a rival group of orcs. The old cults of Gruumsh One-eye had not flourished under the rule of the Obboulds, but neither had they been fully eradicated. The rumors said that yet another group of shamans, following the old warlike ways of goblinkind, were creating unrest and plotting against the king who dared diplomacy and trade with the surrounding kingdoms of humans, elves, and even dwarves, the most ancient and hated enemy of the orcs.

"You killed not one of them," Hralien remarked, glancing around at his warriors who gathered up the five wounded Night Riders. "Is this not in your heart, Drizzt Do'Urden? Do you not strike with surety when you strike to defend the orcs?"

"They are caught, to be justly tried."

"By others."

"That is not my province."

"You would not allow it to be," Hralien said with a wry grin that was not accusatory. "A drow's memories are long, perhaps."

"No longer than a moon elf's."

"My arrow struck the human first, and mortally, I assure you."

"Because you fiercely battle those memories, while I try to mitigate them," Drizzt replied without hesitation, setting Hralien back on his heels. If the elf, startled though he was, took any real offense, he didn't show it.

"Some wounds are not so healed by the passage of a hundred years," Drizzt went on, looking from Hralien to the captured Night Riders. "Wounds felt keenly by some of our captives here, perhaps, or by the grandfather's grandfather of the man who lies dead in the field beyond."

"What of the wounds felt by Drizzt Do'Urden, who did battle with King Obould in the orc's initial sweep of the Spine of the World?" Hralien asked. "Before the settlement of his kingdom and the treaty of Garumn's Gorge? Or who fought again against Obould II in the great war in the Year of the Solitary Cloister?"

Drizzt nodded with every word, unable to deny the truth of it all. He had made his peace with the orcs of Many-Arrows, to a great extent. But still, he would be a liar to himself if he failed to admit a twinge of guilt in battling those who had refused to end the ancient wars and ancient ways, and had continued the fight against the orcs—a war that Drizzt, too, had once waged, and waged viciously.

"A Mithral Hall trade caravan was turned back from Five Tusks," Hralien said, changing his tone as he shifted the subject. "A similar report comes to us from Silverymoon, where one of their caravans was refused entry to Many-Arrows at Ungoor's Gate north of Nesmé. It is a clear violation of the treaty."

"King Obould's response?"

"We are not certain that he even knows of the incidents. But whether he does or not, it is apparent that his shaman rivals have spread their message of the old ways far beyond Dark Arrows Keep."

Drizzt nodded.

"King Obould is in need of your help, Drizzt," Hralien said. "We have walked this road before."

Drizzt nodded in resignation at the unavoidable truth of that statement. There were times when he felt as if the road he walked was not a straight line toward progress, but a circling track, a futile loop. He let that negative notion pass, and reminded himself of how far the region had come—and that in a world gone mad from the Spellplague. Few places in all of Faerûn could claim to be *more* civilized than they had been those hundred years before, but the region known as the Silver Marches, in no small part because of the courage of a succession of orc kings named Obould, had much to be proud of.

His perspective and memories of that time a hundred years gone, before the rise of the Empire of Netheril, the coming of the aboleths, and the discordant and disastrous joining of two worlds, brought to Drizzt thoughts of another predicament so much like the one playing out before him. He remembered the look on Bruenor's face, as incredulous as any expression he had ever seen before or since, when he had presented the dwarf with his surprising assessment and astounding recommendations.

He could almost hear the roar of protest: "Ye lost yer wits, ye durned orc-brained, pointy-eared elf!"

On the other side of the magical barrier, the elf shrieked and Guenhwyvar growled, and Drizzt looked up to see the wizard stubbornly trying to crawl away. Guenhwyvar's great paw thumped against his back, and the panther flexed, causing the elf to drop back to the ground, squirming to avoid the extending claws.

Hralien started to call to his comrades, but Drizzt held his hand up to halt them. He could have walked around the invisible wall, but instead he sprang into the air beside it, reaching his hand as high as he could. His fingers slid over the top and caught a hold, and the drow rolled his back against the invisible surface and reached up with his other hand. A tuck and roll vaulted him feet-over-head over the wall, and he landed nimbly on the far side.

He bade Guenhwyvar to move aside then reached down and pulled the elf wizard to his feet. He was young, as Drizzt had expected—while some older elves and dwarves were inciting the *Casin Cu Calas*, the younger members, full of fire and hatred, were the ones executing the unrest in brutal fashion.

The elf, uncompromising, stared at him hatefully. "You would betray your own kind," he spat.

Drizzt cocked his eyebrows curiously, and tightened his grip on the elf's shirt, holding him firmly. "My own kind?"

"Worse then," the elf spat. "You would betray those who gave shelter and friendship to the rogue Drizzt Do'Urden."

"No," he said.

"You would strike at elves and dwarves for the sake of orcs!"

"I would uphold the law and the peace."

The elf mocked him with a laugh. "To see the once-great ranger siding with orcs," he muttered, shaking his head.

Drizzt yanked him around, stealing his mirth, and tripped him, shoving him backward into the magical wall.

"Are you so eager for war?" the drow asked, his face barely an inch from the elf's. "Do you long to hear the screams of the dying, lying helplessly in fields amidst rows and rows of corpses? Have you ever borne witness to that?"

"Orcs!" the elf protested.

Drizzt grabbed him in both hands, pulled him forward, and slammed him back against the wall. Hralien called to Drizzt, but the dark elf hardly heard it.

"I have ventured outside of the Silver Marches," Drizzt said, "have you? I have witnessed the death of once-proud Luskan, and with it, the death of a dear, dear friend, whose dreams lay shattered and broken beside the bodies of five thousand victims. I have watched the greatest cathedral in the world burn and collapse. I witnessed the hope of the goodly drow, the rise of the followers of Eilistraee. But where are they now?"

"You speak in ridd—" the elf started, but Drizzt slammed him again.

"Gone!" Drizzt shouted. "Gone, and gone with them the hopes of a tamed and gentle world. I have watched once safe trails revert to wilderness, and have walked a dozen-dozen communities that you will never know. They are gone now, lost to the Spellplague or worse! Where are the benevolent gods? Where is the refuge from the tumult of a world gone mad? Where are the candles to chase away the darkness?"

Hralien had quietly moved around the wall and walked up beside Drizzt. He put a hand on the drow's shoulder, but that brought no more than a brief pause in the tirade. Drizzt glanced at him before turning back to the captured elf.

"They are here, those lights of hope," Drizzt said, to both elves. "In the Silver Marches. Or they are nowhere. Do we choose peace or do we choose war? If it is battle you seek, fool elf, then get you gone from this land. You will find death aplenty, I assure you. You will find ruins where once proud cities stood. You will find fields of wind-washed bones, or perhaps the remains of a single hearth, where once an entire village thrived.

"And in that hundred years of chaos, amidst the coming of darkness, few have escaped the swirl of destruction, but we have flourished. Can you say the same for Thay? Mulhorand? Sembia? You say I betray those who befriended me, yet it was the vision of one exceptional dwarf and one exceptional orc that built this island against the roiling sea."

The elf, his expression more cowed, nonetheless began to speak out again, but Drizzt pulled him forward from the wall and slammed him back even harder.

"You fall to your hatred and you seek excitement and glory," the drow said. "Because you do not know. Or is it because you do not care that your pursuits will bring utter misery to thousands in your wake?"

Drizzt shook his head, and threw the elf aside, where he was caught by two of Hralien's warriors and escorted away.

"I hate this," Drizzt admitted to Hralien, quietly so that no one else could hear. "All of it. It is a noble experiment a hundred years long, and still we have no answers."

"And no options," Hralien replied. "Save those you yourself just described. The chaos encroaches, Drizzt Do'Urden, from within and without."

Drizzt turned his lavender eyes to watch the departure of the elf and the captured dwarves.

"We must stand strong, my friend," Hralien offered, and he patted Drizzt on the shoulder and walked away.

"I'm not sure that I know what that means anymore," Drizzt admitted under his breath, too softly for anyone else to hear.

PART 1

THE PURSUIT OF HIGHER TRUTH

THE PURSUIT OF HIGHER TRUTH

One of the consequences of living an existence that spans centuries instead of decades is the inescapable curse of continually viewing the world through the focusing prism employed by an historian.

I say "curse"—when in truth I believe it to be a blessing—because any hope of prescience requires a constant questioning of what is, and a deep-seated belief in the possibility of what can be. Viewing events as might the historian requires an acceptance that my own initial, visceral reactions to seemingly momentous events may be errant, that my "gut instinct" and own emotional needs may not stand the light of reason in the wider view, or even that these events, so momentous in my personal experience, might not be so in the wider world and the long, slow passage of time.

How often have I seen that my first reaction is based on half-truths and biased perceptions! How often have I found expectations completely inverted or tossed aside as events played out to their fullest!

Because emotion clouds the rational, and many perspectives guide the full reality. To view current events as an historian is to account for all perspectives, even those of your enemy. It is to know the past and to use such relevant history as a template for expectations. It is, most of all, to force reason ahead of instinct, to refuse to demonize that which you hate, and to, most of all, accept your own fallibility.

And so I live on shifting sands, where absolutes melt away with the passage of decades. It is a natural extension, I expect, of an existence in which I have shattered the preconceptions of so many people. With every stranger who comes to accept me for who I am instead of who he or she expected me to be, I roil the sands beneath that person's feet. It is a growth experience for them, no doubt, but we are all creatures of ritual and habit and accepted notions of what is and what is not. When true reality cuts against that internalized expectation—when you meet a goodly drow!—there is created an internal dissonance, as uncomfortable as a springtime rash.

There is freedom in seeing the world as a painting in progress, instead of a place already painted, but there are times, my friend . . .

There are times.

And such is one before me now, with Obould and his thousands camped upon the very door of Mithral Hall. In my heart I want nothing more than another try at the orc king, another opportunity to put my scimitar through his yellow-gray skin. I long to wipe the superior grin from his ugly face, to bury it beneath a spray of his own blood. I want him to hurt—to hurt for Shallows and all the other towns flattened beneath the stamp of orc feet. I want him to feel the pain he brought to Shoudra Stargleam, to Dagna and Dagnabbit, and to all the dwarves and others who lay dead on the battlefield that he created.

Will Catti-brie ever walk well again? That, too, is the fault of Obould.

And so I curse his name, and remember with joy those moments of retribution that Innovindil, Tarathiel, and I exacted upon the minions of the foul orc king. To strike back against an invading foe is indeed cathartic.

That, I cannot deny.

And yet, in moments of reason, in times when I sit back against a stony mountainside and overlook that which Obould has facilitated, I am simply not certain.

Of anything, I fear.

He came at the front of an army, one that brought pain and suffering to many people across this land I name as my home. But his army has stopped its march, for now at least, and the signs are visible that Obould seeks something more than plunder and victory.

Does he seek civilization?

Is it possible that we bear witness now to a monumental change in the nature of orc culture? Is it possible that Obould has established a situation, whether he intended this at first or not, where the interests of the orcs and the interests of all the other races of the region coalesce into a relationship of mutual benefit?

Is that possible? Is that even thinkable?

Do I betray the dead by considering such a thing?

Or does it serve the dead if I, if we all, rise above a cycle of revenge and war and find within us—orc and dwarf, human and elf alike—a common ground upon which to build an era of greater peace?

For time beyond the memory of the oldest elves, the orcs have warred with the "goodly" races. For all the victories—and they are countless!—and for all the sacrifices, are the orcs any less populous now than they were millennia ago?

I think not, and that raises the specter of unwinnable conflict. Are we doomed to repeat these wars, generation after generation, unendingly? Are we—elf and dwarf, human and orc alike—condemning our descendants to this same misery, to the pain of steel invading flesh?

I do not know.

And yet I want nothing more than to slide my blade between the ribs of King Obould Many-Arrows, to relish in the grimace of agony on his tusk-torn lips, to see the light dim in his yellow, bloodshot eyes.

But what will the historians say of Obould? Will he be the orc who breaks, at long, long last, this cycle of perpetual war? Will he, inadvertently or not, present the orcs with a path to a better life, a road they will walk—reluctantly at first, no doubt—in pursuit of bounties greater than those they might find at the end of a crude spear?

I do not know.

And therein lies my anguish.

I hope that we are on the threshold of a great era, and that within the orc character, there is the same spark, the same hopes and dreams, that guide the elves, dwarves, humans, halflings, and all the rest. I have heard it said that the universal hope of the world is that our children will find a better life than we.

Is that guiding principle of civilization itself within the emotional make-up of goblinkind? Or was Nojheim, that most unusual goblin slave I once knew, simply an anomaly?

Is Obould a visionary or an opportunist?

Is this the beginning of true progress for the orc race, or a fool's errand for any, myself included, who would suffer the beasts to live?

Because I admit that I do not know, it must give me pause. If I am to give in to the wants of my vengeful heart, then how might the historians view Drizzt Do'Urden?

Will I be seen in the company of those heroes before me who helped vanquish the charge of the orcs, whose names are held in noble esteem? If Obould is to lead the orcs forward, not in conquest, but in civilization, and I am the hand who lays him low, then misguided indeed will be those historians, who might never see the possibilities that I view coalescing before me.

Perhaps it is an experiment. Perhaps it is a grand step along a road worth walking.

Or perhaps I am wrong, and Obould seeks dominion and blood, and the orcs have no sense of commonality, have no aspirations for a better way, unless that way tramples the lands of their mortal, eternal enemies.

But I am given pause.

And so I wait, and so I watch, but my hands are near to my blades.

—Drizzt Do'Urden

CHAPTER
PRIDE AND PRACTICALITY

On the same day that Drizzt and Innovindil had set off for the east to find the body of Ellifain, Catti-brie and Wulfgar had crossed the Surbrin in search of Wulfgar's missing daughter. Their journey had lasted only a couple of days, however, before they had been turned back by the cold winds and darkening skies of a tremendous winter storm. With Catti-brie's injured leg, the pair simply could not hope to move fast enough to out-distance the coming front, and so Wulfgar had refused to continue. Colson was safe, by all accounts, and Wulfgar was confident that the trail would not grow cold during the delay, as all travel in the Silver Marches would come to a near stop through the frozen months. Over Catti-brie's objections, the pair had re-crossed the Surbrin and returned to Mithral Hall.

That same weather front destroyed the ferry soon after, and it remained out of commission though tendays passed. The winter was deep about them, closer to spring than to fall. The Year of Wild Magic had arrived.

For Catti-brie, the permeating cold seemed to forever settle on her injured hip and leg, and she hadn't seen much improvement in her mobility. She could walk with a crutch, but even then every stride made her wince. Still she wouldn't accept a chair with wheels, such as the one the dwarves had fashioned for the crippled Banak Brawn-anvil, and she certainly wanted nothing to do with the contraption

Nanfoodle had designed for her: a comfortable palanquin meant to be borne by four willing dwarves. Stubbornness aside, her injured hip would not support her weight very well, or for any length of time, and so Catti-brie had settled on the crutch.

For the last few days, she had loitered around the eastern edges of Mithral Hall, across Garumn's Gorge from the main chambers, always asking for word of the orcs who had dug in just outside of Keeper's Dale, or of Drizzt, who had at last been seen over the eastern fortifications, flying on a pegasus across the Surbrin beside Innovindil of the Moonwood.

Drizzt had left Mithral Hall with Catti-brie's blessing those tendays before, but she missed him dearly on the long, dark nights of winter. It had surprised her when he hadn't come directly back into the halls upon his return from the west, but she trusted his judgment. If something had compelled him to go on to the Moonwood, then it must have been a good reason.

"I got a hunnerd boys beggin' me to let 'em carry ye," Bruenor scolded her one day, when the pain in her hip was obviously flaring. She was back in the western chambers, in Bruenor's private den, but had already informed her father that she would go back to the east, across the gorge. "Take the gnome's chair, ye stubborn girl!"

"I have my own legs," she insisted.

"Legs that ain't healing, from what me eyes're telling me." He glanced across the hearth to Wulfgar, who reclined in a comfortable chair, staring into the orange flames. "What say ye, boy?"

Wulfgar looked at him blankly, obviously having no comprehension of the conversation between the dwarf and the woman.

"Ye heading out soon to find yer little one?" Bruenor asked. "With the melt?"

"Before the melt," Wulfgar corrected. "Before the river swells."

"A month, perhaps," said Bruenor, and Wulfgar nodded.

"Before Tarsakh," he said, referring to the fourth month of the year.

Catti-brie chewed her lip, understanding that Bruenor had initiated the discussion with Wulfgar for her benefit.

"Ye ain't going with him with that leg, girl," Bruenor stated. "Ye're limpin' about here and never giving the durned thing a chance at mending. Now take the gnome's chair and let me boys carry ye about, and it might be—it just might be—that ye'll be able to go with Wulfgar to find Colson, as ye planned and as ye started afore."

Catti-brie looked from Bruenor to Wulfgar, and saw only the twisting orange flames reflected in the big man's eyes. He seemed lost to them all, she noted, wound up too tightly in inner turmoil. His shoulders were bowed by the weight of guilt, to be sure, and the burden of grief, for he had lost his wife, Delly Curtie, who still lay dead under a blanket of snow on a northern field, as far as they knew.

Catti-brie was no less consumed by guilt over that loss, for it had been her sword, the evil and sentient Khazid'hea, that had overwhelmed Delly Curtie and sent her running out from the safety of Mithral Hall. Thankfully—they all believed—Delly hadn't taken her and Wulfgar's adopted child, the toddler girl, Colson, with her, but had instead deposited Colson with one of the other refugees from the northland, who had crossed the River Surbrin on one of the last ferries to leave before the onslaught of winter. Colson might be in the enchanted city of Silverymoon, or in Sundabar, or in any of a host of other communities, but they had no reason to believe that she had been harmed, or would be.

And Wulfgar meant to find her—it was one of the few declarations that held any fire of conviction that Catti-brie had heard the barbarian make in tendays. He would go to find Colson, and Catti-brie felt it was her duty as his friend to go with him. After they had been turned back by the storm, in no small part because of her infirmity, Catti-brie was even more determined to see the journey through.

Truly Catti-brie hoped that Drizzt would return before that departure day arrived, however. For the spring would surely bring tumult across the land, with a vast orc army entrenched all over the lands surrounding Mithral Hall, from the Spine of the World mountains to the north, to the banks of the Surbrin to the east, and to the passes just north of the Trollmoors in the south. The clouds of war roiled, and only winter had held back the swarms.

When that storm finally broke, Drizzt Do'Urden would be in the middle of it, and Catti-brie did not intend to be riding through the streets of some distant city on that dark day.

"Take the chair," Bruenor said—or said again, it seemed, from his impatient tone.

Catti-brie blinked and looked back at him.

"I'll be needin' both o' ye at me side, and soon enough," Bruenor said. "If ye're to be slowing Wulfgar down in this trip he's needing to make, then ye're not to be going."

"The indignity. . . ." Catti-brie said with a shake of her head.

But as she did that, she overbalanced just a bit on her crutch and lurched to the side. Her face twisted in a pained grimace as shooting pains like little fires rolled through her from her hip.

"Ye catched a giant-thrown boulder on yer leg," Bruenor retorted. "Ain't no indignity in that! Ye helped us hold the hall, and not a one o' Clan Battlehammer's thinking ye anything but a hero. Take the durned chair!"

"You really should," came a voice from the door, and Catti-brie and Bruenor turned to see Regis the halfling enter the room.

His belly was round once again, his cheeks full and rosy. He wore suspenders, as he had of late, and hooked his thumbs under them as he walked, eliciting an air of importance. And truly, as absurd as Regis sometimes seemed, no one in the hall would deny that pride to the halfling who had served so well as Steward of Mithral Hall in the days of constant battle, when Bruenor had lain near death.

"A conspiracy, then?" Catti-brie remarked with a grin, trying to lighten the mood.

They needed to smile more, all of them, and particularly the man seated across from where she stood. She watched Wulfgar as she spoke, and knew that her words had not even registered with him. He just stared into the flames, truly looking inward. The expression on Wulfgar's face, so utterly hopeless and lost, spoke truth to Catti-brie. She began to nod, and accepted her father's offer. Friendship demanded of her that she do whatever she could to ensure that she would be well enough to accompany Wulfgar on his most important journey.

So it was a few days later, that when Drizzt Do'Urden entered Mithral Hall through the eastern door, open to the Surbrin, that Catti-brie spotted him and called to him from on high. "Your step is lighter," she observed, and when Drizzt finally recognized her in her palanquin, carried on the shoulders of four strong dwarves, he offered her a laugh and a wide, wide smile.

"The Princess of Clan Battlehammer," the drow said with a polite and mocking bow.

On Catti-brie's orders, the dwarves placed her down and moved aside, and she had just managed to pull herself out of her chair and collect her crutch, when Drizzt crushed her in a tight and warm embrace.

"Tell me that you're home for a long while," she said after a lingering kiss. "The winter has been cold and lonely."

"I have duties in the field," Drizzt replied. He added, "Of course I do," when Catti-brie smirked helplessly at him. "But yes, I am returned, to Bruenor's side as I promised, before the snows retreat and the gathered armies move. We will know the designs of Obould before long."

"Obould?" Catti-brie asked, for she thought the orc king long dead.

"He lives," Drizzt replied. "Somehow he escaped the catastrophe of the landslide, and the gathered orcs are bound still by the will of that most powerful orc."

"Curse his name."

Drizzt smiled at her, but didn't quite agree.

"I am surprised that you and Wulfgar have already returned," Drizzt said. "What news of Colson?"

Catti-brie shook her head. "We do not know. We did cross the Surbrin on the same morning you flew off with Innovindil for the Sword Coast, but winter was too close on our heels, and brought us back. We did learn that the refugee groups had marched for Silverymoon, at least, and so Wulfgar intends to be off for Lady Alustriel's fair city as soon as the ferry is prepared to run once more."

Drizzt pulled her back to arms' length and looked down at her wounded hip. She wore a dress, as she had been every day, for the tight fit of breeches was too uncomfortable. The drow looked at the crutch the dwarves had fashioned for her, but she caught his gaze with her own and held it.

"I am not healed," she admitted, "but I have rested enough to make the journey with Wulfgar." She paused and reached up with her free hand to gently stroke Drizzt's chin and cheek. "I have to."

"I am no less compelled," Drizzt assured her. "Only my responsibility to Bruenor keeps me here instead."

"Wulfgar will not be alone on this road," she assured him.

Drizzt nodded, and his smile showed that he did indeed take comfort in that. "We should go to Bruenor," he said and started away.

Catti-brie grabbed him by the shoulder. "With good news?"

Drizzt looked at her curiously.

"Your stride is lighter," she remarked. "You walk as if unburdened. What did you see out there? Are the orc armies set to collapse? Are the folk of the Silver Marches ready to rise as one to repel—"

"Nothing like that," Drizzt said. "All is as it was when I departed, except that Obould's forces dig in deeper, as if they mean to stay."

"Your smile does not deceive me," Catti-brie said.

"Because you know me too well," said Drizzt.

"The grim tides of war do not diminish your smile?"

"I have spoken with Ellifain."

Catti-brie gasped. "She lives?" Drizzt's expression showed her the absurdity of that conclusion. Hadn't Catti-brie been there when Ellifain had died, to Drizzt's own blade? "Resurrection?" the woman breathed. "Did the elves employ a powerful cleric to wrest the soul—"

"Nothing like that," Drizzt assured her. "But they did provide Ellifain a conduit to relate to me . . . an apology. And she accepted my own apology."

"You had no reason to apologize," Catti-brie insisted. "You did nothing wrong, nor could you have known."

"I know," Drizzt replied, and the serenity in his voice warmed Catti-brie. "Much has been put right. Ellifain is at peace."

"Drizzt Do'Urden is at peace, you mean."

Drizzt only smiled. "I cannot be," he said. "We approach an uncertain future, with tens of thousands of orcs on our doorstep. So many have died, friends included, and it seems likely that many more will fall."

Catti-brie hardly seemed convinced that his mood was dour.

"Drizzt Do'Urden is at peace," the drow agreed against her unrelenting grin.

He moved as if to lead the woman back to the carriage, but Catti-brie shook her head and motioned instead for him to lead her, crutching, along the corridor that would take them to the bridge across Garumn's Gorge, and to the western reaches of Mithral Hall where Bruenor sat in audience.

"It is a long walk," Drizzt warned her, eyeing her wounded leg.

"I have you to support me," Catti-brie replied, and Drizzt could hardly disagree.

With a grateful nod and a wave to the four dwarf bearers, the couple started away.

* * * * *

So real was his dream that he could feel the warm sun and the cold wind upon his cheeks. So vivid was the sensation that he could smell the cold saltiness of the air blowing down from the Sea of Moving Ice.

So real was it all that Wulfgar was truly surprised when he awoke from his nap to find himself in his small room in Mithral Hall. He closed his eyes again and tried to recapture the dream, tried to step again into the freedom of Icewind Dale.

But it was not possible, and the big man opened his eyes and pulled himself out of his chair. He looked across the room to the bed. He hardly slept there of late, for that had been the bed he'd shared with Delly, his dead wife. On the few occasions he had dared to recline upon it, he had found himself reaching for her, rolling to where she should have been.

The feeling of emptiness as reality invaded his slumber had left Wulfgar cold every time.

At the foot of the bed sat Colson's crib, and looking at it proved even more distressing.

Wulfgar dropped his head in his hands, the soft feel of hair reminding him of his new-grown beard. He smoothed both beard and mustache, and rubbed the blurriness from his eyes. He tried not to think of Delly, then, or even of Colson, needing to be free of his regrets and fears for just a brief moment. He envisioned Icewind Dale in his younger days. He had known loss then, too, and had keenly felt the stings of battle. There were no delusions invading his dreams or his memories that presented a softer image of that harsh land. Icewind Dale remained uncompromising, its winter wind more deadly than refreshing.

But there was something simpler about that place, Wulfgar knew. Something purer. Death was a common visitor to the tundra, and monsters roamed freely. It was a land of constant trial, and with no room for error, and even in the absence of error, the result of any decision often proved disastrous.

Wulfgar nodded, understanding the emotional refuge offered by such uncompromising conditions. For Icewind Dale was a land without regret. It simply was the way of things.

Wulfgar pulled himself from his chair and stretched the weariness from his long arms and legs. He felt constricted, trapped, and as the walls seemed to close in on him, he recalled Delly's pleas to him regarding that very feeling.

"Perhaps you were right," Wulfgar said to the empty room.

He laughed then, at himself, as he considered the steps that had brought him back to that place. He had been turned around by a storm.

He, Wulfgar, son of Beornegar, who had grown tall and strong in the brutal winters of frozen Icewind Dale, had been chased back into the dwarven complex by the threat of winter snows!

Then it hit him. All of it. His meandering, empty road for the last eight years of his life, since his return from the Abyss and the torments of the demon, Errtu. Even after he had gathered up Colson from Meralda in Auckney, had retrieved Aegis-fang and his sense of who he was, and had rejoined his friends for the journey back to Mithral Hall, Wulfgar's steps had not been purposeful, had not been driven by a clear sense of where he wanted to go. He had taken Delly as his wife, but had never stopped loving Catti-brie.

Yes, it was true, he admitted. He could lie about it to others, but not to himself.

Many things came clear at last to Wulfgar that morning in his room in Mithral Hall, most of all the fact that he had allowed himself to live a lie. He knew that he couldn't have Catti-brie—her heart was for Drizzt—but how unfair had he been to Delly and to Colson? He had created a facade, an illusion of family and of stability for the benefit of everyone involved, himself included.

Wulfgar had walked his road of redemption, since Auckney, with manipulation and falsity. He understood that finally. He had been so determined to put everything into a neat and trim little box, a perfectly controlled scene, that he had denied the very essence of who he was, the very fires that had forged Wulfgar son of Beornegar.

He looked at Aegis-fang leaning against the wall then hefted the mighty warhammer in his hand, bringing its crafted head up before his icy-blue eyes. The battles he had waged recently, on the cliff above

Keeper's Dale, in the western chamber, and to the east in the breakout to the Surbrin, had been his moments of true freedom, of emotional clarity and inner calm. He had reveled in that physical turmoil, he realized, because it had calmed the emotional confusion.

That was why he had neglected Delly and Colson, throwing himself with abandon into the defenses of Mithral Hall. He had been a lousy husband to her, and a lousy father to Colson.

Only in battle had he found escape.

And he was still engaged in the self-deception, Wulfgar knew as he stared at the etched head of Aegis-fang. Why else had he allowed the trail to Colson to grow stale? Why else had he been turned back by a mere winter storm? Why else . . . ?

Wulfgar's jaw dropped open, and he thought himself a fool indeed. He dropped the hammer to the floor and swept on his trademark gray wolf cloak. He pulled his backpack out from under the bed and stuffed it with his blankets, then slung it over one arm and gathered up Aegis-fang with the other.

He strode out of his room with fierce determination, heading east past Bruenor's audience chamber.

"Where are you going?" he heard, and paused to see Regis standing before a door in the hallway.

"Out to check on the weather and the ferry."

"Drizzt is back."

Wulfgar nodded, and his smile was genuine. "I hope his journey went well."

"He'll be in with Bruenor in a short while."

"I haven't time. Not now."

"The ferry isn't running yet," Regis said.

But Wulfgar only nodded, as if it didn't matter, and strode off down the corridor, turning through the doors that led to the main avenue that would take him over Garumn's Gorge.

Thumbs hooked in his suspenders, Regis watched his large friend go. He stood there for a long while, considering the encounter, then turned for Bruenor's audience chamber.

He paused after only a few steps, though, and looked back again to the corridor down which Wulfgar had so urgently departed.

The ferry wasn't running.

CHAPTER 2
THE WILL OF GRUUMSH

Grguch blinked repeatedly as he moved from the recesses of the cave toward the pre-dawn light. Broad-shouldered and more than seven feet in height, the powerful half-orc, half-ogre stepped tentatively with his thick legs, and raised one hand to shield his eyes. The chieftain of Clan Karuck, like all of his people other than a couple of forward scouts, had not seen the light of day in nearly a decade. They lived in the tunnels, in the vast labyrinth of lightless caverns known as the Underdark, and Grguch had not undertaken his journey to the surface lightly.

Scores of Karuck warriors, all huge by the standards of the orc race—approaching if not exceeding seven feet and weighing in at nearly four hundred pounds of honed muscle and thick bone—lined the cave walls. They averted their yellow eyes in respect as the great warlord Grguch passed. Behind Grguch came the merciless war priest Hakuun, and behind him the elite guard, a quintet of mighty ogres fully armed and armored for battle. More ogres followed the procession, bearing the fifteen-foot *Kokto Gung Karuck*, the Horn of Karuck, a great instrument with a conical bore and a wide, upturned bell. It was fashioned of *shroomwood*, what the orcs named the hard skin of certain species of gigantic Underdark mushrooms. To the orc warriors looking on, the horn was deserving of, and receiving of, the same respect as the chieftain who preceded it.

Grguch and Hakuun, like their respective predecessors, would have had it no other way.

Grguch moved to the mouth of the cave, and out onto the mountainside ledge. Only Hakuun came up beside him, the war priest signaling the ogres to wait behind.

Grguch gave a rumbling laugh as his eyes adjusted and he noted the more typical orcs scrambling among the mountainside's lower stones. For more than two days, the second orc clan had been frantically keeping ahead of Clan Karuck's march. The moment they'd at last broken free of the confines of the Underdark, their desire to stay far, far away from Clan Karuck grew only more apparent.

"They flee like children," Grguch said to his war priest.

"They *are* children in the presence of Karuck," Hakuun replied. "Less than that when great Grguch stands among them."

The chieftain took the expected compliment in stride and lifted his eyes to survey the wider view around them. The air was cold, winter still gripped the land, but Grguch and his people were not caught unprepared. Layers of fur made the huge orc chieftain appear even larger and more imposing.

"The word will spread that Clan Karuck has come forth," Hakuun assured his chieftain.

Grguch considered the fleeing tribe again and scanned the horizon. "It will be known faster than the words of running children," he replied, and turned back to motion to the ogres.

The guard quintet parted to grant passage to *Kokto Gung Karuck*. In moments, the skilled team had the horn set up, and Hakuun properly blessed it as Grguch moved into place.

When the war priest's incantation was complete, Grguch, the only Karuck permitted to play the horn, wiped the shroomwood mouthpiece and took a deep, deep breath.

A great bass rumbling erupted from the horn, as if the largest bellows in all the world had been pumped by the immortal titans. The low-pitched roar echoed for miles and miles around the stones and mountainsides of the lower southern foothills of the Spine of the World. Smaller stones vibrated under the power of that sound, and one field of snow broke free, creating a small avalanche on a nearby mountain.

Behind Grguch, many of Clan Karuck fell to their knees and began swaying as if in religious frenzy. They prayed to the great

One-eye, their warlike god, for they held great faith that when *Kokto Gung Karuck* was sounded, the blood of Clan Karuck's enemies would stain the ground.

And for Clan Karuck, particularly under the stewardship of mighty Grguch, it had never been hard to find enemies.

* * * * *

In a sheltered vale a few miles to the south, a trio of orcs lifted their eyes to the north.

"Karuck?" asked Ung-thol, a shaman of high standing.

"Could it be any other?" replied Dnark, chieftain of the tribe of the Wolf Jaw. Both turned to regard the smugly smiling shaman Toogwik Tuk as Dnark remarked, "Your call was heard. And answered."

Toogwik Tuk chuckled.

"Are you so sure that the ogre-spawn can be bent to your will?" Dnark added, stealing the smile from Toogwik Tuk's ugly orc face.

His reference to Clan Karuck as "ogre-spawn" rang as a clear reminder to the shaman that they were not ordinary orcs he had summoned from the lowest bowels of the mountain range. Karuck was famous among the many tribes of the Spine of the World—or infamous, actually—for keeping a full breeding stock of ogres among their ranks. For generations untold, Karuck had interbred, creating larger and larger orc warriors. Shunned by the other tribes, Karuck had delved deeper and deeper into the Underdark. They were little known in recent times, and considered no more than a legend among many orc tribes.

But the Wolf Jaw orcs and their allies of tribe Yellow Fang, Toogwik Tuk's kin, knew better.

"They are only three hundred strong," Toogwik Tuk reminded the doubters.

A second rumbling from *Kokto Gung Karuck* shook the stones.

"Indeed," said Dnark, and he shook his head.

"We must go and find Chieftain Grguch quickly," Toogwik Tuk said. "The eagerness of Karuck's warriors must be properly steered. If they come upon other tribes and do battle and plunder . . ."

"Then Obould will use that as more proof that his way is better," Dnark finished.

"Let us go," said Toogwik Tuk, and he took a step forward. Dnark moved to follow, but Ung-thol hesitated. The other two paused and regarded the older shaman.

"We do not know Obould's plan," Ung-thol reminded.

"He has stopped," said Toogwik Tuk.

"To strengthen? To consider the best road?" asked Ung-thol.

"To build and to hold his meager gains!" the other shaman argued.

"Obould's consort has told us as much," Dnark added, and a knowing grin crossed his tusky face, his lips, all twisted from teeth that jutted in a myriad of random directions, turning up with understanding. "You have known Obould for many years."

"And his father before him," Ung-thol conceded. "And I have followed him here to glory." He paused and looked around for effect. "We have not known victory such as this—" he paused again and lifted his arms high—"in living memory. It is Obould who has done this."

"It is the start, and not the end," Dnark replied.

"Many great warriors fall along the road of conquest," added Toogwik Tuk. "That is the will of Gruumsh. That is the glory of Gruumsh."

All three started in surprise as the great bass note of *Kokto Gung Karuck* again resonated across the stones.

Toogwik Tuk and Dnark stood quiet then, staring at Ung-thol, awaiting his decision.

The older orc shaman gave a wistful look back to the southwest, the area where they knew Obould to be, then nodded at his two companions and bade them to lead on.

* * * * *

The young priestess Kna curled around him seductively. Her lithe body slowly slid around the powerful orc, her breath hot on the side of his neck, then the back of his neck, then the other side. But while Kna stared intensely at the great orc as she moved, her performance was not for Obould's benefit.

King Obould knew that, of course, so his smile was double-edged as he stood there before the gathering of shamans and chieftains. He had chosen wisely in making the young, self-absorbed Kna his consort replacement for Tsinka Shinriil. Kna held no reservations. She welcomed the stares of all around as she writhed over King Obould. More than welcomed, Obould knew. She craved them. It was her moment of glory, and she knew that her peers across the kingdom clenched their fists in jealousy. That was her paramount pleasure.

Young and quite attractive by the standards of her race, Kna had entered the priesthood of Gruumsh, but was not nearly as devout or fanatical as Tsinka had been. Kna's god—goddess—was Kna, a purely self-centered view of the world that was so common among the young.

And just what King Obould needed. Tsinka had served him well in her tenure, in bed and out, for she had always spoken in the interests of Gruumsh. Feverishly so. Tsinka had arranged the magical ceremony that had imbued in Obould great prowess both physical and mental, but her devotion was absolute and her vision narrow. She had outlived her usefulness to the orc king before she had been thrown from the lip of the ravine, to fall to her death among the stones.

Obould missed Tsinka. For all of her physical beauty, practiced movements and enthusiasm for the position, Kna was no Tsinka in lovemaking. Nor was Kna possessed of Tsinka's intellect and cunning, not by any means. She could whisper nothing into Obould's ear worth listening to, regarding anything other than coupling. And so she was perfect.

King Obould was clear in his vision, and it was one shared by a collection of steady shamans, most notably a small, young orc named Nukkels. Beyond that group, Obould needed no advice and desired no nay-saying. And most of all, he needed a consort he could trust. Kna was too enamored of Kna to worry about politics, plots and varying interpretations of Gruumsh's desires.

He let her continue her display for a short while longer then gently but solidly pried her from his side and put her back to arms' length. He motioned for her to go to a chair, to which she returned an exaggerated pout. He gave her a resigned shrug to placate her and worked hard to keep his utter contempt for her well suppressed. The orc king motioned again to the chair, and when she hesitated, he forcefully guided her to it.

She started to protest, but Obould held up his huge fist, reminding her in no uncertain terms that she was nearing the limits of his patience. As she settled into a quiet pout, the orc king turned back to his audience, and motioned to Tornfang Brakk, a courier from General Dukka, who oversaw the most important military region.

"The valley known as Keeper's Dale is well secured, God-king," Tornfang reported. "The ground has been broken to prevent easy passage and the structures topping the northern wall of the valley are nearly complete. The dwarves cannot come out."

"Even now?" Obould asked. "Not in the spring, but even now?"

"Even now, Greatness," Tornfang answered with confidence, and Obould wondered just how many titles his people would bestow upon him.

"If the dwarves came forth from Mithral Hall's western doors, we would slaughter them in the valley from on high," Tornfang assured the gathering. "Even if some of the ugly dwarves managed to cross the ground to the west, they would find no escape. The walls are in place, and the army of General Dukka is properly entrenched."

"But can we go in?" asked Chieftain Grimsmal of Clan Grimm, a populous and important tribe.

Obould flashed the impertinent orc a less-than-appreciative glare, for that was the most loaded and dangerous question of all. That was the point of contention, the source of all the whispers and all the arguing between the various factions. Behind Obould they had trampled the ground flat and had marched to glory not known in decades, perhaps centuries. But many were openly asking, to what end? To further conquest and plunder? To the caves of a dwarf clan or to the avenues of a great human or elven city?

As he considered things, however, particularly the whispers among the various shamans and chieftains, Obould came to realize that Grimsmal might have just done him a favor, though inadvertently.

"No," Obould declared solidly, before the bristling could really begin. "The dwarves have their hole. They keep their hole."

"For now," the obstinate Grimsmal dared utter.

Obould didn't answer, other than to grin—though whether it was one of simple amusement or agreement, none could tell.

"The dwarves are out of their hole in the east," reminded another of the gathering, a slight creature in a shaman's garb. "They build through the winter along the ridgeline. They now seek to connect and strengthen walls and towers, from their gates to the great river."

"And foundations along the bank," another added.

"They will construct a bridge," Obould reasoned.

"The foolish dwarves do our work for us!" Grimsmal roared. "They will grant us easier passage to wider lands."

The others all nodded and grinned, and a couple slapped each other on the back.

Obould, too, grinned. The bridge would indeed serve the Kingdom of Many-Arrows. He glanced over at Nukkels, who returned his contented look and offered a slight nod in reply.

Indeed, the bridge would serve, Obould knew, but hardly in the manner that Grimsmal and many of the others, so eager for war, now envisioned.

While the chatter continued around him, King Obould quietly imagined an orc city just to the north of the defenses the dwarves were constructing along the mountain ridge. It would be a large settlement, with wide streets to accommodate caravans, and strong buildings suitable for the storage of many goods. Obould would need to wall it in to protect from bandits, or overeager warrior orcs, so that the merchants who arrived from across King Bruenor's bridge would rest easy and with confidence before beginning their return journey.

The sound of his name drew the orc king from his contemplations, and he looked up to see many curious stares aimed at him. Obviously he had missed a question.

It did not matter.

He offered a calm and disarming smile in response and used the hunger for battle permeating the air around him to remind himself that they were a long, long way from constructing such a city.

But what a magnificent achievement it would be.

* * * * *

"The yellow banner of Karuck," Toogwik Tuk informed his two companions as the trio made their way along a winding, snow-filled valley below the cave that served as the primary exit point for orcs leaving the Underdark.

Dnark and Ung-thol squinted in the midday glare, and both nodded as they sorted out the two yellow pennants shot with red that flew in the stiff, wintry wind. They had known they were getting close, for they had crossed through a pair of hastily abandoned campsites in the sheltered valley. Clan Karuck's march had apparently sent other orcs running fast and far.

Toogwik Tuk led the way up the rocky incline that ramped up between those banners. Hulking orc guards stood to block the way, holding pole arms of various elaborate designs, with side blades and angled spear tips. Half axe and half spear, the weight of the weapons was intimidating enough, but just to enhance their trepidation, the approaching trio couldn't miss the ease with which the Karuck guards handled the heavy implements.

"They are as large as Obould," Ung-thol quietly remarked. "And they are just common guards."

"The orcs of Karuck who do not achieve such size and strength are slave fodder, so it is said," Dnark said.

"And so it is true," Toogwik Tuk said, turning back to the pair. "Nor are any of the runts allowed to breed. They are castrated at an early age, if they are fortunate."

"And my eagerness grows," said Ung-thol, who was the smallest of the trio. In his younger years, he had been a fine warrior, but a wound had left him somewhat infirm, and the shaman had lost quite a bit of weight and muscle over the intervening two decades.

"Rest easy, for you are too old to be worth castrating," Dnark chided, and he motioned for Toogwik Tuk to go and announce them to the guards.

Apparently the younger priest had laid the groundwork well, for the trio was ushered along the trail to the main encampment. Soon after, they stood before the imposing Grguch and his war priest advisor, Hakuun. Grguch sat on a chair of boulders, his fearsome double-bladed battle-axe in hand. The weapon, Rampant by name, was obviously quite heavy, but Grguch easily lifted it before him with one hand. He turned it slowly, so that his guests would get a good view, and a good understanding of the many ways Rampant could kill them. The black metal handle of the axe, which protruded up past the opposing "wing" blades, was shaped in the form of a stretching and turning dragon, its small forelegs pulled in close and the widespread horns on its head presenting a formidable spear tip. At the base, the dragon's long tail curved up and over the grip, forming a guard. Spines extended all along the length so that a punch from Grguch would hit like the stab of several daggers. Most impressive were the blades, the symmetrical wings of the beast. Of shining silver mithral, they fanned out top and bottom, reinforced every finger's-breadth or so by a thin bar of dark adamantine, which created spines top and bottom along each blade. The convex edges were as long as the distance from Dnark's elbow to the tips of his extended fingers, and none of the three visitors had any trouble imagining being cut cleanly in half by a single swipe of Rampant.

"Welcome to Many-Arrows, great Grguch," Toogwik Tuk said with a respectful bow. "The presence of Clan Karuck and its worthy leader makes us greater."

Grguch led his gaze drift slowly across the three visitors then around the gathering to Hakuun. "You will learn the truth of your hopeful claim," he said, his eyes turning back to Toogwik Tuk, "when I have the bones of dwarves and elves and ugly humans to crush beneath my boot."

Dnark couldn't suppress a grin as he looked to Ung-thol, who seemed similarly pleased. Despite their squeamishness at being so badly outnumbered among the fierce and unpredictable tribe, things were going quite well.

* * * * *

Out of the same cavern from which Grguch and Clan Karuck had emerged came a figure much less imposing, save to those folk who held a particular phobia of snakes. Fluttering on wings that seemed more suited to a large butterfly, the reptilian creature wove a swaying, zig-zagging course through the chamber, toward the waning daylight.

The twilight was brighter than anything the creature had seen in a century, and it had to set down inside the cave and spend a long, long while letting its eyes properly adjust.

"Ah, Hakuun, why have you done this?" asked the wizard, who was not really a snake, let alone a flying one. Anyone nearby might have thought it a curious thing to hear a winged snake sigh.

He slithered into a darker corner, and peeked out only occasionally to let his eyes adjust.

He knew the answer to his own question. The only reason the brutes of Clan Karuck would come forth would be for plunder and war. And while war could be an interesting spectacle, the wizard Jack, or Jack the Gnome as he had once been commonly called, really didn't have time for it just then. His studies had taken him deep into the bowels of the Spine of the World, and his easy manipulation of Clan Karuck, from Hakuun's father's father's father's father, had provided him with most excellent cover for his endeavors, to say nothing of the glory it had rained upon Hakuun's miserable little family.

Quite a while later, and only with the last hints of daylight left in the air, Jack slipped up to the cavern exit and peered out over the vast landscape. A couple of spells would allow him to locate Hakuun and the others, of course, but the perceptive fellow didn't need any magic to sense that something was ... different. Something barely distinguishable in the air—a scent or distant sounds, perhaps—pricked at Jack's sensibilities. He had lived on the surface once, far back beyond his memories, before he had fallen in with the illithids and demons in his quest to learn magic more powerful and devious than the typical evocations of mundane spellcasters. He had lived on the surface when he truly was a gnome, something he could hardly claim anymore. He only rarely wore that guise, and had come to understand that physical form really wasn't all that important or defining anyway. He was a blessed thing, he knew, mostly thanks to the illithids, because he had learned to escape the bounds of the corporeal and of the mortal.

A sense of pity came over him as he looked out over the wide lands, populated by creatures so inferior, creatures who didn't understand the truth of the multiverse, or the real power of magic.

That was Jack's armor as he looked out over the land, for he needed such pride to suppress the other, inevitable feelings that whirled in his thoughts and in his heart. For all of his superiority, Jack had spent the last century or more almost completely alone, and while he had found wondrous revelations and new spells in his amazing workshop, with its alchemical equipment and reams of parchments and endless ink and spellbooks he could stack to several times his gnomish height, only by lying to himself could Jack even begin to accept the paradoxical twist of fate afforded him by practical immortality. For while—and perhaps because—he wouldn't die anytime soon of natural causes, Jack was acutely aware that the world was full of mortal danger. Long life had come to mean "more to lose," and Jack had been walled into his secure laboratory as much by fear as by the thick stones of the Underdark.

That laboratory, hidden and magically warded, remained secure even though his unwitting protectors, Clan Karuck, had traveled out of the Underdark. And still, Jack had followed them. He had followed Hakuun, though the pathetic Hakuun was hardly worth following, because, he knew deep inside but wasn't quite ready to admit, he had wanted to come back, to remember the last time he was Jack the Gnome.

He found himself pleasantly surprised by the view. Something tingled in the air around him, something exciting and teeming with possibility.

Perhaps he didn't know the extent of Hakuun's reasoning in allowing Grguch to come forth, Jack thought, and he was intrigued.

CHAPTER
THE SIMPLE QUALITY OF TIMES GONE BY

3

Wulfgar's long, powerful legs drove through the knee-deep—often hip-deep—snow, plowing a path north from the mountain ridge. Rather than perceive the snow as a hindrance, though, Wulfgar considered it a freeing experience. That kind of trailblazing reminded him of the crisp air of home, and in a more practical sense, the snow slowed to a grumbling halt the pair of dwarven sentries who stubbornly pursued him.

More snow fell, and the wind blew cold from the north, promising yet another storm. But Wulfgar did not fear, and his smile was genuine as he drove forward. He kept the river on his immediate right and scrolled through his thoughts all of the landmarks Ivan Boulder-shoulder had told him regarding the trail leading to the body of Delly Curtie. Wulfgar had grilled Ivan and Pikel on the details before they had departed Mithral Hall.

The cold wind, the stinging snow, the pressure on his legs from winter's deep . . . it all felt right to Wulfgar, familiar and comforting, and he knew in his heart that his course was the right one. He drove on all the harder, his stride purposeful and powerful, and no snow drift could slow him.

The calls of protest from Bruenor's kin dissipated into nothingness behind him, defeated by the wall of wind, and very soon the fortifications and towers, and the mountain ridge itself became indistinct black splotches in the distant background.

He was alone and he was free. He had no one on whom he could rely, but no one for whom he was responsible. It was just Wulfgar, son of Beornegar, ranging through the deep winter snow, against the wind of the newest storm. He was just a lone adventurer, whose path was his own to choose, and who had found, to his thrill, a road worth walking.

Despite the cold, despite the danger, despite the missing Colson, despite Delly's death and Catti-brie's relationship with Drizzt, Wulfgar knew only simple joy.

He traveled on long after the dim light had waned to darkness, until the cold night air became too intense for even a proud son of the frozen tundra to bear. He set up camp under the lowest boughs of thick pines, behind insulating walls of snow, where the wind could not find him. He passed the night in dreams of the caribou, and the wandering tribes that followed the herd. He envisioned his friends, all of them, beside him in the shadow of Kelvin's Cairn.

He slept well, and went out early the next day, under the gray sky.

The land was not unfamiliar to Wulfgar, who had spent years in Mithral Hall, and even as he had exited the eastern door of the dwarven complex, he had a good idea of where Ivan and Pikel had found the body of poor Delly. He would get there that day, he knew, but reminded himself repeatedly of the need for caution. He had left friendly lands, and from the moment he had crossed the dwarven battlements on the mountain spur, he was outside the realm of civilization. Wulfgar passed several encampments, the dark smoke of campfires curling lazily into the air, and he didn't need to get close enough to see the campers to know their orc heritage and their malicious intent.

He was glad that the daylight was dim.

The snow began again soon after midday, but it was not the driving stuff of the previous night. Puffy flakes danced lightly on the air, trailing a meandering course to the ground, for there was no wind other than the occasional small whisper of a breeze. Despite having to continually watch for signs of orcs and other monsters, Wulfgar made great progress, and the afternoon was still young when he breached one small rocky rise to look down upon a bowl-shaped dell.

Wulfgar held his breath as he scanned the region. Across the way, beyond the opposite rise, rose the smoke of several campfires, and in the small vale itself Wulfgar saw the remains of an older, deserted encampment. For though the dell was sheltered, the wind had found its way in on the previous day, and had driven the snow to the southeastern reaches, leaving a large portion of the bowl practically uncovered. Wulfgar could clearly see a half-covered ring of small stones, the remains of a cooking pit.

Exactly as Ivan Bouldershoulder had described it.

With a great sigh, the barbarian pulled himself over the ridge and began a slow and deliberate trudge into the dell. He slid his feet along slowly rather than lift them, aware that he might trip over a body buried beneath the foot or so of snow that blanketed the ground. He set a path that took him straight to the cooking pit, then lined himself up as Ivan had described and slowly made his way back out. It took him a long while, but sure enough, he noticed a bluish hand protruding from the edge of the snow.

Wulfgar knelt beside it and reverently brushed back the white powder. It was Delly, unmistakably so, for the deep freeze of winter had only intensified after her fall those months before, and little decomposition had set in. Her face was bloated, but not greatly, and her features were not too badly distorted.

She looked as if she were asleep and at peace, and it occurred to Wulfgar that the poor woman had never known such serenity in all of her life.

A pang of guilt stung him at that realization, for in the end, that truth had been no small part his own fault. He recalled their last conversations, when Delly had subtly and quietly begged him to get her out of Mithral Hall, when she had pleaded with him to free her from the confines of the dwarf-hewn tunnels.

"But I am a stupid one," he whispered to her, gently stroking her face. "Would that you had said it more directly, and yet I fear that still I would not have heard you."

She had given up everything to follow him to Mithral Hall. Truly her impoverished life in Luskan had not been an enviable existence. But still, in Luskan Delly Curtie had friends who were as her family, had a warm bed and food to eat. She had abandoned that much at least for Wulfgar and Colson, and had held up her end of that bargain all the way to Mithral Hall and beyond.

In the end, she had failed. Because of Catti-brie's evil and sentient sword, to be sure, but also because the man she had trusted to stand beside her had not been able to hear and recognize her quiet desperation.

"Forgive me," Wulfgar said, and he bent low to kiss her cold cheek. He rose back to his knees and blinked, for suddenly the dim daylight stung his eyes.

Wulfgar stood.

"Ma la, bo gor du wanak," he said, an ancient barbarian way of accepting resignation, a remark without direct translation to the common tongue.

It was a lament that the world "is as it would be," as the gods would have it, and it was the place of men to accept and discover their best path from what was presented them. Hearing the somewhat stilted and less-flowing tongue of the Icewind Dale barbarians rolling so easily from his lips gave Wulfgar pause. He never used that language anymore, and yet it had come back to him so easily just then.

With the winter thick about him, in the crisp and chill air, and with tragedy lying at his feet, the words had come to him, unbidden and irresistible.

"Ma la, bo gor du wanak," he repeated in a whisper as he looked down at Delly Curtie.

His gaze slid across the bowl to the rising lines of campfire smoke. His expression shifted from grimace to wicked grin as he lifted Aegis-fang into his hands, his current "best path" crystallizing in his thoughts.

Beyond the northern rim of the dell, the ground dropped away sharply for more than a dozen feet, but not far from the ridge sat a small plateau, a single flat-topped jut of stone, like the trunk of a gigantic, ancient tree. The main orc encampment encircled the base of that plinth, but the first thing Wulfgar saw when he charged over the rim of the dell was the single tent and the trio of orc sentries stationed there.

Aegis-fang led the way, trailing the leaping barbarian's cry to the war god Tempus. The spinning warhammer took the closest orc sentry in the chest and blew him across the breadth of the ten-foot diameter pillar, spreading the snow cover like the prow of a speeding ship before dropping him off the back side.

Encumbered by layers of heavy clothing and with only slippery footing beneath, Wulfgar didn't quite clear the fifteen-foot distance, and slammed his shins against the ledge of the pillar, which sent him sprawling into the snow. Roaring with battle-frenzy, thrashing about so that he would present no clear target to the remaining two orcs, the barbarian quickly got his hands under him and heaved himself to his feet. His shins were bleeding but he felt no pain, and he barreled forward at the nearest orc, who lifted a spear to block.

Wulfgar slapped the feeble weapon aside and bore in, grasping the front of the orc's heavy fur wrap. As he simply ran the creature over, Wulfgar caught a second grip down by the orc's groin, and he hoisted his enemy up over his head. He spun toward the remaining orc and let fly, but that last orc dropped low beneath the living missile, who went flailing into the small tent and took it with him in his continuing flight over the far side of the pillar.

The remaining orc took up its sword in both hands, lifting the heavy blade over its head, and charged at Wulfgar with abandon.

He had seen such eagerness many times before in his enemies, for, as was often the case, Wulfgar appeared unarmed. But as the orc came in, Aegis-fang magically reappeared in Wulfgar's waiting grasp, and he jabbed it ahead with one hand. The heavy hammerhead connected solidly on the chest of the charging orc.

The creature stopped as though it had rammed into a stone wall.

Wulfgar drew back Aegis-fang and took it up in both hands to strike again, but the orc made no move at all, just stood there staring at him blankly. He watched as the sword slipped from the creature's grasp, to fall to the ground behind it. Then, before he could strike, the orc simply fell over.

Wulfgar sprinted past it to the edge of the pillar. Below him, orcs scrambled, trying to discern the threat that had come so unexpectedly. One orc lifted a bow Wulfgar's way, but too slowly, for Aegis-fang was already spinning its way. The warhammer crashed through the orc's knuckles and laid the archer low.

Wulfgar leaped from the pillar, right over the nearest duo, who had set spears pointed his way. He crashed among a second group, far less prepared, and drove one down below his descending knee, and knocked two others aside with his falling bulk. He managed to keep his footing somehow, and staggered forward, beyond the reach of the spear-wielders. He used that momentum to flatten the next orc in line with a heavy punch, then grabbed the next and lifted it before him in his run, using its body as a shield as he charged into the raised swords of a pair of confused sentries.

Aegis-fang returned to him, and a mighty strike sent all of that trio flying to the ground. Purely on instinct, Wulfgar halted his momentum and pivoted, Aegis-fang swiping across to shatter the spears and arms of creatures coming in at his back. The overwhelmed orcs fell away in a jumble and Wulfgar, not daring to pause, ran off.

He crashed through the side of a tent, his hammer tearing the deerskin from the wooden supports. He dragged his feet and kicked powerfully, scattering bedrolls and supplies, and a pair of young orcs who crawled off yelping.

That pair was no threat to him, Wulfgar realized, so he didn't pursue, veering instead for the next that raised weapons against him. He came in swinging, rolling his arms in circles above his head. Aegis-fang hummed as it cut through the air. The three orcs fell back, but one tripped and went to the ground. It dropped its weapon and tried to scramble away, but Wulfgar kicked it hard on the hip, sending it sprawling. Stubbornly the orc rolled to its belly and hopped up to all fours, trying to get its feet under it for a dash.

His great muscled arms straining and bulging, Wulfgar halted the spin of Aegis-fang, slid his lead hand up the handle, and jabbed at the orc. The warhammer smacked off the orc's shoulder and cracked into the side of its head, and the creature fell flat to the ground and lay very still.

Wulfgar stomped on it for good measure as he ran past in pursuit of its two companions, who had halted their retreat and stood ready.

Wulfgar roared and lifted Aegis-fang above his head, eagerly accepting the challenge. On he charged . . . but he noted something out of the corner of his eye. He dug in his lead foot, stopped abruptly, and tried to turn. Then he threw himself around, a spear grazing his side painfully. The missile caught in his flying wolf cloak and held fast, hanging awkwardly, its handle dragging on the ground and tangling with Wulfgar's legs as he continued his turn. He could only give it a fraction of his attention, though, for a second spear flew his way. Wulfgar brought Aegis-fang in close to his chest and turned it down at the last moment to crack the spearhead out of line. Still, the missile flipped over the parry and slapped against Wulfgar's shoulder.

As it went over, the back point of the weapon's triangular head cut the barbarian chin to cheek.

And as he lurched away, his leg caught the spear shaft hanging from his cloak.

To his credit, Wulfgar managed to not fall over, but he was off balance, his posture and the positioning of his weapon all wrong, as the two nearer orcs howled and leaped at him.

He drove Aegis-fang across his body, left to right, blocking a sword cut, but more with his arm than with the warhammer. He lifted his lower hand up desperately, turning the warhammer horizontal to parry a spear thrust from the other orc.

But the thrust was a feint, and Wulfgar missed cleanly. As the orc retracted, its smile was all the barbarian needed to see to know that he had no way to stop the second thrust from driving the spear deep into his belly.

He thought of Delly, lying cold in the snow.

* * * * *

Bruenor stood with Catti-brie outside the eastern door of Mithral Hall. North of them, construction was on in full, strengthening the wall that ran from the steep mountainside along the spur all the way to the river. As long as that wall could hold back the orcs, Clan Battlehammer remained connected above ground to the rest of the Silver Marches. The ferry across the River Surbrin, barely a hundred feet from where Bruenor and Catti-brie stood, would be running soon, and it would only be needed for a short while anyway. The abutments of a strong bridge were already in place on both banks.

The orcs could not get at them from the south without many days of forewarning, and such a journey through that broken ground would leave an army vulnerable at many junctures. With the line of catapults, archer posts, and other defensive assault points already set on the banks, particularly across the river, any orc assault using the river for passage would result in utter ruin for the attackers, much as it had for the dwarves of Citadel Felbarr when they had come to join the Battlehammer dwarves in their attempt to secure that most vital piece of ground.

Neither Bruenor nor Catti-brie were looking at the dwarven handiwork at that point, however. Both had their eyes and thoughts turned farther north, to where Wulfgar had unexpectedly gone.

"Ye ready to walk with him to Silverymoon?" Bruenor asked his adopted daughter after a long and uncomfortable silence, for the dwarf knew that Catti-brie harbored the very same feelings of dread as he.

"My leg hurts with every step," the woman admitted. "The boulder hit me good, and I don't know that I'll ever walk easy again."

Bruenor turned to her, his eyes moist. For she spoke the truth, he knew, and the clerics had told him in no uncertain terms. Catti-brie's injuries would never fully heal. The fight in the western entry hall had left her with a limp that she would carry for the rest of her days, and possibly with more damage still. Priest Cordio had confided to Bruenor his fears that Catti-brie would never bear children, particularly given that the woman was nearing the end of her childbearing years anyway.

"But I'm ready for the walk today," Catti-brie said with determination, and without the slightest hesitation. "If Wulfgar crossed over that wall right as we're speaking, I'd turn him to the river that we could be on our way. It is past time that Colson was returned to her father."

Bruenor managed a wide smile. "Ye be quick to get the girl and get ye back," he ordered. "The snows're letting go early this year, I'm thinking, and Gauntlgrym's waiting!"

"You believe that it really was Gauntlgrym?" Catti-brie dared to ask, and it was the first time anyone had actually put the most important question directly to the driven dwarf king. For on their journey back to Mithral Hall, before the coming of Obould, one of the caravan wagons had been swallowed up by a strange sinkhole, one that led, apparently, to an underground labyrinth. Bruenor had immediately proclaimed the place Gauntlgrym, an ancient and long-lost dwarven city, the pinnacle of power for the clan called Delzoun, a common heritage for all the dwarves of the North, Battlehammer, Mirabarran, Felbarran, and Adbarran alike.

"Gauntlgrym," Bruenor said with certainty, a claim he had been making in that tone since his return from the dead. "Moradin put me back here for a reason, girl, and that reason'll be shown to me when

I get meself to Gauntlgrym. There we'll be findin' the weapons we're needing to drive the ugly orcs back to their holes, don't ye doubt."

Catti-brie wasn't about to argue with him, because she knew that Bruenor was in no mood for any debate. She and Drizzt had spoken at length about the dwarf's plan, and about the possibility that the sinkhole had indeed been an entry point to the lost avenues of Gauntlgrym, and she had discussed it at length with Regis, as well, who had been poring over ancient maps and texts. The truth of it was that none of them had any idea whether or not the place was what Bruenor had decided it to be.

And Bruenor wasn't about to argue the point. His litany against the darkness that had settled on the land was a simple one, a single word: Gauntlgrym.

"Durn stubborn fool of a boy," Bruenor muttered, looking back to the north, his mind's eye well beyond the wall that blocked his view. "He's to slow it all down."

Catti-brie started to respond, but found that she could not speak past the lump that welled in her throat. Bruenor was complaining, of course, but in truth, his anger that Wulfgar's rash decision to run off alone into orc-held lands would slow the dwarves' plans was the most optimistic assessment of all.

The woman gave in to her sense of dread for just a moment, and wondered if her duty to her friend would send her off alone across the Surbrin in search of Colson. And in that case, once the toddler had been retrieved, what then?

CHAPTER
BUILDING HIS KINGDOM

4

The beams creaked for a moment, then a great rush of air swept across the onlookers as the counterweights sent the massive neck of the catapult swinging past. The basket released its contents, tri-pointed caltrops, in a line from the highest peak of the arc to the point of maximum momentum and distance.

The rain of black metal plummeted from sight, and King Obould moved quickly to the lip of the cliff to watch them drop to the floor of Keeper's Dale.

Nukkels, Kna, and some of the others shifted uneasily, not pleased to see their god-king standing so near to a two-hundred-foot drop. Any of General Dukka's soldiers, or more likely, proud Chieftain Grimsmal and his guards, could have rushed over and ended the rule of Obould with a simple shove.

But Grimsmal, despite his earlier rumblings of discontent, nodded appreciatively at the defenses that had been set up on the northern ridge overlooking Mithral Hall's sealed western door.

"We have filled the valley floor with caltrops," General Dukka assured Obould. He motioned to the many baskets set beside the line of catapults, all filled with stones ranging in size from a large fist to twice an orc's head. "If the ugly dwarves come forth, we'll shower them with death."

Obould looked down to the southwest, about two-thirds of the way across the broken valley from the dwarven complex, where a line of orcs chopped at the stone, digging a wide, deep trench. Directly to the king's left, atop the cliff at the end of the trench, sat a trio of catapults, all sighted to rake the length of the ravine should the dwarves try to use it for cover against the orcs positioned in the west.

Dukka's plan was easy enough to understand: he would slow any dwarven advance across Keeper's Dale as much as possible, so that his artillery and archers on high could inflict massive damage on the break-out army.

"They came out of the eastern wall with great speed and cunning," Obould warned the beaming general. "Encased in metal carts. A collapsed mountain wall did not slow them."

"From their door to the Surbrin was not far, my king," Dukka dared reply. "Keeper's Dale offers no such sanctuary."

"Do not underestimate them," Obould warned. He stepped closer to General Dukka as he spoke, and the other orc seemed to shrink in stature before him. His voice ominous and loud, so that all could hear, Obould roared out, "They will come out with *fury*. They will have brooms before them to sweep aside your caltrops, and shielding above to block your arrows and stones. They will have folding bridges, no doubt, and your trench will slow them not at all. King Bruenor is no fool, and does not charge into battle unprepared. The dwarves will know exactly where they need to go, and they will get there with all speed."

A long and uncomfortable silence followed, with many of the orcs looking at each other nervously.

"Do you expect them to come forth, my king?" Grimsmal asked.

"All that I expect from King Bruenor is that whatever he chooses to do, he will do it well, and with cunning," Obould replied, and more than one orc jaw fell open to hear such compliments for a dwarf coming forth from an orc king.

Obould considered those looks carefully in light of his disastrous attempt to break into Mithral Hall. He could not let any of them believe that he was speaking from weakness, from memories of his own bad judgment.

"Witness the devastation of the ridge where you now place your catapults," he said, waving his arm out to the west. Where once had stood a ridge line—one atop which Obould had placed allied frost giants and their huge war engines—loomed a torn and jagged crevice of shattered stones. "The dwarves are on their home ground. They know every stone, every rise, and every tunnel. They know how to fight. But *we* . . ." he roared, striding about for maximum effect, and lifting his clawing hands to the sky. He let the words hang in the air for many heartbeats before continuing, "We do not deny them the credit they deserve. We accept that they are formidable and worthy foes, and in that knowledge, we prepare."

He turned directly to General Dukka and Chieftain Grimsmal, who had edged closer together. "We know them, but even against what we have shown to them in conquering this land, they still do not know us. This"—he swept his arm out to encompass the catapults, archers, and all the rest—"they know, and expect. Your preparations are half done, General Dukka, and half done well. Now envision how King Bruenor will try to counter everything you have done, and complete your preparations to defeat that counter."

"B-but . . . my king?" General Dukka stammered.

"I have all confidence in you," Obould said. "Begin by trapping your own entrenchments on the western side of Keeper's Dale, so that if the dwarves reach that goal, your warriors can quickly retreat and leave them exposed on another battlefield of your choosing."

Dukka began to nod, his eyes shining, and his lips curled into a wicked grin.

"Tell me," Obould bade him.

"I can set a second force in the south to get to the doors behind them," the orc replied. "To cut off any dwarf army that charges across the valley."

"Or a second force that appears to do so," said Obould, and he paused and let all around him digest that strange response.

"So they will turn and run back," Dukka answered at length. "And then have to cross yet again to gain the ground they covet."

"I have never wavered in my faith in you, General Dukka," said Obould, and he nodded and even patted the beaming orc on the shoulder as he walked past.

His smile was twofold, and genuine. He had just strengthened the loyalty of an important general, and had impressed the potentially troublesome Grimsmal in the process. Obould knew what played in Grimsmal's mind as he swept up behind the departing entourage. If Obould, and apparently his commanders, could think so far ahead of

King Bruenor, then what might befall any orc chieftain who plotted against the King of Many-Arrows?

Those doubts were the real purpose of his visit to Keeper's Dale, after all, and not any concerns about General Dukka's readiness. For it was all moot, Obould understood. King Bruenor would never come forth from those western doors. As the dwarf had learned in his breakout to the east—and as Obould had learned in trying to flood into Mithral Hall—any such advance would demand too high a cost in blood.

* * * * *

Wulfgar screamed at the top of his lungs, as if his voice alone might somehow, impossibly, halt the thrust of the spear.

A blue-white flash stung the barbarian's eyes, and for a moment he thought it was the burning pain of the spear entering his belly. But when he came out of his blink, he saw the spear-wielding orc flipping awkwardly in front of him. The creature hit the ground limp, already dead, and by the time Wulfgar turned to face its companion that orc had dropped its sword and grasped and clawed at its chest. Blood poured from a wound, both front and back.

Wulfgar didn't understand. He jabbed his warhammer at the wounded orc and missed—another streaking arrow, a bolt of lightning, soared past Wulfgar and hit the orc in the shoulder, throwing it to the ground near its fallen comrade. Wulfgar knew that tell-tale missile, and he roared again and turned to face his rescuer.

He was surprised to see Drizzt, not Catti-brie, holding Taulmaril the Heartseeker.

The drow sprinted toward him, his light steps barely ruffling the blanket of deep snow. He started to nock another arrow, but tossed the bow aside instead and drew forth his two scimitars. He tossed a salute at Wulfgar then darted to the side as he neared, turning into a handful of battle-ready orcs.

"Biggrin!" Drizzt shouted as Wulfgar charged in his wake.

"Tempus!" the barbarian responded.

He put Aegis-fang up behind his head, and let it fly from both hands, the warhammer spinning end-over-end for the back of Drizzt's head.

Drizzt ducked and dropped to his knees at the last moment. The five orcs, following the drow's movements, had no time to react to the spinning surprise. At the last moment, the orcs threw up their arms defensively and tangled each other in their desperation to get out of the way. Aegis-fang took one squarely, and that flying orc clipped another enough to send both tumbling back.

The remaining three hadn't even begun to re-orient themselves to their opponents when the fury of Drizzt fell over them. He skidded on his knees as the hammer flew past, but leaped right back up to his feet and charged forward with abandon, his deadly blades crossing before him, going out wide, then coming back in another fast cross on the backhand. He counted on confusion, and confusion he found. The three orcs fell away in moments, slashed and stabbed.

Wulfgar, still chasing, summoned Aegis-fang back to his waiting hands, then veered inside the drow's turn so that his long legs brought him up beside Drizzt as they approached the encampment's main area of tents, where many orcs had gathered.

But those orcs would not stand against them, and any indecision the porcine humanoids might have had about running away was snapped away a moment later when a giant panther roared from the side.

Weapons went flying, and orcs went running, scattering to the winter's winds.

Wulfgar heaved Aegis-fang after the nearest, dropping it dead in its tracks. He put his head down and plowed on even faster—or started to, until Drizzt grabbed him by the arm and tugged him around.

"Let them go," the drow said. "There are many more about, and we will lose our advantage in the chase."

Wulfgar skidded to a stop and again called his magical warhammer back to his grasp. He took a moment to survey the dead, the wounded, and the fleeing orcs then met Drizzt's gaze and nodded, his bloodlust sated.

And he laughed. He couldn't help it. It came from somewhere deep inside, a desperate release, a burst of protest against the absurdity of his own actions. It came from those distant memories again, of running free in Icewind Dale. He had caught the "Biggrin" reference so easily, understanding in that single name that Drizzt wanted him to throw the warhammer at the back of the drow's head.

How was that even possible?

"Wulfgar has a desire to die?" Drizzt asked, and he, too, chuckled.

"I knew you would arrive. It is what you do."

* * * * *

Kna curled around his arm, rubbing his shoulder, purring and growling as always. Seated at the table in the tent, King Obould seemed not even to notice her, which of course only made her twist, curl, and growl even more intensely.

Across the table, General Dukka and Chieftain Grimsmal understood all too clearly that Kna was their reminder that Obould was above them, in ways they simply could never hope to attain.

"Five blocks free," General Dukka explained, "block" being the orc military term coined by Obould to indicate a column of one thousand warriors, marching ten abreast and one hundred deep. "Before the turn of Tarsakh."

"You can march them to the Surbrin, north of Mithral Hall, in five days," Chieftain Grimsmal remarked. "Four days if you drive them hard."

"I would drive them through the stones for the glory of King Obould!" Dukka replied.

Obould did not appear impressed.

"There is no need of such haste," he said at length, after sitting with a contemplative stare that had the other two chewing their lips in anticipation.

"The onset of Tarsakh will likely bring a clear path to the dwarven battlements," Chieftain Grimsmal dared to reply.

"A place we will not go."

The blunt response had Grimsmal sliding back in his chair, and brought a stupefied blink from Dukka.

"Perhaps I can free six blocks," the general said.

"Five or fifty changes nothing," Obould declared. "The ascent is not our wisest course."

"You know another route to strike at them?" Dukka asked.

"No," said Grimsmal, shaking his head as he looked knowingly at Obould. "The whispers are true, then. King Obould's war is over."

The chieftain wisely kept his tone flat and non-judgmental, but Dukka's wide eyes betrayed the general's shock, albeit briefly.

"We pause to see how many roads are open to us," Obould explained.

"Roads to victory?" asked General Dukka.

"Victory in ways you cannot yet imagine," said Obould, and he wagged his large head and showed a confident and toothy grin. For greater effect, he brought one of his huge fists up on the table before him, and clenched it tightly so that the muscles of his bare forearm bulged and twisted to proportions that pointedly reminded the other orcs of the superiority of this creature. Grimsmal was large by orc standards, and a mighty warrior, which was how he had attained the leadership of his warrior tribe, of course. But even he blanched before the spectacle of Obould's sheer power. Truly it seemed that if the orc king had been holding a block of granite in that hand, he would have easily ground it to dust.

No less overpowering was Obould's expression of supreme confidence and power, heightened by his disciplined detachment to Kna's writhing and purring at his side.

Grimsmal and General Dukka left that meeting having no idea what Obould was planning, but having no doubt of Obould's certainty in that plan. Obould watched them go with a knowing smile that the two would not plot against him. The orc king grabbed Kna and yanked her around before him, deciding that it was time to celebrate.

* * * * *

The body was frozen solid, and Wulfgar and Drizzt could not bend Delly's arms back down against her. Tenderly, Wulfgar took the blankets from his pack and wrapped them around her, keeping her face exposed to the last, as if he wanted her to see his sincere remorse and sorrow.

"She did not deserve this," Wulfgar said, standing straight and staring down at the poor woman. He looked at Drizzt, who stood with Guenhwyvar at his side, one hand on the tuft at the back of the panther's neck. "She had her life in Luskan before I arrived to steal her from it."

"She chose the road with you."

"Foolishly," Wulfgar replied with a self-deprecating laugh and sigh.

Drizzt shrugged as if the point was moot, which of course it was. "Many roads end suddenly, in the wilds and also in the alleyways of Luskan. There is no way of truly knowing where a road will lead until it is walked."

"Her trust in me was misplaced, I fear."

"You did not bring her out here to die," said Drizzt. "Nor did you drive her from the safety of Mithral Hall."

"I did not hear her calls for help. She told me that she could not suffer the dwarven tunnels, but I would not hear."

"And her way was clear across the Surbrin, had that been the route she truly wanted. You are no more to blame for this than is Catti-brie, who did not anticipate the reach of that wicked sword."

The mention of Catti-brie jolted Wulfgar a bit, for he knew that she felt the weight of guilt indeed about Khazid'hea's apparent role in Delly Curtie's tragic death.

"Sometimes what is, just is," said Drizzt. "An accident, a cruel twist of fate, a conjunction of forces that could not have been anticipated."

Wulfgar nodded, and it seemed as if a great weight had been lifted from his broad shoulders. "She did not deserve this," he said again.

"Nor did Dagnabbit, nor did Dagna, nor did Tarathiel, and so many others, like those who took Colson across the Surbrin," said Drizzt. "It is the tragedy of war, the inevitability of armies crashing together, the legacy of orcs and dwarves and elves and humans alike. Many roads end suddenly—it is a reality of which we should all be aware—and Delly could just as easily have fallen to a thief in the dark of Luskan's night, or have been caught in the middle of a brawl in the Cutlass. We know for certain only one thing, my friend, that we will one day share in Delly's fate. If we walk our roads solely to avoid such an inevitability, if we step with too much caution and concern . . ."

"Then we should just as well lie under the snow and let the cold find our bones," Wulfgar finished. He nodded with every word, assuring Drizzt that he needn't worry about the weight of harsh reality bending Wulfgar low.

"You will go for Colson?" Drizzt asked.

"How could I not? You speak of our responsibility to ourselves in choosing our roads with courage and acceptance, yet there remains our responsibility to others. Mine is to Colson. It is the pact I willingly accepted when I took her from Meralda of Auckney. Even if I were assured that she was safe with the goodly refugees who crossed the Surbrin, I could not abandon my promise to Colson's mother, nor to the girl."

"For yourself there is Gauntlgrym?" Wulfgar asked. "Beside Bruenor?"

"That is his expectation, and my duty to him, yes."

Wulfgar gave a nod and scanned the horizon.

"Perhaps Bruenor is right, and Gauntlgrym will show us an end to this war," said Drizzt.

"There will be another war close behind," Wulfgar said with a helpless shrug and chuckle. "It is the way of things."

"Biggrin," Drizzt said, drawing a smile from his large friend.

"Indeed," said Wulfgar. "If we cannot change the way of things, then we are wise to enjoy the journey."

"You knew that I would duck, yes?"

Wulfgar shrugged. "I figured that if you did not, it was—"

"—the way of things," Drizzt finished with him.

They shared a laugh and Wulfgar looked down at Delly once more, his face somber. "I will miss her. She was so much more than she appeared. A fine companion and mother. Her road was difficult for all her days, but she oft found within herself a sense of hope and even joy. My life is lessened with her passing. There is a hole within me that will not be easily filled."

"Which cannot be filled," Drizzt corrected. "That is the thing of loss. And so you will go on, and you will take solace in your memories of Delly, in the good things you shared. You will see her in Colson, though the girl was not of her womb. You will feel her beside you on occasion, and though the sadness will ever remain, it will settle behind treasured memories."

Wulfgar bent down and gently slid his arms beneath Delly and lifted her. It didn't appear as if he was holding a body, for the frozen form did not bend at all. But he hugged her close to his chest and moisture filled his bright blue eyes.

"Do you now hate Obould as much as I do?" Drizzt asked.

Wulfgar didn't reply, but the answer that came fast into his thoughts surprised him. Obould was just a name to him, not even a symbol on which he could focus his inner turmoil. Somehow he had moved past rage and into acceptance.

It is what it is, he thought, echoing Drizzt's earlier sentiments, and Obould diminished to become a circumstance, one of many. An orc, a thief, a dragon, a demon, an assassin from Calimport—it did not matter.

"It was good to fight beside you again," Wulfgar said, and in such a tone as to give Drizzt pause, for the words sounded more like a farewell than anything else.

Drizzt sent Guenhwyvar out to the point, and side-by-side, he and Wulfgar began their trek back to Mithral Hall, with Wulfgar holding Delly close all the way.

CHAPTER
TAKING ADVANTAGE
5

"Clan Grimm has turned north," Toogwik Tuk told his two companions on a clear, calm morning in the middle of Ches, the third month of the year. "King Obould has granted Chieftain Grimsmal a favorable region, a sheltered and wide plateau."

"To prepare?" asked Ung-thol.

"To build," Toogwik Tuk corrected. "To raise the banner of Clan Grimm beside the flag of Many-Arrows above their new village."

"Village?" Dnark asked, spitting the word with surprise.

"King Obould will claim that this is a needed pause to strengthen the lines of supply," Toogwik Tuk said.

"A reasonable claim," said Dnark.

"But one we know is only half true," Toogwik Tuk said.

"What of General Dukka?" asked an obviously agitated Ung-thol. "Has he secured Keeper's Dale?"

"Yes," the other shaman answered.

"And so he marches to the Surbrin?"

"No," said Toogwik Tuk. "General Dukka and his thousands have not moved, though there are rumors that he will assemble several blocks . . . eventually."

Dnark and Ung-thol exchanged concerned glances.

"King Obould would not allow that collection of warriors to filter back to their tribes," Dnark said. "He would not dare."

"But will he send them around to strike at the dwarves at the

Surbrin?" asked Ung-thol. "The dwarf battlements grow higher with each passing day."

"We expected Obould would not proceed," Toogwik Tuk reminded. "Is that not why we coaxed Grguch to the surface?"

Looking at his co-conspirators, Toogwik Tuk recognized that typical doubt right before the moment of truth. The three had long shared their concerns that Obould was veering from the path of conquest, and that was something they, as followers of Gruumsh One-eye, could not suffer. Their shared expectations, however, were that the war was not quite over, and that Obould would strike hard one more time at least, to gain a more advantageous position before his halt.

Leaving the dwarves open to the Surbrin had seemed a more distinct possibility over the past few months, and particularly the past few tendays. The weather was soon to turn, and the appropriate forces were not being moved into a strike position.

Still, in the face of it, the other two couldn't help but be surprised— and concerned, as the weight of their conspiracy settled more heavily on their shoulders.

"Turn them against the elf raiders in the east," Toogwik Tuk said suddenly, jolting his two companions, both of whom looked at him curiously, almost plaintively.

"We had hoped to use Grguch to force the charge to the Surbrin," Toogwik Tuk explained. "But with Obould's waiting to position the warriors, that is not presently an option. But we must offer Grguch some blood."

"Or he will take ours," Ung-thol muttered.

"There have been reports of elf skirmishers along the Surbrin, north of the dwarves," Dnark said, aiming his comment mostly at Ung-thol.

"Grguch and Clan Karuck will build a reputation that will serve them—and us—well when at last it comes to dealing with King Bruenor's troublesome beasts," Toogwik Tuk nudged. "Let us go and bring the Kingdom of Many-Arrows its newest hero."

* * * * *

Like a leaf fluttering silently on a midnight breeze, the dark elf slipped quietly to the side of the darkened stone and mud structure.

The orc guards hadn't noted his quiet passing, nor was he leaving any obvious tracks on the frozen snow.

No corporeal creature could move more stealthily than a trained drow, and Tos'un Armgo was proficient even by the lofty standards of his race.

He paused at the wall and glanced around at the cluster of structures—the village of Tungrush, he knew through the conversations he had overheard from various "villagers." He noted the foundation, even a growing base in several places, of a wall that would eventually ring the compound.

Too late, the drow thought with an evil grin.

He inched toward an opening in the house's back wall, though whether it was an actual window or just a gap that had not yet been properly fitted, he could not tell. Nor did it matter, for the missing stone provided ample egress for the lithe creature. Tos'un slithered in like a snake, walking his hands down the inside of the wall until they braced him against the floor. His roll, like all of his other movements, was executed without a whisper of sound.

The room was nearly pitch black, the meager starlight barely filtering through the many breaks in the stone. A surface dweller would have had little chance of quietly navigating the cluttered place. But to Tos'un, who had lived almost all of his life in the lightless corridors of the Underdark, the place verily glowed with brightness. He stood in the main room, twice the size of the smaller chamber sectioned by an interior wall that extended from the front wall to within three feet of the back. From beyond that partition, he heard snoring.

His two swords, one drow made and the other, the sentient and fabulous Khazid'hea, came out in his hands as he silently approached. At the wall, he peeked in to see a large orc sleeping comfortably, face down on a cot against the house's outer side wall. In the corner near the front of the house rested a large pile of rags.

He meant to quietly slide his sword into the orc's lungs, defeating its shout and finishing it quickly and silently. Khazid'hea, though, had other ideas, and as Tos'un neared and readied the strike, the sword overwhelmed him with a sudden and unexpected burst of sheer outrage.

Down came the blade, through the back of the orc's neck, severing its head and cutting through the wooden frame of the cot with ease, sparking off the floor and drawing a deep line in the hard ground. The cot dropped at the break, clunking down.

Behind Tos'un the rags rose fast, for under them was another orc, a female. Purely on reflex, the drow drove his other arm around, his fine Menzoberranyr sword coming in hard against the female's neck and pinning her up against the wall. That blade could have easily opened her throat, of course, but as he struck, Tos'un, for some reason that had not consciously registered, turned to the flat edge. He had the orc's voice choked off, and a line of blood appeared above the blade, but the creature was not finished.

For Khazid'hea would not suffer that inferior sword to score a kill.

Tos'un shushed the orc, who trembled but did not, could not, resist.

Khazid'hea plunged through her chest, right out her back and into, and through, the stones of the house's front wall.

Surprised by his own movement, Tos'un fast retracted the blade.

The orc stared at him with disbelief. She slipped down to the floor and died with that same expression.

Are you always so hungry? the drow's thoughts asked the sentient sword.

He sensed that Khazid'hea was laughing in response.

It didn't matter anyway, of course. It was just an orc, and even if it had been a superior being, Tos'un Armgo never shied from killing. With the witnesses dispatched, the alarms silenced, the drow went back into the main chamber and found the couple's store of food. He ate and drank, and replenished his pack and his waterskin. He took his time, perfectly at ease, and searched the house for anything that might be of service to him. He even went back into the bedroom, and on a whim, placed the male orc's severed head between its legs, its face pressed into its arse.

He considered his work with a resigned shrug. Like his food, the lonely drow had to take his amusement where he could find it.

He went out soon after, through the same window that had allowed him access. The night was dark—still the time of the drow. He found the orc guards no more alert than when he had come in, and he thought to kill them for their lack of discipline.

A movement in some distant trees caught his attention, however, and the drow was fast to the shadows. It took him some time to realize . . .

There were elves about.

Tos'un wasn't really surprised. Many Moonwood elves had been reconnoitering the various orc settlements and caravan routes. He had been captured by just such a band not so many tendays before, and had thought to join with them after deceiving them into believing that he was not their enemy.

Or was it really a deception? Tos'un hadn't yet decided. Surely a life among the elves would be better than what he had. He'd thought that then, and thought it again with wretched orc food still heavy in his belly.

But it was not an option, he reminded himself. Drizzt Do'Urden was with the elves, and Drizzt knew that he, Tos'un, had been part and party to King Obould's advance. Furthermore, Drizzt would take Khazid'hea from him, no doubt, and without the sword, Tos'un would be vulnerable to the spells of priests, detecting any lies he might need to weave.

Tos'un shook the futile debate from his thoughts before Khazid'hea could weigh in, and tried to get a better idea of how many elves might be watching Tungrush. He tried to pick out more movement, but found nothing substantial. The drow was wiser than to take any sense of relief from that, however, for he knew well that the elves could move with stealth akin to his own. They had, after all, surrounded him once without him ever knowing they were near.

He went out carefully, even calling upon his natural drow abilities and summoning a globe of darkness around him at one point, as he broke past the tree line. He continued his scan afterward, and even did a wide circuit of the village.

The perimeter was thick with elves, so Tos'un melted away into the winter night.

* * * * *

Albondiel's sword cut the air, and cut the throat of the orc. Gasping and clawing, the creature spun and stumbled. An arrow drove into its side, dropping it to the red-stained snow.

Another orc emerged from a house and shouted for the guards.

But the guards were all dead. All of them lay out on the perimeter, riddled with elven arrows. No alarms had sounded. The orcs of the village had not a whisper of warning.

The shouting, frantic orc tried to run, but an arrow drove her to her knees and an elf warrior was fast to her side, his sword silencing her forever.

After the initial assault, no orcs had come out in any semblance of defense. Almost all the remaining orcs were running, nothing more, to the edge of the village and beyond, willy-nilly into the snow. Most soon lay dead well within the village's perimeter, for the elves were ready, and fast and deadly with their bows.

"Enough," Albondiel called to his warriors and to the archers who moved to launch a barrage of death on the remaining fleeing orcs. "Let them run. Their terror works in our favor. Let them spread the word of doom, that more will flee beside them."

"You have little taste for this," noted another elf, a young warrior standing at Albondiel's side.

"I shy not at all from killing orcs," Albondiel answered, turning a stern gaze the upstart's way. "But this is less battle than slaughter."

"Because we were cunning in our approach."

Albondiel smirked and shrugged as if it did not matter. For indeed it did not, the wizened elf understood. The orcs had come, had swept down like a black plague, stomping underfoot all before them. They were to be repelled by any means. It was that simple.

Or was it, the elf wondered as he looked down at his latest kill, an unarmed creature, still gurgling as the last air escaped its lungs. It wore only its nightclothes.

Defenseless and dead.

Albondiel had spoken the truth in his response. He did not shy from battle, and had killed dozens of orcs in combat. Raiding villages, however, left a sour taste in his mouth.

A series of cries from across the way told him that some of the orcs had not fled or come out from their homes. He watched as one emerged from an open door, staggering, bleeding. It fell down dead.

A small one, a child.

With brutal efficiency, the elf raiding party collected the bodies in a large pile. Then they began emptying the houses of anything that would burn, tossing furniture, bedding, blankets, clothes, and all the rest on that same pile.

"Lord Albondiel," one called to him, motioning him to a small house on the village's northern perimeter.

As he approached the caller, Albondiel noted a stain of blood running down the stones at the front of the house, to the left side of the door. Following his summoner's movements, Albondiel saw the hole, a clean gash, through the stones—all the way through to the interior.

"Two were in there, dead before we arrived," the elf explained. "One was beheaded, and the other stabbed against this wall."

"Inside the wall," Albondiel remarked.

"Yes, and by a blade that came right through."

"Tos'un," Albondiel whispered, for he had been in Sinnafain's hunting party when she had captured the drow. The drow who carried Khazid'hea, the sword of Catti-brie. A sword that could cut through solid stone.

"When were they killed?" Albondiel asked.

"Before the dawn. No longer."

Albondiel shifted his gaze outward, beyond the limits of the village. "So he is still out there. Perhaps even watching us now."

"I can send scouts . . ."

"No," Albondiel answered. "There is no need, and I would have none of our people confront the rogue. Be on with our business here, and let us be gone."

Soon after, the pile of rags, wood, and bodies was set ablaze, and from that fire, the elves gathered brands with which to light the thatched roofs. Using fallen trees from the nearby woods, the elves battered down the sides of the burning structures, and any stones that could be pried from the smoking piles were quickly carried to the western side of the village, which was bordered by a long, steep slope, and were thrown down.

What the orcs had created on that windswept hilltop, the elves fast destroyed. To the ground. As if the ugly creatures had never been there.

When they left later that same morning, dark smoke still lifting into the air behind them, Albondiel swept his gaze long and wide across the rugged landscape, wondering if Tos'un might be looking back at him.

He was.

Tos'un Armgo let his gaze linger on the thickest line of black smoke drifting skyward and dissipating into the smothering gray of the continuing overcast. Though he didn't know the specific players in that scene—whether or not Albondiel or Sinnafain, or any of the others he had met, even traveled with, might be up there—they were Moonwood elves. Of that he had no doubt.

They were growing bolder, and more aggressive, and Tos'un knew why. The clouds would soon break, and the wind would shift southward, ferrying the milder breezes of spring. The elves sought to create chaos among the orc ranks. They wanted to inspire terror, confusion, and cowardice, to erode King Obould's foundations before the turn of the season allowed for the orc army to march against the dwarves in the south.

Or even across the river to the east, to the Moonwood, their precious home.

A pang of loneliness stabbed at Tos'un's thoughts and heart as he looked back at the burned village. He would have liked to join in that battle. More than that, the drow admitted, he would have liked departing with the victorious elves.

CHAPTER
FAREWELL
6

A thousand candles flickered on the northern side of the twenty-five foot square chamber, set in rows on a series of steps carved into the wall for just that purpose. A slab of gray stone leaned against the eastern wall, beside the closed wooden door. It had been expertly cut from the center of the floor, and on it, engraved in the Dethek runes of the dwarves:

> DELENIA CURTIE OF LUSKAN AND MITHRAL HALL
> WIFE OF WULFGAR, SON OF KING BRUENOR
> MOTHER OF COLSON
> WHO FELL TO THE DARKNESS OF OBOULD
> IN THE YEAR OF THE UNSTRUNG HARP
> 1371 DALERECKONING
> TO THIS HUMAN
> MORADIN OFFERS HIS CUP
> AND DUMATHOIN WHISPERS HIS SECRETS
> BLESSED IS SHE

Over the hole that had been made when the slab was removed, a stone sarcophagus rested on two heavy wooden beams. A pair of ropes ran out to either side from under it. The box was closed and sealed after Wulfgar paid his final respects.

Wulfgar, Bruenor, Drizzt, Catti-brie, and Regis stood solemnly in a line before the sarcophagus and opposite the candles, while the other guests attending the small ceremony fanned out in a semi-circle behind them. Across from them, the cleric Cordio Muffinhead read prayers to the dead. Wulfgar paid no heed to those words, but used the rhythms of Cordio's resonant voice to find a state of deep contemplation. He recalled the long and arduous road that had brought him there, from his fall in the grasp of the yochlol in the battle for Mithral Hall, to his years of torment at the hands of Errtu. He looked at Catti-brie only once, and regretted what might have been.

What might have been but could not be reclaimed, he knew. There was an old Dwarvish saying: *k'niko burger braz-pex strame*— "too much rubble over the vein"—to describe the point at which a mine simply wasn't worth the effort anymore. So it was with him and Catti-brie. Neither of them could go back. Wulfgar had known that when he had taken Delly as his wife, and he had been sincere in their relationship. That gave him comfort, but it only somewhat mitigated the pain and guilt. For though he had been sincere with Delly, he had not been much of a husband, had not heard her quiet pleas, had not placed her above all else.

Or could he even do that? Were his loyalties to Delly or to Mithral Hall?

He shook his head and pushed that justification away before it could find root. His responsibility was to bring both of those responsibilities to a place of agreement. Whatever his duties to Bruenor and Mithral Hall, he had failed Delly. To hide from that would be a lie, and a lie to himself would destroy him.

Cordio's chanting anesthetized him. He looked at the casket, and he remembered Delly Curtie, the good woman who had been his wife, and who had done so well by Colson. He accepted his own failure and he moved past it. To honor Delly would be to serve Colson, and to make of himself a better man.

Delly forgave him, he knew in his heart, as he would forgive her if the situation had been reversed. That was all they could do in the end, really. Do their best, accept their mistakes, and go on to a better way.

He felt her spirit all around him, and in him. His mind scrolled through images of the woman, flashes of Delly's smile, the tenderness on her face when they finished making love—a look, he knew without asking, that was reserved for him alone.

He recalled a moment when he had observed Delly dancing with Colson, unaware of his presence. In all the time he had known her, never had Wulfgar seen her so animated, so free, so full of life. It was as if, through Colson, and for just that moment, she had found a bit of her own childhood—or the childhood that harsh circumstances had never allowed her to truly experience. That had been Wulfgar's rawest glance into the soul of Delly Curtie, more so even than in their lovemaking.

That was the image that lingered, the image he burned into his consciousness. Forever after, he decided, when he thought of Delly Curtie, he would first envision her dancing with Colson.

A wistful smile creased his face by the time Cordio stopped his chanting. It took Wulfgar a few moments to realize that everyone was looking at him.

"He asked if you wished to say a few words," Drizzt quietly explained to Wulfgar.

Wulfgar nodded and looked around at the dwarves, and at Regis and Catti-brie.

"This is not where Delly Curtie would have chosen to be buried," he said bluntly. "For all of her love for Clan Battlehammer, she was not fond of the tunnels. But she would be . . . she *is* honored that so fine a folk have done this for her."

He looked at the casket and smiled again. "You deserved so much more than life ever offered to you. I am a better man for having known you, and I will carry you with me forever. Farewell, my wife and my love."

He felt a hand clasp his own, and turned to see Catti-brie beside him. Drizzt put his hand over both of theirs, and Regis and Bruenor moved to join in.

Delly deserved better, Wulfgar thought, and I am not deserving of such friends as these.

* * * * *

The sun climbed into the bright blue sky across the Surbrin before them. To the north along the battlements, the hammers rang out, along with a chorus of dwarf voices, singing and whistling as they went about their important work. Across the Surbrin, too, many dwarves and humans were hard at work, strengthening the bridge abutments and pillars and bringing up many of the materials they'd need to properly construct the bridge that summer. For a strong hint of spring was surely in the air that fifth day of Ches, and behind the five friends, rivulets of water danced down the stony mountainside.

"It will be a short window, I am told," Drizzt said to the others. "The river is not yet swollen with the spring melt, and so the ferry can cross. But once the melt is on in full, the pilots do not expect to execute many crossings. If you cross, you may not be able to get back until after the onset of Tarsakh, at least."

"There is no choice in the matter," said Wulfgar.

"It will take you tendays to get to Silverymoon and Sundabar and back anyway," said Regis.

"Especially since my legs aren't ready for running," said Catti-brie. She smiled as she spoke to let the others know that there was no regret or bitterness in her off-handed comment.

"Well, we ain't waitin' for Ches to become an old man," Bruenor grumbled. "If the weather's holding, then we're out for Gauntlgrym in days. I'm not for knowin' how long that's to take, but it'll be tendays, I'm guessing. Might be the whole durned summer."

Drizzt watched Wulfgar in particular, and noted the distance in the man's blue eyes. Bruenor might as well have been talking about Menzoberranzan or Calimport for all Wulfgar seemed to note or to care. He looked outward—to Colson.

And farther, Drizzt knew. It didn't matter to Wulfgar whether or not the Surbrin could be crossed again.

A few moments of silence slipped past, the five friends standing there in the morning sun. Drizzt knew that he should savor that moment, should burn it into his memory. Across from Bruenor, Regis shifted uneasily, and when Drizzt looked that way, he saw the halfling looking back at him, as if at a loss. Drizzt nodded at him and offered an accepting smile.

"The ferry docks," said Catti-brie, turning their attention to the river, where the boat was being quickly off-loaded. "Our road awaits."

Wulfgar nodded for her to lead on and make the arrangements, and with a curious glance at him, she did so, limping slightly and using Taulmaril as a crutch. As she went, Catti-brie kept glancing back, trying to decipher the curious scene. Wulfgar wore a serious expression as he spoke to the three, then he hugged each of them in turn. He ended with his hand firmly grasping Drizzt's wrist, the drow similarly holding him, and the two staring long at each other, with respect and what seemed to Catti-brie to be solemn agreement.

She suspected what that might foretell, but she turned her attention back to the river and the ferry, and cast those suspicions aside.

* * * * *

"Come on, elf," Bruenor said before Wulfgar had even caught up to Catti-brie at the ferry. "I'm wanting to get our maps in order for the trip. No time for wasting!"

Muttering to himself and rubbing his hands together, the dwarf moved back into the complex. Regis and Drizzt waited just a bit longer then turned and followed. They slowed in unison as they neared the open doors and the darkness of the corridor, and turned to look back to the river, and to the sun climbing into the sky beyond.

"Summer cannot come quickly enough for me," said Regis.

Drizzt didn't answer, but his expression wasn't one of disagreement.

"Though I almost fear it," Regis added, more quietly.

"Because the orcs will come?" asked Drizzt.

"Because others may not," said Regis, and he tossed a glance at the departing duo, who had boarded the ferry and were looking to the east, and not back.

Again, Drizzt didn't disagree. Bruenor was too preoccupied to see it, perhaps, but Regis's fears had confirmed Drizzt's suspicions about Wulfgar.

* * * * *

"Pwent's going with us," Bruenor announced to Drizzt and Regis when they caught up to him in his audience chamber later that day. As he spoke, he reached down to the side of his stone throne, lifted a pack, and tossed it to Drizzt.

"Just you three?" Regis asked, but he bit off the question as Bruenor reached down again and brought up a second pack, and tossed it the halfling's way.

Regis gave a little squeak and managed to get out of the way. The pack didn't hit the floor, though, for Drizzt snapped out his hand and plucked it from the air. The drow kept his arm extended, holding the pack out to the startled halfling.

"I'm needin' a sneak. Yerself's a sneak," Bruenor explained. "Besides, ye're the only one who's been into the place."

"Into the place?"

"Ye fell in the hole."

"I was only in there for a few moments!" Regis protested. "I didn't see anything other than the wag—"

"That makes yerself the expert," stated Bruenor.

Regis looked to Drizzt for help, but the drow just stood there holding out the satchel. With a look back to Bruenor and his unrelenting grin, the halfling gave a resigned sigh and took the pack.

"Torgar's coming, too," said Bruenor. "I'm wantin' them Mirabar boys in this from the beginning. Gauntlgrym's a Delzoun place, and Delzoun's including Torgar and his boys."

"Five, then?" asked Drizzt.

"And Cordio's making it six," Bruenor replied.

"In the morning?" asked Drizzt.

"The spring, the first of Tarsakh," Regis argued—rather helplessly, since he was holding a full pack, and since, as he spoke, he noted that Pwent, Torgar, and Cordio all entered the room from a side door, all with heavy packs slung over their shoulders, and Pwent in his full suit of ridged and spiked armor.

"No time better'n this time," said Bruenor. He stood up and gave a whistle, and a door opposite from the one the three dwarves had just used pushed open and Banak Brawnanvil rolled himself out. Behind him came a pair of younger dwarves, carrying Bruenor's mithral armor, his one-horned helmet, and his old and battle-worn axe.

"Seems our friend has been plotting without us," Drizzt remarked to Regis, who didn't seem amused.

"Yerself's got the throne and the hall," Bruenor said to Banak, and he moved down from the dais and tightly clasped his old friend's offered hand. "Ye don't be too good a steward, so that me folk won't want me back."

"Not possible, me king," said Banak. "I'd make 'em take ye back, even if it's just to guard me throne."

Bruenor answered that with a wide, toothy smile, his white teeth shining through his bushy orange-red beard. Few dwarves of Clan Battlehammer, or elsewhere for that matter, would speak to him with such irreverence, but Banak had more than earned the right.

"I'm goin' in peace because I'm knowing that I'm leaving yerself in charge behind me," Bruenor said in all seriousness.

Banak's smile disappeared and he gave his king a grateful nod.

"Come on, then, elf, and yerself, Rumblebelly," Bruenor called, slipping his mithral mail over his head and dropping his battered old one-horned helm on his head. "Me boys've dug us a hole out in the west so that we're not needing to cross all the way back over Garumn's Gorge, then back around the mountain. No time for wasting!"

"Yeah, but I'm not thinking that stoppin' to wipe out a fort o' them orcs is wastin' time," Thibbledorf Pwent remarked as he eagerly led the other two across in front of Drizzt and Regis and over to Bruenor. "Might that we'll find the dog Obould himself and be rid o' the beast all at once."

"Simply wonderful," Regis muttered, taking the pack and slinging it over his shoulder. He gave another sigh, one full of annoyance, when he saw that his small mace was strapped to the flap of the pack. Bruenor had taken care of every little detail, it seemed.

"The road to adventure, my friend," said Drizzt.

Regis smirked at him, but Drizzt only laughed. How many times had he seen that same look from the halfling over the years? Always the reluctant adventurer. But Drizzt knew, and so did everyone else in the room, that Regis was always there when needed. The sighs were just a game, a ritual that somehow allowed Regis to muster his heart and his resolve.

"I am pleased that we have an expert to lead us down this hole," Drizzt remarked quietly as they fell into line behind the trio of dwarves.

Regis sighed.

It occurred to Drizzt as they passed the room where Delly had just been interred that some were leaving who wanted to stay, and some were staying who wanted to leave. He thought of Wulfgar and wondered if that pattern would hold.

CHAPTER

THAT TINGLING FEELING

7

It looked like a simple bear den, a small hole covered by a crisscross of broken branches blanketed by snow. Tos'un Armgo knew better, for he had built that facade. The bear den was at the end of a long but shallow tunnel, chosen because it allowed Tos'un to watch a small work detail composed mostly of goblins, constructing a bridge over a trench they apparently hoped would serve as an irrigation canal through the melt.

Northeast of that, sheltered in a ravine, the elves of the Moonwood plotted. If they decided on an attack, it would come soon, that night or the next day, for it was obvious that they were running short on supplies, and shorter on arrows. Tos'un, following them south to north then northeast, realized that they were heading for their preferred ford across the Surbrin and back to the sheltering boughs of the Moonwood. The drow suspected that they wouldn't ignore a last chance at a fight.

The sun climbed in the sky behind him, and Tos'un had to squint against the painful glare off the wet snow. He noted movement in the sky to the north, and caught a glimpse of a flying horse before it swerved out of sight behind a rocky mountain jag.

The elves favored midday assaults against the usually nocturnal goblins.

Tos'un didn't have to go far to find a fine vantage point for the coming festivities. He slipped into a recess between a pair of high stones, settling back just in time to see the first volley of elven arrows lead the way into the goblin camp. The creatures began howling, hooting, and running around.

So predictable, Tos'un's fingers signaled in the intricate, silent drow code.

Of course, he had seen many goblins in his decades in the Underdark, in Menzoberranzan, where the ugly things were more numerous among the slaves than any other race—other than the kobolds who lived in the channels along the great chasm known as the Clawrift. Goblins could be molded into fierce fighting groups, but the amount of work that required made it hardly worth the effort. Their natural "fight or flight" balance leaned very heavily in the direction of the latter.

And so it was in the valley below him. Goblins rushed every which way, and on came the skilled and disciplined elf warriors, their fine blades gleaming in the sun. It looked to be a fast and uneventful rout.

But then a yellow banner, shot with red so that it looked like the bloodshot eye of an orc, appeared in the west, moving quickly through a pass between a pair of small, round-topped hills. Tos'un peered hard, and harder still as the standard-bearer and its cohorts came into view. He could almost smell them from his perch. They were orcs, but huge by orc standards, even more broad-shouldered than Obould's elite guards, some even bigger than Obould himself.

So caught up in the spectacle, Tos'un stood up and leaned forward, out of the shelter of the stones. He looked back to the rout, and saw that there, too, things had changed, for other groups of those hulking orcs had appeared, some coming up from under the snow near the center of the battle.

"A trap for the elves," the drow whispered in disbelief. A myriad of thoughts flitted through his mind at that realization. Did he want the elves destroyed? Did he care?

He didn't allow himself time to sort through those emotions, though, for the drow realized that he, too, might get swept up in the tumult—and that was something he most certainly did not want.

He looked back to the approaching banner, then to the fight, then back again, measuring the time. With a quick glance all around to ensure his own safety, he rushed out from his perch and back to the hidden tunnel entrance. When he got there, he saw that the battle had been fully joined, and fully reversed.

The elves, badly outnumbered, were on the run. They didn't flee like the goblins, though, and kept their defenses in place against incursions from the brutish orcs. They even managed a couple of stop-and-pivot maneuvers that allowed them to send a volley of arrows at the orc mass.

But that dark wall rolled on after them.

The winged horse appeared again, flying low over the battlefield then climbing gradually as it passed over the orcs, who of course threw a few spears in its direction. The rider and pegasus went up even higher as they glided over the elves.

The rider meant to direct the retreat, obviously, and good fortune sent the winged horse in Tos'un's general direction. As it neared, the drow's eyes widened, for though looking up at the midday sky surely stung his sensitive eyes, he recognized that elf rider, Sinnafain.

For a moment, the drow held his position just inside the tunnel, not sure whether to retreat through the passage or go back out into Sinnafain's view.

Hardly aware of his movements, he came out of that hole and waved at Sinnafain, and when she didn't look his way, he called out to her.

What are you doing? Khazid'hea imparted to him.

The sudden jerk of the reins had the pegasus banking sharply and told Tos'un that Sinnafain had spotted him. He took some comfort in the fact that her next movement was not to draw out her bow.

You would go back to them? Khazid'hea asked and the telepathic communication was edged with no small amount of anger.

Sinnafain brought the winged horse in a slow turn, her eyes locked on the drow the entire time. She was too far away for Tos'un to see her face or fathom what she might be thinking, but still she did not draw her bow. Nor had she signaled to her retreating friends to veer away.

Drizzt will kill you! Khazid'hea warned. *When he takes me from you, you will find yourself defenseless against the truth-finding spells of elf clerics!*

Tos'un lifted the twig barrier that covered his hole, and began motioning to the entrance.

Sinnafain continued to guide the pegasus in a slow circle. When she at last turned back to her companions, Tos'un sprinted off to the side, disappearing into the shadows of the foothills, much to the relief of his demanding sword.

The drow glanced back only one time, to see the elves filtering into the tunnel. He looked up for the pegasus, but it had flown over the ridge and out of sight at that moment.

But Sinnafain had trusted him.

Unbelievably, Sinnafain had trusted him.

Tos'un wasn't sure whether he should take pride in that, or whether his respect for the elves had just diminished.

Perhaps a bit of both.

* * * * *

Sinnafain couldn't track their progress, nor could she join her comrades in the tunnel, obviously, while riding Sunrise. She came back over the high ridge and flew near the entrance of the small cave. She drew out her bow and began peppering the leading edge of the orc advance.

She kept up her barrage even after all the elves had disappeared underground. But the huge orcs carried heavy shields to frustrate such attacks, and Sinnafain could only hope that she had held them back long enough for her friends to escape. She put Sunrise up higher then, and angled back the other way, over the rise once more. She looked for Tos'un as much as for her friends, but there was no sign of the drow.

A long while later, with Sunrise tiring beneath her, the elf was finally able to breathe a sigh of relief, as a flash of white from a copse of trees some distance to the east signaled to her that Albondiel and the other elves had gotten through the tunnel.

Sinnafain took a roundabout route to get to them, not wanting to tip off any orc spotters who might watch her descending from on high, and by the time she got down to the ground, much activity was already underway. Deep in the woods, in a small clearing, the wounded had been laid out side by side, with priests tending them. Another group carried heavy logs and stones to seal the tunnel exit, and the rest had taken to the trees on the perimeter of the copse, setting up a defensive line that allowed them many overlapping angles of fire on approaching enemies.

As she walked Sunrise along a path through the trees, Sinnafain heard whispers of King Obould over and over again, many of the elves certain that he had come. She found Albondiel near the wounded, standing off to the side of the field and sorting the extra packs and weapons.

"You saved many," Albondiel greeted when she approached. "Had you not directed us to that tunnel, more of us would have fallen. Perhaps a complete rout."

Sinnafain thought to mention that it was not her doing, but that of a certain drow, but she kept the thought to herself. "How many were taken down?"

"Four casualties," Albondiel said grimly. He nodded toward the small field, where the quartet of wounded lay on blankets on the snow. "Two of them were wounded seriously, perhaps mortally."

"We . . . *I*, should have seen the trap from on high," Sinnafain said, turning back to the ridge in the east that blocked the view of the battlefield.

"The orc ambush was well set," Albondiel replied. "Those who prepared this battlefield understood our tactics well. They have studied us and learned to counter our methods. Perhaps it is time for us to head back across the Surbrin."

"We are low on supplies," Sinnafain reminded him.

"Perhaps it is time for us to *stay* across the Surbrin," Albondiel clarified.

Again, thoughts of a certain dark elf popped into Sinnafain's mind. Had Tos'un betrayed them? He had fought beside them for a short while, and he knew much of their tactics. Plus, he was a drow, and no race in all the world knew better how to lay an ambush than the treacherous dark elves. Though of course, he had shown the elves the way to escape. With any other race, that alone might serve to dispel Sinnafain's suspicions. But Sinnafain could not allow herself to forget that Tos'un was a dark elf, and no Drizzt Do'Urden, who had proven himself repeatedly over a matter of years. Perhaps Tos'un was playing the elves and orcs against each other for personal gain, or simply for his own amusement.

"Sinnafain?" Albondiel asked, drawing her from her contemplations. "The Surbrin? The Moonwood?"

"You believe that we are finished here?" Sinnafain asked.

"The weather warms, and the orcs will find it easier to move in the coming days. They will be less isolated from each other and so our work here will become more difficult."

"And they have taken note of us."

"It is time to leave," said Albondiel.

Sinnafain nodded and looked to the east. In the distance, the silvery line of the Surbrin could just be seen, flickering out on the horizon.

"Would that we could collect Tos'un on our way," said Sinnafain. "I have much to ask that one."

Albondiel looked at her with surprise for just a few moments then nodded his agreement. Though seemingly out of context, it sounded like a reasonable desire—of course they both knew that they weren't going to catch a drow in those wilds anytime soon.

* * * * *

I know them, Tos'un assured the doubting Khazid'hea. *Dnark is chieftain of an important tribe. I was the one who coaxed him into Obould's coalition before they ever marched from the Spine of the World.*

Much has happened, Khazid'hea reminded him, *between Tos'un and Obould. If these three know of your last encounter with the orc king, they will not welcome you.*

They were not there, Tos'un assured the sword.

They have not heard of the fall of Kaer'lic Suun Wett? Khazid'hea asked. *Can you be certain?*

Even if they have, they are well aware of Obould's temper, Tos'un imparted. *They will accept that he was outraged at Kaer'lic, and so he killed her. Do you believe that any of these orcs have not lost friends to the temper of Obould? And yet they remain loyal to him.*

You risk much.

I risk nothing, Tos'un argued. *If Dnark and his friends know that Obould hunts for me, or if they have concluded that I am in league with the elves, then I . . . then we, will have to kill them. I did not expect that such a result would displease Khazid'hea.*

There, he had communicated the magic words, he knew, for the sword fell silent in his thoughts, and he even sensed eagerness coming from it. He considered the exchange as he made his way down toward the trio of orcs, who had drifted off to the side of the construction area where the unusually large orcs had gathered. He came to the conclusion that he had been paid a compliment, that Khazid'hea did not want to be pried from his grasp.

He chose his path to the three orcs carefully, allowing himself a fast route of escape should the need arise—and he feared it would. Several times he paused to search the surrounding area for any guards he might have missed.

Still some distance from the three, he called out the expected, respectful refrain to the chieftain. "Hail Dnark, may the Wolf Jaw bite strong," he said in his best Orcish, but with no attempt to hide his Underdark drow accent. He watched carefully then to gauge their initial reaction, knowing that to be the bare truth.

All three turned his way, their expressions showing surprise, even shock. Tellingly, however, not one flinched toward a weapon.

"To the throat of your enemy," Tos'un finished the Wolf Jaw tribe's salute. He continued his approach, noting that Ung-thol, the older shaman, visibly relaxed, but that the younger Toogwik Tuk remained very much on edge.

"Well met, again," Tos'un offered, and he climbed the last small rise to gain the sheltered flat ground the trio had staked out. "We have come far from the holes in the Spine of the World, as I predicted to you those months ago."

"Greetings, Tos'un of Menzoberranzan," said Dnark.

The drow measured the chieftain's voice as cautious, and neither warm or cold.

"I am surprised to see you," Dnark finished.

"We have learned the fate of your companions," Ung-thol added.

Tos'un stiffened, and had to consciously remind himself not to grasp his sword hilts. "Yes, Donnia Soldou and Ad'non Kareese," he said. "I have heard their sad fate, and a curse upon the murderous Drizzt Do'Urden."

The three orcs exchanged smug grins. They knew of the murdered priestess, Tos'un realized.

"And pity to Kaer'lic," he said lightly, as if it didn't really matter. "Foolish was she who angered mighty Obould." He found a surprising response to that from Toogwik Tuk, for the young orc's smile disappeared, and his lips grew tight.

"She and you, so it is said," Ung-thol replied.

"I will prove my value again."

"To Obould?" asked Dnark.

The question caught the drow off-balance, for he had no idea of where the chieftain might be going with it.

"Is there another who would seek that value?" he asked, keeping enough sarcasm out of his tone so that Dnark might seize it as an honest question if he so chose.

"There are many above ground now, and scattered throughout the Kingdom of Many-Arrows," said Dnark. He glanced back at the hulking orcs milling around the construction area. "Grguch of Clan Karuck has come."

"I just witnessed his ferocity in routing the cursed surface elves."

"Strong allies," said Dnark.

"To Obould?" Tos'un asked without hesitation, turning the question back in similar measure.

"To Gruumsh," said Dnark with a toothy grin. "To the destruction of Clan Battlehammer and all the wretched dwarves and all the ugly elves."

"Strong allies," said Tos'un.

They are not pleased with King Obould, Khazid'hea said in the drow's mind. Tos'un didn't respond, other than to not disagree. *An interesting turn.*

Again the drow didn't disagree. A tingling feeling came over him, that exciting sensation that befell many of Lady Lolth's followers when they first discovered that an opportunity for mischief might soon present itself.

He thought of Sinnafain and her kin, but didn't dwell on them. The joy of chaos came precisely from the reality that it was often so very easy, and not requiring too much deep contemplation. Perhaps the coming mayhem would benefit the elves, perhaps the orcs, Dnark or Obould, one or both. That was not for Tos'un to determine. His duty was to ensure that no matter which way the tumult broke, he would be in the best position to survive and to profit.

For all of his time with the elves of late, for all of his fantasies of living among the surface folk, Tos'un Armgo remained, first and foremost, drow.

He sensed clearly that Khazid'hea very much approved.

*****

Grguch was not pleased. He stomped across the hillside before the tunnel entrance and all of Clan Karuck fled before him. All except for Hakuun, of course. Hakuun could not flee before Grguch. It was not permitted. If Grguch decided that he wanted to kill Hakuun then Hakuun had to accept that as his fate. Being the shaman of Clan Karuck carried such a responsibility, and it was one that Hakuun's family had accepted throughout the generations—and was one that had cost more than a few of his family their lives.

He knew that Grguch would not cleave him in half, though. The chieftain was angry that the elves had escaped, but the battle could not be called anything but a victory for Clan Karuck. Not only had they stung a few of the elves, but they had sent them running, and had it not been for that troublesome tunnel, the raiding elf band never would have escaped complete and utter ruin.

The hulking brutes of Clan Karuck could not follow them through that tunnel, however, to Grguch's ultimate frustration.

"This will not end here," he said in Hakuun's face.

"Of course not."

"I desired a greater statement to be made in our first meeting with these ugly faerie folk."

"The fleeing elves wore expressions of terror," Hakuun replied. "That will spread back to their people."

"Right before we fall upon them more decisively."

Hakuun paused, expecting the order.

"Plan it," said Grguch. "To their very home."

Hakuun nodded, and Grguch seemed satisfied with that and turned away, barking orders at the others. Elves were just the sort of cowardly creatures to run away and sneak back for quiet murder, of course, and so the chieftain began setting his defenses and his scouts, leaving Hakuun alone with his thoughts.

Or so Hakuun believed.

He flinched then froze when the foot-long serpent landed on his shoulder, and he held his breath, as he always did on those thankfully rare occasions when he found himself in the company of Jaculi—for that was the name that Jack had given him, the name of the winged serpent that Jack wore as a disguise when venturing out of his private workshops.

"I wish that you had informed me of your departure," Jack said in Hakuun's ear.

"I did not want to disturb you," Hakuun meekly replied, for it was hard for him to hold his steadiness with Jack's tongue flicking in his ear, close enough to send one of his forked lightning bolts right through the other side of poor Hakuun's head.

"Clan Karuck disturbs me often," Jack reminded him. "Sometimes I believe that you have told the others of me."

"Never that, O Awful One!"

Jack's laughter came out as a hiss. When he had first begun his domination and deception of the orcs those decades before, pragmatism alone had ruled his actions. But through the years he had come to accept the truth of it: he liked scaring the wits out of those ugly creatures! Truly, that was one of the few pleasures remaining for Jack the Gnome, who lived a life of simplicity and . . . And what? Boredom, he knew, and it stung him to admit it to himself. In the secret corners of his heart, Jack understood precisely why he had followed Karuck out of the caves: because his fear of danger, even of death, could not surmount his fear of letting everything stay the same.

"Why have you ventured out of the Underdark?" he demanded.

Hakuun shook his head. "If the tidings are true then there is much to be gained here."

"For Clan Karuck?"

"Yes."

"For Jaculi?"

Hakuun gulped and swallowed hard, and Jack hiss-laughed again into his ear.

"For Gruumsh," Hakuun dared whisper.

As weakly as it was said, that still gave Jack pause. For all of his domination of Hakuun's family, their fanatical service to Gruumsh had never been in question. It had once taken Jack an afternoon of torture to make one of Hakuun's ancestors—his grandfather, Jack believed, though he couldn't really remember—utter a single word against Gruumsh, and even then, the priest had soon after passed his duties down to his chosen son and killed himself in Gruumsh's name.

As he had in the cave, the gnome wizard sighed. With Gruumsh invoked, he wasn't about to turn Clan Karuck around.

"We shall see," he whispered into Hakuun's ear, and said to himself as well, a resigned acceptance that sometimes the stubborn orcs had their own agenda.

Perhaps he could find some amusement and profit out of it, and really, what did he have to lose? He sniffed the air again, and again sensed that something was different.

"There are many orcs about," he said.

"Tens of thousands," Hakuun confirmed. "Come to the call of King Obould Many-Arrows."

Many-Arrows, Jack thought, a name that registered deep in his memories of long ago. He thought of Citadel Fel . . . Citadel Felb . . . Fel-something-or-other, a place of dwarves. Jack didn't much like dwarves. They annoyed him at least as much as did the orcs, with their hammering and stupid chanting that they somehow, beyond all reason, considered song.

"We shall see," he said again to Hakuun, and noting that the ugly Grguch was fast approaching, Jack slithered down under Hakuun's collar to nestle in the small of his back. Every now and then, he flicked his forked tongue against Hakuun's bare flesh just for the fun of hearing the shaman stutter in his discussion with the beastly Grguch.

PART 2

GAUNTLGRYM

GAUNTLGRYM

I came from the Underdark, the land of monsters. I lived in Icewind Dale, where the wind can freeze a man solid, or a bog can swallow a traveler so quickly that he'll not likely understand what is happening to him soon enough to let out a cry, unless it is one muffled by loose mud. Through Wulfgar I have glimpsed the horrors of the Abyss, the land of demons, and could there be any place more vile, hate-filled, and tormenting? It is indeed a dangerous existence.

I have surrounded myself with friends who will fearlessly face those monsters, the wind and the bog, and the demons, with a snarl and a growl, a jaw set and a weapon held high. None would face them more fearlessly than Bruenor, of course.

But there is something to shake even that one, to shake us all as surely as if the ground beneath our feet began to tremble and break away.

Change.

In any honest analysis, change is the basis of fear, the idea of something new, of some paradigm that is unfamiliar, that is beyond our experiences so completely that we cannot even truly predict where it will lead us. Change. Uncertainty.

It is the very root of our most primal fear—the fear of death—that one change, that one unknown against which we construct elaborate scenarios and "truisms" that may or may not be true at all. These constructions, I think, are an extension of the routines of our lives. We dig ruts with the sameness of our daily paths, and drone and rail against those routines while we, in fact, take comfort in them. We awake and construct our days of habit, and follow the norms we have built fast, solid, and bending only a bit in our daily existence. Change is the unrolled die, the unused *sava* piece. It is exciting and frightening only when we hold some power over it, only when there is a potential reversal of course, difficult though it may be, within our control.

Absent that safety line of real choice, absent that sense of some control, change is merely frightening. Terrifying, even.

An army of orcs does not scare Bruenor. Obould Many-Arrows does not scare Bruenor. But what Obould represents, particularly if the orc king halts his march and establishes a kingdom, and more especially if the other kingdoms of the Silver Marches accept this new paradigm, terrifies Bruenor Battlehammer to the heart of his being and to the core tenets of his faith. Obould threatens more than Bruenor's kin, kingdom, and life. The orc's designs shake the very belief system that binds Bruenor's kin, the very purpose of Mithral Hall, the understanding of what it is to be a dwarf, and the dwarven concept of where the orcs fit into that stable continuum. He would not say it openly, but I suspect that Bruenor hopes the orcs will attack, that they will, in the end, behave in accordance with his expectations of orcs and of all goblinkind. The other possibility is too dissonant, too upsetting, too contrary to Bruenor's very identity for him to entertain the plausibility, indeed the probability, that it would result in less suffering for all involved.

I see before me the battle for the heart of Bruenor Battlehammer, and for the hearts of all the dwarves of the Silver Marches.

Easier by far to lift a weapon and strike dead a known enemy, an orc.

In all the cultures I have known, with all the races I have walked beside, I have observed that when beset by such dissonance, by events that are beyond control and that plod along at their own pace, the frustrated onlookers often seek out a beacon, a focal point—a god, a person, a place, a magical item—which they believe will set all the world aright. Many are the whispers in Mithral Hall that King Bruenor will fix it, all of it, and make everything as it had been before the onslaught of Obould. Bruenor has earned their respect many times over, and wears the mantle of hero among his kin as comfortably and deservedly as has any dwarf in the history of the clan. For most of the dwarves here, then, King Bruenor has become the beacon and focal point of hope itself.

Which only adds to Bruenor's responsibility, because when a frightened people put their faith in an individual, the ramifications of incompetence, recklessness, or malfeasance are multiplied many times over. And so becoming the focus of hope only adds to Bruenor's tension. Because he knows that it is not true, and that their expectations may well be beyond him. He cannot convince Lady Alustriel of Silverymoon or any of the other leaders, not even King Emerus Warcrown of Citadel Felbarr, to march in force against Obould. And to go out alone with Mithral Hall's own forces would lead to the wholesale slaughter of Clan Battlehammer. Bruenor understands that he has to wear the mantle not only of hero, but of savior, and it is for him a terrible burden.

And so Bruenor, too, has engaged in deflection and wild expectation, has found a focal point on which to pin his hopes. The most common phrase he has spoken throughout this winter has been, "Gauntlgrym, elf."

Gauntlgrym. It is a legend among Clan Battlehammer and all the Delzoun dwarves. It is the name of their common heritage, an immense city of splendor, wealth, and strength that represents to every descendant of the Delzoun tribes the apex of dwarven civilization. It is, perhaps, history wound with myth, a likely unintentional lionizing of that which once was. As heroes of old take on more gigantic proportions with each passing generation, so too does this other focal point of hope and pride expand.

"Gauntlgrym, elf," Bruenor says with steady determination. All of his answers lie there, he is certain. In Gauntlgrym, Bruenor will find a path to unravel the doings of King Obould. In Gauntlgrym, he will discover how to put the orcs back in their holes, and more importantly, how to realign the races of the Silver Marches into proper position, into places that make sense to an old, immovable dwarf.

He believes that we found this magical kingdom on our journey here from the Sword Coast. He has to believe that this unremarkable sinkhole in a long-dead pass was really the entrance to a place where he can find his answers.

Otherwise he has to become the answer for his anxious people. And Bruenor knows that their faith is misplaced, for at present, he has no answer to the puzzle that is Obould.

Thus, he says, "Gauntlgrym, elf," with the same conviction that a devout believer will utter the name of his savior god.

We will go to this place, this hole in the ground in a barren pass in the west. We will go and find Gauntlgrym, whatever that may truly mean. Perhaps Bruenor's instincts are correct—could it be that Moradin told him of this in his days of near death? Perhaps we will find something entirely different, but that will still bring to us, to Bruenor, the clarity he needs to find the answers for Mithral Hall.

Fixated and desperate as he is, and as his people are, Bruenor doesn't yet understand that the name he has affixed to our savior is not the point. The point is the search itself, for solutions and for the truth, and not the place he has determined as our goal.

"Gauntlgrym, elf."

Indeed.

—Drizzt Do'Urden

CHAPTER

THE FIRST STRIDES HOME

8

The gates of Silverymoon, shining silver and with bars decorated like leafy vines, were closed, a clear signal that things were amiss in the Silver Marches. Stern-faced guards, elf and human, manned all posts along the city's wall and around a series of small stone houses that served as checkpoints for approaching visitors.

Catti-brie—limping more profoundly from her days on the road—and Wulfgar noted the tense looks coming their way. The woman merely smiled, though, understanding that her companion, nearly seven feet tall and with shoulders broad and strong, could elicit such trepidation even in normal times. Predictably, those nervous guards relaxed and even offered waves as the pair neared, as they came to recognize the barbarian in his trademark wolf-skin cloak and the woman who had often served as liaison between Mithral Hall and Silverymoon.

There was no call for the pair to stop or even slow as they passed the stone structures, and the gate parted before them without request. Several of the sentries near that gate and atop the wall even began clapping for Wulfgar and Catti-brie and more than a few "huzzahs" were shouted as they passed.

"With official word or for pleasure alone?" the commander of the guard asked the couple inside the city gates. He looked at Catti-brie with obvious concern. "Milady, are you injured?"

Catti-brie replied with a dismissive look, as if it did not matter, but the guard continued, "I will provide a coach for you at once!"

"I have walked from Mithral Hall through snow and mud," the woman replied. "I would not deny myself the joy of Silverymoon's meandering ways."

"But..."

"I will walk," Catti-brie said. "Do not deny me this pleasure."

The guard relented with a bow. "Lady Alustriel will be pleased by your arrival."

"And we will be pleased to see her," said Wulfgar.

"With official word from King Bruenor?" the commander asked again.

"With word more personal, but equally pressing," the barbarian answered. "You will announce us?"

"The courier is already on his way to the palace."

Wulfgar nodded his gratitude. "We will walk the ways of Silverymoon, a course not direct, and will arrive at Lady Alustriel's court before the sun has passed its zenith," he explained. "Pleased we are to be here—truly Silverymoon is a welcomed sight and a welcoming city for road-weary travelers. Our business here might well include you and your men as well, commander...."

"Kenyon," said Catti-brie, for she had met the man on many occasions, though briefly at each.

"I am honored that you remember me, Lady Catti-brie," he said with another bow.

"We arrive in search of refugees who have come from Mithral Hall and may have crossed into your fairest of cities," said Wulfgar.

"Many have come," Kenyon admitted. "And many have left. But of course, we are at your disposal, son of Bruenor, on word of Lady Alustriel. Go and secure that word, I bid you."

Wulfgar nodded, and he and Catti-brie moved past the guard station.

With their road-weathered clothes, one with a magical bow as a crutch and the other a giant of a man with a magnificent warhammer strapped across his back, the pair stood out in the city of philosophers and poets, and many a curious look turned their way as they walked the winding, seemingly aimless avenues of the decorated city. As with every visitor to Silverymoon, no matter how many times one traversed the place, their eyes were continually drawn upward, studying the intricate designs and artwork that covered the walls of every building, and upward still, to the tapering spires that topped every structure. Most communities were an expression of utility, with structures built suitable to the elements of their environment and the threats of regional monsters. Cities of commerce were built with wide avenues, port cities with fortified harbors and breakwaters, and frontier towns with thick walls. Silverymoon stood above all of these, for it was an expression of utility, of course, but more than that, an expression of spirit. Security and commerce were facilitated, but they were not paramount to the needs of the soul, where the library was grander than the barracks and the avenues were designed to turn visitors and residents to the most spectacular of views, rather than as efficient straight lines to the marketplace or the rows of houses and mercantiles.

It was hard to arrive in Silverymoon with urgent business, for few could walk swiftly through those streets, and fewer still could focus the mind sufficiently to defeat the intrusions of beauty.

Contrary to Wulfgar's stated expectations, the sun had passed its zenith before Wulfgar and Catti-brie came in sight of Lady Alustriel's wondrous palace, but that was all right, for the experienced guards had informed the Lady of Silverymoon that such would be the case.

"The finest humans of Clan Battlehammer," said the tall woman, coming out from behind the curtains that separated this private section of her palatial audience chamber from the main, public promenade.

There was no overt malice in her humorous remark, though of course the couple standing before her, the adopted son and daughter of King Bruenor, were the only humans of Clan Battlehammer. Wulfgar smiled and chuckled, but Catti-brie didn't quite find that level of mirth within her.

She stared at the great woman, Lady Alustriel, one of the Seven Sisters and leader of magnificent Silverymoon. She only remembered to offer a bow when Wulfgar dipped beside her, and even then, Catti-brie did not lower her head as she bent, staring intently at Alustriel.

For despite herself, Catti-brie was intimidated. Alustriel was nearly six feet tall and undeniably beautiful, by human standards, by elven standards—by any standards. Even the creatures of the higher planes would be pleased by her presence, Catti-brie knew in her heart, for there was a luminescence and gravity about Alustriel that was somehow beyond mortal existence. Her hair was silver and lustrous, and hung thick to her shoulders, and her eyes could melt a man's heart or strip him of all courage at her will. Her gown was a simple affair, green with golden stitching, and just a few emeralds sewn for effect. Most kings and queens wore robes far more decorated and elaborate, of course, but Alustriel didn't need any ornamentation. Any room that she entered was her room to command.

She had never shown Catti-brie anything but kindness and friendship, and the two had been quite warm on occasion. But Catti-brie hadn't seen Alustriel much of late, and she could not help but feel somewhat smaller in the great woman's presence. Once she had been jealous of the Lady of Silverymoon, hearing rumors that Alustriel had been Drizzt's lover, and she had never discerned whether or not that had been the case.

Catti-brie smiled genuinely and laughed at herself, and pushed all of the negative thoughts aside. She couldn't be jealous where Drizzt was concerned anymore, nor could she feel diminished by anyone when she thought of her relationship with the drow.

What did it matter if the gods themselves bowed to Lady Alustriel? For Drizzt had chosen Catti-brie.

To Catti-brie's surprise, Alustriel walked right over and embraced her, and kissed her on the cheek.

"Too many months pass between our visits, milady," Alustriel said, moving Catti-brie back to arms' length. She reached up and pushed back a thick strand of Catti-brie's auburn hair. "How you manage to stay so beautiful, as if the dirt of the road cannot touch you, I will never know."

Catti-brie hardly knew how to reply.

"You could fight a battle with a thousand orcs," Alustriel went on, "slay them all—of course—and bloody your sword, your fist, and your boots. Not even that stain would diminish your glow."

Catti-brie gave a self-deprecating laugh. "Milady, you are too kind," she said. "Too kind for reason, I fear."

"Of course you do, daughter of Bruenor. You are a woman who grew up among dwarves, who hardly appreciated your charms and your beauty. You have no idea of how tall you would stand among those of your own race."

Catti-brie's face twisted a bit in confusion, not quite knowing how to take that.

"And that, too, is part of the charm of Catti-brie," said Alustriel. "Your humility is not calculated, it is intrinsic."

Catti-brie looked no less confused, and that drew a bit of laughter from Wulfgar. Catti-brie shot him a frown to silence him.

"The wind whispers that you have taken Drizzt as your husband," Alustriel said.

Still glancing Wulfgar's way as Alustriel spoke, Catti-brie noted a slight grimace on the barbarian's face—or maybe it was just her imagination.

"You are married?" Alustriel asked.

"Yes," Catti-brie replied. "But we have not celebrated in formal ceremony yet. We will wait for the darkness of Obould to recede."

Alustriel's face grew very serious. "That will be a long time, I fear."

"King Bruenor is determined that it will not."

"Indeed," said Alustriel, and she offered a hopeful little smile and a shrug. "I do hope you will celebrate your joining with Drizzt Do'Urden soon, both in Mithral Hall, and here in Silverymoon, as my honored guests. I will gladly open the palace to you, for many of my subjects would wish well the daughter of good King Bruenor and that most unusual dark elf."

"And many of your court would prefer that Drizzt remain in Mithral Hall," Catti-brie said, a bit more harshly than she had intended.

But Alustriel only laughed and nodded, for it was true enough, and undeniable. "Well, Fret likes him," she said, referring to her favored advisor, a most unusual and uniquely tidy dwarf. "And Fret likes you, and so do I—both of you. If I spent my time worrying over the pettiness and posturing of court lords and ladies, I would turn endless circles of appeasement and apology."

"When you doubt, then trust in Fret," Catti-brie said. She winked and Alustriel gave a hearty laugh and hugged her again.

As she did, she whispered into Catti-brie's ear, "Come here more often, I beg of you, with or without your stubborn dark elf companion."

She stepped up to Wulfgar then and wrapped him in a warm embrace. When she moved back to arms' length, a curious look came over her. "Son of Beornegar," she said quietly, respectfully.

Catti-brie's mouth dropped open in surprise at that, for only recently had Wulfgar been wearing that title more regularly, and it seemed to her as if Alustriel had somehow just discerned that.

"I see contentment in your blue eyes," Alustriel remarked. "You have not been at peace like this ever before—not even when I first met you, those many years ago."

"I was young then, and too strong of spirit," said Wulfgar.

"Can one ever be?"

Wulfgar shrugged. "Too anxious, then," he corrected.

"You hold your strength deeper now, because you are more secure in it, and in how you wish to use it."

Wulfgar's nod seemed to satisfy Alustriel, but Catti-brie just kept looking from the large man to the tall woman. She felt as if they were speaking in code, or half-saying secrets, the other half of which were known only to them.

"You are at peace," said Alustriel.

"And yet I am not," Wulfgar replied. "For my daugh—the girl, Colson, is lost to me."

"She was slain?"

Wulfgar shook his head immediately to calm the gentle woman. "Delly Curtie was lost to the hordes of Obould, but Colson lives. She was sent across the river in the company of refugees from the conquered northern lands."

"Here to Silverymoon?"

"That is what I would know," Wulfgar explained.

Alustriel nodded and stepped back, taking them both in with her protective stare.

"We could go from inn to inn," Catti-brie said. "But Silverymoon is no small city, nor is Sundabar, and there are many more villages about."

"You will remain right here as my guests," Alustriel insisted. "I will call out every soldier of Silverymoon's garrison, and will speak with the merchant guilds. You will have your answer in short time, I promise."

"You are too generous," Wulfgar said with a bow.

"Would King Bruenor, would Wulfgar or Catti-brie, offer any less to me or one of mine if we similarly came to Mithral Hall?"

That simple truth ended any forthcoming arguments from the two grateful travelers.

"We thought that we might travel to some of the common inns and ask around," Catti-brie said.

"And draw attention to your hunt?" Alustriel replied. "Would this person who has Colson wish to give the child back to you?"

Wulfgar shook his head, but Catti-brie said, "We don't know, but it is possible that she would not."

"Then better for you to remain here, as my guests. I have many contacts who frequent the taverns. It is important for a leader to hear the commoners' concerns. The answers you seek will be easily found—in Silverymoon, at least." She motioned to her attendants. "Take them and make them comfortable. I do believe that Fret wishes to see Catti-brie."

"He cannot suffer the dirt of the road upon me," Catti-brie remarked dryly.

"Only because he cares, of course."

"Or because he so despises dirt?"

"That too," Alustriel admitted.

Catti-brie looked to Wulfgar and offered a resigned shrug. She was pleasantly surprised to see him equally at ease with this arrangement. Apparently he understood that their work was better left to Alustriel, and that they could indeed relax and enjoy the respite at the luxurious palace of the Lady of Silverymoon.

"And she came without proper clothing, I'll wager!" came an obviously annoyed voice, a chant that sounded both melodic and sing-song like an elf, and resonant like the bellow of a dwarf—a most unusual dwarf.

Wulfgar and Catti-brie turned to see the fellow, dressed in a fine white gown with bright green trim, enter the room. He looked at Catti-brie and gave a disapproving sigh and a wag of his meticulously manicured stubby finger. Then he stopped and sighed again, and put his chin in one hand, his fingers stroking the thin line of his well-trimmed silver beard as he considered the task of transforming Catti-brie.

"Well met, Fret," Alustriel said. "It would seem that you have your work cut out for you. Do try not to break this one's spirit."

"You confuse spirit with odor, milady."

Catti-brie frowned, but it was hard for her to cover her inner smile.

"Fret would put perfume and bells on a tiger, I do believe," Alustriel said, and her nearby attendants shared a laugh at the dwarf's expense.

"And colored bows and paint for its nails," the tidy dwarf proudly replied. He walked up to Catti-brie, gave a "tsk tsk," and grabbed her by the elbow, pulling her along. "As we appreciate beauty, so it is our divine task to facilitate it. And so I shall. Now come along, child. You've a long bath to suffer."

Catti-brie flashed her smile back at Wulfgar. After their long and arduous journey, she planned to "suffer" it well.

Wulfgar's returned smile was equally genuine. He turned to Alustriel, saluted, and thanked her.

"What might we do for Wulfgar while my scouts seek word of Colson?" Alustriel asked him.

"A quiet room with a view of your fair city," he replied, and he added quietly, "One that faces to the west."

* * * * *

Catti-brie caught up to Wulfgar early that evening on a high balcony of the main turret—one of a dozen that adorned the palace.

"The dwarf has his talents," Wulfgar said.

Catti-brie's freshly washed hair smelled of lilac and springtime. She almost always kept it loose to bounce over her shoulders, but she had one side tied up and the other had a hint of a curl teased into it. She wore a light blue gown that enhanced and highlighted the hue of her eyes, its straps revealing the smooth skin of her delicate shoulders. A white and gold sash was tied around her waist at an angle and a place to accentuate her shapely body. The dress did not go all the way to the floor, and Wulfgar's surprise showed as a smile when he noted that she wasn't wearing her doeskin boots, but rather a pair of delicate slippers, all lace and fancy trim.

"I found meself a choice to let him do it to me or punch him in the nose," Catti-brie remarked, her self-deprecation exaggerated because she allowed just a hint of her Dwarvish accent to come through.

"There is not a part of you that enjoys it?"

Catti-brie scowled at him.

"You would not wish for Drizzt to see you like this?" the barbarian pressed. "You would take no pleasure in the look upon his face?"

"I'll take me pleasure in killing orcs."

"Stop it."

Catti-brie looked at him as if he had slapped her.

"Stop it," Wulfgar repeated. "You need not your boots or your weapons here in Silverymoon, or your dwarf-bred pragmatism and that long-lost accent. Have you looked in the mirror since Fret worked his magic on you?"

Catti-brie snorted and turned away, or started to, but Wulfgar held her with his gaze and his grin.

"You should," he said.

"You are talking foolishness," Catti-brie replied, and her accent was no more.

"Far from that. Is it foolish to enjoy the sights of Silverymoon?" He half-turned and swept his arm out to the deepening gloom in the west, to the twilit structures of the free-form city, with candles burning in many windows. Glowing flames of harmless faerie fire showed on a few of the spires, accenting their inviting forms.

"Did you not allow your mind to wander as we walked through the avenues to this palace?" Wulfgar asked. "Could you help but feel that way with beauty all around you? So why is it any different with your own appearance? Why are you so determined to hide behind mud and simple clothes?"

Catti-brie shook her head. Her lips moved a few times as if she wanted to reply but couldn't find the words.

"Drizzt would be pleased by the sight before him," Wulfgar stated. "I am pleased, as your friend. Quit hiding behind the gruff accent and the road-worn clothing. Quit being afraid of who you are, of who you might dare to be, deep inside. You do not care if someone sees you after a hard day of labor, sweating and dirty. You don't waste your time primping and prettying yourself, and all of that is to your credit. But in times like this, when the opportunity presents itself, do not shy from it, either."

"I feel . . . vain."

"You should simply feel pretty, and be happy with that. If you really are one who cares not what others may think or say, then why would you hide from pleasant thoughts?"

Catti-brie looked at him curiously for a moment, and a smile spread on her face. "Who are you, and what have you done with Wulfgar?"

"The doppelganger is long dead, I assure you," Wulfgar replied. "He was thrown out with the weight of Errtu."

"I have never seen you like this."

"I have never before felt like this. I am content and I know my road. I answer to no one but myself now, and never before have I known such freedom."

"And so you wish to share that with me?"

"With everyone," Wulfgar replied with a laugh.

"I did look in a mirror . . . or two," Catti-brie said, and Wulfgar laughed harder.

"And were you pleased by what you saw?"

"Yes," she admitted.

"And do you wish that Drizzt was here?"

"Enough," she bade him, which of course meant "yes."

Wulfgar took her by the arm and guided her to the railing of the balcony. "So many generations of men and elves have built this place. It is a refuge for Fret and those akin to him, and it is also a place where we all might come from time to time to simply stand and look, and enjoy. That, I think, is the most important time of all. To look inside ourselves honestly and without regret or fear. I could be battling orcs or dragons. I could be digging mithral from the deep mines. I could be leading the hunt in Icewind Dale. But there are times, too few I fear, when this, when standing and looking and just enjoying, is more important than all of that."

Catti-brie wrapped her arm around Wulfgar's waist and leaned her head against his strong shoulder, standing side-by-side, two friends enjoying a moment of life, of perception, of simple pleasure.

Wulfgar draped his arm across her shoulders, equally at peace, and both of them sensed, deep inside, that the moment would be one they would remember for all their days, a defining and lasting image of all they had been through since that fateful day in Icewind Dale when Wulfgar the young warrior had foolishly smacked a tough old dwarf named Bruenor on the head.

They lingered for some time, but the moment was lost as Lady Alustriel came out onto the balcony. The two turned at the sound of her voice, to see her standing with a middle-aged man dressed in the apron of a tavernkeeper.

Alustriel paused when she looked upon Catti-brie, her eyes roaming the woman's form.

"Fret is full of magic, I am told," Catti-brie said, glancing at Wulfgar.

Alustriel shook her head. "Fret finds the beauty, he does not create it."

"He finds it as well as Drizzt finds orcs to slay, or Bruenor finds metal to mine, to be sure," said Wulfgar.

"He has mentioned that he would like to search for the same in Wulfgar, as well."

Catti-brie laughed as Wulfgar chuckled and shook his head. "I've not the time."

"He will be so disappointed," said Alustriel.

"Next time we meet, perhaps," said Wulfgar, and his words elicited a doubting glance from Catti-brie.

She stared at him deeply for a long while, measuring his every expression and movement, and the inflections of his voice. His offer to Fret may or may not have been disingenuous, she knew, but it was moot in any case because Wulfgar had decided that he would never again visit Silverymoon. Catti-brie saw that clearly, and had been feeling it since before they had departed Mithral Hall.

A sense of dread welled up inside her, mingling with that last special moment she had shared with Wulfgar. There was a storm coming. Wulfgar knew it, and though he hadn't yet openly shared it, the signs were mounting.

"This is Master Tapwell of the Rearing Dragon, a fine establishment in the city's lower ward," Alustriel explained. The short, round-bellied man came forward a step, rather sheepishly. "A common respite for visitors to Silverymoon."

"Well met," Catti-brie greeted, and Wulfgar nodded his agreement.

"And to yerselves, Prince and Princess of Mithral Hall," Tapwell replied, dipping a few awkward bows in the process.

"The Rearing Dragon played host to many of the refugees that crossed the Surbrin from Mithral Hall," Alustriel explained. "Master Tapwell believes that a pair who passed through might be of interest to you."

Wulfgar was already leaning forward eagerly. Catti-brie put her hand on his forearm to help steady him.

"Yer girl, Colson," Tapwell said, rubbing his hands nervously over his beer-stained apron. "Skinny thing with straw hair to here?" He indicated a point just below his shoulder, a good approximation of the length of Colson's hair.

"Go on," Wulfgar bade, nodding.

"She came in with the last group, but with her mother."

"Her mother?" Wulfgar looked to Alustriel for an explanation, but the woman deferred to Tapwell.

"Well, she said she was her mother," the tavernkeeper explained.

"What was her name?" Catti-brie asked.

Tapwell fidgeted as if trying to fathom the answer. "I remember her calling the girl Colson clear enough. Her own name was like that. Same beginning, if ye get my meaning."

"Please remember," Wulfgar prompted.

"Cottie?" Catti-brie asked.

"Cottie, yeah. Cottie," said Tapwell.

"Cottie Cooperson," Catti-brie said to Wulfgar. "She was with the group Delly tended in the hall. She lost her family to Obould."

"And Delly gave her a new one," said Wulfgar, but his tone was not bitter.

"You agree with this assessment?" Alustriel asked.

"It does make sense," said Catti-brie.

"This was the last group that crossed the Surbrin before the ferry was closed down, and not just the last group to arrive in Silverymoon," Alustriel said. "I have confirmed that from the guards of Winter Edge themselves. They escorted the refugees in from the Surbrin—all of them—and they, the guards, remain, along with several of the refugees."

"And have you found those refugees to ask them of Cottie and Colson?" asked Catti-brie. "And are Cottie and Colson among those who remain?"

"Further inquiries are being made," Alustriel replied. "I am fairly certain that they will only confirm what we have already discovered. As for Cottie and the child, they left."

Wulfgar's shoulders slumped.

"For Nesmé," Alustriel explained. "Soon after those refugees arrived, a general call came out from Nesmé. They are rebuilding, and offering homes to any who would go and join with them. The place is secure once more—many of the Knights in Silver stand watch with the Riders of Nesmé to ensure that all of the trolls were destroyed or chased back into the Trollmoors. The city will thrive this coming season, well defended and well supplied."

"You are certain that Cottie and Colson are there?" Wulfgar asked.

"I am certain that they were on the caravan that left for Nesmé, only days after they arrived here in Silverymoon. That caravan arrived, though whether Cottie and the child remained with it through the entirety of the journey, I cannot promise. They stopped at several way stations and villages along the route. The woman could have left at any of those."

Wulfgar nodded and looked to Catti-brie, their road clear before them.

"I could fly you to Nesmé upon my chariot," Alustriel offered. "But there is another caravan leaving by midday tomorrow, one that will follow the exact route that Cottie rode, and one in need of more guards. The drivers would be thrilled to have Wulfgar and Catti-brie along for the journey, and Nesmé is only a tenday away."

"And there is nowhere for Cottie to have gone beyond Nesmé," Wulfgar reasoned. "That will do, and well."

"Very good," said Alustriel. "I will inform the lead driver." She and Tapwell took their leave.

"Our road is clear, then," said Wulfgar, and he seemed content with that.

Catti-brie, though, shook her head.

"The southern road is secured and Nesmé is not so far," Wulfgar said to her doubting expression.

"This is not good news, I fear."

"How so?"

"Cottie," Catti-brie explained. "I happened upon her a few times after my wound kept me in the lower tunnels. She was a broken thing, in spirit and in mind."

"You fear that she would harm Colson?" Wulfgar said, his eyes widening with alarm.

"Never that," said Catti-brie. "But I fear that she will clutch the girl too tightly, and will not welcome the reaching hands of Wulfgar."

"Colson is not her child."

"And for some, truth is no more than an inconvenience," Catti-brie replied.

"I will take the child," Wulfgar stated in a tone that left no room for debate.

Aside from that undeniable determination, it struck Catti-brie that Wulfgar had named Colson as "the child," and not as "my child." She studied her friend carefully for a few moments, seeking a deeper read.

But it was not to be found.

CHAPTER 9
AT DESTINY'S DOOR

"I don't like this place."

A trick of the wind, blowing down a channel between a pair of towering snow dunes, amplified Regis's soft-spoken words so that they seemed to fill the space around his four dwarf companions. The words blended with the mourn of the cold breeze, a harmony of fear and lament that seemed so fitting in a place called Fell Pass.

Bruenor, who was too anxious to be anywhere but up front, turned, and appeared as if he was about to scold the halfling. But he didn't. He just shook his head and left it at that, for how could he deny the undeniable?

The region was haunted, palpably so. They had felt it on their journey through the pass the previous spring, moving west to east toward Mithral Hall. That same musty aura remained very much alive in Fell Pass, though the surroundings had been transformed by the season. When they'd first come through, the ground was flat and even, a wide and easily-traversed pass between a pair of distant mountain ranges. Perhaps the winds from both of those ranges continually met here in battle, flattening the ground. Deep snow had since fallen in the teeth of those competing winds, forming a series of drifts that resembled the dunes of the Calim Desert, like a series of gigantic, bright white scallop shells evenly spaced perpendicular to the east-west line that marked the bordering mountain ranges. With the melting and refreezing of the late winter, the top surface of the snow had been crusted with ice, but not enough to bear the weight of a dwarf. Thus they had to make their trudging way along the low points of the still-deep snow, through the channels between the dunes.

Drizzt served as their guide. Running lightly, every now and then chopping a ledge into the snow with one of his scimitars, the drow traversed the dunes as a salmon might skip the waves of a slow river. Up one side and down another he went, pausing at the high points to set his bearings.

It had taken the party of six—Bruenor, Regis, Drizzt, Thibbledorf Pwent, Cordio, and Torgar Hammerstriker—four days to get to the eastern entrance of Fell Pass. They'd kept up a fine pace considering the snow and the fact that they had to circumvent many of King Obould's guard posts and a pair of orc caravans. Once in the pass, even with the scallop drifts, they had continued to make solid progress, with Drizzt scaling the dunes and instructing Pwent where to punch through.

Seven days out, the pace had slowed to a crawl. They were certain they were near to where they'd found the hole that Bruenor believed was the entrance to the legendary dwarven city of Gauntlgrym.

They had mapped the place well on that journey from the west, and had taken note, as Bruenor had ordered, of all the landmarks—the angles to notable mountain peaks north and south, and such. But with the wintry blanket of snow, Fell Pass appeared so different that Drizzt simply could not be certain. The very real possibility that they might walk right past the hole that had swallowed one of their wagons weighed on all of them, particularly Bruenor.

And there was something else there, a feeling hanging in the air that had the hairs on the backs of all their necks tingling. The mournful groan of the wind was full of the laments of the dead. Of that, there was no doubt. The cleric, Cordio, had cast divination spells that told him there was indeed something supernatural about the place, some rift or outsider presence. On the journey to Mithral Hall, Bruenor's priests had urged Drizzt not to call upon Guenhwyvar, for fear of inciting unwanted attention from other extraplanar sources in the process, and once again Cordio had reiterated that point. The Fell

Pass, the dwarf priest had assured his companions, was not stable in a planar sense—though even Cordio admitted that he wasn't really sure what that meant.

"Ye got anything for us, elf?" Bruenor called up to Drizzt. His gruff voice, full of irritation, echoed off the frozen snow.

Drizzt came into view atop the drift to the party's left, the west. He shrugged at Bruenor then stepped forward and began a balanced slide down the glistening white dune. He kept his footing perfectly, and slipped right past the halfling and dwarves to the base of the drift on their other side, where he used its sharp incline to halt his momentum.

"I have snow," he replied. "As much snow as you could want, extending as far as I can see to the west."

"We're goin' to have to stay here until the melt, ain't we?" Bruenor grumbled. He put his hands on his hips and kicked his heavy boot through the icy wall of one mound.

"We will find it," Drizzt replied, but his words were buried by the sudden grumbling of Thibbledorf Pwent.

"Bah!" the battlerager snorted, and he banged his hands together and stomped about, crunching the icy snow beneath his heavy steps. While the others wore mostly furs and layers of various fabrics, Pwent was bedecked in his traditional Gutbuster battle mail, a neck-to-toe suit of overlapping ridged metal plates, spiked at all the appropriate strike zones: fists, elbows, shoulders, and knees. His helmet, too, carried a tall, barbed spike, one that had skewered many an orc in its day.

"Ye got no magic to help me?" Bruenor demanded of Cordio.

The cleric shrugged helplessly. "The riddles of this maze extend beyond the physical, me king," he tried to explain. "Questions asked in spells're getting me nothin' but more questions. I'm knowin' that we're close, but more because I'm feeling that rift with me every spellcasting."

"Bah!" Pwent roared. He lowered his head and rammed through the nearest snow drift, disappearing behind a veil of white that fell behind him as he plowed through to the channel on the other side.

"We'll find it, then," said Torgar Hammerstriker. "If it was here when ye came through, then here it is still. And if me king's thinking it's Gauntlgrym, then nothin's stopping meself from seein' that place."

"Aye and huzzah!" Cordio agreed.

They all jumped as the snow erupted from up ahead. Drizzt's scimitars appeared in his hands as if they had been there all along.

From that break in the dune emerged a snow-encrusted Thibbledorf Pwent, roaring still. He didn't slow, but plowed through the dune across the way, crunching through the icy wall with ease and disappearing from sight.

"Will ye stop it, ye durned fool?" Bruenor chastised, but Pwent was already gone.

"I am certain that we're near the entrance," Drizzt assured Bruenor, and the drow slid his blades away. "We are the right distance from the mountains north and south. Of that, I am sure."

"We are close," Regis confirmed, still glancing all around as if he expected a ghost to leap out and throttle him at any moment. In that regard, Regis knew more than the others, for he had been the one who had gone into the hole after the wagon those months before, and who had encountered, down in the dark, what he believed to be the ghost of a long-dead dwarf.

"Then we'll just keep looking," said Bruenor. "And if it stays in hiding under the snow, its secrets won't be holding, for the melt's coming soon."

"Bah!" they heard Pwent growl from behind the dune to the east and they all scrambled, expecting him to burst through in their midst, and likely with that lethal helmet spike lowered.

The dune shivered as he hit it across the way, and he roared again fiercely. But his pitch changed suddenly, his cry going from defiance to surprise. Then it faded rapidly, as if the dwarf had fallen away.

Bruenor looked at Drizzt. "Gauntlgrym!" the dwarf declared.

Torgar and Cordio dived for the point on the drift behind which they had heard Pwent's cry. They punched through and flung the snow out behind them, working like a pair of dogs digging for a bone. As they weakened the integrity of that section of the drift, it crumbled down before them, complicating their dig. Still, within moments, they came to the edge of a hole in the ground, and the remaining pile of snow slipped in, but seemed to fill the crevice.

"Pwent?" Torgar called into the snow, thinking his companion buried alive.

He leaned over the edge, Cordio stabilizing his feet, and plunged his hand down into the snow pile. That blockage, though, was neither solid nor thick, and had merely packed in to seal the shaft below. When Torgar's hand broke the integrity of the pack, the collected snow broke and fell away, leaving the dwarf staring down into a cold and empty shaft.

"Pwent?" he called more urgently, realizing that his companion had fallen quite far.

"That's it!" Bruenor yelled, rushing up between the kneeling pair. "The wagon went in right there!" As he made the claim, he fell to his knees and brushed aside some more of the snow, revealing a rut that had been made by the wagon wheel those months before. "Gauntlgrym!"

"And Pwent fell in," Drizzt reminded him.

The three dwarves turned to see the drow and Regis feeding out a line of rope that Drizzt had already tied around his waist.

"Get the line, boys!" Bruenor yelled, but Cordio and Torgar were already moving anyway, rushing to secure the rope and find a place to brace their heavy boots.

Drizzt dropped down beside the ledge and tried to pick a careful route, but a cry came up from far below, followed by a high-pitched, sizzling roar that sounded unlike anything any of them had ever heard, like a cross between the screech of an eagle and the hiss of a gigantic lizard.

Drizzt rolled over the lip, turning and setting his hands, and Bruenor dived to add his strength to the rope brace.

"Quickly!" Drizzt instructed as the dwarves began to let out the line. Trusting in them, the drow let go of the lip and dropped from sight.

"There's a ledge fifteen feet down," Regis called, scrambling past the dwarves to the hole. He moved as if he would go right over, but he stopped suddenly, just short of the lip. There he held as the seconds passed, his body frozen by memories of his first journey into the place that Bruenor called Gauntlgrym.

"I'm on the ledge," Drizzt called up, drawing him from his trance. "I can make my way, but keep ready on the rope."

Regis peered over and could just make out the form of the drow in the darkness below.

"Ye be guidin' us, Rumblebelly," Bruenor instructed, and Regis found the fortitude to nod.

A loud crash from far below startled him again, though, followed by a cry of pain and another otherworldly shriek. More noise arose, metal scraping on stone, hissing snakes and eagle screams, and Dwarvish roars of defiance.

Then a cry of absolute terror, Pwent's cry, shook them all to their spines, for when had Thibbledorf Pwent ever cried out in terror?

"What do ye see?" Bruenor called out to Regis.

The halfling peered in and squinted. He could just make out Drizzt, inching down the wall below the ledge. As his eyes adjusted to the gloom, Regis realized it wasn't really a ledge, or a wall, but rather a stalagmite mound that had grown up beside the side of the cave below. He looked back to Drizzt, and the drow dropped from sight. The dwarves behind him gave a yelp and fell over backward as the rope released.

"Set it!" Bruenor yelled at Torgar and Cordio, and the dwarf king charged for the hole, yelling, "What do ye see, Rumblebelly?"

Regis pulled back and turned, shaking his head, but Bruenor wasn't waiting for an explanation anyway. The dwarf dived to the ground and grabbed up the rope, and without hesitation, flung himself over the lip, rapidly descending into the gloom. Back from the hole, Torgar and Cordio grunted from the strain and tried hard to dig their boots in.

Regis swallowed. He heard a grunt and a shriek from far below. Images of a dwarf ghost haunted him and told him to run far away. But Drizzt was down there, Bruenor was down there, Pwent was down there.

The halfling swallowed again and rushed to the hole. He fell to the ground atop the rope and with a glance back at Torgar and Cordio, he disappeared from sight.

* * * * *

As soon as he hit the ledge, Drizzt recognized it for what it was. The tall stalagmite mound rose up at an angle, melding with the sheerer stone of the wall behind him.

Even though he was only fifteen feet down from the lip, Drizzt's sensibilities switched to those of the person he used to be, a creature of the Underdark. He started down tentatively, feeding out the rope behind him, for just a couple of steps.

His eyes focused in the gloom, and he saw the contours of the stalagmite and the floor some twenty feet below. On that floor rested the broken remains of the wagon that had been lost in the journey east those months before. Also on that floor, Drizzt saw a familiar boot, hard and wrapped in metal. Below and to the left, he heard a muffled cry, and the sound of metal scraping on stone, as if an armored dwarf was being dragged.

With a flick of his wrist, Drizzt disengaged himself from the rope, and so balanced was he as he ran down the side of the stalagmite that he not only did not bend low and use his hands, but he drew out both his blades as he descended. He hit the floor in a run, thinking to head off down the narrow tunnel he had spotted ahead and to the right. But his left-hand scimitar, Twinkle, glowed with a blue light, and the drow's keen eyes and ears picked out a whisper of movement and a whisper of sound over by the side wall.

Skidding to a stop, Drizzt whirled to meet the threat, and his eyes went wide indeed when he saw the creature, unlike anything he had ever known, coming out fast for him.

Half again Drizzt's height from head to tail, it charged on strong back legs, like a bipedal lizard, back hunched low and tail suspended behind it, counterbalancing its large head—if it could even be called a head. It seemed no more than a mouth with three equidistant mandibles stretched out wide. Black tusks as large as Drizzt's hands curled inward at the tips of those mandibles, and Drizzt could make out rows of long, sharp teeth running back down its throat, a trio of ridged lines.

Even stranger came the glow from the creature's eyes—three of them—each centered on the flap of mottled skin stretched wide between the respective mandibles. The creature bore down on the drow like some triangular-mouthed snake unhinging its jaw to swallow its prey.

Drizzt started out to the left then reversed fast as the creature swerved to follow. Even with his speed-enhancing anklets, though, the drow could not get far enough back to the right to avoid the turning creature.

The mandibles snapped powerfully, but hit only air as Drizzt leaped and tumbled forward, over the top mandible. He slashed down hard with both hands as he went over, and used the contact to push himself even higher as he executed a twist and brought his feet fast under him. The creature issued a strange roaring, hissing protest—a fitting, otherworldly sound for an otherworldly beast, Drizzt thought.

Tucking and turning, Drizzt planted his feet against the side of the creature's shoulder and kicked out, but the beast was more solid than he'd thought. His strike did no more than bend it away from him at the shoulder as he went out to the side. And that bend, of course, again turned the terrible jaws his way.

But Drizzt flew backward with perfect balance and awareness. As the beast swung around he cut his scimitars across, one-two, scoring hits on the thick muscle and skin of the jaws' connecting flap.

The creature howled again and bit down at the passing blades, its three mandible tips not quite aligning as they clicked together. It opened wide its maw again as it turned to face Drizzt.

His blades worked in a flash, the backhand of Icingdeath slicing the opposing skin flap, and a hard strike of Twinkle passing through the muscle and flesh, then turning straight down to slash the base flap that connected the lower two mandible tips. Drizzt turned the blade just a bit as it connected, and leaned forward hard, forcing the jaws to angle down.

The creature snapped its head back up, accepting the cut, and leaped straight up, turning its back end under so that it landed on its outstretched tail with its hind legs free to claw at its opponent. Formidable indeed were the three claws tipping the feet of those powerful legs, and Drizzt barely dodged back in time to avoid the vicious rake.

Somehow the creature hopped forward in pursuit, using just its tail for propulsion. Its tiny front legs waved frantically in the air as its long, powerful rear legs slashed wildly at the drow.

Drizzt worked his scimitars in a blur to defend, connecting repeatedly, but never too solidly for fear of having a blade torn from his grasp. He retracted a blade and the creature's hind leg flailed free, then he stabbed straight out, piercing its foot.

The creature threw back its head and howled again—from up above there came a crash as a form rolled over the ledge—and Drizzt didn't miss the opportunity offered by the distraction. Rolling around those flailing legs and slashing across with Icingdeath, then with Twinkle in close pursuit, he scored two hits on the creature's thin neck. There was a sucking of air and Drizzt saw the bubbling of blood as his blades passed through flesh.

Not even slowing in his turn as the creature fell silent, then just fell over, the drow sprinted down the tunnel. A roar from behind made him glance back, to see Bruenor flying down the last few feet beside the stalagmite, axe over his head. The dwarf timed his landing perfectly with his overhand chop, driving his axe through the already mortally wounded creature's backbone with a sickening sound.

"Wait here!" Drizzt called to him, and the drow was gone.

* * * * *

Bruenor held on as the creature thrashed in its death throes. It tried to turn around to snap at him, but Drizzt had completely disabled the once-formidable jaws' ability to inflict any real damage. The mandibles flopped awkwardly and without coordination, most of the supporting muscles severed. Similarly, the creature's tail and hind legs exhibited only the occasional spasmodic twitch, for Bruenor's axe had cleaved its spine.

So the dwarf stayed at arms' length, holding his axe out far from his torso to avoid any incidental contact.

"Hurry, elf!" Bruenor called after Drizzt when he glanced to the side and noted Thibbledorf's boot lying on the stone floor. No longer willing to wait out the dying beast, Bruenor leaped atop its back and ripped through tendon and bone as he tugged and yanked his axe free. He thought to run off after Drizzt, but before he even had the weapon set in his hands, a movement to the side caught his eye.

The dwarf watched curiously as a darker patch of shadow coalesced near the side wall and the broken wagon, gradually taking shape—the shape of another of the strange beasts.

It came out hard and fast at him, and Bruenor wisely dropped down behind the fallen creature. On came the second beast, jaws snapping furiously, and the dwarf fell to the stone floor and heaved the fallen creature up as a meaty shield. The dwarf finally saw the damage those strange triangular jaws could inflict, for the ravenous newcomer tore through great chunks of flesh and bone in seconds.

Movement behind Bruenor had him half turning to his right.

"Just me!" Regis called to him before he came around, and the dwarf refocused on the beast before him.

Then Bruenor glanced left, to see Drizzt backing frantically out of the tunnel, his scimitars working fast and independently, each slashing quick lines to hold the snapping mouths of two more creatures at bay.

"Rumblebelly, ye help the elf!" Bruenor called, but when he glanced back, Regis was gone.

Bruenor's foe plowed over its fallen comrade then, and the dwarf king had no time to look for his halfling companion.

* * * * *

Drizzt noticed Regis flattened against the wall as he, and the pair of monsters pursuing him, moved past the halfling.

Regis nodded and waited for a responding nod. As soon as Drizzt offered it, the halfling came out fast and slapped his small mace against the tail of the creature on the left. Predictably, the beast wheeled to snap at this newest foe, but anticipating that, Drizzt moved faster, bringing his right hand blade over and across, cutting a gash across the side of the turning beast's neck.

With a roar of protest, the creature spun back, and the other, seeing the opening, came on suddenly.

But Drizzt was the quicker, and he managed to backstep fast enough to buy the time to realign his blades. He gave an approving nod to Regis as the halfling slipped down the tunnel.

* * * * *

Regis moved deliberately, but nervously, into the darkness, expecting a monster to spring out at him from every patch of shadow. Soon he heard the scraping of metal, and an occasional grumble and Dwarvish curse, and he could tell from the lack of bluster that Thibbledorf Pwent was in serious trouble.

Propelled by that, Regis moved with more speed, coming up to the edge of a side chamber from which issued the terrible, gnashing, metallic sounds. Regis summoned his courage and peeked around the rim of the opening. There in the room, silhouetted by the glow of lichen along the far wall, stood another creature, one larger than the others and easily more than ten feet from maw to tail tip. It stood perfectly still, except that it thrashed its head back and forth. Looking at it from the back, but on a slight angle, Regis could see why it did so. For out of the side of that mouth hung an armored dwarf leg with a dirty bare foot dangling limply at its end. Regis winced, thinking that his friend was being torn apart by that triangular maw. He could picture the black teeth crunching through Pwent's armored shell, tearing his flesh with fangs and ripped metal.

And the dwarf wasn't moving, other than the flailing caused by the limp limbs protruding from the thing's mouth, and no further protests or groans came forth.

Trembling with anger and terror, Regis charged with abandon, leaping forward and lifting high his small mace. But where could he even hit the murderous beast to hurt it?

He got his answer as the creature noticed him, whipping its head around. It was then that the halfling first came to understand the strange head, with its three equidistant eyes set in the middle of each of the skin flaps that connected the mandibles. Purely on instinct, the halfling swung for the nearest eye, and the creature's short forelimbs could not reach forward far enough to block.

The mace hit true, and the flap, taut about the knee and upper leg of the trapped dwarf, had no give that it might absorb the blow. With a sickening *splat*, the eye popped, gushing liquid all over the horrified halfling.

The creature hissed and whipped its head furiously—an attempt to throw the dwarf free.

But Pwent wasn't dead. He had gone into a defensive curl, a "turtle" maneuver that tightened the set of his magnificent armor, strengthening its integrity and hiding its vulnerable seams. As the creature loosened its death grip on him, the dwarf came out of his curl with a defiant snarl. He had no room to punch, or to maneuver his head spike, so he simply thrashed, shaking like a wide-leafed bush in a gale.

The creature lost interest in Regis, and tried to clamp down on the dwarf instead. But too late, for Pwent was in a frenzy, insane with rage.

Finally the creature managed to open wide its maw and angle down, expelling the dwarf. When Pwent came free, Regis's eyes widened to see the amount of damage—torn skin, broken teeth, and blood—the dwarf had inflicted on the beast.

And Pwent was far from done. He hit the ground in a turn that put his feet under him, and his little legs bent, then propelled him right back at the creature, head—and helmet spike—leading. He drove into and through the apex of the jaws, and the dwarf bored on, bending the creature backward. The dwarf punched out, both hands at the same time, launching twin roundhouse hooks that pounded the beast on opposite sides of its neck, fist-spikes digging in. Again and again, the dwarf retracted and punched back hard, both hands together, mashing the flesh.

And the dwarf's legs ground on, pushing the beast backward, up against the side-chamber's wall, and by the time they got there, the creature was not resisting at all, was not pushing back, and without the barrage it would have likely fallen over.

But Pwent kept hitting it, muttering profanities all the while.

* * * * *

Bruenor thrust his axe out horizontally before him, defeating the first attack. He turned the weapon and used it to angle the charging creature aside as he, too, ran ahead, sprinting by the beast to the remains of the wagon. All of the supply crates and sacks had been destroyed, either from the fall or torn apart thereafter, but Bruenor found what he was looking for in an intact portion of the side of the wagon, angling up to about waist height. Knowing the creature to be in full pursuit, the dwarf dived right over that, falling to the floor at its base and rolling to his back, axe up above his head along the ground.

The creature leaped over the planks, not realizing that Bruenor was so close to them until the dwarf's axe hit it hard in the side, cutting a long gash just behind its small, twitching foreleg.

Bruenor fell back flat and continued the momentum to roll him right over, coming back up to his feet. He didn't pause to look over his handiwork, but propelled himself forward, lifting his axe high over one shoulder as he went.

The creature was ready, though, and as the dwarf bore in, it snapped its mouth out at him, and when it had to retract far short of the mark to avoid a swipe of that vicious axe, the creature just fell back on its tail, as the other one had done, and brought up its formidable rear legs.

One blocked Bruenor's next swing, kicking out and catching the axe below the head, while the other lashed out, scraping deep lines on the dwarf's armor. Following that, the creature snapped its upper body forward, the triangular maw biting hard at the dwarf, who only managed at the last instant to get back out of range.

And right back came Bruenor, with a yell and a spit and a downward chop.

The creature rocked back and the axe whipped past cleanly. The creature reversed, coming in behind.

Bruenor didn't stop the axe's momentum and reverse it to parry. Rather, he let it flow through, turning sidelong as the blade came low, then turning some more, daring to roll his back around before the beast in the belief that he would be the quicker.

And so he was.

Bruenor came around, the axe in both hands and at full extension in a great sidelong slash. The creature scrambled to block. Bruenor shortened his grip, bringing the axe head in closer. When the creature kicked out to block, the axe met it squarely, removing one of the three toes and cleaving the blocking foot in half.

The creature threw itself forward, screaming in pain and anger, coming at Bruenor with blind rage. And the dwarf king backed frantically, his axe working to-and-fro to fend off the snapping assaults.

"Elf! I'm needin' ye!" the desperate dwarf bellowed.

* * * * *

Drizzt was in no position to answer. The wound he had inflicted on one of the beasts wasn't quite as serious as he'd hoped, apparently, for that creature showed no signs of relenting. Worse for Drizzt, he had been backed into a wider area, giving the creatures more room to maneuver and spread out before him.

They went wide, left and right, amazingly well coordinated for unthinking beasts—if they were indeed unthinking beasts. Drizzt worked his blades as far to either side as he could, and when that became impractical and awkward, the drow rushed ahead suddenly, back toward the tunnel.

Both creatures turned to chase, but Drizzt reversed even faster, spinning to meet their pursuit with a barrage of blows. He scored a deep gash on the side of one's mouth, and poked the other in its bottom eye.

Up above he heard a crash, and from the side Bruenor called for him. All he could do was look for options.

His gaze followed the trail of falling rocks, to see Torgar Hammerstriker in a wild and overbalanced run down the side of the stalagmite. The dwarf held a heavy crossbow before him, and just before his stumbling sent him into a headlong slide, he let fly a bolt, somehow hitting the creature to Drizzt's right. The crossbow went flying and so did Torgar, crashing and bouncing the rest of the way down.

The creature he had hit stumbled then spun to meet the dwarf's charge. But its jaws couldn't catch up to the bouncing and flailing Torgar, and the dwarf slammed hard against the back and side of the beast, bringing it down in a heap. Dazed beyond sensibility, Torgar couldn't begin to defend himself in that tumble as the creature moved to strike.

But Drizzt moved around the remaining creature and struck hard at the fallen beast, his scimitars slicing at its flesh in rapid succession, tearing deep lines. Drizzt had to pause to fend off the other, but as soon as that attack was repelled, he went back to the first, ensuring that it was dead.

Then the drow smiled, seeing that the tide had turned, seeing the lowered head spike rushing in hard at the standing creature's backside.

Even as Pwent connected, skewering the beast from behind, Drizzt broke off and ran toward the wagon. By the time he got there, he found Bruenor and his opponent in a wild back and forth of snapping and slashing.

Drizzt leaped up to the lip of the wagon side, looking for an opening. Noting him, Bruenor rushed out the other way, and the creature turned with the dwarf.

Drizzt leaped astride its back, his scimitars going to quick and deadly work.

"What in the Nine Hells are them things?" Bruenor asked when the vicious thing at last lay still.

"What *from* the Nine Hells, perhaps," said Drizzt with a shrug.

The two moved back to the center of the room, where Pwent continued pummeling the already dead beast and Regis tended to the dazed and battered Torgar.

"I can't be getting down," came a call from above, and all eyes lifted to see Cordio peering over the entrance, far above. "Ain't no place to set the rope."

"I'll get him," Drizzt assured Bruenor.

With agility that continued to awe, the drow ran up the side of the stalagmite, sliding his scimitars away. At the top, he searched and found his handholds, and between those and the rope, which Cordio had braced once more, Drizzt soon disappeared back out of the hole.

A few moments later, Cordio came down on the rope, gaining to the top of the mound, then, with Drizzt's help, he worked his way gingerly down to the ground. Drizzt came back into the cavern soon after, hanging by his fingertips. He fell purposely, landing lightly atop the stalagmite mound. From there, the drow trotted down to join his friends.

"Stupid, smelly lizards," Pwent muttered as he tried to put his boot back on. The metal bands had been bent, though, crimping the opening in the shoe, and so it was no easy task.

"What were them things?" Bruenor asked any and all.

"Extraplanar creatures," said Cordio, who was inspecting one of the bodies—one of the bodies that was smoking and dissipating before his very eyes. "I'd be keeping yer cat in its statue, elf."

Drizzt's hand went reflexively to his pouch, where he kept the onyx figurine he used to summon Guenhwyvar to the Prime Material Plane. He nodded his agreement with Cordio. If ever he had needed the panther, it would have been in the last fight, and even then, he hadn't dared call upon her. He could sense it, too, a pervasive aura of strange otherworldliness. The place was either truly haunted or somehow dimensionally unstable.

He slipped his hand in the pouch and felt the contours of the panther replica. He hoped the situation wouldn't force him to chance a call to Guenhwyvar, but in glancing around at his already battered companions, he had little confidence that it could be avoided for long.

CHAPTER 10
THE WAY OF THE ORC

The orcs of Clan Yellowtusk swept into the forest from the north, attacking trees as if avenging some heinous crime perpetrated upon them by the inanimate plants. Axes chopped and fires flared to life, and the group, as ordered, made as much noise as they could.

On a hillside to the east, Dnark, Toogwik Tuk, and Ung-thol crouched and waited nervously, while Clan Karuck crept along the low ground behind them and to the south.

"This is too brazen," Ung-thol warned. "The elves will come out in force."

Dnark knew that his shaman's words were not without merit, for they'd encroached on the Moonwood, the home of a deadly clan of elves.

"We will be gone across the river before the main groups arrive," Toogwik Tuk replied. "Grguch and Hakuun have planned this carefully."

"We are exposed!" Ung-thol protested. "If we are seen here on open ground . . ."

"Their eyes will be to the north, to the flames that eat their beloved god-trees," said Toogwik Tuk.

"It is a gamble," Dnark interjected, calming both shamans.

"It is the way of the warrior," said Toogwik Tuk. "The way of the orc. It is something Obould Many-Arrows would have once done, but no more."

Truth resonated in those words to both Dnark and Ung-thol. The chieftain glanced down at the creeping warriors of Clan Karuck, many shrouded by branches they had attached to their dark armor and clothing. Further to the side, tight around the trees of a small copse, a band of ogre javelin throwers held still and quiet, atlatl throwing sticks in hand.

The day could bring disaster, a ruination of all of their plans to force Obould forward, Dnark knew. Or it could bring glory, which would then only push their plans all the more. In any event, a blow struck here would sound like the shredding of a treaty, and that, the chieftain thought, could only be a good thing.

He crouched back low in the grass and watched the scene unfolding before him. He wouldn't likely see the approach of the cunning elves, of course, but he would know of their arrival by the screams of Clan Yellowtusk's sacrificed forward warriors.

A moment later, and not so far to the north, one such cry of orc agony rent the air.

Dnark glanced down at Clan Karuck, who continued their methodical encirclement.

* * * * *

Innovindil could only shake her head in dismay to see the dark lines of smoke rising from the northern end of the Moonwood yet again. The orcs were nothing if not stubborn.

Her bow across her saddle before her, the elf brought Sunset up above the treetops, but kept the pegasus low. The forward scouts would engage the orcs before her arrival, no doubt, but she still hoped to get some shots in from above with the element of surprise working for her.

She banked the pegasus left, toward the river, thinking to come around the back of the orc mob so that she could better direct the battle to her companions on the ground. She went even lower as she broke clear of the thick tree line and eased Sunset's reins, letting the pegasus fly full out. The wind whipped through the elf's blond locks, her hair and cape flapping out behind her, her eyes tearing from the refreshingly chilly breeze. Her rhythm held perfect, posting smoothly with the rise and fall of her steed's powerful shoulders, her balance so centered and complete that she seemed an extension of the pegasus rather than a separate being. She let the fingers of one hand feel the fine design of her bow, while her other hand slipped down to brush the feathered fletching of the arrows set in a quiver on the side of her saddle. She rolled an arrow with her fingers, anticipating when she could let it fly for the face of an orc marauder.

Keeping the river on her left and the trees on her right, Innovindil cruised along. She came up on one hillock and had nearly flown over it by the time she noticed carefully camouflaged forms creeping along.

Orcs. South of the fires and the noise. South of the forward scouts.

The veteran elf warrior recognized an ambush when she saw one. A second group of orcs were set to swing against the rear flank of the Moonwood elves, which meant that the noisemakers and fire-starters in the north were nothing more than a diversion.

Innovindil did a quick scan of the forest beyond and the movement before her, and understood the danger. She took up the reins and banked Sunset hard to the right, flying over a copse of trees that left only a short open expanse to the forest proper. She focused on the greater forest ahead, trying to gauge the fight, the location of the orcs and of her people.

Still, the perceptive elf caught the movements around the trees below her, for she could hardly have missed the brutish behemoths scrambling in the leafless copse. They stood twice her height, with shoulders more than thrice her girth.

She saw them, and they saw her, and they rushed around below her, lifting heavy javelins on notched atlatls.

"Fly on, Sunset!" Innovindil cried, recognizing the danger even before one of the missiles soared her way. She pulled back the reins hard, angling her mount higher, and Sunset, understanding the danger, beat his wings with all his strength and speed.

A javelin cracked the air as it flew past, narrowly missing her, and Innovindil couldn't believe the power behind that throw.

She banked the pegasus left and right, not wanting to present an easy target or a predictable path. She and Sunset had to be at their best in the next few moments, and Innovindil steeled her gaze, ready to meet that challenge.

She couldn't know that she had been expected, and she was too busy dodging huge javelins to take note of the small flying serpent soaring along the treetops parallel to her.

* * * * *

Chieftain Grguch watched the darting and swerving pegasus with amusement and grudging respect. It quickly became clear to him that the ogres would not take the flying pair down, as his closest advisor had predicted. He turned to the prescient Hakuun then, his smile wide.

"This is why I keep you beside me," he said, though he doubted that the shaman, deep in the throes of casting a spell he had prepared precisely for that eventuality, even heard him.

The sight of a ridden pegasus over the previous battle with the elves had greatly angered Grguch, for he had thought on that occasion that his ambush had the raiding group fooled. The flyer had precipitated the elves' escape, Grguch believed, and so he had feared it would happen again—and worse, feared that an elf on high might discover the vulnerable Clan Karuck as well.

Hakuun had given him his answer, and that answer played out in full as the shaman lifted his arms skyward and shouted the last few words of his spell. The air before Hakuun's lips shuddered, a wave of shocking energy blaring forth, distorting images like a rolling ball of water or extreme heat rising from hot stone.

Hakuun's spell exploded around the dodging elf and pegasus, the air itself trembling and quaking in shock waves that buffeted and battered both rider and mount.

Hakuun turned a superior expression his beloved chieftain's way, as if to report simply, "Problem solved."

* * * * *

Innovindil didn't know what hit her, and perhaps more importantly, hit Sunset. They held motionless for a heartbeat, sudden, crackling gusts battering them from all sides. Then they were falling, dazed, but only for a short span before Sunset spread his wings and caught the updrafts.

But they were lower again, too near the ground, and with all momentum stolen. No skill, in rider or in mount, could counter that sudden reversal. Luck alone would get them through.

Sunset whinnied in pain and Innovindil felt a jolt behind her leg.

She looked down to see a javelin buried deep in the pegasus's flank, bright blood dripping out on the great steed's white coat.

"Fly on!" Innovindil implored, for what choice did they have?

Another spear flew past, and another sent Sunset into a sudden turn as it shot up in front of them.

Innovindil hung on for all her life, knuckles whitening, legs clamping the flying horse's flanks. She wanted to reach back and pull out the javelin, which clearly dragged at the pegasus, but she couldn't risk it in that moment of frantic twisting and dodging.

The Moonwood rose up before her, dark and inviting, the place she had known as her home for centuries. If she could just get there, the clerics would tend to Sunset.

She got hit hard on the side and nearly thrown from her perch, unexpectedly buffeted by Sunset's right wing. It hit her again, and the horse dropped suddenly. A javelin had driven through the poor pegasus's wing, right at the joint.

Innovindil leaned forward, imploring the horse for his own sake and for hers, to fight through the pain.

She got hit again, harder.

Sunset managed to stop thrashing and extend his wings enough to catch the updraft and keep them moving along.

As they left the copse behind, Innovindil believed that they could make it, that her magnificent pegasus had enough determination and fortitude to get them through. She turned again to see to the javelin in Sunset's flank—or tried to.

For as Innovindil pivoted in her saddle, a fiery pain shot through her side, nearly taking her from consciousness. The elf somehow settled and turned just her head, and realized then that the last buffet she had taken hadn't been from Sunset's wing, for a dart of some unknown origin hung from her hip, and she could feel it pulsing with magical energy, beating like a heart and flushing painful acid into her side. The closer line of blood pouring down Sunset's flank was her own and not the pegasus's.

Her right leg had gone completely numb, and patches of blackness flitted about her field of vision.

"Fly on," she murmured to the pegasus, though she knew that every stroke of wings brought agony to her beloved equine friend. But they had to get over the forward elf line. Nothing else mattered.

Valiant Sunset rose up over the nearest trees of the Moonwood, and brave Innovindil called down to her people, who she knew to be moving through the trees. "Flee to the south and west," she begged in a voice growing weaker by the syllable. "Ambush! Trap!"

Sunset beat his wings again then whinnied in pain and jerked to the left. They couldn't hold. Somewhere in the back of her mind, in a place caught between consciousness and blackness, Innovindil knew the pegasus could not go on.

She thought that the way before them was clear, but suddenly a large tree loomed where before there had been only empty space. It made no sense to her. She didn't even begin to think that a wizard might be nearby, casting illusions to deceive her. She was only dimly aware as she and Sunset plowed into the tangle of the large tree, and she felt no real pain as she and the horse crashed in headlong, tumbling and twisting in a bone-crunching descent through the branches and to the ground. At one point she caught a curious sight indeed, though it hardly registered: a little, aged gnome with only slight tufts of white hair above his considerable ears and dressed in beautiful shimmering robes of purple and red sat on a branch, legs crossed at the ankles and rocking childlike back and forth, staring at her with an amused expression.

Delirium, the presage to death, she briefly thought. It had to be.

Sunset hit the ground first, in a twisted and broken heap, and Innovindil fell atop him, her face close to his.

She heard his last breath.

She died atop him.

* * * * *

Back on the hillside, the three orcs lost sight of the elf and her flying horse long before the crash, but they had witnessed the javelin strikes, and had cheered each.

"Clan Karuck!" Dnark said, punching his fist into the air, and daring to believe in that moment of elation and victory that the arrival of the half-ogres and their behemoth kin would indeed deliver all the promises of optimistic Toogwik Tuk. The elves and their flying horses had been a bane to the orcs since they had come south, but would any more dare glide over the fields of the Kingdom of Many-Arrows?

"Karuck," Toogwik Tuk agreed, clapping the chieftain on the shoulder, and pointing below.

There, Grguch stood tall, arms upraised. "Take them!" the half-ogre cried to his people. "To the forest!"

With a howl and hoot that brought goosebumps to the chieftain and shamans, the warriors of Clan Karuck leaped up from their concealment and ran howling toward the forest. From the small copse to the south came the lumbering ogres, each with a throw-stick resting on one shoulder, a javelin set in its Y, angled forward and up, ready to launch.

The ground shook beneath their charge, and the wind itself retreated before the force of their vicious howls.

"Clan Karuck!" Ung-thol agreed with his two companions. "And may all the world tremble."

* * * * *

Innovindil's warning cry had been heard, and her people trusted her judgment enough not to question the command. As word filtered through the trees, the Moonwood elves let fly one last arrow and turned to the southwest, sprinting along from cover to cover. Whatever their anger, whatever the temptation of turning back to strike at the orcs in the north, they would not ignore Innovindil.

And true to their beliefs, within a matter of moments, they heard the roars from the east, and realized the trap that their companion had spied. With expert coordination, they tightened their ranks and moved toward the most defensible ground they could find.

Those farthest to the east, a group of a dozen forest folk, were the first to see the charge of Clan Karuck. The enormous half-breeds ran through the trees with wild abandon and frightening speed.

"Hold them," the leader of that patrol told her fellow elves.

Several others looked at her incredulously, but from the majority came nothing but determination. The charge was too ferocious. The other elves moving tree to tree would be overrun.

The group settled behind an ancient, broken, weatherworn wall of piled stones. Exchanging grim nods, they set their arrows and crouched low.

The first huge orcs came into sight, but the elves held their shots. More and more appeared behind the lead runners, but the elves did not break, and did not let fly. The battle wasn't about them, they understood, but about their kin fleeing behind them.

The nearest Clan Karuck warriors were barely five strides from the rock wall when the elves popped up as one, lowered their bows in unison and launched a volley of death.

Orcs shrieked and fell, and the snow before the wall was splattered with red. More arrows went out, but more and more orcs came on. And leaping out before those orcs came a small flaming sphere, and the elves knew what it portended. As one, they crouched and covered against the fireball—one that, in truth, did more damage to the front rank of the charging orcs than to the covering elves, except that it interrupted the stream of the elves' defense.

Clan Karuck fed on the cries of its dying members. Fear was not known among the warriors, who wanted only to die in the service of Gruumsh and Grguch. In a frenzy they defied the rain of arrows and the burning branches falling from the continuing conflagration on high. Some even grabbed their skewered companions and tugged them along as shields.

Behind the wall, the elves abandoned their bows and drew out long, slender swords. In shining mail and with windblown cloaks, most still trailing wisps of smoke and a couple still burning, they met the charge with splendor, strength, and courage.

But Grguch and his minions overran them and slaughtered them, and their weapons gleamed red, not silver, and their cloaks, weighted with blood, would not flap in the breeze.

Grguch led the warriors through the forest a short distance farther, but he knew that he was traveling on elven ground, where defensive lines of archers would sting his warriors from the tops of hills and the boughs of trees, and where powerful spells would explode without warning. He pulled up and raised his open hand, a signal to halt the charge, then he motioned to the south, sending a trio of ogres forward.

"Take their heads," he ordered to his orcs, and nodded back to the stone wall. "We'll pike them along the western bank of the river to remind the faerie folk of their mistake."

Up ahead, some distance already, an ogre cried out in pain. Grguch nodded his understanding, knowing that the elves would regroup quickly—that they probably already had. He looked around at his charges and grinned.

"To the river," he ordered, confident that his point had been made, to Clan Karuck and to the three emissaries who had brought them forth from their tunnels under the Spine of the World.

He didn't know about the fourth non-Karuck onlooker, of course, who had played a role in it all. Jack was back in his Jaculi form, wrapped around the limb of a tree, watching it all unfold around him with mounting curiosity. He would have to have a long talk with Hakuun, and soon, he realized, and he felt a bit of joy then that he had followed Clan Karuck out of the Underdark.

He had long forgotten about the wide world and the fun of mischief.

Besides, he'd never liked elves.

* * * * *

Toogwik Tuk, Ung-thol, and Dnark beamed with toothy grins as they made their way back to orc-held lands.

"We have brought forth the fury of Gruumsh," Dnark said when the trio stood on the western bank of the Surbrin, looking back east at the Moonwood. The sun was low behind them, dusk falling, and the forest took on a singular appearance, as if its tree line was the defensive wall of an immense castle.

"It will remind King Obould of our true purpose," Ung-thol posited.

"Or he will be replaced," said Toogwik Tuk.

The other two didn't even wince at those words, spoken openly. Not after seeing the cunning, the ferocity, and the power of Grguch and Clan Karuck. Barely twenty feet north of their position, an elf head staked upon a tall pike swayed in the wind.

* * * * *

Albondiel's heart sank when he spotted the flash of white against the forest ground. At first he thought it just another patch of snow, but as he came around one thick tree and gained a better vantage point, he realized the truth.

Snow didn't have feathers.

"Hralien," he called in a voice breaking on every syllable. Time seemed to freeze for the shocked elf, as if half the day slid by, but in only a few moments, Hralien was at Albondiel's side.

"Sunset," Hralien whispered and moved forward.

Albondiel summoned his courage and followed. He knew what they would find.

Innovindil still lay atop the pegasus, her arms wrapped around Sunset's neck, her face pressed close to his. From Albondiel's first vantage point when he came around the tree that had abruptly ended Innovindil and Sunset's flight, the scene was peaceful and serene, almost as if his friend had fallen asleep atop her beloved equine friend. Scanning farther down, though, revealed the truth, revealed the blood and the gigantic javelins, the shattered wings and the magical wound of dissolved flesh behind Innovindil's hip.

Hralien bent over the dead elf and gently stroked her thick hair, and ran his other hand over the soft and muscled neck of Sunset.

"They were ready for us," he said.

"Ready?" said Albondiel, shaking his head and wiping the tears from his cheeks. "More than that. They lured us. They anticipated our counterstrike."

"They are orcs!" Hralien protested, rising fast and turning away.

He brought his arms straight out before him, then slowly moved them out wide to either side then behind him, arching his back and lifting his face to the sky as he went. It was a ritual movement, often used in times of great stress and anguish, and Hralien ended by issuing a high-pitched keen toward the sky, a protest to the gods for the pain visited upon his people that dark day.

He collected himself quickly, his grief thrown out for the moment, and spun back at Albondiel, who still kneeled, stroking Innovindil's head.

"Orcs," Hralien said again. "Have they become so sophisticated in their methods?"

"They have always been cunning," Albondiel replied.

"They know too much of us," Hralien protested.

"Then we must change our tactics."

But Hralien was shaking his head. "It is more, I fear. Could it be that they are guided by a dark elf who knows how we fight?"

"We do not know that," Albondiel cautioned. "This was a simple ambush, perhaps."

"One ready for Innovindil and Sunset!"

"By design or by coincidence? You assume much."

Hralien knelt beside his friends, living and dead. "Can we afford not to?"

Albondiel pondered that for a few moments. "We should find Tos'un."

"We should get word to Mithral Hall," said Hralien. "To Drizzt Do'Urden, who will grieve for Innovindil and Sunset. He will understand better the methods of Tos'un, and has already vowed to find the drow."

A shadow passed over them, drawing their attention skyward.

Sunrise circled above them, tossing his head and crying out pitifully for the lost pegasus.

Albondiel looked at Hralien and saw tears streaking his friend's face. He looked back up at the pegasus, but could hardly make out the flying horse through the glare of his own tears in the morning sunlight.

"Get Drizzt," he heard himself whisper.

CHAPTER
MISDIRECTING CLUES
11

"Pack it up and move it out," Bruenor grumbled, slinging his backpack over his shoulder. He snatched up his axe, wrapping his hand around the handle just under the well-worn head. He prodded the hard ground with it as if it were a walking stick as he moved away from the group.

Thibbledorf Pwent, wearing much of his lunch in his beard and on his armor, hopped up right behind, eager to be on his way, and Cordio and Torgar similarly rose to Bruenor's call, though with less enthusiasm, even with a wary glance to each other.

Regis just gave a sigh and looked down at the remainder of his meal, a slab of cold beef wrapped with flattened bread, and with a bowl of thick gravy and a biscuit on the side.

"Always in a hurry," the halfling said to Drizzt, who helped him rewrap the remaining food.

"Bruenor is nervous," said Drizzt, "and anxious."

"Because he fears more monsters?"

"Because these tunnels are not to his expectations or to his liking," the drow explained, and Regis nodded at the revelation.

They had come into the hole expecting to find a tunnel to the dwarven city of Gauntlgrym, and at first, after their encounter with the strange beasts, things had seemed pretty much as they had anticipated, including a sloping tunnel with a worked wall. The other side seemed more natural stone and dirt, as were the ceiling and floor, but that one wall had left no doubt that it was more than a natural cave, and the craftsmanship evident in the fitted stones made Bruenor and the other dwarves believe that it was indeed the work of their ancestors.

But that tunnel hadn't held its promise or its course, and though they were deeper underground, and though they still found fragments of old construction, the trail seemed to be growing cold.

Drizzt and Regis moved quickly to close the distance to the others. With the monsters about, appearing suddenly from the shadows as if from nowhere, the group didn't dare separate. That presented a dilemma a hundred feet along, when Bruenor led them all into a small chamber they quickly recognized to be a hub, with no fewer than six tunnels branching out from it.

"Well, there ye be!" Bruenor cried, hefting his axe and punching it into the air triumphantly. "Ain't no river or burrowing beast made this plaza."

Looking around, it was hard for Drizzt to disagree, for other than one side, where dirt had collapsed into the place, the chamber seemed perfectly circular, and the tunnels too equidistant for it to be a random design.

Torgar fell to his knees and began digging at the hard-packed dirt, and his progress multiplied many times over when Pwent dropped down beside him and put his spiked gauntlets to work. In a few moments, the battlerager scraped stone, and as he worked his way out to the sides, it became apparent that the stone was flat.

"A paver!" Torgar announced.

"Gauntlgrym," Bruenor said to Drizzt and Regis with an exaggerated wink. "Never doubt an old dwarf."

"Another one!" Pwent announced.

"Sure'n the whole place is full o' them," said Bruenor. "It's a trading hub for caravans, or I'm a bearded gnome. Yerself's knowing that," he said to Torgar, and the Mirabarran dwarf nodded.

Drizzt looked past the three dwarves to the fourth, Cordio, who had moved to the wall between a pair of the tunnels and was scraping at the wall. The dwarf nodded as his knife sank in deeper along a crease in the stone behind the accumulated dirt and mud, revealing a vertical line.

"What do ye know?" Bruenor asked, leading Torgar and Thibbledorf over to the cleric.

THE ORC KING

A moment later, as Cordio broke away a larger piece of the covering grime, it became apparent to all that the cleric had found a door. After a few moments, they managed to clear it completely, and to their delight they were able to pry it open, revealing a single-roomed structure behind it. Part of the back left corner had collapsed, taking a series of shelves down with it, but other than that, the place seemed frozen in time.

"Dwarven," Bruenor was saying as Drizzt moved to the threshold.

The dwarf stood off to the side of the small door, examining a rack holding a few ancient metal artifacts. They were tools or weapons, obviously, and Bruenor upended one to examine its head, which could have been the remnants of a pole arm, or even a hoe, perhaps.

"Might be dwarven," Torgar agreed, examining the shorter-handled item beside the one Bruenor had lifted, one showing the clear remains of a spade. "Too old to know for sure."

"Dwarven," Bruenor insisted. He turned and let his gaze encompass the whole of the small house. "All the place is dwarven."

The others nodded, more because they couldn't disprove the theory than because they had reached the same conclusions. The remnants of a table and a pair of chairs might well have been dwarf-made, and seemed about the right size for the bearded folk. Cordio moved around those items to a hearth, and as he began clearing the debris from it and scraping at the stone, that, too, seemed to bolster Bruenor's argument. For there was no mistaking the craftsmanship evident in the ancient fireplace. The bricks had been so tightly set that the passage of time had done little to diminish the integrity of the structure, and indeed it seemed as if, with a bit of cleaning, the companions could safely light a fire.

Drizzt, too, noted that hearth, and paid particular heed to the shallowness of the fireplace, and the funnel shape of the side walls, widening greatly into the room.

"The plaza's a forward post for the city," Bruenor announced as they began moving back out. "So I'm guessing that the city's opposite the tunnel we just came down."

"In the lead!" said Pwent, heading that way at once.

"Good guess on the door," Bruenor said to Cordio, and he patted the cleric on the shoulder before he and Torgar started off after the battlerager.

"It wasn't a guess," Drizzt said under his breath, so that only Regis could hear. And Cordio, for the dwarf glanced back at Drizzt—his expression seeming rather sour, Regis thought—then moved off after his king, muttering, "Wouldn't need pavers this far down."

Regis looked from him to Drizzt, his expression begging answers.

"It was a free-standing house, and not a reinforced cave dwelling," Drizzt explained.

Regis glanced around. "You think there are others, separating the exit tunnels?"

"Probably."

"And what does that mean? There were many free-standing houses in the bowels of Mirabar. Not so uncommon a thing in underground cities."

"True enough," Drizzt agreed. "Menzoberranzan is comprised of many similar structures."

"Cordio's expression spoke of some significance," the halfling remarked. "If this type of structure is to be expected, then why did he wear a frown?"

"Did you note the fireplace?" Drizzt asked.

"Dwarven," Regis replied.

"Perhaps."

"What's wrong?"

"The fireplace was not a cooking pit, primarily," Drizzt explained. "It was designed to throw heat into the room."

Regis shrugged, not understanding.

"We are far enough underground so that the temperature hardly varies," Drizzt informed him, and started off after the others.

Regis paused for just a moment, and glanced back at the revealed structure.

"Should we search this area more completely?" the halfling asked.

"Follow Bruenor," Drizzt replied. "We will have our answers soon enough."

They kept their questions unspoken as they hurried to join up with the four dwarves, which took some time, for the excited Bruenor led them down the tunnel at a hurried pace.

The tunnel widened considerably soon after, breaking into what seemed to be a series of parallel tracks of varying widths continuing in the same general direction. Bruenor moved without hesitation down the centermost of them, but they found it to be a moot choice anyway, since the tunnels interconnected at many junctures. What they soon discerned was that this wasn't so much a series of tunnels as a singular pathway, broken up by pillars, columns, and other structures.

At one such interval, they came upon a low entrance, capped diagonally by a structure that had obviously been made by skilled masons, for the bricks could still be seen, and they held fast despite the passage of centuries and the apparent collapse of the building, which had sent it crashing to the side into another wall.

"Could be a shaft, pitched for a fast descent," Bruenor remarked.

"It's a building that tipped," Cordio argued, and Bruenor snorted and waved his hand dismissively.

But Torgar, who had moved closer, said, "Aye, it is." He paused and looked up. "And one that fell a long way. Or slid."

"And how're ye knowin' that?" Bruenor asked, and there was no mistaking the hint of defiance. He was catching on, obviously, that things weren't unfolding the way he'd anticipated.

Torgar was already motioning them over, and began pointing out the closest corner of the structure, where the edge of the bricks had been rounded, but not by tools.

"We see this in Mirabar all the time," Torgar explained, running a fat thumb over the corner. "Wind wore it round. This place was under the sky, not under the rock."

"There's wind in some tunnels," said Bruenor. "Currents and such blowin' down strong from above."

Torgar remained unconvinced. "This building was up above," he said, shaking his head, "for years and years afore it fell under."

"Bah!" Bruenor snorted. "Ye're guessin'."

"Might be that Gauntlgrym had an aboveground market," Cordio interjected.

Drizzt looked at Regis and rolled his eyes, and as the dwarves moved off, the halfling grabbed Drizzt by the sleeve and held him back.

"You don't believe that Gauntlgrym had an aboveground market?" he asked.

"Gauntlgrym?" Drizzt echoed skeptically.

"You don't believe?"

"More than the market of this place was above ground, I fear," said Drizzt. "Much more. And Cordio and Torgar see it, too."

"But not Bruenor," said Regis.

"It will be a blow to him. One he is not ready to accept."

"You think this whole place was a city above ground?" Regis stated. "A city that sank into the tundra?"

"Let us follow the dwarves. We will learn what we will learn."

The tunnels continued on for a few hundred more feet, but the group came to a solid blockage, one that sealed off all of the nearby corridors. Torgar tapped on that wall repeatedly with a small hammer, listening for echoes, and after inspecting it at several points in all the tunnels, announced to the troop, "There's a big open area behind it. I'm knowin' it."

"Forges?" Bruenor asked hopefully.

Torgar could only shrug. "Only one way we're goin' to find out, me king."

So they set their camp right there, down the main tunnel at the base of the wall, and while Drizzt and Regis went back up the tunnel some distance to keep watch back near the wider areas, the four dwarves devised their plans for safely excavating. Soon after they had shared their next meal, the sound of hammers rang out against the stone, none more urgent than Bruenor's own.

CHAPTER
NESMÉ'S PRIDE
12

"I had hoped to find the woman before we crossed the last expanse to Nesmé," Wulfgar remarked to Catti-brie. Their caravan had stopped to re-supply at a nondescript, unnamed cluster of houses still a couple of days' travel from their destination, and the last such scheduled stop on their journey.

"There are still more settlements," Catti-brie reminded him, for indeed, the drivers had told them that they would pass more secluded lodges in the next two days.

"The houses of hunters and loners," Wulfgar replied. "No places appropriate for Cottie to remain with Colson."

"Unless all the refugees remained together and decided to begin their own community."

Wulfgar replied with a knowing smile, a reflection of Catti-brie's own feelings on the subject, to be sure. She knew as Wulfgar knew that they would find Cottie Cooperson and Colson in Nesmé.

"Two days," Catti-brie said. "In two days, you will have Colson in your arms once more. Where she belongs."

Wulfgar's grim expression, even a little wince, caught her by surprise.

"We have heard of no tragedies along the road," Catti-brie added. "If the caravan bearing Cottie and the others had been attacked, word would have already spread through these outposts. Since we are so close, we can say with confidence that Cottie and Colson reached Nesmé safely."

"Still, I have no love of the place," he said, "and no desire to see the likes of Galen Firth or his prideful companions ever again."

Catti-brie moved closer and put her hand on Wulfgar's shoulder. "We will collect the child and be gone," she said. "Quickly and with few words. We come with the backing of Mithral Hall, and to Mithral Hall we will return with your child."

Wulfgar's face was unreadable, though that, of course, only reaffirmed Catti-brie's suspicions that something was amiss.

The caravan rolled out of the village before the next dawn, wheels creaking against the uneven strain of the perpetually muddy ground. As they continued west, the Trollmoors, the fetid swamp of so many unpleasant beasts, seemed to creep up toward them from the south. But the drivers and those more familiar with the region appeared unconcerned, and were happy to explain, often, that things had quieted since the rout of the trolls by Alustriel's Knights in Silver and the brave Riders of Nesmé.

"The road's safer than it's been in more than a decade," the lead driver insisted.

"More's the pity," one of the regulars from the second wagon answered loudly. "I been hoping a few trolls or bog blokes might show their ugly faces, just so I can watch the work of King Bruenor's kids!"

That brought a cheer from all around, and a smile did widen on Catti-brie's face. She looked to Wulfgar. If he had even heard the remarks, he didn't show it.

Wulfgar and Catti-brie weren't really sure what they might find when their caravan finally came into view of Nesmé, but they knew at once that it was not the same town through which they had traveled on their long-ago journey to rediscover Mithral Hall. Anticipated images of ruined and burned-out homes and shoddy, temporary shelters did not prepare them for the truth of the place. For Nesmé had risen again already, even through the cold winds of winter.

Most of the debris from the troll rampage had been cleared, and newer buildings, stronger, taller, and with thicker walls, replaced the old structures. The double wall surrounding the whole of the place neared completion, and was particularly fortified along the southern borders, facing the Trollmoors.

Contingents of armed and armored riders patrolled the town, meeting the caravan far out from the new and larger gate.

Nesmé was alive again, a testament to the resiliency and determination, and sheer stubbornness that had marked the frontiers of human advancement throughout Faerûn. For all of their rightful negativity toward the place, given their reception those years before, neither Wulfgar nor Catti-brie could hide their respect.

"So much like Ten-Towns," Catti-brie quietly remarked as their wagon neared the gate. "They will not bend."

Wulfgar nodded his agreement, slightly, but he was clearly distracted as he continued to stare at the town.

"They've more people now than before the trolls," Catti-brie said, repeating something the caravan drivers had told the both of them earlier along the road. "Twice the number, say some."

Wulfgar didn't blink and didn't look her way. She sensed his inner turmoil, and knew that it wasn't about Colson. Not only, at least.

She tried one last time to engage him, saying, "Nesmé might inspire other towns to grow along the road to Silverymoon, and won't that be a fitting response to the march of the murderous trolls? It may well be that the northern border will grow strong enough to build a militia that can press into the swamp and be rid of the beasts once and for all."

"It might," said Wulfgar, in such a tone as to show Catti-brie that he hadn't even registered that to which he agreed.

The town gates, towering barriers thrice the height of a tall man and built of strong black-barked logs banded together with heavy straps of metal, groaned in protest as the sentries pulled them back to allow the caravan access to the town's open courtyard. Beyond that defensive wall, Wulfgar and Catti-brie could see that their initial views of Nesmé were no illusion, for indeed the town was larger and more impressive than it had been those years before. It had an official barracks to support the larger militia, a long, two-story building to their left along the defensive southern wall. Before them loomed the tallest structure in town, aside from a singular tower that was under work somewhere in the northwestern quadrant. Two dozen steps led off the main plaza where the wagons parked, directly west of the eastern-facing gates. At the top of those steps ran a pair of parallel, narrow bridges, just a short and defensible expanse, to the impressive front of the new Nesmian Town Hall. Like all the rest of the town, the building was under construction, but like most of the rest, it was ready to stand against any onslaught the Trollmoors in the south, or King Obould in the north, might throw against it.

Wulfgar hopped down from the back of the wagon, then helped Catti-brie to the ground so that she didn't have to pressure her injured hip. She spent a moment standing there, using his offered arm for support, as she stretched the tightness out of her pained leg.

"The folk ye seek could be anywhere in the town," their wagon driver said to them, walking over and speaking quietly.

He alone among the caravan had been in on the real reason Wulfgar and Catti-brie were journeying to Nesmé, for fear that someone else might gossip and send word to Cottie and her friends to flee ahead of their arrival. "They'll not be in any common rooms, as ye saw in Silverymoon, for Nesmé's being built right around the new arrivals. More than half the folk ye'll find here just came from other parts, mostly from lands Obould's darkened with his hordes. Them and some of the Knights in Silver, who remained with the Lady's blessing so that they could get closer to where the fighting's likely to be...."

"Surely there are scribes making note of who's coming in and where they're settling," said Catti-brie.

"If so, ye'll find them in there," said the driver, motioning toward the impressive town hall. "If not, yer best chance is in frequenting the taverns after work's done. Most all the workers find their way to those places—and there're only a few such establishments, and they're all together on one avenue near the southwestern corner. If any're knowing of Cottie, there's the place to find them."

* * * * *

Word spread fast through Nesmé that the arriving caravan had carried with it a couple of extraordinary guards. When the whispers of Catti-brie and Wulfgar reached the ears of Cottie Cooperson's fellow refugees, they knew at once that their friend was in jeopardy.

So by the time Wulfgar and Catti-brie had made their way to the tavern avenue, a pair of concerned friends had whisked Cottie and Colson to the barracks area and the separate house of the town's current leader, Galen Firth.

"He's come to take the child," Teegorr Reth explained to Galen, while his friend Romduul kept Cottie and Colson out in the anteroom.

Galen Firth settled back in his chair behind his desk, digesting it all. It had come as a shock to him, and not a pleasant one, that the human prince and princess of Mithral Hall had arrived in his town. He had assumed it to be a diplomatic mission, and given the principals involved, he had suspected that it wouldn't be a friendly one. Mithral Hall had suffered losses for the sake of Nesmé in the recent battles. Could it be that King Bruenor sought some sort of recompense?

Galen had never been friendly with the dwarves of Mithral Hall or with these two.

"You cannot let him have her," Teegorr implored the Nesmian leader.

"What is his claim?" Galen asked.

"Begging your pardon, sir, but Cottie's been seeing to the girl since she left Mithral Hall. She's taken Colson as her own child, and she's been hurt."

"The child?"

"No, Cottie, sir," Teegorr explained. "She's lost her own—all her own."

"And the child is Wulfgar's?"

"No, not really. He brought the girl to Mithral Hall, with Delly, but then Delly gave her to Cottie."

"With or without Wulfgar's agreement?"

"Who's to say?"

"Wulfgar, I would assume."

"But . . ."

"You assume that Wulfgar has come here to take the child, but could it be that he is merely passing through to check up on her?" Galen asked. "Or might it be that he is here for different reasons—would he even know that your friend Cottie decided to settle in Nesmé?"

"I . . . I . . . I can't be saying for sure, sir."

"So you presume. Very well, then. Let Cottie stay here for now until we can determine why Wulfgar has come."

"Oh, and I thank you for that!"

"But make no mistake, good Teegorr, if Wulfgar's claim is true and he wants the child back, I am bound to honor his claim."

"Your pardon, sir, but Cottie's got twenty folk with her. Good strong hands, who know the frontier and who know how to fight."

"Are you threatening me?"

"No, sir!" Teegorr was quick to reply. "But if Nesmé's not to protect our own, then how are our own to stay in Nesmé?"

"What are you asking?" Galen replied, standing up forcefully. "Am I to condone kidnapping? Is Nesmé to become an outpost for criminals?"

"It's not so simple as that, is all," said Teegorr. "Delly Curtie gave the girl to Cottie, so she's no kidnapper, and not without claim."

That settled Galen Firth back a bit. He couldn't keep the disdain from his face, for it was not a fight he wanted to entertain just then. Clan Battlehammer and Nesmé were not on good terms, despite the fact that the dwarves had sent warriors down to help the Nesmians. In the subsequent sorting of events, the rebuilding of Nesmé had taken precedence over King Bruenor's desire to take the war back to Obould, something that had clearly simmered behind the angry eyes of the fiery dwarf.

And there remained that old issue of the treatment Bruenor and his friends, including Wulfgar and the drow elf Drizzt, had met with on their initial pass through Nesmé those years ago, an unpleasant confrontation that had set Galen Firth and the dwarf at odds.

Neither could Galen Firth keep the wry grin from breaking through his otherwise solemn expression on occasion as he pondered the possibilities. He couldn't deny that there would be a measure of satisfaction in causing grief to Wulfgar, if the opportunity presented itself.

"Who knows that you came here?" Galen asked.

Teegorr looked at him curiously. "To Nesmé?"

"Who knows that you and your friend brought Cottie and the child here to me?"

"Some of the others who crossed the Surbrin beside us."

"And they will not speak of it?"

"No," said Teegorr. "Not a one of us wants to see the child taken from Cottie Cooperson. She's suffered terribly, and now she's found peace—and one that's better for the girl than anything Wulfgar might be offering."

"Wulfgar is a prince of Mithral Hall," Galen reminded. "A man of great wealth, no doubt."

"And Mithral Hall is no place for a man, or a girl—particularly a girl!" Teegorr argued. "Good enough for them dwarves, and good for them. But it's no place for a human girl to grow."

Galen Firth rose up from his seat. "Keep her here," he instructed. "I will go and see my old friend Wulfgar. Perhaps he is here for reasons other than the girl."

"And if he is?"

"Then you and I never had this discussion," Galen explained.

He set a pair of guards outside the anteroom, with orders that no one should enter, and he gathered up a couple of others in his wake as he headed out across the darkening town to the taverns and the common rooms. As he expected, he found Wulfgar and Catti-brie in short order, sitting at a table near the bar of the largest of the taverns, and listening more than speaking.

"You have come to join our garrison!" Galen said with great exaggeration as he approached. "I always welcome strong arms and a deadly bow."

Wulfgar and Catti-brie turned to regard him, their faces, particularly the large barbarian's, hardening upon recognition.

"We have need for a garrison of our own in Mithral Hall," Catti-brie replied politely.

"The orcs have not been pushed back," Wulfgar added, his sharp tone reminding Galen Firth that Galen himself, and his insistence on Nesmé taking precedence, had played no minor role in the decision to not dislodge King Obould.

The other folk in the town knew that as well, and didn't miss the reference, and all in the tavern hushed as Galen stood before the two adopted children of King Bruenor Battlehammer.

"Everything in its time," Galen replied, after looking around to ensure his support. "The Silver Marches are stronger now that Nesmé has risen from the ruins." A cheer started around him, and he raised his voice in proclamation, "For never again will the trolls come forth from the mud to threaten the lands west of Silverymoon or the southern reaches of your own Mithral Hall."

Wulfgar's jaw tightened even more at the notion that Nesmé was serving as Mithral Hall's vanguard, particularly since Mithral Hall's efforts had preserved what little had remained of Nesmé's population.

Which was exactly the effect Galen Firth had been hoping for, and he grinned knowingly as Catti-brie put her hand on Wulfgar's enormous forearm in an effort to keep him calm.

"We had no word that we would be so graced," Galen said. "Is it customary among Clan Battlehammer for emissaries to arrive unannounced?"

"We are not here on the business of Bruenor," said Catti-brie, and she motioned for Galen Firth to sit down beside her, opposite Wulfgar.

The man did pull out the chair, but he merely turned it and put his foot up on it, which made him tower over the two even more. Until, that is, Wulfgar rose to his feet, his nearly seven foot frame, his giant shoulders, stealing that advantage.

But Galen didn't back down. He stared hard at Wulfgar, locking the man's gaze. "Then why?" he asked, his voice lower and more insistent.

"We came in as sentries for a caravan," Catti-brie said.

Galen glanced down at her. "The children of Bruenor hire out as mercenaries?"

"Volunteers doing our part in the collective effort," Catti-brie answered.

"It was a way to serve others as we served our own needs," Wulfgar said.

"To come to Nesmé?" asked Galen.

"Yes."

"Why, if not for Brue—"

"I have come to find a girl, Colson, who was taken from Mithral Hall," Wulfgar stated.

" 'Taken'? Wrongly?"

"Yes."

Behind Wulfgar, several people bustled about. Galen recognized them as friends of Teegorr and Cottie, and expected that there might soon be trouble—which he didn't think so dire a possibility. In truth, the man was interested in testing his strength against that of the legendary Wulfgar, and besides, he had enough guards nearby to ensure that there would be no real downside to any brawl.

"How is it that a child was abducted from Mithral Hall," he asked, "and ferried across the river by Bruenor's own? What dastardly plot turned that result?"

"The girl's name is Colson," Catti-brie intervened, as Wulfgar and Galen Firth leaned in closer toward each other. "We have reason to believe that she has come to Nesmé. In fact, that seems most assured."

"There are children here," Galen Firth admitted, "brought in with the various groups of displaced people, who have come to find community and shelter."

"No one can deny that Nesmé has opened her gates to those in need," Catti-brie replied, and Wulfgar shot a glare her way. "A mutually beneficial arrangement for a town that grows more grand by the day."

"But there is a child here that does not belong in Nesmé, nor to the woman who brought her here," Wulfgar insisted. "I have come to retrieve that girl."

Someone moved fast behind Wulfgar, and he spun, quick as an elf. He brought his right arm across, sweeping aside a two-handed grab by one of Cottie's friends, then turned the arm down, bringing the fool's arms with it. Wulfgar's left hand snapped out and grabbed the man by the front of his tunic. In the blink of an astonished eye, Wulfgar had the man up in the air, fully two feet off the ground, and shook him with just the one hand.

The barbarian turned back on Galen Firth, and with a flick of his arm sent the shaken fool tumbling aside.

"Colson is leaving with me. She was wrongly taken, and though I bear no ill will"—he paused and turned to let his penetrating gaze sweep the room—"to any of those who were with the woman to whom she was entrusted, and no ill will toward the woman herself—surely not!—I will leave with the girl rightfully returned."

"How did she get out of Mithral Hall, a fortress of dwarves?" an increasingly annoyed Galen Firth asked.

"Delly Curtie," said Wulfgar.

"Wife of Wulfgar," Catti-brie explained.

"Was she not then this child's mother?"

"Adopted mother, as Wulfgar is Colson's adopted father," said Catti-brie.

Galen Firth snorted, and many in the room muttered curses under their breath.

"Delly Curtie was under the spell of a powerful and evil weapon," Catti-brie explained. "She did not surrender the child of her own volition."

"Then she should be here to swear to that very thing."

"She is dead," said Wulfgar.

"Killed by Obould's orcs," Catti-brie added. "For after she handed the child to Cottie Cooperson, she ran off to the north, to the orc lines, where she was found, murdered and frozen in the snow."

Galen Firth did grimace a bit at that, and the look he gave to Wulfgar was almost one tinged with sympathy. Almost.

"The weapon controlled her," said Catti-brie. "Both in surrendering the child and in running to certain doom. It is a most foul blade. I know well, for I carried it for years."

That brought more murmurs from around the room and a look of astonishment from Galen. "And what horrors did Catti-brie perpetrate under the influence of such a sentient evil?"

"None, for I controlled the weapon. It did not control me."

"But Delly Curtie was made of stuff less stern," said Galen Firth.

"She was no warrior. She was not raised by dwarves."

Galen Firth didn't miss the pointed reminder of both facts, of who these two were and what they had behind their claim.

He nodded and pondered the words for a bit, then replied, "It is an interesting tale."

"It is a demand that will be properly answered," said Wulfgar, narrowing his blue eyes and leaning even more imposingly toward the leader of Nesmé. "We do not ask you to adjudicate. We tell you the circumstance and expect you to give back the girl."

"You are not in Mithral Hall, son of Bruenor," Galen Firth replied through gritted teeth.

"You deny me?" Wulfgar asked, and it seemed to all that the barbarian was on the verge of a terrible explosion. His blue eyes were wide and wild.

Galen didn't back down, though he surely expected an attack.

And again Catti-brie intervened. "We came to Nesmé as sentries on a caravan from Silverymoon, as a favor to Lady Alustriel," she explained, turning her shoulder and putting her arm across the table to block Wulfgar, though of course she couldn't hope to slow his charge, should it come. "For it was Lady Alustriel, friend of King Bruenor Battlehammer, friend of Drizzt Do'Urden, friend of Wulfgar and of Catti-brie, who told us that Colson would be found in Nesmé."

Galen Firth tried to hold steady, but he knew he was giving ground.

"For she knows Colson well, and well she knows of Colson's rightful father, Wulfgar," Catti-brie went on. "When she heard our purpose in traveling to Silverymoon, she put all of her assets at our disposal, and it was she who told us that Cottie Cooperson and Colson had traveled to Nesmé. She wished us well on our travels, and even offered to fly us here on her fiery chariot, but we felt indebted and so we agreed to travel along with the caravan and serve as sentries."

"Would not a desperate father take the quicker route?" asked Galen Firth, and around him, heads bobbed in agreement.

"We did not know that the caravan bearing Colson made it to Nesmé, or whether perhaps the hearty and good folk accompanying the child decided to debark earlier along the road. And that is not for you to decide in any case, Galen Firth. Do you deny Wulfgar's rightful claim? Would you have us go back to Lady Alustriel and tell her that the proud folk of Nesmé would not accede to the proper claim of Colson's own father? Would you have us return at once to Silverymoon and to Mithral Hall with word that Galen Firth refused to give Wulfgar his child?"

"Adopted child," remarked one of the men across the way.

Galen Firth didn't register that argument. The man had thrown him some support, but only because he obviously needed it at that moment. That poignant reminder had him squaring his shoulders, but he knew that Catti-brie had delivered a death blow to his obstinacy. For he knew that she spoke the truth, and that he could ill afford to anger the Lady of Silverymoon. Whatever might happen between King Bruenor and Galen would not likely ill affect Nesmé, for the dwarves would not come south to do battle, but for Lady Alustriel to take King Bruenor's side was another matter entirely. Nesmé needed Silverymoon's support. No caravan would travel to Nesmé that did not originate in, or at least pass through, the city of Lady Alustriel.

Galen Firth was no fool. He did not doubt the story of Catti-brie and Wulfgar, and he had seen clearly the desperation on Cottie Cooperson's face when he had left her in the barracks. That type of desperation was borne of knowing that she had no real claim, that the child was not hers.

For of course, Colson was not.

Galen Firth looked over his shoulder to his guards. "Go and fetch Cottie Cooperson and the girl," he said.

Protests erupted around the room, with men shaking their fists in the air.

"The child is mine!" Wulfgar shouted at them, turning fiercely, and indeed, all of those in front stepped back. "Would any of you demand any less if she was yours?"

"Cottie is our friend," one man replied, rather meekly. "She means the girl no harm."

"Fetch your own child, then," said Wulfgar. "Relinquish her, or him, to me in trade!"

"What foolish words are those?"

"Words to show you your own folly," said the big man. "However good Cottie Cooperson's heart, and I do not doubt your claim that she is worthy both as a friend and a mother, I cannot surrender to her a girl that is my own. I have come for Colson, and I will leave with Colson, and any man who stands in my way would do well to have made his peace with his god."

He snapped his arm in the air before him and called to Aegis-fang, and the mighty warhammer appeared magically in his grasp. With a flick, Wulfgar rapped the hammer atop a nearby table, shattering all four legs and dropping the kindling to the floor.

Galen Firth gasped in protest, and the one guard behind him reached for his sword—and stared down the length of an arrow set on Catti-brie's Taulmaril.

"Which of you will come forward and deny my claim to Colson?" Wulfgar asked the group, and not surprisingly, his challenge was met with silence.

"You will leave my town," Galen Firth said.

"We will, on the same caravan that brought us in," Catti-brie replied, easing her bow back to a rest position as the guard relinquished his grip on the sword and raised his hands before him. "As soon as we have Colson."

"I intend to protest this to Lady Alustriel," Galen Firth warned.

"When you do," said Catti-brie, "be certain to explain to Lady Alustriel how you almost incited a riot and a tragedy by playing the drama out before the hot humors of men and women who came to your town seeking naught but refuge and a new home. Be certain to tell Lady Alustriel of Silverymoon of your discretion, Galen Firth, and we will do likewise with King Bruenor."

"I grow tired of your threats," Galen Firth said to her, but Catti-brie only smiled in reply.

"And I long ago tired of you," Wulfgar said to the man.

Behind Galen Firth, the tavern door opened, and in came Cottie Cooperson holding Colson and pulled along by a guard. Outside the door two men jostled with another pair of guards, who would not let them enter.

The question of Wulfgar's claim was answered the moment Colson came into the room. "Da!" the toddler cried, verily leaping out of Cottie's grasp to get to the man she had known as her father for all her life. She squealed and squirmed and reached with both her arms for Wulfgar, calling for her "Da!" over and over again.

He rushed to her, dropping Aegis-fang to the ground, and took her in his arms then gently, but forcefully, removed her from Cottie's desperate grasp. Colson made no movement back toward the woman at all, but crushed her da in a desperate hug.

Cottie began to tremble, to cry, and her desperation grew by the second. In a few moments, she went down to her knees, wailing.

And Wulfgar responded, dropping to one knee before her. With his free hand, he lifted her chin and brushed back her hair, then quieted her with soft words. "Colson has a mother who loves her as much as you loved your own children, dear woman," he said.

Behind him, Catti-brie's eyes widened with surprise.

"I can take care o' her," Cottie wailed.

Wulfgar smiled at her, brushed her hair back again, then rose. He called Aegis-fang to his free hand and stalked past Galen Firth, snickering in defiance of the man's glare. As he went through the door, Cottie's two companions, for all their verbal protests, parted before him, for few men in all the world would dare stand before Wulfgar, son of Beornegar, a warrior whose legend had been well earned.

"I will speak with our drivers," Catti-brie informed Wulfgar when they exited the inn, with a chorus of shouts and protests echoing behind them. "We should be on our way as soon as possible."

"Agreed," said Wulfgar. "I will wait for the wagons to depart."

Catti-brie nodded and started for the door of a different tavern, where she knew the lead driver to be. She stopped short, though, as she considered the curious answer, and turned back to regard Wulfgar.

"I will not be returning to Silverymoon," Wulfgar confirmed.

"You can't be thinking of going straight to Mithral Hall with the child. The terrain is too rough, and in the hands of orcs for much of the way. The safest road back to Mithral Hall is through Silverymoon."

"It is, and so you must go to Silverymoon."

Catti-brie stared at him hard. "Are you planning to stay here, that Cottie Cooperson can help with Colson?" she said with obvious and pointed sarcasm. To her ultimate frustration, she couldn't read Wulfgar's expression. "You've got family in the hall. I'll be there for you and for the girl. I'm knowing that it will be difficult for you without Delly, but I won't be on the road anytime soon, and be sure that the girl will be no burden to me."

"I will not return to Mithral Hall," Wulfgar stated bluntly, and a gust of wind would have likely knocked Catti-brie over at that moment. "Her place is with her mother," Wulfgar went on. "Her real mother. Never should I have taken her, but I will correct that error now, in returning her where she belongs."

"Auckney?"

Wulfgar nodded.

"That is halfway across the North."

"A journey I have oft traveled and one not fraught with peril."

"Colson has a home in Mithral Hall," Catti-brie argued, and Wulfgar was shaking his head even as the predictable words left her mouth.

"Not one suitable for her."

Catti-brie licked her lips and looked from the girl to Wulfgar, and she knew that he might as well have been speaking about himself at that moment.

"How long will you be gone from us?" the woman dared to ask.

Wulfgar's pause spoke volumes.

"Ye cannot," Catti-brie whispered, seeming very much like a little girl with a Dwarvish accent again.

"I have no choice before me," Wulfgar replied. "This is not my place. Not now. Look at me!" He paused and swept his free hand dramatically from his head to his feet, encompassing his gigantic frame. "I was not born to crawl through dwarven tunnels. My place is the tundra. Icewind Dale, where my people roam."

Catti-brie shook her head with every word, in helpless denial. "Bruenor is your father," she whispered.

"I will love him to the end of my days," Wulfgar admitted. "His place is there, but mine is not."

"Drizzt is your friend."

Wulfgar nodded. "As is Catti-brie," he said with a wistful smile. "Two dear friends who have found love, at long last."

Catti-brie mouthed, "I'm sorry," but she couldn't bring herself to actually speak the words aloud.

"I am happy for you both," said Wulfgar. "Truly I am. You complement each other's every movement, and I have never heard your laughter more full of contentment, nor Drizzt's. But this was not as I had wanted it. I am happy for you—both, and truly. But I cannot stand around and watch it."

The admission took the woman's breath away. "It doesn't have to be like this," she said.

"Do not be sad!" Wulfgar roared. "Not for me! I know now where my home is, and where my destiny lies. I long for the song of Icewind Dale's chill breeze, and for the freedom of my former life. I will hunt caribou along the shores of the Sea of Moving Ice. I will battle goblins and orcs without the restraints of political prudence. I am going home, to be among my own people, to pray at the graves of my ancestors, to find a wife and carry on the line of Beornegar."

"It is too sudden."

Again Wulfgar shook his head. "It is as deliberate as I have ever been."

"You have to go back and talk to Bruenor," Catti-brie said. "You owe him that."

Wulfgar reached under his tunic, produced a scroll, and handed it to her. "You will tell him for me. My road is easier west from here than from Mithral Hall."

"He will be outraged!"

"He will not even be in Mithral Hall," Wulfgar reminded. "He is out to the west with Drizzt in search of Gauntlgrym."

"Because he is in dire need of answers," Catti-brie protested. "Would you desert Bruenor in these desperate days?"

Wulfgar chuckled and shook his head. "He is a dwarf king in a land of orcs. Every day will qualify as you describe. There will be no end to this, and if there is an end to Obould, another threat will rise from the depths of the halls, perhaps, or from Obould's successor. This is the way of things, ever and always. I leave now or I wait until the situation is settled—and it will only be settled for me when I have crossed to Warrior's Rest. You know the truth of it," he said with a disarming grin, one that Catti-brie could not dismiss. "Obould today, the drow yesterday, and something—of course something—tomorrow. That is the way of it."

"Wulfgar . . ."

"Bruenor will forgive me," said the barbarian. "He is surrounded by fine warriors and friends, and the orcs will not likely try again to capture the hall. There is no good time for me to leave, and yet I know that I cannot stay. And every day that Colson is apart from her mother is a tragic day. I understand that now."

"Meralda gave the girl to you," Catti-brie reminded him. "She had no choice."

"She was wrong. I know that now."

"Because Delly is dead?"

"I am reminded that life is fragile, and often short."

"It is not as dark as you believe. You have many here who support . . ."

Wulfgar shook his head emphatically, silencing her. "I loved you," he said. "I loved you and lost you because I was a fool. It will always be the great regret of my life, the way I treated you before we were to be wed. I accept that we cannot go back, for even if you were able and willing, I know that I am not the same man. My time with Errtu left marks deep in my soul, scars I mean to erase in the winds of Icewind Dale, running beside my tribe, the Tribe of the Elk. I am content. I am at peace. And never have I been more certain of my road."

Catti-brie shook her head with every word, in helpless and futile denial, and her blue eyes grew wet with tears. This wasn't how it was supposed to be. The five Companions of the Hall were together again, and they were supposed to stay that way for all their days.

"You said that you support me, and so I ask you to now," said Wulfgar. "Trust in my judgment, in that I know what course I must follow. I take with me my love for you and for Drizzt and for Bruenor and for Regis. That is ever in the heart of Wulfgar. I will never let the image of you and the others fade from my thoughts, and never let the lessons I have learned from all of you escape me as I walk my road."

"Your road so far away."

Wulfgar nodded. "In the winds of Icewind Dale."

CHAPTER 13

A CITY UNDWARVEN

The six companions stood just inside the opening they had carved through the stone, their mouths uniformly agape. They had their backs to the wall of a gigantic cavern that held a magnificent and very ancient city. Huge structures rose up all around them: a trio of stepped pyramids to their right and a beautifully crafted series of towers to their left, all interconnected with flying walkways, and every edge adorned with smaller spires, gargoyles, and minarets. A collection of smaller buildings sat before them, around an ancient pond that still held brackish water and many plants creeping up around its stone perimeter wall. The plants near the pool and scattered throughout the cavern, the common Underdark luminous fungi, provided a minimal light beyond the torches held by Torgar and Thibbledorf, and of course Regis, who would not let his go. The pool and surrounding architecture hardly held their attention at that moment, though, for beyond the buildings loomed the grandest structure of all, a domed building—a castle, cathedral, or palace. Many stone stairs led up to the front of the place, where giant columns stood in a line, supporting a heavy stone porch. In the shadowy recesses, the six could make out gigantic doors.

"Gauntlgrym," Bruenor mouthed repeatedly, and his eyes were wet with tears.

Less willing to make such a pronouncement, Drizzt instead continued to survey the area. The ground was broken, but not excessively, and he could see that the entire area had been paved with flat stones, shaped and fitted to define specific avenues winding through the many buildings.

"The dwarves had different sensibilities then," Regis remarked, and fittingly, Drizzt thought.

Indeed, the place was unlike any dwarven city he had known. No construction under Kelvin's Cairn in Icewind Dale, or in Mirabar, Felbarr, or Mithral Hall, approached the height of even the smallest of the many grand structures around them, and the main building before them loomed larger even than the individual stalagmite-formed great houses of Menzoberranzan. That building was more suited to Waterdeep, he thought, or to Calimport and the marvelous palaces of the pashas.

As the overwhelming shock and awe faded a bit, the dwarves fanned out and moved away from the wall. Drizzt focused on Torgar, who went down to one knee and began scraping between the edges of two flagstones. He brought up a bit of dirt and tasted it then spat it aside, nodding his head and wearing an expression of concern.

Drizzt looked ahead to Bruenor, who seemed oblivious to his companions, walking zombielike toward the giant structure as if pulled by unseen forces.

And indeed the dwarf king was, Drizzt understood. He was tugged forward by pride and by hope, that it truly was Gauntlgrym, the fabulous city of his ancestors, glorious beyond his expectations, and that he would somehow find answers to the question of how to defeat Obould.

Thibbledorf Pwent walked behind Bruenor, while Cordio moved near to Torgar, the latter two striking up a quiet conversation.

One of doubt, Drizzt suspected.

"Is it Gauntlgrym?" Regis asked the drow.

"We will learn soon enough," Drizzt replied and started after Bruenor.

But Regis grabbed him by the arm, forcing him to turn back around.

"It doesn't sound like you believe it is," the halfling said quietly.

Drizzt scanned the cavern, inviting Regis to follow his gaze. "Have you ever seen such structures as these?"

"Of course not."

"No?" Drizzt asked. "Or is it that you have never seen such structures as these in such an environment as this?"

"What do you mean?" Regis asked, but his voice trailed away and his eyes widened as he finished, and Drizzt knew that he had caught on.

The pair scurried to catch up to Torgar and Cordio, who were fast gaining on the front two.

"Check the buildings as we pass," Bruenor instructed, motioning to Pwent and Torgar. "Elf, ye take the flank, and Rumblebelly come close up to me and Cordio."

As they moved by doorways, Pwent and Torgar alternately kicked them in, or rushed in through those that were already opened, as Bruenor continued his march, but more slowly, toward the huge structure, with Regis seemingly glued to his side. Cordio, though, kept hanging back, close enough to get to any of the other three dwarves in a hurry.

Drizzt, moving out into the shadows on the right flank, watched them all with quick glances while focusing his attention primarily on the deeper shadows. He wanted to unravel the mystery of the place, of course, but his main concern was ensuring that no current monstrous residents of the strange city made a sudden and unexpected appearance. Drizzt had been a creature of the Underdark long enough to know that few places so full of shelter would remain uninhabited for long.

"A forge!" Thibbledorf Pwent called from one building—one that had an open back, Drizzt noted, much like a smithy in the surface communities. "I got me a forge!"

Bruenor paused for just a moment before starting again for the huge building, his grin wide and his pace quicker. The other dwarves and Regis, even the stupidly grinning Pwent, hurried to catch up, and by the time Bruenor put his foot on the bottom step, all five were grouped together.

The stairs were wider than they were tall, and while they rose up a full thirty feet, they extended nearly twice that to Bruenor's left and right. Over at the very edge to the right, Drizzt moved fast to get up ahead of the others. Silent as a shadow and nearly invisible in the dim light, Drizzt rushed along, and Bruenor had barely taken his tenth step up when Drizzt crested the top, coming under the darker shadows of the pillared canopy.

And in there, the drow saw that they were not alone, and that danger was indeed waiting for his friends, for behind one of the centermost pillars loomed a behemoth unlike any Drizzt had even seen. Tall and sinewy, the hairless humanoid was blacker than a drow, if that was possible. It stood easily thrice Drizzt's height, perhaps four times, and exuded an aura of tremendous power, the strength of a mountain giant, monstrous and brutish despite its lean form.

And it moved with surprising speed.

*****

Perched in the rafters of the canopy behind and above Drizzt, another beast of darkness studied the approaching group. Batlike in appearance, but huge and perfectly black, the nightwing took note of the movements, particularly those of the drow elf and the behemoth, a fellow denizen of the Plane of Shadow, a fearsome creature known as a nightwalker.

*****

"Bruenor!" Drizzt cried as the giant started moving, and at the sound of his warning the dwarves reacted at once, particularly Thibbledorf Pwent, who leaped defensively before his king.

And when the giant, black-skinned nightwalker appeared, twenty feet of muscle and terror, Thibbledorf Pwent met its paralyzing gaze with a whoop of battlerager delight, and charged.

He got about three strides up the stairs before the nightwalker bent and reached forward, with long arms more akin in proportion to those of a great ape than to a human. Giant black hands clamped about the ferocious dwarf, long fingers fully engulfing him. Kicking and thrashing like a child in his father's arms, Pwent lifted off the ground.

Behind him, Bruenor could not move quickly enough to stop the hoist, and Cordio fell to spellcasting, and Regis and Torgar didn't move at all, both of them captured by the magical gaze of the powerful giant, both of them standing and trembling and gasping for breath.

That would have been the sudden end of Thibbledorf Pwent, surely, for the nightwalker could turn solid stone to dust in the crush of its tremendous grasp, but from the stairs above and to the right came Drizzt Do'Urden, leaping high, scimitars drawn. He executed a vicious double slash across the upper left arm of the nightwalker, his magical blades tearing through flesh and muscle.

In its lurch, the nightwalker dropped its left hand away, and so lost half the vice with which to crush the wildly flailing dwarf. So the behemoth took the second best option and instead of crushing Thibbledorf Pwent, it flung him high and far.

Pwent's cry changed pitch like the screech of a diving hawk, and he slammed hard against the front of the porch's canopy, some forty feet from the ground. He somehow kept the presence of mind to smash his spiked gauntlets against that facing, and luck was with him as one caught fast in a seam in the stone and left him hanging helplessly, but very much alive.

Down below, Drizzt landed on the stairs, more than a dozen feet below where he had begun his leap, and only his quickness and great agility kept him from serious harm, as he scrambled down the steps to absorb his momentum, even keeping the presence of mind to swat Torgar with the flat of one blade as he rushed past.

Torgar blinked and came back to his senses, just a bit, and turned to regard the running drow.

Drizzt finally stopped his run and swung around, to see Bruenor darting between the nightwalker's legs, his axe chopping hard against one. The behemoth roared—a strange and otherworldly howl that changed pitch multiple times, as if several different creatures had been given voice through the same horn. Again the nightwalker moved with deceiving speed, twisting and turning, lifting one foot and slamming it down at the dwarf.

But Bruenor saw it coming and threw himself back the other way, and even managed to whack at the other leg as he tumbled past. The nightwalker hit only stone with its stomp, but it cracked and crushed that stone.

Drizzt charged to join his friend, but noted a movement to his right that he could not dismiss. Looking past the thrashing, cursing, hanging Thibbledorf, he saw the gigantic, batlike creature drop from the canopy, spreading black wings fully forty feet across as it commenced its swoop. The air shimmered in front of it before it ever really began, though. It sent forth a wave of devastating magical energy that struck the drow with tremendous force.

Drizzt felt his heart stop as if it had been grabbed by a giant hand. Blood came from his eyes and blackness filled his vision. He staggered and stumbled, and as the nightwing came on, he knew he was helpless. He did see, but didn't consciously register, Thibbledorf Pwent curling up against the canopy, tucking his feet against the stone.

* * * * *

Torgar Hammerstriker, proud warrior from Mirabar, whose family had served the various Marchions of Mirabar for generations, and who had bravely marched from that city to Mithral Hall, pledging allegiance to King Bruenor, could not believe his fright. Torgar Hammerstriker, who had leaped headlong into an army of orcs, who had battled giants and giant mottled worms, who had once fought a dragon, cursed himself for being held in the paralysis of fear from the black-skinned behemoth.

He saw Drizzt stagger and stumble, and noted the swoop of the giant batlike creature. But he went for Bruenor, only for Bruenor, his king, his great-axe held high.

Beside him as he sped past, Cordio Muffinhead cast the first of his spells, throwing a wave of magic out at Bruenor that infused the dwarf king with added strength so that with his next swing, his many-notched axe bit in a little deeper. Cordio, too, turned to meet the rush of the nightwing, and deduced immediately that it had somehow rendered Drizzt helpless. The dwarf began another spell, but doubted he could cast it in time.

But Thibbledorf Pwent loosed his own type of spell, a battlerager dweomer, indeed. With a roar of defiance, the already battered dwarf shoved off with all his strength, his powerful legs tearing free his embedded hand spikes with a terrible screeching noise. Pwent flew out and up backward from the canopy and executed a half-twist, half-somersault as he went.

He came around as the nightwing glided under him, and he punched out, one fist after another, latching on with forged metal spikes.

The nightwing dipped under the dwarf's weight as he crashed down on its back, then it shrieked in protest. It finished with a great intake of breath, and Pwent felt it grow cold beneath him—not as if in death, but magically so, as if he had leaped not on a living, giant bat, but upon the Great Glacier itself.

The nightwing started to swing its head, but Pwent moved faster, tucking his chin and snapping every muscle in his body to propel himself forward and down, driving his head spike into the base of the nightwing's skull. The sheer power of the dwarf's movement straightened the creature's head back out and facing forward as the nightwing executed its magic, breathing a cone of freezing air before it.

Unfortunately for the humanoid giant, it stood right in the path of the devastating cone of cold.

The behemoth roared in protest and thrashed its arms to block the blinding and painful breath. White frost appeared all over the black skin of its head, arms, and chest, and strictly on reflex the giant punched out as the frantic nightwing fluttered past, scoring a solid slam against the base of its wing that sent both bat and dwarf into a fast-spinning plummet. They soared over the stairs and off toward the towers, skipped off the top of one building and barreled into another, crashing down in a tangled heap.

Thibbledorf Pwent never stopped shouting, cursing, or thrashing.

* * * * *

Drizzt fought through the pain and wiped the blurriness from his bloodied eyes. He had no time to go after Pwent and the giant shadowy bat. None of them did, for the black-skinned giant was far from defeated.

Bruenor and Torgar raced across the stairs, swatting at the treelike legs with their masterwork weapons, and indeed several gashes showed on those legs, and from them issued grayish ooze that smoked as it dribbled to the ground. But they would have to hit the giant a hundred times to fell it, Drizzt realized, and if the behemoth connected solidly on either of them but once. . . .

Drizzt winced as the nightwalker kicked out, just clipping the dodging Torgar, but still hitting him hard enough to send him bouncing down the stone stairs, his axe flying from his grasp. Knowing that

Bruenor couldn't stand alone against the beast, Drizzt started for him, but stumbled, still weak and wounded, disoriented from the magical attack of the flying creature.

The drow felt another magical intrusion then, a wave of soothing, healing energy, and as he renewed his charge Bruenor's way, he managed a quick glance, a quick nod of appreciation, to Cordio.

As he did, he noted Regis simply walking away, muttering to himself, as if oblivious to the events unfolding around him.

As with Pwent, though, the drow had no time to concern himself with it, and when he refocused on his giant target, he winced in fear, for the behemoth chopped down its huge hand, leaving a trail of blackness hanging in the air, and more than opaque, that blackness had dimension.

A magical gate. And one with shapes already moving within its inviting swirls.

Drizzt took heart as Bruenor scored a solid hit, nearly tripping up the giant as it lifted a foot to stomp at him. The nightwalker howled and grabbed at its torn foot, giving Bruenor time to move safely aside, and more importantly, giving Torgar time to begin his charge back up the stairs, limping though he was.

Drizzt, though, had stopped his own advance. The warnings of the priests echoing in his thoughts, the drow pulled forth his onyx figurine. He could see the dangers clearly, the instability of the region, the appearance of a gate to the Plane of Shadow. But as the first wraith-like form began to slide through that smoky portal, Drizzt knew they could not win without help.

"Come to me, Guenhwyvar!" he yelled, and dropped the statue to the stone. "I need you."

"Drizzt, no!" Cordio cried, but it was too late, already the gray mist that would become the panther had begun to form.

Torgar sprinted by the drow, taking the stairs two at a time. He veered from his path to the behemoth to intercept the first floating, shadowy creature to emerge from the gate, which resembled an emaciated human dressed in tattered dark gray robes. Torgar leaped at it with a great two-handed swipe of his axe, and the creature, a dread wraith, met that with a sweep of its arm, trailing tendrils of smoke.

The axe struck home and the creature's hand slapped across the dwarf's shoulder, its permeating and numbing touch reaching into Torgar and leaching his life-force. Blanching, weaker, Torgar growled through the sudden weariness and pulled back his axe, spinning a complete circuit the other way and coming around with a second chop that bludgeoned the dread wraith straight back into the smoky portal.

But another was taking its place, and Torgar's legs shook beneath him. He hadn't the strength to charge, so he tried to firm himself up to meet the newest wraith's approach.

Leaving Drizzt with a dilemma, to be sure, for while Torgar obviously needed his help, so did Bruenor up above, where the giant was moving deliberately, cutting off the dwarf's avenues of escape.

But the choice didn't materialize, for there came a flash of blackness and time seemed to stand still for many long heartbeats.

Light turned to dark and dark to light, so that the giant seemed to become a brighter gray in hue, as did Drizzt, and the dwarves' faces darkened. Everything reversed, torches flaring black, and the hush of surprise engulfed the creatures of shadow and the companions alike.

Guenhwyvar's roar broke the spell.

When Drizzt turned to see his beloved companion, his hope turned to horror, for Guenhwyvar, whiter than Drizzt or the behemoth, seemed only half-formed, and she elongated as she leaped for the second emerging wraith, as if she were somehow dragging her magical gate with her very form. She hit the wraith and went back into the shadow portal with it, and as those two portals merged into a weird weave of conflicting energies, there came another blinding burst of black energy. The wraith hissed in protest, and Guenhwyvar's roar flooded with pain.

The behemoth howled, too, its agony obvious. The portal stretched, twisted, and reached out to grab at the gigantic creature of shadow, as if to bring it home.

No, Drizzt realized, his eyes straining to make sense through the myriad of free-flowing shapes, not to bring it home but as if to engulf the giant and swallow it, and the behemoth's howls only confirmed that the assault of the twisting portals was no pleasant embrace.

The giant proved the stronger, though, and the portals winked out, and the light returned to normal torch- and lichen light, and all was as it had been before the giant had enacted its gate and Drizzt had responded with one of his own.

Except that the behemoth was clearly wounded, clearly off-balance and staggering. And not everyone had been frozen by the stunning events of the merging gates and the dizzying reversals of light and dark.

Far up the stairs, King Bruenor Battlehammer seized the moment of opportunity. He came down like a rolling boulder, skipped out to the edge of a stair, and leaped as high and as far as his short legs would carry him.

Drizzt charged at the behemoth, demanding its attention with a wild flurry of his blades and a piercing battle cry, and so the giant was fully focused on him when Bruenor's axe, clutched in both his hands, cracked into its spine.

The behemoth threw its shoulders back in pain and surprise, its elbows tucked against its ribs, its forearms and long fingers flailing and grabbing at the empty air.

Drizzt's charge became real, focused, and he went right for the giant's most obviously injured leg, his scimitars digging many lines as he quick-stepped past.

The behemoth whirled to follow the movements of the drow, and Bruenor could not hold on. His axe remained deep into the giant's back as the dwarf flew off down the stairs. He crashed in a twisted mess, but Cordio was there at once, infusing him with waves of magical healing.

The giant grimaced and staggered, and Drizzt easily got out of reach. He turned fast, thinking to charge right back in.

But he paused when he saw a tell-tale mist reappearing by the small figurine lying on the stairs.

The giant set itself again. It tried to reach back to extract the dwarf's axe, but the placement prevented it from getting any grip. Down below, Torgar tried to join in, but his legs gave out and he slumped to the stone. No help would come soon from Bruenor, either, Drizzt could see, nor from Cordio, who attended the dwarf king. And Regis was nowhere to be seen.

Giving up on the axe, the behemoth turned its hateful glare at Drizzt. The drow felt a wave of energy flow forth, and for just an instant, he forgot where he was or what was happening. In that split second, he even thought about leaping down at the dwarves, somehow envisioning them as mortal enemies.

But the spell, a dizzying enchantment of confusion, could not take hold on the veteran dark elf the way it had so debilitated Regis, and Drizzt leaped down to the side, coming to the same level as the giant, surrendering the higher ground to limit the giant's attack options. Better to force it to reach for him, he thought, and better still for it to try to stomp or kick at him.

The giant did just that, lifting its leg, and Guenhwyvar did just as Drizzt wanted and sprang upon the one planted leg, raking at the back of the behemoth's knee.

In charged Drizzt, forcing the giant to twist, or try to twist, to keep pace. The drow's magical anklets allowed him to accelerate suddenly past the stomping foot, and he reversed immediately, spinning and slashing at the back of the leading leg. The giant twisted and tried to kick, but Guenhwyvar clamped powerful jaws on the back of its knee, feline fangs tearing deep into dark muscle.

That leg buckled. Arms flailing, the giant fell over backward down the stairs, landing with a tremendous, stone-crunching crash, and just missing crushing poor unconscious Torgar.

Drizzt sprinted and leaped atop it, running down its length to reach its neck before it could bring its arms in to fend him off. Drizzt found less resistance than he expected, for the giant's fall had driven Bruenor's axe in all the deeper, severing its spine.

The behemoth was helpless, and Drizzt showed it no mercy. He crossed its massive chest. Its head was back due to the angle of the stairs, leaving its neck fully exposed.

He leaped from the gurgling, dying behemoth a moment later, landing gracefully on the stairs in full run, angling toward where the batlike creature and Pwent had tumbled. It was quiet there, the fight apparently ended, and Drizzt winced when he saw a leathery wing flop, thinking the monster still alive.

But it was just Pwent, he saw, grumbling as he extracted himself from the broken body.

Drizzt veered back the way they'd come, thinking to go after Regis, but before he could even begin, Regis appeared between the buildings, walking back swiftly toward the group, his mace in hand, his chubby cheeks flushed with embarrassment.

"It took me strength, me king," Torgar Hammerstriker was saying when Drizzt, Guenhwyvar in tow, moved back to the three dwarves.

"Like it pulled me spine right out."

"A wraith," explained Cordio, who was still working on the battered Bruenor, bandaging a cut along the dwarf king's scalp. "Their chilling touch steals yer inner strength—and it can suren kill ye to death if it gets enough o' the stuff from ye! Take heart, for ye'll be fine in a short bit."

"As will me king?" Torgar asked.

"Bah!" Bruenor snorted. "Got me a bigger bounce fallin' off me throne after a proper blessing to Moradin. A night o' the holy mead's hurtin' me more than that thing e'er could!"

Torgar moved over to the dead giant and tried to lift its shoulder. He looked back at the others, shaking his head. "Gonna be a chore for ten in gettin' back yer axe," he said.

"Then take yer own and cut yer way through the durned thing," Bruenor ordered.

Torgar considered the giant, then looked to his great-axe. He gave a "hmm" and a shrug, spat in both his hands, and hoisted the weapon. "Won't take long," he promised. "But take care with yer axe when I get it for ye, for the handle's sure to be slick."

"Nah, it crusts when it dries," came a voice from the side, and the group turned to regard Thibbledorf Pwent, who certainly knew of what he spoke. For Pwent was covered in blood and gore from the thrashing he had given the batlike monster, and a piece of the creature's skull was still stuck to his great head spike, with gobs of bloody brain sliding slowly down the spike's stem. To emphasize his point, Pwent held up his hand and clenched and unclenched his fist, making sounds both sloppy wet and crunchy.

"And what happened to yerself?" Pwent demanded of Regis as the halfling approached. "Ye find something to hit back there, did ye?"

"I don't know," the halfling honestly answered.

"Bah, let off the little one," Bruenor told Pwent, and he included all the others as he swept his gaze around. "Ain't nothing chasing Rumblebelly off."

"I don't know what happened," Regis said to Bruenor, and he looked at the dead giant and shrugged. "For any of it."

"Magic," said Drizzt. "The creatures were possessed of more than physical prowess, as is typical of extraplanar beings. One of those spells attacked the mind. A disorienting dweomer."

"True enough, elf," Cordio agreed. "It delayed me spellcasting."

"Bah, but I didn't feel nothing," said Pwent.

"Attacked the *mind*," Bruenor remarked. "Yerself was well defended."

Pwent paused and pondered that for a few moments before bursting into laughter.

"What is this place?" Torgar asked at length, finding the strength to rise and walk, taking in the sights, the sculpture, the strange designs.

"Gauntlgrym," Bruenor declared, his dark eyes gleaming with intensity.

"Then yer Gauntlgrym was a town above the ground," said Torgar, and Bruenor glared at him.

"This place was above ground, me king," Torgar answered that look. "All of it. This building and those, too. This plaza, set with stones to protect from the mud o' the spring melt. . . ." He looked at Cordio, then Drizzt, who nodded his agreement. "Something must've melted the tundra beneath the whole of it. Turned it all to mud and sank this place from sight."

"And the melts bring water, every year," Cordio added, pointing to the north. "Washing away the mud, bucket by bucket, but leaving the stones behind."

"Yer answer's in the ceiling," Torgar explained, pointing up. "Can ye get a light up there, priest?"

Cordio nodded and moved away from Bruenor. He began casting again, gently waving his arms, creating a globe of light up at the cavern's ceiling, right at the point where it joined in with the top of the great building before them. Some tell-tale signs were revealed with that light, confirming Torgar's suspicions.

"Roots," the Mirabarran dwarf explained. "Can't be more than a few feet o' ground between that roof and the surface. And these taller buildings're acting like supports to keep that ceiling up. The tangle o' roots and the frozen ground're doin' the rest. Whole place sank, I tell ye, for these buildings weren't built for the Underdark."

Bruenor looked at the ceiling, then at Drizzt, but the drow could only nod his agreement.

"Bah!" Bruenor snorted. "Gauntlgrym was akin to Mirabar, then, and ye're for knowin' that. So this must be the top o' the place, with more below. All we need be looking for is a shaft to take us to the lower levels, akin to that rope and come-along dumbwaiter ye got in Mirabar. Now let's see what this big place is all about—important building, I'm thinking. Might be a throne room."

Torgar nodded and Pwent ran up in front of Bruenor to lead the way up the stairs, with Cordio close on his heels. Torgar, though, lagged behind, something Drizzt didn't miss.

"Not akin to Mirabar," the dwarf whispered to Drizzt and Regis.

"A dwarf city above ground?" Regis asked.

Torgar shrugged. "I'm not for knowing." He reached to his side and pulled an item from his belt, one he had taken from the smithy he had found back across the plaza. "Lots of these and little of anything else," he said.

Regis sucked in his breath, and Drizzt nodded his agreement with the dwarf's assessment of the muddy catastrophe that had hit the place. For in his hand, Torgar held an item all too common on the surface and all too rare in the Underdark: a horseshoe.

At Drizzt's insistence, he, and not the noisy Thibbledorf, led the way into the building with Guenhwyvar beside him. The drow and panther filtered out to either side of the massive, decorated doors—doors filled with color and gleaming metal much more indicative of a construction built under the sun. The drow and his cat melted into the shadows of the great hall that awaited them, moving with practiced coordination. They sensed no danger. The place seemed still and long dead.

It was no audience chamber, though, no palace for a dwarf king. When the others came in and they filled the room with torchlight, it became apparent that the place had been a library and gallery, a place of art and learning.

Rotted scrolls filled ancient wooden shelves all around the room and along the walls, interspersed with tapestries whose images had long ago faded, and with sculptures grand and small alike.

Those sculptures set off the first waves of alarm in the companions, particularly in Bruenor, for while some depicted dwarves in their typically heroic battle poses and regalia, others showed orc warriors standing proud. And more than one depicted orcs in other dress, in flowing robes or with pen in hand.

The most prominent of all stood upon a dais at the far end of the room, directly across from the doors. The image of Moradin, stocky and strong, was quite recognizable to the dwarves.

So was the image of Gruumsh One-eye, god of the orcs, standing across from him, and while the two were shown eyeing each other with expressions that could be considered suspicious, the simple fact that they were not shown with Moradin standing atop the vanquished Gruumsh's chest elicited stares of disbelief on the faces of all four dwarves. Thibbledorf Pwent even babbled something undecipherable.

"What place was this?" Cordio asked, giving sound to the question that was on all their minds. "What hall? What city?"

"Delzoun," muttered Bruenor. "Gauntlgrym."

"Then she's no place akin to the tales," said Cordio, and Bruenor shot a glare his way.

"Grander, I'm saying," the priest quickly added.

"Whatever it was, it was grand indeed," said Drizzt. "And beyond my expectations when we set out from Mithral Hall. I had thought we would find a hole in the ground, Bruenor, or perhaps a small, ancient settlement."

"I telled ye it was Gauntlgrym," Bruenor replied.

"If it is, then it is a place to do your Delzoun heritage proud," said the drow. "If it is not, then let us discover other accomplishments of which you can be rightly proud."

Bruenor's stubborn expression softened a bit at those words, and he offered Drizzt a nod and moved off deeper into the room, Thibbledorf at his heel. Drizzt looked to Cordio and Torgar, both of whom nodded their appreciation of his handling of the volatile king.

It was not Gauntlgrym, all three of them knew—at least, it was not the Gauntlgrym of dwarven legend. But what then?

There wasn't much to salvage in the library, but they did find a few scrolls that hadn't fully succumbed to the passage of time. None of them could read the writing on the ancient paper, but there were a few items that could give hints about the craftsmanship of the former residents, and even one tapestry that Regis believed could be cleaned enough to reveal some hints of its former depictions. They gathered their hoard together with great care, rolling and tying the tapestry and softly packing the other items in bags that had held the food they had thus far consumed.

They were done scouring the hall in less than an afternoon's time, and finished with a cursory and rather unremarkable examination of the rest of the cavern for just as long after that. Abruptly, and at Bruenor's insistence, so ended their expedition. Soon after, they climbed back up through the hole that had brought them underground and were greeted by a late winter's quiet night. At the next break of dawn they began their journey home, where they hoped to find some answers.

CHAPTER

POSSIBILITIES

14

King Obould normally liked the cheering of the many orcs that surrounded his temporary palace, a heavy tent set within a larger tent, set within a larger tent. All three were reinforced with metal and wood, and their entrances opened at different points for further security. Obould's most trusted guards, heavily armored and with great gleaming weapons, patrolled the two outer corridors.

The security measures were relatively new, as the orc king cemented his grip and began to unfold his strategy—a plan, the cheering that day only reminded him, that might not sit well with the warlike instincts of some of his subjects. He had already waged the first rounds of what he knew would be his long struggle among the stones of Keeper's Dale. His decision to stand down the attack on Mithral Hall had been met with more than a few mutterings of discontent.

And that had only been the beginning, of course.

He moved along the outer ring of his tent palace to the opened flap and looked out on the gathering on the plaza of the nomadic orc village. At least two hundred of his minions were out there, cheering wildly, thrusting weapons into the air, and clapping each other on the back. Word had come in of a great orc victory in the Moonwood, tales of elf heads spiked on the riverbank.

"We should go there and see the heads," Kna said to Obould as she curled at his side. "It is a sight that would fill me with lust."

Obould swiveled his head to regard her, and he offered a smile, knowing that stupid Kna would never understand it to be one of pity.

Out in the plaza, the cheering grew a backbone chant: "Karuck! Karuck! Karuck!"

It was not unexpected. Obould, who had received word of the fight in the east the previous night, before the public courier had arrived, motioned to the many loyalists he had set in place, and on his nod, they filtered into the crowd.

A second chant bubbled up among the first, "Many-Arrows! Many-Arrows! Many-Arrows!" And gradually, the call for kingdom overcame the cheer for clan.

"Take me there and I will love you," Kna whispered in the orc king's ear, tightening her hold on his side.

Obould's bloodshot eyes narrowed as he turned to regard her again. He brought his hand up to grab the back of her hair and roughly bent her head back so that she could see the intensity on his face. He envisioned those elf heads he'd heard of, set on tall pikes. His smile widened as he considered putting Kna's head in that very line.

Misconstruing his intensity as interest, the consort grinned and writhed against him.

With almost godlike strength, Obould tugged her from his side and tossed her to the ground. He turned back to the plaza and wondered how many of his minions—those not in his immediate presence—would add the chant of Many-Arrows to the praises of Clan Karuck as word of the victory spread throughout the kingdom.

* * * * *

The night was dark, but not to the sensitive eyes of Tos'un Armgo, who had known the blackness of the Underdark. He crouched by a rocky jag, looking down at the silvery snake known as the Surbrin River, and more pointedly at the line of poles before it.

The perpetrators had moved to the south, along with the prodding trio of Dnark, Ung-thol, and the upstart young Toogwik Tuk. They had talked of attacking the Battlehammer dwarves at the Surbrin.

Obould would not be pleased to see such independence among his ranks. And strangely, the drow wasn't overly thrilled at the prospect himself. He'd personally led the first orc assault on that dwarven position, infiltrating and silencing the main watchtower before the orc tide swept Clan Battlehammer back into its hole.

It had been a good day.

So what had changed, wondered Tos'un. What had left him with such melancholy when battle was afoot, particularly a battle between orcs and dwarves, two of the ugliest and smelliest races he had ever had the displeasure of knowing?

As he looked down at the river, he came to understand. Tos'un was a drow, had been raised in Menzoberranzan, and held no love for his surface elf cousins. The war between the surface and Underdark elves was among the fiercest rivalries in the world, a long history of dastardly deeds and murderous raids that equaled anything the continually warring demons of the Abyss and devils of the Nine Hells could imagine. Cutting out the throat of a surface elf had never presented Tos'un with a moral dilemma, surely, but there was something about the current situation, about those heads, that unnerved him, that filled him with a sense of dread.

As much as he hated surface elves, Tos'un despised orcs even more. The idea that orcs could have scored such a victory over elves of any sort left the drow cold. He had grown up in a city of twenty thousand dark elves, and with probably thrice that number of orc, goblin, and kobold slaves. Was there, perhaps, a Clan Karuck in their midst, ready to spike the heads of the nobles of House Barrison Del'Armgo or even of House Baenre?

He scoffed at the absurd notion, and reminded himself that surface elves were weaker than their drow kin. This group fell to Clan Karuck because they deserved it, because they were weak or stupid, or both.

Or at least, that's what Tos'un told himself over and over again, hoping that repetition would provide comfort where reason could not. He looked to the south, where the receding pennants of Clan Karuck had long been lost to the uneven landscape and the darkness. Whatever he might tell himself about the slaughter in the Moonwood, deep inside the true echoes of his heart and soul, Tos'un hoped that Grguch and his minions would all die horribly.

* * * * *

The sound of dripping water accompanied the wagon rolling east from Nesmé, as the warm day nibbled at winter's icy grip. Several times the wagon driver grumbled about muddy ruts, even expressing his hope that the night would be cold.

"If the night's warm, we'll be walking!" he warned repeatedly.

Catti-brie hardly heard him, and hardly noticed the gentle symphony of the melt around her. She sat in the bed of the wagon, with her back up against the driver's seat, staring out to the west behind them.

Wulfgar was out there, moving away from her. Away forever, she feared.

She was full of anger, full of hurt. How could he leave them with an army of orcs encamped around Mithral Hall? Why would he ever want to leave the Companions of the Hall? And how could he go without saying farewell to Bruenor, Drizzt, and Regis?

Her mind whirled through those questions and more, trying to make sense of it all, trying to come to terms with something she could not control. It wasn't the way things were supposed to be! She had tried to say that to Wulfgar, but his smile, so sure and serene, had defeated her argument before it could be made.

She thought back to the day when she and Wulfgar had left Mithral Hall for Silverymoon. She remembered the reactions of Bruenor and Drizzt—too emotional for the former and too stoic for the latter, she realized.

Wulfgar had told them. He'd said his good-byes before they set out, whether in explicit terms or in hints they could not miss. It hadn't been an impulsive decision brought about by some epiphany that had come to him on the road.

Catti-brie grimaced through a sudden flash of anger, at Bruenor and especially at Drizzt. How could they have known and not have told her?

She suppressed that anger quickly, and realized that it had been Wulfgar's choice. He had waited to tell her until after they'd recovered Colson. Catti-brie nodded as she considered that. He'd waited because he knew that the sight of the girl, the girl who had been taken from her mother and was to be returned, would make things more clear for Catti-brie.

"My anger isn't for Wulfgar, or any of them," she whispered.

"Eh?" asked the driver, and Catti-brie turned her head and gave him a smile that settled him back to his own business.

She held that smile as she turned back to stare at the empty west, and squinted, putting on a mask that might counter the tears that welled within. Wulfgar was gone, and if she sat back and considered his reasons, she knew she couldn't fault him. He was not a young man any longer. His legacy was still to be made, and time was running short. It would not be made in Mithral Hall, and even in the cities surrounding the dwarven stronghold, the people, the humans, were not kin to Wulfgar in appearance or in sensibility. His home was Icewind Dale. His people were in Icewind Dale. In Icewind Dale alone could he truly hope to find a wife.

Because Catti-brie was lost to him. And though he bore her no ill will, she understood the pain he must have felt when he looked upon her and Drizzt.

She and Wulfgar had had their moment, but that moment had passed, had been stolen by demons, both within Wulfgar and in the form of the denizens of the Abyss. Their moment had passed, and there seemed no other moments for Wulfgar to find in the court of a dwarf king.

"Farewell," Catti-brie silently mouthed to the empty west, and never had she so meant that simple word.

* * * * *

He bent low to bring Colson close to the flowering snowdrops, their tiny white bells denying the snow along the trail. The first flowers, the sign of coming spring.

"For Ma, Dell-y," Colson chattered happily, holding the first syllable of Delly's name for a long heartbeat, which only tugged all the more at Wulfgar's heart. "Flowvers," she giggled, and she pulled one close to her nose.

Wulfgar didn't correct her lisp, for she beamed as brightly as any "flowvers" ever could.

"Ma for flowvers." Colson rambled, and she mumbled through a dozen further sounds that Wulfgar could not decipher, though it was apparent to him that the girl thought she was speaking in cogent sentences. Wulfgar was sure that Colson made perfect sense to Colson, at least!

There was a little person in there—Wulfgar only truly realized at that innocent moment. A thinking, rational individual. She wasn't a baby anymore, wasn't helpless and unwitting.

The joy and pride that brought to Wulfgar was tempered, to be sure, by his realization that he would soon turn Colson over to her mother, to a woman the girl had never known in a land she had never called home.

"So be it," he said, and Colson looked at him and giggled, and gradually Wulfgar's delight overcame his sense of impending dread. He felt the season in his heart, as if his own internal, icy pall had at last been lifted. Nothing could change that overriding sensation. He was free. He was content. He knew in his heart that what he was doing was good, and right.

As he bent lower to the flower, he noted something else: a fresh print in the mud, right on the edge of the hardened snow. It had come from a shoddily-wrapped foot, and since it was so far from any town, Wulfgar recognized it at once as the print of a goblinkin's foot. He stood back up and glanced all around.

He looked to Colson and smiled comfortingly, then hustled along down the broken trail, his direction, fortunately, opposite the one the creature had taken. He wanted no battle that day, or any other day Colson was in his arms.

All the more reason to get the child back where she belonged.

Wulfgar hoisted the girl onto his broad shoulder and whistled quietly for her as his long legs carried them swiftly down the road, to the west.

Home.

* * * * *

North of Wulfgar's position, four dwarves, a halfling, and a drow settled around a small fire in a snowy dell. They had stopped their march early, that they could better light a fire to warm some stones that would get them more comfortably through the cold night. After briskly rubbing their hands over the dancing orange flames, Torgar, Cordio, and Thibbledorf set off to find the stones.

Bruenor hardly noticed their departure, for his gaze had settled on the sack of scrolls and artifacts, and on a tied tapestry lying nearby.

While Regis began preparing their supper, Drizzt just sat and watched his dwarf friend, for he knew that Bruenor was churning inside, and that he would soon enough need to speak his mind.

As if on cue, Bruenor turned to the drow. "Thought I'd find Gauntlgrym and find me answers," he said.

"You don't know whether you've found them or not," Drizzt reminded.

Bruenor grunted. "Weren't Gauntlgrym, elf. Not by any o' the legends o' the place. Not by any stories I e'er heard."

"Likely not," the drow agreed.

"Weren't no place I ever heared of."

"Which might prove even more important," said Drizzt.

"Bah," Bruenor snorted half-heartedly. "A place of riddles, and none that I'm wanting answered."

"They are what they are."

"And that be?"

"Hopefully revealed in the writings we took."

"Bah!" Bruenor snorted more loudly, and he waved his hands at Drizzt and at the sack of scrolls. "Gonna get me a stone to warm me bed," he muttered, and started away. "And one I can bang me head against."

The last remark brought a grin to Drizzt's face, reminding him that Bruenor would follow the clues wherever they led, whatever the implications. He held great faith in his friend.

"He's afraid," Regis remarked as soon as the dwarf was out of sight.

"He should be," Drizzt replied. "At stake are the very foundations of his world."

"What do you think is on the scrolls?" Regis asked, and Drizzt shrugged.

"And those statues!" the halfling went on undeterred. "Orcs and dwarves, and not in battle. What does it mean? Answers for us? Or just more questions?"

Drizzt thought about it for just a moment, and was nodding as he replied, "Possibilities."

PART 3

A WAR WITHIN A WAR

A WAR WITHIN A WAR

We construct our days, bit by bit, tenday by tenday, year by year. Our lives take on a routine, and then we bemoan that routine. Predictability, it seems, is a double-edged blade of comfort and boredom. We long for it, we build it, and when we find it, we reject it.

Because while change is not always growth, growth is always rooted in change. A finished person, like a finished house, is a static thing. Pleasant, perhaps, or beautiful or admirable, but not for long exciting.

King Bruenor has reached the epitome, the pinnacle, the realization of every dream a dwarf could fathom. And still King Bruenor desires change, though he would refuse to phrase it that way, admitting only his love of adventure. He has found his post, and now seeks reasons to abandon that post at every turn. He seeks, because inside of him he knows that he must seek to grow. Being a king will make Bruenor old before his time, as the old saying goes.

Not all people are possessed of such spirits. Some desire and cling to the comfort of the routine, to the surety that comes with the completion of the construction of life's details. On the smaller scale, they become wedded to their daily routines. They become enamored of the predictability. They calm their restless souls in the confidence that they have found their place in the multiverse, that things are the way they are supposed to be, that there are no roads left to explore and no reason to wander.

On the larger scale, such people become fearful and resentful—sometimes to extremes that defy logic—of anyone or anything that intrudes on that construct. A societal change, a king's edict, an attitude shift in the neighboring lands, even events that have nothing to do with them personally can set off a reaction of dissonance and fear. When Lady Alustriel initially allowed me to walk the streets of Silverymoon openly, she found great resistance. Her people, well protected by one of the finest armies in all the land and by a leader whose magical abilities are renowned throughout the world, did not fear Drizzt Do'Urden. Nay, they feared the change that I represented. My very presence in Silverymoon infringed upon the construct of their lives, threatened their understanding of the way things were, threatened the way things were supposed to be. Even though, of course, I posed no threat to them whatsoever.

That is the line we all straddle, between comfort and adventure. There are those who find satisfaction, even fulfillment, in the former, and there are those who are forever seeking.

It is my guess, and can only be my guess, that the fears of the former are rooted in fear of the greatest mystery of all, death. It is no accident that those who construct the thickest walls are most often rooted firmly, immovably, in their faith. The here and now is as it is, and the better way will be found in the afterlife. That proposition is central to the core beliefs that guide the faithful, with, for many, the added caveat that the afterlife will only fulfill its promise if the here and now remains in strict accord with the guiding principles of the chosen deity.

I count myself among the other group, the seekers. Bruenor, too, obviously so, for he will ever be the discontented king. Catti-brie cannot be rooted. There is no sparkle in her eyes greater than the one when she looks upon a new road. And even Regis, for all his complaints regarding the trials of the road, wanders and seeks and fights. Wulfgar, too, will not be confined. He has seen his life in

Mithral Hall and has concluded, rightfully and painfully, that there is for him a better place and a better way. It saddens me to see him go. For more than a score of years he has been my friend and companion, a trusted arm in battle and in life. I miss him dearly, every day; and yet when I think of him, I smile for him. Wulfgar has left Mithral Hall because he has outgrown all that this place can offer, because he knows that in Icewind Dale he will find a home where he will do more good—for himself and for those around him.

I, too, hold little faith that I will live out my days in Bruenor's kingdom. It is not just boredom that propels my steps along paths unknown, but a firm belief that the guiding principle of life must be a search not for what is, but for what could be. To look at injustice or oppression, at poverty or slavery, and shrug helplessly, or worse to twist a god's "word" to justify such states, is anathema to the ideal, and to me, the ideal is achieved only when the ideal is sought. The ideal is not a gift from the gods, but a promise from them.

We are possessed of reason. We are possessed of generosity. We are possessed of sympathy and empathy. We have within us a better nature, and it is one that cannot be confined by the constructed walls of anything short of the concept of heaven itself. Within the very logic of that better nature, a perfect life cannot be found in a world that is imperfect.

So we dare to seek. So we dare to change. Even knowing that we will not get to "heaven" in this life is no excuse to hide within the comfort of routine. For it is in that seeking, in that continual desire to improve ourselves and to improve the world around us, that we walk the road of enlightenment, that we eventually can approach the gods with heads bowed in humility, but with confidence that we did their work, that we tried to lift ourselves and our world to their lofty standards, the image of the ideal.

—Drizzt Do'Urden

CHAPTER
CONVERGENCE OF CRISES
15

Magical horses striding long, the fiery chariot cut a line of orange across the pre-dawn sky. Flames whipped in the driving wind, but for the riders they did not burn. Standing beside Lady Alustriel, Catti-brie felt that wind indeed, her auburn hair flying wildly behind her, but the bite of the breeze was mitigated by the warmth of Alustriel's animated cart. She lost herself in that sensation, allowing the howl of the wind to deafen her thoughts as well. For a short time, she was free to just exist, under the last twinkling stars with all of her senses consumed by the extraordinary nature of the journey.

She didn't see the approaching silver line of the Surbrin, and was only vaguely aware of a dip in altitude as Alustriel brought the conjured chariot down low over the water, and to a running stop on the ground outside the eastern door of Mithral Hall.

Few dwarves were out at that early hour, but those who were, mostly those standing guard along the northern wall, came running and cheering for the Lady of Silverymoon. For of course they knew it was she, whose chariot had graced them several times over the past few months.

Their cheering grew all the louder when they noted Alustriel's passenger, the Princess of Mithral Hall.

"Well met," more than one of the bearded folk greeted.

"King Bruenor's not yet returned," said one, a grizzled old sort, with one eye lost and patched over, and half his great black beard torn away. Catti-brie smiled as she recognized the fierce and fiercely loyal Shingles McRuff, who had come to Mithral Hall beside Torgar Hammerstriker. "Should be along any day."

"And be knowin' that ye're all welcome, and that ye'll find all the hospitality o' Mithral Hall for yerself," another dwarf offered.

"That is most generous," said Alustriel. She turned and looked back to the east as she continued, "More of my people—wizards from Silverymoon—will be coming in throughout the morn, on all manner of flight, some self-propelled and some riding ebony flies, and two on broomsticks and another on a carpet. I pray your archers will not shoot them down."

"Ebony flies?" Shingles replied. "Flying on bugs, ye mean?"

"Big bugs," said Catti-brie.

"Would have to be."

"We come armed with spells of creation, for we wish to see the bridge across the Surbrin opened and secure as soon as possible," Alustriel explained. "For the sake of Mithral Hall and for all the goodly kingdoms of the Silver Marches."

"More well met, then!" bellowed Shingles, and he led yet another cheer.

Catti-brie moved toward the back edge of the chariot, but Alustriel took her by the shoulder. "We can fly out to the west and seek King Bruenor," she offered.

Catti-brie paused and looked that way, but shook her head and replied, "He will return presently, I'm sure."

Catti-brie accepted Shingles's offered hand, and let the dwarf ease her down to the ground. Shingles was quick to Alustriel, similarly helping her, and the Lady, though not injured as was Catti-brie, graciously accepted. She moved back from her cart and motioned for the others to follow.

Alustriel could have simply dismissed the flaming chariot and the horses made of magical fire. Dispelling her own magic was easy work, of course, and the fiery team and cart alike would have flared for an instant before they winked into blackness, a final puff of smoke drifting and dissipating into the air.

But Lady Alustriel had been using that particular spell for many years, and had put her own flavor into it, both in the construction of the cart and team and in the dismissal of the magic. Figuring that

THE ORC KING

the dwarves could use a bit of spirit-lifting, the powerful wizardess performed her most impressive variation of the dispelling.

The horse team snorted and reared, flames shooting from swirling, fiery nostrils. As one, they leaped into the air, straight up, the cart lurching behind them. Some twenty feet off the ground, the many sinews of fire that held the form broke apart, orange tendrils soaring every which way, and as they reached their limits, exploded with deafening bangs, throwing showers of sparks far and wide.

The dwarves howled with glee, and Catti-brie, for all of her distress, couldn't contain a giggle.

When it ended a few heartbeats later, their ears ringing with the echoes of the retorts, their eyes blinking against the sting of the brilliant flashes, Catti-brie offered an appreciative smile to her friend and driver.

"It was just the enchantment they needed," she whispered, and Alustriel replied with a wink.

They went into Mithral Hall side-by-side.

* * * * *

Early the next morning, Shingles again found himself in the role of official greeter in the region east of the hall's eastern gate, for it was he who first caught up with the six adventurers returning from the place Bruenor had named Gauntlgrym. The old Mirabarran dwarf had directed the watch overnight, and was sorting out assignments for the workday, both along the fortifications on the northern mountain spur and at the bridge. No stranger to the work of wizards, Shingles repeatedly warned his boys to stay well back when Alustriel's gang came out to work their dweomers. When word came that King Bruenor and the others had returned, Shingles moved fast to the south to intercept them.

"Did ye find it, then, me king?" he asked excitedly, giving voice to the thoughts and whispers of all the others around him.

"Aye," Bruenor replied, but in a tone surprisingly unenthusiastic. "We found something, though we're not for knowing if it's Gauntlgrym just yet." He motioned to the large sack that Torgar carried, and the rolled tapestry slung over Cordio's shoulder. "We've some things for Nanfoodle and me scholars to look over. We'll get our answers."

"Yer girl's come home," Shingles explained. "Lady Alustriel flew her in on that chariot o' fire. And the Lady's here, too, along with ten Silverymoon wizards, all come to work on the bridge."

Bruenor, Drizzt, and Regis exchanged glances as Shingles finished.

"Me girl alone?" Bruenor asked.

"With the Lady."

Bruenor stared at Shingles.

"Wulfgar's not returned with 'em," the old Mirabarran dwarf said. "Catti-brie said nothing of it, and I didn't think it me place to ask."

Bruenor looked to Drizzt.

"He is far west," the drow said quietly, and Bruenor inadvertently glanced out that way then nodded.

"Get me to me girl," Bruenor instructed as he started off at a swift pace for Mithral Hall's eastern door.

They found Catti-brie, Lady Alustriel, and the Silverymoon wizards not far down the corridor inside, the lot of them having spent the night in the hall's easternmost quarters. After a quick and polite greeting, Bruenor begged the Lady's pardon, and Alustriel and her wizards quickly departed the hall, heading for the Surbrin bridge.

"Where's he at?" Bruenor asked Catti-brie when it was just the two of them, Drizzt, and Regis.

"You're knowing well enough."

"Ye found Colson, then?"

Catti-brie nodded.

"And he's taking her home," Bruenor stated.

Another nod. "I offered to journey with him," Catti-brie explained, and she glanced at Drizzt and was relieved to see him smile at that news. "But he would not have me along."

"Because the fool ain't for coming back," said Bruenor, and he spat and stalked off. "Durned fool son of an over-sized orc."

Drizzt motioned to Regis to go with Bruenor, and the halfling nodded and trotted away.

"I think Bruenor is right," Catti-brie said, and she shook her head in futile denial, then rushed over and wrapped Drizzt in a tight hug and kissed him deeply. She put her head on his shoulder, not relenting a bit in her embrace. She sniffed back tears.

"He knew that Wulfgar would not likely return," Drizzt whispered.

Catti-brie pushed him back to arms' length. "As did yourself, but you didn't tell me," she said.

"I honored Wulfgar's wishes. He was not sure of where his road would lead, but he did not wish discussion of it all the way to Silverymoon and beyond."

"If I had known along our road, I might've been able to change his mind," Catti-brie protested.

Drizzt gave her a helpless look. "More the reason to not tell you."

"You agree with Wulfgar's choice?"

"I think it is not my place to agree or to argue," Drizzt said with a shrug.

"You think it's his place to be deserting Bruenor at this time of—?"

"This time or any time."

"How can you say that? Wulfgar is family to us, and he just left . . ."

"As you and I did those years ago, after the drow war when Wulfgar fell to the yochlol," Drizzt reminded her. "We longed for the road and so we took to the road, and left Bruenor to his hall. For six years."

That reminder seemed to deflate Catti-brie's ire quite a bit. "But now Bruenor's got an army of orcs on his doorstep," she protested, but with far less enthusiasm.

"An army that will likely be there for years to come. Wulfgar told me that he could not see his future here. And truly, what is there for him here? No wife, no children."

"And it pained him to look upon us."

Drizzt nodded. "Likely."

"He told me as much."

"And so you wear a mantle of guilt?"

Catti-brie shrugged.

"It doesn't suit you," Drizzt said. He drew her in close once more, and gently pushed her head onto his shoulder. "Wulfgar's road is Wulfgar's own to choose. He has family in Icewind Dale, if that is where he decides to go. He has his people there. Would you deny him the chance to find love? Should he not sire children, who will follow his legacy of leadership among the tribes of Icewind Dale?"

Catti-brie didn't respond for a long while then merely said, "I miss him already," in a voice weak with sorrow.

"As do I. And so too for Bruenor and Regis, and all else who knew him. But he isn't dead. He did not fall in battle, as we feared those years ago. He will follow his road, to bring Colson home, as he sees fit, and then perhaps to Icewind Dale. Or perhaps not. It might be that when he is away, Wulfgar will come to realize that Mithral Hall truly is his home, and turn again for Bruenor's halls. Or perhaps he'll take another wife, and return to us with her, full of love and free of pain."

He pushed Catti-brie back again, his lavender eyes locking stares with her rich blue orbs. "You have to trust in Wulfgar. He has earned that from us all many times over. Allow him to walk whatever road he chooses, and hold confidence that you and I, and Bruenor and Regis, all go with him in his heart, as we carry him in ours. You carry with you guilt you do not deserve. Would you truly desire that Wulfgar not follow his road for the sake of mending your melancholy?"

Catti-brie considered the words for a few heartbeats, then managed a smile. "My heart is not empty," she said, and she came forward and kissed Drizzt again, with urgency and passion.

* * * * *

"Whate'er ye're needin', ye're gettin'," Bruenor assured Nanfoodle as the gnome gently slid one of the parchment scrolls out of the sack. "Rumblebelly here is yer slave, and he'll be running to meself and all me boys at the command o' Nanfoodle."

The gnome began to unroll the document, but winced and halted, hearing the fragile parchment crackle.

"I will have to brew oils of preservation," he explained to Bruenor. "I dare not put this under bright light until it's properly treated."

"Whate'er ye need," Bruenor assured him. "Ye just get it done, and get it done quick."

"How quick?" The gnome seemed a bit unnerved by that request.

"Alustriel's here now," said Bruenor. "She's to be working on the bridge for the next few days, and I'm thinkin' that if them scrolls're saying what I'm thinkin' they're saying, it might be good for Alustriel to go back to Silverymoon muttering and musing on the revelations."

But Nanfoodle shook his head. "It will take me more than a day to prepare the potions—and that's assuming that you have the ingredients I will require." He looked to Regis. "Bat guano forms the base."

"Wonderful," the halfling muttered.

"We'll have it or we'll get it," Bruenor promised him.

"It will take more than a day to brew anyway," said Nanfoodle. "Then three days for it to set on the parchment—at least three. I'd rather it be five."

"So four days total," said Bruenor, and the gnome nodded.

"Just to prepare the parchments for examination," Nanfoodle was quick to add. "It could take me tendays to decipher the ancient writing, even with my magic."

"Bah, ye'll be faster."

"I cannot promise."

"Ye'll be faster," Bruenor said again, in a tone less encouraging and more demanding. "Guano," he said to Regis, and he turned and walked from the room.

"Guano," Regis repeated, looking at Nanfoodle helplessly.

"And oil from the smiths," said the gnome. He drew another scroll from the sack and placed it beside the first, then put his hands on his hips and heaved a great sigh. "If they understood the delicacy of the task, they would not be so impatient," he said, more to himself than to the halfling.

"Bruenor is well past delicacy, I'm guessing," said Regis. "Too many orcs about for delicacy."

"Orcs and dwarves," muttered the gnome. "Orcs and dwarves. How is an artist to do his work?" He heaved another sigh, as if to say "if I must," and moved to the side of the room, to the cabinet where he kept his mortar and pestle, and assorted spoons and vials.

"Always rushing, always grumbling," he griped. "Orcs and dwarves, indeed!"

* * * * *

The companions had barely settled into their chambers in the dwarven hall west of Garumn's Gorge when word came that yet another unexpected visitor had arrived at the eastern gate. It wasn't often that elves walked through King Bruenor's door, but those gates were swung wide for Hralien of the Moonwood.

Drizzt, Catti-brie, and Bruenor waited impatiently in Bruenor's audience chamber for the elf.

"Alustriel and now Hralien," Bruenor said, nodding with every word. "It's all coming together. Once we get the words from them scrolls, we'll get both o' them to agree that the time's now for striking them smelly orcs."

Drizzt held his doubts private and Catti-brie merely smiled and nodded. There was no reason to derail Bruenor's optimism with an injection of sober reality.

"We know them Adbar and Felbarr boys'll fight with us," Bruenor went on, oblivious to the detachment of his audience. "If we're getting the Moonwood and Silverymoon to join in, we'll be puttin' them orcs back in their holes in short order, don't ye doubt!"

He rambled on sporadically for the next few moments, until at last Hralien was led into the chamber and formally introduced.

"Well met, King Bruenor," the elf said after the list of his accomplishments and titles was read in full. "I come with news from the Moonwood."

"Long ride if ye've come just to break bread," said Bruenor.

"We have suffered an incursion from the orcs," Hralien explained, talking right past Bruenor's little jest. "A coordinated and cunning attack."

"We know yer pain," Bruenor replied, and Hralien bowed in appreciation.

"Several of my people were lost," Hralien went on, "elves who should have known the birth and death of centuries to come." He looked squarely at Drizzt as he continued, "Innovindil among them."

Drizzt's eyes widened and he gasped and slumped back, and Catti-brie brought her arm across his back to support him.

"And Sunset beneath her," said Hralien, his voice less steady. "It would appear that the orcs had anticipated her arrival on the field, and were well prepared."

Drizzt's chest pumped with strong, gasping breaths. He looked as if he was about to say something, but no words came forth and he had the strength only to shake his head in denial. A great emptiness washed through him, a cold loss and callous reminder of the harsh immediacy of change, a sudden and irreversible reminder of mortality.

"I share your grief," Hralien said. "Innovindil was my friend, beloved by all who knew her. And Sunrise is bereaved, do not doubt, for the loss of Innovindil and of Sunset, his companion for all these years."

"Durned pig orcs," Bruenor growled. "Are ye all still thinkin' we should leave them to their gains? Are ye still o' the mind that Obould's kingdom should stand?"

"Orcs have attacked the Moonwood for years uncounted," Hralien replied. "They come for wood and for mischief, and we kill them and send them running. But their attack was better this time—too much so for the simplistic race, we believe." As he finished, he was again looking directly at Drizzt, so much so that he drew curious stares from Bruenor and Catti-brie in response.

"Tos'un Armgo," Drizzt reasoned.

"We know him to be in the region, and he learned much of our ways in his time with Albondiel and Sinnafain," Hralien explained.

Drizzt nodded, determination replacing his wounded expression. He had vowed to hunt down Tos'un when he and Innovindil had returned Ellifain's body to the Moonwood. Suddenly that promise seemed all the more critical.

"A journey full o' grief is a longer ride by ten, so the sayin' goes," said Bruenor. "Ye make yerself comfortable, Hralien o' the Moonwood. Me boys'll see to yer every need, and ye stay as long as ye're wantin'. Might be that I'll have a story for ye soon enough—one that'll put us all in better stead for ridding ourselves o' the curse of Obould. A few days at the most, me friends're tellin' me."

"I am a courier of news, and have come with a request, King Bruenor," the elf explained, and he gave another respectful and appreciative bow. "Others will journey here from the Moonwood to your call, of course, but my own road is back through your eastern door no later than dawn tomorrow." Again he looked Drizzt in the eye. "I hope I will not be alone."

Drizzt nodded his agreement to go out on the hunt before he even turned to Catti-brie. He knew that she would not deny him that.

* * * * *

The couple were alone in their room soon after, and Drizzt began to fill his backpack.

"You're going after Tos'un," Catti-brie remarked, but did not ask.

"Have I a choice?"

"No. I only wish that I were well enough to go with you."

Drizzt paused in his packing and turned to regard her. "In Menzoberranzan, they say, *Aspis tu drow bed n'tuth drow*. 'Only a drow can hunt a drow.'"

"Then hunt well," said Catti-brie, and she moved to the side wardrobe to aid Drizzt in his preparations. She seemed not upset with him in the least, which was why she caught Drizzt completely off his guard when she quietly asked, "Would you have married Innovindil when I am gone?"

Drizzt froze, and slowly mustered the courage to turn and look at Catti-brie. She wore a slight smile and seemed quite at ease and comfortable. She moved to their bed and sat on the edge, and motioned for Drizzt to join her.

"Would you have?" she asked again as he approached. "Innovindil was very beautiful, in body and in mind."

"It is not something I think about," said Drizzt.

Catti-brie's smile grew wider. "I know," she assured him. "But I am asking you to consider it now. Could you have loved her?"

Drizzt thought about it for a few moments then admitted, "I do not know."

"And you never wondered about it at all?"

Drizzt's thoughts went back to a moment he had shared with Innovindil when the two of them were out alone among the orc lines. Innovindil had nearly seduced him, though only to let him see more clearly his feelings for Catti-brie, whom he had thought dead at the time.

"You could have loved her, I think," Catti-brie said.

"You may well be right," he said.

"Do you think she thought of you in her last moments?"

Drizzt's eyes widened in shock at the blunt question, but Catti-brie didn't back down.

"She thought of Tarathiel, likely, and what was," he answered.

"Or of Drizzt and what might have been."

Drizzt shook his head. "She would not have looked there. Not then. Likely her every thought was for Sunset. To be an elf is to find the moment, the here and now. To revel in what is with knowledge and acceptance that what will be, will be, no matter the hopes and plans of any."

"Innovindil would have had a fleeting moment of regret for Drizzt, and potential love lost," Catti-brie said.

THE ORC KING

Drizzt didn't disagree, and couldn't, given the woman's generous tone and expression. Catti-brie wasn't judging him, wasn't looking for reasons to doubt him. She confirmed that a moment later, when she laughed and put her hand up to stroke his cheek.

"You will outlive me by centuries, in all likelihood," she explained. "I understand the implications of that, my love, and what a selfish fool I would be if I expected you to remain faithful to a memory. Nor would I want—nor do I want—that for you."

"It doesn't mean that we have to speak of it," Drizzt retorted. "We know not where our roads will lead, nor which of us will outlive the other. These are dangerous times in a dangerous world."

"I know."

"Then is this something we should bother to discuss?"

Catti-brie shrugged, but gradually her smile dissipated and a cloud crossed her fair features.

"What is it?" Drizzt asked, and lifted his hand to turn her to face him directly.

"If the dangers do not end our time together, how will Drizzt feel, I wonder, in twenty years? Or thirty?"

The drow wore a puzzled expression.

"You will still be young and handsome, and full of life and love to give," Catti-brie explained. "But I will be old and bent and ugly. You will stay by my side, I am sure, but what life will that be? What lust?"

It was Drizzt's turn to laugh.

"Can you look at a human woman who has seen the turn of seventy years and think her attractive?"

"Are there not couples of humans still in love after so many years together?" Drizzt asked. "Are there not human husbands who love their wives still when seventy is a birthday passed?"

"But the husbands are not usually in the springtime of their lives."

"You err because you pretend that it will happen overnight, in the snap of fingers," Drizzt said. "That is far from the case, even for an elf looking upon the human lifespan. Every wrinkle is earned, my love. Day by day, we spend our time together, and the changes that come will be well earned. In your heart you know that I love you, and I have no doubt but that my love will grow with the passage of years. I know your heart, Catti-brie. You are blissfully predictable to me in some ways, never so in others. I know where your choices will be, time and again, and ever are they on the right side of justice and integrity."

Catti-brie smiled and kissed him, but Drizzt broke it off fast and pushed her back.

"If a dragon's fiery breath were to catch up with me, and scar my skin hideously, blind me, and keep about me a stench of burnt flesh, would Catti-brie still love me?"

"Wonderful thought," the woman said dryly.

"Would she? Would you stand beside me?"

"Of course."

"And if I thought otherwise, at all, then never would I have desired to be your husband. Do you not similarly trust in me?"

Catti-brie grinned and kissed him again, then pushed him on his back on the bed.

The packing could wait.

* * * * *

Early the next morning, Drizzt leaned over the sleeping Catti-brie and gently brushed her lips with his own. He stared at her for a long while, even while he walked from the bed to the door. He at last turned and nearly jumped back in surprise, for set against the door was Taulmaril, the Heartseeker, Catti-brie's bow, and lying below it was her magical quiver, one that never ran out of arrows. For a moment, Drizzt stood confused, until he noticed a small note on the floor by the quiver. From a puncture in its side, he deduced that it had been pressed onto the top of the bow but had not held its perch.

He knew what it said before he ever brought it close enough to read the scribbling.

He looked back at Catti-brie once more. She couldn't be with him in body, perhaps, but with Taulmaril in his hand, she'd be there in spirit.

Drizzt slung the bow over his shoulder then retrieved the quiver and did likewise. He looked back once more to his love then left the room without a sound.

CHAPTER 16

TOOGWIK TUK'S PARADE

The warriors of Clan Karuck paraded onto the muddy plaza centering a small orc village one rainy morning, the dreary overcast and pounding rain doing nothing to diminish the glory of their thunderous march.

"Stand and stomp!" the warriors sang in voices that resonated deeply from their massive half-ogre chests. "Smash and crush! All for the glory of One-eye Gruumsh!"

Yellow pennants flapping in the wind, waves of mud splattering with every coordinated step, the clan came on in tight and precise formation, their six flags moving, two-by-two, in near perfect synchronization. The curious onlookers couldn't help but notice the stark contrast between the huge half-ogre, half-orcs and the scores of orcs from other tribes that had been swept up into their wake from the first villages through which Chieftain Grguch had marched.

Only one full-blooded orc marched with Grguch, a young and fiery shaman. Toogwik Tuk wasted no time as the villagers gathered. He moved out in front as Grguch halted his march.

"We are fresh from victory in the Moonwood!" Toogwik Tuk proclaimed, and every orc along the eastern reaches of Obould's fledgling kingdom knew well that hated place. Thus, predictably, a great cheer greeted the news.

"All hail Chieftain Grguch of Clan Karuck!" Toogwik Tuk

proclaimed, and that was met with an uncomfortable pause until he added, "For the glory of King Obould!"

Toogwik Tuk glanced back to Grguch, who nodded his agreement, and the young shaman started the chant, "Grguch! Obould! Grguch! Obould! Grguch! Grguch! Grguch!"

All of Clan Karuck fell in quickly with the cadence, as did the orcs who had already joined in with the march, and the villagers' doubts were quickly overwhelmed.

"As Obould before him, Chieftain Grguch will bring the judgment of Gruumsh upon our enemies!" Toogwik Tuk cried, running through the mob and whipping them into frenzy. "The snow retreats, and we advance!" With every glorious proclamation, he took care to add, "For the glory of Obould! By the power of Grguch!"

Toogwik Tuk understood well the weight that had settled on his shoulders. Dnark and Ung-thol had departed for the west to meet with Obould regarding the new developments, and it fell squarely upon Toogwik Tuk to facilitate Grguch's determined march to the south. Clan Karuck alone would not stand against Obould and his thousands, obviously, but if Clan Karuck carried along with them the orc warriors from the dozen villages lining the Surbrin, their arrival on the field north of King Bruenor's fortifications would carry great import—enough, so the conspirators hoped, to coerce the involvement of the army Obould had likely already positioned there.

That sort of rabble rousing had been Toogwik Tuk's signature for years. His rise through the ranks to become the chief shaman of his tribe—almost all of whom were dead, crushed in the mysterious, devastating explosion of a mountain ridge north of Keeper's Dale—had been expedited by precisely that talent. He knew well how to manipulate the emotions of the peasant orcs, to conflate their present loyalties with what he wanted their loyalties to be. Every time he mentioned Obould, he was quick to add the name Grguch. Every time he spoke of Gruumsh, he was quick to add the name of Grguch. Mingle them, say them together enough times so that his audience would unwittingly add "Grguch" whenever they heard the names of the other two.

His energy again proved infectious, and he soon had all of the villagers hopping about and chanting with him, always for the glory of Obould, and always by the power of Grguch.

Those two names needed to be intimately linked, the three conspirators had decided before Dnark and Ung-thol had departed. To even hint against Obould after such dramatic and sweeping victories as the orc king had brought would have spelled a fast end to the coup. Even considering the disastrous attempt to enter Mithral Hall's western gate, or the loss of the eastern ground between the dwarven halls and the Surbrin, or the stall throughout winter and the whispers that it might be longer than that, the vast majority of orcs spoke of Obould in the hushed tones usually reserved for Gruumsh himself. But Toogwik Tuk and two companions planned to move the tribes to oppose their king, one baby-step at a time.

"By the power of Grguch!" Toogwik Tuk cried again, and before the cheer could erupt, he added, "Will the dwarven wall hold against a warrior who burned the Moonwood?"

Though he expected a cheer, Toogwik Tuk was answered with looks of suspicion and confusion.

"The dwarves will flee before us," the shaman promised. "Into their hole they will run, and we will control the Surbrin for King Obould! *For the glory of King Obould!*" he finished, screaming with all his power.

The orcs around him cheered wildly, insanely.

"By the power of Grguch!" the not-quite-so-out-of-control Toogwik Tuk cleverly added, and many of the villagers, so used to the chant by then, shouted the words right along beside him.

Toogwik Tuk glanced back at Chieftain Grguch, who wore a most satisfied grin.

Another step taken, Toogwik Tuk knew.

Taking many offered supplies, Clan Karuck soon resumed their march, and a new pennant flew among the many in the mob behind them, and another forty warriors eagerly melded into Chieftain Grguch's trailing ranks. With several larger villages before them, both the chieftain and his shaman spokesman expected that they would number in the thousands when they at last reached the dwarven wall.

Toogwik Tuk held faith that when they smashed that wall, the cries for Grguch would be louder than those for Obould. The next cheers he led would hold fewer references to the glory of Obould and more to the glory of Gruumsh. But he would not lessen the number of his claims that all of it was being wrought by the power of Grguch.

* * * * *

Jack could see that the sprout of hair on one side of Hakuun's misshapen, wart-covered nose tingled with nervous energy as he walked out from the main host, among dark pines and broken fir trees.

"By sprockets and elemental essences, that was exciting, wasn't it?"

The orc shaman froze in place at the all-too-familiar voice, composed himself with a deep breath that greatly flared his nostrils, and slowly turned to regard a curious little humanoid in brilliant purple robes sitting on a low branch, swinging his feet back and forth like a carefree child. The form was new to Hakuun. Oh, he knew what a gnome was, indeed, but he had never seen Jaculi in that state before.

"That young priest is so full of spirit," Jack said. "I almost walked out and joined in with Grguch myself! Oh, what a grand march they have planned!"

"I didn't ask you to come up here," Hakuun remarked.

"Did you not?" said Jack, and he hopped down from the tree and brushed the twigs from his fabulous robes. "Tell me, Shaman of Clan Karuck, what am I to think when I peer out from my work to find that the one to whom I have bestowed such great gifts has run off?"

"I did not run off," Hakuun insisted, trying to keep his voice steady, though he was visibly near panic. "Often does Clan Karuck go hunting."

Hakuun gave ground as the gnome walked up to him. Jack continued to advance as Hakuun retreated.

"But this was no ordinary excursion."

Hakuun looked at Jack with dull curiosity, obviously not understanding him.

"No ordinary *hunt*," Jack explained.

"I have told you."

"Of Obould, yes, and of his thousands," said Jack. "A bit of mischief and a bit of loot to be found, so you said. But it is more than that, is it not?"

Again Hakuun wore a puzzled expression.

Jack snapped his stubby fingers in the air and whirled away. "Do you not feel it, shaman?" he asked, his voice full of excitement. "Do you not recognize that this is no ordinary hunt?"

Jack spun back on Hakuun to measure his response, and still he saw that the shaman wasn't quite catching on. For Jack, so perceptive and cunning, had deduced the subtext of Toogwik Tuk's speech, and the implications it offered.

"Perhaps it is just my own suspicion," the gnome said, "but you must tell me all that you know. Then we should speak with that spirited young priest."

"I have told you . . ." Hakuun protested. His voiced trailed off and he retreated a step, knowing what awful thing was about to befall him.

"No, I mean that you must tell me everything," Jack said, all humor gone from his voice and his expression as he took a step toward the shaman. Hakuun shrank back, but that only made Jack stride more purposefully.

"Ah, you do forget," the gnome said as he closed the gap. "All that I have done for you, and so little have I asked in return. With great power, Hakuun, comes great expectations."

"There is nothing more," the shaman started to plead, and he held up his hands.

Jack the Gnome wore a mask of evil. He said not a word, but pointed to the ground. Hakuun shook his head feebly and continued to wave, and Jack continued to point.

But it was no contest, the outcome never in doubt. With a slight whimper, Hakuun, the mighty shaman of Clan Karuck, the conduit between Grguch and Gruumsh, prostrated himself on the ground, face down.

Jack looked straight ahead and lowered his arms to his sides as he quietly mouthed the words to his spell. He thought of the mysterious illithids, the brilliant mind flayers, who had taught him so much of one particular school of magic.

His robes fluttered only briefly as he shrank, then they and all his other gear melded into his changing form. In an instant Jack the Gnome was gone and a sightless rodent padded across the ground on four tiny feet. He went up to Hakuun's ear and sniffed for a few moments, hesitating simply because he recognized how uncomfortable it was making the cowering creature.

Then Jack the Gnome-cum-brain mole crawled into Hakuun's ear and disappeared from sight.

Hakuun shuddered and jerked in agonized spasms as the creature burrowed deeper, through the walls of his inner ear and into the seat of his consciousness. The shaman forced himself up to all fours as he began to gag. He vomited and spat, though of course the feeble defenses of his physical body could not begin to dislodge his unwelcome guest.

A few moments later, Hakuun staggered to his feet.

There, said the voice of Jack in his head. *Now I better understand the purpose of this adventure, and together we will learn the extent of this spirited young shaman's plans.*

Hakuun didn't argue—there was no way he could, of course. And for all his revulsion and pain, Hakuun knew that with Jack inside him, he was much more perceptive, and many times more powerful.

A private conversation with Toogwik Tuk, Jack instructed, and Hakuun could not disagree.

* * * * *

Even with their sensitive elf ears, Drizzt and Hralien could only make out the loudest chants from the gathered orcs. Still, the purpose of the march became painfully obvious.

"They are the ones," Hralien remarked. "The yellow banner was seen in the Moonwood. It appears that their numbers have . . ."

He paused as he looked over at his companion, who didn't seem to be listening. Drizzt crouched, perfectly still, his head turned back to the south, toward Mithral Hall.

"We have already passed several orc settlements," the drow said a few heartbeats later. "No doubt this march will cross through each."

"Swelling their numbers," Hralien agreed, and Drizzt finally looked at him.

"And they'll continue southward," the drow reasoned.

Hralien said, "This may be renewed aggression brewing. And I fear that there is an instigator."

"Tos'un?" said Drizzt. "I see no dark elf among the gathering."

"He's likely not far afield."

"Look at them," Drizzt said, nodding his chin in the direction of the chanting, cheering orcs. "If Tos'un did instigate this madness, could he still be in control of it?"

It was Hralien's turn to shrug. "Do not underestimate his cunning," the elf warned. "The attack on the Moonwood was well-coordinated, and brutally efficient."

"Obould's orcs have surprised us at every turn."

"And they were not without drow advisors."

The two locked stares at that remark, a cloud briefly crossing Drizzt's face.

"I truly believe that Tos'un orchestrated the attack on the Moonwood," Hralien said. "And that he is behind this march, wherever it may lead."

Drizzt glanced back to the south, toward Bruenor's kingdom.

"It may well be that their destination is Mithral Hall," Hralien conceded. "But I beg you to continue on the road that led you out of Bruenor's depths. For all our sakes, find Tos'un Armgo. I will shadow these orcs, and will give ample warning to King Bruenor should it become necessary—and I will err on the side of caution. Trust me in this, I beg, and free yourself for this most important task."

Drizzt looked from the gathered orcs back toward Mithral Hall yet again. He envisioned a battle fought along the Surbrin, fierce and vicious, and felt the pangs of guilt in considering that Bruenor and Regis, perhaps even Catti-brie and the rest of Clan Battlehammer, would yet again be fighting for their survival without him by their side. He winced as he saw again the fall of the tower at Shallows, with Dagnabbit, whom he had then thought to be Bruenor, tumbling down to his death atop it.

He took a deep breath and turned back to the orc frenzy, the chanting and dancing continuing unabated. If a dark elf from Barrison Del'Armgo, one of the most formidable Houses of Menzoberranzan, was to blame then the orcs would no doubt prove many times more formidable than they appeared. Drizzt nodded grimly, his responsibility and thus his path clear before him.

"Follow their every move," he bade Hralien.

"On my word," the elf replied. "Your friends will not be caught unprepared."

The orcs moved along soon after, and Hralien shadowed their southwestern march, leaving Drizzt alone on the mountainside. He considered going down to the orc village and snooping around, but decided that Tos'un, if he was about, would likely be along the periphery, among the stones, as was Drizzt.

"Come to me, Guenhwyvar," the drow commanded, drawing forth the onyx figurine. When the gray mist coalesced into the panther, Drizzt sent her out hunting. Guenhwyvar could cover a tremendous amount of ground in short order, and not even a lone drow could escape her keen senses.

Drizzt, too, set off, moving deliberately but with great caution in the opposite direction from the panther, who was already cutting across the wake of the departing army. If Hralien's guess was correct and Tos'un Armgo was directing the orcs from nearby, Drizzt held all faith that he would soon confront the rogue.

His hands went to his scimitars as he considered Khazid'hea, Catti-brie's sword, the weapon that had fallen into the hands of Tos'un. Any drow warrior was formidable. A warrior of a noble House likely more so. Even thinking in those respectful terms, Drizzt consciously reminded himself that the drow noble was even more potent, for those who underestimated Khazid'hea usually wound up on the ground.

In two pieces.

* * * * *

Interesting, Jack said to Hakuun's mind when they walked away from their quiet little meeting with Toogwik Tuk, one in which Jack had used the power of magical suggestion to complement Hakuun's spells of lie detection, allowing the dual being to extract much more honest answers from Toogwik Tuk than the young shaman had ever meant to offer. *So the conspirators have not brought you here to enhance Obould's forces.*

"We must tell Grguch," Hakuun whispered.

Tell him what? That we have come to do battle?

"That our venture into the Moonwood and now against the dwarves will likely anger Obould."

Inside his head, Hakuun could feel Jack laughing. *Orcs plotting against orcs,* Jack silently related. *Orcs manipulating orcs to plot against orcs. All of this will be surprising news to old Chieftain Grguch, I am sure.*

Hakuun's determined stride slowed, his tailwind stolen by Jack's cynical sarcasm—sarcasm effective only because it held the ring of truth.

Let the play play, said Jack. *The plots of the conspirators will be bent to our favor when we need them to be. For now, all the risk is theirs, for Clan Karuck is unwitting. If they have played the part of fools to even consider such a plot, their fall will be enjoyable to witness. If they are not fools, then all to our gain.*

"Our gain?" said Hakuun, emphasizing Jack's inclusion into it all.

"For as long as I am interested," Hakuun's voice replied, though it was Jack who controlled it.

A not-so-subtle reminder, Hakuun understood, of who was leading whom.

CHAPTER
DEFINING GRUUMSH
17

Chieftain Dnark did not miss the simmer behind King Obould's yellow eyes whenever the orc king's glance happened his and Ung-thol's way. Obould was continually repositioning his forces, which all of the chieftains understood was the king's way of keeping them in unfamiliar territory, and thus, keeping them dependent upon the larger kingdom for any real sense of security. Dnark and Ung-thol had rejoined their clan, the tribe of the Wolf Jaw, only to learn that Obould had summoned them to work on a defensive position north of Keeper's Dale, not far from where Obould had settled to ride out the fleeting days of winter.

As soon as Obould had met Wolf Jaw at the new site, the wise and perceptive Dnark understood that there had been more to that movement than simple tactical repositioning, and when he'd first met the orc king's gaze, he had known beyond doubt that he and Ung-thol had been the focus of Obould's decision.

The annoying Kna squirmed around his side, as always, and shaman Nukkels kept to a respectful two paces behind and to his god-figure's left. That meant that Nukkels's many shamans were filtered around the common warriors accompanying the king. Dnark presumed that all of the orcs setting up Obould's three-layered tent were fanatics in the service of Nukkels.

Obould launched into his expected tirade about the importance of the mountain ridge upon which the tent was being erected, and how the fate of the entire kingdom could well rest upon the efforts of Clan Wolf Jaw in properly securing and fortifying the ground, the tunnels, and the walls. They had heard it all before, of course, but Dnark couldn't help but marvel at the rapt expressions on the faces of his minions as the undeniably charismatic king wove his spell yet again. Predictability didn't diminish the effect, and that, the chieftain knew, was no small feat.

Dnark purposely focused on the reactions of the other orcs, in part to keep himself from listening too carefully to Obould, whose rhetoric was truly hard to resist—sometimes so much so that Dnark wondered if Nukkels and the other priests weren't weaving a bit of magic of their own behind the notes of Obould's resonating voice.

Wound in his contemplations, it took a nudge from Ung-thol to get Dnark to realize that Obould had addressed him directly. Panic washing through him, the chieftain turned to face the king squarely, and he fumbled for something to say that wouldn't give away his obliviousness.

Obould's knowing smile let him know that nothing would suffice.

"My pennant will be set upon the door of my tent when it is ready for private audience," the orc king said—said again, obviously. "When you see it, you will come for a private parlay."

"Private?" Dnark dared ask. "Or am I to bring my second?"

Obould, his smile smug indeed, looked past him to Ung-thol. "Please do," he said, and it seemed to Dnark the enticing purr of a cat looking to sharpen its claws.

Wearing a smug and superior smile, Obould walked past him, carrying Kna and with Nukkels scurrying in tow. Dnark scanned wider as the king and his entourage moved off to the tent, noting the glances from the king's warriors filtering across his clan, and identifying those likely serving the priests. If it came to blows, Dnark would have to direct his own warriors against the magic-wielding fanatics, first and foremost.

He winced as he considered that, seeing the futility laid bare before him. If it came to blows with King Obould and his guard, Dnark's clan would scatter and flee for their lives, and nothing he could say would alter that.

He looked to Ung-thol, who stared at Obould without blinking, watching the king's every receding step.

Ung-thol knew the truth of it as well, Dnark realized, and wondered—not for the first time—if Toogwik Tuk hadn't led them down a fool's path.

"The flag of Obould is on the door," Ung-thol said to his chieftain a short while later.

"Let us go, then," said Dnark. "It would not do to keep the king waiting."

Dnark started off, but Ung-thol grabbed him by the arm. "We must not underestimate King Obould's network of spies," the shaman said. "He has sorted the various tribes carefully throughout the region, where those more loyal to him remain watchful of others he suspects. He may know that you and I were in the east. And he knows of the attack on the Moonwood, for Grguch's name echoes through the valleys, a new hero in the Kingdom of Many-Arrows."

Dnark paused and considered the words, then began to nod.

"Does Obould consider Grguch a hero?" Ung-thol asked.

"Or a rival?" asked Dnark, and Ung-thol was glad that they were in agreement, and that Dnark apparently understood the danger to them. "Fortunately for King Obould, he has a loyal chieftain"— Dnark patted his hand against his own chest—"and wise shaman who can bear witness here that Chieftain Grguch and Clan Karuck are valuable allies."

With a nod at Ung-thol's agreeing grin, Dnark turned and started for the tent. The shaman's grin faded as soon as Dnark looked away. None of it, Ung-thol feared, was to be taken lightly. He had been at the ceremony wherein King Obould had been blessed with the gifts of Gruumsh. He had watched the orc king break a bull's neck with his bare hands. He had seen the remains of a powerful drow priestess, her throat bitten out by Obould after the king had been taken down the side of a ravine in a landslide brought about by a priestess's earth-shaking enchantment. Watching Grguch's work in the east had been heady, invigorating and inspiring, to be sure. Clan Karuck showed the fire and mettle of the very best orc warriors, and the priest of Gruumsh could not help but feel his heart swell with pride at their fast and devastating accomplishments.

But Ung-thol was old enough and wise enough to temper his elation and soaring hopes against the reality that was King Obould Many-Arrows.

As he and Dnark entered the third and final off-set entrance into Obould's inner chamber, Ung-thol was only reminded of that awful reality. King Obould, seeming very much the part, sat on his throne on a raised dais, so that even though he was seated, he towered over any who stood before him. He wore his trademark black armor, patched back together after his terrific battle with the drow, Drizzt Do'Urden. His greatsword, which could blaze with magical fire at Obould's will, rested against the arm of his throne, within easy reach.

Obould leaned forward at their approach, dropping one elbow on his knee and stroking his chin. He didn't blink as he measured the steps of the pair, his focus almost exclusively on Dnark. Ung-thol hoped that his wrath, if it came forth, would be equally selective.

"Wolf Jaw performs brilliantly," Obould greeted, somewhat dissipating the tension.

Dnark bowed low at the compliment. "We are an old and disciplined clan."

"I know that well," said the king. "And you are a respected and feared tribe. It is why I keep you close to Many-Arrows, so that the center of my line will never waver."

Dnark bowed again at the compliment, particularly the notion that Wolf Jaw was feared, which was about as high as orc praise ever climbed. Ung-thol considered his chieftain's expression when he came back up from that bow. When the smug Dnark glanced his way, Ung-thol shot him a stern but silent retort, reminding him of the truth of Obould's reasoning. He was keeping Wolf Jaw close, indeed, but Dnark had to understand that Obould's aim was more to keep an eye on the tribe than to shore up his center. After all, there was no line of battle, so there was no center to fortify.

"The winter was favorable to us all," said Dnark. "Many towers have been built, and miles of wall."

"Every hilltop, Chieftain Dnark," said Obould. "If the dwarves or their allies come against us, they will have to fight over walls and towers on every hilltop."

Dnark glanced at Ung-thol again, and the cleric nodded for him to let it go at that. There was no need to engage Obould in an argument of defensive versus offensive preparations, certainly. Not with their schemes unfolding in the east.

"You were gone from your tribe," Obould stated, and Ung-thol started and blinked, wondering if the perceptive Obould had just read his mind.

"My king?" Dnark asked.

"You have been away in the east," said Obould. "With your shaman."

Dnark had done a good job keeping his composure, Ung-thol believed, but then the shaman winced when Dnark swallowed hard.

"There are many rogue orcs left over from the fierce battles with the dwarves," Dnark said. "Some strong and seasoned warriors, even shamans, have lost all their kin and clan. They have no banner."

As soon as he spoke the words, Dnark shrank back a step, for a murderous scowl crossed Obould's powerful features. At either side of the tent chamber, guards bristled, a couple even growling.

"They have no banner?" Obould calmly—too calmly—asked.

"They have the flag of Many-Arrows, of course," Ung-thol dared to interject, and Obould's eyes widened then narrowed quickly as he regarded the shaman. "But your kingdom is arranged by tribe, my king. You send tribes to the hills and the vales to do the work, and those who have lost their tribes know not where to go. Dnark and other chieftains are trying to sweep up the rogues to better organize your kingdom, so that you, with great plans opening wide before your Gruumsh-inspired visions, are not cluttered by such minor details."

Obould eased back in his throne and the moment of distress seemed to slip back from the edge of disaster. Of course with Obould, whose temper had left uncounted dead in his murderous wake, none could be sure.

"You were in the east," Obould said after many heartbeats had passed. "Near the Moonwood."

"Not so near, but yes, my king," said Dnark.

"Tell me of Grguch."

The blunt demand rocked Dnark back on his heels and crippled his denial as he replied with incredulity, "Grguch?"

"His name echoes through the kingdom," said Obould. "You have heard it."

"Ah, you mean Chieftain Grguch," Dnark said, changing the inflection of the name to put emphasis on the "Gr," and acting as if Obould's further remarks had spurred recognition. "Yes, I have heard of him."

"You have met him," said Obould, his tone and the set of his face conveying that his assertion was not assumption, but known fact.

Dnark glanced at Ung-thol, and for a moment the shaman thought his chieftain might just turn on his heel and flee. And indeed, Ung-thol wanted to do the same. Not for the first time and not for the last time, he wondered how they could have been foolish enough to dare conspire against King Obould Many-Arrows.

A soft chuckle from Dnark settled Ung-thol, though, and reminded him that Dnark had risen through difficult trials to become the chieftain of an impressive tribe—a tribe that even then surrounded Obould's tent.

"Chieftain Grguch of Clan Karuck, yes," Dnark said, matching Obould's stare. "I witnessed his movement through Teg'ngun's Dale near the Surbrin. He was marching to the Moonwood, though we did not know that at the time. Would that I had, for I would have enjoyed witnessing his slaughter of the foolish elves."

"You approve of his attack?"

"The elves have been striking at your minions in the east day after day," said Dnark. "I think it good that the pain of battle was taken to their forest, and that the heads of several of the creatures were placed upon pikes at the river's edge. Chieftain Grguch did you a great service. I had thought his assault on the Moonwood to be at your command."

He ended with an inflection of confusion, even suspicion, craftily turning the event back upon the orc king.

"Our enemies do not avoid their deserved punishment," Obould said without hesitation.

At Dnark's side, Ung-thol realized that his companion's quick-thinking had likely just saved both their lives. For King Obould would not kill them and tacitly admit that Grguch had acted independent of the throne.

"Chieftain Grguch and Clan Karuck will serve the kingdom well," Dnark pressed. "They are as fierce as any tribe I have ever seen."

"They breed with ogres, I am told."

"And carry many of the brutes along to anchor their lines."

"Where are they now?"

"In the east, I expect," said Dnark.

"Near the Moonwood still?"

"Likely," said Dnark. "Likely awaiting the response of our enemies. If the ugly elves dare cross the Surbrin, Chieftain Grguch will pike more heads on the riverbank."

Ung-thol eyed Obould carefully through Dnark's lie, and he easily recognized that the king knew more than he was letting on. Word of Grguch's march to the south had reached Obould's ear. Obould knew that the chieftain of Clan Karuck was a dangerous rival.

Ung-thol studied Obould carefully, but the cunning warrior king gave little more away. He offered some instructions for shoring up the defense of the region, included a punishing deadline, then dismissed the pair with a wave of his hand as he turned his attention to the annoying Kna.

"Your hesitance in admitting your knowledge of Grguch warned him," Ung-thol whispered to Dnark as they left the tent and crossed the muddy ground to rejoin their clan.

"He pronounced it wrong."

"You did."

Dnark stopped and turned on the shaman. "Does it matter?"

CHAPTER 18
THE SURBRIN BRIDGE

The wizard held his hand out, fingers locked as if it were the talon of a great hunting bird. Sweat streaked his forehead despite the cold wind, and he locked his face into a mask of intensity.

The stone was too heavy for him, but he kept up his telekinetic assault, willing it into the air. Down at the riverbank, dwarf masons on the far bank furiously cranked their come-alongs, while others rushed around the large stone, throwing an extra strap or chain where needed. Still, despite the muscle and ingenuity of the dwarf craftsmen, and magical aid from the Silverymoon wizard, the floating stone teetered on the brink of disaster.

"Joquim!" another citizen of Silverymoon called.

"I . . . can't . . . hold . . . it," the wizard Joquim grunted back, each word forced out through gritted teeth.

The second wizard shouted for help and rushed down to Joquim's side. He had little in the way of telekinetic prowess, but he had memorized a dweomer for just that eventuality. He launched into his spellcasting and threw his magical energies out toward the shaking stone. It stabilized, and when a third member of the Silverymoon contingent rushed over, the balance shifted in favor of the builders. It began to seem almost effortless as the combination of dwarf and wizard guided the stone out over the rushing waters of the River Surbrin.

With a dwarf on the end of a beam guiding the way, the team with the come-alongs positioned the block perfectly over the even larger stones that had already been set in place. The guide dwarf called for a hold, rechecked the alignment, then lifted a red flag.

The wizards eased up their magic gradually, slowly lowering the block.

"Go get the next one!" the dwarf yelled to his companions and the wizards on the near bank. "Seems the Lady's almost ready for this span!"

All eyes turned to the work at the near bank, the point closest to Mithral Hall, where Lady Alustriel stood on the first length of span over the river, her features serene as she whispered the words of a powerful spell of creation. Cold and strong she appeared, almost godlike above the rushing waters. Her white robes, highlighted in light green, blew about her tall and slender form. There was hardly a gasp of surprise when a second stone span appeared before her, reaching out to the next set of supports.

Alustriel's arms slipped down to her sides and she gave a deep exhale, her shoulders slumping as if her effort had thrown out more than magical strength.

"Amazing," Catti-brie said, coming up beside her and inspecting the newly conjured slab.

"The Art, Catti-brie," Alustriel replied. "Mystra's blessings are wondrous indeed." Alustriel turned a sly look her way. "Perhaps I can tutor you."

Catti-brie scoffed at the notion, but coincidentally, as she threw her head back, she twisted her leg at an angle that sent a wave of pain rolling through her damaged hip, and she was reminded that her days as a warrior might indeed be at their end—one way or another.

"Perhaps," she said.

Alustriel's smile beamed genuine and warm. The Lady of Silverymoon glanced back and motioned to the dwarf masons, who flooded forward with their tubs of mortar to seal and smooth the newest span.

"The conjured stone is permanent?" Catti-brie asked as she and Alustriel moved back down the ramp to the bank.

Alustriel looked at her as if the question was completely absurd. "Would you have it vanish beneath the wheels of a wagon?"

They both laughed at the flippant response.

"I mean, it is real stone," the younger woman clarified.

"Not an illusion, to be sure."

"But still the stuff of magic?"

Alustriel furrowed her brow as she considered the woman. "The stone is as real as anything the dwarves could drag in from a quarry, and the dweomer that created it is permanent."

"Unless it is dispelled," Catti-brie replied, and Alustriel said, "Ah," as she caught on to the woman's line of thought.

"It would take Elminster himself to even hope to dispel the work of Lady Alustriel," another nearby wizard interjected.

Catti-brie looked from the mage to Alustriel.

"A bit of an exaggeration, of course," Alustriel admitted. "But truly, any mage of sufficient power to dispel my creations would also have in his arsenal evocations that could easily destroy a bridge constructed without magic."

"But a conventional bridge can be warded against lightning bolts and other destructive evocations," Catti-brie reasoned.

"As this one shall be," promised Alustriel.

"And so it will be as safe as if the dwarves had . . ." Catti-brie started, and Alustriel finished the thought with her, "dragged the stones from a quarry."

They shared another laugh, until Catti-brie added, "Except from Alustriel."

The Lady of Silverymoon stopped cold and turned to stare directly at Catti-brie.

"It is an easy feat for a wizard to dispel her own magic, so I am told," Catti-brie remarked. "There will be no wards in place to prevent you from waving your hands and making expanse after expanse disappear."

A wry grin crossed Alustriel's beautiful face, and she cocked an eyebrow, an expression of congratulations for the woman's sound and cunning reasoning.

"An added benefit should the orcs overrun this position and try to use the bridge to spread their darkness to other lands," Catti-brie went on.

"Other lands like Silverymoon," Alustriel admitted.

"Do not be quick to sever the bridge to Mithral Hall, Lady," Catti-brie said.

"Mithral Hall is connected to the eastern bank through tunnels in any case," Alustriel replied. "We will not abandon your father, Catti-brie. We will never abandon King Bruenor and the valiant dwarves of Clan Battlehammer."

Catti-brie's responding smile came easy to her, for she didn't doubt a word of the pledge. She glanced back at the conjured slabs and nodded appreciatively, both for the power in creating them and the strategy of Alustriel in keeping the power to easily destroy them.

* * * * *

The late afternoon sun reflected moisture in Toogwik Tuk's jaundiced brown eyes, for he could hardly contain his tears of joy at the ferocious reminder of what it was to be an orc. Grguch's march through the three remaining villages had been predictably successful, and after Toogwik Tuk had delivered his perfected sermon, every able-bodied orc warrior of those villages had eagerly marched out in Grguch's wake. That alone would have garnered the fierce chieftain of Clan Karuck another two hundred soldiers.

But more impressively, they soon enough discovered, came the reinforcements from villages through which they had not passed. Word of Grguch's march had spread across the region directly north of Mithral Hall, and the war-thirsty orcs of many tribes, frustrated by the winter pause, had rushed to the call.

As he crossed the impromptu encampment, Toogwik Tuk surveyed the scores—no, hundreds—of new recruits. Grguch would hit the dwarven fortifications with closer to two thousand orcs than one thousand, by the shaman's estimation. Victory at the Surbrin was all but assured. Could King Obould hope to hold back the tide of war after that?

Toogwik Tuk shook his head with honest disappointment as he considered the once-great leader. Something had happened to Obould. The shaman wondered if it might have been the stinging defeat Bruenor's dwarves had handed him in his ill-fated attempt to breach Mithral Hall's western door. Or had it been the loss of the conspiring dark elves and Gerti Orelsdottr and her frost giant minions? Or perhaps it had come about because of the loss of his son, Urlgen, in the fight on the cliff tops north of Keeper's Dale.

Whatever the cause, Obould hardly seemed the same fierce warrior who had led the charge into Citadel Adbar, or who had begun his great sweep south from the Spine of the World only a few months before. Obould had lost his understanding of the essence of the orc. He had lost the voice of Gruumsh within his heart.

"He demands that we wait," the shaman mused aloud, staring out at the teeming swarm, "and yet they come by the score to the promise of renewed battle with the cursed dwarves."

Never more certain of the righteousness of his conspiracy, the shaman moved quickly toward Grguch's tent. Obould no longer heard the call of Gruumsh, but Grguch surely did, and after the dwarves were smashed and chased back into their holes, how might King Obould claim dominion over the chieftain of Clan Karuck? And how might Obould secure fealty from the tens of thousands of orcs he had brought forth from their holes with promises of conquest?

Obould demanded they sit and wait, that they till the ground like peasant human farmers. Grguch demanded of them that they sharpen their spears and swords to better cut the flesh of dwarves.

Grguch heard the call of Gruumsh.

The shaman found the chieftain standing on the far side of a small table, surrounded by two of his Karuck warlords and with a much smaller orc standing across from them and manipulating a pile of dirt and stones that had been set upon the table. As he neared, Toogwik Tuk recognized the terrain being described by the smaller orc, for he had seen the mountain ridge that stretched from the eastern end of Mithral Hall down to the Surbrin.

"Welcome, Gruumsh-speaker," Grguch greeted him. "Join us."

Toogwik Tuk moved to an open side of the table and inspected the scout's work, which depicted a wall nearly completed to the Surbrin and a series of towers anchoring it.

"The dwarves have been industrious throughout the winter," said Grguch. "As you feared. King Obould's pause has given them strength."

"They will anticipate an attack like ours," the shaman remarked.

"They have witnessed no large movements of forces to indicate it," said Grguch.

"Other than our own," Toogwik Tuk had to remind him.

But Grguch laughed it off. "Possibly they have taken note of many orcs now moving nearer to their position," he agreed. "They may expect an attack in the coming tendays."

The two Karuck warlords beside the brutish chieftain chuckled at that.

"They will never expect one this very night," said Grguch.

Toogwik Tuk's face dropped into a sudden frown, and he looked down at the battlefield in near panic. "We have not even sorted out our forces . . ." he started to weakly protest.

"There is nothing to sort," Grguch replied. "Our tactic is swarm fodder and nothing more."

"Swarm fodder?" asked the shaman.

"A simple swarm to and through the wall," said Grguch. "Darkness is our ally. Speed and surprise are our allies. We will hit them as a wave flattens the ridge of a boot print on a beach."

"You know not the techniques of the many tribes who have come into the fold."

"I don't need to," Grguch declared. "I don't need to count my warriors. I don't need to place them in lines and squares, to form reserves and ensure that our flanks are protected back far enough to prevent an end run by our enemies. That is the way of the dwarf." He paused and looked around at the stupidly grinning warlords and the excited scout. "I see no dwarves in this room," he said, and the others laughed.

Grguch looked back at Toogwik Tuk. His eyes went wide, as if in alarm, and he sniffed at the air a couple of times. "No," he declared, looking again to his warlords. "I *smell* no dwarves in this room."

The laughter that followed was much more pronounced, and despite his reservations, Toogwik Tuk was wise enough to join in.

"Tactics are for dwarves," the chieftain explained. "Discipline is for elves. For orcs, there is only . . ." He looked directly at Toogwik Tuk.

"Swarm fodder?" the shaman asked, and a wry grin spread on Grguch's ugly face.

"Chaos," he confirmed. "Ferocity. Bloodlust and abandon. As soon as the sun has set, we begin our run. All the way to the wall. All the way to the Surbrin. All the way to the eastern doors of Mithral Hall. Half, perhaps more than half, of our warriors will find tonight the reward of glorious death."

Toogwik Tuk winced at that, and silently berated himself. Was he beginning to think more like Obould?

Grguch reminded him of the words of Gruumsh One-eye. "They will die with joy," the chieftain promised. "Their last cry will be of elation and not agony. And any who die otherwise, with regret or with sorrow or with fear, should have been slaughtered in sacrifice to Gruumsh before our attack commenced!"

The sudden volume and ferocity of his last proclamation set Toogwik Tuk back on his heels and had both the Clan Karuck warlords and guards at the perimeter of the room growling and gnashing their teeth. For a brief moment, Toogwik Tuk almost reconsidered his call to the deepest holes to rouse Chieftain Grguch.

Almost.

"There has been no sign from the dwarves that they know of our march," Grguch told a great gathering later that day, when the sunlight began to wane. Toogwik Tuk noted the dangerous priest Hakuun standing at his side, and that gave the younger shaman pause. He got the feeling that Hakuun had been watching him all along.

"They do not see the doom that has come against them," Grguch ordered. "Do not shout out, but run. Run fast to the wall, without delay, and whispering praise for Gruumsh with every stride."

There were no lines or coordinated movements, just a wild charge begun miles from the goal. There were no torches to light the way, no magical lights conjured by Toogwik Tuk or the other priests of Gruumsh. They were orcs, after all, raised in the upper tunnels of the lightless Underdark.

The night was their ally, the dark their comfort.

*****

Once, when he was a child, Hralien had found a large pile of sand down by one of the Moonwood's two lakes. From a distance, that mound of light-colored sand had seemed discolored with streaks of red, and as he moved closer, young Hralien realized that the streaks weren't discolored sand, but were actually moving upon the surface of the mound. Being young and inexperienced, he had at first feared that he had happened upon a tiny volcano, perhaps.

On closer inspection, though, the truth had come clear to him, for the pile of sand had been an ant mound, and the red streaks were lines of the six-legged creatures marching to and fro.

Hralien thought of that long-ago experience as he witnessed the charge of the orcs, swarming the small, rocky hills north of King Bruenor's eastern defenses. Their movements seemed no less frenetic, and truly their march appeared no less determined. Given their speed and intensity, and the obstacle that awaited them barely two miles to the south, Hralien recognized their intent.

The elf bit his lip as he remembered his promise to Drizzt Do'Urden. He looked south, sorting out the landscape and recalling the trails that would most quickly return him to Mithral Hall.

Then he was running, and fearing that he could not keep his promise to his drow friend, for the orc line stretched ahead of him and the creatures had not far to travel. With great grace and agility, Hralien sprang from stone to stone. He leaped up and grabbed a low tree branch and swung out across a narrow chasm, landing lightly on the other side and in a full run. He moved with hardly a whisper of sound, unlike the orcs, whose heavy steps echoed in his keen elf's ears.

He knew that he should be cautious, for he could ill afford the delay if he happened into a fight. But neither could he slow his run and carefully pick his path, for some of the orcs were ahead of him, and the dwarves would need every heartbeat of warning he could give them. So he ran on, leaping and scrambling over bluffs and through low dales, where the melting snow had streamed down and pooled in clear, cold pockets. Hralien tried to avoid those pools as much as possible, for they often concealed slick ice. But even with his great dexterity and sharp vision, he occasionally splashed through, cringing at the unavoidable sound.

At one point, he heard an orc cry out, and feared that he had been spotted. Many strides later, he realized that the creature was just calling to a companion, a stark reminder that the lead runners and scouts of the brutish force were all around him.

Finally he left the sounds of orcs behind, for though the brutes could move with great speed, they could not match the pace of a dexterous elf, even across such broken ground.

Soon after, coming up over a rocky rise, Hralien caught sight of squat stone towers in the south, running down from tall mountains to the silvery, moonlit snake that was the River Surbrin.

"Too soon," the elf whispered in dismay, and he glanced back as if expecting Obould's entire army to roll over him. He shook his head and winced, then sprinted off for the south.

* * * * *

"We will have it completed within the tenday," Alustriel said to Catti-brie, the two sitting with some of the other Silverymoon wizards around a small campfire. One of the wizards, a robust human with thick salt and pepper hair and a tightly trimmed goatee, had conjured the flames and was playing with them, casting cantrips to change their color from orange to white to blue and red. A second wizard, a rather eccentric half-elf with shiny black hair magically streaked by a bloom of bright red locks, joined in and wove enchantments to make the red flames form into the shape of a small dragon. Seeing the challenge, the first wizard likewise formed blue flames, and the two spellcasters set their fiery pets into a proxy battle. Almost immediately, several other wizards began excitedly placing their bets.

Catti-brie watched with amusement and interest—more than she would have expected, and Alustriel's words to her about dabbling in the dark arts flitted unbidden through her thoughts. Her experience with wizards was very limited, and mostly involved the unpredictable and dangerously foolish Harpell family from Longsaddle.

"Asa Havel will win," Alustriel whispered to her, leaning in close and indicating the half-elf wizard who had manipulated the red flame. "Duzberyl is far more powerful at manipulating fire, but he has taxed his powers to their limit this day conjuring bright hot flames to seal the stone. And Asa Havel knows it."

"So he challenged," Catti-brie whispered back. "And his friends know, too, so they wager."

"They would wager anyway," Alustriel explained. "It is a matter of pride. Whatever is lost here will be reclaimed soon enough in another challenge."

Catti-brie nodded and watched the unfolding drama, the many faces, elf and human alike, glowing in varying shades and hues in the uneven light, turning blue as the blue dragon leaped atop the red, but then drifting back, green and yellow and toward a feverish red as Asa Havel's drake filtered up through Duzberyl's and gradually gained supremacy. It was all good-natured, of course, but Catti-brie didn't miss the intensity etched onto the faces of the combatants and onlookers alike. It occurred to her that she was looking into an entirely different world. She could relate it to the drinking games, and the arm-wrestling and sparring that so often took place in the taverns of Mithral Hall, for though the venue was different, the emotions were not. Still, there remained enough of a difference to intrigue her. It was a battle of strength, but of mental strength and concentration, and not of muscle and intestinal fortitude.

"Within a month, you could form flames into such shapes, yourself," Alustriel teased.

Catti-brie looked at her and laughed dismissively, but that hardly hid her interest.

She looked back to the fire just in time to see Duzberyl's blue roll over and consume Asa Havel's red, contrary to Alustriel's prediction. The backers of both wizards gasped in surprise and Duzberyl gave a yelp that was more shock than of victory. Catti-brie's gaze turned to Asa Havel, and her surprise turned to confusion.

The half-elf was not looking at the fight, and seemed oblivious to the fact that his dragon had been consumed by the human's blue. He stared out to the north, his sea-blue eyes scanning high above the flames. Catti-brie felt Alustriel turn beside her, then stand. The woman glanced over her shoulder, up at the dark wall, but shook her head slightly in confusion, seeing nothing out of the ordinary. Beside her, Alustriel cast a minor spell.

Other wizards rose and peered out to the north.

"An elf has come," Alustriel said to Catti-brie. "And the dwarves are scrambling."

"It's an attack," Asa Havel announced, rising and moving past the two women. He looked right at Alustriel and the princess of Mithral Hall and asked, "Orcs?"

"Prepare for battle," Alustriel said to her contingent. "Area spells to disrupt any charge."

"We have little left this day," Duzberyl reminded her.

In response, Alustriel reached inside one of the folds of her robes and drew forth a pair of slender wands. She half-turned and tossed

THE ORC KING

one to Duzberyl. "Your necklace, too, if needed," she instructed, and the human nodded and brought a hand to a gaudy choker he wore, its golden links set with large stones like rubies of varying sizes, including one so large that Catti-brie couldn't have closed her fist around it.

"Talindra, to the gates of the dwarven halls," Alustriel said to a young elf female. "Warn the dwarves and help them sort the battle."

The elf nodded and took a few fast steps to the west, then disappeared with a flash of blue-white light. A second flash followed almost instantly, over near the hall's eastern gates, transporting Talindra to her assigned position, the surprised Catti-brie assumed, for she couldn't actually see the young elf.

She turned back to hear Alustriel positioning Asa Havel and another pair. "Secure fast passage to the far bank, should we need it. Prepare enough to carry any dwarves routed from the wall."

Catti-brie heard the first shouts from the wall, followed by the blare of horns, many horns, from beyond to the north. Then came the blare of one that overwhelmed all the others, a resonating, low-pitched grumble that shook the stones beneath Catti-brie's feet.

"Damn Obould to the Nine Hells," Catti-brie whispered, and she grimaced at the realization that she had loaned Taulmaril to Drizzt. She looked over at Alustriel. "I haven't my bow, or a sword. A weapon, please? Conjure one or produce one from a deep pocket."

To Catti-brie's surprise, the Lady of Silverymoon did just that, pulling yet another wand from inside her robes. Catti-brie took it, not knowing what to make of the thing, and when she looked back at Alustriel, the tall woman was tugging a ring from her finger.

"And this," she said, handing over the thin gold band set with a trio of sparkling diamonds. "I trust you are not already in the possession of two magical rings."

Catti-brie took it and held it pressed between her thumb and index finger, her expression dumbfounded.

"The command word for the wand is 'twell-in-sey,' " Alustriel explained. "Or 'twell-in-sey-sey' if you wish to loose two magical bolts."

"I don't know . . ."

"Anyone can use it," Alustriel assured her. "Point it at your target and speak the word. For the bigger orcs, choose two."

"But..."

"Put the ring on your finger and open your mind to it, for it will impart to you its dweomers. And know that they are powerful indeed." With that, Alustriel turned away, and Catti-brie understood that the lesson was at its end.

The Lady of Silverymoon and her wizards, except for those working near the river preparing a magical escape to the far bank, headed off for the wall, nearly all of them drawing forth wands or rods, or switching rings and other jewelry. Catti-brie watched it all with an undeniable sense of excitement, so much so that she was trembling so badly she could hardly line up the ring to slip it on her finger.

Finally she did, and she closed her eyes and took a deep breath. She felt as if she were looking up at the heavens, to see stars shooting across the darkened night sky, to see flashes of brilliance so magnificent that it seemed to her as if the gods must be throwing bolts at each other.

The first sounds of battle shook her from her contemplation. She opened her eyes and nearly fell over due to dizziness from the sudden change, as if she had just stepped back to solid ground from the Astral Plane.

She started after Alustriel, inspecting the wand, and garnered quickly which end to hold from a leather strap wrapped diagonally as a hand grip. At least she hoped it was the right end, and she winced at the thought of unloading enchanted bolts of magic into her own face. She dismissed the worry, noting that she wasn't gaining much on Alustriel, and noting more pointedly that the dwarves at the wall scrambled and yelled for support in many places already. She dropped her arms down beside her and ran as fast as her battered hip would allow.

"Twell-in-sey," she whispered, trying to get the inflection correct. She did.

The wand discharged and a red dart of energy burst forth, snapping into the ground with a hiss right before her running feet. Catti-brie yelped and stumbled, nearly falling over. She caught her balance and her composure, and was glad that no one seemed to notice.

On she ran, or tried to, but a wave of hot fire ran up her leg and nearly toppled her yet again. She looked down to her boot, smoking and charred on the side just back of her little toe. She paused again and composed herself, taking heart that the wound was not too severe, and thanking Moradin himself that Lady Alustriel hadn't given her a wand of lightning bolts.

* * * * *

The orc gained the wall in a wild rush, stabbing powerfully at the nearest dwarf, who seemed an easy kill as he was busy driving a second orc back over the wall and into the darkness.

But that dwarf, Charmorffe Dredgewelder of Fine Family Yellowbeard—so named because none of the Dredgewelders was ever known to have a yellow beard—was neither particularly surprised nor particularly impressed by the aggressive move. Trained under Thibbledorf Pwent himself, having served more than a score of years in the Gutbuster Brigade, Charmorffe had faced many a finer foe than that pathetic creature.

As Charmorffe had never gotten familiar with a formal buckler, his plate-shielded arm swooped down to intercept the spear, blocking it solidly and sweeping it back behind him as he turned. That same movement brought his cudgel swinging around, and a quick three-step forward caught the overbalanced orc cleanly in range. The creature grunted, as did the dwarf, as the cudgel slammed it right behind the shoulder, launching it into a dive and spin forward, right off the ten-foot parapet.

As the path before him cleared, Charmorffe looked down the tip of an arrow set on a short bow. He yelped and fell over backward, buckling at both his knees, and as soon as he was clear, Hralien let fly. The missile hummed through the air right above the dwarf, and splattered into the chest of an orc that had been sneaking up on him from behind.

As soon as his back hit the stone, Charmorffe snapped all of his muscles forward, throwing his arms up high, and brought himself right back to his feet.

"That's twice I'm owin' ye, ye durned elf!" the dwarf protested. "First for savin' us all, and now for savin' meself!"

"I did neither, good dwarf," Hralien replied, running across the parapet to the waist-high wall, where he set his bow to work immediately. "I've faith that Clan Battlehammer is more than able to save itself."

He shot off an arrow as he spoke, but as soon as he finished, a large orc rose into the air right before him, sword ready to strike a killing blow. The orc landed lightly on the wall top and struck, but a spinning cudgel hit both the sword and the orc, turning its blow harmlessly short. And when the orc managed to hold its balance and throw itself forward at Hralien, it too was intercepted, by a flying Charmorffe Dredgewelder. The dwarf connected with a shoulder block, driving the orc tight against the wall. The orc began raining ineffective blows upon the dwarf's back for Charmorffe's powerful legs kept grinding, pressing in even tighter.

Hralien stabbed the orc in the eye with an arrow.

The elf jumped back fast, though, set the arrow and let fly, point blank into yet another orc flying up to the top of the wall. Hralien hit it squarely, and though its feet landed atop the narrow rail, the jolt of the hit dropped it right back off.

Charmorffe leaped up and clean-and-jerked the thrashing orc up high over his head. The dwarf threw himself into the wall, which hit him about mid chest, and snapped forward, tossing the orc over. As he went forward, Charmorffe solved the riddle, for just below him, and off to both sides as well, stood ogres, their backs tight against the wall. As each bent low and cupped its hands down near the ground, another orc ran up and stepped into that brace. A slight toss by the ogres had orcs sailing up over the wall.

"Pig-faced goblin kissers," Charmorffe growled. He turned and shouted, "Rocks over the wall, boys! We got ogres playing as ladders!"

Hralien rushed up beside Charmorffe, leaned far out and shot an arrow into the top of the nearest ogre's head. He marveled at his handiwork, then saw it all the more clearly as a fireball lit up the night, down to the east of his position, closer to the Surbrin where the wall was far from complete.

When Hralien looked that way, he thought their position surely lost, for though Alustriel and her wizards had entered the fray, a mass of huge orcs and larger foes swarmed across the defenses.

"Run for Mithral Hall, good dwarf," the elf said.

"That's what I be thinking," said Charmorffe.

THE ORC KING

* * * * *

Duzberyl ambled toward the wall, grumbling incessantly. "Two hundred pieces of gold for this one alone," he muttered, pulling another glittering red jewel from his enchanted necklace. He reached back and threw it at the nearest orcs, but his estimate of distance in the low light was off and the jewel landed short of the mark. Its fiery explosion still managed to engulf and destroy a couple of the creatures, and the others fell back in full flight, shrieking with every stride.

But Duzberyl griped all the more. "A hundred gold an orc," he grumbled, glancing back at Alustriel, who was far off to the side. "I could hire an army of rangers to kill ten times the number for one-tenth the cost!" he said, though he knew she was too far away to hear him.

And she wasn't listening anyway. She stood perfectly still, the wind whipping her robes. She lifted one arm before her, a jeweled ring on her clenched fist sparking with multicolored light.

Duzberyl had seen that effect before, but still he was startled when a bolt of bright white lightning burst forth from Alustriel's ring, splitting the night. The powerful wizard's aim was, as always, right on target, her bolt slamming an ogre in the face as it climbed over the wall. Hair dancing wildly, head smoking, the brute flew back into the darkness as Alustriel's bolt bounced away to hit another nearby attacker, an orc that seemed to simply melt into the stone. Again and again, Alustriel's chain lightning leaped away, striking orc or ogre or half-ogre, sending foes flying or spinning down with smoke rising from bubbling skin.

But every vacancy was fast-filled, ten attackers for every one that fell, it seemed.

The apparent futility brought a renewed growl to Duzberyl's chubby face, and he stomped along to a better vantage point.

* * * * *

Limping from foot and hip, Catti-brie watched it all with equal if not greater frustration, for at least Alustriel and her wizards were equipped to battle the monsters. The woman felt naked without her bow, and even with the gifts Alustriel had offered, she believed that she would prove more a burden than an asset.

She considered removing herself from the front lines, back to the bridge where she might prove of some use to Asa Havel in directing the retreat, should it come to that. That in mind, she glanced back—and noted a small group of orcs sprinting along the riverbank toward the distracted wizards.

Catti-brie thrust forth the wand, but brought it back and punched out with her other fist instead. The ring's teeming magical energies called out to her and she listened, and though she didn't know exactly the effects of her call, she followed the magical path toward the strongest sensation of stored energy.

The ring jolted once, twice, thrice, each burst sending forth a fiery ball at Catti-brie's targets. Like twinkling little stars, they seemed, as if the ring had reached up to the heavens and pulled celestial bodies down for its wielder to launch at her enemies. At great speed, they shot out across the night, leaving fiery trails, and when they reached the orc group, they exploded into larger blasts of consuming flames.

Orcs shrieked and scrambled frantically, and more than one leaped into the river to be washed away by cold, killing currents. Others rolled on the ground, trying to douse the biting flames, and when that failed, they ran off like living torches into the dark night, only to fall a few steps away, to crumble and burn on the frozen ground.

It lasted only a heartbeat, but seemed like much longer to Catti-brie, who stood transfixed, breathing hard, her eyes wide with shock. With a thought, she had blown apart nearly a score of orcs. As if they were nothing. As if she were a goddess, passing judgment on insignificant creatures. Never had she felt such power!

At that moment, if someone had asked Catti-brie the Elvish name of her treasured longbow, she would not have recalled it.

* * * * *

"It's not to hold!" Charmorffe cried to Hralien, and a swipe of the dwarf's heavy cudgel sent another orc flying aside.

Hralien wanted to shout back words of encouragement, but his view of the battlefield, since he wielded a weapon that made it incumbent upon him to seek a wider perspective, was more complete, and he understood that the situation was even worse than Charmorffe likely believed.

Few dwarves came forth from Mithral Hall and a host of orcs poured through the lower, uncompleted sections of the defensive wall. Huge orcs, some two feet taller and more than a hundred pounds heavier than the dwarves. Among them were true ogres, though it was hard for Hralien to distinguish where some of the orcs ended and the clusters of ogres began.

More orcs came up over the wall, launched by their ogre step-stools, putting pressure on the dwarves and preventing them from organizing a coordinated defense against the larger mass rolling in from the east.

"It's not to hold!" Charmorffe yelled again, and the words rang true. Hralien knew that the end was coming fast. The wizards intervened—one fireball then another, and a lightning chain that left many creatures smoking on the ground. But that wouldn't be enough, and Hralien understood that the wizards had been at their magical work all day long and had little power left to offer.

"Start the retreat," the elf said to Charmorffe. "To Mithral Hall!"

Even as he spoke, the orc mass surged forward, and Hralien feared that he and Charmorffe and the others had waited too long.

* * * * *

"By the gods, and the gemstone vendors!" Duzberyl roared, watching the sudden break in the dwarven line, the bearded folk sprinting back to the west along the wall, leaping down from the parapets and veering straight for Mithral Hall's eastern door. All semblance of a defensive posture had flown, creating a full and frantic retreat.

And it wouldn't be enough, the wizard calculated, for the orcs, hungry for dwarf blood, closed with every stride. Duzberyl grimaced as a dwarf was swallowed in the black cloud of the orc horde.

The portly wizard ran, and he reached up to his necklace, grasping the largest stone of all. He tore it free, cursed the gemstone merchant again for good measure, and heaved it with all his strength.

The magical grenade hit the base of the wall just behind the leading orcs, and exploded, filling the area, even up onto the parapet, with biting, killing fires. Those monsters immediately above and near the blast charred and died, while others scrambled in an agonized and horrified frenzy, flames consuming them as they ran. Panic hit the orc line, and the dwarves ran free.

* * * * *

"Mage," Grguch muttered as he alighted on the wall some distance back of the enormous fireball.

"Of considerable power," said Hakuun, who stood beside him, having blessed himself and Grguch with every conceivable ward and enhancement.

The chieftain turned back and fell prone on the parapet railing. "Hand it up," he called down to the ogre who had flipped him up, indicating a weapon. A moment later, Grguch stood again on the wall, hoisting on one shoulder a huge javelin at the end of an atlatl.

"Mage," Grguch grumbled again with obvious disgust.

Hakuun held up a hand, motioning for the chieftain to pause. Then, from inside the orc priest, Jack the Gnome cast a most devious enchantment on the head of the missile.

Grguch grinned and brought his shoulder back, shifting the angle of the ten-foot missile. As Hakuun cast a second, complimentary spell upon the intended victim, Grguch launched the spear with all his might.

* * * * *

The stubborn orc lurched toward her, one of its legs still showing flashes of biting flame.

Catti-brie didn't flinch, didn't even start as the orc awkwardly threw a spear her way. She kept her eyes locked on the creature, met its gaze and its hate, and slowly lifted her wand.

She wished at that moment that she had Khazid'hea at her side, that she could engage the vile creature in personal combat. The orc took another staggering step, and Catti-brie uttered the command word.

The red missile sizzled into the orc's chest, knocking it backward. Somehow it held its balance and even advanced another step. Cattibrie said the last word of the trigger twice, as she had been schooled, and the first red missile knocked the orc back yet again, and the second dropped it to the ground where it writhed for just a heartbeat before laying very still.

Catti-brie stood calm and motionless for a few moments, steadying herself. She turned back to the wall, and blinked against the bursts of fiery explosions and the sharp cuts of lightning bolts, a fury that truly left her breathless. In her temporary blindness, she almost expected that the battle had ended, that the wizardly barrage had utterly destroyed the attackers as she had laid low the small group by the river.

But there came the largest blast of all, a tremendous fireball some distance back along the wall to the west, toward Mithral Hall. Catti-brie saw the truth of it, saw the dwarves, and one elf, in desperate retreat, saw all semblance of defense stripped from the wall, buried under the trampling boots of a charging orc horde.

The wall was lost. All from Mithral Hall to the Surbrin was lost. Even Lady Alustriel was withdrawing, not quite in full flight, but in a determined retreat.

Looking past Alustriel, Catti-brie noted Duzberyl. For a moment, she wondered why he, too, was not in retreat, until she realized that he stood strangely, leaning too far back for his legs to support him, his arms lolling limply at his sides.

One of the other wizards threw a lightning bolt—a rather feeble one—and in the flash, Catti-brie saw the huge javelin that had been driven half of its ten-foot length through his chest, its tip buried into the ground, pinning the wizard in that curious, angular stance.

*****

"We have them routed! Now is the moment of victory!" a frustrated Hakuun said as he stood alone behind the charging horde. He wanted to go with them, or to serve as Jaculi's conduit, as he often had, to launch a barrage of devastating magic.

But Jaculi would not begin that barrage, and worse, the uninvited parasite interrupted him every time he tried to use his more conventional shaman's magic.

A temporary moment, to be sure, Jack said in his thoughts.

"What foolishness . . . ?"

That is Lady Alustriel, Jack explained. *Alustriel of the Seven Sisters. Do not draw her attention!*

"She is running!" Hakuun protested.

She will know me. She will recognize me. She will turn loose her army and all of her wizards and all of her magic to destroy me, Jack explained. *It is an old grudge, but one that neither I nor she has forgotten! Do nothing to draw her attention.*

"She is running! We can kill her," said Hakuun.

Jack's incredulous laughter filled his head with dizzying volume, so much so that the shaman couldn't even start off after Grguch and the others. He just stood there, swaying, as the battle ended around him.

Inside Hakuun's head, Jack the brain mole breathed a lot easier. In truth, he had no idea if Alustriel remembered the slight he had given her more than a century earlier. But he surely remembered her wrath from that dangerous day, and it was nothing that Jack the Gnome ever wanted to see again.

* * * * *

One of Lady Alustriel's wizards ran past Catti-brie at that moment, shouting, "Be quick to the bridge!"

Catti-brie shook her head, but she knew it to be a futile denial. Mithral Hall hadn't expected an assault of such ferocity so soon. They had been lulled by a winter of inaction, by the many reports that the bulk of the orc army remained in the west, near to Keeper's Dale, and by the widespread rumors that King Obould had settled in place, satisfied with his gains.

"To the Nine Hells with you, Obould," she cursed under her breath. "I pray that Drizzt won't kill you, only that I may find the pleasure myself."

She turned and started for the bridge with as much speed as she could muster, stepping awkwardly, as each time she brought her right foot forward, she felt the pangs from her damaged hip, and each time she placed that foot onto the ground, she was reminded by a burning sting of her foolishness with the magical wand.

When another wizard running by skidded to a stop beside her and offered her shoulder, Catti-brie, for all her pride and all her determination to not be a burden, gratefully accepted. If she had refused a hand, she would have fallen to the back of the line and likely would have never made it to the bridge.

Asa Havel greeted the returning contingent, directing them to floating disks of glowing magic that hovered nearby. As each seat filled, the wizard who had created it climbed aboard, but for a few moments, none started out across the river, for none wanted to leave the fleeing dwarves.

"Be gone!" Alustriel ordered them, coming in at the end of the line and with orc pursuit not far behind. "Because of Duzberyl's sacrifice, the retreating dwarves will make the safety of the hall, and I have sent a whisper on the wind to Talindra to instruct them to hold fast their gates and wait for morning. Across the river for us, to the safety of the eastern bank. Let us prepare our spells for a morning reprisal that will leave our enemies melted between the river and King Bruenor's hall."

Many heads nodded in agreement, and as Alustriel's eyes flashed with the sheerest intensity, Catti-brie could only wonder what mighty dweomers the Lady of Silverymoon would cast upon the foolish orcs when dawn revealed them.

Seated on the edge of a disk, her feet dangling just inches above the cold and dark rushing waters of the Surbrin, Catti-brie stared back at Mithral Hall with a mixture of emotions, not least among them guilt, and fear for her beloved home and for her beloved husband. Drizzt had gone to the north, and the army had descended from that direction. Yet he had not returned in front of the marching force with a warning, she knew, for she had not seen the lightning arrows of Taulmaril streaking through the night sky.

Catti-brie looked down at the water and steeled her thoughts and her heart.

Asa Havel, sitting beside her, put a hand on her shoulder. When she looked at the half-elf, he offered a warm and comforting smile. That smile turned a bit mischievous, and he nodded down to her torn boot. Catti-brie followed his gaze then looked back up at him, her face flushed with embarrassment.

But the elf nodded and shrugged, and lifted his red and black hair by his left ear, turning his head to catch the moonlight so that she could take note of a white scar running up the side of his head. He took her wand and assumed a pensive pose, tapping it against the side of his face, in line with the scar.

"You won't err like that again," he assured her with a playful wink, handing the wand back. "And take heart, for your impressive meteor shower gave us the time to complete the floating disks."

"It wasn't mine. It came from the ring Lady Alustriel loaned to me."

"However you accomplished it, your timing and your calm action saved our efforts. You will find a role in the morning."

"When we avenge Duzberyl," Catti-brie said grimly.

Asa Havel nodded, and added, "And the dwarves who no doubt fell this dark night."

The shouting across the river ended soon after, silenced by a resounding *bang* as Mithral Hall slammed shut her eastern door. But as the wizards and Catti-brie set their camp for the evening, they heard more commotion across the dark water. The orcs scrambled around the towers and the wizards' previous encampment, tearing and smashing and looting, their grunts and assaults punctuated by the occasional *crack* of a thrown boulder hitting the bridge abutments, and bouncing into the water.

Others settled down to sleep, but Catti-brie remained sitting, staring back at the darkness, where an occasional fire sprang to life, consuming a tent or some other item.

"I had an extra spellbook over there," one wizard grumbled.

"Aye, and I, the first twenty pages of a spell I was penning," said another.

"And I, my finest robes," a third wailed. "Oh, but orcs will burn for this!"

A short while later, a rustle from the other direction, back to the east, turned Catti-brie and the few others who hadn't yet settled in for the night. The woman rose and limped across to stand beside Alustriel, who greeted the Felbarran contingent as they rushed in to investigate the night's tumult.

"We'd set off for Winter Edge to quarry more stones," explained the leader, a squat and tough old character with a white beard and eyebrows so bushy that they hid his eyes. "What in the grumble of a dragon's belly hit ye?"

"Obould," Catti-brie said before Alustriel could respond.

"So much then for the good intentions," said the Felbarran dwarf. "Never thought them dogs'd sit quiet on the ground they'd taken. Mithral Hall get breached?"

"Never," said Catti-brie.

"Good enough then," said the dwarf. "We'll push 'em back north o' the wall in short order."

"In the morning," said Alustriel. "My charges are preparing their spells. I have ears and a voice in Mithral Hall to coordinate the counterattack."

"Might be then that we'll kill 'em all and not let any be running," said the dwarf. "More's the fun!"

"Set your camp by the river, and order your forces into small and swift groups," Alustriel explained. "We will open magical gates of transport to the other bank and your speed and coordination in entering the battlefield will prove decisive."

"Pity them orcs, then," said the dwarf, and he nodded and bowed, then stormed off, barking orders at his grim-faced forces.

He had barely gone a few strides, though, when there came a tremendous crash from across the way, followed by wild orc cheering.

"A tower," Alustriel explained to the surprised stares of all around her.

Catti-brie cursed under her breath.

"We will extend our time at Mithral Hall," the Lady of Silverymoon promised her. "Our enemies have exploited a vulnerability that cannot be allowed to hold. We will sweep the orcs back to the north and chase them far from the doors."

"Then finish the bridge," another nearby wizard offered, but Alustriel was shaking her head.

"The wall first," she explained. "Our enemies did us a favor by revealing our weakness. Woe to all in the North if the orcs had taken this ground after the bridge's completion. So our first duty after they are expelled is to complete and fortify that wall. Any orc excursion back to Mithral Hall's eastern door must come at a great cost to them, and must provide the time for us to disassemble the bridge. We will finish the wall and then we will finish the bridge."

"And then?" Catti-brie asked, and Alustriel and the other wizards looked at her curiously.

"You will return to Silverymoon?" Catti-brie asked.

"My duties are there. What else would you suggest?"

"Obould has shown his hand," Catti-brie replied. "There is no peace to be found while he is camped north of Mithral Hall."

"You ask me to rally an army," said Alustriel.

"Have we a choice?"

Alustriel paused and considered the woman's words. "I know not," she admitted. "But let us first concentrate on the battle at hand." She turned to the nearby wizards. "Sleep well, and when you awaken, prepare your most devastating evocations. Join with each other when you open your spellbooks, and coordinate your efforts and complement your spells. I want these orcs utterly destroyed. Let their folly serve as a warning that will keep their kin at bay long enough for us to strengthen the defenses."

Many nods came back at her, along with a sudden and unexpected shout, "For Duzberyl!"

"Duzberyl!" another cried, and another, and even those Silverymoon wizards who had settled down for the night rose and joined in the chant. Soon enough, even the Felbarran dwarves joined in, though none of them knew what a "Duzberyl" might be.

It didn't matter.

More than once that night, Catti-brie awoke to the sound of a thunderous crash from across the river. That only steeled her determination, though, and each time, she fell back asleep with Lady Alustriel's promise in her thoughts. They would pay the orcs back in full, and then some.

The preparations began before dawn, wizards ruffling the pages of their spellbooks, dwarves sharpening weapons. With a wave of yet another wand, Lady Alustriel turned herself into an owl, and flew off silently to scout out the coming battlefield.

She returned in mere moments, and reverted to her human form as the first rays of dawn crept across the Surbrin, revealing to all the others what Alustriel had returned to report.

Spellbooks snapped shut and the dwarves lowered their weapons and tools, moving to the riverbank and staring in disbelief.

Not an orc was to be seen.

Alustriel set them to motion, her minions opening dimensional doors that soon enough got all of them, dwarf, wizard, and Catti-brie alike, across the Surbrin, the last of them crossing even as Mithral

Hall's eastern door banged open and King Bruenor himself led the charge out from the stronghold.

But all they found were a dozen dead dwarves, stripped naked, and a dead wizard, still standing, held in place by a mighty javelin.

The wizards' encampment had been razed and looted, as had the small shacks the dwarf builders had used. An assortment of boulders lay around the base of the damaged bridge abutment, and all of the towers and a good portion of the northern wall had been toppled.

And not an orc, dead or alive, was anywhere to be found.

CHAPTER 19
AN ORC KING'S CONJECTURE

"By all the glories of Gruumsh!" Kna squealed happily when the reports of the victory at the Surbrin made their way like wildfire back to King Obould's entourage. "We have killed the dwarves!"

"We have stung them and left them vulnerable," said the messenger who had come from the battle, an orc named Oktule, who was a member of one of the many minor tribes that had been swept up in the march of Chieftain Grguch—a name Oktule used often, Obould had sourly noted. "Their walls are reduced and the winter is fast receding. They will have to work through the summer, building as they defend their position at the Surbrin."

The orcs all around began to cheer wildly.

"We have severed Mithral Hall from their allies!"

The cheering only increased.

Obould sat there, digesting it all. He knew that Grguch hadn't done any such thing, for the cunning dwarves had tunnels under the Surbrin, and many others that stretched far to the south. Still, it was hard to dismiss the victory, from both practical and symbolic terms. The bridge, had it been completed, would have provided a comfortable and easy approach to Mithral Hall from Silverymoon, Winter Edge, the Moonwood, and the other surrounding communities, and an easy way for King Bruenor to continue doing his profitable business.

Of course, one orc's victory was another orc's setback. Obould, too, had wanted to claim a piece of the Surbrin bridge, but not in such a manner, not as an enemy. And certainly not at the cost of assuring the mysterious Grguch all the glory. He fought hard to keep the scowl from his face. To go against the tide of joy then was to invite suspicion, perhaps even open revolt.

"Chieftain Grguch and Clan Karuck did not hold the ground?" he asked, not so innocently, for he knew well the answer.

"Lady Alustriel and a gang of wizards were with the dwarves," Oktule explained. "Chieftain Grguch expected that the whole of the dwarven hall would come forth with the morning light."

"No doubt with King Bruenor, Drizzt Do'Urden, and the rest of that strange companionship at its head," Obould muttered.

"We did not have the numbers to hold against that," Oktule admitted.

Obould glanced past the messenger to the gathered crowd. He saw more trepidation on their faces than anything else, along with an undercurrent of . . . what? Suspicion?

The orc king stood up and stretched to his full height, towering over Oktule. He looked up and let his gaze sweep in the mob then said with a wicked grin, "A great victory anyway!"

The cheering reached new heights, and Obould, his anger beginning to boil within him, used that opportunity to steal off into his tent, the ever-present Kna and the priest Nukkels following close behind.

Inside the inner chamber, Obould dismissed all of his guards.

"You, too," Kna snapped at Nukkels, errantly presuming that the glorious news had excited her partner as it had her.

Nukkels grinned at her and looked to Obould, who confirmed his suspicions.

"You, too," Obould echoed, but aimed the comment at Kna and not the priest. "Be gone until I summon you back to my side."

Kna's yellow eyes widened in shock, and she instinctively moved to Obould's side and began to curl sensually around him. But with one hand, with the strength of a giant, he yanked her away.

"Do not make me ask you again," he said slowly and deliberately, as if he were a parent addressing a child. With a flick of his wrist he sent Kna skipping and tumbling backward, and she kept scrambling away, her eyes wide with shock as she locked her stare on Obould's frightening expression.

"We must commune with Gruumsh to determine the next victory,"

Obould said to her, purposely softening his visage. "You will play with Obould later."

That seemed to calm the idiot Kna a bit, and she even managed a smile as she exited the chamber.

Nukkels started to talk then, but Obould stopped him with an upraised hand. "Give Kna time to be properly away," the king said loudly. "For if my dear consort inadvertently overhears the words of Gruumsh, the One-eye will demand her death."

As soon as he finished, a rustling just to the side of the exit confirmed his suspicions that his foolish Kna had been thinking to eavesdrop. Obould looked at Nukkels and sighed.

"An informative idiot, at least," the priest offered, and Obould could only shrug. Nukkels began spellcasting, waving his arms and releasing wards to silence the area around himself and Obould.

When he finished, Obould nodded his approval and said, "I have heard the name of Chieftain Grguch far too often of late. What do you know of Clan Karuck?"

It was Nukkels's turn to shrug. "Half-ogres, say the rumors, but I cannot confirm. They are not known to me."

"And yet they heard my call."

"Many tribes have come forth from the deep holes of the Spine of the World, seeking to join in the triumph of King Obould. Surely Clan Karuck's priests could have heard of our march through communion with Gruumsh."

"Or from mortal voices."

Nukkels mulled that over for a bit. "There has been a chain of whispers and shouts, no doubt," he replied cautiously, for Obould's tone hinted at something more nefarious.

"He comes forth and attacks the Moonwood then sweeps south and overruns the dwarves' wall. For a chieftain who lived deep in the holes of the distant mountains, Grguch seems to know well the enemies lurking on the borders of Many-Arrows."

Nukkels nodded and said, "You believe that Clan Karuck was called here with purpose."

"I believe I would be a fool not to find out if that was the case," Obould replied. "It is no secret that many have disagreed with my decision to pause in our campaign."

"Pause?"

"As far as they know."

"So they bring forth an instigator, to drive Obould forward?"

"An instigator, or a rival?"

"None would be so foolish!" the priest said with proper and prudent astonishment.

"Do not overestimate the intelligence of the masses," Obould said. "But whether as an instigator or a rival, Grguch has brought trouble to my designs. Perhaps irreparable damage. We can expect a counterattack from King Bruenor, I am sure, and from many of his allies if we are unlucky."

"Grguch stung them, but he left," Nukkels reminded the king. "If they see his strike as bait, Bruenor will not be so foolish as to come forth from his defended halls."

"Let us hope, and let us hope that we can quickly contain this eager chieftain. Send Oktule back to Grguch, with word that I would speak to him. Offer an invitation to Clan Karuck for a great feast in honor of their victories."

Nukkels nodded.

"And prepare yourself for a journey, my trusted friend," Obould went on, and that reference took Nukkels off-guard, for he had only known Obould for a short time, and had only spoken directly to the orc king since Obould had climbed back up from the landslide that had nearly killed him and the dark elf.

"I would go to Mithral Hall itself for King Obould Many-Arrows," Nukkels replied, standing straight and determined.

Obould grinned and nodded, and Nukkels knew that his guess had been correct. And his answer had been sincere and well-placed—and expected, since it had, after all, come from the king's "trusted friend."

"Shall I invite Kna and your private guard to return to you, Great One?" Nukkels asked, bowing low.

Obould paused for a moment then shook his head. "I will call for them when they are needed," he told the priest. "Go and speak with Oktule. Send him on his way, and return to me this night, with your own pack readied for a long and trying road."

Nukkels bowed again, turned, and swiftly departed.

* * * * *

"Ah, but it's good that ye're here, Lady," Bruenor said to Alustriel when they met out by the wall. Catti-brie stood beside the Lady of Silverymoon, with Regis and Thibbledorf Pwent close behind Bruenor.

Not far away, Cordio Muffinhead and another dwarf priest went to work immediately on the poor, impaled Duzberyl, extricating the dead wizard as gently as possible.

"Would that we could have done more," Alustriel replied solemnly. "Like your kin, we were lulled by the passing months of quiet, and so the orc assault caught us by surprise. We had not the proper spells prepared, for our studies have focused on working the Surbrin Bridge to completion."

"Ye did a bit o' damage to the pigs, and got most o' me boys back to the hall," said Bruenor. "Ye did good by us, and we're not for forgettin' that."

Alustriel responded with a bow. "And now that we know, we will not be caught unawares again," she promised. "Our efforts on the bridge will be slowed, of course, as half our magical repertoire each day will be focused on spells for defending the ground and repelling invaders. And indeed, we will have just a small crew at the bridge until the wall and towers are repaired and completed. The bridge will serve no useful purpose until—"

"Bah!" Bruenor snorted. "The point's all moot. We seen the truth o' Obould, suren as there is any. Put all yer spells for orc-killing—excepting them ye'll be needin' to get yer Knights in Silver across the Surbrin. When we're done with the damned orcs, we can worry about the bridge and the wall, though I'm thinkin' we won't be needing much of a wall!"

Behind him, Thibbledorf Pwent snorted, as did several others, but Alustriel just looked at him curiously, as if she didn't understand. As her expression registered to Bruenor, his own face became a scowl of abject disbelief. That look only intensified as he noted Catti-brie's wince at Alustriel's side, confirmation that he wasn't misreading the Lady of Silverymoon.

"Ye're thinkin' we're to dig in and let Obould play it as Obould wants?" the dwarf asked.

"I advise caution, good king," Alustriel said.

"Caution?"

"The orcs did not hold the ground," Alustriel noted. "They struck and then they ran—likely to evoke just such a response from you. They would have you roar out of Mithral Hall, all full of fight and rage. And out there"—she motioned to the wild north—"they would have their battle with you on the ground of their own choosing."

"Her words make sense," Catti-brie added, but Bruenor snorted again.

"And if they're thinking that Clan Battlehammer's to come out alone, then I'm thinkin' their plan to be a good one," Bruenor said. "But what a trap they'll find when the trap they spring closes on all the force o' the Silver Marches. On Alustriel's wizards and the Knights in Silver, on Felbarr's thousands and Adbar's tens o'! On Sundabar's army, guided in on Obould's flank by them Moonwood elves, who're not too fond o' the damned orcs, in case ye're missing the grumbles."

Alustriel drew her lips very tight, as clear a response as she could possibly give.

"What?" Bruenor roared. "Ye're not for calling them? Not now? Not when we seen what Obould's all about? Ye hoped for a truce, and now ye're seein' the truth o' that truce! What more're ye needing?"

"It is not a matter of evidence, good dwarf," Alustriel replied, calmly and evenly, though her voice rang much thinner than usual. "It is a matter of practicality."

"Practicality, or cowardice?" Bruenor demanded.

Alustriel accepted the barb with a light, resigned shrug.

"Ye said ye'd be standin' with me boys when we needed ye," Bruenor reminded.

"They will . . ." Catti-brie started to say, but she shut up fast when Bruenor snapped his scowl her way.

"Ye're friendship's all pretty when it's words and building, but when there's blood. . . ." Bruenor accused, and Alustriel swept her arm out toward Duzberyl, who lay on the ground with Cordio praying over him.

"Bah, so ye got caught in one fight, but I'm not talking about one!" Bruenor kept on. "Lost me a dozen good boys last night."

"All the Silver Marches weep for your dead, King Bruenor."

"I ain't askin' ye to weep!" Bruenor screamed at her, and all around, work stopped, and dwarf, human, and elf—including Hralien—stood and stared at the outraged king of Mithral Hall and the great Lady of Silverymoon, who not a one of them had ever imagined could be yelled at in such a manner. "I'm askin' ye to fight!" the unrelenting Bruenor fumed on. "I'm askin' ye to do what's right and send yer armies—*all* yer durned armies! Obould's belongin' in a hole, and ye're knowing that! So get yer armies, and get all the armies, and let's put him where he belongs, and let's put the Silver Marches back where the Silver Marches're belonging!"

"We will leave all the ground between Mithral Hall and the Spine of the World stained with the blood of dwarves and men and elves," Alustriel warned. "Obould's thousands are well en—"

"And well meaning to strike out until they're stopped!" Bruenor shouted over her. "Ye heared o' the Moonwood and their dead, and now ye're seein' this attack with yer own eyes. Ye can't be doubtin' what that foul orc's got in his head."

"But to go out from defensive positions against that force—"

"Is to be our only choice, now or tomorrow, or me and me boys'll forever be on yer point, fighting Obould one bridge, one door at a time," said Bruenor. "Ye think we're to take their hits? Ye think we can be keeping both our doors always sealed and secured, and our tunnels, too, lest the durned pigs tunnel in and pop up in our middle?"

Bruenor's eyes narrowed, his expression taking on a clear look of suspicion. "Or would that arrangement please Alustriel and all th' others about? Battlehammer dwarves'll die, and that's suitin' ye all, is it?"

"Of course not," Alustriel protested, but her words did little to soften the scowl of King Bruenor.

"Me girl beside ye just got back from Nesmé, and what a fine job yer knights've done pushing them trolls back into the swamp," Bruenor went on. "Seems Nesmé's grander than afore the attacks, mostly because o' yer own work—and don't that make Lady Alustriel proud?"

"Father," Catti-brie warned, shocked by the sarcasm.

"But then, them folk're more akin to yer own, in looks and thoughts."

"We should continue this discussion in private, King Bruenor," said Alustriel.

Bruenor snorted at her and waved his hand, turned on his heel, and stomped away, Thibbledorf Pwent in tow.

Regis remained, and he turned a concerned look at Alustriel then at Catti-brie.

"He will calm down," Regis said unconvincingly.

"Not so sure I'm wantin' him to," Catti-brie admitted, and she glanced at Alustriel.

The Lady of Silverymoon had nothing more than helplessly upraised hands in reply, and so Catti-brie limped off after her beloved father.

"It is a dark day, my friend Regis," Alustriel said when the woman had gone.

Regis's eyes popped open wide, surprised at being directly addressed by one of Alustriel's stature.

"This is how great wars begin," Alustriel explained. "And do not doubt that no matter the outcome, there will be no winners."

* * * * *

As soon as the priest had gone, Obould was glad of his decision not to call in his entourage. He needed to be alone, to vent, to rant, and to think things through. He knew in his heart that Grguch was no ally, and had not arrived by accident. Ever since the disaster in the western antechamber of Mithral Hall and the pushback of Proffit's troll army, the orcs and dwarves had settled into a stalemate—and it was one that Obould welcomed. But one that he welcomed privately, for he knew that he was working against the traditions, instincts, and conditioning of his warrior race. No voices of protest came to him directly, of course—he was too feared by those around him for that kind of insolence—but he heard the rumbles of discontent even in the grating background of praises thrown his way. The restless orcs wanted to march on, back into Mithral Hall, across the Surbrin to Silverymoon and Sundabar, and particularly Citadel Felbarr, which they had once, long ago, claimed as their own.

"The cost . . ." Obould muttered, shaking his head.

He would lose thousands in such an endeavor—even if he only tried to dislodge fierce King Bruenor. He would lose tens of thousands if he went farther, and though he would have loved nothing more than to claim the throne of Silverymoon as his own, Obould understood that if he had gathered all the orcs from all the holes in all the world, he could not likely accomplish such a thing.

Certainly he might find allies—more giants and dark elves, perhaps, or any of the other multitude of races and monsters that lived solely for the pleasure of fighting and destruction. In such an alliance, though, he could never reign, nor could his minions ever gain true freedom and self-determination.

And even if he did manage greater conquests with his orc minions, even if he widened the scope of the Kingdom of Many-Arrows, the lessons of history had taught him definitively that the center of such a kingdom could never hold. His reach was long, his grip iron strong. Long and strong enough to hold the perimeters of the Kingdom of Many-Arrows? Long and strong enough to fend off Grguch and any potential conspirators who had coaxed the fierce chieftain to the surface?

Obould clenched his fist mightily as that last question filtered through his mind, and he issued a long and low growl then licked his lips as if tasting the blood of his enemies.

Were Clan Karuck even his enemies?

The question sobered him. He was getting ahead of the facts, he realized. A ferocious and aggressive orc clan had arrived in Many-Arrows, and had taken up the fight independently, as orc clans often did, and with great and glorious effect.

Obould nodded as he considered the truth of it and realized the limits of his conjecture. In his heart, though, he knew that a rival had come, and a very dangerous one at that.

Reflexively, the orc king looked to the southwest, the direction of General Dukka and his most reliable fighting force. He would need another courier, he realized immediately. As Oktule went to summon Grguch, as Nukkels traveled to King Bruenor's Court with word of truce, so he would need a third, the fastest of the three, to go and retrieve Dukka and the warriors. For the dwarves might soon counterattack, and likely would be joined by the dangerous and outraged Moonwood elves.

Or more likely, Clan Karuck would need to be taught a lesson.

CHAPTER 20

ON SQUIGGLES AND EMISSARIES

With but one hand, for the chieftain was no minor warrior, Dnark pushed Oktule to the side and stepped past him to the edge of a mountain-view precipice overlooking King Obould's encampment. A group of riders exited that camp, moving swiftly to the south, and without the banner of Many-Arrows flying from their midst.

"War pigs, and armored," the shaman Ung-thol remarked. "Elite warriors. Obould's own."

Dnark pointed to a rider in the middle of the pack, and though they were far away and moving farther, his headdress could still be seen.

"The priest, Nukkels," Ung-thol said with a nod.

"What does this mean?" Oktule asked, his tone concurring with his body posture to relate his discomfort. Young Oktule had been chosen as a courier from the east because of his speed and stamina, but he had not the experience or the wisdom to fathom all that was going on around him.

The chieftain and his shaman turned as one to regard the orc. "It means that you should tell Grguch to proceed with all caution," Dnark said.

"I do not understand."

"King Obould might not welcome him with the warmth promised in the invitation," Dnark explained.

"Or might greet him with more warmth than promised," Ung-thol quipped.

Oktule stared at them, his jaw hanging open. "King Obould is angry?"

That brought a laugh from the two older and more worldly orcs.

"You know Toogwik Tuk?" Ung-thol asked.

Oktule nodded. "The preacher orc. His words showed me to the glory of Grguch. He proclaimed the power of Chieftain Grguch and the call of Gruumsh to bring war to the dwarves."

Dnark chuckled and patted the air with his hand, trying to calm the fool. "Deliver your words to Chieftain Grguch as your king demanded," he said. "But seek out Toogwik Tuk first and inform him that a second courier went out from Obould's"—then he quickly corrected himself—"*King* Obould's camp, this one riding to the south."

"What does it mean?" Oktule asked again.

"It means that King Obould expects trouble," Ung-thol interrupted, stopping Dnark before he could respond. "Toogwik Tuk will know what to do."

"Trouble?" asked Oktule.

"The dwarves will likely counterattack, and more furious will they become when they learn that both King Obould and Chieftain Grguch are in the same place."

Oktule began to nod stupidly, catching on.

"Be off at once," Dnark told him, and the young orc spun on his heel and rushed away. A signal from Dnark sent a couple of guards off with him, to escort him on his important journey.

As soon as they were gone, the chieftain and the shaman turned back to the distant riders.

"Do you really believe that Obould would send an emissary to the Battlehammer dwarves?" Ung-thol asked. "Has he become so cowardly as that?"

Dnark nodded through every word, and when Ung-thol glanced over at him, he replied, "We should find out."

* * * * *

"Ye tell Emerus that we'll be lookin' for all he's to bring," Bruenor said to Jackonray Broadbelt and Nikwillig, the emissaries from Citadel Felbarr.

"The bridge'll be ready soon, I'm told," Jackonray replied.

THE ORC KING

"Forget the durned bridge!" Bruenor snapped, startling everyone in the room with his unexpected outburst. "Alustriel's wizards'll be working more on the wall for the next days. I'm wanting an army here afore the work's even begun on the bridge again. I'm wanting Alustriel to see Felbarr side-by-side with Mithral Hall, that when we're walking out that gate, she'll know the time for talkin's over and the time for fightin's come."

"Ah," Jackonray replied, nodding, a smile spreading on his hairy and toothy face. "So I'm seeing why Bruenor's the king. Ye've got me respect, good King Bruenor, and ye've got me word that I'll shove King Emerus out the durned tunnel door meself if it's needin' to be!"

"Ye're a good dwarf. Ye do yer kin proud."

Jackonray bowed so low that his beard brushed the ground, and he and Nikwillig left in a rush—or started to, until Bruenor's call turned them fast around.

"Go out through the eastern gate, under the open sky," Bruenor instructed with a wry grin.

"Quicker through the tunnels," Nikwillig dared to argue.

"Nah, ye go out and tell Alustriel that I'm wantin' the two o' ye put outside o' Felbarr in a blink," Bruenor explained, and snapped his stubby fingers in the air to accentuate his point. All around Bruenor, dwarves began to chuckle.

"Never let it be said that a Battlehammer don't know a good joke when he's seein' one," Bruenor remarked, and the chuckles turned to laughter.

Jackonray and Nikwillig left in a rush, giggling.

"Let Alustriel play a part in her own trap," Bruenor said to Cordio, Thibbledorf, and Banak Brawnanvil, who had a specially designed throne right beside Bruenor's own, a place of honor for the heroic leader who had been crippled in the orc assault.

"Suren she's to be scrunching up her pretty face," Banak said.

"When Mithral Hall and Citadel Adbar march right past her working wizards, to be sure," Bruenor agreed. "But she'll be seeing, too, that the time's past hiding from Obould's dogs. He's wantin' a fight and we're for givin' him one—one that'll take him all the way back where he came from, and beyond."

The room erupted in cheering, and Banak reached out to grab

Bruenor's offered hand, clasping tight in a shake of mutual respect and determination.

"Ye stay here and take the rest o' the audiences," Bruenor instructed Banak. "I'm for seeing Rumblebelly and the littler one. There's clues in them scrolls we brought back, or I'm a bearded gnome, and I'm wantin' all the tricks and truths we can muster afore we strike out against Obould."

He hopped down from his throne and from the dais, motioning for Cordio to follow and for Thibbledorf to stand as Banak's second.

"Nanfoodle told me that the runes on them scrolls weren't nothing he'd e'er seen," Cordio said to Bruenor as they started out of the audience chamber. "Squiggles in places squiggles shouldn't be."

"The littler one'll straighten 'em out, don't ye doubt. As clever as any I've ever seen, and a good friend o' the clan. Mirabar's lost a lot when Torgar and his boys come our way, and they lost a lot when Nanfoodle and Shoudra come looking for Torgar and his boys."

Cordio nodded his agreement and left it at that, following Bruenor down the corridors and stairwells to a small cluster of secluded rooms where Nanfoodle had set up his alchemy lab and library.

* * * * *

No one in the tribe knew if it had gotten its name through its traditional battle tactics, or if the succession of chieftains had fashioned the tactics to fit the name. Whatever the cause-effect, their peculiar battle posture had been perfected through generations. Indeed, the leaders of Wolf Jaw selected orcs at a young age based on size and speed to find the appropriate place in the formation each might best fit.

Choosing the enemy and the battleground was more important even than that, if the dangerous maneuver was to work. And no orc in the tribe's history had been better at such tasks than the present chieftain, Dnark of the Fang. He was descended from a long line of point warriors, the tip of the fangs of the wolf jaw that snapped over its enemies. For years, young Dnark had spearheaded the top line of the V formation, sliding out along the left flank of an intended target, while another orc, often a cousin of Dnark's, led the right, or bottom, jaw. When the lines stretched to their limit, Dnark would swing his assault group to a sharp right, forming a fang, and he and his counterpart would join forces, sealing the escape route at the rear of the enemy formation.

As chieftain, though, Dnark anchored the apex. His jaws of warriors went out north and south of the small encampment, and when the signals came back to the chieftain, he led the initial assault, moving forward with his main battle group.

They did not charge, and did not holler and hoot. Instead, they approached calmly, as if nothing was amiss—and indeed, why would King Obould's shaman advisor suspect anything different?

The camp did stir at the approach of so large a contingent, with calls for Nukkels to come forth from his tent.

Ung-thol put his hand on Dnark's arm, urging restraint. "We do not know his purpose," the shaman reminded.

Nukkels appeared a few moments later, moving to the eastern end of the small plateau he and his warriors had used for their pause. Beside him, Obould's powerful guards lifted heavy spears.

How Dnark wanted to call for the charge! How he wanted to lead the way up the rocky incline to smash through those fools!

But Ung-thol was there, reminding him, coaxing him to patience.

"Praise to King Obould!" Dnark called out, and he took his tribe's banner from an orc to the side and waved it around. "We have word from Chieftain Grguch," he lied.

Nukkels held up his hand, palm out at Dnark, warning him to hold back.

"We have no business with you," he called down.

"King Obould does not share that belief," Dnark replied, and he began his march again, slowly. "He has sent us to accompany you, as more assurance that Clan Karuck will not interfere."

"Interfere with what?" Nukkels shouted back.

Dnark glanced at Ung-thol, then back up the rise. "We know where you are going," he bluffed.

It was Nukkels's turn to look around at his entourage. "Come in alone, Chieftain Dnark," he called. "That we might plot our next move."

Dnark kept moving up the slope, calm and unthreatening, and he did not bid his force to lag behind.

"Alone!" Nukkels called more urgently.

Dnark smiled, but otherwise changed not a thing. The orcs beside Nukkels lifted their spears.

It didn't matter. The bluff had played its part, allowing Dnark's core force to close nearly half the incline to Nukkels. Dnark held up his hands to Nukkels and the guards then turned to address his group—ostensibly to instruct them to wait there.

"Kill them all—except for Nukkels and the closest guards," he instructed instead, and when he turned back, he had his sword in hand, and he raised it high.

The warriors of Clan Wolf Jaw swept past him on either side, those nearest swerving to obstruct their enemies' view of their beloved chieftain. More than one of those shield orcs died in the next moments, as spears flew down upon them.

But the jaws of the wolf closed.

By the time Dnark got up to the plateau, the fighting was heavy all around him and Nukkels was nowhere to be found. Angered by that, Dnark threw himself into the nearest battle, where a pair of his orcs attacked a single guard, wildly and ineffectively.

Obould had chosen his inner circle of warriors well.

One of the Wolf Jaw orcs stabbed in awkwardly with his spear, but the guard's sword swept across and shattered the hilt, launching it out to confuse the attacker's companion. With the opening clear, the guard retracted and stepped forward for the easy kill.

Except that Dnark came in fast from the side and hacked the fool's sword arm off at the elbow.

The guard howled and half-turned, falling to its knees and clutching its stump. Dnark stepped in and grabbed it by the hair, tugging its head back, opening its neck for a killing strike.

And always before, the chieftain of Clan Wolf Jaw would have taken that strike, would have claimed that kill. But he held back his sword and kicked the guard in the throat instead, and as it fell away, he instructed his two warriors to make sure that the fallen enemy didn't die.

Then he went on to the next fight in a long line of battles.

When the skirmish on the plateau ended, though, Shaman Nukkels was not to be found, either among the seven prisoners or the score of dead. He had gone off the back end at the first sign of trouble, so said witnesses.

Before Dnark could begin to curse that news, however, he found that his selections for the fangs of the formation had done his own legacy proud, for in they marched, Nukkels and a battered guard prodded before them with spears.

"Obould will kill you for this," Nukkels said when presented before Dnark.

Dnark's left hook left the shaman squirming on the ground.

* * * * *

"The symbol is correct," Nanfoodle proudly announced. "The pattern is unmistakable."

Regis stared at the large copy of the parchment, its runes separated and magnified. On Nanfoodle's instruction, the halfling had spent the better part of a day transcribing each mark to that larger version then the pair had spent several days cutting out wooden stencils for each—even for those that seemed to hold an obvious correlation to the current Dwarvish writing.

Mistaking that tempting lure, accepting the obvious runes for what they supposed them to be, Dethek runes of an archaic orc tongue called Hulgorkyn, had been their downfall through all of their early translation attempts, and it wasn't until Nanfoodle had insisted that they treat the writing from the lost city as something wholly unrecognizable that the pair had begun to make any progress at all.

If that was indeed what they were making.

Many other stencils had been crafted, multiple representations of every Dwarvish symbol. Then had come the trial and error—and error, and error, and error—for more than a day of painstaking rearranging and reevaluation. Nanfoodle, no minor illusionist, had cast many spells, and priests had been brought in to offer various auguries and inspired insights.

Thirty-two separate symbols appeared on the parchment, and while a thorough statistical analysis had offered hints of potential correlations to the traditional twenty-six runes of Dethek, the fact that none of those promising hints added up to anything substantial made much of that analysis no more than guesswork.

Gradually, though, patterns had taken shape, and spells seemed to confirm the best guesses time and time again.

More than a tenday into the work, an insight from Nanfoodle—after hearing all of Regis's stories of the strange city—proved to be the tipping point. Instead of using Dwarvish as his basis for the analysis, he decided upon a double-basis and began incorporating the Orcish tongue—in which, of course, he was fluent. More stencils were cut, more combinations explored.

Early one morning, Nanfoodle presented Regis with his completed conclusion for translation, a correlative identifying every symbol on the parchment, some that mirrored current Dwarvish or Orcish lettering.

The halfling went to work over the transcribed, larger-lettered parchment, diligently placing above each symbol the stencil Nanfoodle believed correlative. Regis didn't pause at all to consider familiar patterns, but simply placed them all as fast as he could.

Then he stepped back and stood up on the high bench Nanfoodle had placed beside the work table. The gnome was already there, staring back incredulously, his mouth hanging open, and when he took his place beside Nanfoodle, Regis understood.

For the gnome's guesses had been correct, obviously, and the translation of the text was clear to see, and to read. It wasn't unknown for orcs to steal and incorporate Dethek runes, of course, as was most evident with Hulgorkyn. But there was something more than that, a willful blending of related but disparate languages in a balanced manner, one that indicated compromise and coordination between dwarf and orc linguists.

The translation was laid bare for them to see. Digesting the words, however, proved more difficult.

"Bruenor won't like this," Regis remarked, and he glanced around as if expecting the dwarf king to crash into the room in a tirade at any moment.

"It is what it is," Nanfoodle replied. "He will not like it, but he must accept it."

Regis looked back at the translated paragraph and read again the words of the orc philosopher Duugee.

"You place too much value in reason," the halfling muttered.

PART 4

STEPPING BACK FROM ANGER

STEPPING BACK
FROM ANGER

The questions continue to haunt me. Are we watching the birth of a civilization? Are the orcs, instead of wanting us dead, wishing to become more like us, with our ways, our hopes, our aspirations? Or was that wish always present in the hearts of the primitive and fierce race, only they saw not how to get to it? And if this is the case, if the orcs are redeemable, tamable, how then are we best to facilitate the rise of their more civilized culture? For that would be an act of great self-defense for Mithral Hall and all of the Silver Marches.

Accepting the premise of a universal desire among rational beings, a commonality of wishes, I wonder, then, what might occur should one kingdom stand paramount, should one city-state somehow attain unquestioned superiority over all the rest. What responsibilities might such predominance entail? If Bruenor has his way, and the Silver Marches rise up and drive Obould's orcs from the land and back to their individual tribes, what will be our role, then, in our resulting, unquestioned dominance?

Would the moral road be the extermination of the orcs, one tribe at a time? If my suspicions regarding Obould are correct, then that I cannot reconcile. Are the dwarves to become neighbors or oppressors?

It is all premised on a caveat, of course, on a hunch—or is it a deep-rooted prayer in the renegade soul of Drizzt Do'Urden? I desperately want to be right about Obould—as much as my personal desires might urge me to kill him!—because if I am, if there is in him a glint of rational and acceptable aspirations, then surely the world will benefit.

These are the questions for kings and queens, the principal building blocks of the guiding philosophies for those who gain power over others. In the best of these kingdoms—and I name Bruenor's among that lot—the community moves constantly to better itself, the parts of the whole turn in harmony to the betterment of the whole. Freedom and community live side-by-side, a tandem of the self and the bigger tapestry. As those communities evolve and ally with other like-minded kingdoms, as roads and trade routes are secured and cultures exchanged, what of the diminishing few left behind? It is incumbent, I believe, for the powerful to bend and grasp the hand of the weak, to pull them up, to share in the prosperity, to contribute to the whole. For that is the essence of community. It is to be based on hope and inspiration and not on fear and oppression.

But there remains the truth that if you help an orc to stand, he will likely stab your heart on the way to his feet.

Ah, but it is too much, for in my heart I see the fall of Tarathiel and want to cut the vicious orc king apart! It is too much because I know of Innovindil's fall! Oh, Innovindil, I pray you do not think less of me for my musing!

I feel the sting of paradox, the pain of the irresolvable, the stark and painful imperfections of a world of which I secretly demand perfection. Yet for all the blemishes, I remain an optimist, that in the end the ideal will prevail. And this too I also know, and it is why my weapons sit comfortably in my hands. Only from a position of unquestioned strength can true change be facilitated. For it is not in the hands of a rival to affect change. It is not in the hands of the weaker to grant peace and hope to the stronger.

I hold faith in the kingdom of common voices that Bruenor has created, that Alustriel has similarly created in Silverymoon. I believe that this is the proper order of things—though perhaps with some refining yet to be found—for theirs are kingdoms of freedom and hope, where individual aspirations are encouraged and the common good is shared by all, in both benefit and responsibility. How different are these two places from the darkness of Menzoberranzan, where the power of House presided over the common good of the community, and the aspirations of the individual overwhelmed the liberty, even the life, of others.

My belief in Mithral Hall as nearer the ideal brings with it a sense of Mithral Hall's responsibilities, however. It is not enough to field armies to thwart foes, to crush our enemies under the stamp of well-traveled dwarven boots. It is not enough to bring riches to Mithral Hall, to expand power and influence, if said power and influence is to the benefit only of the powerful and influential.

To truly fulfill the responsibilities of predominance, Mithral Hall must not only shine brightly for Clan Battlehammer, but must serve as a beacon of hope for all of those who glimpse upon it. If we truly believe our way to be the best way, then we must hold faith that all others—perhaps even the orcs!—will gravitate toward our perspectives and practices, that we will serve as the shining city on the hill, that we will influence and pacify through generosity and example instead of through the power of armies.

For if it is the latter, if dominance is attained and then maintained through strength of arm alone, then it is no victory, and it cannot be a permanent ordering. Empires cannot survive, for they lack the humility and generosity necessary to facilitate true loyalty. The wont of the slave is to throw off his shackles. The greatest aspiration of the conquered is to beat back their oppressors. There are no exceptions to this. To the victors I warn without doubt that those you conquer will never accept your dominion. All desire to emulate your better way, even if the conquered agree with the premise, will be overwhelmed by grudge and humiliation and a sense of their own community. It is a universal truth, rooted in tribalism, perhaps, and in pride and the comfort of tradition and the sameness of one's peers.

And in a perfect world, no society would aspire to dominance unless it was a dominance of ideals. We believe our way is the right way, and thus we must hold faith that others will gravitate similarly, that our way will become their way and that assimilation will sheathe the swords of sorrow. It is not a short process, and it is one that will be played out in starts and stops, with treaties forged and treaties shattered by the ring of steel on steel.

Deep inside, it is my hope that I will find the chance to slay King Obould Many-Arrows.

Deeper inside, it is my prayer that King Obould Many-Arrows sees the dwarves standing higher on the ladder in pursuit of true civilization, that he sees Mithral Hall as a shining city on the hill, and that he will have the strength to tame the orcs long enough for them to scale the rungs of that same ladder.

—Drizzt Do'Urden

CHAPTER
PUTTING HIS WORLD TOGETHER
21

The wagon rocked, sometimes soothing, sometimes jarring, as it rolled along the rocky path, heading north. Sitting on the open bed and looking back the way they had come, Wulfgar watched the skyline of Luskan recede. The many points of the wizard's tower seemed like a single blur, and the gates were too far for him to make out the guards pacing the city wall.

Wulfgar smiled as he considered those guards. He and his accomplice Morik had been thrown out of Luskan with orders never to return, on pain of death, yet he had walked right into the city, and at least one of the guards had surely recognized him, even tossing him a knowing wink. No doubt Morik was in there, too.

Justice in Luskan was a sham, a scripted play for the people to make them feel secure and feel afraid and feel empowered over the specter of death itself, however the authorities decided was timely.

Wulfgar had debated whether or not to return to Luskan. He wanted to join in with a caravan heading north, for that would serve as his cover, but he feared exposing Colson to the potential dangers of entering the forbidden place. In the end, though, he found that he had no real choice. Arumn Gardpeck and Josi Puddles deserved to learn of Delly Curtie's sad end. They had been friends of the woman's for years, and far be it from Wulfgar to deny them the information.

The tears shed by all three—Arumn, Josi, and Wulfgar—had felt right to the barbarian. There was so much more to Delly Curtie than the easy, clichéd idea that many in Luskan had of her, and that Wulfgar had initially bought into himself. There was an honesty and an honor beneath the crust that circumstance had caked over Delly. She'd been a good friend to all three, a good wife to Wulfgar, and a great mother to Colson.

Wulfgar tossed off a chuckle as he considered Josi's initial reaction to the news, the small man practically launching himself at Wulfgar in a rage, blaming the barbarian for the loss of Delly. With little effort, Wulfgar had put him back in his seat, where he had melted into his folded arms, his shoulders bobbing with sobs—perhaps enhanced by too many drinks, but likely sincere, for Wulfgar had never doubted that Josi had secretly loved Delly.

The world rolled along, stamping its events into the books of history. What was, was, Wulfgar understood, and regrets were not to be long held—no longer than the lessons they imparted regarding future circumstance. He was not innocent of Josi's accusations, though not to the extent the distraught man had taken them, surely.

But what was, was.

After one particularly sharp bounce of the wagon, Wulfgar draped his arm over Colson's shoulder and glanced down at the girl, who was busying herself with some sticks Wulfgar had tied together to approximate a doll. She seemed content, or at least unbothered, which was the norm for her. Quiet and unassuming, asking for little and accepting less, Colson just seemed to go along with whatever came her way.

That road had not been fair so far in her young life, Wulfgar knew. She had lost Delly, by all measures her mother, and nearly as bad, Wulfgar realized, she had suffered the great misfortune of being saddled with him as her surrogate father. He stroked her soft, wheat-colored hair.

"Doll, Da," she said, using her moniker for Wulfgar, one that he had heard only a couple of times over the last tendays.

"Doll, yes," he said back to her, and tousled her hair.

She giggled, and if ever a sound could lift Wulfgar's heart....

And he was going to leave her. A momentary wave of weakness flushed through him. How could he even think of such a thing?

"You don't remember your Ma," he said quietly, not expecting a response as Colson went back to her play. But she looked up at him, beaming a huge smile.

"Dell-y. Ma," she said.

Wulfgar felt as if her little hand had just flicked against his heart. He realized how poor a father he had been to her. Urgent business filled his every day, it seemed, and Colson was always placed behind the necessities. She had been with him for many months, and yet he hardly knew her. They had traveled hundreds of miles to the east, and then back west, and only on that return trip had he truly spent time with Colson, had he tried to listen to the child, to understand her needs, to hug her.

He gave a helpless and self-deprecating chuckle and patted her head again. She looked up at him with that unending smile, and went immediately back to her doll.

He hadn't done right by her, Wulfgar knew. As he had failed Delly as a husband, so he had failed Colson as her father. "Guardian" would be a better term to describe his role in the child's life.

So he was on that road that would pain him greatly, but in the end it would give to Colson all that she deserved and more.

"You are a princess," he said to her, and she looked up at him again, though she knew not what it meant.

Wulfgar responded with a smile and another pat, and turned his eyes back toward Luskan, wondering if he would ever travel that far south again.

* * * * *

The village of Auckney seemed to have changed not at all in the three years since Wulfgar had last seen it. Most of his last visit, of course, had been spent in the lord's dungeon, an accommodation he hoped to avoid a second time. It amused him to think of how his time with Morik had so ingratiated him to the towns of that region, where the words "on pain of death" seemed to accompany his every departure.

Unlike those guards in Luskan, though, Wulfgar suspected that Auckney's crew would follow through with the threat if they figured out who he was. So for the sake of Colson, he took great pains to disguise himself as the trading caravan wound its way along the rocky road in the westernmost reaches of the Spine of the World, toward the Auckney gate. He wore his beard much thicker, but his stature alone distinguished him from the great majority of the populace, being closer to seven feet tall than to six, and with shoulders wide and strong.

He bundled his traveling cloak tight around him and kept the cowl up over his head—not an unusual practice in the early spring in that part of the world, where the cold winds still howled from on high. When he sat, which was most of the time, he kept his legs tucked in tight so as not to emphasize the length of the limbs, and when he walked, he crouched and hunched his shoulders forward, not only disguising his true height somewhat, but also appearing older, and more importantly, less threatening.

Whether through his cleverness, or more likely sheer luck and the fact that he was accompanied by an entire parade of merchants in that first post-winter caravan, Wulfgar managed to get into the town easily enough, and once past the checkpoint, he did his best to blend in with the group at the circled wagons, where kiosks were hastily constructed and goods displayed to the delight of the winter-weary townsfolk.

Lord Feringal Auck, seeming as petulant as ever, visited on the first full day of the caravan faire. Dressed in impractical finery, including puffy pantaloons of purple and white, the foppish man strutted with a perpetual air of contempt turning up his thin, straight nose. He glanced at goods but never seemed interested enough to bother—though his attendants often returned to purchase particular pieces, obviously for the lord.

Steward Temigast and the gnome driver—and fine fighter—Liam Woodgate, stood out among those attendants. Temigast, Wulfgar trusted, but he knew that if Liam spotted him, the game was surely up.

"He casts an impressive shadow, don't he?" came a sarcastic voice from behind, and Wulfgar turned to see one of the caravan drivers looking past him to the lord and his entourage. "Feringal Auck. . . ." the man added, chuckling.

"I am told that he has a most extraordinary wife," Wulfgar replied.

"Lady Meralda," the man answered, rather lewdly. "As pretty as the moon and more dangerous than the night, with hair blacker than the darkest of 'em and eyes so green that ye're thinking yerself to be in a summer's meadow whenever she glances yer way. Aye, but every man doing business in Auckney would want to bed that one."

"Have they children together?"

"A son," the man answered. "A strong and sturdy lad, and with features favoring his mother and not the lord, thank the gods. Little lord Ferin. All in the town celebrated his first birthday just a month ago, and from what I'm hearing, they'll be buying extra stores to replenish that which they ate at the feast. Finished off their winter stores, by some accounts, and there's more truth than lie to those, judging by the coins that've been falling all the morning."

Wulfgar glanced back at Feringal and his entourage as they wound their way along the far side of the merchant caravan.

"And here we feared that the market'd be thinner with the glutton Lady Priscilla gone."

That perked up Wulfgar's ears, and he turned fast on the man. "Feringal's . . . ?"

"Sister," the man confirmed.

"Died?"

The man snorted and didn't seem the least bit bothered by that possibility, something that Wulfgar figured anyone who had ever had the misfortune of meeting Priscilla Auck would surely appreciate.

"She's in Luskan—been there for a year. She went back with this same caravan after our market here last year," the man explained. "She never much cared for Lady Meralda, for 'twas said she'd had Feringal's ear until he married that one. I'm not for knowing what happened, but that Priscilla's time in Castle Auck came to an end soon after the marriage, and when Meralda got fat with Feringal's heir, she likely knew her influence here would shrink even more. So she went to Luskan, and there she's living, with enough coin to keep her to the end of her days, may they be mercifully short."

"Mercifully for all around her, you mean?"

"That's the way they tell it, aye."

Wulfgar nodded and smiled, and that genuine grin came from more than the humor at Priscilla's expense. He looked back at Lord Feringal and narrowed his crystalline blue eyes, thinking that one major obstacle, the disagreeable Lady Priscilla, had just been removed from his path.

"If Priscilla was at Castle Auck, as much as he'd be wanting to leave, Lord Feringal wouldn't dare be out without his wife at his side. He wouldn't leave them two together!" the man said.

"I would expect that Lady Meralda would wish to visit the caravan more than would the lord," Wulfgar remarked.

"Ah, but not until her flowers bloom."

Wulfgar looked at him curiously.

"She's put in beds of rare tulips, and they're soon to bloom, I'm guessing," the man explained. " 'Twas so last year—she didn't come down to the market until our second tenday, not until the white petals were revealed. Put her in a fine, buying mood, and finer still, for by that time, we knew that Lady Priscilla would be journeying from Auckney with us."

He began to laugh, but Wulfgar didn't follow the cue. He stared across the little stone bridge to the small island that housed Castle Auck, trying to remember the layout and where those gardens might be. He took note of a railing built atop the smaller of the castle's square keeps. Wulfgar glanced back at Feringal, to see the man making his way out of the far end of the market, and with the threat removed, Wulfgar also set out, nodding appreciatively at the merchant, to find a better vantage point for scouting the castle.

Not long after, he had his answer, spotting the form of a woman moving along the flat tower's roof, behind the railing.

* * * * *

There were no threats to Auckney. The town had known peace for a long time. In that atmosphere, it was no surprise to Wulfgar to learn that the guards were typically less than alert. Even so, the big man had no idea how he might get across that little stone bridge unnoticed, and the waters roiling beneath the structure were simply too cold for him to try to swim—and besides, both the near bank and the island upon which the castle stood had sheer cliffs that rose too steeply from the pounding surf below.

He lingered long by the bridge, seeking the answer to his dilemma, and he finally came to accept that he might have to simply wait for those flowers to bloom, so he could confront Lady Meralda in the market. That thought didn't sit well with him, for in that setting he would almost surely need to face Lord Feringal and his entourage as well. It would be easier if he could speak with Meralda first, and alone.

He leaned against the wall of a nearby tavern one afternoon, staring out at the bridge and taking note of the guards' maneuvers. They weren't very disciplined, but the bridge was so narrow that they didn't have to be. Wulfgar stood up straight as a coach rambled across the structure, heading out of the castle.

Liam Woodgate wasn't driving. Steward Temigast was.

Wulfgar stroked his beard and weighed his options, and purely on instinct—for he knew that if he considered his movements, he would lose heart—he gathered up Colson and moved out to the road, to a spot where he could intercept the wagon out of sight of the guards at the bridge, and most of the townsfolk.

"Good trader, do move aside," Steward Temigast bade him, but in a kindly way. "I've some paintings to sell and I wish to see the market before the light wanes. Dark comes early to a man of my age, you know."

The old man's smile drifted to nothingness as Wulfgar pulled back the cowl of his cloak, revealing himself.

"Always full of surprises, Wulfgar is," Temigast said.

"You look well," Wulfgar offered, and he meant it. Temigast's white hair had thinned a bit, perhaps, but the last few years had not been rough on the man.

"Is that. . . . ?" Temigast asked, nodding to Colson.

"Meralda's girl."

"Are you mad?"

Wulfgar merely shrugged and said, "She should be with her mother."

"That decision was made some three years ago."

"Necessary at the time," said Wulfgar.

Temigast sat back on his seat and conceded the point with a nod.

"Lady Priscilla is gone from here, I am told," said Wulfgar, and Temigast couldn't help but smile—a reassurance to Wulfgar that his measure of the steward was correct, that the man hated Priscilla.

"To the joy of Auckney," Temigast admitted. He set the reins on the seat, and with surprising nimbleness climbed down and approached Wulfgar, his hands out for Colson.

The girl shoved her hand in her mouth and whirled away, burying her face in Wulfgar's shoulder.

"Bashful," Temigast said. Colson peeked out at him and he smiled all the wider. "And she has her mother's eyes."

"She is a wonderful girl, and sure to become a beautiful woman," said Wulfgar. "But she needs her mother. I cannot keep her with me. I am bound for a land that will not look favorably on a child, any child."

Temigast stared at him for a long time, obviously unsure of what he should do.

"I share your concern," Wulfgar said to him. "I never hurt Lady Meralda, and never wish to hurt her."

"My loyalty is to her husband, as well."

"And what a fool he would be to refuse this child."

Temigast paused again. "It is complicated."

"Because Meralda loved another before him," said Wulfgar. "And Colson is a reminder of that."

"Colson," said Temigast, and the girl peeked out at him and smiled, and the steward's whole face lit up in response. "A pretty name for a pretty girl." He grew more serious as he turned back to Wulfgar, though, and asked bluntly, "What would you have me do?"

"Get us to Meralda. Let me show her the beautiful child her daughter has become. She will not part with the girl again."

"And what of Lord Feringal?"

"Is he worthy of your loyalty and love?"

Temigast paused and considered that. "And what of Wulfgar?"

Wulfgar shrugged as if it did not matter, and indeed, regarding his obligation to Colson, it did not. "If he desires to hang me, he will have to—"

"Not that," Temigast interrupted, and looked at Colson.

Wulfgar's shoulders slumped and he heaved a deep sigh. "I know what is right. I know what I must do, though it will surely break my heart. But it will be a temporary wound, I hope, for in the passing months and years, I will rest assured that I did right by Colson, that I gave her the home and the chance she deserved, and that I could not provide."

Colson looked at Temigast and responded to his every gesture with a delighted smile.

"Are you certain?" the steward asked.

Wulfgar stood very straight.

Temigast glanced back at Castle Auck, at the short keep where Lady Meralda kept her flowers. "I will return this way before nightfall," he said. "With an empty carriage. I can get you to her, perhaps, but I disavow myself of you from that point forward. My loyalty is not to Wulfgar, not even to Colson."

"One day it will be," said Wulfgar. "To Colson, I mean."

Temigast was too charmed by the girl to disagree.

* * * * *

One hand patted the soft soil at the base of the stem, while the fingers of Meralda's other hand gently brushed the smooth petals. The tulips would bloom soon, she knew—perhaps even that very evening.

Meralda sang to them softly, an ancient rhyme of sailors and explorers lost in the waves, as her first love had been taken by the sea. She didn't know all the words, but it hardly mattered, for she hummed to fill in the holes in the verses and it sounded no less beautiful.

A slap on the stone broke her song, though, and the woman stood up suddenly and retreated a fast step when she noted the prongs of a ladder. Then a large hand clamped over the lip of the garden wall, not ten feet from her.

She brushed back her thick black hair, and her eyes widened as the intruder pulled his head up over the wall.

"Who are you?" she demanded, retreating again, and ignoring his shushing plea.

"Guards!" Meralda called, and turned to run as the intruder shifted. But as his other hand came up, she found herself frozen in place, rooted as if she was just another plant in her carefully cultivated garden. In the man's other hand was a young girl.

"Wulfgar?" Meralda mouthed, but had not the breath to say aloud.

He put the girl down inside, and Colson turned shyly away from Meralda. Wulfgar grabbed the wall with both hands and hauled himself over. The girl went to his leg and wrapped one arm around it, the thumb of her other hand going into her mouth as she continued to shy away.

"Wulfgar?" Meralda asked again.

"Da!" implored Colson, reaching up to Wulfgar with both hands. He scooped her up and set her on his hip, then pulled back his cowl, revealing himself fully.

"Lady Meralda," he replied.

"You should not be here!" Meralda said, but her eyes betrayed her words, for she stared unblinkingly at the girl, at her child.

Wulfgar shook his head. "Too long have I been away."

"My husband would not agree."

"It is not about him, nor about me," Wulfgar said, his calm and sure tone drawing her gaze back to him. "It is about her, your daughter."

Meralda swayed, and Wulfgar was certain that a slight breeze would have knocked her right over.

"I have tried to be a good father to her," Wulfgar explained. "I had even found her a woman to serve as her mother, though she is gone now, taken by foul orcs. But it is all a ruse, I know."

"I never asked—"

"Your husband's actions demanded it," Wulfgar reminded her, and she went silent, her gaze locking once more on the shy child, who had buried her face in her da's strong shoulder.

"My road is too arduous," Wulfgar explained. "Too dangerous for the likes of Colson."

"Colson?" Meralda echoed.

Wulfgar merely shrugged.

"Colson . . ." the woman said softly, and the girl looked her way only briefly and flashed a sheepish smile.

"She belongs with her mother," Wulfgar said. "With her real mother."

"I had thought her father had demanded her to raise as his princess in Icewind Dale," came a sharp retort from the side, and all three turned to regard the entrance of Lord Feringal. The man twisted his face tightly as he moved near to his wife, all the while staring hatefully at Wulfgar.

Wulfgar looked to Meralda for a clue, but found nothing on her shocked face. He struggled to figure out which way to veer the conversation, when Meralda unexpectedly took the lead.

"Colson is not his child," the Lady of Auckney said. She grabbed

Feringal by the hands and forced him to look at her directly. "Wulfgar never ravished—"

Before she could finish, Feringal pulled one of his hands free and lifted a finger over her lips to silence her, nodding his understanding.

He knew, Meralda realized and so did Wulfgar. Feringal had known all along that the child was not Wulfgar's, not the product of a rape.

"I took her to protect your wife . . . and you," Wulfgar said after allowing Feringal and Meralda a few heartbeats to stare into each other's eyes. Feringal turned a scowl his way, to which Wulfgar only shrugged. "I had to protect the child," he explained.

"I would not . . ." Feringal started to reply, but he stopped and shook his head then addressed Meralda instead. "I would not have hurt her," he said, and Meralda nodded.

"I would not have continued our marriage, would not have borne you an heir, if I had thought differently," Meralda quietly replied.

Feringal's scowl returned as he glanced back at Wulfgar. "What do you want, son of Icewind Dale?" he demanded.

Some noise to the side clued Wulfgar in to the fact that the Lord of Auckney hadn't come to the garden alone. Guards waited in the shadows to rush out and protect Feringal.

"I want only to do what is right, Lord Feringal," he replied. "As I did what I thought was right those years ago." He shrugged and looked at Colson, the thought of parting with her suddenly stabbing at his heart.

Feringal stood staring at him.

"The child, Colson, is Meralda's," Wulfgar explained. "I would not cede her to another adoptive mother without first determining Meralda's intent."

"Meralda's intent?" Feringal echoed. "Am I to have no say?"

As the lord of Auckney finished, Meralda put a hand to his cheek and turned him to face her directly. "I cannot," she whispered.

Again Feringal silenced her with a finger against her lips, and turned back to Wulfgar. "There are a dozen bows trained upon you at this moment," he assured the man. "And a dozen guards ready to rush out and cut you down, Liam Woodgate among them—and you know that he holds no love for Wulfgar of Icewind Dale. I warned you that you return to Auckney only under pain of death."

A horrified expression crossed Meralda's face, and Wulfgar squared his shoulders. His instincts told him to counter the threat, to bring Aegis-fang magically to his hand and explain to the pompous Feringal in no uncertain terms that in any ensuing fight, he, Feringal, would be the first to die.

But Wulfgar held his tongue and checked his pride. Meralda's expression guided him, and Colson, clutching his shoulder, demanded that he diffuse the situation and not escalate a threat into action.

"For the sake of the girl, I allow you to flee, straightaway," Feringal said, and both Wulfgar and Meralda widened their eyes with shock.

The lord waved his hands dismissively at Wulfgar. "Be gone, foul fool. Over the wall and away. My patience wears thin, and when it is gone, the whole of Auckney will fall over you."

Wulfgar stared at him for a moment then looked at Colson.

"Leave the girl," Feringal demanded, lifting his voice for the sake of the distant onlookers, Wulfgar realized. "She is forfeit, a princess of Icewind Dale no more. I claim her for Auckney, by Lady Meralda's blood, and do so with the ransom of Wulfgar's promise that the tribes of Icewind Dale will never descend upon my domain."

Wulfgar spent a moment digesting the words, shaking his head in disbelief all the while. When it all sorted out, he dipped a quick and respectful bow to the surprising Lord Feringal.

"Your faith in your husband and your love for him were not misplaced," he said quietly to Meralda, and he wanted to laugh out loud and cry all at the same time, for never had he expected to see such growth in the foppish lord of that isolated town.

But for all of Wulfgar's joy at the confirmation that he had been right to return there, the price of his, and Feringal's, generosity could not be denied.

Wulfgar pulled Colson out to arms' length then brought her in and hugged her close, burying his face in her soft hair. "This is your mother," he whispered, knowing that the child wouldn't begin to understand. He was reminding himself, though, for he needed to do that. "Your ma will always love you. I will always love you."

He hugged her even closer and kissed her on the cheek then stood fast and offered a curt nod to Feringal.

Before he could change his mind, before he surrendered to the tearing of his heart, Wulfgar thrust Colson out at Meralda, who gathered her up. He hadn't even let go of the girl when she began to cry out, "Da! Da!" reaching back at him plaintively and pitifully.

Wulfgar blinked away his tears, turned, and went over the wall, dropping the fifteen feet and landing on the grass below in a run that didn't stop until he had long crossed through Auckney's front gates.

A run that carried with every step the frantic cries of "Da! Da!"

"You did the right thing," he said to himself, but he hardly believed it. He glanced back at Castle Auck and felt as if he had just betrayed the one person in the world who had most trusted him and most needed him.

CHAPTER

THE PRACTICAL MORALITY

22

Certain that no orcs were about, for he could hear their revelry far over a distant hill, Tos'un Armgo settled against a natural seat of stone. Or perhaps it wasn't natural, he mused, situated as it was in the middle of a small lea, roughly circular and sheltered by ancient evergreens. Perhaps some former occupant had constructed the granite throne, for though there were other such stones scattered around the area, the placement of those two, seat and back, was perhaps a bit too convenient.

Whatever and however it had come to be, Tos'un appreciated the chair and the view it afforded him. He was a creature of the nearly lightless Underdark, where no stars shone, where no ceiling was too far above, too vast and distant, otherworldly or extraplanar, even. The canopy that floated above him every night was far beyond his experience, reaching into places that he did not know he possessed. Tos'un was a drow, and a drow male, and in that role his life remained solidly grounded in the needs of the here-and-now, in the day-to-day practicality of survival. As his goals were ever clear to him, based on simple necessity, so his limitations stayed crystalline clear as well—the boundaries of House walls and the cavern that was Menzoberranzan. For all of his life, the limits of Tos'un's aspirations hung over him as solidly as the ceiling of Menzoberranzan's stone cavern.

But those limitations were one of the reasons he had abandoned his House on their journey back to Menzoberranzan after the stunning defeat at the hands of Clan Battlehammer and Mithral Hall. Aside from the chaos that was surely to ensue following that catastrophe, when Matron Yvonnel Baenre herself had been cut down, Tos'un understood that whatever the reshuffling that chaos resolved, his place was set. Perhaps he would have died in the House warfare—as a noble, he made a fine trophy for enemy warriors, and since his mother thought little of him, he would have no doubt wound up on the front lines of any fight. But even had he survived, even had House Barrison Del'Armgo used the vulnerability of the suddenly matron-less House Baenre to ascend to the top rank in Menzoberranzan's hierarchy, Tos'un's life would be as it had always been, as he could not dare hope it would be anything but.

So he had seized the opportunity and had fled, not in search of any particular opportunity, not to follow any ambition or fleeting dream. Why had he fled, then, he wondered as he sat there under the stars?

You will be king, promised a voice in his head, startling Tos'un from his contemplations.

Without a word, with hardly a thought, the drow climbed out of the seat and took a few steps across the meadow. The snow had settled deep on that spot not long ago, but had melted, leaving spongy, muddy ground behind. A few steps from the throne, Tos'un unstrapped his sword belt and lay it upon the ground, then went back to his spot and leaned back, letting his thoughts soar up among the curious points of light.

"Why did I flee?" he asked himself quietly. "What did I desire?"

He thought of Kaer'lic, Donnia, and Ad'non, the drow trio he had joined up with after wandering aimlessly for tendays. Life with them had been good. He had found excitement and had started a war—a proxy war, which was the best kind, after all. It had been heady and clever and great fun, right up until the beastly Obould had bitten the throat out of Kaer'lic Suun Wett, sending Tos'un on the run for his life.

But even that excitement, even controlling the destiny of an army of orcs, a handful of human settlements, and a dwarven kingdom, had been nothing Tos'un had ever desired or even considered, until circumstance had dangled it before him and his three co-conspirators.

No, he realized in that moment of clarity, sitting under a canopy so foreign to his Underdark sensibilities. No tangible desire had brought him from the ranks of House Barrison Del'Armgo. It was, instead, the desire to eliminate the boundaries, the need to dare to dream, whatever dream may come to him. Tos'un and the other three drow—even Kaer'lic, despite her subservience to Lady Lolth—had run to their freedom for no reason more than to escape from the rigid structure of drow culture.

The irony of that had Tos'un blinking repeatedly as he sat there. "The rigid structure of drow culture," he said aloud, just to bask in the irony. For drow culture was premised on the tenets of Lady Lolth, the Spider Queen, the demon queen of chaos.

"Controlled chaos, then," he decided with a sharp laugh.

A laugh that was cut short as he noted movement in the trees.

Never taking his eyes from that spot, Tos'un rolled backward from the stone seat, flipping to his feet in a crouch with the stone between him and the shadowy form—a large, feline form—filtering in and out of the darker lines of the tree trunks.

The drow eased his way to the edge of the stone nearest his discarded sword belt, preparing his dash. He held still, though, not wanting to alert the creature to his presence.

But then he stood taller, blinking, for the great cat seemed to diminish, to dematerialize into a dark mist that filtered away to nothingness. For just a moment, Tos'un wondered if his imagination was playing tricks on him in that strange environment, under a sky that he had still not grown accustomed to or comfortable with.

When he realized the truth of the beast, when he recalled its origins, the drow leaped out from the stone, dived into a forward roll retrieving his belt as he went, and came up so perfectly that he had already buckled it in place before he stood once more.

Drizzt's cat! his thoughts screamed.

Pray that it is! came the unexpected and unasked for answer from his intrusive sword. *A glorious victory is at hand!*

Tos'un winced at the thought. *In Lolth's favor . . .* he imparted to the sword, recalling Kaer'lic's fears about Drizzt Do'Urden.

The priestess had been terrified at the prospect of battling the rogue from Menzoberranzan, fearing, with solid reasoning, that the trouble Drizzt had brought upon the drow city was just the sort of chaos that pleased Lady Lolth. Add to that Drizzt's uncanny luck and almost supernatural proficiency with the blade, and the idea that he was secretly in the favor of Lolth seemed not so far-fetched.

And Tos'un, for all of his irreverence, understood well that anyone who crossed Lolth's will could meet a most unpleasant end.

All of those thoughts followed his intentional telepathic message to Khazid'hea, and the sword went strangely quiet for the next few moments. Indeed, to Tos'un's sensibilities, everything seemed to go strangely quiet. He strained his eyes in the direction of the pines where he had last seen the feline shape, his hands wringing on the hilt of Khazid'hea and his other, drow-made sword. Every passing moment drew him farther into the shadows. His eyes, his ears, his sense of smell, every instinct within him honed in on that spot where the cat had disappeared as he tried desperately to discern where it had gone.

And so he nearly leaped out of his low, soft boots when a voice behind him, speaking in the drow language with perfect Menzoberranyr inflection, said, "Guenhwyvar was tired, so I sent her home to rest."

Tos'un whirled, slashing the empty air with his blades as if he believed the demon Drizzt to be right behind him.

The rogue drow was many steps away, though, standing easily, his scimitars sheathed, his forearms resting comfortably on their respective hilts.

"A fine sword you carry, son of Barrison Del'Armgo," Drizzt said, nodding toward Khazid'hea. "Not drow made, but fine."

Tos'un turned his hand over and regarded the sentient blade for a moment before turning back to Drizzt. "One I found in the valley, below . . ."

"Below where I fought King Obould," Drizzt finished, and Tos'un nodded.

"You have come for it?" Tos'un asked, and in his head, Khazid'hea simmered and imparted thoughts of battle.

Leap upon him and cut him down! I would drink the blood of Drizzt Do'Urden!

Drizzt noted Tos'un's uncomfortable wince, and suspected that Khazid'hea had been behind the grimace. Drizzt had carried the annoying sentient blade long enough to understand that its ego simply would not let it remain silent through any conversation. The way Tos'un had measured his cadence, as if he was listening to the sound of his own words coming back at him in an echo from a stone wall, revealed the continual intrusions of the ever-present Khazid'hea.

"I have come here to see this curiosity I find before me," Drizzt replied. "A son of Barrison Del'Armgo, living on the surface world, alone."

"Akin to yourself."

"Hardly," Drizzt said with a chuckle. "I carry my surname out of habit alone, and toward no familiarity or relationship with the House of Matron Malice."

"As I have abandoned my own House," Tos'un insisted, again in that stilted cadence.

Drizzt wasn't about to argue with that much of his claim, for indeed it seemed plausible enough—though of course, the events that drove Tos'un from the ranks of his formidable House might be anything but exculpatory. "To trade service to a matron mother for service to a king," Drizzt remarked. "For both of us, it seems."

Whatever Tos'un meant to reply, he bit it back and tilted his head to the side, searching the statement, no doubt.

Drizzt didn't hide his wry and knowing grin.

"I serve no king," Tos'un insisted, and with speed enough and force enough to prevent any interruptions from the intrusive blade.

"Obould names himself a king."

Tos'un shook his head, his face curling into a snarl.

"Do you deny your part in the conspiracy that prompted Obould to come south?" Drizzt asked. "I have had this conversation with two of your dead companions, of course. Or do you deny your partnering with the pair I killed? Recall that I saw you standing with the priestess when I came to battle Obould."

"Where was I, a Houseless rogue, to turn?" Tos'un replied. "I happened upon the trio of which you speak in my wandering. Alone and without hope, they offered me sanctuary, and that I could not refuse. We did not raid your dwarf friends, nor any human settlements."

"You prompted Obould and brought disaster upon the land."

"Obould was coming with his thousands with no prompt from us—from my companions, for I had no part in that."

"So you would have to say."

"So I do say. I serve no orc king. I would kill him if given the chance."

"So you would have to say."

"I watched him bite out the throat of Kaer'lic Suun Wett!" Tos'un roared at him.

"And I killed your other two friends," Drizzt was quick to reply. "By your reasoning, you would kill me if given the chance."

That gave Tos'un pause, but only for a moment. "Not so," he said.

But he winced again as Khazid'hea emphatically shot, *Do not let him strike first!* into his thoughts.

The sword continued its prompting, egging Tos'un to leap forward and dispatch Drizzt, as the drow continued, "There is no honor in Obould, no honor in the smelly orcs. They are *iblith*."

Again his comments were broken, his cadence uneven, and Drizzt knew that Khazid'hea was imploring him. Drizzt took a slight step and shift to Tos'un's right, for in that hand he held Khazid'hea.

"You may be correct in your assessment," Drizzt replied. "But then, I found little honor in your two friends before I killed them." He half-expected his words to prompt a charge, and shifted his hands appropriately nearer his hilts, but Tos'un stayed in place.

He just stood there, trembling, waging an inner battle against the sword's murderous intent, Drizzt surmised.

"The orcs have gone on the attack once again," Drizzt remarked, and his tone changed, and his thoughts went dark, as he reminded himself of the fate of Innovindil. "In the Moonwood and against the dwarves."

"They are old enemies." Tos'un replied, as if the whole news was matter-of-fact and hardly unexpected.

"Spurred by instigators who revel in chaos—indeed, who worship a demon queen who thrives on a state of utter confusion."

"No," Tos'un answered flatly. "If you are referring to me—"

"Are there other drow about?"

"No, and no," said Tos'un.

"You would have to say that."

"I fought beside the Moonwood elves."

"Why would you not, in the service of chaos? I doubt that you care which side wins this war, as long as Tos'un realizes his gain."

The drow shook his head, unconvinced.

"And in the Moonwood, " Drizzt continued, "the orcs' attacks were cunning and coordinated—more so than one might expect from a band of the dimwitted goblinkin." As he finished, Drizzt's scimitars appeared in his hands as if they had simply materialized there, so fast and fluid was his motion. Again he sidled to his left, reminding himself that Tos'un was a drow warrior, trained at Melee-Magthere, likely under the legendary Uthegental. House Barrison Del'Armgo's warriors were known for their ferocity and straightforward attacks. Formidable, to be sure, Drizzt knew, and he could not forget for one instant that sword Tos'un carried.

Drizzt went to the right, trying to keep Tos'un using only short strokes with Khazid'hea, a weapon powerful enough to perhaps sever one of Drizzt's enchanted blades if swung with enough weight behind the blow.

"There is a new general among them, an orc most cunning and devious," Tos'un replied, his face twisting with every word—arguing against the intrusions of Khazid'hea, Drizzt clearly recognized.

That obvious truth of Tos'un's inner struggle had Drizzt somewhat hesitant, for why would this drow, if everything Drizzt presumed was true, be arguing against the murderous sword?

Before his thoughts could even go down that road, however, Drizzt thought again of Innovindil, and his face grew very dark. He turned his blades over and back again, anxious to exact revenge for his lost friend.

"More cunning than a warrior trained in Melee-Magthere?" he asked. "More devious than one raised in Menzoberranzan? More hateful of elves than a drow?"

Tos'un shook his head through all of the questions. "I was with the elves," he argued.

"And you deceived them and ran—and ran with knowledge of their tactics."

"I killed none as I left, though I surely could—"

"Because you are more cunning than that," Drizzt interrupted. "I would expect nothing less from a son of House Barrison Del'Armgo. You knew that if you struck and murdered some in your escape, the elves of the Moonwood would have understood the depths of your depravity and would have known that an attack was soon to befall them."

"I did not," Tos'un said, shaking his head helplessly. "None of . . ." He stopped and grimaced as Khazid'hea assaulted his thoughts.

He will take from you his friend's sword! Without me, your lies will not withstand the interrogations of the elf clerics. They would know your heart.

Tos'un found it hard to breathe. He was trapped in a way he never wanted, facing a foe he believed he could not defeat. He couldn't run away from Drizzt as he had Obould.

Kill him! Khazid'hea demanded. *With me in your grasp, Drizzt Do'Urden will fall. Take his head to Obould!*

"No!" Tos'un shot back audibly—and Drizzt smiled in understanding—instinctively recoiling from the orc king, an emotion that Khazid'hea surely understood.

Then take his head to Menzoberranzan, the sword offered, and again Tos'un's reasoning argued, for he hadn't the strength to return to the drow city alone along the unmerciful corridors of the Underdark.

But again the sword had the answers waiting. *Promise Dnark the friendship of Menzoberranzan. He will give you warriors to accompany you to the city, where you will betray them and assume your place as a hero of Menzoberranzan.*

Tos'un tightened his grip on both his swords and thought of Kaer'lic's warning regarding Drizzt. Before Khazid'hea could even begin to argue, though, the drow did it for himself, for Kaer'lic's warning that Drizzt might be in the graces of Lolth had been but a suspicion, and an outlandish one at that, but that mortal predicament standing before him loomed all too real.

And Drizzt watched it all, and recognized many of the fears and emotions playing through Tos'un's thoughts, and so when the son of House Barrison Del'Armgo leaped toward him, his scimitars rose in a sudden and effortless cross before him.

Tos'un executed a double-thrust wide, Khazid'hea and his other sword stabbing past the axis of Drizzt's blades. Drizzt threw his hands out wide to their respective sides, the called-for defense, each of his blades taking one of Tos'un's.

Advantage taken, Drizzt went for the greater stance offered by his curved blades. A more conventional warrior would have reversed the thrust back at his opponent, but Tos'un, expecting that, would have been too quick on the retreat for any real advantage to be realized. So Drizzt turned his scimitars over Tos'un's swords, using the curve of his blades to draw the swords in tighter, that he could send them out with more authority and perhaps even knock his foe off-balance enough that he could score a quick kill.

He rolled the scimitars over with a snap of his wrists.

But Khazid'hea....

Tos'un countered by jamming the powerful sword hard into the hilt of Drizzt's scimitar—and the impossibly sharp blade cut in, catching a hold that halted Drizzt's move. Tos'un pressed forward with his right and stepped back with his left, keeping perfect balance as he disengaged his left from Drizzt's rolling blade.

Seeing disaster, Drizzt reversed suddenly, bringing Icingdeath, his right-hand blade, across hard instead of ahead, which would have left him off-balance and lunging. He drove Twinkle down hard directly away from the terrible blade of Khazid'hea, for that was the only chance to disengage before the mighty sword cut half of Twinkle's crosspiece away. Tos'un followed until the disengagement, then thrust forward at Drizzt, of course, and Icingdeath came across in the last instant, scraping along Khazid'hea's blade, shearing a line of sparks into the air.

Drizzt was half-turned, though, and Tos'un stabbed forward with his left for the ranger's exposed side.

But Twinkle came up from under Drizzt's other arm, neatly picking off the attack, and Drizzt uncrossed his arms suddenly, Icingdeath slashing back across to knock Tos'un's sword aside. Twinkle slapped back against Khazid'hea with equal fury. Tos'un leaped back, as did Drizzt, the two again circling, taking a measure of each other.

He was good, Drizzt realized. Better than he had anticipated. He managed a glance at Twinkle to note the clear tear where Khazid'hea had struck, and noted, too, a nick on Icingdeath's previously unblemished blade.

Tos'un came ahead with a lazy thrust, a feint and a sudden flurry, leading with his left then rattling off several quick blows with Khazid'hea. He moved forward with every strike, forcing Drizzt to block and not dodge. Every time Khazid'hea slapped against one of his blades, Drizzt winced, fearing that the awful sword would cut right through.

He couldn't play it Tos'un's way, he realized. Not with Khazid'hea in the mix. He couldn't use a defensive posture, as he normally would against a warrior who had trained under Uthegental, an overly aggressive sort that would allow him to simply let Tos'un's rage wear him out.

As soon as the attacks of Khazid'hea played out, Drizzt sprang forward, putting his blades up high and rolling his hands in a sudden blur. Over and over went his scimitars, as he rolled his hands left and right, striking rapidly at Tos'un from varying angles.

Tos'un's defense mirrored Drizzt's movements, hands rolling, blades turning in and out, rolling over each other with equal harmony.

Drizzt kept in tight and kept the strokes short, not willing to let Tos'un put any weight behind Khazid'hea. He thought that to be Tos'un's only possible advantage, the sheer viciousness and power of that sword, and without it, Drizzt, who had defeated the greatest weapons master of Menzoberranzan, would find victory.

But Tos'un matched his rolling fury, anticipated his every move, and even managed several short counterstrikes that interrupted Drizzt's rhythm, and one that nearly got past Drizzt's sudden reversal and defense and would have surely gutted him. Surprised, Drizzt pressed the attack even more, rolling his hands more widely, changing the angles of attack more dramatically.

He slashed—one, two, three—downward at Tos'un's left shoulder, spun suddenly as the last parry sounded, and turned lower as he went so that as he came around, both his swords tore for Tos'un's right side. He expected a down-stroke parry from Khazid'hea, but Tos'un turned inside the attack, bringing his drow blade across to block. As he turned, he stabbed Khazid'hea back and down over his right shoulder.

Drizzt ducked the brunt of it, but felt the bite as the sword sliced down his shoulder blade, leaving a long and painful gash. Drizzt ran straight out from the engagement and dived forward in a roll, turning as he came up to face the pursuing Tos'un.

It was Tos'un's turn, and he came on with fury, stabbing and slashing, spinning completely around and with perfect balance and measured speed.

Ignoring the pain and the warm blood running down the right side of his back, Drizzt matched that intensity, parrying left and right, up and down, the blades ringing in one long note as they clanged and scraped. With every parry of Khazid'hea, Drizzt caught the sword more softly, retreating his own blade upon contact, as he might catch a thrown sec to avoid breaking it. That was more taxing, though, more precise and time-consuming, and the necessity of such a concentrated defense prevented him from regaining the momentum and the offense.

Around and around the sheltered lea they went, Tos'un pressing, not tiring, and growing more confident with every strike.

He had a right to do so, Drizzt had to admit, for he fought brilliantly, fluidly, and only then did Drizzt begin to understand that Tos'un had done with Khazid'hea that which Drizzt had refused to allow. Tos'un was letting the sword infiltrate his thoughts, was following the instincts of Khazid'hea as if they were his own. They had found a complementary relationship, a joining of sword and wielder.

Worse, Drizzt realized, Khazid'hea knew him, knew his movements as intimately as a lover, for Drizzt had wielded the sword in a desperate fight against King Obould.

He understood then, to his horror, how Tos'un had so easily anticipated his rollover and second throw move after the initial cross and parry. He understood then, to his dilemma, his inability to set up a killing strike. Khazid'hea knew him, and though the sword couldn't read his thoughts, it had taken a good measure of the fighting techniques of Drizzt Do'Urden. Just as damaging, since Tos'un had apparently given over to Khazid'hea's every intrusion, the sword and the trained drow warrior had found a symbiosis, a joining of knowledge and instinct, of skill and understanding.

For a fleeting moment, Drizzt wished that he had not dismissed Guenhwyvar, as tired as she had been after finally leading him to Tos'un Armgo.

A fleeting moment indeed, for Tos'un and Khazid'hea came on again, hungrily, the drow stabbing high and low simultaneously then spinning his blades over in a cross, and back again with a pair of backhand slashes.

Drizzt backed as Tos'un pursued. He parried about half the strikes—mostly those of the less dangerous drow blade—and dodged the other half cleanly. He offered no counters, allowing Tos'un to press, as he tried to find the answers to the riddle of the drow warrior and his mighty sword.

Back he stepped, parrying a slash. Back he stepped again, and he knew that he was running out of room, that the stone throne was near. He began to parry more and retreat less, his steps slowing and becoming more measured, until he felt at last the thick granite of the throne behind his trailing heel.

Apparently sensing that Drizzt had run out of room, Tos'un came forward more aggressively, executing a double thrust low. Surprised by the maneuver, Drizzt launched a double-cross down, the appropriate parry, where he crossed his scimitars down over the two thrusting swords. Drizzt had long ago solved the riddle of that maneuver. Before, the defender could hope for no advantage beyond a draw.

Tos'un would know that, he realized in the instant it took him to begin the second part of his counter, kicking his foot through the upper cross of his down-held blades, and so when Tos'un reacted, Drizzt already had his improvisation ready.

He kicked for Tos'un's face, so it appeared. Tos'un leaned back and drove his swords straight up, his intent to knock the kicking Drizzt, already in an awkward maneuver, off his balance.

But Drizzt shortened his kick, which could have no more than glanced Tos'un's face anyway, and changed the angle of his momentum upward then used Tos'un's push from below to bolster that directional change. Drizzt leaped right up and tucked in a tight turn that spun him head-over-heels to land lightly atop the seat of the stone throne, and it was Tos'un who overbalanced as the counterweight disappeared in a back flip, the drow staggering back a step.

Typical of an Armgo, Tos'un growled and came right back in, slashing across, which Drizzt hopped easily. Up above, Drizzt had the advantage, but Tos'un tried to use sheer aggressiveness to dislodge him from the seat, slashing and stabbing with abandon. One swipe cut across short of Drizzt, who threw back his hips, and sent Khazid'hea hard into the back of the stone throne. With a crack and a spark, the sword slashed through, leaving a gouge in the granite.

"I will not let you win, and I will not let you flee!" Drizzt cried in that moment, when the stone, though it hadn't stopped the sword, surely broke Tos'un's rhythm.

Drizzt went on the offensive, hacking down at Tos'un with powerful and straightforward strokes, using his advantageous angle to put his weight behind every blow. Tos'un tried to not retreat as a drum roll of bashing blades landed against his upraised swords, sending shivers of numbness down his arms, but Drizzt had him defending against angles varying too greatly for him to ever get his feet fully under him. Soon he had no choice but to fall back, stumbling, and Drizzt was there, leaping from the seat and coming down with a heavy double chop of his blades that nearly took Tos'un's swords from his hands.

"I will not let you win!" Drizzt cried again, throwing out the words in a release of all his inner strength as he backhanded across with Icingdeath, smashing Tos'un's drow-made sword out to the side.

And that was the moment when Drizzt could have ended it, for Twinkle's thrust, turn, and out-roll had Khazid'hea too far to the side to stop the second movement of Icingdeath, a turn and stab that would have plunged the blade deep into Tos'un's chest.

Drizzt didn't want the kill, for all the rage inside him for Innovindil. He played his trump.

"I will again wield the magnificent Khazid'hea!" he cried, disengaging instead of pressing his advantage. He went back just a couple of steps, and only for a few heartbeats—long enough to see a sudden wave of confusion cross Tos'un's face.

"Give me the sword!" Drizzt demanded.

Tos'un cringed, and Drizzt understood. For he had just given Khazid'hea what it had long desired, had just spoken the words Khazid'hea could not ignore. Khazid'hea's loyalty was to Khazid'hea alone, and Khazid'hea wanted, above all else, to be wielded by Drizzt Do'Urden.

Tos'un stumbled, hardly able to bring his blades up in defense as Drizzt charged in. In came Twinkle, in came Icingdeath, but not the blades. The hilts smashed Tos'un's face, one after another. Both Tos'un's swords went flying, and he went with them, back and to the ground. He recovered quickly, but not quickly enough. Drizzt's boot slammed down upon his chest and Icingdeath came to rest against his neck, its diamond edge promising him a quick death if he struggled.

"You have so much to answer for," Drizzt said to him.

Tos'un fell back and gave a great exhale, his whole body relaxing with utter resignation, for he could not deny that he was truly doomed.

CHAPTER
BLACK AND WHITE
23

Nanfoodle lifted one foot and drew little circles on the floor with his toes. Standing with his hands clasped behind his back, the gnome presented an image of uncertainty and trepidation. Bruenor and Hralien, who had been sitting discussing their next moves when Nanfoodle and Regis had entered the dwarf's private quarters, looked at each other with confusion.

"Well if ye can't get it translated, then so be it," Bruenor said, guessing at the source of the gnome's consternation. "But ye're to keep working on it, don't ye doubt!"

Nanfoodle looked up, glanced at Regis, then bolstered by Regis's nod, turned back to the dwarf king and squared his shoulders. "It is an ancient language, based on the Dwarvish tongue," he explained. "It has roots in Hulgorkyn, perhaps, and Dethek runes for certain."

"Thought I'd recognized a couple o' the scribbles," Bruenor replied.

"Though it is more akin to the proper Orcish," Nanfoodle explained, and Bruenor gasped.

"Dworcish?" Regis remarked with a grin, but he was the only one who found any humor in it.

"Ye're telling me that the durned orcs took part of me Delzoun ancestors' words?" Bruenor asked.

Nanfoodle shook his head. "How this language came about is a mystery whose answer is beyond the parchments you brought to me.

From what I can tell of the proportion of linguistic influence, you've juxtaposed the source and add."

"What in the Nine Hells are ye babblin' about?" Bruenor asked, his voice beginning to take on an impatient undercurrent.

"Seems more like old Dwarvish with added pieces from old Orcish," Regis explained, drawing Bruenor's scowl his way and taking it off of Nanfoodle, who seemed to be withering before the unhappy dwarf king with still the most important news forthcoming.

"Well, they needed to talk to the dogs to tell them what's what," said Bruenor, but both Regis and Nanfoodle shook their heads with every word.

"It was deeper than that," Regis said, stepping up beside the gnome. "The dwarves didn't borrow orc phrases, they integrated the language into their own."

"Something that would have taken years, even decades, to come into being," said Nanfoodle. "Such language blending is common throughout the history of all the races, but it occurs, every time, because of familiarity and cultural bonds."

Silence came back at the pair, and Bruenor and Hralien looked to each other repeatedly. Finally, Bruenor found the courage to ask directly, "What are ye saying?"

"Dwarves and orcs lived together, side-by-side, in the city you found," said Nanfoodle.

Bruenor's eyes popped open wide, his strong hands slapped against the arms of his chair, and he came forward as if he meant to leap out and throttle both the gnome and the halfling.

"For years," Regis added as soon as Bruenor settled back.

The dwarf looked at Hralien, seeming near panic.

"There is a town called Palishchuk in the wastes of Vaasa on the other side of Anauroch," the elf said with a shrug, as if the news was not as unexpected and impossible as it seemed. "Half-orcs, one and all, and strong allies with the goodly races of the region."

"*Half-orcs?*" Bruenor roared back at him. "Half-orcs're half-humans, and that lot'd take on a porcupine if the durned spines didn't hurt so much! But we're talkin' me kin here. Me ancestors!"

Hralien shrugged again, as if it wasn't so shocking, and Bruenor stopped sputtering long enough to catch the fact that the elf might be having a bit of fun with the revelation, at the dwarf's expense.

"We don't know that these were your ancestors," Regis remarked.

"Gauntlgrym's the home o' Delzoun!" Bruenor snapped.

"This wasn't Gauntlgrym," said Nanfoodle, after clearing his throat. "It wasn't," he reiterated when Bruenor's scowl fell over him fully.

"What was it, then?"

"A town called Baffenburg," said Nanfoodle.

"Never heared of it."

"Nor had I," the gnome replied. "It probably dates from around the time of Gauntlgrym, but it was surely not the city described in your histories. Not nearly that size, or with that kind of influence."

"That which we saw of it was probably the extent of the main town," Regis added. "It wasn't Gauntlgrym."

Bruenor fell back in his seat, shaking his head and muttering under his breath. He wanted to argue, but had no facts with which to do so. As he considered things, he recognized that he'd never had any evidence that the hole in the ground led to Gauntlgrym, that he had no maps that indicated the ancient Delzoun homeland to be anywhere near that region. All that had led him to believe that it was indeed Gauntlgrym was his own fervent desire, his faith that he had been returned to Mithral Hall by the graces of Moradin for that very purpose.

Nanfoodle started to talk, but Bruenor silenced him and waved both him and Regis away.

"This does not mean that there is nothing of value . . ." Regis started to say, but again, Bruenor waved his hand, dismissing them both—then dismissing Hralien with a gesture, as well, for at that terrible moment of revelation, with orcs attacking and Alustriel balking at decisive action, the crestfallen dwarf king wanted only to be alone.

* * * * *

"Still here, elf?" Bruenor asked when he saw Hralien inside Mithral Hall the next morning. "Seeing the beauty o' dwarf ways, then?"

Hralien shared the dwarf king's resigned chuckle. "I am interested in watching the texts unmasked. And I would be re—" He stopped and studied Bruenor for a moment then added, "It is good to see you in such fine spirits this day. I had worried that the gnome's discovery from yesterday would cloak you in a dour humor."

Bruenor waved a hand dismissively. "He's just scratched the scribblings. Might be that some dwarves were stupid enough to trust the damned orcs. Might be that they paid for it with their city and their lives—and that might be a lesson for yer own folk and for Lady Alustriel and the rest of them that's hesitating in driving Obould back to his hole. Come with me, if ye're wantin', for I'm on me way to the gnome now. He and Rumblebelly have worked the night through, on me orders. I'm to take their news to Alustriel and her friends out working on the wall. Speak for the Moonwood in that discussion, elf, and let's be setting our plans together."

Hralien nodded and followed Bruenor through the winding tunnels and to the lower floors, and a small candlelit room where Regis and Nanfoodle were hard at work. Parchment had been spread over several tables, held in place by paperweights. The aroma of lavender permeated the room, a side-effect from Nanfoodle's preservation potions that had been carefully applied to each of the ancient writings, and to the tapestry, which had been hung on one wall. Most of its image remained obscured, but parts of it had been revealed. That vision made Bruenor cringe, for the orcs and dwarves visible in the drawing were not meeting in battle or even in parlay. They were together, intermingled, going about their daily business.

Regis, who sat off to the side transcribing some text, greeted the pair as they entered, but Nanfoodle didn't even turn around, hunched as he was over a parchment, his face pressed close to the cracked and faded page.

"Ye're not looking so tired, Rumblebelly," Bruenor greeted accusingly.

"I'm watching a lost world open before my eyes," he replied. "I'm sure that I will fall down soon enough, but not now."

Bruenor nodded. "Then ye're saying that the night showed ye more o' the old town," he said.

"Now that we have broken the code of the language, the pace improves greatly," said Nanfoodle, never turning from the parchment he was studying. "You retrieved some interesting texts on your journey."

Bruenor stared at him for a few heartbeats, expecting him to elaborate, but soon realized that the gnome was fully engulfed by his work once more. The dwarf turned to Regis instead.

"The town was mostly dwarves at first," Regis explained. He hopped up from his chair and moved to one of the many side tables, glanced at the parchment spread there, and moved along to the next in line. "This one," he explained, "talks about how the orcs were growing more numerous. They were coming in from all around, but most of the dwarven ties remained to places like Gauntlgrym, which was of course belowground and more appealing to a dwarf's sensibilities."

"So it was an unusual community?" Hralien asked.

Regis shrugged, for he couldn't be certain.

Bruenor looked to Hralien and nodded smugly in apparent vindication, and certainly the elf and the halfling understood that Bruenor did not want his history intertwined with that of the foul orcs!

"But it was a lasting arrangement," Nanfoodle intervened, finally looking up from the parchment. "Two centuries at least."

"Until the orcs betrayed me ancestors," Bruenor insisted.

"Until something obliterated the town, melting the permafrost and dropping the whole of it underground in a sudden and singular catastrophe," Nanfoodle corrected. "And not one of orc making. Look at the tapestry on the wall—it remained in place after the fall of Baffenburg, and certainly it would have been removed if that downfall had been precipitated by one side or the other. I don't believe that there were 'sides,' my king."

"And how're ye knowing that?" Bruenor demanded. "That scroll tellin' ye that?"

"There is no indication of treachery on the part of the orcs—at least not near the end of the arrangement," the gnome explained, hopping down from his bench and moving to yet another parchment across from the table where Regis stood. "And the tapestry . . . Early on, there were problems. A single orc chieftain held the orcs in place beside the dwarves. He was murdered."

"By the dwarves?" Hralien asked.

"By his own," said Nanfoodle, moving to another parchment. "And a time of unrest ensued."

"Seemin' to me that the whole time was a time of unrest," Bruenor said with a snort. "Ye can't be living with damned orcs!"

"Off and on unrest, from what I can discern," Nanfoodle agreed. "And it seemed to get better through the years, not worse."

"Until the orcs brought an end to it," Bruenor grumbled. "Suddenly, and with orc treachery."

"I do not believe . . ." Nanfoodle started to reply.

"But ye're guessin', and not a thing more," said Bruenor. "Ye just admitted that ye don't know what brought the end."

"Every indication—"

"Bah! But ye're guessing."

Nanfoodle conceded the point with a bow. "I would very much like to go to this city and build a workshop there, in the library. You have uncovered something fascinating, King Bru—"

"When the time's for it," Bruenor interrupted. "Right now I'm seeing the call of them words. Get rid of Obould and the orcs'll fall apart, as we were expecting from the start. This is our battle call, gnome. This is why Moradin sent me back here and told me to go to that hole, Gauntlgrym or not!"

"But that's not . . ." Nanfoodle started to argue, but his voice trailed away, for it was obvious that Bruenor paid him no heed.

His head bobbing with excitement and vigor, Bruenor had already turned to Hralien. He swatted the elf on the shoulder and swept Hralien up in his wake as he quick-stepped from the room, pausing only to berate Nanfoodle, "And I'm still thinking it's Gauntlgrym!"

Nanfoodle looked helplessly at Regis. "The possibilities. . . ." the gnome remarked.

"We've all our own way of looking at the world, it would seem," Regis answered with a shrug that seemed almost embarrassed for Bruenor.

"Is this find not an example?"

"Of what?" asked Regis. "We do not even know how it ended, or why it ended."

"Drizzt has whispered of the inevitability of Obould's kingdom," Nanfoodle reminded him.

"And Bruenor is determined that it will not be. The last time I looked, Bruenor, and not Drizzt, commanded the army of Mithral Hall and the respect of the surrounding kingdoms."

"A terrible war is about to befall us," said the gnome.

"One begun by King Obould Many-Arrows," the halfling replied.

Nanfoodle sighed and looked at the many parchment sheets spread around the room. It took all his willpower to resist the urge to rush from table to table and crumble them to dust.

* * * * *

"His name was Bowug Kr'kri," Regis explained to Bruenor, presenting more of the deciphered text to the dwarf king.

"An orc?"

"An orc philosopher and wizard," the halfling replied. "We think the statues we saw in the library were of him, and maybe his disciples."

"So he's the one who brought the orcs into the dwarf city?"

"We think."

"The two of ye do a lot o' thinking for so little answering," Bruenor growled.

"We have only a few old texts," Regis replied. "It's all a riddle, still."

"Guesses."

"Speculation," said Regis. "But we know that the orcs lived there with the dwarves, and that Bowug Kr'kri was one of the leaders of the community."

"Any better guesses on how long that town lived? Ye said centuries, but I'm not for believin' ye."

Regis shrugged and shook his head. "It had to be over generations. You saw the structures, and the language."

"And how many o' them structures were built by the dwarfs afore the orcs came in?" Bruenor asked with a sly smile.

Regis had no answer.

"Might've been a dwarf kingdom taken down by trusting the damned orcs," Bruenor said. "Fool dwarfs who took much o' the orc tongue to try to be better neighbors to the treacherous dogs."

"We don't think—"

"Ye think too much," Bruenor interrupted. "Yerself and the gnome're all excited about finding something so different than that which we're knowin' to be true. If ye're just finding more o' the same, then it's just more o' the same. But if ye're findin' something to make yer eyes go wide enough to fall out o' their holes, then that's something to dance about."

"We didn't invent that library, or the statues inside it," Regis argued, but he was talking into as smug and sure an expression as he had ever seen. And he wasn't sure, of course, that Bruenor's reasoning was wrong, for indeed, he and Nanfoodle were doing a lot of guessing. The final puzzle picture was far from complete. They hadn't even yet assembled the borders of the maze, let alone filled in the interior details.

Hralien walked into the room then, answering a summons Bruenor had sent out for him earlier.

"It's coming clear, elf," Bruenor greeted him. "That town's a warning. If we're following Alustriel's plans, we're to wind up a dead and dust-covered artifact for a future dwarf king to discover."

"My own people are as guilty as is Alustriel in wanting to find a stable division, King Bruenor," Hralien admitted. "The idea of crossing the Surbrin to do battle with Obould's thousands is daunting—it will not be attempted without great sorrow and great loss."

"And what's to be found by sitting back?" Bruenor asked.

Hralien, who had just lost a dozen friends in an orc assault on the Moonwood, and had just witnessed first-hand the attack on the dwarven wall, didn't need to use his imagination to guess the answer to that question.

"We can't be fightin' them straight up," Bruenor reasoned. "That's the way o' doom. Too many o' the stinking things." He paused and grinned, nodding his hairy head. "Unless they're attacking us, and in bits and pieces. Like the group that went into the Moonwood and the one that come over me wall. If we were ready for them, then there'd be a lot o' dead orcs."

Hralien gave a slight bow in agreement.

"So Drizzt was right," said Bruenor. "It's all about the one on top. He tried to get rid of Obould, and almost did. That'd've been the answer, and still is. If we can just get rid o' the durned Obould, we'll be tearing it all down."

"A difficult task," said Hralien.

"It's why Moradin gave me back to me boys," said Bruenor. "We're goin' to kill him, elf."

" 'We're'?" asked Hralien. "Are you to spearhead an army to strike into the heart of Obould's kingdom?"

THE ORC KING

"Nah, that's just what the dog's wantin'. We'll do it the way Drizzt tried it. A small group, better'n . . ." He paused and a cloud passed over his face.

"Me girl won't be going," Bruenor explained. "Too hurt."

"And Wulfgar has left for the west," said Hralien, catching on to the source of Bruenor's growing despair.

"They'd be helpin', don't ye doubt."

"I do not doubt at all," Hralien assured him. "Who, then?"

"Meself and yerself, if ye're up for the fight."

The elf gave a half-bow, seeming to agree but not fully committing, and Bruenor knew he'd have to be satisfied with that.

The dwarf looked over to Regis, who nodded with increased determination, his face as grim as his cherubic features would allow.

"And Rumblebelly there," the dwarf said.

Regis took a step back, shifting uncomfortably as Hralien cast a doubtful look his way.

"He's knowing how to find his place," Bruenor assured the elf. "And he's knowin' me fightin' ways, and them o' Drizzt."

"We will collect Drizzt on our road?"

"Can ye think o' anyone ye'd want beside ye more than the drow?"

"Indeed, no, unless it was Lady Alustriel herself."

"Bah!" Bruenor snorted. "Ye won't be getting that one to agree. Meself and a few o' me boys, yerself and Drizzt, and Rumblebelly."

"To kill Obould."

"Crush his thick skull," said Bruenor. "Me and some o' me best boys. We'll be cuttin' a quiet way, right to the head o' th' ugly beast, and then let it fall where it may."

"He is formidable," Hralien warned.

"Heared the same thing about Matron Baenre o' Menzoberranzan," Bruenor replied, referring to his own fateful strike that had decapitated the drow city and ended the assault on Mithral Hall. "And we got Moradin with us, don't ye doubt. It's why he sent me back."

Hralien's posture and expression didn't show him to be completely convinced by any of it, but he nodded his agreement just the same.

"Ye help me find me drow friend," Bruenor said to him, seeing that unspoken doubt. "Then ye make yer mind up."

"Of course," Hralien agreed.

Off to the side, Regis shifted nervously. He wasn't afraid of adventuring beside Bruenor and Drizzt, even if it would be behind orc lines. But he did fear that Bruenor was reading it all wrong, and that their mission would turn out badly, for them perhaps, and for the world.

* * * * *

The gathering fell quiet when Banak Brawnanvil looked Bruenor in the eye and declared, "Ye're bats!"

Bruenor, however, didn't blink. "Obould's the one," he said evenly.

"Not doubtin' that," replied the irrepressible Banak, who seemed to tower over Bruenor at that moment despite the fact that he was confined to a sitting position because of his injury in the orc war. "So send Pwent and yer boys to go and get him, like ye're wantin'."

"It's me own job."

"Only because ye're a thick-headed Battlehammer!"

A few gasps filtered about the room at that proclamation, but they were diffused by a couple of chortles, most notably from the priest Cordio. Bruenor turned on Cordio with a scowl, but it fast melted against the reality of Banak's words. Truer words regarding the density of Bruenor's skull, Cordio—and Bruenor—knew, had never been spoken.

"Was meself that went to Gauntlgrym," Bruenor said. He snapped his head to Regis's direction, as if expecting the halfling to argue that it wasn't Gauntlgrym. Regis, though, wisely stayed silent. "Was meself that anchored the retreat from Keeper's Dale. Was meself that battled Obould's first attack in the north." He was gaining speed and momentum, not to *bang drums for meself*, as the dwarven saying went, but to justify his decision that he would personally lead the mission. "Was meself that went to Calimport to bring back Rumblebelly. Was meself that cut the damned Baenre in half!"

"I drunk enough toasts to ye to appreciate the effort," said Banak.

"And now I'm seeing one more task afore me."

"The King o' Mithral Hall's plannin' to march off behind an orc army and kill the orc king," Banak remarked. "And if ye're caught on the way? Won't yer kin here be in fine straits then in trying to bargain with Obould?"

"If ye're thinkin' I'm to be caught livin', then ye're not knowing what it is to be a Battlehammer," Bruenor retorted. "Besides, ain't no different than if Drizzt got himself caught already, or any o' the rest of us. Ye're not for changing yer ways with orcs for meself any more than ye would for any of our boys."

Banak started to respond, but really had no answer for that.

"Besides, besides," Bruenor added, "once I'm walking out that gate, I'm not the king o' Mithral Hall, which is the whole point in us being here, now ain't it?"

"I'll be yer steward, but no king is Banak," the crippled Brawnanvil argued.

"Ye'll be me steward, but if I'm not returning then yerself is the Ninth King o' Mithral Hall and don't ye be doubting it. And not a dwarf here would agree with ye if ye were."

Bruenor turned and led Banak's gaze around the room with his own, taking in the solemn nods of all the gathering, from Pwent and his Gutbusters to Cordio and the other priests to Torgar and the dwarves from Mirabar.

"This is why Moradin sent me back," Bruenor insisted. "It's me against Obould, and ye're a fool betting if ye're betting on Obould!"

That elicited a cheer around the room.

"Yerself and the drow?" Banak asked.

"Me and Drizzt," Bruenor confirmed. "And Rumblebelly's up for it, though me girl's in no place for it."

"Ye telled her that, have ye?" Banak asked with a snicker that was echoed around the room.

"Bah, but she can't be running, if running we're needing, and she'd not ever put her friends in a spot o' staying behind to protect her," said Bruenor.

"Then ye ain't telled her," said Banak, and again came the snorts.

"Bah!" Bruenor said, throwing up his hands.

"So yerself, Drizzt, and Regis," said Banak. "And Thibbledorf Pwent?"

"Try to stop me," Pwent replied, and the Gutbuster brigade cheered.

"And Pwent," said Bruenor, and the Gutbusters cheered again. Nothing seemed to excite that group quite so much as the prospect of one of their own walking off on an apparent suicide mission.

"Begging yer pardon, King Bruenor," Torgar Hammerstriker said from the other side of the room. "But me thinking is that the Mirabar boys should be represented on yer team, and me thinking's that meself and Shingles here"—he reached to the side and pulled forward the scarred old warrior, Shingles McRuff—"be just the two to do Mirabar proud."

As he finished, the other five Mirabarran dwarves in the room exploded into cheers for their mighty leader and the legendary Shingles.

"Make it seven, then," Cordio Muffinhead added. "For ye can't be goin' on a march for Moradin without a priest o' Moradin, and I'm that priest."

"Eight, then," Bruenor corrected, "for I'm thinking that Hralien o' the Moonwood won't be leaving us after we find Drizzt."

"Eight for the road and eight for Obould!" came the cheer, and it grew louder as it was repeated a second then a third time.

Then it ended abruptly, as a scowling Catti-brie came in through the door, staring hard at Bruenor with a look that had even the doubting Banak Brawnanvil looking at the dwarf king with sympathy.

"Go and do what needs doin'," Bruenor instructed them all, his voice suddenly shaky, and as the others scattered through every door in the room, Catti-brie limped toward her father.

"So you're going for Obould's head, and you're to lead it?" she asked.

Bruenor nodded. "It's me destiny, girl. It's why Moradin put me back here."

"Regis brought you back, with his pendant."

"Moradin let me go from his hall," Bruenor insisted. "And it was for a reason!"

Catti-brie stared at him long and hard. "So now you're to go out, and to take my friend Regis with you, and to take my husband with you. But I'm not welcome?"

"Ye can't run!" Bruenor argued. "Ye can hardly walk more than a few dozen yards. If we're turning from orcs, then are we to wait for yerself?"

"There'll be less turning from orcs if I'm there."

"Not for doubtin' that," said Bruenor. "But ye know ye can't do it. Not now."

"Then wait for me."

Bruenor shook his head. Catti-brie's lips grew tight and she blinked her blue eyes as if fighting back tears of frustration.

"I could lose all of you," she whispered.

Bruenor caught on then that part of her difficulty at least had to do with Wulfgar. "He'll come back," the dwarf said. "He'll walk the road that's needin' walking, but don't ye doubt that Wulfgar'll be coming back to us."

Catti-brie winced at the mention of his name, and her expression showed her to be far less convinced of that than was her father.

"But will you?" she asked.

"Bah!" Bruenor snorted, throwing up a hand as if the question was ridiculous.

"And will Regis come back? And Drizzt?"

"Drizzt is out there already," Bruenor argued. "Are ye doubtin' him?"

"No."

"Then why're ye doubting me?" asked Bruenor. "I'm out for doing the same thing Drizzt set out to do afore the winter. And he went out alone! I won't be out there alone, girl, and ye'd be smarter if ye was worrying about the damned orcs."

Catti-brie continued to look at him, and had no answer.

Bruenor opened wide his arms, inviting her to a hug that she could not resist. "Ye won't be alone, girl. Ye won't ever be alone," he whispered into her ear.

He understood fully her frustration, for would his own have been any less if he was to be left out of such a mission, when all of his friends were to go?

Catti-brie pulled back from him far enough to look him in the eye and ask, "Are you sure of this?"

"Obould's got to die, and I'm the dwarf to kill him," said Bruenor.

"Drizzt tried, and failed."

"Well Drizzt'll try again, but this time he's got friends trying with him. When we come back to ye, the orc lines'll be breaking apart. Ye'll find plenty o' fighting then, to be sure, and most of it outside our own doors. But the orcs'll be scattered and easy to kill. Take me bet now, girl, that I'll kill more than yerself."

"You're going out now, and getting a head start," Catti-brie answered, her face brightening a bit.

"Bah, but I won't count the ones I'm killing on the road," said Bruenor. "When I get back here and the orcs come on, as they're sure'n to do when Obould's no more, then I'll be killing more orcs than Catti-brie's to fell."

Catti-brie wore a sly grin. "I'll have me bow back from Drizzt then," she said, assuming a Dwarvish accent as she threw out the warning. "Every arrow's taking one down. Some'll take down two, or might even be three."

"And every swipe o' me axe is cutting three in half," Bruenor countered. "And I'm not for tiring when there're orcs to cut."

The two stared at each other without blinking as each extended a hand to shake on the bet.

"The loser represents Mithral Hall at the next ceremony in Nesmé," Catti-brie said, and Bruenor feigned a grimace, as though he hadn't expected the stakes to be quite so high.

"Ye'll enjoy the journey," the dwarf said. He smiled and tried to pull back, but Catti-brie held his hand firmly and stared him in the eye, her expression solemn.

"Just get back to me, alive, and with Drizzt, Regis, and the others alive," she said.

"Plannin' on it," said Bruenor, though he didn't believe it any more than did Catti-brie. "And with Obould's ugly head.

Catti-brie agreed. "With Obould's head."

CHAPTER

TAKING CARE IN WHAT THEY WISHED FOR

24

Clan Wolf Jaw lined both sides of the trail, their formidable array of warriors stretching out for hundreds of feet, beyond the bend and out of Chieftain Grguch's line of sight. None moved to block the progress of Clan Karuck, or to threaten the hulking orcs in any way, and Grguch recognized the pair who did step out in the middle of the trail.

"Greetings again, Dnark," Grguch said. "You have heard of our assault on the ugly dwarves?"

"All the tribes of Many-Arrows have heard of the glory of Grguch's march," Dnark answered, and Grguch smiled, as did Toogwik Tuk, who stood to the side and just behind the ferocious chieftain.

"You march west," remarked Dnark, glancing back over his shoulder. "To the invitation of King Obould?"

Grguch spent a few moments looking over Dnark and his associate, the shaman Ung-thol. Then the huge orc warrior glanced back at Toogwik Tuk and beyond him, motioning to a trio of soldiers, two obviously of Clan Karuck, with wide shoulders and bulging muscles, and a third that Dnark and Ung-thol had parted company with just a few days earlier.

"Obould has sent an emissary, requesting parlay," Grguch explained. Behind him, Oktule saluted the pair and bowed repeatedly.

"We were there among King Obould's entourage when Oktule was sent forth," Dnark replied. "Know you, though, that he was not the only emissary sent out that day." He finished and met Grguch's hard stare for a few heartbeats, then motioned behind to the Wolf Jaw ranks. Several warriors stepped out, dragging a beaten and battered orc. They took him around Dnark, and on his signal closed half the distance to Grguch before dropping their living cargo unceremoniously onto the dirt.

Priest Nukkels groaned as he hit the ground, and squirmed a bit, but Ung-thol and Dnark had done their work extremely well and there was no chance of him getting up from the ground.

"An emissary sent to you?" Grguch asked. "But you said that you were with Obould."

"No," Toogwik Tuk explained, reading correctly the smug expressions worn by his co-conspirators. He stepped forward, daring to pass Grguch as he moved toward the battered priest. "No, this is Nukkels," he explained, looking back at Grguch.

Grguch shrugged, for the name meant nothing to him.

"King Obould's advisor," Toogwik Tuk explained. "He would not be sent to deliver a message to Chieftain Dnark. No, not even to Chieftain Grguch."

"What?" Grguch demanded, and though his tone was calm and even, there remained behind it a hint of warning to Toogwik Tuk to tread lightly, where he seemed on the verge of insult.

"This emissary was for no orc," Toogwik Tuk explained. He looked to Dnark and Ung-thol. "Nor was he heading north, to Gerti Orelsdottr, was he?"

"South," Dnark answered.

"Southeast, precisely," added Ung-thol.

Toogwik Tuk could barely contain his amusement—and his elation that King Obould had so perfectly played into their plans. He turned to Grguch, certain of his guess. "Priest Nukkels was sent by King Obould to parlay with King Bruenor Battlehammer."

Grguch's face went stone cold.

"We believe the same," said Dnark, and he moved forward to stand beside Toogwik Tuk—and to ensure that Toogwik Tuk did not claim an overdue amount of the credit for that revelation. "Nukkels has resisted our . . . methods," he explained, and to accentuate his point, he stepped over and kicked the groaning Nukkels hard in the ribs, sending him into a fetal curl. "He has offered many explanations for his journey, including that of going to King Bruenor."

"This pathetic dwarf-kisser in the dirt was sent by Obould to meet with Bruenor?" Grguch asked incredulously, as if he could not believe his ears.

"So we believe," Dnark answered.

"It is easy enough to discern," came a voice from behind, among Clan Karuck's ranks. All turned, Grguch with a wide, knowing smile, to see Hakuun step forward to stand beside his chieftain. "Would you like me to question the emissary?" Hakuun asked.

Grguch laughed and glanced around, motioning at last to a dark cluster of trees off to the side of the path. Dnark began signaling to his ranks for orcs to drag the prisoner over, but Grguch cut him short as Hakuun launched into a spell. Nukkels contorted as if in pain, and curled up on the ground—until he was not on the ground, but floating in the air. Hakuun walked for the trees, and Nukkels drifted behind him.

* * * * *

Away from the others, Hakuun obediently put his ear in line with that of Nukkels. The transfer took only a moment, with Jack the brain mole slipping out of Hakuun's ear and into Nukkels's.

As he realized what was happening to him, Nukkels began thrashing wildly in the air, but with nothing to orient him, with no pull of gravity to keep him upright or even on his side, he began to spin—which dizzied him, of course, and only made Jack's intrusion that much easier.

Jack came back out, and back into his more usual host a short while later, having ripped Nukkels's brain of every detail. He knew, and soon Hakuun knew, of Obould's true designs, confirming the fears of the trio who had summoned Clan Karuck from the bowels of the Spine of the World.

"Obould seeks peace with the dwarves," Hakuun remarked in disbelief. "He wants the war to be at its end."

A very un-orc orc, said the voice in his head.

"He defiles the will of Gruumsh!"

As I said.

Hakuun stalked out of the tree cluster, Jack's magic yanking the shivering, slobbering, floating Nukkels along behind him. When Hakuun got back to the others on the trail, he waved Nukkels in and let him drop hard to the ground.

"He was bound for King Bruenor," the shaman of Clan Karuck stated. "To undo the damage wrought by Chieftain Grguch and Clan Karuck."

"Damage?" Grguch asked, furrowing his thick brow. "Damage!"

"As we explained to you upon your arrival," said Ung-thol.

"It is as our friends have told us," Hakuun confirmed. "King Obould has lost his heart for war. He wishes no further battle with Clan Battlehammer."

"Cowardice," spat Toogwik Tuk.

"Has he found enough spoils to return to his home?" Grguch asked, his tone mocking and derogatory.

"He has conquered empty rocks," Dnark proclaimed. "All that is of value lies within the halls of the Battlehammer dwarves, or across the river in the realm of Silverymoon. But Obould—" he paused, turned, and kicked Nukkels hard—"Obould would parlay with Bruenor. He would seek a treaty!"

"With *dwarves?*" Grguch bellowed.

"Exactly that," said Hakuun, and Grguch nodded, having seen Hakuun at his work too many times to doubt a word he spoke.

Ung-thol and Toogwik Tuk exchanged knowing grins. It was all for show, all to rouse the rabble around the two chieftains, to garner outrage at the utter ridiculousness of the apparent designs of Obould.

"And he would parlay with Grguch," Dnark reminded the ferocious orc chieftain. "He would summon you to his side to gain your approval. Or perhaps to scold you for attacking the elves and dwarves."

Grguch's bloodshot eyes opened wide and a great snarl rumbled behind his trembling lips. He seemed as if he would leap forward and bite off Dnark's head, but the Chieftain of Wolf Jaw did not relent. "Obould intends to show Grguch who controls the Kingdom of Many-Arrows. He will coax you to join his way, so certain is he that he follows the true vision of Gruumsh."

"To parlay with dwarves?" Grguch roared.

"Cowardice!" Dnark cried.

Grguch stood there, clenching his fists, the muscles in his neck straining, his chest and shoulders bulging as if their sinewy power could not be contained by the orc's skin.

"Oktule!" he cried, wheeling to face the orc who had arrived with King Obould's invitation.

The emissary shrank back, as did every orc around him.

"Come here," Grguch demanded.

Oktule, trembling and sweating, gave a quick shake of his head and stumbled back even more—or would have, had not a pair of Clan Karuck's powerful warriors grabbed him by the arms and walked him forward. He tried to dig his feet in, but they just dragged him, depositing him before the wild gaze of Chieftain Grguch.

"King Obould would scold me?" Grguch asked.

A line of wetness ran down poor Oktule's leg, and he shook his head again—though whether in response to the question or in simple, desperate denial, no one around could tell. He focused on Dnark, pleading with the chieftain who knew that his role was unwitting.

Dnark laughed at him.

"He would scold me?" Grguch said again, louder. He leaned forward, towering over the trembling Oktule. "You did not tell me that."

"He would not . . . he . . . he . . . he told me to come to get you," Oktule stammered.

"That he might scold me?" Grguch demanded, and Oktule seemed about to faint.

"I did not know," the pathetic courier protested meekly.

Grguch whirled to regard Dnark and the others, his expression brightening as if he had just sorted everything out. "To gain the favor of Bruenor, Obould would have to offer something," Grguch realized. He spun back on Oktule and slapped him with a backhand across the face, launching him to the side and to the ground.

Grguch turned on Dnark again, his smile wry, nodding his head knowingly. "He would offer to Bruenor the head of the warrior who struck against Mithral Hall, perhaps."

Behind him, Oktule gulped.

"Is there truth in that?" Dnark asked Nukkels, and he kicked the prone orc hard again.

Nukkels grunted and groaned, but said nothing decipherable.

"It is reasonable," Ung-thol said, and Dnark quickly nodded, neither of them wishing to let Grguch calm from his self-imposed frenzy. "If Obould wishes to convince Bruenor that the attack was not of his doing, he would have to prove his claim."

"With the head of Grguch?" the chieftain of Clan Karuck asked as he turned to Hakuun, and Grguch laughed as if it was all absurd.

"The foolish priest showed me nothing of this," Hakuun admitted. "But if Obould truly wishes peace with Bruenor, and he does, then Chieftain Grguch has quickly become . . . an inconvenience."

"It is past time I meet this Obould fool, that I can show him the truth of Clan Karuck," said Grguch, and he gave a little laugh, clearly enjoying the moment. "It may be unfortunate that you interrupted the journey of the one in the dirt," he said, nodding toward the still-squirming Nukkels. "Greater would be King Bruenor's surprise and fear when he looked into that basket, I say! I would pay in women and good gold to see the face of the dwarf when he pulled out Obould's head!"

The orcs of Clan Karuck began to howl at that, but Dnark, Ungthol, and Toogwik Tuk just looked at each other solemnly and with nods of understanding. For there it was, the conspiracy spoken clearly, openly proclaimed, and there could be no turning back. They offered their nods of thanks to Hakuun, who remained impassive, the part of him that was Jack the Gnome not wishing to even acknowledge their existence, let alone allow them the illusion that they were somehow his peers.

Grguch hoisted his two-bladed axe, but paused then set it aside. Instead, he drew a long and wicked knife from his belt and glanced back to the Karuck orcs standing around Oktule. His smile was all the impetus those orcs needed to drag the poor courier forward.

Oktule's feet dug small trenches in the wet spring ground. He shook his head in denial, crying, "No, no, please no!"

Those pleas only seemed to spur Grguch on. He strode behind Oktule and grabbed a handful of the fool's hair, roughly yanking his head back, exposing his throat.

Even the orcs of Oktule's own clan joined in the cheering and chanting, and so he was doomed.

He screamed and shrieked in tones preternatural in their sheer horror. He thrashed and kicked and fought as the blade came against the soft skin of his throat.

Then his screams became watery, and Grguch bore him to the ground, face down, the chieftain's knees upon his back, pinning him, while Grguch's arm pumped furiously.

When Grguch stood up again, presenting Oktule's head to the frenzied gathering, the three conspirators shared another glance, and each took a deep and steadying breath.

Dnark, Toogwik Tuk, and Ung-thol had made a deal with as brutal a creature as any of them had ever known. And they knew, all three, that there was more than a passing chance that Chieftain Grguch would one day present their heads for the approval of the masses.

They had to be satisfied with the odds, however, because the other choice before them was obedience to Obould, and Obould alone. And that course of cowardice they could not accept.

* * * * *

"There will be nothing subtle about Grguch's challenge to Obould," Ung-thol warned his comrades when the three were alone later that same night. "Diplomacy is not his way."

"There is no time for diplomacy, nor is there any need," said Toogwik Tuk, who clearly stood as the calmest and most confident of the trio. "We know the options before us, and we chose our road long ago. Are you surprised by Grguch and Clan Karuck? They are exactly as I portrayed them to you."

"I am surprised by their ... efficiency," said Dnark. "Grguch walks a straight line."

"Straight to Obould," Toogwik Tuk remarked with a snicker.

"Do not underestimate King Obould," warned Dnark. "That he sent Nukkels to Mithral Hall tells us that he understands the true threat of Grguch. He will not be caught unawares."

"We cannot allow this to become a wider war," Ung-thol agreed. "Grguch's name is great among the orcs in the east, along the Surbrin, but the numbers of warriors there are few compared to what Obould commands in the west and the north. If this widens in scope, we will surely be overwhelmed."

"Then it will not," Toogwik Tuk said. "We will confront Obould with his small group around him, and Clan Karuck will overwhelm him and be done with it. He does not have the favor of Gruumsh—have we any doubt of that?"

"His actions do not echo the words of Gruumsh," Ung-thol reluctantly agreed.

"If we are certain of his actions," said Dnark.

"He will not march against Mithral Hall!" Toogwik Tuk snarled at them. "You have heard the whimpers of Nukkels! Grguch's priest confirmed it."

"Did he? Truly?" Dnark asked.

"Or is it all a ruse?" Ung-thol posed. "Is Obould's pause a feint to fully unbalance our enemies?"

"Obould will not march," Toogwik Tuk protested.

"And Grguch will not be controlled," said Dnark. "And are we to believe that this half-ogre creature will hold the armies of Many-Arrows together in a unified march for wider glory?"

"The promise of conquest will hold the armies together far better than the hope of parlay with the likes of King Bruenor of the dwarves," Toogwik Tuk argued.

"And that is the truth," said Dnark, ending the debate. "And that is why we brought Clan Karuck forth. It unfolds before us now exactly as we anticipated, and Grguch meets and exceeds every expectation. Now that we are finding that which we decided we wished to find, we must hold fast to our initial beliefs that led us to this point. It is not the will of Gruumsh that his people should pause when great glory and conquest awaits. It is not the will of Gruumsh that his people should parlay with the likes of King Bruenor of the dwarves. Never that! Obould has pushed himself beyond the boundaries of decency and common sense. We knew that when we called to Clan Karuck, and we know that now." He turned his head and spat upon Nukkels, who lay unconscious and near death in the mud. "We know that with even more certainty now."

"So let us go and witness Grguch as he answers the summons of Obould," said Toogwik Tuk. "Let us lead the cheers to King Grguch, as he leads our armies against King Bruenor."

Ung-thol still wore doubts on his old and wrinkled face, but he looked to Dnark and shared in his chieftain's assenting nod.

In a tree not far away, a curious winged snake listened to it all with amusement.

CHAPTER
POLITICS AND ALLIANCES
25

Raised in Menzoberranzan, a male drow in the matriarchal city of Menzoberranzan, Tos'un Armgo didn't as much as grimace when Drizzt tugged his arms back hard and secured the rope on the other side of the large tree. He was caught, with nowhere to run or hide. He glanced to the side—or tried to, for Drizzt had expertly looped the rope under his chin to secure him against the tree trunk—where Khazid'hea rested, stabbed into a stone by Drizzt. He could feel the sword calling to him, but he couldn't reach out to it.

Drizzt studied Tos'un as if he understood the silent pleas exchanged between drow and sentient sword—and likely, he did, Tos'un realized.

"You have nothing further to gain or lose," Drizzt said. "Your day in the service of Obould is done."

"I have not been in his service for many tendays," Tos'un stubbornly argued. "Not since before the winter. Not since that day you battled him, and even before that, truth be told."

"Truth told by a son of House Barrison Del'Armgo?" Drizzt asked with a scoff.

"I have nothing to gain or lose, just as you said."

"A friend of mine, a dwarf named Bill, would speak with you about that," Drizzt said. "Or whisper at you, I should say, for his throat was expertly cut to steal the depth of his voice."

Tos'un grimaced at that inescapable truth, for he had indeed cut a dwarf's throat in preparation for Obould's first assault on Mithral Hall's eastern door.

"I have other friends who might have wished to speak with you, too," said Drizzt. "But they are dead, in no small part because of your actions."

"I was fighting a war," Tos'un blurted. "I did not understand—"

"How could you not understand the carnage to which you contributed? Is that truly your defense?"

Tos'un shook his head, though it would hardly turn to either side.

"I have learned," the captured drow added. "I have tried to make amends. I have aided the elves."

Despite himself and his intentions that he would bring no harm to his prisoner, Drizzt slapped Tos'un across the face. "You led them to the elves," he accused.

"No," said Tos'un. "No."

"I have heard the details of the raid."

"Facilitated by Chieftain Grguch of Clan Karuck, and a trio of conspirators who seek to force Obould back to the road of conquest," said Tos'un. "There is more afoot here than you understand. Never did I side with those who attacked the Moonwood, and who have marched south, I am sure, with intent to strike at Mithral Hall."

"Yet you just said that you were no ally of Obould," Drizzt reasoned.

"Not of Obould, nor of any other orc," said Tos'un. "I admit my role, though it was a passive one, in the early stages, when Donnia Soldou, Ad'non Kareese, and Kaer'lic Suun Wett decided to foster an alliance between Obould and his orcs, Gerti Orelsdottr and her giants, and the two-headed troll named Proffit. I went along because I did not care—why would I care for dwarves, humans, and elves? I am drow!"

"A point I have never forgotten, I assure you."

The threat took much of Tos'un's bluster, but he pressed on anyway. "The events surrounding me were not my concern."

"Until Obould tried to kill you."

"Until I was chased away by the murderous Obould, yes," said Tos'un. "And into the camp of Albondiel and Sinnafain of the Moonwood."

"Whom you *betrayed*," Drizzt shouted in his face.

"From whom I escaped, though I was not their captive," Tos'un yelled back.

"Then why did you run?"

"Because of you!" Tos'un cried. "Because of that sword I carried, who knew that Drizzt Do'Urden would never allow me to keep it, who knew that Drizzt Do'Urden would find me among the elves and strike me down for possessing a sword that I had found abandoned in the bottom of a ravine."

"That is not why, and you know it," said Drizzt, backing off just a step. " 'Twas I who lost the sword, recall?"

As he spoke he glanced over at Khazid'hea, and an idea came to him. He wanted to believe Tos'un, as he had wanted to believe the female, Donnia, when he had captured her those months before.

He looked back at Tos'un, smiled wryly, and said, "It is all opportunity, is it not?"

"What do you mean?"

"You ally with Obould as he gains the upper hand. But he is held at bay, and you face his wrath. So you find your way to Sinnafain and Albondiel and the others and think to create new opportunities where your old ones have ended. Or to recreate the old ones, at the expense of your new 'friends.' Once you have gained their trust and learned their ways, you again have something to offer to the orcs, something that will perhaps bring Obould back to your side."

"By helping Grguch? You do not understand."

"But I shall," Drizzt promised, moving off to the side, toward Khazid'hea. Without hesitation, he grabbed the sword by the hilt. Metal scraped and screeched as he withdrew the blade from the stone, but Drizzt didn't hear that, for Khazid'hea already invaded his thoughts.

I had thought you lost to me.

But Drizzt wasn't listening to any of that, had not the time for it. He forced his thoughts into the sword, demanding of Khazid'hea a summary of its time in the hands of Tos'un Armgo. He did not coddle the sword with promises that together they would find glory. He did not offer to the sword anything. He simply asked of it, *Were you in the Moonwood? Have you tasted the blood of elves?*

Sweet blood . . . Khazid'hea admitted, but with that thought came to Drizzt a sense of a time long past. And the sword had not been in the Moonwood. Of that much, the drow was almost immediately certain.

In light of Khazid'hea's open admission of its fondness for elf blood, Drizzt considered the unlikely scenario that Tos'un could have been an integral part of the planning for that raid and yet still have remained on the western side of the Surbrin. Would Khazid'hea have allowed that participation from afar, knowing that blood was to be spilled, and particularly since Khazid'hea had been in Tos'un's possession when he had been with the elves?

Drizzt glanced back at the captured drow and considered the relationship between Tos'un and the sword. Had Tos'un so dominated Khazid'hea?

As that very question filtered through Drizzt's thoughts, and thus was offered to the telepathic sword, Khazid'hea's mocking response chimed in.

Drizzt put the sword down for a few moments to let it all sink in. When he retrieved the blade, he directed his questioning toward the newcomer.

Grguch, he imparted.

A fine warrior. Fierce and powerful.

A worthy wielder for Khazid'hea? Drizzt asked.

The sword didn't deny it.

More worthy than Obould? Drizzt silently asked.

The feeling that came back at him seemed not so favorably impressed. And yet, Drizzt knew that King Obould was as fine a warrior as any orc he had ever encountered, as fine as Drizzt himself, whom the sword had long coveted as a wielder. Though not of that elite class, Catti-brie, too, was a fine warrior, and yet Drizzt knew from his last experience with the sword that she had fallen out of Khazid'hea's favor, as she opted to use her bow far too often for Khazid'hea's ego.

A long time passed before Drizzt set the sword down once again, and he was left with the impression that the ever-bloodthirsty Khazid'hea clearly favored Grguch over Obould, and just for the reasons that Tos'un had said. Obould was not pressing for conquest and battle.

Drizzt looked at Tos'un, who rested as comfortably as could be expected given his awkward position tied to the tree. Drizzt could not dismiss the plausibility of Tos'un's claims, all of them, and perhaps, whether through heartfelt emotion or simple opportunity, Tos'un was not now an enemy to him and his allies.

But after his experiences with Donnia Soldou—indeed, after his experiences with his own race from the earliest moments of his conscious life, Drizzt Do'Urden wasn't about to take that chance.

* * * * *

The sun had long set, the dark night made murkier by a fog that curled up from the softening snow. Into that mist disappeared Bruenor, Hralien, Regis, Thibbledorf Pwent, Torgar Hammerstriker and Shingles McRuff of Mirabar, and Cordio the priest.

On the other side of the ridgeline, behind the wall where Bruenor's dwarves and Alustriel's wizards worked vigilantly, Catti-brie watched the receding group with a heavy heart.

"I should be going with them," she said.

"You cannot," said her companion, Lady Alustriel of Silverymoon. The tall woman moved nearer to Catti-brie and put her arm around the woman's shoulders. "Your leg will heal."

Catti-brie looked up at her, for Alustriel was nearly half a foot taller than she.

"Perhaps this is a sign that you should consider my offer," Alustriel said.

"To train in wizardry? Am I not too old to begin such an endeavor?"

Alustriel laughed dismissively at the absurd question. "You will take to it naturally, even though you were raised by the magically inept dwarves."

Catti-brie considered her words for a moment, but soon turned her attention to the view beyond the wall, where the fog had swallowed her father and friends. "I had thought that you would walk beside my father, as he bade," she said, and glanced over at the Lady of Silverymoon.

"As you could not, neither could I," Alustriel replied. "My position prevented me from it as fully as did your wounded leg."

"You do not agree with Bruenor's goal? You would side with Obould?"

"Surely not," said Alustriel. "But it is not my place to interject Silverymoon in a war."

"You did exactly that when you and your Knights in Silver rescued the wandering Nesmians."

"Our treaties with Nesmé demanded no less," Alustriel explained. "They were under attack and running for their lives. Small friends we would be if we did not come to them in their time of need."

"Bruenor sees it just that way right now," said Catti-brie.

"Indeed he does," Alustriel admitted.

"So he plans to eradicate the threat. To decapitate the orc army and send them scattering."

"And I hope and pray that he succeeds. To have the orcs gone is a goal agreed upon by all the folk of the Silver Marches, of course. But it is not my place to bring Silverymoon into this provocative attack. My council has determined that our posture is to remain defensive, and I am bound to abide by their edicts."

Catti-brie shook her head and did not hide her disgusted look. "You act as if we are in a time of peace, and Bruenor is breaking that peace," she said. "Does a needed pause in the war because of the winter's snows cancel what has gone before?"

Alustriel hugged the angry woman a bit tighter. "It is not the way any of us wish it to be," she said. "But the council of Silverymoon has determined that Obould has stopped his march, and we must accept that."

"Mithral Hall was just attacked," Catti-brie reminded. "Are we to sit back and let them strike at us again and again?"

Alustriel's pause showed that she had no answer for that. "I cannot go after Obould now," she said. "In my role as leader of Silverymoon, I am bound by the decisions of the council. I wish Bruenor well. I hope with all my heart and soul that he succeeds and that the orcs are chased back to their holes."

Catti-brie calmed, more from the sincerity and regret in Alustriel's tone than from her actual words. Alustriel had helped, despite her refusal to go along, for she had given to Bruenor a locket enchanted to lead the dwarf toward Drizzt, an identical locket to the one she had given to Catti-brie many years before when she, too, had gone off to find a wandering Drizzt.

"I hope that Bruenor is correct in his guess," Alustriel went on, trepidation in her voice. "I hope that killing Obould will bring the results he desires."

Catti-brie didn't reply, but just stood there and absorbed the words. She couldn't bring herself to believe that Obould, who had started the war, might actually have become a stabilizing force, and yet she could not deny her doubts.

*****

The two orcs stood under a widespread maple, the sharp, stark lines of its branches not yet softened by the onset of buds. They talked and chuckled at their own stupidity, for they were completely lost, and far separated from their kin at the small village. A wrong turn on a trail in the dark of night had put them far afield, and they had long ago abandoned the firewood they had come out to collect.

One lamented that his wife would beat him red, to warm him up so he could replace the fire that wouldn't last half the night.

The other laughed and his smile lingered long after his mirth was stolen by an elven arrow, one that neatly sliced into his companion's temple. Standing in confusion, grinning simply because he hadn't the presence of mind to remove his own smile, the orc didn't even register the sudden *thump* of heavy boots closing in fast from behind him. He was caught completely unawares as the sharp tip of a helmet spike drove into his spine, tearing through muscle and bone, and blasted out the front of his chest, covered in blood and pieces of his torn heart.

He was dead before Thibbledorf Pwent straightened, lifting the orc's flopping body atop his head. The dwarf hopped around, looking for more enemies. He saw Bruenor and Cordio scrambling in the shadows south of the maple, and noted Torgar and Shingles farther to the east. With Hralien in the northwest, and Regis following in the shadows behind Pwent, the group soon surmised that the pair had been out alone.

"Good enough, then," said Bruenor, nodding his approval. He held up the locket Alustriel had given him. "Warmer," he explained. "Drizzt is nearby."

"Still north?" Hralien asked, coming in under the maple to stand beside Bruenor.

"Back from where ye just walked," Bruenor confirmed, holding forth his fist, which held the locket. "And getting warmer by the step."

A curious expression showed on Bruenor's face. "And getting warmer as we're standin' here," he explained to the curious glances that came his way.

"Drizzt!" Regis cried an instant later.

Following the halfling's pointing finger, the others spied a pair of dark elves coming toward them, with Tos'un bound and walking before their friend.

"Taked ye long enough to find him, eh?" Thibbledorf Pwent said with a snort. He bent and slapped his leg for effect, which sent the dead orc flopping weirdly.

Drizzt stared at the bloody dwarf, at the cargo he carried on his helmet spike. Realizing that there was simply nothing he might say against the absurdity of that image, he just prodded Tos'un on, moving to the main group.

"They hit the wall east of Mithral Hall," Hralien explained to Drizzt. "As you had feared."

"Aye, but know that we sent them running," Bruenor added.

Drizzt's confused expression didn't change as he scanned the group.

"And now we're out for Obould," Bruenor explained. "I'm knowing ye were right, elf. We got to kill Obould and break it all apart, as ye thought afore when ye went after him with me girl's sword."

"We're out for him?" Drizzt asked doubtfully, looking past the small group. "You've brought no army, my friend."

"Bah, an army'd just muddle it all," Bruenor said with a wave of his hand.

It wasn't hard for Drizzt to catch the gist of that, and in considering it for a moment, in considering Bruenor's leadership methodology, he realized that he should not be the least bit surprised.

"We wish to get to Obould, and it seems that we have a captive who might aid in exactly that," Hralien remarked, stepping up before Tos'un.

"I have no idea where he is," Tos'un said in his still-stinted command of the Elvish tongue.

"You would have to say that," said Hralien.

"I helped you . . . your people," Tos'un protested. "Grguch had them caught in the failed raid and I showed them the tunnel that took them to safety."

"True," Hralien replied. "But then, isn't that what a drow would do? To gain our trust, I mean?"

Tos'un's shoulders sagged and he lowered his eyes, for he had just fought that same battle with Drizzt, and there seemed no way for him to escape it. Everything he had done leading up to that point could be interpreted as self-serving, and for the benefit of a larger and more nefarious plot.

"Ye should've just killed him and been done with it," Bruenor said to Drizzt. "If he's not for helping us then he's just slowing us down."

"Meself'll be there for the task in a heartbeat, me king!" Pwent shouted from the side, and all eyes turned to see the dwarf, bent low with head forward, backing through the narrow opening between a pair of trees. Pwent set the back of the dead orc's thighs against one trunk, the poor creature's shoulder blades against another, and with a sudden burst, the dwarf tugged backward. Bones and gristle popped and ground as the barbed spike tore back through, freeing the dwarf of his dead-weight burden.

Pwent stumbled backward and fell to his rump, but hopped right back to his feet and bounced around to face the others, shaking his head so vigorously that his lips flapped. Then, with a smile, Pwent brought his hands up before him, palms facing out, extended thumbs touching tip-to-tip, lining up his charge.

"Turn the dark-skinned dog just a bit," he instructed.

"Not just yet, good dwarf," Drizzt said, and Pwent straightened, disappointment clear on his face.

"Ye thinkin' to take him along?" Bruenor asked, and Drizzt nodded.

"We could divert our course to the Moonwood, or back to Mithral Hall," Hralien offered. "We would lose no more than a day or so, and would be rid of our burden."

But Drizzt shook his head.

"Easier just to kill him," said Bruenor, and to the side, Pwent began scraping his feet across the ground like a bull readying for a charge.

"But not wiser," Drizzt said. "If Tos'un's claims are true, he might prove to be a valuable asset to us. If not, we have lost nothing because we have risked nothing." He looked to his fellow drow. "If you do not deceive us, on my word I will let you leave when we are done."

"You cannot do this," said Hralien, drawing all eyes his way. "If he has committed crimes against the Moonwood, his fate is not yours alone to decide."

"He has not," Drizzt assured the elf. "He was not there, for Khazid'hea was not there."

Bruenor yanked Drizzt aside, pulling him away from the others. "How much o' this is yer way o' hoping for a drow akin to yerself?" the dwarf asked bluntly.

Drizzt shook his head, with sincerity and certainty. "On my word, Bruenor, this I do because I think it best for us and our cause—whatever that cause may be."

"What's that meaning?" the dwarf demanded. "We're for killing Obould, don't ye doubt!" He raised his voice with the proclamation, and the others all looked his way.

Drizzt didn't argue. "Obould would kill Tos'un if given the chance, as Obould murdered Tos'un's companion. We will gamble nothing with Tos'un, I promise you, my friend, and the possibility of gain cannot be ignored."

Bruenor looked long and hard at Drizzt then glanced back at Tos'un, who stood calmly, as if resigned to his fate—whatever that fate may be.

"On my word," Drizzt said.

"Yer word's always been good enough, elf," said Bruenor. He turned and started back for the others, calling to Torgar and Shingles as he went. "Think yerselves are up to guardin' a drow?" he asked, or started to, for as soon as his intent became clear, Drizzt interrupted him.

"Let Tos'un remain my responsibility," he said.

Again Bruenor granted Drizzt his wish.

CHAPTER 26
CROSSROAD

Wulfgar lingered around the outskirts of Auckney for several days. He didn't dare show his face in the town for fear that connecting himself to the new arrival at Castle Auck would put undue pressure on Lord Feringal, and create dangerous ramifications for Colson. But Wulfgar was a man comfortable in the wilds, who knew how to survive through the cold nights, and who knew how to keep himself hidden.

Everything he heard about the lord and lady's new child brought him hope. One of the prevalent rumors whispered by excited townsfolk hinted that the girl was Feringal's and Meralda's own, and that she had been born in a sleep-state from which they had never expected her to awaken. And what joy now for the couple and the town that the child had recovered!

Another rumor attached Colson to barbarian nobility, and claimed that her presence with Lord Feringal ensured security for the folk of Auckney—a wonderful thing in the tough terrain of the frozen North.

Wulfgar absorbed it all with a growing sense that he had done well for Colson, for himself, and for Delly. Truly he had a hole in his heart that he never expected to fill, and truly he vowed that he would visit Auckney and Colson in the coming years. Feringal would have no reason to dismiss him or arrest him as time passed, after all, and indeed Wulfgar might find a level of bargaining power in the future, since he knew the truth of the girl's parentage. Lord Feringal wouldn't want him for an enemy, physically or politically.

That was the barbarian's hope, the one thing that kept him from breaking down and rushing back into the town to "rescue" Colson.

He continued to linger, to listen and to watch, for on more than one occasion he chanced to see Colson out with her new parents. He was truly amazed and heartened to see how quickly the young girl had adapted to her new surroundings and new parents, from afar at least. Colson smiled as often as she had in Mithral Hall, and she seemed at ease holding Meralda's hand and walking along in the woman's shadow.

Similarly, the love Meralda held for her could not be denied. The look of serenity on her face was everything Wulfgar had hoped it would be. She seemed complete and content, and in addition to those promising appearances, what gave Wulfgar more hope still was the posture of Lord Feringal whenever he was near to the girl. There could be no doubt that Feringal had grown greatly in character over the years. Perhaps it was due to the support of Meralda, a woman Wulfgar knew to be possessed of extraordinary integrity, or perhaps it was due to the absence of Feringal's shrill sister.

Whatever the cause, the result was clear for him to see and hear, and every day he lingered near to Auckney was a day in which he grew more certain of his decision to return the child to her rightful mother. It did Wulfgar's heart good, for all the pain still there, to think of Colson in Meralda's loving arms.

So many times he wanted to run into Auckney to tell Colson that he loved her, to crush her close to him in his arms and assure her that he would always love her, would always protect her. So many times he wanted to go in and simply say goodbye. Her cries of "Da!" still echoed in his mind and would haunt him for years and years, he knew.

But he could not go in, and so as the days became a tenday, Wulfgar melted away down the mountain road to the east, the way he had come. The next day, he arrived at the end of the eastern pass, where the road ran south through the foothills to Luskan, and north to the long dale that traversed the Spine of the World and opened up into Icewind Dale.

Wulfgar turned neither way at first. Instead he crossed the trail and scaled a rocky outcropping that afforded him a grand view of the rolling lands farther to the east. He perched upon the stone and let his mind's eye rove beyond the physical limitations of his vision, imagining the landscape as it neared Mithral Hall and his dearest friends. The place he had called home.

He turned suddenly back to the west, thinking of his daughter and realizing just how badly he missed her—much more so than he'd anticipated.

Then back to the east went his thoughts and his eyes, to the tomb of Delly, lying cold in Mithral Hall.

"I only ever tried to do the best I could," he whispered as if talking to his dead wife.

It was true enough. For all of his failures since his return from the Abyss, Wulfgar had tried to do the best he could manage. It had been so when he'd first rejoined his friends, when he'd failed and assaulted Catti-brie after a hallucinatory dream. It had been so during his travels with Morik, through Luskan and up to Auckney. So many times had he failed during those dark days.

Looking west then looking east, Wulfgar accepted the responsibility for all of those mistakes. He did not couch his admission of failure with self-serving whining about the trials he had suffered at the claws of Errtu. He did not make excuses for any of it, for there were none that could alter the truth of his behavior.

All he could do was do the best he could in all matters before him. That was what had led him to retrieve Delly's body. It was the right thing to do. That was what had led him not only to retrieve Colson from Cottie and the refugees, but to bring her home to Meralda. It was the right thing to do.

And now?

Wulfgar had thought he'd sorted it all out, had thought his plans and road determined. But with the stark reality of those plans before him, he was unsure. He knelt upon the stone and prayed to Delly for guidance. He called upon her ghost to show him the way.

Was Obould pounding on the doors of Mithral Hall yet again?

Bruenor might need him, he knew. His adoptive father, who had shown him nothing but love for all those years, might need his strength in the coming war. Wulfgar's absence could result in Bruenor's death!

The same could be true of Drizzt, or Regis, or Catti-brie. They might find themselves in situations in the coming days where only Wulfgar could save them.

"Might," Wulfgar said, and as he heard the word, he recognized that that would forever be the case. They might need him as he might need any of them, or all of them. Or perhaps even all of them together would one day soon be overcome by a black tide like the one of Obould.

"Might," he said again. "Always might."

Aside from the grim possibilities offered by the nearly perpetual state of war, however, Wulfgar had to remind himself of important questions. What of his own needs? What of his own desires? What of his own legacy?

He was approaching middle age.

Reflexively, Wulfgar turned from the east to face north, looking up the trail that would lead him to Icewind Dale, the land of his ancestors, the land of his people.

Before he could fully turn that way, however, he looked back to the east, toward Mithral Hall, and envisioned Obould the Awful towering over Bruenor.

CHAPTER
TRUST, AND VERIFY
27

"This Toogwik Tuk is aggressive," Grguch said to Hakuun, and to Jack, though of course Grguch didn't know that. They stood off to the side of the gathering force as it realigned itself for a march to the west. "He would have us wage war with Obould."

"He claims that Obould would wage war with us," the shaman agreed after a quick internal dialogue with Jack.

Grguch grinned as if nothing in the world would please him more. "I like this Toogwik Tuk," he said. "He speaks with Gruumsh."

"Are you not curious as to why Obould halted his march?" Hakuun asked, though the question had originated with Jack. "His reputation is for ferocity, but he builds walls instead of tearing them down."

"He fears rivals," Grguch assumed. "Or he has grown comfortable. He walks away from Gruumsh."

"You do not intend to convince him otherwise."

Grguch grinned even more wickedly. "I intend to kill him and take his armies. I speak to Gruumsh, and I will please Gruumsh."

"Your message will be blunt, or coaxed at first?"

Grguch looked at the shaman curiously then motioned with his chin toward a bag set off to the side, a sack that held Oktule's head.

A wry smile widened on Hakuun's face. "I can strengthen the message," he promised, and Grguch was pleased.

Hakuun looked back over his shoulder and spoke a few arcane words, strung together with dramatic inflection. Jack had predicted all of it, and had already worked the primary magic for it. Out of the shadows walked Oktule, headless and grotesque. The animated zombie strode stiff-legged to the sack and shifted aside the flaps. It stood straight a moment later and moved slowly toward the pair, cradling its lost head in both hands at its midsection.

Hakuun looked to Grguch and shrugged sheepishly. The chieftain laughed.

"Blunt," he said. "I only wish that I might view Obould's face when the message is delivered."

Inside Hakuun's head, Jack whispered, and Hakuun echoed to Grguch, "It can be arranged."

Grguch laughed even louder.

With a bellow of *"Kokto Gung Karuck,"* Grguch's orc force, a thousand strong and growing, began its march to the west, the clan of the Wolf Jaw taking the southern flank, Clan Karuck spearheading the main mass.

In the very front walked the zombie Oktule, holding a message for Obould.

* * * * *

They heard the resonating grumble of *"Kokto Gung Karuck,"* and from a high mountain ridge not far northeast of Mithral Hall, Drizzt, Bruenor, and the others saw the source of that sound, the march of Clan Karuck and its allies.

"It is Grguch," Tos'un told the group. "The conspirators are leading him to Obould."

"To fight him?" Bruenor asked.

"Or to convince him," said Tos'un.

Bruenor snorted at him, but Tos'un just looked at Drizzt and Hralien and shook his head, unwilling to concede the point.

"Obould has shown signs that he wishes to halt his march," Drizzt dared say.

"Tell it to the families of me boys who died at the wall a couple o' nights ago, elf," Bruenor growled.

"That was Grguch, perhaps," Drizzt offered, careful to add the equivocation.

"That was orcs," Bruenor shot back. "Orcs is orcs is orcs, and th' only thing they're good for is fertilizing the fields. Might that their rotting bodies'll help grow trees to cover the scars in yer Moonwood," he added, addressing Hralien, who blanched and rocked back on his heels.

"To cover the blood of Innovindil," Bruenor added, glaring at Drizzt.

But Drizzt didn't back from the stinging comment. "Information is both our weapon and our advantage," he said. "We would do well to learn more of this march, its purpose, and where it might turn next." He looked down and to the north, where the black swarm of Grguch's army was clear to see along the rocky hills. "Besides, our trails parallel anyway."

Bruenor waved his hand dismissively and turned away, Pwent following him back to the food spread out at the main encampment.

"We need to get closer to them," Drizzt told the remaining half a dozen. "We need to learn the truth of their march."

Regis took a deep breath as Drizzt finished, for he felt the weight of the task on his shoulders.

"The little one will be killed," Tos'un said to Drizzt, using the drow language, Low Drow, that only he and Drizzt understood.

Drizzt looked at him hard.

"They are warriors, fierce and alert," Tos'un explained.

"Regis is more than he seems," Drizzt replied in the same Underdark language.

"So is Grguch." As he finished, Tos'un glanced at Hralien, as if to invite Drizzt to speak to the elf for confirmation.

"Then I will go," said Drizzt.

"There is a better way," Tos'un replied. *"I know of one who can walk right in and speak with the conspirators."*

That gave Drizzt pause, an expression of doubt clouding his face and obvious to everyone nearby.

"Ye plannin' to tell us what ye're talking about?" Torgar said impatiently.

Drizzt looked at him then back at Tos'un. He nodded, to both.

After a brief private conversation with Cordio, Drizzt pulled Tos'un off to the side to join the priest.

"Ye sure?" Cordio asked Drizzt when they were alone. "Ye're just gonna have to kill him."

Tos'un tensed at the words, and Drizzt fought hard to keep the smile from his face.

"He might be full o' more information that we can coax out o' him," Cordio went on, playing his role perfectly. "Might be that a few tendays o' torture'll bring us answers about Obould."

"Or lies to stop the torture," Drizzt replied, but he ended the forthcoming debate with an upraised hand, for it didn't matter anyway. "I am sure," he said simply, and Cordio heaved an "oh-if-I-must" sigh, the perfect mix of disgust and resignation.

Cordio began to chant and slowly dance around the startled Tos'un. The dwarf cast a spell—a harmless dweomer that would have cured any diseases that Tos'un might have contracted, though of course, Tos'un didn't know that, and recognized only that the dwarf had sent some magical energy into his body. Another harmless spell followed, then a third, and with each casting, Cordio narrowed his eyes and sharpened his inflection just a bit more, making it all seem quite sinister.

"The arrow," the dwarf commanded, holding a hand out toward Drizzt though his intense stare never left Tos'un.

"What?" Drizzt asked, and Cordio snapped his fingers impatiently. Drizzt recovered quickly and drew an arrow from his magical quiver, handing it over as demanded.

Cordio held it up before his face and chanted. He waggled the fingers of his free hand over the missile's wicked tip. Then he moved it toward Tos'un, who shrank back but did not retreat. The dwarf lifted the arrow up to Tos'un's head then lowered it.

"The head, or the heart?" he asked, turning to Drizzt.

Drizzt looked at him curiously.

"Telled ye it was a good spell," Cordio lied. "Not that it'll much matter with that durned bow o' yers. Blast his head from his shoulders or take out half his chest? Yer choice."

"The head," said the amused drow. "No, the chest. Shoot center mass...."

"Ye can't miss either way," the dwarf promised.

Tos'un stared hard at Drizzt.

"Cordio has placed an enchantment upon you," Drizzt explained as Cordio continued to chant and wave the arrow before Tos'un's slender chest. The dwarf ended by tapping the arrowhead against the drow, right over his heart.

"This arrow is now attuned to you," Drizzt said, taking the arrow from the dwarf. "If it is shot, it will find your heart, unerringly. You cannot dodge it. You cannot deflect it. You cannot block it."

Tos'un's look was skeptical.

"Show 'im, elf," Cordio said.

Drizzt hesitated for effect.

"We're shielded from the damned orcs," the priest insisted. "Show 'im."

Looking back at Tos'un, Drizzt still saw doubt, and that he could not allow. He drew Taulmaril from his shoulder, replaced the "enchanted" arrow in his quiver and took out a different one. As he set it, he turned and targeted, then let fly at a distant boulder.

The magical bolt split the air like a miniature lightning bolt, flashing fast and true. It cracked into the stone and blasted through with a sharp retort that had Regis and the other dwarves jumping with surprise. It left only a smoking hole in the stone where it had hit.

"The magic of the surface dwellers is strange and powerful, do not doubt," Drizzt warned his fellow drow.

"Ye ain't got a chest plate thick enough," Cordio added, and he tossed an exaggerated wink at Tos'un then turned with a great laugh and ambled away.

"What is this about?" Tos'un asked in the drow tongue.

"You wish to play the role of scout, so I will let you."

"But with the specter of death walking beside me."

"Of course," said Drizzt. *"Were it just me, I might trust you."*

Tos'un tilted his head, curious, trying to get a measure of Drizzt.

"Fool that I am," Drizzt added. *"But it is not just me, and if I am to entrust you with this, I need to ensure that my friends will not be harmed by my decision. You hinted that you can walk right into their camp."*

"The conspirators know that I am no friend of Obould's."

"Then I will allow you to prove your worth. Go and learn what you may. I will be near, bow in hand."

"To kill me if I deceive you."

"To ensure the safety of my friends."

Tos'un began to slowly shake his head.

"You will not go?" Drizzt asked.

"You need not do any of this, but I understand," Tos'un replied. *"I will go as I offered. You will come to know that I am not deceiving you."*

By the time the two dark elves got back to the rest of the group, Cordio had informed the others of what had transpired, and of the plan going forward. Bruenor stood with his hands on his hips, clearly unconvinced, but he merely gave a "harrumph" and turned away, letting Drizzt play out his game.

* * * * *

The two drow set off from the others after nightfall, moving through the shadows with silent ease. They picked their way toward the main orc encampment, dodging guards and smaller camps, and always with Tos'un several steps in the lead. Drizzt followed with Taulmaril in hand, the deadly "enchanted" arrow set on its string—at least, Drizzt hoped he had taken out the same arrow Cordio had played with, or that if he had not, Tos'un hadn't noticed.

As they neared the main group, crossing along the edge of a clearing that was centered by a large tree, Drizzt whispered for Tos'un to stop. Drizzt paused for a few heartbeats, hearing the rhythm of the night. He waved for Tos'un to follow out to the tree. Up Drizzt went, so gracefully that it seemed as if he had walked along a fallen log rather than up a vertical trunk. On the lowest branch, he paused and looked around then turned his attention on Tos'un below.

Drizzt dropped a sword belt, both of Tos'un's weapons sheathed.

You would trust me? the son of House Barrison Del'Armgo signaled up with his fingers, using the intricate silent language of the drow.

Drizzt's answer was simple, and reflected on his impassive expression. *I have nothing to lose. I care nothing for that sword—it destroys more than it helps. You will drop it and your other blade to the ground when you return to the tree, or I will retrieve it from the grasp of the dying orc who took it from you after I put an arrow through your heart.*

Tos'un stared at him long and hard, but had no retort against the simple and straightforward logic. He looked down at the sword belt, at the hilt of Khazid'hea, and truly he was glad to have the sword back in hand.

He disappeared into the darkness a moment later, and Drizzt could only hope that his guess regarding Tos'un's veracity had been correct. For there had been no spell, of course, Cordio's grand exhibition being no more than an elaborate ruse.

*****

Tos'un was truly torn as he crossed the orc lines to the main encampment. Known by the Wolf Jaw orcs sprinkled among the Clan Karuck sentries, he had no trouble moving in, and found Dnark and Ung-thol easily enough.

"I have news," he told the pair.

Dnark and Ung-thol exchanged suspicious looks. "Then speak it," Ung-thol bade him.

"Not here." Tos'un glanced around, as if expecting to find spies behind every rock or tree. "It is too important."

Dnark studied him for a few moments. "Get Toogwik . . ." he started to say to Ung-thol, but Tos'un cut him short.

"No. For Dnark and Ung-thol alone."

"Regarding Obould."

"Perhaps," was all the drow would answer, and he turned and started away. With another look at each other, the two orcs followed him into the night, all the way back to the edge of the field where Drizzt Do'Urden waited in a tree.

"My friends are watching," Tos'un said, loudly enough for Drizzt, with his keen drow senses, to hear.

Drizzt tensed and drew back Taulmaril, wondering if he was about to be revealed.

Tos'un would die first, he decided.

"Your friends are dead," Dnark replied.

"Three are," said Tos'un.

"You have made others. I salute you."

Tos'un shook his head with disgust at the pathetic attempt at sarcasm, wondering why he had ever suffered such creatures to live.

"There is a sizable drow force beneath us," he explained, and the two orcs, predictably, blanched. "Watching us—watching you."

He let that hang there for a few heartbeats, watching the two shift uncomfortably.

"Before she died, Kaer'lic called to them, to Menzoberranzan, my home. There was glory and wealth to be found, she promised them, and that call from a priestess of Lady Lolth could not go unheeded. And so they have come, to watch and to wait, at first. You are advancing toward Obould."

"Ob—*King* Obould," Dnark corrected rather stiffly, "has summoned Chieftain Grguch to his side."

Tos'un wore a knowing grin. "The drow hold no love for Obould," he explained, and indeed, it seemed to Drizzt as if the orc chieftain relaxed a bit at that.

"You go to pay fealty? Or to wage war?"

The two orcs looked at each other again.

"King Obould summoned Clan Karuck, and so we go," Ung-thol said with clear determination.

"Grguch attacked the Moonwood," Tos'un replied. "Grguch attacked Mithral Hall. Without Obould's permission. He will not be pleased."

"Perhaps . . ." Dnark started.

"He will not be pleased at all," Tos'un interrupted. "You know this. It is why you brought Clan Karuck forth from their deep hole."

"Obould has no heart for the fight," Dnark said with a sudden sneer. "He has lost the words of Gruumsh. He would barter and . . ." He stopped and took a deep breath, and Ung-thol picked up the thought.

"Perhaps the presence of Grguch will inspire Obould and remind him of his duty to Gruumsh," the shaman said.

"It will not," said Tos'un. "And so my people watch and wait. If Obould wins, we will travel back to the lower Underdark. If Grguch prevails, perhaps there is cause for us to come forth."

"And if Obould and Grguch join together to sweep the northland?" Dnark asked.

Tos'un laughed at the preposterous statement.

Dnark laughed, too, after a moment.

"Obould has forgotten the will of Gruumsh," Dnark said bluntly. "He sent an emissary to parlay with the dwarves, to beg forgiveness for Grguch's attack."

Tos'un could not hide his surprise.

"An emissary who never arrived, of course," the orc chieftain explained.

"Of course. And so Grguch and Dnark will remind Obould?"

The orc didn't reply.

"You will kill Obould, and replace him with Grguch, for the will of Gruumsh?"

No answer again, but it was apparent from the posture and expressions of the two orcs that the last remark hit closer to the truth.

Tos'un smiled at them and nodded. "We will watch, Chieftain Dnark. And we will wait. And I will take great pleasure in witnessing the death of Obould Many-Arrows. And greater pleasure in taking the head of King Bruenor and crossing the River Surbrin to lay waste to the wider lands beyond."

The drow gave a curt bow and turned away. "We are watching," he warned as he started off. "All of it."

"Listen for the Horn of Karuck," Dnark said. "When you hear it blow, know that King Obould nears the end of his reign."

Tos'un didn't so much as offer a glance up at Drizzt as he crossed the clearing to the far side, but soon after the orcs had headed back to their encampment, the rogue drow returned to the base of the tree.

"Your belt," Drizzt whispered down, but Tos'un was already undoing it. He let it fall to the ground and stepped back.

Drizzt hopped down and retrieved it.

"You might have prepared them to say as much," Drizzt remarked. "Ask the sword."

Drizzt looked down at Khazid'hea skeptically. "It is not to be trusted."

"Then demand of it," said Tos'un.

But Drizzt merely slung the sword belt over his shoulder, motioning for Tos'un to lead the way back to the waiting dwarves.

Whatever Tos'un's position, whether it was out of a change of heart or simple pragmatism, Drizzt had no reason to doubt what he had heard, and one statement in particular kept repeating in his thoughts, the orc's claim that Obould had "sent an emissary to parlay with the dwarves, to beg forgiveness for Grguch's attack."

Obould would not march. For the orc king, the war was at its end. But for many of his subjects, apparently, that was not so pleasing a thought.

CHAPTER

FOR THE GREATER GOOD

28

The scout pointed to a trio of rocky hills in the northwest, a few miles away. "Obould's flag flies atop the centermost," he explained to Grguch, Hakuun, and the others. "He has rallied his clan around him in a formidable defense."

Grguch nodded and stared toward his distant enemy. "How many?"

"Hundreds."

"Not thousands?" the chieftain asked.

"There are thousands south of his position, and thousands north," the scout explained. "They could close before us and shield King Obould."

"Or swing around and trap us," said Hakuun, but in a tone that showed he was not overly concerned—for Jack, answering that particular question through Hakuun's mouth, held little fear of being trapped by orcs.

"If they remain loyal to King Obould," Toogwik Tuk dared interject, and all eyes turned his way. "Many are angry at his decision to halt his march. They have come to know Grguch as a hero."

Dnark started as if to speak, but changed his mind. He had caught Grguch's attention, though, and when the fierce half-orc, half-ogre turned his gaze Dnark's way, Dnark said, "Do we even know that Obould intends to do battle? Or will he just posture and paint with pretty words? Obould rules through wit and muscle. He will see the wisdom of coaxing Grguch."

"To build walls?" the chieftain of Clan Karuck said with a dismissive snicker.

"He will not march!" Toogwik Tuk insisted.

"He will speak enough words of war to create doubt," said Dnark.

"The only word I wish to hear from the coward Obould is 'mercy,'" Grguch stated. "It pleases me to hear a victim beg before he is put to my axe."

Dnark started to respond, but Grguch held up his hand, ending any further debate. With a scowl that promised only war, Grguch nodded to Hakuun, who commanded forth the grotesque zombie of Oktule, still holding its head before it.

"This is our parlay," Grguch said. He swung his gaze out to the side, where the battered Nukkels hung by his ankles from poles suspended across the broad shoulders of a pair of ogres. "And our advanced emissary," Grguch added with a wicked grin.

He took up his dragon-fashioned axe and stalked toward Nukkels, who was too beaten and dazed to even register his approach. Nukkels did see the axe, though, at the last moment, and he gave a pathetic yelp as Grguch swung it across, cleanly severing the rope and dropping Nukkels on his head to the ground.

Grguch reached down and hoisted the shaman to his feet. "Go to Obould," he ordered, turning Nukkels around and shoving him toward the northwest so ferociously that the poor orc went flying headlong to the ground. "Go and tell Obould the Coward to listen for the sound of *Kokto Gung Karuck.*"

Nukkels staggered back to his feet and stumbled along, desperate to be away from the brutal Karuck orcs.

"Tell Obould the Coward that Grguch has come and that Gruumsh is not pleased," Grguch shouted after him, and cheers began to filter through all of the onlookers. "I will accept his surrender . . . perhaps."

That sent the Karuck orcs and ogres into a frenzy, and even Toogwik Tuk beamed in anticipation. Dnark, though, looked at Ung-thol.

This conspiracy had been laid bare, to the ultimate fruition. This was real, suddenly, and this was war.

THE ORC KING

* * * * *

"Grguch comes with many tribes in his wake," Obould said to General Dukka. "To parlay?"

He and Obould's other commanders stood on the centermost of the three rocky hills. The foundations of a small keep lined the ground behind the orc leader, and three low walls of piled stones ringed the hill. The other two hills were similarly outfitted, though the defenses were hardly complete. Obould looked over his shoulder and motioned to his attendants, who brought forth the battered, nearly dead Nukkels.

"He's already spoken, it would seem," the orc king remarked.

"Then it will be war within your kingdom," the general replied, and his doubts were evident for all to hear.

Doubts offered for his benefit, Obould recognized. He didn't blink as he stared at Dukka, though others around him gasped and whispered.

"They are well-supported at their center," Dukka explained. "The battle will be fierce and long."

They are well-supported indeed, Obould thought but did not say.

He offered a slight nod of appreciation to Dukka, for he read easily enough between Dukka's words. The general had just warned him that Grguch's fame had preceded him, and that many in Obould's ranks had grown restless. There was no doubt that Obould commanded the superior forces. He could send orcs ten-to-one against the march of Clan Karuck and its allies. But with the choice laid bare before them, how many of those orcs would carry the banner of Obould, and how many would decide that Grguch was the better choice?

But there was no question among those on the three hills, Obould understood, for there stood Clan Many-Arrows, his people, his slavish disciples, who would follow him into Lady Alustriel's own bedroom if he so commanded.

"How many thousands will die?" he asked Dukka quietly.

"And will not the dwarves come forth when the opportunity is seen?" the general bluntly replied, and again Obould nodded, for he could not disagree.

A part of Obould did want to reach out and throttle Dukka for the assessment and for the lack of complete obedience and loyalty, but he knew in his heart that Dukka was right. If Dukka's force, more than two thousand strong, joined battle on the side of Clan Karuck and her allies, the fight could well shift before first blood was spilled.

Obould and his clan would be overwhelmed in short order.

"Hold my flank from the orcs who are not Karuck," Obould asked of his general. "Let Gruumsh decide which of us, Obould or Grguch, is more worthy to lead the kingdom forward."

"Grguch is strong with Gruumsh, so they say," Dukka warned, and a cloud crossed over Obould's face. But Dukka broke a smile before that cloud could become a full scowl. "You have chosen wisely, and for the good of the Kingdom of Many-Arrows. Grguch is strong with Gruumsh, it is said, but Obould protects the minions of the One-eye."

"Grguch is strong," the orc king said, and he brought his greatsword from its scabbard strapped diagonally across his back. "But Obould is stronger. You will learn."

General Dukka eyed that sword for a long while, recalling the many occasions when he had seen it put to devastating use. Gradually, he began to nod then to grin.

"Your flanks will be secure," he promised his king. "And any fodder prodded before Grguch's clan will be swept clean before they reach the hill. Clan Karuck alone will press the center."

* * * * *

"Ye lost yer wits, ye durned orc-brained, pointy-eared elf!" Bruenor bellowed and stomped the ground in frustration. "I come out here to kill the beast!"

"Tos'un speaks the truth."

"I ain't for trusting drow elfs, exceptin' yerself!"

"Then trust me, for I overheard much of his conversation with the orc conspirators. Obould dispatched an emissary to Mithral Hall to forbid the attack."

"Ye don't know what Tos'un telled them orcs to say afore they got out to ye."

"True enough," Drizzt conceded, "but I suspected that which Tos'un reports long before I ever caught up to him. Obould's pause has run too long."

"He attacked me wall! And the Moonwood. Are ye so quick in forgetting Innovindil?"

The accusation rocked Drizzt back on his heels, and he winced, profoundly stung. For he had not forgotten Innovindil, not at all. He could still hear her sweet voice all around him, coaxing him to explore his innermost thoughts and feelings, coaching him on what it was to be an elf. Innovindil had given to him a great and wondrous gift, and in that gift, Drizzt Do'Urden had found himself, his heart and his course. With her lessons, offered in the purest friendship, Innovindil had solidified the sand beneath Drizzt' Do'Urden's feet, which had been shifting unsteadily for so many years.

He hadn't forgotten Innovindil. He could see her. He could smell her. He could hear her voice and the song of her spirit.

But her demise was not the work of Obould, he was certain. That terrible loss was the consequence of the *absence* of Obould, a prelude to the chaos that would ensue if that new threat, the beast Grguch, assumed command of Obould's vast and savage army.

"What are ye askin' me for, elf?" Bruenor said after the long and uncomfortable pause.

"It wasn't Gauntlgrym."

Bruenor locked his gaze, unblinking.

"But it was beautiful, was it not?" Drizzt asked. "A testament—"

"An abomination," Bruenor interrupted.

"Was it? Would Dagna and Dagnabbit think it so? Would Shoudra?"

"Ye ask me to dishonor them!"

"I ask you to honor them with the most uncommon courage, will and vision. In all the recorded and violent histories of all the races, there are few who could claim such."

Bruenor tightened his grip on his many-notched axe and lifted it before him.

"No one doubts the courage of King Bruenor Battlehammer," Drizzt assured the dwarf. "Any who witnessed your stand against the tide of orcs on the retreat into Mithral Hall places you among the legends of dwarf warriors, and rightly so. But I seek in you the courage *not* to fight."

"Ye're bats, elf, and I knowed ye'd be nothing but trouble when I first laid eyes on ye on the side o' Kelvin's Cairn."

Drizzt drew out Twinkle and Icingdeath and tapped them on either side of Bruenor's axe.

"I'll be watchin' the fight afore us," Bruenor promised. "And when I find me place in it, don't ye be blocking me axe, where'er it's aimed."

Drizzt snapped his scimitars away and bowed before Bruenor. "You are my king. My counsel has been given. My blades are ready."

Bruenor nodded and started to turn away, but stopped abruptly and swiveled his head back at Drizzt, a sly look in his eye. "And if ye send yer durned cat to pin me down, elf, I'll be cooking kitty, don't ye doubt."

Bruenor stomped away and Drizzt looked back at the probable battlefield, where the distant lines of orcs were converging. He pulled the onyx figurine from his belt pouch and summoned Guenhwyvar to his side, confident that the fight would ensue long before the panther began to tire.

Besides, he needed the surety of Guenhwyvar, the nonjudgmental companionship. For as he had asked for courage from Bruenor, so Drizzt had demanded it of himself. He thought of Tarathiel and Shoudra and all the others, dead now because of the march of Obould, dead at Obould's own hand. He thought of Innovindil, always he thought of Innovindil, and of Sunset, and he knew that he would carry that pain with him for the rest of his life. And though he could logically remove that last atrocity from the bloody hands of Obould, would any of it have happened in the Moonwood, in Mithral Hall, in Shallows and Nesmé, and all throughout the Silver Marches, had not Obould come forth with designs of conquest?

And yet, there he was, asking for uncommon courage from Bruenor, betting on Tos'un, and gambling with all the world, it seemed.

He brought his hand down to stroke Guenhwyvar's sleek black coat, and the panther sat down then collapsed onto her belly, her tongue hanging out between her formidable fangs.

"If I am wrong, Guenhwyvar, my friend, and to my ultimate loss, then I ask of you this one thing: dig your claws deep into the flesh of

King Obould of the orcs. Leave him in agony upon the ground, dying of mortal wounds."

Guenhwyvar gave a lazy growl and rolled to her side, calling for a scratching on her ribs.

But Drizzt knew that she had understood every word, and that she, above all others, would not let him down.

CHAPTER 29

DWARVEN KING, DWARVEN ARROW

Shingles and Torgar stood quietly, staring at Bruenor, letting him lead without question, while an eager Pwent hopped around them. Cordio kept his eyes closed, praying to Moradin—and to Clangeddin, for he understood that the road to battle was clear. For Hralien, there showed only grim determination, and beside him, the bound Tos'un matched that intensity. Regis shifted from foot to foot nervously. And Drizzt, who had just delivered the assessment that battle was soon to be joined, and that the time had come for them to either leave or engage, waited patiently.

All focus fell to Bruenor, and the weight of that responsibility showed clearly on the face of the agitated dwarf. He had brought them there, and on his word they would either flee to safety or leap into the jaws of a tremendous battle—a battle they could not hope to win, or likely even survive, but one that they might, if their gods blessed them, influence.

* * * * *

To the south, Obould saw Dukka's force rolling forward like a dark cloud, streaming toward a line of orcs moving west to flank the hills. The clan of the Wolf Jaw, he knew, and he nodded and growled softly, imagining all the horrors he would inflict upon Dnark when his business with Grguch was over.

Confident that General Dukka would keep Wolf Jaw at bay, Obould focused his gaze directly to the east, where rising dust showed the approach of a powerful force, and yellow banners shot with red proclaimed Clan Karuck. The orc king closed his eyes and fell within his thoughts, imagining again his great kingdom, full of walls and castles, and teeming cities of orcs living under the sun and sharing fully in the bounty of the world.

Kna's shriek brought him from his quiet meditation, and as soon as he opened his eyes, Obould understood her distress.

An orc approached, a zombie orc, holding its head plaintively in its hands before it. Before any of his warriors and guards could react, Obould leaped the low wall before him and charged down, drawing his greatsword as he went. A single swing cleaved the zombie in half and sent the head flying.

So it was, the orc king knew as he executed the swing. Grguch had stated his intent and Obould had answered. There was no more to be said.

Not so far to the east, a great horn blared.

* * * * *

From over the very next ridge came the sound of a skirmish, orc against orc.

"Obould and Grguch," Tos'un stated.

In the distance to the northeast, a great horn, *Kokto Gung Karuck*, sounded.

"Grguch," Drizzt agreed.

Bruenor snorted. "I can't be asking any o' ye to come with me," he started.

"Bah, but just ye try to stop us," said Torgar, with Shingles nodding beside him.

"I would travel to the Abyss itself for a try at Obould," Hralien added.

Beside him, Tos'un shook his head.

"Obould's to be found on them hills," Bruenor said, waving his axe in the general direction of the trio of rocky mounds they had determined to be Obould's main encampment. "And I'm meaning to get there. Right through, one charge, like an arrow shot from me girl's bow. I'm not for knowing how many I'll be leavin' in me wake. I'm not for knowin' how I'm getting back out after I kill the dog. And I'm not for caring."

Torgar slapped the long handle of his greataxe across his open palm, and Shingles banged his hammer against his shield.

"We'll get ye there," Torgar promised.

The sounds of battle grew louder, some close and some distant. The great horn blew again, its echoes vibrating the stones beneath their feet.

Bruenor nodded and turned to the next ridge, but hesitated and glanced back, focusing his gaze on Tos'un. "Me elf friend told me that ye done nothing worth killin' ye over," he said. "And Hralien's agreeing. Get ye gone, and don't ye e'er give me a reason to regret me choice."

Tos'un held his hands out wide. "I have no weapons."

"There'll be plenty for ye to find in our wake, but don't ye be following too close," Bruenor replied.

With a helpless look to Drizzt, then to all the others, Tos'un gave a bow and walked back the way they had come. *"Grguch is your nightmare, now,"* he called to Drizzt, in the drow tongue.

"What's that?" Bruenor asked, but Drizzt only smiled and walked over to Hralien.

"I'll be moving fast beside Bruenor," the drow explained, handing Tos'un's weapon belt over. "If any are to escape this, it will be you. Beware this sword. Keep it safe." He glanced over at Regis, clearly nervous. "This will not unravel the way we had intended. Our run will be frantic and furious, and had we known the lay of the land and the orc forces, Bruenor and I would have come out—"

"Alone, of course," finished the elf.

"Keep the sword safe," Drizzt said again, though he looked not at Khazid'hea, but at Regis as he spoke, a message all too clear for Hralien.

"And live to tell our tale," the drow finished, and he and Hralien clasped hands.

"Come on, then!" Bruenor called.

He scraped his boots in the dirt to clear them of mud, and adjusted his one-horned helmet and his foaming mug shield. He started off at a brisk walk, but Thibbledorf Pwent rushed up beside him, and past him, and swept Bruenor up in his eagerness.

They were in full charge before they crested the ridge.

They found the fighting to the west of them, back toward Obould's line, but there were orcs aplenty right below, running eagerly to battle—so eagerly that Pwent had already lowered his head spike before the nearest one turned to regard the intruders.

That orc's scream became a sudden gasp as the helmet spike prodded through its chest, and a lip-flapping head wag from Pwent sent the mortally wounded creature flying aside. The next two braced for the charge, ready to dive aside, but Pwent lifted his head and leaped at them, spiked gauntlets punching every which way.

* * * * *

Drizzt and Bruenor veered to the right, where orc reinforcements rushed past the trees and the stones. Torgar and Shingles ran straight ahead off their wake, following Pwent in his attempt to punch through this thin flank and toward the main engagement, which was still far to the north.

With his long strides, Drizzt moved ahead of Bruenor. He lifted Taulmaril, holding the bow horizontal before his chest, for the orcs were close enough and plentiful enough that he didn't even need to aim. His first shot took one in the chest and blasted it backward and to the ground. His second went through another orc so cleanly that the creature hardly jerked, and Drizzt thought for a moment that he had somehow missed—he even braced for a counter.

But blood poured forth, chest and back, and the creature died where it stood, too fast for it to even realize that it should fall over.

"Bend right!" Bruenor roared, and Drizzt did, sidestepping as the dwarf charged past him, barreling into the next group of orcs, shield bashing and axe flying left, right, and center.

With a single fluid movement, Drizzt shouldered the bow and drew forth his scimitars, and went in right behind Bruenor. Dwarf and drow found themselves outnumbered three to one in short order.

The orcs never had a chance.

THE ORC KING

* * * * *

Regis didn't argue as Hralien pulled him to the side, still well behind the other six and moving from cover to cover.

"Protect me," the elf bade as he put up his longbow and began streaming arrows at the plentiful orcs.

His little mace in hand, Regis was in no position to argue—though he suspected that Drizzt had arranged it for his protection. For Hralien, Regis knew, was the one Drizzt most expected to escape the insanity.

His anger at the drow for pushing him to the side of the fight lasted only the moment it took Regis to view the fury of the engagement. To the right, Pwent spun, punched, butted, kicked, kneed, and elbowed with abandon, knocking orcs aside with every twist and turn.

But they were orcs of Wolf Jaw, warriors all, and not all of the blood on the battlerager was from an orc.

Back-to-back behind him, Torgar and Shingles worked with a precision wrought of years of experience, a harmony of devastating axe-work the pair had perfected in a century of fighting together as part of Mirabar's vaunted watch. Every routine ended with a step—either left or right, it didn't seem to matter—as each dwarf behind moved in perfect complement to keep the defense complete.

"Spear, down!" Torgar yelled.

He ducked, unable to deflect the missile. It flew over his head, apparently to crack through the back of Shingles's skull, but hearing the warning, old Shingles threw his shield up behind his head at the last instant, turning the crude spear aside.

Shingles had to fall away as the orc before him seized the opening.

But of course there was no opening, as Shingles rolled out to the side and Torgar came in behind him with a two-handed slash that disemboweled the surprised creature.

Two orcs took its place and Torgar got stabbed in the upper arm—which only made him madder, of course.

Regis swallowed hard and shook his head, certain that if he'd followed the charge, he'd already have been dead. He nearly fainted as he saw an orc, stone axe high for a killing blow, close in on Shingles, an angle that neither dwarf could possibly block.

But the orc fell away, an arrow deep in its throat.

That startled Regis from his shock, and he looked up to Hralien, who had already set another arrow and swiveled back the other way.

For there Bruenor and Drizzt worked their magic, as only they could. Drizzt's scimitars spun in a blur, too quick for Regis to follow their movements, which he measured instead by the angles of the orcs falling away from the furious drow. What Bruenor couldn't match in finesse, he made up for with sheer ferocity, and it occurred to Regis that if Thibbledorf Pwent and Drizzt Do'Urden collided with enough force to meld them into a single warrior, the result would be Bruenor Battlehammer.

The dwarf sang as he cut, kicked, and bashed. Unlike the other trio, who seemed stuck in a morass and tangle of orcs, Drizzt and Bruenor kept moving across and to the north, chopping and slashing and dancing away. At one point, a group of orcs formed in their path, and it seemed as if they would be stopped.

But Hralien's arrows broke the integrity of the orc line, and a flying black panther crashed into the surprised creatures, scattering them and sending them flying.

Drizzt and Bruenor ran by, breaking clear of the conflict.

At first, that thought panicked Regis. Shouldn't the two turn back to help Pwent and the others? And shouldn't he and Hralien hurry to keep up?

He looked at the elf and realized it wasn't about them, any of them. It was about Bruenor getting to Obould, about Bruenor killing Obould.

Whatever the cost.

* * * * *

Cordio wanted to keep up with Bruenor, to protect his beloved king at all costs, but the priest could not pace the fiery dwarf and his drow companion, and once he noted the harmony of their movements, attacks and charges, he recognized that he would likely only get in their way.

He turned for the dwarf trio instead, angling to get into the melee near to Torgar, whose right arm drooped low from a nasty stab.

Still fighting fiercely, the Mirabarran dwarf nevertheless grunted his approval as Cordio reached toward him, sending waves of magical healing energy into him. When Torgar turned to note his appreciation more directly, he saw that Cordio's help hadn't come without cost, for the priest had sacrificed his own position against one particularly large and nasty orc for the opportunity to help Torgar. Cordio bent low under the weight of a rain of blows against his fine shield.

"Pwent!" Torgar roared, motioning for the priest as the battlerager turned his way.

"For Moradin!" came Pwent's roar and he disengaged from the pair he was battering and charged headlong for Cordio.

The two orcs gave close chase, but Torgar and Shingles intercepted and drove them aside.

By the time Pwent reached Cordio, the priest was back to an even stance against the orc. No novice to battle, Cordio Muffinhead had covered himself with defensive enchantments and had brought the strength of his gods into his arms, swinging his flail with powerful strokes.

That didn't slow Pwent, of course, who rushed past the startled priest and leaped at the orc.

The orc's sword screeched against Pwent's wondrous armor, but it hardly bit through before Pwent slammed against the orc and began to thrash, the ridges on his plate mail tearing apart the orc's leather jerkin and slicing into its flesh beneath. With a howl of pain, the orc tried to disengage, but a sudden left and right hook from Pwent's spiked gauntlets held it in place like harvest corn.

Cordio used the opportunity to cast some healing magic into the battlerager, though he knew that Pwent wouldn't feel any difference. Pwent didn't really seem to feel pain.

* * * * *

The back of the small clearing dipped even lower, down into a dell full of boulders and a few scraggly tree skeletons. Drizzt and Bruenor rushed through, leaving their fighting companions behind, and with his longer strides, Drizzt took the lead.

Their goal was to avoid battle while they closed the ground to the trio of rocky hills and King Obould. As they came up the far side of the dell, they saw the orc king, picking him out from the flames engulfing his magical greatsword.

An ogre tumbled away from him then he shifted back and stabbed up over his shoulder, skewering another ten-foot behemoth. With strength beyond all reason, Obould used his sword to pull that ogre right over his shoulder and send it spinning down the side of the hillock.

All around him the battle raged, as Clan Karuck and Clan Many-Arrows fought for supremacy.

And in truth, with Obould and his minions holding the high ground, it didn't seem as if it would be much of a fight.

But then a fireball exploded, intense and powerful, right behind the highest wall on the hill to Obould's left, the northernmost of the three, and all of the Many-Arrows archers concealed there flailed about, immolated by the magical flames. They shrieked and they died, curling up on the ground in blackened, smoking husks.

Clan Karuck warriors swarmed over the stones.

"What in the Nine Hells...?" Bruenor asked Drizzt. "Since when are them orcs throwing fireballs?"

Drizzt had no answer, other than to reinforce his feelings about the entire situation, simply by stating, "Grguch."

"Bah!" Bruenor snorted, so predictably, and the pair ran on.

* * * * *

"Keep to the high ground," Hralien instructed Regis as he led the halfling along to the east. They pulled up amidst a boulder tumble, beside a single maple tree, Hralien sighting targets and lifting his bow.

"We have to go and join them!" Regis cried, for the four dwarves moved out of sight over the near ridge of the dell.

"No time!"

Regis wanted to argue, but the frantic hum of Hralien's bowstring, the elf firing off arrow after arrow, denied him his voice. More orcs swarmed along before them from the east, and a darker cloud had formed in the west as a vast army began its approach.

Regis cast a plaintive gaze to the north, where Drizzt and Bruenor had gone, where Cordio, Pwent, and the others had run. He believed that he would never see his friends again. Drizzt had done it, he knew. Drizzt had put him with Hralien, knowing that the

THE ORC KING

elf would likely find a way out, where there could be no retreat for Drizzt and Bruenor.

Bitterness filled the back of Regis's throat. He felt betrayed and abandoned. In the end, when the circumstances had grown darkest, he had been set aside. Logically he could understand it all—he was, after all, no hero. He couldn't fight like Bruenor, Drizzt, and Pwent. And with so many orcs around, there really wasn't any way for him to hide and strike from points of opportunity.

But that did little to calm the sting.

He nearly jumped out of his boots when a form rose up beside him, an orc springing from concealment. Purely on instinct, Regis squealed and shouldered the thing, knocking it off-balance just enough so that its stab at Hralien only grazed the distracted archer.

Hralien turned fast, smashing his bow across the orc's face. The bow flew free as the orc tumbled, Hralien going for his sword.

Regis lifted his mace to finish the orc first, except that as he retracted his arm for the strike, something grabbed him and yanked that arm back viciously. He felt his shoulder pop out of joint. His hand went numb as his mace fell away. He managed to half turn then to duck, bringing his other arm up over his head defensively as he noted the descent of a stone hammer.

A blinding explosion spread over the back of his head, and he had no idea of whether his legs had buckled or simply been driven straight into the ground as he fell face-down in the stony dirt. He felt a soft boot come in tight against his ear and heard Hralien battling above him.

He tried to put his hands under him, but one arm would not move to his call, and the attempt sent waves of nauseating agony through him. He managed to lift his head, just a bit, and tasted the blood streaming down from the back of his skull as he half-turned to try to get his bearings.

He was back on the ground again, though he knew not how. Cold fingers reached up at him, as if from the ground itself. He had his eyes open, but the darkness crept in from the edges.

The last thing he heard was his own ragged breathing.

* * * * *

Orc armor proved no match for the fine elven sword as Hralien slid the blade deep into the chest of the newest attacker, who held a stone hammer wet with Regis's blood.

The elf slashed out to the side, finishing the first one, who stubbornly tried to regain its footing, then spun to meet the charge of a third creature coming in around the tree. His sword flashed across, turning the orc's spear in against the bark and knocking the creature off balance. The tree alone stopped it from falling aside, but that proved an unfortunate thing for the orc, as Hralien leaped out to the side and stabbed back in, catching the creature through the armpit.

It shrieked and went into a frenzy, spinning and stumbling away, grabbing at the vicious wound.

Hralien let it go, turning back to Regis, who lay so very still on the cold ground. More orcs had spotted him, he knew. He had no time. He grabbed the halfling as gently as he could and slid him down into a depression at the base of the maple, between two large roots. He kicked dirt and twigs and leaves, anything he could find to disguise the poor halfling. Then, for the sake of the fallen Regis, Hralien grabbed up his bow and sprang away, running again to the east.

Orcs closed on him from behind and below. More rose up before him, running at an angle to prevent him from going over the ridge to the south.

Hralien dropped his second sword belt, the one Drizzt had given him, and threw aside his bow, needing to be nimble.

He charged ahead, desperate to put as much ground between himself and Regis as possible, in the faint hope that the orcs would not find the wounded halfling. The run lasted only a few strides, though, as Hralien skidded to a stop, turning frantically to bring his sword around to deflect a flying spear. Swords came in at him from every angle, orcs closing for the kill. Hralien felt the hot blood of his elders coursing through his veins. All the lessons he had learned in two centuries of life flooded through him, driving him on. There was no thought, only instinct and reaction, his shining sword darting to block, angling to turn a spear and stabbing ahead to force an attacker into a short retreat.

Beautiful was his dance, magnificent his turns, and lightning-quick his thrusts and ripostes.

But there were too many—too many for him to even consider them separately as he tried to find some answer to the riddle of the battle.

Images of Innovindil flitted through his mind, along with those others he had lost so recently. He took hope in the fact that they had gone before him, that they would greet him in Arvandor when a single missed block let a sword or a spear slip through.

Behind him, back the way he had come, Regis sank deeper into the cold darkness. And not so far away, perhaps halfway to the tree, a black hand closed over Khazid'hea's hilt.

* * * * *

They had intended to follow in the wake of Bruenor and Drizzt, but the four dwarves found the route blocked by a wall of orcs. They came out of the dell to the east instead, and there, too, they met resistance.

"For Mirabar and Mithral Hall!" Torgar Hammerstriker called, and shoulder to shoulder with his beloved and longtime friend Shingles, the leader of the Mirabarran exodus met the orcs.

To the side of them, Thibbledorf Pwent snarled and bit and found within himself yet another frenzy. Flailing his arms and legs, and butting his head so often that his forward movements seemed the steps of a gawky, long-necked seabird, Pwent had the orcs on that side of the line in complete disarray. They threw spears at him, but so intent were they on getting out of his way that they threw as they turned, and thus with little or no effect.

It couldn't hold, though. Too many orcs stood before them, and they would have to pile the orc bodies as thick as the walls of a dwarf-built keep before they could even hope to find a way through.

Bruenor and Drizzt were lost to them, as was any route that would get them back to the south and the safety of Mithral Hall. So they did what dwarves do best, they fought to gain the highest ground.

Cordio wanted to tap some offensive magic, to stun the orcs with a blast of shocking air, perhaps, or to hold a group in place so that Torgar and Shingles could score quick kills. But blood flowed freely from all the dwarves in short order, and the priest could not keep up with the wounds, though his every spell cast was one of healing. Cordio was filled with Moradin's blessing, a priest of extraordinary power and piety. It occurred to him, though, that Moradin himself was not possessed of enough magical healing to win that fight. They were known, the clear spectacle of the most-hated enemy in the midst of the orcs, and behind the immediate fighting, the ugly creatures stalked all around them, preparing to overwhelm them.

Not a dwarf was afraid, though. They sang to Moradin and Clangeddin and Dumathoin. They sang of bar wenches and heavy mugs of ale, of killing orcs and giants, of chasing dwarf ladies.

And Cordio led a song to King Bruenor, of the fall of Shimmergloom and the reclamation of Mithral Hall.

They sang and they fought. They killed and they bled, and they looked continually to the north, where Bruenor their king had gone.

For all that mattered was that they had served him well that day, that they had given him enough time and enough of a distraction to get to the hills and to end, once and for all, the threat of Obould.

* * * * *

Hralien felt the sting of a sword across his forearm, and though the wound was not deep, it was telling. He was slowing, and the orcs had caught on to the rhythms of his dance.

He had nowhere to run.

An orc to his right came on suddenly, he thought, and he spun to meet the charge—then saw that it was no charge at all, for the tip of a sword protruded from the falling creature's chest.

Behind the orc, Tos'un Armgo retracted Khazid'hea and leaped out to the side. An orc lifted its shield to block, but the sword went right through the shield, right through the arm, and right through the side of the creature's chest.

Before it had even fallen away, another orc fell to Tos'un's second weapon, an orc-made sword.

Hralien had no time to watch the spectacle or to even consider the insanity of it all. He spun back and took down the nearest orc, who seemed dumbfounded by the arrival of the drow. On the elves pressed, light and dark, and orcs fell away, or threw their weapons and ran away, and soon the pair faced off, Hralien drawing a few much-needed deep breaths.

"Clan Wolf Jaw," Tos'un explained to Hralien. "They fear me."

"With good reason," Hralien replied.

The sound of battle to the north, and the sound of dwarf voices lifted in song, stole their conversation, and before Tos'un could begin to clarify, he found that he did not have to, for Hralien led their run down from the ridgeline.

CHAPTER
OLD AND NEW BEFORE HIM
30

It had to come down to the two of them, for among the orcs, struggles within and among tribes were ultimately personal.

King Obould leaped atop a stone wall and plunged his sword into the belly of a Karuck ogre. He stared the behemoth in the face, grinning wickedly as he called upon his enchanted sword to burst into flame.

The ogre tried to scream. Its mouth stretched wide in silent horror.

Obould only smiled wider and held his sword perfectly still, not wanting to hurry the death of the ogre. Gradually, the dimwitted behemoth leaned back, back, then slid off the blade, tumbling down the hill, wisps of smoke coming from the already cauterized wound.

Looking past it, Obould saw one of his guards, an elite Many-Arrows warrior, go flying aside, broken and torn. Tracing its flight back to the source, he saw another of his warriors, a young orc who had shown great promise in the battles with the Battlehammer dwarves, leap back. The warrior stood still for a curiously long time, his arms out wide.

Obould stared at his back, shaking his head, not understanding, until a huge axe swept up from in front of the warrior, then cut down diagonally with tremendous, jolting force, cleaving the warrior in half, left shoulder to right hip. Half the orc fell away, but the other half stood there for a few long heartbeats before buckling to the ground.

And there stood Grguch, swinging his awful axe easily at the end of one arm.

Their eyes met, and all the other orcs and ogres nearby, Karuck and Many-Arrows alike, took their battles to the side.

Obould stretched his arms out wide, fires leaping from the blade of his greatsword as he held it aloft in his right hand. He threw back his head and bellowed.

Grguch did likewise, axe out wide, his roar echoing across the stones, the challenge accepted. Up the hill he ran, hoisting his axe in both hands and bringing it back over his left shoulder.

Obould tried for the quick kill, feigning a defensive posture, but then leaping down at the approaching chieftain and stabbing straight ahead. Across came Grguch's axe with brutal and sudden efficiency, the half-ogre chopping short to smash his dragon-winged weapon against Obould's blade. He turned it sidelong as he swiped, the winged blades perpendicular to the ground, but so strong was the beast that the resistance as he brought the axe across didn't slow his swing in the least. By doing it that way, his blade obscuring nearly three feet top-to-bottom, Grguch prevented Obould from turning his greatsword over the block.

Obould just let his sword get knocked out to his left, and instead of letting go with his right hand, as would be expected, the cunning orc let go with his left, allowing him to spin in behind the cut of Grguch's axe. He went forward as he went around, lowering his soon-leading left shoulder as he collided with Grguch.

The pair slid down the stony hill, and to Obould's amazement, Grguch did not fall. Grguch met his heavy charge with equal strength.

He was taller than Obould by several inches, but Obould had been blessed by Gruumsh, had been given the strength of the bull, a might of arm that had allowed him to bowl over Gerti Orelsdottr of the frost giants.

But not Grguch.

The two struggled, their weapon arms, Obould's right and Grguch's left, locked at one side. Obould slugged Grguch hard in the face, snapping his head back, but as he recoiled from that stinging blow, Grguch snapped his head forward, inside the next punch, and crunched his forehead into Obould's nose.

They clutched, they twisted, and they postured, and both tried to shove back at the same time, sending themselves skidding far apart.

Right back they went with identical blows, axe and sword meeting with tremendous force, so powerfully that a gout of flames flew free of Obould's sword and burst into the air.

* * * * *

"As Tos'un told us," Drizzt said to Bruenor as they slipped between fights to come in view of the great struggle.

"Think they'd forget each other and turn on us, elf?" Bruenor asked hopefully.

"Likely not—not Obould, at least," Drizzt replied dryly, stealing Bruenor's mirth, and he led the dwarf around a pile of stones that hadn't yet been set on the walls.

"Bah! Ye're bats!"

"Two futures clear before us," Drizzt remarked. "What does Moradin say to Bruenor?"

Before Bruenor could answer, as Drizzt came around the pile, a pair of orcs leaped at him. He snapped up both his blades and threw himself backward, quickstepping across Bruenor's field of vision and dragging the bloodthirsty orcs with him.

The dwarf's axe came crashing down, and then there was one.

And that orc twisted and half-turned, startled by Bruenor and never imagining that Drizzt could be nimble enough to reverse his field so quickly.

The orc got hit four times by Drizzt's scimitars, and Bruenor creased its skull for good measure, and the pair rambled along.

Before them, much closer, Obould and Grguch clutched again, and traded a series of brutal punches that splattered blood from both faces.

"Two roads before us," Drizzt said, and he looked at Bruenor earnestly.

The dwarf shrugged then tapped his axe against Drizzt's scimitars. "For the good o' the world, elf," he said. "For the kids o' me kin and me trust for me friends. And ye're still bats."

* * * * *

Every swing brought enough force to score a kill, every cut cracked through the air. They were orcs, one half ogre, but they fought as giants, titans even, gods among their respective people.

Bred for battle, trained in battle, hardened as his skin had calloused, and propped by magical spells from Hakuun, and secretly from Jack the Gnome, Grguch moved his heavy axe with the speed and precision with which a Calimport assassin might wield a dagger. None in Clan Karuck, not the largest and the strongest, questioned Grguch's leadership role, for none in that clan would dare oppose him. With good reason, Obould understood all too quickly, as the chieftain pressed him ferociously.

Blessed by Gruumsh, infused with the strength of a chosen being, and veteran of so many battles, Obould equaled his opponent, muscle for muscle. And unlike so many power-driven warriors who could smash a weapon right through an opponent's defenses, Obould combined finesse and speed with that sheer strength. He had matched blades with Drizzt Do'Urden, and overmatched Wulfgar with brawn. And so he met Grguch's heavy strikes with powerful blocks, and so he similarly pressed Grguch with mighty counterstrikes that made the chieftain's arms strain to hold back the deadly greatsword.

Grguch rushed around to Obould's left, up the hill a short expanse. He turned back from that higher ground and drove a tremendous overhand chop down at the orc king, and Obould nearly buckled under the weight of the blow, his feet sliding back dangerously beneath him.

Grguch struck again, and a third time, but Obould went out to the side suddenly, and that third chop cut nothing but air, forcing Grguch down the hill a few quick steps.

They stood even again, and with the miss, Obould gained an offensive posture. Both hands grasping his sword, he smashed it in from the right then the left then right again. Grguch moved to a solely defensive posture, axe darting left and right to block.

Obould quickened the pace, slashing with abandon, allowing Grguch no chance for a counter. He brought forth fire on his blade then winked it out with a thought—and brought it forth again, just to command more of his opponent's attention, to further occupy Grguch.

Left and right came the greatsword, then three overhead chops, battering Grguch's blocking blade, sending shivers through the chieftain's muscled arms. Obould did not tire, and more furious came his strikes, backing his opponent.

Grguch was no longer looking for an opening to counter, Obould knew. Grguch tried only to find a way to disengage, to put them back on even ground.

Obould wouldn't give it to him. The chieftain was worthy, indeed, but in the end, he was no Obould.

A blinding flash and a thunderous retort broke the orc king's momentum and rhythm, and as he recovered from the initial, stunning shock of it, he realized that he had lost more than advantage. His legs twitched and could hardly hold him upright. His greatsword trembled violently and his teeth chattered so uncontrollably that he tore strips of skin from the inside of his mouth.

A wizard's lightning bolt, he understood somewhere deep in the recesses of his dazed mind, and a mighty one.

His block of Grguch's next attack was purely coincidental, his greatsword fortunately in the way of the swing. Or maybe Grguch had aimed for the weapon, Obould realized as he staggered back from the weight of the blow, fighting to hold his balance with every stumbling, disoriented step.

He offered a better attempt to block the next sidelong swing, turning to the left and presenting his sword at a perfect angle to intercept the flying axe.

A perfect parry, except that Obould's twitching legs gave out under the weight of the blow. He skidded half-backward and half-sidelong down the hill and went down to one knee.

Grguch hit his sword again, knocking it aside, and as the chieftain stepped forward, bringing his blade back yet again, Obould realized that he had little defense.

A booted foot stomped hard on the back of Obould's neck, driving him low, and he tried to turn and lash out at what he deemed to be a new attacker.

But Bruenor Battlehammer's target was not Obould, and he had used the battered and dazed orc king merely as a springboard to launch himself at his real quarry.

Grguch twisted frantically to get his axe in line with the dwarf's weapon, but Bruenor, too, turned as he flew, and his buckler, emblazoned with the foaming mug of Clan Battlehammer, crashed hard into Grguch's face, knocking him back.

Grguch leaped up and came right back at Bruenor with a mighty chop, but Bruenor rushed ahead under the blow, butting his one-horned helmet into Grguch's belly and sweeping his axe up between the orc chieftain's legs. Grguch leaped, and Bruenor grabbed and leaped back and over with him, the pair flying away and tumbling down the hill. As they unwound, Grguch, caught with his back to the dwarf, rushed away and shoulder-rolled over the hill's lowest stone wall.

Bruenor pursued furiously, springing atop the wall, then leaping from it, swooping down from on high with a mighty chop that sent the blocking Grguch staggering backward.

The dwarf pressed, axe and shield, and it took Grguch many steps before he could begin to attain even footing with his newest enemy.

Back on the hill, Obould stubbornly gained his feet and tried to follow, but another crackling lightning bolt flattened him.

* * * * *

Hralien darted out in front as the pair crossed the narrow channel. He leaped a stone, started right, then rolled back left around the trunk of a dead tree, coming around face up against an unfortunate orc, whose sword was still angled the other way to intercept his charge. The elf struck hard and true, and the orc fell away, mortally wounded.

Hralien retracted the blade as he ran past the falling creature, which left his sword arm out behind him.

As his sword pulled free, a sudden sting broke the elf's grasp on it, and he glanced back in shock to see Tos'un flipping the blade over between his two swords. With amazing dexterity, the drow slid his own sword into its sheath and caught Hralien's flipping weapon by the hilt.

"Treacherous dog!" Hralien protested as the dark elf moved in behind him, prodding him along.

"Just shut up and run," Tos'un scolded him.

Hralien stopped, though, and the tip of Khazid'hea nicked him. Tos'un's hand came against his back then, and shoved him roughly forward.

"Run!" he demanded.

Hralien stumbled forward and Tos'un didn't let him dig in, keeping up and pushing him along with every stride.

* * * * *

Drizzt hated breaking away from Bruenor with both the orc leaders so close, but the magic-using orc, nestled in a mixed copse of evergreen and deciduous trees to the east of Obould's defenses, demanded his attention. Having lived and fought beside the wizards of the drow school Sorcere, who were skilled in the tactics of wizardry combined with sword-fighters, Drizzt understood the danger of those thunderous, blinding lightning bolts.

And there was something more, some nagging suspicion in Drizzt's thoughts. How had the orcs taken Innovindil and Sunset from the sky? That puzzle had nagged at Drizzt since Hralien had delivered the news of their fall. Did he have his answer?

The wizard wasn't alone, for he had set other orcs, large Karuck half-ogre orcs, around the perimeter of the copse. One of them confronted Drizzt as he reached the tree line, leaping forward with a growl and a thrusting spear.

But Drizzt had no time for such nonsense, and he shifted, throwing himself to the left, and brought both of his scimitars down and back to the right, double-striking the spear and driving it harmlessly aside. Drizzt continued right past the off-balance spear-wielder, lifting Twinkle expertly to slash a line across the orc's throat.

As that one fell away, though, two more charged at the drow, from left and right, and the commotion also drew the attention of the wizard, still some thirty feet away.

Drizzt pasted an expression of fear on his face, for the benefit of the wizard, then darted out to the right, quick-stepping to intercept the charging orc. He turned as they came together, rolling right around and to the left, tilting his shoulders out of horizontal as he turned so that his sweeping blades lifted the orc's sword up high.

Drizzt sprinted right for the trunk of a nearby tree, both orcs closing. He ran up it and leaped off, threw his head and shoulders back, and tucked into a tight somersault. He landed lightly, exploding into a barrage of whirling blades, and one orc fell away, the other running off to the side.

Drizzt came out from behind the tree as he pursued, to see the orc wizard waggling his fingers in spellcasting, aiming his way.

It was exactly as Drizzt had planned, for the surprise on the wizard orc's face was both genuine and delicious as Guenhwyvar crashed in from the side, bearing the creature to the ground.

* * * * *

"For the lives of your dwarven friends," Tos'un explained, pushing the stubborn elf forward. The surprising words diminished Hralien's resistance, and he did not fight against the shift when the flat of Tos'un's blade turned him, angling him more directly to the east.

"The Wolf Jaw standard," Tos'un explained to the elf. "Chieftain Dnark and his priest."

"But the dwarves are in trouble!" Hralien protested, for not far away, Pwent and Torgar and the others fought furiously against an orc force thrice their number.

"To the head of the serpent!" Tos'un insisted, and Hralien could not disagree.

He began to understand as they passed several orcs, who glanced at the dark elf deferentially and did not try to intercept them.

They sprinted around some boulders and broken ground, down past a cluster of thick pines and across a short expanse to the heart of Dnark's army. Tos'un spotted the chieftain immediately, Toogwik Tuk and Ung-thol at his side as expected.

"A present for Dnark," the drow called at the stunned expressions, and he pushed Hralien harder, nearly toppling the elf.

Dnark waved some guards toward Hralien to take the elf from Tos'un.

"General Dukka and his thousands approach," Dnark called to the drow. "But we will not fight until it is settled between the chieftains."

"Obould and Grguch," Tos'un agreed, and as the orc guards approached, he went past Hralien.

"Left hip," the dark elf whispered as he crossed past Hralien, and he brushed close enough for the surface elf to feel the hilt of his own belted sword.

Tos'un paused and nodded at both the orcs, drawing their attention and giving Hralien ample time to draw forth the blade. And so Hralien did, and even as the orc guards noted it and called out in protest, the flash of elven steel left them dead.

Tos'un stumbled away from Hralien, stumbled toward Dnark's group, looking back and scrambling as if fleeing the murderous elf. He turned fully as he put his feet under him, and saw that Toogwik Tuk had begun spellcasting, with Dnark directing other orcs toward Hralien.

"Back to the elf and finish him!" Dnark protested as Tos'un continued his flight. "Dukka is coming and we must prepare . . ."

But Dnark's voice trailed off as he finished, as he came to realize that Tos'un, that treacherous drow, wasn't running away from the elf, but was, in fact, charging at him.

Standing at Dnark's left, Toogwik Tuk gasped as Khazid'hea rudely interrupted his spellcasting, biting deep into his chest. To Chieftain Dnark's credit, he managed to get his shield up to block Tos'un's other blade as it came in at him. He couldn't anticipate the power of Khazid'hea, though, for instead of yanking the blade out of Toogwik Tuk's chest, Tos'un just drove it across, the impossibly fine edge of the sword known as Cutter slicing through bone and muscle as easily as if it were parting water. The blade came across just under Dnark's shoulder, and before the chieftain even realized the attack enough to spin away, his left arm was taken, falling free to the ground.

Dnark howled and dropped his weapon, reaching across to grab at the blood spurting from his stumped shoulder. He fell back and to the ground, thrashing and roaring empty threats.

But Tos'un wasn't even listening, turning to strike at the nearest orcs. Not Ung-thol, though, for the shaman ran away, taking a large portion of Dnark's elite group with him.

"The dwarves!" Hralien called to the drow, and Tos'un followed the Moonwood elf. He forced back his nearest attackers with a blinding, stabbing routine, then angled away, turning back toward Hralien, who had already swung around in full charge toward the dell in the west.

* * * * *

Bruenor rolled his shield forward, picking off a swing, then advanced, turning his shoulders and rolling his axe at the dodging Grguch. He swung his shield arm up to deflect the next attack, and swiped his axe across underneath it, forcing Grguch to suck in his gut and throw back his hips.

On came the dwarf, pounding away with his shield, slashing wildly with his axe. He had the much larger half-ogre off balance, and knew from the craftsmanship and sheer size of Grguch's axe that he would do well to keep it that way!

The song of Moradin poured from his lips. He swung across and reversed in a mighty backhand, nearly scoring a hit, then charged forward, shield leading. That is why he had been returned to his people, Bruenor knew in his heart. That was the moment when Moradin needed him, when Clan Battlehammer needed him.

He threw out the confusion of the lost city and its riddles, of Drizzt's surprising guesses. None of that mattered—it was he and that newest, fiercest foe, battling to the death, old enemies locked in mortal combat. It was the way of Moradin and the way of Gruumsh, or at least, it was the way it had always been.

Light steps propelled the dwarf, spinning, advancing and retreating out of every swing and every block with perfect balance, using his speed to keep his larger, stronger foe slightly off balance.

Every time Grguch tried to wind up for a mighty stroke of that magnificent axe, Bruenor moved out of range, or came in too close, or too far to the same side as the retracted weapon, shortening Grguch's strike and stealing much of its power.

And always Bruenor's axe slashed at the orc. Always, the dwarf had Grguch twisting and dodging, and cursing.

Like sweet music to Bruenor's ears did those orc curses sound.

In utter frustration, Grguch leaped back and roared in protest, bringing his axe up high. Bruenor knew better than to pursue, dropping one foot back instead, then rushing back and to the side, under the branch of a leafless maple.

Grguch, too outraged by the frustrating dwarf to hold back, rushed forward and swung with all his might anyway—and the dragon-axe crashed right through that thick limb, splintering its base and driving it back at the dwarf. Bruenor threw up his shield at the last second, but the weight of the limb sent him staggering backward.

THE ORC KING

By the time he recovered, Grguch was there, roaring still, his axe cutting a line for Bruenor's skull.

Bruenor ducked and threw up his shield, and the axe hit it solidly—too solidly! The foaming mug shield, that most recognizable of Mithral Hall's artifacts, split in half, and below it, the bone in Bruenor's arm cracked, the weight of the blow driving the dwarf to his knees.

Agony burned through Bruenor's body, and white flashes filled his vision.

But Moradin was on his lips, and Moradin was in his heart, and he scrambled forward, slashing his axe with all his might, forcing Grguch before him in his frenzy.

* * * * *

Pwent, Torgar, and Shingles formed a triangle around Cordio. The priest directed their movements, mostly coordinating Shingles and Torgar with the wild leaps and surges of the unbridled fury that was Thibbledorf Pwent. Pwent had never viewed battle in terms of defensive formations. To his credit, though, the wild-eyed battlerager did not completely compromise the integrity of their defensive stand, and the bodies of dead orcs began to pile up around them.

But more took the places of the fallen—many more, an endless stream. As weapon arms drooped from simple weariness, the three frontline dwarves took more and more hits, and Cordio's spells of healing came nearly constant from his lips, depleting his magical energies.

They couldn't keep it up for much longer, all three knew, and even Pwent suspected that it would be their last, glorious stand.

The orc immediately before Torgar rushed forward suddenly. The Mirabarran dwarf turned the long handle of his axe at the last moment to deflect the creature aside, and only when it started to fall away did Torgar recognize that it was already mortally wounded, blood pouring from a deep wound in its back.

As the dwarf turned to face any other nearby orcs, he saw the way before him cleared of enemies, saw Hralien and Tos'un fighting side by side. They backed as Torgar shifted to his right, moving beside Shingles, and the defensive triangle became two, two and one, and with an apparent escape route open to the east. Hralien and Tos'un started that flight, Cordio bringing the others in behind.

But they became bogged down before they had ever really started, as more and more orcs joined the fray—orcs thirsty for vengeance for their fallen chieftain, and orcs simply thirsty for the taste of dwarf and elf blood.

* * * * *

The panther's claws raked the fallen orc's body, but Jack's wards held strong and Guenhwyvar did little real damage. Even as Guenhwyvar thrashed, Hakuun began to mouth the words of a spell as Jack took control.

Guenhwyvar understood well the power of wizards and priests, though, and the panther clamped her jaws over the orc's face, pressing and twisting. Still the wizard's defensive wards held, diminishing the effect. But Hakuun began to feel the pain, and knowing that the magical shields were being torn asunder, the orc panicked.

That mattered little to Jack, safe within Hakuun's head. Wise old Jack was worldly enough to recognize Guenhwyvar for what she was. In the shelter of Hakuun's thick skull, Jack calmly went about his task. He reached into the Weave of magical energy, found the nearby loose ends of enchanting emanations, and tied them together, filling the area with countering magical force.

Hakuun screamed as panther claws tore through his leather tunic and raked lines of blood along his shoulder. The cat retracted her huge maw, opened wide and snapped back at his face, and Hakuun screamed louder, certain that the wards were gone and that the panther would crush his skull to dust.

But that head dissipated as the panther bit down, and gray mist replaced the dispelled Guenhwyvar.

Hakuun lay there, trembling. He felt some of the magical wards being renewed about his disheveled frame.

Get up, you idiot! Jack screamed in his thoughts.

The orc shaman rolled to his side and up to one knee. He struggled to stand then stumbled away and back to the ground as a shower of sparks exploded beside him, a heavy punch knocking him backward.

He collected his wits and looked back in surprise to see the drow lifting a bow his way.

A second lightning-arrow streaked in, exploding, throwing him backward. But inside of Hakuun, Jack was already casting, and while the shaman struggled, one of his hands reached out, answering the drow's third shot with a bolt of white-hot lightning.

When his blindness cleared, Hakuun saw that his enemy was gone. Destroyed to a smoking husk, he hoped, but only briefly, as another arrow came in at him from a different angle.

Again Jack answered with a blast of his own, followed by a series of stinging magical missiles that weaved through the trees to strike at the drow.

Dual voices invaded Hakuun's head, as Jack prepared another evocation and Hakuun cast a spell of healing upon himself. He had just finished mending the panther's fleshy tear when the stubborn drow hit him with another arrow.

He felt the magical wards flicker dangerously.

"Kill him!" Hakuun begged Jack, for he understood that one of those deadly arrows, maybe the very next one, was going to get through.

* * * * *

They had fought minor skirmishes, as anticipated, but nothing more, as word arrived along the line that Grguch and Obould had met in battle. Never one to play his hand fully, General Dukka moved his forces deliberately and with minimal risk. However things turned out, he intended to remain in power.

The Wolf Jaw orcs gave ground to Dukka's thousands, rolling down the channel on Obould's southern flank like floodwaters.

Always ready for a fight, Dukka stayed near the front, and so he was not far away when he heard a cry from the south, along the higher ridge, and when he heard the sound of battle to the northeast, and to the north, where he knew Obould to be. Lightning flashes filled the air up there, and Dukka could only imagine the carnage.

* * * * *

His arm ached and hung practically useless, and Bruenor understood that if he lost his momentum, he would meet a quick and unpleasant end. So he didn't relent. He drove on and on, slashing away with his many-notched axe, driving the oversized orc before him.

The orc could hardly keep up, and Bruenor scored minor hits, clipping him across one hand and nicking his thigh as he spun away.

The dwarf could win. He knew he could.

But the orc began calling out, and Bruenor understood enough Orcish to understand that he called for help. Not just orc help, either, the dwarf saw, as a pair of ogres moved over at the side of his vision, lifting heavy weapons.

Bruenor couldn't hope to win against all three. He thought to drive the orc leader back before him, then break off and head back the other way—perhaps Drizzt was finished with the troublesome wizard.

But the dwarf shook his head stubbornly. He had come to win against Obould, of course, until his dark-skinned friend had shown him another way. He had never expected to return to Mithral Hall, had guessed from the start that his reprieve from Moradin's halls had been temporary, and for a single purpose.

That purpose stood before him in the form of one of the largest and ugliest orcs he had ever had the displeasure to lay eyes on.

So Bruenor ignored the ogres and pressed his attack with even more fury. He would die, and so be it, but that bestial orc would fall before him.

His axe pounded with wild abandon, cracking against the blocking weapon of his opponent. He drew a deep line in one of the heads on Grguch's axe then nearly cracked through the weapon's handle when the orc brought it up horizontally to intercept a cut.

Bruenor had intended that cut to be the coup de grace, though, and he winced at the block, expecting that his time was over, that the ogres would finish him. He heard them off to the side, stalking in, growling . . . screaming.

Before him, the orc roared in protest, and Bruenor managed to glance back as he wound up for another strike.

One of the ogres had fallen away, its leg cleaved off at the hip. The other had turned away from Bruenor, to battle King Obould.

"Bah! Haha!" Bruenor howled at the absurdity of it all, and he brought his axe in at the same chopping downward angle, but more to his right, more to his opponent's left. The orc shifted appropriately and blocked, and Bruenor did it again, and again more to his right.

The orc decided to change the dynamics, and instead of just presenting the horizontal handle to block, he angled it down to his left. Since Bruenor was already leaning that way, there was no way for him to avoid the rightward slide.

The huge orc howled, advantage gained.

* * * * *

The orc had dispelled Guenhwyvar! From its back, claws and fangs digging at it, the orc had sent Drizzt's feline companion back to the Astral Plane.

At least, that's what the stunned drow prayed had happened, for when he had finished with the pair of orcs at the trees, he had come in sight just in time to watch his friend dissolve into smoky nothingness.

And that orc, so surprising, so unusual for one of the brutish race, had taken the hits of Drizzt's arrows, and had met his barrage with lightning-bolt retorts that had left Drizzt dazed and wounded.

Drizzt continued to circle, firing as he found opportunities between the trees. Every shot hit the mark, but every arrow was stopped just short, exploding into multicolored sparks.

And every arrow was met with a magical response, lightning and insidious magic missiles, from which Drizzt could not hide.

He went into the thickness of some evergreens, only to find other orcs already within. Bow in hand instead of his scimitars, and still dazed from the magical assaults, Drizzt had no intention of joining combat at that difficult moment, and so he cut to his right, back away from the magic-using orc, and ran out of the copse.

And just in time, for without regard to its orc comrades, the wizard dropped a fireball on those trees, a tremendous blast that instantly consumed the copse and everyone within.

Drizzt continued his run farther to the side before turning back at the orc. He dropped Taulmaril and drew forth his blades, and he thought of Guenhwyvar, and called out plaintively for his lost cat.

In sight of the wizard again, Drizzt dived behind a tree.

A lightning bolt split it down the middle before him, opening the ground to the orc wizard again, stealing Drizzt's protective wall, and so he ran on, to the side again.

"I won't run out of magic, foolish drow!" the orc called—and in High Drow, with perfect inflection!

That unnerved Drizzt almost as much as the magical barrage, but Drizzt accepted his role, and suspected that Bruenor was no less hard-pressed.

He swung out away from the orc wizard then veered around, finding a direct path to his enemy that would take him under a widespread maple and right beside another cluster of evergreens.

He roared and charged. He saw a tell-tale movement beside him, and grinned as he recognized it.

Drizzt reached inside himself as the wizard began casting, and summoned a globe of absolute darkness before him, between him and the mage.

Into the darkness went Drizzt. To his right, the evergreens rustled, as if he had cut fast and leaped out that way.

* * * * *

Dull pain and cold darkness filled Regis's head. He was far from consciousness, and sliding farther with every passing heartbeat. He knew not where he was, or what had put him there, in a deep and dark hole.

Somewhere, distantly, he felt a heavy thud against his back, and the jolt sent lines of searing pain into the halfling.

He groaned then simply let it all go.

The sensation of flying filled him, as if he had broken free of his mortal coil and was floating . . . floating.

* * * * *

"Not so clever, drow," Jack said through Hakuun's mouth as they both noted the movement in the limbs of the evergreens. A slight turn had the fiery pea released from Jack's spell lofting out that way, and an instant later, those evergreens exploded into flames, with, Jack and Hakuun both presumed, the troublesome drow inside.

THE ORC KING

But Drizzt had not gone out to his right. That had been Guenhwyvar, re-summoned from the Astral Plane by his call, heeding his quiet commands to serve her role as diversion. Guenhwyvar had gone across right behind Drizzt to leap into the evergreens, while Drizzt had tumbled headlong, gaining momentum, into the darkness.

In there, he had leaped straight up, finding the maple's lowest branch.

"Be gone, Guen," he whispered as he ran along that branch, feeling the heat of the flames to his side. "Please be gone," he begged as he came out of the blackness, bearing down on the wizard, who was still looking at the evergreens, still apparently oblivious to Drizzt.

The drow came off the branch in a leaping somersault, landing lightly in a roll before the orc, who nearly jumped out of his boots and threw his hands up defensively. As Drizzt came out of that roll, he sprang and rolled again, going right past the orc, right over the orc's shoulder as he turned back upright.

Anger drove him, memories of Innovindil. He told himself that he had solved the riddle, that that creature had been the cause.

Fury driving his arms, he slashed back behind him and down with Icingdeath as he landed, and felt the blade slash hard through the orc's leather tunic and bite deeply into flesh. Drizzt skidded to an abrupt stop and pirouetted, slashing hard with Twinkle, gashing the back-bending orc across the shoulder blades. Drizzt stepped back toward him, moving around him on the other side, and cut Twinkle down hard across the creature's exposed throat, driving it to the ground on its back.

He moved for the kill, but stopped short, realizing that he needn't bother. A growl from over by the burning pines showed him that Guenhwyvar hadn't heeded his call to be gone, but neither had the panther, so swift and clever, been caught in the blast.

Relief flooded through Drizzt, but with the diversion, he didn't take notice of a small winged snake slithering out of the dead orc's ear.

* * * * *

Bruenor's axe slid down hard to the side, and Bruenor stumbled that way. He saw the huge orc's face twist in glee, in the belief of victory.

But that was exactly the look he had hoped for.

For Bruenor was not stumbling, and had forced the angled block for that very reason, to disengage his axe quickly and down to the side, far to the right of his target. In his stumble, Bruenor was really just re-setting his stance, and he spun away from the orc, daring to turn his back on it for a brief moment.

In that spin, Bruenor sent his axe in a roundabout swing at the end of his arm, and the orc, readying a killing strike, could not redirect his heavy two-bladed axe in time.

Bruenor whirled around, his axe flying out wide to the right, setting himself in a widespread stance, ready to meet any attack.

None came, for his axe had torn the orc's belly as it had come around, and the creature crumbled backward, holding its heavy axe in its right hand, but clutching at its spilling entrails with its left.

Bruenor stalked forward and began battering it once more. The orc managed to block a blow, then a second, but the third slipped past and gashed its forearm, tearing its hand clear of its belly.

Guts spilled out. The orc howled and tried to back away.

But a flaming sword swept in over Bruenor's one-horned helmet and cut Grguch's misshapen head apart.

* * * * *

Guenhwyvar's roar saved him, for Drizzt glanced back at the last moment, and ducked aside just in time to avoid the brunt of the winged snake's murderous lightning strike. Still the bolt clipped the drow, and lifted him into the air, flipping him over more than a complete rotation, so that he landed hard on his side.

He bounced right back up, though, and the winged snake dropped to the ground and darted for the trees.

But the curved edge of a scimitar hooked under it and flipped it into the air, where Drizzt's other blade slashed against it.

Against it, but not through it, for a magical ward prevented the cut—though the force of the blade surely bent the serpent over it!

Undeterred, for that mystery within a mystery somehow confirmed to Drizzt his suspicions about Innovindil's fall, the drow growled and pushed on. Whether his guess was accurate or not hardly mattered, for Drizzt transformed that rage into blinding, furious action. He flipped the serpent again, then went into a frenzy, slashing left, right, left, right, over and over again, holding the serpent aloft by the sheer speed and precision of his repeated hits. He didn't slow, he didn't breathe, he simply battered away with abandon.

The creature flapped its wings, and Drizzt scored a hit at last, cutting up and nearly severing one where it met the serpent's body.

Again the drow went into a fury, slashing back and forth, and he ended by turning one blade around the torn snake. He fell into a short run and turn behind that strike and used his scimitar to fling the snake out far.

In mid-air, the snake transformed, becoming a gnome as it hit the ground in a roll, turning as it came up and slamming its back hard against a tree.

Drizzt relaxed, convinced that the tree was the only thing holding the surprising creature upright.

"You summoned . . . the panther . . . back," the gnome said, his voice weak and fading.

Drizzt didn't reply.

"Brilliant diversion," the gnome congratulated.

A curious expression came over the diminutive creature, and it held up one trembling hand. Blood poured from out of his robe's voluminous sleeve, though it did not stain the material—material that showed not a tear from the drow's assault.

"Hmm," the gnome said, and looked down, and so did Drizzt, to see more blood pouring out from under the hem of the robe, pooling on the ground between the little fellow's boots.

"Good garment," the gnome noted. "Know you a mage worthy?"

Drizzt looked at him curiously.

Jack the Gnome shrugged. His left arm fell off then, sliding out of his garment, the tiny piece of remaining skin that attached it to his shoulder tearing free under the dead weight.

Jack looked at it, Drizzt looked at it, and they looked at each other again.

And Jack shrugged. And Jack fell face down. And Jack the Gnome was dead.

CHAPTER
GARUMN'S GORGE
31

Bruenor tried to stand straight, but the pain of his broken arm had him constantly twitching and lowering his left shoulder. Directly across from him, King Obould stared hard, the fingers of his hand kneading the hilt of his gigantic sword. Gradually that blade inched down toward the ground, and Obould dismissed its magical flames.

"Well, what of it, then?" Bruenor asked, feeling the eyes of orcs boring into him from all around.

Obould let his gaze sweep across the crowd, holding them all at bay. "You came to me," he reminded the dwarf.

"I heared ye wanted to talk, so I come to talk."

Obould's expression showed him to be less than convinced. He glanced up the hill, motioning to Nukkels the priest, the emissary, who had never made it near to Bruenor's court.

Bruenor, too, looked up at the battered shaman, and the dwarf's eyes widened indeed when Nukkels was joined by another orc, dressed in decorated military garb, who carried a bundle of great interest to Bruenor. The two orcs walked down to stand beside their king, and the second, General Dukka, dropped his cargo, a bloody and limp halfling, at Obould's feet.

All around them, the orcs stirred, expecting the fight to erupt anew.

But Obould silenced them with an upraised hand, as he looked

Bruenor in the eye. Before him, Regis stirred, and Obould reached down and with surprising gentleness, lifted the halfling to his feet.

Regis could not stand on his own, though, his knees buckling. But Obould held him upright and motioned to Nukkels. Immediately, the shaman cast a spell of healing over the halfling, and though it only marginally helped, it was enough for Regis to stand at least. Obould pushed him toward Bruenor, but again, without any evident malice.

"Grguch is dead," Obould proclaimed to all around, ending as he locked stares with Bruenor. "Grguch's path is not the way."

Beside Obould, General Dukka stood firm and nodded, and Bruenor and Obould both understood that the orc king had all the support he needed, and more.

"What are you wantin', orc?" Bruenor asked, and he held his hand up as he finished, looking past Obould.

Many orcs turned, Obould, Dukka, and Nukkels included, to see Drizzt Do'Urden standing calmly, Taulmaril in hand, arrow resting at ease on its string, and with Guenhwyvar beside him.

"What are ye wanting?" Bruenor asked again as Obould turned back.

The dwarf already knew, of course, and the answer was one that filled him with both hope and dread.

Not that he was in any position to bargain.

* * * * *

"It won't make her more than a surcoat, elf," Bruenor said as Drizzt folded up the fabulous garment of Jack the Gnome, wrapping it over a few rings and other trinkets he had taken from the body.

"Give it to Rumblebelly," said Bruenor, and he propped Regis up a bit more, for the halfling leaned on him heavily.

"A wizard's . . . robe," the still-groggy Regis slurred. "Not for me."

"Not for me girl, neither," Bruenor declared.

But Drizzt only smiled and tucked the fairly won gains into his pack.

Somewhere in the east, fighting erupted again, a reminder to them all that not everything was settled quite yet, with remnants of Clan Karuck still to be rooted out. The distant battle sounds also reminded them that their friends were still out there, and though Obould, after conferring with Dukka, had assured them that four dwarves, an elf, and a drow had gone back over the southern ridge when Dukka's force had sent Wolf Jaw running, the relief of the companions showed clearly on their faces when they came in sight of the bedraggled, battered, and bloody sextet.

Cordio and Shingles ran to take Regis off of Bruenor's hands, while Pwent fell all over himself, hopping around Bruenor with unbridled glee.

"Thought ye was sure'n dead," Torgar said. "Thought we were suren dead, to boot. But them orcs held back and let us run south. I'm not for knowin' why."

Bruenor looked at Drizzt then at Torgar and the others. "Not sure that I'm knowin' why, meself," he said, and he shook his head helplessly, as if none of it made any sense to him. "Just get me home. Get us all home, and we'll figure it out."

It sounded good, of course, except that one of the group had no home to speak of, none in the area, at least. Drizzt stepped past Bruenor and the others and motioned for Tos'un and Hralien to join him off to the side.

Back with the others, Cordio tended to Bruenor's broken arm, which of course had Bruenor cursing him profusely, while Torgar and Shingles tried to figure out the best way to repair the king's broken shield, an artifact that could not be left in two pieces.

"Is it in your heart, or in your mind?" Drizzt asked his fellow drow when the three of them were far enough away.

"Your change, I mean," Drizzt explained when Tos'un did not immediately answer. "This new demeanor you wear, these possibilities you see before you—are they in your heart, or in your mind? Are they born of feelings, or is it pragmatism that guides your actions?"

"He was dismissed and running free," Hralien said. "Yet he came back to save me, perhaps to save us all."

Drizzt nodded his acceptance of that fact, but it didn't change his posture as he continued to stare at Tos'un.

"I do not know," Tos'un admitted. "I prefer the elves of the Moonwood to Obould's orcs. That much I can tell you. And I will not go against the Moonwood elves, on my word."

"The word of a drow," Drizzt remarked, and Hralien snorted at the absurdity of the statement, given the speaker.

Drizzt held his hand out, and motioned toward the sentient sword belted on Tos'un's hip. With only a moment's hesitation, Tos'un drew the blade and handed it over.

"I cannot allow him to keep it," Drizzt explained to Hralien.

"It is Catti-brie's sword," the elf agreed, but Drizzt shook his head.

"It is a corrupting, evil, sentient being," Drizzt said. "It will feed the doubts of Tos'un and play into his fears, hoping to incite him to spill blood." To Hralien's surprise, Drizzt handed it over to him. "Nor does Catti-brie wish it returned to Mithral Hall. Take it to the Moonwood, I beg, for your wizards and priests are better able to deal with such weapons."

"Tos'un will be there," Hralien warned, and he glanced at the wandering drow and nodded, and relief showed clearly on Tos'un's face.

"Perhaps your wizards and priests will be better able to discern the heart and mind of the dark elf, too," said Drizzt. "If trust is gained then return the sword to him. It is a choice beyond my judgment."

"Elf! Ye done jabberin'?" Bruenor called. "I'm wanting to go see me girl."

Drizzt looked to Hralien and Tos'un in turn. "Indeed," he offered. "Let us all go home."

* * * * *

The wind howled out its singular, mournful note, a constant blow that sounded to Wulfgar of home.

He stood on the northeastern slopes of Kelvin's Cairn, not far below the remnants of the high ridge once known as Bruenor's Climb, looking out over the vast tundra, where the snows had receded once more.

Slanting light crossed the flat ground, the last rays of day sparkling in the many puddles dotting the landscape.

Wulfgar stayed there, unmoving, as the last lights faded, as the stars began to twinkle overhead, and his heart leaped again when a distant campfire appeared out in the north.

His people.

His heart was full. This was his place, his home, the land where he would build his legacy. He would assume his rightful place among the Tribe of the Elk, would take a wife and live as his father, his grandfather, and all of his ancestors had lived. The simplicity of it, the lack of the deceitful trappings of civilization, welcomed him, heart and soul.

His heart was full.

The son of Beornegar had come home.

* * * * *

The dwarven hall in the great chamber known as Garumn's Gorge, with its gently arcing stone bridge and the new statue of Shimmergloom the shadow dragon, ridden to the bottom of the gorge to its death by heroic King Bruenor, had never looked so wondrous. Torches burned throughout the hall, lining the gorge and the bridge, their firelight changing through the spectrum of colors due to the enchantments of Lady Alustriel's wizards.

On the western side of the gorge before the bridge stood hundreds of Battlehammer dwarves, all dressed in their full, shining armor, pennants flying, spear tips gleaming in the magical light. Across from them stood a contingent of orc warriors, not nearly as well-outfitted, but standing with equal discipline and pride.

Dwarf masons had constructed a platform at the center of the long bridge, and on it had built a three-tiered fountain. Nanfoodle's alchemy and Alustriel's wizards had done their work there, as well, for the water danced to the sound of haunting music, its flowing streams glowing brightly and changing colors.

Before the fountain, on a mosaic of intricate tiles fashioned to herald that very day, stood a mithral podium, and on it rested a pile of identical parchments, pinned by weights sculpted into the form of a dwarf, an elf, a human, and an orc. The bottom paper of that pile had been sealed atop the podium, to remain there throughout the coming decades.

Bruenor stepped out from his line and walked the ten strides to the podium. He looked back to his friends and kin, to Banak in his chair, sitting impassive and unconvinced, but unwilling to argue with Bruenor's decision. He matched stares with Regis, who solemnly nodded, as did Cordio. Beside the priest, Thibbledorf Pwent was too distracted to return Bruenor's look. The battle-rager, as clean as anyone in the hall had ever seen him, swiveled his head around, sizing up any threats that might materialize from the strange gathering—or maybe, Bruenor thought with a grin, looking for Alustriel's dwarf friend, Fret, who had forced a bath upon Pwent.

To the side lay Guenhwyvar, majestic and eternal, and beside her stood Drizzt, calm and smiling, his mithral shirt, his belted weapons, and Taulmaril over his shoulder, reminding Bruenor that no dwarf had ever known a better champion. In looking at him, Bruenor was amazed yet again at how much he had come to love and trust that dark elf.

Just as much, Bruenor knew, as his gaze slipped past Drizzt to Catti-brie, his beloved daughter, Drizzt's wife. Never had she looked as beautiful to Bruenor as she did just then, never more sure of herself and comfortable in her place. She wore her auburn hair up high on one side, hanging loosely on the other, and it caught the light of the fountain, reflected off the rich, silken colors of her blouse, the garment of the gnome wizard. It had been a full robe on the gnome, of course, but it reached only to mid-thigh on Catti-brie, and while the sleeves had nearly covered the gnome's hands, they flared halfway down Catti-brie's delicate forearms. She wore a dark blue dress under the blouse, a gift from Lady Alustriel, her new tutor—working through Nanfoodle—that reached to her knees and matched exactly the blue trim of her blouse. High boots of black leather completed the outfit, and seemed so appropriate for Catti-brie, as they were both delicate and sturdy all at once.

Bruenor chuckled, recalling so many images of Catti-brie covered in dirt and in the blood of her enemies, dressed in simple breeches and tunic, and fighting in the mud. Those times were gone, he knew, and he thought of Wulfgar.

So much had changed.

Bruenor looked back to the podium and the treaty, and the extent of the change weakened his knees beneath him.

Along the southern rim of the center platform stood the other dignitaries: Lady Alustriel of Silverymoon, Galen Firth of Nesmé, King Emerus Warcrown of Citadel Felbarr—looking none too pleased, but accepting King Bruenor's decision—and Hralien of the Moonwood. More would join in, it was said, including the great human city of Sundabar and the largest of the dwarven cities in the region, Citadel Adbar.

If it held.

That thought made Bruenor look across the podium to the other principal, and he could not believe that he had allowed King Obould Many-Arrows to enter Mithral Hall. Yet there stood the orc, in all his terrible splendor, with his black armor, ridged and spiked, and his mighty greatsword strapped diagonally across his back.

Together they walked to opposite sides of the podium. Together they lifted their respective quills.

Obould leaned forward, but even though he was a foot and a half taller, his posture did not diminish the splendor and strength of King Bruenor Battlehammer.

"If ye're e'er to deceive . . ." Bruenor started to whisper, but he shook his head and let the thought drift away.

"It is no less bitter for me," Obould assured him.

And still they signed. For the good of their respective peoples, they put their names to the Treaty of Garumn's Gorge, recognizing the Kingdom of Many-Arrows and forever changing the face of the Silver Marches.

Calls went out from the gorge, and horns blew along the tunnels of Mithral Hall. And there came a greater blast, a rumble and resonance that vibrated through the stones of the hall and beyond, as the great horn once known as *Kokto Gung Karuck,* a gift from Obould to Bruenor, sounded from its new perch on the high lookout post above Mithral Hall's eastern door.

The world had changed, Bruenor knew.

EPILOGUE

"How different might the world now be if King Bruenor had not chosen such a course with the first Obould Many-Arrows," Hralien asked Drizzt. "Better, or worse?"

"Who can know?" the drow replied. "But at that time, a war between Obould's thousands and the gathered armies of the Silver Marches would have changed the region profoundly. How many of Bruenor's people would have died? How many of your own, who now flourish in the Glimmerwood in relative peace? And in the end, my friend, we do not know who would have prevailed."

"And yet here we stand, a century beyond that ceremony, and can either of us say with absolute truth that Bruenor chose correctly?"

He was right, Drizzt knew, to his ultimate frustration. He reminded himself of the roads he had walked over the last decades, of the ruins he had seen, of the devastation of the Spellplague. But in the North, instead of that, because of a brave dwarf named Bruenor Battlehammer, who threw off his baser instincts, his hatred and his hunger for revenge, in light of what he believed to be the greater good, the region had known a century and more of relative peace. More peace than ever it had known before. And that while the world around had fallen to shadow and despair.

Hralien started away, but Drizzt called after him.

"We both supported Bruenor on that day when he signed the Treaty of Garumn's Gorge," he reminded. Hralien nodded as he turned.

"As we both fought alongside Bruenor on the day he chose to stand beside Obould against Grguch and the old ways of Gruumsh," Drizzt added. "If I recall that day correctly, a younger Hralien was so taken by the moment that he chose to place his trust in a dark elf, though that same drow had marched to war against Hralien's people only months before."

Hralien laughed and held up his hands in surrender.

"And what resulted from that trust?" Drizzt asked. "How fares Tos'un Armgo, husband of Sinnafain, father of Teirflin and Doum'wielle?"

"I will ask him when I return to the Moonwood," the beaten Hralien replied, but he managed to get in the last arrow when he directed Drizzt's gaze to the prisoners they had taken that day.

Drizzt conceded the point with a polite nod. It wasn't over. It wasn't decided. The world rolled on around him, the sand shifted under his feet.

He reached down to pet Guenhwyvar, needing to feel the comfort of his panther friend, the one constant in his surprising life, the one great hope along his ever-winding road.

R.A. SALVATORE

FORGOTTEN REALMS

The New York Times Best-Selling Author!

An Excerpt

THE PIRATE KING

II

TRANSITIONS

Regis glanced around nervously. The agreement was for Obould to come out with a small contingent, but it was clear to the halfling that the orc had unilaterally changed that deal. Scores of orc warriors and shamans had been set all over main encampment, hiding behind rocks or in crevices, cunningly concealed and prepared for easy and swift egress.

As soon as Elastul's emissaries had delivered the word that the Arcane Brotherhood meant to move on the Silver Marches, and that enlisting Obould would be their first endeavor, the orc king's every move had been increasingly aggressive. Lady Alustriel and King Bruenor had reached out to Obould immediately, but so too had Obould begun to reach out to them. In the four years since the treaty of Garumn's Gorge, there hadn't been all that much contact between the various kingdoms, dwarf and orc, and indeed, most of that contact had come in the form of skirmishes along disputed boundaries.

But they had joined in their first common mission since Bruenor and his friends, Regis among them, had traveled north to help Obould stave off a coup by a vicious tribe of half-ogre orcs.

Or had they? The question nagged at Regis as he continued to glance around. Ostensibly, they had agreed to come together to meet the brotherhood's emissaries with a show of united force, but a disturbing possibility nagged at the halfling. Suppose Obould instead planned to use his overwhelming number in support of the erinyes emissary and against Regis and his friends?

"You would not have me risk the lives of King Bruenor and his princess Catti-brie, student of Alustriel, would you?" came Obould's voice from behind, shattering the halfling's train of thought. Regis sheepishly turned to regard the massive humanoid, dressed in his fabulous overlapping black armor with its abundant and imposing spikes, and with that tremendous greatsword strapped across his back.

"I—I know not what you mean," Regis stammered, feeling naked under the knowing gaze of this unusual, and unusually perceptive, orc.

Obould laughed at him and turned away, leaving the halfling less than assured.

Several of the forward sentries began calling then, announcing the arrival of the outsiders. Regis rushed forward and to the side to get a good look, and when he did spy the newcomers a few moments later, his heart leaped into his throat.

A trio of beautiful, barely-dressed women led the way up the path, one stepping proudly in front flanked left and right by her entourage. Tall, statuesque, with beautiful skin, they seemed almost angelic to Regis, for from behind their strong but delicate shoulders, they each sprouted a pair of shining white feathered wings. Everything about them spoke of otherworldliness, from their natural—or supernatural—charms, like hair too lustrous and eyes a bit too shining, to their adornments such as the fine swords and delicate rope, all magically glowing in a rainbow of hues, carried on belts twined of shining gold and silver fibers that sparkled as if enchanted.

It would have been easy to confuse these women with the goodly celestials, had it not been for their escort. For behind them came a mob of gruesome and beastly warriors, the barbazu. Each carried a saw-toothed glaive, great tips waving in the light as the hunched, green-skinned creatures shuffled behind their leaders. They were also known as bearded devils because of a shock of facial hair that ran ear to ear down under their jawline, beneath a toothy mouth far too wide for their otherwise emaciated faces. Scattered about their ranks were their pets, the lemure, oozing, fleshy creatures that had no more definable shape than that of a lump of molten stone, continually rolling, spreading and contracting to propel them forward.

The group, nearly two-score by Regis's count, moved steadily up the rock path toward Obould, who had climbed to the top to directly intercept them. Just a dozen paces before him the leading trio motioned for their shock troops to stay and came forward as a group, again with same one—a most striking and alluring creature with stunning too-red hair and too-red eyes and too-red lips—taking the point.

"You are Obould, I am sure," she purred, striding forward to stand right before the imposing orc, and though he was more than half a foot taller than her and twice her weight, she did not seem diminished before him.

"Nyphithys, I assume," Obould replied.

The she-devil smiled, showing teeth blindingly white and dangerously sharp.

"We are honored to speak with King Obould Many-Arrows," the devil said, her red eyes twinkling coyly. "Your reputation has spread across Faerûn. Your kingdom brings hope to all orcs."

"And hope to the Arcane Brotherhood, it would seem," Obould said, as Nyphithys's gaze drifted over to the side, where Regis remained half-hidden by a large rock. The erinyes grinned again— and Regis felt his knees go weak—before finally, mercifully, looking back to the imposing orc king.

"We make no secret of our wishes to expand our influence," she admitted. "Not to those with whom we wish to ally, at least. To others. . . ." Her voice trailed off as she again looked Regis's way.

"He is a useful infiltrator," Obould remarked. "One whose loyalty is to whoever pays him the most gold. I have much gold."

Nyphithys's accepting nod seemed less than convincing.

"Your army is mighty, by all accounts," said the devil. "Your healers capable. Where you fail is in the arcane Art, which leaves you dangerously vulnerable to mages, who are so prevalent in Silverymoon."

"And this is what the brotherhood offers," Obould reasoned.

"We can more than match Alustriel's power."

"And so with you behind me, the Kingdom of Many-Arrows will overrun the Silver Marches."

Regis's knees went weak again at Obould's proclamation. The halfling's thoughts screamed of double-cross, and with his friends so dangerously exposed—and with himself so obviously doomed!

"It would be a beautiful coupling," the erinyes said, and ran her delicate hand across Obould's massive chest.

"A coupling is a temporary arrangement."

"A marriage, then," said Nyphithys.

"Or an enslavement."

The erinyes stepped back and looked at him curiously.

"I would provide you the fodder to absorb the spears and spells of your enemies," Obould explained. "My orcs would become to you as those barbezu."

"You misunderstand."

"Do I, Nyphithys?" Obould said, and it was his turn to offer a toothy grin.

"The brotherhood seeks to enhance trade and cooperation."

"Then why do you approach me under the cloak of secrecy? All the kingdoms of the Silver Marches value trade."

"Surely you do not consider yourself kin and kind with the dwarves of Mithral Hall, or with Alustriel and her delicate creatures. You are a god among orcs. Gruumsh adores you—I know this, as I have spoken with him."

Regis, who was growing confident again at Obould's strong rebuke, winced as surely as did Obould himself when Nyphithys made that particular reference.

"Gruumsh has guided the vision that is Many-Arrows," Obould replied after a moment of collecting himself. "I know his will."

Nyphithys beamed. "My master will be pleased. We will send—"

Obould's mocking laughter stopped her, and she looked at him both curiously and skeptically.

"War brought us to this, our home," Obould explained. "But peace sustains us."

"Peace with dwarves?" the devil asked incredulously.

Obould stood firm and did not bother to reply.

"My master will not be pleased."

"He will exact punishment upon me?"

"Be careful what you wish for, king of orcs," the devil warned. "Your puny kingdom is no match for the weight of the Arcane Brotherhood."

"Who ally with devils and will send forth a horde of barbezu to entangle my armies while their overwizards rain death upon us?"

Obould asked, and it was Nyphithys's turn to stand firm. "While my own allies support my ranks with elven arrows, dwarven war machines, and Lady Alustriel's own knights and wizards," the orc said and drew out his greatsword, willing its massive blade to erupt with fire as it came free of its sheath.

To Nyphithys and her two erinyes companions, none of whom were smiling, he yelled, "Let us see how my orc fodder fares against your barbezu and flesh beasts!"

From all around, orcs leaped out of hiding. Brandishing swords and spears, axes and flails, they howled and rushed forward, and the devils, ever eager for battle, fanned out and met the charge with one of their own.

Available in Hardcover

October 2008

from

THE ABYSSAL PLAGUE

From the molten core of a dead universe

Hunger
Spills a seed of evil

Fury
So pure, so concentrated, so infectious

Hate
Its corruption will span worlds

The Temple of Yellow Skulls
Don Bassingthwaite

Sword of the Gods
Bruce R. Cordell

Under the Crimson Sun
Keith R.A. DeCandido

Oath of Vigilance
James Wyatt

Shadowbane
Erik Scott de Bie

Find these novels at your favorite bookseller.
Also available as ebooks.

DungeonsandDragons.com

Dungeons & Dragons, D&D, Wizards of the Coast, and their respective logos are trademarks of Wizards of the Coast LLC in the U.S.A. and other countries. ©2011 Wizards.

DUNGEONS & DRAGONS

An ancient time, an ancient place...
When magic fills the world and terrible monsters roam the wilderness...
It is a time of heroes, of legends, of dungeons and dragons...

THE MARK OF NERATH
Bill Slavicsek

THE SEAL OF KARGA KUL
Alex Irvine

UNTOLD ADVENTURES
Short stories by Alan Dean Foster, Kevin J. Anderson,
Jay Lake, Mike Resnick, and more

THE LAST GARRISON
Matthew Beard
December 2011

Bringing the world of Dungeons & Dragons alive,
find these great novels at your favorite bookseller.
Also available as ebooks.

DungeonsandDragons.com

DUNGEONS & DRAGONS, D&D, WIZARDS OF THE COAST, and their
respective logos are trademarks of Wizards of the Coast
LLC in the U.S.A. and other countries. ©2011 Wizards.

EPIC STORIES
UNFORGETTABLE CHARACTERS
UNBEATABLE VALUE
OMNIBUS EDITIONS — THREE BOOKS IN ONE

FORGOTTEN REALMS

Empyrean Odyssey
Thomas M. Reid

The Last Mythal
Richard Baker
(Ebook Exclusive)

Ed Greenwood Presents Waterdeep I

Ed Greenwood Presents Waterdeep II
December 2011

DRAGONLANCE

Dragonlance Legends
Margaret Weis & Tracy Hickman
September 2011

EBERRON

Draconic Prophecies
James Wyatt
October 2011
(Ebook Exclusive)

Find these great books at your favorite bookseller.

DungeonsandDragons.com

Dungeons & Dragons, D&D, Forgotten Realms, Dragonlance, Eberron, Wizards of the Coast, and their respective logos are trademarks of Wizards of the Coast LLC in the U.S.A. and other countries. ©2011 Wizards.

VIE FOR GLORY
NEVERWINTER

GAUNTLGRYM
Neverwinter Saga, Book I
R.A. SALVATORE

NEVERWINTER
Neverwinter Saga, Book II
R.A. SALVATORE

BRIMSTONE ANGELS
Legends of Neverwinter
ERIN M. EVANS
November 2011

NEVERWINTER
RPG for PC
Coming in 2011

NEVERWINTER CAMPAIGN SETTING
For the D&D® Roleplaying Game
August 2011

THE LEGEND OF DRIZZT
Neverwinter Tales
Comic Books Written by R.A. Salvatore & Geno Salvatore
August 2011

THE LEGEND OF DRIZZT™
Cooperative Board Game
October 2011

Find these great products at your favorite bookseller or game shop.
DungeonsandDragons.com

NEVERWINTER, DUNGEONS & DRAGONS, D&D, WIZARDS OF THE COAST, their respective logos and THE LEGEND OF DRIZZT are trademarks of Wizards of the Coast LLC in the U.S.A. and other countries. ©2011 Wizards.

WELCOME TO THE DESERT WORLD OF ATHAS, A LAND RULED BY A HARSH AND UNFORGIVING CLIMATE, A LAND GOVERNED BY THE ANCIENT AND TYRANNICAL SORCERER KINGS. THIS IS THE LAND OF

DARK·SUN

CITY UNDER THE SAND
Jeff Mariotte

UNDER THE CRIMSON SUN
Keith R.A. DeCandido

DEATH MARK
Robert Schwalb
NOVEMBER 2011

ALSO AVAILABLE AS EBOOKS!

THE PRISM PENTAD
Troy Denning's classic DARK SUN series revisited! Check out the great new editions of *The Verdant Passage*, *The Crimson Legion*, *The Amber Enchantress*, *The Obsidian Oracle*, and *The Cerulean Storm*.

DUNGEONS & DRAGONS, D&D, Dark Sun, WIZARDS OF THE COAST, and their respective logos are trademarks of Wizards of the Coast LLC in the U.S.A. and other countries. ©2011 Wizards.

WELCOME TO LUSKAN

A gargoyle leaped off a balcony from above, swooping down at him, leathery wings wide, clawed hands and feet raking wildly.

The drow dived into a roll, somehow maneuvered out to the side when the gargoyle angled its wings to intercept, and came back to his feet with such force that he sprang high into the air, his blades working in short and devastating strokes. So completely did he overwhelm the creature that it actually hit the ground before he did, already dead.

"Huzzah for Drizzt Do'Urden!" cried a voice above all the cheering, a voice that Drizzt surely knew, and he took heart that Arumn Gardpeck, proprietor of the Cutlass, was among the ranks.

Magical anklets enhancing his speed, Drizzt sprinted for the central tower of the great structure in short, angled bursts, and often with long, diving rolls. He held only one scimitar then, his other hand clutching an onyx figurine. "I need you," he called to Guenhwyvar, and the weary panther, home on the Astral Plane, heard.

ENJOY IT WHILE IT LASTS!

"The fighting is entertaining as always, and a twist at the end . . . promises an interesting future for Drizzt and his companions."
—Bookspot Central on *The Pirate King*

"Fans of Salvatore and the FORGOTTEN REALMS (world) will certainly want to pick this book up and see the changes that are happening. Some of those changes surprised me quite a bit, so I can really only guess what will happen in the next book. *(The Pirate King)* is a book that I whole-heartedly recommend to those who are this far along in the series. Only time will tell what is in store for Drizzt and the FORGOTTEN REALMS (world)."
—The Beezer Review on *The Pirate King*

. . . breathes new life into the stereotypical creatures of the milieu: the motivations of his villains make sense without violating the traditions of the game. His heroes face dilemmas deeper than merely how to slay their foes. Salvatore has long used his dark elf protagonist to reflect on issues of racial prejudice . . . and this novel is no exception.
—Paul Brink, *School Library Journal* on *The Thousand Orcs*

FORGOTTEN REALMS

R.A. SALVATORE

TRANSITIONS

The Orc King

The Pirate King

The Ghost King

THE HUNTER'S BLADES TRILOGY

The Thousand Orcs

The Lone Drow

The Two Swords

THE LEGEND OF DRIZZT*

Homeland

Exile

Sojourn

The Crystal Shard

Streams of Silver

The Halfling's Gem

The Legacy

Starless Night

Siege of Darkness

Passage to Dawn

The Silent Blade

The Spine of the World

Sea of Swords

THE SELLSWORDS

Servant of the Shard

Promise of the Witch-King

Road of the Patriarch

THE CLERIC QUINTET

Canticle

In Sylvan Shadows

Night Masks

The Fallen Fortress

The Chaos Curse

R.A. SALVATORE

FORGOTTEN REALMS

THE PIRATE KING

TRANSITIONS II

Wizards of the Coast

The Pirate King
Transitions, Book II

©2009 Wizards of the Coast LLC

All characters in this book are fictitious. Any resemblance to actual persons, living or dead, is purely coincidental.

This book is protected under the copyright laws of the United States of America. Any reproduction or unauthorized use of the material or artwork contained herein is prohibited without the express written permission of Wizards of the Coast LLC.

Published by Wizards of the Coast LLC

FORGOTTEN REALMS, WIZARDS OF THE COAST, DUNGEONS & DRAGONS, D&D, and their respective logos are trademarks of Wizards of the Coast LLC in the U.S.A. and other countries.

Printed in the U.S.A.

Cover art by Todd Lockwood
Map by Todd Gamble

Original Hardcover Edition First Printing: October 2008
First Paperback Printing: July 2009

9 8 7 6 5 4 3

ISBN: 978-0-7869-5144-4
ISBN: 978-0-7869-5265-6 (e-book)
620-24051740-001-EN

The sale of this book without its cover has not been authorized by the publisher. If you purchased this book without a cover, you should be aware that neither the author nor the publisher has received payment for this "stripped book."

U.S., CANADA,	EUROPEAN HEADQUARTERS
ASIA, PACIFIC, & LATIN AMERICA	Hasbro UK Ltd
Wizards of the Coast LLC	Caswell Way
P.O. Box 707	Newport, Gwent NP9 0YH
Renton, WA 98057-0707	GREAT BRITAIN
+1-800-324-6496	Save this address for your records.

Visit our web site at www.wizards.com

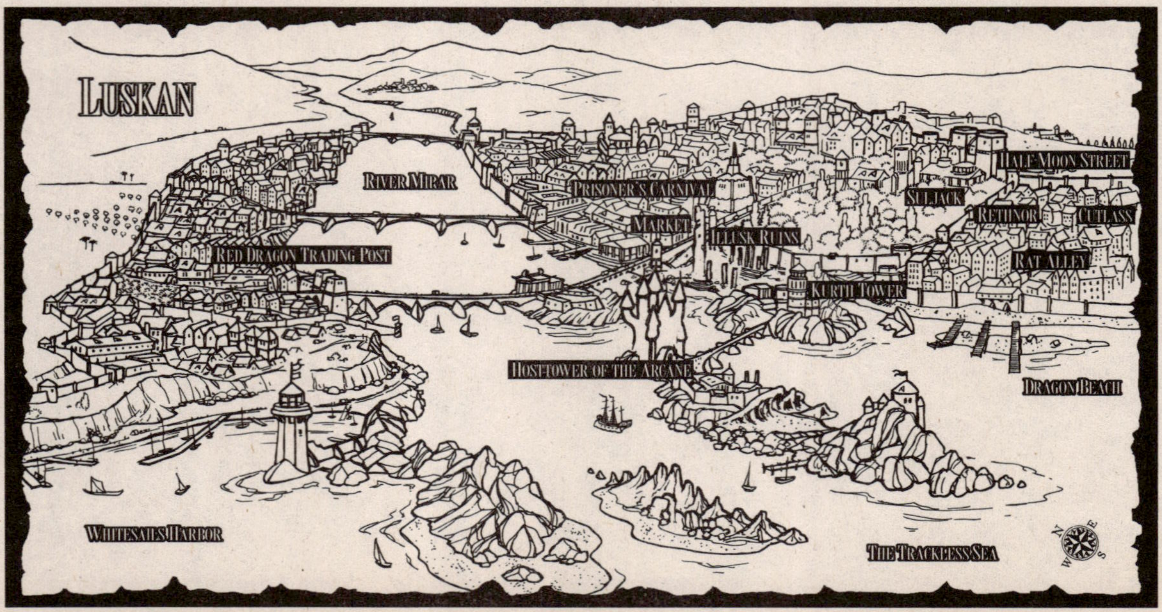
Luskan
River Mirar
Prisoner's Carnival
Half-Moon Street
Suljack
Rethnor
Cutlass
Market
Illusk Ruins
Red Dragon Trading Post
Rat Alley
Kurth Tower
Host Tower of the Arcane
Dragon Beach
Whitesails Harbor
The Trackless Sea
N
E
S
W

PRELUDE

Suljack, one of the five high captains ruling Luskan and a former commander of one of the most successful pirate crews ever to terrorize the Sword Coast, was not easily intimidated. An extrovert who typically bellowed before he considered his roar, his voice often rang loudest among the ruling council. Even the Arcane Brotherhood, who many knew to be the true power in the city, were hard-pressed to cow him. He ruled Ship Suljack, and commanded a solid collection of merchants and thugs from Suljack Lodge, in the south central section of Luskan. It was not a showy or grand place, certainly nothing to match the strength of High Captain Taerl's four-spired castle, or High Captain Kurth's mighty tower, but it was well-defended and situated comfortably near the residence of Rethnor, Suljack's closest ally among the captains.

Still, Suljack found himself on unsteady ground as he walked into the room in Ten Oaks, the palace of Ship Rethnor. The old man Rethnor wasn't there, and wasn't supposed to be. He spoke through what seemed to be the least intimidating man in the room, the youngest of his three sons.

But Suljack knew that appearances could be deceiving.

Kensidan, a small man, well-dressed in dull gray and black tones, and well-groomed, with his hair cut short in all the appropriate angles and clips, sat with a leg crossed over one knee in a comfortable chair in the center-back of the plain room. He was sometimes called "The Crow," as he always wore a high-collared black cape, and high black shoes that tied tightly halfway up his calf. He walked with an awkward gait, stiff-legged like a bird. Put that together with his long, hooked nose, and any who saw him would immediately understand the nickname, even a year ago, before he'd first donned the high-collared cape. Any minor wizard could easily discern that there was magic in that garment, powerful magic, and such items were often reputed to affect changes on their bearer. As with the renowned girdle of dwarvenkind, which gradually imparted the characteristics of a dwarf to its wearer, so too Kensidan's cloak seemed to be acting upon him. His gait grew a bit more awkward, and his nose a bit longer and more hooked.

His muscles were not taut, and his hands were not calloused. Unlike many of Rethnor's men, Kensidan didn't decorate his dark brown hair. He carried nothing flashy at all on his person. Furthermore, the cushions of the seat made him appear even smaller, but somehow, inexplicably, all of it seemed to work for him.

Kensidan was the center of the room, with everyone leaning in to hear his every soft-spoken word. And whenever he happened to twitch or shift in his seat, those nearest him inevitably jumped and glanced nervously around.

Except, of course, for the dwarf who stood behind and to the right of Kensidan's chair. The dwarf's burly arms were crossed over his barrel chest, their flowing lines of corded muscles broken by the black, beaded braids of his thick beard. His weapons stabbed up diagonally behind him, spiked heads dangling at the end of glassteel chains. No one wanted a piece of that one, not even Suljack. Kensidan's "friend," recently imported muscle from the east, had waged a series of fights along the docks that had left any and all opposing him dead or wishing they were.

"How fares your father?" Suljack asked Kensidan, though he hadn't yet pried his eyes from the dangerous dwarf. He took his seat before and to the side of Kensidan.

"Rethnor is well," Kensidan answered.

"For an old man?" Suljack dared remark, and Kensidan merely nodded.

"There is a rumor that he wishes to retire, or that he already has," Suljack went on.

Kensidan put his elbows on the arms of his chair, finger-locked his hands together, and rested his chin upon them in a pensive pose.

"Will he announce you as his replacement?" Suljack pressed.

The younger man, barely past his mid-twenties, chuckled a bit at that, and Suljack cleared his throat.

"Would that eventuality displease you?" asked the Crow.

"You know me better than that," Suljack protested.

"And what of the other three?"

Suljack paused to consider that for a moment then shrugged. "It's not unexpected. Welcomed? Perhaps, but with a wary eye turned your way. The high captains live well, and don't wish to upset the balance."

"Their ambition falls victim to success, you mean."

Again Suljack shrugged and said lightheartedly, "Isn't enough ever enough?"

"No," Kensidan answered simply, with blunt and brutal honesty, and once again Suljack found himself on shifting sands.

Suljack glanced around at the many attendants then dismissed his own. Kensidan did likewise—except for his dwarf bodyguard. Suljack looked past the seated man sourly.

"Speak freely," Kensidan said.

Suljack nodded toward the dwarf.

"He's deaf," Kensidan explained.

"Can't hear a thing," the dwarf confirmed.

Suljack shook his head. What he meant to say needed saying, he told himself, and so he started, "You are serious about going after the brotherhood?"

Kensidan sat expressionless, emotionless.

"There are more than a hundred wizards who call the Hosttower home," Suljack announced.

No response, not a whit.

"Many of them archmages."

"You presume that they speak and act with a singular mind," said Kensidan finally.

"Arklem Greeth holds them fast."

"No one holds a wizard fast," Kensidan replied. "Theirs is the most selfish and self-serving of professions."

"Some say that Greeth has cheated death itself."

"Death is a patient opponent."

Suljack blew out a frustrated sigh. "He consorts with devils!" he blurted. "Greeth is not to be taken lightly."

"I take no one lightly," Kensidan assured him, a clear edge to his words.

Suljack sighed again and managed to calm himself. "I'm wary of them, is all," he explained more quietly. "Even the people of Luskan know it now, that we five high captains, your father among us, are puppets to the master Arklem Greeth. I've been so long under his thumb I've forgotten the feel of wind breaking over the prow of my own ship. Might be that it's time to take back the wheel."

"Past time. And all we need is for Arklem Greeth to continue to feel secure in his superiority. He weaves too many threads, and only a few need unravel to unwind his tapestry of power."

Suljack shook his head, clearly less than confident.

"Thrice Lucky is secured?" Kensidan asked.

"Maimun sailed this morning, yes. Is he to meet with Lord Brambleberry of Waterdeep?"

"He knows what he is to do," Kensidan replied.

Suljack scowled, understanding that to mean that Suljack need not know. Secrecy was power, he understood, though he was far too emotional a thug to ever keep a secret for long.

It hit Suljack then, and he looked at Kensidan with even more respect, if that was possible. Secrecy was the weight of the man, the pull that had everyone constantly leaning toward him. Kensidan had many pieces in play, and no one saw more than a few of them.

That was Kensidan's strength. Everyone around him stood on shifting sand, while he was rooted in bedrock.

"So it's Deudermont, you say?" Suljack asked, determined to at least begin weaving the young man's threads into some sensible pattern. He shook his head at the irony of that possibility.

"Sea Sprite's captain is a true hero of the people," Kensidan replied. "Perhaps the only hero for the people of Luskan, who have no one to speak for them in the halls of power."

Suljack smirked at the insult, reminding himself that if it were a barb aimed at him then logic aimed it at Kensidan's own father as well.

"Deudermont is unbending in principle, and therein lies our opportunity," Kensidan explained. "He is no friend of the brotherhood, surely."

"The best war is a proxy war, I suppose," said Suljack.

"No," Kensidan corrected, "the best war is a proxy war when no one knows the true power behind it."

Suljack chuckled at that, and wasn't about to disagree. His laughter remained tempered, however, by the reality that was Kensidan the Crow. His partner, his ally . . . a man he dared not trust.

A man from whom he could not, could never, escape.

* * * * *

"Suljack knows enough, but not too much?" Rethnor asked when Kensidan joined him a short while later.

Kensidan spent a few moments studying his father before nodding his assent. How old Rethnor looked these days, with his pallid skin sagging below his eyes and down his cheeks, leaving great flopping jowls. He had thinned considerably in the last year or so, and his skin, so leathery from years at sea, had little resilience left. He walked stiff-legged and bolt upright, for his back had locked securely in place. And when he talked, he sounded as if he had his mouth stuffed with fabric, his voice muffled and weak.

"Enough to throw himself on my sword," Kensidan replied, "but he will not."

"You trust him?"

Kensidan nodded. "He and I want the same thing. We have no desire to serve under the thumb of Arklem Greeth."

"As I have, you mean," Rethnor retorted, but Kensidan was shaking his head even as the old man spoke the words.

"You put in place everything upon which I now build," he said. "Without your long reach, I wouldn't dare move against Greeth."

"Suljack appreciates this, as well?"

"Like a starving man viewing a feast at a distant table. He wants a seat at that table. Neither of us will feast without the other."

"You're watching him closely, then."

"Yes."

Rethnor gave a wheezing laugh.

"And Suljack is too stupid to betray me in a manner that I couldn't anticipate," Kensidan added, and Rethnor's laugh became a quick scowl.

"Kurth is the one to watch, not Suljack," said Kensidan.

Rethnor considered the words for a few moments, then nodded his agreement. High Captain Kurth, out there on Closeguard Island and so close to the Hosttower, was possibly the strongest of the five high captains, and surely the only one who could stand one-to-one against Ship Rethnor. And Kurth was so very clever, whereas, Rethnor had to admit, his friend Suljack often had to be led to the trough with a carrot.

"Your brother is in Mirabar?" Rethnor asked.

Kensidan nodded. "Fate has been kind to us."

"No," Rethnor corrected. "Arklem Greeth has erred. His Mistresses of the South Tower and North Tower both hold vested interests in his planned infiltration and domination of their homeland, interests that are diametrically opposed. Arklem Greeth is too prideful and cocksure to recognize the insecurity of his position—I doubt he understands Arabeth Raurym's anger."

"She is aboard *Thrice Lucky*, seeking *Sea Sprite*."

"And Lord Brambleberry awaits Deudermont at Waterdeep," Rethnor stated, nodding in approval.

Kensidan the Crow allowed a rare smile to crease his emotionless facade. He quickly suppressed it, though, reminding himself of the dangers of pride. Surely, Kensidan had much to be proud of. He was a juggler with many balls in the air, seamlessly and surely spinning their orbits. He was two steps ahead of Arklem Greeth in the east, and facilitating unwitting allies in the south. His considerable investments—bags of gold—had been well spent.

"The Arcane Brotherhood must fail in the east," Rethnor remarked.

"Maximum pain and exposure," Kensidan agreed.

"And beware Overwizard Shadowmantle," the old high captain warned, referring to the moon elf, Valindra, Mistress of the North Tower. "She will become incensed if Greeth is set back in his plans for dominion over the Silver Marches, a place she loathes."

"And she will blame Overwizard Arabeth Raurym of the South Tower, daughter of Marchion Elastul, for who stands to lose as much as Arabeth by Arklem Greeth's power grab?"

Rethnor started to talk, but he just looked upon his son, flashed a smile of complete confidence, and nodded. The boy understood it, all of it.

He had overlooked nothing.

"The Arcane Brotherhood must fail in the east," he said again, only to savor the words.

"I will not disappoint you," the Crow promised.

PART 1

WEAVING THE TAPESTRY

WEAVING THE TAPESTRY

A million, million changes—uncountable changes!—every day, every heartbeat of every day. That is the nature of things, of the world, with every decision a crossroad, every drop of rain an instrument both of destruction and creation, every animal hunting and every animal eaten changing the present just a bit.

On a larger level, it's hardly and rarely noticeable, but those multitude of pieces that comprise every image are not constants, nor, necessarily, are constant in the way we view them.

My friends and I are not the norm for the folk of Faerûn. We have traveled half the world, for me both under and above. Most people will never see the wider world outside of their town, or even the more distant parts of the cities of their births. Theirs is a small and familiar existence, a place of comfort and routine, parochial in their church, selective in their lifelong friends.

I could not suffer such an existence. Boredom builds like smothering walls, and the tiny changes of everyday existence would never cut large enough windows in those opaque barriers.

Of my companions, I think Regis could most accept such a life, so long as the food was plentiful and not bland and he was given some manner of contact with the goings-on of the wider world outside. I have often wondered how many hours a halfling might lie on the same spot on the shore of the same lake with the same un-baited line tied to his toe.

Has Wulfgar moved back to a similar existence? Has he shrunk his world, recoiling from the harder truths of reality?

It's possible for him, with his deep emotional scars, but never would it be possible for Catti-brie to go with him to such a life of steadfast routine. Of that I'm most certain. The wanderlust grips her as it grips me, forcing us along the road—even apart along our separate roads, and confident in the love we share and the eventual reunions.

And Bruenor, as I witness daily, battles the smallness of his existence with growls and grumbles. He is the king of Mithral Hall, with riches untold at his fingertips. His every wish can be granted by a host of subjects loyal to him unto death. He accepts the responsibilities of his lineage, and fits that throne well, but it galls him every day as surely as if he was tied to his kingly seat. He has often found and will often find again excuses to get himself out of the hall on some mission or other, whatever the danger.

He knows, as Catti-brie and I know, that stasis is boredom and boredom is a wee piece of death itself.

For we measure our lives by the changes, by the moments of the unusual. Perhaps that manifests itself in the first glimpse of a new city, or the first breath of air on a tall mountain, a swim in a river cold from the melt or a frenzied battle in the shadows of Kelvin's Cairn. The unusual experiences are those that create the memories, and a tenday of memories is more life than a year of routine. I remember my first sail aboard *Sea Sprite*, for example, as keenly as my first kiss from Catti-brie, and though that journey lasted mere tendays in a life more than three-quarters of the way through a century, the memories of that voyage play out more vividly than some of the years I spent in House Do'Urden, trapped in the routine of a drow boy's repetitive duties.

It's true that many of the wealthier folk I have known, lords of Waterdeep even, will open their purses wide for a journey to a far off place of respite. Even if a particular journey does not go as anticipated for them, with unpleasant weather or unpleasant company, or foul food or even minor illnesses, to a one, the lords would claim the trip worth the effort and the gold. What they valued most for their trouble and treasure was not the actual journey, but the memory of it that remained behind, the memory of it that they will carry to their graves. Life is in the experiencing, to be sure, but it's just as much in the recollection and in the telling!

Contrastingly, I see in Mithral Hall many dwarves, particularly older folk, who revel in the routine, whose every step mirrors those of the day before. Every meal, every hour of work, every chop with the pick or bang with the hammer follows the pattern ingrained throughout the years. There is a game of delusion at work here, I know, though I wouldn't say it aloud. It's an unspoken and internal logic that drives them ever on in the same place. It's even chanted in an old dwarven song:

> *For this I did on yesterday*
> *And not to Moradin's Hall did I fly*
> *So's to do it again'll keep me well*
> *And today I sha'not die.*

The logic is simple and straightforward, and the trap is easily set, for if I did these things the day before and do these same things today, I can reasonably assume that the result will not change.

And the result is that I will be alive tomorrow to do these things yet again.

Thus do the mundane and the routine become the—false—assurance of continued life, but I have to wonder, even if the premise were true, even if doing the same thing daily would ensure immortality, would a year of such existence not already be the same as the most troubling possibility of death?

From my perspective, this ill-fated logic ensures the opposite of that delusional promise! To live a decade in such a state is to ensure the swiftest path to death, for it is to ensure the swiftest passage of the decade, an unremarkable recollection that will flitter by without a pause, the years of mere existence. For in those hours and heartbeats and passing days, there is no variance, no outstanding memory, no first kiss.

To seek the road and embrace change could well lead to a shorter life in these dangerous times in Faerûn. But in those hours, days, years, whatever the measure, I will have lived a longer life by far than the smith who ever taps the same hammer to the same familiar spot on the same familiar metal.

For life is experience, and longevity is, in the end, measured by memory, and those with a thousand tales to tell have indeed lived longer than any who embrace the mundane.

—Drizzt Do'Urden

CHAPTER 1
FAIR WINDS AND FOLLOWING SEAS

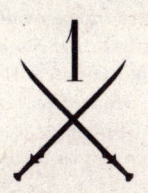

Sails billowing, timbers creaking, water spraying high from her prow, *Thrice Lucky* leaped across the swells with the grace of a dancer. All the multitude of sounds blended together in a musical chorus, both invigorating and inspiring, and it occurred to young Captain Maimun that if he had hired a band of musicians to rouse his crew, their work would add little to the natural music all around them.

The chase was on, and every man and woman aboard felt it, and heard it.

Maimun stood forward and starboard, holding fast to a guide rope, his brown hair waving in the wind, his black shirt half unbuttoned and flapping refreshingly and noisily, bouncing out enough to show a tar-black scar across the left side of his chest.

"They are close," came a woman's voice from behind him, and Maimun half-turned to regard Overwizard Arabeth Raurym, Mistress of the South Tower.

"Your magic tells you so?"

"Can't you feel it?" the woman answered, and gave a coy toss of her head so that her waist-length red hair caught the wind and flipped back behind her. Her blouse was as open as Maimun's shirt, and the young man couldn't help but look admiringly at the alluring creature.

He thought of the previous night, and the night before that, and before that as well—of the whole enjoyable journey. Arabeth had promised him a wonderful and exciting sail in addition to the rather large sum she'd offered for her passage, and Maimun couldn't honestly say that she'd disappointed him. She was around his age, just past thirty, intelligent, attractive, sometimes brazen, sometimes coy, and just enough of each to keep Maimun and every other man around her off-balance and keenly interested in pursuing her. Arabeth knew her power well, and Maimun knew that she knew it, but still, he couldn't shake himself free of her.

Arabeth stepped up beside him and playfully brushed her fingers through his thick hair. He glanced around quickly, hoping none of the crew had seen, for the action only accentuated that he was quite young to be captaining a ship, and that he looked even younger. His build was slight, wiry yet strong, his features boyish and his eyes a delicate light blue. While his hands were calloused, like those of any honest seaman, his skin had not yet taken on the weathered, leathery look of a man too much under the sparkling sun.

Arabeth dared to run her hand under the open fold of his shirt, her fingers dancing across his smooth skin to the rougher place where skin and tar had melded together, and it occurred to Maimun that he typically kept his shirt open just a bit more for exactly the reason of revealing a hint of that scar, that badge of honor, that reminder to all around that he had spent most of his life with a blade in his hand.

"You are a paradox," Arabeth remarked, and Maimun merely smiled. "Gentle and strong, soft and rough, kind and merciless, an artist and a warrior. With your lute in hand, you sing with the voice of the sirens, and with your sword in hand, you fight with the tenacity of a drow weapons master."

"You find this off-putting?"

Arabeth laughed. "I would drag you to your cabin right now," she replied, "but they are close."

As if on cue—and Maimun was certain Arabeth had used some magic to confirm her prediction before she'd offered it—a crewman from the crow's nest shouted down, "Sails! Sails on the horizon!"

"Two ships," Arabeth said to Maimun.

"Two ships!" the man in the nest called down.

THE PIRATE KING

"*Sea Sprite* and *Quelch's Folly*," said Arabeth. "As I told you when we left Luskan."

Maimun could only chuckle helplessly at the manipulative wizard. He reminded himself of the pleasures of the journey, and of the hefty bag of gold awaiting its completion.

He thought, too, in terms bitter and sweet, of *Sea Sprite* and Deudermont, his old ship, his old captain.

* * * * *

"Aye, Captain, that's Argus Retch or I'm the son of a barbarian king and an orc queen," Waillan Micanty said. He winced as he finished, reminding himself of the cultured man he served. He scanned Deudermont head to toe, from his neatly trimmed beard and hair to his tall and spotless black boots. The captain showed more gray in his hair, but still not much for a man of more than fifty years, and that only made him appear more regal and impressive.

"A bottle of the finest wine for Dhomas Sheeringvale, then," Deudermont said in a light tone that put Micanty back at ease. "Against all of my doubts, the information you garnered from him was correct and we've finally got that filthy pirate before us." He clapped Micanty on the back and glanced back over his shoulder and up to *Sea Sprite*'s wizard, who sat on the edge of the poop deck, his skinny legs dangling under his heavy robes. "And soon in range of our catapult," Deudermont added loudly, catching the attention of the mage, Robillard, "if our resident wizard there can get the sails straining."

"Cheat to win," Robillard replied, and with a dramatic flourish he waggled his fingers, the ring that allowed him control over a fickle air elemental sending forth another mighty gust of wind that made *Sea Sprite*'s timbers creak.

"I grow weary of the chase," Deudermont retorted, his way of saying that he was eager to finally confront the beastly pirate he pursued.

"Less so than I," the wizard replied.

Deudermont didn't argue that point, and he knew that the benefit of Robillard's magic filling the sails was mitigated by the strong following winds. In calmer seas, *Sea Sprite* could still rush along, propelled by the wizard and his ring, while their quarry would typically flee at a crawl. The captain clapped Micanty on the shoulder and led him to the side, in view of *Sea Sprite*'s new and greatly improved catapult. Heavily banded in metal strapping, the dwarven weapon could heave a larger payload. The throwing arm and basket strained under the weight of many lengths of chain, laid out for maximum extension by gunners rich in experience.

"How long?" Deudermont asked the sighting officer, who stood beside the catapult, spyglass in hand.

"We could hit her now with a ball of pitch, mighten be, but getting the chains up high enough to shred her sails . . . That'll take another fifty yards closing."

"One yard for every gust," Deudermont said with a sigh of feigned resignation. "We need a stronger wizard."

"You'd be looking for Elminster himself, then," Robillard shot back. "And he'd probably burn your sails in some demented attempt at a colorful flourish. But please, hire him on. I would enjoy a holiday, and would enjoy more the sight of you swimming back to Luskan."

This time Deudermont's sigh was real.

So was Robillard's grin.

Sea Sprite's timbers creaked again, forward-leaning masts driving the prow hard against the dark water.

Soon after, everyone on the deck, even the seemingly-dispassionate wizard, waited with breath held for the barked command, "Tack starboard!"

Sea Sprite bent over in a water-swirling hard turn, bending her masts out of the way for the aft catapult to let fly. And let fly she did, the dwarven siege engine screeching and creaking, hurling several hundred pounds of wrapped metal through the air. The chains burst open to near full length as they soared, and whipped in above the deck of *Quelch's Folly*, slashing her sails.

As the wounded pirate ship slowed, *Sea Sprite* tacked hard back to port. A flurry of activity on the pirate's deck showed her archers preparing for the fight, and *Sea Sprite*'s crack crew responded in kind, aligning themselves along the port rail, composite bows in hand.

But it was Robillard who, by design, struck first. In addition to constructing the necessary spells to defend against magical attacks, the wizard used an enchanted censer and brought forth a denizen from the Elemental Plane of Air. It appeared like a waterspout, but with hints of a human form, a roiling of air powerful enough to suck up and hold water within it to better define its dimensions. Loyal and obedient because of the ring Robillard wore, the cloud-like pet all but invisibly floated over the rail of *Sea Sprite* and glided toward *Quelch's Folly*.

Captain Deudermont lifted his hand high and looked to Robillard for guidance. "Alongside her fast and straight," he instructed the helmsman.

"Not to rake?" Waillan Micanty asked, echoing perfectly the sentiments of the helmsman, for normally *Sea Sprite* would cripple her opponent and come in broadside to the pirate's taffrail, giving *Sea Sprite*'s archers greater latitude and mobility.

Robillard had convinced Deudermont of a new plan for the ruffians of *Quelch's Folly*, a plan more straightforward and more devastating to a crew deserving of no quarter.

Sea Sprite closed—archers on both decks lifted their bows.

"Hold for me," Deudermont called along his line, his hand still high in the air.

More than one man on *Sea Sprite*'s deck rubbed his arm against his sweating face; more than one rolled eager fingers over his drawn bowstring. Deudermont was asking them to cede the initiative, to let the pirates shoot first.

Trained, seasoned, and trusting in their captain, they obliged.

And so Argus's crew let fly . . . right into the suddenly howling winds of Robillard's air elemental.

The creature rose up above the dark water and began to spin with such suddenness and velocity that by the time the arrows of Argus's archers cleared their bows, they were soaring straight into a growing tornado, a water spout. Robillard willed the creature right to the side of *Quelch's Folly*, its winds so strong that they deterred any attempt to reload the bows.

Then, with only a few yards separating *Sea Sprite* from the pirate, the wizard nodded to Deudermont, who counted down from three—precisely the time Robillard needed to simply dismiss his elemental and the winds with it. Argus's crew, mistakenly thinking the wind to be as much a defense as a deterrent to their own attacks, had barely moved for cover when the volley crossed deck to deck.

* * * * *

"They are good," Arabeth remarked to Maimun as the two stared into a scrying bowl she had empowered to give them a close-up view of the distant battle. Following the barrage of arrows, a second catapult shot sent hundreds of small stones raking the deck of *Quelch's Folly*. With brutal efficiency, *Sea Sprite* sidled up to the pirate ship, grapnels and boarding planks flying.

"It will be all but over before we get there," Maimun said.

"Before *you* get there, you mean," Arabeth said with a wink. She cast a quick spell and faded from sight. "Put up your proper pennant, else *Sea Sprite* sinks you beside her."

Maimun laughed at the disembodied voice of the invisible mage and started to respond, but a flash out on the water told him that Arabeth had already created a dimensional portal to rush away.

"Up Luskan's dock flag!" Maimun called to his crew.

Thrice Lucky was in a wonderful position, for she had no outstanding crimes or warrants against her. With a flag of Luskan's wharf above her, stating a clear intent to side with Deudermont, she would be well-received.

And of course Maimun would side with Deudermont against Argus Retch. Though Maimun, too, was considered a "pirate" of sorts, he was nothing akin to the wretched Retch—whose last name had been taken with pride, albeit misspelled. Retch was a murderer, and took great pleasure in torturing and killing even helpless civilians.

Maimun wouldn't abide that, and part of the reason he had agreed to take Arabeth out was to see, at long last, the downfall of the dreadful pirate. He realized he was leaning over the rail. His greatest pleasure would be crossing swords with Retch himself.

But Maimun knew Deudermont too well to believe that the battle would last that long.

"Take up a song," the young captain, who was also a renowned bard, commanded, and his crew did just that, singing rousing praises to *Thrice Lucky*, warning her enemies, "Beware or be swimming!"

THE PIRATE KING

Maimun shook his thick brown locks from his face, his light blue eyes—orbs that made him look much younger than his twenty-nine years—squinting as he measured the fast-closing distance.

Deudermont's men were already on the deck.

* * * * *

Robillard found himself quickly bored. He had expected better out of Argus Retch, though he'd wondered for a long time if the man's impressive reputation had been exaggerated by the ruthlessness of his tactics. Robillard, formerly of the Hosttower of the Arcane, had known many such men, rather ordinary in terms of conventional intelligence or prowess, but seeming above that because they were unbounded by morality.

"Sails port and aft!" the man in the crow's nest shouted down.

Robillard waved his hand, casting a spell to enhance his vision, his gaze locking on the pennant climbing the new ship's rigging.

"Thrice Lucky," he muttered, noting young Captain Maimun standing mid-rail. "Go home, boy."

With a disgusted sigh, Robillard dismissed Maimun and his boat and turned his attention to the fight at hand.

He brought his pet air elemental back to him then used his ring to enact a spell of levitation. On his command, the elemental shoved him across the expanse toward *Quelch's Folly*. He visually scoured the deck as he glided in, seeking her wizard. Deudermont and his crack crew weren't to be outdone with swords, he well knew, and so the only potential damage would be wrought by magic.

He floated over the pirate's rail, caught a rope to halt his drift, and calmly reached out to tap a nearby pirate, releasing a shock of electrical magic as he did. That man hopped weirdly once or twice, his long hair dancing crazily, then he fell over, twitching.

Robillard didn't watch it. He glanced from battle to battle, and anywhere it seemed as though a pirate was getting the best of one of Deudermont's men, he flicked his finger in that direction, sending forth a stream of magical missiles that laid the pirate low.

But where was her wizard? And where was Retch?

"Cowering in the hold, no doubt," Robillard muttered to himself.

He released the levitation spell and began calmly striding across the deck. A pirate rushed at him from the side and slashed his saber hard against the wizard, but of course Robillard had well-prepared his defenses for any such crude attempts. The saber hit his skin and would have done no more against solid rock, a magical barrier blocking it fully.

Then the pirate went up into the air, caught by Robillard's elemental. He flew out over the rail, flailing insanely, to splash into the cold ocean waters.

A favor for an old friend? Came a magical whisper in Robillard's ear, and in a voice he surely recognized.

"Arabeth Raurym?" he mouthed in disbelief, and in sadness, for what might that promising young lass be doing at sea with the likes of Argus Retch?

Robillard sighed again, dropped another pair of pirates with a missile volley, loosed his air elemental on yet another group, and moved to the hatch. He glanced around then "removed" the hatch with a mighty gust of wind. Using his ring again to buoy him, for he didn't want to bother with a ladder, the wizard floated down belowdecks.

* * * * *

What little fight remained in Argus Retch's crew dissipated at the approach of the second ship, for *Thrice Lucky* had declared her allegiance with Deudermont. With expert handling, Maimun's crew brought their vessel up alongside *Quelch's Folly,* opposite *Sea Sprite,* and quickly set their boarding planks.

Maimun led the way, but he didn't get two steps from his own deck before Deudermont himself appeared at the other end of the plank, staring at him with what seemed a mixture of curiosity and disdain.

"Sail past," *Sea Sprite*'s captain said.

"We fly Luskan's banner," Maimun replied.

Deudermont didn't blink.

"Have we come to this, then, my captain?" Maimun asked.

"The choice was yours."

"'The choice,'" Maimun echoed. "Was it to be made only

with your approval?" He kept approaching as he spoke, and dared hop down to the deck beside Deudermont. He looked back at his hesitant crew, and waved them forward.

"Come now, my old captain," Maimun said, "there is no reason we cannot share an ocean so large, a coast so long."

"And yet, in such a large ocean, you somehow find your way to my side."

"For old times' sake," Maimun said with a disarming chuckle, and despite himself, Deudermont couldn't suppress his smile.

"Have you killed the wretched Retch?" Maimun asked.

"We will have him soon enough."

"You and I, perhaps, if we're clever," Maimun offered, and when Deudermont looked at him curiously, he added a knowing wink.

Maimun motioned Deudermont to follow and led him toward the captain's quarters, though the door had already been ripped open and the anteroom appeared empty.

"Retch is rumored to always have a means of escape," Maimun explained as they crossed the threshold into the private room, exactly as Arabeth had instructed Maimun to do.

"All pirates do," Deudermont replied. "Where is yours?"

Maimun stopped and regarded Deudermont out of the corner of his eye for a few moments, but otherwise let the jab pass.

"Or are you implying that you have an idea where Retch's escape might be found?" Deudermont asked when his joke flattened.

Maimun led the captain through a secret door and into Retch's private quarters. The room was gaudily adorned with booty from a variety of places and with a variety of designs, rarely complimentary. Glass mixed with metalwork, fancy-edge and block, and a rainbow of colors left onlookers more dizzy than impressed. Of course, anyone who knew Captain Argus Retch, with his red-and-white striped shirt, wide green sash, and bright blue pants, would have thought the room perfectly within the wide parameters of the man's curious sensibilities.

The moment of quiet distraction also brought a revelation to the two—one that Maimun had expected. A conversation from below drifted through a small grate in the corner of the room, and the sound of a cultured woman's voice fully captured Deudermont's attention.

"I care nothing for the likes of Argus Retch," the woman said. "He is an ugly and ill-tempered dog, who should be put down."

"Yet you are here," a man's voice—Robillard's voice—answered.

"Because I fear Arklem Greeth more than I fear *Sea Sprite,* or any of the other pretend pirate hunters sailing the Sword Coast."

"Pretend? Is this not a pirate? Is it not caught?"

"You know *Sea Sprite* is a show," the woman argued. "You are a facade offered by the high captains so the peasants believe they're being protected."

"So the high captains approve of piracy?" asked an obviously doubting Robillard.

The woman laughed. "The Arcane Brotherhood operates the pirate trade, to great profit. Whether the high captains approve or disapprove is not important, because they don't dare oppose Arklem Greeth. Feign not your ignorance of this, Brother Robillard. You served at the Hosttower for years."

"It was a different time."

"Indeed," the woman agreed. "But now is as now is, and now is the time of Arklem Greeth."

"You fear him?"

"I'm terrified of him, and horrified of what he is," the woman answered without the slightest hesitation. "And I pray that someone will rise up and rid the Hosttower of him and his many minions. But I'm not that person. I take pride in my prowess as an overwizard and in my heritage as daughter of the marchion of Mirabar."

"Arabeth Raurym," Deudermont mouthed in recognition.

"But I wouldn't involve my father in this, for he is already entangled with the brotherhood's designs on the Silver Marches. Luskan would be well-served by being rid of Arklem Greeth—even Prisoner's Carnival might then be brought back under lawful and orderly control. But he will outlive my children's children's children—or out-exist them, I mean, since he long ago stopped drawing breath."

"Lich," Robillard said quietly. "It's true, then."

"I am gone," Arabeth answered. "Do you intend to stop me?"

"I would be well within my province to arrest you here and now."

"But will you?"

Robillard sighed, and up above, Deudermont and Maimun heard a quick chant and the sizzle of magical release as Arabeth spirited away.

The implications of her revelations—rumors made true before Deudermont's very ears—hung silently in the air between Deudermont and Maimun.

"I don't serve Arklem Greeth, if that's what you're wondering," Maimun said. "But then, I am no pirate."

"Indeed," replied an obviously unconvinced Deudermont.

"As a soldier is no murderer," said Maimun.

"Soldiers can be murderers," Deudermont deadpanned.

"So can lords and ladies, high captains and archmages, pirates and pirate hunters alike."

"You forgot peasants," said Deudermont. "And chickens. Chickens can kill, I've been told."

Maimun tipped his fingers against his forehead in salute and surrender.

"Retch's escape?" Deudermont asked, and Maimun moved to the back of the cabin. He fumbled about a small set of shelves there, moving trinkets and statues and books alike, until finally he smiled and tugged a hidden lever.

The wall pulled open, revealing an empty shaft.

"An escape boat," Maimun reasoned, and Deudermont started for the door.

"If he knew it was *Sea Sprite* pursuing him, he is long gone," Maimun said, and Deudermont stopped. "Retch is no fool, nor is he loyal enough to follow his ship and crew to the depths. He no doubt recognized that it was *Sea Sprite* chasing him, and relieved himself of his command quietly and quickly. These escape boats are clever things; some submerge for many hours and are possessed of magical propulsion that can return them to a designed point of recall. You can take pride, though, for the escape boats are often referred to as 'Deuderboats.'"

Deudermont's eyes narrowed.

"It's something, at least," Maimun offered.

Deudermont's handsome face soured and he headed through the door.

"You won't catch him," Maimun called after him. The young man—bard, pirate, captain—sighed and chuckled helplessly, knowing full well that Retch was likely already back in Luskan, and knowing the ways of Kensidan, his employer, he wondered if the notorious pirate wasn't already being compensated for sacrificing his ship.

Arabeth had come out there for a reason, to have that conversation with Robillard within earshot of Captain Deudermont. It all started to come together for clever Maimun. Kensidan was soon to be a high captain, and the ambitious warlord was working hard to change the very definition of that title.

Despite his deep resentment, Maimun found himself glancing at the door through which Deudermont had exited. Despite his falling out with his former captain, he felt uneasy about the prospect of this too-noble man being used as a pawn.

And Arabeth Raurym had just seen to that.

* * * * *

"She was a good ship—best I ever had," Argus Retch protested.

"Best of a bad lot, then," Kensidan replied. He sat—he was always sitting, it seemed—before the blustering, gaudy pirate, his dark and somber clothing so in contrast to Argus Retch's display of mismatched colors.

"Salt in your throat, ye damned Crow!" Retch cursed. "And lost me a good crew, too!"

"Most of your crew never left Luskan. You used a band of wharf-rats and a few of your own you wished to be rid of. Captain Retch, don't play me for a fool."

"W-well . . . well," Retch stammered. "Well, good enough, then! But still a crew, and still workin' for me. And I lost *Folly*! Don't you forget that."

"Why would I forget that which I ordered? And why would I forget that for which you were compensated?"

"Compensated?" the pirate blustered.

Kensidan looked at Retch's hip, where the bag of gold hung.

"Gold's all well and fine," Retch said, "but I need a ship, and

I'm not for finding one with any ease. Who'd sell to Argus Retch, knowing that Deudermont got his last and is after him?"

"In good time," said Kensidan. "Spend your gold on delicacies. Patience. Patience."

"I'm a man of the sea!"

Kensidan shifted in his seat, planting one elbow on the arm of the chair, forearm up. He pointed his index finger and rested his temple against it, staring at Retch pensively, and with obvious annoyance. "I can put you back to sea this very day."

"Good!"

"I doubt you'll think so."

The deadpan clued Retch in to Kensidan's true meaning. Rumors had been filtering around Luskan that several of Kensidan's enemies had been dropped into the deep waters outside the harbor.

"Well, I can be a bit patient, no doubt."

"No doubt," Kensidan echoed. "And it will be well worth your time, I assure you."

"You'll get me a good ship?"

Kensidan gave a little chuckle. "Would *Sea Sprite* suffice?"

Argus Retch's bloodshot eyes popped open wide and the man seemed to simply freeze in place. He stayed like that for a very long time—so long that Kensidan simply looked past him to several of Rethnor's lieutenants who stood against the walls of the room.

"I'm sure it will," Kensidan said, and the men laughed. To Retch, he added, "Go and play," and he waved the man away.

As Retch exited through one door, Suljack came in through another.

"Do you think that wise?" the high captain asked.

The Crow shrugged and smirked as if it hardly mattered.

"You intend to give him *Sea Sprite*?"

"We're a long way from having *Sea Sprite*."

"Agreed," said Suljack. "But you just promised . . ."

"Nothing at all," said Kensidan. "I asked if he thought *Sea Sprite* would suffice, nothing more."

"Not to his ears."

Kensidan chuckled as he reached over the side of his seat to retrieve his glass of whiskey, along with a bag of potent leaves and shoots. He downed the drink in one gulp and brought the leaves up below his nose, inhaling deeply of their powerful aroma.

"He'll brag," Suljack warned.

"With Deudermont looking for him? He'll hide."

Suljack's shake of his head revealed his doubts, but Kensidan brought his herbs up beneath his nose again and seemed not to care.

Seemed not to care because he didn't. His plans were flowing exactly as he had predicted.

"Nyphithys is in the east?"

Kensidan merely chuckled.

CHAPTER

DEFYING EXPECTATIONS

2

The large moonstone hanging around Catti-brie's neck glowed suddenly and fiercely, and she brought a hand up to clench it.

"Devils," said Drizzt Do'Urden. "So Marchion Elastul's emissary wasn't lying."

"Telled ye as much," said the dwarf Torgar Hammerstriker, who had been of Elastul's court only a few short years before. "Elastul's a shooting pain in a dwarf's arse, but he's not so much the liar, and he's wanting the trade. Always the trade."

"Been more than five years since we went through Mirabar on our road that bringed us home," King Bruenor Battlehammer added. "Elastul lost a lot to our passing, and his nobles ain't been happy with him for a long time. He's reachin' out to us."

"And to him," Drizzt added, nodding down in the direction of Obould, master of the newly formed Kingdom of Many-Arrows.

"The world's gone Gutbuster," Bruenor muttered, a phrase referring to his wildest guardsmen and which Bruenor had aptly appropriated as a synonym for "crazy."

"Better world, then," Thibbledorf Pwent, leader of said guardsmen, was quick to respond.

"When we're done with this, ye're going back to Mirabar," Bruenor said to Torgar. Torgar's eyes widened and he blanched at the notion. "As me own emissary. Elastul done good and we're needing to tell him he done good. And not one's better for telling him that than Torgar Hammerstriker."

Torgar seemed less than convinced, to be sure, but he nodded. He had pledged his loyalty to King Bruenor and would follow his king's commands without complaint.

"Business here first, I'm thinking," Bruenor said.

The dwarf king looked at Catti-brie, who had turned to stare off in the direction the gemstone amulet indicated. The westering sun backlit her, reflecting off the red and purple blouse she wore, a shirt that had once been the magical robes of a gnome wizard. Bruenor's adopted daughter was in her late thirties—not old in the counting of a dwarf, but near middle-aged for a human. And though she still had that luminescence, a beauty that radiated from within, luster to her auburn hair and the sparkle of youth in her large blue eyes, Bruenor could see the changes that had come over her.

She had Taulmaril the Heartseeker, her deadly bow, slung over one shoulder, though of late, Drizzt was the one with that bow in hand. Catti-brie had become a wizard, and one with a tutor as fine as any in the land. Alustriel herself, the Lady of Silverymoon and of the famed Seven Sisters, had taken Catti-brie in as a student shortly after the stalemated war between Bruenor's dwarves and King Obould's orcs. Other than the bow, Catti-brie carried only a small dagger, one that seemed hardly used as it sat on her hip. An assortment of wands lined her belt, though, and she wore a pair of powerfully enchanted rings, including one that she claimed could bring the stars themselves down from the sky upon her enemies.

"They're not far," she said in a voice still melodic and filled with wonder.

"They?" asked Drizzt.

"Such a creature would not travel alone—certainly not for a meeting with an orc of Obould's ferocious reputation." Catti-brie reminded him.

"But escorted by other devils, not a more common guard?"

Catti-brie shrugged, tightened her grip on the amulet, and concentrated for a few moments then nodded.

"A bold move," said Drizzt, "even when dealing with an orc. How confident must the Arcane Brotherhood be to allow devils to openly walk the land?"

"Less confident tomorrow than today's all I'm knowing," muttered Bruenor. He moved down to the side of the stony hill that afforded him the best view of Obould's encampment.

"Indeed," Drizzt agreed, throwing a wink at Catti-brie before moving down beside the dwarf. "For never would they have calculated that King Bruenor Battlehammer would rush to the aid of an orc."

"Just shut yer mouth, elf," Bruenor grumbled, and Drizzt and Catti-brie shared a smile.

* * * * *

Regis glanced around nervously. The agreement was for Obould to come out with a small contingent, but it was clear to the halfling that the orc had unilaterally changed that plan. Scores of orc warriors and shamans had been set around the main camp, hiding behind rocks or in crevices, cunningly concealed and prepared for swift egress.

As soon as Elastul's emissaries had delivered the word that the Arcane Brotherhood meant to move on the Silver Marches, and that enlisting Obould would be their first endeavor, the orc king's every maneuver had been aggressive.

Too aggressive? Regis wondered.

Lady Alustriel and Bruenor had reached out to Obould, but so too had Obould begun to reach out to them. In the four years since the treaty of Garumn's Gorge, there hadn't been all that much contact between the various kingdoms, dwarf and orc, and indeed, most of that contact had come in the form of skirmishes along disputed boundaries.

But they had come to join in their first common mission since Bruenor and his friends, Regis among them, had traveled north to help Obould stave off a coup attempt by a vicious tribe of half-ogre orcs.

Or had they? The question nagged at Regis as he continued to glance around. Ostensibly, they had agreed to come together to meet the brotherhood's emissaries with a show of united force, but a disturbing possibility nagged at the halfling. Suppose Obould instead planned to use his overwhelming numbers in support of the fiendish emissary and against Regis and his friends?

"You wouldn't have me risk the lives of King Bruenor and his princess Catti-brie, student of Alustriel, would you?" came Obould's voice from behind, shattering the halfling's train of thought.

Regis sheepishly turned to regard the massive humanoid, dressed in his overlapping black armor with its abundant and imposing spikes, and with that tremendous greatsword strapped across his back.

"I-I know not what you mean," Regis stammered, feeling naked under the knowing gaze of the unusually perceptive orc.

Obould laughed at him and turned away, leaving the halfling less than assured.

Several of the forward sentries began calling then, announcing the arrival of the outsiders. Regis rushed forward and to the side to get a good look, and when he did spy the newcomers a few moments later, his heart leaped into his throat.

A trio of beautiful, barely-dressed women led the way up the path. One stepped proudly in front, flanked left and right by her entourage. Tall, statuesque, with beautiful skin, they seemed almost angelic to Regis, for from behind their strong but delicate shoulders, they each sprouted a pair of shining white feathered wings. Everything about them spoke of otherworldliness, from their natural—or supernatural!—charms, like hair too lustrous and eyes too shining, to their adornments such as the fine swords and delicate rope, all magically glowing in a rainbow of hues, carried on belts twined of shining gold and silver fibers that sparkled with enchantments.

It would have been easy to confuse these women with the goodly celestials, had it not been for their escort. For behind them came a mob of gruesome and beastly warriors, the barbazu. Each carried a saw-toothed glaive, great tips waving in the light as the hunched, green-skinned creatures shuffled behind their leaders. Barbazu were also known as "bearded devils" because of a shock of facial hair that ran ear to ear down under their jawline, beneath a toothy mouth far too wide for their otherwise emaciated-looking faces. Scattered amongst their ranks were their pets, the lemure, oozing, fleshy creatures that had no more definable shape than that of a lump of molten stone, continually rolling, spreading, and contracting to propel themselves forward.

The group, nearly two score by Regis's count, moved steadily up the rock path toward Obould, who had climbed to the top to directly intercept them. Just a dozen paces before him the leading trio motioned for their shock troops to hold and came forward as a group, again with the same one, a most striking and alluring creature with stunning too-red hair, too-red eyes, and too-red lips, taking the point.

"You are Obould, I am sure," the erinyes purred, striding forward to stand right before the imposing orc, and though he was more than half a foot taller than her and twice her weight, she didn't seem diminished before him.

"Nyphithys, I assume," Obould replied.

The she-devil smiled, showing teeth blindingly white and dangerously sharp.

"We're honored to speak with King Obould Many-Arrows," the devil said, her red eyes twinkling coyly. "Your reputation has spread across Faerûn. Your kingdom brings hope to all orcs."

"And hope to the Arcane Brotherhood, it would seem," Obould said, as Nyphithys's gaze drifted over to the side, where Regis remained half-hidden by a large rock. The erinyes grinned again—and Regis felt his knees go weak—before finally, mercifully, looking back to the imposing orc king.

"We make no secret of our wishes to expand our influence," she admitted. "Not to those with whom we wish to ally, at least. To others. . . ." Her voice trailed off as she again looked Regis's way.

"He is a useful infiltrator," Obould remarked. "One whose loyalty is to whoever pays him the most gold. I have much gold."

Nyphithys's accepting nod seemed less than convinced.

"Your army is mighty, by all accounts," said the devil. "Your healers capable. Where you fail is in the Art, which leaves you dangerously vulnerable to the mages that are so prevalent in Silverymoon."

"And this is what the Arcane Brotherhood offers," Obould reasoned.

"We can more than match Alustriel's power."

"And so with you behind me, the Kingdom of Many-Arrows will overrun the Silver Marches."

Regis's knees went weak again at Obould's proclamation.

The halfling's thoughts screamed of double-cross, and with his friends so dangerously exposed—and with himself so obviously doomed!

"It would be a beautiful coupling," the erinyes said, and ran her delicate hand across Obould's massive chest.

"A coupling is a temporary arrangement."

"A marriage, then," said Nyphithys.

"Or an enslavement."

The erinyes stepped back and looked at him curiously.

"I would provide you the fodder to absorb the spears and spells of your enemies," Obould explained. "My orcs would become to you as those barbezu."

"You misunderstand."

"Do I, Nyphithys?" Obould said, and it was his turn to offer a toothy grin.

"The brotherhood seeks to enhance trade and cooperation."

"Then why do you approach me under the cloak of secrecy? All the kingdoms of the Silver Marches value trade."

"Surely you don't consider yourself kin and kind with the dwarves of Mithral Hall, or with Alustriel and her delicate creatures. You are a god among orcs. Gruumsh adores you—I know this, as I have spoken with him."

Regis, who was growing confident again at Obould's strong rebuke, winced as surely as did Obould himself when Nyphithys made that particular reference.

"Gruumsh has guided the vision that is Many-Arrows," Obould replied after a moment of collecting himself. "I know his will."

Nyphithys beamed. "My master will be pleased. We will send . . ."

Obould's mocking laughter stopped her, and she looked at him with both curiosity and skepticism.

"War brought us to this, our home," Obould explained, "but peace sustains us."

"Peace with *dwarves?*" the devil asked.

Obould stood firm and didn't bother to reply.

"My master will not be pleased."

"He will exact punishment upon me?"

"Be careful what you wish for, king of orcs," the devil warned.

"Your puny kingdom is no match for the magic of the Arcane Brotherhood."

"Who ally with devils and will send forth a horde of barbezu to entangle my armies while their overwizards rain death upon us?" Obould asked, and it was Nyphithys's turn to stand firm.

"While my own allies support my ranks with elven arrows, dwarven war machines, and Lady Alustriel's own knights and wizards," the orc said and drew out his greatsword, willing its massive blade to erupt with fire as it came free of its sheath.

To Nyphithys and her two erinyes companions, none of whom were smiling, he yelled, "Let us see how my orc fodder fares against your barbezu and flesh beasts!"

From all around, orcs leaped out of hiding. Brandishing swords and spears, axes and flails, they howled and rushed forward, and the devils, ever eager for battle, fanned out and met the charge.

"Fool orc," Nyphithys said. She pulled out her own sword, a wicked, straight-edged blade, blood red in color, and took her strange rope from her belt as well, as did her sister erinyes devils. "Our promise to you was of greater power than you will ever know!"

To the sides of the principals, orcs and lesser devils crashed together in a sudden torrent of howls and shrieks.

Obould came forward with frightening speed, his sword driving for the hollow between Nyphithys's breasts. He roared with victory, thinking the kill assured.

But Nyphithys was gone—just gone, magically disappeared, and so were her sisters.

"Fool orc," she called down to him from above, and Obould whirled and looked up to see the three devils some twenty feet off the ground, their feathered wings beating easily, holding them aloft and steady against the wind.

A bearded devil rushed at the seemingly distracted orc king, but Obould swept around at the last moment, his flaming greatsword cutting a devastating arc, and the creature fell away . . . in pieces.

As he turned back to regard Nyphithys, though, a rope slapped down around him. A magical rope, he quickly discerned, as it began to entwine him of its own accord, wrapping with blinding speed and the strength of a giant constrictor snake around his torso and limbs. Before he even began sorting that out, a second rope hit him and began to enwrap him, as each of Nyphithys's fellow erinyes, flanking their alluring leader, caught him in their extended magical grasp.

"Destroy them all!" Nyphithys called down to her horde. "They are only orcs!"

* * * * *

"Only orcs!" a bearded devil echoed, or tried to, for it came out "only or-*glul*," as a spike blasted through the devil's spine and lungs, exploding out its chest with a spray of blood and gore.

"Yeah, ye keep tellin' yerself that," said Thibbledorf Pwent, who had leaped down from a rocky abutment head first—helmet spike first—upon the unsuspecting creature. Pwent pulled himself to his feet, yanking the flailing, dying devil up over his head as he went. With a powerful jerk and twitch, he sent the creature flying away. "It'll make ye feel better," he said after it then he howled and charged at the next enemy he could find.

"Slow down, ye durned stoneheaded pile o' road apples!" Bruenor, who was more gingerly making his way down the same abutment, called after Pwent, to no avail. "So much for formations," the dwarf king grumbled to Drizzt, who rushed by with a fluid gait, leaping down ledge to ledge as easily as if he were running across flat tundra.

The drow hit the ground running. He darted off to the side and fell into a sidelong roll over a smooth boulder, landing solidly on his feet and with his scimitars already weaving a deadly pattern before him. Oozing lemures bubbled and popped under the slashes of those blades as Drizzt fell fully into his dance. He stopped, and whirled around just in time to double-parry the incoming glaive of a barbezu. Not wanting to fully engage the saw-toothed weapon, Drizzt instead slapped it with a series of shortened strikes, deflecting its thrust out wide.

His magical anklets enhancing his strides, the drow rushed in behind the glaive, Icingdeath and Twinkle, his trusted blades, making short work of the bearded devil.

"I got to get me a fast pony," Bruenor grumbled.

THE PIRATE KING

"War pig," one of the other dwarves coming down, another Gutbuster, corrected.

"Whatever's about," Bruenor agreed. "Anything to get me in the fight afore them two steal all the fun."

As if on cue, Pwent roared, "Come on, me boys! There's blood for spillin'!" and all the Gutbusters gave a great cheer and began raining down around Bruenor. They leaped from the stones and crashed down hard, caring not at all, and rolled off as one with all the frenzy of a tornado in an open market.

Bruenor sighed and looked at Torgar, the only other one left beside him at the base of the abutment, who couldn't suppress a chuckle of his own.

"They do it because they love their king," the Mirabarran dwarf remarked.

"They do it because they want to hit things," Bruenor muttered. He glanced over his shoulder, back up the rocks, to Catti-brie, who was crouched low, using a stone to steady her aim.

She looked down at Bruenor and winked then nodded forward, leading the dwarf's gaze to the three flying erinyes.

A dozen orc missiles reached up at Nyphithys and her sisters in the few moments Bruenor regarded them, but not one got close to penetrating the skin of the devils, who had enacted magical shields to prevent just such an attack.

Bruenor looked back to Catti-brie, who winked again and drew back far on her powerfully enchanted bow. She let fly a sizzling, lightning-like arrow that flashed brilliantly, cutting the air.

Nyphithys's magical shield sparked in protest as the missile slashed in, and to the devil's credit, the protection did deflect Catti-brie's arrow—just enough to turn it from the side of Nyphithys's chest to her wings. White feathers flew in a burst as the missile exploded through one wing then the other. The devil, her face a mask of surprise and agony, began to twist in a downward spiral.

"Good shot," Torgar remarked.

"Wasting her time with that stupid wizard stuff. . . ." Bruenor replied.

A cacophony of metallic clangs turned them both to the side, to see Drizzt backing furiously, skipping up to the top of rocks, leaping from one to another, always just ahead of one or another of a multitude of glaives slashing at him.

"Who's wasting time?" the dark elf asked between desperate parries.

Bruenor and Torgar took the not-so-subtle hint, hoisted their weapons, and ran in support.

From on high, another arrow flashed, splitting the air just to the side of Drizzt and splitting the face of the bearded devil standing before him.

Bruenor's old, notched axe took out the devil chasing the drow from the other side, and Torgar rushed past the drow, shield-blocking another glaive aside, and as he passed, Drizzt sprinted in behind him to slash out the surprised devil's throat.

"We kill more than Pwent and his boys do, and I'm buying the ale for a year and a day," Bruenor cried, charging in beside his companions.

"Ten o' them, three of us," Torgar reminded his king as another arrow from Taulmaril blasted a lemure that roiled toward them.

"Four of us," Bruenor corrected with a wink back at Catti-brie, "and I'm thinking I'll make that bet!"

* * * * *

Either unaware or uncaring for the fall of Nyphithys, the other erinyes tightened their pressure and focus on Obould. Their magical ropes had wrapped him tightly and the devils pulled with all their otherworldly might in opposing directions to wrench and tear the orc king and lift him from the ground.

But they weren't the only ones possessed of otherworldly strength.

Obould let the ropes tighten around his waist, and locked his abdominal muscles to prevent them from doing any real damage. He dropped his greatsword to the ground, slapped his hands on the ropes running diagonally from him, and flipped them over and around once to secure his grasp. While almost any other creature would have tried to free itself from the grasp of two devils, Obould welcomed it. As soon as he was satisfied with his grip, his every muscle corded against the tightening rope and the pull of the erinyes, the orc began a series of sudden and brutal downward tugs.

Despite their powerful wings, despite their devilish power, the erinyes couldn't resist the pull of the mighty orc, and each tug reeled them down. Working like a fisherman, Obould's every muscle jerked in synch, and he let go of the ropes at precisely the right moment to grasp them higher up.

Around him the battle raged and Obould knew that he was vulnerable, but rage drove him on. Even as a barbezu approached him, he continued his work against the erinyes.

The barbezu howled, thinking it had found an opening, and leaped forward, but a series of small flashes of silver whipped past Obould's side. The barbezu jerked and gyrated, trying to avoid or deflect the stream of daggers. Obould managed a glance back to see the halfling friend of Bruenor shrugging, almost apologetically, as he loosed the last of his missiles.

That barrage wasn't about to stop a barbezu, of course, but it did deter the devil long enough. Another form, lithe and fast, rushed past Regis and Obould. Drizzt leaped high as he neared the surprised bearded devil, too high for the creature to lift its saw-toothed glaive to intercept. Drizzt managed to stamp down on the flat of its heavy blade as he descended, and he skipped right past the barbezu, launching a knee into its face for good measure as he soared by. That knee was more to slow his progress than to defeat the creature, though it caught the devil off guard. The real attack came from behind, Drizzt spinning around and putting his scimitars to deadly work before the devil could counter with any semblance of a defense.

The wounded barbezu, flailing crazily, looked around for support, but all around it, its comrades were crumbling. The orcs, the Gutbusters, and Bruenor's small group simply overwhelmed them.

Obould saw it, too, and he gave another huge tug, pulling down the erinyes. Barely a dozen feet from the ground, the devils recognized their doom. As one, they unfastened their respective ropes in an attempt to soar away, but before they could even get free of their own entanglement, a barrage of spears, stones, knives, and axes whipped up at them. Then came a devastating missile at the devil fluttering to Obould's left. A pair of dwarves, hands locked between them, made a platform from which jumped one Thibbledorf Pwent. He went up high enough to wrap the devil in a great hug, and the wild dwarf immediately went into his frenzied gyrations, his ridged armor biting deep and hard.

The erinyes screamed in protest, and Pwent punched a spiked gauntlet right through her face.

The two fell like a stone. Pwent expertly twisted to put the devil under him before they landed.

* * * * *

"You know not what you do, drow," Nyphithys said as Drizzt, fresh from his kill of the barbezu, approached. The devil's wings hung bloody and useless behind her, but she stood steadily, and seemed more angry than hurt. She held her sword in her left hand, her enchanted rope, coiled like a whip, in her right.

"I have battled and defeated a marilith and a balor," Drizzt replied, though the erinyes laughed at him. "I do not tremble."

"Even should you beat me, you will be making enemies more dangerous than you could ever imagine!" Nyphithys warned, and it was Drizzt's turn to laugh.

"You don't know my history," he said dryly.

"The Arcane Brotherhood—"

Drizzt cut her short. "Would be a minor House in the city of Menzoberranzan, where all the families looked long to see the end of me. I do not tremble, Nyphithys of Stygia, who calls Luskan her home."

The devil's eyes flashed.

"Yes, we know your name," Drizzt assured her. "And we know who sent you."

"Arabeth," Nyphithys mouthed with a hiss.

The name meant nothing to Drizzt, though if she had added Arabeth's surname, Raurym, he would have made the connection to Marchion Elastul Raurym, who had indeed tipped them off.

"At least I will see the end of you before I am banished to the Nine Hells," Nyphithys declared, and she raised her right arm, letting free several lengths of rope, and snapped it like a whip at Drizzt.

THE PIRATE KING

He moved before she ever came forward, turning sidelong to the snapping rope. He slashed at it with Icingdeath, his right-hand blade, turned fully to strike it higher up with a backhanded uppercut of Twinkle in his left hand, then came around again with Icingdeath, slashing harder.

And around he went again, and again, turning three circles that had the rope out wide, and shortened its length with every powerful slash.

As he came around the fourth time, he met Nyphithys's thrusting sword with a slashing backhand parry.

The devil was ready for it, though, and she easily rolled her blade over the scimitar and thrust again for Drizzt's belly as he continued his turn.

Drizzt was ready for her to be ready for it, though, and Icingdeath came up under the long sword, catching it with its curved back edge. The dark elf completed the upward movement, rotating his arm up and out, throwing Nyphithys's blade far and high to his right.

Before the devil could extract her blade, Drizzt did a three-way movement of perfect coordination, bringing Twinkle snapping up and across to replace its companion blade in keeping the devil's sword out of the way, stepping forward and snapping his right down and ahead, its edge coming in tight against the devil's throat.

He had her helpless.

But she kept smiling.

And she was gone—just gone—vanished from his sight.

Drizzt whirled around and fell into a defensive roll, but relaxed somewhat when he spotted the devil, some thirty feet away on an island of rock a few feet up from his level.

"Fool drow," she scolded. "Fools, all of you. My masters will melt your land to ash and molten stone!"

A movement to the side turned her, to see Obould stalking her way.

"And you are the biggest fool of all," she roared at him. "We promised you power beyond anything you could ever imagine."

The orc took three sudden and furious strides then leaped as only Obould could leap, a greater leap than any orc would even attempt, a leap that seemed more akin to magical flight.

41

Nyphithys didn't anticipate it. Drizzt didn't, either. And neither did Bruenor or Catti-brie, who was readying an arrow to try to finish off the devil. She quickly deduced that there was no need for it, when Obould cleared the remaining distance and went high enough to land beside Nyphithys. He delivered his answer by transferring all of his momentum into a swing of his powerful greatsword.

Drizzt winced, for he had seen that play before. He thought of Tarathiel, his fallen friend, and pictured the elf in Nyphithys's place as she was shorn in half by the orc's mighty, fiery blade.

The devil fell to the stone, in two pieces.

* * * * *

"By Moradin's own mug," said Thibbledorf Pwent, standing between Bruenor and Regis. "I'm knowin' he's an orc, but I'm likin' this one."

Bruenor smirked at his battlerager escort, but his gaze went right back to Obould, who seemed almost godlike standing up on that stone, his foe, vanquished, at his feet.

Realizing that he had to react, Bruenor stalked the orc's way. "She'd have made a fine prisoner," he reminded Obould.

"She makes a better trophy," the orc king insisted, and he and Bruenor locked their typically angry stares, the two always seeming on the verge of battle.

"Don't ye forget that we came to help ye," said Bruenor.

"Don't you forget that I let you," Obould countered, and they continued to stare.

Over to the side, Drizzt found his way to Catti-brie. "Been four years," the woman lamented, watching the two rival kings and their unending growling at each other. "I wonder if I will live long enough to see them change."

"They're staring, not fighting," Drizzt replied. "You already have."

CHAPTER
TO DARE TO DREAM
3

A few years earlier, *Sea Sprite* would have just sent *Quelch's Folly* to the ocean floor and sailed on her way in search of more pirates. And *Sea Sprite* would have found other pirates to destroy before she needed to sail back into port. *Sea Sprite* could catch and destroy and hunt again with near impunity. She was faster, she was stronger, and she was possessed of tremendous advantages over those she hunted in terms of information.

A catch, though, was becoming increasingly rare, though pirates were plentiful.

A troubled Deudermont paced the deck of his beloved pirate hunter, occasionally glancing back at the damaged ship he had put in tow. He needed the assurance. Like an aging gladiator, Deudermont understood that time was fast passing him by, that his enemies had caught up to his tactics. The ship in tow alleviated those fears somewhat, of course, like a swordsman's win in the arena. And it would bring a fine payoff in Waterdeep, he knew.

"For months now I have wondered. . . ." Deudermont remarked to Robillard when he walked near the wizard, seated on his customary throne behind the mainmast, a dozen feet up from the deck. "Now I know."

"Know what, my captain?" Robillard asked with obviously feigned interest.

"Why we don't find them."

"We found one."

"Why we don't more readily find them," the captain retorted to his wizard's unending dry humor.

"Pray tell." As he spoke, Robillard apparently caught on to the intensity of Deudermont's gaze, and he didn't look away.

"I heard your conversation with Arabeth Raurym," Deudermont said.

Robillard replaced his shock with an amused grin. "Indeed. She is an interesting little creature."

"A pirate who escaped our grasp," Deudermont remarked.

"You would have had me put her in chains?" the wizard asked. "You are aware of her lineage, I presume."

Deudermont didn't blink.

"And her power," Robillard added. "She is an overwizard of the Hosttower of the Arcane. Had I tried to detain her, she would have blown the ship out from under our boarding party, yourself included."

"Isn't that exactly the circumstance for which you were hired?"

Robillard smirked and let the quip pass.

"I don't like that she escaped," Deudermont said. He paused and directed Robillard's gaze to starboard.

The sun dipped below the ocean horizon, turning a distant line of clouds fiery orange, red, and pink. The sun was setting, but at least it was a beautiful sight. Deudermont couldn't dismiss the symbolism of the sunset, given his feelings as he considered the relative inefficiency of *Sea Sprite* of late, those nagging suspicions that his tactics had been successfully countered by the many pirates running wild along the Sword Coast.

He stared at the sunset.

"The Arcane Brotherhood meddles where they should not," he said quietly, as much to himself as to Robillard.

"You would expect differently?" came the wizard's response.

Deudermont managed to tear his eyes from the natural spectacle to regard Robillard.

"They have always been meddlesome," Robillard explained. "Some, at least. There are those—I counted myself among them— who simply wanted to be left alone to our studies and experiments.

We viewed the Hosttower as a refuge for the brilliant. Sadly, others wish to use that brilliance for gain or for dominance."

"This Arklem Greeth creature."

"Creature? Yes, a fitting description."

"You left the Hosttower before he arrived?" Deudermont asked.

"I was still among its members as he rose to prominence, sadly."

"Do you count his rise among your reasons for leaving?"

Robillard considered that for a moment then shrugged. "I don't believe Greeth alone was the catalyst for the changes in the tower, he was more a symptom. But perhaps the fatal blow to whatever honor remained at the Hosttower."

"Now he supports the pirates."

"Likely the least of his crimes. He is an indecent creature."

Deudermont rubbed his tired eyes and looked back to the sunset.

* * * * *

Three days later, *Sea Sprite* and *Quelch's Folly*—whose name had been purposely marred beyond recognition—put into Waterdeep Harbor. They were met by eager wharf hands and the harbormaster himself, who also served as auctioneer for the captured pirate ships Deudermont and a very few others brought in.

"Argus Retch's ship," he said to Deudermont when the captain walked down from *Sea Sprite*. "Tell me ye got him in yer hold, and me day'll be brighter."

Deudermont shook his head and looked past the harbormaster, to a young friend of his, Lord Brambleberry of the East Waterdeep nobility. The man moved swiftly, with a boyish spring still in his step. He had passed the age of twenty, but barely, and while Deudermont admired his youth and vigor, and indeed believed that he was looking at a kindred spirit—Brambleberry so reminded him of himself at that age—he sometimes found the young man too eager and anxious to make a name for himself. Such rushed ambition could lead to a premature visit to the Fugue Plane, Deudermont knew.

"Ye killed him, then, did ye?" the harbormaster asked.

"He was not aboard when we boarded," Deudermont explained. "But we've a score of pirate prisoners for your gaolers."

"Bah, but I'd trade the lot of them for Argus Retch's ugly head," the man said and spat. Deudermont nodded quickly and walked by him.

"I heard that your sails had been sighted, and was hoping that you would put in this day," Lord Brambleberry said as the captain neared. He extended his hand, which Deudermont grasped in a firm shake.

"You wish to get in an early bid on Retch's ship?" Deudermont asked.

"I may," the young nobleman replied. He was taller than most men—as tall as Deudermont—with hair the color of wheat in a bright sun and eyes that darted to and fro with inquisitiveness and not wariness, as if there was too much of the world yet to be seen. He had thin and handsome features, again so much like Deudermont, and unblemished skin and clean fingernails bespeaking his noble birthright.

"May?" asked Deudermont. "I had thought you intended to construct a fleet of pirate hunters."

"You know I do," the young lord replied. "Or did. I fear that the pirates have learned to evade such tactics." He glanced at *Quelch's Folly* and added, "Usually."

"A fleet of escort ships, then," said Deudermont.

"A prudent adjustment, Captain," Brambleberry replied, and led Deudermont away to his waiting coach.

They let the unpleasant talk of pirates abate during their ride across the fabulous city of Waterdeep. The city was bustling that fine day, and too noisy for them to speak and be heard without shouting.

A cobblestone drive led up to Brambleberry's estate. The coach rolled under an awning and the attendants were fast to open the door and help the lord and his guest climb out. Inside the palatial dwelling, Brambleberry went first to the wine rack, a fine stock of elven vintages. Deudermont watched him reach to the lower rack and pull forth one bottle, then another, examining the label and brushing away the dust.

Brambleberry was retrieving the finest of his stock, Deudermont realized and smiled in appreciation, and also in recognizing that the Lord Brambleberry must have some important revelations waiting for him if he was reaching so deep into his liquid treasure trove.

They moved up to a comfortable sitting room, where a hearth blazed and fine treats had been set out on a small wooden table set between two plush chairs.

"I have wondered if we should turn to defensive measures, protecting the merchant ships, instead of our aggressive pirate hunts," Brambleberry said almost as soon as Deudermont took his seat.

"It's no duty I would wish."

"There is nothing exciting about it—particularly not for *Sea Sprite*," Brambleberry agreed. "Since any pirates spying such an escort would simply raise sail and flee long before any engagement. The price of fame," he said, and lifted his glass in toast.

Deudermont tapped the glass and took a sip, and indeed the young lord had provided him with a good vintage.

"And what has been the result of your pondering?" Deudermont asked. "Are you and the other lords convinced of the wisdom of escorts? It does sound like a costly proposition, given the number of merchant ships sailing out of your harbor every day."

"Prohibitive," the lord agreed. "And surely unproductive. The pirates adjust, cleverly and with . . . assistance."

"They have friends," Deudermont agreed.

"Powerful friends," said Lord Brambleberry.

Deudermont started the next toast, and after his sip asked, "Are we to dance around in circles, or are you to tell me what you know or what you suspect?"

Brambleberry's eyes flashed with amusement and he grinned smugly. "Rumors—perhaps merely rumors," he said. "It's whispered that the pirates have found allies in the greater powers of Luskan."

"The high captains, to a one, once shared their dishonorable profession, to some degree or another," said Deudermont.

"Not them," said the still elusive Brambleberry. "Though it wouldn't surprise me to learn that one or another of the high captains had an interest, perhaps financial, with a pirate or two. Nay, my friend, I speak of a more intimate and powerful arrangement."

"If not the high captains, then...."

"The Hosttower," said Brambleberry.

Deudermont's expression showed his increased interest.

"I know it's surprising, Captain," Brambleberry remarked, "but I have heard whispers, from reliable places, that the Hosttower is indeed involved in the increasing piracy of late—which would explain your more limited successes, and those of every other authority trying to track down and rid the waters of the scum."

Deudermont rubbed his chin, trying to put it all in perspective.

"You don't believe me?" Brambleberry asked.

"Quite the contrary," the captain replied. "Your words only confirm similar information I have recently received."

With a wide smile, Brambleberry reached again for his wineglass, but he paused as he lifted it, and stared at it intently.

"These were quite expensive," he said.

"Their quality is obvious."

"And the wine contained within them is many times more precious." He looked up at Deudermont.

"What would you have me say?" the captain asked. "I'm grateful to share in such luxury as this."

"That is my whole point," Brambleberry said, and Deudermont's face screwed up with confusion.

"Look around you," the Waterdhavian nobleman bade him. "Wealth—unbelievable wealth. All mine by birthright. I know that you have been well-rewarded for your efforts these years, good Captain Deudermont, but if you were to collect all of your earnings combined, I doubt you could afford that single rack of wine from which I pulled our present drink."

Deudermont set his glass down, not quite knowing how to respond, or how Brambleberry wanted him to respond. He easily suppressed his nagging, prideful anger and bade the man to continue.

"You sail out and bring down Argus Retch, through great effort and at great risk," Brambleberry went on. "And you come here with his ship, which I might purchase at a whim, with a snap of my fingers, and at a cost to my fortune that wouldn't be noticed by any but the most nitpicking of coin-counters."

"We all have our places," Deudermont replied, finally catching on to where the man was heading.

"Even if those places are not attained through effort or justice," said Brambleberry. He gave a self-deprecating chuckle. "I feel that I'm living a good life and the life of a good man, Captain. I treat my servants well, and seek to serve the people."

"You are a well-respected lord, and for good reason."

"And you are a hero, in Luskan and in Waterdeep."

"And a villain to many others," the captain said with a grin.

"A villain to villains, perhaps, and to no others. I envy you. And I salute you and look up to you," he added, and lifted his glass in toast, finally. "And I would trade places with you."

"Tell your staff and I will tell my crew," Deudermont said with a laugh.

"I jest with you not at all," Brambleberry replied. "Would that it were so simple. But we know it's not, and I know that to follow in your footsteps will be a journey of deeds, not of birthright. And not of purchases. I would have the people speak of me, one day, as they now speak of Captain Deudermont."

To Deudermont's surprise, Brambleberry threw his wineglass against the hearth, shattering it.

"I have earned none of this, other than by the good fortune of my birth. And so you see, Captain, I'm determined to put this good fortune to work. Yes, I will purchase Argus Retch's ship from you, to make three in my fleet, and I will sail them, crewed by mercenaries, to Luskan—beside you if you'll join me—and deal such a blow to those pirates sailing the Sword Coast as they have never before known. And when we're done, I will turn my fleet loose to the seas, hunting as *Sea Sprite* hunts, until the scourge of piracy is removed from the waters."

Deudermont let the proclamation hang in the air for a long while, trying to wind his thoughts along the many potential paths, most of them seeming quite disastrous.

"If you mean to wage war on the Hosttower, you will be facing a formidable foe—and a foe no doubt supported by the five high captains of Luskan," he finally replied. "Do you mean to start a war between Waterdeep and the City of Sails?"

"No, of course not," said Brambleberry. "We can be quieter than that."

"A small force to unseat Arklem Greeth and his overwizards?" Deudermont asked.

"Not just any small force," Brambleberry promised. "Waterdeep knows no shortage of individuals of considerable personal power."

Deudermont sat there staring as the heartbeats slipped past.

"Consider the possibilities, Captain Deudermont," Brambleberry begged.

"Are you not being too anxious to make your coveted mark, my young friend?"

"Or am I offering you the opportunity to truly finish that which you started so many years ago?" Brambleberry countered. "To deal a blow such as this would ensure that all of your efforts these years were far more than a temporary alleviation of misery for the merchants sailing the Sword Coast."

Captain Deudermont sat back in his chair and lifted his glass before him to drink. He paused, though, seeing the flickering fire in the hearth twisting through the facets of the crystal.

He couldn't deny the sense of challenge, and the hope of true accomplishment.

CHAPTER 4
FISHING FOR MEMORIES

"It was a prime example of the good that can come through cooperation," Drizzt remarked, and his smirk told Regis that he was making the lofty statement more to irk Bruenor than to make any profound philosophical point.

"Bah, I had to choose between orcs and demons . . ."

"Devils," the halfling corrected and Bruenor glared at him.

"Between orcs and *devils*," the dwarf king conceded. "I picked the ones what smelled better."

"You were bound to do so," Regis dared say, and it was his turn to toss a clever wink Drizzt's way.

"Bah, the Nine Hells I was!"

"Shall I retrieve the Treaty of Garumn's Gorge that we might review the responsibilities of the signatories?" Drizzt asked.

"Yerself winks at him and I put me fist into yer eye, then I toss Rumblebelly down the hallway," Bruenor warned.

"You cannot blame them for being surprised that King Bruenor would go to the aid of an orc," came a voice from the door, and the three turned as one to watch Catti-brie enter the room.

"Don't ye join them," Bruenor warned.

Catti-brie bowed with respect. "Fear not," she said. "I've come for my husband, that he can see me on my way."

"Back to Silverymoon for more lessons with Alustriel?" Regis asked.

"Beyond that," Drizzt answered for her as he walked across to take her arm. "Lady Alustriel has promised Catti-brie a journey that will span half the continent and several planes of existence." He looked at his wife and smiled with obvious envy.

"And how long's that to take?" Bruenor demanded. He had made it no secret to Catti-brie that her prolonged absences from Mithral Hall had created extra work for him, though in truth, the woman and everyone else who had heard the dwarf's grumbling had understood it to be his way of admitting that he sorely missed Catti-brie without actually saying the words.

"She gets to escape another Mithral Hall winter," Regis said. "Have you room for a short but stout companion?"

"Only if she turns you into a toad," Drizzt answered and led Catti-brie away.

*****

Later that same day, Regis walked outside of Mithral Hall to the banks of the River Surbrin. His remark about winter had reminded him that the unfriendly season was not so far away, and indeed, though the day was glorious, the wind swept down from the north, blustery and cold, and the leaves on the many trees across the river were beginning to show the colors of autumn.

Something in the air that day, the wind or the smell of the changing season, reminded Regis of his old home in Icewind Dale. He had more to call his own in Mithral Hall, and security—for where could be safer than inside the dwarven hall?—but the things he'd gained did little to alleviate the halfling's sense of loss for what had been. He had known a good life in Icewind Dale. He'd spent his days fishing for knucklehead trout from the banks of Maer Dualdon. The lake had given him all he needed and more, with water and food—he knew a hundred good recipes for cooking the delicious fish. And few could carve their skulls more wonderfully than Regis. His trinkets, statues, and paperweights had earned him a fine reputation among the local merchants.

Best of all, of course, was the fact that his "work" consisted mostly of lying on the banks of the lake, a fishing line tied to his toe.

With that in mind, Regis spent a long time walking along the riverbank, north of the bridge, in search of the perfect spot. He finally settled on a small patch of grass, somewhat sheltered from the north wind by a rounded gray stone, but one not high enough to shade him at all. He took great care in getting his line out to just the right spot, a quieter pool around the edge of a stony jut in the dark water. He used a heavy weight, but even that wouldn't hold if he put the line into the main flow of the river; the strong currents would wash it far downstream.

He waited a few moments, and confident that his location would hold steady, he removed a shoe, looped the line around his big toe, and dropped his pack to use as a pillow. He had barely settled down and closed his eyes when a noise from the north startled him.

He recognized the source before he even sat up to look beyond the rounded stone.

Orcs.

Several young ones had gathered at the water's edge. They argued noisily—why were orcs always so boisterous?—about fishing lines and fishing nets and where to cast and how to cast.

Regis almost laughed aloud at himself for his bubbling annoyance, for he understood his anger even as he felt it. They were orcs, and so he was angry. They were orcs, and so he was impatient. They were orcs, and so his first reaction had to be negative.

Old feelings died hard.

Regis thought back to another time and another place, recalling when a group of boys and girls had begun a noisy splash fight not far from where he had cast his line in Maer Dualdon. Regis had scolded them that day, but only briefly.

As he thought of it, he couldn't help grin, remembering how he had then spent a wonderful afternoon showing those youngsters how to fish, how to play a hooked knucklehead, and how to skin a catch. Indeed, that long-ago night, the group of youngsters had arrived at Regis's front door, at his invitation, to see some of his carvings and to enjoy a meal of trout prepared only as Regis knew how.

Among so many uneventful days on the banks of Maer Dualdon, that one stood out in Regis's memory.

He considered the noisy orc youngsters again, and laughed as he watched them try to throw a net—and wind up netting one young orc girl instead.

He almost got up, thinking to go and offer lessons as he had on that long ago day in Icewind Dale. But he stopped when he noticed the boundary marker between his spot and the orcs. Where the mountain spilled down to the Surbrin marked the end of Mithral Hall and the beginning of the Kingdom of Many-Arrows, and across that line, Regis could not go.

The orcs noticed him, then, just as he scowled. He lifted a hand to wave, and they did likewise, though more than a little tentatively.

Regis settled back behind the stone, not wanting to upset the group. One day, he thought, he might be able to go up there and show them how to throw a net or cast a line. One day soon, perhaps, given the relative peace of the past four years and the recent cooperative ambush that had destroyed a potential threat to the Silver Marches.

Or maybe he would one day wage war against those very orc youngsters, kill one with his mace or be taken in the gut by another's spear. He could picture Drizzt dancing through that group then and there, his scimitars striking with brilliant precision, leaving the lot of them squirming and bleeding on the rocks.

A shudder coursed the halfling's spine, and he shook away those dark thoughts.

They were building something there, Regis had to believe. Despite Bruenor's stubbornness and Obould's heritage, the uneasy truce had already become an accepted if still uneasy peace, and it was Regis's greatest hope that every day that passed without incident made the prospect of another dwarf-orc war a bit more remote.

A tug on the line had him sitting up, and once he had the line in hand, he scrambled to his feet, working the line expertly. Understanding that he had an audience, he took his time landing the fish, a fine, foot-long ice perch.

When at last he landed it, he held it up to show the young orcs, who applauded and waved enthusiastically.

"One day I will teach you," Regis said, though they were too far away—and upwind and with a noisy river bubbling by—and could not hear. "One day."

Then he paused and listened to his own words and realized that he was musing about orcs. Orcs. He had killed orcs, and with hardly a care. A moment of uncomfortable regret seized the halfling, followed quickly by a sense of complete confusion. He suppressed all of that, but only momentarily, by going back to work on his line, putting it back out in the calmer waters of the pool.

Orcs.

Orcs!

Orcs?

* * * * *

"Bruenor wishes to speak with you?" Catti-brie asked Drizzt when he returned to their suite of rooms late one night, only to be met by Bruenor's page with a quiet request. A tenday had passed since the fight with the devils and the situation had calmed considerably.

"He is trying to sort through the confusion of our recent adventure."

"He wants you to go to Mirabar with Torgar Hammerstriker," Catti-brie reasoned.

"It does seem ridiculous," Drizzt replied, agreeing with Catti-brie's incredulous tone. "In the best of times, and the most secure, Marchion Elastul would not grant me entrance."

"A long way to hike to camp out on the cold ground," Catti-brie quipped.

Drizzt moved up to her, grinning wickedly. "Not so unwelcome an event if I bring along the right bedroll," he said, his hands sliding around the woman's waist as he moved even closer.

Catti-brie laughed and responded to his kiss. "I would enjoy that."

"But you cannot go," Drizzt said, moving back. "You have a grand adventure before you, and one you would not wisely avoid."

"If you ask me to go with you, I will."

Drizzt stepped back, shaking his head. "A fine husband I would be to do so! I have heard hints of some of the wonders Alustriel has planned for you throughout the next few months, I could not deny you that for the sake of my own desires."

"Ah, but don't you understand how alluring it is to know that your desires for me overwhelm that absolute sense of right and wrong that is so deeply engrained into your heart and soul?"

Drizzt fell back at that and stared at Catti-brie, blinking repeatedly. He tried to respond several times, but nothing decipherable came forth.

Catti-brie let her laughter flow. "You are insufferable," she said, and danced across the room from Drizzt. "You spend so much time wondering how you *should* feel that you rarely ever simply *do* feel."

Knowing he was being mocked, Drizzt crossed his arms over his chest and turned his confused stare into a glare.

"I admire your judgment, all the while being frustrated by it," Catti-brie said. "I remember when you went into Biggrin's cave those many years ago, Wulfar at your side. It was not a wise choice, but you followed your emotions instead of your reason. What has happened to that Drizzt Do'Urden?"

"He has grown older and wiser."

"Wiser? Or more cautious?" she asked with a sly grin.

"Are they not one and the same?"

"In battle, perhaps," Catti-brie replied. "And since that is the only arena in which you have ever been willing to take a chance...."

Drizzt blew a helpless sigh.

"A span of a few heartbeats can make for a greater memory than the sum of a mundane year," Catti-brie continued.

Drizzt nodded his concession. "There are still risks to be had." He started for the door, saying, "I will try to be brief, though I suspect your father will wish to talk this through over and over again." He glanced back as he grabbed the handle and pulled the door open, shaking his head and smiling.

His expression changed when he considered his wife.

She had unfastened the top two buttons of her colorful shirt and stood looking at him with a sly and inviting expression. She gave a little grin and shrug, and chewed her bottom lip teasingly.

"It wouldn't be a wise choice to keep the king waiting," she said in a voice far too innocent.

Drizzt nodded, paused, and slammed and locked the door.

"I'm his son by marriage now," he explained, gliding across the room, his sword belt falling to the floor as he went. "The king will forgive me."

"Not if he knew what you were doing to his daughter," Catti-brie said as Drizzt wrapped her in a hug and tumbled down to the bed with her.

* * * * *

"If Marchion Elastul will not grant me entrance, I will walk past his gates and along my road," Drizzt was saying when Catti-brie entered Bruenor's chambers later on that night.

Regis was there as well, along with Torgar Hammerstriker and his Mirabarran companion, Shingles McRuff.

"He's a stubborn one," Shingles agreed with Drizzt after giving a nod to Catti-brie. "But ye've a longer road by far."

"Oh?" Catti-brie asked.

"He's for Icewind Dale," Bruenor explained. "Him and Rumblebelly."

Catti-brie stepped back at the surprising news and looked to Drizzt for an explanation.

"Me own decision," Bruenor said. "We're hearing that Wulfgar's settled back there, so I'm thinking that Drizzt and Rumblebelly might be looking in on him."

Catti-brie considered it for a few moments then nodded her agreement. She and Drizzt had discussed a journey to Icewind Dale to see their old friend. Word had come to Mithral Hall not long after the signing of the Treaty of Garumn's Gorge that Wulfgar was well and back in Icewind Dale, and Catti-brie and Drizzt had immediately begun plotting how they might go to him.

But they had delayed, for Wulfgar's sake. He didn't need to see them together. He had left Mithral Hall to start anew, and it wouldn't be fair for them to remind him of the life he could have had with Catti-brie.

"I will be back in Mithral Hall before your return," Drizzt promised her.

"Maybe," Catti-brie replied, but with an accepting smile.

"Both of our roads are fraught with adventure," Drizzt said.

"And neither of us would have it any other way," Catti-brie agreed. "I expect that's why we're in love."

"Ye're knowing that other people are in the room, I'm guessin'," Bruenor said rather gruffly, and the two looked at the dwarf to see him shaking his head and rolling his eyes.

CHAPTER 5
THE GREATER OF TWO EVILS

With a sigh, Bellany Tundash rolled over to the side, away from her lover. "You ask too many questions, and always at the wrong moments," she complained.

The small man, Morik by name, scrambled over to sit beside her on the edge of the bed. They looked like two cut of the same cloth, petite and dark-haired, only Bellany's eyes shone with a mischievousness and luster that had been lacking from Morik's dark orbs of late. "I take an interest in your life," he explained. "I find the Hosttower of the Arcane . . . fascinating."

"You're looking for a way to rob it, you mean."

Morik laughed, paused and considered the possibility, then shook his head at the absurdity of the thought and remembered why he was there. "I can undo any trap ever made," he boasted. "Except those of trickster wizards. Those traps, I leave alone."

"Well, every door has one," Bellany teased, and she poked Morik hard in the chest. "Ones that would freeze you, ones that would melt you . . ."

"Ah, so if I just open two doors simultaneously. . . ."

"Ones that would jolt you so forcefully you would bite out that feisty tongue!" Bellany was quick to add.

In response, Morik leaned over, nibbled her ear and gave her a little lick, drawing a soft moan.

"Then do tell me all the knowledge that I need to keep it," he whispered.

Bellany laughed and pulled away. "This is not about you at all," she replied. "This is about that smelly dwarf. Everything seems to be about him of late."

Morik rested back on his elbows. "He is insistent," he admitted.

"Then kill him."

Morik's laugh was one of incredulity.

"Then I will kill him—or get one of the overwizards to do it. Valindra . . . Yes, she hates ugly things and hates dwarves most of all. She will kill the little fellow."

Morik's expression grew deadly serious, so much so that Bellany didn't chuckle at her own clever remark and instead quieted and looked back at him in all seriousness.

"The dwarf is not the problem," Morik explained, "though I've heard he's devastating in battle."

"More boast than display, I wager," said Bellany. "Has he even fought anyone since his arrival in Luskan?"

Again Morik stopped her with a serious frown. "I know who it is he serves," he said. "And know that he wouldn't serve them if his exploits and proficiency were anything less than his reputation. I warn you because I care for you. The dwarf and his masters are not to be taken lightly, not to be threatened, and not to be ignored."

"It sounds as if I should indeed inform Valindra," said Bellany.

"If you do, I will be dead in short order. And so will you."

"And so will Valindra, I suppose, if you're correct in your terror-filled assessment. Do you really believe the high captains, any or all together, are of more than a pittance of concern to the Hosttower?"

"This has nothing to do with the high captains," Morik assured her.

"The dwarf has been seen with the son of Rethnor."

Morik shook his head.

"Then who?" she demanded. "Who are these mysterious ringleaders who seek information about the Hosttower? And if they are a threat, then why should I answer any of your questions?"

"Enemies of some within the tower, I would guess," Morik calmly answered. "Though not necessarily enemies of the tower, if you can see the distinction."

"Enemies of mine, perhaps."

"No," Morik answered. "Be glad you have my ear, and I yours." As he said it, Morik leaned in and bit Bellany on the ear softly. "I will warn you if anything is to come of this."

"Enemies of my friends," the woman said, pulling away forcefully, and for the first time, there seemed no playfulness in her tone.

"You have few friends in the Hosttower," Morik reminded her. "That's why you come down here so often."

"Perhaps down here, I simply feel superior."

"To me?" Morik asked with feigned pain. "Am I just an object of lust for you?"

"In your prayers."

Morik nodded and smiled lewdly.

"But you still haven't given me any reason to help you," Bellany replied. "Other than to forestall your own impending death, I mean."

"You wound me with every word."

"It's a talent. Now answer."

"Because the Hosttower does not recruit from outside the Hosttower, other than acolytes," said Morik. "Think about it. You have spent the better part of a decade in the Hosttower, and yet you are very low in the hierarchy."

"Wizards tend to stay for many, many years. We're a patient lot, else we would not be wizards."

"True, and those who come in with some heritage of power behind their name—Dornegal of Baldur's Gate, Raurym of Mirabar—tend to fill all the vacancies that arise higher up the chain of power. But were the Hosttower to suffer many losses all at once. . . ."

Bellany smirked at him, but her sour expression couldn't hide the sparkle of intrigue in her dark eyes.

"Besides, you'll help me because I know the truth of Montague Gale, who didn't die in an accident of alchemy."

Bellany narrowed her eyes. "Perhaps I should have eliminated the only witness," she said, but there was no real threat in her voice. She and Morik competed on many levels—in their lovemaking most of all—but try as either might to deny the truth of their relationship, they both knew they were more than lovers; they were in love.

"And in so doing eliminate the finest lover you've ever known?" Morik asked. "I think not."

Bellany had no immediate answer, but after a pause, she said in all seriousness, "I don't like that dwarf."

"You would like his masters even less, I assure you."

"Who are they?"

"I care too much about you to tell you. Just get what I need and get far out of the way when I tell you to."

After another pause, Bellany nodded.

* * * * *

They called him "the general" because among all the mid-level battle-mages at the Hosttower, Dondom Maealik was considered the finest. His repertoire was dominated by evocations, of course, and he could throw lightning bolts and fireballs more intense than any but the overwizards and the Archmage Arcane Arklem Greeth himself. And Dondom sprinkled in just enough defensive spells—transmutations that could blink him away to safety, an abjuration to make his skin like stone, various protection auras and misdirection dweomers—so that on a battlefield, he always seemed one step ahead of any adversary. Some of his maneuvers were the stuff of growing legend at the Hosttower, like the time he executed a dimensional retreat at the last second to escape a mob of orc warriors, who were left swinging at empty air before Dondom engulfed them in a conflagration that melted them to a one.

This night, though, because of information passed through a pair of petite, dark-haired lovers, Dondom's adversaries knew exactly what spells he had remaining in his daily repertoire, and had already put in place a plethora of countermeasures.

He came out of a tavern that dark night, after having tipped a few too many to end off a day of hard work at the Hosttower—a day when he had exhausted all but a few of his available spells.

The dwarf came out of an alleyway two doors down and fell into cadence with the walking wizard. He made no attempt to cover his heavy footsteps, and Dondom glanced back, though still he tried to hide the fact that he knew he was being followed. The wizard picked up his pace and the dwarf did likewise.

"Idiot," Dondom muttered under his breath, for he knew that it was the same dwarf who'd been heckling him inside the tavern earlier that night. The unpleasant fellow had professed vengeance when he'd been escorted out, but Dondom was surprised—pleasantly so!—to learn that there was more than bluster to the ugly little fellow.

Dondom considered his remaining spells and nodded to himself. As he neared the next alleyway, he broke into a run, propelling himself around the corner where he pulled up fast and traced a line on the ground. He had only a few heartbeats, and his head buzzed from too much liquor, but Dondom knew the incantation well, for most of his research occurred on distant planes.

The line on the ground glowed in the darkness. Both ends of it rolled into the center, then climbed into the air, drawing a column taller than Dondom by well over a foot. That vertical slice of energy cut through the planar continuum, splitting to two and moving out from each other. In between loomed a darkness more profound than the already black shadows.

But the dwarf wouldn't notice, Dondom knew.

The wizard settled his portal into place, and nodded as the glowing lines fast disappeared. Then Dondom ran down the alley, hoping he would hear the dwarf's screams.

* * * * *

Another form came out of the shadows as soon as the wizard had departed. With equal deftness, the lithe creature created a second magical gate, right in front of Dondom's, and dismissed the original as soon as the second was secure.

A dark hand waved on the street, motioning the dwarf to continue.

The dwarf had to take a deep breath. He trusted his boss—well, as much as anyone could trust a creature of that particular . . . persuasion, but traveling to the lower planes didn't come with many assurances, no matter who was doing the assuring.

But he was a good soldier, and besides, what worse could happen to him than all that had already transpired? He picked up his pace and came around the alleyway entrance in full run, yelling so that the clever wizard would know he'd gone through the gate.

* * * * *

"Ruffian," Dondom muttered as he strolled back to review his handiwork—and to dismiss the gate so that the obstinate and ugly dwarf—or one of the foul denizens of the Abyss—didn't somehow figure out how to get back through. The last thing Dondom wanted was to feel the wrath of Arklem Greeth for loosing demons onto the streets of Luskan. Or it was the next to the last thing he wanted, Dondom realized as he walked around and waved his hand to dispel his magic.

The gate didn't close.

The dwarf walked calmly back out onto the street and said, "Hate those places."

"H-how did you . . ." Dondom stuttered.

"Just went in to get me dog," said the dwarf. "Every dwarf's needin' a dog, don't ya know." He shoved his thumb and index finger against his lips and blew a shrill whistle.

Dondom more forcefully willed his gate to close—but it wasn't his gate. "You fool!" he cried at the dwarf. "What have you done?"

The dwarf pointed at his own chest. "Me?"

With a strange shriek, half roar of outrage, half squeal of fear, Dondom launched into spellcasting, determined to blow the vile creature into nothingness.

He stammered, though, as a second creature came forth from the blackness of the gate. It stepped out bent way over, for that was the only way it could fit through the man-sized portal, its horned head leading the way. Even in the dark of night, the bluish hue of its skin was apparent, and when it stood to full height, some twelve feet, Dondom nearly fainted.

"A—a glabrezu," he whispered, his gaze locked on the demon's lower arms—it sported two sets—that ended in large pincers.

"I just call him 'Poochie,'" said the dwarf. "We play a game."

With a howl, Dondom spun around and ran.

"Yeah, that's it!" cried the dwarf. To the demon, he commanded, "Fetch."

A fine sight greeted those revelers exiting the many taverns on Whiskey Row at that moment of the evening. Out of an alleyway came a wizard of the Hosttower, flailing his arms, screaming indecipherably. With his long and voluminous sleeves he looked rather like a frantic, wounded bird.

Behind him came the dwarf's dog, a twelve-foot, bipedal, four-armed, blue-skinned demon, taking one stride for the wizard's three and gaining ground easily.

"Teleport! Teleport!" Dondom shrieked. "Yes I must! Or blink . . . phase in and out . . . find a way."

That last word came out in a long, rolling syllable, covering several octaves, as one of the demon's pincers clamped around his waist and easily lifted him off the ground. He looked like a wounded bird that had gained a bit of altitude, except that he was moving backward, back into the alley.

And into the gate.

"I could've just smacked him in the skull," the dwarf said to his master's friend, a strange one who wasn't really a wizard but could do so many wizardly things.

"You bore me," came the reply he always got from that one.

"Haha!"

The gate blinked out, and the lithe, dark creature moved into the shadows—and probably blinked out, too. The dwarf walked along his merry way, the heads of his glassteel morningstars bouncing at the ends of their chains behind his shoulders.

He found himself smiling more often these days. There might not have been enough bloodletting for his tastes, but life was good.

* * * * *

"He wasn't a bad sort," Morik said to Kensidan. He tried to look the man in the eye as he spoke, but he always had trouble doing that with the Crow.

Morik held a deep-seated, nagging fear that Kensidan was possessed of some magical charming power, that his gaze would set even his most determined adversary whimpering at his feet. That skinny little man with soft arms and knobby knees that he always kept crossed, that shrinking runt who had done nothing noteworthy in his entire life, held such power over all those around him... and that was a group, Morik knew, that included several notorious killers. They all served the Crow. Morik didn't understand it, and yet he, too, found himself thoroughly intimidated every time he stood in the room, before that chair, looking down at a knobby knee.

Kensidan was more than the son of Rethnor. He was the brains behind Rethnor's captaincy. Too smart, too clever, too much the *sava* master. Imposing as he seemed when he sat, when he stood up and walked that awkward gait, his cloak collar up high, his black boots laced tightly halfway up his skinny shins, Kensidan appeared even more intimidating. It made no logical sense, but somehow that frailty played off as the exact opposite, an unfathomable and ultimately deadly strength.

Behind the chair, the dwarf stood quietly, picking at his teeth as if all was right in the world. Bellany didn't like the dwarf, which was no surprise to Morik, who wondered if anyone had ever liked that particular dwarf.

"Dondom was a dangerous sort, by your own word," the Crow answered in those quiet, even, too controlled tones that he had long-ago perfected—probably in the cradle, Morik mused. "Too loyal to Arklem Greeth and a dear friend to three of the tower's four overwizards."

"You feared that if Dondom allied with Arklem Greeth then his friends who might otherwise stay out of the way would intervene on behalf of the archmage arcane," Morik reasoned, nodding then finally looking Kensidan in the eye.

To find a disapproving stare.

"You twist and turn into designs of which you have no knowledge, and no capacity to comprehend," Kensidan said. "Do as you are bid, Morik the Rogue, and no more."

"I'm not just some unthinking lackey."

"Truly?"

Morik couldn't match the stare and couldn't hold the line of defiance, either. Even if he somehow summoned the courage to deny the terrible Crow and run free of him, there was the not-so-little matter of those other puppeteers. . . .

"You have no one to blame for your discomfort but yourself," Kensidan remarked, seeming quite amused by it all. "Was it not you who planted the seeds?"

Morik closed his eyes and cursed the day he'd ever met Wulfgar, son of Beornegar.

"And now your garden grows," said Kensidan. "And if the fragrance is not to your liking . . . well, you cannot pull the flowers, for they have thorns. Thorns that make you sleep. Deadly thorns."

Morik's eyes darted to and fro as he scanned the room for an escape route. He didn't like where the conversation was leading; he didn't like the smile that had creased the face of the dangerous dwarf standing behind Kensidan.

"But you need not fear those thorns," Kensidan said, startling the distracted rogue. "All you need to do is continue feeding them."

"And they feast on information," Morik managed to quip.

"Your lady Bellany is a fine chef," Kensidan remarked. "She will enjoy her ascent when the garden is in full bloom."

That put Morik a bit more at ease. He had been commanded to Kensidan's court by one he dared not refuse, but the tasks he had been assigned the last few months had come with promises of great rewards. And it wasn't so difficult a job, either. All he had to do was continue his love affair with Bellany, which was reward enough in itself.

"You need to protect her," he blurted as his thoughts shifted to the woman. "Now, I mean."

"She is not in jeopardy," the Crow replied.

"You've used the information she passed to the detriment of several powerful wizards of the Hosttower."

Kensidan considered that for a moment then smiled again, wickedly. "If you wish to describe being carried through a gate to the Abyss in the clutches of a glabrezu as 'detrimental,' so be it. I might have used a different word."

"Without Bellany—" Morik started to say, but Kensidan finished for him.

"The end result would be a battle far more bloody and far more dangerous for everyone who lives in Luskan. Think not that you are instrumental to my designs, Morik the Rogue. You are a convenience, nothing more, and would do well to keep it that way."

Morik started to reply several times, but found no proper retort, looking all the while, as he was, at the evilly grinning dwarf.

Kensidan waved him away and turned to an aide, striking up a conversation on an entirely different subject. He paused after only a few words, shot Morik a warning glare, and waved him away again.

Back out on the street, walking briskly and cursing under his breath, Morik the Rogue again damned the day he'd met the barbarian from Icewind Dale. All the while, though, he secretly hoped he would soon be blessing that day, for as terrified as he was of his masters, their promises of rewards were neither inconsequential nor hollow. Or so he hoped.

CHAPTER
EXPEDIENCE
6

"Bruenor is still angry with him," Regis said to Drizzt. Torgar and Shingles had moved out ahead of them to look for familiar trails, for the dwarves believed they were nearing their old home city of Mirabar.

"No."

"He holds grudges for a long, long time."

"And he loves his adopted children," Drizzt reminded the halfling. "Both of them. True, he was angry when first he learned that Wulfgar had left, and at a time when the world seemed dark indeed."

"We all were," said Regis.

Drizzt nodded and didn't disagree, though he knew the halfling was wrong. Wulfgar's departure had saddened him, but hadn't angered him, for he understood it all too well. Carrying the grief of a dead wife, one he had let down terribly by missing all her signs of misery, had bowed his shoulders. Following that, Wulfgar had to watch Catti-brie, the woman he had once dearly loved, wed his best friend. Circumstance had not been kind to Wulfgar, and had wounded him profoundly.

But not mortally, Drizzt knew, and he smiled despite the unpleasant memories. Wulfgar had come to accept the failures of his past and bore nothing but love for the other Companions of the Hall. But he had decided to look forward, to find his place, his wife, his family, among his ancient people.

So when Wulfgar departed for the east, Drizzt harbored no anger, and when word had arrived back in Mithral Hall that following autumn that Wulfgar was back in Icewind Dale, the news lifted Drizzt's heart.

He couldn't believe that four years had passed. It seemed like only a day, and yet, when he thought of Wulfgar, it seemed as though he hadn't been beside his friend in a hundred years.

"I hope he is well," Regis stated, and Drizzt nodded.

"I hope he is alive," Regis added, and Drizzt patted his friend on the shoulder.

"Today," Torgar Hammerstriker announced, coming up over a rocky rise. He pointed back behind him and to the left. "Two miles for a bird, four for a dwarf." He paused and grinned. "Five for a fat halfling."

"Who ate too much of last night's rations," Shingles McRuff added, moving up to join his old friend.

"Then let us be quick to the gates," Drizzt remarked, stealing the mirth with his serious tone. "I wish to be long away before the fall of night if Marchion Elastul holds true to his former ways."

The two dwarves exchanged concerned looks, their excitement at returning to their former home tempered by the grim reminder that they had left under less than ideal circumstances those years before. They, along with many of their kin, more than half the dwarves of Mirabar, had deserted Elastul and his city over a dispute concerning King Bruenor. Over the last three years, many more Mirabarran dwarves, *Delzoun* dwarves, had come to Mithral Hall to join them, and not all of the hundreds formerly of Mirabar that called Bruenor their king had agreed with Torgar's decision to trust the emissary and return.

More than one had warned that Elastul would throw Torgar and Shingles in chains.

"He won't make ye walk away," Torgar said with determination. "Elastul's a stubborn one, but he's no fool. He's wanting his eastern trade route back. He never thinked that Silverymoon and Sundabar would side with Mithral Hall."

"We shall see," was all Drizzt would concede, and off they went at a swift pace.

They passed through the front gates of Mirabar soon after, hustled in by excited guards both dwarf and human. They were greeted by cheers—even Drizzt, who had been denied entrance just a few short years earlier when King Bruenor had returned to Mithral Hall. Before any of the companions could even digest the pleasant surprise the four found themselves before Elastul himself, a highly unusual circumstance.

"Torgar Hammerstriker, never did I expect to see you again," the old marchion—and indeed, he seemed much, much older than when Torgar had left—said with a tone as warm as the dancing licks of faerie fire.

Torgar, ever mindful of his place, bowed low, as did Shingles. "We come to ye as emissaries of King Bruenor Battlehammer of Mithral Hall, both in appreciation of your warning to us and in reply to yer request for an audience."

"Yes, and I hear that went quite well," said Elastul. "With the emissary of the Arcane Brotherhood, I mean."

"Devil feathers all over the field," Torgar assured him.

"You were there?" asked Elastul, and Torgar nodded. "Holding up the pride of Mirabar, I hope."

"Don't ye go there," the dwarf replied, and Regis sucked in his breath. "Was one day I'd get me to the Nine Hells and back, singing for Mirabar all the while. Me axe's for Bruenor now and Mithral Hall, and ye're knowin' as much and knowin' it's not to change."

For a brief moment, Elastul seemed as if he were about to shout at Torgar, but he suppressed his anger. "Mirabar is not the city you left, my old friend," he said instead, and again Drizzt sensed that the sweetness of his tone was tearing the old marchion apart behind his facade. "We have grown, in understanding if not in size. Witness your dark-skinned friend, here, standing before my very throne."

Torgar snickered. "If ye was any more generous, Moradin himself'd drop down and kiss ye."

Elastul's expression soured at the dwarf's sarcasm, but he worked hard to bring himself back to a neutral posture.

"I'm serious in my offer, Torgar Hammerstriker," he said. "Full amnesty for you and any of the others who went over to Mithral Hall. You may return to your previous status—indeed, I will grant you a commendation and promotion within the ranks of the Shield of Mirabar, because it was your courageous determination that forced me to look beyond my own walls and beyond the limitations of a view too parochial."

Torgar bowed again. "Then thank me and me boys by accepting what is, and what's going to be," he said. "I come for Bruenor, me king and me friend. And all hopes o' Mithral Hall are that we're both for lettin' past . . . unpleasantness, pass. The orcs're tamed well enough and the route's an easy one for yer own trade east and ours back west."

Elastul slumped back in his throne and seemed quite deflated, again on the verge of screaming. He looked at Drizzt instead and said, "Welcome to Mirabar, Drizzt Do'Urden. It's far past time that you enjoyed the splendors of my most remarkable city."

Drizzt bowed and replied, "I have heard of them often, and am honored."

"You have unfettered access, of course," Elastul said. "All of you. And I will prepare a treaty for King Bruenor that you may take and deliver before the blows of the northern winds bury those easy routes under deep snows."

He motioned for them to go and they were more than happy to oblige, with Torgar muttering to Drizzt as they walked out of the audience chamber's door, "He's needing the trade . . . badly."

The city's reaction to Torgar and Shingles proved to be as mixed as the structures of the half above-ground, half below-ground city. For every two smiling dwarves, the former Mirabarrans found the scowl of another obviously harboring feelings of betrayal, and few of the many humans in the upper sections even looked at Torgar, though their eyes surely weighed uncomfortably on the shoulders of a certain dark elf.

"It was all a ruse," Regis remarked after one old woman spat on the winding road as Drizzt passed her by.

"Not all of it," Drizzt answered, though Shingles was nodding and Torgar wore a disgusted look.

"They expected we would come, and practiced for it," Regis argued. "They hustled us right in to see Elastul, not because he was so thrilled at our arrival, but because he wanted to greet us before we knew the extent of Mirabar's grudge."

"He let us in, and most o' me kin'll be glad for it," Torgar said. "The pain's raw. When me and me boys left, we cut open a wound long festerin' in the town."

"Uppity dwarves, huzzah," Shingles deadpanned.

"The wound will heal," said Drizzt. "In time. Elastul has placed a salve on it now by greeting us so warmly." As he finished, he gave a slight bow and salute to a couple of elderly men who glared at him with open contempt. His disarming greeting brought a harrumph of disgust from the pair, and they turned away in a huff.

"The voice of experience," Regis dryly observed.

"I'm no stranger to scorn," Drizzt agreed. "Though my charm wins them over every time."

"Or yer blades cut them low," said Torgar.

Drizzt let it go with a chuckle. He knew already that it would be the last laugh the four would share for some time. The reception in Mirabar, Elastul's promise of hospitality notwithstanding, would fast prove counterproductive to Bruenor's designs.

Very soon after the group descended the great lift to the town's lower reaches, where the dwarves proved no less scornful of Drizzt than had the humans above. The drow had seen enough.

"We've a long road and a short season remaining," Drizzt said to Torgar and Shingles. "Your city is as wondrous as you've oft told me, but I fear that my presence here hinders your desire to bring good will from Mithral Hall."

"Bah, but they'll shut their mouths!" Torgar insisted, and he seemed to be winding himself into a froth. Drizzt put a hand on his shoulder.

"This is for King Bruenor, not for you and not for me," the drow explained. "And my reason is not false. The trail to Icewind Dale fast closes, often before winter proper, and I would see my old and dear friend before the spring melt."

"We're leaving already?" Regis put in. "I've been promised a good meal."

"And so ye're to get one," said Torgar, and he steered them toward the nearest tavern.

But Drizzt grabbed him by the arm and pulled him up short, and Torgar turned to see the drow shaking his head. "There's likely to be a commotion that will do none of us any good."

"Getting dark outside," Torgar argued.

"It has been dark every night since we left Mithral Hall, as expected," the drow replied with a disarming grin. "I don't fear the night. Many call it the time of the drow, and I am, after all. . . ."

"But I'm not, and I'm hungry," Regis argued.

"Our packs are half full!"

"With dry bread and salted meat. Nothing juicy and tender and . . ."

"He'll moan all the way to Icewind Dale," Torgar warned.

"Long road," Shingles added.

Drizzt knew he was defeated, so he followed the dwarves into the common room. It was as expected, with every eye turning on Drizzt the moment he walked through the door. The tavernkeeper gave a great sigh of resignation; word had gone out from Elastul that the drow must be served, Drizzt realized.

He didn't argue, nor did he press the point, allowing Torgar and Shingles to go to the bar to get the food while he and Regis settled at the most remote table. The four spent the whole of their meal suffering the glares of a dozen other patrons. If it bothered Regis at all, he didn't show it, for he never looked up from his plate, other than to scout out the next helping.

It was no leisurely meal, to be sure. The tavernkeeper and his serving lady showed great efficiency in producing the meal and cleaning the empty plates.

That suited Drizzt, and when the last of the bones and crumbs were removed and Regis pulled out his pipe and began tapping it on the table, the drow put his hand atop it, holding it still. He held still, too, the halfling's gaze.

"It's time to go," he said.

"Mirabar won't open her gates at this hour," Torgar protested.

"I'm betting they will," Drizzt replied, "to let a dark elf leave."

Torgar was wise enough to refuse that bet, and as the gates of the city above swung open, Drizzt and Regis said farewell to their two dwarf companions and went out into the night.

"That bothers me more than it bothers you, doesn't it?" Regis asked as the city receded into the darkness behind them.

"Only because it costs you a soft bed and good food."

"No," the halfling said, in all seriousness.

Drizzt shrugged as if it didn't matter, and of course, to him it didn't. He had found similar receptions in so many surface communities, particularly during his first years on the World Above, before his reputation had spread before him. The mood of Mirabar, though the folk harbored resentment against the dwarves and Mithral Hall as well, had been light compared to Drizzt's early days—days when he dared not even approach a city's gates without an expectation of mortal peril.

"I wonder if Ten-Towns is different now," Regis remarked some time later, as they set their camp in a sheltered dell.

"Different?"

"Bigger, perhaps. More people."

Drizzt shook his head, thinking that unlikely. "It's a difficult journey through lands not easily tamed. We will find Luskan a larger place, no doubt, unless plague or war has visited it, but Icewind Dale is a land barely touched by the passage of time. It is now as it has been for centuries, with small communities surviving on the banks of the three lakes and various tribes of Wulfgar's people following the caribou, as they have beyond memory."

"Unless war or a plague has left them empty."

Drizzt shook his head again. "If any or all of the ten towns of Icewind Dale were destroyed, they would be rebuilt in short order and the cycle of life and death is returned to balance."

"You sound certain."

That brought a smile to the drow's face. There was indeed something comforting about the perpetuity of a land like Icewind Dale, some solace and a sense of belonging in a place where traditions reached back through the generations, where the rhythms of nature ruled supreme, where the seasons were the only timepiece that really mattered.

"The world is grounded in places like Icewind Dale," Drizzt said, as much to himself as to Regis. "And all the tumult of Luskan and Waterdeep, prey to the petty whims of transient, short-lived rulers, cannot take root there. Icewind Dale serves no ruler, unless it be Toril herself, and Toril is a patient mistress." He looked at Regis and grinned to lighten the mood. "Perhaps a thousand years from now, a halfling fishing the banks of Maer Dualdon will happen upon a piece of ancient scrimshaw, and will see the mark of Regis upon it."

"Keep talking, friend," Regis replied, "and Bruenor and your wife will wonder, years hence, why we didn't return."

CHAPTER 7

FAITH IN THE BETTER ANGELS

"We go with the rising sun and the morning tide," Lord Brambleberry said to the gathering in the great room of his estate, "to deal a blow to the pirates as never before!"

The guests, lords and ladies all, lifted their crystal goblets high in response, but only after a moment of whispering and shrugging, for Brambleberry's invitation had mentioned nothing about any grand adventure. Those shrugs fast turned to nods as the news settled in, however, for rumors had been growing around "impatient Lord Brambleberry" for many months. He had made no secret of his desire to transform good fortune into great deed.

Up to that point, though, his blather had been considered the typical boasting of almost any young lord of Waterdeep, a game to impress the ladies, to create stature where before had been only finery. Many in the room carried reputations as worthy heroes, after all, though some of them had never set foot outside of Waterdeep, except traveling in luxury and surrounded by an army of private guards. Some other lords with actual battlefield credentials to their names had gained such notoriety over the bodies of hired warriors, only arriving on the scene of a victory after the fact for the heroic pose to be captured on a painter's canvas.

There were real heroes in the room, to be sure. Morus Brokengulf the Younger, paladin of great renown and well-earned reputation, had just returned to Waterdeep to inherit his family's vast holdings.

He stood talking to Rhiist Majarra, considered the greatest bard of the city, perhaps of the entire Sword Coast, though he'd barely passed his twentieth year. Across the way from them, the ranger Aluar Zendos, "who could track a shadow at midnight," and the famous Captain Rulathon tapped glasses of fine wine and commiserated of great adventures and heroic deeds. These men, usually the least boastful of the crowd, knew the difference between the posers and the doers, and often relished in such gossip, and up to that moment they had been evenly split on which camp the striking young Lord Brambleberry would ultimately inhabit.

It was hard not to take him seriously at that moment, however, for standing beside the young Brambleberry was Captain Deudermont of *Sea Sprite*, well known in Waterdeep and very highly considered among the nobility. If Brambleberry sailed with Deudermont, his adventure would be no ruse. Those true heroes in the room offered solemn nods of approval to each other, but quietly, for they didn't want to spoil the excited and humorously inane conversations erupting all across the hall, squealed in the corners under cover of the rousing symphony or whispered on the dance floor.

Roaming the floor, Deudermont and Robillard took it all in; the wizard even cast an enchantment of clairaudience so that they could better spy on the amusing exchanges.

"He's not satisfied with wealth and wine," one lady of court whispered. She stood in the corner near a table full of tallglasses, which she not-so-gracefully imbibed one after another.

"He'll add the word 'hero' to his title or they'll put him in the cold ground for trying," said her friend, with hair bound up in a woven mound that climbed more than a foot above her head.

"To get such fine skin dirty at the feet of an ogre...." another decried.

"Or bloody at the end of a pirate's sword," yet another lamented. "So much the pity."

They all stopped chattering at once, all eyes going to Brambleberry, who swept across their field of view on the dance floor, gracefully twirling a pretty young thing. That brought a collective sigh from the four, and the first remarked, "One would expect the older and wiser lords to temper this one. So much a waste!"

"So much to lose."

"The young fool."

"If he is in need of physical adventure. . . ." the last said, ending in a lewd smile, and the others burst out in ridiculous tittering.

* * * * *

The wizard waved his hand to dismiss the clairaudience dweomer, having heard more than enough.

"Their attitude makes it difficult to take the young lord's desires seriously," Robillard remarked to Deudermont.

"Or easier to believe that our young friend needs more than this emptiness to sustain him," the captain answered. "Obviously he needs no further laurels to be invited to any of their beds. Which is a blessing, I say, for there is nothing more dangerous than a young man trying to hero himself into a lady's arms."

Robillard narrowed his eyes as he turned to his companion. "Spoken like a young man I knew in Luskan, so many years ago, when the world was calmer and my life held a steady cadence."

"Steady and boring," Deudermont replied without hesitation. "You remember that young man well because of the joy he has brought to you, stubborn though you have been through it all."

"Or perhaps I just felt pity for the fool."

With a helpless chuckle, Deudermont lifted his tallglass, and Robillard tapped it with his own.

* * * * *

Without fanfare, the four ships glided out of Waterdeep Harbor to the wider waters of the Sea of Swords the next morning. No trumpets heralded their departure, no crowds gathered on the docks to bid them farewell, and even the Chaplain Blessing for favorable winds and gentle swells was kept quiet, held aboard each ship instead of the common prayer on the wharves with sailors and dockhands alike.

From the deck of *Sea Sprite,* Robillard and Deudermont regarded the skill and discipline, or lack thereof, of Brambleberry's three ships as they tried to form a tight squadron. At one point, all three nearly collided. The quick recovery left Brambleberry's flagship, formerly *Quelch's Folly,* and since lettered with the additional *"—Justice,"* with tangled rigging. Brambleberry had wanted to rename the ship entirely, but Deudermont had dissuaded him. Such practices were considered bad luck, after all.

"Keep us well back," Deudermont ordered his helmsman. "And to port. Always in the deeper water."

"Afraid that we might have to dodge their wreckage?" Robillard quipped.

"They are warriors, not seamen," Deudermont replied.

"If they fight as well as they sail, they'll be corpses," Robillard said and looked out to sea, leaning on the rail. He added, "Probably will be anyway," under his breath, but loudly enough so that Deudermont heard.

"This adventure troubles you," said Deudermont. "More than usual, I mean. Do you fear Arklem Greeth and your former associates so much?"

Robillard shrugged and let the question hang in the air for a few heartbeats before replying, "Perhaps I fear the absence of Arklem Greeth."

"How so? We know now what we have suspected for some time. Surely the people of the Sword Coast will be better off without such treachery."

"Things are not always as simple as they seem."

"I ask again, how so?"

Robillard merely shrugged.

"Or is it that you hold some affinity for your former peer?"

Robillard turned to look at the captain and said, "He is a beast . . . a lich, an abomination."

"But you fear his power."

"He is not a foe to be taken lightly, nor are his minions," the wizard replied. "But I'm assured that our young Lord Brambleberry there has assembled a capable and potent force, and, well, you have me beside you, after all."

"Then what? What do you mean when you say that you fear the *absence* of Greeth? What do you know, my friend?"

"I know that Arklem Greeth is the absolute ruler of Luskan. He has established his boundaries."

"Yes, and extended them to pirates running wild along the Sword Coast."

"Not so wild," said Robillard. "And need I remind you that the five high captains who appear to rule Luskan once skirted similar boundaries?"

"Shall we explain to the next shipwrecked and miserable victims we happen across, good and decent folk who just watched family and friends murdered, that the pirates who scuttled them were operating within acceptable boundaries?" asked Deudermont. "Are we to tolerate such injustice and malevolence out of some fear of an unknown future?"

"Things are not always as simple as they seem," Robillard said again. "The Hosttower of the Arcane, the Arcane Brotherhood itself, might not be the most just and deserving rulers of Luskan, but we have seen the result of their rule: Peace in the city, if not in the seas beyond. Are you so confident that without them, Luskan can steer better course?"

"Yes," Deudermont declared. "Yes, indeed."

"I would expect such surety from Brambleberry."

"I have lived my life trying to do right," said Deudermont. "And it's not for fear of any god or goddess, nor of the law and its enforcers. I follow that course because I believe that doing good will bring about good results."

"The wide world is not so easily controlled."

"Indeed, but do you not agree that the better angels of man will win out? The world moves forward to better times, times of peace and justice. It's the nature of humanity."

"But it's not a straight road."

"I grant you that," said Deudermont. "And the twists and turns, the steps backward to strife, are ever facilitated by creatures like Arklem Greeth, by those who hold power but should not. They drive us to darkness when men do nothing, when bravery and honor is in short supply. They are a suffocating pall on the land, and only when brave men lift that pall can the better angels of men stride forward."

"It's a good theory, a goodly philosophy," said Robillard.

"Brave men must act of their heart!" Deudermont declared.

"And of their reason," Robillard warned. "Strides on ice are wisely tempered."

"The bold man reaches the mountaintop!"

Robillard thought, but didn't say, or falls to his death.

"You will fight beside me, beside Lord Brambleberry, against your former brother wizards?"

"Against those who don't willingly come over to us, yes," Robillard answered. "My oath of loyalty is to you, and to *Sea Sprite*. I have spent too many years saving you from your own foolishness to let you die so ingloriously now."

Deudermont clapped his dearest friend on the shoulder and moved to the rail beside him, leading Robillard's gaze back out to the open sea. "I do fear that you may be right," he conceded. "When we defeat Arklem Greeth and end the pirate scourge, the unintended consequences might include the retirement of *Sea Sprite*. We'll have nothing left to hunt, after all."

"You know the world better than that. There were pirates before Arklem Greeth, there are pirates in the time of Greeth, and there will be pirates when his name is lost to the ashes of history. Better angels, you say, and on the whole, I believe—or at least I pray—that you are correct. But it's never the whole that troubles us, is it? It's but a tiny piece of humanity who sail the Sword Coast as pirates."

"A tiny piece magnified by the powers of the Hosttower."

"You may well be right," said Robillard. "And you may well be wrong, and that, my friend, is my fear."

Deudermont held fast to the rail and kept his gaze to the horizon, unblinking though the sun had broken through and reflected brilliantly off the rolling waters. It was a good man's place to act for the cause of justice. It was a brave man's place to battle those who would oppress and do harm to helpless innocents. It was a leader's place to act in concert with his principles and trust enough in those principles to believe that they would lead him and those who followed him to a better place.

Those were the things Deudermont believed, and he recited them in his mind as he stared at the brilliant reflections on the waters he loved so dearly. He had lived his life, had shaped his own code of conduct, through his faith in the dictums of a good and brave leader, and they had served him well as he in turn had served so well the people of Luskan, Waterdeep, and Baldur's Gate.

Robillard knew the Hosttower and the ways of the Arcane

Brotherhood, and so Deudermont would indeed defer to him on the specifics of their present enemy.

But Captain Deudermont would not shy from the duty he saw before him, not with the opportunity of having eager Lord Brambleberry and his considerable resources sailing beside him.

He had to believe that he was right.

CHAPTER 8
SMOTHERED BY A SECURITY BLANKET

"Perhaps I'm just getting older and harder to impress," Regis said to Drizzt as they walked across a wide fields of grass. "She's not so great a city, not near the beauty of Mithral Hall—and surely not Silverymoon—but I'm glad they let you in through the gates, at least. Folk are stubborn, but it gives me hope that they can learn."

"I was no more impressed by Mirabar than you were," Drizzt replied, tossing a sidelong glance at his halfling friend. "I had long heard of her wonders, but I agree they're lacking beside Mithral Hall. Or maybe it's just that I like the folk who live in Mithral Hall better."

"It's a warmer place," Regis decided. "From the king on down. But still, you must be glad of your acceptance in Mirabar."

Drizzt shrugged as though it didn't matter, and of course, it didn't. Not to him, anyway; he could not deny his hope that Marchion Elastul would truly make peace with Mithral Hall and his lost dwarves. That development could only bode well for the North, particularly with an orc kingdom settled on Mithral Hall's northern border.

"I'm more glad that Bruenor found the courage to go to Obould's aid for a cause of common good," the drow remarked. "We've seen a great change in the world."

"Or a temporary reprieve."

Again Drizzt shrugged, but the gesture was accompanied by a look of helpless resignation. "Every day Obould holds the peace is a day of greater security than we could have expected. When his hordes rushed down from the mountains, I believed we would know nothing but war for years on end. When they surrounded Mithral Hall, I feared we would be driven from the place forever more. Even in the first months of stalemate, I, like everyone else, expected that it would surely descend into war and misery."

"I still expect it."

Drizzt's smile showed that he didn't necessarily disagree. "We stay vigilant for good reason. But every passing day makes that future just a bit less certain. And that's a good thing."

"Or is every passing day nothing more than another day Obould prepares to finish his conquest?" Regis asked.

Drizzt draped his arm over the halfling's shoulders.

"Am I too cynical for fearing such?" Regis asked.

"If you are, then so am I, and so is Bruenor—and Alustriel, who has spies working all through the Kingdom of Many-Arrows. Our experience with the orcs is long and bitter, full of treachery and war. To think that all we've known to be true is not necessarily an absolute is unsettling and almost incomprehensible, and so to walk the road of acceptance and peace often takes more courage than the way of the warrior."

"It always is more complicated than it seems, isn't it?" Regis asked with a wry grin. "Like you, for example."

"Or like a halfling friend of mine who fishes with one foot and flees with the other, fights with a mace in his right hand and pickpockets an unsuspecting fool with his left, and all the while manages to keep his belly full."

"I have a reputation to uphold," Regis answered, and handed Drizzt back the purse he'd just lifted from the drow's belt.

"Very good," Drizzt congratulated. "You almost had it off my belt before I felt your hand." As he took the purse, he handed Regis back the unicorn-headed mace he'd deftly slid from the halfling's belt as the rogue was lifting his purse.

Regis shrugged innocently. "If we steal one-for-one, I will end up with the more valuable items of magic."

Drizzt looked across the halfling and out to the north, leading

Regis's gaze to a huge black panther moving their way. Drizzt had summoned Guenhwyvar from her Astral home that afternoon and let her go to run a perimeter around them. He hadn't brought the panther forth much of late, not needing her in the halls of King Bruenor and not wanting to spark some tragic incident with any of the orcs in Obould's kingdom, who might react to such a sight as Guenhwyvar with a volley of spears and arrows.

"It's good to be on the road again," Regis declared as Guenhwyvar loped up beside him, opposite Drizzt. He ruffled the fur on the back of the great cat's neck and Guenhwyvar tilted her head and her eyes narrowed to contented slits of approval.

"And you are complicated, as I said," Drizzt remarked, viewing this rarely seen side of his comfort-loving friend.

"I believe I was the one to say that," Regis corrected. "You just applied it to me. And it's not that I'm a complicated sort. It's just that I ever keep my enemies confused."

"And your friends."

"I use you for practice," said the halfling, and as he gave a rather vigorous rub of Guenhwyvar's neck, the panther let out a low growl of approval that resonated across the dales and widened the eyes of every deer within range.

The fields of tall grass and wild flowers gave way to cultivated land as the sun neared the horizon before them. In the waning twilight, with farmhouses and barns dotting both sides, the path had become a road. The companions spotted a familiar hill in the distance, one sporting the zigzagging silhouette of a house magnificent and curious, with many towers tall and thin, and many more short and squat. Lights burned in every window.

"Ah, but what mysteries might the Harpells have in store for us this visit?" Drizzt asked.

"Mysteries for themselves as well, no doubt," said Regis. "If they haven't all killed each other by accident by now."

As lighthearted as the quip was meant to be, it held an undeniable ring of truth for them both. They'd known the eccentric family of wizards for many years, and never had visited, or been visited by, any of the clan, particularly one Harkle Harpell, without witnessing some strange occurrence. But the Harpells were good friends of Mithral Hall. They had come to the call of Bruenor when the drow of Menzoberranzan assaulted his kingdom, and had fought valiantly among the dwarven ranks. Their magic lacked predictability, to be sure, but there was no shortage of power behind it.

"We should go straight to the Ivy Mansion," Drizzt said as darkness closed in on the small town of Longsaddle. Even as he finished speaking, almost in response, it seemed, a shout of anger erupted in the stillness, followed by an answering bellow and a cry of pain. Without hesitation, the drow and halfling turned and headed that way, Guenhwyvar trotting beside them. Drizzt's hands stayed near his sheathed scimitars, but he didn't draw them.

Another shout, words too distant to be decipherable, followed by a cheer, followed by a cacophony of shouted protests . . .

Drizzt sprinted out ahead of Regis. He scrambled down a long embankment, picking a careful route over fallen branches and between the tightly-packed trees. He broke out of the copse and skidded to a stop, surprised.

"What is it?" Regis asked, stumbling down past him, and the halfling would have gone headlong into a small pond had Drizzt not caught him by the shoulder and held him back.

"I don't remember this pond," Drizzt said, and glanced back in the general direction of the Ivy Mansion to try to get his bearings. "I don't believe it was here the last time I came through, though it was only a couple of years back."

"A couple of years is an eternity where the Harpells are concerned," Regis reminded him. "Had we come here and found a deep hole where the town had once stood, would you have been surprised? Truly?"

Drizzt was only half listening. He moved to a clear, flat space and noted the dark outline of a forested island and the light of a larger fire showing through breaks in the thick foliage.

Another ruckus of arguing sounded from the island.

Cheers came from the right bank, the protests from the left, both groups hidden from Drizzt's view by thick foliage, with only a few campfire lights twinkling through the leaves.

"What?" the perplexed Regis asked, a simple question that accurately reflected Drizzt's confusion as well. The halfling poked Drizzt's arm and pointed back to the left, to the outline of a boat dock with several craft bobbing nearby.

"Be gone, Guenhwyvar," Drizzt commanded his panther companion. "But be ready to return to me."

The cat began to pace in a tight circle, moving faster and faster, and dissipating into a thick gray smoke as she returned to her extraplanar home. Drizzt replaced her small onyx likeness in his belt pouch and rushed to join Regis at the dock. The halfling already had a small rowboat unmoored and was readying the oars.

"A spell gone awry?" Regis asked as yet another yell of pain sounded from the island.

Drizzt didn't answer, but for some reason, didn't think that to be the case. He motioned Regis aside and took up the oars himself, pulling strongly.

Then they heard more than bickering and screams. Whimpers filled in the gaps between the arguing, along with feral snarls that prompted Regis to ask, "Wolves?"

It was not a large lake and Regis soon spotted a dock at the island. Drizzt worked to keep the boat in line with it. They glided in unnoticed and scrambled onto the wharf. A path wound up from it between trees, rocks, and thick brush, which rustled almost constantly from some small animals rushing to and fro. Drizzt caught sight of a fluffy white rabbit hopping away.

He dismissed the animal with a shake of his head and pressed onward, and once over a short rise, he and Regis finally saw the source of the commotion.

And neither understood a bit of it.

A man, stripped to the waist, stood in a cage constructed of vertical posts wrapped with horizontal ropes. Three men dressed in blue robes sat behind him and to the left, with three in red robes similarly seated, only behind and to the right. Directly before the caged man stood a beast, half man and half wolf, he seemed, with a canine snout but eyes distinctly human. He jumped about, appearing on the very edge of control, snarling, growling, and chomping his fangs right in front of the wide eyes of the terrified prisoner.

"Bidderdoo?" Drizzt asked.

"Has to be," said Regis, and he stepped forward—or tried to, for Drizzt held him back.

"No guards," the drow warned. "The area is likely magically warded."

The werewolf roared in the poor prisoner's face, and the man recoiled and pleaded pathetically.

"You *did!*" the werewolf growled.

"He had to!" shouted one of the blue-robed men.

"Murderer!" argued one wearing red robes.

Bidderdoo whirled and howled, ending the conversation abruptly. The Harpell werewolf spun back to the prisoner and began chanting and waving his arms.

The man cried out in alarm and protest.

"What . . . ?" Regis asked, but Drizzt had no answer.

The prisoner's babbling began to twist into indecipherable grunts and groans, pain interspersed with protest. His body began to shake and quiver, his bones crackling.

"Bidderdoo!" Drizzt yelled, and all eyes save those of the squirming, tortured man and the concentrating Harpell wizard, snapped the drow's way.

"Dark elf!" yelled one of the blue-robed onlookers, and all of them fell back, one right off his seat to land unceremoniously on the ground.

"Drow! Drow!" they yelled.

Drizzt hardly heard them, his lavender eyes popping open wide as he watched the prisoner crumble before him, limbs transforming, fur sprouting.

"No stew will ever be the same," Regis muttered helplessly, for no man remained in the wood and rope prison.

The rabbit, white and fluffy, yipped and yammered, as if trying to form words that would not come. Then it leaped away, easily passing through the wide ropes as it scurried for the safety of the underbrush.

Spell completed, the werewolf snarled and howled as it spun on the intruders. But the creature quickly calmed, and in a voice too cultured for such a hairy and wild mein said, "Drizzt Do'Urden! Well met!"

"I want to go home," Regis mumbled at Drizzt's side.

* * * * *

A warm fire burned in the hearth, and there was no denying the comfort of the overstuffed chair and divan set before it, but Drizzt didn't recline or even sit, and felt little of the room's warmth.

They had been ushered into the Ivy Mansion, accompanied by the almost continual flash of lightning bolts, searing the darkness with hot white light on either side of the pond below. Shouts of protest dissipated under the magical explosions, and the howl of a lone wolf—a lone *were*wolf—silenced them even more completely.

The people of Longsaddle had come to understand the dire implications of that howl, apparently.

For some time, Drizzt and Regis paced or sat in the room, with only an occasional visit by a maid asking if they wanted more to eat or drink, to which Regis always eagerly nodded.

"That seemed very un-Harpell-like," he mentioned to Drizzt between bites. "I knew Bidderdoo was a fierce one—he killed Uthegental of House Barrison Del'Armgo, after all—but that was simply tor—"

"Justice," interrupted a voice from the door, and the pair turned to see Bidderdoo Harpell enter from the hallway. He no longer looked the werewolf, but rather like a man who had seen much of life—too much, perhaps. He stood in a lanky pose that made him look taller than his six-foot frame, and his hair, all gray, stood out wildly in every conceivable direction, giving the impression that it had not been combed or even finger-brushed in a long, long time. Strangely, though, he was meticulously clean-shaven.

Regis seemed to have no answer as he looked at Drizzt.

"Harsher justice than we would expect to find at the hands of the goodly Harpells," Drizzt explained for him.

"The prisoner meant to start a war," Bidderdoo explained. "I prevented it."

Drizzt and Regis exchanged expressions full of doubt.

"Fanaticism requires extreme measures," the Harpell werewolf—a curse of his own doing due to a badly botched polymorph experiment—explained.

"This is not the Longsaddle I have known," said Drizzt.

"It changed quickly," Bidderdoo was fast to agree.

"Longsaddle, or the Harpells?" Regis asked, crossing his arms over his chest and tapping his foot impatiently.

The answer, "Both," came from the hallway, and even the outraged halfling couldn't hold his dour posture and expression at the sound of the familiar voice. "One after the other, of course," Harkle Harpell explained, bounding in through the door.

The lanky wizard was dressed all in robes, three shades of blue, ruffled and wrinkled, with sleeves so long they covered his hands. He wore a white beret topped by a blue button that matched the darkest hue of his robes, as did his dyed beard, which had grown—with magical assistance, no doubt—to outrageous proportions. One long braid ran down from Harkle's chin to his belt, flanked by two short, thick scruffs of wiry hair hanging below each jowl. The hair on his head had gone gray, but his eyes held the same luster and eagerness the friends had seen flash so many times in years gone by—usually right before some Harkle-precipitated disaster had befallen them all.

"The town changed first," Regis remarked.

"Of course!" said Harpell. "You don't think we enjoy this, do you?" He bounded over to Drizzt and took the drow's hand in a great shake—or started to before wrapping Drizzt in a powerful embrace that nearly lifted him off the ground.

"It's grand to see you, my old pirate-hunting companion!" Harkle boomed.

"Bidderdoo seemed to enjoy his work," Regis said, cutting Harkle's turn toward him short.

"You come to pass judgment after so short a time?" Bidderdoo replied.

"I know what I saw," said the halfling, not backing down an inch.

"What you saw without context, you mean," said Bidderdoo.

Regis glared at him then turned his judgment upon Harkle.

"You understand, of course," Harkle said to Drizzt, seeking support. But he found little in the drow's rigid expression.

Harkle rolled his eyes and sighed then nearly fell over as one of his orbs kept on rolling, over and over, in its socket. After a few moments, the discombobulated wizard slapped himself hard on the side of the head, and the eye steadied into place.

"My orbs have never been the same since I went to look in on Bruenor," he quipped with an exaggerated wink, referring, of course, to the time he'd accidentally teleported just his eyes to Mithral Hall to roll around on Bruenor's audience chamber floor.

"Indeed," said Regis, "and Bruenor bids you to never do so in such a manner ever again."

Harkle looked at him curiously for a few moments then burst out laughing. Apparently thinking the tension gone, the wizard moved to wrap Regis in a tight hug.

The halfling stopped him with an upraised hand. "We make peace with orcs while the Harpells torture humans."

"Justice, not torture," Harkle corrected. "Torture? Hardly that!"

"I know what I saw," said the halfling, "And I saw it with both of my eyes in my head and neither of them rolling around in circles."

"There are a lot of rabbits on that small island," Drizzt added.

"And do you know what you would have seen if we hadn't dealt harshly with men like that priest Ganibo?"

"Priest?" both Drizzt and Regis said together.

"Aren't they all and aren't they always?" Bidderdoo answered with obvious disgust.

"More than our share of them, to be sure," Harkle agreed. "We're a tolerant bunch here in Longsaddle, as you know."

"As we *knew*," said Regis, and it was Bidderdoo who rolled his eyes, though having never botched a teleportation like his bumbling cousin, his eyes didn't keep rolling.

"Our acceptance of . . . strangeness . . ." Harkle started.

"Embrace of strangeness, you mean," said Drizzt.

"What?" the wizard asked, and looked curiously at Bidderdoo before catching on and giving a burst of laughter. "Indeed, yes!" he said. "We who so play in the extremes of Mystra's Weave are not so fast to judge others. Which invited trouble to Longsaddle."

"You are aware of the disposition of Malarites in general, yes?" Bidderdoo clarified.

"Malarites?" Drizzt asked.

"The worshipers of Malar?" asked the more surface-worldly Regis.

"A battle of gods?" Drizzt asked.

"Worse," said Harkle. "A battle of followers."

Drizzt and Regis looked at him curiously.

"Different sects of the same god," Harkle explained. "Same god with different edicts, depending on which side you ask—and oh, but they'll kill you if you disagree with their narrow interpretations of their beast god's will! And how these Malarites always disagree, with each other and with everyone else. One group built a chapel on the eastern bank of Pavlel. The other on the western bank."

"Pavlel? The lake?"

"We named it after him," said Harkle.

"In memoriam, no doubt," Regis said.

"Well, we don't really know," Harkle replied. "Since he and the mountain flew off together."

"Of course," said the halfling who knew he shouldn't be surprised.

"The blue-robed and red-robed onlookers at the . . . punishment," said Drizzt.

"Priests of Malar all," Bidderdoo replied. "One side witnessing justice, the other accepting consequences. It's important that we make a display of such punishment to deter future acts."

"He burned down a house," Harkle explained. "With a family inside."

"And so he was punished," Bidderdoo added.

"By being polymorphed into a rabbit?" asked Regis.

"At least they can't hurt anyone in that state," said Bidderdoo.

"Except for that one," Harkle corrected. "The one with the big teeth, who could jump so high!"

"Ah, him," Bidderdoo agreed. "That rabbit was smokepowder! It seemed as if he was possessed of the edge of a vorpal weapon, that one, giving nasty bites!" He turned to Drizzt. "Can I borrow your cat?"

"No," the drow replied.

Regis growled with frustration. "You turned him into a rabbit!" he shouted, as if there could be no suitable reply.

Bidderdoo shook his head solemnly. "He remains happy and with bountiful leaves, brush, and flowers on the island."

"Happy? Is he man or rabbit? Where is his mind?"

"Somewhere in between, at this point, I would expect," Bidderdoo admitted.

"That's ghastly!" Regis protested.

"Time's passage will align his thoughts with his new body."

"To live as a rabbit," said Regis.

Bidderdoo and Harkle exchanged concerned, and guilty, glances.

"You killed him!" Regis shouted.

"He is very much alive!" Harkle protested.

"How can you say that?"

Drizzt put a hand on the halfling's shoulder, and when he looked up to meet the drow's gaze, Drizzt shook his head slowly, backing him down.

"Would that we could simply obliterate them all, that Longsaddle would know her days of old," Bidderdoo mumbled and left the room.

"The task that has befallen us is not a pleasant one," Harkle said. "But you don't understand..."

Drizzt motioned for him to stop, needing no further elaboration, for indeed, the drow did understand the untenable situation that had descended upon his friends, the Harpells. A foul taste filled his throat and he wanted to scream in protest of it all, but he didn't. Truly there was nothing to say, and nothing left for him to see in Longsaddle.

He informed Harkle, "We're traveling down the road to Luskan and from there to Icewind Dale."

"Ah, Luskan!" said Harkle. "I was to apprentice there once, long ago, but for some reason, they wouldn't let me into the famed Hosttower. A pity." He sighed profoundly and shook his head, but brightened immediately, as Harkle always did. "I can get you there in an instant," he said, snapping his fingers in such dramatic fashion, waving his hand with such zest, that he knocked over a lamp.

Or would have, except that Drizzt, his speed enhanced by magical anklets, darted forward in a blur, caught the lamp, and righted it.

"We prefer to walk," the drow said. "It's not so far and the weather is clear and kind. It's not the destination that matters most, after all, but the journey."

"True, I suppose," Harkle muttered, seeming disappointed for just a moment before again brightening. "But then, we could not have dragged *Sea Sprite* across the miles to Carradoon, could we?"

"Fog of fate?" Regis asked Drizzt, recalling the tale of how Drizzt and Catti-brie wound up in a landlocked lake with Captain Deudermont and his oceangoing pirate hunter. Harkle Harpell had created a new enchantment, which, as expected, had gone terribly awry, transporting the ship and all aboard her to a landlocked lake in the Snowflake Mountains.

"I have a new one!" Harkle squealed. Regis blanched and fell back, and Drizzt waved his hands to shut down the wizard before he could fully launch into spellcasting.

"We will walk," the drow said again. He looked down at Regis and added, "At once," which brought a curious expression from the halfling.

They were out of Longsaddle soon after, hustling down the road to the west, and despite Drizzt's determined stride, Regis kept pausing and glancing left and right, as if expecting the drow to turn.

"What is it?" Drizzt finally asked him.

"Are we really leaving?"

"That was our plan."

"I thought you meant to come out of town then circle back in to better view the situation."

Drizzt gave a helpless little chuckle. "To what end?"

"We could go to the island."

"And rescue rabbits?" came the drow's sarcastic reply. "Do not underestimate Harpell magic—their silliness belies the strength of their enchantments. For all the folly of Fog of Fate, not many wizards in the world could have so warped Mystra's Weave to teleport an entire ship and crew. We go and collect the rabbits, but then what? Seek audience of Elminster, who perhaps alone might undue the dweomer?"

Regis stammered, logically cornered.

"And to what end?" Drizzt asked. "Should we, new to the scene, interject ourselves in the Longsaddle's justice?" Regis started to argue, but Drizzt cut him short. "What might Bruenor do to one who burned a family inside a house?" the drow asked. "Do you think his justice would be less harsh than the polymorph? I think it might come at the end of a many-notched axe!"

"This is different," Regis said, shaking his head in obvious frustration. Clearly the sight of a man violently transformed into a rabbit had unnerved the halfling profoundly. "You cannot . . . that's not what the Harpells . . . Longsaddle shouldn't . . ." Regis stammered, looking for a focus for his frustration.

"It's not what I expected, and no, I'm not pleased by it."

"But you will accept it?"

"It's not my choice to make."

"The people of Longsaddle call out to you," Regis said.

The drow stopped walking and moved to a boulder resting on the side of the trail, where he sat down, gazing back the way they'd come.

"These situations are more complicated than they appear," he said. "You grew up among the pashas of Calimport, with their personal armies and thuggish ways."

"Of course, but that doesn't mean I accept the same thing from the Harpells."

Drizzt shook his head. "That's not my point. In their respective neighborhoods, how were the pashas viewed?"

"As heroes," Regis said.

"Why?"

Regis leaned back against a stone, a perplexed look on his face.

"In the lawless streets of Calimport, why were thugs like Pasha Pook seen as heroes?"

"Because without them, it would have been worse," Regis said, and caught on.

"The Harpells have no answer to the fanaticism of the battling priests, and so they respond with a heavy hand."

"You agree with that?"

"It's not my place to agree or disagree," said Drizzt. "The Harpells are the lid on a boiling cauldron. I don't know if their choice of justice is the correct one, but I suspect from what we were told that without that lid, Longsaddle would know strife beyond anything you or I can imagine. Sects of opposing gods battling for supremacy can be terrifying indeed, but when the fight is between two interpretations of the same god, the misery can reach new proportions. I saw this intimately in my youth, my friend. You cannot imagine the fury of opposing matron mothers, each convinced that she, and not her enemy, spoke the will of Lolth!

"You would have me descend upon Longsaddle and use my influence, even my blades, to somehow alter the situation. But what would that, even if I could accomplish anything, which I strongly doubt, loose upon the common folk of Longsaddle?"

"Better to let Bidderdoo continue his brutality?" Regis asked.

"Better to let the people with a stake in the outcome determine their own fate," Drizzt answered. "We've not the standing or the forces to better the situation in Longsaddle."

"We don't even know what that situation really is."

Drizzt took a deep, steadying breath, and said, "I know enough to recognize that if the problems in Longsaddle are not as profound as I—as we—fear, then the Harpells will find their way out of it. And if it is as dangerous then there's nothing we can do to help. However we intervene, one or even both sides will see us as meddling. Better that we go on our way. I think we are both unnerved by the unusual nature of the Harpells' justice, but I have to say that there is a temperate manner to it."

"Drizzt!"

"It is not a permanent punishment, for Bidderdoo can undo that which he has enacted," the drow explained. "He is neutering the warring offenders by rendering them harmless—unless, of course, he is turning the other side into carrots."

"That's not funny."

"I know," Drizzt admitted with an upraised hand and a smirk. "But who are we to intervene, and haven't the Harpells earned our trust?"

"You trust in what you saw?"

"I trust that if the situation alters and calls for a recanting of the justice delivered, the Harpells will undo the transformations and return the no-doubt shaken and hopefully repentant men to their respective places. Easier that than the dwarves of Mithral Hall sewing a head back on a criminal there."

Regis sighed and seemed to let it all go. "Can we stop back here on our return to Mithral Hall?"

"Do you want to?"

"I don't know," Regis answered honestly, and he too looked back toward the distant town, profound disappointment on his normally cheery face. "It's like Obould Many-Arrows," Regis mumbled.

Drizzt looked at him curiously.

"Everything is like Obould lately," the halfling went on. "Always the best of a bad choice."

"I will be certain to relay your feelings to Bruenor."

Regis stared blankly for just a moment then a grin widened and widened until it was followed by a belly-laugh, both heartfelt and sadly resigned.

"Come along," Drizzt bade him. "Let us go and see if we can save the rest of the world."

And so the two friends lightened their steps and headed down the western trail, oblivious to the prophecy embedded in Drizzt Do'Urden's joke.

CHAPTER 9
THE CITY OF SAILS

Pymian Loodran burst out the tavern door, arms flailing with terror. He fell as he turned, tearing the skin on one knee, but he hardly slowed. Scrambling, rolling, and finally getting back to his feet, he sprinted down the way. Behind him, out of the tavern, came a pair of men dressed in the familiar robes of the Hosttower of the Arcane, white with broad red trim, talking as if nothing was amiss.

"You don't believe he's fool enough to enter his own house," one said.

"You accepted the bet," the other reminded.

"He will flee for the gate and the wider road beyond," the first insisted, but even as he finished the other pointed down the road to a three-story building. The terrified man ascended an outside stairway on all fours, grabbing and pulling at the steps.

The first wizard, defeated, handed over the wand. "May I open the door, at least?" he asked.

"I would be an unappreciative victor to deny you at least some enjoyment," his friend replied.

They made their way without rushing, even though the stairway moved back along an alleyway and away from the main road, so the hunted man had passed out of sight.

"He resides on the second floor?" the first wizard asked.

"Does it matter?" said the second, to which the first nodded and smiled.

As they reached the alleyway, they came in sight of the second story door. The first wizard pulled out a tiny metal rod and began to mutter the first words of a spell.

"High Captain Kurth's man," his companion interrupted. He motioned with his chin across to the other side of the street where a large-framed thug had exited a building and taken a particular interest in the two wizards.

"Very fortunate," the first replied. "It's always good to give a reminder to the high captains." And he went right back to his spellcasting.

A few heartbeats later, a sizzling lightning bolt rent the air between the wizard and the door, blasting the flimsy wooden portal from its hinges and sending splinters flying into the flat.

The second wizard, already deep in chanting to activate the wand, took careful aim and sent a small globe of orange fire leaping up to the opening. It disappeared into the flat and a blood-curdling, delicious scream told both wizards that the fool knew it for what it was.

A fireball.

A moment later, one that no doubt seemed like an eternity to the fugitive in the flat—and his wife and children, too, judging from the chorus of screams coming forth from the building—the spell burst to life. Flames roared out the open door, and out every window and every unsealed crack in the wall as well. Though not a concussive blast, the magical fire did its work hungrily, biting at the dry wood of the old building, engulfing the entire second floor and roaring upward to quickly engulf the third.

As the wizards admired their handiwork, a young boy appeared on the third story balcony, his back and hair burning. Out of his mind with pain and terror, he leaped without hesitation, thumping down with bone-cracking force against the alleyway cobblestones.

He lay moaning, broken, and probably dying.

"A pity," said the first wizard.

"It's the fault of Pymian Loodran," the second replied, referring to the fugitive who had had the audacity to steal the purse of a lower-ranking acolyte from the Hosttower. The young mage had indulged too liberally of potent drink, making him easy prey, and the rogue Loodran had apparently been unable to resist.

Normally, Loodran's offense would have gotten him arrested and dragged to Prisoner's Carnival, where he likely would have survived, though probably without all of his fingers. But Arklem Greeth had decided that it was time for a show of force in the streets. The peasants were becoming a bit more bold of late, and worse, the high captains seemed to be thinking of themselves as the true rulers of the city.

The two wizards turned back to regard Kurth's scout, but he had already melted into the shadows, no doubt to run screaming to his master.

Arklem Greeth would be pleased.

"This work invigorates and wearies me at the same time," the second said to the first, handing him back his wand. "I do love putting all of my practice into true action." He glanced down the alley, where the boy lay unmoving, though still quietly groaning. "But . . ."

"Take heart, brother," the other said, leading him away. "The greater purpose is served and Luskan is at peace."

The fire burned through the night, engulfing three other structures before the area residents finally contained it. In the morning, they dug out eleven bodies, including that of Pymian Loodran, who had been so proud the day before when he had brought a chicken and fresh fruit home to his hungry family. A real chicken! A real meal, their first that was not just moldy bread and old vegetables in more than a year.

The first real meal his young daughter had ever known.

And the last.

* * * * *

"If I wanted to speak with Rethnor's brat, I'd've come here looking for him!" said Duragoe, a ranking captain in the Ship of High Captain Baram. He finished his rant and moved as if to strike the Ship Rethnor soldier who had tried to divert him to Kensidan's audience chamber, but held the slap when he noted the dreaded Crow himself entering the small antechamber with a look on his face that showed he'd heard every word.

"My father has passed the daily business onto my shoulders,"

Kensidan said calmly. In the other room, out of sight of Duragoe, High Captain Suljack quietly snickered. "If you wish to speak with Ship Rethnor, your discussion is with me."

"Me orders from High Captain Baram are to speak with Rethnor hisself. Ye'd deny a high captain a direct audience with another of his ilk, would ye?"

"But you are not a high captain."

"I'm his appointed speaker."

"As am I, to my father."

That seemed to fluster the brutish Duragoe a bit, but he shook his head vigorously—so much so that Kensidan almost expected to see bugs flying out of his ears—and brought one of his huge hands up to rub his ruddy face. "And yerself'll take me words to Rethnor, so he's getting it second-hand . . ." he tried to argue.

"Third-hand, if your words are Baram's words relayed to you."

"Bah yerself," Duragoe fumed. "I'm to say them exactly as Baram told me to say them!"

"Then say them."

"But I'm not for liking that ye're to then take them to yer father that we might get something done!"

"If anything is to be done due to your request, good Duragoe, the action will be at my command, not my father's."

"Are ye calling yerself a high captain, then?"

"I have done no such thing," Kensidan was wise to reply. "I handle my father's daily business, which includes speaking to the likes of you. If you wish to deliver High Captain Baram's concerns, then please do so, and now. I have much else to do this day."

Duragoe looked around and rubbed his grizzled and ruddy face again. "In there," he demanded, pointing to the room behind the young Kensidan.

Kensidan held up a hand to keep the man at bay and walked back just inside the audience chamber's door. "Be gone. We have private matters to discuss," he called, ostensibly to the guards within, but also to give Suljack the time he needed to move to the next room, from which he could eavesdrop on the whole conversation.

He motioned for Duragoe to follow him into the audience chamber and took his seat on the unremarkable, but tallest, chair in the room.

"Ye smell the smoke?" Duragoe asked.

A thin smile creased Kensidan's face, purposely tipping his hand that he was pleased to see that another of the high captains had taken note of the devastation the two Hosttower enforcers had rained upon a section of Luskan the previous night.

"Not a funny thing!" Duragoe growled.

"High Captain Baram told you to say that?" Kensidan asked.

Duragoe's eyes widened and his nostrils flared as if he was on the verge of catastrophe. "My captain lost a valuable merchant in that blaze," Duragoe insisted.

"And what would you ask Rethnor to do about that?"

"We're looking to find out which high captain the crook who brought the fires of justice down was working for," Duragoe explained. "Pymian Loodran's his name."

"I'm certain that I have never heard that name before," said Kensidan.

"And yer father's to say the same?" a skeptical Duragoe asked.

"Yes," came the even response. "And why would you care? Pymian Loodran is dead, correct?"

"And how would ye be knowing that if ye don't know the name?" the suspicious Duragoe asked.

"Because I was told that a pair of wizards burned down a house into which had fled a man who had angered the Hosttower of the Arcane," came the reply. "I assume the target of their devastation didn't escape, though I care not whether he did or not. Is it recompense you seek from the high captain who employed this Loodran fool, if indeed any high captain did so?"

"We're looking to find out what happened."

"That you can file a grievance at the Council of Five, and no doubt attach a weight of gold to repair your mercantile losses?"

"Only be fair. . . ." Duragoe said.

" 'Fair' would be for you to take up your grievance with the Hosttower of the Arcane and Arklem Greeth," said Kensidan. The Crow smiled again as the tough Duragoe shrank at the mere mention of the mighty archmage arcane.

"The events of last night, the manner and extent of the punishment exacted, were decided by Arklem Greeth or his enforcers," Kensidan reasoned. He sat back comfortably and crossed his thin legs at the knee, and even though Duragoe remained standing, he seemed diminished by the casual, dismissive posture of the acting high captain. "Whatever this fool—what did you name him? Loodran?—did to exact the ire of the Hosttower is another matter all together. Perhaps Arklem Greeth has a case to present against one of the high captains, should it be discovered that this fool indeed was in the employ of one, though I doubt that to be the case. Still, from the perspective of High Captain Baram, the perpetrator of his loss was none other than Arklem Greeth."

"We don't see it that way," Duragoe said with amusing vigor— amusing only because it reinforced the man's abject terror at the thought of bringing his bluster to the feet of the archmage arcane.

Kensidan shrugged. "You have no claim with Ship Rethnor," he said. "I know not of this fool, Loodran, nor does my father."

"Ye haven't even asked him," Duragoe said with a growl and an accusatory point of his thick finger.

Kensidan brought his hands up before his face, tapped his fingertips a couple of times, then folded the hands together, staring all the while at Duragoe, and without the slightest hint of a blink.

Duragoe shrank back even more, as if he had realized for the first time that he might be in enemy territory, and that he might be wise to take greater care before throwing forth his accusations. He glanced left and right nervously, sweat showing at his temples, and his breathing became noticeably faster.

"Go and tell High Captain Baram that he has no business with Ship Rethnor regarding this matter," Kensidan explained. "We know nothing of it beyond the whispers filtering through the streets. That is my last word on the subject."

Duragoe started to respond, but Kensidan cut him short with a sharp and loud, "Ever."

The thug straightened and tried to regain a bit of his dignity. He looked around again, left and right, to see Ship Rethnor soldiers entering the room, having heard Kensidan's declaration that their discussion was at its end.

"And pray do tell High Captain Baram that if he wishes to discuss any matters with Ship Rethnor in the future, then Kensidan will be pleased to host him," Kensidan said.

Before the flustered Duragoe could respond, the Crow turned to a pair of guards and motioned them to escort the visitor away.

As soon as Duragoe had exited the room, High Captain Suljack came back in through a side door. "Good fortune to us that Arklem Greeth overplayed his hand, and that this man, Loodran, happened to intersect with one of Baram's merchants," he said. "Baram's not an easy one to bring to our side. A favorable coincidence with favorable timing."

"Only a fool would leave necessary good fortune to coincidence at a critical time," Kensidan not-so-cryptically replied.

Behind him, the tough dwarf with the morningstars giggled, drawing a concerned look from High Captain Suljack, who had long ago realized that the son of Rethnor was many steps ahead of his every move.

"*Sea Sprite* will put in today at high tide," Kensidan said, trying not to grin as Suljack tried hard not to look surprised, "along with Lord Brambleberry of Waterdeep and his fleet."

"Int'resting times," High Captain Suljack managed to sputter.

* * * * *

"We could have gone straight to Icewind Dale," Regis remarked as he and Drizzt passed through the heavily guarded gate of Luskan. The halfling looked back over his shoulder as he spoke, eyeing the guards with contempt. Their greeting at the gate had not been warm, but condescending and full of suspicion regarding Regis's dark-skinned companion.

Drizzt didn't look back, and if he was bothered at all by the icy reception, he didn't show it.

"I never would have believed that my friend Regis would choose a hard trail over a comfortable bed in a city full of indulgences," the drow said.

"I'm weary from the comments, always the comments," Regis said. "And the looks of derision. How can you ignore it? How many times do you have to prove your worth and value?"

"Why should the ignorance of a pair of guards in a city that is not my home concern me at all?" Drizzt replied. "Had they not allowed us through, as with Mirabar when we ventured through there with Bruenor on our way to Mithral Hall, then their actions affect me and my friends, and so yes, that is a concern. But we're past the gate, after all. Their stares at my back don't invade my body, and wouldn't even if I were not wearing this fine mithral shirt."

"But you have been nothing other than a friend and ally to Luskan!" Regis protested. "You sailed with *Sea Sprite* for years, to their benefit. And that was not so long ago."

"I knew neither of the sentries."

"But they had to know you—your reputation at least."

"If they believed I was who I said I was."

Regis shook his head in frustration.

"I don't have to prove my worth and value to any but those I love," Drizzt said to him, dropping his arm across the halfling's shoulders. "And that I do by being who I am, with confidence that those I love appreciate the good and accept the bad. Does anything else really matter? Do the looks of guards I don't know and who don't know me truly affect the pleasures, the triumphs, and the failings of my life?"

"I just get angry . . ."

Drizzt pulled him close and laughed, appreciating the support. "If I ever get such a scornful look from you, Bruenor, or Catti-brie, then I will fret," the drow said.

"Or from Wulfgar," Regis remarked, and indeed that did put a bit of weight into Drizzt's stride, for he didn't truly know what to expect when he glanced upon his barbarian friend again.

"Come," he said, veering down the first side street. "Let us enjoy the comforts of the Cutlass and prepare for the road beyond."

"Drizzt Do'Urden! Huzzah!" a man on the opposite side of the road cheered, recognizing the drow who had served so well with the hero Captain Deudermont. Drizzt returned his wave and smile.

"And does that affect you more than the scornful looks from the guards?" Regis slyly asked.

Drizzt considered his answer for a few heartbeats, recognizing the trap of inconsistency and hypocrisy Regis had lain before him. If nothing really mattered other than the opinions of his friends, then such logic and insistence would need to include the positive receptions as well as the negative.

"Only because I allow it to," the drow answered.

"Because of vanity?"

Drizzt shrugged and laughed. "Indeed."

Soon after, they went into the Cutlass, a rather unremarkable tavern serving the docks of Luskan, particularly the returning or visiting merchant crews. So close to the harbor, it was not hard to understand the moniker given to Luskan: the City of Sails. Many tall ships were tied beside her long wharves, and many more sat at anchor out in the deeper waters—so many, it seemed to Drizzt, that the whole of the city could just up and sail away.

"I have never had the wanderlust for ocean voyages," Regis said, and when Drizzt tore his eyes from the spectacle of the harbor, he found the halfling staring up at him knowingly.

Drizzt merely smiled in reply and led his friend into the tavern.

More than one mug lifted to toast the pair, particularly Drizzt, who had a long history there. Still, most of the many patrons of the bustling place gave no more than a casual glance at the unusual pair, for few in the Cutlass were not considered unusual elsewhere.

"Drizzt Do'Urden, in the black flesh," the portly proprietor said as the drow came up to the bar. "What brings you back to Luskan after these long years?" He extended a hand, which Drizzt grasped and shook warmly.

"Well met, Arumn Gardpeck," he replied. "Perhaps I have returned merely to see if you continued to ply your trade—I take comfort that some things ever remain the same."

"What else would an old fool like me do?" Arumn replied. "Have you sailed in with Deudermont, then?"

"Deudermont? Is *Sea Sprite* in port?"

"Aye, and with a trio of ships of a Waterdhavian lord beside her," Arumn replied.

"And spoiling for a fight," said one of the patrons, a thin and weasely little man leaning heavily on the bar, as if needing its support.

"You remember Josi Puddles," Arumn said as Drizzt turned to regard the speaker.

"Yes," Drizzt politely replied, though he wasn't so sure he did remember. To Josi, he added, "If Captain Deudermont is indeed seeking a battle, then why has he come ashore?"

"Not a fight with pirates this time," Josi replied, despite Arumn shaking his head for the man to shut up, and nodding his chin in the direction of various patrons who seemed to be listening a bit too intently. "Deudermont is looking for a bigger prize!" Josi ended with a laugh, until he finally noticed Arumn's scowl, whereupon he shrugged innocently.

"There's talk of a fight coming in Luskan," Arumn explained quietly, leaning in close so that only Drizzt and Regis—and Josi, who similarly leaned in—could hear. "Deudermont sailed in with an army, and there's talk that he's come here with purpose."

"His army's not one for fighting on the open seas," Josi said more loudly, drawing a hush from Arumn.

The two quieted as Drizzt and Regis exchanged glances, neither knowing what to make of the news.

"We're going north, straightaway," Regis reminded Drizzt, and though the drow nodded, albeit half-heartedly, the halfling suddenly wasn't so sure of his claim.

"Deudermont will be glad to see you," Arumn said. "Thrilled, I'd bet."

"And if he sees you, you will stay and fight beside him," Regis said with obvious resignation. "I'd bet."

Drizzt chuckled but held quiet.

He and Regis left the Cutlass early the next morning, supposedly for Icewind Dale, but on a route that took them down by Luskan's docks, where *Sea Sprite* sat in her customary, honorary berth.

Drizzt met with Captain Deudermont and the brash young Lord Brambleberry before noon.

And the two companions from Mithral Hall didn't leave the City of Sails that day.

PART 2

MORAL GROUNDING

MORAL GROUNDING

I put Regis at ease as we walked out of Longsaddle. I kept my demeanor calm and assuring, my stride solid and my posture forward-leaning. Yet inside, my stomach churned and my heart surely ached. What I saw in the once-peaceful village shook me profoundly. I had known the Harpells for years, or thought so, and I was pained to see that they were walking a path that could well lead them to a level of authoritarian brutishness that would have made the magistrates at Luskan's wretched Prisoner's Carnival proud.

I cannot pretend to judge the immediacy and criticality of their situation, but I can certainly lament the potential outcome I so clearly recognized.

I wonder, then, where is the line between utilitarian necessity and morality? Where does one cross that line, and more importantly, when, if ever, is the greater good not served by the smaller victories of, or concessions to, basic standards of morality?

This world in which I walk often makes such distinctions based on racial lines. Given my dark elf heritage, I certainly know and understand that. Moral boundaries are comfortably relaxed in the concept of "the other." Cut down an orc or a drow with impunity, indeed, but not so a dwarf, a human, an elf?

What will such moral surety do in light of King Obould should he consider his unexpected course? What did such moral surety do in light of myself? Is Obould, am I, an anomaly, the exception to a hard and fast rule, or a glimpse of wider potential?

I know not.

Words and blades, I kept in check in Longsaddle. This was not my fight, since I had not the time, the standing, or the power to see it through to any logical conclusion. Nor could I and Regis have done much to alter the events at hand. For all their foolishness, the Harpells are a family of powerful magic-users. They didn't ask the permission or the opinion from a dark elf and halfling walking a road far from home.

Is it pragmatism, therefore, to justify my lack of action, and my subsequent assurances to Regis, who was so openly troubled by what we had witnessed?

I can lie to him—or at least, conceal my true unease—but I cannot do so to myself. What I saw in Longsaddle wounded me profoundly; it broke my heart as much as it shocked my sensibilities.

It also reminded me that I am one small person in a very large world. I hold in reserve my hope and faith in the general weal of the family Harpell. This is a good and generous family, grounded in morality if not in common sense. I cannot consider myself so wrong in trusting in them. But still . . .

Almost in answer to that emotional turmoil, I now find a situation not so different waiting for me in Luskan, but one from a distinctly opposing perspective. If Captain Deudermont and this young Waterdhavian lord are to be believed, then the authorities in Luskan have gone over to a dangerous place. Deudermont intends to lead something not quite a revolution, since the Hosttower of the Arcane is not the recognized leadership of the city.

Is Luskan now what Longsaddle will become as the Harpells consolidate their power with clever polymorphs and caged bunnies? Are the Harpells susceptible to the same temptations and hunger for greater power that has apparently infected the hierarchy of the Hosttower? Is this a case of better natures prevailing? My fear is that in any ruling council where the only check against persecuting power is the better nature of the ruling principles is doomed to eventual, disastrous failure. And so I ride with Deudermont as he begins his correction of that abuse.

Here, too, I find myself conflicted. It is not a lament for Longsaddle that drives me on in Luskan; I accept the call because of the man who calls. But my words to Regis were more than empty comforts. The Harpells were behaving with brutality, it seemed, but I hold no doubt that the absence of suffocating justice would precipitate a level of wild and uncontrollable violence between the feuding clerics.

If that is true, then what will happen in Luskan without the power behind the throne? It is well understood that the Arcane Brotherhood keeps under its control the five high captains, whose individual desires and goals are often conflicting. These high captains were all men of violence and personal power before their ascent. They are a confederation whose individual domains have never been subservient to the betterment of the whole of Luskan's populace.

Captain Deudermont will wage his battle against the Hosttower. I fear that defeating Arklem Greeth will be the easier task than replacing the control exerted by the archmage arcane.

I will be there beside Deudermont, one small person in a very large world. And as we take actions that will no doubt hold important implications for so many people, I can only hope that Deudermont and I, and those who walk with us, will create good results from good desires.

If so, should I reverse my steps and return to Longsaddle?

—Drizzt Do'Urden

CHAPTER 10
TACTICS AND FIREBALLS

"Brilliant thought, this battling against wizards!" Regis said, ending in a shriek as he dived aside and behind a water trough. A lightning bolt blasted out the distant building's open front door, digging a small trench across the ground just to the side of where Regis had been.

"They are annoying," Drizzt said, accentuating his point by popping up from behind a barrel and letting fly three arrows in rapid succession from Taulmaril. All three, magically sizzling like lightning bolts of their own, disappeared into the darkness of the house and popped loudly against some unseen surface within.

"We should move," Regis remarked. "He—or they—know where we are."

Drizzt shook his head, but dived low and cried out as a second bolt of lightning came forth. It hit the barrel in front of him, blasting it to kindling and sending out a thick spray of foamy beer.

Regis started to cry out for his friend, but stopped when he discovered that Drizzt, moving with speed enhanced by magical anklets, was already crouching beside him.

"You may be right," the drow conceded.

"Call Guenhwyvar, at the least!" Regis said, but Drizzt was shaking his head through every word.

Guenhwyvar had fought beside them throughout the night, and the Astral panther had limitations on the time she could spend on the Prime Material Plane. Exceeding those limitations rendered Guenhwyvar a feeble and pained companion.

Regis glanced back down the road the other way, at a column of black smoke that rose into the late afternoon sky. "Where is Deudermont?" he lamented.

"Fighting at the Harbor Cross bridge, as we knew he would be."

"Some should have pushed through to our aid!"

"We're forward scouts," Drizzt reminded. "It was not our place to engage."

"Forward scouts in a battle that came too swiftly," Regis remarked.

Only the day before, Drizzt and Regis sat in Deudermont's cabin on *Sea Sprite*, none of them sure there would even be a fight. But apparently, over the course of the afternoon, the captain had communicated with one or more of the high captains, and had received a reply to his and Lord Brambleberry's offer. They'd received an answer from the Hosttower, as well. In fact, had not the ever-vigilant Robillard intercepted that reply with a diffusion of magical energies, seaman Waillan Micanty would have been turned into a frog.

And so it was on, suddenly and brutally, and the Luskan Guard, their loyalties split between the five high captains, had made no overt moves to hinder Deudermont's circuitous march.

They had gone north first, past the ruins of ancient Illusk and the grand open market of Luskan to the banks of the Mirar River. To cross out onto the second island, Cutlass by name, and assault the Hosttower directly would have been a foolish move, for the Arcane Brotherhood had established safehouses and satellite fortresses all over the city. Deudermont meant to shrink Arklem Greeth's perimeter of influence, but every step was proving difficult indeed.

"Let us hope we can extract ourselves from this unwanted delay," Drizzt remarked.

Regis turned his cherubic but frowning face up at Drizzt, recognizing from the drow's tone that his words were a not so subtle reminder of why they had been spotted by the wizard in the house in the first place.

"I was thirsty," Regis muttered under his breath, eliciting a grin from Drizzt and a sidelong glance at the shattered beer barrel that had so lured the halfling scout into the open.

"Wars will do that to you," Drizzt replied, ending in another yelp and shoving Regis down beside him as a third lightning bolt shot forth, skimming in across the top of the trough and taking out one of the higher boards in the process. Even as the ground shook beneath them from the retort, water began to drain out onto them.

Regis rolled one away, Drizzt the other, the drow coming up to one knee. "Drink up," he said, putting his bow to use again, first through the open door, then shattering a glass window and another on the second floor for good measure. He kept drawing and letting fly, his magical quiver forever replenishing his supply of enchanted missiles.

A different sort of missile came forth from the house, though, a trio of small pulses of magical light, spinning over each other, bending and turning and sweeping unerringly for Drizzt.

One split off at the last moment as the retreating drow tried futilely to dodge. It veered right into Regis's chest, singeing his vest and sending a jolt of energy through him.

Drizzt took his two hits with a grimace and a growl, and turned around to send an arrow at the window from which the missiles had flown. As he let fly, he envisioned his path to the house, looking for barriers against the persistent magical barrage. He sent another magical arrow flying. It hit the doorjamb and exploded with a shower of magical sparks.

Using that as cover, the drow sprinted at an angle to the right side of the street, heading behind a group of barrels.

He thought he would make it, expecting to dive past another lightning stroke, as he lowered his head and sprinted full out. He felt foolish for so overbalancing, though, as he saw a pea of flame gracefully arc out of the second floor window.

"Drizzt!" Regis cried, seeing it too.

And the halfling's friend was gone, just gone, when the fireball exploded all around the barrels and the front of the building backing them.

*****

Sea Sprite tacked hard against the current at the mouth of the Mirar River. Occasional lightning bolts reached out at her from the northern bank, where a group of Hosttower wizards fought desperately to hold back Brambleberry's forces at the northern, longer span of Harbor Cross, the westernmost bridge across the Mirar.

"We would need to lose a score of men to each wizard downed, you claimed, if we were to have any chance," Deudermont remarked to Robillard, who stood beside him at the rail. "But it would seem that Lord Brambleberry has chosen his soldiers well."

Robillard let the sarcasm slip past as he, too, tried to get a better summation of the situation unfolding before them. Parts of the bridge were aflame, but the fires seemed to be gaining no real traction. One of Brambleberry's wizards had brought up an elemental from the Plane of Water, a creature that knew no fear of such fires.

One of the enemy wizards had responded with an elemental summoning of his own, a great creature of the earth, a collection of rock, mud, and grassy turf that seemed no more than a hillside come to life, sprouting arms of connected stone and dirt with boulder hands. It splashed into the river to do battle, its magical consistency strong enough to keep the waters from washing its binding dirt away, and both sides of the battle seemed intent on the other's elemental proxy—or proxies as more wizards brought forth their own otherworldly servants.

A trumpet sounded on the southern end of Harbor Cross, from Blood Island, and out from Brambleberry's position came a host of riders, all in shining armor, banners flying, spear tips glistening in the morning sun.

"Idiots," Robillard muttered with a shake of his head as they charged out onto the wide bridge.

"Harder to port!" Deudermont shouted to his crew, recognizing, as had Robillard, that Brambleberry's men needed support. *Sea Sprite* groaned under the strain as she listed farther, the river waters pounding into her broadside, threatening to drive her against one of the huge rocks that dotted the banks of the Mirar. She couldn't hold her position, of course, but she didn't need to. Her crack

THE PIRATE KING

catapult team had a ball of fiery pitch away almost immediately, cutting through the wind.

A barrage of lightning bolts, capped by a fireball, slammed the bridge, and the riders disappeared in a cloud of smoke, flame, and blinding flashes.

When they re-emerged, a bit fewer in number, battered and seeming much less eager and much less proud, they were heading back the way they'd come.

Any sense of victory the Hosttower wizards might have felt, though, was short-lived, as *Sea Sprite's* shot thundered into the side of one of the structures they used for cover, one of several compounds that had been identified as secret safehouses for the Arcane Brotherhood. The wooden building went up in flames, and wizards scrambled for safety.

Brambleberry's men charged across the bridge once more.

"Fight the current!" Deudermont implored his crew as his ship groaned back the other way, barely holding her angle.

A second ball of pitch went flying, and though it fell short, it splattered up against the barricades used by the enemy, creating more smoke, more screaming, and more confusion.

Deudermont's knuckles whitened as he grasped the rail, cursing at the less-than-favorable winds and tide. If he could just get *Sea Sprite's* archers in range, they could quickly turn the tide of the fight.

The captain winced and Robillard gave an amused but helpless chuckle, as the leading edge of Brambleberry's assault hit a stream of evocation magic. Missiles of glowing energy, lightning bolts, and a pair of fireballs burst upon them, sending men writhing and flailing to the ground, or leaping from the bridge, which shook under the continuing thunder of the earth elemental's pounding.

"Just take her near to the wharf and debark!" the captain cried, and to Robillard, he added, "Bring it up."

"You wanted to hold our surprise," the wizard replied.

"We cannot lose this battle," Deudermont said. "Not like this. Brambleberry stands in sight of the Luskan garrison, and they are watching intently, knowing not where to join in. And the young lord has the Hosttower behind him and soon to awaken to the fighting."

"He has two secured bridges and the roads around the ruins of Illusk," Robillard reminded the captain. "And a busy marketplace as buffer."

"The Hosttower wizards need not cross to the mainland. They can strike at him from the northern edge of Closeguard."

"They're not on Closeguard," Robillard argued. "High Captain Kurth's men block the bridges, east and west."

"We don't know that Kurth's men would even try to slow the wizards," Deudermont stubbornly replied. "He has not professed his loyalty."

The wizard shrugged, gave another of his all-too-common sighs, and faced the northern bank. He began chanting and waving his arms. Recognizing that the Hosttower kept several safehouses in the northern district, Robillard and some of Brambleberry's men had set up a wharf just below the waves, but far enough out into the river for *Sea Sprite* to get up beside it safely. As Robillard ignited the magical dweomers he had set on the bridge, the front poles of the makeshift dock rose up out of the dark waters, guiding the helmsman.

Still, *Sea Sprite* wouldn't have been able to tack enough to make headway and come alongside, but again, Robillard provided the answer. He snapped his fingers, propelling himself through a dimensional gate back to his customary spot on the raised deck behind the mainsail. He reached into his ring, first to bring up gusts of wind to help fill the sails then to communicate with his own elemental from the Plane of Water. *Sea Sprite* lurched and bucked, the river slamming in protest against her starboard side. The elemental set itself against the port side and braced with its otherworldly strength.

The catapult crew let fly a third missile, and a fourth right behind.

On the bridge, Brambleberry's forces pushed hard against the magic barrage and the leading edge managed to get across just as *Sea Sprite* slid in behind the secret, submerged wharf, a hundred yards downriver. Planks went out beside the securing ropes, and the crew wasted no time in scrambling to the rail.

Robillard closed his eyes, trusting fully in his detection spell, and sensed for the magic target. Still with his eyes closed, the wizard loosed a searing line of lightning into the water just before the wharf's guide poles. His shot proved precise, severing the locking chain of the wharf. Buoyed by a line of empty barrels, free of its shackles, the wharf lifted up and broke the water with a great splash and surge. The crew poured down.

"Now we have them," Deudermont cried.

He had barely finished speaking, though, when a great crash sounded upriver, as a span of the century-old Harbor Cross Bridge collapsed into the Mirar.

"Back to stations!" Deudermont yelled to those crewmen still aboard. The captain, though, ran to the nearest plank and scrambled over the rail, not willing to desert his crewmen who had already left the ship. "Port! Port!" he cried for his ship to flee.

"By the giggling demons," Robillard cursed, and as soon as Deudermont hit the wharf running, the wizard commanded his elemental to let go the ship and slide under it to catch the drifting flotsam. Then he helped free *Sea Sprite* by pulling a wand and shooting a line of lightning at the heavy rope tying her off forward, severing it cleanly.

Before the crew aft could even begin to free that second heavy rope, *Sea Sprite* swung around violently to the left, and a pair of unfortunate crewmen flipped over the rail to splash into the cold Mirar.

Sputtering curses, the wizard blinked himself to the taffrail and blasted the second rope apart.

The first pieces of the shattered bridge expanse swept down at them. Robillard's elemental deflected the bulk, but a few got through, chasing *Sea Sprite* as she glided away toward the harbor.

Robillard ordered his elemental to rush up and push her along. He breathed a sigh of relief as he saw his friend Deudermont get off the makeshift dock, right before a large piece of the fallen bridge slammed against it, shattering its planking and destroying its integrity, as it, too, became another piece of wreckage. Barrels and dock planks joined the sweep of debris.

Robillard had to stay with the ship, at least long enough for his summoned monster to assist *Sea Sprite* safely out of the river mouth and into quieter waters. He never took his eyes off of Deudermont, though, thinking that his dearest friend was surely doomed, trapped as he was on the northern bank with only a fraction of Brambleberry's forces in support, and a host of angry wizards against them.

* * * * *

Drizzt saw it coming, a little burning ball of flame, enticing as a candlelight, gentle and benign.

He knew better, though, and knew, too, that he couldn't hope to get out of its explosive range. So he threw his shoulders back violently and kicked his feet out in front of him, and didn't even try to break his fall as he slammed down on his back. He even resisted the urge to throw his arms out wide to somehow mitigate the fall, instead curling them over his face, hands grasping his cloak to wrap it around him.

Even covered as he was with the wet clothing and cloak, the darkness flew away when the fireball exploded, and hot flames bit at Drizzt, igniting a thousand tiny fires in his body. It lasted only an instant, mercifully, and winked out as immediately as it had materialized. Drizzt knew he couldn't hesitate—the wizard could strike at him again within the span of a few heartbeats, or if another wizard was inside the house, a second fireball might already be on its way.

He rolled sidelong away from his enemy to put out the little fires burning on his cloak and clothing, and even left the cloak smoldering on the ground when he leaped back to his feet. Again Drizzt ran full out, leaning forward in complete commitment to his goal, a tight strand of birch trees. He dived in headlong, rolling to a sitting position and curling up, expecting another blast.

Nothing happened.

Gradually, Drizzt uncoiled and looked back Regis's way, to see the halfling still crouched in the muddied ground behind the damaged water trough.

Regis's little hands flashed the rough letters of the drow silent alphabet, approximating the question, *Is he gone?*

His arsenal is depleted, perhaps, Drizzt's fingers replied.

Regis shook his head—he didn't understand.

THE PIRATE KING

Drizzt signaled again, more slowly, but the halfling still couldn't make sense of the too-intricate movements.

"He may be out of spells," the drow called quietly, and Regis nodded enthusiastically—until a rumble from inside the distant house turned them both that way.

Trailing a line of fire that charred the floorboards, it came through the open door, a great beast comprised entirely of flame: orange, red, yellow, and white when it swirled more tightly. It seemed vaguely bipedal, but had no real form, as the flames would commit to nothing but moving forward, and with purpose.

When it cleared the door, leaving smoking wood at every point of the jamb, it grew to its full, gigantic proportions, towering over the distant companions, mocking them with its intensity and its size.

A fiery monstrosity from the Elemental Plane of Fire.

Drizzt sucked in his breath and lifted Taulmaril, not even thinking to go to his more trusted scimitars. He couldn't fight the creature in close; of all the four primary elemental beasts, fire was the type any melee warrior was least capable of battling. Its flames burned with skin-curling intensity, and the strike of a scimitar, though it could hurt the beast, would heat the weapon as well.

Drizzt drew back and let fly, and the arrow disappeared into the swirl of flames.

The fire elemental swung around toward him and roared, the sound of a thousand trees crackling, then spat forth a line of flames that immediately set the birch stand aflame.

"How do we fight it?" Regis cried, and yelped as the elemental scorched the trough he hid behind, filling the air with thick steam.

Drizzt didn't have an answer. He shot off another arrow, and again had no way of knowing if it scored any damage on the creature or not.

Then, on instinct, the drow angled his bow to the side and let fly a third, right past the elemental to slam into, and punch through, the wall of the structure housing the wizard.

A cry from inside told him that he had startled the mage, and the sudden and angry turn of the fire elemental, back toward the house, confirmed what the drow had hoped.

He fired off a continual stream, then, a volley placed all around the wooden structure, blasting hole after hole and without discernable pattern. He judged his effect by the motions of the elemental, gliding one stride toward him, then one back at the wizard. For controlling such a beast was no easy feat, and one that required absolute concentration. And if that control was lost, Drizzt knew, the summoned creature would almost always take out its rage upon the summoner.

More arrows flashed into the house but to less effect; Drizzt needed to actually score a hit on the mage to turn the elemental fully.

But he didn't, and he soon recognized that the creature was inevitably edging his way. The wizard had adjusted.

Drizzt kept up the barrage anyway, and began moving away as he fired, confident that he could turn and outdistance the creature, or at least get to the water's edge, where the Mirar would protect him from the elemental's fury. He turned and glanced to the water trough, thinking to tell Regis to run.

But the halfling was already gone.

The wizard was protected from the arrows, Drizzt realized as the elemental bore down on him with renewed enthusiasm. The drow fired off a pair of shots into it for good measure then turned and sprinted back the way he'd come, around the edge of the building hit by the same fireball that had nearly melted him, which was burning furiously.

"Clever wizard," he heard himself muttering as he almost ran headlong into a giant web that stretched from building to building in the alleyway. He spun to see the elemental blocking the exit, its flames licking the structures to either side.

"Have at it, then," Drizzt said to the beast and drew his scimitars.

He couldn't really speak to a creature from an elemental plane, of course, but it seemed to Drizzt as if the monster heard him, for as he finished, the elemental rushed forward, its fiery arms sweeping ferociously.

Drizzt ducked the first swing then leaped out to his right just ahead of the second, running up the wall—and feeling that its integrity was diminished by the fires roaring within—and spinning into a back somersault. He came down in a spin, scimitars slashing across, backhand leading forehand, and both sent puffs of flame into the air as they slashed against the life-force that held those flames together into a physical, solid creature.

That second weapon, Icingdeath, sent a surge of hope through Drizzt, for its properties were not only affording him some substantial protection from flames, as it had done against the wizard's fireball, but the frostbrand scimitar took a particular pleasure in inflicting cold pain upon creatures with affinity to fire. The fire elemental shook off Twinkle's backhand hit, as it had all but ignored the shots from Taulmaril, but when Icingdeath connected, the creature seemed to burn less bright. The elemental whirled away and seemed to shrink in on itself, spinning around tightly.

Its flames burned brighter, white hot, and the creature came out enraged and huge once more.

Drizzt met its charge with a furious flurry of whirling blades. He shortened Twinkle's every stroke, using that blade to fend off the elemental's barrage of punches. He followed every strike with Icingdeath, knowing that he was hurting the elemental.

But not killing it.

Not anytime soon at least, and despite the protection of Icingdeath, Drizzt felt the heat of the magnificent, deadly beast. More than that, the power of the elemental's swings could fell an ogre even without the fiery accompaniment.

The elemental stomped its foot and a circular gout of flames rushed out from the point of impact, sweeping past Drizzt and making him hop in surprise.

The creature came forward and let fly a sweeping right hook, and Drizzt fell low, barely escaping the hit, which smashed hard into the burning building, crushing through the wooden wall.

From that hole came a blast of fire, and as it retracted, Drizzt leaped for the broken wood. He planted his foot on the bottom rim of the opening and came up flat against the wall, but only for the brief second it took him to swing his momentum and leap away into a backward somersault and turn, and as he came around, climbing higher across the alleyway, he somehow managed to sheathe his blades and catch on to the rim of the opposite building's roof. He ignored the stun of the impact as he crashed against the structure and scrambled, lifting his legs just above another heavy, fiery slug.

As fast as he went, though, the elemental was faster. It didn't climb the wall in any conventional sense, but just fell against it and swirled up over itself, rising as flames would climb a dry tree. Even as Drizzt stood tall on the roof, so did the elemental, and that building, too, was fully involved.

The elemental shot a line of flames at Drizzt, who dived aside, but still got hit—and though Icingdeath helped him avoid the brunt of the burn, he surely felt that sting!

Worse, the roof was burning behind him, and the elemental sent out another line, and another, all designed, Drizzt recognized, to seal off his avenues of escape.

The elemental hadn't done that in the alley, the drow realized as he drew out his scimitars yet again. The creature was smart enough to recognize a web, and knew that such an assault would have freed its intended prey. This creature was not dumb.

"Wonderful," Drizzt muttered.

* * * * *

"To the bridge!" Deudermont ordered, running from the collapsing wharf to the collection of rocks and crates, stone walls and trees his crewmen were using as cover. "We have to turn the wizards from Brambleberry's men."

"We be fifteen strong!' one man shouted back at him. "Or fifteen *weak,* I'm saying!"

"Two fireballs from extinction," said another, a fierce woman from Baldur's Gate who, for the last two years, had led almost every boarding charge.

Deudermont didn't disagree with their assessments, but he knew, too, that there was no other choice before them. With the collapse of the bridge, the Hosttower wizards had gained the upper hand, but despite the odds, Brambleberry's leading ranks had nowhere to retreat. "If we flee or if we wait, they die," the captain explained, and when he charged northeast along the river's northern bank, not one of the fifteen sailors hesitated before following.

Their charge turned into a series of stops and starts as the wizards

THE PIRATE KING

took note of them and began loosing terrible blasts of magic their way. Even with the volume of natural and manmade cover available to them, it occurred to Deudermont that his entire force might be wiped out before they ever got near the bridge.

And worse, Brambleberry's force could not make progress, as every attempt to break out from the solid structures at the edge of the bridge was met with fire and ice, electricity and summoned monsters. The earth elemental was finally brought down by the coordinated efforts of many soldiers and friendly wizards, but another beast, demonic in nature, rushed out from the enemy wizards' position to take its place before any of Brambleberry's men had even begun to cheer the earth beast's fall.

Deudermont looked downriver, hoping to witness the return of *Sea Sprite*, but she was far into the harbor by then. He looked forlornly to the southeast, to Blood Island, where Brambleberry and the bulk of his forces remained, and was not encouraged to see that the young lord had only then begun to swing his forces back to the bridge that would bring them to the south-bank mainland and Luskan's market, where they could march up the riverbank and cross along the bridge farther to the east.

This would be a stinging defeat, the captain reasoned, with many men lost and few of the Hosttower's resources captured or destroyed.

Even as he began to rethink his assault, considering that perhaps he and his men should hunker down and wait for Brambleberry, a shout to the north distracted him.

The mob rushing to enter the fray, men and dwarves with an assortment of weapons, terrified him. The northwestern section of Luskan was known as the Shield, the district housing merchants' storehouses and assembling grounds for visiting caravans from Luskan's most important trading partner, the city of Mirabar. And the marchion of Mirabar was known to have blood connections among the Hosttower's highest ranks.

But the rumors of a rift between Mirabar and the Arcane Brotherhood were apparently true. Deudermont saw that as soon as it became obvious that the new force entering the fray was no ally of the Hosttower wizards. They swept toward the wizards' position, leading with a volley of sling bullets, spears, and arrows that brought howls of protest from the wizards and a chorus of cheers from Brambleberry's trapped warriors.

"Onward!" the captain cried. "They are ours!"

Indeed they were, at least those poor lesser mages who didn't possess the magical ability to fly or teleport from the field. Enemies closed in on them from three sides, and the wizards fleeing east, the only open route, could not hope to get past the next bridge before Brambleberry swept across and cut them off.

* * * * *

The fire elemental reared up to its full height, towering over the drow, who used the moment to rush ahead and sting it with Icingdeath before running back the other way as the great arms flashed in powerful swipes.

Thinking pursuit imminent, Drizzt cut to the side and dived headlong into a roll, turning halfway into the circuit in case he had to continue right over the edge of the building.

The elemental, though, didn't pursue. Instead it roared off the other way, burning a line over the front edge of the building, then down into the street where it left a scarred trail back to the house from which it had emerged.

* * * * *

"It's a pretty gem," the wizard agreed, staring stupidly at the little ruby pendant the halfling had spinning at the end of a chain. On every rotation, the gem caught the light, bending it and transforming it into the wizard's fondest desires.

Regis giggled and gave it another spin, deftly moving it back from the wizard's grabbing hand. "Pretty, yes," he said.

His smile disappeared, and so did the gem, scooped up into his hand in the blink of an astonished wizard's eye.

"What are you doing?" the mage asked, seeming sober once more. "Where did it . . . ?" His eyes widened with horror, and he started to say, "What have you done?" as he spun back toward the door just in time to see his angry elemental rushing into the house.

"Stay warm," Regis said, and he fell backward out of the same window through which he'd entered, hitting the alleyway in a roll and running along with all speed.

Fire puffed out every window in the house, and between the wooden planks as well. Regis came back into the street. Drizzt, smoke wafting from his shoulders and hair, emerged from the front door of the house behind the battered water trough.

They met in the middle of the road, both turning back to the house that served as battleground between the wizard and his pet. Booms of magical thunder accompanied the crackle of burning beams. The roar of flames, given voice by the elemental, howled alongside the screams of the terrified wizard. The outer wall froze over suddenly, hit by some magical, frosty blast, only to melt and steam almost immediately as the fire elemental's handiwork won the contest.

It went on for a few moments before the house began to fall apart. The wizard staggered out the front door, his robes aflame, his hair burned away, his skin beginning to curl.

The elemental, defeated, didn't come out behind him, but the man could hardly call it a victory as he toppled face down in the road. Regis and Drizzt ran to him, patting out the flames and rolling him over.

"He won't live for long without a priest," the halfling said.

"Then we must find him one," Drizzt replied, and looked back to the southwest, where Deudermont and Brambleberry assaulted the bridge. Smoke rose along with dozens of screams, the ring of metal, and the booming of magic.

Regis blew a long sigh as he answered, "I think most of the priests are going to be busy for a while."

CHAPTER
THE ARCHMAGE ARCANE
11

The building resembled a tree, its arms lifting up like graceful branches, tapering to elegant points. Because of the five prominent spires, one for each compass point and a large central pillar, the structure also brought to mind a gigantic hand.

In the centermost spire of the famous Hosttower of the Arcane, Arklem Greeth looked out upon the city. He was a robust creature, rotund and with a thick and full gray beard and a bald head that gave him the appearance of a jolly old uncle. When he laughed, if he wanted to, it came from a great belly that shook and jiggled with phony but hearty glee. When he smiled, if he pretended to, great dimples appeared and his whole face brightened.

Of course Arklem Greeth had an enchantment at his disposal that made his skin look positively flushed with life, the epitome of health and vigor. He was the Archmage Arcane of Luskan, and it wouldn't do to have people put off by his appearance, since he was, after all, a skeletal, undead thing, a lich who had cheated death. Magical illusions and perfumes hid the more unpleasant aspects of his decaying corporeal form well enough.

Fires burned in the north—he knew them to be the largest collection of his safehouses. Several of his wizards were likely dead or captured.

The lich gave a cackling laugh—not his jolly one, but one of wicked and perverse enjoyment—wondering if he might soon find them in the netherworld and bring them back to his side, even more powerful than they had been in life.

Beneath that laughter, though, Arklem Greeth seethed. The Luskar guards had allowed it to happen. They had turned their backs on law and order for the sake of the upstart Captain Deudermont and that miserable Waterdhavian brat, Brambleberry. The Arcane Brotherhood would have to repay the Brambleberry family, to be sure. Every one of them would die, Arklem Greeth decided, from the oldest to the infants.

A sharp knock on his door broke through the lich's contemplation.

"Enter," he called, never looking back. The door magically swung open.

In rushed the young wizard Tollenus the Spike. He nearly tripped and fell on his face as he crossed the threshold, he was so excited and out of sorts.

"Archmage, they have attacked us," he gasped.

"Yes, I am watching the smoke rise," said an unimpressed Greeth. "How many are dead?"

"Seven, at least, and more than two-score of our servants," the Spike answered. "I know not of Pallindra or Honorus—perhaps they managed to escape as did I."

"By teleporting."

"Yes, Archmage."

"Escape? Or flee?" Greeth asked, turning slowly to stare at the flustered young man. "You left without knowing the disposition of your superior, Pallindra?"

"Th-there was nothing..." the Spike stuttered. "All was—was lost..."

"Lost? To a few warriors and half a ship's crew?"

"Lost to the Mirabarrans!" the Spike cried. "We thought victory ours, but the Mirabarrans..."

"Do tell."

"They swept upon us like a great wave, m-men and dwarves alike," the Spike stammered. "We had little power remaining to us in the way of destructive magic, and the hearty dwarves could not be slowed."

He kept rambling with the details of their last stand, but Greeth tuned him out. He thought of Nyphithys, his darling erinyes, lost to him in the east. He had tried to summon her, and when that had failed, had brought from the lower planes one of her associates, who had told him of the betrayal of King Obould of the orcs and the interference of that wretched Bruenor Battlehammer and his friends.

Arklem Greeth had long wondered how such an ambush had been so carefully planned. He had feared that he had completely underestimated that Obould creature, or the strength of the truce between Many-Arrows and Mithral Hall. He wondered if it hadn't been a bit more than that strange alliance, though.

And now the Shield of Mirabar in Luskan had surprisingly joined into a fight that the Luskar guards had avoided.

A curious thought crossed Arklem Greeth's mind.

That thought had a name: Arabeth Raurym.

* * * * *

"They will be compensated," Lord Brambleberry assured the angry guard captain, who had followed the Waterdhavian lord all the way from Blood Island to the Upstream Span, the northern and westernmost of Luskan's three Mirar bridges. "Houses can be rebuilt."

"And children can be re-birthed?" the man snapped back.

"There will be unfortunate circumstances," said Brambleberry. "It's the way of battle. And how many were killed by my forces and how many by the Hosttower's wizards with their wild displays of magic?"

"None would have died if you hadn't started the fight!"

"My good captain, some things are worth dying for."

"Shouldn't that be the choice of him what's dying?"

Lord Brambleberry smirked at the man, but really had no response. He wasn't pleased at the losses incurred around the Harbor Cross Bridge. A fire had broken out just north of their perimeter and several homes had been reduced to smoldering ruin. Innocent Luskar had died.

The guard captain's forward-leaning posture weakened when Captain Deudermont walked over to stand beside Lord Brambleberry.

"Is there a problem?" the legend of Luskan asked.

"N-no, Mr. Deudermont," the guard stammered, for he was clearly intimidated. "Well, yes, sir."

"It pains you to see smoke over your city," Deudermont replied. "It tears at my heart as well, but the worm must be cut from the apple. Be glad that the Hosttower is on a separate island."

"Yes, Mr. Deudermont." The guard captain gave one more curt look at Lord Brambleberry then briskly turned and marched away to join his men and their rescue work at the site of the battle.

"His resistance was less strident than I'd anticipated," Brambleberry said to Deudermont. "Your reputation here makes this much easier."

"The fight has only just begun," the captain reminded him.

"Once we have them driven into the Hosttower, it will go quickly," Brambleberry said.

"They're wizards. They won't be held back by lines of men. We'll be looking over our shoulders for the entirety of the war."

"Then make it a short one," the eager Waterdhavian lord said. "Before my neck stiffens."

He offered a wink and a bow and hurried away, nearly bumping into Robillard, who was coming Deudermont's way.

"Pallindra is among the dead, and that is no small loss for the Hosttower, and an even greater one for Arklem Greeth, personally, for she was known to be fiercely loyal to him," Robillard reported. "And our scout of questionable heritage . . ."

"His name is Drizzt," Deudermont said.

"Yes, that one," the wizard replied. "He defeated a wizard by name of Huantar Seashark, paramount among the Hosttower at summoning elementals and demons—even elder elementals and demon lords."

"Paramount? Even better than Robillard?" Deudermont said to lighten the wizard's typically dour mood.

"Be not a fool," Robillard replied, drawing a wide smile from Deudermont, who took note that Robillard hadn't actually answered the question. "Huantar's prowess would have served Arklem Greeth well when our flames tickle at his towers."

"Then it's a day of great victory," Deudermont reasoned.

"It's the day we awakened the beast. Nothing more."

"Indeed," Deudermont replied, though in a tone that showed neither agreement nor concession, but rather more of a detached amusement as the captain looked past Robillard and nodded.

Robillard turned to see Drizzt and Regis coming down the road, the drow with a tattered cloak over one arm.

"You found a fine battle, I'm told," Deudermont called to them as they neared.

"Those two words rarely go together," said the drow.

"I like him more all the time," Robillard said so that only Deudermont could hear, and the captain snorted.

"Come, let us four retire to a warm hearth and warmer brandy, that we might exchange tales," said Deudermont.

"And cake," Regis said. "Never forget the cake."

* * * * *

"Cause or effect?" Arklem Greeth asked quietly as he padded down the hallway leading to the chambers of the Overwizard of the South Spire.

Beside him Valindra Shadowmantle, Overwizard of the North Tower, widely considered to be next in line to succeed Arklem Greeth—which of course was a rather useless tribute, since the lich planned to live forever—gave a derisive snort. She was a tiny thing, much shorter than Greeth and with a lithe moon elf frame that was many times more diminutive than the archmage arcane's burly and bloated animated vessel.

"No, truly," Arklem Greeth went on. "Did the Mirabarrans join in the battle against Pallindra and our safehouse because of the rumors that we had threatened to intervene with the stability of the Silver Marches? Or was their interference part of a wider revolt against the Arcane Brotherhood? Cause or effect?"

"The latter," Valindra replied with a flip of her long and lustrous black hair, so clear in contrast to eyes that seemed as if they had stolen all the blue from the waters of the Sword Coast. "The Mirabarrans would have joined in the fight against us whether Nyphithys had gone to Obould or not. This betrayal has Arabeth's stench all over it."

"Of course you would say that of your rival."

"Do you disagree?" the forceful elf said without the slightest hesitation, and Arklem Greeth gave a wheezing chuckle. It wasn't often that anyone had the courage to speak to him so bluntly—in fact, beyond Valindra's occasional outbursts, he couldn't remember the last person who had done so. Someone he had subsequently murdered, no doubt.

"You would then imply that Overwizard Raurym sent word ahead of the meeting between Nyphithys and King Obould," reasoned the lich. "Following your logic, I mean."

"Her treachery is not so surprising, to me at least."

"And yet you too have your roots in the Silver Marches," Greeth said with a wry grin. "In the Moonwood, I believe, and among the elves who wouldn't be pleased to see the Arcane Brotherhood bolster King Obould."

"All the more reason for you to know that I did not betray you," said Valindra. "I have made no secret of my feelings for my People. And it was I who first suggested to you that the Arcane Brotherhood would do well to stake a claim in the bountiful North."

"Perhaps only so that you could foil me later and weaken my position," said Greeth. "And that after you had gained my favor with your prodding for the spread of our influence. Clever of you to insinuate yourself as my heir apparent before leading me to a great chasm, yes?"

Valindra stopped abruptly and Arklem Greeth had to turn and look back to look at her. She stood with one arm on her hip, the other hanging at her side, and her expression absent any hint of amusement.

The lich laughed all the louder. "You are offended that I credit you with such potential for deviousness? Why, if half of what I said were true, you would be a credit to the twisted dealings of the dark elves themselves! It was a compliment, girl."

"Half was true," Valindra replied. "Except that I wouldn't be so clever to desire anything good to befall the Silver Marches or the worthless fools of the Moonwood. Were I to love my homeland, I might take your words as a compliment, though I insist I would have come up with something a bit less transparent than the plot you lay at my feet. But I take no pleasure in the loss of Nyphithys and the setback for the Arcane Brotherhood."

Arklem Greeth stopped smiling at the sheer bitterness and venom in the elf woman's words. He nodded somberly. "Arabeth Raurym, then," he said. "The cause for this troubling and costly effect."

"Her heart has ever remained in Mirabar," said Valindra, and under her breath, she added, "The little wretch."

Arklem Greeth smiled again when he heard that, having already turned back for the door to the South Tower. He recited a quiet incantation and waved a thick hand at the door. The locks clicked and humming sounds of various pitches emanated from all around the portal. At last, the heavy bar behind the door fell away with a clang and the portal swung open toward Arklem Greeth and Valindra, revealing a darkened room beyond.

The archmage arcane stared into the black emptiness for a few moments before turning back to regard the elf as she walked up beside him.

"Where are the guards?" the Overwizard of the South Tower asked.

Arklem Greeth lifted a fist up before his face and summoned around it a globe of purple, flickering flames. With that faerie fire "torch" thrust before him, he strode into the south tower.

The pair went up room by room, the stubborn and confident lich ignoring Valindra's continual complaints that they should go and find an escort of capable battle-mages. The archmage arcane whispered an incantation into every torch on the walls, so that soon after he and Valindra had made their way out of the room, the enchanted torches would burst into flame behind them.

They found themselves outside the door to Arabeth's private quarters not long after, and there the lich paused to consider all they had seen, or had not seen.

"Did you notice an absence of anything?" he asked his companion.

"People," Valindra dryly replied.

Arklem Greeth smirked at her, not appreciating the levity. "Scrolls," he explained. "And rods, staves, and wands, and any other magical implements. Not a spellbook to be found. . . ."

"What might it mean?" Valindra asked, seeming more curious.

"That the chamber beyond this door is equally deserted," said

Greeth. "That our guesses about Arabeth ring true, and that she knew that we knew."

He ended with a grimace and spun back at Arabeth's door, waving his hand forcefully its way as he completed another spell, one that sent the reinforced, many-locked door flinging wide.

Revealing nothing but darkness behind.

With a growl, Valindra started past Greeth, heading into the room, but the archmage arcane held out his arm and with supernatural power held the elf back. She started to protest, but Arklem Greeth held up the index finger of his free hand over pursed lips, and again added the power of supernatural dominance, hushing the woman as surely as he had physically gagged her.

He looked back into the darkness, as did Valindra, only it wasn't as pitch black as before. In the distance to the left, a soft light glowed and a tiny voice lessened the emptiness.

Arklem Greeth strode in, Valindra on his heel. He cast a spell of detection and moved slowly, scanning for glyphs and other deadly wards. He couldn't help but pick up his pace, though, as he came to understand the light source as a crystal ball set on a small table, and came to recognize the voice as that of Arabeth Raurym.

The lich walked up to the table and stared into the face of his missing overwizard.

"What is she doing out of . . . ?" Valindra started to ask as she, too, came to recognize Arabeth, but Arklem Greeth waved his hand and snarled in her direction. Her words caught in her throat so fully that she fell back, choking.

"Well met, Arabeth," he said to the crystal ball. "You didn't inform me that you and your associate wizards would be leaving the Hosttower."

"I didn't know that your permission was required for an overwizard to leave the tower," Arabeth replied.

"You knew enough to leave an active scrying ball in place to greet any visitors," Greeth replied. "And who but I would deign to enter your chambers without permission?"

"Perhaps that permission has been given to others."

Arklem Greeth paused and considered the sly comment, the veiled threat that Arabeth had co-conspirators within the Hosttower.

"There is an army assembled against you," Arabeth went on.

"Against us, you mean."

The woman in the crystal ball paused and didn't blink. "Captain Deudermont leads them, and that is no small thing."

"I tremble at the thought," Arklem Greeth replied.

"He is a hero of Luskan, known to all," Arabeth warned. "The high captains will not oppose him."

"Good, then they won't get in my way," said Arklem Greeth. "So pray tell me, daughter of Mirabar, in this time of trial for the Hosttower, why is one of my overwizards unavailable to me?"

"The world changes around us," Arabeth said, and Arklem Greeth took note that she seemed a bit shaken, that as the reality of her choice opened wide before her, as expected as that eventuality had to be, doubts nibbled at her arrogant surety. "Deudermont has arrived with a Waterdhavian lord, and an army trained specifically in tactics for battling wizards."

"You know much of them."

"I made it a priority to learn."

"And you have not once addressed me by my title, Overwizard Raurym. Not once have you spoken to me as the archmage arcane. What am I to garner from your lack of protocol and respect, to say nothing of your conspicuous absence in this, our time of trial?"

The woman's face grew stern.

"Traitor," said Valindra, who had at last rediscovered her magically muted voice. "She has betrayed us!"

Arklem Greeth turned a condescending look over the perceptive elf.

"Tell me then, daughter of Mirabar," the archmage arcane said, seeming amused, "have you fled the city? Or do you intend to side with Captain Deudermont?"

As he finished, he closed his eyes and sent more than his thoughts or voice into the crystal ball. He sent a piece of his life essence, his very being, the undead and eternal power that had held Arklem Greeth from passing into the netherworld.

"I choose self-preservation, whatever course that—" She stopped and winced, then coughed and shook her head. It seemed as if she would simply topple over. The fit passed, though, and she steadied herself and looked back at her former master.

The crystal ball went black.

"She will run, the coward," said Valindra. "But never far enough...."

Arklem Greeth grabbed her and tugged her along, hustling her out of the room. "Wraithform, at once!" he instructed, and he cast the enchantment upon himself, his body flattening to a two-dimensional form. He slipped through a crack in the wall then through the floor, rushing swiftly and in a nearly straight line back to the main section of the Hosttower with the similarly flattened Valindra close behind.

And not a moment too soon, both learned as they slipped out of a crease in the tower's main audience chamber just as the south tower was wracked by a massive, fiery explosion.

"The witch!" Valindra growled.

"Impressive witch," Greeth said.

All around them, other wizards began scrambling, shouting out warnings of fire in the south tower.

"Summon your watery friends," Arklem Greeth said to them all, calmly, almost amused, as if he truly enjoyed the spectacle. "Perhaps I have at last found a worthy challenge in this Deudermont creature, and in the allies he has inspired," he said to Valindra, who stood with her jaw hanging open in disbelief.

"Arabeth Raurym is still in the city," he told her. "In the northern section, with the Shield of Mirabar. I looked through her eyes, albeit briefly," he explained as she started to ask the obvious question. "I saw her heart, too. She means to fight against us, and has gathered an impressive number of our lesser acolytes to join her. I'm wounded by their lack of loyalty, truly."

"Archmage Arcane, I fear you don't understand," Valindra said. "This Captain Deudermont is not to be taken—"

"Don't tell me how I should take him!" Arklem Greeth shouted in her face, his dead eyes going wide and flashing with inner fires that came straight from the Nine Hells.

"I will take him roasted and basted before this is through, or I will devour him raw! The choice is mine, and mine alone. Now go and oversee the fighting in the south tower. You bore me with your fretting. We have been issued a challenge, Valindra Shadowmantle. Are you not up to fighting it?"

"I am, Archmage Arcane!" the moon elf cried. "I only feared—"

"You feared I didn't understand the seriousness of this conflict."

"Yes," Valindra said, or started to say, before she gasped as an unseen magical hand grabbed at her throat and lifted her to her tip-toes then right off the ground.

"You are an overwizard of the Hosttower of the Arcane," Arklem Greeth said. "And yet, I could snap your neck with a thought. Consider your power, Valindra, and lose not your confidence that it's considerable."

The woman squirmed, but could not begin to break free.

"And while you are remembering who you are, while you consider your power and your present predicament, let that remind you of who I am." He finished with a snort and Valindra went flying away, stumbling and nearly falling over.

With a last look at the grumbling archmage arcane, Valindra ran for the south tower.

Arklem Greeth didn't watch her go. He had other things on his mind.

CHAPTER

SAVA, FIVE-AND-A-HALF WAYS

12

"My bilge rats are grumbling!" High Captain Baram protested, referring to the peasants who lived in the section of the city that was his domain, the northeastern quadrant of Luskan south of the Mirar. "I can't have fires taking down their hovels, now can I? Your war's not a cheap thing!"

"*My* war?" old Rethnor replied, leaning back in his chair. Kensidan sat beside him, his chair pushed back from the table, as was the protocol, and with his thin legs crossed as always.

"Word's out that you provoked Deudermont from the start," Baram insisted. He was the heaviest of the five high captains by far, and the tallest, though in their sailing days, he was the lightest of the bunch, a twig of a man, thinner even than the fretful Taerl, who very much resembled a weasel.

A bit of grumbling ensued around the table, but it ended when the most imposing of the five interjected, "I heard it, too."

All eyes turned to regard High Captain Kurth, a dark man, second oldest of the five high captains, who seemed always cloaked in shadow. That was due in part to his grizzled beard, which seemed perpetually locked in two days' growth, but more of that shadowy cloak was a result of the man's demeanor. He alone among the five lived out on the river, on Closeguard Island, the gateway to Cutlass Island, which housed the Hosttower of the Arcane. With such a strategic position in the current conflict, many believed that Kurth held the upper hand.

From his posture, it seemed to Kensidan that Kurth agreed with that assessment.

Never a boisterous or happy man, Kurth seemed all the more grim, and understandably so. His domain, though relatively unscathed so far, seemed most in peril.

"Rumors!" Suljack insisted, pounding his fist on the table, a display that brought a knowing smile to Kensidan's face. The perceptive son of Rethnor realized then where Baram and Kurth had heard the rumor. Suljack was not the most discreet of men, nor the most intelligent.

"These rumors are no doubt due to my father's—" Kensidan began, but such an outcry came at him as to stop him short.

"Ye're not for talking here, Crow!" Baram cried.

"Ye come and ye sit quiet, and be glad that we're letting ye do that!" Taerl, the third of the five, agreed, his large head bobbing stupidly at the end of his long, skinny neck—a neck possessed of the largest Adam's apple Kensidan had ever seen. Standing beside Taerl, Suljack wore an expression of absolute horror and rubbed his face nervously.

"Have you lost your voice, Rethnor?" High Captain Kurth added. "I've been told that you've turned your Ship over to the boy, all but formally. If you're wishing him to speak for you here, then mayhaps it's time for you to abdicate."

Rethnor's laugh was full of phlegm, a clear reminder of the man's failing health, and it did more to heighten the tension than to alleviate it. "My son speaks for Ship Rethnor, because his words come from me," he said, seemingly with great difficulty. "If he utters a word that I don't like, I will say so."

"High captains alone may speak at our gathering," Baram insisted. "Am I to bring all my brats and have them blabber at all of Taerl's brats? Or maybe our street captains, or might that Kurth could bring a few of his island whores. . . ."

Kensidan and Rethnor exchanged looks, the son nodding for his father to take the lead.

"No," Rethnor said to the others, "I have not yet surrendered my Ship to Kensidan, though the day be fast approaching." He began to cough and hock and continued for a long while—long enough for more than one of the others to roll his eyes at the not-so-subtle reminder that they might have been able to listen to a young, strong voice instead of all that ridiculous wheezing.

"It's not my war," Rethnor said at last. "I did nothing *to* Deudermont or *for* him. The archmage arcane has brought this on himself. In his supreme confidence, he has overreached—his work with the pirates has become too great an annoyance for the lords of Waterdeep. Solid information tells that he has made no friend of Mirabar, either. It's all perfectly reasonable, a pattern that has played out time and again through history, all across Faerûn."

A long pause ensued, where the old man seemed to be working hard to catch his breath. After another coughing session, he continued, "What is more amazing are the faces of my fellow high captains."

"It's a startling turn-around!" Baram protested. "The south spire of the Hosttower is burning. There is smoke rising from the northern section of the city. Powerful wizards lay dead in our streets."

"Good. A cleansing leaves opportunity, a truth not reflected in these long and frightened faces."

Rethnor's remark left three of the others, including Suljack, staring wide-eyed. Kurth, though, just folded his hands on his lap and stared hard at old Rethnor, ever his most formidable opponent. Even back in their sailing days, the two had often tangled, and none of that had changed when they traded their waterborne ships for their respective "Ships" of state.

"My bilge rats—" Baram protested.

"Will grump and complain, and in the end accept what is offered to them," said Rethnor. "They have no other choice."

"They could rise up."

"And you would slaughter them until the survivors sat back down," said Rethnor. "View this as an opportunity, my friends. Too long have we sat on our hands while Arklem Greeth reaps and rapes the wealth of Luskan. He pays us well, indeed, but our gains are a mere pittance beside his own."

"Better the archmage arcane, who knows and lives for Luskan . . ." Baram started, but stopped as a few others began to chuckle at his curious choice of words.

"He knows Luskan," Baram corrected, joining in the mirth with a grin of his own. "Better him than some Waterdhavian lord."

"This Brambleberry idiot has no designs on Luskan," said Rethnor. "He is a young lord, borne to riches, who fancies himself a hero, and nothing more. I doubt he will survive his folly, and even should he, he will take his thousand bows and seek ten thousand more cheers in Waterdeep."

"Which is leaving us with Deudermont," said Taerl. "He fancies nothing, and already has a greater reputation than Brambleberry'd ever imagine."

"True, but not to our loss," Rethnor explained. "Should Deudermont prevail, the people of Luskan would all but worship him."

"Some already do that," said Baram.

"Many do, if the numbers o' his swelling ranks are to be told," Taerl corrected. "I'd not've thought folks would dare follow anyone against the likes o' Arklem Greeth, but they are."

"And at no cost to us," said Rethnor.

"You would want Deudermont as ruler above us five, then?" asked Baram.

Rethnor shrugged. "Do you really think him as formidable as Arklem Greeth?"

"He has the numbers—*growing* numbers—and so he might prove to be," Taerl replied.

"In this fight, perhaps, but Arklem Greeth has the resources to see where Deudermont cannot see, and to kill quickly where Deudermont would need to send an army," said Rethnor, again after a long pause. It was obvious that the man was nearing the limit of his stamina. "For our purposes, we wouldn't be worse off with Deudermont at the head of Luskan, even openly, as Arklem Greeth is secretly."

He ended with a fit of coughing as the other high captains exchanged curious glances, some seeming intrigued, others obviously simmering.

Kensidan stood up and moved to his father. "The meeting is ended," he announced, and he called a Ship Rethnor guard over to thump his ailing father on the back in the hopes that they could extract some of that choking phlegm.

THE PIRATE KING

"We haven't even answered the question we came to discuss," Baram protested. "What are we to do with the city guard? They're getting eager, and they don't rightly know which side to join. They sat in their barracks on Blood Island and let Deudermont march through, and the northern span of the Harbor Cross fell into the water!"

"We do nothing with them," Kensidan replied, and Taerl shot him an angry look then turned to Kurth for support. Kurth, though, just sat there, hands folded, expression hidden behind his dark cloud.

"My father will not allow those guards who heed Ship Rethnor's call, at least, to act," the Crow explained. "Let Deudermont and Arklem Greeth have their fight, and we will join in as it decisively turns."

"For the winner, of course," Taerl reasoned in sarcastic tones.

"It's not our fight, but that does not mean that it cannot be our spoils," Suljack said. He looked at Kensidan, seeming quite proud of his contribution.

"The archmage arcane will turn the whole of the guard against Deudermont," Kurth warned.

"And against us for not doing just that!" Taerl added.

"Then . . . why . . . hasn't he?" Rethnor shouted between gasps and coughs.

"Because they won't listen to him," Suljack added at Kensidan's silent prompting. "They won't fight against Deudermont."

"Just what Luskan needs," Kurth replied with a heavy sigh. "A hero."

* * * * *

"Unexpected allies from every front," Deudermont announced to Robillard, Drizzt, and Regis. Lord Brambleberry had just left them, heading for a meeting with Arabeth Raurym and the Mirabarran dwarves and humans who had unexpectedly thrown in with Brambleberry and Deudermont in their fight against Arklem Greeth. "The first battles have been waged in the Hosttower and we have not even crossed to Closeguard Isle yet."

"It's going better than we might have hoped," Drizzt agreed, "but these are wizards, my friend, and never to be underestimated."

"Arklem Greeth has a trick or ten ready for us, I don't doubt," said Deudermont. "But with an overwizard and her minions now on our side, we can better anticipate and so better defeat such tricks. Unless, of course, this Arabeth Raurym is the first of those very deceptions...."

He said it in jest, but his glance at Robillard showed anything but levity.

"She isn't," the wizard assured him. "Her betrayal of the Hosttower is genuine, and not unexpected. It was she, I'm sure—and so is Arklem Greeth—who betrayed the Arcane Brotherhood's advances into the Silver Marches. No, her survival depends upon Arklem Greeth losing, and losing everything."

"She has put everything on the line for our cause."

"Or for her own," Robillard replied.

"So be it," said Deudermont. "In any case, her defection brings us needed strength to ensure the destruction of the Hosttower's perverse leader."

"And then what?" Regis asked.

Deudermont stared hard at Regis and replied, "What do you mean? You cannot support the rule of Arklem Greeth, who is not even alive. His very existence is a perversion!"

Regis nodded. "All true, I expect," he replied. "I only wonder..." He looked to Drizzt for support, but then just shook his head, not believing himself qualified to get into such a debate with Captain Deudermont.

Deudermont smiled at him then moved to pour wine into four tallglasses, handing them around.

"Follow your heart and do what is good and just, and the world will be aright," Deudermont said, and lifted his glass in toast.

The others joined in, though the tapping of glasses was not enthusiastic.

"Enough time has passed," Deudermont said after a sip. He referred to Lord Brambleberry's bidding that he should go and join Brambleberry with Arabeth and the Mirabarrans. His intentional delay in going was a calculated stutter in bringing in the leadership, to keep the balance of power on Brambleberry's side. He and Deudermont were more impressive introduced separately than together.

Drizzt motioned to Regis to go with the captain. "The Mirabarrans will not yet understand my new relationship with their marchion," Drizzt said. "Go and represent Bruenor's interests at this meeting."

"I don't know Bruenor's interests," Regis quipped.

Drizzt tossed a wink at Deudermont. "He trusts the good captain," the drow said.

"Trusting the good captain's heart and trusting his judgment might be two entirely different matters, wouldn't you agree?" Robillard said to Drizzt when the other two had gone. He dumped his remaining wine into the hearth and moved to a different bottle, a stronger liquor, to refill his glass, and to fill another one for Drizzt, who gingerly accepted it.

"You don't trust his judgment?" the drow asked.

"I fear his enthusiasm."

"You loathe Arklem Greeth."

"More so because I know him," Robillard agreed. "But I know Luskan, too, and recognize that she is not a town predisposed to peace and law."

"What will we have when the smothering mantle of the Hosttower is removed?" asked Drizzt.

"Five high captains of questionable demeanor—men Captain Deudermont would have gladly killed at sea had he caught them in their swaggering days of piracy. Perhaps they have settled into reasonable and capable leaders, but . . ."

"Perhaps not," Drizzt offered, and Robillard lifted his glass in solemn agreement.

"I know the devil who rules Luskan, and the limits of his demands and depravations. I know his thievery, his piracy, his murder. I know the sad injustice of Prisoner's Carnival, and how Greeth cynically uses it to keep the peasants terrified even as they're entertained. What I don't know is what devil will come after Greeth."

"So believe in Captain Deudermont's premise," the drow offered. "Do what is good and just, and trust that the world will be aright."

"I like the open seas," Robillard replied. "Out there, I find clear demarcations of right and wrong. There is no real twilight out there, and no dawn light filtered by mountains and trees. There is light and there is darkness."

"To simplicity," Drizzt said with another tip of his glass.

Robillard looked out the window to the late afternoon skyline. Smoke rose from several locations, adding to the gloom.

"So much gray out there," the wizard remarked. "So many shades of gray...."

* * * * *

"I didn't think you would have the courage to come here," High Captain Kurth said when Kensidan, seeming so much the Crow, walked unescorted into his private parlor. "You could disappear...."

"And how would that benefit you?"

"Perhaps I just don't like you."

Kensidan laughed. "But you like what I have allowed to take place."

"What you have allowed? You speak for Ship Rethnor now?"

"My father accepts my advice."

"I should kill you for simply admitting that. It's not your prerogative to so alter the course of my life, whatever promise of better things you might expect."

"This need not affect you," Kensidan said.

Kurth snorted. "To get to the Hosttower, Brambleberry's forces will have to cross Closeguard. By allowing that, I'm taking sides. You and the others can hide and wait, but you—or your father—have forced a choice upon me that threatens my security. I don't like your presumption."

"Don't allow them passage," Kensidan replied. "Closeguard is your domain. If you tell Deudermont and Brambleberry that they cannot pass, then they will have to sail to the Hosttower's courtyard."

"And if they win?"

"You have my assurance—the assurance of Ship Rethnor—that we will speak on your behalf with Captain Deudermont should he ascend to lead Luskan. There will be no residual acrimony toward Ship Kurth for your reasonable decision."

"In other words, you expect me to be in your debt."

"No . . ."

"Do not play me for a fool, young man," said Kurth. "I was indenturing would-be leaders before your mother spread her legs. I know the price of your loyalty."

"You misjudge me, and my Ship," said Kensidan. "When Arklem Greeth is no more, the high captains will find a new division of spoils. There is only one among that group, outside of Ship Rethnor, who is truly formidable, and who will be able seize the right opportunity."

"Flattery . . ." Kurth said with a derisive snort.

"Truth, and you know it."

"I know that you said 'outside of Ship Rethnor' and not 'other than Rethnor,' " Kurth remarked. "It's official then, though secret, that Kensidan captains that Ship."

Kensidan shook his head. "My father is a great man."

"Was," Kurth corrected. "Oh, take no offense at a statement you know to be true," he added when Kensidan bristled, like a Crow ruffling the feathers of its black wings. "Rethnor recognizes it, as well. He is wise to know when it's time to pass along the reins of power. Whether or not he chose wisely is another matter entirely."

"Flattery . . ." Kensidan said, mocking Kurth's earlier tone.

Kurth cracked a smile at that.

"How long has Suljack suckled at your teat, boy?" Kurth asked. "You should coach him to stop looking at you for approval whenever he makes a suggestion or statement favorable to your position."

"He sees the potential."

"He is an idiot, and you know him to be just that."

Kensidan didn't bother replying to the obvious. "Captain Deudermont and Lord Brambleberry chart their own course," he said. "Ship Rethnor neither encourages nor dissuades them, but seeks only to find profit in the wake."

"I don't believe you."

Kensidan shrugged.

"Will Arklem Greeth believe you if he proves victorious?"

"Will Captain Deudermont understand your refusal to allow passage across Closeguard if he wins the fight?"

"Should we just draw sides now and be done with it?"

"No," Kensidan answered with a tone of finality that stopped Kurth cold. "No, none of us are served in this fight. In the aftermath, likely, but not in the fight. If you throw in with Greeth against Deudermont, and with the implication that you would then use a successful Arklem Greeth against Ship Rethnor, then I . . . then my father would need to throw in with Deudermont to prevent such an outcome. Suljack will follow our lead. Baram and Taerl would find themselves isolated if they followed yours, you being out here on Closeguard, don't you think? Neither of them would stand against Brambleberry and Deudermont for a few days, and how much help would the wretch Arklem Greeth send them, after all?"

Kurth laughed. "You have it all charted, it seems."

"I see the potential for gain. I hedge against the potential for loss. My father raised no fool."

"Yet you are here, alone."

"And my father didn't send me out this day without an understanding of High Captain Kurth, a man he respects above all others in Luskan."

"More flattery."

"Deserved, I'm told. Was I misinformed?"

"Go home, young fool," Kurth said with a wave of his hand, and Kensidan was more than happy to oblige.

You heard that? Kensidan asked the voice in his head as soon as he had exited the high captain's palace, making his way with all speed to the bridge, where his men waited.

Of course.

The assault on the Hosttower will be much more difficult by sea.

High Captain Kurth will allow passage, the voice assured him.

CHAPTER 13

THE NOOSE AND THE DEAD MEN

"Help me! They want to kill me!" the man cried.

He ran to the base of the stone tower, where he began pounding on the ironbound wooden door. Though he wore no robes, the nondescript fellow was known to be a wizard.

"Out of spells and tricks, then?" one of the sentries called down. Beside the sentry, his companion chuckled then elbowed him and nodded for him to look out across the square to the approaching warrior.

"Wouldn't want to be this one," the second sentry said.

The first looked down at the desperate wizard. "Threw a few bolts at that one, did you? I'm thinking I'd rather punch my fist through a wasp nest."

"Let me in, you fools!" the wizard yelled up. "He'll kill me."

"We're not doubting that."

"He is a drow!" the wizard yelled. "Can you not see that? You would side with a dark elf against one of your own race?"

"Aye, a drow by the name of Drizzt Do'Urden," the second sentry shouted back. "And he's working for Captain Deudermont. You wouldn't expect us to go against the master of *Sea Sprite*, would you?"

The wizard started to protest, but stopped as reality settled in. The guards weren't going to help him. He rolled his back to the door so he could face the approaching drow. Drizzt came across the square, weapons in hand, his expression emotionless.

"Well met, Drizzt Do'Urden," one of the sentries called down as the drow stopped a few steps from the whimpering wizard. "If you're thinking to kill him, then let us turn away so that we can't bear witness against you." The other sentry laughed.

"You are caught, fairly and fully," Drizzt said to the frantic man. "Do you accept that?"

"You have no right!"

"I have my blades, you have no spells remaining. Need I ask you again?"

Perhaps it was the deathly calm of Drizzt's tone, or the laughter of the amused sentries, but the wizard found a moment of strength then, and straightened against the door, squaring his shoulders to his adversary. "I am an overwizard of the Hosttower of . . ."

"I know who you are, Blaskar Lauthlon," Drizzt replied. "And I witnessed your work. There are dead men back there, by your hand."

"They attacked my position! My companions are dead . . ."

"You were offered quarter."

"I was bade to surrender, and to one who has no authority."

"Few in Luskan would agree with that, I fear."

"Few in Luskan would suffer a drow to live!"

Drizzt chuckled at that. "And yet, here I am."

"Be gone from this place at once!" Blaskar yelled. "Or feel the sting of Arklem Greeth!"

"I ask only one more time," said Drizzt. "Do you yield?"

Blaskar straightened his shoulders again. He knew his fate, should he surrender.

He spat at Drizzt's feet—feet that moved too quickly to be caught by the spittle, slipping back a step then rushing forward with blinding speed. Blaskar shrieked as the drow's blades came up and closed on him. Above, the guards also cried out in surprise, though their yelps seemed more full of glee than fear.

Drizzt's scimitars hummed in a cross, then a second, one blade stabbing left past Blaskar's head to prod the door, the other cutting the air just above the man's brown hair. The flurry went on for many moments, scimitars spinning, Drizzt spinning, blades slashing at every conceivable angle.

Blaskar yelled a couple of times. He tried to cover up, but really had no way to avoid any of the drow's stunningly swift, sure movements. When the barrage ended, the wizard stood in a slight crouch, arms tight against him and afraid to move, as if expecting that pieces of his extremities would simply fall away.

But he hadn't been touched.

"What?" he said, before realizing that the show had been merely to put Drizzt into just the right position.

The drow, much closer to Blaskar than when the flurry began, punched out, and the pommel of Icingdeath smashed hard into the overwizard's face, slamming him up against the door.

He held his balance for just a moment, shooting an accusatory look and pointing a finger at Drizzt before crumbling to the ground.

"Bet that hurt," said one of the sentries from above.

Drizzt looked up to see that four men, not two, stared down at him, admiring his handiwork.

"I thought you'd cut him to bits," said one, and the others laughed.

"Captain Deudermont will arrive here soon," Drizzt replied. "I expect you will open the door for him."

The sentries all nodded. "Only four of us here," one mentioned, and Drizzt looked at him curiously.

"Most aren't at their posts," another explained. "They're watching over their families as the battles draw near."

"We got no orders to join in for either side," said the third.

"Nor to stay out," the last added.

"Captain Deudermont fights for justice, for all of Luskan," Drizzt said to them. "But I understand that your choice, should you make it, will be based on pragmatism."

"Meaning?" asked the first.

"Meaning that you have no desire to be on the side that loses," Drizzt said with a grin.

"Can't argue that."

"And I cannot blame you for it," said the drow. "But Deudermont will prevail, don't doubt. Too long has the Hosttower cast a dark shadow over Luskan. It was meant to be a shining addition to the beauty of the city, but under the control of the lich Greeth, it has become a tombstone. Join with us, and we'll take the fight to Greeth's door—and through it."

"Do it fast, then," said one of the men, and he motioned out toward the wider city, where fires burned and smoke clouded nearly every street, "before there's nothing left to win."

* * * * *

A woman ran screaming out onto the square, flames biting at her hair and clothing. She tried to drop and roll, but merely dropped and squirmed as the fire consumed her.

More screams emanated from the house she'd run from, and flashes of lightning left thundering reports. An upper story window shattered and a man came flying out, waving his arms wildly all the way to the hard ground. He pulled himself up, or tried to, but fell over, grasping at a torn knee and a broken leg.

A wizard appeared at the window from which the man had fallen, and pointed a slender wand down at him, sneering with wicked glee.

A hail of arrows arched above the square from rooftops across the way, and the wizard staggered back into the room, killed by the unexpected barrage.

The battle raged with missiles magical and mundane. A group of warriors charged across the square at the house, only to be driven back by a devastating volley of magical flame and lightning.

A second magical volley rose up just south of the house, aimed at it, and despite all the wards of the Hosttower wizards trapped inside, a corner of the building roared in flames.

From a large palace some distance to the northwest, High Captains Taerl and Suljack watched it all with growing fascination.

"It's the same tale each time," Suljack remarked.

"No less than twenty o' Deudermont's followers dead," Taerl replied, to which Suljack merely shrugged.

"Deudermont will replace archers and swordsmen far more readily than Arklem Greeth will find wizards to throw fireballs at them," Suljack said. "This is to end the same way all of them have, with Deudermont's men drawing out every ounce of magical energy from Greeth's wizards then rushing over them.

"And look out in the harbor," he went on, pointing to the masts of four ships anchored in the waterway between Fang and Harbor Arm Islands, and between Fang Island and Cutlass Island, which housed the Hosttower. "Word is that Kurth's shut the Sea Tower down, so it can't oppose *Sea Sprite*, or anyone else that tries to put in on southern Cutlass. Deudermont's already got Greeth blocked east, west, and north, and south'll be closed within a short stretch. Arklem Greeth's not long for the world, or not long for Luskan, at least."

"Bah, but ye're not remembering the power o' that one!" Taerl protested. "He's the archmage arcane!"

"Not for long."

"When those boys get close to the Hosttower, you'll see how long," Taerl argued. "Kurth won't let them cross Closeguard, and going at Arklem Greeth by sea alone will fill the harbor with bodies, whether Sea Tower's to oppose them or not. More likely, Greeth's wanting Sea Tower empty so that Deudermont and his boys'll foolishly walk onto Cutlass Island and he can sink their ships behind them."

"Nothing foolish about Captain Deudermont," Suljack reminded his companions, something every living man who ever sailed the Sword Coast knew all too well. "And nothing weak about that dog Robillard who walks beside him. If this was just Brambleberry, I'd be thinking you're right, friend."

A loud cheer went up across the way, and Suljack and Taerl looked across to see Deudermont riding down one of the side streets, the crowd swelling behind him. Both high captains turned to the wizards' safehouse, knowing the fight would be over all too soon.

"He's to win, I tell you," said Suljack. "We should all just throw in with him now and ride the wind that's filling Deudermont's sails."

The stubborn Taerl snorted and turned away, but Suljack grabbed him and turned him right back, pointing to a group of men flanking Deudermont. They wore the garb of city guards, and seemed as enthusiastic as the men Brambleberry had brought along from Waterdeep—more so, even.

"Your boys," Suljack said with a grin.

"Their choice, not me own," the high captain protested.

"But you didn't stop them," Suljack replied. "Some of Baram's boys are down there, too."

Taerl didn't respond to Suljack's knowing grin. The fight for Luskan was going exactly as Kensidan had predicted, to Arklem Greeth's ultimate dismay, no doubt.

* * * * *

"Fires in the east, fires in the north," Valindra said to Arklem Greeth, the two of them looking out from the Hosttower to the same scene as Taerl and Suljack, though from an entirely different direction and an entirely different perspective.

"Anyone of worth to us will have the spells needed to get back to the Hosttower," Greeth replied.

"Only those skilled in such schools," said Valindra. "Unlike Blaskar—we have not heard from him."

"My mistake in appointing him overwizard," said Greeth. "As it was my mistake in ever trusting that Raurym creature. I will see her dead before this is ended, don't you doubt that."

"I don't, but I wonder to what end."

Arklem Greeth turned on her fiercely, but Valindra Shadowmantle didn't back down.

"They press us," she said.

"They will not cross Closeguard and we can fend them off from the rocky shores of Cutlass," Greeth replied. "Station our best invokers and our most clever illusionists to every possible landing point, and guard their positions with every magical fortification you can assemble. Robillard and whatever other wizards Deudermont holds at his disposal are not to be taken lightly, but as they are aboard ship and we're on solid ground, the advantage is ours."

"For how long?"

"For as long as need be!" Arklem Greeth yelled, his undead eyes glowing with inner fires. He calmed quickly, though, and nodded, conceding, "You are correct, of course. Deudermont and Brambleberry will be relentless and patient as long as Luskan accepts them. Perhaps it's time we turn that game back on them."

"You will speak with the high captains?"

Arklem Greeth scoffed before she ever finished the question. "With Kurth, perhaps, or perhaps not. Are you so certain those foolish pirates are not in fact behind this peasant uprising?"

"Deudermont learned of our complicity in the piracy along the Sword Coast, I'm told."

"And suddenly found a willing ally in Brambleberry, and a willing traitor in Arabeth Raurym? Convenience is often a matter of careful planning, and as soon as I'm finished with the idiot Deudermont, I intend to have a long discussion with each of the high captains. One I doubt any of them will enjoy."

"And until then?"

"Allow that to be my concern," Arklem Greeth told her. "You see to the defense of Cutlass Island. But first pry Overwizard Rimardo from his library in the east tower and bid him go and learn what has happened to Blaskar. And remind our muscular friend that if he is too busy shaking hands, he'll have one less arm available for casting spells."

"Are you sure I shouldn't go find Blaskar while Rimardo prepares the defenses?"

"If Rimardo is too stupid or distracted to do his work correctly, I would rather have the consequences befall him when I'm not standing right behind him," said the lich. He grinned wickedly, taking Valindra's measure with his undressing stare. "Besides, you only wish to go that you might find an opportunity to unearth our dear Arabeth. Nothing would please you more than destroying that one, yes?"

"Guilty as charged, Archmage."

Arklem Greeth lifted a cold hand to cup Valindra's narrow elf chin. "If I were only alive," he said wistfully. "Or perhaps, if you were only dead."

Valindra swallowed hard at that one, and fell back a step, out of Greeth's deathly cold grasp. The archmage arcane cackled his wheezing laugh.

"It's time to punish them," he said. "Arabeth Raurym most of all."

*****

Late that night, Arklem Greeth, a gaseous and insubstantial cloud, slipped out of the Hosttower of the Arcane. He drifted across Closeguard Island and resisted the urge to go into Kurth Tower and disturb the high captain's sleep.

Instead, he went right past the structure and across the bridge to the mainland, to Luskan proper. Just off the bridge, he turned left, north, and entered an overgrown region of brambles, creepers, broken towers, and general disrepair: Illusk, the only remaining ruins of an ancient city. It wasn't more than a couple of acres—at least above ground. There was much more below, including damp old tunnels reaching out to Closeguard Island, and to Cutlass Island beyond that. The place smelled of rotting vegetation, for Illusk also served as a dump for waste from the open market just to the north.

Illusk was entirely unpleasant to the sensibilities of the average man. To the lich, however, there was something special there. It was the place where Arklem Greeth had at last managed the transformation from living man to undead lich. In that ancient place with its ancient graves, the boundary between life and death was a less tangible barrier. It was a place of ghosts and ghouls, and the people of Luskan knew that well. Among the Hosttower's greatest accomplishments, the first real mark the wizards had put upon Luskan during its founding so long ago, was an enchantment of great power that kept the living dead in their place, in Illusk. That was a favor that had, of course, elicited great favor among the people of the City of Sails for the founders of the Hosttower of the Arcane.

Arklem Greeth had studied that dweomer in depth before his transformation, and though he too was an undead thing, the power of the dweomer could not touch him.

He came back to corporeal form in the center of the ruins, and sensed immediately that he was being watched by a hungry ghoul, but the realization only humored him. Few undead creatures would dare approach a lich of his power, and fewer still could refuse to approach him if he so beckoned.

Still grinning wickedly, Arklem Greeth moved to the northwestern tip of the ruins, on the banks of the Mirar. He unfastened a large belt pouch and carefully pulled it open, revealing powdered bone.

Arklem Greeth walked along the bank to the south, chanting softly and sprinkling the bone dust as he went. He took greater care when he came around to the southern edge of the ruins, making certain he wasn't being watched. It took him some time, and a second belt pouch full of bone dust, to pace the entirety of the cordoned area—to set the countering magic in place.

The ghouls and ghosts were free. Greeth knew it, but they didn't.

He went to a mausoleum near the center of the ruins, the very structure in which he'd completed his transformation so long ago. The door was heavily bolted and locked, but the lich rattled off a spell that transformed him once more into a gaseous cloud and he slipped through a seam in the door. He turned corporeal immediately upon entering, wanting to feel the hard, wet stones of the ancient grave beneath his feet.

He padded down the stairs, his undead eyes having no trouble navigating through the pitch dark. On the landing below, he found the second portal, a heavy stone trapdoor. He reached his arm out toward it, enacted a spell of telekinesis, and reached farther with magical fingers, easily lifting the block aside.

Down he went, into the dank tunnel, and there he sent out his magical call, gathered the ghouls and ghosts, and told them of their freedom.

And there, when the monsters had gone, Arklem Greeth placed one of his most prized items, an orb of exceptional power, an artifact he had created to reach into the netherworld and bring forth the residual life energies of long dead individuals.

Cities of men had been situated on that location for centuries, and before the cities, tribes of barbarians had settled there. Each settlement had been built upon the bones of the previous—the bones of the buildings, and the bones of the inhabitants.

Called by the orb of Arklem Greeth, the latter part of the foundation of Luskan began to stir, to awaken, to rise.

CHAPTER
FOLLOW THE SCREAMS
14

"Drizzt? Drizzt?" a nervous Regis asked. With his eyes fixated on the door of the house across the lane, he reached back to tug at his friend's sleeve. "Drizzt?" he asked again, flailing his hand around. He finally caught on to the truth and turned around to see that his friend was gone.

Across the lane, the woman screamed again, and the tone of her shriek, bloodcurdling and full of primal horror, told Regis exactly what was happening there. The halfling summoned his courage and took up his little mace in one hand, his ruby pendant in the other. As he forced himself across the lane, calling softly for Drizzt with every step, he reminded himself of the nature of his enemy and let the useless pendant drop back to the end of its chain.

The screaming was replaced by gasping and whimpering and the shuffling of furniture as Regis neared the house. He saw the woman rush by a window to the right of the door, her arm whipping out behind her—likely upending a chair to slow her pursuer.

Regis darted to that window and saw that her impromptu missile had some effect, tripping up a wretched ghoul.

Regis fought hard trying to breathe at the sight of the hideous thing. It had once been a man, but was hardly recognizable now, with its emaciated appearance, skin stretched tight over bone, lips rotted away to reveal fangs clotted with strips of freshly devoured flesh. The ghoul grabbed the chair in both hands, nails as long as fingers scraping at the wood, and brought it up to its mouth. Snarling and grumbling with rage, needing to bite something, it seemed, the ghoul tore into the chair before flinging it aside.

The woman screamed again.

The ghoul charged, but so intent was it on the woman that it never noticed the small form crouched on the window pane.

As the ghoul rushed past, Regis leaped out. Both hands clutching his mace, he used his flight and all his strength to whip the weapon across the back of the passing ghoul's head. Bone crackled and withered skin tore free. The ghoul stumbled and fell off to the side, crashing down amidst more chairs.

Regis, too, landed hard, overbalanced from his heavy swing. He caught himself quickly, though, and set with a wide stance facing the fallen ghoul, praying that he had hit it hard enough to keep it down.

No such luck—the ghoul pulled itself back up and turned its lipless grin at the halfling.

"Come on, then, and be done with it," Regis heard himself say, and as if in response, the ghoul leaped at him.

The halfling batted aside its flailing arms, knowing that the poison and filth, the essence of undeath in those clawlike fingernails could render a man or halfling immobile. Back and forth he whipped his mace, slapping against the ghoul's arms, defeating the weight of every attack.

But he still got scratched, and felt his knees wobble against the vile poison. And while his swings were stinging the ghoul, perhaps, he wasn't really hurting it.

Desperation drove Regis to new tactics and he dived in between the ghoul's wide swings, repeatedly bashing his mace about the undead monster's face and chest.

He felt the tearing of his shoulders, arms and back, felt the weakness of paralyzation creeping through him like the cold of death. But he stubbornly resisted the urge to fall down, and kept swinging, kept pounding.

Then his strength was gone and he crumbled to the floor.

The ghoul fell in front of him, its head a mass of blasted pulp.

The woman was holding Regis then, though he couldn't feel her touch. He heard her grateful thanks then her renewed scream of terror as she leaped past him and ran for the door.

Regis couldn't turn to follow her movements. He stared helplessly forward, then saw only their legs—four legs, two ghouls. He tried to find comfort in the knowledge that his paralysis likely meant that he wouldn't feel the wretched things eating him.

*****

"Out to the streets!" Deudermont yelled, running along a lane, his forces behind him, and Robillard beside him. "Come out, one and all! There is safety in unity!"

The people of Luskan heard that call and ran to it, though some houses echoed only with screams. Deudermont directed his soldiers into those houses, to battle ghouls and rescue victims.

"Arklem Greeth freed them from Illusk," Robillard said. He'd been grumbling since sunset, since the onslaught of undead. "He seeks to punish the Luskar for allowing us, his enemies, to take the streets."

"He will only turn the whole of the town against him," Deudermont growled.

"I doubt the monster cares," said Robillard. He stopped and turned, and Deudermont paused to regard him then followed his gaze to a balcony across the way. A group of children hustled into view then disappeared into a different door. Behind them came a pair of hungry ghouls, drooling and slavering.

A bolt of lightning reached out from Robillard, forking into two streaks as it neared the balcony, each fork blasting a monster.

The smoking husks, the former ghouls, fell dead on the balcony as the blackened wood behind them smoldered.

Deudermont was glad to have Robillard on his side.

"I will kill that lich," Robillard muttered.

The captain didn't doubt him.

*****

Drizzt ran along the street, searching for his companion. He'd charged into a building, following the screams, but Regis had not followed.

The streets were dangerous. Too dangerous.

Drizzt nodded to Guenhwyvar, who padded along the rooftops, shadowing his movements. "Find him, Guen," he bade, and the panther growled and sprang away.

Across the way, a woman burst out of a house, staggering, bleeding, terrified. Drizzt instinctively charged for her, expecting pursuit.

When none came, when he realized the proximity of that house to where he'd left Regis, a sickly feeling churned in the dark elf's gut.

He didn't pause to question the woman, guessing that she wouldn't have been able to answer with any coherence anyway. He didn't pause at all. He sprinted flat out for the door, then veered when he noticed an open window—no ghoul would have paused to open a window, and the air was too cold for any to have simply been left wide.

Drizzt knew as he leaped to the sill what he would find inside, and only prayed that he wasn't too late.

He crashed atop a ghoul bent over a small form. A second ghoul slashed at him as he and the other went tumbling aside, scoring a tear on Drizzt's forearm. He ached from that, but his elf constitution rendered him impervious to the debilitating touch of such a creature, and he gave it no thought as he hit the floor in a roll. He slammed the wall, willingly, using the barrier to redirect his momentum and allow him to squirm back to his feet as the ghoul bore down hard.

Twinkle and Icingdeath went to fast work before him, much as Regis had parried with his little mace. But those blades, in those hands, proved far more effective. The ghoul's arms were deflected then they were slashed to pieces before they went falling to the floor.

Out of the corner of his eye, Drizzt saw Regis, poor Regis, lying in blood, and the image enraged him like none before. He drove into the standing ghoul, blades stabbing, poking into the emaciated creature with wet, sickly sounds. Drizzt hit it a dozen times, thrusting his blades with such force that they burst right through the creature's back.

He retracted as the ghoul fell against a wall. Likely, it was already dead, but that didn't slow the outraged drow. He brought his blades back and sent them into complimentary spins and began slashing at the ghoul instead of stabbing it. Skin ripped in great lines, showing gray bones and dried-up entrails.

He kept beating the creature even when he heard its companion approach from behind.

That ghoul leaped upon him, claws slashing for Drizzt's face.

They never got close, for even as the ghoul leaped atop him, the drow ducked low and the creature flipped right over him to slam against its destroyed friend.

Drizzt held his swing as a dark form flew in through the window, the great panther slamming the animated corpse, driving the ghoul to the floor under a barrage of slashing claws and tearing fangs.

Drizzt ran to Regis, dropping his blades and skidding down to his knees. He cradled Regis's head and stared into his wide-open eyes, hoping to see a flash of life left there. Yet another ghoul charged at him, but Guenhwyvar leaped over him as he crouched with Regis and hit the thing squarely, blasting it back into the other room.

"Get me out of here," Regis, seeming so near to death, whispered breathlessly.

* * * * *

In Luskan, they came to call the next two tendays the Nights of Endless Screams. No matter how many ghouls and other undead monsters Deudermont and his charges destroyed, more appeared as the sun set the next evening.

Terror fast turned to rage for the folk of Luskan, and that rage had a definite focus.

Deudermont's work moved all the faster, despite the nocturnal terrors, and almost every able bodied man and woman of Luskan marched with him as he flushed the Hosttower's wizards out of their safehouses, and soon there were thirty ships, not four, anchored in a line facing Cutlass Island.

"Arklem Greeth stepped too far," Regis said to Drizzt one morning. From his bed where he was slowly and painfully recovering, the halfling could see the harbor and the ships, and from beneath his window he could hear the shouts of outrage against the Hosttower. "He thought to cow them, but he only angered them."

"There is a moment when a man thinks he's going to die when he's terrified," Drizzt replied. "Then there is a moment when a man is sure he's going to die when he's outraged. That moment, upon the Luskar right now, is the time of greatest courage and the time when enemies should quiver in fear."

"Do you think Arklem Greeth is quivering?"

Drizzt, staring out at the distant Hosttower and its ruined and charred southern arm, thought for a moment then shook his head. "He is a wizard, and wizards don't scare easily. Nor do they always see the obvious, for their thoughts are elsewhere, on matters less corporeal."

"Remind me to repeat that notion to Catti-brie," said Regis.

Drizzt turned a sharp stare at him. "There are still hungry ghouls to feed," he reminded, and Regis snickered all the louder, but held his belly in pain from the laughter.

Drizzt turned back to the Hosttower. "And Arklem Greeth is a lich," he added, "immortal, and unconcerned with momentary triumphs or defeats. Win or lose, he assumes he will fight for Luskan again when Captain Deudermont and his ilk are dust in the ground."

"He won't win," said Regis. "Not this time."

"No," Drizzt agreed.

"But he'll flee."

Drizzt shrugged as if it didn't matter, and in many ways, it didn't.

"Robillard says he'll kill the lich," said Regis.

"Then let us pray for Robillard's success."

* * * * *

"What?" Deudermont asked Drizzt when he noticed the drow looking at him curiously from across the breakfast table. Diagonal to both, Robillard, whose mouth was full of food, chuckled and brought a napkin over his lips.

Drizzt shrugged, but didn't hide his smile.

"What do you . . . what do both of you know that I don't?" the captain demanded.

"I know we spent the night fighting ghouls," Robillard said through his food. "But you know that, too."

"Then what?" asked Deudermont.

"Your mood," Drizzt replied. "You're full of morning sunshine."

"Our struggles go well," Deudermont replied, as if that should have been obvious. "Thousands have rallied behind us."

"There is a reason for that," said Robillard.

"And that's why you're in such a fine mood—the reason, not the reinforcements," said Drizzt.

Deudermont looked at them both in complete puzzlement.

"Arklem Greeth has erased the shades of gray—or has colored them more darkly, to be precise," said Drizzt. "Any doubts you harbored regarding this action in Luskan have been cast away because of the lich's actions at Illusk. As Arklem Greeth stripped the magical boundary that held the monsters at bay, so did he peel away the heavy pall of doubt from Captain Deudermont's shoulders."

Deudermont turned his stare upon Robillard, but the wizard's expression only supported Drizzt's words.

The good captain slid his chair back from the table and stared out across the battered city. Several fires still burned in parts of Luskan, their smoke feeding the perpetual gloom. Wide, flat carts moved along the streets, their drivers solemnly clanging bells as a call for the removal of bodies. Those carts, some moving below Deudermont's window, carried the bodies of many dead.

"I knew Lord Brambleberry's plan would exact a heavy price from the city, yes," the captain admitted. "I see it—I smell it!—every day, as do you. And you speak truly. It has weighed heavily upon me." He kept looking out as he spoke, and the others followed his gaze across the dark roads and buildings.

"This is much harder than sailing a ship," Deudermont said, and Drizzt glanced at Robillard and smiled knowingly, for he knew that Deudermont was going down the same philosophical path as had the wizard those tendays ago when the revolt against the Hosttower had first begun. "When you're hunting pirates, you know your actions are for the greater good. There's little debate to be had beyond the argument of sink them and let them drown out there in the emptiness, or return them to Luskan or Waterdeep for trial. There are no hidden designs behind the actions of pirates—none that would change my actions toward them, at least. Whether they serve the greed of a master or of their own black hearts, my fight with them remains grounded in absolute morality."

"To the joys of political expediency," Robillard said, lifting a mug of breakfast tea in toast. "Here, I mean, in an arena far more complicated and full of half-truths and hidden designs."

"I watch Prisoner's Carnival with utter revulsion," said Deudermont. "More than once I fought the urge to charge the stage and cut down the torturing magistrate, and all the while I knew that he acted under the command of the lawmakers of Luskan. High Captain Taerl and I once nearly came to blows over that whole grotesque scene."

"He argued that the viciousness was necessary to maintain order, of course," said Robillard.

"And not without conviction," Deudermont replied.

"He was wrong," said Drizzt, and both turned to him with surprise.

"I had thought you skeptical of our mission here," said Deudermont.

"You know that I am," Drizzt replied. "But that doesn't mean I disagree that some things, at least, needed to change. But that is not my place to decide in all of this, as you and many others are far more familiar with the nature and character of Luskan than I. My blade is for Captain Deudermont, but my fears remain."

"As do mine," said Robillard. "There are hatreds here, and designs, plots, and rivalries that run deeper than a distaste for Arklem Greeth's callous ways."

Deudermont held up his hand for Robillard to stop, and shifted his open palm toward Drizzt when the drow started to cut in.

"I'm not without consternation," he said, "but I will not surrender my faith that right action makes right result. I cannot surrender that faith, else who am I, and what has my life been worth?"

"A rather simple and unfair reduction," the always-sarcastic wizard replied.

"Unfair?"

"To you," Drizzt answered for Robillard. "You and I have not walked so different a road, though we started from vastly different places. Meddlers, both, we be, and always with the hope that our meddling will leave in our wake a more beautiful tapestry than that we first encountered." Drizzt heard the irony in his own words as he spoke them, a painful reminder that he had chosen not to meddle in Longsaddle, where his meddling might have been needed.

"Me with pirates and you with monsters, eh?" the captain said with a grin, and it was his turn to lift a cup of tea in toast. "Easier to kill pirates, and easier still to kill orcs, I suppose."

Given the recent events in the North, Drizzt nearly snorted his tea out of his nose at that, and it took him a long moment to catch his breath and clear his throat. He held up his hand to deflect the curious looks coming at him from both his companions, not wanting to muddy the conversation even more with tales of the improbable treaty between Kings Bruenor and Obould, dwarf and orc. The drow's expectations of absolutism had been thoroughly flattened of late, and so he was both heartened by and fearful of his friend's unwavering faith.

"Beware the unintended consequences," Robillard said.

But Captain Deudermont looked back out over the city and shrugged that away. A bell clanged below the window, followed by a call for the dead. The course had been set. The captain's gaze drifted to Cutlass Island and the treelike structure of the Hosttower, the masts of so many ships behind it across the harbor and the river.

The threat of the ghouls had diminished. Robillard's wizard friends were on the verge of recreating the seal around Illusk, and most of the creatures had been utterly destroyed.

It was time to take the fight to the source, and that, Deudermont feared, would exact the greatest cost of all.

CHAPTER 15
FROM THE SHADOWS

The ground shaking beneath his bed awakened High Captain Kurth one dismal morning. As soon as he got his bearings and realized he wasn't dreaming, the former pirate acted with the reflexes of a warrior, rolling off the side of his bed to his feet while in the same movement grabbing his sword belt from the bed pole and slapping it around his waist.

"You will not need that," came a quiet, melodic voice from the shadows across the large, circular room, the second highest chamber in Kurth Tower. As his dreams faded and the moment of alarm passed, Kurth recognized the voice as one that had visited him unbidden twice before in that very room.

The high captain gnashed his teeth and considered spinning and throwing one of the many daggers set in his sword belt.

This is no enemy, he reminded himself, though without much conviction, for he wasn't certain who the mysterious visitor really was.

"The western window," the voice said. "It has begun."

Kurth moved to that window and pulled open the heavy drapes, flooding the room with the dawn's light. He looked in the direction from which the voice had sounded, hoping to catch a glimpse of its source from the shadows, but that edge of his chamber defied the morning light and remained as dark as a moonless midnight—magic, Kurth was certain, and potent magic, indeed. The tower had been sealed against magical intrusion by Arklem Greeth himself. And yet, there was the visitor—again!

Kurth turned back to the west, to the slowly brightening ocean.

A dozen boulders and balls of pitch drew fiery lines in the air, flying fast for the Hosttower, or for various parts of the rocky shore of Cutlass Island.

"See?" asked the voice. "It is as I have assured you."

"Rethnor's son is a fool."

"A fool who will prevail," the voice replied.

It was hard to argue that possibility, given the line of ships throwing their missiles at Cutlass Island. Their work was meticulous. They threw in unison and with concentrated aim. He counted fifteen ships firing, though there might have been a couple more hidden from view. In addition, another group of wide, low boats ferried along the line then back to Whitesails Harbor to get more ammunition.

Whitesails Harbor!

The reality hit Kurth hard. Whitesails served as the harbor for Luskan's navy, a flotilla under the auspices, supposedly, of the five high captains as directed by the Hosttower. The ships at Whitesails were the pretty front to the ugly piracy behind Luskan's riches. Deudermont knew those pirates, and they knew him, and many of them hated him and had lost friends to *Sea Sprite*'s exploits on the open seas.

Despite that, the nagging thought—reinforced as more and more masts lined up beside *Sea Sprite* and Brambleberry's warships—was that the Luskar sailors might well desert. As improbable as it seemed, he couldn't deny what he saw with his own eyes. Luskan's fleet, and the men and women of Whitesails, were directly involved in supporting the bombardment of the Hosttower of the Arcane. The men and women of Luskan's fleet were in open revolt against Arklem Greeth.

"The fool with his undead," Kurth muttered.

Arklem Greeth had pushed too hard, too wickedly. He had crossed a line and had driven the whole of the city against him. The high captain kept his gaze to the northwest, to Whitesails Harbor, and though he couldn't make out much from that distance, he

THE PIRATE KING

clearly saw the banner of Mirabar among many on the quayside. He imagined Mirabarran dwarves and men working hard to load the courier ships with rocks and pitch.

Full of anxiety, Kurth turned angrily at the hidden visitor. "What do you demand of me?"

"Demand?" came the reassuring reply, in a tone that seemed truly surprised by the accusation. "Nothing! I . . . we, are not here to demand, but to advise. We watch the wave of change and measure the strength of the rocks against which that wave will break. Nothing more."

Kurth scoffed at the obvious understatement. "So, what do you see? And do you truly understand the strength of those rocks to which you so poetically refer? Do you grasp the power of Arklem Greeth?"

"We have known greater foes, and greater allies. Captain Deudermont has an army of ten thousand to march against the Hosttower."

"And what do you see in that?" Kurth demanded.

"Opportunity."

"For that wretch Deudermont."

A chuckle came from the darkness. "Captain Deudermont has no understanding of the forces he will unwittingly unleash. He knows good and evil, but nothing more, but we—and you—see shades of gray. Captain Deudermont will scale to unstable heights in short order. His absolutes will rally the masses of Luskan, then will send them into revolt."

Kurth shrugged, unconvinced, and fearful of the reputation and power of Captain Deudermont. He suspected that those mysterious outside forces, that hidden character who had visited him twice before, never threateningly, but never comfortably, were sorely underestimating the good captain and the loyalty of those who would follow him.

"I see the rule of law, heavy and cumbersome," he said.

"We see the opposite," said the voice. "We see five men of Luskan who will collect the spoils set free when the Hosttower falls. We see only two of those five who are wise enough to separate the copper from the gold."

Kurth paused and considered that for a while. "A speech you

give to Taerl, Suljack, and Baram, too, no doubt," he replied at length.

"Nay. We have visited none of them, and come to you only because the son of Rethnor, and Rethnor himself, insist that you are the most worthy."

"I'm flattered, truly," Kurth said dryly. He did well to hide his smile and his suspicion, for whenever his "guest" so singled him out as one of importance, it occurred to him that his guest might indeed be a spy from the Hosttower, even Arklem Greeth himself, come to test the loyalty of the high captains in difficult times. It was Arklem Greeth, after all, who had strengthened the magical defenses of Kurth Tower and Closeguard Island a decade before. What wizard would be powerful enough to circumvent defenses set in place by the archmage arcane, but the archmage arcane himself? What wizard in Luskan could claim the power of Arklem Greeth? None who were not in the Hosttower, as far as Kurth knew, would even be close, other than that Robillard beast who sailed with Deudermont, and if his guest was Robillard, that raised the banner of duplicity even higher.

"You will be flattered," the voice responded, "when you come to understand the sincerity behind the claim. Rethnor and Kensidan will show outward respect to all of their peers—"

"It's Rethnor's Ship alone, unless and until he formally cedes it to Kensidan," Kurth insisted. "Quit referring to that annoying Crow as one whose word is of any import."

"Spare us both your quaint customs, for they are a ridiculous assertion to me, and a dangerous delusion for you. Kensidan's hand is in every twist of that which you see before you: the Mirabarrans, the Waterdhavians, Deudermont himself, and the defection of a quarter of Arklem Greeth's forces."

"You openly admit that to me?" Kurth replied, the implication being that he could wage war on Ship Rethnor for such a reality.

"You needed to hear it to know it?"

Kurth narrowed his eyes as he stared into the darkness. The rest of the room had brightened considerably, but still no daylight touched that far corner—or ever would unless his guest willed it to be so.

"Arklem Greeth's rule is doomed, this day," the voice said. "Five men will profit most from his fall, and two of those five are wise enough and strong enough to recognize it. Is one of those two too stubborn and set in his ways to grasp the chest of jewels?"

"You ask me for a declaration of loyalty," Kurth replied. "You ask me to disavow my allegiance to Arklem Greeth."

"I ask nothing of you. I help to explain to you that which is occurring outside your window, and show you paths I think wise. You walk those paths or you do not of your own volition."

"Kensidan sent you here," Kurth accused.

A telling pause ensued before the voice answered, "He didn't, directly. It's his respect for you that guided us here, for we see the possible futures of Luskan and would prefer that the high captains, above all, above Deudermont and above Arklem Greeth, prevailed."

Just as Kurth started to respond, the door to his room burst open and his most trusted guards rushed in.

"The Hosttower is under bombardment!" one cried.

"A vast army gathers at our eastern bridge, demanding passage!" said the other.

Kurth glanced to the shadows—to where the shadows had been, for they were gone, completely.

So was his guest, whoever that guest might have been.

* * * * *

Arabeth and Robillard walked along *Sea Sprite*'s rail before the line of archers, waggling their fingers and casting devious, countering enchantments on the piles of arrows at each bowman's feet.

The ship lurched as her aft catapult let fly a large ball of pitch. It streaked through the air, unerringly for the Hosttower's westernmost limb, where it hit and splattered, launching lines of fire that lit up bushes and already scorched grass at the base of the mighty structure.

But the tower itself had repelled the strike with no apparent ill effects.

"The archmage arcane defends it well," Arabeth remarked.

"Each hit takes from his defenses, and from him," Robillard

replied. He bent low and touched another pile of arrows. Their silvery tips glowed for just a moment before going dim again. "Even the smallest of swords will wear through the strongest warrior's shield if they tap it enough."

Arabeth looked to the Hosttower and laughed aloud, and Robillard followed her gaze. The ground all around the five-limbed structure was thick with boulders, ballista bolts, and smoldering pitch. *Sea Sprite* and her companion vessels had been launching non-stop against Cutlass Island throughout the morning, and at Robillard's direction, all of their firepower had been directed at the Hosttower itself.

"Do you think they will respond?" Arabeth asked.

"You know Greeth as well as I do," Robillard answered. He finished with the last batch of arrows, waited for Arabeth to do likewise, then led her back to his usual perch behind the mainsail. "He will grow annoyed and will order his defenders along the shore to lash out."

"Then we will make them pay."

"Only if we're quick enough," Robillard replied.

"Every one of them will be guarded by spells to counter a dozen arrows," said the woman of Mirabar.

"Then every one will be hit by thirteen," came Robillard's dry reply.

Sea Sprite shuddered again as a rock flew out, along with ten others from the line, all soaring in at the Hosttower with such precision and timing that a pair collided before they reached their mark and skipped harmlessly away. The others shook the ground around the place, or smacked against the Hosttower's sides, to be repelled by its defensive magic.

Robillard looked to the north where one of Brambleberry's boats eased a bit closer against the strong currents of the Mirar.

"Sails!" Robillard cried, and *Sea Sprite*'s crew flipped the lines, unfurling fast.

From the rocks of the northwestern tip of Cutlass Island, a pair of lightning bolts reached out at Brambleberry's ship, scorching her side, tearing one of her sails. With the strong and favorable current, though, the ship was able to immediately reverse direction.

Even as *Sea Sprite* leaned and splashed to life, Robillard and

Arabeth filled her sails with sudden and powerful winds. They didn't even take the time to pull up the anchor, but just cut the line, and *Sea Sprite* turned straight in, bucking the currents with such jolting force that all aboard had to grab on and hold tight.

Arklem Greeth's wizards focused on Brambleberry's boat for far too long, as Robillard had hoped, and by the time the Hosttower contingent noticed the sudden charge of *Sea Sprite*, she was close enough so that those on her deck could see the small forms scrambling across the rocks and ducking for whatever cover they could find.

From a more southern vantage on Cutlass Island, a lightning bolt streaked out at *Sea Sprite*, but she was too well warded to be slowed by the single strike. Her front ballista swiveled and threw a heavy spear at the point from which that attack had emanated, and as *Sea Sprite* began her broadside turn, her prow bending to straight north in a run up the coast, the crack catapult crew on her aft deck had another ball of pitch flying away. It splattered among the rocks and several men and women scrambled up from the burning ground, one engulfed in flame, all screaming.

And those weren't even the primary targets, which were to starboard, trying to hide as a bank of archers the length of *Sea Sprite*'s main deck and three deep lifted and bent their bows.

Three separate volleys went in, enchanted arrows all, skipping off the stones or striking against the defensive magic shields Greeth's minions had raised.

But as Robillard had predicted, more arrows found their way than could be defeated by the enchantments, and another Hosttower wizard fell dead on the stones.

Lightning bolts and arrows reached out at *Sea Sprite* from the rocky coastline. Boulders and balls of pitch flew out from the ship line in response, followed by a devastating barrage of arrows as *Sea Sprite* veered due west and sped away with the fast current.

Robillard nodded his approval.

"One dead, perhaps, or perhaps two," said Arabeth. "It's difficult work."

"Another one Arklem Greeth cannot afford to lose," Robillard replied.

"Our tricks will catch fewer and fewer. Arklem Greeth will teach his forces to adapt."

"Then we will not let him keep up with our evolving tricks," Robillard said, and nodded his chin toward the line of ships, all of whom were pulling up anchor. One by one, they began to glide to the south.

"Sea Tower," Robillard explained, referring to the strong guard tower on southern Cutlass Island. "It would cost Arklem Greeth too much energy to have it as fortified as the Hosttower, so we'll bombard it to rubble, and destroy every other defensible position along the southern coast of the island."

"There are few places to land even a small boat in those rocky waters," Arabeth replied. "Sea Tower was built so that defenders could assault any ships attempting to enter the southern mouth of the Mirar, and not as a defense for Cutlass Island."

Robillard's deadpan expression quieted her, for of course he knew all of that. "We're tightening the noose," he explained. "I expect that those inside the Hosttower are growing more uncomfortable by the hour."

"We nibble at the edges when we must bite out the heart of the place," Arabeth protested.

"Patience," said Robillard. "Our final fight with the lich will be brutal—no one doubts that. Hundreds will likely die, but hundreds more will surely perish if we attack before we prepare the battlefield. The people of Luskan are on our side. We own the streets. We have Harbor Arm and Fang Island fully under our control. Whitesails Harbor sides with us. Captain's Court is ours, and Illusk has been rendered quiescent once again. The Mirar bridges are ours."

"Those that remain," said Arabeth, to which Robillard chuckled.

"Arklem Greeth hasn't a safehouse left in the city, or if he does, his minions there are huddled in a dark basement, trembling—rightfully so!—in fear. And when we have bombed Sea Tower to rubble, and have chased off or killed all of his minions he placed in the southern reaches of Cutlass, Arklem Greeth will need to look south, on his own shores, as well. Unrelenting bombardment, unrelenting pressure, and keep clear in your mind that if we lose ten men—nay, fifty!—for every Arcane Brotherhood wizard we slay, Captain Deudermont will claim victory in a rout."

Arabeth Raurym considered the older and wiser wizard's words for some time before nodding her agreement. Above all else, she wanted the archmage arcane dead, for she knew with certainty that if he wasn't killed, he would find a way to kill her—a horrible, painful way, no doubt.

She looked south as *Sea Sprite* came around Fang Island, to see that the other ships were already lining up to begin the bombardment of Sea Tower.

Sea Sprite's bell rang and the men tacked accordingly to slow her as a trio of ammunition barges from Whitesails Harbor turned around the horn of Harbor Arm Island and crossed in front of her. Arabeth looked over to regard Robillard and could almost hear the calculations playing out behind his eyes. He had orchestrated every piece of the day's action—the bombardment, the trap and attack, and the turn south, complete with supply lines—to the most minute detail.

She understood how Deudermont had gained such a glorious reputation hunting the ever-elusive pirates of the Sword Coast. He had surrounded himself with the finest crew she had ever seen, and standing beside him was the wizard Robillard, so calculating and so very, very deadly.

A shiver ran along Arabeth's spine, but it was one of hope and reassurance as she reminded herself that Robillard and *Sea Sprite* were on her side.

* * * * *

From his eastern balcony, High Captain Kurth and his two closest advisors, one the captain of his guard and the other a high-ranking commander in Luskan's garrison, watched the gathering of thousands at the small bridge that linked Closeguard Island to the city. Deudermont was there, judging from the banners, and Brambleberry as well, though their ships were active in the continuing, unrelenting bombardment of Cutlass Island to the west.

For a moment, Kurth envisioned the whole of the invading army enveloped in the flames of a gigantic Arklem Greeth fireball, and it was not an unpleasant mental image—briefly, at least, until he considered the practical ramifications of having a third of Luskan's populace lying dead and charred in the streets.

"A third of the populace. . . ." he said aloud.

"Aye, and most o' me soldiers in the bunch," said Nehwerg, who had once commanded the garrison at Sea Tower, which was even then crumbling under a constant rain of boulders.

"They could have ten times that number and not get across, unless we let them," insisted Master Shanty, Kurth Tower's captain of the guard.

The high captain chuckled at the ridiculous, empty boast. He could make Deudermont and the others pay dearly for trying to cross to Closeguard—he could even drop the bridge, which his engineers had long ago rigged for just such an eventuality—but to what gain and to what end?

"There's yer bird," Nehwerg grumbled, and pointed down at a black spec flapping past the crowd and climbing higher in the eastern sky. "The man's got no dignity, I tell ya."

Kurth chuckled again and reminded himself that Nehwerg served a valuable purpose for him, and that the man's inanity was a blessing and not a curse. It wouldn't do to have such a personal liaison to the Luskar garrison who could think his way through too many layers of intrigue, after all.

The black bird, the Crow, closed rapidly on Kurth's position, finally alighting on the balcony railing. It hopped down, and flipped its wings over as it did, enacting the transformation back to a human form.

"You said you would be alone," Kensidan said, eyeing the two soldiers hard.

"Of course my closest advisors are well aware of this particular aspect of your magical cloak, son of Rethnor," Kurth replied. "Would you expect that I wouldn't have told them?"

Kensidan didn't reply, other than to let his gaze linger a bit longer on the two before turning it to Kurth, who motioned for them all to enter his private room.

"I'm surprised you would ask to see me at this tense time," Kurth said, moving to the bar and pouring a bit of brandy for himself and Kensidan. When Nehwerg made a move toward the drink, Kurth

THE PIRATE KING

turned him back with a narrow-eyed glare.

"It was not Arklem Greeth," said Kensidan, "nor one of his lackeys. You need know that."

Kurth looked at him curiously.

"Your shadowy visitor," Kensidan explained. "It was not Greeth, not an ally of Greeth in any way, and not a mage of the Arcane Brotherhood."

"Bah, but who's he talking about?" demanded Nehwerg, and Master Shanty stepped up beside his high captain. Kurth impatiently waved them both back.

"How do you . . . ?" Kurth started to ask, but stopped short and just smirked at the surprising, dangerous upstart.

"No wizard outside of Arklem Greeth's inner circle could penetrate the magical defenses he has set in place in Kurth Tower," Kensidan said as if reading Kurth's mind.

Kurth tried hard to not look impressed, and just held his smirk, inviting the Crow to continue.

"Because it was no wizard," Kensidan said. "There is another type of magic involved."

"Priests are no match for the web of Arklem Greeth," Kurth replied. "Do you think him foolish enough to forget the schools of those divinely inspired?"

"And no priest," said Kensidan.

"You're running out of magic-users."

Kensidan tapped the side of his head and Kurth's smirk turned back into an unintentional, intrigued expression.

"A mind mage?" he asked quietly, a Luskar slang for those rare and reputably powerful practitioners of the concentration art known as psionics. "A monk?"

"I had such a visitor months ago, when first I started seeing the possibilities of Captain Deudermont's future," Kensidan explained, taking the glass from Kurth and settling into a chair in front of the room's generous hearth, which had only been lit a few minutes earlier and wasn't yet throwing substantial heat.

Kurth took the seat across from Rethnor's son and motioned for Nehwerg and Master Shanty to stand a step behind him.

"So the machinations of this rebellion, the inspiration even, came from outside Luskan?" Kurth asked.

Kensidan shook his head. "This is a natural progression, a response to the overreaching of Arklem Greeth both on the high seas, where Deudermont roams, and in the east, in the Silver Marches."

"Which all came together in this 'coincidental' conglomeration of opponents lining up against the Hosttower?" Kurth asked, doubt dripping from every sarcastic word.

"I don't believe in coincidence," Kensidan replied.

"And yet, here we are. Do you admit that Kensidan's hand, that Ship Rethnor's hands, are in this?"

"Up to our elbows . . . our shoulders, perhaps," Kensidan said with a laugh, and lifted his glass in toast. "I didn't create this opportunity, but neither would I let it pass."

"You, or your father?"

"He is my advisor—you know as much."

"A startling admission, and a dangerous one," said Kurth.

"How so? Have you heard the rumble on the island to your west? Have you seen the gathering at the gates of Closeguard Bridge?"

Kurth considered that for a moment, and it was his turn to tip his glass to his companion.

"So Arklem Greeth has frayed the many strings, and Kensidan of Ship Rethnor has worked to weave them into something to his own benefit," said Kurth.

Kensidan nodded.

"And these others? Our shadowy visitors?"

Kensidan rubbed his long and thin fingers over his chin. "Consider the dwarf," he said.

Kurth stared at him curiously for a few moments, recalling the rumors from the east regarding the Silver Marches. "King Bruenor? The dwarf King of Mithral Hall works for the fall of Luskan?

"No, not Bruenor. Of course it's not Bruenor, who, by all reports, has troubles enough to keep him busy in the east, thank the gods."

"But it's Bruenor's strange friend who rides with Deudermont," said Kurth.

"Not Bruenor," Kensidan replied. "He has no place or part in any of this, and how the dark elf happened back to Deudermont's side I neither know nor care."

"Then what dwarves? The Ironspur Clan from the mountains?"

"Not dwarves," Kensidan corrected. "Dwarf. You know of my recent acquisition . . . the bodyguard?"

Kurth nodded, finally catching on. "The creature with the unusual morningstars, yes. How could I not know? The one whose ill-fashioned rhymes grate on the nerves of every sailor in town. He has brawled in every tavern in Luskan over the last few months, mostly over his own wretched poetry, and from what my scouts tell me, he's a far better fighter than he is a poet. Ship Rethnor strengthened her position on the street greatly with that one. But he is tied to all of this?" Kurth waved his arm out toward the western window, where the sound of the bombardment had increased yet again.

Kensidan nodded his chin at Master Shanty and Nehwerg, staring all the while into Kurth's dark eyes.

"They are trusted," Kurth assured him.

"Not by me."

"You have come to my Ship."

"To advise and to offer, and not under duress, and nor under duress shall I stay."

Kurth paused and seemed to be taking it all in, glancing from his guest to his guards. It was obvious to Kensidan that the man was intrigued, though, and so it came as no surprise when he turned at last to the two guards and ordered them out of the room. They protested, but Kurth would hear none of it and waved them away.

"The dwarf was a gift to me from these visitors, who take great interest in establishing strong trading ties with Luskan. They are here for commerce, not conquest—that is my hope at least. And my belief, for were they openly revealed, we would be facing greater lords of Waterdeep than Brambleberry, do not doubt, and King Bruenor, Marchion Elastul of Mirabar, and Lady Alustriel of Silverymoon wouldn't be far behind with their own armies."

Kurth felt a bit more perplexed and defensive, and a lot less intrigued.

"These events were not their doing, but they watch closely, and advise me and my father, as they have visited you," said Kensidan, hoping that naming Rethnor almost as an afterthought had slipped past the perceptive Kurth. The man's arched eyebrow showed that it had not, however, and Kensidan silently berated himself and promised that he would do better in the future. Ship Rethnor wasn't yet officially his. Not officially.

"So you hear voices in the shadows, and these bring you confidence," Kurth said. He held up his hand as Kensidan tried to interrupt and continued, "Then we're back at the initial square of the board, are we not? How do you know your friends in the shadows aren't agents of Arklem Greeth? Perhaps the cunning lich has decided it's time to test the loyalties of his high captains. Are you too young to see the dangerous possibilities? And wouldn't that make you the biggest fool of all?"

Kensidan held up his open palm and finally managed to silence the man. He slowly reached under his strange black cloak and produced a small glass item, a bottle, and within it stood the tiny figure of a tiny man.

No, not a figure, Kurth realized. His eyes widened as the poor soul trapped within shifted about.

Kensidan motioned to the hearth. "May I?"

Kurth responded with a puzzled expression, which Kensidan took as permission. He flung the bottle into the hearth, where it smashed against the back bricks.

The tiny man enlarged, bouncing around the low-burning logs before catching his bearings and his balance enough to roll back out, taking ash and one burning log with him.

"By the Nine Hells!" the man protested, batting at his smoldering gray cloak. Blood dripped from several wounds on his hands and face and he reached up and pulled a small shard of glass out of his cheek. "Don't ever do that to me again!" he cried, still flustered and waving his arms. It seemed then as if he had at last caught his bearings, and only then he realized where he was and who was seated before him. The blood drained from his face.

"Are you settled?" Kensidan asked.

The thoroughly flustered little man toed the log beside him and brushed it back into the fireplace, but didn't otherwise respond.

"High Captain Kurth, I give you Morik," Kensidan explained. "Morik the Rogue, to those who know him enough to care. His lady is a mage in the Hosttower—perhaps that is why he's found a place in all this."

Morik looked anxiously from man to man, dipping many short bows.

Kensidan drew Kurth's gaze with his own. "Our visitors are not agents of Arklem Greeth," he said, before turning to the pathetic little man and motioning for him to begin. "Tell my friend your story, Morik the Rogue," Kensidan bade him. "Tell him of your visitors those years ago. Tell him of the dark friends of Wulfgar of Icewind Dale."

* * * * *

"I told ye they wouldn't get across without a row," Baram insisted to his fellow high captains, Taerl and Suljack. The three stood atop the southwest tower of High Captain Taerl's fortress, looking directly west to the bridge to Kurth's Closeguard Island and the great open square south of Illusk where Deudermont and Lord Brambleberry had gathered their mighty army.

"They will," Suljack replied. "Kensi—Rethnor said they will, and so they will."

"That Crow boy is trouble," said Baram. "He'll bring down Rethnor's great Ship before the old man passes on."

"The gates will open," Suljack replied, but very quietly. "Kurth can't refuse. Not this many, not with almost all of Luskan knocking."

"Hard to be denyin' that number," Taerl said. "Most o' the city's walking with Deudermont."

"Kurth won't go against Arklem Greeth—he's more sense than that," Baram replied. "Deudermont's fools'll be swimming or sailing if they want to get to the Hosttower."

Even as Baram spoke, some of High Captain Kurth's sentries rushed up to the bridge and began throwing the locks. To Baram's utter shock, and to Taerl's as well, despite his words, the gates of the Kurth Tower compound pulled open and Kurth's guards stepped back, offering passage.

"A trick!" Baram protested, leaping to his feet. "She's got to be a trick! Arklem Greeth's bidding them on that he can destroy them."

"He'll have to kill half the city, then," Suljack said.

Deudermont's banner led the way across the small bridge with more than five thousand in his wake. Out in the harbor beyond Cutlass Island, sails appeared and anchors climbed from the water. The fleet began to creep in, boulders and pitch leading the way.

The noose tightened.

CHAPTER 16
ACCEPTABLE LOSSES

Valindra Shadowmantle's green eyes opened wide as she noted the approaching mob. She turned to rush to Arklem Greeth's chambers, but found the lich standing behind her, wearing a wicked grin.

"They come," Valindra gasped. "All of them."

Arklem Greeth shrugged as if he was hardly concerned. Gripped by her fear, the archmage's casual reaction served only to anger Valindra.

"You have underestimated our enemies at every turn!" she screamed, and several lesser wizards nearby sucked in their breath and turned away, pretending not to have heard.

Arklem Greeth laughed at her.

"You find this amusing?" she replied.

"I find it . . . predictable," Greeth answered. "Sadly so, but alas, the cards were played long ago. A Waterdhavian lord and the hero of the Sword Coast, the hero of Luskan, aligned against us. People are so fickle and easy to sway; it's no wonder that they rally to the empty platitudes of an idiot like Captain Deudermont."

"Because you raised the undead against them," Valindra accused.

The lich laughed again. "Our options were limited from the beginning. The high captains, cowards all, did little to hold back the mounting tide of invasion. I feared we could never depend upon those fools, those thieves, but again alas, you accept what you have and make the best of it."

Valindra stared at her master, wondering if he'd lost his mind. "The whole of the city is rallied against us," she cried. "Thousands! They gather on Closeguard, and will fight their way across."

"We have good wizards guarding our bridge."

"And they have powerful spellcasters among their ranks, as well," said Valindra. "If Deudermont wanted, he could send the least of his warriors against us, and our wizards would expend their energies long before he ran out of fodder."

"It will be amusing to watch," Arklem Greeth said, grinning all the wider.

"You have gone mad," Valindra stated, and beyond Arklem Greeth several lesser wizards shuffled nervously as they went about their assigned tasks, or at least, feigned going about them.

"Valindra, my friend," Greeth said, and he took her by the arm and walked her deeper into the structure of the Hosttower, away from the disquieting sights in the east. "If you play this correctly, you will find great entertainment, a fine practice experience, and little loss," the archmage arcane explained when they were alone. "Deudermont wants my head, not yours."

"The traitor Arabeth is with him, and she is no ally of mine."

The lich waved the notion away. "A minor inconvenience and nothing more. Let them lay the blame fully upon Arklem Greeth—I welcome the prestige of such notoriety."

"You seem to care little about anything at the moment, Archmage," the overwizard replied. "The Hosttower itself is in dire peril."

"It will fall to utter ruin," Arklem Greeth predicted with continuing calm.

Valindra held out her hands and stuttered repeatedly, unable to fashion a response.

"All things fall, and all things can be rebuilt from the rubble," the lich explained. "Surely they're not going to destroy me—or you, if you're sufficiently cunning. I'm nimble enough to survive the likes of Deudermont, and will take great enjoyment in watching the 'reconstruction' of Luskan when he proclaims his victory."

"Why did we ever allow it to come to such a state as this?"

Arklem Greeth shrugged. "Mistakes," he admitted. "My own, as well. I struck out for the Silver Marches at precisely the worst time, it would seem, though by coincidence and bad luck, or more devious coordination on the part of my enemies, I cannot know. Mirabar turned against us, as have even the orcs and their fledgling king. Deudermont and Brambleberry on their own would prove to be formidable opponents, I don't doubt, but with such an alignment of enemies mounting against us, it would do us ill to remain in Luskan. Here we are immobile, an easy target."

"How can you say such things?"

"Because they are true. Aha! I know not all of the conspirators behind this uprising, but surely there are traitors among the ranks of those I thought allies."

"The high captains."

Arklem Greeth shrugged again. "Our enemies are vast, it would seem—even more so than the few thousand who flock to Deudermont's side. They are merely fodder, as you said, while the real power behind this usurpation lays hidden and in wait. We could fight them hard and stubbornly, I expect, but in the end, that would prove to be the more dangerous course for those of us who really matter."

"We are to just run away?"

"Oh no!" Greeth assured her. "Not *just* run away. Nay, my friend, we're going to inflict such pain upon the people of Luskan this day that they will long remember it, and while they may call my abdication a victory, that notion will prove short lived when winter blows in mercilessly on the many households missing a father or mother. And their victory will not claim the most coveted prize, rest assured, for I have long anticipated this eventuality, and long prepared."

Valindra relaxed a bit at that assurance.

"Their victory will reveal the conspirators," said Greeth, "and I will find my way back. You put too much value in this one place, Valindra, this Hosttower of the Arcane. Have I not taught you that the Arcane Brotherhood is much greater than what you see in Luskan?"

"Yes, my master," the elf wizard replied.

"So take heart!" said Arklem Greeth. He cupped her chin in

his cold, dead fingers and made her look up into his soulless eyes. "Enjoy the day—ah the excitement! I surely will! Use your wiles, use your magic, use your cunning to survive and escape . . . or to surrender."

"Surrender?" she echoed. "I don't understand."

"Surrender in a manner that exonerates you enough so that they don't execute you, of course." Arklem Greeth laughed. "Blame me—oh, please do! Find your way out of this, or trust in me to come and retrieve you. I surely will. And from the ashes we two will find enjoyment and opportunity, I promise. And more excitement than we have known in decades!"

Valindra stared at him for a few moments then nodded.

"Now be gone from this multi-limbed target," said Greeth. "Get to the coast and our wizards set in defense, and take your shots as you find them. Make them hurt, Valindra, all of them, and hold faith in your heart and in your magnificent mind that this is a temporary setback, one intended to lead to ultimate and enduring victory."

"When?"

The simple question rocked Arklem Greeth back on his heels a bit, for Valindra's tone had made it clear that she understood that her timetable and that of a lich might not be one and the same.

"Go," he bade her, and nodded toward the door. "Make them hurt."

Half-dazed with confusion, Valindra Shadowmantle, Overwizard of the North Tower, in many eyes the second ranking wizard of the great Hosttower of the Arcane of Luskan, ambled toward the door of the mighty structure, fully believing that when she left it, she would never again enter. It was all too overwhelming, these dramatic and dangerous changes.

* * * * *

They crossed the bridge from Closeguard to Cutlass in full charge, banners flying, swords banging against shields, voices raised in hearty cheers.

On the other side of the bridge loomed the eastern wall of the Hosttower's courtyard, ground unblemished by the naval bombardment, and atop that wall, two score wizards crouched and waited, accompanied by a hundred apprentices armed with bows and spears.

They unleashed their fury as one, with the leading edge of Brambleberry's forces barely a dozen running strides from the wall. Men and ladders went up in flames, or flew away under the jolt of lightning bolts. Spears and arrows banged against shields and armor, or found a seam and sent an enemy writhing and screaming to the ground.

But Lord Brambleberry had brought wizards of his own, mages who had enacted wards on shield and man alike, who had brought forth watery elementals to quickly defeat the fireballs' flames. Men and women died or fell to grave wounds, to be sure, but not nearly to the devastating effect the Hosttower's front line of defense had hoped, and needed.

Volleys of arrows skipped in off the battlements, and concentrations of lightning blasts shook the wall, chipping and cracking the stone. The front row of Brambleberry's forces parted and through the gap ran a concentration of strong men wielding heavy hammers and picks. Lightning blasts led them to specific points on the wall, where they went to work, smashing away, further weakening the integrity of the structure.

"Pressure the top!" Lord Brambleberry yelled, and his archers and wizards let fly a steady stream of devastation, keeping the Hosttower defenders low.

"What ho!" one hammer team commander cried, and his group fell back as some of the Waterdhavian wizards heard the beckon and sent a trio of powerful blasts at the indicated spot. The first rebounded off the broken stone and sent the commander himself flying to the ground. The second bolt, though, broke through, sending stone chips flying into the courtyard, and the third blew out the section's support, dropping blocks and creating an opening through which a man could easily pass.

"What ho!" another team leader called from another spot, and a different trio of wizards was ready to finish the work of the sledges.

At the same time, far to the left and right, ladders went up against the walls. Initial resistance from the defenders fast gave way to calls for retreat.

The Hosttower's first line of defense had killed Brambleberry's men a dozen to one or more, but the swarm of Luskar, following Brambleberry and Deudermont, enraged by the ghouls sent by Arklem Greeth, and excited by the smell of blood and battle, rolled through.

* * * * *

As soon as the charge across the bridge had begun, the warships, too, went into swift action. Knowing that the Hosttower's focus had to be on the eastern wall, half a dozen vessels weighed anchor and filled their sails, crashing in against the current. They let fly long and far, over the western wall and courtyard to the Hosttower itself, or even beyond it to the eastern courtyard. Crewed by a bare minimum of sailors and gunners, they knew their role as one of diversion and pressure, to keep the defenders outside of the Hosttower confused and frightened, and perhaps even to score a lucky throw and kill a few in the process.

To the south of them, another half a dozen ships led by *Sea Sprite* sailed for the battered surrounds of Sea Tower, leading their assault with pitch and arrows, littering the rocky shore with destruction in case any of the Hosttower's wizards lay in wait there.

More than one such defender showed himself, either lashing out with a lightning bolt, or trying to flee back to the north.

Robillard and Arabeth welcomed such moments, and though both hoped to hold their greatest energies for the confrontation with Arklem Greeth and the main tower, neither could resist the temptation to reply to magic with greater evocations of their own.

"Hold and lower!" ordered Robillard, who remained in command of *Sea Sprite* while Deudermont rode at Brambleberry's side.

The ship dropped her sails and the anchor splashed into the dark waters as other crewmen ran to the smaller boats she carried and put them over the side. Taking their cues from *Sea Sprite*, the other five ships acted in concert.

"Sails south!" the man in the crow's nest shouted down to Robillard.

Eyes wide, the wizard ran aft and grabbed the rail hard, leaning out to get a better view of the leading craft, then of another two ships sailing hard their way.

"*Thrice Lucky,*" Arabeth said, coming up beside the wizard. "That's Maimun's ship."

"And what side does he choose?" Robillard wondered. He murmured through a quick spell and tapped thumb and forefinger against his temples, imbuing his eyes with the sight of an eagle.

It was indeed Maimun leading the way, the man standing forward at the prow of *Thrice Lucky,* his crew readying boats behind him. More tellingly, the ship's catapult was neither armed nor manned, and no archers stood ready.

"The boy chose well," Robillard said. "He sails with us."

"How can you know?" Arabeth asked. "How can you be certain enough to continue the landing?"

"Because I know Maimun."

"His heart?"

"His purse," Robillard clarified. "He knows the force arrayed against Arklem Greeth and understands that the Hosttower cannot win this day. A fool he would be to stand back and let the city move on without his help, and Maimun is many things, but a fool is not among them."

"Three ships," Arabeth warned, looking at the trio expertly navigating the familiar waters under full sail, and closing with great speed. "As our crews disembark, they could do profound damage. We should hold three at full strength to meet them if they attack."

Robillard shook his head. "Maimun chose well," he said. "He is a vulture seeking to pick the bones of the dead, and he understands which bones will be meatier this day."

He turned and strode back amidships, waving and calling for his crew to continue. He enacted another spell as he neared the gangplank and gingerly hopped down onto the water—onto and not into, for he didn't sink beneath the waves.

Arabeth copied his movements and stood beside him on the rolling sea. Side by side, they walked swiftly toward the rocky shore, small boats overcrowded with warriors bobbing all around them.

Two of the newcomers dropped sail near the fleet and *Sea*

Sprite, their crews similarly manning the smaller boats. But one, *Thrice Lucky*, sailed past, weaving in through the narrow, rocky channel.

"The young pirate knows his craft," Valindra marveled.

"He learned from Deudermont himself," said Robillard. "A pity that's all he learned."

* * * * *

The wall had fallen in short order, but Lord Brambleberry's forces quickly came to realize that the defenders of the Hosttower had fallen back by design. The wall defense had been set only so the tower's wizards could have time to prepare.

As the fierce folk of Luskan crashed into the courtyard, the full fury of the Hosttower of the Arcane fell upon them. Such a barrage of fire, lightning, magical bolts, and conical blasts of frost so intense they froze a man's blood solid fell over them that of the first several hundred who crossed the wall, nine of ten died within a few heartbeats.

Among those survivors, though, were Deudermont and Brambleberry, protected from the intense barrage by powerful Waterdhavian wizards. Because the pennants of their leaders still stood, the rest of the army continued its charge undeterred. The second volley didn't match the first in intensity or duration, and the warriors pushed on.

Undead rose from the ground before them, ghouls, skeletons, and rotting corpses given a grim semblance of life. And from the tower came golems and gargoyles, magical animations sent to turn back the tide.

The folk of Luskan didn't turn in fear, didn't run in horror, with the undead monsters only bitterly reminding them of why they'd joined the fight in the first place. And while Lord Brambleberry was there astride a large roan stallion, a spectacular figure of strength, two others inspired them even more.

First was Deudermont, sitting tall on a blue-eyed paint mare. Though he was no great rider, his mere presence brought hope to the heart of every commoner in the city.

And there was the other, the friend of Deudermont. As the

explosions lessened and the Hosttower's melee force came out to meet the charge, so it became the time of Drizzt.

With quickness that mocked allies and foes alike, with anger solidly grounded in the image of his halfling friend lying injured on a bed, the drow burst through the leading ranks and met the enemy monsters head on. He whirled and twirled, leaped and spun through a line of ghouls and skeletons, leaving piles of torn flesh and shattered bones in his wake.

A gargoyle leaped off a balcony from above, swooping down at him, leathery wings wide, clawed hands and feet raking wildly.

The drow dived into a roll, somehow maneuvered out to the side when the gargoyle angled its wings to intercept, and came back to his feet with such force that he sprang high into into the air, his blades working in short and devastating strokes. So completely did he overwhelm the creature that it actually hit the ground before he did, already dead.

"Huzzah for Drizzt Do'Urden!" cried a voice above all the cheering, a voice that Drizzt surely knew, and he took heart that Arumn Gardpeck, proprietor of the Cutlass, was among the ranks.

Magical anklets enhancing his speed, Drizzt sprinted for the central tower of the great structure in short, angled bursts, and often with long, diving rolls. He held only one scimitar then, his other hand clutching an onyx figurine. "I need you," he called to Guenhwyvar, and the weary panther, home on the Astral Plane, heard.

Lightning and fire rained down around Drizzt as he continued his desperate run, but every blast came a little farther behind him.

* * * * *

"He moves as if time itself has slowed around him," Lord Brambleberry remarked to Deudermont when they, like everyone else on the field, took note of the dark elf's spectacular charge.

"It has and it does," Deudermont replied, wearing a perfectly smug expression. Lord Brambleberry hadn't taken well to hearing that a drow was joining his ranks, but Deudermont hoped Drizzt's exploits would earn him some inroads into the previously unwelcoming city of Waterdeep.

He'd be making quite an impression on the minions of Arklem Greeth in short order, as well, by Deudermont's calculations.

If he hadn't already.

Even more importantly, Drizzt's charge had emboldened his comrades, and the line moved inexorably for the tower, accepting the blasts and assaults from wizards, smashing the reaching arms of skeletons and ghouls, shooting gargoyles from the air with so many arrows they darkened the sky.

"Many will die," Brambleberry said, "but the day is ours."

Watching the progress of the insurgent army, Deudermont couldn't really disagree, but he knew, too, that they were battling mighty wizards, and any proclamations of victory were surely premature.

* * * * *

Drizzt came around the side of the main structure, skidding to a fast stop, his face a mask of horror, for he found himself wide open to a balcony on which stood a trio of wizards, all frantically waving their arms in the midst of some powerful spellcasting.

Drizzt couldn't turn, couldn't dodge, and had no apparent or plausible defense.

* * * * *

Resistance at the Sea Tower proved almost nonexistent, and the force of Robillard, Arabeth, and the sailors quickly secured the southern end of Cutlass Island. To the north, fireballs and lightning bolts boomed, cheers rose in combination with agonized screams, and horns blew.

Valindra Shadowmantle watched it all from concealment in a cubby formed of Sea Tower's fallen blocks.

"Come on, then, lich," she whispered, for though the magical display seemed impressive, it was nothing of the sort that could result in the explosive ending Arklem Greeth had promised her.

Which made her doubt his other promise to her, that all would be put aright in short order.

Valindra was no novice to the ways and depths of the Art. Her lightning bolts didn't drop men shaking to the ground, but sent their souls to the Fugue Plane and their bodies to the ground in smoldering heaps.

She looked to the beach, where the sailors were putting up their boats and preparing to march north to join the battle.

Valindra knew she could kill many of them, then and there, and when she noted the wretched Arabeth Raurym among their ranks, her desire to do so multiplied many times over, though the sight of the mighty Robillard beside the wretched Mirabarran witch tempered that somewhat.

But she held her spells in check and looked to the north, where the sound of battle—and the horns of Brambleberry and the Luskar insurgents—grew ever stronger.

Would Arklem Greeth be able to save her if she struck against Arabeth and Robillard? Would he even try?

Her doubts holding her back, Valindra stared and pictured Arabeth lying dead on the ground—no, not dead, but writhing in the agony of a slow, burning, mortal wound.

"You surprise me," said a voice behind her, and the overwizard froze in place, eyes going wide. Her thoughts whirled as she tried to discern the speaker, for she knew that she had heard that voice before.

"Your judgment, I mean," the speaker added, and Valindra recognized him then, and spun around to face the pirate Maimun—or more specifically, to face the tip of his extended blade.

"You have thrown in with . . . them?" Valindra asked incredulously. "With *Deudermont?*"

Maimun shrugged. "Seemed better than the alternative."

"You should have stayed at sea."

"Ah, yes, to then sail in and claim allegiance with whichever side won the day. That is the way you would play it, isn't it?"

The moon elf mage narrowed her eyes.

"You reserve your magic when so many targets present themselves," Maimun added.

"Prudence is not a fault."

"Perhaps not," said the grinning young pirate captain. "But 'tis better to join in the fight with the apparent winner than to claim allegiance when the deed is done. People, even celebratory victors, resent hangers-on, you know."

"Have you ever been anything but?"

"By the seas, a vicious retort!" Maimun replied with a laugh. "Vicious . . . and desperate."

Valindra moved to brush the blade away from her face, but Maimun deftly flipped it past her waving hand and poked her on the tip of her nose.

"Vicious, but ridiculous," the pirate added. "There were times when I found that trait endearing in you. Now it's simply annoying."

"Because it reeks of truth."

"Ah, but dear, beautiful, wicked Valindra, I can hardly be called an opportunist now. I have an overwizard in my grasp to prove my worth. A prisoner I suspect a certain Lady Raurym will greatly covet."

Valindra's gaze threw daggers at the slender man. "You claim me as a prisoner?" she asked, her voice low and threatening.

Maimun shrugged. "So it would seem."

Valindra's face softened, a smile appearing. "Maimun, foolish child, for all your steel and all your bluster, I know you won't kill me." She stepped aside and reached for the blade.

And it jumped back from her hand and came forward with sudden brutality, stabbing her hard in the chest, drawing a gasp and a whimper of pain. Maimun pulled the stroke up short, but his words cut deeper.

"Mithral, not steel," he corrected. "Mithral through your pretty little breast before the next beat of your pretty little heart."

"You have . . . chosen," Valindra warned.

"And chosen well, my prisoner."

* * * * *

Guenhwyvar leaped past Drizzt to shield him from the slings and arrows of enemies, from blasts magical and mundane. Lightning bolts reached down from the balcony as Guenhwyvar soared up toward it, and though they stung her, they didn't deter her.

On the scarred field below, Drizzt stumbled forward and

regained his balance and looked on with admiration and deep love for his most trusted friend who had, yet again, saved him.

Saved him and vanquished his enemies all at once, the drow noted with a wince, as flailing arms and horrified expressions appeared to him every so often from around the ball of black fury.

He had no time to dwell on the scene, though, for more undead creatures approached him, and more gargoyles swooped down from above.

And lightning roared and his allies died in their charge behind him. But they kept coming, outraged at the lich and his ghoulish emissaries. A hundred died, two hundred died, five hundred died, but the wave rolled for the beach and wouldn't be deterred.

In the middle of it all rode Deudermont and Brambleberry, urging their charges on, seeking battle side by side wherever it could be found.

Drizzt spotted their banners, and whenever he found a moment's reprieve, he glanced back at them, knowing they would eventually lead him to the most coveted prize of all, to the lich whose defeat would end the carnage.

It was to Drizzt's complete surprise, then, that Arklem Greeth did indeed come upon the field to face his foes, but not straightaway to Deudermont and Brambleberry, but straightaway to Drizzt Do'Urden.

He appeared as no more than a thin black line at first, which widened and flattened to a two-dimensional image of the archmage arcane then filled out to become Arklem Greeth in person.

"They are always full of surprises," the archmage said, considering the drow from about five strides away. Grinning wickedly, he lifted his hands and waggled his fingers.

Drizzt sprinted at him with blinding speed, intent on taking him down before he could complete the spell. He dived at the powerful wizard, scimitars leading, and driving right through the image of the lich.

It was just an image—an image masking a magical gate through which tumbled the surprised dark elf. He tried to stop, skidding along the ground, and when it was obvious that he was caught, on pure instinct and a combination of desperate hope and the responsibility of friendship, he tore free his belt pouch and threw it back behind him.

Then he was tumbling in the darkness, a wretched, sulfuric smell thickening around him, great dark shapes moving through the smoky shadows of a vast, dark field of sharp-edged rocks and steaming lines of blood red lava.

Gehenna . . . or the Nine Hells . . . or the Abyss . . . or Tarterus. . . . He didn't know, but it was one of the lower planes, one of the homes of the devils and demons and other wicked creatures, a place in which he could not long survive.

He didn't even have his bearings or his feet back under him when a black beast, dark as the shadows, leaped upon him from behind.

* * * * *

"Pathetic," Arklem Greeth said, shaking his head, almost disappointed that the champion of the lords who had come against him had been so easily dispatched.

Staying close to the central tower, the archmage arcane moved along and spotted the banners of his principle enemies, the invading Lord Brambleberry, so far from home, and the fool Deudermont, who had turned the city against him.

He studied the field for a short while, mentally measuring the distance with supernatural precision. The tumult all around him, the screaming, dying, and explosions, seemed distant and unremarkable. A spear flew his way and struck solidly, except that his magical protections simply flattened its metal tip and dropped it harmlessly to the ground before it got near to his undead flesh.

He didn't even wince. His focus remained on his principle enemies.

Arklem Greeth rubbed his hands together eagerly, preparing his spells.

In a flash he was gone, and when he stepped through the other side of the dimensional portal in the midst of a fighting throng, he tapped his thumbs together before him and brought forth a fan of fire, driving away friend and foe alike. Then he thrust his hands out wide to his sides and from each came a mighty forked lightning bolt, angled down to thump into the ground with such force that men and zombies, dwarves and ghouls went bouncing wildly away, leaving Arklem Greeth alone in his own little field of calm.

Everyone noticed him—how could they not?—for his display of power and fury was so far beyond anything that had been brought to the field thus far, by either Brambleberry or the Hosttower.

Barely controlling their mounts at that point, both Brambleberry and Deudermont turned to regard their foe.

"Kill him!" Brambleberry cried, and even as the words left his mouth, so too came the next of Arklem Greeth's magical barrages.

All around the two leaders, the ground churned and broke apart, soil spraying, rocks flying, roots tearing. Down they tumbled side by side, their horses twisting and breaking around them. Brambleberry's landed atop him with a sickening cracking of bones, and though he was luckier to fall aside from his thrashing and terrified horse, Deudermont still found himself at the bottom of a ten-foot hole, thick with mud and water.

Up above, Arklem Greeth wasn't finished. He ignored the sudden reversal his assault on Brambleberry, and particularly upon beloved Deudermont, had wrought in the army around them, their fear quickly turning to outrage aimed at Greeth alone. Like the one point of calm in a world gone mad, Arklem Greeth followed his earth-shaking spell with an earthquake that had all around him stumbling and falling. The line of the tremor was aimed perfectly for the loose mounds at the sides of the chasm he had created. He meant to bury the Waterdhavian lord and the good captain alive.

All around them realized it, though, and came at Greeth with fury, a roiling throng of outrage closing in on him from every side, throwing spears and rocks—even swords—anything to distract or wound that being of ultimate evil.

"Fools, all," the archmage arcane muttered under his breath.

With one last burst of power that broke apart one side of the deep hole, Greeth fell back into his wraithform, flattening to two dimensions. He narrowed to a black line and slipped down into the ground, running swiftly through narrow cracks until he stood again in his own chamber in the Hosttower of the Arcane.

Exhaustion followed him there, for the lich had not utilized such a sudden and potent barrage of magic in many, many years. He heard the continuing roar outside his window and didn't need to go there to understand that any gains he'd made would prove temporary.

Dropping the leaders had not turned the mob, but had only incensed it further.

There were simply too many. Too many fools . . . too much fodder.

"Fools all," he said again, and he thought of Valindra out along the southern rocks of Cutlass Island. He hoped she was dead already.

With a heavy sigh that crackled across the collection of hardened mucus in Arklem Greeth's unbreathing lungs, the lich went to his private stash of potent drinks—drinks he had created himself, fashioned mostly of blood and living things. Drinks that, like the lich himself, transcended death. He took a long, deep sip of one potent mixture.

He thought of his decades at the Hosttower, a place he had so long called home. He knew that was over, for the time being at least, but he could wait.

And he could make it hurt.

The chamber would come with him—he had fashioned it with magic for just such a sudden and violent transportation, for he had known from the moment he'd achieved lichdom that the day would surely befall him when he'd have to abandon his tower home. But he, and the part he most coveted, would be saved.

The rest would be lost.

Arklem Greeth moved through a small trapdoor, down a ladder to a tiny secret room where he kept one of his most prized possessions: a staff of incredible power. With that staff, a younger, living Arklem Greeth had waged great battles, his fireballs and lightning bolts greater in number and intensity. With that staff, full of its own power to taste of Mystra's Weave, he had escaped certain doom many times on those occasions when his own magical reservoir had been drained.

He rubbed a hand over its burnished wood, considering it as he would an old friend.

It was set in a strange contraption of Greeth's design. The staff itself was laid across a pyramid-shaped stone, the very center of the six-foot long staff right at the narrow tip of the great block. Hanging from chains at either end of the staff were two large metal bowls, and up above those bowls, over the staff and on stout stands of thick iron, sat two tanks of dense silver liquid.

With another sigh, Greeth reached up and pulled a central cord, one that uncorked plugs from the mercury-filled reservoirs, and dropped out chutes directly over the corresponding bowls.

The heavy fluid metal began to flow, slowly and teasingly dripping into the bowls, like the sands of an hourglass counting down the end of the world.

Such staves as that, so full of magical energy, could not be broken without a cataclysmic release.

Arklem Greeth went back to his secure but mobile chamber with confidence that the explosion would send him exactly where he wanted to go.

* * * * *

They were winning the field, but the Luskar and their Waterdhavian allies didn't feel victorious, not with their leaders Brambleberry and Deudermont buried! They set a defensive perimeter around the churned area, and many fell over the loose dirt, digging with sword and dagger, or bare hands. A torn fingernail elicited no more than a grimace among the determined, frantic group. One man inadvertently drove his dagger through his own hand, but merely growled as he went back to tearing at the ground for his beloved Captain Deudermont.

Fury rained upon the field: fire and lightning, monsters undead and magically created. The Luskar matched that fury; they were fighting for their very lives, for their families. There could be no retreat, no withdrawal, and to a man and woman they knew it.

So they fought, and fired their arrows at the wizards on the balconies, and though they died ten-to-one, perhaps more, it seemed that their advance could not be halted.

But then it was, with the snap of a magical staff.

* * * * *

Someone tugged hard at his arm, and Deudermont gasped his first breath in far too long a time as another hand scraped the dirt away from his face.

Through bleary eyes, he saw his rescuers, a woman brushing his face, a strong man yanking at his one extended arm, and with such force that Deudermont feared he would pull his shoulder right out of its socket.

His thoughts went to Brambleberry, who had fallen beside him, and he took heart to see so many clawing at the ground, so much commotion to rescue the Waterdhavian lord. Though he was still fully immersed in the soil, other than that one extended arm, Deudermont somehow managed to nod, and even smile at the woman cleaning off his face.

Then she was gone—a wave of multicolored energy rolled out like a ripple on a pond, crossing over Deudermont with the sound of a cyclone.

The sleeve burned from his extended arm, his face flushed with stinging warmth. It seemed to go on for many, many heartbeats, then came the sound of crashing, like trees falling. Deudermont felt the ground rumble three or four times—too close together for him to accurately take a count.

His arm fell limp to the ground. As he regained his sensibilities, Deudermont saw the boots of the man who had been tugging at his arm. The captain couldn't turn his head enough to follow up the legs, but he knew the man was dead.

He knew that the field was dead.

Too still.

And too quiet, so suddenly, as if all the world had ended.

* * * * *

Robillard kept his forces tight and organized as they made their way north along Cutlass Island. He was fairly certain that they'd meet no resistance until they got within the Hosttower's compound, but he wanted the first response from his force to be coordinated and devastating. He assured those around him that they would clear every window, every balcony, every doorway on the North Spire with their first barrage.

Behind Robillard came Valindra, her arms tightly bound behind her back, flanked by Maimun and Arabeth.

"The archmage arcane falls this day," Robillard remarked quietly, so that only those close to him could hear.

"Arklem Greeth is more than ready for you," Valindra retorted.

Arabeth reacted with a suddenness that shocked the others, spinning a left hook into the face of their moon elf captive. Valindra's head jolted back and came forward, blood showing below her thin, pretty nose.

"You will pay for—" Valindra warned, or started to, until Arabeth hit her again, just as viciously.

Robillard and Maimun looked to each other incredulously, but then both just grinned at Arabeth's initiative. They could clearly see the years of enmity between the two overwizards, and separately reasoned that the taller and more classically beautiful Valindra had often been a thorn in Arabeth's side.

Each man made a mental note to not anger the Lady Raurym.

Valindra seemed to get the message as well, for she said no more.

Robillard led them up a tumble of boulders to get a view over the wall. The fighting was thick and vicious all around the five-spired tower. The ship's wizard quickly formulated an approach to best come onto the field, and was about to relay it to his charges when the staff broke.

The world seemed to fall apart.

Maimun saved Robillard that day, the young pirate reacting with amazing agility to pull the older wizard down behind the rocks beside him. Similarly, Arabeth rescued Valindra, albeit inadvertently, for as she, too, dived back, she brushed the captive enough to send her tumbling down as well.

The wave of energy rolled over them. Rocks went flying and several of Robillard's force fell hard, more than one mortally wounded. They were on the outer edge of the blast and so it passed quickly. Robillard, Maimun, and Arabeth all scrambled to their feet quickly enough to peer over and witness the fall of the Hosttower itself. The largest, central pillar, Greeth's own, was gone, as if it had either been blown to dust or had simply vanished—and it truth, it was a bit of both. The four armlike spires, the once graceful limbs, tumbled down, crashing in burning heaps and billowing clouds of angry gray dust.

The warriors on the field, man and monster alike, had fallen in neat rows, like cut timber, and though groans and cries told Robillard and the others that some had survived, none of the three believed for a heartbeat that number to be large.

"By the gods, Greeth, what have you done?" Robillard asked into the empty and suddenly still morning air.

Arabeth gave a sudden cry of dismay and fell back, and neither Maimun nor Robillard considered her quickly enough to stop her as she leaped down at the face-down and battered Valindra and drove a dagger deep into the captured wizard's back.

"No!" Robillard cried at her when he realized her action. "We need . . ." He stopped and grimaced as Arabeth retracted the blade and struck again, and again, and Valindra's screams became muffled with blood.

Maimun finally got to Arabeth and pulled her back; Robillard called for a priest.

He waved back the first of the clerics that came forward, though, knowing that it was too late, and that others would need his healing prayers.

"What have you done?" Robillard asked Arabeth, who sobbed, but looked at the devastated field, not at her gruesome handiwork.

"It was better than she deserved," Arabeth replied.

Glancing over his shoulder at the utter devastation of the Hosttower of the Arcane, and the men and women who had gone against it, Robillard found it hard to disagree.

CHAPTER
CONSEQUENCE
17

The irony of pulling a battered, but very much alive Deudermont from the ground was not lost on Maimun, who considered how many others—they were all around him on the devastated field—would soon be put *into* the ground, and because of the decisions of that very same captain.

"Don't kick a man who's lying flat, I've been told," Maimun muttered, and Robillard and Arabeth turned to regard him, as well as the half-conscious Deudermont. "But you're an idiot, good captain."

"Watch your tongue, young one," Robillard warned.

"Better to remain silent than speak the truth and offend the powerful, yes Robillard?" Maimun replied with a sour and knowing grin.

"Remind me why *Sea Sprite* didn't sink *Thrice Lucky* on the many occasions we've seen you at sea," the wizard threatened. "I seem to forget."

"My charm, no doubt."

"Enough, you two," Arabeth scolded, her voice trembling with every syllable. "Look around you! Is this travesty all about *you*? About your petty rivalry? About placing blame?"

"How can it not be about who's to blame?" Maimun started to argue, but Arabeth cut him short with a vicious scowl.

"It's about those scattered on this field, nothing more," she said, her voice even. "Alive and dead . . . in the Hosttower and without."

Maimun swallowed hard and glanced at Robillard, who seemed equally out of venom, and indeed, Arabeth's argument was difficult to counter given the carnage around them. They finished extracting Deudermont at the same time that another rescue team called out that they had located Lord Brambleberry.

The ground covering him had saved him from the explosion, but had smothered him in the process. The young Waterdhavian lord, so full of ambition and vision, and the desire to earn his way, was dead.

There would be no cheering that day, and even if there had been, it would have been drowned out by the cries of anguish and agony.

Work went on through the night and into the next day, separating dead from wounded, tending to those who could be helped. Guided by Robillard, assault teams went into each of the four fallen spires of the destroyed Hosttower, and more than a few of Arklem Greeth's minions were pulled from the rubble, all surrendering without a struggle, no fight left in them—not after seeing the unbridled evil of the man they'd once called the archmage arcane.

The cost had been horrific—more than a third of the population of the once-teeming city of Luskan was dead.

But the war was over.

* * * * *

Captain Deudermont shook his head solemnly.

"What does that mean?" Regis yelled at him. "You can't just say he's *gone!*"

"Many are just gone, my friend," Deudermont explained. "The blast that took the Hosttower released all manner of magical power, destructive and altering. Men were burned and blasted, others transformed, and others, many others, banished from this world. Some were utterly destroyed, I'm told, their very souls disintegrated into nothingness."

"And what happened to Drizzt?" Regis demanded.

"We cannot know. He is not to be found. Like so many. I'm sorry. I feel this loss as keenly as—"

"Shut up!" Regis yelled at him. "You don't know anything! Robillard tried to warn you—many did! You don't know anything! You chose this fight and look at what it has gotten you, what it has gotten us all!"

"Enough!" Robillard growled at the halfling, and he moved threateningly at Regis.

Deudermont held him back, though, understanding that Regis's tirade was wrought of utter grief. How could it not be? Why should it not be? The loss of Drizzt Do'Urden was no small thing, after all, particularly not to the halfling that had spent the better part of the last decades by the dark elf's side.

"We could not know the desperation of Arklem Greeth, or that he was capable of such wanton devastation," Deudermont said, his voice quiet and humble. "But the fact that he was capable of it, and willing to do it, only proves that he had to be removed, by whatever means the people of Luskan could muster. He would have rained his devastation upon them sooner or later, and in more malicious forms, no doubt. Whether freeing the undead from the magical bindings of Illusk or using his wizards to slowly bleed the city into submission, he was no man worthy of being the leader of this city."

"You act as if this city is worthy of having a leader," Regis said.

"They stood arm in arm to win," Deudermont scolded, growing excited—so much so that the priest attending him grabbed him by the shoulders to remind him that he had to stay calm. "Every family in Luskan feels grief as keen as your own. Doubt that not at all. The price of their freedom has been high indeed."

"Their freedom, their fight," the halfling spat.

"Drizzt marched with me willingly," Deudermont reminded Regis. That was the last of it, though, as the priest forcibly guided the captain out of the room.

"You throw guilt on the shoulders of a man already bent low by its great weight," Robillard said.

"He made his choices."

"As did you, as did I, and as did Drizzt. I understand your

pain—Drizzt Do'Urden was my friend, as well—but does your anger at Captain Deudermont do anything to alleviate it?"

Regis started to answer, started to protest, but stopped and fell back on his bed. What was the point?

Of anything?

He thought of Mithral Hall and felt that it was past time for him to go home.

* * * * *

He couldn't even make out their physical shapes, as they seemed no more than extensions of the endless shadows that surrounded him. Nor could he distinguish the many natural weapons that each of the demonic creatures seemed to possess, and so all of his fighting was purely on instinct, purely on reaction.

There was no victory to be found. He would stay alive only as long as his reactions and reflexes remained fast enough to fend off the gathering cloud of monsters, only as long as his arms held the strength to keep his scimitars high enough to block a serpentine head from tearing out his throat, or a clublike fist from bashing in the side of his skull.

He needed a reprieve, but there was none. He needed to escape, but knew that was just as unlikely.

So he fought, blades and growls denying his own mortality. Drizzt fought and ran, and fought some more and ran some more, always seeking a place of refuge.

And finding only more battle.

A large black shape rose before him, six arms coming at him in an overwhelming barrage, and with overwhelming strength. Knowing better than to try to stand against it, Drizzt dived to the ground to the side, thinking to roll to his feet and rush around to attack the creature from another angle.

But it had prepared for him, and when he hit the ground, he found his momentum stolen by a thick puddle of sticky mucus.

The creature rushed over to him, rising to its full height, twice that of a tall man. It lifted all six of its thunderous arms out wide and high, and bellowed in anticipation of victory.

Drizzt wriggled an arm free and stabbed it hard in the leg, but that would hardly slow the beast.

When Guenhwyvar crashed into the side of its lupine head, though, all thoughts of finishing off the drow fled, as both panther and demon flew away.

Drizzt wasted no time in extracting himself from the muck, muttering thanks to Guenhwyvar all the while. How lifted his spirits had been when he'd realized the identity of his first encounter in that hellish place, when he'd realized that Guenhwyvar had followed him through Arklem Greeth's gate. Together they had defeated every foe thus far, and as Drizzt closed in on the fallen behemoth, scimitars swinging, another demon found its premature victory cries muffled by its own blood.

Drizzt paused to crouch beside Guenhwyvar, though he knew they had to move along, and quickly.

He had been so pleased to see her, so hopeful that his rescue was at hand by his dearest of companions, but he had come to regret that Guenhwyvar had come through, for she was as trapped as he, and surely as doomed.

* * * * *

"Well, now, there's a good one," Queaser said to Skerrit through a mouth half-full of twisted yellow teeth. "I'll get us a good bit for this, I'd be guessin'."

"What'd ye find then, ye dirty cow?" Skerrit replied with an equally wretched grin, and one made worse since he was between bites of some rancid meat he had found in the pocket of a dead soldier.

Queaser motioned for Skerrit to come closer—the field was full of looting thugs, after all—and showed him an onyx figurine beautifully crafted into the likeness of a great black cat.

"Heh, but we should be thanking Deudermont for bringing so much opportunity our way, I'm thinking," said a very pleased Skerrit. "Three-hands'll give us a purse o' gold for that one."

Queaser laughed and stuffed the figurine into a pouch under his dirty and ragged vest, instead of the large, bulging sack where he and Skerrit had placed the more mundane booty.

"Let's get away," Queaser reasoned. "If they're to catch us with the coin and the belts, that's our loss, but I'm not for wanting this treasure tucked into the pocket of a Luskar guard."

"Get her sold," Skerrit agreed. "There'll be more to find on the field tomorrow night, and the night after that, and after that again."

The two wretches shuffled across the dark field. Somewhere in the darkness, a wounded woman, not yet found by the rescue teams, moaned pitifully, but they ignored the plea and went on their profitable way.

CHAPTER
ASCENSION AND SALVATION
18

"You are recovering well," Robillard said to Deudermont the next morning, a brilliantly sunny one, quite rare in Luskan that time of year. In response, the captain held up his injured arm, clenched his hand, and nodded. "Or would be, if we could quiet the din," Robillard added. He moved to the room's large window, which overlooked a wide square, and pulled aside a corner of the heavy curtain.

Out in the square, a great cheer arose.

Robillard shook his head and sighed then turned back to see Deudermont sitting up on the edge of his bed.

"My waistcoat, if you would," Deudermont said.

"You should not . . ." Robillard replied, but without much conviction, for he knew the captain would never heed his warning. The resigned wizard went from the window to the dresser and retrieved his friend's clothes.

Deudermont followed him, albeit shakily.

"You're sure you're ready for this?" the wizard asked, helping with the sleeves of a puffy white shirt.

"How many days has it been?"

"Only three."

"Do we know the count of the dead? Has Drizzt been found?"

"Two thousand, at least," Robillard answered. "Perhaps half

again that number." Deudermont winced from more than pain as Robillard slid the waistcoat along his injured arm. "And no, I fear that Arklem Greeth's treachery marked the end of our drow friend," Robillard added. "We haven't found as much as a dark-skinned finger. He was right near the tower when it exploded, I'm told."

"Quick and without pain, then," said Deudermont. "That's something we all hope for." He nodded and shuffled to the window.

"I expect Drizzt hoped for it to come several centuries from now," Robillard had to jab as he followed.

Propelled as much by anger as determination, Deudermont grabbed the heavy curtain and pulled it wide. Still using only his uninjured arm, he tugged the window open and stepped into clear view of the throng gathered in the square.

Below him on the street, the people of Luskan, so battered and bereaved, so weary of battle, oppression, thieves, murderers, and all the rest, cheered wildly. More than one of the gathering fainted, overcome by emotion.

"Deudermont is alive!" someone cried.

"Huzzah for Deudermont!" another cheered.

"A third of them dead and they cheer for me," Deudermont said over his shoulder, his expression grim.

"It shows how much they hated Arklem Greeth, I expect," Robillard replied. "But look past the square, past the hopeful faces, and you will see that we haven't much time."

Deudermont did just that, and took in the ruin of Cutlass Island. Even Closeguard had not escaped the weight of the blast, with many of the houses on the western side of the island flattened and still smoldering. Beyond Closeguard, in the harbor, a quartet of masts protruded from the dark waves. Four ships had been damaged, and two fully lost.

All across the city signs of devastation remained, the fallen bridge, the burned buildings, the heavy pall of smoke.

"Hopeful faces," Deudermont remarked of the crowd. "Not satisfied, not victorious, just hopeful."

"Hope is the back of hate's coin," Robillard warned and the captain nodded, knowing all too well that it was past time for him to get out of his bed and get to work.

He waved to the crowd and moved back into his room, followed by the frenzied cheers of desperate folk.

* * * * *

"It's worth a thousand gold if it's worth a plug copper," Queaser argued, shaking the figurine in front of the unimpressed expression of Rodrick Fenn, the most famous pawnbroker in Luskan. Languishing beside the many others who dealt with the minor rogues and pirates of the city, Rodrick had only recently come into prominence, mostly because of the vast array of exotic goods he'd somehow managed to wrangle. A large bounty had been offered for information regarding Rodrick's new source.

"I'll give ye three gold, and ye'll be glad to get it," Rodrick said.

Queaser and Skerrit exchanged sour looks, both shaking their heads.

"You should pay him to take it from you," said another in the store, who seemed an unassuming enough patron. In fact, he had been invited by Rodrick for just such a transaction, since Skerrit had tipped off Rodrick the night before regarding the onyx figurine.

"What d'ye know of it?" Skerrit demanded.

"I know that it was Drizzt Do'Urden's," Morik the Rogue replied. "I know that you hold a drow item, and one the dark elves will want returned. I wouldn't wish to be the person caught with it, to be sure."

Queaser and Skerrit looked at each other again, then Queaser scoffed and waved a hand dismissively at the rogue.

"Think, you fools," said Morik. "Consider who—what—ran beside Drizzt into that last battle." Morik gave a little laugh. "You've managed to place yourself between legions of drow and Captain Deudermont . . . oh, and King Bruenor of Mithral Hall, as well, who will no doubt seek that figurine out. Congratulations are in order." He ended his sarcastic stream with a mocking laugh, and made his way toward the door.

"Twenty pieces of gold, and be glad for it," Rodrick said. "And I'll be turning it over to Deudermont, don't you doubt, and hoping he'll repay me—and if I'm in a good mood, I might tell him that the two of you came to me so that I could give it back to him."

Queaser looked as if he was trying to say something, but no words came out.

"Or I'll just go to Deudermont and make his search a bit easier, and you'll be glad that I sent him and that I had no way to tell any dark elves instead."

"Ye're bluffing," Skerrit insisted.

"Call it, then," Rodrick said with a wry grin.

Skerrit turned to Queaser, but the suddenly pale man was already handing the figurine over.

The two left quickly, passing Morik, who was outside leaning against the wall beside the door.

"You chose well," the rogue assured them.

Skerrit got in his face. "Shut yer mouth, and if ye're ever for telling anyone other than what Rodrick's telling them, then know we're to find ye first and do ye under."

Morik shrugged, an exaggerated movement that perfectly covered the slide of his hand. He went back into Rodrick's shop as the two hustled away.

"I'll be wanting my gold back," Rodrick greeted him, but the smiling Morik was already tossing the pouch the pawnbroker's way. Morik walked over to the counter and Rodrick handed him the statue.

"Worth more than a thousand," Rodrick muttered as Morik took it.

"If it keeps the bosses happy, it's worth our very lives," the rogue replied, and he tipped his hat and departed.

* * * * *

"Governor," Baram spat with disgust. "They're wanting him to be governor, and he's to take the call, by all accounts."

"And well he should," Kensidan replied.

"And this don't bother ye?" Baram asked. "Ye said we'd be finding power when Greeth was gone, and now Greeth's gone and all I'm finding are widows and brats needing food. I'll be emptying half of me coffers to keep the folk of Ship Baram in line."

"Consider it the best investment of your life," High Captain Kurth answered before Kensidan could. "No Ship lost more than my own."

"I lost most of me guards," Taerl put in. "Ye lost a hundred common folk and a score of houses, but I lost fighters. How many of yers marched alongside Deudermont?"

His bluster couldn't hold, though, as Kurth fixed him with a perfectly vicious glare.

"Deudermont's ascension was predictable and desirable," Kensidan said to them all to get the meeting of the five back on track. "We survived the war. Our Ships remain intact, though battered, as Luskan herself is battered. That will mend, and this time, we will not have the smothering strength of the Hosttower holding us in check at every turn. Be at ease, my friends, for this has gone splendidly. True, we could not fully anticipate the devastation Greeth wrought, and true, we have many more dead than we expected, but the war was mercifully short and favorably concluded. We could not ask for a better stooge than Captain Deudermont to serve as the new puppet governor of Luskan."

"Don't underestimate him," Kurth warned. "He is a hero to the people, even to those fighters who serve in our ranks."

"Then we must make sure that the next few tendays shine a different light upon him," said Kensidan. As he finished, he looked at his closest ally, Suljack, and saw the man frowning and shaking his head. Kensidan wasn't quite sure what that might mean, for in truth, Suljack had lost the most soldiers in the battle, with nearly all of his Ship marching beside Deudermont and a good many of them killed at the Hosttower.

* * * * *

"Well enough to get out of bed, I would say," a voice accosted Regis. He lay in his bed, half asleep, feeling perfectly miserable both emotionally and physically. He could deal with his wounds a lot easier than with the loss of Drizzt. How was he going to go back to Mithral Hall and face Bruenor? And Catti-brie!

"I feel better," he lied.

"Then do sit up, little one," the voice replied, and that gave

Regis pause, for he didn't recognize the speaker and saw no one when he looked around the room.

He sat up quickly then, and immediately focused on a darkened corner of the room.

Magically darkened, he knew.

"Who are you?" he asked.

"An old friend."

Regis shook his head.

"Fare well on your journey...." the voice said and the last notes of the sentence faded away to nothingness, taking the magical darkness with it.

Leaving a revelation that had Regis gawking with surprise and trepidation.

* * * * *

He knew that he was nearing the end, and that there was no way out. Guenhwyvar, too, would perish, and Drizzt could only pray that her death on that alien plane, removed from the figurine, wouldn't be permanent, that she would, as she had on the Prime Material Plane, simply revert to her Astral home.

The drow cursed himself for leaving the statuette behind.

And he fought, not for himself, for he knew that he was doomed, but for Guenhwyvar, his beloved friend. Perhaps she would find her way home through sheer exhaustion, as long as he could keep her alive long enough.

He didn't know how many hours, days, had passed. He had found bitter nourishment in giant mushrooms and in the flesh of some of the strange beasts that had come against him, but both had left him sickly and weak.

He knew he was nearing the end, but the fighting was not.

He faced a six-armed monstrosity, every lumbering swing from its thick arms heavy enough to decapitate him. Drizzt was too quick for those swipes, of course, and had he been less weary, his foe would have been an easy kill. But the drow could hardly hold his scimitars aloft, and his focus kept slipping. Several times, he managed to duck away just in time to avoid a heavy punch.

"Come on, Guen," he whispered under his breath, having set the fiendish beast up for a sidelong strike from the panther's position on a rocky outcropping to the right. Drizzt heard a growl, and grinned, expecting Guenhwyvar to fly in for the kill.

But Drizzt got hit, and hard, instead, a flying tackle that flung him away from the beast and left him rolling in a tangle with another powerful creature.

He didn't understand—it was all he could do to hold onto his scimitars, let alone try to bring them to bear.

But then the muddy ground beneath him became more solid, and a stinging light blinded him, and though his eyes could not adjust to see anything, he realized from another familiar growl that it was Guenhwyvar who had tackled him.

He heard a friendly voice, a welcomed voice, a cry of glee.

He got hit with another flying tackle almost as soon as he'd extricated himself from the jumble with Guen.

"How?" he asked Regis.

"I don't know and I don't care!" the halfling responded, hugging Drizzt all the tighter.

* * * * *

"Kurth is right," High Captain Rethnor warned his son. "Underestimate Captain Deudermont... *Governor* Deudermont, at our peril. He is a man of actions, not words. You were never at sea, and so you don't understand the horror that filled men's eyes when the sails of *Sea Sprite* were spotted."

"I have heard the tales, but this is not the sea," Kensidan replied.

"You have it all figured out," Rethnor said, his mocking tone unmistakable.

"I remain agile in my ability to adapt to whatever comes our way."

"But for now?"

"For now, I allow Kurth to run rampant on Closeguard and Cutlass, and even in the market area. He and I will dominate the streets easily enough, with Suljack playing my fool."

"Deudermont may disband Prisoner's Carnival, but he will raise a strong militia to enforce the laws."

"His laws," Kensidan replied, "not Luskan's."

"They are one and the same now."

"No, not yet, and not ever if we properly pressure the streets," said Kensidan. "Turmoil is Deudermont's enemy, and lack of order will eventually turn the people against him. If he pushes too hard, he will find all of Luskan against him, as Arklem Greeth realized."

"It's a fight you want?" Rethnor said after a contemplative pause.

"It's a fight I insist upon," his conniving son answered. "For now, Deudermont makes a fine target for the anger of others, while Ship Kurth and Ship Rethnor rule the streets. When the breaking point is reached, a second war will erupt in Luskan, and when it's done . . ."

"A free port," said Rethnor. "A sanctuary for . . . merchant ships."

"With ready trade in exotic goods that will find their way to the homes of Waterdhavian lords and to the shops of Baldur's Gate," said Kensidan. "That alone will keep Waterdeep from organizing an invasion of the new Luskan, for the self-serving bastard nobles will not threaten their own playthings. We'll have our port, our city, and all pretense of law and subservience to the lords of Waterdeep be damned."

"Lofty goals," said Rethnor.

"My father, I only seek to make you proud," Kensidan said with such obvious sarcasm that old Rethnor could only laugh, and heartily.

* * * * *

"I'm not easy with this disembodied voice arriving in the darkness," Deudermont said. "But pleased I am, beyond anything, to see you alive and well."

"Well is a relative term," the drow replied. "But I'm recovering—though if you ever happen to travel to the plane of my imprisonment, take care to avoid the mushrooms."

Deudermont and Robillard laughed at that, as did Regis, who was standing at Drizzt's side, both of them carrying their packs for the road.

"I have acquaintances on Luskan's streets," Drizzt reasoned. "Some not even of my knowing, but friends of a friend."

"Wulfgar," said Deudermont. "Perhaps it was that Morik character he ran beside—though he's not supposed to be in Luskan, on pain of death."

Drizzt shrugged. "Whatever good fortune brought Guenhwyvar's statue to Regis, it's good fortune I will accept."

"True enough," said the captain. "And now you are bound for Icewind Dale. Are you sure that you cannot stay the winter, for I've much to do, and your help would serve me well."

"If we hurry, we can beat the snows to Ten-Towns," said Drizzt.

"And you will return to Luskan in the spring?"

"We would be sorry friends indeed if we didn't," Regis answered.

"We will return," Drizzt promised.

With handshakes and bows, the pair left *Sea Sprite*, which served as the governor's palace until the devastation in the city could be sorted out and a new location, formerly the Red Dragon Inn on the northern bank of the Mirar, could be properly secured and readied.

The enormity of the rebuilding task ahead of Luskan was not lost on Drizzt and Regis as they walked through the city's streets. Much of the place had been gutted by flames and so many had died, leaving one empty structure after another. Many of the larger homes and taverns had been confiscated by order of Governor Deudermont and set up as hospitals for the many, many wounded, or as often as not as morgues to hold the bodies until they could be properly identified and buried.

"The Luskar will do little through the winter, other than to try to find food and warmth," Regis remarked as they passed a group of haggard women huddled in a doorway.

"It will be a long road," Drizzt agreed.

"Was it worth the cost?" the halfling asked.

"We can't yet know."

"A lot of folk would disagree with you on that," Regis remarked, nodding in the direction of the new graveyard north of the city.

"Arklem Greeth was intolerable," Drizzt reminded his friend. "If the city can withstand the next few months, a year perhaps, with the rebuilding in the summer, then Deudermont will do well by them, do not doubt. He will call in every favor from every Waterdhavian lord, and goods and supplies will flow fast to Luskan."

"Will it be enough, though?" Regis asked. "With so many of the healthy adults dead, how many of their families will even stay?"

Drizzt shrugged helplessly.

"Perhaps we should stay and help through the winter," said Regis, but Drizzt was shaking his head.

"Not everyone in Luskan accepts me, Deudermont's friend or not," the drow replied. "We didn't instigate their fight, but we helped the correct side win it. Now we must trust them to do what's right—there's little we can do here now. Besides, I want to see Wulfgar again, and Icewind Dale. Its been too long since I've looked upon my first true home."

"But Luskan . . ." Regis started.

Drizzt interrupted with an upraised hand.

"Was it really worth it?" Regis pressed anyway.

"I have no answers, nor do you."

They passed out of the city's northern gate then, to the half-hearted cheers of the few guardsmen along the wall and towers.

"Maybe we could get them all to march to Longsaddle next," Regis remarked, and Drizzt laughed, almost as helplessly as he had shrugged.

PART 3

HARMONY

HARMONY

I am often struck by the parallel courses I find in the wide world. My life's road has led me to many places, back and forth from Mithral Hall to the Sword Coast, to Icewind Dale and the Snowflake Mountains, to Calimport and to the Underdark. I have come to know the truth of the old saying that the only constant is change, but what strikes me most profoundly is the similarity of direction in that change, a concordance of mood, from place to place, in towns and among people who have no, or at least only cursory, knowledge of each other.

I find unrest and I find hope. I find contentment and I find anger. And always, it seems, I'm met with the same general set of emotions among the people from place to place. I understand there is a rationality to it all, for even peoples remote from each other will share common influences: a difficult winter, a war in one land that affects commerce in another, whispers of a spreading plague, the rise of a new king whose message resonates among the populace and brings hope and joy even to those far removed from his growing legend. But still, I often feel as though there is another realm of the senses. As a cold winter might spread through Icewind Dale and Luskan, and all the way to the Silver Marches, so too, it seems, does mood spiderweb the paths and roads of the Realms. It's almost as if there is a second layer of weather, an emotional wave that rolls and roils its way across Faerûn.

There is trepidation and hopeful change in Mithral Hall and the rest of the Silver Marches, a collective holding of breath where the coin of true peace and all-out war spins on its edge, and not dwarf nor elf nor human nor orc knows on which side it will land. There is a powerful emotional battle waging between the status quo and the desire to embrace great and promising change.

And so I found this same unsettling dynamic in Longsaddle, where the Harpells are engaged in a similar state of near disaster with the rival factions of their community. They hold the coin fast, locked in spells to conserve what is, but the stress and strain are obvious to all who view.

And so I found this same dynamic in Luskan, where the potential change is no less profound than the possible—and none too popular—acceptance of an orc kingdom as a viable partner in the league of nations that comprise the Silver Marches.

A wave of unrest and edginess has gripped the land, from Mithral Hall to the Sword Coast—palpably so. It's as if the people and races of the world have all at once declared the unacceptability of their current lot in life, as if the sentient beings have finished their collective exhale and are now taking in a new breath.

I head to Icewind Dale, a land of tradition that extends beyond the people who live there, a land of constants and of constant pressure. A land not unaccustomed to war, a land that knows death intimately. If the same breath that brought Obould from his hole, that brought out ancient hatreds among the priests of Longsaddle, that led to the rise of Deudermont and the fall of Arklem Greeth, has filled the unending winds of Icewind Dale, then I truly fear what I may find there, in a place where the smoke of a gutted homestead is almost as common as the smoke of a campfire, and where the howl of the wolf is no less threatening than the war cry of a barbarian, or the battle call of an orc, or the roar of a white dragon. Under the constant struggle to simply survive, Icewind Dale is on edge even in those times when the world is in a place of peace and contentment. What might I find there now, when my road has passed through lands of strife and battle?

I wonder sometimes if there is a god, or gods, who play with the emotions of the collective of sentient beings as an artist colors a canvas. Might there be supernatural beings watching and taking amusement at our toils and tribulations? Do these gods wave giant wands of envy or greed or contentment or love over us all, that they can then watch at their pleasure, perhaps even gamble on the outcome?

Or do they, too, battle amongst themselves, reflections of our own failures, and their victories and failures similarly extend to us, their insignificant minions?

Or am I simply taking the easier route of reasoning, and ascribing what I cannot know to some irrationally defined being or beings for the sake of my own comfort? This trail, I fear, may be no more than warm porridge on a wintry morning.

Whatever it is, the weather or the rise of a great foe, folk demanding to partake of advancements in comfort or the sweep of a plague, or some unseen and nefarious god or gods at play, or whether, perhaps, the collective I view is no more than an extension of my own inner turmoil or contentment, a projection of Drizzt upon the people he views . . . whatever it may be, this collective emotion seems to me a palpable thing, a real and true motion of shared breath.

—Drizzt Do'Urden

CHAPTER

THE WIND IN THEIR EARS

19

It happened imperceptibly, a delicate transition that touched the memories and souls of the companions as profoundly as it reverberated in their physical senses. For as the endless and mournful wind of Icewind Dale filled their ears, as the smell of the tundra filled their noses, as the cold northern air tickled their skin, and as the sheet of wintry white dazzled their eyes, so too did the aura of the place, the primal savagery, the pristine beauty, fill their thoughts, so too did the edge of catastrophe awaken their conflicting fears.

That was the true power of the dale, exemplified by the wind, always the wind, the constant reminder of the paradox of existence, that one was always alone and never alone, that communion ended at senses' edge and yet that the same communion never truly ended.

They walked side-by-side, without speaking, but not in silence. They were joined by the wind of Icewind Dale, in the same place and same time, and whatever thoughts they each entertained separately could not fully escape the bond of awareness forced by Icewind Dale itself upon all who ventured there.

They crossed out of the pass through the Spine of the World and onto the wider tundra one bright and shining morning, and found that the snows were not yet too deep, and the wind not yet too cold. In a few days, if the weather held, they would arrive in

Ten-Towns, the ten settlements around the three deep lakes to the north. There, Regis had once found sanctuary from the relentless pursuit of Pasha Pook, a former employer, from whom he had stolen the magical ruby pendant he still wore. There, the beleaguered and weary Drizzt Do'Urden had at last found a place to call home, and the friends he continued to hold most dear.

For the next few days, they held wistfulness in their eyes and fullness in their hearts. Around their small campfire each night they spoke of times past, of fishing Maer Dualdon, the largest of the lakes; of nights on Kelvin's Cairn, the lone mountain above the caves where Bruenor's clan had lived in exile, where the stars seemed so close that one could grasp them; and questions of immortality seemed crystalline clear. For one could not stand on Bruenor's Climb on Kelvin's Cairn, amidst the stars on a cold and crisp Icewind Dale night and not feel a profound connection to eternity.

The trail, known simply as "the caravan route," ran almost directly northeast to Bryn Shander, the largest of the ten settlements, the accepted seat of power for the region and the common marketplace. Bryn Shander was favorably located within the meager protection of a series of rolling hillocks and nearly equidistant to the three lakes, Maer Dualdon to the northwest, Redwaters to the southeast and Lac Dinneshere, the easternmost of the lakes. Along the same line as the caravan route, just half a day's walk northeast of Bryn Shander, loomed the dormant volcano Kelvin's Cairn, and before it, the valley and tunnels that once, and for more than a century, had housed Clan Battlehammer.

Nearly ten thousand hearty souls lived in those ten settlements, all but those in Bryn Shander on the banks of one of the three lakes.

The approach of a dark elf and a halfling elicited excitement and alarm in the young guards manning Bryn Shander's main gate. To see anyone coming up the caravan route at such a late date was a surprise, but to have one of those approaching be an elf with skin as black as midnight . . . !

The gates closed fast and hard, and Drizzt laughed aloud—loud enough to be heard, though he and Regis were still many yards away.

"I told you to keep your hood up," Regis scolded.

"Better they see me for what I am before we're in range of a longbow."

Regis took a step away from the drow, and Drizzt laughed again, and so did the halfling.

"Halt and be recognized!" a guard shouted at them in a voice too shaky to truly be threatening.

"Recognize me, then, and be done with this foolishness," Drizzt called back, and he stopped in the middle of the road barely twenty strides from the wooden stockade wall. "How many years must one live among the folk of Ten-Towns before the lapse of a few short years so erases the memory of men?"

A long pause ensued before a different guard called out, "What is your name?"

"Drizzt Do'Urden, you fool!" Regis yelled back. "And I am Regis of Lonelywood, who serves King Bruenor in Mithral Hall."

"Can it be?" yet another voice cried out.

The gates swung open as quickly and as forcefully as they had closed.

"Apparently their memories are not as short as you feared," Regis remarked.

"It's good to be home," the drow replied.

* * * * *

The snow-covered trees muffled the wind's mournful song as Regis silently padded through them down to the banks of the partially frozen lake a few days later. Maer Dualdon spread out wide before him, gray ice, black ice, and blue water. One boat bobbed at the town of Lonelywood's longest wharf, not yet caught fast by the winter. From dozens of small houses nestled in the woods, single lines of smoke wafted into the morning air.

Regis was at peace.

He moved to the water's edge, where a small patch remained unfrozen, and dropped a tiny chunk of ice into the lake, then watched as the ripples rolled out from the impact, washing little bits of water onto the surrounding ice. His mind took him through those ripples and into the past. He thought of fishing—this had been his favorite spot. He told himself it would be a good thing to come back one summer and again set his bobber in the waters of Maer Dualdon.

Hardly thinking of the action, he reached into a small sack he had tied to his belt and produced a palm-sized piece of white bone, the famous skull that gave the trout of Icewind Dale their name. From his other hip pouch, he produced his carving knife, and never looking down at the bone, his eyes gazing across the empty lake, he went to work. Shavings fell as the halfling worked to free that which he knew to be in the bone, for that was the true secret of scrimshaw. His art wasn't to carve the bone into some definable shape, but to free the shape that was already in there, waiting for skilled and delicate fingers to show it to the world.

Regis looked down and smiled as he came to understand the image he was freeing, one so fitting for him at that moment of reflection on what had once been, of good times spent among good friends in a land so beautiful and so deadly all at once.

He lost track of time as he stood there reminiscing and sculpting, and soaking in the beauty and the refreshing chill. Half in a daze, half in the past, Regis nearly jumped out of his furry boots when he glanced down again and saw the head of a gigantic cat beside his hip.

His little squeak became a call of, "Guenhwyvar!" as the startled halfling tried to catch his breath.

"She likes it here, too," Drizzt said from the trees behind him, and he turned to watch his drow friend's approach.

"You could have called out a warning," Regis said, and he noted that in his startled jump, he'd nicked his thumb with the sharp knife. He brought it up to suck on the wound, and was greatly relieved to learn that his scrimshaw had not been damaged.

"I did," Drizzt replied. "Twice. You've the wind in your ears."

"It's not so breezy here."

"Then the winds of time," said Drizzt.

Regis smiled and nodded. "It's hard to come here and not want to stay."

"It's a more difficult place than Mithral Hall," said Drizzt.

"But a more simple one," Regis answered, and it was Drizzt's turn to smile and nod. "You met with the spokesmen of Bryn Shander?"

Drizzt shook his head. "There was no need," he explained. "Proprietor Faelfaril knew well of Wulfgar's journey through Ten-Towns four years ago. I learned everything we need from the innkeeper."

"And it saved you the trouble of the fanfare you knew would accompany your return."

"As you avoided it by jumping a wagon north to Lonelywood," Drizzt retorted.

"I wanted to see it again. It was my home, after all, and for many, many years. Did fat old Faelfaril mention any subsequent visits by Wulfgar?"

Drizzt shook his head. "Our friend came through, praise Tempus, but very briefly before going straightaway out to the tundra, to rejoin his people. The folk of Bryn Shander heard one other mention of him, just one, a short time after that, but nothing definitive and nothing that Faelfaril remembers well."

"Then he is out there," Regis said, nodding to the northeast, the open lands where the barbarians roamed. "I'd wager he's the king of them all by now."

Drizzt's expression showed he didn't agree. "Where he went, where he is, is not known in Bryn Shander, and perhaps Wulfgar has become chieftain of the Tribe of the Elk, his people. But the tribes are no longer united, and have not been for years. They have only occasional and very minor dealings with the folk of Ten-Towns at all, and Faelfaril assured me that were it not for the occasional campfires seen in the distance, the folk of Ten-Towns wouldn't even know that they were constantly surrounded by wandering barbarians."

Regis furrowed his brow in consternation.

"But neither do they fear the tribes, as they once did," Drizzt said. "They coexist, and there is relative peace, and that is no small legacy of our friend Wulfgar."

"Do you think he's still out there?"

"I know he is."

"And we're going to find him," said Regis.

"Poor friends we would be if we didn't."

"It's getting cold," the halfling warned.

"Not as cold as the ice cave of a white dragon."

Regis rubbed Guenhwyvar's strong neck and chuckled helplessly. "You'll get me there, too, before this is all done," he said, "or I'm an unbearded gnome."

"Unbearded?" Drizzt asked and Regis shrugged.

"Works for Bruenor the other way," he said.

"A furry-footed gnome, then," Drizzt offered.

"A hungry halfling," Regis corrected. "If we're going out there, we'll need ample supplies. Buy some saddlebags for your cat, or bend your back, elf."

Laughing, Drizzt walked over and draped his arm around Regis's sturdy shoulders, and started turning the halfling to leave. Regis resisted, though, and instead forced Drizzt to pause and take a good long look at Maer Dualdon.

He heard the drow sigh deeply, and knew he'd been taken by the same nostalgic trance, by memories of the years they had known in the simple, beautiful, and deadly splendors of Icewind Dale.

"What are you carving?" Drizzt asked after a long while.

"We'll both know when it reveals itself," Regis answered, and Drizzt accepted that inescapable truth with a nod.

They went out that very afternoon, packs heavy with food and extra clothing. They made the base of Kelvin's Cairn as twilight descended, and found shelter in a shallow cave, one that Drizzt knew very well.

"I'm going up tonight," Drizzt informed Regis over supper.

"To Bruenor's Climb?"

"To where it was before the collapse, yes. I will stoke the fire well before I go, I promise, and leave Guenhwyvar beside you until I return."

"Let it burn low, and keep or release the cat as she needs," Regis answered. "I'm going with you."

Surprised, but pleasantly so, Drizzt nodded. He kept Guenhwyvar by his side as he and Regis made a silent ascent to the top of Kelvin's Cairn. It was a difficult climb, with few trails, and those along icy rocks, but less than an hour later, the companions stepped out from behind one overhang to find that they had reached the peak. The tundra spread wide before them, and stars twinkled all around them.

The three of them stood there in communion with Icewind

Dale, in harmony with the cycles of life and death, in contemplation of eternity and a oneness of being with all the great universe, for a long time. They took great comfort in feeling so much a part of something larger than themselves.

And somewhere in the north, a campfire flared to life, seeming like another star.

They each wondered silently if Wulfgar might be sitting beside it, rubbing the cold from his strong hands.

A wolf howled from somewhere unseen, and another answered, then still more took up the nighttime song of Icewind Dale.

Guenhwyvar growled softly, not angered, excited, or uneasy, but simply to speak to the heavens and the wind.

Drizzt crouched beside her and looked across her back to meet Regis's stare. Each knew well what the other was thinking and feeling and remembering, and there was no need at all for words, so none were spoken.

It was a night that they, all three, would remember for the rest of their lives.

CHAPTER

THE BETTER NATURES OF MEN

20

"This was not my intent," Captain Deudermont told the gathered Luskar, his strong voice reaching out through the driving rain. "My life was the sea, and perhaps will be again, but for now I accept your call to serve as governor of Luskan."

The cheering overwhelmed the drumbeat of raindrops.

"Marvelous," Robillard muttered from the back of the stage—the stage built for Prisoner's Carnival, the brutal face of Luskan justice.

"I have sailed to many lands and seen many ways," Deudermont went on and many in the crowd demanded quiet of their peers, for they wanted to savor the man's every word. "I have known Waterdeep and Baldur's Gate, Memnon and faraway Calimport, and every port in between. I have seen far better leaders than Arklem Greeth—" the mere mention of the name brought a long hiss from the thousands gathered—"but never have I witnessed a people stronger in courage and character than those I see before me now," the governor went on, and the cheering erupted anew.

"Would that they would shut up that we might be done with this, and out of the miserable rain," Robillard grumbled.

"Today I make my first decree," the governor declared, "that this stage, that this abomination known as Prisoner's Carnival, is now and forever ended!"

The response—some wild cheering, many curious stares, and more than a few sour expressions—reminded Deudermont of the enormity of the task before him. The carnival was among the most barbaric circuses Deudermont had ever witnessed, where men and women, some guilty, some probably not, were publicly tortured, humiliated, even gruesomely murdered. In Luskan, many called it entertainment.

"I will work with the high captains, who will leave our long-ago battles out to sea, I'm sure," Deudermont moved along. "Together we will forge from Luskan a shining example of what can be, when the greater and common good is the goal, and the voices of the least are heard as strongly as those of the nobility."

More cheering made Deudermont pause yet again.

"He is an optimistic sort," muttered Robillard.

"And why not?" asked Suljack, who sat beside him, the lone high captain who had accepted the invitation to sit on the dais behind Deudermont, and had only committed to do so at the insistence of Kensidan. Being out there, listening to Deudermont, and to the cheers coming back at the dais from the throng of Luskar, had Suljack sitting taller and leaning this way and that with some enthusiasm.

Robillard ignored him and leaned forward. "Captain," he called, getting Deudermont's attention. "Would you have half your subjects fall ill from the wet and cold?"

Deudermont smiled at the not-so-subtle hint.

"Go to your homes, now, and take heart," Deudermont bade the crowd. "Be warm, and be filled with hope. The day has turned, and though Talos the Storm Lord has not yet heard, the skies are brighter in Luskan!"

That brought the loudest cheering of all.

* * * * *

"Three times he put me to the bottom," Baram growled, watching with Taerl from a balcony across the way. "Three times that dog Deudermont and his fancy *Sea Sprite*, curse her name, dropped me ship out from under me, and one of them times, 'e got me landed in Prisoner's Carnival." He pulled up his sleeve, showing a series of burn scars where he'd been prodded with a hot poker. "Cost me more to bribe me way out than it cost for a new ship."

"Deudermont's a dog, to be sure," Taerl agreed. He smiled as he finished, nudged his partner, and pointed down to the back of the square, where most of the city's magistrates huddled under an awning. "Not a one o' them's happy at the call for the end o' their fun."

Baram snorted as he considered the grim expressions on the faces of the torturers. They reveled in their duties; they called Prisoner's Carnival a necessary evil for the administration of justice. But Baram, who had sat in the cells of the limestone holding caves, who had been paraded across that stage, who had paid two of them handsomely to get his reduced sentence—he should have been drawn and quartered for the pirate he was—knew they had all profited from bribes, as well.

"I'm thinking that the rain's fitting for the day's events," Baram remarked. "Lots o' storm clouds in Luskan's coming days."

"Ye'd not be thinking that looking at the fool Suljack, sitting there all a'titter at the dog Deudermont's every word," Taerl said, and Baram issued a low growl.

"He's looking for a way to up himself on Deudermont's sleeve," Taerl went on. "He knows he's the least among us, and now's thinking himself to be the cleverest."

"Too clever by half," Baram said, and there was no missing the threatening tone in his voice.

"Chaos," Taerl agreed. "Kensidan wanted chaos, and claimed we five would be better for it, eh? So let's us be better, I say."

* * * * *

As gently as a father lifting an injured daughter, the lich scooped the weathered body of Valindra Shadowmantle into his arms. He cradled her close, that dark and rainy evening, the same day Deudermont had made his "I am your god" speech to the idiot peasants of Luskan.

He didn't use the bridge to cross from blasted Cutlass Island to Closeguard, but simply walked into the water. He didn't need air, nor did Valindra, after all. He moved into an underwater cave beneath the rim of Closeguard then to the sewer system that took him to the mainland, under his new home: Illusk, where he placed Valindra gently in a curtained bed of soft satin and velvet.

When he poured an elixir down her throat a short while later, the woman coughed out the rain, blood, and seawater. Groggily, she sat up and found that her breathing was hard to come by. She forced the air in and out of her lungs, taking in the many unfamiliar and curious smells as she did. She finally settled and glanced through a crack in the canopy.

"The Hosttower . . ." she rasped, straining with every word. "We survived. I thought the witch had killed . . ."

"The Hosttower is gone," Arklem Greeth told her.

Valindra looked at him curiously then struggled to the edge of the bed and parted the canopy, glancing around in confusion at what looked like the archmage arcane's bedchamber in the Hosttower. She ended by turning her puzzled expression to the lich.

"Boom," he said with a grin. "It's gone, destroyed wholly and utterly, and many of Luskan with it, curse their rotting corpses."

"But this is your room."

"Which was never actually *in* the Hosttower, of course," Arklem Greeth sort of explained.

"I entered it a thousand times!"

"Extradimensional travel . . . there is magic in the world, you know."

Valindra smirked at his sarcasm.

"I expected it would come to this one day," Arklem Greeth explained with a chuckle. "In fact, I hoped for it." He looked up at Valindra's stunned expression and laughed all the louder before adding, "People are so fickle. It comes from living so short and miserable a life."

"So then where are we?"

"Under Illusk, our new home."

Valindra shook her head at every word. "This is no place for me. Find me another assignment within the Arcane Brotherhood."

It was Arklem Greeth's turn to shake his head. "This is your place, as surely as it is my own."

"Illusk?" the moon elf asked with obvious consternation and dismay.

"You haven't yet noted that you're not drawing breath, except to give sound to your voice," said the lich, and Valindra looked at him curiously. Then she looked down at her own pale and unmoving breast, then back to him with alarm.

"What have you done?" she barely managed to whisper.

"Not I, but Arabeth," Arklem Greeth replied. "Her dagger was well-placed. You died before the Hosttower exploded."

"But you resurrected . . ."

Greeth was still shaking his head. "I am no wretched priest who grovels before a fool god."

"Then what?" Valindra asked, but she knew. . . .

He had expected the terrorized reaction that followed, of course, for few people welcome lichdom in so sudden—and unbidden—a manner.

He returned her horror with a smile, knowing that Valindra Shadowmantle, his beloved, would get past the shock and recognize the blessing.

* * * * *

"Events move quickly," Tanally, one of Luskan's most prestigious guards, warned Deudermont. The governor had invited Tanally and many other prominent guards and citizens to meet with him in his quarters, and had bade them to speak honestly and forthrightly.

The governor was certainly getting what he'd asked for, to the continual groaning of Robillard, who sat at the window at the back of the spacious room.

"As well they must," Deudermont replied. "Winter will be fast upon us, and many are without homes. I will not have my people—*our* people—starving and freezing in the streets."

"Of course not," Tanally agreed. "I didn't mean to suggest—"

"He means other events," said Magistrate Jerem Boll, formerly a leading adjudicator of the defunct Prisoner's Carnival.

"People will think to loot and scavenge," Tanally clarified.

Deudermont nodded. "They will. They will scavenge for food,

so that they won't starve and die. And for that, what? Would you have me serve them up to Prisoner's Carnival for the delight of other starving people?"

"You risk the breakdown of order," Magistrate Jerem Boll warned.

"Prisoner's Carnival epitomized the lack of order!" Deudermont shot back, raising his voice for the first time in the long and often contentious discussion. "Don't sneer at my observation. I witnessed Luskan's meting out of justice for much of my adult life, and know of more than a few who met a grisly and undeserved fate at the hands of the magistrates."

"And yet, under that blanket, the city thrived," said Jerem Boll.

"Thrived? Who is it that thrived, Magistrate? Those with enough coin to buy their way free of your 'carnival'? Those with enough influence that the magistrates dare not touch them, however heinous their affronts?"

"You should take care how you refer to those people," Jerem Boll replied, his voice going low. "You speak of the core of Luskan's power, of the men who allowed their folk to join in your impetuous march to tear down the most glorious structure that this city—nay, the most glorious structure that any city in the north has ever known!"

"A glorious structure ruled by a lich who loosed undead monsters randomly about the streets," Deudermont reminded him. "Would there have been a seat at Prisoner's Carnival for Arklem Greeth, I wonder? Other than a position of oversight, I mean."

Jerem Boll narrowed his gaze, but didn't respond, and on that sour note, the meeting was adjourned.

"What?" Deudermont asked of the surly-faced Robillard when they were alone. "You don't agree?"

"When have I ever?"

"True enough," Deudermont admitted. "Luskan must start anew, and quickly. Forgiveness is the order of the day—it has to be! I will issue a blanket pardon to everyone not directly affiliated with the Arcane Brotherhood who fought against us on the side of the Hosttower. Confusion and fear, not malice, drove their resistance. And even for those who threw in their lot with the brotherhood, we will adjudicate with an even hand."

Robillard chuckled,

"I doubt many knew the truth of Arklem Greeth, and probably, and justifiably, saw Lord Brambleberry and me as invaders."

"In a sense," said the wizard.

Deudermont shook his head at the dry and unending sarcasm, and wondered again why he kept Robillard at his side for all those years. He knew the answer, of course, and it came more from exactly that willingness to disagree than the wizard's formidable skill in the Art.

"The life of the typical Luskar was no more than a prison sentence," Deudermont said, "awaiting the formality of Prisoner's Carnival, or joining in with one of the many street gangs. . . ."

"Gangs, or Ships?"

Deudermont nodded. He knew the wizard was right, and that the thuggery of Luskan had emanated from six distinct locations. One was down now, with Arklem Greeth blown away, but the other five, the Ships of the high captains, remained.

"And though they fought with you, or not against you at least, are you to doubt that some—Baram comes to mind—haven't quite forgiven you for past . . . meetings?"

"If he decides to act upon that old score, let us hope that he's as poor a fighter on land as he was at sea," said Deudermont, and even Robillard cracked a smile at that.

"Do you even understand the level of risk you're taking here— and in the name of the folk you claim to serve?" Robillard asked after a short pause. "These Luskar have known only iron rule for decades. Under the fist of Arklem Greeth and the high captains, their little wars remained little wars, their crimes both petty and murderous were rewarded with harsh retribution, either by a blade in the alley or, yes, by Prisoner's Carnival. The sword was always drawn, ready to slash anyone who got too far out of the boundaries of acceptable behavior—even if that behavior was never acceptable to you. Now you retract that sword and—"

"And show them a better way," Deudermont insisted. "We have seen commoners leading better lives across the wide world, in Waterdeep and even in the wilder cities to the south. Are there any so ill-structured as the Luskan of Arklem Greeth?"

"Waterdeep has its own iron fists, Captain," Robillard reminded him. "The power of the lords, both secret and open, backed by the Blackstaff, is so overwhelming as to afford them nearly complete control of day to day life in the City of Splendors. You cannot compare cities south of here to Luskan. This place has only commerce. Its entire existence settles on its ability to attract merchants, including unsavory types, from Ten-Towns in Icewind Dale to the dwarves of Ironspur to Mirabar and the Silver Marches to the ships that put into her harbors and yes, to Waterdeep as well. Luskan is not a town of noble families, but of rogues. She is not a town of farmers, but of pirates. Do I truly need to explain these truths to you?"

"You speak of *old* Luskan," the stubborn Deudermont replied. "These rogues and pirates have taken homes, have taken wives and husbands, have brought forth children. The transition began long before Brambleberry and I sailed north from Waterdeep. That is why the people so readily joined in against the drawn sword, as you put it. Their days in the darkness are ended."

"Only one high captain accepted the invitation to sit with you for your acceptance speech, and he, Suljack, is considered the least among them."

"The least, or the wisest?"

Robillard laughed. "Wisdom is not something Suljack has oft been accused of, I'm sure."

"If he sees the future of Luskan united, then it's a mantle he will wear more often," Deudermont insisted.

"So says the governor."

"So he does." Deudermont insisted. "Have you no faith in the spirit of humanity?"

Robillard scoffed loudly at that. "I've sailed the same seas you have, Captain. I saw the same murderers and pirates. I've seen the nature of men, indeed. The spirit of *humanity?*"

"I believe in it. Optimism, good man! Shake off your surliness and take heart and take hope. Optimism trumps pessimism, and—"

"And reality slaughters one and justifies the other. Problems are not often simply matters of perception."

"True enough," Deudermont conceded, "but we can shape that reality if we're clever enough and strong enough."

"And optimistic enough," Robillard said dryly.

"Indeed," the captain, the governor, beamed against that unending sarcasm.

"The spirit of humanity and brotherhood," came another dry remark.

"Indeed!"

And wise Robillard rolled his eyes.

CHAPTER 21
THE UNFORGIVING ICEWIND DALE

The rocks provided only meager shelter from the relentlessly howling wind. North of Kelvin's Cairn, out on the open tundra, Drizzt and Regis appreciated having found any shelter at all. Somehow the drow managed to get a fire started, though the flames engaged in so fierce a battle with the wind that they seemed to have little heat left over for the companions.

Regis sat uncomplaining, working his little knife fast over a piece of knucklehead bone.

"A cold night indeed," Drizzt remarked.

Regis looked up to see his friend staring at him curiously, as if expecting that Regis would launch into a series of complaints, as, he had to admit, had often been his nature. For some reason even he didn't understand—perhaps it was the feeling of homecoming, or maybe the hope that he would soon see Wulfgar again—Regis wasn't miserable in the wind and certainly didn't feel like grumbling.

"It's the north sea wind come calling," the halfling said absently, still focused on his scrimshaw. "And it's here for the season, of course." He looked up at the sky and confirmed his observation. Far fewer stars shone, and the black shapes of clouds moved swiftly from the northwest.

"Then even if we find Wulfgar's tribe in the morning as we had hoped, we'll not likely get out of Icewind Dale in time to beat the first deep snows," said Drizzt. "We're stuck here for the duration of the winter."

Regis shrugged, strangely unbothered by the thought, and went on with his carving.

A few moments later, Drizzt chuckled, drawing the halfling's eyes up to see the drow staring at him.

"What?"

"You feel it, too," said Drizzt.

Regis paused in his carving and let the drow's words sink in. "A lot of years, a lot of memories."

"And most of them grand."

"And even the bad ones, like Akar Kessell and the Crystal Shard, worth retelling," Regis agreed. "So when we're all gone, even Bruenor dead of old age, will you return to Icewind Dale?"

The question had Drizzt blinking and leaning back from the fire, his expression caught somewhere between confusion and alarm. "It's not something I prefer to think about," he replied.

"I'm asking you to do that very thing."

Drizzt shrugged and seemed lost, seemed almost as if he were drowning. "With all the battles ahead of us, what makes you believe I'll outlive you all?"

"It's the way of things, or could well be . . . elf."

"And if I'm cut down in battle, and the rest with me, would *you* return to Icewind Dale?"

"Bruenor would likely bind me to Mithral Hall to serve the next king, or to serve as steward until a king might be found."

"You'll not escape that easily, my little friend."

"But I asked first."

"But I demand of you an answer before I offer my own."

Drizzt started to settle in stubbornly, crossing his arms over his chest, and Regis blurted out, "Yes!" before he could assume his defiant posture.

"Yes," the halfling said again. "I would return if I had no duties elsewhere. I cannot think of a better place in all the world to live."

"You don't much sound like the Regis who used to button up tight against the winter's chill and complain at the turn of the first leaf of Lonelywood."

"My complaining was . . ."

"Extortion," Drizzt finished. "A way to ensure that Regis's hearth was never short of logs, for those around you could not suffer your whining."

Regis considered the playful insult for a moment, then shrugged in acceptance, not about to disagree. "And the complaints were borne of fear," he explained. "I couldn't believe this was my home—I couldn't appreciate that this was my home. I came here fleeing Pasha Pook and Artemis Entreri, and had no idea I would remain here for so long. In my mind, Icewind Dale was a waypoint and nothing more, a place to set that devilish assassin off my trail."

He gave a little laugh and shake of his head as he looked back down at the small statue taking shape in his hand. "Somewhere along the way, I came to know Icewind Dale as my home," he said, his voice growing somber. "I don't think I understood that until I came back here just now."

"It might be you're just weary of the battles and tribulations of Mithral Hall," said Drizzt, "with Obould so close and Bruenor in constant worry."

"Perhaps," Regis conceded, but he didn't seem convinced. He looked back up at Drizzt and offered a sincere smile. "Whatever the reason, I'm glad we're here, we two together."

"On a cold winter's night."

"So be it."

Drizzt looked at Regis with friendship and admiration, amazed at how much the halfling had grown over the last few years, ever since he had taken a spear in battle several years before. That wound, that near-death experience, had brought a palpable change over Drizzt's halfling friend. Before that fight on the river, far to the south, Regis had always shied from trouble, and had been very good at fleeing, but from that point on, when he'd recognized, admitted, and was horrified to see that he had become a dangerous burden to his heroic friends, the halfling had faced, met, and conquered every challenge put before him.

"I think it'll snow tonight," Regis said, looking up at the lowering and thickening clouds.

"So be it," Drizzt replied with an infectious grin.

* * * * *

Surprisingly, the wind let up before dawn, and though Regis's prediction of snow proved accurate, it was not a driving and unpleasant storm. Thick flakes drifted down from above, lazily pirouetting, dodging and darting on their way to the whitened ground.

The companions had barely started on their way when they saw again the smoke of campfires, and as they neared the camp, still before midday, Drizzt recognized the standards and knew that they had indeed found the Tribe of the Elk, Wulfgar's people.

"Just the Elk?" Regis remarked, and cast a concerned look up at Drizzt at the apparent confirmation of what they had been told in Bryn Shander. When they'd left for Mithral Hall, the barbarians of Icewind Dale had been united, all tribes in one. That seemed not to be the case anymore, both from the small size of the encampment and from the fact of that one, and only one, distinguished banner.

They approached slowly, side by side, hands up, palms out in an unthreatening manner.

Smiles and nods came back at them from the men sitting watch on the perimeter; they were recognized still in that place, and accepted as friends. The vigilant sentries didn't leave their positions to go over and greet them, but did wave, and motion them through.

And somehow signaled ahead to the people in the camp, Drizzt and Regis realized from the movements of the main area. It was set in the shelter of a shallow dell, so there was no way they had been spotted from within the collection of tents before they'd crested the surrounding hillock, and yet the camp was all astir, with people rushing about excitedly. A large figure, a huge man with corded muscles and wisdom in his seasoned eyes, stood in the center of all the commotion, flanked by warriors and priests.

He wore the headdress of leadership, elf-horned and decorated, and he was well-known to Drizzt and Regis.

But to their surprise, it was not Wulfgar.

"You stopped the wind, Drizzt Do'Urden," Berkthgar the Bold said in his strong voice. "Your legend is without end."

Drizzt accepted the compliment with a polite bow. "You are well, Berkthgar, and that gladdens my heart," the drow said.

"The seasons have been difficult," the barbarian admitted. "Winter has been the strongest, and the filthy goblins and giants ever-present. We have suffered many losses, but my people have fared best among the tribes."

Both Regis and Drizzt stiffened at that admission, particularly of the losses, and particularly in light of the fact that it was not Wulfgar standing before them, and that he was nowhere to be seen.

"We survive and we go on," Berkthgar added. "That is our heritage and our way."

Drizzt nodded solemnly. He wanted to ask the pressing question, but he held his tongue and let the barbarian continue.

"How fares Bruenor and Mithral Hall?" Berkthgar asked. "I pray to the spirits that you didn't come to tell me that this foul orc king has won the day."

"Nay, not tha—" Drizzt started to say, but he bit it off and looked at Berkthgar with curiosity. "How do you know of King Obould and his minions?"

"Wulfgar, son of Beornegar, returned to us with many tales to share."

"Then where is he?" Regis blurted, unable to contain himself. "Out hunting?"

"None are out hunting."

"Then where?" the halfling demanded, and such a voice came out of his diminutive form as to startle Berkthgar and all the others, even Drizzt.

"Wulfgar came to us four winters ago, and for three winters, he remained among the people," Berkthgar replied. "He hunted with the Tribe of the Elk, as he always should have. He shared in our food and our drink. He danced and sang with the people who were once his own, but no more."

"He tried to take your crown, but you wouldn't let him!" Regis said, trying futilely to keep any level of accusation out of his voice. He knew he'd failed miserably at that, however, when Drizzt elbowed him in the shoulder.

"Wulfgar never challenged me," Berkthgar replied. "He had no place to challenge my leadership, and no right."

"He was once your leader."

"Once."

The simple answer set the halfling back on his heels.

"Wulfgar forgot the ways of Icewind Dale, the ways of our people," Berkthgar said, addressing Drizzt directly and not even glancing down at the upset halfling. "Icewind Dale is unforgiving. Wulfgar, son of Beornegar, didn't need to be told that. He offered no challenge."

Drizzt nodded his understanding and acceptance.

"He left us in the first draw of light and dark," the barbarian explained.

"The spring equinox," Drizzt explained to Regis. "When day and night are equal."

He turned to Berkthgar and asked directly, "Was it demanded of him that he leave?"

The chieftain shook his head. "Too long are the tales of Wulfgar. Great sorrow, it is, for us to know that he is of us no more."

"He thought he was coming home," said Regis.

"This was not his home."

"Then where is he?" the halfling demanded, and Berkthgar shook his head solemnly, having no answer.

"He didn't go back to Ten-Towns," Regis said, growing more animated as he became more alarmed. "He didn't go back to Luskan. He couldn't have without stopping through Ten—"

"The Son of Beornegar is dead," Berkthgar interrupted. "We're not pleased that it came to this, but Icewind Dale wins over us all. Wulfgar forgot who he was, and forgot where he came from. Icewind Dale does not forgive. He left us in the first draw of light and dark, and we found signs of him for many tendays. But they are gone, and he is gone."

"Are you certain?" Drizzt asked, trying to keep the tremor out of his pained voice.

Berkthgar slowly blinked. "Our words with the people of the three lakes are few," he explained. "But when sign of Wulfgar faded from the tundra of Icewind Dale, we asked of him among them. The little one is right. Wulfgar did not go back to Ten-Towns."

"Our mourning is passed," came a voice from behind Berkthgar and the barbarian leader turned to regard the man who had disregarded custom by speaking out. A nod from Berkthgar showed forgiveness for that, and when they saw the speaker, Drizzt and Regis understood the sympathy, for Kierstaad, grown into a strong man, had ever been a devout champion of the son of Beornegar. No doubt for Kierstaad, the loss of Wulfgar was akin to the loss of his father. None of that pain showed in his voice or his stance, however. He had proclaimed the mourning of Wulfgar passed, and so it simply was.

"You don't know that he's dead," Regis protested, and both Berkthgar and Kierstaad, and many others, scowled at him. Drizzt hushed him with a little tap on the shoulder.

"You know the comforts of a hearth and a bed of down," Berkthgar said to Regis. "We know Icewind Dale. Icewind Dale does not forgive."

Regis started to protest again, but Drizzt held him back, understanding well that resignation and acceptance was the way of the barbarians. They accepted death without remorse because death was all too near, always. Not a man or woman there had not known the specter of death—of a lover, a parent, a child, or a friend.

And so the drow tried to show the same stoicism when he and Regis took their leave of the Tribe of the Elk soon after, walking the same path that had brought them so far out from Ten-Towns. The facade couldn't hold, though, and the drow couldn't hide his wince of pain. He didn't know where to turn, where to look, who to ask. Wulfgar was gone, lost to him, and the taste proved bitter indeed. Black wings of guilt fluttered around him as he walked, images of the look on Wulfgar's face when first he'd learned that Catti-brie was lost to him, betrothed to the drow he called his best friend. It had been no one's fault, not Drizzt's nor Catti-brie's, nor Wulfgar's, for Wulfgar had been lost to them for years, trapped in the Abyss by the balor Errtu. In that time, Drizzt and Catti-brie had fallen in love, or had at last admitted the love they had known for years, but had muted because of their obvious differences.

When Wulfgar had returned from the dead, there was nothing they could do, though Catti-brie had surely tried.

And so it was circumstance that had driven Wulfgar from the Companions of the Hall. Blameless circumstance, Drizzt tried hard to tell himself as he and Regis walked without speaking through the continuing gentle snowfall. He wasn't about to convince himself, but it hardly mattered anyway. All that mattered was that Wulfgar was lost to him forever, that his beloved friend was no more and his world had diminished.

Beside him, the muffling aspect of the snow and breeze did little to hide Regis's sniffles.

CHAPTER 22

PARADISE . . . DELAYED

"Ah, but ye're a thief!" the man accused, poking his finger into the chest of the one who he believed had just pocketed the wares.

"Speak on yer own!" the other shouted back. "The merchant here's pointin' to *yer* vest and not me own."

"And he's wrong, because yerself took it!"

"Says a fool!"

The first man retracted his finger, balled up his fist, and let fly a heavy punch for the second's face.

The other was more than ready, though, dropping low beneath the awkward swing and coming up fast and hard to hit his opponent in the gut.

And not with just a fist.

The man staggered back, clutching at his spilling entrails. "Ah, but he sticked me!" he cried.

The knife-wielder came up straight and grinned, then stabbed his opponent again then a third time for good measure. Though screams erupted all across the open market of Luskan, with guards scrambling every which way, the attacker very calmly stepped over and wiped his blade on the shirt of the bent-over man.

"Fall down and die then, like a good fellow," he said to his victim. "One less idiot walking the streets with the name of Captain Suljack on his sputtering lips."

"Murderer!" a woman screamed at the knifeman as his victim fell to the street at his feet.

"Bah! But th' other one struck first!" a man in the crowd shouted.

"Nay, but just a fist!" another one of Suljack's men protested, and the shouting man replied by punching him in the face.

As if on cue, and indeed it was—though only those working for Baram and Taerl understood that cue—the market exploded into violent chaos. Fights broke out at every kiosk and wagon. Women screamed and children ran to better vantage points, so they could watch the fun.

From every corner, the city guards swooped in to restore order. Some shouted orders, but others countermanded those with opposing commands, and the fighting only widened. One furious guard captain ran into the midst of an opposing group, whose leader had just negated his call for a group of ruffians to stand down.

"And who are you with, then?" the leader of that group demanded of the guard captain.

"With Luskan, ye fool," he retorted.

"Bah, there ain't no Luskan," the thug retorted. "Luskan's dead—there's just the Five Ships."

"What nonsense escapes your flapping lips?" the guard captain demanded, but the man didn't relent.

"Ye're a Suljack man, ain't ye?" he accused. The guard captain, who was indeed affiliated with Ship Suljack, stared at him incredulously.

The man slugged him in the chest, and before he could respond, two others pulled back his arms so that the thug could continue the beating uninterrupted.

The melee went on for a long while, until a sharp boom of thunder, a resounding and reverberating blast of explosive magic, drew everyone's attention to the eastern edge of the market. There stood Governor Deudermont, with Robillard, who had thrown the lightning signal, right beside him. All the crew of *Sea Sprite* and the remainder of Lord Brambleberry's men stood shoulder to shoulder behind them.

"We've no time for this!" the governor shouted. "We stand together against the winter, or we fall!"

A rock flew at Deudermont's head, but Robillard caught it with a spell that gracefully and harmlessly moved it aside.

The fighting broke out anew.

From a balcony at Taerl's castle, Baram and Taerl watched it all with great amusement.

"He wants to be the ruler, does he?" Baram spat over the rail as he leaned on it and stared intently out at the hated Deudermont. "A wish he's to come to regret."

"Note the guards," Taerl added. "As soon as the fighting started, they moved to groups of their own Ship. Their loyalty's not to Deudermont or Luskan, but to a high captain."

"It's our town," Baram insisted. "And I've had enough of Governor Deudermont already."

Taerl nodded his agreement and watched the continuing fracas, one that he and Baram had incited with well-paid, well-fed, and well-liquored proxies. "Chaos," he whispered, smiling all the wider.

*****

"Oh, it's you," Suljack said as the tough dwarf moved through his door and into his private chambers. "What news from Ship Rethnor?"

"A great fight in the market," the dwarf replied.

Suljack sighed and wearily rubbed a hand over his face. "Fools," he said. "They'll not give Deudermont a chance—the man will do great things for Luskan, and for our trade."

The dwarf shrugged as though he hardly cared.

"Now's not the time for us to be fighting among ourselves," Suljack remarked, and paced the room, still rubbing at his face. He stopped and turned on the dwarf. "It's just as Kensidan predicted. We been battered but we'll come out all the better."

"Some will. Some won't"

Suljack looked at Kensidan's bodyguard curiously at that remark. "Why are you here?" he asked.

"That fight in the market weren't random," said the dwarf. "Ye're to be finding more than a few o' yer boys hurtin'—might be a few dead, too."

"*My* boys?"

"Slow on the upkeep, eh?" asked the dwarf.

Again Suljack stared at him with a thoroughly puzzled expression and asked, "Why are you here?"

"To keep ye alive."

The question set the high captain back on his heels. "I'm a high captain of Luskan!" he protested. "I have a guard of my—"

"And ye're needin' more help than meself'll bring ye if you're still thinking the fight in the market to be a random brawl."

"Are you saying that my men were targeted?"

"Said it twice, if ye was smart enough to hear."

"And Kensidan sent you here to protect me?"

The dwarf threw him an exaggerated wink.

"Preposterous!" Suljack yelled.

"Ye're welcome," said the dwarf, and he plopped down in a seat facing the room's only door and stared at it without blinking.

* * * * *

"They found three bodies this morning," Robillard reported to Deudermont at the next sunrise. They sat in the front guest hall of the Red Dragon Inn, which had come to serve as the official Governor's Palace. The room boasted wide, strong windows, reinforced with intricate iron work, which looked out to the south, to the River Mirar and the main section of Luskan across it. "Only three today, so I suppose that's a good thing. Unless, of course, the Mirar swept ten times that number out into the bay."

"Your sarcasm knows no end."

"It's an easy thing to criticize," Robillard replied.

"Because what I try to do here is a difficult thing."

"Or a foolish thing, and one that will end badly."

Deudermont got up from the breakfast table and walked across the room. "I'll not argue this same point with you every morning!"

"And still, every morning will be just like this—or worse," Robillard replied. He moved to the window and looked out into the distance of Luskan's market. "Do you think the merchants will come out today? Or will they just cancel the next tenday's work and pack up their wagons for Waterdeep?"

"They've still much to sell."

"Or to have pilfered in the next fight, which should be in a few hours, I would guess."

"The guards will be thick about the market this day."

"Whose? Baram's? Suljack's?"

"Luskan's!"

"Of course, foolish of me to think otherwise," said Robillard.

"You cannot deny that High Captain Suljack sat on the dais," Deudermont reminded. "Or that his men shouldered up to us when the market fighting died away."

"Because his men were getting clobbered," Robillard replied with a chuckle. "Which might be due to his sitting on that dais. Have you thought of that?"

Deudermont sighed and waved his hand at the cynical wizard. "Have *Sea Sprite*'s crew visible in the market as well," he instructed. "Order them to stay close to each other, but to be a very obvious presence. The show of force will help."

"And Brambleberry's men?"

"For tomorrow," Deudermont replied.

"They may be gone by then," Robillard said. The captain looked at him with surprise. "Oh, have you not heard?" the wizard asked. "Lord Brambleberry's veteran and cultured warriors have had quite enough of this uncouth City of Sails and intend to head back to their own City of Splendors before the winter closes the boat lanes. I don't know when they'll go, but have heard some remark that the next favorable tide wouldn't be soon enough."

Deudermont sighed and dropped his head in his hand. "Offer them bonuses if they will remain through the winter," he said.

"Bonuses?"

"Large ones—as much as we can afford."

"I see. You will spend all our gold on your folly before you admit you were wrong."

Deudermont's head snapped up and around so he could glare at the wizard. *"Our* gold?"

"Yours, my captain," Robillard said with a deep bow.

"I was not wrong," said Deudermont. "Time is our ally."

"You will need more tangible allies than that."

"The Mirabarrans . . ." Deudermont said.

"They have closed their gates," Robillard replied. "Our merchant friends from Mirabar suffered greatly when the Hosttower exploded. Many dwarves went straight to Moradin's Halls. You'll not see them on the wall with Luskan's city guard anytime soon."

Deudermont felt and looked old indeed at that moment of great trial. He sighed again and muttered, "The high captains . . ."

"You will need them," Robillard agreed.

"We already have Suljack."

"The one least respected by the other four, of course."

"It's a start!" Deudermont insisted.

"And the others will surely come along to our side, since you know some of them so well already," Robillard said with mock enthusiasm.

Even Deudermont couldn't help but chuckle at that quip. Oh yes, he knew them. He had sunk the ships of at least two of the remaining four beneath them.

"My crew has never let me down," Deudermont said.

"Your crew fights pirates, not cities," came the reminder, stealing any comfort the already beleaguered governor might have garnered from his last remark.

Even Robillard recognized the man's despair and showed him some sympathy. "The remnants of the Hosttower. . . ."

Deudermont looked at him curiously.

"Arabeth and the others," Robillard explained. "I will put them in and around the crew in the market square, in their full Hosttower regalia."

"There is great bitterness against those insignias," Deudermont warned.

"A calculated risk," the wizard admitted. "Surely there are many in Luskan who would see any and all members of the Hosttower destroyed, but surely, too, there are many who recognize the role that Arabeth played in securing the victory we achieved, however great the cost. I wouldn't send her and her lessers out alone, to be sure, but among our crew, with your approval bolstering them, she and hers will serve us well."

"You trust her?"

"No, but I trust in her judgment, and now she knows that her existence here is predicated on the victory of Captain . . . of *Governor* Deudermont."

Deudermont considered the reasoning for a moment then nodded his agreement. "Send for her."

* * * * *

Arabeth Raurym left Deudermont's palace later that same day, pulling her cloak tight against the driving rain. She padded down the puddle-filled street, sweeping up attendants from every corner and alley until the full contingent of eleven former Hosttower wizards marched as a group. It wouldn't do for any of them to be out alone, with so many of Luskan's folk nursing fresh wounds at the hands of their previous comrades. Not a person in Luskan spoke of the Hosttower of the Arcane with anything but venom, it seemed.

She gave her orders as they walked, and as soon as they linked up with *Sea Sprite*'s crew, just north of Illusk, Arabeth took her leave. She cast an enchantment upon herself, reducing her size, making her look like a small girl, and moved southeast into the city, heading straight for Ten Oaks.

To her relief, she was not recognized or bothered, and soon stood before the seated Kensidan, taking note that his newest—and reputedly strongest—bodyguard, that curious and annoying dwarf, was nowhere to be seen.

"Robillard understands the precarious perch upon which Deudermont stands," she reported. "They will not be caught unawares."

"How can they not understand when half the city is in conflict, or burning?"

"Blame Taerl and Baram," Arabeth reminded him.

"Blame them, or credit them?"

"You wanted Deudermont as a figurehead, to give credibility and bona fides to Luskan," the overwizard said.

"If Baram and Taerl decide to openly oppose Deudermont, all the better for those wise enough to pick up the pieces," Kensidan replied. "Whichever side proves victorious."

"You don't sound like you hold any doubts."

"I wouldn't bet against the captain of *Sea Sprite*. Of course, the battleground has changed quite dramatically."

"I wouldn't bet against whichever side Ships Kurth and Rethnor join."

"Join?" the son of Ship Rethnor asked.

Arabeth nodded, smiling as if she knew something Kensidan hadn't yet deduced.

"You wish to remain neutral in this fight, and savor the opportunities," Arabeth explained. "But one side—Deudermont's, I predict—will not grow weaker in the conflict. Nay, he will strengthen his hand, and dangerously so."

"I have considered that possibility."

"And if you allow it, will Deudermont's reign be any different than that of Arklem Greeth?"

"He isn't a lich. That's a start."

Arabeth folded her arms over her chest at the snide comment.

"We will see how it plays out," Kensidan said. "We will allow them—all three of them—their play, as long as it doesn't interfere with my own."

"Your shield guard is with Suljack?"

"I applaud your skill at deduction."

"Good," Arabeth said. "Taerl and Baram are not in good spirits toward Suljack, not after he sat behind Deudermont on the stage."

"I didn't think they would be, hence. . . ."

"You put him there? Surely you knew that Baram would go out of his mind with rage at the thought of Deuder—" She paused and a smile widened across her fair face as she sorted it all out. "Kurth could threaten you, but you don't think that likely—not, at least, until the rest of the city has sorted under the new hierarchy. With that confidence, the only threats to your gains would be Deudermont, who is now far too busy in simply trying to maintain some semblance of order, and an alliance of the lesser high captains, particularly Baram and Taerl, neither of whom have been fond of Ship Rethnor."

"I'm sure that Kurth is as pleased as I am that Baram and Taerl have revealed such anger at Suljack, poor Suljack," Kensidan remarked.

"You've been saying you intended to profit from the chaos," Arabeth replied with obvious admiration. "I didn't know that you meant to control that chaos."

"If I did control it, it wouldn't truly be chaos, now would it?"

"Herd it, then, if not control it."

"I would be a sorry high captain if I didn't work to ensure that the situation would lean in favor of my Ship."

Arabeth assumed a pose that was as much one of seduction as of petulance, with one hand on a hip thrust forward and a wicked little grin on her face. "But you are not a high captain," she said.

"Yes," Kensidan replied, seeming distant and unmoved. "Let us make sure that everyone understands the truth of that statement. I'm just the son of Ship Rethnor."

Arabeth stepped forward and knelt on the chair, straddling Kensidan's legs. She put a hand on each of his shoulders and drove him back under her weight as she pressed forward.

"You're going to rule Luskan even as you pretend that you don't," she whispered, and Kensidan didn't respond, though his expression certainly didn't disagree. "Kensidan the Pirate King."

"You find that alluring," he started to say, until Arabeth buried him in a passionate kiss.

CHAPTER
BECOMING ONE
23

He stood against the snow.

It was not a gentle tumble of flakes, as with the previous storm, but a wind-whipped blizzard of stinging ice and bitter cold.

He didn't fight it. He accepted it. He took it into himself, into his very being, as if becoming one with the brutal surroundings. His muscles tensed and clenched, forcing blood into whitened limbs. He squinted, but refused to shut his eyes against the blow, refused to turn any of his senses off to the truth of Icewind Dale and the deadly elements—deadly to strangers, to foreigners, to weak southerners, to those who could not become one with the tundra, one with the frozen north wind.

He had defeated the spring, the muddy melt, when a man could disappear into a bog without a trace.

He had defeated the summer, the gentlest weather, but the time when the beasts of Icewind Dale came out in force, seeking food—and human flesh was a delicacy to most—to feed their young.

His defeat of autumn neared completion, with the first cold winds and first brutal blizzards. He had survived the brown bears, seeking to fatten their bellies before settling into their caves. He had survived the goblins, orcs, and orogs that challenged him for the meager pickings on the last hunt of the caribou.

And he would defeat the blizzard, the wind that could freeze a man's blood solid in his limbs.

But not this man. His heritage wouldn't allow it. His strength and determination wouldn't allow it. Like his father's father's father's father before him, he was of Icewind Dale.

He didn't fight the northwestern wind. He didn't deny the ice and the snow. He took them in as a part of himself, for he was greater than a man. He was a son of the tundra.

For hours he stood unmoving on a high rock, muscles braced against the wind, snow piling around his feet, then his ankles, then his long legs. The whole world became a dreamlike haze as ice covered his eyes. His hair and beard glistened with icicles, his heavy breath filled the air before him with fog, the cloud fast smashed apart by the driving pellets of ice and snow.

When he at last moved, even the howl of the wind could not muffle the sound of crunching and cracking. A deep, deep breath broke him free of the frozen natural shirt of ice, and he extended his arms out to his sides, hands clenching powerfully as if he were grasping and crushing the storm around him.

He threw his head back, staring up into the gray ceiling of heavy clouds, and let out a long, low roar, a primal grumble that came from his belly and denied Icewind Dale its prize.

He was alive. He had beaten the storm. He had beaten three seasons and knew that he was ready for the fourth and most trying.

Though piled to his thighs, the snow slowed him hardly at all as his powerful muscles drove him along. He stalked down the trails of the rocky hill, stepping sure-footed across patches bare of snow but thick with ice, and pounding right through the drifts, some taller than his nearly seven foot frame, as easily as a sword slashing a sheet of dried old parchment.

He came to the ledge above the entrance to a cave he had entered once, long, long ago. He knew it was inhabited again, for he had seen goblins, and the greater beast they named as their chieftain.

But still the cave was to be his winter home.

He dropped down lightly to a large stone that had been placed to partially cover the entrance. A dozen creatures with levers had moved it into place, but he alone, using nothing but his muscles—muscles made hard by the wind and the cold—braced himself and easily shoved the rock aside.

A pair of goblins began to whoop and holler at the intrusion, their cries of warning turning fast to terror as the icy giant stepped into their doorway, blocking the meager daylight.

Like a beast out of nightmares, he strode in, slapping aside their small and insignificant spears. He caught one goblin by the face and easily hoisted it from the ground with one arm. He shook it violently, all the while fending off the pathetic stabs of its companion, and when it at last stopped resisting, he smashed it hard into the wall of rock.

The second creature squealed and fled, but he threw the first into it, taking it down in a heap.

He stalked past, crushing the life out of the second goblin with a single heavy stomp to the back of its skinny neck.

Several of the creatures, females, too, presented themselves in the next room, some cowering, but they would find no mercy from the giant. A trio of small spears flew at him, only one connecting, striking him right in the chest, right in the thick of the curious gray fur cape he wore. The spear hit bone—the skull of the creature from which the cape had been fashioned, an unrecognizable thing under a layer of ice and snow. The spear had not the weight, nor the weight behind the throw, to penetrate, and it hung there, stuck in the folds and slowing the enraged giant not at all.

He caught a goblin in his huge hand, lifted it easily, and flung it across the chamber. It smashed into stone and fell still.

Others tried to run away, and he caught one and threw it. Then another went flying. With their backs to the wall, a pair of goblins found courage and turned to meet him, thrusting their spears to fend him off.

The giant tugged the spear from his cape, brought it up and bit it mid-shaft, tearing it in two, and advanced. With his batons, he slapped aside the spears, furiously, wildly, with speed and agility that seemed out of place in a man of his size and strength.

Again and again, he pushed the spears aside and closed, and he moved suddenly, swiftly, bashing the spears out wide and reversing his hands as he lurched forward, stabbing the batons into the chest of the respective goblins. He rolled his hands under and lifted the squealing creatures on the end of those batons, and slammed them together once and again, as one fell squirming and shrieking to the floor.

The other, stabbed by the sharp end of the spear, hung there in agony and the giant dropped it low and suddenly reversed, shoving it straight up as the spear slid deeper into its chest. He tossed the dying thing aside and stomped down on its fallen companion.

He stalked off in pursuit of the chieftain, the champion.

It was larger than he, a verbeeg, a true giant and not a man. It carried a heavy, spiked club and he held nothing in his hands.

But he didn't hesitate. He barreled right in, lowering his shoulder, accepting the hit of the club with the confidence that his charge would steal the energy from the swing.

His powerful legs drove on with fury, with the rage of the storm, the strength of Icewind Dale. He drove the verbeeg backward several strides and only the wall stopped his progress.

The spiked club fell aside and the verbeeg began slamming him with its mighty fists. One blew the air from his lungs, but he ignored the pain as he had ignored the bite of the cold wind.

The man leaped back and straightened, his balled fists exploding upward before him, slamming the verbeeg hard and breaking the grapple.

Giant and man reset immediately and crashed together like rutting caribou. The crack of bone against bone echoed through the cave and the few goblins who stayed around to watch, perplexed by the titanic battle, gasped to realize that had any of them been caught between those crashing behemoths, it would surely have been crushed to death.

Chins on shoulders, giant and man each clasped the other around the back and pressed with all his might. No punches or kicks mattered anymore. It was no contest of agility, but of sheer strength. And in that, the goblins took heart, and believed that their verbeeg leader could not be beaten.

Indeed, the giant, two feet taller, hundreds of pounds heavier, seemed to gain an advantage, and the man started to bend under the press, his legs began to tremble.

On the giant pushed, the timbre of its growl going from determination to victory as the mighty man bent.

But he was of the tundra, he was Icewind Dale. By birth and

by heritage, he was Icewind Dale—indomitable, indefatigable, timeless, and unbending. His legs locked, as sturdy as young oaks, and the verbeeg could press no more.

"I . . . am . . . the . . . son . . . of . . ." he began, driving the giant back to even, and after a grunt and a renewed push that had him gaining more ground, he finished, ". . . Icewind . . . Dale!"

He roared and drove on. "I am the son of Icewind Dale!" he cried, and roared and roared and forced his arms downward, bending the stubborn verbeeg to a more upright, less powerful stance.

"I am the son of Icewind Dale!" he yelled again, and the goblins yelped and fled, and the verbeeg groaned.

He growled and pushed on with more fury and stunning strength. He bent the verbeeg awkwardly and it tried to twist away, but he had it and he pressed relentlessly. Bones started to crack.

"I am the son of Icewind Dale!" he cried, and his legs churned as he twisted and bent the giant. He had it down to its knees, bending it backward, shoulders leaning. A sudden and violent thrust and roar ended the resistance, shattering the verbeeg's spine.

Still the man drove on. "I am the son of Icewind Dale!" he proclaimed again.

He stepped back and grabbed the groaning, dying giant by the throat and the crotch and lifted it above him as he stood, as easily as if it weighed no more than one of its goblin minions.

"I am the son of Beornegar!" the victor cried, and he threw the verbeeg against the wall.

CHAPTER 24
AN ADVISOR NO MORE

"You're keeping Suljack alive?" old Rethnor asked Kensidan as they walked together along the decorated halls of the palace of Ship Rethnor.

"I gave him the dwarf," Kensidan replied. "I was beginning to find the little beast annoying anyway. He was starting to speak in rhymes—something his former master warned me about."

"*Former* master?" the old man said with a wry grin.

"Yes, father, I agree," the Crow replied with a self-deprecating chuckle. "I trust them only because I know that our best interests converge and lead us to the same place."

Rethnor nodded.

"But I cannot allow Baram and Taerl to kill Suljack—and I believe they want to do that very thing after seeing him on the dais with Deudermont."

"Sitting behind Deudermont has angered them so?"

"No, but it has presented the two with an opportunity they shan't pass up," Kensidan explained. "Kurth has bottled up his forces on Closeguard Island, riding out the storm. I've no doubt that he is instigating many of the fights on the mainland, but he wants the corpse of Luskan a bit more dead before he swoops upon her like a hungry vulture. Baram and Taerl believe that I'm wounded at present, because I was so strongly in Deudermont's court, and also, of course, because there has been no formal transition of power from you to me. To their thinking, the destruction of the Hosttower caused such devastation across the city that even my own followers are reeling and unsure, and so won't follow my commands into battle."

"Now why would Baram and Taerl think such a thing about the loyal footsoldiers of Ship Rethnor?" the high captain asked.

"Why indeed?" replied the coy Kensidan, and Rethnor nodded again, smiling widely, the grin revealing that he thought his son played it perfectly.

"So you and Kurth have closed up," Rethnor said. "You didn't even appear at Deudermont's inauguration. Any gains to be made on the street by the other three lesser high captains have to be made now, and quickly, before either of you two, or Deudermont, comes out and crushes it all. Just to add a bit of fire to that smokepowder, you put Suljack on the stage with Deudermont, all the excuse that Taerl and Baram need."

"Something like that, yes."

"But don't let them get to him," Rethnor warned. "You'll be needing Suljack before this mess has ended. He's a fool, but a useful one."

"The dwarf will keep him safe. For now."

They came to the intersection of hallways leading to their respective rooms then, and parted ways, but not before Rethnor leaned over and kissed Kensidan on the forehead, a sign of great respect.

The old man shuffled down the corridor and through his bedroom door. "My son," he whispered, full of contentment.

He knew then, without doubt, that he had chosen right in turning Ship Rethnor over to Kensidan, instead of his other son, Bronwin, who was hardly ever in the city of late. Bronwin had been a disappointment to Rethnor, for he never seemed to be able to look beyond his most immediate needs, for treasure or for women, nor did he show any capacity for patience in satiating his many hungers. But Kensidan, the one they called the Crow, had more than made up for Bronwin's failings. Kensidan was every bit as cunning as his father, indeed, and probably even more so.

Rethnor lay down with that thought in mind, and it was a good last thought.

For he never awakened.

* * * * *

He hustled her along the rain-soaked dark streets, taking great pains to keep the large cloak wrapped about her. He constantly glanced around—left, right, behind them—and more than once put a hand to the dagger at his belt.

Lightning split the sky and revealed many other people out in the torrent, huddled in alleyways and under awnings, or, pathetically, in the jamb of a doorway, as if trying to draw comfort out of mere proximity to a house.

The couple finally got to the dock section, leaving the houses behind, but that was even more dangerous terrain, Morik knew, for though fewer potential assailants watched their passage, so too did fewer potential witnesses.

"He went out—all the boats went out to moor so they wouldn't get cracked against the wharves," Bellany said to him, her voice muffled by the wet cloak. "Stupid plan."

"He didn't, and he wouldn't," Morik replied. "He's my coin and I've his word."

"A pirate's word."

"An honorable man's word," Morik corrected, and he felt vindicated indeed when he and Bellany turned a corner of a rather large storehouse to see one ship still in tight against the docks, bucking the breakers that rolled in on the front of the gathering storm. One after another, those storms assaulted Luskan, a sure sign that the wind had changed and winter was soon to jump the Spine of the World and bring her fury to the City of Sails.

The couple hustled down to the wharves, resisting the urge to sprint in the open across the boardwalk. Morik kept them to the shadows until they reached the nearest point to *Thrice Lucky*'s berth.

They waited in the deep shadows of the inner harbor storehouses until another lightning strike creased the sky and lit the area, and they looked left and right. Seeing no one, Morik grabbed Bellany's arm and sprinted straight for the ship, feeling vulnerable indeed as he and his beloved ran along the open pier.

When they got to the boarding plank, they found Captain Maimun himself, lantern in hand, waiting for them.

"Be quick, then," he said. "We're out now, or we're riding it out against the dock."

Morik let Bellany lead the way up the narrow wooden ramp, and went with her onto the deck and into Maimun's personal quarters.

"A drink?" the captain asked, but Morik held up his hand, begging off.

"I haven't the time."

"You're not coming out to mooring with us?"

"Kensidan won't have it," Morik explained. "I don't know what's going on, but he's pulling us all into Ten Oaks this night."

"You'd trust your beautiful lady to a rogue like me?" Maimun asked. "Should I be offended?" As he spoke of her, both he and Maimun turned to Bellany, and she fit that description indeed at that moment. Bathed in the light of many candles, her black hair soaked, her skin sparkling with raindrops, there was no other way to describe the woman as she pulled herself out of her heavy woolen weathercloak.

She tossed her wet hair out of her face casually, a movement that had both men fully entranced, and looked to them curiously, surprised to see them staring at her.

"Is there a problem?" she asked, and Maimun and Morik both laughed, which only confused the woman even more.

Maimun motioned toward her with the bottle and Bellany eagerly nodded.

"It must be very difficult out there if you're willing to sit aboard a ship in a storm," Maimun remarked as he handed her a glass of whiskey.

Bellany drained it in a single gulp and handed the glass back for a refill.

"I'm not with Deudermont and won't be," Bellany explained as Maimun poured. "Arabeth Raurym won the fight with Valindra, and Arabeth is no matron of mine."

"And if a former inhabitant of the Hosttower of the Arcane is not with Deudermont, then she's surely dead," Morik added. "Some have found refuge with Kurth on Closeguard Island."

"Mostly those who worked closely with him over the years, and I hardly know the man," Bellany said.

"I thought Deudermont had granted amnesty to all who fought with Arklem Greeth?" Maimun asked.

"For what it's worth, he did," said Morik.

"And it's worth a lot to the many attendants and non-practitioners who came out of the rubble of the Hosttower," said Bellany. "But for we who wove spells under the direction of Arklem Greeth, who are seen as members of the Arcane Brotherhood and not just the Hosttower, there is no amnesty—not with the common Luskar, at least."

Maimun handed her back her refilled glass, which she sipped instead of gulping. "Order has broken down across the city," the young captain said. "This was the fear of many when Deudermont and Brambleberry's intent became apparent. Arklem Greeth was a beast, and it was precisely that inhumanity and viciousness that kept the five high captains, and their men below them, in line. When the city rallied to Deudermont that day in the square, even I came to think that maybe, just maybe, the noble captain was strong enough of character and reputation to pull it off."

"He's running out of time," said Morik. "You'll find the murdered in every alley."

"What of Rethnor?" Maimun asked. "You work for him."

"Not by choice," said Bellany, and Morik's scowl at her was quite revealing to the perceptive young pirate captain.

"I'm not for knowing what Rethnor intends," Morik admitted. "I do as I'm told to do, and don't poke my nose into places it doesn't belong."

"That's not the Morik I know and love," said Maimun.

"Truth be told," Bellany agreed.

But Morik continued to shake his head. "I know what Rethnor's got behind him, and knowing that, I'm smart enough to just do as I'm told to do."

A call from the deck informed them that the last lines were about to be cast off.

"And you were told to return to Ship Rethnor this night," Maimun reminded Morik, leading him to the door. The rogue paused long enough to give Bellany a kiss and a hug.

"Maimun will keep you safe," he promised her, and he looked at his friend, who nodded and held up his glass in response.

"And you?" Bellany replied. "Why don't you just stay out here?"

"Because then Maimun couldn't keep any of us safe," Morik replied. "I'll be all right. If there's one thing I know as truth in all of this chaos, it's that Ship Rethnor will survive, however the fates weigh on Captain Deudermont."

He kissed her again, bundled up his cloak against the deepening storm, and rushed from *Thrice Lucky*. Morik waited at the docks just long enough to see the crew expertly push and row the ship far enough from the wharves to safely moor then he ran off into the rainy night. When he returned to Ship Rethnor Morik learned that the high captain had quietly passed away, and Kensidan the Crow was fully at the helm.

* * * * *

They entered from the continuing rain in a single and solemn line, moving through the entry rooms of Rethnor's palace to the large ballroom where the high captain lay in state.

All of the remaining four high captains attended, with Suljack the first to arrive, Kurth the last, and Baram and Taerl, tellingly, entering together.

Kensidan had assembled them, all four, in his private audience chamber when word arrived that the governor of Luskan had come to pay his respects.

"Bring him," Kensidan said to his attendant.

"He is not alone," the woman replied.

"Robillard?"

"And some others of *Sea Sprite*'s crew," the attendant explained.

Kensidan waved her away as if it didn't matter. "I tell you four now, before Deudermont joins us, that Ship Rethnor is mine. It was given to me before my father passed on, with all his blessings."

"Ye changing the name, are ye? Ship Crow?" Baram joked, but Kensidan stared at him hard and elicited a nervous cough.

"Any of you who think that perhaps Ship Rethnor is vulnerable now would be wise to think otherwise," Kensidan said, biting off the last word as the door opened and Governor Deudermont walked in, the ever-vigilant and ever-dangerous Robillard close behind. The others of *Sea Sprite* didn't enter, but were likely very close nearby.

"You have met Luskan's newest high captain?" Kurth asked him, motioning toward Kensidan.

"I didn't know it to be an inherited position," Deudermont said.

"It is," was Kensidan's curt response.

"So if the good Captain Deudermont passes on, I get Luskan then?" Robillard quipped, and he shrugged as Deudermont cast him an unappreciative look for the sentiment.

"Doubtin' that," said Baram.

"If you are to be the five high captains of Luskan, then so be it," said Deudermont. "I care not how you manage the titles as of now. What I care about is Luskan, and her people, and I expect the same from you all, as well."

The five men, unused to being spoken to in that manner and tone, all grew more attentive up, Baram and Taerl bristling openly.

"I ask for peace and calm, that the city can rebound from a trying struggle," said Deudermont.

"One yerself started, and who asked ye?" Baram replied.

"The people asked me," Deudermont retorted. "Your people among them—your people who marched with Lord Brambleberry and I to the gates of the Hosttower."

Baram had no answer.

But Suljack did, enthusiastically. "Aye, and Captain Deudermont's givin' us a chance to make Luskan the envy of the Sword Coast," he declared, surprising even Deudermont with his energy. But not surprising Kensidan, who had bid him to do that very thing, and not surprising Kurth, who offered a sly grin at Kensidan as the fool Suljack rambled on.

"My people are tiring and hurting bad," he said. "The war was tough on them, on us all, and now's the time for hoping for better and working together to get better. Know that Ship Suljack's with you, Governor, and we won't be fighting unless it's to save our own lives."

"My appreciation," Deudermont replied with a bow, his

expression showing as much suspicion as gratitude, which was not lost on the perceptive Kensidan.

"If you will pardon me, Governor, I'm here to bury my father, not to discuss politics," said Kensidan, and he motioned to the door.

With a bow, Deudermont and Robillard departed, joining some others of their crew who had been stationed right outside the door. Suljack went next, then Baram and Taerl together, as they had entered, both grumbling unhappily.

"This passing changes nothing," Kurth paused to remark to the Crow as he moved to leave. "Except that you have lost a valuable advisor." He gave a little knowing laugh and left the room.

"I'm not much liking that one," the dwarf behind Kensidan's chair remarked a moment later.

Kensidan shrugged. "Be quick to Suljack," he ordered. "Baram and Taerl will be even more angry with him after he so openly pledged with Deudermont."

"What o' Kurth?"

"He won't move against me. He sees where this is leading, and he awaits the destination."

"Ye sure?"

"Sure enough to tell you again to get to Suljack's side."

The dwarf gave an exaggerated sigh and thumped past the chair. "Getting a little tired o' being telled what to do," he mumbled under his breath, drawing a grin from Kensidan.

A few moments later, half the room where Kensidan sat alone darkened.

"You heard it all?" he stated as much as asked.

"Enough to know that you continue to put your friend in dire peril."

"And that displeases you?"

"It encourages us," said the voice of the unseen, the never-seen, speaker. "This is bigger than one alliance, of course."

"The dwarf will protect him," Kensidan replied, just to show that maybe it wasn't bigger than his alliance with Suljack.

"Don't doubt that," the voice assured him. "Half of Luskan's garrison would be killed trying to get past that one."

"And if more than that come, and Suljack is killed?" Kensidan asked.

"Then he will be dead. That is not the question. The question is what will Kensidan then do if his ally is lost?"

"I have many inroads to Suljack's followers," the head of Ship Rethnor replied. "None of them will form allegiance to Baram or Taerl, nor will I let them forgive those two for killing Suljack."

"The fighting will continue, then? Beware, for Kurth understands the depth of your trickery here."

The dwarf walked back into the room at that moment, his eyes widening at the darkness, at the unexpected visitation by his true masters.

Kensidan watched him just long enough to gauge his reaction then answered, "The chaos is Deudermont's worst enemy. My city guards don't report to their posts, nor do many, many others. Deudermont can give great speeches and make wonderful promises, but he cannot control the streets. He cannot keep the peasants safe. But I can keep mine safe, and Kurth his, and so on."

Beside him, the dwarf laughed, though he bit it off when Kensidan turned to regard him. "True enough," the head of Ship Rethnor admitted. " 'Tis the trap of competitive humanity, you see. Few men are content if others have more to be content about."

"How long will you let it proceed?" asked the voice in the darkness.

Kensidan shrugged. "That is up to Deudermont."

"He's stubborn to the end."

"Good enough," Kensidan said with a shrug.

The dwarf laughed again as he moved behind the chair to retrieve his forgotten weathercloak.

"I hope you live up to your reputation," Kensidan said to him as he passed by again.

"Been looking for something to hit for a long time," the dwarf replied. "Might even have a rhyme or two ready for me first battle."

Someone in the darkness groaned, and the dwarf laughed even louder and all but skipped from the room.

CHAPTER

VISION OF THE PAST

25

"We soon have to turn to Ten-Towns," Drizzt informed Regis one morning.

They were out on the tundra, and had been for a tenday since their departure from Berkthgar and the Tribe of the Elk. They both knew they should have gone back to one of the towns with winter coming in so fast and hard. Prudence demanded such, for Icewind Dale winters were indeed deadly.

But they had stayed out, roaming from the Sea of Moving Ice to the south, and the foothills of the Spine of the World. They had encountered two other tribes, and had been greeted cordially, if not warmly, by both. Neither had any word of Wulfgar, however, and indeed had counted him dead.

"He's not out here," Regis said after a while. "He must have gone south, out of the dale."

Drizzt nodded, or tried to, but so unconvincing was he that his motion seemed more a head shake of denial.

"Wulfgar was too upset at the revelation, embarrassed even, and so he went right past Ten-Towns," Regis went on stubbornly. "When he lost his past, he lost his home, and so he could not bear to remain here."

"And he traveled past Luskan?"

"We don't know that Wulfgar avoided Luskan. He might have gone in—perhaps he signed on with a ship and is sailing the southern Sword Coast, out by Memnon or even Calimport. Wouldn't he be amused to see us huddled in a snowstorm looking for him?"

Drizzt shrugged. "It's possible," he admitted, but again, his tone and posture conveyed no confidence.

"Whatever happened, we've seen no sign that he's out here, alone or with anyone else," said Regis. "He left Icewind Dale. He walked right past Ten-Towns last spring and moved south through the dale—or maybe he's back in that little fiefdom, Auckney was its name, with Colson! Yes, that's . . ."

Drizzt held up his hand to stop the rambling halfling. He, they, had no idea what had happened to Wulfgar, or to Colson for that matter, since she had left the Silver Marches with him but was not with him when he entered Ten-Towns those years ago. Perhaps Regis was correct, but more likely, Berkthgar, who understood Icewind Dale and who knew the turmoil within Wulfgar, had deduced it correctly.

So many men had ventured out alone on the tundra, to simply disappear—into a bog, under the snow, into the belly of a monster. . . . Wulfgar wouldn't have been the first, surely, nor would he be the last.

"We make for Ten-Towns today," Drizzt informed the halfling.

The dark elf stared up at the heavy gray sky, and knew that yet another snow was fast approaching, and one that would be colder and more driven by the winds—one that could kill them.

Regis started to argue, but just nodded and gave a sigh. Wulfgar was lost to them.

The pair set out forlornly, Regis following closely in Drizzt's trail—which wasn't much of a path in the snow, since the drow verily ran atop it—across the flat, white emptiness. Many times even Drizzt, who knew Icewind Dale so well, had to pause for a long while to regain his bearings.

By midday, the snow had begun to fall, lightly at first, but it steadily worsened, along with the howl of the northwestern gale. The pair bundled their cloaks tighter and leaned forward, pressing on.

"We should find a cave!" Regis shouted, his voice tiny against the wind.

Drizzt turned back and nodded, but before he turned forward again, Regis gave a yelp of alarm.

In the blink of an eye, Drizzt whirled, scimitars in hand, just in time to see a huge spear descend through the storm and drive into the ground just a few feet in front of him. He jumped back and tried to spot the thrower, but found his eyes drawn instead to the quivering weapon stuck into the ground before him.

The head of a verbeeg was tied to it, dangling at the end of a leather strap at the back of the spear.

Drizzt moved to it, glancing all around, and up, expecting a volley of similar missiles at any moment.

The giant head rolled over the spear shaft with the gusts of wind, lolling back and forth, staring at Drizzt with empty, dead eyes. Its forehead was curiously scarred. Drizzt used Twinkle to brush aside its thick shock of hair to get a better look.

"Wulfgar," Regis muttered, and Drizzt turned to regard him. The halfling stared at the verbeeg's scarred forehead.

"Wulfgar?" Drizzt replied. "This is a verb—"

"The pattern," Regis said, pointing to the scar.

Drizzt examined it more closely, and sucked in his breath with anticipation. The scar, a brand, really, was jumbled and imperfect, but Drizzt could make out the overlapping symbols of three dwarf gods—the same etching that Bruenor had carved into the head of Aegis-fang! Wulfgar, or someone else holding Aegis-fang, had used that warhammer's head to brand that verbeeg.

Drizzt stood up straight and looked all around. In the storm, the thrower could not have been too far away, particularly if he wanted to be sure he didn't skewer either Drizzt or Regis.

"Wulfgar!" he yelled, and it echoed off the nearby stones, but died quickly under the muffling blanket of falling snow and howling wind.

"It was him!" Regis cried, and he, too, began shouting for their lost friend.

But no voice came back to them, save the echoes of their own.

Regis continued to shout for a while, until Drizzt, grinning knowingly, finally halted him.

"What?" the halfling asked.

"I know this place—I should have thought of this before."

"Thought of what?"

"A cave, not so far away," Drizzt explained. "A place where Wulfgar and I first fought side-by-side."

"Against verbeegs," Regis said, catching on as he looked back to the spear.

"Against verbeegs," Drizzt confirmed.

"Looks like you didn't kill them all."

"Come along," Drizzt bade him.

The drow found his bearings then called in Guenhwyvar and sent her off and running in search of the cave. Her roars led them through the mounting storm, and though the distance was not far, no more than a few hundred yards, it took the pair some time to at last come to the opening of a deep, dark cave. Drizzt moved just inside and spent a long while standing there staring into the deeper darkness, letting his eyes adjust. He replayed that long ago battle as he did, trying to remember the twists and turns of the tunnels of Biggrin's Lair.

He took Regis by the hand and started in, for the halfling couldn't see nearly as well as the drow in unlit caverns. At the first intersection, a turn down to their left, they saw that not all the caverns were unlit.

Drizzt motioned for Guenhwyvar to lead and for Regis to stay put, and drew his blades. He moved cautiously and silently, one slow, short step at a time. Ahead of him, Guenhwyvar reached the lit chamber, the fire within silhouetting her so clearly he saw her ears go up and her muscles relax as she trotted in, out of his view.

He picked up his pace, replacing his blades in their sheaths. At the chamber entrance, he had to squint against the bright flames.

He hardly recognized the man sitting on the far side of that fire, hardly recognized that it was a man at all at first, for with all the layers of furs, he surely could have passed for a giant himself.

Of course, such had often been said of Wulfgar, son of Beornegar.

Drizzt started in, but Regis rushed past him, crying, "Wulfgar!" with great joy.

The man managed a smile back through his thick blond beard at the exuberant halfling.

"We thought you were dead," Regis gushed.

"I was," Wulfgar answered. "Perhaps I still am, but I'm nearly back to life." He pulled himself up straight but didn't stand as Drizzt and Regis neared. The barbarian motioned to two furs he had set out for them to sit upon.

Regis looked curiously to Drizzt for some answers, and the drow, more versed in the way of the barbarians, seconded Wulfgar's motion and took his own seat opposite the man.

"I have beaten three of the seasons," Wulfgar explained. "But the most difficult now steps before me in challenge."

Regis started to question the curious wording, but Drizzt stopped him with an upraised hand, and led by example as they waited for Wulfgar to tell his tale.

"Colson is back with her mother in Auckney," Wulfgar began. "As it should be."

"And her father, the foolish lord?" Drizzt asked.

"His foolishness has been tempered by the companionship of a fine woman, it seems," Wulfgar answered.

"It must have pained you," Regis remarked, and Wulfgar nodded slightly.

"When I traveled from Auckney to the main north-south trail, I didn't know which way I would turn. I fear I have abandoned Bruenor, and that is no small thing."

"He fares well," Drizzt assured his friend. "He misses you dearly, but his kingdom is at peace."

"At peace, with a host of orcs outside his northern door?" said Wulfgar, and it was Drizzt's turn to nod.

"The peace will not hold, and Bruenor will know war again," Wulfgar predicted.

"It's possible," the drow replied. "But because he showed patience and tolerance, any outbreak of war by the orcs will be met by Mithral Hall and a host of mighty allies. Had Bruenor continued the war against Obould, he would have fought it alone, but now, should it come to blows. . . ."

"May the gods keep him, and all of you, safe," Wulfgar said. "But what brought you here?"

"We journeyed to Mirabar as emissaries of Bruenor," the drow explained.

"Since we were in your neighborhood...." Regis quipped, an assertion made funny by its ridiculousness—Mirabar was nowhere near Icewind Dale.

"We all wanted to know how you fared," Drizzt said.

"All?"

"We two, Bruenor, and Catti-brie." The drow paused to measure Wulfgar's expression, but to his relief saw no pain there. "She is well," he added, and Wulfgar smiled.

"Never did I doubt otherwise."

"Your father will return here soon to visit you," Regis assured the man. "Should he look for this cave?"

Wulfgar smiled at that. "Seek the banner of the elk," he replied.

"They think you dead," the halfling said.

"And so I was. But Tempus has been kind and has allowed me a rebirth in this place, his home."

He paused, and his crystal blue eyes, so much like the autumn sky of Icewind Dale, flashed. Regis started to say something, but Drizzt held him back.

"I made errors upon my return—too many," the barbarian said somberly a few heartbeats later. "Icewind Dale does not forgive, and does not often offer a second chance to correct a mistake. I had forgotten who I was and who my people were, and most of all, I had forgotten my home."

He paused and stared into the flames for what seemed like an hour. "Icewind Dale challenged me," he said quietly, as if speaking more to himself than to his friends. "Tempus dared me to remember who I was, and the price of failure would be—will be—my life.

"But I have won thus far," he said, looking up at the pair. "I survived the bears and hunters of the spring, the bottomless bogs of the summer, and the last frenzy of feeding in the autumn. I made this my home and painted it with the blood of the goblinkind and giantkin who lived here."

"We saw," Regis said dryly, but his smile was not infectious—not to Wulfgar at least.

"I will defeat the winter, my quest will be at an end, and I will return to the Tribe of the Elk. I remember now. I am again the son of Icewind Dale, the son of Beornegar."

"They will have you back," Drizzt stated.

Wulfgar paused for a long while, and finally nodded his agreement, though slowly. "My people will forgive me."

"You will claim leadership again?" Regis asked.

Wulfgar shook his head. "I will take a wife and have as many children as we can. I will hunt the caribou and kill the goblins. I will live as my father lived, and his father before him, as my children will live and their children after them. There is peace in that, Drizzt, and comfort and joy and endlessness."

"There are many handsome women among your kin," Drizzt said. "Who wouldn't be proud to be the wife of Wulfgar, son of Beornegar?"

Regis scrunched up his face as he regarded the drow after that curious comment, but when he looked over at Wulfgar, he saw that Drizzt's words had apparently been well-spoken.

"I would have married more than a year ago," Wulfgar said. "There is one . . ." His voice trailed off with a little laugh. "I was not worthy."

"Perhaps she is still available," Drizzt offered, and Wulfgar smiled again, and nodded.

"But they think you dead," Regis blurted, and Drizzt scowled at him.

"I was dead," Wulfgar said. "On the day I left, I had never truly returned. Berkthgar knew it. They all knew it. Icewind Dale does not forgive."

"You had to earn your way back to this life," said Drizzt.

"I am again the son of Beornegar."

"Of the Tribe of the Elk—after the winter," said Drizzt, and he offered a sincere nod and smile of understanding.

"And you will not forget your friends?" Regis asked, breaking the silent communication between Drizzt and Wulfgar, both turning to regard him. "Well?" he said stubbornly. "Is there no place in the life of the son of Beornegar for those who once knew him and loved him? Will you forget your friends?"

The halfling's warmth melted the ice from Wulfgar's face, and he grinned widely. "How could I ever?" he asked. "How could anyone forget Drizzt Do'Urden, and the dwarf king of Mithral Hall, who was as my father for all those years? How could I forget the woman who taught me how to love, and who showed me such sincerity and honesty?"

Drizzt squirmed a bit at that reminder that it was his relationship with Catti-brie that had driven Wulfgar from them. But there was no malice, no regret, in Wulfgar's eyes. Just calm nostalgia and peace—peace as Drizzt hadn't seen in him in many, many years.

"And who could ever forget Regis of Lonelywood?" Wulfgar asked.

The halfling nodded appreciatively. "I wish you would come home," he whispered.

"I am home, at long last," said Wulfgar.

Regis shook his head and wanted to argue, but no words escaped the lump in his throat.

"You will one day challenge for the leadership of your tribe," Drizzt said. "It's the way of Icewind Dale."

"I am old among them now," Wulfgar replied. "There are many young and strong men."

"Stronger than the son of Beornegar?" Drizzt said. "I think not."

Wulfgar nodded in silent appreciation.

"You will one day challenge, and will again lead the Tribe of the Elk," Drizzt predicted. "Berkthgar will serve you loyally, as you will serve him until that day arrives, until you are again comfortable among the people and among the dale. He knows that."

Wulfgar shrugged. "I have yet to defeat the winter," he said. "But I will return to them in the spring, after the first draw of light and dark. And they will accept me, as they tried to accept me when first I returned. From there, I don't know, but I do know, with confidence, that ever will you be welcome among my people, and we will rejoice at your visits."

"They were gracious to us even without you there," Drizzt assured him.

Wulfgar again stared into the fire for a long, long while, deep in thought. Then he rose and moved to the back of the chamber, returning with a thick piece of meat. "I share my meal with you this night," he said. "And give you my ear. Icewind Dale will not be angry at me for hearing of that which I left behind."

"A meal for a tale," Regis remarked.

"We will leave at dawn's first light," Drizzt assured Wulfgar, and that drew a startled expression from Regis. Wulfgar, though, nodded in gratitude.

"Then tell me of Mithral Hall," he said. "Of Bruenor and Catti-brie. Of Obould—he is dead now, I hope."

"Not remotely," said Regis.

Wulfgar laughed, skewered the meat, and began to slow roast it.

They spent many hours catching up on the last four years, with Drizzt and Regis doing most of the talking, Drizzt running the litany of events and Regis adding color to every incident. They told him of Bruenor's grudging acceptance of the Treaty of Garumn's Gorge, for the good of the region, and of Obould's fledgling and tentative kingdom. Wulfgar just shook his head in obvious disapproval. They told him of Catti-brie's new endeavors alongside Lady Alustriel, turning to the Art, and surprisingly, the barbarian seemed quite pleased with the news, though he did quip, "She should bear your children."

With much prodding, Wulfgar finally related his own adventures, the road with Colson that led to Auckney and his decision that her mother should raise her—and his insistence and relief that the foolish lord of Auckney went along with the decision.

"She is better off by far," he said. "Her blood is not the blood of Icewind Dale, and here she would not have thrived."

Regis and Drizzt exchanged knowing looks, recognizing the open wound in Wulfgar's heart.

Regis was fast to change the subject at Wulfgar's next pause, telling of Deudermont's war in Luskan, of the fall of the Hosttower and the devastation that was general throughout the City of Sails.

"I fear that he moved too boldly, too swiftly," Drizzt remarked.

"But he is beloved," Regis argued, and a brief discussion and debate ensued about whether or not their friend had done the right thing. It was brief, because both quickly realized that Wulfgar cared little for the fate of Luskan. He sat there, his expression distant, rubbing his hands along the thick, sleek fur of Guenhwyvar, who lay beside him.

So Drizzt turned the discussion to times long past, to the first time he and Wulfgar had come to the verbeegs' lair, and to their walks up Bruenor's Climb on Kelvin's Cairn. They replayed their adventures, those long and trying roads they had walked and sailed, the many fights, the many pleasures. They were still talking, though the conversation slowed as the fire burned low, when Regis fell fast asleep, right there on a little fur rug on the stone floor.

He awoke to find Drizzt and Wulfgar already up, sharing breakfast.

"Eat quickly," Drizzt said to him. "The storm has subsided and we must be on our way."

Regis did so, silently, and a short while later, the three said their good-byes at the edge of Wulfgar's temporary home.

Wulfgar and Drizzt clasped hands firmly, eyes locking in deep and mutual respect. They fell into a tight hug, a bond that would last forever, then broke apart, Drizzt turning for the brightness outside. Wulfgar slapped Guenhwyvar on the rump as she trotted by.

"Here," Regis said to him, and held out a piece of scrimshaw he'd been working for some time.

Wulfgar took it carefully and lifted it up before his eyes, his smile widening as he recognized it as a carving of the Companions of the Hall: Wulfgar and Drizzt, Cattie-brie and Bruenor, Regis and Guenhwyvar, side-by-side, shoulder-to-shoulder. He chuckled at the likeness of Aegis-fang in his miniature's hand, at the sculpture of Bruenor's axe and Catti-brie's bow—a bow carried by Drizzt, he noted as he examined the scrimshaw.

"I will keep it against my heart and in my heart for the rest of my days," the barbarian promised.

Regis shrugged, embarrassed. "If you lose the piece," he offered, "well, if it's in your heart then you never can."

"Never," Wulfgar agreed, and he lifted Regis in a crushing hug.

"You will find your way back to Icewind Dale," he said in the halfling's ear. "I will surprise you on the banks of Maer Dualdon. Perhaps I will even take the moment to bait your hook."

The sun, meager though it was, seemed all the brighter to Regis and Drizzt that morning, as it reflected off the brilliant whiteness of new-fallen snow, glistening in their moist eyes.

PART 4

PRINCIPLES AND PRAGMATISM

PRINCIPLES

AND PRAGMATISM

They are two men I love dearly, two men I truly respect, and as such, I'm amazed when I step back and consider the opposite directions of the roads of Wulfgar and Deudermont. Indeed, they are both true warriors, yet they have chosen different foes to battle.

Deudermont's road, I think, was wrought of frustration. He has spent more than two decades sailing the Sword Coast in pursuit of pirates, and no person in the memories of old elves has ever been so successful at such a dangerous trade. All honors were bestowed upon *Sea Sprite* when she put in to any of the major cities, particularly the all-important Waterdeep. Captain Deudermont dined with lords, and could have taken that title at his whim, bestowed by the grateful noblemen of Waterdeep for his tireless and effective service.

But for all that, it was upon learning the truth of the newest pirate advances, that the Hosttower of the Arcane supported them with magic and coin, that Captain Deudermont had to face the futility of his lifelong quest. The pirates would outlive him, or at least, they would not soon run out of successors.

Thus was Deudermont faced with an untenable situation and a lofty challenge indeed. He didn't shy, he didn't sway, but rather took his ship straight to the source to face this greater foe.

His reaction to a more terrible and wider world was to fight for control of that which seemed uncontrollable. And with such courage and allies, he may actually succeed, for the specter of the Hosttower of the Arcane is no more, Arklem Greeth is no more, and the people of Luskan have rallied to Deudermont's noble cause.

How different has been Wulfgar's path. Where Deudermont turned outward to seek greater allies and greater victories, Wulfgar turned inward, and returned his thoughts to a time and place more simple and straightforward. A time and place no less harsh or dangerous, to be sure, but one of clear definition, and one where a victory does not mean a stalemate with a horde of orcs, or a political concession for the sake of expediency. In Wulfgar's world, in Icewind Dale, there is no compromise. There is perfection of effort, of body, of soul, or there is death. Indeed, even absent mistakes, even if perfection is achieved, Icewind Dale can take a man, any man, at a whim. Living there, I know, is the most humbling of experiences.

Still, I have no doubt that Wulfgar will defeat Icewind Dale's winter season. I have no doubt that upon his return to the Tribe of the Elk at the spring equinox, he will be greeted as family and friend, to be trusted. I have no doubt that Wulfgar will one day again be crowned as chief of his tribe, and that, should a terrible enemy rise up in the dale, he will stand forward, with all the inspired tribes gratefully at his back, cheering for the son of Beornegar.

His legend is secured, but hardly fully written.

So one of my friends battles a lich and an army of pirates and sorcerers, while the other battles inner demons and seeks definition of a scattered and unique existence. And there, I think, rests the most profound difference in their respective roads. For Deudermont is secure in his time and place, and reaches from solid foundation to greater endeavors. He is confident and comfortable with, above all others, Deudermont. He knows his pleasures and comforts, and knows, too, his enemies within and without. Because he understands his limitations, so he can find the allies to help him step beyond them. He is, in spirit, that which Wulfgar will become, for only after one has understanding and acceptance of the self can one truly affect the external.

I have looked into the eyes of Wulfgar, into the eyes of the son of Beornegar, into the eyes of the son of Icewind Dale.

I fear for him no longer—not in body, not in soul.

And yet, even though Wulfgar seeks as a goal to be where Deudermont already resides, it's Deudermont for whom I now fear. He steps with confidence and so he steps boldly, but in Menzoberranzan we had a saying, *"Noet z'hin lil'avinsin."*

"Boldly stride the doomed."

—Drizzt Do'Urden

CHAPTER 26

LUSKAN'S LONG WINTER NIGHT

The man walked down the alley, glancing left and right. He knew he was right to be careful, for the cargo he would soon carry was among the most precious of commodities in Luskan that harsh winter.

He moved to a spot on the wall, one that seemed unremarkable, and knocked in a specific manner, three short raps, a pause, two short raps, a pause, and a final heavy thud.

The boards of the house parted, revealing a cleverly concealed window.

"Yeah?" asked the grumpy old man within. "Who ye for?"

"Seven," the man replied, and he handed over a note sealed with the mark of Ship Rethnor, cupping it around seven small chips, like those often used as substitutions for gold and silver in gambling games along the docks. Those too bore Ship Rethnor's mark.

"Seven, ye say?" replied the old man inside. "But I'm knowin' ye, Feercus Oduuna, and knowin' that ye got no wife and no brats, no brothers and naught but the one sister. That adds to two, if me brain's not gone too feeble."

"Seven chips," Feercus argued.

"Five bought, pocket-picked, or taken from a dead man?"

"If bought, then what's the harm?" Feercus argued. "I'm not stealing from my brothers of Ship Rethnor, nor killing them to take their chips!"

"So ye admit ye bought 'em?"

Feercus shook his head.

"Kensidan's not looking kindly on any black marketeering here, I'm telling ye for yer own sake."

"I offered to retrieve the goods for five others," Feercus explained. "Me sister and me, and Darvus's family, with no living man to come and no child old enough to trust to do it."

"Ah, and what might ye be getting from Missus Darvus in exchange for yer helpfulness?" the old codger asked.

Feercus flashed a lewd smile.

"More than that, if I'm knowin' Feercus— and I am," the old man said. "Ye're taking part o' the bargain in flesh, I'm not doubting, but ye're getting a fill for yer pocket, too. How much?"

"Has Kensidan outlawed that as well?"

"Nay."

"Then . . ."

"How much?" the old man insisted. "And I'll be asking Darvus's widow, and I'm knowin' her well, so ye best be tellin' me true."

Feercus glanced around again then sighed and admitted, "Four silver."

"Two for me," said the old man, holding out his hand. When Feercus didn't immediately hand over the coins, he wagged his fingers impatiently. "Two, or ye're not eating."

With a grumbled curse under his breath, Feercus handed over the coins. The old man retreated into the storehouse, and Feercus watched as he put seven small bags into a single sack, then returned and handed them out the window.

Again Feercus glanced around.

"Someone follow ye here?" the old man asked.

Feercus shrugged. "Lots of eyes. Baram or Taerl's men, I expect, as they're not eating so well."

"Kensidan's got guards all about the Ship," the old man assured him. "Baram and Taerl wouldn't dare to move against him, and Kurth's been paid off with food. Likely them eyes ye're seeing are the watching guards—and don't ye doubt that they'll not be friends o' Feercus, if Feercus is stealing or murdering them who're under the protection of Kensidan!"

Feercus held up the sack. "For widow Darvus," he said, and

slung it over his shoulder as he started away. He hadn't gone more than a step when the window's shutter banged closed, showing no more than an unremarkable wall once more.

Gradually, Feercus managed to take his thoughts off the watching eyes he knew to be peering out from every alley and window, and from many of the rooftops, as well. He thought of his cargo, and liked the weight of it. Widow Darvus had promised him that she had some spices to take the tanginess out of the curious meat Kensidan handed out to all under his protection—and many more had come under his protection, swearing fealty to Ship Rethnor, throughout that cold and threadbare winter. Between that and the strange, thick mushrooms, Feercus Oduuna expected a wonderful meal that evening.

He promised himself that he wouldn't get too greedy and eat it all, and that his sister, all alone in her house since her husband and two children had died in the explosion of the Hosttower, would get more than her one-seventh share.

He glanced back once as he exited the alley, whispering his sincere thanks for the generosity of High Captain Kensidan.

* * * * *

In another part of Luskan, not far from the road Feercus traveled, several men stood on a street corner, a fire blazing between them over which they huddled for warmth. One man's stomach growled from emptiness and another punched him in the shoulder for the painful reminder.

"Ah, keep it quiet," he said.

"And how am I to stop it?" the man with the grumbling belly replied. "The rat I ate last night didn't go near to filling me, and I been throwin' up more of it than I put down!"

"All our bellies're grumbling," a third man said.

"Baram's got food coming out tonight, so he says," a fourth piped in hopefully.

"Won't be near enough," said the first, who punched the other's shoulder again. "Never near enough. I ain't been so hungry in all my days, not even when out on the water, days and days in a dead wind."

"A pity we're not for eating man flesh," the third said with a pathetic chuckle. "Lots o' fat bodies out on Cutlass Island, eh?"

"A pity we're not working for Rethnor, ye mean," said the first, and the others all snapped surprised glances his way. Such words could get a man killed in short order.

"Ain't even Rethnor—Rethnor's dead, so they're saying," said another.

"Aye, it's that boy o' his, the sneaky one they call the Crow," said the first. "He's gettin' food. Not knowing how, but he's gettin' it and feedin' his boys well this winter. I'm thinking that Baram'd be smart to stop arguing with him and start gettin' us some of that food!"

"And I'm thinking ye're talkin'll of us dead in an alley," one of the others said in a tone that offered no room for argument. As much a threat as a warning, the harsh comment ended the discussion abruptly and the group went back to rubbing their hands, saying nothing, but with their bellies doing enough complaining to aptly relay their foul sentiments.

* * * * *

The mood in the Cutlass was fine that night—a small gathering, but of men who had eaten well and who had fed their families properly, and all thanks to the generosity of the son of Rethnor.

Behind the bar, Arumn Gardpeck noticed a couple of new faces that night, as he was now seeing quite regularly. He nudged his friend and most reliable customer, Josi Puddles, and nodded his chin toward the new pair who sat in a corner.

"I'm not liking it," Josi slurred after glancing that way. "It's our tavern."

"More patrons, more coin," Arumn replied.

"More trouble, you mean," said Josi, and as if on cue, Kensidan's dwarf walked in and moved right up to Arumn.

The dwarf followed their gazes to the corner then said to Arumn, "From the avenue called Setting Sun," he said.

"Taerl's men, then," Josi replied.

"Or Kensidan's now, eh?" Arumn said to the dwarf, sliding the usual brew his way.

The dwarf nodded, his eyes never leaving the two men as he brought the flagon to his lips and drained it in a single draw, ale spilling out over his black, beaded beard. He stayed there for some time, staring and hardly listening to the continuing conversation between Josi and Arumn. Every so often, he motioned for another ale, which Arumn, who was eating quite well thanks to the generosity of Kensidan, was happy to supply.

Finally the two men departed and the dwarf drained one last flagon and followed them out into the street. He wasn't far behind when he exited, despite pausing for his last drink, because the pair had to pause as well to retrieve their weapons as they left. On Kensidan's command, weapons weren't allowed inside Arumn's establishment. That rule didn't apply to Kensidan's personal bodyguard of course, and so the dwarf had not been similarly slowed.

He made no effort to conceal the fact that he was following the pair, one of whom stupidly glanced back several times. The dwarf thought they would confront him out in the street, with so many witnesses around, but to his surprise and delight, the pair slipped down a dark and narrow alleyway instead.

Grinning, he eagerly followed.

"Far enough," said a voice from the darkness beyond. Following the sound, the dwarf made out a single silhouette standing by a pile of refuse. "I'm not liking yer staring, black-beard, and liking yer following even less."

"Ye're for calling Captain Taerl's guards on me, I'm guessing," the dwarf replied, and he saw the man shift uncomfortably at the reminder that he was not on his home turf.

"H-here on—on Rethnor's invitation," the man stammered.

"Here to eat, ye mean."

"Aye, as invited."

"Nay, friend," the dwarf said. "Rethnor's welcoming them looking for a Ship to crew, not them looking to come in, eat, and go home to tell th' other high captains. Ye're a man o' Taerl, and good enough for ye."

"Switching," the man blurted.

"Bwahahaha," the dwarf taunted. "Ye been here five times now, yerself and yer hiding friend. And five times ye been on the road back home. A lot o' yer boys, too. Ye think we're for feeding ye, do ye?"

"I-I'm paying well," the man stammered.

"For what's not for sale," said the dwarf.

"If they're for selling, then it's for sale," said the man, but the dwarf crossed his burly arms over his chest and shook his head slowly.

From the roof to the dwarf's left came the man's companion, leaping down from on high, dagger thrust before him as if he thought himself a human spear. He apparently figured that he had the dwarf by surprise, an easy kill.

So did his friend, down the alley, who started a whoop of victory, one that ended abruptly as the dwarf exploded into motion, throwing his arms forward and over his head and springing a backward somersault. As he went over, he deftly pulled out his twin morningstars, and he landed solidly on the balls of his feet, leaning forward so that he easily reversed his momentum and plowed forward.

With surprising agility, the diving man managed to adjust to his complete miss and tuck into a fairly nimble roll that brought him right back to his feet. He spun, slashing with his dagger to keep the dwarf at bay.

The spiked head of a morningstar met that extended hand, and if the blow wasn't enough to shatter it, a coating on the ball exploded with magical power. The dagger, a misshapen and twisted thing, flew away, along with three fingers.

The man howled in agony and punched out with other hand as he brought the wounded one in close.

But again the dwarf was way ahead of him. As his first, right-hand morningstar swiped across to take the knife, his left arm went over his head, his second weapon spinning the same way as the first. Executing the block easily, the dwarf stepped forward and down. The punch went over his head as his second morningstar whipped around, the spiked head reaching out at the end of its black chain to take the man on the side of the knee.

The crack of bone drowned out the squeal of pain and the man's leg buckled and he flopped down to the ground.

His charging friend nearly tripped over him, but somehow held his balance, brandishing sword and dagger at the low-crouched dwarf. He thrust and slashed wildly, trying to overwhelm the dwarf with sheer ferocity.

And he almost got through the clever parries, but only because the dwarf was laughing too hard to more properly defend.

Frantic, trying hard to block out the pitiful crying of his broken friend, the man stabbed again, rushing forward.

He hit nothing, for the dwarf, in perfect balance, slipped out to the side.

"Ye're starting to try me patience," the dwarf warned. "Ye might be leaving with just a beating."

Too terrified to even comprehend that he had just been offered his life, the man spun and threw himself at the dwarf.

By the time the second morningstar ball smashed him on the side of his ribs, crunching them to dust, he realized his mistake. By the time that second ball smacked him again, in the head, he knew nothing at all.

His friend howled all the louder when the swordsman fell dead before him, his brains spilling out all over the cobblestones.

He was still howling when the dwarf grabbed him by the front of his shirt and with frightening strength stood him upright and smashed him against the wall.

"Ye're not listening to me, boy," the dwarf said several times, until the man finally shut up.

"Now ye get back to Setting Sun and ye tell Taerl's boys that this ain't yer place," said the dwarf. "If ye're with Taerl then ye ain't with Rethnor, and if ye ain't with Rethnor, then go and catch yerself some rats to eat."

The man gasped for breath.

"Ye hear me?" the dwarf asked, giving him a rough shake, and though it was with just one hand, the man couldn't have any more resisted it than he could the pull of a strong horse.

He nodded stupidly and the dwarf flung him down to the ground. "Crawl out o' here, boy. And if ye're meaning to crawl back, then do it with a pledge to Ship Rethnor."

The man replied, "Yes, yes, yes, yes . . ." over and over again as the dwarf calmly walked out of the alleyway, tucking his twin morningstars diagonally into their respective sheaths on his back as he went, and seeming as if nothing at all had just happened.

*****

"You don't have to enjoy it so much," Kensidan said to the dwarf a short while later.

"Then pay me more."

Kensidan gave a little laugh. "I told you not to kill anyone."

"And I telled yerself that if they're drawing steel, I'm drawing blood," the dwarf replied.

Kensidan continued to chuckle and waved his hand in concession.

"They're getting' desperate," the dwarf said. "Not enough food in most quarters for Baram and Taerl."

"Good. I wonder how fondly they look upon Captain Deudermont now?"

"Governor, ye mean."

Kensidan rolled his eyes.

"Yer friend Suljack's getting more than them other two," said the dwarf. "If ye was to send him a bit o' ours on top o' what he's getting from Deudermont, he might be climbing up behind yerself and Kurth."

"Very astute," Kensidan congratulated.

"Been playing politics since afore yer daddy's daddy found his first breath," the dwarf replied.

"Then I would think you smart enough to understand that it's not in my interest to prop Suljack to new and greater heights."

The dwarf looked at Kensidan curiously for just a moment, then nodded. "Ye're making him Deudermont's stooge."

Kensidan nodded.

"But he's to take it to heart," the dwarf warned.

"My father has spent years protecting him, often from himself," said Kensidan. "It's past time for Suljack to prove he's worthy of our efforts. If he can't understand his true role beside Deudermont, then he's beyond my aid."

"Ye could tell him."

"And I would likely be telling Baram and Taerl. I don't think that's a good thing."

"How hard're ye meaning to press them?" the dwarf asked.

"Deudermont's still formidable, and if they're throwing in with him . . ."

"Baram hates Deudermont to his soul," Kensidan assured the dwarf. "I count on you to gauge the level of discontent on the streets. We want to steal some of their men, but only enough to make sure that those two will understand their place when the arrows start flying. It's not in my interest to weaken them to anarchy, or to chase them to Deudermont's side for fear of their lives."

The dwarf nodded.

"And no more killing," Kensidan said. "Run the intruders out, show them a way to more and better food. Break a few noses. But no more killing."

The dwarf put his hands on his hips, thoroughly flustered by the painful command.

"You will have all the fighting you desire and more when Deudermont makes his move," Kensidan promised.

"Ain't no more fightin' than I'm desiring."

"The spring, early on," Kensidan replied. "We keep Luskan alive through the winter, but just barely. When the ships and the caravans don't arrive in the early spring, the city will disintegrate around the good capt—*governor*. His promises will ring as hollow as the bellies of his minions. He will be seen not as savior, but as a fraud, a flame without heat on a cold winter's eve."

And so it went through Luskan's long winter night. Supplies reached out from Ship Rethnor to Closeguard Island and Kurth, to Suljack and even a bit to Deudermont's new palace, fashioned from the former Red Dragon Inn, north of the river. From Deudermont, what little he had to spare, supplies went out to the two high captains in dire need, though never enough, of course, and to the Mirabarrans holed up in the Shield. And as the winter deepened, Suljack, prodded by Kensidan, came to spend more and more time by Deudermont's side.

The many ships riding out the winter in port got their food from Kurth, as Kensidan ceded to him control of the quay.

The coldest months passed, and were not kind to battered Luskan, and the people looked with weary eyes and grumbling bellies to the lengthening days, too weary and too hungry to truly hope for reprieve.

* * * * *

"I won't do it," Maimun said, and Kurth's eyes widened with surprise.

"A dozen ships, heavily laden and hardly guarded," the high captain argued. "Could a pirate ask for more?"

"Luskan needs them," said Maimun. "Your people fared well throughout the winter, but the folk on the mainland. . . ."

"Your crew ate well."

Maimun sighed, for indeed Kurth had been kind to the men and women of *Thrice Lucky*.

"You mean to drive Deudermont from power," the perceptive young pirate captain said. "Luskan looks to the sea and to the south, praying for food, and grain to replant the fields. There is not enough livestock in the city to support a tenth of the people living here, though only half of what Luskan once was remains."

"Luskan is not a farming community."

"What, then?" Maimun asked, but he knew the answer well enough.

Kurth and Kensidan wanted a free port, a place of trade where no questions would ever be asked, where pirates could put in and answer only to other pirates, where highwaymen could fence jewels and hide kidnap victims until the ransom arrived. Something had happened over the winter, Maimun knew, some subtle shift. Before the onset of the northern winds, the two plotting high captains had been far more cautious in their approach. In their apparent plan, Deudermont would rule Luskan and they would find ways around him.

Now they seemed to want the town for their own, in full.

"I won't do it," the young pirate captain said again. "I cannot so punish Luskan, whatever the expected outcome."

Kurth looked at him hard, and for a moment, Maimun expected that he would have to fight his way out of the tower.

"You are far too full of presumptions and assumptions," Kurth said to him. "Deudermont has his Luskan, and it serves us well to keep him here."

Maimun knew the lie for what it was, but he didn't let on, of course.

"The food will arrive from Waterdeep's fleet, but it will come through Closeguard and not through Deudermont's palace," Kurth explained. "And the ground caravans belong to Kensidan, again not to Deudermont. The people of Luskan will be grateful. Deudermont will be grateful, if we're clever. I had thought you to be clever."

Maimun had no answer to the high captain's scenario. Maimun knew Deudermont as well as any who were not currently crewing *Sea Sprite*, and he doubted the captain would ever be so foolish as to think Kurth and Kensidan the saviors of Luskan. Stealing for the reward was the oldest and simplest of pirate tricks, after all:

"I offered *Thrice Lucky* the flagship role as a tribute," Kurth said. "An offer, not an order."

"Then I politely refuse."

Kurth nodded slowly and Maimun's hand slid down to his belted sword, with all expectation that he was about to be killed.

But the blow never came, and the young pirate captain left Closeguard Island a short while later, making all haste back to his ship.

Back in Kurth's chamber, a globe of darkness appeared in a far corner, signaling that the high captain was not alone.

"He would have been a big help," Kurth explained. "*Thrice Lucky* is swift enough to get inside the firing line of Waterdeep's fleet."

"The defeat of the Waterdhavian flotilla is well in hand," the voice from the darkness assured him. "For the right price, of course."

Kurth gave a sigh and rubbed his hand over his sharp features, considering the cost against the potential gain. He considered many times in those moments that Kensidan would certainly handle the land caravan, that Kensidan was walking ever more boldly and more powerfully in no small part because of the food those strangers in the darkness were providing.

"See to it," he agreed.

CHAPTER
CIVILIZATION'S MELT
27

"A tenday and a half," Regis complained as he and Drizzt made their way down the trail south of Bryn Shander.

"These storms can arrive anytime for the next two months," Drizzt replied. "Neither of us wants another two months in Ten-Towns." As he finished, he cast a sidelong glance at his companion to note the expected wistfulness in Regis's large eyes. It had not been a bad winter in Ten-Towns for the two of them, though the snow fell deep and the wind blew hard all those months. Still, strong too were the fires in the common rooms, and the many friendly conversations overwhelmed the wintry wind.

But as the winter waned, Drizzt had grown increasingly impatient. His business with Wulfgar was done, and he was satisfied that he would see his barbarian friend again, in better times.

He wanted to go home. His heart ached for Catti-brie, and though the situation had seemed stable, he couldn't help but fear for his friend Bruenor, living as he was under the shadow of twenty thousand orcs.

The drow ranger set a strong pace down the uneven trail, where mud had refrozen and melted many times over the past few days. Patches of snow had clung stubbornly to the ground, behind every rock and filling every crevice. It was indeed early to be making such a journey through the Spine of the World, but Drizzt knew that to wait was to walk through deeper and more stubborn mud.

Over the months, Icewind Dale had filled their sensibilities again, rekindling old memories and experiences, and bringing forth many of the lessons their years there had taught them. They wouldn't lose their way among familiar landmarks. They wouldn't be caught unaware by tundra yetis or bands of goblins.

As Regis had feared, they awoke the next morning to find the air filled with snow, but Drizzt didn't lead the way to a cave.

"It will not be a strong storm," he assured the halfling repeatedly as they trudged along, and through good instinct or simply good fortune, his prediction proved correct.

Within a few days, they had made the trail through the Spine of the World, and soon after they entered the pass, the wind diminished considerably and not even the long shadows of the tall mountains to either side of them could cover the signs that spring fast approached.

"Do you think we'll meet the Luskar caravan?" Regis asked more than once, for his belt pouches bulged with scrimshaw and he was eager to get first pickings from the Luskar goods.

"Too early," Drizzt always answered, but as they crossed the miles through the mountain range, every step bringing them closer to the warming breezes of spring, his tone became more hopeful with each response. After all, in addition to the welcome sound of new voices and the luxuries such a caravan might offer, a strong and early showing by Luskan in Icewind Dale would go a long way toward calming Drizzt's anxieties about the depth and endurance of Deudermont's victory.

As they neared the southern end of the mountain pass, the trail widened and broke off in several directions.

"To Auckney, and Colson," Drizzt explained to Regis as they crossed one trail climbing up to the west. "Two days of marching," he answered in response to the halfling's questioning gaze. "Two days there and two days back."

"Straight to Luskan, then, for some sales and some food for the road east," Regis replied. "Or is it possible that we might find a former Hosttower associate—or Robillard, yes Robillard!—to fly us home on a magical chariot?"

Drizzt chuckled in reply, and wished it were so. "We will arrive back at Mithral Hall in good time," he said, "if you can stride longer with those short legs."

On they went, down out of the foothills, and soon after breaking camp one brilliant morning, they came over a rocky rise in sight of the City of Sails.

Their hearts didn't lift.

Smoke hung low and thick over Luskan, and even from a distance, the companions could see that large swaths of the city were still but blackened husks. It had not been a kind winter in Deudermont's city, if indeed it remained Deudermont's city.

Regis didn't complain as Drizzt picked up their pace, almost trotting down the winding road. They passed many farms north of the city but noted surprisingly little activity, though the melt had progressed enough south of the Spine of the World for the early preparations of spring planting to begin. When it became apparent that they wouldn't make the city that day, Drizzt veered off the road and led Regis to the door of one such farmhouse. He rapped loudly, and when the door swung open, the woman noted the black skin of her unexpected and hardly typical guest, and she jumped in surprise and gave a little yelp.

"Drizzt Do'Urden, at your service," Drizzt said with a polite bow. "Back from Ten-Towns in Icewind Dale to visit my good friend Captain Deudermont."

The woman seemed to ease considerably, for surely anyone that close to Luskan had heard of Drizzt Do'Urden even before his exploits beside Deudermont in throwing down Arklem Greeth.

"If it's shelter ye're seeking, then put up in the barn," she said.

"The barn would be most hospitable," said Drizzt, 'but truly it's more good conversation and news of Luskan that would do we weary travelers good."

"Bah, but what news? News o' yer friend the governor?"

Drizzt couldn't suppress a smile at hearing Deudermont still referred to as governor. He nodded his assent.

"What's to tell, then?" asked the woman. "He gets his cheers, but don't he? And oh, but that one can wag a pretty tongue. A great feeder o' the pig, none's doubting."

"But . . . ?" Drizzt prompted, catching the prissy sarcasm sharpening her voice.

"But not so much for feedin' them that's feedin' the pigs, eh?" she said. "And not so quick with the grain we're needin' for the fields."

Drizzt looked south toward Luskan.

"I'm sure the captain will see to it as soon as he is able," Regis offered.

"Which?" the woman asked, and Regis realized that his use of Deudermont's old title had been taken to mean one of Luskan's high captains, and that inadvertent misunderstanding, given the woman's suddenly hopeful tone, had hinted to both Regis and Drizzt that Deudermont had not yet established control over those five.

"So, are ye to be stayin'?" the woman asked after a lengthy silence.

"Aye, the barn," Drizzt replied, turning to face her again and putting on a supremely pleasant and cheery expression as he did.

The pair were out the next morning before the cock crowed, trotting fast down the road all the way to Luskan's North Gate—Luskan's *unguarded* North Gate, they realized to their surprise. The ironclad door was neither locked nor barred, and not a voice of protest came at them from either of the towers flanking it as they pushed it open and crossed into the city.

"To the Cutlass, or the Red Dragon?" Regis asked, moving to the wide stone stairway of the Upstream Span bridge, which opened up into the northern section of the city wherein lay Deudermont's makeshift palace. But Drizzt shook his head and marched straight down the span, crossing the Mirar with Regis skipping at his heels.

"The market," he explained. "The level of activity there will tell us much of Luskan's winter before we rendezvous with Deudermont."

"I think we've already seen too much of it," Regis muttered.

Glancing left and right, it was hard for Drizzt to argue the sentiment. The city was a battered place, with many buildings crumbling, many more burned out, and with haggard folk covered in dirty layers of rags milling about the streets. The unmistakable look of hunger played on their dark faces, the profound hopelessness that could only be stamped by months of misery.

"Have ye seen the caravan, then?" came the quickly familiar

question soon after the pair stepped off the Upstream Span and into the city proper.

"Luskan's caravan north to Ten-Towns?" Regis asked.

The man looked at him incredulously, so much so that Regis's heart sank.

"Waterdeep's," he corrected the halfling. "A caravan's coming, don't ye know? And a great fleet of ships with food and warm clothes, and grain for the fields and pigs for the barn! Have ye seen it, boy?"

"Boy?" Regis echoed, but the man was too lost in his rambling to notice and pause for even a breath.

"Have ye seen the caravan? Oh, but she's to be a big one, they're saying! Enough food for to fill our bellies through the summer and the winter next. And all from Lord Brambleberry's people, they're saying."

All around the old man, people nodded and attempted, at least, to cheer a bit, though the sound was surely pathetic.

Barely three blocks into the city and still a long way from the market, Drizzt had seen enough. He turned Regis around and made for Dalath's Span, the remaining usable bridges across the Mirar, the closest to the harbor and the Red Dragon.

When at last they arrived at Deudermont's "palace," the companions found warm greetings and wide smiles. The guards ushered them right to the inner chambers, where Deudermont and Robillard met with a surly red-bearded dwarf Drizzt remembered from the Mirabarran contingent at the battle of the Hosttower.

"If we're interrupting . . ." Drizzt started to apologize, but Deudermont cut him short, leaping up from his seat and saying, "Nonsense! It's a good day in Luskan when Drizzt and Regis return."

"And Luskan's needing some good days," the dwarf remarked.

"And some meetings are better off interrupted," Robillard mumbled.

The dwarf turned on him sharply, drawing a smirk and a shrug from the cynical wizard.

"Aye," the dwarf said, "and some meetings go on longer than all what's needed saying's been said."

"Beautifully if confusedly expressed," said Robillard.

"Ah, but it might be a wizard's addled brain's what's needing unrattling," said the dwarf. "A good shake—"

"A flaming dwarf. . . ." Robillard added.

The dwarf growled and Deudermont sidled between the two. "Tell your fellows that their help through the winter was most appreciated," he said to the dwarf. "And when the first caravan arrives from the Silver Marches, we hope you will find your way to more generosity."

"Aye, soon as our own bellies ain't growling," the dwarf agreed, and with a final glare at Robillard and a tip of his wide-brimmed hat to Drizzt and Regis, he took his leave.

"It's good you have returned," Deudermont said, moving over to offer a handshake to his two friends. "I trust the Icewind Dale winter was no more harsh than what we suffered here."

"The city is battered," said Drizzt.

"And hungry," Regis added.

"Every priest in Luskan toils away throughout every day in prayers to their gods, creating food and drink," Deudermont said. "But their efforts are not nearly enough. Over at the Shield, the Mirabarrans tightened their belts considerably through the months, rationing their supplies, for they alone in Luskan had storehouses properly prepared for the winter."

"Not alone," Robillard corrected, and there was no missing the edge in his tone.

Deudermont conceded the point with a nod. "Some of the high captains seem to have avenues of securing food. All praise to Suljack, who has funneled good meat through this palace to the citizens, even to those who were not of his Ship."

"He's an idiot," said Robillard.

"He is a fine example to the other four," Deudermont quickly argued. "He puts Luskan above Ship, and alone among them, it seems, is wise enough to understand that the fate of Luskan will ultimately determine the fate of their private little empires."

"You have to act, and quickly," said Drizzt. "Or Luskan will not survive."

Deudermont nodded his agreement with every word. "A flotilla has left Waterdeep, and a great caravan winds its way up from the south, both laden with food and grain, and with soldiers to aid in calming the city. The lords of Waterdeep have rallied around the work of the late Lord Brambleberry, that his efforts will not be in vain."

"They don't want one of their own to look as stupid as the whispers make him out to be," Robillard clarified, and even Drizzt couldn't help but chuckle at that. "Expect too much from the flotilla and caravan at your peril," the wizard warned Deudermont. "They're laden well with food, no doubt, but a few dozen sellswords would be a dozen or two more than I'll be willing to wager they've offered. They have a way of looking more generous than they actually are, these lords."

Deudermont didn't bother to argue the point. "They will both arrive within the next couple of tendays, say the scouts. I secured a promise of extra food from our dwarf friend Argithas of Mirabar. The Mirabarrans agreed to accelerate their tithing to the city in anticipation of the re-supply, though their storehouses are near empty. Mirabar has stood strong with me through the winter—I would bid you to relay our gratitude to Marchion Elastul when you return to the Silver Marches."

Drizzt nodded.

"What choice did they have?" Robillard asked. "We're the only acre of sanity left in Luskan!"

"The caravans—" said Deudermont.

"Are a temporary reprieve."

Deudermont shook his head. "We will use the example of Suljack to enlist the other four," he reasoned. "They will end their foolish warring and support the city or their people will turn against them, as the whole of the city turned against Arklem Greeth."

"The people on the streets appear desperate," said Regis, and Deudermont nodded.

"The times are hard," he replied. "The relief of summer will allow them to look beyond their misery and seek long-term solutions to the ills of the city. Those solutions lie with me and not with the high captains, unless those old seadogs are smart enough to understand the needs of the city beyond their own narrow streets."

"They're not," Robillard assured him. "And we'd do well to climb on *Sea Sprite* and sail back to Waterdeep."

"I would go without food for a winter and more if only I heard a word of encouragement from Robillard," Deudermont remarked with a heavy sigh.

The wizard snickered, threw his arm across the back of his chair, and turned away.

"Enough of our misery," Deudermont said. "Tell me of Icewind Dale, and of Wulfgar. Did you find him?"

Drizzt's smile surely answered before the drow began to recant his tale of the journey.

CHAPTER
PRESSURE
28

The small bit of water they had put in the pot bubbled and steamed away, its aroma eliciting many licks of anticipation. The dark meat, twenty pounds of basted perfection, glistened from the surface burns of fast cooking, for not a one of the band of highwaymen was willing to wait the hours to properly prepare the unexpected feast.

The moment the cook announced it was done, the group began tearing at it eagerly, ripping off large chunks and shoving them into hungry mouths so that their cheeks bulged like rodents storing food for the winter. Every now and then one or another paused just long enough to lift a toast to Ship Rethnor, who had supplied them so well. And all that the generous son of the recently-deceased high captain had asked for in return was that the band waylay a caravan, and with all proceeds of the theft going to the highwaymen.

"They give us food for taking food," one rogue observed with a chuckle.

"And give us help in taking it," another agreed, indicating a small keg of particularly effective poison.

So they cheered and they ate, and they laughed and cheered some more for the son of Ship Rethnor.

The next morning, they watched from a series of low forested hills as the expected caravan, more than two dozen wagons, wound its way up the road from the south. Many guards accompanied the train—proud Waterdhavian soldiers—and even several wizards.

"Remember that we've a whole tenday," Sotinthal Magree, the leader of the Luskar band, told his fellows. "Sting and run, sting and run—wear them down day after day."

The others nodded as one. They didn't have to kill all of the guards. They didn't have to stop all of the wagons. If less than half of the wagons and less than half of the supplies got through to Luskan, Ship Rethnor would be satisfied and the highwaymen would share in the bounty.

That morning, a volley of crossbow quarrels flew out at the teams of the last two wagons in line, horses and guards alike. From a safe distance and with light crossbows, such an attack would hardly have bothered the seasoned travelers, but even the slightest scratch from a poisoned quarrel brought down even the largest of the draft horses.

The group of guards that charged out at the attackers similarly found their numbers halved with a second, more concentrated volley. Minor wounds proved devastating. Strong men crumbled to the ground in a deep and uncompromising sleep.

The crossbowmen melted into the woods before any close engagement could begin and from the other side of the road, a small group of grenadiers found their openings and charged the weakest spans of the caravan, hurling their fiery missiles of volatile oil and running off in fast retreat.

When some guards gave chase they found themselves caught in a series of spring traps, swinging logs and deviously buried spikes, all tipped, once again, with that devious poison.

By the end of the encounter, two wagons and their contents were fully engulfed in flames and two others damaged so badly that the Waterdhavians had to strip one to salvage the other. The caravan had lost several horses to flames or to injuries caused when the sleeping poison had sent them falling to the ground. A trio of guards had been murdered in the woods.

"They've no plan for the likes of us," Sotinthal told his men that night as they shadowed the caravan. "Like the dwarf told us they wouldn't. They're thinking that all the folk north of Waterdeep would welcome their passing and the food and grain they're bringing. A straight-on attack by monsters? Aye. A hungry band o' highwaymen? Aye. But not the likes of us—well fed and not needing their goods, well rewarded and not needing to fight them straight up."

He ended with a laugh that proved infectious around the campfire, and he wondered what tricks he and his fellows might use on the caravan the following day.

The next night, Sotinthal congratulated himself again, for the heavy boulder his men had rolled down the hill had taken out another wagon, destroying two of its wheels and spilling sacks of grain across the ground.

Their biggest cheer of all came three nights later, when a well-placed fiery arrow had lit up the oil-soaked understructure of a small bridge across a fast-moving stream, taking two wagons in the ensuing blaze and leaving five stranded on one side of the water, the men of the dozen-and-four on the other side staring helplessly.

Over the next two days, Sotinthal's men picked away at the Waterdhavians as they tried to find a ford or rebuild some measure of a bridge that could get the rest of their wagons across the stream.

The leader of the highwaymen knew the battered Waterdhavians were approaching their breaking point, and he was not surprised, though surely elated, when they simply ferried the supplies back over the stream to the south, overloaded the remaining wagons, and set off to the south, back to Waterdeep.

Kensidan would pay him well indeed.

* * * * *

"He is in her mind," the voice in the shadows said to Arklem Greeth. "Calming her, reminding her that her life remains and that eternity allows her to pursue that which she longs."

The lich resisted the urge to dispel the darkness and view the speaker, if only to confirm his guess about his identity. He looked over at poor Valindra Shadowmantle, who seemed at peace for the first time since he'd resurrected her consciousness inside her dead body. Arklem Greeth knew well the shock of death, and of undeath. After his own transformation to lichdom, he had battled many of the same anxieties and losses that had so unsettled Valindra, and of course he had spent many years in preparation for that still-shocking moment.

Valindra's experience had been far more devastating to the poor elf. Her heritage alone meant that she had expected several more centuries of life; with elves, the craving for immortality was not nearly as profound a thing as the desperation of short-lived humans. Thus, Valindra's transformation had nearly broken the poor soul, and would likely have turned her into a thing of utter and unrelenting hatred had not the voice in the shadows and his associate unexpectedly intervened.

"He tells me that the effort to keep her calm will be great indeed," the voice said.

"As will the price, no doubt," Arklem Greeth said.

Soft laughter came back at him. "What is your intent, Archmage?"

"With?"

"Luskan."

"What remains of Luskan, you mean," Arklem Greeth replied, in a tone that indicated he hardly cared.

"You remain within the city walls," said the voice. "Your heart is here."

"It was a profitable location, well-situated for the Arcane Brotherhood," the lich admitted.

"It can be again."

Despite not wanting to play his hand, Arklem Greeth couldn't help but lean forward.

"Not as it was, to be sure, but in other ways," said the voice.

"All we have to do is kill Deudermont. Is that what you are asking of me?"

"I'm asking nothing, except that your plans remain known to me."

"That is not nothing," said Arklem Greeth. "In many circles, such a price would be considered extravagant."

"In some circles, Valindra Shadowmantle would lose her mind."

Arklem Greeth had no answer to that. He glanced again at his beloved.

"Deudermont is well-guarded," said the voice. "He is not vulnerable while still in Luskan. The city is under considerable stress, as you might expect, and Deudermont's future as governor will depend upon his ability to feed and care for the people. So he has turned to his friends in Waterdeep, by land and by sea."

"You ask me to be a highwayman?"

"I told you that I asked nothing other than to know your plans as you evolve them," said the voice. "I had thought that one such as you, who need not draw air, who feels not the cold of the sea, would be interested to know that your hated enemy Deudermont is desperately awaiting the arrival of a flotilla from Waterdeep. It is presently sailing up the coast and the soft belly of supply ships is too well guarded for any pirates to even think of attacking."

Arklem Greeth sat perfectly still, digesting the information. He looked again at Valindra.

"My friend is not in her mind any longer," said the voice, and Arklem Greeth sharpened his focus on the undead woman, and was greatly encouraged as she didn't melt into a well of despair.

"He has shown her possibilities," said the voice. "He will return to her to reinforce the message and help her through this difficult time."

Arklem Greeth turned to the magical darkness. "I'm grateful," he said, and sincerely.

"You will have many years to repay us," said the voice, and it melted away as the darkness dissipated.

Arklem Greeth went to his beloved Valindra, and when she didn't respond to him, he sat and draped an arm around her.

His thoughts, though, sailed out to sea.

* * * * *

"It has not been a good winter," Deudermont admitted to Drizzt and Regis in the palace that day. "Too many dead men, too many shattered families."

"And during it all, the idiots fought each other," Robillard interjected. "They should have been out fishing and hunting, preparing the harvested crops and pooling their supplies. But would they?" He scoffed and waved his hand at the city beyond the window. "They fought amongst themselves—high captains posturing, guildless rogues murdering. . . ."

Drizzt listened to every word, but never took his eyes off Deudermont, who stared out the window and winced at every one of Robillard's points. There was no disagreement—how could there be, with smoke rising from every quarter of Luskan and with bodies practically lining the streets? There was something else in Deudermont's posture that, even more than the words, revealed to Drizzt how brutal the winter had been. The weight of responsibility bowed the captain's shoulders, and worse, Drizzt realized, was breaking his heart.

"The winter has passed," the drow said. "Spring brings new hope, and new opportunities."

Deudermont finally turned, and brightened just a bit. "There are promising signs," he said, but Robillard scoffed again. "It's true! High Captain Suljack sat behind me on that day when I was appointed as governor, and he has stood behind me since. And Baram and Taerl have hinted at coming around to a truce."

"Only because they have some grudge with Ship Rethnor and fear the new leader of that crew, this creature Kensidan, whom they call the Crow," said Robillard. "And only because Ship Rethnor ate well through the winter, but the only food Baram and Taerl could find came from the rats or came through us."

"Whatever the reason," Deudermont replied. "The Mirabarrans suffered greatly in the explosion of the Hosttower and have not opened the gates of the Shield District to the new Luskan, but with the spring, they may be persuaded to look toward the opportunities before us instead of the problems behind us. And we will need them this trading season. I expect Marchion Elastul will let the food flow generously, and on credit."

Drizzt and Regis exchanged concerned looks at that, neither overly impressed by the goodness of Elastul's heart. They had dealt with the man several times in the past, after all, and more often than not, had left the table shaking their heads in dismay.

"Elastul's daughter, Arabeth, survived the war and may help us in that," Deudermont said, obviously noting their frowns.

"It's all about food," Robillard said. "Who has it and who will share it, whatever the price. You speak of Baram and Taerl, but they're our friends only because we have the dark meat and the fungus."

"Curiously put," said Drizzt.

"From Suljack," Robillard explained, "who gets it from his friend in Ship Rethnor. Suljack has been most generous, while that young high captain of Rethnor ignores us as if we don't exist."

"He is unsure, like the Mirabarrans, perhaps," Regis offered.

"Or he is too sure of his position," Robillard said in a grim tone that Kensidan, had he heard, would have certainly taken as a warning.

"The spring will be our friend," Deudermont said as the door opened and his attendant indicated that dinner was served. "Caravans will arrive by land and by sea, laden with goods from the grateful lords of Waterdeep. With that bargaining power in my hands, I will align the city behind me and drag the high captains along, or I will rouse the city behind me and be rid of them."

"I hope for the latter," Robillard said, and Drizzt and Regis were not surprised.

They moved into the adjacent room and sat at Deudermont's finely appointed table, while attendants brought out trays of the winter's unexpected staple.

"Eat well, and may Luskan never be hungry again!" Deudermont toasted with his feywine, and all the others cheered that thought.

Drizzt gathered up knife and fork and went to work on the large chunk of meat on his plate, and even as that first morsel neared his lips, a familiar sensation came over him. The consistency of the meat, the smell, the taste. . . .

He looked at the side dish that ringed his main course, light brown mushrooms speckled with dots of purple.

He knew them. He knew the meat—deep rothé.

The drow fell back in his chair, mouth hanging open, eyes unblinking. "Where did you get this?"

"Suljack," Deudermont replied.

"Where did he get it?"

"Kensidan, likely," said Robillard as both he, Deudermont, and Regis stared at Drizzt curiously.

"And he?"

Robillard shrugged and Deudermont admitted, "I know not."

But Drizzt was afraid that he did.

*****

If Valindra Shadowmantle's corpse had indeed been animated, she didn't show it those hours subsequent to the strangers' visit in Arklem Greeth's subterranean palace. She didn't sway, didn't moan, didn't blink her dead eyes, and any attempts to reach the woman were met with utter emptiness.

"But it will pass," Arklem Greeth told himself repeatedly as he moved through the sewers beneath Illusk and Closeguard Island, collecting allies for his journey.

All the while, he considered the intruders to his subterranean palace. How had they so easily gotten past his many wards and glyphs? How had they even known that his extradimensional room had been anchored down there in the sewers? What magic did they possess? Psionics, he knew, from the one who had entered Valindra's consciousness to calm her, but were they truly powerful enough in those strange arts to utilize them to neuter his own skilled magical wards? An involuntary shudder coursed Greeth's spine—the first time anything like that had happened in his decades of lichdom—but it was true. Arklem Greeth feared the visitors who had come unbidden, and Arklem Greeth rarely feared anything.

That fear, as much as his hatred for Captain Deudermont, drove the lich along his course.

With an army of unbreathing, undead monsters behind him, Arklem Greeth went out into the harbor then out to sea, steadily, tirelessly moving south. He found more of his unbreathing soldiers in the deeper waters—ugly lacedon ghouls—and easily brought them under his sway. The undead were his to control. Skeletons and zombies, ghouls and ghasts, wights and wraiths proved no match for his superior and dominating willpower.

Arklem Greeth swept them up in his wake, continuing south all the while, paralleling the shore as he knew the Waterdhavian ships would do. His army needed no rest in the depths, where day and night were not so different. With their webbed, clawing hands, the lacedons moved with great speed, weaving through the watery depths with the grace of dolphins and the impunity of a great shark or whale. They stayed low, far from the surface, sliding past the reeds and weeds, crossing low over reefs, where even the mighty and fierce eels stayed deep in their holes to avoid the undead things. Only through a great expenditure of magic could Arklem Greeth hope to pace the aquatic ghouls, and so he commanded a pair to tow him along with them. Every so often, the powerful lich opened dimensional doors, transporting himself and his ghoulish coachmen far ahead of the undead army, that he would note the ships long before engaging them.

Well-versed in the ways of the ocean, Greeth suspected that the ships might be near when he first spotted the inevitable companions of any such flotilla: a lazily-swimming and circling school of hammerhead sharks, common as vultures along the perilous Sword Coast.

Greeth could have led his lacedon army wide of the small group, but the lich had grown bored of the long journey. He willed his escorts in a straight-line ascent toward the school, and he started the festivities by rolling forth a ball of lightning at the nearest sharks. They popped and jerked at the sparking intrusion, a pair hung stunned in the water and several others darted fast out of sight in the murky water.

The lacedons swam furiously past Greeth, their hunger incited. They tore into the closest sharks, and the stunned pair thrashed and rolled. A ghoulish arm was torn free, and floated down past the amused Arklem Greeth. He watched as another lacedon, clamped firmly in the jaws of a hammerhead, was shaken to pieces.

But the undead could not be intimidated, and they swarmed the shark with impunity, their claws slashing through its tough skin, filling the dark water with blood.

The school came on in full, a frenzy of biting and tearing, a bloodlust that made ghoul and shark alike a target for those razor teeth.

Greeth stayed safely to the side, reveling in the fury, the primal orgy, the ecstasy and agony of life and pain, death and undeath. He measured his losses, the ghouls bitten in half, the limbs torn asunder, and when he finally reached the point of balance between voyeuristic pleasure and practical consideration, he intervened in a most definitive way, conjuring a cloud of poison around the entirety of the battlefield.

The lacedons were immune, of course. The sharks fled or died, violently and painfully.

It took great concentration for Greeth to control the bloodthirsty ghouls, to keep them from pursuing, to put them back in line and on course, but soon enough the undead army moved along as if nothing had transpired.

But Greeth knew that they were even more anxious and eager than normal, that their hunger consumed them.

Thus, when at last those ships floated over Arklem Greeth's army, Greeth was well-prepared and his beastly army was more than ready to strike.

In the dark of night, the ships at half-sail and barely moving in still air and calm waters, Arklem Greeth turned his forces loose. Three score lacedons swam up beneath one boat like a volley of swaying arrows. One by one, they disappeared out of the water, and the archmage arcane could only imagine them scaling the side of the low, cargo-laden ship, padding softly onto the deck where half-asleep lookouts yawned with boredom.

The lich lamented that he wouldn't hear their dying screams.

He knew soon after that his ghoulish soldiers were tearing apart the crew and rigging, for the ship above him turned awkwardly and without apparent purpose.

A second ship came in fast, as Arklem Greeth had expected, and it was his to intercept. Many ships of the great ports were well-guarded from magical attacks, of course, with wards all along their decks and hull.

But those defenses were almost always exclusively above or just below the waterline.

The lich led the way in to the bottom of the ship with a series of small magical arrows. He concentrated his firing and soon the water near his target points hissed and fizzed as the arrows pumped acid into the old wood of the hull. By the time Arklem Greeth arrived at the spot, he could easily punch his hand through the compromised planks.

From that hand flew a small fiery pea, arcing up into the hull before exploding into a raging fireball.

Again the lich could only imagine the carnage, the screams and confusion!

In moments, men began diving into the water, and his lacedons, their job complete on the first ship, plunged in behind. What beauty those creatures showed in their simple and effective technique, swimming up gracefully below the splashing sailors, tearing at their ankles, and dragging them down to watery deaths.

The ship he had fireballed continued on its course, not slowing in the least as it reached the first target. Arklem Greeth couldn't resist. He swam up and poked his head out of the water, and nearly cackled with glee in watching the tangled ships share the hungry fire.

More ships approached from every direction. More desperate men jumped into the water and the lacedons dragged them down.

All the darkness echoed with horrified screams. Arklem Greeth picked a second target and turned it, too, into a great fiery disaster. Calls for calm and composure could not match the terror of that night. Some ships dropped sail and clustered together, while others tried to run off under full sail, committing the fatal error of separating from their companion vessels.

For they couldn't outrun the lacedons.

The ghouls fed well that night.

CHAPTER 29
WRONG CHOICE

"There's not enough," Suljack complained to Kensidan after the most recent shipment of food had arrived. "Barely half of the last load."

"Two-thirds," Kensidan corrected.

"Ah, we're running low, then?"

"No."

The flat answer hung in the air for a long while. Suljack studied his young friend, but Kensidan didn't blink, didn't smirk, gave no expression at all.

"We're not running low?" Suljack asked.

Kensidan didn't blink and didn't answer.

"Then why two-thirds, if that's what it was?"

"It's all you need," Kensidan replied. "More than you need, judging from the load you dropped at the Red Dragon Inn. I trust that Deudermont paid you well for the effort."

Suljack licked his lips nervously. "It's for the better."

"For whose better? Mine? Yours?"

"Luskan's," said Suljack.

"What does that even mean?" asked Kensidan. "Luskan's? For the betterment of Luskan? What is Luskan? Is it Taerl's Luskan, or Baram's? Kurth's or Rethnor's?"

"It's no time to be thinking of it like that," Suljack insisted. "We're one now, for the sake of all."

"One, behind Deudermont."

"Aye, and it was you that put me behind him that day when he became governor—and you should've been there! Then you'd know. The people ain't caring about which high captain's which, or about which streets're whose. They're needing food, and Deudermont's helping."

"Because you're giving my supplies to Deudermont."

"I'm giving them to Luskan. We've got to stand as one."

"We knew the winter would be difficult when we goaded Deudermont to attack the Hosttower," said Kensidan. "You do remember we did that, yes? You do understand the purpose of it all, yes?"

"Aye, I know it all full well, but things've changed now. The city's desperate."

"We knew it would be."

"But not like this!" Suljack insisted. "Little kids starving dead in their mother's arms . . . I could sink a ship and watch her crew drown and not think a bit about it—you know it—but I can't be watching that!"

Kensidan shifted in his chair and brought one hand up to cup his chin. "So Deudermont is the savior of Luskan? This is your plan?"

"He's the governor, and through it all, the people are with him."

"With him all the more if he's doling out food to them, I would expect," said Kensidan. "Am I to expect him to be a friend to Ship Rethnor when Baram and Taerl unite against me? Am I to expect those now growing more loyal to Deudermont to turn from him to support my work?"

"He's feeding them."

"So am I!" Kensidan shouted, and all the guards in the room turned sharply, unused to hearing such volatility from the always-composed son of Rethnor. "As suits me, as suits us."

"You want me to stop supplying him."

"Brilliant deduction—you should apply to the Hosttower, if we ever revive it. What I want more is for you to remember who you are, who we are, and the point of all of this trouble and planning."

Suljack couldn't help himself as he slowly shook his head. "Too many fallen," he said quietly, talking to himself more than to Kensidan. "Too high a price. Luskan stands as one, or falls."

He looked up, into the eyes of an obviously unimpressed Crow.

"If you've not the stomach for this," Kensidan began, but Suljack held up his hand to defeat the notion before it could be fully expressed.

"I will give him less," he said.

Kensidan started to respond, sharply, but bit it off. He turned to one of his attendants instead, and said, "Get the other third of Suljack's supplies packed on a wagon."

"Good man!" Suljack congratulated. "Luskan stands as one, and she'll get through this time of pain."

"I'm giving them to you," Kensidan said, his tone biting. "To you. They are yours to do with as you see fit, but remember our purpose in all of this. Remember why we put Deudermont together with Brambleberry, why we let the good captain know of the Hosttower's involvement with the pirates, why we tipped the Silver Marches to the advances of the Arcane Brotherhood. Those events were planned with purpose—you alone among my peers know that. So I give to you your rations, in full, and you are to do with them as you judge best."

Suljack started to respond, but bit it off and stood taking a long measure of Kensidan. But again, of course, the Crow assumed an unreadable posture and expression. With a nod and a smile of gratitude, Suljack left the room.

The dwarf slowly followed, letting the high captain get long out of earshot before he whispered to Kensidan, "He's to choose Deudermont."

"Wrong choice," Kensidan replied.

The dwarf nodded and continued out behind Suljack.

* * * * *

Amid the cries and the men rushing around, Suljack ran to the window overlooking the dark street, the dwarf close behind.

"Baram or Taerl?" the high captain asked Phillus, one of his most trusted guards, who knelt beside a second window, bow in hand.

"Might be both," the man replied.

"Too many," said another of the guards in the room.

"Both, then," said another.

Suljack rubbed his hands across his face, trying to comprehend the meaning of it all. The second shipment had arrived from Ship Rethnor earlier that same day, but it had come with a warning that High Captains Baram and Taerl were growing increasingly angry with the arrangements.

Suljack had decided to send the excess food to Deudermont anyway.

Directly below him in the street, the fighting had all but ended, with the combatants moving off to the alleyways, Suljack's men in pursuit, and the stripped and shattered wagons lay in ruins.

"Why would they do this?" the high captain asked.

"Might be that they're not liking yerself climbing over them in Deudermont's favor," said the dwarf. "Or might be that both o' them're still hating Deudermont o' *Sea Sprite* too much to agree with yer choices."

Suljack waved him to silence. Of course he knew all of that reasoning, but still it shocked him to think that his peers would strike out so boldly at a time of such desperation, even with relief reportedly well on its way.

He came out of his contemplation at the sound of renewed fighting across the street below him, and just down an alleyway. When one man came into view, looking back and down the alley, Phillus put up his bow and took deadly aim.

"Baram, or Taerl?" Suljack asked as Phillus let fly.

The arrow struck true. The man let out a howl and staggered back under cover, just as another man, one of Suljack's, came screaming out of the alley, blood streaming from a dozen wounds.

"That's M'Nack!" Phillus cried, referring to a favored young soldier of the Ship.

"Go! Go! Go!" Suljack yelled to his guards, and they all ran from the room, except for the dwarf and Phillus. "Kill any who come out in pursuit," Suljack instructed his deadly archer, who nodded and held his bow steady.

As the room all but cleared, Suljack went closer to the window, pulling it open and peering out intently. "Baram, Taerl, or both?" he asked quietly, his gaze roving the street, looking for some hint.

Across the way, the man Phillus had pegged stumbled out and away. A second arrow shot off, but missed the staggering thief, though it came close enough to make the man turn and look up at the source.

Suljack's jaw dropped open when he recognized the minor street thug. "Reth—?" he started to ask when he heard a thump to the side.

He turned to see Phillus lying on the floor, his head split open, a familiar spiked morningstar lying beside him.

He turned farther to see the dwarf, holding Phillus's bow, drawn and set.

"Wh—?" he started to ask as the dwarf let fly, the arrow driving into Suljack's gut and taking his breath. He staggered and fought to stand as the dwarf calmly reloaded and shot him again.

On the ground and crying, Suljack started to crawl away. He managed to gasp, "Why?"

"Ye forgot who ye were," the dwarf said, and put a third arrow into him, right in the shoulder blade.

Suljack continued to crawl, gasping and crying loudly,

A fourth arrow nicked his spine and stabbed into his kidney.

"Ye're just making it hurt more," the dwarf calmly explained, his voice distant, as if coming from far, far away.

Suljack hardly felt the next arrow, or the one after that, but he somehow knew that he wasn't moving anymore. He tried futilely to cry out, but found one last fleeting hope when he heard the dwarf cry out, "Murder!"

He managed to shift his head far enough to see the dwarf holding Phillus up in the air, and with three short running strides, he launched the already-dead guard crashing through the window to plummet to the hard street below. Phillus's broken bow, the dwarf having snapped it in half, followed in short order.

The last thing Suljack saw before darkness closed was the dwarf sliding down beside him. The last thing he heard was the dwarf crying out, "Murder! He shot the boss! Phillus the dog shot the boss! Oh, murder!"

CHAPTER 30
DEUDERMONT'S GAUNTLET

Three spears flew down the alley almost simultaneously, all thrown with great anger and strength. Desperate defenders angled bucklers to deflect or at least minimize the impact. But the spears never made it to the opposing lines, for a lithe figure sprang from an open window, tumbled to the street, and a pair of curved blades worked fast to chop at the missiles as they passed, driving them harmlessly aside.

The defenders cheered, thinking a new and mighty ally had come, and the spearmen cursed, seeing their impending doom in the fiery eyes and spinning blades of the deadly dark elf.

"What madness is this?" Drizzt demanded, turning repeatedly to encompass all the combatants with his accusation.

"Be asking *them!*" cried one of the spearmen. "Them who killed Suljack!"

"Be asking *them!*" the leader of the defenders retorted. "Them who came to wage war!"

"Murderers!" cried a spearman.

"By your lies!" came the response.

"The city is dying around you!" Drizzt cried. "Your disputes can be resolved, but not until . . ." He ended there since, with another cry of, "Murderers!" the spearmen flooded into the alleyway and charged. On the opposite side, the defenders responded with, "Lying thieves!" and similarly rushed.

Leaving Drizzt caught in the middle.

Suljack, or Taerl? The question swirled in Drizzt's thoughts as the choice became urgent. With which Ship would he side? Whose claim was stronger? How could he assume the role of judge with so little information? All of those thoughts and troubling questions played through his mind in the few heartbeats he had before being crushed between the opposing forces, and the only answer he could fathom was that he could not choose.

He belted his scimitars and ran to the side of the alleyway, springing upon the wall and pulling himself up out of harm's way. He found a perch on a windowsill and turned to watch helplessly, shaking his head.

Fury drove the Suljack crew. Those behind the leading wall of flesh who couldn't punish their enemies in melee threw any missiles they could find: spears, daggers, even pieces of wood or stone they managed to tear from neighboring buildings.

Taerl's defenders seemed no less resolute, if more controlled, forming a proper shield wall to defend the initial collision, showing patience as the rage of the attackers played out.

Drizzt didn't have the detachment necessary to admire or criticize either side's tactics, and didn't have the heart to even begin to predict which side would win. He knew in his gut that the outcome was assured, that all of Luskan would surely lose.

Only his quick instincts and reflexes saved his life as one of Suljack's men, unable to get a clear shot at Taerl's defenders, instead lifted his crossbow at Drizzt and let fly. The drow dodged at the last instant, but still got slashed across the back of his shoulder before his mithral shirt turned the bolt. The effort nearly sent him tumbling from his perch.

His hand went to his scimitar, and his eyes discerned a path down the wall and to the alleyway near the archer.

But pity overruled his anger, and he responded instead by calling upon his hereditary power to create a globe of darkness around the fool with the crossbow. Drizzt understood that he had no place in that fight, that he could accomplish nothing positive with combatants who were beyond reason. The weight of that tugged at him as he scaled the building to the roof and made off from the alley, trying to leave the screams of rage and pain behind him.

They were before him as well, however, just two streets down, where two mobs had engaged in a vicious, confused battle along the avenue separating the Ships of Baram and Taerl. As he ran along the rooftops above them, the drow tried to make out the allegiance of the fighters, but whether it was Ship Baram against Ship Taerl, or Suljack against Baram, or a continuation of Suljack and Taerl's fight, or perhaps even another faction all together, he couldn't tell.

Off in the distance, halfway across the city, near the eastern wall, flames lit up the night.

* * * * *

"Triple the guard at the mainland bridge," High Captain Kurth instructed one of his sergeants. "And set patrols to walk the length and breadth of the shoreline."

"Aye!" replied the warrior, clearly understanding the urgency as the sounds of battle drifted to Closeguard Island, along with the smell of smoke. He ran from the room, taking a pair of soldiers with him.

"It's mostly Taerl and Suljack's crews, I'm told," another of the Kurth sergeants informed the high captain.

"Baram's in it thick," another added.

"It's mostly the kid o' Rethnor, from my guess," said another of the men, moving to stand beside Kurth as he looked out to the mainland, where several fires blazed brightly.

That prompted a disagreement among the warriors, for though rumors abounded about Kensidan's influence in the fighting, the idea that Taerl and Baram had gone against Suljack without prompting was not so far-fetched, particularly given the common knowledge that Suljack had thrown in with Deudermont.

Kurth ignored the bickering. He knew full well what was going on in Luskan, who was pulling the strings and inciting the riots. "Will there be anything left when that fool Crow is through?" he mumbled under his breath.

"Closeguard," answered the sergeant standing beside him, and after a moment's thought, Kurth nodded appreciatively at the man.

A stark cry, a shriek, from outside the room ended the bickering and interrupted Kurth's contemplation. He turned, his eyes and the eyes of every man and woman in the room widening with shock as an uninvited guest entered.

"You live!" one man cried, and Kurth snickered at the irony of that notion.

Arklem Greeth had not "lived" in decades.

"Be at ease," the lich said to all around, holding up his hands in an unthreatening manner. "I come as a friend."

"The Hosttower was blasted apart!" the man beside Kurth shouted.

"'Twas beautiful, yes?" the lich responded, smiling with his yellow teeth. He tightened up almost immediately, though, and turned directly to High Captain Kurth. "I would speak with you."

A dozen swords leveled on Arklem Greeth.

"I understand and accept that you had no real choice but to open the bridges," said Arklem Greeth, but not a sword lowered at the assurance.

"How are you alive, and why are you here?" Kurth asked, and he had to work very hard to keep the tremor from his voice.

"As no enemy, surely," the lich replied. He looked around at the stubborn warriors and gave a profound, but breathless, sigh. "If I came to do ill, I would have engulfed the lowest floor of this tower in flames and would have assailed you with a magical barrage that would have killed half of your Ship before you ever realized the source," he said. "Please, my old friend. You know me better than to think I would need to get you alone to be rid of you."

Kurth spent a long while staring at the lich. "Leave us," he instructed his guards, who bristled and muttered complaints, but eventually did as they were told.

"Kensidan sent you?" Kurth asked when he was alone with the lich.

"Who?" Arklem Greeth replied, and he laughed. "No. I doubt the son of Rethnor knows I survived the catastrophe on Cutlass Island. Nor do I believe he would be glad to hear the news."

Kurth cocked his head just a bit, showing his intrigue and a bit of confusion.

"There are others watching the events in Luskan, of course," said Arklem Greeth.

"The Arcane Brotherhood," reasoned Kurth.

"Nay, not yet. Other than myself, of course, for once more, and sooner than I expected by many years, I find myself intrigued by this curious collection of rogues we call a city. No, my friend, I speak of the voices in the shadows. 'Twere they who guided me to you now."

Kurth's eyes flashed.

"It will end badly for Captain Deudermont, I fear," said Arklem Greeth.

"And well for Kensidan and Ship Rethnor."

"And for you," Arklem Greeth assured him.

"And for you?" Kurth asked.

"It will end well," said the lich. "It already has, though I seek one more thing."

"The throne of Luskan?" Kurth asked.

Arklem Greeth again broke out in that wheezing laugh. "My day in public here is done," he admitted. "I accepted that before Lord Brambleberry sailed into the Mirar. It's the way of things, of course. Expected, accepted, and well planned for, I assure you. I could have defeated Brambleberry, likely, but in doing so, I would have invoked the wrath of the Waterdhavian lords, and thus caused more trouble for the Arcane Brotherhood than the minor setback we received here."

"Minor setback?" Kurth indignantly replied. "You have lost Luskan!"

Greeth shrugged, and Kurth's jaw clenched in anger. "Luskan," said again, giving the name great weight.

"It is but one city, rather unremarkable," said Greeth.

"Not so," Kurth replied, calling him on his now-obvious bluff. "It is a hub of a great wheel, a center of weight for regions of riches, north, east and south, and with the waterways to move those riches."

"Be at ease, friend," said Greeth, patting his hands in the air. "I do not diminish the value of your beloved Luskan."

Kurth's expression aptly reflected his disagreement with that assessment.

"Only because I know our loss here to be a temporary thing," Greeth explained. "And because I expect that the city will remain in hands competent and reasonable," he added with a deferential and thoroughly disarming bow toward Kurth.

"And so you plan to leave?" Kurth asked, not quite sorting it all out. He could hardly believe, after all, that Arklem Greeth—the fearsome and ultimately deadly archmage arcane—would willingly surrender the city.

The lich shrugged, a collection of mucus and seawater in its lungs crackling with the movement. "Perhaps. But before I go away, I wish to repay a certain traitorous wizard. Two, actually."

"Arabeth Raurym," Kurth reasoned. "She plays both sides of the conflict, moving between Deudermont and Ship Rethnor."

"Until she is dead," said the lich. "Which I very much intend."

"And the other?"

"Robillard of *Sea Sprite*," the lich said in a tone as close to a sneer as the breathless creature could imitate. "Too long have I suffered the righteous indignation of that fool."

"Neither death would sadden me," Kurth agreed.

"I wish you to facilitate that," said Arklem Greeth, and Kurth lifted an eyebrow. "The city unravels. Deudermont's dream will falter, and very soon."

"Unless he can find food and—"

"Relief will not come," the lich insisted. "Not soon enough, at least."

"You seem to know much for one who has not shown himself in Luskan for many months. And you seem to be quite certain in your assurances."

"Voices in the shadows. . . ." Arklem Greeth replied with a sly smile. "Let me tell you of our observant and little-seen allies."

Kurth nodded and the lich spoke openly, only confirming that which Morik the Rogue, at Kensidan's bidding, had already explained. The high captain did well to hide his consternation at the further unwelcome evidence of yet another powerful player in the tug-of-war that was Luskan, particularly a player with a reputation so vile and unpredictable. Not for the first time did High Captain Kurth question Kensidan's judgment in helping to facilitate the Luskan disaster.

And not for the last time, either, he thought as Arklem Greeth told his dark tale of lacedon ghouls and murdered sailors.

* * * * *

"We act now or we lose Luskan," Governor Deudermont announced to Robillard, Drizzt, Regis, and some of his other commanders almost as soon as Drizzt delivered the news of the melee in the streets. "We must calm them until the caravans arrive."

"They will hear no reason," said Drizzt.

"Simpletons," Robillard muttered.

"They seek a focus for their frustrations," said Deudermont. "They are hungry and frightened, and grieving. Every family has suffered great losses."

"You overestimate the spontaneity of the moment," Robillard warned. "They are being goaded . . . and supplied."

"The high captains," Deudermont replied, and the wizard shrugged at the obvious answer.

"Indeed," the governor continued. "The four fools construct small empires within the city and posture now with swords."

Drizzt glanced at the luncheon platters still set on the table, and the scraps of meat—of deep rothé meat—and he wondered if there was even more posturing going on than the infighting of the high captains. He kept his fears silent, though, as he had when they'd first surfaced at dinner the previous night. He had no idea who had opened the trade channels necessary to get deep rothé and Underdark mushrooms, or with whom that enterprising high captain might be trading, but there was chaos in Luskan, and Drizzt's life experiences associated that state with one race in particular.

"We must act immediately," Deudermont announced. He turned to Robillard. "Go to the Mirabarrans and bid them to reinforce and keep safe the Red Dragon Inn."

"We're leaving?" Regis asked.

"To *Sea Sprite*, I pray," said Robillard.

"We need to cross the bridge," Deudermont answered. "Our place now is in Luskan proper. The Mirabarrans can control the north bank. Our duty is to step into the middle of the fighting and force the competing high captains back to their respective domains."

"One Ship is without her captain," Drizzt reminded him.

"And there we will go," Deudermont decided. "To Suljack's palace, which I will declare as the temporary Governor's Residence, and we will ally with his people in their time of need."

"Before the vultures can tear the carcass of Ship Suljack to bits?" Regis asked.

"Precisely."

"Sea Sprite would be a better choice," said the wizard.

"Enough, Robillard! You weary me."

"Luskan is already dead, Captain," the wizard added. "You haven't the courage to see it clearly."

"The Mirabarrans?" Deudermont asked in a sharper tone, and Robillard bowed and said no more, leaving the room immediately and the Red Dragon soon after to enlist the men and dwarves of the Shield District.

"We will announce our presence in no uncertain terms," Deudermont explained when the wizard was gone. "And will fight to protect any and all who need us. Through strength of resolve and sword we will hold Luskan together until the supplies arrive, and we will demand fealty to the city and not the Ship."

It was obvious that he was thinking on his feet. "Call in the magistrates and all of the city guard," he said, speaking as much to himself as to anyone else. "We will show them stakes. Now is the time for us to stand strong and resolute, the time to rally the city around us and force the high captains to acquiesce to the greater good." He paused and looked directly at Drizzt, showing the drow his strength before squarely laying down the gauntlet.

"Or they will lose their standing," he said. "We will dissolve the ship of any who will not swear fealty to the office of governor."

"To you, you mean," said Regis.

"No, to the office and to the city. They are bigger than any man who occupies the seat."

"A bold statement," said Drizzt. "Lose their standing?"

"They had their chance to show their value to Luskan throughout the long winter night," Deudermont steadfastly replied. "Other than Suljack, to a one, they failed."

The meeting adjourned on that grim note.

* * * * *

" 'E's on our side, what?" one of the soldiers formerly of Ship Suljack who had just signed on with Deudermont asked his companion when they exited the palace to join the fighting, only to spot Drizzt Do'Urden at work on a couple of Baram's ruffians.

"Aye, and that's why meself's noddin' yes to Deudermont," said the other.

The first nodded back as they watched the drow in action. One of Baram's boys took an awkward swing, apparently trying to cut the drow's legs out from under him, but Drizzt nimbly jumped, snapping a kick in the man's face as he came over.

The second thug came in hard with a straight thrust from the side, but the drow's scimitars beat him to the mark. One blade crossed to easily drive the thug's sword out wide, the other stabbed straight out, driving right against the man's throat. Drizzt then swept his free blade back across in time to loop it over the other ruffian's blade as it came up from its low position. A twist and flick of the drow's wrist had that one flying free and the suddenly unarmed ruffian, like his friend who stood immobilized with a sharp tip against his throat, was caught.

"The fight is done for you," Drizzt announced to the pair, and neither was in a position to disagree.

The two men rushed down the alley to join the drow, skidding to an abrupt stop as Drizzt turned a wary eye on them.

"We're with Deudermont!" they yelled together.

"Just signed up," one clarified.

"These two are fairly caught," Drizzt explained, and turned to his prisoners. "I will have your words of honor that you are out of the fight, or I will spill your lifeblood here and now."

Baram's boys looked at each other helplessly, then offered undying oaths as Drizzt prodded with his blades.

"Take them to the eastern wing of the first floor," Drizzt instructed the new Deudermont recruits. "No harm is to come to them."

"But they're with Baram!" one protested.

"Was them what killed Suljack!" said the other.

Drizzt silenced them with an even stare. "They're caught. Their fight is ended. And when this foolishness is done, they will again become a part of Luskan, a city that has seen far too much death."

"Oh yes, yes, Mister Regis, sir," a voice interrupted, and all five at Drizzt's encounter glanced to see Regis entering the far end of the alleyway. A pair of thugs—Taerl's boys—trailed him stupidly, their eyes locked on a particularly fascinating ruby that Regis spun at the end of a chain.

"No more fightin' for me," said the other hypnotized fool.

Regis walked right by Drizzt and the others, offering a profound sigh at the inanity of it all.

"We win by preserving the heart and soul of Luskan," Drizzt explained to the thoroughly confused new recruits. "Not by killing everyone who's not now with our cause." Drizzt nodded to the still-armed ruffian to drop his blade, and when he didn't immediately respond, the drow prodded him again in the throat. His blade fell to the cobblestones. With his scimitars, Drizzt then guided the pair to the new recruits. "Take them to the eastern wing."

"Prisoners," one of the new recruits said, nodding.

"Aye," said the other, and they started off, the captured thugs before them and following the same line as Regis and his two captives.

Despite the enormity of the calamity around them—the streets around Deudermont's new palace were thick with fighting, as both Baram and Taerl, at least, had come against the governor fully—Drizzt couldn't help but chuckle, particularly at Regis and his effective tactics.

That grin was blown away a few moments later, however, when Drizzt ran to the far end of the alleyway, arriving just in time to see the less subtle Robillard engulf an entire building in a massive fireball. Screams emanated from inside the burning structure and one man leaped out of a second story window, his clothing fully aflame.

Despite his and Deudermont's hopes to keep the battle as bloodless as possible, Drizzt understood that before the fight was over, many more Luskar would lie dead.

THE PIRATE KING

The drow rubbed his weary eyes and blew a long and resigned sigh. Not for the first time and not for the last, he wished he could rewind time to when he and Regis had first arrived in the city, before Deudermont and Lord Brambleberry had begun their fateful journey.

CHAPTER

THE PROVERBIAL STRAW

31

Deudermont, Robillard, Drizzt, Regis, and the others gathered in the governor's war room shared a profound sense of dread from the look on Waillan Micanty's face as he entered the room.

"Waterdhavian flotilla came in," the man said.

"And . . . ?" Deudermont prompted.

"One boat," Micanty replied.

"One?" Robillard growled.

"Battered, and with her crew half dead," Micanty reported. "All that's left of the flotilla. Some turned back, most are floating empty or have been sent to the bottom."

He paused, but no one in the room had the strength to ask a question or offer a response, or even, it seemed, to draw breath.

"Was lacedons, they said," Micanty went on. "Sea ghouls. Scores of 'em. And something bigger and stronger, burning ships with fire that came up from the deep."

"Those ships were supposed to be *guarded!*" Robillard fumed.

"Aye, and so they were," Waillan Micanty replied, "but not from below. Hundreds of men dead and most all of the supplies lost to the waves."

Deudermont slipped into his chair, and it seemed to Drizzt that if he had not, he might have just fallen over.

"The folk of Luskan won't like this," Regis remarked.

"The supplies were our bartering card," Deudermont agreed.

"Perhaps we can use the sea ghouls as a new, common enemy," Regis offered. "Tell the high captains that we have to join together to win back the shipping lanes."

Robillard scoffed loudly.

"It's something!" the halfling protested.

"It's everything, perhaps," Deudermont agreed, to Regis's surprise most of all.

"We have to stop this warring," the governor went on, addressing Robillard most of all. "Declare a truce and sail side-by-side against these monstrosities. We can sail all the way to Waterdeep and fill our holds with—"

"You've lost your mind," Robillard interrupted. "You think the four high captains will join an expedition that will only secure *your* power?"

"For their own good as well," the governor argued. "To save Luskan."

"Luskan is already dead," said Robillard.

Drizzt wanted to argue with the wizard, but found no words to suffice.

"Send word to the high captains for parlay," Deudermont ordered. "They will see the wisdom in this."

"They will not!" Robillard insisted.

"We have to try!" Deudermont shouted back and the wizard scoffed again and turned away.

Regis sent a concerned look Drizzt's way, but the drow had little comfort to offer him. They both had spent the previous day battling in the streets around Suljack's palace, and both knew that Luskan teetered on the brink of disaster, if indeed she wasn't already there. The only mitigating factor seemed to be the wealth of supplies streaming up from Waterdeep, and if most of those were not to arrive. . . .

"We have to try," Deudermont said again, his tone and timbre more quiet, even, and controlled.

But there was no mistaking the desperation and fear embedded in that voice.

* * * * *

Baram and Taerl wouldn't come to him personally, but sent a single emissary to deliver their message. Kurth and Kensidan didn't even answer his request for a parlay.

Deudermont tried to put a good face on the rejection, but whenever he thought that Robillard or Drizzt weren't looking his way, he sighed.

"Twenty-seven?" Robillard asked in a mocking tone. "A whole day of fighting, a dozen men dead or near it on our side, and all we've got to show for our work are twenty-seven prisoners, and not a one of them pledging to our cause?"

"But all agreeing that they're out of the fight, so if we win . . ." Drizzt started to reply.

Robillard cut him off with a smirk and said, "If?"

Drizzt cleared his throat and glanced at Deudermont, then went on, "When we win, these men will join with us. Luskan need not be burned to the ground. Of that much, I'm sure."

"That isn't much, Drizzt," Robillard said, and the drow could only shrug, having little evidence to prove the wizard wrong. They had held Suljack's palace that first day, but the enemy seemed all around them, and several of the adjoining streets were fully under the control of Baram and Taerl. They had indeed lost at least twelve fighters, and who knew how many more had been killed out in the streets near the palace?

Deudermont couldn't win a war of attrition. He didn't have thousands behind him, unlike when he'd gone against Arklem Greeth. The supplies might have renewed that faith in him, but the main source had been destroyed at sea and nothing else had arrived.

Regis entered the war room then to announce the arrival of Baram and Taerl's ambassador. Deudermont sprang out of his seat and rushed past the other two, urging Regis along to the audience chamber.

The man, a scruffy-looking sea dog with a hairline that had receded to the back of his scalp, wild gray strands hanging all about him, waited for them, picking his nose as Deudermont entered the room.

"Don't waste me time," he said, flicking something off to the floor and staring at Deudermont the way a big dog might look upon a cornered rodent—hardly the usual look Captain Deudermont of *Sea Sprite* was used to seeing from such a bilge rat.

"Baram and Taerl should have come and saved you the trouble then," Deudermont replied, taking a seat before the man. "They had my word that no harm would befall them."

The man snickered. "Same word ye gived to Suljack, not a doubt."

"You believe I was involved in the death of Suljack?" Deudermont asked.

The man shrugged as if it hardly mattered. "Baram and Taerl ain't no fools, like Suljack," he said. "They'd be needing more than yer word to believe the likes of Captain Deudermont."

"They project their own sense of honor upon me, it would seem. I'm a man of my word," he paused and motioned for the man to properly introduce himself.

"Me own name ain't important, and I ain't for tellin' it to the likes o' yerself."

Behind Deudermont, Robillard laughed and offered, "I can discover it for you, Cap—Governor."

"Bah, no one'd tell ye!" the ambassador said with a growl.

"Oh, you would tell me, and do not doubt it," the wizard replied. "Perhaps I would even etch it on your gravestone, if we bothered to get you a gravesto—"

"So much for yer word, eh Captain?" the sea dog said with a broken-toothed grin, just as Deudermont held up his hand to silence the troublesome Robillard.

"Baram and Taerl sent you here to hear my offer," said Deudermont. "Tell them . . ."

The filthy ambassador started laughing and shaking his head. "Nothing they want to hear," he interrupted. "They sent me here with *their* offer. Their only offer." He stared at Deudermont intensely. "Captain, get on yer *Sea Sprite* and sail away. We're givin' ye that, and it's more than ye deserve, ye fool. But be knowing that we're givin' ye it on yer word that ye'll not e'er again sink any ship what's carrying the colors o' Luskan,"

Deudermont's eyes widened then narrowed dangerously.

"That's yer deal," the sea dog said.

"I'm going to burn this city to rubble," Robillard growled under his breath, but then he shook his head and added, "Take the offer, Captain. To the Nine Hells with Luskan."

Beside Robillard, Drizzt and Regis exchanged concerned glances, and both of them were thinking the same thing, that maybe it was time for Deudermont to admit that he could not succeed in the City of Sails, as he'd hoped. They had been out on the streets the previous day, after all, and had seen the scale of the opposition.

For a long while, the room lay silent. Deudermont put his chin in his hand and seemed deep in thought. He didn't look back to his three friends, nor did he pay any heed at all to the ambassador, who stood tapping his foot impatiently.

Finally, the governor of Luskan sat up straight. "Baram and Taerl err," he said.

"Only deal ye're gettin'," said the pirate.

"Go and tell your bosses that Luskan will not go to the Nine Hells, but that they surely shall," said Deudermont. "The people of Luskan have entrusted me to lead them to a better place, and to that place we will go."

"And where might all these people be?" the pirate asked with dripping sarcasm. "Might they be shooting arrows at ye're boys even as we're talkin'?"

"Be gone to your masters," said Deudermont. "And know that if I see your ugly face again, I will surely kill you."

The threat, delivered so calmly, seemed to unsettle the man, and he staggered backward a few steps, then turned and rushed from the room.

"Secure a route from here to the wharves," Deudermont instructed his friends. "If we're forced into retreat, it will be to *Sea Sprite*."

"We could just walk there, openly," said Robillard, and he pointed at the door through which the ambassador had just exited.

"If we leave, it will be a temporary departure," Deudermont promised. "And woe to any ship we see flying Luskan's colors. And woe to the high captains when we return, Waterdhavian lords at our side."

* * * * *

"The reports from the street are unequivocal," Kensidan announced. "This is it. There will be no pause. Deudermont wins or he loses this day."

"He loses," came the voice from the shadows. "There is no relief on the way from Waterdeep."

"I don't underestimate that one, or his powerful friends," said the Crow.

"Don't underestimate his powerful enemies," the voice replied. "Kurth succeeded in defeating the flotilla, though no ships from Luskan got near to it."

That turned Kensidan away from the window, to peer at the globe of darkness.

"Kurth has an ally," the voice explained. "One Deudermont believes destroyed. One who does not draw breath, save to find his voice for powerful magical dweomers."

The Crow considered the cryptic clues for a moment then his eyes widened and he seemed as near to panic as anyone had ever seen him. "Greeth," he mumbled.

"Arklem Greeth himself," said the voice. "Seeking revenge on Deudermont."

The Crow began to stalk the room, eyes darting all around.

"Arklem Greeth will not challenge you," the voice in the darkness promised. "His days of ruling Luskan are at an end. He accepted this before Deudermont moved on the Hosttower."

"But he aligns with Kurth. Whatever your assurances regarding the archmage arcane, you cannot make the same with regard to Kurth!"

"The lich will not go against us, whatever High Captain Kurth might ask of him," the unseen speaker said with confidence.

"You cannot know that!"

A soft chuckle came from the darkness, one that ended any further debate on the subject, and one that sent a shiver coursing Kensidan's spine, a reminder of who it was he was dealing with, of who he had trusted—trusted!—throughout his entire ordeal.

"Move decisively," the voice prompted. "You are correct in your assessment that this day determines Luskan's future. There is nothing but the angled wall of a corner behind you now."

CHAPTER
THE ONE I WOULD KILL
32

"We should be on the shore with the captain!" one woman cried.

"Aye, we can't be letting him fight that mob alone!" said another of *Sea Sprite*'s increasingly impatient and upset crew. "Half the city's come against him."

"We were told to guard *Sea Sprite*," Waillan Micanty shouted above them all. "Captain Deudermont put no 'unless' in our orders! He said stay with *Sea Sprite* and keep her safe, and that's what we're to do—all of us!"

"While he gets himself killed?"

"He's got Robillard with him, and Drizzt Do'Urden," Waillan argued back, and the mention of those two names did seem to have a calming effect on the crew. "He'll get to us if he needs to get to us—and what a sorry bunch of sailors we'd be to lose the ship and his one chance at escaping!

"Now, to your stations, one and all," he ordered. "Turn your eyes to the sea and the many pirates moored just outside the harbor."

"They all fought *with* us," a crewman remarked.

"Aye, against Arklem Greeth," said Waillan. "And most of those coming against Captain Deudermont now marched with him to the Hosttower. The game's changed, so be on your guard."

There was a bit of grumbling, but *Sea Sprite*'s veteran crew scurried back to their respective watch and gunnery posts and most managed to tear their eyes from the signs of fighting in the city proper to focus again on any possible threats to their own position.

And not a moment too soon, for Waillan Micanty had barely finished speaking when the crewman in the crow's nest shouted down, "Starboard!" Then clarified, "The water line!" as Micanty and others rushed to the rail.

As chance would have it, the first lacedon scaling *Sea Sprite*'s hull pulled over the rail right in front of Micanty himself, who met it with a heavy slash of his saber.

"Ghouls!" he cried. "Ghouls aboard *Sea Sprite!*"

And so came Arklem Greeth's horrid minions, splashing out of the water all around the pirate hunter. Crewmen rushed to and fro, weapons drawn, determined to cut the beasts down before they could get a foothold, for if the lacedons managed to get onto the deck, they all knew that their own ranks would quickly thin. Waillan Micanty led the way, bludgeoning and cutting ghoul after ghoul, rushing from starboard to port just in time to drive back over the rail the first of the lacedons attacking that side of the vessel.

"Too many!" came a cry from aft, near the catapult, and Waillan turned to see ghouls standing up straight on the deck, and to see a pair of the catapult crew fall paralyzed to the deck. His gaze immediately went out to the deeper waters and the many ships anchored there. The catapult was down. *Sea Sprite* was vulnerable.

He charged the breach, calling for crewmen to join him, but when one rushed into his wake, Waillan, recognizing the terrible danger, stopped the woman. "Contact Robillard," he bade her. "Tell him of our situation."

"We can win," the woman, an apprentice of Robillard's, replied.

But Waillan was hearing none of it. "Now! Tell him!"

The mage nodded reluctantly, her gaze still locked on the fight on the aft deck. She did turn, though, and scrambled down the bulkhead.

Sitting invisibly in *Sea Sprite*'s hold, Arklem Greeth watched her move to the crystal ball with great anticipation and amusement.

* * * * *

"The same force that destroyed the Waterdhavian flotilla," Deudermont remarked when Robillard relayed the predicament of *Sea Sprite*. "Perhaps they followed the one surviving ship to us."

The wizard considered the reasoning for a moment then nodded, but he was thinking of much more sinister possibilities given the nature and coordination of the lacedon attack, and the fact that it was occurring right in Luskan Harbor, where such attacks were unprecedented.

"Go to them and clear *Sea Sprite*," Deudermont bade his friend.

"We have our own problems here, Captain," Robillard reminded him, but it was clear from his tone that he didn't really disagree with Deudermont's command.

"Be quick then," said the captain. "Above all else, that ship must remain secure!"

Robillard glanced at the door leading to the stairs and the palace's front exit. "I will go, and hopefully return at once," the wizard announced. "But only on your promise that you will find Drizzt Do'Urden and stay tight to his side."

Deudermont couldn't suppress a grin. "I survived for many years without him, and without you," he said.

"True, and your old arms aren't nearly as swift with your sword anymore," the wizard replied without hesitation. He threw the captain a wink and collected his gear then began casting a spell to transport him to *Sea Sprite*'s deck.

* * * * *

High Captain Baram slapped aside the frantic scout and took a clearer look at the influx swarming through the square just three blocks from Suljack's palace and Deudermont.

Taerl rushed up beside him, similarly holding his breath, for they both knew at once the identity of the new and overpowering force that had come on the scene. Ship Rethnor was about to join the fight in full.

"For us, or for Deudermont?" Taerl asked. Even as he finished, one small group of Baram's boys inadvertently charged out in front of Rethnor's swarm. Baram's eyes widened, and Taerl let out a gasp.

But the dwarf leading the way for Rethnor engaged those men with words, not morningstars, and as the forces parted, Ship Rethnor's contingent angling off to the side, the two high captains found their hoped-for answer.

Ship Rethnor had come out in full against Deudermont.

* * * * *

"Oh oh," Regis said from his perch on a low roof overlooking an alley from which Drizzt had just chased a trio of Taerl's ruffians.

Drizzt started to ask the halfling for a clarification, but when he saw the look on Regis's face, he just ran to the spot, leaped and spun to catch the trim of the roof in a double backhanded grasp then curled and tucked his legs, rolling them right up over him to the roof. As soon as he set himself up there, he understood the halfling's sentiments.

Like a swarm of ants, Ship Rethnor's warriors streamed along several of the streets, chasing Deudermont's forces before them with ease.

"And out there," Regis remarked pointing to the northwest.

Drizzt's heart sank lower when he followed that motion, for the gates on Closeguard Island were open once more, High Captain Kurth's forces streaming onto and across the bridge. Looking back to Kensidan's fighters, it wasn't hard to figure out which side Kurth favored.

"It's over," said Drizzt.

"Luskan's dead," Regis agreed. "And we've got to get Deudermont out of here."

Drizzt gave a shrill whistle and a moment later Guenhwyvar leaped from rooftop to rooftop to join him.

"Go to the docks, Guen," the drow bade the panther. "Find a route for me."

Guenhwyvar gave a short growl and leaped away.

"Let us hope that Robillard has a spell of transportation available and ready," Drizzt explained to Regis. "If not, Guen will lead us." He jumped down to the alleyway and helped slow Regis's descent as the halfling came down behind him. They turned back the way they had come, picking the fastest route to the palace, toward a service door for the kitchen.

They had barely gone a few steps, though, when they found the way blocked by a most strange-looking dwarf.

"I once met me Drizzit the drow," he chanted. "The two of us suren did have a row. He did dart and did sting, how his blades they did sing, till me morningstars landed a blow!"

Drizzt and Regis stared at him open-mouthed.

"Bwahahahaha!" the dwarf bellowed.

"What a curious little beast," Regis remarked.

* * * * *

Robillard landed on the deck of *Sea Sprite* holding up a gem that spread forth a most profound and powerful light, as if he had brought a piece of the sun with him. All around him, lacedons cowered and shrieked, their greenish-gray skin curling and shriveling under the daunting power of that sunlike beacon.

"Kill them while they cower!" Waillan Micanty shouted out, seeing so many of the crew stunned by the sudden and dominating appearance of their heroic wizard.

"Drive them off!" another man shouted, and his gaff hook tore into a ghoul as it shielded its burning eyes from the awful power of the gemstone.

All over the deck, the veteran crew turned the tide of the battle, with many lacedons simply leaping overboard to get away from the awful brightness and many more falling to deadly blows of sword and club and gaff hook.

Robillard sought out Micanty and handed him the brilliant gem. "Clear the ship," he told the dependable sailor. "And prepare to get us out of the harbor and to open waters. I'm off for Deudermont."

He started casting a teleport spell to return him to the palace then, but nearly got knocked off his feet as *Sea Sprite* shuddered under the weight of a tremendous blast. Licks of flame poked up from the deck planks, and Robillard understood then the blast to be magical, and to have come from *Sea Sprite*'s own hold!

Without a word to Micanty, the wizard rushed to the bulkhead and threw it wide. He leaped down the stairs and saw his apprentice at once, lying charred and quite dead beside the burning table upon which still sat the crystal ball. Robillard's gaze darted all about—and stopped cold when he saw Arklem Greeth, sitting comfortably on a stack of grain sacks.

"Oh, do tell me that you expected me," the lich said. "Certainly you were smart enough to realize that I hadn't destroyed myself in the tower."

Robillard, his mouth suddenly very dry, started to answer, but just shook his head.

* * * * *

With great reluctance, Captain Deudermont headed out of his audience chamber toward the kitchen and the service door, where he knew Drizzt to be. For the first time in a long time, the captain's thoughts were out to sea, to *Sea Sprite* and his many crewmen still aboard her. He couldn't begin to guess what had precipitated the attack of undead monsters, but surely it seemed too detrimental and coordinated with the fighting in the streets to have been a coincidence.

A shout from a corridor on his left stopped Deudermont and brought him back to the moment.

"Intruders in the palace!" came the cry.

Deudermont drew out his sword and started down that corridor, but only a couple of steps. He had promised Robillard, and not out of any thought for his own safety. It was not his place, it could not be his place, to engage in street fights unless there was some hope of winning out.

Somewhere in the vast array of rooms behind him, a window shattered, then another.

Enemies were entering Suljack's palace, and Deudermont had not the force to repel them.

He turned fast again, cursing under his breath and speeding for the kitchen.

The form came at him from the side, from a shadow, and the captain only noticed it out of the corner of his eye. He spun with catlike grace, swiping his sword across in a gradual arc that perfectly parried the thrusting spear. A sudden reversal sent the sword slashing back down across the chest of his attacker, opening a wide gash and sending the man crashing back into the shadows, gurgling with pain.

Deudermont rushed away. He needed to link up with Drizzt and Regis, and with them pave an escape route for those loyal to his cause.

He heard a commotion in the kitchen and kicked open the door, sword at the ready.

Too late, Deudermont knew, as he watched a cook slide to the floor off the end of a sword, clutching at the mortal wound in his chest. Deudermont followed that deadly line to the swordsman, and couldn't hide his surprise at the garish outfit of the flamboyant man. He wore a puffy and huge red-and-white striped shirt, tied by a green sash that seemed almost a wall between the bright colors of the shirt and the even brighter blue of the man's pants. His hat was huge and plumed, and Deudermont could only imagine the wild nest of hair crimped beneath it, for the man's beard nearly doubled the size of his head, all black and wild and sticking out in every direction.

"We're knowin' yer every move then, ain't we Captain Deudermont?" the pirate asked, licking his yellow teeth eagerly.

"Argus Retch," Deudermont replied. "So, the reports of your insult to good taste weren't exaggerated after all."

The pirate cackled with laughter. "Paid good gold for these," he said, and wiped his bloody sword across his pants—and though the blade did wipe clean, his obviously magical pants showed not a spot of the blood.

Deudermont resisted the urge to reply with a snide comment regarding the value of such an outfit and the possible fashion benefits of soiling the damned ugly thing, but he held his tongue. There would be no bargaining with the pirate, obviously, nor did the captain want to—particularly since a man loyal to Deudermont, an innocent man, lay dead at Retch's feet.

In reply, then, Deudermont presented his sword.

"Ye got no crew to command here, Captain," Argus Retch answered in response, lifting his own blade and drawing out a long dirk in his other hand. "Oh, but ye're the best at maneuverin' ships, ain't ye? Let's see how you turn a blade!" With that, he leaped forward, stabbing with his sword, and when that got deflected aside, he turned with the momentum and slashed his dirk across wildly.

Deudermont leaned back out of range of that swipe and quickly brought his sword before him, managing a thrust of his own that didn't get near to hitting the pirate, but managed to steal Retch's offensive initiative and force him back on his heels. The pirate went down low then, legs wide, blades presented forward, but wide apart, as well.

He began to circle in measured steps.

Deudermont turned with him, watching for some tell, some sign that the man would explode into an aggressive attack once more, and also take in the room, the battlefield. He noted the island counter, all full of cooking pots and bowls, and the narrow cabinets lined side-to-side along the side wall.

Retch's jaw clenched and Deudermont noted it clearly, and so he was hardly surprised as the pirate leaped forward, sword stabbing.

Deudermont easily slipped beside the cooking island, and Retch's succeeding dagger swipe missed by several feet.

"Stand still and fight me, ye dog!" Retch bellowed in protest, giving chase around the island.

Deudermont grinned at him, egging him on. The captain continued his retreat down the backside of the island, then around to the front, putting himself between the island and the row of cabinets.

Retch pursued, growling and slashing.

Deudermont stopped and let him close, but only so that he could grab the nearest cabinet with his free left hand and topple it forward, to fall right in front of the pirate. Retch leaped it, only to bang against the second cabinet as it similarly toppled, then the fourth, Deudermont having safely retreated past the third without pulling it down.

"I knew ye was a coward!" Retch cried, ending in a sputter as Deudermont used the moment while the pirate dodged the falling cabinet to swing his sword low and hard across the top of the island, smashing bowls and sending liquid and powdery flour flying at Argus Retch. The pirate waved his hands, futilely trying to block, and wound up with his face powdered in white, with several wet streaks along one cheek. His beard, too, lost its black hue in the flour storm.

Sputtering and spitting, he came forward, and turned his shoulder to rush sidelong past as Deudermont reached out for yet another cabinet to topple.

But Deudermont didn't pull down the cabinet. Instead he used Retch's defensive turn and the line of his free hand to step forward. He executed a quick double parry, sword and dirk, then stepped inside Retch's sword reach and slugged the pirate hard in the face.

Retch's nose cracked and blood poured forth to cake with the flour on his lip.

Deudermont started back, or seemed to, but in truth, he was merely rotating his shoulders, having reached back and turned his own sword expertly.

Retch came forward in outraged pursuit, thinking to stab the captain with his dagger, and shouting, "Curse ye, cheatin' dog!"

At least, that's what he meant to say, but he found his dagger going right by the captain and his words choked short as Deudermont's fine sword drove up under his jaw, through his mouth and into his brain, and right through that with such force as to lift the hat right from Argus Retch's head.

Deudermont did get stuck by the dagger for his daring move, but there was no strength behind the strike, for the pirate was already dead.

Still, Retch kept that surprised and outraged, wide-eyed expression for a long few heartbeats before falling forward, past the dodging captain, to land face-down on the floor.

"I wish I had the time to extend our battle, Argus Retch," Deudermont said to the corpse, "but I've business to attend to more important than satisfying the sense of fair play from the likes of you."

* * * * *

"Good that ye're slowin'! Ye'd be smarter to be rowin', cause this way ye ain't goin', ye know?" the dwarf bellowed, apparently amusing himself beyond all reason as he ended with a howling, "Bwahahahaha!"

"Oh, do kill him," Regis said to Drizzt.

"The fight is over, good dwarf," Drizzt said.

"I ain't thinking that," replied the dwarf.

"I'm going to get my captain, to usher him away," Drizzt explained. "Luskan is not for Deudermont, so it has been decided by the Luskar themselves. Thus, we go. There is no reason to continue this madness."

"Nah," the dwarf spouted, unconvinced. "I been wantin' to test me morningstars against the likes o' Drizzt Do'Urden since I heared yer name, elf. And I been hearin' yer name too many times." He drew his morningstars from over his shoulders.

Drizzt scimitars appeared in his hands as if they had been there all along.

"Bwahahahaha!" the dwarf roared in laughing applause. "As quick as they're saying, are ye?"

"Quicker," Drizzt promised. "And again I offer you this chance to be gone. I've no fight with you."

"Now there's a wager I'm willin' to take," said the dwarf, and he came forward, laughing maniacally.

CHAPTER

SUNSET IN LUSKAN

33

There could be no mistaking the Crow's forward leaning posture as he approached Arabeth Raurym, who had been summoned to his audience chamber at Ten Oaks.

Where lie your loyalties?" he asked.

Arabeth tried to keep her own posture firm and aggressive, but failed miserably as the small but strangely intimidating young man strode toward her. "Are you threatening me, an Overwizard of the Hosttower of the Arcane?"

"The what?"

"The achievement still merits respect!" said Arabeth, but her voice faltered just a bit when she noted that the Crow had drawn a long, wicked dagger. "Back, I warn you . . ."

She retreated a few quick steps and began waving her arms and chanting. Kensidan kept the measure of his approach and seemed in no hurry to interrupt her spellcasting. Arabeth blasted him full force with a lightning bolt, one that should have lifted him out of his high boots, however tight the lacing, and sent him flying across the room to slam into the back wall, a blast that should have burned a hole into him and sent his black hair to dancing, a blast that should have sent his heart to trembling before stopping all together.

Nothing happened.

The lightning burst out from Arabeth's fingers, then just . . . stopped.

* * * * *

Arabeth's face crinkled in a most unflattering expression and she gave a little cry and stumbled to her right, toward the door.

At that moment, Kensidan, tingling with power, knew he'd been right to trust the voices in the darkness all along. He rushed forward just enough to tap Arabeth on the shoulder as she rushed past, and in that touch, he released all of the energy of her lightning bolt, energy that had been caught and held.

The woman flew through the air, but not so far, for she had enacted many wards before entering the room and much of the magic was absorbed. Of more concern, a globe of blackness appeared at the door, blocking her way. She gave a little yelp and staggered off to the side again, the Crow laughing behind her.

Three figures stepped out from the globe of darkness.

Kensidan watched Arabeth all the while, grinning as her eyes opened, as she tried to scream, and stumbled again, falling to the floor on her behind.

The second of the dark elves thrust his hands out toward her, and the woman's screams became an indecipherable babble as a wave of mental energy rushed through her, jumbling her thoughts and sensibilities. She continued her downward spiral to lay on the floor, babbling and curling up like a frightened child.

"What is your plan?" said the leader of the drow, the one with the gigantic plumed hat and the foppish garb. "Or do you intend to have others fight all of your battles this day?"

Kensidan nodded, an admission that it did indeed seem that way. "I must make my mark for the greater purpose we intend," he agreed.

"Well said," the drow replied.

"Deudermont is mine," the high captain promised.

"A formidable foe," said the drow. "And one we might be better off allowing to run away."

Kensidan didn't miss that the psionicist gave his master a curious, almost incredulous look at that. A free Deudermont wouldn't give up the fight, and would surely return with many powerful allies.

"We shall see," was all the Crow could promise. He looked

to Arabeth. "Don't kill her. She will be loyal . . . and pleasurable enough."

The drow with the big hat tipped it at that, and Kensidan nodded his gratitude. Then he flipped his cloak up high to the sides and as it descended, Kensidan seemed to melt beneath its dropping black wings. Then he was a bird, a large crow. He flew to the sill of his open window and leaped off for Suljack's palace, a place he knew quite well.

"He will be a good ally," Kimmuriel said to Jarlaxle, who had resumed the helm of Bregan D'aerthe. "As long as we never trust him."

A wistful and nostalgic sigh escaped Jarlaxle's lips as he replied, "Just like home."

* * * * *

Any thoughts Regis had of rushing in to help his friend disappeared when Drizzt and this curious dwarf joined in battle, a start so furious and brutal that the halfling figured it to be over before he could even draw his—in light of the titanic struggle suddenly exploding before him—pitiful little mace.

Morningstar and scimitar crossed in a dizzying series of vicious swings, more a matter of the combatants trying to get a feel for each other than either trying to land a killing blow. What stunned Regis the most was the way the dwarf kept up with Drizzt. He had seen the dark elf in battle many times, but the idea that the short, stout, thick-limbed creature swinging unwieldy morningstars could pace him swing for swing had the halfling gaping in astonishment.

But there it was. The dwarf's weapon hummed across and Drizzt angled his blade, swinging opposite, just enough to force a miss. He didn't want to connect a thin scimitar to one of those spiked balls.

The morningstar head flew past and the dwarf didn't pull it up short, but let it swing far out to his left to connect on the wall of the alleyway, and when it did, the ensuing explosion revealed that there was more than a little magic in that weapon. A huge chunk of the building blasted away, leaving a gaping hole.

Pulling his own swing short, his feet sped by his magical

anklets, Drizzt saw the opening and charged ahead, only wincing slightly at the crashing blast when the morningstar hit the wooden wall.

But the slight wince was too much; the momentary distraction too long. Regis saw it and gasped. The dwarf was already into his duck and turn as the spiked ball took out the wall, coming fast around, his left arm at full extension, his second morningstar head whistling out as wide as it could go.

If his opponent hadn't been a dwarf, but a taller human, Drizzt likely would have had his left leg caved in underneath him, but as the morningstar head came around a bit lower, the drow stole his own forward progress in the blink of a surprised eye and threw himself into a leap and back flip.

The morningstar hit nothing but air, the drow landing lightly on his feet some three strides back from the dwarf.

Again, against a lesser opponent, there would have been a clear opening then. The great twirling swing had brought the dwarf to an overbalanced and nearly defenseless state. But so strong was he that he growled himself right out of it. He ran a couple of steps straight away from Drizzt, diving into a forward roll and turning as he did so that when he came up, over, and around, he was again directly squared to the drow.

More impressively, even as he came up straight, his arms already worked the morningstars, creating a smooth rhythm once again. The balls spun at the ends of their respective chains, ready to block or strike.

"How do you hurt him?" Regis asked incredulously, not meaning for Drizzt to hear.

The drow did hear, though, as was evidenced by his responding shrug as he and the dwarf engaged yet again. They began to circle, Drizzt sliding to put his back along the wall the morningstar had just demolished, the dwarf staying opposite.

It was the look on Drizzt's face as he turned the back side of that circle that alerted Regis to trouble, for the drow suddenly broke concentration on his primary target, his eyes going wide as he looked Regis's way.

Purely on instinct, Regis snapped out his mace and spun, swinging wildly.

He hit the thrusting sword right before it would have entered his back. Regis gave a yelp of surprise, and still got cut across his left arm as he turned. He fell back against the wall, his desperate gaze going to Drizzt, and he found himself trying to yell out, "No!" as if all the world had suddenly turned upside down.

For Drizzt had started to sprint Regis's way, and so quick was he that against almost any enemy, he would have been able to cleanly disengage.

But that dwarf wasn't any enemy, and Regis could only stare in horror as the dwarf's primary hand weapon, the one that had blown so gaping a hole in the building, came on a backhand at the passing drow.

Drizzt sensed it, or anticipated it, and he dived into a forward roll.

He couldn't avoid the morningstar, and his roll went all the faster for the added momentum.

Amazingly, the blow didn't prove lethal, though, and the drow came right around in a full run at Regis's attacker—who, spying his certain doom, tried to run away.

He didn't even begin his turn, backstepping still, when Drizzt caught him, scimitars working in a blur. The man's sword went flying in moments, and he fell back and to the ground, his chest stabbed three separate times.

He stared at the drow and at Regis for just a moment before falling flat.

Drizzt spun as if expecting pursuit, but the dwarf was still far back in the alleyway, casually spinning his morningstars.

"Get to Deudermont," Drizzt whispered to Regis, and he tucked one scimitar under his other arm and put his open hand out and low. As soon as Regis stepped into it, Drizzt hoisted him up to grab onto the low roof of the shed and pull himself over as Drizzt hoisted him to his full outstretched height.

The drow turned the moment Regis was out of sight, scimitars in hand, but still the dwarf had not approached.

"Could've killed ye to death, darkskin," the dwarf said. "Could've put me magic on the ball that clipped ye, and oh, but ye'd still be rollin'! Clear out o' the streets and into the bay, ye'd still be rollin'! Bwahahahaha!"

Regis looked to Drizzt, and was shocked to see that his friend was not disagreeing.

"Or I could've just chased ye down the hall," the dwarf went on. "Quick as ye were rid o' that fool wouldn't've been quick enough to set yerself against the catastrophe coming yer way from behind!"

Again, the drow didn't disagree. "But you didn't," Drizzt said, walking slowly back toward his adversary. "You didn't enact the morningstar's magic and you didn't pursue me. Twice you had the win, by your own boast, and twice you didn't take it."

"Bah, wasn't fair!" bellowed the dwarf. "What's the fun in that?"

"Then you have honor," said Drizzt.

"Got nothin' else, elf."

"Then why waste it?" Drizzt cried. "You are a fine warrior, to be sure. Join with me and with Deudermont. Put your skills—"

"What?" the dwarf interrupted. "To the cause of good? There ain't no cause of good, ye fool elf. Not in the fightin'. There's only them wantin' more power, and the killers like yerself and meself helpin' one side or the other side—they're both the same side, ye see—climb to the top o' the hill."

"No," said Drizzt. "There is more."

"Bwahahahaha!" roared the dwarf. "Still a young one, I'm guessin'!"

"I can offer you amnesty, here and now," said Drizzt. "All past crimes will be forgiven, or at least . . . not asked about."

"Bwahahahaha!" the dwarf roared again. "If ye only knowed the half of it, elf, ye wouldn't be so quick to put Athrogate by yer side!" And with that, he charged, yelling, "Have at it!"

Drizzt paused only long enough to look up at Regis and snap, "Go!"

Regis had barely clambered two crawling steps up the steep roof when he heard the pair below come crashing together.

* * * * *

"Scream louder," the Crow ordered, and he twisted his dagger deeper into the belly of the woman, who readily complied.

A moment later, Kensidan, giggling at his own cleverness, tossed the pained woman aside, as the door to the room crashed open and

Captain Deudermont, diverted by the screams from his rush to the kitchen service door of Suljack's palace, charged in.

"Noble to a fault," said Kensidan. "And with the road of retreat clear before you. I suppose I should salute you, but alas, I simply don't feel like it."

Deudermont's gaze went from the injured woman to the son of Rethnor, who reclined casually against a window sill.

"Have you taken in the view, Captain?" Kensidan asked. "The fall of the City of Sails . . . It's a marvelous thing, don't you think?"

"Why would you do this?" Deudermont asked, coming forward in cautious and measured steps.

"I?" Kensidan replied. "It was not Ship Rethnor that went against the Hosttower."

"That fight is ended, and won."

"This fight is that fight, you fool," said Kensidan. "When you decapitated Luskan, you set into motion this very struggle for power."

"We could have joined forces and ruled from a position of justice."

"Justice for the poor—ah, yes, that is the beauty of your rhetoric," Kensidan replied in a mocking tone, and he hopped up from the window sill and drew his sword to compliment the long dagger. "And has it not occurred to the captain of a pirate hunter that not all the poor of Luskan are so deserving of justice? Or that there are afoot in the city many who wouldn't prosper as well under such an idyllic design?"

"That is why I needed the high captains, fool," Deudermont countered, spitting every word.

"Can you be so innocent, Deudermont, as to believe that men like us would willingly surrender power?"

"Can you be so cynical, Kensidan, son of Rethnor, as to be blind to the possibilities of the common good?"

"I live among pirates, so I fought them with piracy," Kensidan replied.

"You had a choice. You could have changed things."

"And you had a choice. You could have minded your own business. You could have left Luskan alone, and now, more recently, you could have simply gone home. You accuse me of pride and greed for not following you, but in truth, it's your own pride that blinded you to the realities of this place you would remake in your likeness, and your own greed that has kept you here. A tragedy, indeed, for here you will die, and Luskan will steer onto a course even farther from your hopes and dreams."

On the floor, the woman groaned.

"Let me take her out of here," Deudermont said.

"Of course," Kensidan replied. "All you have to do is kill me, and she's yours."

Without any further hesitation, Captain Deudermont launched himself forward at the son of Rethnor, his fine sword cutting a trail before him.

Kensidan tried to execute a parry with his dagger, thinking to bring his sword to bear for a quick kill, but Deudermont was far too fast and practiced. Kensidan wound up only barely tapping the thrusting sword with his dagger before flailing wildly with his own sword to hardly move Deudermont's aside.

The captain retracted quickly and thrust again, pulled up short before another series of wild parry attempts, then thrust forth again.

"Oh, but you are good!" said Kensidan.

Deudermont didn't let up through the compliment, but launched another thrust then retracted and brought his sword up high for a following downward strike.

Kensidan barely got his sword up horizontally above him to block, and as he did, he turned, for his back was nearing a wall. The weight of the blow had him scrambling to keep his feet.

Deudermont methodically pursued, unimpressed by the son of Rethnor's swordsmanship. In the back of his mind, he wondered why the young fool would dare to come against him so. Was his hubris so great that he fancied himself a swordsman? Or was he faking incompetence to move Deudermont off his guard?

With that warning ringing in his thoughts, Deudermont moved at his foe with a flurry, but measured every strike so he could quickly revert to a fully defensive posture.

But no counterattack came, not even when it seemed as if he had obviously overplayed his attacks.

The captain didn't show his smile, but the conclusion seemed inescapable: Kensidan was no match for him.

The woman groaned again, bringing rage to Deudermont, and he assured himself that his victory would strike an important blow for the retribution he would surely bring with him on his return to the City of Sails.

So he went for the kill, skipping in fast, smashing Kensidan's sword out wide and rolling his blade so as to avoid the awkward parry of the dagger.

Kensidan leaped straight up in the air, but Deudermont knew he would have him fast on his descent.

Except that Kensidan didn't come down.

Deudermont's confusion only multiplied as he heard the thrum of large wings above him and as one of those large black-feathered appendages batted him about the head, sending him staggering aside. He turned and waved his sword to fend him off, but Kensidan the Crow wasn't following.

He set down with a hop on three-toed feet, a gigantic, man-sized crow. His bird eyes regarded Deudermont from several angles, head twitching left and right to take in the scene.

"A nickname well-earned," Deudermont managed to say, trying hard to parse his words correctly and coherently, trying hard not to let on how off balance the man's sudden transformation into the outrageous creature had left him.

The Crow skipped his way and Deudermont presented his sword defensively. Wings going wide, the Crow leaped up, clawed feet coming forward, black wings assaulting Deudermont from either side. He slashed at one, trying to fall back, and did manage to dislodge a few black feathers.

But the Crow came on with squawking fury, throwing forward his torso and feet as he beat his wings back. Deudermont tried to bring his sword in to properly fend the creature off. Six toes, widespread, all ending with lethal talons clawed at him.

He managed to nick one of the feet, but the Crow dropped it fast out of harm's way, while the other foot slipped past the captain's defenses and caught hold of his shoulder.

The wings beat furiously, the Crow changing his angle as he raked that foot down, tearing the captain from left shoulder to right hip.

Deudermont brought his sword slashing across, but the creature was too fast and too nimble, and the taloned foot slipped out of his reach. The bird came forward and pecked the captain hard in the right shoulder, sending him flying to the ground, stealing all sensation and strength from his sword arm.

A wing beat and a leap had the Crow straddling the fallen man. Deudermont tried to roll upright, but the next peck hit him on the head, slamming him back to the floor.

Blood poured down from his brow across his left eye and cheek, but more than that, opaque liquid blurred the captain's sight as, thoroughly dazed, he faded in and out of consciousness.

* * * * *

Regis kept his head down, focusing solely on the task before him. Crawling on hands and knees, picking each handhold cautiously but expediently, the halfling made his way up the steep roof.

"Have to get to Deudermont," he told himself, pulling himself along, increasing his pace as he gained confidence with the climb. He finally hit his stride and was just about to look up when he bumped into something hard. High, black boots filled his vision.

Regis froze and slowly lifted his gaze, up past the fine fabric of well-tailored trousers, up past a fabulously crafted belt buckle, a fine gray vest and white shirt, to a face he never expected.

"You!" he cried in dismay and horror, desperately throwing his arms up before his face as a small crossbow leveled his way.

The exaggerated movement cost the halfling his balance, but even the unexpected tumble didn't save him from being stuck in the neck by the quarrel. Down the roof Regis tumbled, darkness rushing up all around him, stealing the strength from his limbs, stealing the light from his eyes, stealing even his voice as he tried to cry out.

* * * * *

The dwarf's swings didn't come any slower as he rejoined battle against Drizzt. And Drizzt quickly realized that the dwarf wasn't even breathing hard. Using his anklets to speed his steps, Drizzt pushed the issue, scampering to the left, then right back around the dwarf, and out and back suddenly as the furious little creature spun to keep up.

The drow worked a blur of measured strikes, and exaggerated steps, forcing the stubby-limbed dwarf to rush every which way.

The flurry went on and on, scimitars rolling one over the other, morningstars spinning to keep pace, and even, once in a while, to offer a devious counterstroke. And still Drizzt pressed, rushing left and back to center, right and all the way around, forcing the dwarf to continually reverse momentum on his heavier weapons.

But Athrogate did so with ease, and showed no labored breath, and whenever a thrust or parry connected, weapon to weapon, Drizzt was reminded of the dwarf's preternatural strength.

Indeed, Athrogate possessed it all: speed, stamina, strength, and technique. He was as complete a fighter as Drizzt had ever battled, and with weapons to equal Drizzt's own. The first morningstar kept coating over with some explosive liquid, and the second head leaked a brownish fluid. The first time that connected in a parry against Icingdeath, Drizzt was sure he felt the scimitar's fear. He brought the blade back for a quick inspection as he broke away, angling for a new attack, and noted dots of brown on is shining metal. It was rust, he realized, and realized, too, that only the mighty magic of Icingdeath had saved the blade from rotting away in his hand!

And Athrogate just kept howling, "Bwahahahaha!" and charging on with abandon.

Seeming abandon, because never, ever, did the dwarf abandon his defensive technique.

He was good. Very good.

But so was Drizzt Do'Urden.

The dark elf slowed his attacks and let Athrogate gain momentum, until it was the dwarf, not the drow, pressing the advantage.

"Bwahahahaha!" Athrogate roared, and sent both his morningstars into aggressive spins, low and high, working one down, the other up in a dizzying barrage that nearly caught up to the dodging, parrying drow.

Drizzt measured every movement, his eyes moving three steps ahead. He thrust into the left, forcing a parry, then went with that block to send his scimitar out wide but in an arcing movement that brought it back in again, sweeping down at his shorter opponent's shoulder.

Athrogate was up to the task of parrying, as Drizzt knew he would be, bringing his left-hand morningstar flying up across his right shoulder to defeat the attack.

But it wasn't really an attack, and Icingdeath snuck in for a stab at Athrogate's side. The dwarf yelped and leaped back, clearing three long strides. He laughed again, but winced, and brought his hand down against his rib. When he brought that hand back up, both Drizzt and he understood that the drow had drawn first blood.

"Well done!" he said, or started to, for Drizzt leaped at him, scimitars working wildly.

Drizzt rolled them over each other in a punishing alternating downward and straightforward slash, keeping them timed perfectly so that one morningstar could not defeat them both, and keeping them angled perfectly so that Athrogate had to keep his own weapons at a more awkward and draining angle, up high in front of his face.

The dwarf's grimace told Drizzt that his stab in the ribs had been more effective than Athrogate pretended, and holding his arms up in such a manner was not comfortable at all.

The drow kept up the roll and pressed the advantage, driving Athrogate ever backward, both combatants knowing that one slip by Drizzt would do no more than put them back at an even posture, but one slip by Athrogate would likely end the fight in short order.

The dwarf wasn't laughing anymore.

Drizzt pressed him even harder, growling with every rolling swing, backing Athrogate back down the alley the way Drizzt had come, away from the palace.

Drizzt caught the movement out of the corner of his eye, a small form rolling limply off the roof. Without a whimper, without a cry of alarm, Regis, tumbled to the ground and lay still.

Athrogate seized the distraction for his advantage, and cut back and to his right, then smashed his morningstar across to bat the drow's chopping scimitar out far to the side with such force—and an added magical explosion—that Drizzt had to disengage fully and

THE PIRATE KING

scamper to the opposite wall to simply hold onto the blade.

Drizzt got a look at Regis, lying awkwardly twisted in the alleyway's gutter. Not a sound, not a squirm, not a whimper of pain....

He was somewhere past pain; it seemed to Drizzt as if his spirit had already left his battered body.

And Drizzt couldn't go to him. Drizzt, who had chosen to return to Luskan, to stand with Deudermont, couldn't do anything but look at his dear friend.

* * * * *

At sea, it's said that danger can be measured by the scurry of the rats, and if that model held true, then the battle between Robillard and Arklem Greeth in the hold of *Sea Sprite* ranked right up alongside beaching the boat on the back of a dragon turtle.

All manner of evocations flew out between the dueling wizards, fire and ice, magical energy of different colors and inventive shapes. Robillard tried to keep his spells more narrow in scope, aiming *just* for Arklem Greeth, but the lich was as full of hatred for *Sea Sprite* herself as he was for his old peer in the Hosttower. Robillard threw missiles of solid magic and acidic darts. Greeth responded with forked lightning bolts and fireballs, filling the hold with flame.

Robillard's work on the hull with magical protections and wards, and all manner of alchemical mixtures, had been as complete and as brilliant as the work of any wizard or team of wizards had ever put on any ship, but he knew with every mighty explosion that Arklem Greeth tested those wards to their fullest and beyond.

With every fireball, a few more residual flames burned for just a few heartbeats longer. Every successive lightning bolt thumped the planking out a bit wider, and a little more water managed to seep in.

Soon enough, the wizards stood among a maelstrom of destruction, water up to their ankles, *Sea Sprite* rocking hard with every blast.

Robillard knew he had to get Arklem Greeth out of his ship. Whatever the cost, whatever else might happen, he had to move the spell duel to another place. He launched into a mighty spell, and as he cast it, he threw himself at Greeth, thinking that both he and his adversary would be projected into the Astral Plane to finish the insanity.

Nothing happened, for the archmage arcane had already applied a dimensional lock to the hold.

Robillard staggered as he realized that he was not flying on another plane of existence, as he had anticipated. He threw his arms up defensively as he righted himself, for Arklem Greeth brought in a gigantic disembodied fist that punched at him with the force of a titan.

The blow didn't break through the stoneskin dweomer of mighty Robillard, but it did send him flying back to the other end of the hold. He hit the wall hard, but felt not a thing, landing lightly on his feet and launching immediately into another lightning bolt.

Arklem Greeth, too, was already into a new casting, and his spell went off right before Robillard's, creating a summoned wall of stone halfway between the combatants.

Robillard's lightning bolt hit that stone with such tremendous force that huge chunks flew, but the bolt also rebounded into the wizard's face, throwing him again into the wall behind him.

And he had exhausted his wards. He felt that impact, and felt, too, the sizzle of his own lightning bolt. His heart palpitated, his hair stood on end. He kept his awareness just enough to realize that *Sea Sprite* was listing badly as a result of the tremendous weight of Arklem Greeth's summoned wall. From up above he heard screaming, and he knew that more than one of *Sea Sprite*'s crew had fallen overboard as a result.

Across the way, beyond the wall, Arklem Greeth cackled with delight, and in looking at the wall, Robillard understood that the worst was yet to come. For Greeth had offset it on the floor and had lined it along with the length and not the breadth of the ship, but he had not anchored it!

So as *Sea Sprite* listed under the great weight, so too leaned the wall, and it was beginning to tip.

Robillard realized that he couldn't stop it, so he found a moment of intense concentration instead and focused on his most-hated enemy. The wall fell, clearing the ground between the wizards, and Robillard let fly another devastating lightning blast.

So intent was he on his stone wall tumbling into *Sea Sprite*'s side planking, crashing through the wood, that Arklem Greeth never saw the bolt coming. He flew backward under the power of the stroke and hit the wall even as the side of the hull broke open and Luskan Harbor rushed in.

Robillard beat the rush of water, launching himself upon Arklem Greeth. Energy crackled through his hands, one electrical discharge after another.

Arklem Greeth fought back physically, tearing at Robillard with undead hands.

They held their death grip on each other as the sea turned *Sea Sprite* farther on her side, taking her down into the harbor. Spell after spell leaped from Robillard's fingers into the lich, blasting away at his magical defenses, and when those were finally beaten, as was his very life-force, still Arklem Greeth merely held on.

The lich didn't need to breathe, but Robillard surely did.

The pitch of the sinking ship sent them out through the hole in the hull, tumbling amidst the debris, rocks, and weeds of Luskan Harbor.

Robillard felt his ears pop under the pressure and knew his lungs wouldn't be far behind. But he held on, determined to end the struggle at whatever cost. The sight of *Sea Sprite*, the wreckage of his beloved *Sea Sprite*, spurred him on and he resisted the urge to break free of Arklem Greeth and focused instead on continuing his electrical barrage on the lich—even though every powerful discharge stung him as well in the conducting water.

It seemed like a dozen, dozen spells. It seemed like his lungs would surely burst. It seemed like Arklem Greeth was mocking him.

But the lich simply let go, and the face the surprised Robillard looked into was dead, not undead.

Robillard shoved away and kicked off the bottom, determined not to die in the arms of the hideous Arklem Greeth. Instinctively he clawed for the surface, and saw the water growing lighter above him.

But he knew he wouldn't make it.

* * * * *

"*Sea Sprite!*" more than one sailor of *Thrice Lucky*, and of every other ship moored in the area, cried out in astonishment. To those men and women, friend and enemy of Deudermont's ship alike, the sight before them seemed impossible.

The waves took *Sea Sprite* and smashed her up on a line of rocks, just one rail of her glorious hull and her three distinctive masts protruding from the dark waters of Luskan Harbor.

It could not be. In the minds of those who knew the ship as friend or foe, the loss of *Sea Sprite* proved no less traumatic than the disintegration of the Hosttower of the Arcane, a sudden and unimaginable change in the landscape that had shaped their lives.

"*Sea Sprite!*" they cried as one, pointing and jumping.

Morik the Rogue and Bellany rushed to *Thrice Lucky*'s rail to take in the awful scene.

"What are we to do?" Morik asked incredulously. "Where is Maimun?" He knew the answer, and so did many others echoing that very sentiment, for their captain had gone ashore less than an hour earlier.

Some crewmen called for lifelines, to weigh anchor to rush to the aid of the crew in the water. Bellany did likewise and started for a lifeboat, but Morik grabbed her by the shoulder and spun her to face him.

"Make me fly!" he bade her, and she looked at him curiously.

"Give me flight!" he screamed. "You've done it before!"

"Flight?"

"Do it!"

Bellany rubbed her hands together and tried to focus, tried to remember the words as the insanity around her only multiplied. She reached out and touched Morik on the shoulder and the man leaped up to the rail and out from the ship.

He didn't fall into the water, though, but flew out across the bay. He scanned, trying to figure out where he was most needed, then cut across for the downed vessel herself, fearing that some of the crew might be trapped aboard her.

Then he crossed over a form in the water, just under the surface but sinking fast, and willed himself to stop. He slapped his hand down, plunging it through the waves, and grabbed hard on the fine fabric of a wizard's robes.

THE PIRATE KING

* * * * *

"Ah, the glorious pain," Kensidan taunted. Deudermont again tried to pull himself up and the Crow pecked him hard on the forehead, slamming him back to the floor.

The room's door banged open. "No!" cried a voice familiar to both men. "Let him go!"

"Are you mad, young pirate?" the Crow cackled as he turned to regard Maimun. He spun back and slammed Deudermont hard again, smashing him flat to the floor.

Maimun responded with a sudden and brutal charge, flashing sword leading the way. Kensidan beat his wings and tried to extricate himself from the close quarters, but Maimun's fury was too great and his advantage too sudden and complete. The wings battered around the perimeter of the fight, but Maimun's sword cut a narrower and more direct line.

In the span of a few heartbeats, Maimun had Kensidan pinned at the end of his blade, and when Kensidan tried to turn the sword with his beak, Maimun got the blade inside the Crow's mouth.

Given that awkward and devastating clutch, Kensidan could offer no further resistance.

Maimun, breathing hard, clearly outraged, held the pose and the pin for a long breath. "I give you your life," he said finally, easing the blade just a bit. "You have the city—there will be no challenge. I will go, and I'm taking Captain Deudermont with me."

Kensidan looked over at the battered and bloody form of Deudermont and started to cackle, but Maimun stopped that with a prod of his well-placed blade.

"You will allow us clear passage to our ships, and for our ships out of Luskan Harbor."

"He is already dead, fool, or soon enough to be!" the Crow argued, slurring every word, as he spouted them around the hard steel of a fine blade.

The words nearly buckled Maimun's knees. His thoughts swirled back in time to his first meeting with the captain. He had stowed away on *Sea Sprite,* fleeing a demon intent on his destruction. Deudermont had allowed him to stay. *Sea Sprite*'s crew, generous to a fault, had not abandoned him when they'd learned the truth of his ordeal, even when they discerned that having Maimun aboard made them targets of the powerful demon and its many deadly allies.

Captain Deudermont had saved young Maimun, without a doubt, and had taken him under his wing and trained him in the ways of the sea.

And Maimun had betrayed him. Though he had never expected it to come to so tragic an end, the young pirate captain could not deny the truth. Paid by Kensidan, Maimun had sailed Arabeth to *Quelch's Folly*. Maimun had played a role in the catastrophe that had befallen Luskan, and in the catastrophe that had lain Captain Deudermont low before him.

Maimun turned back sharply on Kensidan and pressed the sword in tighter. "I will have your word, Crow, that I will be allowed free passage, with Deudermont and *Sea Sprite* beside me."

Kensidan stared at him hatefully with those black crow eyes. "Do you understand who I am now, young pirate?" he replied slowly, and as evenly as the prodding blade allowed. "Luskan is mine. I am the Pirate King."

"And you're to be the dead Pirate King if I don't get your word!" Maimun assured him.

But even as Maimun spoke, Kensidan all but disappeared beneath him, almost instantly reverting to the form of a small crow. He rushed out from under the overbalanced Maimun and with a flap of his wings, fluttered up to light on the windowsill across the room.

Maimun wrung his hands on his sword hilt, grimacing in frustration as he turned to regard the Crow, expecting that his world had just ended.

"You have my word," Kensidan said, surprising him.

"I have nothing with which to barter," Maimun stated.

The Crow shrugged, a curious movement from the bird, but one that conveyed the precise sentiment clearly enough. "I owe Maimun of *Thrice Lucky* that much, at least," said Kensidan. "So we will forget this incident, eh?"

Maimun could only stare at the bird.

"And I look forward to seeing your sails in my harbor again," Kensidan finished, and he flew away out the window.

Maimun stood there stunned for a few moments then rushed to Deudermont, falling to his knees beside the broken man.

* * * * *

His first attacks after seeing Regis fall were measured, his first defenses almost half-hearted. Drizzt could hardly find his focus, with his friend lying there in the gutter, could hardly muster the energy necessary to stand his ground against the dwarf warrior.

Perhaps sensing that very thing, or perhaps thinking it all a ploy, Athrogate didn't press in those first few moments of rejoined battle, measuring his own strikes to gain strategic advantage rather than going for the sudden kill.

His mistake.

For Drizzt internalized the shock and the pain, and as he always had before, took it and turned the tumult into a narrowly-focused burst of outrage. His scimitars picked up their pace, the strength of his strikes increasing proportionately. He began to work Athrogate as he had before the fall of Regis, moving side to side and forcing the dwarf to keep up.

But the dwarf did match his pace, fighting Drizzt to a solid draw strike after thrust after slash.

And what a glorious draw it was to any who might have chanced to look on. The combatants spun with abandon, scimitars and morningstars humming through the air. Athrogate hit a wall again, the spiked ball smashing the wood to splinters. He hit the cobblestones before the backward-leaping drow and crushed them to dust.

And there Drizzt scored his second hit, Twinkle nicking Athrogate's cheek and taking away one of his great beard's braids.

"Ah, but ye'll pay for that, elf!" the dwarf roared, and on he came.

To the side, Regis groaned.

He was alive.

He needed help.

Drizzt turned away from Athrogate and fled across the alleyway, the dwarf in close pursuit. The drow leaped to the wall, throwing his shoulders back and planting one foot solidly as if he meant to run right up the side of the structure.

Or, to Athrogate's discerning and seasoned battle sensibilities, to flip a backward somersault right over him.

The dwarf pulled up short and whirled, shouting "Bwaha! I'm knowin' that move!"

But Drizzt didn't fly over him and come down in front of him, and the drow, who had not used his planted foot to push off, and who had not brought his second foot up to further climb, replied, "I know you know."

From behind the turned dwarf, down the alley, Guenhwyvar roared, like an exclamation point to Drizzt's victory.

For indeed the win was his; he could only pray that Regis was not beyond his help. Icingdeath slashed down at Athrogate's defenseless head, surely a blow that would split the dwarf's head apart. He took little satisfaction in that win as his blade connected against Athrogate's skull, as he felt the transfer of deadly energy.

But the dwarf didn't seem to even feel it, no blood erupted, and Drizzt's blade didn't bounce aside.

Drizzt had felt that curious sensation before, as if he had landed a blow without consequence.

Still, he didn't sort it out quickly enough, didn't understand the source.

Athrogate spun, morningstars flying desperately. One barely clipped Drizzt's blade, but in that slightest of touches, a great surge of energy exploded out of the dwarf and hurled Drizzt back against the wall with such force that his blades flew from his hands.

Athrogate closed, weapons flying with fury.

Drizzt had no defense. Out of the corner of one eye, he noted the rise of a spiked metal ball, glistening with explosive liquid.

It rushed at his head, the last thing he saw.

EPILOGUE

"Don't you die! Don't you die on me!" Maimun cried, cradling Deudermont's head. "Damn you! You can't die on me!"

Deudermont opened his eyes—or one, at least, for the other was crusted closed by dried blood.

"I failed," he said.

Maimun hugged him close, shaking his head, choking up.

"I have been . . . a fool," Deudermont gasped, no strength left in him.

"No!" Maimun insisted. "No. You tried. For the good of the people, you tried."

And something strange came over young Maimun in that moment, a revelation, an epiphany. He was speaking on Deudermont's behalf at that moment, trying to bring some comfort in a devastating moment of ultimate defeat, but as he spoke the words, they resonated within Maimun himself.

For Deudermont had indeed tried, had struck out for the good of those who had for years, in some cases for all their lives, suffered under the horror of Arklem Greeth and the five corrupt high captains. He had tried to be rid of the awful Prisoner's Carnival, to be rid of the pirates and the lawlessness that had left so many corpses in its bloody wake.

Maimun's own accusations against Deudermont, his claims that Deudermont's authoritarian nature was no better for the people he claimed to serve than were the methods of the enemies he tried to defeat, rang hollow to the young pirate in that moment of great pain. He felt unsure of himself, as if the axioms upon which he had built his adult life were neither as resolute nor as morally pure, and as if Deudermont's imposition of order might not be so absolutely bad, as he had believed.

"You tried, Captain," he said. "That is all any of us can ever do."

He ended with a wail, for he realized that the captain had not heard him, that Captain Deudermont, who had been as a father to him in years past, was dead.

Sobbing, Maimun gently stroked the captain's bloody face. Again he thought of their first meeting, of those early, good years together aboard *Sea Sprite*.

With a growl of defiance, Maimun cradled Deudermont, shoulders and knees, and gently lifted the man into his arms as he stood straight.

He walked out of Suljack's palace, onto Luskan's streets, where the fighting had strangely quieted as news of the captain's demise began to spread.

Head up, eyes straight ahead, Maimun walked to the dock, and he waited patiently, holding Deudermont all the while, as a small boat from *Thrice Lucky* was rowed furiously to retrieve him.

* * * * *

"Oh, but what a shot ye took on yer crown, and if yer head's hurting as much as me own, then suren yer head's hurtin' more'n ever ye've known! Bwahahaha!"

The dwarf's rhyming words drew Drizzt out of the darkness, however much he wanted to avoid them. He opened his groggy eyes, to find himself sitting in a comfortably-adorned room—a room in the Red Dragon Inn, he realized, a room in which he and Deudermont had shared several meals and exchanged many words.

And there was the dwarf, Athrogate, his adversary, sitting calmly across from him, weapons tucked into their sheaths across his back.

Drizzt couldn't sort it out, but then he remembered Regis. He bolted upright, eyes scanning the room, hands going to his belt.

His blades were not there. He didn't know what to think.

And his confusion only heightened when Jarlaxle Baenre and Kimmuriel Oblodra walked into the room.

It made sense, of course, given Drizzt's failed—psionically blocked—strike against Athrogate, and he placed then the moment when he had felt that strange sensation of his energy being absorbed before, in a fight with Artemis Entreri, a fight overseen by this very pair of drow.

Drizzt fell back, a bitter expression clouding his face. "I should have guessed your handiwork," he grumbled.

"Luskan's fall?" Jarlaxle asked. "But you give me too much credit—or blame, my friend. What you see around you was not my doing."

Drizzt eyed the mercenary with clear skepticism.

"Oh, but you wound me with your doubts!" Jarlaxle added, heaving a great sigh. He calmed quickly and moved to Drizzt, taking a chair with him. He flipped it around and sat on it backward, propping his elbows on the high back and staring Drizzt in the eye.

"We didn't do this," Jarlaxle insisted.

"My fight with the dwarf?"

"We did intervene in that, of course," the drow mercenary admitted. "I couldn't have you destroying so valuable an asset as that one."

"And yes, you surely could have," Kimmuriel muttered, speaking in the language of the drow.

"All of it, I mean," Jarlaxle went on without missing a beat. "This was not our doing, but rather the work of ambitious men."

"The high captains," Drizzt reasoned, though he still didn't believe it.

"And Deudermont," Jarlaxle added. "Had he not surrendered to his own foolish ambition. . . ."

"Where is he?" Drizzt demanded, sitting up tall once more.

Jarlaxle's expression grew grim and Drizzt held his breath.

"Alas, he has fallen," Jarlaxle explained. "And *Sea Sprite* lays wrecked on rocks in the harbor, though most of her crew have escaped the city aboard another ship."

Drizzt tried not to sink back, but the weight of Deudermont's death fell heavily on his shoulders. He had known the man for so many years, had considered him a dear friend, a good man, a great leader.

"This was not my work," Jarlaxle insisted, forcing Drizzt to look him in the eye. "Nor the work of any of my band. On my word."

"You lurked around its edges," Drizzt accused, and Jarlaxle offered a conciliatory shrug.

"We meant to . . . indeed, we *mean* to, make the most of the chaos," Jarlaxle said. "I'll not deny my attempt to profit, as I would have tried had Deudermont triumphed."

"He would have rejected you," Drizzt spat, and again, Jarlaxle shrugged.

"Likely," he conceded. "Then perhaps it's best for me that he didn't win. I didn't create the end, but I will certainly exploit it."

Drizzt glared at him.

"But I'm not without some redeeming qualities," Jarlaxle reminded. "You are alive, after all."

"I would have won the fight outright, had you not intervened," Drizzt reminded him.

"That fight, perhaps, but what of the hundred following?"

Drizzt just continued to glare, unrelenting—until the door opened and Regis, battered, but very much alive, and seeming quite well considering his ordeal, stepped into the room.

* * * * *

Robillard stood at the rail of *Thrice Lucky*, staring back at the distant skyline of Luskan.

"Was Morik the Rogue who plucked you from the waves," Maimun said to him, walking over to join him.

"Tell him I won't kill him, then," Robillard replied. "Today."

Maimun chuckled, though there remained profound sadness behind his laugh, at the unrelenting sarcasm of the dour wizard. "Do you think *Sea Sprite* might be salvaged?" he asked

"Do I care?"

Maimun found himself at a loss to reply to the blunt answer, though he suspected it to be more an expression of anger and grief than anything else.

"Well, if you manage it, I can only hope that you and your crew will be too busy exacting revenge upon Luskan to chase the likes of me across the waves," the young pirate remarked.

Robillard looked at him, finally, and managed a smirk. "Neither fight seems worth a pile of rotting fish," he said, and he and Maimun looked at each other deeply then, sharing the moment of painful reality.

"I miss him, too," Maimun said.

"I know you do, boy," said Robillard.

Maimun put a hand on Robillard's shoulder, then walked away, leaving the wizard to his grief. Robillard had guaranteed him safe passage for *Thrice Lucky* through Waterdeep, and he trusted the wizard's words.

What the young pirate didn't trust at that moment were his own instincts. Deudermont's fall had hit him profoundly, had made him think, for the first time in many years, that the world might be more complicated than his idealistic sensibilities had allowed.

* * * * *

"We could not have asked for a better outcome," Kensidan insisted to the gathering at Ten Oaks. Baram and Taerl exchanged doubtful looks, but Kurth nodded his agreement with the Crow's assessment.

The streets of Luskan were quiet again, for the first time since Deudermont and Lord Brambleberry had put into the docks. The high captains had retreated to their respective corners; only Suljack's former domain remained in disarray.

"The city is ours" Kensidan said.

"Aye, and half of it's dead, and many others have run off," Baram replied.

"Unwanted and unnecessary fodder," said Kensidan. "We who remain, control. None who don't trade for us or fight for us or otherwise work for us belong here. This is no city for families and mundane issues. Nay, my comrades, Luskan is a free port now. A true free port. The only true free port in all the world."

"Can we survive without the institutions of a real city?" Kurth asked. "What foes might come against us, I wonder?"

"Waterdeep? Mirabar?" Taerl asked.

Kensidan grinned. "They will not. I have already spoken to the dwarves and men of Mirabar who live in the Shield District. I explained to them the benefits of our new arrangement, where exotic goods shall pass through Luskan's gates, in and out, without restriction, without question. They expressed confidence that Marchion Elastul would go along, as has his daughter, Arabeth. The other kingdoms of the Silver Marches will not pass over Mirabar to get to us." He looked slyly to Kurth as he added, "They will accept the profits with feigned outrage, if any at all."

Kurth offered an agreeing grin in return.

"And Waterdeep will muster no energy to attack us," Kensidan assured them. "To what end would they? What would be their gain?"

"Revenge for Brambleberry and Deudermont," said Baram.

"The rich lords, who will get richer by trading with us, will not wage war over that," Kensidan replied. "It is over. Arklem Greeth and the Arcane Brotherhood have lost. Lord Brambleberry and Captain Deudermont have lost. Some would say that Luskan herself has lost, and by the old definition of the City of Sails, I could not disagree.

"But the new Luskan is ours, my friends, my comrades," he went on, his ultimately calm demeanor, his absolute composure, lending power to his claims. "Outsiders will call us lawless because we care not for the minor matters of governance. Those who know us well will call us clever because we four will profit beyond anything we ever imagined possible."

Kurth stood up, then, staring at Kensidan hard. But only for a moment, before his face cracked into a wide smile, and he lifted his glass of rum in toast, "To the City of Sails," he said.

The other three joined in the toast.

* * * * *

Beneath the City of Sails, Valindra Shadowmantle sat unblinking, but hardly unthinking. She had felt it, the demise of Arklem Greeth, stabbing at her as profoundly as any dagger ever could. The two were linked, inexorably, in undeath, she as the unbreathing child of the master lich, and so his fall had stung her.

She at last turned her head to the side, the first movement she'd made in many days. There on a shelf, from within the depths of a hollowed skull, it sparkled—and with more than simple reflection of the enchanted light set in the corners of the decorated chamber.

Nay, that light came from inside the gem, the phylactery. That sparkle was the spark of life, of undeath existence, of Arklem Greeth.

With great effort, her skin and bones crackling at the first real movement in so many days, Valindra stood and walked stiff-legged over to the skull. She rolled it onto its side and reached in to retrieve the phylactery. Lifting it to her eyes, Valindra stared intently, as if trying to discern the tiny form of the lich.

But it appeared as just a gem with an inner sparkle, a magical light.

Valindra knew better. She knew that she held the spirit, the life energy, of Arklem Greeth in her hand.

To be resurrected into undeath, a lich once more, or to be destroyed, utterly and irrevocably?

Valindra Shadowmantle smiled and for just a brief moment, forgot her calamity and considered the possibilities.

He had promised her immortality, and more importantly, he had promised her power.

Perhaps that was all she had left.

She stared at the phylactery, the gemstone prison of her helpless master, feeling and basking in her power.

* * * * *

"It's all there," Jarlaxle insisted to Drizzt on the outskirts of Luskan as evening fell.

Drizzt eyed him for just a moment before slinging the pack over his shoulder.

"If I meant to keep anything, it would have been the cat, certainly," Jarlaxle said, looking over, and leading Drizzt's gaze to Guenhwyvar, who sat contentedly licking her paws. "Perhaps someday you'll realize that I'm not your enemy."

Regis, his face all bruised and bandaged from his fall, snorted at that.

"Well, I didn't mean for you to roll off the roof!" Jarlaxle answered. "But of course, I had to put you to sleep, for your own sake."

"You didn't give me everything back," Regis snarled at him.

Jarlaxle conceded the point with a shrug and a sigh. "Almost everything," he replied. "Enough for you to forgive me my one indulgence—and rest assured that I have replaced it with gems more valuable than anything it would have garnered on the open market."

Regis had no answer.

"Go home," Jarlaxle bade them both. "Go home to King Bruenor and your beloved friends. There is nothing left for you to do here."

"Luskan is dead," Drizzt said.

"To your sensibilities, surely so," Jarlaxle agreed. "Beyond resurrection."

Drizzt stared at the City of Sails for a few moments longer, digesting all that had transpired. Then he turned, draped an arm over his halfling friend, and led Regis away, not looking back.

"We can still save Longsaddle, perhaps," Regis offered, and Drizzt laughed and gave him an appreciative shake.

Jarlaxle watched them go until they were out of sight. Then he reached into his belt pouch to retrieve the one item he had taken from Regis: a small scrimshaw statue the halfling had sculpted into the likeness of Drizzt and Guenhwyvar.

Jarlaxle smiled warmly and tipped his great cap to the east, to Drizzt Do'Urden.

R.A. SALVATORE

THE GHOST KING

III
TRANSITIONS

An Excerpt

THE GHOST KING

Drizzt Do'Urden slipped out of his bedroll and reached his bare arms up high, fingers wide, stretching to the morning sky. It was good to be on the road, out of Mithral Hall, after the dark winter. It was good to smell the fresh, crisp air, absent the smoke of the forges, and to feel the wind across his shoulders and through his long, thick white hair.

It was good to be alone with his wife.

The dark elf rolled his head in wide circles, stretching his neck. He reached up high again while he knelt there on his blankets. The breeze was chill across his naked form, but he didn't mind, it invigorated him and made him feel alive with sensation.

He slowly moved to stand, exaggerating every movement to flex and stretch away the hard ground that had served as his mattress, then paced away from the small encampment and outside the ring of boulders to catch a view of Catti-brie.

Dressed only in her colorful magical blouse, which had once been the enchanted robes of a gnome wizard, she was up on a hill not far away, her palms together in front of her in a pose of deep concentration. Drizzt marveled at her simple charm, for the colorful shift reached only to mid-thigh, and Catti-brie's natural beauty was neither diminished nor outshone by the finely-crafted garment.

They were on the road back to Mithral Hall from the city of Silverymoon, where Catti-brie's wizard mentor, the great Lady

Alustriel, ruled. It had not been a good visit. Something was in the air, something dangerous and frightening, some feeling among the wizards that all was not well with the Weave of magic. Reports and whispers coming in from all over Faerûn spoke of spells gone horribly awry, of magic misfiring or not firing at all, of brilliant spellcasters falling to apparent insanity.

Alustriel had noted that she feared the integrity of Mystra's Weave itself, the very source of arcane energy, and the look on her face, ashen, was something Drizzt had never before witnessed from her, not even when the drow had come to Mithral Hall those many years ago, not even when King Obould and his great horde had crawled from their mountain holes in murderous frenzy. It was indeed a crestfallen and fearful look that Drizzt had never thought possible on the face of that renowned champion, one of the Seven Sisters, Chosen of Mystra, beloved ruler of mighty Silverymoon.

Vigilance, observance, and meditation were Alustriel's orders of the day, as she and all others scrambled to try to decipher what in the Nine Hells might be happening, and Catti-brie, less than a decade a wizard, but still showing great promise in that endeavor, had taken those orders to heart.

That's why she had risen so early, Drizzt knew, and had moved out from the distractions of the encampment and his presence, to be alone with her meditation.

He smiled as he watched her, her auburn hair still rich in color and thick to her shoulders, blowing in the breeze, her form, a bit thicker with age, perhaps, but still so beautiful and inviting to him, swaying gently with her thoughts.

She slowly reached her hands out wide as if in invitation to magic, the sleeves of her blouse covering only to her elbows, and Drizzt smiled as she lifted off the ground, floating up a couple of feet in easy levitation. Purple flames of faerie fire flickered to life across her body, appearing as extensions of the purple fabric of the blouse, as if its magic joined with her in a symbiotic completion, and a magical gust of wind buffeted her more forcefully, sending her auburn mane out wide behind her.

Drizzt could see that she was immersing herself in simple spells, in safe magic, trying to create more intimacy with the Weave as she contemplated the fears Alustriel had relayed.

A flash of lightning in the distance startled Drizzt and he turned fast toward it as a rumble of thunder followed.

He crinkled his brow in confusion. The dawn was cloudless, but lightning it had been, reaching from high in the sky to the ground, apparently, for he saw the crackling blue bolt continuing along the distant terrain.

Drizzt had been on the surface for forty-five years, but he had never seen any natural phenomenon quite like that. He had witnessed terrific storms from the deck of Captain Deudermont's *Sea Sprite*, had watched a dust storm engulf the Calim Desert, had seen a snow squall pile knee-deep on the ground in an hour's time. He had even seen the rare event known as ball lightning once, in Icewind Dale, and he figured the sight before him to be some variant on that peculiar energy.

But the lightning traveled in a straight line, leaving behind a curtain of blue-white, shimmering energy. He couldn't gauge its speed, other than to note that the curtain of blue fire expanded behind it.

It appeared to be crossing to the north of his position. He glanced up at Catti-brie, floating and glowing on the hilltop in the east, and wondered whether he should disturb her meditation to point out the phenomenon. He glanced back at the line of lightning and his lavender eyes widened in shock to find that it had accelerated suddenly, and had changed course, angling more in his direction.

He turned from the lightning to Catti-brie, to realize that it was running straight at her!

"Cat!" Drizzt yelled and started running that way.

She seemed not to hear.

Magical anklets sped Drizzt on his way, his legs moving in a blur. But the lightning was faster, and he could only cry out again and again as it sizzled past him. He could feel its teeming energy. His hair flew wildly from the proximity of the powerful charge, white strands dancing out to the side.

"Cat!" he yelled to the floating, glowing woman. "Catti-brie! Run!"

She was too deep in her meditation, though she did seem to respond, just a bit, turning her head to glance at Drizzt.

But too late, and her eyes widened just as the speeding ground lightning engulfed her. Blue sparks flew from her outstretched arms, her fingers jerking spasmodically, her form jolting with powerful discharges.

The tip of the strange lightning stayed there for a few heartbeats, then continued past, leaving the still-floating woman in the shimmering blue curtain of its wake.

"Cat," Drizzt gasped, scrambling desperately across the stones. By the time he got there, the curtain was moving past, leaving a scarred line still crackling with power along the ground.

Catti-brie still floated above it, still trembled and jerked, and Drizzt held his breath as he neared her, to see that her eyes had rolled up into her head, showing only white.

He grabbed her hand and felt the sting of electrical discharge. But he didn't let go and he stubbornly pulled her aside of the scarred line. He hugged her close and tried unsuccessfully to pull her down to the ground.

"Catti-brie," Drizzt begged. "Don't you leave me!"

* * * * *

He leaned up against a dead tree, a twisted silhouette whose shadow looked like the skeleton of a man who reached, pleading, to the gods. Jarlaxle didn't climb it—the old tree likely wouldn't have held his weight anyway—but instead remained standing, leaning against the rough trunk.

He let his mind fall away from his surroundings, let it fall within. Memories blended with sensations in the gentle swirl of Reverie. He felt his own heartbeat, the blood rushing through his veins. He felt the rhythms of the world, like a gentle breathing beneath his feet, and he embraced the sensation of a connection to the earth, as if he had grown roots into the deep rock. At the same time, he experienced a sensation of weightlessness, as if he was floating, as the wonderful relaxation of Reverie swept through his mind and body.

Only there was Jarlaxle free. Reverie was his refuge.

I will find you, drow.

Hephaestus was there with him, waiting for him. In his mind,

Jarlaxle saw again the fiery eyes of the beast, felt the hot breath and the hotter hatred.

Be gone. You have no quarrel with me, the dark elf silently replied.

I have not forgotten!

'Twas your own breath that broke the shard, Jarlaxle reminded.

Through your trickery, clever drow. I have not forgotten. You blinded me, you weakened me, you destroyed me!

That last clause struck Jarlaxle as odd, not just because the dragon obviously wasn't "destroyed," but because he still had the distinct feeling that it wasn't Hephaestus—but it was Hephaestus!

Another image came into Jarlaxle's thoughts, that of a bulbous-headed creature with tentacles waving menacingly from its face.

I know you. I will find you, the dragon went on. *You who stole from me the pleasures of the flesh and life. You who stole from me the sweet taste of food and the pleasure of touch.*

So the dragon is dead, Jarlaxle thought.

Not I! Him! the voice that resonated like Hephaestus roared in his mind. *I was blind, and slept in darkness! Too intelligent for death! Consider the enemies you have made, drow! Consider that a king will find you—has found you!*

That last thought came through with such ferocity, and such terrible implications, that it startled Jarlaxle from his Reverie. He glanced all around frantically, as if expecting a dragon to swoop down upon him and melt his camp into the dirt with an explosion of fiery breath, or an illithid to materialize and blast him with a cone of psionic energy that would scramble his mind forever.

But the night was quiet under the moon's pale glow.

Too quiet, Jarlaxle believed, like the hush of a predator. Where were the frogs, the night birds, the beetles?

Something shifted down to the west, catching Jarlaxle's attention. He scanned the small field, seeking the source—a rodent of some sort, likely.

But there was nothing, just the uneven grasses dancing in the moonlight on the gentle night breeze.

Something moved again, and Jarlaxle swept his gaze back across the field, even reached up and lifted his eyepatch so that he could more distinctly focus. Across the field stood a shadowy, huddled figure, bowing and waving its arms. It occurred to the drow that it was not a living man, but a wraith or a specter or a lich.

On the field between them, a flat stone shifted. Another, standing upright, slid to a greater angle.

Jarlaxle took a step toward the field.

The moon disappeared behind a dark cloud and the darkness deepened. But Jarlaxle was a creature of the Underdark, blessed with eyes that could see in the most meager light. In the nearly lightless caverns far below the stone, a patch of luminous lichen would glow to his eyes like a high-burning torch. So even in the moments while the moon hid, he saw that standing stone shift again, ever so slightly, as if something scrabbled at its base below the ground.

"A graveyard . . ." he whispered, finally recognizing the flat stones as markers. Even as he spoke, the moon came clear, brightening the field, and something churned in the dirt beside the shifting stone.

A hand—a skeletal hand.

October 2009

FORGOTTEN REALMS

RICHARD LEE BYERS

BROTHERHOOD OF THE GRIFFON

NOBODY DARED TO CROSS CHESSENTA...

BOOK I
The Captive Flame

BOOK II
Whisper of Venom
NOVEMBER 2010

BOOK III
The Spectral Blaze
JUNE 2011

...WHEN THE RED DRAGON WAS KING.

"This is Thay as it's never been shown before... Dark, sinister, foreboding and downright disturbing!"
—Alaundo, Candlekeep.com on Richard Byers's *Unclean*

ALSO AVAILABLE AS E-BOOKS!
Follow us on Twitter @WotC_Novels

FORGOTTEN REALMS, DUNGEONS & DRAGONS, WIZARDS OF THE COAST, and their respective logos are trademarks of Wizards of the Coast LLC in the U.S.A. and other countries. Other trademarks are property of their respective owners. ©2010 Wizards.

FORGOTTEN REALMS

The New York Times BEST-SELLING AUTHOR

RICHARD BAKER

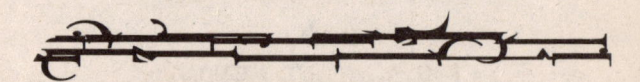

BLADES OF THE MOONSEA

"... it was so good that the bar has been raised.
Few other fantasy novels will hold up to it, I fear."
—Kevin Mathis, d20zines.com on *Forsaken House*

Book I
Swordmage

Book II
Corsair

Book III
Avenger
March 2010

Enter the Year of the Ageless One!

A DUNGEONS & DRAGONS NOVEL

Forgotten Realms, Dungeons & Dragons, Wizards of the Coast, and their respective logos are trademarks of Wizards of the Coast LLC in the U.S.A. and other countries. ©2009 Wizards.

WELCOME TO THE DESERT WORLD
OF ATHAS, A LAND RULED BY A HARSH
AND UNFORGIVING CLIMATE, A LAND
GOVERNED BY THE ANCIENT AND
TYRANNICAL SORCERER KINGS.
THIS IS THE LAND OF

DARK SUN
WORLD

CITY UNDER THE SAND
Jeff Mariotte
OCTOBER 2010

*Sometimes lost knowledge is
knowledge best left unknown.*

FIND OUT WHAT YOU'RE MISSING IN THIS
BRAND NEW DARK SUN® ADVENTURE BY
THE AUTHOR OF *COLD BLACK HEARTS*.

ALSO AVAILABLE AS AN E-BOOK!
THE PRISM PENTAD
Troy Denning's classic *DARK SUN*
series revisited! Check out the great new editions of
*The Verdant Passage, The Crimson Legion,
The Amber Enchantress, The Obsidian Oracle,*
and *The Cerulean Storm.*

Follow us on Twitter @WotC_Novels

DARK SUN, DUNGEONS & DRAGONS, WIZARDS OF THE COAST, and their respective logos are trademarks of Wizards of the Coast LLC in the U.S.A. and other countries. Other trademarks are property of their respective owners. ©2010 Wizards.

RETURN TO A WORLD OF PERIL, DECEIT, AND INTRIGUE, A WORLD REBORN IN THE WAKE OF A GLOBAL WAR.

EBERRON

TIM WAGGONER'S
LADY RUIN

She dedicated her life to the nation of Karrnath. With the war ended, and the army asleep—waiting—in their crypts, Karrnath assigned her to a new project: find a way to harness the dark powers of the Plane of Madness.

REVEL IN THE RUIN
DECEMBER 2010

ALSO AVAILABLE AS AN E-BOOK!

Follow us on Twitter @WotC_Novels

EBERRON, DUNGEONS & DRAGONS, WIZARDS OF THE COAST, and their respective logos are trademarks of Wizards of the Coast LLC in the U.S.A. and other countries. Other trademarks are property of their respective owners. ©2010 Wizards.

Dungeons & Dragons

From the Ruins of Fallen Empires, A New Age of Heroes Arises

It is a time of magic and monsters, a time when the world struggles against a rising tide of shadow. Only a few scattered points of light glow with stubborn determination in the deepening darkness.

It is a time where everything is new in an ancient and mysterious world.

Be There as the First Adventures Unfold.

The Mark of Nerath
Bill Slavicsek
August 2010

The Seal of Karga Kul
Alex Irvine
December 2010

The first two novels in a new line set in the evolving world of the Dungeons & Dragons® game setting. If you haven't played . . . or read D&D® in a while, your reintroduction starts in August!

ALSO AVAILABLE AS E-BOOKS!
Follow us on Twitter @WotC_Novels

A Dungeons & Dragons Novel

Dungeons & Dragons, Wizards of the Coast, and their respective logos, and D&D are trademarks of Wizards of the Coast LLC in the U.S.A. and other countries. Other trademarks are property of their respective owners. ©2010 Wizards.

FORGOTTEN REALMS

R.A. SALVATORE & GENO

STONE OF TYMORA TRILOGY

Sail the treacherous seas of the Forgotten Realms® world with Maimun, a boy who couldn't imagine how unlucky it would be to be blessed by the goddess of luck. Chased by a demon, hunted by pirates, Maimun must discover the secret of the Stone of Tymora, before his luck runs out!

Book 1 *The Stowaway*
Hardcover: 978-0-7869-5094-2
Paperback: 978-0-7869-5257-1

Book 2 *The Shadowmask*
Hardcover: 978-0-7869-5147-5
Paperback: available June 2010: 978-0-7869-5501-5

Book 3 *The Sentinels*
Hardcover: available September 2010: 978-0-7869-5505-3
Paperback: available in Fall 2011

"An exciting new tale from R.A. Salvatore, complete with his famously pulse-quickening action scenes and, of course, lots and lots of swordplay. If you're a fan of fantasy fiction, this book is not to be missed!"
—Kidzworld on *The Stowaway*

Follow us on Twitter @WotC_Novels

A DUNGEONS & DRAGONS NOVEL

FORGOTTEN REALMS, DUNGEONS & DRAGONS, WIZARDS OF THE COAST, and their respective logos are trademarks of Wizards of the Coast LLC in the U.S.A. and other countries. Other trademarks are property of their respective owners ©2010 Wizards.

WIZARDS OF THE COAST
Books for Young Readers

YOU ARE THE GHOST KING.

After a long while, Hephaestus settled back on his haunches, surveying the scene and trying to make sense of it all. The crawling lightning reached the cavern's far wall, the rock surface suddenly sparkling as if holding a thousand little stars. Through the curtain of blue light came the undead liches moving into a semi-circle before Hephaestus. They prayed in their ancient and long-forgotten languages and kept their horrid visages low, directed humbly at the floor.

Hephaestus's gaze went back to the blue fire, the strand of Mystra's Weave made visible, all but solid. He thought again of his last memories of sight, when he had brought forth his fiery breath over a drow and an illithid, and over the Crystal Shard. Dragonfire had detonated the mighty relic and had filled Hephaestus's eyes with brilliant, blinding light.

Then a cold wave of emptiness had slain him, had rotted the scales and the flesh from his bones.

DEATH DOES NOT RULE YOU.
YOU RULE DEATH.

"A fast-paced, heartrending book, *The Ghost King* is a must-read for any fans of the Drizzt Do'Urden stories and a welcome read for general fantasy enthusiasts."
—Ryan Van Cleave, *California Literary Review*

"There is only so much I can say about *(The Ghost King)*. You have to read it for yourself. It's good. Seriously. Probably R.A. Salvatore's best work. I cried like a baby. It took several tries to get through the last dozen pages."
—Jeff Preston, *Flames Rising*

"*(The Ghost King)* really leaves you on a sad, depressing note. I'm not giving away anything, but I know people who have teared up and cried about it. After going in, knowing what happens, I even got a little upset. It's so powerful and written so well. Even the last line, ". . . for guests who never came," was just so powerful and sad that you couldn't believe it."
—Travizzt's Reviews

FORGOTTEN REALMS

R.A. SALVATORE

TRANSITIONS
The Orc King
The Pirate King
The Ghost King

THE HUNTER'S BLADES TRILOGY
The Thousand Orcs
The Lone Drow
The Two Swords

THE LEGEND OF DRIZZT*
Homeland
Exile
Sojourn
The Crystal Shard
Streams of Silver
The Halfling's Gem
The Legacy
Starless Night
Siege of Darkness
Passage to Dawn
The Silent Blade
The Spine of the World
Sea of Swords

THE SELLSWORDS
Servant of the Shard
Promise of the Witch-King
Road of the Patriarch

THE CLERIC QUINTET
Canticle
In Sylvan Shadows
Night Masks
The Fallen Fortress
The Chaos Curse

R.A. SALVATORE

FORGOTTEN REALMS

THE GHOST KING

TRANSITIONS III

THE GHOST KING
Transitions, Book III

©2010 Wizards of the Coast LLC

All characters in this book are fictitious. Any resemblance to actual persons, living or dead, is purely coincidental.

This book is protected under the copyright laws of the United States of America. Any reproduction or unauthorized use of the material or artwork contained herein is prohibited without the express written permission of Wizards of the Coast LLC.

Published by Wizards of the Coast LLC

FORGOTTEN REALMS, DUNGEONS & DRAGONS, D&D, WIZARDS OF THE COAST, and their respective logos are trademarks of Wizards of the Coast LLC in the U.S.A. and other countries.

Printed in the U.S.A.

Cover art by Todd Lockwood
Map by Todd Gamble

Original Hardcover Edition First Printing: October 2009
First Mass Market Paperback Printing: July 2010

9 8 7 6 5 4 3 2

ISBN: 978-0-7869-5499-5
620-25393000-001-EN

The Library of Congress has catalogued the hardcover edition as follows:

Salvatore, R. A., 1959-
 The ghost king / R.A. Salvatore.
  p. cm. -- (Transitions ; bk. 3)
 ISBN 978-0-7869-5233-5
 1. Drizzt Do'Urden (Fictitious character)--Fiction. 2. Forgotten realms (Imaginary place)--Fiction. I. Title.
 PS3569.A462345G47 2009
 813'.54--dc22

2009016151

The sale of this book without its cover has not been authorized by the publisher. If you purchased this book without a cover, you should be aware that neither the author nor the publisher has received payment for this "stripped book."

U.S., CANADA, ASIA, PACIFIC, & LATIN AMERICA Wizards of the Coast LLC P.O. Box 707 Renton, WA 98057-0707 +1-800-324-6496	EUROPEAN HEADQUARTERS Hasbro UK Ltd Caswell Way Newport, Gwent NP9 0YH GREAT BRITAIN Save this address for your records.

Visit our web site at www.wizards.com

To Diane, of course, the love of my life who has walked through these years beside me and my dreams, and I beside her and hers.

But there is someone else who gets a big thank you for this book—five someones actually. This calling I have found, this purpose in my life, takes me places. It is my duty to let it, to follow it. Sometimes those journeys are not to places I want to go. Sometimes it hurts. When I finished *Mortalis,* the fourth book of my DemonWars series, during a terrible time in my life, I stated that I hoped I would never write a book like that again (though I considered it the best piece I had ever written), that I would never again have to go to that dark place.

When I started *The Ghost King,* I knew I had to go there, yet again. These characters, these friends of twenty years, demanded no less of me. And so I have spent the last months watching three videos, songs of my past from the band and songstress that have walked beside me for most of my life.

Stevie Nicks once asked in a song, "Has anyone ever written anything for you? And in your darkest hours, do you hear me sing?"

Ah, Ms. Nicks, you have been writing songs for me since my high school years in the 1970s, though you don't know it. You were there with me during those lonely and confusing days in high school, those awakening moments of college. I watched the sun rise over Fitchburg State College, sitting in my car and waiting for my class to begin, to the sounds of "The Chain." You were there with me during that blizzard in 1978 when I found the works of Tolkien and a whole new way of expressing myself suddenly came into view. You were there with me when I met the woman who would be my wife, and on the morning after our wedding, and at the births of our three children.

You went with us to hockey games and horse shows. To your concert at Great Woods went my family, and my brother even as he neared the end of his life.

And you were there with me as I wrote this book. "Sisters of the Moon," "Has Anyone Ever Written Anything for You?" and "Rhiannon," all three, the songs that took me through my darkest hours and now let me go back to that place, because my friends of two decades, the Companions of the Hall, demanded no less of me.

So thank you, Stevie Nicks, and Fleetwood Mac, for writing the music of my life.

—R. A. Salvatore

Welcome to Faerûn, a land of magic and intrigue, brutal violence and divine compassion, where gods have ascended and died, and mighty heroes have risen to fight terrifying monsters. Here, millennia of warfare and conquest have shaped dozens of unique cultures, raised and leveled shining kingdoms and tyrannical empires alike, and left long forgotten, horror-infested ruins in their wake.

A LAND OF MAGIC

When the goddess of magic was murdered, a magical plague of blue fire—the Spellplague—swept across the face of Faerûn, killing some, mutilating many, and imbuing a rare few with amazing supernatural abilities. The Spellplague forever changed the nature of magic itself, and seeded the land with hidden wonders and bloodcurdling monstrosities.

A LAND OF DARKNESS

The threats Faerûn faces are legion. Armies of undead mass in Thay under the brilliant but mad lich king Szass Tam. Treacherous dark elves plot in the Underdark in the service of their cruel and fickle goddess, Lolth. The Aboleth Sovereignty, a terrifying hive of inhuman slave masters, floats above the Sea of Fallen Stars, spreading chaos and destruction. And the Empire of Netheril, armed with magic of unimaginable power, prowls Faerûn in flying fortresses, sowing discord to their own incalculable ends.

A LAND OF HEROES

But Faerûn is not without hope. Heroes have emerged to fight the growing tide of darkness. Battle-scarred rangers bring their notched blades to bear against marauding hordes of orcs. Lowly street rats match wits with demons for the fate of cities. Inscrutable tiefling warlocks unite with fierce elf warriors to rain fire and steel upon monstrous enemies. And valiant servants of merciful gods forever struggle against the darkness.

FORGOTTEN REALMS

A LAND OF
UNTOLD ADVENTURE

THE BARONIES OF ERLKAZAR
PRE-SPELLPLAGUE
N
W
E
S
RUINS OF CASTLE TRINITY
NIGHTGLOW
IMPRESK
BYERNADINE
SPIRIT SOARING
ORMATH
IMPRESK LAKE
LHESHAYL
CARRADOON
SHALANE
CARRELATH
SURKH
SHALANE LAKE
GOLCONDA
LLORBAUTH
THE DEEPWASH
DUHINARIM
AHLARKHEM
MOUNT NOBLESSE
FIVE SPEARS HOLD
SARADUSH
TANISTAN
TIBOLD

PRELUDE

The dragon issued a low growl and flexed his claws in close, curling himself into a defensive crouch. His eyes were gone, having been lost to the brilliant light bursting from a destroyed artifact, but his draconian senses more than compensated.

Someone was in his chamber—Hephaestus knew that beyond a doubt—but the beast could neither smell nor hear him.

"Well?" the dragon asked in his rumbling voice, barely a whisper for the beast, but it reverberated and echoed off the stone walls of the mountain cavern. "Have you come to face me or to hide from me?"

I am right here before you, dragon, came the reply—not audibly, but in the wyrm's mind.

Hephaestus tilted his great horned head at the telepathic intrusion and growled.

You do not remember me? You destroyed me, dragon, when you destroyed the Crystal Shard.

"Your cryptic games do not impress me, drow!"

Not drow.

That gave Hephaestus pause, and the sockets that once—not so long ago—housed his burned-out eyes widened.

"Illithid!" the dragon roared, and he breathed forth his murderous, fiery breath at the spot where he'd once destroyed the mind flayer and its drow companion, along with the Crystal Shard, all at once.

The fire blazed on and on, bubbling stone, heating the entire room. Many heartbeats later, fire still flowing, Hephaestus heard in his mind, *Thank you.*

Confusion stole the remaining breath from the dragon—confusion that lasted only an instant before a chill began to creep into the air around him, began to seep through his red scales. Hephaestus didn't like the cold. He was a creature of flame and heat and fiery anger, and the high frosts bit at his wings when he flew out of his mountain abode in the wintry months.

But this cold was worse, for it was beyond physical frost. It was the utter void of emptiness, the complete absence of the heat of life, the last vestiges of Crenshinibon spewing forth the necromantic power that had forged the mighty relic millennia before.

Icy fingers pried under the dragon's scales and permeated his flesh, leaching the life-force from the great beast.

Hephaestus tried to resist, growling and snarling, tightening sinewy muscles as if trying to repel the cold. A great inhale got the dragon's inner fires churning, not to breathe forth, but to fight cold with heat.

The crack of a single scale hitting the stone floor resounded in the dragon's ears. He swiveled his great head as if to view the calamity, though of course, he couldn't see.

But Hephaestus could feel . . . the rot.

Hephaestus could feel death reaching into him, reaching through him, grasping his heart and squeezing.

His inhale puffed out in a gout of cold flame. He tried to draw in again, but his lungs would not heed the call. The dragon started to swing his head forward, but his neck gave out halfway and the great horned head bounced down onto the floor.

Hephaestus had perceived only darkness around him since the first destruction of the Crystal Shard, and now he felt the same inside.

Darkness.

* * * * *

Two flames flickered to life, two eyes of fire, of pure energy, of pure hatred.

And that alone—sight!—confused the blind Hephaestus. He could see!

But how?

The beast watched a blue light, a curtain of crawling lightning, crackle and sizzle its way across the slag floor. It had crossed the point of ultimate devastation, where the mighty artifact had long ago blasted loose its layers and layers of magic to blind Hephaestus, then again more recently, that very day, to emanate waves of murderous necromantic energy to assail the dragon and . . . ?

And do what? The dragon recalled the cold, the falling scales, the profound sensation of rot and death. Somehow he could see again, but at what cost?

Hephaestus drew a deep breath, or tried to, but only then did the dragon realize that he was not drawing breath at all.

Suddenly terrified, Hephaestus focused on the point of cataclysm, and as the strange curtain of blue magic thinned, the beast saw huddled forms, once contained within, dancing about the remnants of their artifact home. Stooped low, backs hunched, the apparitions—the seven liches who had created the mighty Crenshinibon—circled and chanted ancient words of power long lost to the realms of Faerûn. A closer look revealed the many different backgrounds of these men of ancient times, the varied cultures and features from all across the continent. But from afar, they appeared only as similar huddled gray creatures, ragged clothes dripping dullness as if a gray mist flowed from their every movement. Hephaestus recognized them for what they were: the life force of the sentient artifact.

But they had been destroyed in the first blast of the Crystal Shard!

The beast did not lift his great head high on his serpentine neck to breathe forth catastrophe on the undead. He watched, and he measured. He took note of their cadence and tone, and recognized their desperation. They wanted to get back into their home, back into Crenshinibon, the Crystal Shard.

The dragon, curious yet terrified, let his gaze focus on that empty vessel, on the once mighty artifact that he had inadvertently annihilated at the cost of his own eyes.

And he had destroyed it a second time, he realized. Unknown to him, there had remained residual power in the Crystal Shard, and when the tentacle-headed illithid had goaded him, he'd breathed forth fires that had again assaulted the Crystal Shard.

Hephaestus swiveled his head around. Rage engulfed the creature even more, a horror-filled revulsion that turned instantly from dismay to pure anger.

For his great and beautiful shining red scales were mostly gone, scattered about the floor. A few dotted the beast's mostly skeletal form here and there, pathetic remnants of the majesty and power he had once shown. He lifted a wing, a beautiful wing that had once allowed Hephaestus to sail effortlessly across the high winds curling up from the Snowflake Mountains to the northwest.

Bones, torn leathery tatters, and nothing more adorned that blasted appendage.

Once a beast of grandeur, majesty, and terrible beauty, reduced to a hideous mockery.

Once a dragon, earlier that very day a dragon, reduced to . . . what? Dead? Alive?

How?

Hephaestus looked at his other broken and skeletal wing to realize that the blue plane of strange magical power had crossed it. Looking more closely within that nearly opaque curtain, Hephaestus noted a second stream of crackling energy, a greenish dart within the blue field, backtracking and sparking inside the curtain. Low to the ground, that visible tether of energy connected the wing of the dragon to the artifact, joining Hephaestus to the Crystal Shard he thought he had long ago destroyed.

Awaken, great beast, said the voice in his head, the voice of the illithid, Yharaskrik.

"You did this!" Hephaestus roared. He started to growl, but

was struck, suddenly and without warning, by a stream of psionic energy that left him babbling in confusion.

You are alive, the creature within that energy told him. *You have defeated death. You are greater than before, and I am with you to guide you, to teach you powers beyond anything you have ever imagined.*

With a burst of rage-inspired strength, the beast rose up on his legs, head high and swiveling to take in the cavern. Hephaestus dared not remove his wing from the magical curtain, fearing that he would again know nothingness. He scraped his way across the floor toward the dancing apparitions and the Crystal Shard.

The huddled and shadowy forms of the undead stopped their circling and turned as one to regard the dragon. They backed away—whether out of fear or reverence, Hephaestus could not determine. The beast approached the shard, and a clawed foreleg moved forward gingerly to touch the item. As soon as his skeletal digits closed around it, a sudden compulsion, an overwhelming calling, compelled Hephaestus to swing his forelimb up, to smash the Crystal Shard into the center of his skull, right above his fiery eyes. Even as he performed that movement, Hephaestus realized that Yharaskrik's overwhelming willpower was compelling him so.

Before he could avenge that insult, however, Hephaestus's rage flew away. Ecstasy overwhelmed the dragon, a release of tremendous power and overwhelming joy, a wash of oneness and completeness.

The beast shuffled back. His wing left the curtain, but Hephaestus felt no horror at that realization, for his newfound sentience and awareness, and restored life energy, did not diminish.

No, not *life* energy, Hephaestus realized.

Quite the opposite . . . precisely the opposite.

You are the Ghost King, Yharaskrik told him. *Death does not rule you. You rule death.*

After a long while, Hephaestus settled back on his haunches, surveying the scene and trying to make sense of it all. The crawling lightning reached the cavern's far wall, the rock surface suddenly sparkling as if holding a thousand little stars. Through the curtain came the undead liches moving into a semi-circle before Hephaestus. They prayed in their ancient and long-forgotten languages and kept their horrid visages low, directed humbly at the floor.

He could command them, Hephaestus realized, but he chose to let them grovel and genuflect before him, for the beast was more concerned with the wall of blue energy dissecting his cavern.

What could it be?

"Mystra's Weave," the liches whispered, as if reading his every thought.

The Weave? Hephaestus thought.

"The Weave . . . collapsing," answered the chorus of liches. "Magic . . . wild."

Hephaestus considered the wretched creatures as he tried to piece together the possibilities. The apparitions of the Crystal Shard were the ancient wizards who had imbued the artifact with their own life-forces. At its essence, Crenshinibon radiated necromantic dweomers.

Hephaestus's gaze went back to the curtain, the strand of Mystra's Weave made visible, all but solid. He thought again of his last memories of sight, when he had brought forth his fiery breath over a drow and an illithid, and over the Crystal Shard. Dragonfire had detonated the mighty relic and had filled Hephaestus's eyes with brilliant, blinding light.

Then a cold wave of emptiness had slain him, had rotted the scales and the flesh from his bones. Had that spell . . . whatever it was . . . brought down a piece of Mystra's Weave?

"The strand was here before you breathed," the apparitions explained, reading his thoughts and dispelling that errant notion.

"Brought from the first fires that shattered the shard," Hephaestus said.

No, Yharaskrik said in the dragon's mind. *The strand released the necromancy of the ruined shard, giving me sentience once more and reviving the apparitions in their current state.*

And you invaded my sleep, Hephaestus accused.

I am so guilty, the illithid admitted. *As you destroyed me in that long-lost time, so I have returned to repay you.*

"I will destroy you again!" Hephaestus promised.

You cannot, for there is nothing to destroy. I am disembodied thought, sentience without substance. And I seek a home.

Before Hephaestus could even register that notion for what it was—a clear threat—another wave of psionic energy, much more insistent and overwhelming, filled his every synapse, his every thought, his every bit of reason with a buzzing and crackling distortion. He couldn't even think his name let alone respond to the intrusion as the powerful mind of the undead illithid worked its way into his subconscious, into every mental fiber that formulated the dragon's psyche.

Then, as if a great darkness were suddenly lifted, Hephaestus understood—everything.

What have you done? he telepathically asked the illithid. But the answer was there, waiting for him, in his own thoughts.

For Hephaestus needn't ask Yharaskrik anything ever again. Doing so would be no more than pondering the question himself.

Hephaestus was Yharaskrik and Yharaskrik was Hephaestus.

And both were Crenshinibon, the Ghost King.

Hephaestus's great intellect worked backward through the reality of his present state and the enthusiasm of the seven liches as his thoughts careened and at last convened, spurring him to certainty. The strand of blue fire, how ever it had come to be, had tied him to Crenshinibon and its lingering necromantic powers. Those powers were remnants but still mighty, he realized as the Crystal Shard pulsed against his skull. It had fused there, and the necromantic energy had infused the remains of Hephaestus's physical coil.

Thus he had risen, not in resurrection, but in undeath.

The apparitions bowed to him, and he understood their thoughts and intentions as clearly as they heard his own. Their sole purpose was to serve.

Hephaestus understood himself to be a sentient conduit between the realms of the living and the dead.

The blue fire crawled out of the far wall and etched along the floor. It crossed over where the Crystal Shard had lain, and over where Hephaestus's wingtip had been. In the span of a few heartbeats, it exited the chamber altogether, leaving the place dim, with only the dancing orange flames of the liches' eyes, Hephaestus's eyes, and the soft green glow of Crenshinibon.

But the beast's power did not diminish with its passing, and the apparitions still bowed.

He was risen.

A dracolich.

PART 1

UNWEAVING

UNWEAVING

Where does reason end and magic begin? Where does reason end and faith begin? These are two of the central questions of sentience, so I have been told by a philosopher friend who has gone to the end of his days and back again. It is the ultimate musing, the ultimate search, the ultimate reality of who we are. To live is to die, and to know that you shall, and to wonder, always wonder.

This truth is the foundation of the Spirit Soaring, a cathedral, a library, a place of worship and reason, of debate and philosophy. Her stones were placed by faith and magic, her walls constructed of wonderment and hope, her ceiling held up by reason. There, Cadderly Bonaduce strides in profundity and demands of his many visitors, devout and scholarly, that they do not shy from the larger questions of existence, and do not shield themselves and buffet others with unreasoned dogma.

There is now raging in the wider world a fierce debate—just such a collision between reason and dogma. Are we no more than the whim of the gods or the result of harmonic process? Eternal or mortal, and if the former, then what is the relationship of that which is forever more, the soul, to that which we know will feed the worms? What is the next progression for consciousness and spirit, of self-awareness and—or—the loss of individuality in the state of oneness with all else? What is the relationship between the answerable and the unanswerable, and what does it bode if the former grows at the expense of the latter?

Of course, the act of simply asking these questions raises troubling possibilities for many people, acts of punishable heresy for others, and indeed even Cadderly once confided in me that life would be simpler if he could just accept what is, and exist in the present. The irony of his tale is not lost on me. One of the most prominent priests of Deneir, young Cadderly remained skeptical even of the existence of the god he served. Indeed he was an agnostic priest, but one mighty with powers divine. Had he worshipped any god other than Deneir, whose very tenets encourage inquisition, young Cadderly likely would never have found any of those powers, to heal or to invoke the wrath of his deity.

He is confident now in the evermore, and in the possibility of some Deneirrath heaven, but still he questions, still he seeks. At Spirit Soaring, many truths—laws of the wider world, even of the heavens above—are being unraveled and unrolled for study and inquisition. With humility and courage, the scholars who flock there illuminate details of the scheme of our reality, argue the patterns of the multiverse and the rules that guide it, indeed, realign our very understanding of Toril and its relationship to the moon and the stars above.

For some, that very act bespeaks heresy, a dangerous exploration into the realms of knowledge that should remain solely the domain of the gods, of beings higher than us. Worse, these frantic prophets of doom warn, such ponderings and impolitic explanations diminish the gods themselves and turn away from faith those who need to hear the word. To philosophers like Cadderly, however, the greater intricacy, the greater complexity of the multiverse only elevates his feelings for his god. The harmony of nature, he argues, and the beauty of universal law and process bespeak a brilliance and a notion of infinity beyond that realized in blindness or willful, fearful ignorance.

To Cadderly's inquisitive mind, the observed system supporting divine law far surpasses the superstitions of the Material Plane.

For many others, though, even some of those who agree with Cadderly's search, there is an undeniable level of discomfort.

I see the opposite in Catti-brie and her continued learning and understanding of magic. She takes comfort in magic, she has said, because it cannot be explained. Her strength in faith and spirituality climbs beside her magical prowess. To have before you that which simply is, without explanation, without fabrication and replication, is the essence of faith.

I do not know if Mielikki exists. I do not know if any of the gods are real, or if they are actual beings, whether or not they care about the day-to-day existence of one rogue dark elf. The precepts of Mielikki—the morality, the sense of community and service, and the appreciation for life—are real to me, are in my heart. They were there before I found Mielikki, a name to place upon them, and they would remain there even if indisputable proof were given to me that there was no actual being, no physical manifestation of those precepts.

Do we behave out of fear of punishment, or out of the demands of our heart? For me, it is the latter, as I would hope is true for all adults, though I know from bitter experience that such is not often the case. To act in a manner designed to catapult you into one heaven or another would seem transparent to a god, any god, for if one's heart is not in alignment with the creator of that heaven, then . . . what is the point?

And so I salute Cadderly and the seekers, who put aside the ethereal, the easy answers, and climb courageously toward the honesty and the beauty of a greater harmony.

As the many peoples of Faerûn scramble through their daily endeavors, march through to the ends of their respective lives, there will be much hesitance at the words that flow from Spirit Soaring, even resentment and attempts at sabotage. Caddery's personal journey to explore the cosmos within the bounds of his own considerable intellect will no doubt foster fear, in particular of the most basic and terrifying concept of all, death.

From me, I show only support for my priestly friend. I remember my nights in Icewind Dale, tall upon Bruenor's Climb, more removed from the tundra below, it seemed, than from the stars above. Were my ponderings there any less heretical than the work of Spirit Soaring? And if the result for Caddery and those others is anything akin to what I knew on that lonely mountaintop, then I recognize the strength of Cadderly's armor against the curses of the incurious and the cries of heresy from less enlightened and more dogmatic fools.

My journey to the stars, among the stars, at one with the stars, was a place of absolute contentment and unbridled joy, a moment of the most peaceful existence I have ever known.

And the most powerful, for in that state of oneness with the universe around me, I, Drizzt Do'Urden, stood as a god.

—Drizzt Do'Urden

CHAPTER 1
VISITING A DROW'S DREAMS

I will find you, drow.

The dark elf's eyes popped open wide, and he quickly attuned his keen senses to his physical surroundings. The voice remained clear in his mind, invading his moment of quiet Reverie.

He knew the voice, for with it came an image of catastrophe all too clear in his memories, from perhaps a decade and a half before.

He adjusted his eye patch and ran a hand over his bald head, trying to make sense of it. It couldn't be. The dragon had been destroyed, and nothing, not even a great red wyrm like Hephaestus, could have survived the intensity of the blast when Crenshinibon had released its power. Or even if the beast had somehow lived, why hadn't it arisen then and there, where its enemies would have been helpless before it?

No, Jarlaxle was certain that Hephaestus had been destroyed.

But he hadn't dreamed the intrusion into his Reverie. Of that, too, Jarlaxle was certain.

I will find you, drow.

It had been Hephaestus—the telepathic impartation into Jarlaxle's Reverie had brought the image of the great dragon to him clearly. He could not have mistaken the weight of that voice. It had startled him from his meditation, and he had instinctively retreated from it and forced himself back into the present, to his physical surroundings.

He regretted that almost immediately, and calmed long enough to hear the contented snoring of his dwarf companion, to ensure that all around him was secure, then he closed his eyes once more and turned his thoughts inward, to a place of meditation and solitude.

Except, he was not alone.

Hephaestus was there waiting for him. He envisioned the dragon's eyes, twin flickers of angry flame. He could feel the beast's rage, simmering and promising revenge. A contented growl rumbled through Jarlaxle's thoughts, the smirk of the predator when the prey was at hand. The dragon had found him telepathically, but did that mean it knew where he was physically?

A moment of panic swept through Jarlaxle, a moment of confusion. He reached up and touched his eye patch, wearing it that day over his left eye. Its magic should have stopped Hephaestus's intrusion, should have shielded Jarlaxle from all scrying or unwanted telepathic contact. But he was not imagining it. Hephaestus was with him.

I will find you, drow, the dragon assured him once more.

"Will" find him, so therefore had not yet found him . . .

Jarlaxle threw up his defenses, refusing to consider his current whereabouts in the recognition of why Hephaestus kept repeating his declaration. The dragon wanted him to consider his position so the beast could telepathically take the knowledge of his whereabouts from him.

He filled his thoughts with images of the city of Luskan, of Calimport, of the Underdark. Jarlaxle's principal lieutenant in his powerful mercenary band was an accomplished psionicist, and had taught Jarlaxle much in the ways of mental trickery and defense. Jarlaxle brought every bit of that knowledge to bear.

Hephaestus's psionically-imparted growl, turning from satisfaction to frustration, was met by Jarlaxle's chuckle.

You cannot elude me, the dragon insisted.

Aren't you dead?

I will find you, drow!
Then I will kill you again.

Jarlaxle's matter-of-fact, casual response elicited a great rage from the beast—as the drow had hoped—and with that emotion came a momentary loss of control by the dragon, which was all Jarlaxle needed.

He met that rage with a wall of denial, forcing Hephaestus from his thoughts. He shifted the eye patch to his right eye, his touch awakening the item, bringing forth its shielding power more acutely.

That was the way with many of his magical trinkets of late. Something was happening to the wider world, to Mystra's Weave. Kimmuriel had warned him to beware the use of magic, for reports of disastrous results from even simple castings had become all too commonplace.

The eye patch did its job, though, and combined with Jarlaxle's clever tricks and practiced defenses, Hephaestus was thrown far from the drow's subconscious.

Eyes open once more, Jarlaxle surveyed his small encampment. He and Athrogate were north of Mirabar. The sun had not yet appeared, but the eastern sky was beginning to leak its pre-dawn glow. The two of them were scheduled to meet, clandestinely, with Marchion Elastul of Mirabar that very morning, to complete a trading agreement between the self-serving ruler and the coastal city of Luskan. Or more specifically, between Elastul and Bregan D'aerthe, Jarlaxle's mercenary—and increasingly mercantile—band. Bregan D'aerthe used the city of Luskan as a conduit to the World Above, trading goods from the Underdark for artifacts from the surface realms, ferrying valuable and exotic baubles to and from the drow city-state of Menzoberranzan.

The drow scanned their camp, set in a small hollow amid a trio of large oaks. He could see the road, quiet and empty. From one of the trees a cicada crescendoed its whining song, and a bird cawed as if in answer. A rabbit darted through the small grassy lea on the downside of the camp, fleeing with sharp turns and great leaps as if terrified by the weight of Jarlaxle's gaze.

The drow slipped down from the low crook in the tree, rolling off the heavy limb that had served as his bed. He landed silently on magical boots and wove a careful path out of the copse to get a wider view of the area.

"And where're ye goin', I'm wantin' to be knowin'?" the dwarf called after him.

Jarlaxle turned on Athrogate, who still lay on his back, wrapped in a tangled bedroll. One half-opened eye looked back at him.

"I often ponder which is more annoying, dwarf, your snoring or your rhyming."

"Meself, too," said Athrogate. "But since I'm not much hearing me snoring, I'll be choosing the word-song."

Jarlaxle just shook his head and turned to walk away.

"I'm still asking, elf."

"I thought it wise to search the grounds before our esteemed visitor arrives," Jarlaxle replied.

"He'll be getting here with half the dwarfs o' Mirabar's Shield, not for doubting," said Athrogate.

True enough, Jarlaxle knew. He heard Athrogate shuffle out of his bedroll and scramble to his feet.

"Prudence, my friend," the drow said over his shoulder, and started away.

"Nah, it's more'n that," Athrogate declared.

Jarlaxle laughed helplessly. Few in the world knew him well enough to so easily read through his tactical deflections and assertions, but in the years Athrogate had been at his side, he had indeed let the dwarf get to know something of the true Jarlaxle Baenre. He turned and offered a grin to his dirty, bearded friend.

"Well?" Athrogate asked. "Yer words I'm taking, but what's got ye shaking?"

"Shaking?"

Athrogate shrugged. "It be what it be, and I see what it be."

"Enough," Jarlaxle bade him, holding his hands out in surrender.

"Ye tell me or I'll rhyme at ye again," the dwarf warned.

"Hit me with your mighty morningstars instead, I beg you."

Athrogate planted his hands on his hips and stared at the dark elf hard.

"I do not yet know," Jarlaxle admitted. "Something . . ." He reached around and retrieved his enormous, wide-brimmed hat, patted it into shape, and plopped it atop his head.

"Something?"

"Aye," said the drow. "A visitor, perhaps in my dreams, perhaps not."

"Tell me she's a redhead."

"Red scales, more likely."

Athrogate's face crinkled in disgust. "Ye need to dream better, elf."

"Indeed."

*****

"My daughter fares well, I trust," Marchion Elastul remarked. He sat in a great, comfortable chair at the heavy, ornately decorated table his attendants had brought from his palace in Mirabar, surrounded by a dozen grim-faced dwarves of Mirabar's Shield. Across from him, in lesser thrones, sat Jarlaxle and Athrogate, who stuffed his face with bread, eggs, and all manner of delicacies. Even for a meeting in the wilderness, Elastul had demanded some manner of civilized discourse, which, to the dwarf's ultimate joy, had included a fine breakfast.

"Arabeth has adapted well to the changes in Luskan, yes," Jarlaxle answered. "She and Kensidan have grown closer, and her position within the city continues to expand in prominence and power."

"That miserable Crow," Elastul whispered with a sigh, referring to High Captain Kensidan, one of the four high captains who ruled the city. He knew well that Kensidan had become the dominant member of that elite group.

"Kensidan won," Jarlaxle reminded him. "He outwitted Arklem Greeth and the Arcane Brotherhood—no small feat!—and convinced the other high captains that his course was the best."

"I would have preferred Captain Deudermont."

Jarlaxle shrugged. "This way is more profitable for us all."

"To think that I'm sitting here dealing with a drow elf," Elastul lamented. "Half of my Shield dwarves would prefer that I kill you rather than negotiate with you."

"That would not be wise."

"Or profitable?"

"Nor healthy."

Elastul snorted, but his daughter Arabeth had told him enough about the creature Jarlaxle for him to know that the drow's quip was only half a joke, and half a deadly serious threat.

"If Kensidan the Crow and the other three high captains learn of our little arrangement here, they will not be pleased," Elastul said.

"Bregan D'aerthe does not answer to Kensidan and the others."

"But you do have an arrangement with them to trade your goods through their markets alone."

"Their wealth grows considerably because of the quiet trade with Menzoberranzan," Jarlaxle replied. "If I decide it convenient to do some dealing outside the parameters of that arrangement, then . . . I am a merchant, after all."

"A dead one, should Kensidan learn of this."

Jarlaxle laughed at the assertion. "A weary one, more likely, for what shall I do with a surface city to rule?"

It took a moment for the implications of that boast to sink in to Elastul, and the possibility brought him little amusement, for it served as a reminder and a warning that he dealt with dark elves.

Very dangerous dark elves.

"We have a deal, then?" Jarlaxle asked.

"I will open the tunnel to Barkskin's storehouse," Elastul replied, referring to a secret marketplace in the Undercity of Mirabar, the dwarf section. "Kimmuriel's wagons can move in through there alone, and none shall be allowed beyond the entry hall. And I expect the pricing exactly as we discussed, since the cost to me in merely keeping the appropriate guards alert for drow presence will be no small matter."

" 'Drow presence?' Surely you do not expect that we will deign to move further into your city, good marchion. We are quite content with the arrangement we have now, I assure you."

"You are a drow, Jarlaxle. You are never 'quite content.' "

Jarlaxle simply laughed, unwilling and unable to dispute that point. He had agreed to personally broker the deal for Kimmuriel, who would oversee the set-up of the operation, since Jarlaxle's wanderlust had returned and he wanted some time away from Luskan. In truth, Jarlaxle had to admit to himself that he wouldn't really be surprised at all to return to the North after a few months on the road and find Kimmuriel making great inroads in the city of Mirabar, perhaps even becoming the true power in the city, using Elastul or whatever other fool he might prop up to give him cover.

Jarlaxle tipped his great hat, then, and rose to leave, signaling Athrogate to follow. Snorting like a pig on a truffle, the dwarf kept stuffing his mouth, egg yolk and jam splattering his great black beard, a braided and dung-tipped mane.

"It has been a long and hungry road," Jarlaxle commented to Elastul.

The marchion shook his head in disgust. The dwarves of Mirabar's Shield, however, looked on with pure jealousy.

* * * * *

Jarlaxle and Athrogate had marched more than a mile before the dwarf stopped belching long enough to ask, "So, we're back for Luskan?"

"No," Jarlaxle replied. "Kimmuriel will see to the more mundane details now that I have completed the deal."

"Long way to ride for a short talk and a shorter meal."

"You ate through half the morning."

Athrogate rubbed his considerable belly and issued a belch that scared a flock of birds from a nearby tree, and Jarlaxle gave a helpless shake of his head.

"My tummy hurts," the dwarf explained. He rubbed his belly

and burped again, several times in rapid succession. "So we're not back to Luskan. Where, then?"

That question gave Jarlaxle pause. "I am not sure," he said honestly.

"I won't be missing the place," said Athrogate. He reached over his shoulder and patted the grip of one of his mighty glassteel morningstars, which he kept strapped diagonally on his back, handles up high, their spiked ball heads bouncing behind his shoulders as he bobbed along the trail. "Ain't used these in months."

Jarlaxle, staring absently into the distance, simply nodded.

"Well, wherever we're to go, if even ye're to know, I'm thinkin' and talkin', it's better ridin' than walkin'. Bwahaha!" He reached into a belt pouch where he kept a black figurine of a war boar that could summon a magical mount to his side. He started to take it out, but Jarlaxle put a hand over his and stopped him.

"Not today," the drow explained. "Today, we meander."

"Bah, but I'm wantin' a bumpy road to shake a few belches free, ye damned elf."

"Today we walk," Jarlaxle said with finality.

Athrogate looked at him with suspicion. "So ye're not for knowin' where we're to be goin'."

The drow looked around at the rough terrain and rubbed his slender chin. "Soon," he promised.

"Bah! We could've gone back into Mirabar for more food!" Athrogate blanched as he finished, though, a rare expression indeed for the tough dwarf, for Jarlaxle fixed him with a serious and withering glare, one that reminded him in no uncertain terms who was the leader and who the sidekick.

"Good day for a walk!" Athrogate exclaimed, and finished with a great belch.

They set their camp only a few miles northeast of the field where they had met with Marchion Elastul, on a small ridge among a line of scraggly, short trees, many dead, others nearly leafless. Below them to the west loomed the remains of an old farm, or perhaps a small village, beyond a short rocky field splashed with flat, cut stones, most lying but some standing on end, leading

THE GHOST KING

Athrogate to mutter that it was probably an old graveyard.

"That or a pavilion," Jarlaxle replied, hardly caring.

Selûne was up, dancing in and out of the many small clouds that rushed overhead. Under her pale glow, Athrogate was soon snoring contentedly, but for Jarlaxle, the thought of Reverie was not welcomed.

He watched as the shadows under the moon's pale glow began to shrink, disappear, then stretch toward the east as the moon passed overhead and started its western descent. Weariness crept in upon him, and he resisted it for a long while.

The drow silently berated himself for his foolishness. He couldn't stay present and alert forever.

He leaned against a dead tree, a twisted silhouette whose shadow looked like the skeleton of a man who reached, pleading, to the gods. Jarlaxle didn't climb it—the old tree likely wouldn't have held his weight—but instead remained standing, leaning against the rough trunk.

He let his mind fall away from his surroundings, let it fall inward. Memories blended with sensations in the gentle swirl of Reverie. He felt his own heartbeat, the blood rushing through his veins. He felt the rhythms of the world, like a gentle breathing beneath his feet, and he embraced the sensation of a connection to the earth, as if he had grown roots into the deep rock. At the same time, he experienced a sensation of weightlessness, as if he were floating, as the wonderful relaxation of Reverie swept through his mind and body.

Only there was Jarlaxle free. Reverie was his refuge.

I will find you, drow.

Hephaestus was there with him, waiting for him. In his mind, Jarlaxle saw again the fiery eyes of the beast, felt the hot breath and the hotter hatred.

Be gone. You have no quarrel with me, the dark elf silently replied.

I have not forgotten!

'Twas your own breath that broke the shard, Jarlaxle reminded the creature.

Through your trickery, clever drow. I have not forgotten. You blinded me, you weakened me, you destroyed me!

That last clause struck Jarlaxle as odd, not just because the dragon obviously wasn't destroyed, but because he still had the distinct feeling that it wasn't Hephaestus he was communicating with—but it was Hephaestus!

Another image came into Jarlaxle's thoughts, that of a bulbous-headed creature with tentacles waving menacingly from its face.

I know you. I will find you, the dragon went on. *You who stole from me the pleasures of life and the flesh. You who stole from me the sweet taste of food and the pleasure of touch.*

So the dragon is dead, Jarlaxle thought.

Not I! Him! the voice that resonated like Hephaestus roared in his mind. *I was blind, and slept in darkness! Too intelligent for death! Consider the enemies you have made, drow! Consider that a king will find you—has found you!*

That last thought came through with such ferocity and such terrible implications that it startled Jarlaxle from his Reverie. He glanced around frantic, as if expecting a dragon to swoop down upon him and melt his camp into the dirt with an explosion of fiery breath, or an illithid to materialize and blast him with psionic energy that would scramble his mind forever.

But the night was quiet under the moon's pale glow.

Too quiet, Jarlaxle believed, like the hush of a predator. Where were the frogs, the night birds, the beetles?

Something shifted down to the west, catching Jarlaxle's attention. He scanned the field, seeking the source—a rodent of some sort, likely.

But he saw nothing, just the uneven grasses dancing in the moonlight on the gentle night breeze.

Something moved again, and Jarlaxle swept his gaze across the abandoned stones littering the field, reached up and lifted his eye patch so he could more distinctly focus. Across the field stood a shadowy, huddled figure, bowing and waving its arms. It occurred to the drow that it was not a living man, but a wraith or a specter or a lich.

In the open ground between them, a flat stone shifted. Another, standing upright, tilted to a greater angle.

Jarlaxle took a step toward the ancient markers.

The moon disappeared behind a dark cloud and the darkness deepened. But Jarlaxle was a creature of the Underdark, blessed with eyes that could see in the most meager light. In the nearly lightless caverns far below the stone, a patch of luminous lichen would glow to his eyes like a high-burning torch. Even in those moments when the moon hid, he saw that standing stone shift again, ever so slightly, as if something scrabbled at its base below the ground.

"A graveyard . . ." he whispered, finally recognizing the flat stones as markers and understanding Athrogate's earlier assessment. As he spoke, the moon came clear, brightening the field. Something churned in the dirt beside the shifting stone.

A hand—a skeletal hand.

A greenish blue crackle of strange ground lightning blasted tracers across the field. In that light, Jarlaxle saw many more stones shifting, the ground churning.

I have found you, drow! the beast whispered in Jarlaxle's thoughts.

"Athrogate," Jarlaxle called softly. "Awaken, good dwarf."

The dwarf snored, coughed, belched, and rolled to his side, his back to the drow.

Jarlaxle slipped a hand crossbow from the holster on his belt, expertly drawing back the string with his thumb as he moved. He focused on a particular type of bolt, blunted and heavy, and the magical pouch beside the holster dispensed it into his hand as he reached for it.

"Awaken, good dwarf," the drow said again, never taking his gaze from the field. A skeletal arm grasped at the empty air near the low-leaning headstone.

When Athrogate did not reply, Jarlaxle leveled the hand crossbow and pulled the trigger.

"Hey, now, what's the price o' bacon!" the dwarf yelped as the bolt thumped him in the arse. He rolled over and scrambled like a tipped crab, but jumped to his feet. He began circling back and forth with short hops on bent legs, rubbing his wounded bum all the while.

"What do ye know, elf?" he asked at length.

"That you are indeed loud enough to wake the dead," Jarlaxle replied, motioning over Athrogate's shoulder toward the stone-strewn field.

Athrogate leaped around.

"I see . . . dark," he said. As he finished, not only did the moon break free of the clouds, but another strange lightning bolt arced over the field like a net of energy had been cast over it. In the flash, whole skeletons showed themselves, standing free of their graves and shambling toward the tree-lined ridge.

"Coming for us, I'm thinking!" Athrogate bellowed. "And they look a bit hungry. More than a bit! Bwahaha! Starved, I'd wager!"

"Let us be gone from this place, and quickly," said Jarlaxle. He reached into his belt pouch and produced an obsidian statue of a gaunt horse with twists like fire around its hooves.

Athrogate nodded and did likewise, producing his boar figurine.

They both dropped their items and called forth their steeds together, an equine nightmare for Jarlaxle, snorting smoke and running on hooves of flame, and a demonic boar for Athrogate that radiated heat and belched the fire of the lower planes. Jarlaxle was first up in his seat, turning his mount to charge away, but he looked over his shoulder to see Athrogate take up his twin morningstars, leap upon the boar, and kick it into a squealing charge straight down at the graveyard.

"This way's faster!" the dwarf howled, and he set the heavy balls of his weapons spinning at the ends of their chains on either side. "Bwahaha!"

"Oh, Lady Lolth," Jarlaxle groaned. "If you sent this one to torment me, then know that I surrender, and just take him back."

Athrogate charged straight down onto the field, the boar kicking and bucking. Another green flash lit up the stony meadow before him, showing dozens of walking dead climbing from the torn earth, lifting skeletal hands at the approaching dwarf.

Athrogate bellowed all the louder and clamped his powerful legs tightly on the demon-boar. Seeming no less crazy than its bearded rider, the boar charged straight at the walking horde, and the dwarf sent his morningstars spinning. All around him they worked, heavy glassteel balls smashing against bone, breaking off reaching fingers and arms, shattering ribs with powerful swipes.

The boar beneath him gored, kicked, and plowed through the mindless undead that closed in hungrily. Athrogate drove his heels in hard against the boar's flanks and it leaped straight up and brought forth the fires of the lower planes, a burst of orange flame blasting out beneath its hooves as it landed, boiling into a radius half again wider than the dwarf was tall and curling up in an eruption of flame. The grass all around Athrogate smoked, licks of flame springing to life on the taller clumps.

While the flames bit at the nearest skeletons, they proved little deterrence to those coming from behind. The creatures closed, showing not the slightest sign of fear.

An overhead swing from Athrogate brought a morningstar down atop a skull, exploding it in a puff of white powder. He swung his other morningstar in a wide sweep, back to front, clipping three separate reaching skeletal arms and taking them off cleanly.

The skeletons seemed not to notice or care, and kept coming. Closing, always closing.

Athrogate roared all the louder against the press, and increased the fury of his swings. He didn't need to aim. The dwarf couldn't have missed smashing bones if he tried. Clawing fingers reached out at him, grinning skulls snapped their jaws.

Then the boar shrieked in pain. It hopped and sent out another circle of flames, but the unthinking skeletons seemed not to notice as their legs blackened. Clawing fingers raked the boar, sending it into a bucking frenzy, and Athrogate was thrown wide, clearing the front row of skeletons, but many more rushed at him as he fell.

* * * * *

Jarlaxle hated this kind of fight. Most of his battle repertoire, both magical and physical, was designed to misdirect, to confuse, and to keep his opponent off-balance.

You couldn't confuse a brainless skeleton or zombie.

With a great sigh, Jarlaxle plucked the huge feather from his hat and threw it to the ground, issuing commands to the magical item in an arcane language. Almost immediately, with a great puff of smoke, the feather became a gigantic flightless bird, a diatryma, ten feet tall and with a neck as thick as a strong man's chest.

Responding to Jarlaxle's telepathic commands, the monstrous bird charged onto the field and buffeted the undead with its short wings, pecking them to pieces with its powerful beak. The bird pushed through the throng of undead, kicking and buffeting and pecking with abandon. Every attack rattled a skeleton to pieces or smashed a skull to powder.

But more rose from the torn soil, and they closed and clawed.

On the side of the ridge, Jarlaxle casually slipped a ring onto his finger and drew a thin wand from his pack.

He punched out with the ring and its magic extended and amplified his strike many times over, blowing a path of force through the nearest ranks of skeletons, sending bones flying every which way. A second punch shattered three others as they tried to close from his left flank.

His immediate position secured, the drow lifted the wand, calling upon its powers to bring forth a burst of brilliantly shining light, warm and magical and ultimately devastating to the undead creatures.

Unlike the flames of the magical boar, the wand's light could not be ignored by the skeletons. Where fire could but blacken their bones, perhaps wound them slightly, the magical light struck at the core of the very magic that gave them animation, countering the negative energy that had lifted them from the grave.

Jarlaxle centered the burst in the area where Athrogate had fallen, and the dwarf's expected yelp of surprise and pain—pain from stinging eyes—sounded sweet to the drow.

He couldn't help but laugh when the dwarf finally emerged from the rattle of collapsing skeletons.

The fight, however, remained far from won. More and more skeletons continued to rise and advance.

Athrogate's boar was gone, slain by the horde. The magic of the figurine could not produce another creature for several hours. Jarlaxle's bird, too, had fallen victim to slashing digits and was being torn asunder. The drow lifted his fingers to the band on his hat, where the nub of a new feather was beginning to sprout. But several days would pass before another diatryma could be summoned.

Athrogate turned as if he meant to charge into another knot of skeletons, and Jarlaxle yelled, "Get back here!"

Still rubbing his stinging eyes, the dwarf replied, "There be more to hit, elf!"

"I will leave you, then, and they will tear you apart."

"Ye're askin' me to run from a fight!" Athrogate yelled as his morningstars pulverized another skeleton that reached for him with clawing hands.

"Perhaps the magic that raised these creatures will lift you up as a zombie," Jarlaxle said as he turned his nightmare around, facing up the ridge. Within a few heartbeats, he heard mumbling behind him as Athrogate approached. The dwarf huffed and puffed beside him, holding the onyx boar figurine and muttering.

"You cannot call another one now," Jarlaxle reminded him, extending a hand that Athrogate grasped.

The dwarf settled behind the drow on the nightmare's back and Jarlaxle kicked the steed away, leaving the skeletons far, far behind. They rode hard, then more easily, and the dwarf began to giggle.

"What do you know?" the drow asked, but Athrogate only bellowed with wild laughter.

"What?" Jarlaxle demanded, but he couldn't spare the time to properly look back, and Athrogate sounded too amused to properly answer.

When they finally reached a place where they could safely stop, Jarlaxle pulled up abruptly and turned around.

There sat Athrogate, red-faced with laughter as he held a skeletal hand and forearm, the fingers still clawing in the air before him. Jarlaxle leaped from the nightmare, and when the dwarf didn't immediately follow, the drow dismissed the steed, sending Athrogate falling to the ground through an insubstantial swirl of black smoke.

But Athrogate still laughed as he thumped to the ground, thoroughly amused by the animated skeletal arm.

"Be rid of that wretched thing!" Jarlaxle said.

Athrogate looked at him incredulously. "Thought ye had more imagination, elf," he said. He hopped up and unstrapped his heavy breastplate. As soon as it fell aside, the dwarf reached over his shoulder with the still-clawing hand and gave a great sigh of pleasure as the fingers scratched his back. "How long do ye think it'll live?"

"Longer than you, I hope," the drow replied, closing his eyes and shaking his head helplessly. "Not very long, I imagine."

"Bwahaha!" Athrogate bellowed, then, "Aaaaaaaah."

* * * * *

"The next time we face such creatures, I expect you to follow my lead," Jarlaxle said to Athrogate the next morning as the dwarf fiddled once more with his skeletal toy.

"Next time? What do ye know, elf?"

"It was not a random event," the drow admitted. "I have been visited, twice now, in my Reverie by a beast I had thought destroyed, but one that has somehow transcended death."

"A beast that brought up them skeletons?"

"A great dragon," Jarlaxle explained, "to the south of here and . . ." Jarlaxle paused, not really certain where Hephaestus's lair was. He had gone there, but magically with a teleportation spell. He knew the general features of that distant region, but not the specifics of the lair, though he thought of someone who would surely know the place. "Near to the Snowflake Mountains," he finished. "A great dragon whose thoughts can reach across hundreds of miles, it seems."

"Ye thinking we need to run farther?"

Jarlaxle shook his head. "There are great powers I can enlist in defeating this creature."

"Hmm," said the dwarf.

"I just have to convince them not to kill us first."

"Hmm."

"Indeed," said the drow. "A mighty priest named Cadderly, a Chosen of his god, who promised me death should I ever return."

"Hmm."

"But I will find a way."

"So ye're sayin', and so ye're prayin', but I'm hoping I'm not the one what'll be payin'."

Jarlaxle glared at the dwarf.

"Well, then ye can't be going back where ye're wanting—though I canno' be thinking why ye're wanting what ye're wantin'! To go to a place where the dragons are hauntin'!"

The glare melted into a groan.

"I know, I know," said Athrogate. "No more word-songin'. But that was a good one, what?"

"Needs work," said the drow. "Though considerably less so than your usual efforts."

"Hmm," said the dwarf, beaming with pride.

CHAPTER 2
THE BROKEN CONTINUUM

Drizzt Do'Urden slipped out of his bedroll and reached his bare arms up high, fingers wide, stretching to the morning sky. It was good to be on the road, out of Mithral Hall after the dark winter. It was invigorating to smell the fresh, crisp air, absent the smoke of the forges, and to feel the wind across his shoulders and through his long, thick white hair.

It was good to be alone with his wife.

The dark elf rolled his head in wide circles, stretching his neck. He reached up high again, kneeling on his blankets. The breeze was chill across his naked form, but he didn't mind. The cool wind invigorated him and made him feel alive with sensation.

He slowly moved to stand, exaggerating every movement to flex away the kinks from the hard ground that had served as his mattress, then paced away from the small encampment and outside the ring of boulders to catch a view of Catti-brie.

Dressed only in her colorful magical blouse, which had once been the enchanted robe of a gnome wizard, she stood on a hillside not far away, her palms together in front of her in a pose of deep concentration. Drizzt marveled at her simple charm. The colorful shift reached only to mid-thigh, and Catti-brie's natural beauty was neither diminished nor outshone by the finely crafted garment.

They were on the road back to Mithral Hall from the city of Silverymoon, where Catti-brie's wizard mentor, the great Lady Alustriel, ruled. It had not been a good visit. Something was in the air, something dangerous and frightening, some feeling among the wizards that all was not well with the Weave of magic. Reports and whispers from all over Faerûn spoke of spells gone horribly awry, of magic misfiring or not firing at all, of brilliant spellcasters falling to apparent insanity.

Alustriel had admitted that she feared for the integrity of Mystra's Weave itself, the very source of arcane energy, and the look on her face, ashen, was something Drizzt had never before witnessed from her, not even when the drow had gone to Mithral Hall those many years ago, not even when King Obould and his great horde had crawled from their mountain holes in murderous frenzy. It was indeed a crestfallen and fearful look that Drizzt would never have thought possible on the face of that renowned champion, one of the Seven Sisters, Chosen of Mystra, beloved ruler of mighty Silverymoon.

Vigilance, observation, and meditation were Alustriel's orders of the day, as she and all others scrambled to try to discern what in the Nine Hells might be happening, and Catti-brie, less than a decade a wizard but showing great promise, had taken those orders to heart.

That's why she had risen so early, Drizzt knew, and had moved away from the distractions of the encampment and his presence, to be alone with her meditation.

He smiled as he watched her, her auburn hair still rich in color and thick to her shoulders, blowing in the breeze, her form, a bit thicker with age, perhaps, but still so beautiful and inviting to him, swaying gently with her thoughts.

She slowly spread her hands out wide as if in invitation to magic, the sleeves of her blouse reaching only to her elbows. Drizzt smiled as she rose from the ground, floating upward a few feet in easy levitation. Purple flames of faerie fire flickered to life across her body, appearing as extensions of the violet fabric of the blouse, as if its magic joined with her in a symbiotic completion.

A magical gust of wind buffeted her, blowing her auburn mane out wide behind her.

Drizzt could see that she was immersing herself in simple spells, in safe magic, trying to create more intimacy with the Weave as she contemplated the fears Alustriel had relayed.

A flash of lightning in the distance startled Drizzt and he jerked his head toward it as a rumble of thunder followed.

He crinkled his brow in confusion. The dawn was cloudless, but lightning it had been, reaching from high in the sky to the ground, for he saw the crackling blue bolt lingering along the distant terrain.

Drizzt had been on the surface for forty-five years, but he had never seen any natural phenomenon quite like that. He had witnessed terrific storms from the deck of Captain Deudermont's *Sea Sprite*, had watched a dust storm engulf the Calim Desert, had seen a squall pile snow knee-deep on the ground in an hour's time. He had even seen the rare event known as ball lightning once, in Icewind Dale, and he figured the sight before him to be some variant of that peculiar energy.

But this lightning traveled in a straight line, and trailed behind it a curtain of blue-white, shimmering energy. He couldn't gauge its speed, other than to note that the curtain of blue fire expanded behind it.

It appeared to be crossing the countryside to the north of his position. He glanced up at Catti-brie, floating and glowing on the hilltop to the east, and he wondered whether he should disturb her meditation to point out the phenomenon. He glanced at the line of lightning and his lavender eyes widened in shock. It had accelerated suddenly and had changed course, angling in his direction.

He turned from the lightning to Catti-brie, to realize that it was running straight at her!

"Cat!" Drizzt yelled, and started running.

She seemed not to hear.

Magical anklets sped Drizzt on his way, his legs moving in a blur. But the lightning was faster, and he could only cry out again and again as it sizzled past him. He could feel its teeming energy.

His hair rose up wildly from the proximity of the powerful charge, white strands floating on all sides.

"Cat!" he yelled to the hovering, glowing woman. "Catti-brie! Run!"

She was deep in her meditation, though she did seem to react, just a bit, turning her head to glance at Drizzt.

But too late. Her eyes widened just as the speeding ground lightning engulfed her. Blue sparks flew from her outstretched arms, her fingers jerking spasmodically, her form jolting with powerful discharges.

The edge of the strange lightning remained for a few heartbeats, then continued onward, leaving the still-floating woman in the shimmering blue curtain of its wake.

"Cat," Drizzt gasped, scrambling desperately across the stones. By the time he got there, the curtain was moving along, leaving a scarred line crackling with power on the ground.

Catti-brie still floated above it, still trembled and jerked. Drizzt held his breath as he neared her, to see that her eyes had rolled up into her head, showing only white.

He grabbed her hand and felt the sting of electrical discharge. But he didn't let go and he stubbornly pulled her aside of the scarred line. He hugged her close and tried unsuccessfully to pull her down to the ground.

"Catti-brie," Drizzt begged. "Don't you leave me!"

A thousand heartbeats or more passed as Drizzt held her, then the woman finally relaxed and gently sank from her levitation. Drizzt leaned her back to see her face, his heart skipping beats until he saw that he was staring into her beautiful blue eyes once more.

"By the gods, I thought you lost to me," he said with a great sigh of relief, one that he bit short as he noted that Catti-brie wasn't blinking. She wasn't really looking at him at all, but rather looking past him. He glanced over his shoulder to see what might be holding her interest so intently, but there was nothing.

"Cat?" he whispered, staring into her large eyes—eyes that did not gaze back at him nor past him, but into nothingness, he realized.

He gave her a shake. She mumbled something he could not decipher. Drizzt leaned closer.

"What?" he asked, and shook her again.

She lifted off the ground several inches, her arms reaching out wide, her eyes rolling back into her head. The purple flames began anew, as did the crackling energy.

Drizzt moved to hug her and pull her down again, but he fell back in surprise as her entire form shimmered as if emanating waves of energy. Helplessly the drow watched, mesmerized and horrified.

"Catti-brie?" he asked, and as he looked into her white eyes, he realized that something was different, very different! The lines on her face softened and disappeared. Her hair seemed longer and thicker—even her part changed to a style Catti-brie had not worn for years! And she seemed a bit leaner, her skin a bit tighter.

Younger.

" 'Twas a bow that found meself in the halls of a dwarven king," she said, or something like that—Drizzt could not be certain—and in a distinctly Dwarvish accent, like she'd once had when her time had been spent almost exclusively with Bruenor's clan in the shadows of Kelvin's Cairn in faraway Icewind Dale. She still floated off the ground, but the faerie fire and the crackling energy dissipated. Her eyes focused and returned to normal, those rich, deep blue orbs that had so stolen Drizzt's heart.

"Heartseeker, yes," Drizzt said. He stepped back and pulled the mighty bow from his shoulder, presenting it to her.

"Can't be fishing Maer Dualdon with a bow, though, and so it's Rumblebelly's line I'm favorin'," she said, still looking into the distance and not at Drizzt.

Drizzt crinkled his face in confusion.

The woman sighed deeply. Her eyes rolled back into her head, showing only white to Drizzt. The flames and energy reappeared and a gust of wind came up from nowhere, striking only Catti-brie, as if those waves of energy that had come forth from her were returning to her being. Her hair, her skin, her age—all returned, and her colorful garment stopped blowing in the unfelt wind.

The moment passed and she settled to the ground, unconscious once more.

Drizzt shook her again, called to her many times, but she seemed not to notice. He snapped his fingers in front of her eyes, but she didn't even blink. He started to lift her, to carry her toward the camp so they could hurry on their way to Mithral Hall, but as he extended her arm, he saw a tear in her magical blouse just behind the shoulder. Then he froze as he noticed bruises under the fabric. With a shiver of panic, Drizzt gently slid the ripped section aside.

He sucked in his breath in fear and confusion. He had seen Catti-brie's bare back a thousand times, had marveled at her unblemished, smooth skin. But it was marked, scarred even, in the distinctive shape of an hourglass as large as Drizzt's fist. The lower half was almost fully discolored, the top showing only a small sliver of bruising, as if almost all of the counting sand had drained.

With trembling fingers, Drizzt touched it. Catti-brie did not react.

"What?" he whispered helplessly.

He carried Catti-brie along briskly, her head lolling as if she were half-asleep.

CHAPTER 3

REASONING THE INDECIPHERABLE

It was a place of soaring towers and sweeping stairways, of flying buttresses and giant, decorated windows, of light and enlightenment, of magic and reason, of faith and science. It was Spirit Soaring, the work of Cadderly Bonaduce, Chosen of Deneir. Cadderly the Questioner, he had been labeled by his brothers of Deneir, the god who demanded such inquiry and continual reason from his devoted.

Cadderly had raised the grand structure from the ruins of the Edificant Library, considered by many to be the most magnificent library in all of Faerûn. Indeed, architects from lands as far and varied as Silverymoon and Calimport had come to the Snowflake Mountains to glimpse this creation, to marvel in the flying buttresses—a recent innovation in the lands of Faerûn, and never before on so grand a scale. The work of magic, of divine inspiration, had formed the stained glass windows, and also rendered the great murals of scholars at work in their endless pursuit of reason.

Spirit Soaring had been raised as a library and a cathedral, a common ground where scholars, mages, sages, and priests might gather to question superstition, to embrace reason. No place on the continent so represented the wondrous joining of faith and science, where one need not fear that logic, observation, and experimentation might take a learner away from edicts of the divine. Spirit

Soaring was a place where truth was considered divine, and not the other way around.

Scholars did not fear to pursue their theories there. Philosophers did not fear to question the common understanding of the pantheon and the world. Priests of any and all gods did not fear persecution there, unless the very concept of rational debate represented persecution to a closed and small mind.

Spirit Soaring was a place to explore, to question, to learn—about everything. There, discussions of the various gods of the world of Toril always bordered on heresy. There, the nature of magic was examined, and so there, at a time of fear and uncertainty, at the time of the failing Weave, rushed scholars from far and wide.

And Cadderly greeted them, every one, with open arms and shared concern. He looked like a very young man, much younger than his forty-four years. His gray eyes sparkled with youthful luster and his mop of curly brown hair bounced along his shoulders. He moved like a much younger man, loose and agile, a distinctive spring in his step. He wore a typical Deneirrath outfit, tan-white tunic and trousers, and added his own flair with a light blue cape and a wide-brimmed hat, blue to match the cape, with a red band, plumed on the right side.

The time was unsettling, the magic of the world possibly unraveling, yet Cadderly Bonaduce's eyes reflected excitement more than dread. Cadderly was forever a student, his mind always inquisitive, and he did not fear what was simply not yet explained.

He just wanted to understand it.

"Welcome, welcome!" He greeted a trio of visitors one bright morning, who were dressed in the green robes of druids.

"Young Bonaduce, I presume," said one, an old graybeard.

"Not so young," Cadderly admitted.

"I knew your father many years ago," the druid replied. "Am I right in assuming that we will be welcomed here in this time of confusion?"

Cadderly looked at the man curiously.

"Cadderly still lives, correct?"

"Well, yes," Cadderly answered, then grinned and asked, "Cleo?"

"Ah, your father has told you of . . . me . . ." the druid answered, but he ended with wide eyes, stuttering, "C-Cadderly? Is that you?"

"I had thought you lost in the advent of the chaos curse, old friend!" Cadderly said.

"How can you be . . . ?" Cleo started to ask, in utter confusion.

"Were you not destroyed?" the youthful-seeming priest asked. "Of course you weren't—you stand here before me!"

"I wandered in the form of a turtle, for years," Cleo explained. "Trapped by insanity within the animal coil I most favored. But how can you be Cadderly? I had heard of Cadderly's children, who should be as old . . ."

As he spoke, a young man walked up to the priest. He looked very much like Cadderly, but with exotic, almond-shaped eyes.

"And here is one," Cadderly explained, sweeping his son to him with an outstretched arm. "My oldest son, Temberle."

"Who looks older than you," Cleo remarked dryly.

"A long and complicated story," said the priest. "Connected to this place, Spirit Soaring."

"You are wanted in the observatory, Father," Temberle said with a polite salute to the new visitors. "The Gondsmen are declaring supremacy again, as gadget overcomes magic."

"No doubt, both factions think I side with their cause."

Temberle shrugged and Cadderly breathed a great sigh.

"My old friend," Cadderly said to Cleo, "I should like some time with you, to catch up."

"I can tell you of life as a turtle," Cleo deadpanned, drawing a smile from Cadderly.

"We have many points of view in Spirit Soaring at the time, and little agreement," Cadderly explained. "They're all nervous, of course."

"With reason," said another of the druids.

"And reason is our only way through this," said Cadderly. "So welcome, friends, and enter. We have food aplenty, and discussion aplenty more. Add your voices without reserve."

The three druids looked to each other, the other two nodding approvingly to Cleo. "As I told you it would be," Cleo said. "Reasonable priests, these Deneirrath." He turned to Cadderly, who bowed, smiled widely, and took his leave.

"You see?" Cadderly said to Temberle as the druids walked past into Spirit Soaring. "I have told you many times that I am reasonable." He patted his son on the shoulder and followed after the druids.

"And every time you do, Mother whispers in my ear that your reasonableness is based entirely on what suits your current desires," Temberle said after him.

Cadderly skipped a step and seemed almost to trip. He didn't look back, but laughed and continued on his way.

* * * * *

Temberle left the building and walked to the southern wall, to the great garden, where he was to meet with his twin sister, Hanaleisa. The two had planned a trip that morning to Carradoon, the small town on the banks of Impresk Lake, a day's march from Spirit Soaring. Temberle's grin widened as he approached the large, fenced garden, catching sight of his sister with his favorite uncle.

The green-bearded dwarf hopped about over a row of newly-planted seeds, whispering words of encouragement and waving his arms—one severed at his elbow—like a bird trying to gain altitude in a gale. This dwarf, Pikel Bouldershoulder, was most unusual for his kind for having embraced the ways of the druids—and for many other reasons, most of which made him Temberle's favorite uncle.

Hanaleisa Maupoissant Bonaduce, looking so much like a younger version of their mother, Danica, with her strawberry blond hair and rich brown eyes, almond-shaped like Temberle's own, looked up from the row of new plantings and grinned at her brother, as clearly amused by Pikel's gyrations as was Temberle.

"Uncle Pikel says he'll make them grow bigger than ever," Hanaleisa remarked as Temberle came through the gate.

"Evah!" Pikel roared, and Temberle was impressed that he had apparently learned a new word.

"But I thought that the gods weren't listening," Temberle dared say, drawing an "Ooooh" of consternation and a lot of finger-wagging from Pikel.

"Faith, brother," said Hanaleisa. "Uncle Pikel knows the dirt."

"Hee hee hee," said the dwarf.

"Carradoon awaits," said Temberle.

"Where is Rorey?" Hanaleisa asked, referring to their brother Rorick, at seventeen, five years their junior.

"With a gaggle of mages, arguing the integrity of the magical strands that empower the world. I expect that when this strangeness is ended, Rorey will have a dozen powerful wizards vying to serve as his mentor."

Hanaleisa nodded at that, for she, like Temberle, knew well their younger brother's propensity and talent at interjecting himself into any debate. The young woman brushed the dirt from her knees and slapped her hands together to clean them.

"Lead on," she bade her brother. "Uncle Pikel won't let my garden die, will you?"

"Doo-dad!" Pikel triumphantly proclaimed and launched into his rain dance . . . or fertility dance . . . or dance of the sunshine . . . or whatever it was that he danced about. As always, the Bonaduce twins left their Uncle Pikel with wide, sincere smiles splayed on their young faces, as it had been since their toddler days.

* * * * *

Her forearms and forehead planted firmly on the rug, the woman eased her feet from the floor, drawing her legs perpendicular to her torso. With great grace, she let her legs swing wide to their respective sides, then pulled them together as she straightened in an easy and secure headstand.

Breathing softly, in perfect balance and harmony, Danica

turned her hands flat and pressed up, rising into a complete handstand. She posed as if underwater, or as if gravity itself could not touch her in her deep meditative state. She moved even beyond that grace, seeming as if some wire or force pulled her upward as she rose up from palms to fingers.

She stood inverted, perfectly still and perfectly straight, immune to the passage of time, unstrained. Her muscles did not struggle for balance, but firmly held her in position so her weight pressed down uniformly onto her strong hands. She kept her eyes closed, and her hair, showing gray amidst the strawberry hues, hung to the floor.

She was deep in the moment, deep within herself. Yet she sensed an approach, a movement by the door, and she opened her eyes just as Ivan Bouldershoulder, yellow-bearded brother of Pikel, poked his hairy head through.

Danica opened her eyes to regard the dwarf.

"When all their magic's gone, yerself and meself'll take over the world, girl," he said with an exaggerated wink.

Danica rolled down to her toes and gracefully stood upright, turning as she went so that she still faced the dwarf.

"What do you know, Ivan?" she asked.

"More'n I should and not enough to be sure," he replied. "Yer older brats went down to Carradoon, me brother's telling me."

"Temberle enjoys the availability of some young ladies there, or so I've heard."

"Ah," the dwarf mused, and a very serious look came over him. "And what o' Hana?"

Danica laughed at him. "What of her?"

"She got some boy sniffin' around?"

"She's twenty-two years old, Ivan. That would be her business."

"Bah! Not until her Uncle Ivan gets to talk to the fool, it won't!"

"She can handle herself. She's trained in the ways of—"

"No, she can'no'!"

"You don't show the same concern for Temberle, I see."

"Bah. Boys'll do what boys're supposed to be doin', but they best not be doin' it to me girl, Hana!"

Danica put a hand up over her mouth in a futile attempt to mask her laughter.

"Bah!" Ivan said, waving his hand at her. "I'm takin' that girl to Bruenor's halls, I am!"

"I don't think she'd agree to that."

"Who's askin'? Yer young ones be runnin' wild, they be!"

He continued to grumble, until the laughing Danica finally managed to catch her breath long enough to inquire, "Was there something you wished to ask me?"

Ivan stared at her blankly for a moment, confused and flustered. "Yeah," he said, though he seemed uncertain. After another moment of reflection, he added, "Where's the little one? Me brother was thinkin' o' jogging down to Carradoon, and he missed them older brats when they left."

"I haven't seen Rorick all day."

"Well, he didn't go with Temberle and Hana. Is it good by yerself that he goes with his uncle?"

"I cannot think of a safer place for any of my children to be, good Ivan."

"Aye, and that's what's what," the dwarf agreed, hooking his thumbs under the suspenders of his breeches.

"I fear that I cannot say the same for my future children-in-law, however. . . ."

"Just the son-in-law," Ivan corrected with a wink.

"Don't break anything," Danica begged. "And don't leave any marks."

Ivan nodded, then brought his hands together and cracked his knuckles loudly. With a bow, he took his leave.

Danica knew Ivan was harmless, at least as far as suitors to her daughter were concerned. It occurred to her just then that Hanaleisa would have a hard time indeed maintaining any relationships with Ivan and Pikel hovering over her.

Or maybe, those two would serve as a good test of a young man's intentions. His heart would surely have to be full for him to stick around once the dwarves started in on him.

Danica giggled and sighed contentedly, reminding herself that, other than the few years they had been away serving King Bruenor in Mithral Hall, Ivan and Pikel Bouldershoulder had been the best guardians any child could ever know.

* * * * *

The shadowy being, once Fetchigrol the archmage of a great and lost civilization, didn't even recognize himself by that name, having long ago abandoned his identity in the communal joining ritual that had forged the Crystal Shard. He had known life; had known undeath as a lich; had known a state of pure energy as part of the Crystal Shard; had known nothingness, obliteration.

And even from that last state, the creature that was once Fetchigrol had returned, touched by the Weave itself. No more was he a free-willed spirit, but merely an extension, an angry outreach of that curious triumvirate of power that had melded into a singular malevolent force in a fire-blasted cavern many miles to the southeast.

Fetchigrol served the anger of Crenshinibon-Hephaestus-Yharaskrik, of the being they had become, the Ghost King.

And like all seven of the shadowy specters, Fetchigrol searched the night, seeking those who had wronged his masters. In the lower reaches of the Snowflake Mountains, overlooking a large lake shining under the moonlight to the west, and on a trail leading deeper into the mountains and to a great library, he sensed that he was close.

When he heard the voices, a thrill coursed Fetchigrol's shadowy substance, for above all, the undead specter sought an outlet for his malevolence, a victim of his hatred. He drifted to the deeper shadows behind a tree overlooking the path as a pair of young humans came into view, walking tentatively in the dim light among the roots that crisscrossed the trail.

They passed right before him, not noticing at all—though the young woman did cock her head curiously and shiver.

How the undead creature wanted to leap out and devour them! But Fetchigrol was too far removed from their world, was too much within the Shadowfell, the intruding realm of shadow and darkness that had come to Faerûn. Like his six brothers, he had not the substance to affect material creatures.

Only spirits. Only the diminishing life energies of the dead.

He followed the pair down the mountain until they at last found a place they deemed suitable for an encampment. Confident that they would stay there at least until pre-dawn, the malevolent spirit rushed into the wilds, seeking a vessel.

He found it only a couple of miles from the young humans' camp, in the form of a dead bear, its half-rotted carcass teeming with maggots and flies.

Fetchigrol bowed before the beast and began to chant, to channel the power of the Ghost King, to call to the spirit of the bear.

The corpse stirred.

* * * * *

His steps slow, his heart heavier than his weary limbs, Drizzt Do'Urden crossed the Surbrin River Bridge. The eastern door of Mithral Hall was in sight, as were members of Clan Battlehammer, scurrying to join him as he bore his burden.

Catti-brie lay listless in his arms, her head lolling with every step, her eyes open but seeing nothing.

And Drizzt's expression, so full of fear and sadness, only added to that horrifying image.

Calls to "Get Bruenor!" and "Open the doors and clear the road!" led Drizzt through that back door, and before he had gone ten strides into Mithral Hall, a wagon bounced up beside him and a group of dwarves helped get him and the listless Catti-brie into the back.

Only then did Drizzt realize how exhausted he was. He had walked for miles with Catti-brie in his arms, not daring to stop, for she needed help he could not provide. Bruenor's priests would know what to do, he'd prayed, and so the dwarves who gathered around repeatedly assured him.

The driver pushed the team hard across Garumn's Gorge and down the long and winding tunnels toward Bruenor's chambers.

Word had passed ahead, and Bruenor was in the hall waiting for them. Regis and many others stood beside him as he paced anxiously, wringing his strong hands or pulling at his great beard, softened to orange by the gray that dulled its once-fiery red.

"Elf?" Bruenor called. "What d'ye know?"

Drizzt nearly crumbled under the desperate tone in his dear friend's voice, for he couldn't offer much in the way of explanation or hope. He summoned as much energy as he could and flipped his legs over the side rail of the wagon, dropping lightly to the floor. He met Bruenor's gaze and managed a slight and hopeful nod. He struggled to keep up that optimism as he moved around the wagon and dropped the gate, then gathered his beloved Catti-brie in his arms.

Bruenor was at his side as Drizzt hoisted her. The dwarf's eyes widened and his hands trembled as he tried to reach up and touch his dear daughter.

"Elf?" he asked, his voice barely a whisper, and so shaky that the short word seemed multisyllabic.

Drizzt looked at him, and there he froze, unable to shake his head or offer a smile of hope.

Drizzt had no answers.

Catti-brie had somehow been touched by wild magic, and as far as he could tell, she was lost to them, was lost to the reality around her.

"Elf?" Bruenor asked again, and he managed to run his fingers across his daughter's soft face.

* * * * *

She stood perfectly still, staring at the jutting limb of the dead tree, her hands up before her, locked in striking form. Hanaleisa, so much her mother's daughter, found her center of peace and strength.

She could have reached up and grasped the end of the branch, then used her weight and leverage to break it free. But what would have been the fun in that?

So instead, the tree became her opponent, her enemy, her challenge.

"Hurry up, the night grows cold!" Temberle called from their camp near the trail.

Hanaleisa allowed no smile to crease her serious visage, and blocked out her brother's call. Her concentration complete, she struck with suddenness and with sheer power, striking the branch near the trunk with a left jab then a right cross, once, twice, then again with a snapping left before falling back into a defensive lean, lifting her leg for a jolting kick.

She rose up in a spinning leap and snapped out a strike that severed the end of the branch much farther out from the trunk, then again to splinter the limb in the middle. She finished with another leaping spin, bringing her leg up high and wide then dropping it down hard on the place she had already weakened with her jabs.

The limb broke away cleanly, falling to the ground in three neat pieces.

Hanaleisa landed, completely balanced, and brought her hands in close, fingers touching. She bowed to the tree, her defeated opponent, then scooped the broken firewood and started for the camp as her brother called out once more.

She had gone only a few steps before she heard a shuffling in the forest, not far away. The young woman froze in place, making not a sound, her eyes scouring the patches of moonlight in the darkness, seeking movement.

Something ambled through the brush, something heavy, not twenty strides away, and heading, she realized, straight for their camp.

Hanaleisa slowly bent her knees, lowering herself to the ground, where she gently and silently placed the firewood, except for one thick piece. She stood and remained very still for a moment, seeking the sound again to get her bearings. With great agility she brought her feet up one at a time and removed her boots, then padded off, walking lightly on the balls of her bare feet.

She soon saw the light of the fire Temberle had managed to get going, then noted the form moving cumbersomely before her, crossing between her and that firelight, showing itself to be a large creature indeed.

Hanaleisa held her breath, trying to choose her next move, and quickly, for the creature was closing on her brother. She had been trained by her parents to fight and fight well, but never before had she found herself with lethal danger so close at hand.

The sound of her brother's voice, calling her name, "Hana?" jarred her from her contemplation. Temberle had heard the beast, and indeed, the beast was very close to him, and moving with great speed.

Hanaleisa sprinted ahead and shouted out to catch the creature's attention, fearing that she had hesitated too long. "Your sword!" she cried to her brother.

Hanaleisa leaped up as she neared the beast—a bear, she realized—and caught a branch overhead, then swung out and let go, soaring high and far, clearing the animal. Only then did Hanaleisa understand the true nature of the monster, that it was not just a bear that might be frightened away. She saw that half of its face had rotted away, the white bone of its skull shining in the moonlight.

She struck down as she passed over it, her open palm smacking hard against the snout as the creature looked up to react. The solid blow jolted the monster, but did not stop its swipe, which clipped Hanaleisa as she flew past, sending her into a spin.

She landed lightly but off balance and stumbled aside, and just in time as Temberle raced past her, greatsword in hand. He charged straight in with a mighty thrust and the sword plunged through the loose skin on the undead creature's back and cracked off bone.

But the bear kept coming, seeming unbothered by the wound, and walked itself right up the blade to Temberle, its terrible claws out wide, its toothy maw opened in a roar.

Hanaleisa leaped past Temberle, laying flat out in mid-air and double-kicking the beast about the shoulders and chest. Had it been a living bear, several hundred pounds of muscle and tough hide and thick bone, she wouldn't have moved it much, of course, but its undead condition worked in her favor, for much of the creature's mass had rotted away or been carried off by scavengers.

The beast stumbled back, sliding down the greatsword's blade enough for Temberle to yank it free.

"Slash, don't stab!" Hanaleisa reminded him as she landed on her feet and waded in, laying forth a barrage of kicks and punches. She batted aside a swatting paw and got behind the swipe of deadly claws, then rattled off a series of heavy punches into the beast's shoulders.

She felt the bone crunching under the weight of those blows, but again, the beast seemed unbothered and launched a backhand that forced the young woman to retreat.

The bear went on the offensive, and it attacked with ferocity, moving to tackle the woman. Hanaleisa scrambled back, nearly tripping over an exposed root, then getting caught against a birch stand.

She cried out in fear as the beast fell over her, or started to, until a mighty sword flashed in the moonlight above and behind it, coming down powerfully across the bear's right shoulder and driving through.

The undead beast howled and pursued the dodging Hanaleisa, crashing into the birch stand and taking the whole of it down beneath its bulky, tumbling form. It bit and slashed as if it had its enemy secured, but Hanaleisa was gone, out the side, rolling away.

The bear tried to follow, but Temberle moved fast behind it, relentlessly smashing at it with his heavy greatsword. He chopped away chunks of flesh, sending maggots flying and smashing bones to powder.

Still the beast came on, on all fours and down low, closing on Hanaleisa.

She fought away her revulsion and panic. She placed her back against a solid tree and curled her legs, and as the beast neared, jaws open to bite at her, she kicked out repeatedly, her heel smashing the snout again and again.

Still the beast drove in, and still Temberle smashed at it, and Hanaleisa kept on kicking. The top jaw and snout broke away, hanging to the side, but still the animated corpse bore down!

At the last moment, Hanaleisa threw herself to the side and backward into a roll. She came around to her feet, every instinct telling her to run away.

She denied her fear.

The bear turned on Temberle ferociously. His sword crashed down across its collarbone, but the monster swatted it with such strength that it tore the sword from Temberle's hand and sent it flying away.

Up rose the monster to its full height, its arms raised to the sky, ready to drop down upon the unarmed warrior.

Hanaleisa leaped upon its back and with the momentum of her charge, with every bit of focus and concentration, with all the strength of her years of training as a monk behind her strike, drove her hand—index and middle fingers extended like a blade—at the back of the beast's head.

She felt her fingers break through the skull. She retracted and punched again and again, pulverizing the bone, driving her fingers into the beast's brain and tearing pieces out.

The bear swung around and Hanaleisa went flying into the trees, crashing hard through a close pair of young elms, bouncing from one to the other, her momentum pushing her so she fell to the ground right behind them.

But as she slid down the narrowing gap, her ankle caught. Desperate, she looked at the approaching monster.

She saw the sword descend behind it, atop its skull, splitting the head in half and driving down the creature's neck.

And still it kept coming! Hanaleisa's eyes widened with horror. She couldn't free her foot!

But it was only the undead beast's momentum that propelled it forward, and it crashed into the elms and fell to the side.

Hanaleisa breathed easier. Temberle rushed up and helped her free her foot, then helped her stand. She was sore in a dozen places—her shoulder was surely bruised.

But the beast was dead—again.

"What evil has come to these woods?" the young woman asked.

"I don't..." Temberle started to answer, but he stopped. Both he and his sister shivered, their eyes going wide in surprise. A sudden coldness filled the air around them.

They heard a hissing sound, perhaps laughter, and jumped back to back into a defensive posture, as they had been trained.

The chill passed, and the laughter receded.

In the firelight of their nearby camp, they saw a shadowy figure drift away.

"What was that?" Temberle asked.

"We should go back," Hanaleisa breathlessly replied.

"We're much closer to Carradoon than Spirit Soaring."

"Then go!" Hanaleisa said, and the pair rushed to the camp and scooped up their gear.

Each took a burning branch to use as a torch, then started along the trail. Cold pockets of air found them repeatedly as they ran, with hissing laughter and patches of shadow darker than the darkest night shifting around them. They heard animals screech in fear and birds flutter from branches.

"Press on," each urged the other repeatedly, and they whispered more insistently when at last their torches burned away and the darkness closed in tightly.

They didn't stop running until they reached the outskirts of the town of Carradoon, dark and asleep on the shores of Impresk Lake, still hours before the dawn. They knew the proprietor at Cedar Shakes, a fine inn nearby, and went right to the door, rapping hard and insistently.

"Here, now! What's the racket at this witching hour?" came a sharp response from a window above. "What and wait, ho! Is that Danica's kids?"

"Let us in, good Bester Bilge," Temberle called up. "Please, just let us in."

They relaxed when the door swung open. Cheery old Bester Bilge pulled them inside, telling Temberle to throw a few logs on the low-burning hearth and promising a strong drink and some warm soup in short order.

Temberle and Hanaleisa looked to each other with great relief, hoping they had left the cold and dark outside.

They couldn't know that Fetchigrol had followed them to Carradoon and was even then at the old graveyard outside the town walls, planning the carnage to come with the next sunset.

CHAPTER
A CLUE IN THE RIFT
4

Athrogate held the skeletal arm aloft. He grumbled at its inactivity, and gave it a little shake. The fingers began to claw once more and the dwarf grinned and reached the bony arm over his shoulder, sighing contentedly as the scraping digits worked at a hard-to-reach spot in the middle of his itchy back.

"How long ye think it'll last, elf?" he asked.

Jarlaxle, too concerned to even acknowledge the dwarf's antics, just shrugged and continued on his meandering way. The drow wasn't sure where he was going. Any who knew Jarlaxle would have read the gravity of the situation clearly in his uncertain expression, for rarely, if ever, had anyone ever witnessed Jarlaxle Baenre perplexed.

The drow realized that he couldn't wait for Hephaestus to come to him. He didn't want to encounter such a foe on his own, or with only Athrogate at his side. He considered returning to Luskan—Kimmuriel and Bregan D'aerthe could certainly help—but his instincts argued against that. Once again, he would be allowing Hephaestus the offensive, and would be pitted against a foe that could apparently raise undead minions to his command with ease.

Above all else, Jarlaxle wanted to take the fight to the dragon, and he believed that Cadderly might well prove the solution to his troubles. But how could he enlist the priest, who was surely no willing ally of the dark elves? Except one particular dark elf.

And wouldn't it be grand to have Drizzt Do'Urden and some of his mighty friends along for the hunt?

But how?

So at Jarlaxle's direction, the pair traveled eastward, meandering across the Silver Marches toward Mithral Hall. It would take them easily a tenday, and Jarlaxle wasn't sure he had that kind of time to spare. He resisted Reverie that first day, and when night came, he meditated lightly, standing on a precarious perch.

A cold breeze found him, and as he shifted to curl against it, he slipped from the narrow log upon which he stood and the resulting stumble startled him. His hand already in his pocket, Jarlaxle pulled forth a fistful of ceramic pebbles. He spun a quick circle, spreading them around, and as each hit the ground, it broke open and the enchantment within, dweomers of bright light, spewed forth.

"What the—?" Athrogate cried, startled from his sleep by the sudden brightness.

Jarlaxle paid him no heed. He moved fast after a shadowy figure racing away from the magical light, a painful thing to undead creatures. He threw another light bomb ahead of the fleeing, huddled form, then another as it veered toward a shadowy patch.

"Hurry, dwarf!" the drow called, and he soon heard Athrogate huffing and puffing in pursuit. As soon as Athrogate passed him, Jarlaxle drew out a wand and brought forth a burst of brighter and more powerful light, landing it near the shadowy form. The creature shrieked, an awful, preternatural keening that sent a shiver coursing down Jarlaxle's spine.

That howl didn't slow Athrogate in the least, and the brave dwarf charged in with abandon, his morningstars spinning in both hands, arms outstretched. Athrogate called upon the enchantment of the morningstar in his right hand and explosive oil oozed over its metallic head. The dwarf leaped at the cowering creature and swung with all his might, thinking to end the fight with a single, explosive smite.

The morningstar hit nothing substantial, just hummed through the empty night.

Then Athrogate yelped in pain as a sharp touch hit his shoulder, a point of sudden and burning agony. He fell back, swinging with abandon, his morningstars crisscrossing, again hitting nothing.

The dwarf saw the specter's dark, cold hands reaching toward him, so he tried a different tactic. He swung his morningstars in from opposite sides, aiming the heads to collide directly in the center of the shadowy darkness.

Jarlaxle watched the battle with a curious eye, trying to gauge this foe. The specter was a minion of Hephaestus, obviously, and he knew well the usual qualities of incorporeal undead denizens.

Athrogate's weapon should have harmed it, at least some—the dwarf's morningstars were heavily enchanted. Even the most powerful undead creatures, the ones that existed on both the Prime Material Plane and a darker place of negative energy, should not have such complete immunity to his assault.

Jarlaxle winced and looked away when Athrogate's morningstar heads clanged together, the volatile oil exploding in a blinding flash, a concussive burst that forced the dwarf to stumble backward.

When the drow looked again, the specter seemed wholly unbothered by the burst. Jarlaxle took note of something unusual. Precisely as the morningstar heads collided, the specter seemed to diminish. In the moment of explosion, the creature appeared to vanish or shrink.

As the undead creature approached the dwarf, it grew substantial again, those dark hands reaching forth to inflict more cold agony.

"Elf! I can't be hitting the damned thing!" The dwarf howled in pain and staggered back.

"More oil!" Jarlaxle yelled, a sudden idea coming to him. "Smash them together again."

"That hurt, elf! Me arms're numb!"

"Do it!" Jarlaxle commanded.

He fired off his wand again, and the burst of light caused the specter to recoil, buying Athrogate a few heartbeats. Jarlaxle pulled off his hat and reached inside, and as Athrogate swung mightily with his opposing morningstars, the drow pulled forth a flat circle of cloth, like the black lining of his hat. He threw it out and it spun, elongating as it sailed past the dwarf.

The morningstars collided in another explosion, throwing Athrogate backward again. The specter, as Jarlaxle expected, faded, began to diminish to nothingness—no, not to nothingness, but to some other plane or dimension.

And the fabric circle, the magical extra-dimensional pocket created by the power of Jarlaxle's enchanted hat, fell over the spot.

The sudden glare caused by waves of energy—purple, blue, and green—rolled forth from the spot, pounding out a hum of sheer power.

The fabric of the world tore open.

Jarlaxle and Athrogate floated, weightless, staring at a spot that was once a clearing in the trees but seemed to have been replaced with . . . starscape.

"What'd'ye do, elf!" the dwarf cried, his voice modulating in volume as if carried on gigantic intermittent winds.

"Stay away from it!" Jarlaxle warned, and he felt a slight push at his back, compelling him toward the starry spot, the rift, he knew, to the Astral Plane.

Athrogate began to flail wildly, suddenly afraid, for he was not far from that dangerous place. He began to spin head over heels and all around, but the gyrations proved irrelevant to his inexorable drift toward the stars.

"Not like that!" Jarlaxle called.

"How, ye stupid elf?"

For Jarlaxle, the solution was easy. His drift carried him beside a tree, still rooted solidly in the firmament. He grabbed on with one hand and held himself easily in place, and knew that an easy push would propel him away from the rift. That was exactly what it was, Jarlaxle knew, a tear in the fabric of the Prime Material Plane, the result of mixing the energies of two extra-dimensional spaces. For Jarlaxle, who carried items of holding that created extra-dimensional pockets larger than their apparent capacity, a pair of belt pouches that did the same, and several other trinkets that could facilitate similar dweomers, the consequences of mingling them was not unknown or unexpected.

What surprised him, though, was that his extra-dimensional hole had reacted in such a way with that shadowy being. All he'd hoped to do was trap the thing within the magical hole when it tried to flow back into the plane of the living.

"Throw something at it!" Jarlaxle cried, and as Athrogate lifted his arm as if to launch one of his morningstars, the drow added, "Something you never need to retrieve!"

Athrogate held his throw at the last moment then pulled his heavy pack off his back. He waited until he spun around, then heaved it at the rift. The opposite reaction sent the dwarf floating backward, away from the tear—far enough for Jarlaxle to take a chance with a rope. He threw an end out toward Athrogate, close enough for the dwarf to grasp, and as soon as Athrogate held on, the drow tugged hard and brought the dwarf sailing toward him, then right past.

Jarlaxle took note that Athrogate drifted only a few feet before exiting the area of weightlessness and falling hard to his rump. His eyes never leaving the curious starscape that loomed barely ten strides away, Jarlaxle pushed himself back and dropped to stand beside Athrogate as the dwarf pulled himself to his feet.

"What'd ye do?" the dwarf asked in all seriousness.

"I have no idea," Jarlaxle replied.

"Worked, though," Athrogate offered.

Jarlaxle, not so certain of that, merely smirked.

They kept watch over the rift for a short while, and gradually the phenomenon dissipated, the wilderness returning to its previous firmament with no discernable damage. All was as it had been, except that the specter was gone.

* * * * *

"Still going east?" Athrogate asked as he and Jarlaxle started out the next day.

"That was the plan."

"The plan to win."

"Yes."

"I'm thinkin' we won last night," the dwarf said.

"We defeated a minion," Jarlaxle explained. "It has always been my experience that defeating a minion of a powerful foe only makes that foe angrier."

"So we should've let the shadow thing win?"

Jarlaxle's sigh elicited a loud laugh from Athrogate.

On they went through the day, and at camp that night, Jarlaxle dared to allow himself some time in Reverie.

And there, in his own subconscious, Hephaestus found him again.

Clever drow, the dracolich said in his mind. *Did you truly believe you could so easily escape me?*

Jarlaxle threw up his defenses in the form of images of Menzoberranzan, the great Underdark city. He concentrated on a distinct memory, of a battle his mercenary band had waged on behalf of Matron Mother Baenre. In that fight, a much younger Jarlaxle had engaged two separate weapons masters right in front of the doors of Melee-Magthere, the drow school of martial training. It was perhaps the most desperate struggle Jarlaxle had ever known, and one he would not have survived were it not for the intervention of a third weapons master, one of a lower-ranked House—House Do'Urden, actually, though that battle had been fought many decades before Drizzt drew his first breath.

That memory had long been crystallized in the mind of Jarlaxle Baenre, with images distinct and clear, and a level of tumult enough to keep his thoughts occupied. And with such emotional mental churning, the drow hoped he wouldn't surrender his current position to the intrusive Hephaestus.

Well done, drow! Hephaestus congratulated him. *But it will not matter in the end. Do you truly believe you can so easily hide from me? Do you truly believe your simple, but undeniably clever trick, would destroy one of the Seven?*

One of *what* 'Seven'? Jarlaxle asked himself.

He put the question to the back of his mind quickly and resumed his mental defense. He understood that his bold stand did little or nothing to shake the confidence of Hephaestus, but he remained certain that the hunting dragon wasn't making much headway. Then a notion occurred to him and he was jolted from his confrontation with the dragon, and from his Reverie entirely. He stumbled away from the tree upon which he was leaning.

"The Seven," he said, and swallowed hard, trying to recall all that he had learned about the origins of the Crystal Shard—

—and the seven liches who had created it.

"The Seven . . ." Jarlaxle whispered again, and a shiver ran up his spine.

* * * * *

Jarlaxle set the pace even swifter the next day, nightmare and hell boar running hard along the road. When they saw the smoke of an encampment not far ahead, Jarlaxle pulled to a halt.

"Orcs, likely," he explained to the dwarf. "We are near the border of King Obould's domain."

"Let's kill 'em, then."

Jarlaxle shook his head. "You must learn to exploit your enemies, my hairy little friend," he explained. "If these are Obould's orcs, they are not enemies of Mithral Hall."

"Bah!" Athrogate said, and spat on the ground.

"We go to them not as enemies, but as fellow travelers," Jarlaxle ordered. "Let us see what we might learn." Noting the disappointment on Athrogate's face, he added, "But do keep your morningstars near at hand."

It was indeed a camp of Many Arrow orcs, who served Obould, and though they sprang to readiness, brandishing weapons, at the casual approach of the curious pair—dwarf and drow—they held their arrows.

"We are travelers from Luskan," Jarlaxle greeted them in perfect command of Orcish, *"trade emissaries to King Obould and King Bruenor."* Out of the corner of his mouth, he bade Athrogate to

remain calm and to keep his mount's pace steady and slow. *"We have good food to share,"* Jarlaxle added. *"And better grog."*

"What'd'ye tell 'em?" Athrogate asked, seeing the porcine soldiers brighten and nod at one another.

"That we're all going to get drunk together," Jarlaxle whispered back.

"In a pig's fat rump!" the dwarf protested.

"Wherever you please," the drow replied. He slid down from his saddle and dismissed his hell-spawned steed. "Come, let us learn what we may."

It all started rather tentatively, with Jarlaxle producing both food and "grog" aplenty. The drink went over well with the orcs, even more so when the dwarf spat out his first taste of it with disgust. He looked to Jarlaxle as if dumbstruck, as if he never could have imagined anything potent tasting so wretched. Jarlaxle responded with a wink and held out his flask to replenish Athrogate's mug, but with a different mixture, the dwarf noted.

Gutbuster.

Not another word of complaint came from Athrogate.

"You friends with Drizzt Do'Urden?" one of the orcs asked Jarlaxle, the creature's tongue loosened by the drink.

"You know of him?" the drow replied, and several of the orcs nodded. *"As do I! I have met him many times, and fought beside him on occasion—and woe to those who stand before his scimitars!"*

That last bit didn't go over well with the orcs, and one of them growled threateningly.

"Drizzt is wounded in his heart," said the orc, and the creature grinned as if that fact pleased him immensely.

Jarlaxle stared hard and tried to decipher that notion. "Catti-brie?"

"A fool now," the orc explained. *"Touched by magic. Daft by magic."*

A couple of the others chuckled.

The Weave, Jarlaxle realized, for he was not ignorant of the traumatic events unfolding around him. Luskan, too, a city that once housed the Hosttower of the Arcane and still named many of the wizards of that place as citizens—and allies of Bregan D'aerthe—had certainly been touched by the unraveling Weave.

"Where is she?" Jarlaxle asked, and the orc shrugged as if it hardly cared.

But Jarlaxle surely did, for a plan was already formulating. To defeat Hephaestus, he needed Cadderly. To enlist Cadderly, he needed Drizzt. Could it be that Catti-brie, and so Drizzt, needed Cadderly as well?

* * * * *

"Guenhwyvar," the young girl called. Her eyes leveled in their sockets, showing their rich blue hue.

Drizzt and Bruenor stood dumbfounded in the small chamber, staring at Catti-brie, whose demeanor had suddenly changed to that of her pre-teen self. She had floated off the bed again, rising as her eyes rolled to white, purple flames and crackling energy dancing all around her, her thick hair flowing in a wind neither Drizzt nor Bruenor could feel.

Drizzt had seen this strange event before, and had warned Bruenor, but when his daughter's posture and demeanor, everything about the way she held herself, had changed so subtly, yet dramatically, Bruenor nearly fell over with weakness. Truly she seemed a different person at that moment, a younger Catti-brie.

Bruenor called to her, his voice thick with desperation and remorse, but she seemed not to notice.

"Guenhwyvar?" she called again.

She seemed to be walking then, slowly and deliberately, though she didn't actually move. She held out one hand as if toward the cat—the cat who wasn't there.

Her voice was gentle and quiet when she asked, "Where's the dark elf, Guenhwyvar? Can ye take me to him?"

"By the gods," Drizzt muttered.

"What is it, elf?" Bruenor demanded.

The young girl straightened, then slowly turned away from the pair. "Be ye a drow?" she asked. Then she paused, as though she heard a response. "I've heard that drow be evil, but ye don't seem so to me."

"Elf?" Bruenor begged.

"Her first words to me," Drizzt whispered.

"Me name's Catti-brie," she said, still talking to the wall away from the pair. "Me dad is Bruenor, King o' Clan Battlehammer."

"She's on Kelvin's Cairn," said Bruenor.

"The dwarves," Catti-brie said. "He's not me real dad. Bruenor took me in when I was just a babe, when me real parents were . . ." She paused and swallowed hard.

"The first time we met, on Kelvin's Cairn," Drizzt breathlessly explained, and indeed he was hearing the woman, then just a girl, exactly as he had that unseasonably warm winter's day on the side of a faraway mountain.

Catti-brie looked over her shoulder at them—no, not at them, but above them. "She's a beautiful ca—" she started to say, but she sucked in her breath suddenly and her eyes rolled up into her head and her arms went out to her sides. The unseen magical energy rushed back into her once more, shaking her with its intensity.

And before their astonished eyes, Catti-brie aged once again.

By the time she floated down to the floor, both Drizzt and Bruenor were hugging her, and they gently moved her to her bed and laid her down.

"Elf?" Bruenor asked, his voice thick with desperation.

"I don't know," replied the trembling Drizzt. He tried to fight back the tears. The moment Catti-brie had recaptured was so precious to him, so burned into his heart and soul. . . .

They sat beside the woman's bed for a long while, even after Regis came in to remind Bruenor that he was due in his audience chamber. Emissaries had arrived from Silverymoon and Nesmé, from Obould and from the wider world. It was time for Bruenor Battlehammer to be king of Mithral Hall again.

But leaving his daughter there on her bed was one of the toughest things Bruenor Battlehammer had ever done. To the dwarf's great relief, after ensuring that the woman was sleeping soundly, Drizzt went out with him, leaving the reliable Regis to watch over her.

* * * * *

The black-bearded dwarf stood in line, third from the front, trying to remember his lines. He was an emissary, a formal representative to a king's court. It was not a new situation to Athrogate, for he had once lived a life that included daily audiences with regional leaders.

Once, long ago.

"Don't rhyme," he warned himself quietly, for as Jarlaxle had pointed out, any of his silly word games would likely tip off Drizzt Do'Urden to the truth about the disguised dwarf. He cleared his throat loudly, wishing he had his morningstars with him, or some other weapon that might get him out of there if his true identity were discovered.

The first representative had his audience with the dwarf king and moved out of the way.

Athrogate rehearsed his lines again, telling himself that it was really simple, assuring himself that Jarlaxle had prepared him well. He went through the routine over and over.

"Come forward, then, fellow dwarf," King Bruenor said, startling Athrogate. "I've too much to do to be sittin' here waitin'!"

Athrogate looked at the seated Bruenor, then at Drizzt Do'Urden, who stood behind the throne. As he locked gazes with Drizzt, he saw a hint of recognition, for they had matched weapons eight years before, during the fall of Deudermont's Luskan.

If Drizzt saw through his disguise, the drow hid it well.

"Well met, King Bruenor, for all the tales I heared of ye," Athrogate greeted enthusiastically, coming forward to stand before the throne. "I'm hopin' that ye're not put out by me coming to see yerself directly, but if I'm returning to me kinfolk without having had me say to yerself, then suren they'd be chasing me out!"

"And where might home be, good . . . ?"

"Stuttgard," Athrogate replied. "Stuttgard o' the Stone Hills Stuttgard Clan."

Bruenor looked at him curiously and shook his head.

"South o' the Snowflakes, long south o' here," the dwarf bluffed.

"I am afraid that I know not of yer clan, or yer Stone Hills," said Bruenor. He glanced at Drizzt, who shrugged and shook his head.

"Well, we heard o' yerself," Athrogate replied. "Many're the songs o' Mithral Hall sung in the Stone Hills!"

"Good to know," Bruenor replied, then he prompted the emissary with a rolling motion of his hand, obviously in a rush to be done with the formalities. "And ye're here to offer trade, perhaps? Or to set the grounds for an alliance?"

"Nah," said Athrogate. "Just a dwarf walkin' the world and wantin' to meet King Bruenor Battlehammer."

The dwarf king nodded. "Very well. And ye're wishing to remain with us in Mithral Hall for some time?"

Athrogate shrugged. "Was heading east, to Adbar," he said. "Got some family there. I was hopin' to come to Mithral Hall on me return back to the west, and not plannin' to stop through now. But on the road, I heared whispers about yer girl."

That perked Bruenor up, and the drow behind him as well.

"What of me girl?" Bruenor asked, suspicion thick in his voice.

"Heared on the road that she got touched by the falling Weave o' magic."

"Ye heared that, did ye?"

"Aye, King Bruenor, so I thought I should come through as fast as me short legs'd be taking me."

"Ye're a priest, then?"

"Nah, just a scrapper."

"Then why? What? Have ye anything to offer me, Stuttgard o' the Stone Hills?" Bruenor said, clearly agitated.

"A name, and one I think ye're knowin'," said Athrogate. "Human name o' Cadderly."

Bruenor and Drizzt exchanged glances, then both stared hard at the visitor.

"His place's not too far from me home," Athrogate explained. "I went right through it on me way here, o' course. Oh, but he's got a hunnerd wizards and priests in there now, all trying to get what's what, if ye get me meaning."

"What about him?" Bruenor asked, obviously trying to remain calm but unable to keep the urgency out of his tone—or out of his posture, as he leaned forward in his throne.

"He and his been workin' on the problems," Athrogate explained. "I thinked ye should know that more'n a few that been brain-touched by the Weave've gone in there, and most've come out whole."

Bruenor leaped up from his seat. "Cadderly is curing those rendered foolish by the troubles?"

Athrogate shrugged. "I thinked ye'd want to be knowin'."

Bruenor turned fast to Drizzt.

"A month and more of hard travel," the drow warned.

"Magical items're working," Bruenor replied. "We got the wagon me boys're building for Silverymoon journeys. We got the zephyr shoes . . ."

Drizzt's eyes lit up at the reference, for indeed the dwarves of Clan Battlehammer had been working on a solution to their isolation, even before the onset of magical afflictions. Without the magical teleportation of their neighboring cities, or creations of magic like Lady Alustriel's flying chariots of fire, the dwarves had taken to a more mundane solution, constructing a wagon strong enough to handle the bumps and stones of treacherous terrain. They had sought out magical assistance for teams that might be pulling the vehicle.

The drow was already starting off the dais before Bruenor could finish his sentence. "On my way," Drizzt said.

"Can I wish ye all me best, King Bruenor?" Athrogate asked.

"Stuttgard o' the Stone Hills," Bruenor repeated, and he turned to the court scribe. "Write it down!"

"Aye, me king!"

"And know that if me girl finds peace in Spirit Soaring, that I'll be visiting yer clan, good friend," Bruenor said, looking back to

Athrogate. "And know that ye're fore'er a friend o' Mithral Hall. Ye stay as long as ye're wantin', and all costs fall to meself! But beggin' yer pardon, the time's for me to be goin'."

He bowed fast and was running out of the room before Athrogate could even offer his thanks in reply.

* * * * *

Full of energy and enthusiasm for the first time in a few long days, the hope-filled Drizzt and Bruenor charged down the hall toward Catti-brie's door. They slowed abruptly as they neared, seeing the sizzling purple and blue streaks of energy slipping through the cracks in the door.

"Bah, not again!" Bruenor groaned. He beat Drizzt to the door and shoved it open.

There was Catti-brie, standing in mid air above the bed, her arms out to her sides, her eyes rolled to white, trembling, trembling. . . .

"Me girl . . ." Bruenor started to say, but he bit back the words when he noted Regis against the far wall, curled up on the floor, his arms over his head.

"Elf!" Bruenor cried, but Drizzt was already running to Catti-brie, grabbing her and pulling her down to the bed. Bruenor grumbled and cursed and rushed over to Regis.

Catti-brie's stiffness melted as the fit ended, and she fell limp into Drizzt's arms. He eased her down to a sitting position and hugged her close, and only then did he notice the desperate Regis.

The halfling flailed wildly at Bruenor, slapping the dwarf repeatedly and squirming away from Bruenor's reaching hands. Clearly terrified, he seemed to be looking not at the dwarf, but at some great monster.

"Rumblebelly, what're ye about?" Bruenor asked.

Regis screamed into the dwarf's face in response, a primal explosion of sheer terror. As Bruenor fell back, the halfling scrambled away, rising up to his knees, then to his feet. He ran headlong, face-first, into the opposite wall. He bounced back and fell with a groan.

"Oh, by the gods," said Bruenor, and he reached down and scooped something up from the floor. He turned to Drizzt and presented the item for the drow to see.

It was the halfling's ruby pendant, the enchanted gemstone that allowed Regis to cast charms upon unwitting victims.

Regis recovered from his self-inflicted wallop and leaped to his feet. He screamed again and ran past Bruenor, flailing his arms insanely. When Bruenor tried to intercept him, the halfling slapped him and punched him, pinched him and even bit him, and all the while Bruenor called to him, but Regis seemed not to hear a word. The dwarf might as well have been a demon or devil come to eat the little one for dinner.

"Elf!" Bruenor called. Then he yelped and fell back, clutching his bleeding hand.

Regis sprinted for the door. Drizzt beat him there, hitting him with a flying tackle that sent them both into a roll into the hall. In that somersault, Drizzt deftly worked his hands so that when they settled, he was behind Regis, his legs clamped around the halfling's waist, his arms knifed under Regis's, turning and twisting expertly to tie the little one in knots.

There was no way for Regis to break out, to hit Drizzt, or to squirm away from him. But that hardly slowed his frantic gyrations, and didn't stop him from screaming insanely.

The hallway began to fill with curious dwarves.

"Ye got a pin stuck in the little one's arse, elf?" one asked.

"Help me with him!" Drizzt implored.

The dwarf came over and reached for Regis, then quickly retracted his hand when the halfling tried to bite it.

"What in the Nine Hells?"

"Just ye take him!" Bruenor yelled from inside the room. "Ye take him and tie him down—and don't ye be hurting him!"

"Yes, me king!"

It took a long time, but finally the dwarves dragged the thrashing Regis away from Drizzt.

"I could slug him and put him down quiet," one offered, but Drizzt's scowl denied that course of action.

"Take him to his chamber and keep him safe," the drow said. He went back into the room, closing the door behind him.

"She didn't even notice," Bruenor explained as Drizzt sat on the bed beside Catti-brie. "She's not knowing the world around her."

"We knew that," Drizzt reminded.

"Not even a bit! Nor's the little one now."

Drizzt shrugged. "Cadderly," he reminded the dwarf king.

"For both o' them," said the dwarf, and he looked at the door. "Rumblebelly used the ruby on her."

"To try to reach her," Drizzt agreed.

"But she reached him instead," the dwarf said.

CHAPTER 5
ANGRY DEAD

"It will be at Spirit Soaring," the Ghost King proclaimed.

The specter chasing Jarlaxle had worked out the drow's intentions even before the clever dark elf's dastardly trick had sent the creature on its extraplanar journey. And anything the specters knew, so knew the dracolich.

The enemies of Hephaestus, Yharaskrik, and mostly of Crenshinibon would congregate there, in the Snowflake Mountains, where a pair of the Ghost King's specters were already causing mischief.

Then there would be only one more, the human southerner. The Crystal Shard knew he could be found, though not as easily as Jarlaxle. After all, Crenshinibon had shared an intimate bond with the dark elf for many tendays. With Yharaskrik's psychic powers added to the shard's, locating the familiar drow had proven as simple as it was necessary. Jarlaxle had become the focus of anger that served to bring the trio of mighty beings together, united in common cause. The human, however tangential, would be revealed soon enough.

Besides, to at least one of the three vengeful entities— the dragon—the coming catastrophe would be enjoyable.

To Yharaskrik, the destruction of its enemies would be practical and informative, a worthy test for the uncomfortable but likely profitable unification.

And Crenshinibon, which served as conduit between the wildly passionate dragon and the ultimately practical mind flayer, would share in all the sensations the destruction of Jarlaxle and the others would bring to both of them.

* * * * *

"Uncle Pikel!" Hanaleisa called when she saw the green-bearded dwarf on a street in Carradoon late the next morning. He was dressed in his traveling gear, which meant that he carried a stick and had a cooking pot strapped on his head as a helmet.

Pikel flashed her a big smile and called into the shop behind him. As the dwarf advanced to give Hanaleisa a great hug, Hanaleisa's younger brother Rorick exited the shop.

"What are you doing here?" she called over Pikel's shoulder as her grinning sibling approached.

"I told you I wanted to come along."

"Then spent the rest of the morning arguing with wizards about the nature of the cosmos," Hanaleisa replied.

"Doo-dad!" Pikel yelled, pulling back from the young woman, and when both she and Rorick looked at him curiously, he just added, "Hee hee hee."

"He has it all figured out," Rorick explained, and Hanaleisa nodded.

"And do the wizards and priests have it all figured out as well?" Hanaleisa asked. "Because of your insights, I mean?"

Rorick looked down.

"They kicked you out," Hanaleisa reasoned.

"Because they couldn't stand to be upstaged by our little brother, no doubt!" greeted Temberle, rounding the corner from the blacksmith he'd just visited. His greatsword had taken a nasty nick the previous night when bouncing off the collarbone of the undead bear.

Rorick brightened a bit at that, but when he looked up at his brother and sister, an expression of confusion came over him. "What happened?" he asked, noting that Temberle had his greatsword in hand and was examining the blade.

"You left Spirit Soaring late yesterday?" Temberle asked.

"Midday, yes," Rorick answered. "Uncle Pikel wanted to use the tree roots to move us down from the mountains, but father overruled that, fearing the unpredictability and instability of magic, even druidic."

"Doo-dad," Pikel said with a giggle.

"I wouldn't be traveling magically either," said Hanaleisa. "Not now."

Pikel folded his arm and stump over his chest and glared at her.

"So you camped in the forest last night?" Temberle went on.

Rorick answered with a nod, not really understanding where his brother might be going, but Pikel apparently caught on a bit, and the dwarf issued an "Ooooh."

"There's something wrong in those woods," said Temberle.

"Yup, yup," Pikel agreed.

"What are you talking about?" Rorick asked, looking from one to the other.

"Brr," Pikel said, and hugged himself tightly.

"I slept right through the night," said Rorick. "But it wasn't that cold."

"We fought a zombie," Hanaleisa explained. "A zombie bear. And there was something else out there, haunting the forest."

"Yup, yup," Pikel agreed.

Rorick looked at the dwarf, curious. "You didn't say anything was amiss."

Pikel shrugged.

"But you felt it?" Temberle asked.

The dwarf gave another, "Yup, yup."

"So you did battle—*real* battle?" Rorick asked his siblings, his intrigue obvious. The three had grown up in the shadow of a great library, surrounded by mighty priests and veteran wizards. They had heard stories of great battles, most notably the fight their parents had waged against the dreaded chaos curse and against their own grandfather, but other than the few times when their parents had been called away for battle, or their dwarf uncles had gone to serve King Bruenor of Mithral Hall, the lives of the Bonaduce children had been soft and peaceful. They had trained vigorously in martial arts—hand-fighting and sword-fighting—and in the ways of the priest, the wizard, and the monk. With Cadderly and Danica as their parents, the three had been blessed with as comprehensive and exhaustive an education as any in Faerûn could ever hope for, but in practical applications of their lessons, particularly fighting, the three were neophytes indeed, completely untested until the previous night.

Hanaleisa and Temberle exchanged concerned looks.

"Tell me!" Rorick pressed.

"It was terrifying," his sister admitted. "I've never been so scared in my entire life."

"But it was exciting," Temberle added. "And as soon as the fight began, you couldn't think about being afraid."

"You couldn't think about anything," said Hanaleisa.

"Hee hee hee," Pikel agreed with a nod.

"Our training," said Rorick.

"We are fortunate that our parents, and our uncles," said Hanaleisa, looking at the beaming Pikel, "didn't take the peace we've known for granted, and taught us—"

"To fight," Temberle interrupted.

"And to react," said Hanaleisa, who was always a bit more philosophical about battle and the role that martial training played in a wider world view. She was much more akin to her mother in that matter, and that was why she had foregone extensive training with the sword or the mace in favor of the more disciplined and intimate open-hand techniques employed by Danica's order. "Even one who knew how to use a sword well would have been killed in the forest last night if his mind didn't know how to tuck away his fears."

"So you felt the presence in the forest, too," Temberle said to Pikel.

"Yup."

"It's still there."

"Yup."

"We have to warn the townsfolk, and get word to Spirit Soaring," Hanaleisa added.

"Yup, yup." Pikel lifted his good arm before him and straightened his fingers, pointing forward. He began swaying that hand back and forth, as if gliding like a fish under the waters of Impresk Lake. The others understood that the dwarf was talking about his plant-walking, even before he added with a grin, "Doo-dad."

"You cannot do that," Hanaleisa said, and Temberle, too, shook his head.

"We can go out tomorrow, at the break of dawn," he said. "Whatever it is out there, it's closer to Carradoon than to Spirit Soaring. We can get horses to take us the first part of the way—I'm certain the stable masters will accompany us along the lower trails."

"Moving fast, we can arrive before sunset," Hanaleisa agreed.

"But right now, we've got to get the town prepared for whatever might come," said Temberle. He looked at Hanaleisa and shrugged. "Though we don't really know what is out there, or even if it's still there. Maybe it was just that one bear we killed, a wayward malevolent spirit, and now it's gone."

"Maybe it wasn't," said Rorick, and his tone made it clear that he hoped he was right. In his youthful enthusiasm, he was more than a little jealous of his siblings at that moment—a misplaced desire that would soon enough be corrected.

* * * * *

"Probably wandering around for a hundred years," muttered one old water-dog—a Carradoon term for the many wrinkled fishermen who lived in town. The man waved his hand as if the story was nothing to fret about.

"Eh, but the world's gone softer," another in the tavern lamented.

"Nay, not the world," yet another explained. "Just our part of it, living in the shadow of them three's parents. We've been civilized, I'm thinking!"

That brought a cheer, half mocking, half in good will, from the many gathered patrons.

"The rest of the world's grown tougher," the man continued. "It'll get to us, and don't you doubt it."

"And us older folk remember the fights well," said the first old water-dog. "But I'm wondering if the younger ones, grown up under the time of Cadderly, will be ready for any fights that might come."

"His kids did well, eh?" came the reply, and all in the tavern cheered and lifted tankards in honor of the twins, who stood at the bar.

"We survived," Hanaleisa said loudly, drawing the attention of all. "But likely, some sort of evil is still out there."

That didn't foster the feeling of dread the young woman had hoped for, but elicited a rather mixed reaction of clanking mugs and even laughter. Hanaleisa looked at Temberle, and they both glanced back when Pikel bemoaned the lack of seriousness in the crowd with a profound, "Ooooh."

"Carradoon should post sentries at every gate, and along the walls," Temberle shouted. "Start patrols through the streets, armed and with torches. Light up the town, I beg you!"

Though his outburst attracted some attention, all eyes turned to the tavern door as it banged open. A man stumbled in, crying out, "Attack! Attack!" More than his shouts jarred them all, though, for filtering in behind the stranger came cries and screams, terrified and agonized.

Tables upended as the water-dogs leaped to their feet.

"Uh-oh," said Pikel, and he grabbed Temberle's arm with his hand and tapped Hanaleisa with his stump before they could intervene. They had come to the tavern to warn people and to organize them, but Pikel was astute enough to realize the folly of the latter intention.

Temberle tried to speak anyway, but already the various crews of the many Carradden fishing boats were organizing, calling for groups to go to the docks to retrieve weapons, putting together gangs to head into the streets.

"But, people . . ." Temberle tried to protest. Pikel tugged at him insistently.

"Shhh!" the dwarf cautioned.

"The four of us, then," Hanaleisa agreed. "Let's see where we can be of help."

They exited alongside a score of patrons, though a few remained behind—fishing boat captains, mostly—to try to formulate some sort of strategy. With a few quick words, Pikel tucked his black oaken cudgel—his magical shillelagh—under his half-arm and waggled his fingers over one end, conjuring a bright light that transformed the weapon into a magical, fire-less torch.

Less than two blocks from the tavern door, back toward the gateway through which they had entered Carradoon, the four learned what all the tumult was about. Rotting corpses and skeletons swarmed the streets. Human and elf, dwarf and halfling, and many animal corpses roamed freely. The dead walked—and attacked.

Spotting a family trying to escape along the side of the wide road, the group veered that way, but Rorick stopped short and cried out, then stumbled and pulled up his pant leg. As Pikel moved his light near, trickles of blood showed clearly, along with something small and thrashing. Rorick kicked out and the attacking creature flew to the side of the road.

It flopped weirdly back at him, a mess of bones, skin, and feathers.

"A bird," Hanaleisa gasped.

Pikel ran over and swung the bright end of his cudgel down hard, splattering the creature onto the cobblestones. The light proved equally damaging to the undead thing, searing it and leaving it smoldering.

"Sha-la-la!" Pikel proudly proclaimed, lifting his club high. He turned fast, adjusting his cooking pot helmet as he did so, and launched himself into the nearest alleyway. As soon as the light of the cudgel crossed the alley's threshold, it revealed a host of skeletons swarming at the dwarf.

Temberle threw his arm around his brother's back and propped him up, hustling him back the way they had come, calling for the fleeing Carradden family to catch up.

"Uncle Pikel!" Hanaleisa cried, running to support him.

She pulled up short as she neared the alleyway, assaulted by the sound of crunching bones and by bits of rib and skull flying by. Pikel's light danced wildly, as if a flame in a gale, for the doo-dad dwarf danced wildly, too. It was as ferocious a display as Hanaleisa had ever seen, and one she had never imagined possible from her gentle gardener uncle.

She refocused her attention back down the street, to the retreating family, a couple and their trio of young children. Trusting in Pikel to battle the creatures in the alley, though he was outnumbered many times over, the woman sprinted away, crossing close behind the family. Hanaleisa threw herself at two skeletons moving in close pursuit. She hit them hard with a flat-out body block, knocking them back several steps, and she tucked and turned as she fell to land easily on her feet.

Hanaleisa went up on the ball of one foot and launched into a spinning kick that drove her other foot through the ribcage of an attacker. With a spray of bone chips, she tugged her foot out, then, without bringing it down and holding perfect balance, she leaned back to re-angle her kick, and cracked the skeleton in its bony face.

Still balanced on one foot, Hanaleisa expertly turned and kicked again, once, twice, a third time, into the chest of the second skeleton.

She sprang up and sent her back foot into a high circle kick before the skeleton's face, not to hit it, but as a distraction, for when she landed firmly on both feet, she did so leaning forward, in perfect position to launch a series of devastating punches at her foe.

With both skeletons quickly dispatched, Hanaleisa backed away, pursuing the family. To her relief, Pikel joined her as she passed the alleyway. Side by side, the two grinned, pivoted back, and charged into the pursuing throng of undead, feet, fists, and sha-la-la pounding.

More citizens joined them in short order, as did Temberle, his greatsword shearing down skeletons and zombies with abandon.

But there were so many!

The dead had risen from a cemetery that had been the final resting place for many generations of Carradden. They rose from a thick forest, too, where the cycle of life worked relentlessly to feed the hunger of such a powerful and malignant spell. Even near the shores of Impresk Lake, under the dark waters, skeletons of fish—thousands of them thrown back to the waters after being cleaned on the decks of fishing boats—sprang to unlife and knifed up hard against the undersides of dark hulls, or swam past the boats and flung themselves out of the water and onto the shore and docks, thrashing in desperation to destroy something, anything, alive.

And standing atop the dark waters, Fetchigrol watched. His dead eyes flared to life in reflected orange as a fire grew and consumed several houses. Those eyes flickered with inner satisfaction whenever a cry of horror rang out across the dark, besieged city.

He sensed a shipwreck not far away, many shipwrecks, many long-dead sailors.

* * * * *

"I'm all right!" Rorick insisted, trying to pull his leg away from his fretting Uncle Pikel.

But the dwarf grabbed him hard with one hand, a grip that could hold back a lunging horse, and waggled his stumpy arm at the obstinate youngster.

They were back in the tavern, but nothing outside had calmed. Quite the opposite, it seemed.

Pikel bit down on a piece of cloth and tore off a strip. He dipped it into his upturned cookpot-helmet, into which he'd poured a bit of potent liquor mixed with some herbs he always kept handy.

"We can't stay here," Temberle called, coming in the door. "They approach."

Pikel worked fast, slapping the bandage against Rorick's bloody shin, pinning one end with his half-arm and expertly working the other until he had it knotted. Then he tightened it down with his teeth on one end, his hand on the other.

"Too tight," Rorick complained.

"Shh!" scolded the dwarf.

Pikel grabbed his helmet and dropped it on his head, either forgetting or ignoring the contents, which splashed down over his green hair and beard. If that bothered the dwarf, he didn't show it, though he did lick at the little rivulets streaming down near his mouth. He hopped up, shillelagh tucked securely under his stump, and pulled Rorick up before him.

The young man tried to start away fast, but he nearly fell over with the first step on his torn leg. The wound was deeper than Rorick apparently believed.

Pikel was there to support him, though, and they rushed out behind Temberle. Hanaleisa was outside waiting, shaking her head.

"Too many," she explained grimly. "There's no winning ground, just retreat."

"To the docks?" Temberle asked, looking at the flow of townsfolk in that direction and seeming none too pleased by that prospect. "We're to put our backs to the water?"

Hanaleisa's expression showed that she didn't like that idea any more than he, but they had no choice. They joined the fleeing townsfolk and ran on.

They found some organized defense forming halfway to the docks and eagerly found positions among the ranks. Pikel offered an approving nod as he continued past with Rorick, toward a cluster of large buildings overlooking the boardwalk and wharves. Built on an old fort, it was where the ship captains had decided to make their stand.

"Fight well for mother and father," Hanaleisa said to Temberle. "We will not dishonor their names."

Temberle smiled back at her, feeling like a veteran already.

They got their chance soon enough, their line rushing up the street to support the last groups of townsfolk trying hard to get ahead of the monstrous pursuit. Fearlessly, Hanaleisa and Temberle charged among the undead, smashing and slashing with abandon.

Their efforts became all the more devastating when Uncle Pikel joined them, his bright cudgel destroying every monster that ventured near.

Despite their combined power, the trio and the rest of the squad fighting beside them were pushed back, moving inexorably in retreat. For every zombie or skeleton they destroyed, it seemed there were three more to take its place. Their own line thinned whenever a man or woman was pulled down under the raking and biting throng.

And those unfortunate victims soon enough stood up, fighting for the other side.

Horrified and weak with revulsion, their morale shattered as friends and family rose up in undeath to turn against them, the townsfolk gave ground.

They found support at the cluster of buildings, where they had no choice but to stand and fight. Eventually, even that defense began to crumble.

Hanaleisa looked to her brother, desperation and sadness in her rich brown eyes. They couldn't retreat into the water, and the walls of the buildings wouldn't hold back the horde for long. She was scared, and so was he.

"We have to find Rorick," Temberle said to his dwarf uncle.

"Eh?" Pikel replied.

He didn't understand that the twins only wanted to make sure that the three siblings were together when they died.

CHAPTER
THE POLITICS OF ENGAGEMENT
6

It was the last thing Bruenor Battlehammer wanted to hear just then.

"Obould's angry," Nanfoodle the gnome explained. "He thinks we're to blame for the strange madness of magic, and the silence of his god."

"Yeah, we're always to blame in that one's rock-head," Bruenor grumbled back. He looked at the door leading to the corridor to Garumn's Gorge and the Hall's eastern exit, hoping to see Drizzt. Morning had done nothing to help Catti-brie or Regis. The halfling had thrashed himself to utter exhaustion and since languished in restless misery.

"Obould's emissary—" Nanfoodle started to say.

"I got no time for him!" Bruenor shouted.

Across the way, several dwarves observed the uncharacteristic outburst. Among them was General Banak Brawnanvil, who watched from his chair. He'd lost the use of his lower body in the long-ago first battle with Obould's emerging hordes.

"I got no time!" Bruenor yelled again, though somewhat apologetically. "Me girl's got to go! And Rumblebelly, too!"

"I will accompany Drizzt," Nanfoodle offered.

"The Nine Hells and a tenth for luck ye will!" Bruenor roared at him. "I ain't for leaving me girl!"

"But ye're the king," one of the dwarves cried.

"And the whole world is going mad," Nanfoodle answered.

Bruenor simmered, on the edge of an explosion. "No," he said finally, and with a nod to the gnome, who had become one of his most trusted and reliable advisors, he walked across the room to stand before Banak.

"No," Bruenor said again. "I ain't the king. Not now."

A couple of dwarves gasped, but Banak Brawnanvil nodded solemnly, accepting the responsibility he knew to be coming.

"Ye've ruled the place before," said Bruenor. "And I'm knowin' ye can do it again. Been too long since I seen the road."

"Ye save yer girl," the old general replied.

"Can't give ye Rumblebelly to help ye this time," Bruenor went on, "but the gnome here's clever enough." He looked back at Nanfoodle, who couldn't help but smile at the unexpected compliment and the trust Bruenor showed in him.

"We've many good hands," Banak agreed.

"Now don't ye be startin' another war with Obould," Bruenor instructed. "Not without me here to swat a few o' his dogs."

"Never."

Bruenor clapped his friend on the shoulder, turned, and started to walk away. A large part of him knew that his responsibilities lay there, where Clan Battlehammer looked to him to lead, particularly in that suddenly troubling time. But a larger part of him denied that. He was the king of Mithral Hall, indeed, but he was the father of Catti-brie and the friend of Regis, as well.

And little else seemed to matter at that dark moment.

He found Drizzt at Garumn's Gorge, along with as smelly and dirty a dwarf as had ever been known.

"Ready to go, me king!" Thibbledorf Pwent greeted him with enthusiasm. The grisly dwarf hopped to attention, his creased battle armor, all sharpened plates and jagged spikes, creaking and squealing with the sudden motion.

Bruenor looked at the drow, who just closed his eyes, long ago having quit arguing with the likes of the battlerager.

"Ready to go?" Bruenor asked. "With war brewing here?"

Pwent's eyes flared a bit at that hopeful possibility, but he resolutely shook his head. "Me place is with me king!"

"Brawnanvil's the Steward o' Mithral Hall while I'm gone."

A flash of confusion in the dwarf's eyes couldn't take hold. "With me King Bruenor!" Pwent argued. "If ye're for the road, Pwent and his boys're for the road!"

At that proclamation, a great cheer came up and several nearby doors banged open. The famed Gutbuster Brigade poured into the wide corridor.

"Oh no, no," Bruenor scolded. "No, ye ain't!"

"But me king!" twenty Gutbusters cried in unison.

"I ain't taking the best brigade Faerûn's e'er known away from Steward Brawnanvil in this troubled time," said Bruenor. "No, but I can't." He looked Pwent straight in the eye. "None o' ye. Ain't got room in the wagon, neither."

"Bah! We'll run with ye!" Pwent insisted.

"We're goin' on magical shoes and we ain't got no magical boots for the lot of ye to keep up," Bruenor explained. "I ain't doubtin' that ye'd all run till ye drop dead, but that'd be the end of it. No, me friend, yer place is here, in case that Obould thinks it's time again for war." He gave a great sigh and looked to Drizzt for support, muttering, "Me own place is here."

"And you'll be back here swiftly," the drow promised. "Your place now is on the road with me, with Catti-brie and Regis. We've no time for foolishness, I warn. Our wagon is waiting."

"Me king!" Pwent cried. He waved his brigade away, but hustled after Drizzt and Bruenor as they quickly moved to the tunnels that would take them to their troubled friends.

In the end, only four of them left Mithral Hall in the wagon pulled by a team of the best mules that could be found. It wasn't Pwent who stayed behind, but Regis.

The poor halfling wouldn't stop thrashing, fending off monsters that none of them could see, and with all the fury and desperation of a halfling standing on the edge of the pit of the Abyss itself. He couldn't eat. He couldn't drink. He wouldn't stop swinging and kicking and biting for a moment, and no words reached his ears to any effect. Only through the efforts of a number of attendants were the dwarves able to get any nourishment into him at all, something that could never have been done on a bouncing wagon moving through the wilds.

Bruenor argued taking him anyway, to the point of hoarseness, but in the end, it was Drizzt who said, "Enough!" and led the frustrated Bruenor away.

"Even if the magic holds, even if the wagon survives," Drizzt said, "it will be a tenday and more to Spirit Soaring and an equal time back. He'll not survive."

They left Regis in a stupor of exhaustion, a broken thing.

"He may recover with the passage of time," Drizzt explained as they hustled along the tunnels and across the great gorge. "He was not touched directly by the magic, as was Catti-brie."

"He's daft, elf!"

"And as I said, it may not hold. Your priests will reach him—" Drizzt paused and skidded to a stop "—or I will."

"What do ye know, elf?" Bruenor demanded.

"Go and ready the wagon," Drizzt instructed, "but wait for me."

He turned and sprinted back the way they'd come, all the way to Regis's room, where he burst in and dashed to the small coffer atop the dresser. With trembling hands, Drizzt pulled forth the ruby pendant.

"What're ye about?" asked Cordio Muffinhead, a priest of high repute, who stood beside the halfling.

Drizzt held up the pendant, the enchanting ruby spinning enticingly in the torchlight. "I have an idea. Pray, wake the little one, but hold him steady, all of you."

They looked at the drow curiously, but so many years together had taught them to trust Drizzt Do'Urden, and they did as he bade them.

Regis came awake thrashing, his legs moving as if he were trying to run away from some unseen monster.

Drizzt moved his face very close to the halfling, calling to him, but Regis gave no sign of hearing his old friend.

The drow brought forth the ruby pendant and set it spinning right before Regis's eyes. The sparkles drew Drizzt inside, so alluring and calming, and a short while later, within the depths of the ruby, he found Regis.

"Drizzt," the halfling said aloud, and also in Drizzt's mind. *"Help me."*

Drizzt got only the slightest glimpse of the visions tormenting Regis. He found himself in a land of shadow—the very Plane of Shadow, perhaps, or some other lower plane—with dark and ominous creatures coming at him from every side, clawing at him, open maws full of sharpened teeth biting at his face. Clawed hands slashed at him along the periphery of his vision, always just a moment ahead of him. Instinctively, Drizzt's free hand went to a scimitar belted at his hip and he cried out and began to draw it forth.

Something hit him hard, throwing him aside, right over the bed he couldn't see. It sent him tumbling to a floor he couldn't see.

In the distance, Drizzt heard the clatter of something bouncing across the stone floor and knew it to be the ruby pendant. He felt a burning sensation in his forearm and closed his eyes tightly to grimace away the pain. When he opened his eyes again, he was back in the room, Cordio standing over him. He looked at his arm to see a trickle of blood where it had caught against his half-drawn scimitar as he tumbled.

"What—?" he started to ask the dwarf.

"Apologies, elf," said Cordio, "but I had to ram ye. Ye was seein' monsters like the little one there, and drawing yer blade . . ."

"Say no more, good dwarf," Drizzt replied, pulling himself up to a sitting position and bringing his injured arm in front of him, pressing hard to try to stem the flow of blood.

"Get me a bandage!" Cordio yelled to the others, who were hard at work holding down the thrashing Regis.

"He's in there," Drizzt explained as Cordio wrapped his arm. "I found him. He called out for help."

"Yeah, that we heared."

"He's seeing monsters—shadowy things—in a horrible place."

Another dwarf came over and handed the ruby pendant to Cordio, who presented it to Drizzt, but the drow held up his hand.

"Keep it," Drizzt explained. "You might find a way to use it to reach him, but do take care."

"Oh, I'll be having a team o' Gutbusters ready to knock me down in that case," Cordio assured him.

"More than that," said Drizzt. "Take care that you can escape the place where Regis now resides." He looked with great sympathy at his poor halfling friend, for the first time truly appreciating the horror Regis felt with every waking moment.

Drizzt caught up to Bruenor in the eastern halls. The king sat on the bench of a fabulous wagon of burnished wood and solid wheels, with a sub-carriage that featured several strong springs of an alloy Nanfoodle had concocted, almost as strong as iron, but not nearly as brittle. The wagon showed true craftsmanship and pride, a fitting representation of the art and skill of Mithral Hall.

The vehicle wasn't yet finished, though, for the dwarves had planned an enclosed bed and perhaps an extension bed for cargo behind, with a greater harness that would allow a team of six or eight. But upon Bruenor's call for urgency, they had cut the work short and fitted low wooden walls and a tailgate quickly. They had brought out their finest team of mules, young and strong, fitting them with magical horseshoes that would allow them to move at a swift pace throughout the entirety of a day.

"I found Regis in his nightmares," Drizzt explained, climbing up beside his friend. "I used the ruby on him, as he did with Catti-brie."

"Ye durned fool!"

Drizzt shook his head. "With all caution," he assured his companion.

"I'm seein' that," Bruenor said dryly, staring at the drow's bandaged arm.

"I found him and he saw me, but only briefly. He is living in the realm of nightmares, Bruenor, and though I tried to pull him back with me, I could not begin to gain ground. Instead, he pulled me in with him, a place that would overwhelm me as it has him. But there is hope, I believe." He sighed and mouthed the name they had attached to that hope, "Cadderly." That notion made Bruenor drive the team on with more urgency as they rolled out of Mithral Hall's eastern gate, turning fast for the southwest.

Pwent moved up to ride on the seat with Bruenor. Drizzt ran scout along their flanks, though he often had to climb aboard the wagon and catch his breath, for it rolled along without the need to rest the mules. Through it all, Catti-brie sat quietly in the back, seeing nothing that they could see, hearing nothing that they could hear, lost and alone.

* * * * *

"Ye're knowin' them well," Athrogate congratulated Jarlaxle later that day when the pair, lying on top of a grassy knoll, spied the wagon rambling down the road from the northeast.

Jarlaxle's expression showed no such confidence, for he had been caught completely by surprise at the quick progress the wagon had already made; he hadn't expected to see Bruenor's party until the next morning.

"They'll drive the mules to exhaustion in a day," he mumbled, shaking his head.

Off in the distance, a dark figure moved among the shadows, and Jarlaxle knew it to be Drizzt.

"Running hard for their hurt friend," Athrogate remarked.

"There is no power greater than the bonds they share, my friend," said the drow. He finished with a cough to clear his throat, and to banish the wistfulness from his tone. But not quickly enough, he realized when he glanced at Athrogate, to keep the dwarf from staring at him incredulously.

"Their sentiments are their weakness," Jarlaxle said, trying to be convincing. "And I know how to exploit that weakness."

"Uh-huh," said Athrogate, then he gave a great "Bwahaha!"

Jarlaxle could only smile.

"We goin' down there, or we just following?"

Jarlaxle thought about it for a moment, then surprised himself and the dwarf by hopping up from the grass and brushing himself off.

* * * * *

"Stuttgard o' the Stone Hills?" Bruenor asked when the wagon rolled around a bend in the road to reveal the dwarf standing in their way. "I thought ye was stayin' in Mithral . . ." he called as he eased the wagon to a stop before the dwarf. His voice trailed off as he noted the dwarf's impressive weapons, a pair of glassteel morningstars bobbing behind his sturdy shoulders. Suspicion filled Bruenor's expression, for Stuttgard had shown no such armament in Mithral Hall. His suspicion only grew as he considered how far along the road he was already—for Stuttgard to have arrived meant that the dwarf must have departed Mithral Hall immediately after meeting with Bruenor.

"Nah, but well met again, King Bruenor," Athrogate replied.

"What're ye about, dwarf?" Bruenor asked. Beside Bruenor, Pwent stood flexing his knees, ready to fight.

A growl from the side turned them all to look that way, and up on a branch in the lone tree overlooking the road perched Guenhwyvar, tamping her paws as if she meant to spring down upon the dwarf.

"Peace, good king," Athrogate said, patting his hands calmly in the air before him. "I ain't no enemy."

"Nor are you Stuttgard of the Stone Hills," came a call from farther along the road, behind Athrogate and ahead of the wagon.

Bruenor and Pwent looked past Stuttgard and nodded, though they couldn't see their drow companion. Stuttgard glanced over his shoulder, knowing it to be Drizzt, though the drow was too concealed in the brush to be seen.

"I should have recognized you at Bruenor's court," Drizzt called.

"It's me morningstars," Stuttgard explained. "I'm lookin'

bigger with them, so I'm told. Bwahaha! Been a lot o' years since we crossed weapons, eh Drizzt Do'Urden?"

"Who is he?" Bruenor called to Drizzt, then he looked straight at the dwarf in the road and said, "Who are ye?"

"Where is he?" Drizzt called out in answer, drawing looks of surprise from both Bruenor and Pwent.

"He's right in front o' us, ye blind elf!" Pwent called out.

"Not him," Drizzt replied. "Not . . . Stuttgard."

"Ah, but suren me heart's to fall, for me worthy drow me name can't recall," said the dwarf in the road.

"Where is who?" Bruenor demanded of Drizzt, anger and impatience mounting

"He means me," another voice answered. On the side of the road opposite Guenhwyvar stood Jarlaxle.

"Oh, by Moradin's itchy arse," grumbled Bruenor. "Scratched it, he did, and this one fell out."

"A pleasure to see you again as well, King Bruenor," Jarlaxle said with a bow.

Drizzt came out of the brush then, moving toward the group. The drow had no weapons drawn—indeed, he leaned his bow over his shoulder as he went.

"What is it, me king?" Pwent asked, glancing nervously from the dwarf to Jarlaxle. "What?"

"Not a fight," Bruenor assured him and disappointed him at the same time. "Not *yet* a fight."

"Never that," Jarlaxle added as he moved beside his companion.

"Bah!" Pwent snorted.

"What's this about?" Bruenor demanded.

Athrogate grumbled as Drizzt walked by, and gave a lamenting shake of his head, his braided beard rattling as its small beads bounced.

"Athrogate," Drizzt whispered as he passed, and the dwarf howled in laughter.

"Ye're knowin' him?" asked Bruenor.

"I told you about him. From Luskan." He looked at Jarlaxle. "Eight years ago."

The drow mercenary bowed. "A sad day for many."

"But not for you and yours."

"I told you then and I tell you now, Drizzt Do'Urden. The fall of Luskan, and of Captain Deudermont, was not the doing of Bregan D'aerthe. I would have been as happy dealing with him—"

"He never would have dealt with the likes of you and your mercenaries," Drizzt interrupted.

Jarlaxle didn't finish his thought, just held his hands out wide, conceding the point.

"And what's this about?" Bruenor demanded again.

"We heard of your plight—of Catti-brie's," Jarlaxle explained. "The right road is to Cadderly, so I had my friend here go in—"

"And lie to us," said Drizzt.

"It seemed prudent in the moment," Jarlaxle admitted. "But the right road *is* to Cadderly. You know that."

"I don't know anything where Jarlaxle is concerned," Drizzt shot back, even as Bruenor nodded. "If this is all you claim, then why would you meet us out here on the road?"

"Needin' a ride, not to doubt," Pwent said, and his bracers screeched as they slid together when he crossed his burly arms over his chest.

"Hardly that," the drow replied, "though I would welcome the company." He paused and looked at the mules then, obviously surprised at how fresh they appeared, given that they had already traveled farther than most teams would go in two days.

"Magical hooves," Drizzt remarked. "They can cover six days in one."

Jarlaxle nodded.

"Now he's wanting a ride," Pwent remarked, and Jarlaxle did laugh at that, but shook his head.

"Nay, good dwarf, not a ride," the drow explained. "But there is something I would ask of you."

"Surprising," Drizzt said dryly.

"I am in need of Cadderly, too, for an entirely different reason," Jarlaxle explained. "And he will be in need of me, or will be glad that I am there, when he learns of it. Unfortunately, my last visit with the mighty priest did not fare so well, and he requested that I not return."

"And ye're thinking that he'll let ye in if ye're with us," Bruenor reasoned, and Jarlaxle bowed.

"Bah!" snorted the dwarf king. "Ye better have more to say than that."

"Much more," Jarlaxle replied, looking more at Drizzt than Bruenor. "And I will tell you all of it. But it is a long tale, and we should not tarry, for the sake of your wife."

"Don't ye be pretendin' that ye care about me girl!" Bruenor shouted, and Jarlaxle retreated a step.

Drizzt saw something then, though Bruenor was too upset to catch it. True pain flashed in Jarlaxle's dark eyes; he did care. Drizzt thought back to the time Jarlaxle had allowed him, with Catti-brie and Artemis Entreri, to escape from Menzoberranzan, one of the many times Jarlaxle had let him walk away. Drizzt tried to put it all in the context of the current situation, to reveal the possible motives behind Jarlaxle's actions. Was he lying, or was he speaking the truth?

Drizzt felt it the latter, and that realization surprised him.

"What're ye thinking, elf?" Bruenor asked him.

"I would like to hear the story," Drizzt replied, his gaze never leaving Jarlaxle. "But hear it as we travel along the road."

Jarlaxle nudged Athrogate, and the dwarf produced his boar figurine at the same time that Jarlaxle reached into his pouch for the obsidian nightmare. A moment later, their mounts materialized and Bruenor's mules flattened their ears and backed nervously away.

"What in the Nine Hells?" Bruenor muttered, working hard to control the team.

On a signal from Jarlaxle, Athrogate guided his boar to the side of the wagon, to take up a position in the rear.

"I want one o' them!" Thibbledorf Pwent said, his eyes wide with adoration as the fiery demon boar trotted past. "Oh, me king!"

Jarlaxle reined his nightmare aside and moved it to walk beside the wagon. Drizzt scrambled over that side to sit on the rail nearest him. Then he called to Guenhwyvar.

The panther knew her place. She leaped down from the tree, took a few running strides past Athrogate, and leaped into the wagon bed, curling up defensively around the seated Catti-brie.

"It is a long road," Drizzt remarked.

"It is a long tale," Jarlaxle replied.

"Tell it slowly then, and fully."

The wagon wasn't moving, and both Drizzt and Jarlaxle looked at Bruenor, the dwarf staring back at them with dark eyes full of doubt.

"Ye sure about this, elf?" he asked Drizzt.

"No," Drizzt answered, but then he looked at Jarlaxle, shook his head, and changed his mind. "To Spirit Soaring," he said.

"With hope," Jarlaxle added.

Drizzt turned his gaze to Catti-brie, who sat calmly, fully withdrawn from the world around her.

CHAPTER
NUMBERING THE STRANDS
7

"This is futile!" cried Wanabrick Prestocovin, a spirited young wizard from Baldur's Gate. He shoved his palms forward on the table before him, ruffling a pile of parchment.

"Easy, friend," said Dalebrentia Promise, a fellow traveler from the port city. Older and with a large gray beard that seemed to dwarf his skinny frame, Dalebrentia looked the part of the mage, and even wore stereotypical garb: a blue conical hat and a dark blue robe adorned with golden stars. "We are asked to respect the scrolls and books of Spirit Soaring."

A few months earlier, Wanabrick's explosion of frustration would have been met by a sea of contempt in the study of the great library, where indeed, the massive collections of varied knowledge from all across Faerûn, pulled together by Cadderly and his fellows, were revered and treasured. Tellingly, though, as many wizards, sages, and priests in the large study nodded their agreement with Wanabrick as revealed their scorn at his outburst.

That fact was not lost on Cadderly as he sat across the room amidst his own piles of parchment, including one on which he was working mathematical equations to try to inject predictability and an overriding logic into the seeming randomness of the mysterious events.

His own frustrations were mounting, though Cadderly did

well to hide them, for that apparent randomness seemed less and less like a veil to be unwound and more and more like an actual collapse of the logic that held Mystra's Weave aloft. The gods were not all dark, had not all gone silent, unlike the terrible Time of Troubles, but there was a palpable distance involved in any divine communion, and an utter unpredictability to spellcasting, divine or wizardly.

Cadderly rose and started toward the table where the trio of Baldur's Gate visitors studied, but he purposely put a disarming smile on his face, and walked with calm and measured steps.

"Your pardon, good Brother Bonaduce," Dalebrentia said as he neared. "My friend is young, and truly worried."

Wanabrick turned a wary eye at Cadderly. His face remained tense despite Cadderly's calm nod.

"I don't blame you, or Spirit Soaring," Wanabrick said. "My anger, it seems, is as unfocused as my magic."

"We're all frustrated and weary," Cadderly said.

"We left three of our guild in varying states of insanity," Dalebrentia explained. "And a fourth, a friend of Wanabrick's, was consumed in his own fireball while trying to help a farmer clear some land. He cast it long—I am certain of it—but it blew up before it ever left his hand."

"The Weave is eternal," Wanabrick fumed. "It must be . . . stable and eternal, else all my life's work is naught but a cruel joke!"

"The priests do not disagree," said a gnome, a disciple of Gond.

His support was telling. The Gondsmen, who loved logic and gears, smokepowder and contraptions built with cunning more than magic, had been the least affected by the sudden troubles.

"He is young," Dalebrentia said to Cadderly. "He doesn't remember the Time of Troubles."

"I am not so young," Cadderly replied.

"In mind!" Dalebrentia cried, and laughed to break the tension. The other two Baldurian wizards, one middle-aged like Cadderly and the other even older than Dalebrentia, laughed as well. "But so many of us who feel the creak of knees on a rainy morning do not much sympathize, good rejuvenated Brother Bonaduce!"

Even Cadderly smiled at that, for his journey through age had been a strange one indeed. He had begun construction of Spirit Soaring after the terrible chaos curse had wrought the destruction of its predecessor, the Edificant Library. Using magic given him by the god Deneir—nay, not given him, but channeled through him—Cadderly had aged greatly, to the point of believing that the construction would culminate with his death as an old, old man. He and Danica had accepted that fate for the sake of Spirit Soaring, the magnificent tribute to reason and enlightenment.

But the cost had proven a temporary thing, perhaps a trial of Deneir to test Cadderly's loyalty to the cause he professed, the cause of Deneir. After the completion of Spirit Soaring, the man had begun to grow younger physically—much younger, even younger than his actual age. He was forty-four, but appeared as a man in his young twenties, younger even than his twin children. That strange journey to physical youth, too, had subsequently stabilized, Cadderly believed, and he appeared to be aging more normally with the passage of the past several months.

"I have traveled the strangest of journeys," Cadderly said, putting a comforting hand on Wanabrick's shoulder. "Change is the only constant, I fear."

"But surely not like this!" Wanabrick replied.

"So we hope," said Cadderly.

"Have you found any answers, good priest?" Dalebrentia asked.

"Only that Deneir works as I work, writing his logic, seeking reason in the chaos, applying rules to that which seems unruly."

"And without success," Wanabrick said, somewhat dismissively.

"Patience," said Cadderly. "There are answers to be found, and rules that will apply. As we discern them, so too will we understand the extent of their implications, and so too will we adjust our thinking, and our spellcasting."

The gnome at a nearby table began to clap his hands at that, and the applause spread throughout the great study, dozens of mages and priests joining in, most soon standing. They were not cheering for him, Cadderly knew, but for hope itself in the face of their most frightening trial.

"Thank you," Dalebrentia quietly said to Cadderly. "We needed to hear that."

Cadderly looked at Wanabrick, who stood with his arms crossed over his chest, his face tight with anxiety and anger. The wizard did manage a nod to Cadderly, however.

Cadderly patted him on the shoulder again and started away, nodding and smiling to all who silently greeted him as he passed.

Outside the hall, the priest gave a sigh full of deep concern. He hadn't lied when he'd told Dalebrentia that Deneir was hard at work trying to unravel the unraveling, but he hadn't relayed the whole truth, either.

Deneir, a god of knowledge and history and reason, had answered Cadderly's prayers of communion with little more than a sensation of grave trepidation.

* * * * *

"Keep faith, friend," Cadderly said to Wanabrick later that same night, when the Baldurian contingent departed Spirit Soaring. "It's a temporary turbulence, I'm sure."

Wanabrick didn't agree, but he nodded anyway and headed out the door.

"Let us hope," Dalebrentia said to Cadderly, approaching him and offering his hand in gratitude.

"Will you not stay the night at least, and leave when the sun is bright?"

"Nay, good brother, we have been away too long as it is," Dalebrentia replied. "Several of our guild have been touched by the madness of the pure Weave. We must go to them and see if anything we have learned here might be of some assistance. Again, we thank you for the use of your library."

"It's not my library, good Dalebrentia. It's the world's library. I am merely the steward of the knowledge contained herein, and humbled by the responsibilities the great sages put upon me."

"A steward, and an author of more than a few of the tomes, I note," Dalebrentia said. "And truly we are all better off for your stewardship, Brother Bonaduce. In these troubled times, to find a place where great minds might congregate is comforting, even if not overly productive on this particular occasion. But we are dealing with unknowns here, and I am confident that as the unraveling of the Weave, if that is what it is, is understood, you will have many more important works to add to your collection."

"Any that you and your peers pen would be welcome," Cadderly assured him.

Dalebrentia nodded. "Our scribes will replicate every word spoken here today for Spirit Soaring, that in times to come when such a trouble as this visits Faerûn again, Tymora forefend, our wisdom will help the worried wizards and priests of the future."

They held their handshake throughout the conversation, each feeding off the strength of the other, for both Cadderly—so wise, the Chosen of Deneir—and Dalebrentia—an established mage even back in the Time of Troubles some two decades before—suspected that what they'd all experienced of late was no temporary thing, that it might lead to the end of Toril as they knew it, to turmoil beyond anything they could imagine.

"I will read the words of Dalebrentia with great interest," Cadderly assured the man as they finally broke off their handshake, and Dalebrentia moved out into the night to join his three companions.

They were a somber group as their wagon rolled slowly down Spirit Soaring's long cobblestone entry road, but not nearly as much so as when they had first arrived. Though they had found nothing solid to help them solve the troubling puzzle that lay before them, it was hard to leave Spirit Soaring without some measure of hope. Truly the library had become as magnificent in content as it was in construction, with thousands of parchments and tomes donated from cities as far away as Waterdeep and Luskan, Silverymoon, and even from great Calimport, far to the south. The place carried an aura of lightness and hope, a measure of greatness and promise, as surely as any other structure in all the lands.

Dalebrentia had climbed into the wagon beside old Resmilitu, while Wanabrick rode the jockey box with Pearson Bluth, who drove the two ponies.

"We will find our answers," Dalebrentia said, mostly to the fuming Wanabrick, but for the sake of all three.

Hooves clacking and wheels bouncing across the cobblestones were the only sounds that accompanied them down the lane. They reached the packed dirt of the long road that would lead them out of the Snowflakes to Carradoon.

The night grew darker as they moved under the thick canopy of overhanging tree limbs. The woods around them remained nearly silent—strangely so, they would have thought, had they bothered to notice—save for the occasional rustle of the wind through the leaves.

The lights of Spirit Soaring receded behind them, soon lost to the darkness.

"Bring up a flame," Resmilitu bade the others.

"A light will train enemies upon us," Wanabrick replied.

"We are four mighty wizards, young one. What enemies shall we fear this dark and chilly night?"

"Not so chilly, eh?" Pearson Bluth said, and glanced over his shoulder.

Though the driver's statement was accurate, he and the other two noted with surprise that Resmilitu hugged his arms around his chest and shivered mightily.

"Pop a light, then," Dalebrentia bade Wanabrick.

The younger wizard closed his eyes and waggled his fingers through a quick cantrip, conjuring a magical light atop his oaken staff. It flared to life, and Resmilitu nodded, though it shed no heat.

Dalebrentia moved to collect a blanket from the bags in the wagon bed.

Then it was dark again.

"Ah, Mystra, you tease," said Pearson Bluth, as Wanabrick offered stronger curses to the failure.

A moment later, Pearson's good nature turned to alarm. The darkness grew more intense than the night around them, as if Wanabrick's dweomer had not only failed, but had transformed somehow into an opposing spell of darkness. The man pulled the team to a stop. He couldn't see the ponies, and couldn't even see Wanabrick sitting beside him. He had no way of knowing if they, too, were engulfed in the pitch blackness.

"Damn this madness!" Wanabrick cried.

"Oh, but you've erased the stars themselves," said Dalebrentia in as light-hearted a tone as he could manage, confirming that the back of the wagon, too, had fallen victim to the apparent reversal of the dweomer.

Resmilitu cried out then through chattering teeth, "So chill!" and before the others could react to his call, they felt it too, a sudden, unnatural coldness, profound and to the bone.

"What?" Pearson Bluth blurted, for he knew as the others knew that the chill was no natural phenomenon, and he felt as the others felt a malevolence in that coldness, a sense of death itself.

Resmilitu was the first to scream out in pain as some unseen creature came over the side of the wagon, its raking hands clawing at the old mage.

"Light! Light!" cried Dalebrentia.

Pearson Bluth moved to heed that call, but the ponies began to buck and kick and whinny terribly. The poor driver couldn't hold the frantic animals in check. Beside him, Wanabrick waved his arms, daring to dive into the suddenly unpredictable realm of magic for an even greater enchantment. He brought forth a bright light, but it lasted only a heartbeat—enough to reveal the hunched and shadowy form assailing Resmilitu.

The thing was short and squat, a misshapen torso of black flesh and wide shoulders, with a head that looked more like a lump without a neck. Its legs were no more than flaps of skin tucked under it, but its arms were long and sinewy, with long-fingered, clawing hands. As Resmilitu rolled away, the creature followed by propelling itself with those front limbs, like a legless man dragging himself.

"Be gone!" cried Dalebrentia, brandishing a thin wand of burnished wood tipped in metal. He sent forth its sparkling bolts of pure energy just as Wanabrick's magical light winked out.

The creature wailed in pain, but so too did poor Resmilitu, and the others heard the tearing of the old wizard's robes.

"Be gone!" Dalebrentia cried again—the trigger phrase for his wand—and they heard the release of the missiles even though they couldn't see any flash in the magical darkness.

"More light!" Dalebrentia cried.

Resmilitu cried out again, and so did the creature, though it sounded more like a shriek of murderous pleasure than of pain.

Wanabrick threw himself over the seat atop the fleshy beast and began thrashing and pounding away with his staff to try to dislodge it from poor Resmilitu.

The monster was not so strong, and the wizard managed to pry one arm free, but then Pearson Bluth screamed out from in front, and the wagon lurched to the side. It rolled out of the magical darkness at that moment, and the light atop Wanabrick's oaken staff brightened the air around them. But the wizards took little solace in that, for the terrified team dragged the wagon right off the road, to go bouncing down a steep embankment. They all tried to hold on, but the front wheels turned sharply and dug into a rut, lifting the wagon end over end.

Wood splintered and the mages screamed. Loudest of all came the shriek of a mule as its legs shattered in the roll.

Dalebrentia landed hard in some moss at the base of a tree, and he was certain he'd broken his arm. He fought through the pain, however, forcing himself to his knees. He glanced around quickly for his lost wand but found instead poor Resmilitu, the fleshy beast still atop him, tearing at his broken frame in a frenzy.

Dalebrentia started for him, but fell back as a blast of lightning blazed from the other side, lifting the shadowy beast right off his old friend and throwing it far into the night. Dalebrentia looked to Wanabrick to nod his approval.

But he never managed that nod. Looking at the man, the magically-lit staff lying near him, Dalebrentia saw the shadowy beasts crawling in behind the younger mage, huddled, fleshy beasts coming on ravenously.

To the side, Pearson Bluth stumbled into view, a beast upon his back, one of its arms wrapped around his neck, its other hand clawing at his face.

Dalebrentia fell into his spellcasting and brought forth a fiery pea, thinking to hurl it past Wanabrick, far enough so its explosion would catch the approaching horde but not engulf his friend.

But the collapsing Weave deceived the old mage. The pea had barely left his hand when it exploded. Waves of intense heat assailed Dalebrentia and he fell back, clutching at his seared eyes. He rolled around wildly on the ground, trying to extinguish the flames, too far lost to agony to even hear the cries of his friends, and those of the fleshy beasts, likewise shrieking in burning pain.

Somewhere in the back of his mind, old Dalebrentia could only hope that his fireball had eliminated the monsters and had not killed his companions.

His hopes for the former were dashed a heartbeat later when a clawed hand came down hard against the side of his neck, the force of the blow driving a dirty talon through his skin. Hooked like a fish, blinded and burned by his own fire and battered from the fall, Dalebrentia could do little to resist as the shadowy beast tugged at him.

* * * * *

Had he remained at the door where he'd sent the wizards off more than an hour before, Cadderly might have seen the sudden burst of fire far down the mountain trail, with one tall pine going up in flames like the fireworks the priest had often used to entertain his children in their younger days. But Cadderly had gone back inside as soon as the four from Baldur's Gate had departed.

Their inability to discover anything pertinent had spurred the priest to his meditation, to try again to commune with Deneir, the god who might, above all others in the pantheon, offer some clues to the source of the unpredictable and troubling events.

He sat in a small room lit only by a pair of tall candles, one to either side of the blanket he had spread on the floor. He sat cross-legged on that blanket, hands on his knees, palms facing up. For a long while, he focused only on his breathing, making his inhalations and exhalations the same length, using the count to clear his mind of all worry and trials. He was alone in his cadence, moving away from the Prime Material Plane and into the realm of pure thought, the realm of Deneir.

He'd done the same many times since the advent of the troubles, but never to great effect. Once or twice, he thought he had reached Deneir, but the god had flitted out of his thoughts before any clear pictures might emerge.

This time, though, Cadderly felt Deneir's presence keenly. He pressed on, letting himself fall far from consciousness. He saw the starscape all around him, as if he floated among the heavens, and he saw the image of Deneir, the old scribe, sitting in the night sky, long scroll spread before him, chanting, though Cadderly could not at first make out the words.

The priest willed himself toward his god, knowing that good fortune was on his side, that he had entered that particular region of concentration and reason in conjunction with the Lord of All Glyphs and Images.

He heard the chant.

Numbers. Deneir was working the *Metatext*, the binding logic of the multiverse.

Gradually, Cadderly began to discern the slightly-glowing strands forming a net in the sky above him and Deneir, the blanket of magic that gave enchantment to Toril. The Weave. Cadderly paused and considered the implications. Was it possible that the *Metatext* and the Weave were connected in ways more than philosophical? And if that were true, since the Weave was obviously flawed and failing, could not the *Metatext* also be flawed? No, that could not be, he told himself, and he moved his focus back to Deneir.

Deneir was numbering the strands, Cadderly realized, was giving them order and recording the patterns on his scroll. Was he somehow trying to infuse the failing Weave with the perfect logic and consistency of the *Metatext?* The thought thrilled the priest. Would his god, above all others, be the one to repair the rents in the fabric of magic?

He wanted to implore his god, to garner some divine inspiration and instruction, but Cadderly realized, to his surprise, that Deneir was not there to answer his call to commune, that Deneir had not brought him to that place. No, he had arrived at that place and time as Deneir had, by coincidence, not design.

He drifted closer—close enough to look over Deneir's shoulder as the god sat there, suspended in emptiness, recording his observations.

The parchment held patterns of numbers, Cadderly noted, like a great puzzle. Deneir was trying to decode the Weave itself, each strand by type and form. Was it possible that the Weave, like a spider's web, was comprised of various parts that sustained it? Was it possible that the unraveling, if that's what the time of turbulence truly was, resulted from a missing supporting strand?

Or a flaw in the design? Surely not that!

Cadderly continued to silently watch over Deneir's shoulder. He committed to memory a few sequences of the numbers, so he could record them later when he was back in his study. Though certainly no god, Cadderly still hoped he might discern something in those sequences that he could then communicate back to Deneir, to aid the Scribe of Oghma in his contemplations.

When at last Cadderly opened his physical eyes again, he found the candles still burning beside him. Looking at them, he deduced that he had been journeying the realm of concentration for perhaps two hours. He rose and moved to his desk, to transcribe the numbers he had seen, the representation of the Weave.

The collapsing Weave.

Where were the missing or errant strands? he wondered.

* * * * *

Cadderly hadn't seen the firelight down the mountain trail, but Ivan Bouldershoulder, out collecting wood for his forge, surely had.

"Well, what mischief's about?" the dwarf asked. He thought of his brother, then, and realized that Pikel would be angry indeed to see so majestic a pine go up in a pillar of flame.

Ivan moved to a rocky outcropping to gain a better vantage. He still couldn't make out much down the dark trails, but his new position put the wind in his face, and that breeze carried with it screams.

The dwarf dropped his pack beside the hand-sled on which rested the firewood, adjusted his helmet, which was adorned with great deer antlers, and hoisted Splitter, his double-bladed battle-axe, so named—by Ivan, after Cadderly had enchanted it with a powerfully keen edge—for its work on logs and goblin skulls alike. Without so much as a glance back at Spirit Soaring, the yellow-bearded dwarf ran down the dark trails, his short legs propelling him at a tremendous pace.

Fleshy beasts of shadow were feeding on the bodies of the Baldurian wizards by the time he arrived.

Ivan skidded to an abrupt halt, and the nearest creatures noticed him and came on, dragging themselves with their long forelimbs.

Ivan thought to retreat, but only until he heard a groan from one of the wizards.

"Well, all righty then!" the dwarf decided, and he charged at the beasts, Splitter humming as he slashed it back and forth with seeming abandon. The keen axe sheared through black skin with ease, spilling goo from the shrieking crawlers. They were too slow to get ahead of those powerful swipes, and too stupid to resist their insatiable hunger and simply flee.

One after another fell to Ivan, splattering with sickly sounds as Splitter eviscerated them. The dwarf's arms did not tire and his swings did not slow, though the beasts did not stop coming for a long, long while.

When finally there seemed nothing left to hit, Ivan rushed to the nearest mage, the oldest of the group.

"No helpin' that one," he muttered when he rolled Resmilitu over to find his neck torn out.

Only one of them wasn't quite dead. Poor Dalebrentia lay shivering, his skin all blistered, his eyes tightly closed.

"I got ye," Ivan whispered to him. "Ye hold that bit o' life and I'll get ye back to Cadderly."

With that and a quick glance around, the dwarf set Splitter in place across his back and bent low to slide one hand under Dalebrentia's knees, the other under his upper back. Before he lifted the man, though, Ivan felt such a sensation of coldness—not the cold of winter, but something more profound, as if death itself stood behind him.

He turned, slowly at first, as he reached around to grasp his weapon.

A shadowy form stood nearby, staring at him. Unlike the fleshy beasts that lay dead all around him—indeed, the four mages had also killed quite a few—it appeared more like a man, old and hunched over.

Such a cold chill went through Ivan then that his teeth began to chatter. He wanted to call out to the man, or shadow, or specter, or whatever it was, but found that he could not.

And found that he didn't have to.

Images of a long-ago time swirled in Ivan's mind, of dancing with his six mighty friends around an artifact of great power.

Images of a red dragon came clear to him, so clear that he began to duck as if the beast circled right above his head.

An image of another creature erased the others, an octopus-headed monstrosity with tentacles waggling under its chin like the braided strands of an old dwarf's beard.

A name was whispered into his ear, carried on unseen breezes. "Yharaskrik."

Ivan stood up straight, lifting Dalebrentia in his arms.

Then he dropped the man to the ground before him, lifted his heavy boot, and pressed it down on Dalebrentia's throat until the wheezing and the squirming stopped.

With a satisfied grin, Ivan, who was not Ivan, looked all

around. He held out his hand toward each of the Baldurian wizards in turn, and each rose up to his call.

Throats torn, arms half-eaten, great holes in their bellies, it did not matter. For Ivan's call was the echo of the Ghost King, and the Ghost King's call beckoned souls from the land of the dead with ease.

His four gruesome bodyguards behind him, Ivan Bouldershoulder started off along the trails, moving farther away from Spirit Soaring.

He didn't reach his intended location that night. Instead, he found a cave nearby where he and his bodyguards could spend the daylight hours.

There would be plenty of time to kill when the darkness fell once more.

CHAPTER
BATTLE OF THE BLADE AND OF THE MIND
8

Hanaleisa snap-kicked to the side, breaking the tibia of a skeleton that had gotten inside the reach of Temberle's greatsword. The young woman leaned low to her left, raising her right leg higher, and kicked again, knocking the skull off the animated skeleton as it turned toward her.

At the same time, she punched out straight at a second target, her flying fist making a grotesque splattering sound as it smashed through the rotting chest of a zombie.

The blow would have knocked the breath from any man, but zombies have no need for breath. The creature continued its lumbering swing, its heavy arm slamming against Hanaleisa's blocking left arm and shoulder, driving her a step to her right, closer to her brother.

Exhausted after a long night of fighting, Hanaleisa found a burst of energy yet again, stepping forward and rocking the zombie with a barrage of punches, kicks, and driving knees. She ignored the gory results of every blow, almost all of them punching through rotting skin and breaking brittle bones, leaving holes through which fell rotted organs and clusters of maggots. Again and again the woman pounded the zombie until at last it fell away.

Another lumbered up—an inexhaustible line of enemies, it seemed.

Temberle's greatsword cut across in front of Hanaleisa just before she advanced to meet the newest foe. Temberle hit the creature just below the shoulder, taking its arm, and the sword plowed through ribs with ease, throwing the zombie aside.

"You looked like you needed to catch your breath," Hanaleisa's brother explained. Then he yelped, his move to defend Hanaleisa costing him a parry against the next beast closing with him. His right arm bloody from a long, deep wound, he stepped back fast and punched out with the pommel of his sword, slamming and jolting the skeleton.

Then Hanaleisa was there. She leaped up and ahead, rising between the skeleton closing on her and the one battling Temberle. Hanaleisa kicked out to the sides, both feet flying wide. With a jolting rattle of bones, the two skeletons flew apart.

Hanaleisa landed lightly, rising up on the ball of her left foot and spinning a powerful circle-kick into the gut of the next approaching zombie.

Her foot went right through it, and when she tried to retract, she discovered herself hooked on the monster's spine. She pulled back again, having little choice, and found herself even more entangled as the zombie, not quite destroyed by the mighty blow, reached and clawed at her.

Temberle's sword stabbed in hard from the side, taking the monster in the face and skewering it.

Hanaleisa stumbled back, still locked with the corpse. "Protect me!" she yelled to her brother, but she bit the words back sharply as she noted Temberle's arm covered in blood, and with more streaming from the wound. As he clenched his sword to swing again, his forearm muscles tightening, blood sprayed into the air.

Hanaleisa knew he couldn't go on for long. None of them could. Exhausted and horrified, and with their backs almost against the wall of the wharf's storehouse, they needed a break from the relentless assault, needed something to give them time to regroup and bandage themselves—or Temberle would surely bleed to death.

Finally pulling free and leaping to both feet, Hanaleisa glanced around for Pikel, or for an escape route, or for anything that might give her hope. All she saw was yet another defender being pulled down by the undead horde, and a sea of monsters all around them.

In the distance, just a few blocks away, more fires leaped to angry life as Carradoon burned.

With a sigh of regret, a grunt of determination, and a sniffle to hold back her tears, the young woman went back into the fray ferociously, pounding the monster nearest her and the one battling Temberle with blow after blow. She leaped and spun, kicked and punched, and her brother tried to match her.

But his swings were slowing as his blood continued to drain.

The end was coming fast.

* * * * *

"They're too heavy!" a young girl complained, straining to lift a keg with little success. Suddenly, though, it grew lighter and rose up through the trapdoor as easily as if it were empty. Indeed, when she saw that no one was pushing from below, the girl did glance underneath at the bottom of the keg, thinking its whiskey must have all drained out.

On the roof nearby, Rorick kept his focus, commanding an invisible servant to hold fast to the keg and help the little one. It wasn't much of a spell, but Rorick wasn't yet much of a wizard, and in times of unpredictable and often backfiring magic, he dared not attempt more difficult tricks.

He found satisfaction in his efforts, though, reminding himself that leaders needed to be clever and thoughtful, not just strong of arm or Art. His father had never been the greatest of fighters, and it wasn't until near the end of the troubles that had come to Edificant Library that Cadderly had truly come into his own Deneir-granted power. Still, Rorick wished he'd trained more the way his sister and brother had. Leaning heavily on a walking stick, his ankle swollen and pus oozing from the dirty wound, he was reminded with every pained step that he really wasn't much of a warrior.

I'm not much of a wizard, either, he thought, and he winced as his unseen servant dissipated. The girl, overbalanced with the keg, tumbled down. The side of the container broke open and whiskey spilled over the corner of the storehouse roof.

"What now, then?" a sailor asked, and it took Rorick a moment to realize that the man, far older and more seasoned than he, was speaking to him, was looking to him for direction.

"Be a leader," Rorick mumbled under his breath, and he pointed toward the front of the storehouse, to the edge of the low roof, where below the battle was on in full.

*****

"Doo-dad!" came a familiar cry from far to Hanaleisa's right, much beyond Temberle. She started to glance that way, but saw movement up above and fell back, startled.

Out over the heads of the defenders came the whiskey kegs—by the dozen! They sailed out and crashed down, some atop zombies and other wretched creatures, others smashing hard on the cobblestones.

"What in the—?" more than one surprised defender cried out, Temberle included.

"Doo-dad!" came the emphatic answer.

All the defenders looked that way to see Pikel charging at them. His right arm was stretched out to the side, shillelagh pointed at the horde. The club threw sparks, and at first the bright light alone kept the undead back from Pikel, clearing the way as he continued his run. But more importantly, those sparks sizzled out to the spilled alcohol, and nothing burned brighter than Carradden whiskey.

The dwarf ran on, the enchanted cudgel spitting its flares, and flames roared up in response.

Despite her pain, despite her fear for her brothers, Hanaleisa couldn't help but giggle as the dwarf passed, his stumpy arm flapping like the wing of a wounded duck. He was not running, Hanaleisa saw—he was skipping.

An image of a five-year-old Rorick skipping around her mother's garden outside Spirit Soaring, sparkler in hand, flashed in Hanaleisa's mind, and a sudden contentment washed over her, as if she was certain that Uncle Pikel would make everything all right.

She shook the notion away quickly, though, and finished off a nearby monster that was caught on their side of the fire wall. Then she ran to Temberle, who was already calling out to organize the retreat. Hanaleisa reached into her pouch and pulled forth some clean cloth, quickly tying off Temberle's torn arm.

And not a moment too soon. Her brother nodded appreciatively, then swooned. Hanaleisa caught him and called for help, directing a woman to retrieve Temberle's greatsword, for she knew—they all knew—he would surely need it again, and very soon.

Into the storehouse they went, a line of weary and battered defenders—battered emotionally as much as physically, perhaps even more so, for they knew to a man and woman that their beloved Carradoon was unlikely to survive the surprise onslaught.

* * * * *

"You saved us all," Hanaleisa said to Rorick a short while later, when they were all together once more.

"Uncle Pikel did the dangerous work," Rorick said, nodding his chin toward the dwarf.

"Doo-dad, hee hee hee," said the dwarf. He presented his shillelagh and added, "Boom!" with a shake of his hairy head.

"We're not saved yet," Temberle said from a small window overlooking the carnage on the street. Conscious again, but still weakened, the young man's voice sounded grim indeed. "Those fires won't last for long."

It was true, but the whiskey-fueled conflagration had turned the battle and saved their cause. The stupid undead knew no fear and had kept coming on, their rotting clothes and skin adding fuel to the flames as they crumpled and burned atop their fellows.

But a few stragglers were getting through, scratching at the storehouse walls, battering the planks, and the fires outside were burning low.

One zombie walked right through the fires and came out ablaze. Still it advanced, right to the storehouse door, and managed to pound its fists a few times before succumbing to the flames. And as bad luck would have it, those flames licked at the wood. They wouldn't have been of consequence, except from the roof above, one of the kegs had overturned, spilling its volatile contents across the roof and down the side.

Several people screamed as the corner of the storehouse flared up. Some went to try to battle the flames, but to no avail. Worse, the keg throwers hadn't emptied about a third of the whiskey stocks from the storehouse. Whiskey was one of Carradoon's largest exports—boats sailed out with kegs of the stuff almost every tenday.

More than a hundred people were in that storehouse, and panic spread quickly as the flames licked up over their heads to the roof, fanning across the ceiling.

"We've got to get out!" one man called.

"To the docks!" others yelled in agreement, and the stampede for the back door began in full.

"Uh oh," said Pikel.

Temberle hooked Rorick's arm over his shoulder and the brothers leaned heavily on each other for support as they moved toward the exit, both calling for Hanaleisa and Pikel to follow.

Pikel started to move, but Hanaleisa grabbed him by the arm and held him back.

"Eh?"

Hanaleisa pointed to a nearby keg and rushed for it. She popped the top and hoisted it, then ran to the front door, where skeletons and zombies pounded furiously. With a look back at Pikel, Hanaleisa began splashing the keg's contents all along the wall.

"Hee hee hee," Pikel agreed, coming up beside her with a keg of his own. First he lifted it to his lips for a good long swallow, but then he ran along the wall, splashing whiskey all over the floor and the base of the planks.

Hanaleisa looked across the storehouse. The brave townsfolk had regained a measure of calm and were moving swiftly and orderly out onto the docks.

The heat grew quickly. A beam fell from the roof, dropping a line of fire across the floor.

"Hana!" Rorick cried from the back of the storehouse.

"Get out!" she screamed at him. "Uncle Pikel, come along!"

The dwarf charged toward her and hopped the fallen beam alongside her, both heading fast for the door.

More fiery debris tumbled from the ceiling, and the whiskey-soaked side wall began to burn furiously. The flames spread up the walls behind them.

But the undead hadn't broken through, Hanaleisa realized when she reached the exit. "Go!" she ordered Pikel, and pushed him through the door. To the dwarf's horror, to the horror of her brothers, and to the horror of everyone watching, Hanaleisa turned and sprinted back into the burning building.

Smoke filled her nostrils and stung her eyes. She could barely see, but she knew her way. She leaped the beam burning in the middle of the floor, then ducked and rolled under another that tumbled down from above.

She neared the front door, and just as she leaped for it, a nearby keg burst in a ball of fire, causing another to explode beside it. Hanaleisa kicked out at the heavy bar sealing the door, all her focus and strength behind the blow. She heard the wood crack beneath her foot, and a good thing that was, for she had no time to follow the move. At that moment, the fires reached the whiskey she and Pikel had poured out, and Hanaleisa had to sprint away to avoid immolation.

But the door was open, and the undead streamed in hungrily, stupidly.

More kegs exploded and half the roof caved in beside her, but Hanaleisa maintained her focus and kept her legs moving. She could hardly see in the heavy smoke, and tripped over a burning beam, painfully smashing her toes in the process.

She scrambled along, quickly regaining her footing.

More kegs exploded, and fiery debris flew all around her. The smoke grew so thick that she couldn't get her bearings. She couldn't see the doorway. Hanaleisa skidded to a halt, but she couldn't afford to stop. She sprinted ahead once more, crashing into some piled crates and overturning them.

She couldn't see, she couldn't breathe, she had no idea which way was out, and she knew that any other direction led to certain death.

She spun left and right, started one way, then fell back in dismay. She called out, but her voice was lost in the roar of the flames.

In that moment, horror turned to resignation. She knew she was doomed, that her daring stunt had succeeded at the cost of her life.

So be it.

The young woman dropped down onto all fours and thought of her brothers. She hoped she had bought them the time they needed to escape. Uncle Pikel would lead them to safety, she told herself, and she nodded her acceptance.

* * * * *

To his credit, Bruenor didn't say anything. But it was hard for Thibbledorf Pwent and Drizzt not to notice his continual and obviously uncomfortable glances to either side, where Jarlaxle and Athrogate weaved in and out of the trees on their magical mounts.

"He's the makings of a Gutbuster," remarked Pwent, who sat beside Bruenor on the wagon's jockey box, while Drizzt walked along beside them. The Gutbuster nodded his hairy chin toward Athrogate. "Bit too clean, me's thinkin', but I'm likin' that pig o' his. And them morningstars!"

"Gutbusters play with drow, do they?" Bruenor replied, but before the sting of that remark could sink in to Pwent, Drizzt beat him to the reply with, "Sometimes."

"Bah, elf, ye ain't no drow, and ain't been one, ever," Bruenor protested. "Ye know what I'm meaning."

"I do," Drizzt admitted. "No offense intended, so no offense taken. But neither do I believe that Jarlaxle is what you've come to expect from my people."

"Bah, but he ain't no Drizzt."

"Nor was Zaknafein, in the manner you imply," Drizzt responded. "But King Bruenor would have welcomed my father into Mithral Hall. Of that, I'm sure."

"And this strange one's akin to yer father, is he?"

Drizzt looked through the trees to see Jarlaxle guiding his hellish steed along, and he shrugged, honestly at a loss. "They were friends, I've been told."

Bruenor paused for a bit and similarly considered the strange creature that was Jarlaxle, with his outrageously plumed hat. Everything about Jarlaxle seemed unfamiliar to the parochial Bruenor, everything spoke of the proverbial "other" to the dwarf.

"I just ain't sure o' that one," the dwarf king muttered. "Me girl's in trouble here, and ye're asking me to trust the likes o' Jarlaxle and his pet dwarf."

"True enough," Drizzt admitted. "And I don't deny that I have concerns of my own." Drizzt hopped up and grabbed the rail behind the seat so he could ride along for a bit. He looked directly at Bruenor, demanding the dwarf's complete attention. "But I also know that if Jarlaxle had wanted us dead, we would likely already be walking the Fugue Plain. Regis and I would not have gotten out of Luskan without his help. Catti-brie and I would not have been able to escape his many warriors outside of Menzoberranzan those years ago, had he not allowed it. I have no doubt that there's more to his offer to help us than his concern for us, or for Catti-brie."

"He's got some trouble o' his own," said Bruenor, "or I'm a bearded gnome! And bigger trouble than that tale he telled about needing to make sure the Crystal Shard was gone."

Drizzt nodded. "That may well be. But even if that is true, I like our chances better with Jarlaxle beside us. We wouldn't even have turned toward Spirit Soaring and Cadderly, had not Jarlaxle sent his dwarf companion to Mithral Hall to suggest it."

"To lure us out!" Bruenor snapped back, rather loudly.

Drizzt patted one hand in the air to calm the dwarf. "Again, my friend, if that was only to make us vulnerable, Jarlaxle would have ambushed us on the road right outside your door, and there we would remain, pecked by the crows."

"Unless he's looking for something from ye," Bruenor argued. "Might still be a pretty ransom on Drizzt Do'Urden's head, thanks to the matron mothers of Menzoberranzan."

That was possible, Drizzt had to admit to himself, and he glanced over his shoulder at Jarlaxle once more, but eventually shook his head. If Jarlaxle had wanted anything like that, he would have hit the wagon with overwhelming force outside of Mithral Hall, and easily enough captured all four, or whichever of them might have proven valuable to his nefarious schemes. Even beyond that simple logic, however, there was within Drizzt something else: an understanding of Jarlaxle and his motives that surprised Drizzt every time he paused to consider it.

"I do not believe that," Drizzt replied to Bruenor. "Not any of it."

"Bah!" Bruenor snorted, hardly seeming convinced, and he snapped the reins to coax the team along more swiftly, though they had already put more than fifty miles behind them that day, with half-a-day's riding yet before them. The wagon bounced along comfortably, the dwarven craftsmanship more than equal to the task of the long rides. "So ye're thinking he's just wanting us for a proper introduction to Cadderly? Ye're buying his tale, are ye? Bah!"

It was hard to find a proper response to one of Bruenor's "bahs," let alone two. But before Drizzt could even try, a scream from the back of the wagon ended the discussion.

The three turned to see Catti-brie floating in the air, her eyes rolled back to show only white. She hadn't risen high enough to escape the tailgate of the wagon, and was being towed along in her weightless state. One of her arms rose to the side, floating in the air as if in water, as they had seen before during her fits, but her other arm was forward, her hand turned and grasping as if she were presenting a sword before her.

Bruenor pulled hard on the reins and flipped them to Pwent, heading over the back of the seat before the Gutbuster even caught them. Drizzt beat the dwarf to the wagon bed, the agile drow leaping over the side in a rush to grab Catti-brie's left arm before she slipped over the back of the rail. The drow raised his other hand toward Bruenor to stop him, and stared intently at Catti-brie as she played out what she saw in her mind's eye.

Her eyes rolled back to show their deep blue once more.

Her right arm twitched, and she winced. Her focus seemed to be straight ahead, though given her distant stare, it was hard to be certain. Her extended hand slowly turned, as if her imaginary sword was being forced into a downward angle. Then it popped back up a bit, as if someone or something had slid off the end of the blade. Catti-brie's breath came in short gasps. A single tear rolled down one cheek, and she quietly mouthed, "I killed her."

"What's she about, then?" Bruenor asked.

Drizzt held his hand up to silence the dwarf, letting it play out. Catti-brie's chin tipped down, as if she were looking at the ground, then lifted again as she raised her imaginary sword.

"Suren she's looking at the blood," Bruenor whispered. He heard Jarlaxle's mount galloping to the side, and Athrogate's as well, but he didn't take his eyes off his beloved daughter.

Catti-brie sniffled hard and tried to catch her breath as more tears streamed down her face.

"Is she looking into the future, or the past?" Jarlaxle asked.

Drizzt shook his head, uncertain, but in truth, he was pretty sure he recognized the scene playing out before him.

"But she's floated up and almost o'er the aft. I ain't for sayin', but that one's daft," said Athrogate.

Bruenor did turn to the side then, throwing a hateful look at the dwarf.

"Beggin' yer pardon, good King Bruenor," Athrogate apologized. "But that's what I'm thinking."

Catti-brie began to sob and shake violently. Drizzt had seen enough. He pulled the woman close, hugging her and whispering into her ear.

And the world darkened for the drow. For just an instant, he saw Catti-brie's victim, a woman wearing the robes of the Hosttower of the Arcane, a mage named Sydney, he knew, and he knew then without doubt the incident his beloved had just replayed.

Before he could fully understand that he saw the body of the first real kill Catti-brie had ever known, the first time she had felt her victim's blood splash on her own skin, the image faded from his mind and he moved deeper, as if through the realm of death and into . . .

Drizzt did not know. He glanced around in alarm, looking not at the wagon and Bruenor, but at a strange plain of dim light and dark shadows, and dark gray—almost black— fog wafting on unfelt breezes.

They came at him there, in that other place, dark, fleshy beasts like legless, misshapen trolls, pulling themselves along with gangly, sinewy arms, snarling through long, pointed teeth.

Drizzt turned fast to put his back to Catti-brie and went for his scimitars as the first of the beasts reached out to claw at him. Even the glow of Twinkle seemed dark to his eyes as he brought the blade slashing down. But it did its work, taking the thing's arm at the elbow. Drizzt slipped forward behind the cut, driving Icingdeath into the torso of the wretched creature.

He came back fast the other way and spun around. To his horror, Catti-brie was not there. He sprinted out, bumping hard into someone, then tripped and went rolling forward. Or he tried to roll, but discovered that the ground was several feet lower than he'd anticipated, and he landed hard on his lower back and rump, rattling his teeth.

Drizzt stabbed and slashed furiously as the dark beasts swarmed over him. He managed to get his feet under him and came up with a high leap, simply trying to avoid the many slashing clawed hands.

He landed in a flurry and a fury, blades rolling over each other with powerful and devastating strokes and stabs, and wild slashes that sent the beasts falling away with terrible shrieks and screeches, three at a time.

"Catti-brie!" he cried, for he could not see her, and he knew that they had taken her!

He tried to go forward, but heard a call from his right, and just as he spun, something hit him hard, as if one of the beasts had leaped up and slammed him with incredible force.

He lost a scimitar as he flew backward a dozen feet and more, and came down hard against some solid object, a tree perhaps, where he found himself stuck fast—completely stuck, as if the fleshy beast or whatever it was that had hit him had just turned to goo as it had engulfed him. He could move only one hand and couldn't see, could hardly breathe.

Drizzt tried to struggle free, thinking of Catti-brie, and he knew the fleshy black beasts were closing in on him.

CHAPTER 9
A TIME FOR HEROES

A light appeared, a bright beacon cutting through the smoke, beckoning her. Hanaleisa felt its inviting warmth, so different from the bite of the fire's heat. It called to her, almost as if it were enchanted. When she at last burst out the door, past the thick smoke, rolling out onto the wharves, Hanaleisa was not surprised to see a grinning Uncle Pikel standing there, holding aloft his brilliantly glowing shillelagh. She tried to thank him, but coughed and gagged on the smoke. Nearly overcome, she managed to reach Pikel and wrap him in a great hug, her brothers coming in to flank her, patting her back to help her dislodge the persistent smoke.

After a long while, Hanaleisa finally managed to stop coughing and stand straight. Pikel quickly ushered them all away from the storehouse, as more explosions wracked it, kegs of Carradden whiskey still left to explode.

"Why did you go in there?" Rorick scolded her once the immediate danger was past. "That was foolish!"

"Tut tut," Pikel said to him, waggling a finger in the air to silence him.

A portion of the roof caved in with a great roar, taking down part of the wall with it. Through the hole, the four saw the continuing onslaught of the undead, the unthinking monsters willingly walking in the door after Hanaleisa had opened it. They were fast falling, consumed by the flames.

"She invited them in," Temberle said to his little brother. "Hana bought us the time we'll need."

"What are they doing?" Hanaleisa asked, looking past her brothers toward the wharves, her question punctuated by coughs. The question was more of surprise than to elicit a response, for the answer was obvious. People swarmed aboard the two small fishing vessels docked nearby.

"They mean to ferry us across the lake to the north, to Byernadine," Temberle explained, referring to the lakeside hamlet nearest to Carradoon.

"We haven't the time," Hanaleisa replied.

"We haven't a choice," Temberle said. "They have good crews here. They'll get more boats in fast."

Shouting erupted on the docks. It escalated into pushing and fighting as desperate townsfolk scrambled to get aboard the first two boats.

"Sailors only!" a man shouted above the rest, for the plan had been to fill those two boats with experienced fishermen, who could then retrieve the rest of the fleet.

But the operation wasn't going as planned.

"Cast her off!" many people aboard one of the boats shouted, while others still tried to jump on board.

"Too many," Hanaleisa whispered to her companions, for indeed the small fishing vessel, barely twenty feet long, had not near the capacity to carry the throng that had packed aboard her. Still, they threw out the lines and pushed her away from the wharf. Several people went into the water as she drifted off, swimming hard to catch her and clinging desperately to her rail, which was barely above the cold waters of Impresk Lake.

The second boat went out as well, not quite as laden, and the square sails soon opened as they drifted out from shore. So packed was the first boat that the crewmen aboard couldn't even reach the rigging, let alone raise sail. Listing badly, weaving erratically, her movements made all on shore gasp and whisper nervously, while the shouting and arguing on the boat only increased in desperation.

Already, many were shaking their heads in dismay and expecting catastrophe when the situation fast deteriorated. The people in the water suddenly began to scream and thrash about. Skeletal fish knifed up to stab hard into them like thrown knives.

The fishing boat rocked as the many hangers-on let go, and people shrieked as the waters churned and turned red with blood.

Then came the undead sailors, rising up to some unseen command. Bony hands gripped the rails of both low-riding ships, and people aboard and on shore cried out in horror as the skeletons of long-dead fishermen began to pull themselves up from the dark waters.

The panic on the first boat sent several people splashing overboard. The boat rocked and veered with the shifting weight, turning uncontrollably—and disastrously. Similarly panicked, the sailors on the second boat couldn't react quickly enough as the first boat turned toward her. They crashed together with the crackle of splintering wood and the screams of scores of townsfolk realizing their doom. Many went into the water, and as the skeletons scrambled aboard, many others had no choice but to leap into Impresk Lake and try to swim to shore.

Long had men plied the waters of Impresk Lake. Its depths had known a thousand thousand turns of the circle of life. Her deep bed churned with the rising dead, and her waters roiled as more skeletal fish swarmed the splashing Carradden.

And those on the wharves, Hanaleisa, her bothers, and Uncle Pikel as well, could only watch in horror, for not one of the eighty-some people who had boarded those two boats made it back to shore alive.

"Now what?" Rorick cried, his face streaked with tears, his words escaping through such profound gasps that he could hardly get them out.

Indeed, everyone on the wharves shared that horrible question. Then the storehouse collapsed with a great fiery roar. Many of the undead horde were destroyed in that conflagration, thanks to the daring of Hanaleisa, but many, many more remained. And the townsfolk were trapped with their backs to the water, a lake they dared not enter.

Rag-tag groups ran to the north and south as all semblance of order broke down. A few boat crews managed to band together along the shore, and many townsfolk followed in their protective wake.

Many more looked to the children of Cadderly and Danica, those two so long the heroes of the barony. In turn, the three siblings looked to the only hope they could find: Uncle Pikel.

Pikel Bouldershoulder accepted the responsibility with typical gusto, punching his stump into the air. He tucked his cudgel under that shortened arm and began to hop around, tapping his lips with one finger and mumbling, "umm" over and over again.

"Well, what then?" a fishing boat captain cried. Many people closed in on the foursome, looking for answers.

"We find a spot to defend, and we order our line," Temberle said after looking to Pikel for answers that did not seem to be forthcoming. "Find a narrow alleyway. We cannot remain down here."

"Uh-uh," Pikel disagreed, even as the group began to organize its retreat.

"We can't stay here, Uncle Pikel!" Rorick said to the dwarf, but the indomitable Pikel just smiled back at him.

Then the green-bearded dwarf closed his eyes and tapped his shillelagh against the boardwalk, as if calling to the ground beneath. He turned left, to the north, then hesitated and turned back before spinning to the north again and dashing off at a swift pace.

"What's he doing?" the captain and several others asked.

"I don't know," Temberle answered, but he and Rorick hooked arms again and started after.

"We ain't following the fool dwarf blindly!" the captain protested.

"Then you're sure to die," Hanaleisa answered without hesitation.

Her words had an effect, for all of them swarmed together in Pikel's wake. He led them off the docks and onto the north beach, moving fast toward the dark rocks that sheltered Carradoon's harbor from the northern winds.

"We can't get over those cliffs!" one man complained.

"We're too near the water!" another woman cried, and indeed, a trio of undead sailors came splashing at them, forcing Temberle and Hanaleisa and other warriors to protect their right flank all the way.

All the way to an apparent dead end, where the rocky path rose up a long slope, then ended at a drop to the stone-filled lake.

"Brilliant," the captain complained, moving near Pikel. "Ye've killed us all, ye fool dwarf!"

It surely seemed as if he spoke the truth, for the undead were in pursuit and the group had nowhere left to run.

But Pikel was unbothered. He stood on the edge of the drop, beside a swaying pine, and closed his eyes, chanting his druidic magic. The tree responded by lowering a branch down before him.

"Hee hee hee," said Pikel, opening his eyes and handing the branch to Rorick, who stood beside him.

"What?" the young man asked.

Pikel nodded to the drop, and directed Rorick's gaze to a cave at the back of the inlet.

"You want me to jump down there?" Rorick asked, incredulous. "You want me to *swing* down?"

Pikel nodded, and pushed him off the ledge.

The screaming Rorick, guided by the obedient tree, was set down—as gently as a mother lays her infant in its crib—on a narrow strip of stone beside the watery inlet. He waited there for the captain and two others, who came down on the next swing, before heading toward the cave.

Pikel was the last one off the ledge, with a host of zombies and skeletons closing in as he leaped. Several of the monsters jumped after him, only to fall and shatter on the stones below.

His cudgel glowing brightly, Pikel moved past the huddled group and led the way into the cave, which at first glance seemed a wide, high, and shallow chamber, ankle deep with water. But Pikel's instincts and his magical call to the earth had guided him well. On the back wall of that shallow cave was a sidelong corridor leading deeper into the cliffs, and deeper still into the Snowflake Mountains.

Into that darkness went two score of Carradoon's survivors, half of them capable fighters, the other half frightened citizens, some elderly, some too young to wield a weapon. Just a short while into the retreat, they came to a defensible spot where the corridor ended at a narrow chimney, and through that chimney was another chamber.

There they decided to make their first camp, a circle of guards standing at the cave entrance, which they covered with a heavy stone, and more guarding the two corridors that led out of the chamber, deeper into the mountains.

No more complaints were shouted Uncle Pikel's way.

* * * * *

Jarlaxle slid his wand away, shouting to Athrogate, "Just his face!"

The drow leaped from his mount to the back of the wagon, charging right past Bruenor, who was down on one knee, his right hand grasping his left shoulder in an attempt to stem the flow of spraying blood.

Twinkle had cut right through the dwarf's fine armor and dug deeply into the flesh beneath.

Jarlaxle seized Catti-brie just as she floated over the back of the wagon, having been jostled hard by the thrashing and running Drizzt. Jarlaxle pulled her in and hugged her closely, as Drizzt had done, and started that same journey to insanity.

Jarlaxle knew the distortions for what they were, the magic of his eye patch fighting back the deception. So he held Catti-brie and whispered softly to her as she sobbed. Gradually, he was able to ease her down to the floorboards of the wagon, moving her to a sitting position against the side wall.

He turned away, shaking his head, to find Thibbledorf Pwent

hard at work tearing off Bruenor's blood-soaked sleeve.

"Ah, me king," the battlerager lamented.

"He's breathing," Athrogate called from the side of the trail, where Drizzt remained stuck fast by the viscous glob Jarlaxle's wand had launched at him. "And seethin', thrashing and slashin', not moving at all but wantin' to be bashin'!"

"Don't ask," Jarlaxle said as both Bruenor and Pwent looked Athrogate's way, then questioningly back at Jarlaxle.

"What just happened?" Bruenor demanded.

"To your daughter, I do not know," Jarlaxle admitted. "But when I went to her, I was drawn through her into a dark place." He glanced furtively at Drizzt. "A place where our friend remains, I fear."

"Regis," Bruenor muttered. He looked at Jarlaxle, but the drow was staring into the distance, lost in thought. "What d'ya know?" Bruenor demanded, but Jarlaxle just shook his head.

The drow mercenary looked at Catti-brie again and thought of the sudden journey he had taken when he'd touched her. It was more than an illusion, he believed. It was almost as if his mind had walked into another plane of existence. The Plane of Shadow, perhaps, or some other dark region he hoped never to visit again.

But even on that short journey, Jarlaxle hadn't really gone away, as if that plane and the Prime Material Plane had overlapped, joined in some sort of curious and dangerous rift.

He thought about the specter he'd encountered when Hephaestus had come looking for him, of the dimensional hole he had thrown over the creature, and of the rift to the Astral Plane that he'd inadvertently created.

Had that specter, that huddled creature, been physically passing back and forth from Toril to that shadowy dimension?

"It's real," he said quietly.

"What?" Bruenor and Pwent demanded together.

Jarlaxle looked at them and shook his head, not sure how he could explain what he feared had come to pass.

* * * * *

"He's calming down," Athrogate called from the tree. "Asking for the girl, and talking to me."

With Pwent's help, Bruenor pulled himself to his feet and went with the drow and the dwarf to Drizzt's side.

"What're ye about, elf?" Bruenor asked when he got to Drizzt, who was perfectly helpless, stuck fast against the tree.

"What happened?" the drow ranger replied, his gaze fixed on Bruenor's arm.

"Just a scratch," Bruenor assured him.

"Bah, but two fingers higher and ye'd have taken his head!" Athrogate cut in, and both Bruenor and Jarlaxle glared at the brash dwarf.

"I did—?" Drizzt started to ask, but he stopped and scowled with a perplexed look.

"Just like back at Mithral Hall," muttered Bruenor.

"I know where Regis is," Drizzt said, looking up with alarm. He was sure the others could tell that he was even more afraid for his little friend at that dark moment. And his face twisted with more fear and pain when he glanced over at Catti-brie. If Regis's mind had inadvertently entered and been trapped in that dark place, then Catti-brie was surely caught between the two worlds.

"Yerself came back, elf, and so'll the little one," Bruenor assured him.

Drizzt wasn't so confident of that. He had barely set his toes in that umbral dimension, but with the ruby, Regis had entered the very depths of Catti-brie's mind.

Jarlaxle flicked his wrist, and a dagger appeared in his hand. He motioned for Athrogate to move aside, and stepped forward, bending low, carefully cutting Drizzt free.

"If you mean to go mad again, do warn me," Jarlaxle said to Drizzt with a wink.

Drizzt neither replied nor smiled. His expression became darker still when Athrogate walked over, holding the drow's lost scimitar, red with the blood of his dearest friend.

PART 2

PRYING THE RIFT

PRYING THE RIFT

I know she is in constant torment, and I cannot go to her. I have seen into the darkness in which she resides, a place of shadows more profound and more grim than the lower planes. She took me there, inadvertently, when I tried to offer some comfort, and there, in so short a time, I nearly broke.

She took Regis there, inadvertently, when he tried to reach her with the ruby, and there he broke fully. He threw the drowning Catti-brie a rope and she pulled him from the shore of sanity.

She is lost to me. Forever, I fear. Lost in an oblivious state, a complete emptiness, a listless and lifeless existence. And those rare occasions when she is active are perhaps the most painful of all to me, for the depth of her delusions shines all too clearly. It's as if she's reliving her life, piecemeal, seeing again those pivotal moments that shaped this beautiful woman, this woman I love with all my heart. She stood again on the side of Kelvin's Cairn back in Icewind Dale, living again the moment when first we met, and while that to me is among my most precious of memories, that fact made seeing it play out again through the distant eyes of my love even more painful.

How lost must my beloved Catti-brie be to have so broken with the world around her?

And Regis, poor Regis. I cannot know how deeply into that darkness Catti-brie now resides, but it's obvious to me that Regis went fully into that place of shadows. I can attest to the convincing nature of his delusions, as can Bruenor, whose shoulder now carries the scar of my blade as I fought off imaginary monsters. Or were they imaginary? I cannot begin to know. But that is a moot point to Regis, for to him they are surely real, and they're all around him, ever clawing at him, wounding him and terrifying him relentlessly.

We four—Bruenor, Catti-brie, Regis, and I—are representative of the world around us, I fear. The fall of Luskan, Captain Deudermont's folly, the advent of Obould—all of it were but the precursors. For now we have the collapse of that which we once believed eternal, the unraveling of Mystra's Weave. The enormity of that catastrophe is easy to see on the face of the always calm Lady Alustriel. The potential results of it are reflected in the insanity of Regis, the emptiness of Catti-brie, the near-loss of my own sanity, and the scar carried by King Bruenor.

More than the wizards of Faerûn will feel the weight of this dramatic change. How will diseases be quelled if the gods do not hear the desperate pleas of their priests? How will the kings of the world fare when any contact to potential rivals and allies, instead of commonplace through divination and teleportation, becomes an arduous and lengthy process? How weakened will be the armies, the caravans, the small towns, without the potent power of magic-users among their ranks? And what gains will the more base races, like goblins and orcs, make in the face of such sudden magical weakness? What druids will tend the fields? What magic will bolster and secure the exotic structures of the world? Or will they fall catastrophically as did the Hosttower of the Arcane, or long-dead Netheril?

Not so long ago, I had a conversation with Nanfoodle the gnome in Mithral Hall. We discussed his cleverness in funneling explosive gasses under the mountain ridge where Obould's giant allies had set up devastating artillery. Quite an engineering feat by the gnome and his crew of dwarves, and one that blew the mountain ridge apart more fully than even a fireball from Elminster could have done. Nanfoodle is much more a follower of Gond, the god of inventions, than he is a practitioner of the Art. I asked him about that, inquiring as to why he tinkered so when so much of what he might do could be accomplished more quickly by simply touching the Weave.

I never got an answer, of course, as that is not Nanfoodle's wont. Instead, he launched into a philosophical discussion of the false comfort we take in our dependence on, and expectation of, "that which is."

Never has his point been more clear to me than it is now, as I see "that which is" collapsing around us all.

Do the farmers around the larger cities of Faerûn, around Waterdeep and Silverymoon, know how to manage their produce without the magical aid of the druids? Without such magical help, will they be able to meet the demands of the large populations in those cities? And that is only the top level of the problems that will arise should magic fail! Even the sewers of Waterdeep are complicated affairs, built over many generations, and aided at certain critical points, since the city has so expanded, by the power of wizards, summoning elementals to help usher away the waste. Without them—what?

And what of Calimport? Regis has told me often that there are far too many people there, beyond any sensible number for which the ocean and desert could possibly provide. But the fabulously rich Pashas have supplemented their natural resources by employing mighty clerics to summon food and drink for the markets, and mighty wizards to teleport in fresh sustenance from faraway lands.

Without that aid, what chaos might ensue?

And, of course, in my own homeland of Menzoberranzan, it is magic that keeps the kobolds enslaved, magic that protects the greater Houses from their envious rivals, and magic that holds together the threads of the entire society. Lady Lolth loves chaos, they say, and so she may see it in the extreme if that magic fades!

The societies of the world have grown over the centuries. The systems we have in place have evolved through the many generations, and in that evolution, I fear, we have long forgotten the basic foundations of society's structures. Worse, perhaps, even re-learning those lost arts and crafts will not likely suffice to meet the needs of lands grown fatter and more populous because of the magical supplements to the old ways. Calimport could never have supported her enormous population centuries ago.

Nor could the world, a much wider place by far, have attained such a level of singularity, of oneness, of community, as it has now. For people travel and communicate to and with distant lands much more now than in times long past. Many of the powerful merchants in Baldur's Gate are often seen in Waterdeep, and vice versa. Their networks extend over the leagues because their wizards can maintain them. And those networks are vital in ensuring that there will be no war between such mighty rival cities. If the people of Baldur's Gate are dependent upon the craftsmen and farmers of Waterdeep, then they will want no war with that city!

But what happens if it all collapses? What happens if "that which is" suddenly is not? How will we cope when the food runs out, and the diseases cannot be defeated through godly intervention?

Will the people of the world band together to create new realities and structures to fulfill the needs of the masses?

Or will all the world know calamity, on a scale never before seen?

The latter, I fear. The removal of "that which is" will bring war and distance and a world of pockets of civilization huddled defensively in corners against the intrusion of murderous insanity.

I look helplessly at Catti-brie's lifelessness, at Regis's terror, and at Bruenor's torn shoulder and I fear that I am seeing the future.

—Drizzt Do'Urden

CHAPTER 10

BEARDED PROXY

"You garner too much enjoyment from so simple a trick," Hephaestus said to his companion in a cave south of Spirit Soaring.

"It is a matter of simple efficiency and expedience, dragon, from which I take no measure of enjoyment," Yharaskrik answered in the voice of Ivan Bouldershoulder, whose body the illithid had come to reside in—partially, at least.

Any who knew Ivan would have scratched their heads in surprise at the strange accent in the dwarf's gravelly voice. A closer inspection would only have added to the onlooker's sense of strangeness, for Ivan stood too calmly. He refrained from tugging at the hairs of his great yellow beard, shifting from one foot to the other, or thumping his hands against his hips or chest, as was typical.

"I am still within you," Yharaskrik added. "Hephaestus, Crenshinibon, and Yharaskrik as one. Holding this dwarf under my control allows me to give external voice to our conversations, though that is rarely a good thing."

"While you are reading my every thought," the dragon replied, no small amount of sarcasm in his tone, "you have externalized a portion of your consciousness to shield your own thoughts from me."

The dwarf bowed.

"You do not deny it?" Hephaestus asked.

"I am in your consciousness, dragon. You know what I know. Any question you ask of me is rendered rhetorical."

"But we are no longer fully joined," Hephaestus protested, and the dwarf chuckled. The dragon's confusion was apparent. "Are you not wise enough to segment your thoughts into small compartments, some within and some, in the guise of that ugly little dwarf, without?"

The Yharaskrik in Ivan's body bowed again. "You flatter me, great Hephaestus. Trust that we are inexorably joined. I could no more hurt you than harm myself, for to do to one is truly to do to the other. You know this is true."

"Then why did you reach out to the dwarf, this proxy host?"

"Because for you, particularly, who have never known such mental intimacy," the illithid answered, "it can become confusing as to where one voice stops and the other begins. We might find ourselves battling for control of the body we both inhabit, working each other to exhaustion over the simplest of movements. It is better this way."

"So you say."

"Look within yourself, Hephaestus."

The dracolich did exactly that and for a long while did not reply. Finally, he looked the dwarf straight in the eye and said, "It is a good thing."

Yharaskrik bowed again. He glanced to the side of the chamber, past the four animated corpses of the Baldurian wizards, to the pair of huddled creatures in the deeper shadows.

"As Crenshinibon has externalized parts of itself," the illithid said in the dwarf's voice.

Fetchigrol stepped forward before Hephaestus could respond. "We are Crenshinibon," the specter said. "Now we are apart in body, sundered by the magic of the falling Weave, but we are one in thought."

Hephaestus nodded his gigantic head, but Yharaskrik, who had felt a strange evolution over the last few days, disagreed. "You are not," the illithid argued. "You are tentacles of the squid, but there is independence in your movements."

"We do as we are commanded," Fetchigrol protested, but it rang hollow to the Ghost King. The illithid was correct in his assessment. The seven apparitions were gaining a small measure of independent thought once more, though neither feared that the Ghost King could be threatened by such an occurrence.

"You are fine soldiers for the cause of Crenshinibon," said Yharaskrik. "Yet within the philosophy that guides you there is independence, as you have shown here in these mountains."

The specter let out a low groan.

"We exist in two worlds," Yharaskrik explained. "And a third, because of Crenshinibon, because of the sacrifice of Fetchigrol and his six brethren. How easy it was for you, how easy it is for us all, to reach into the realm of death and bring forth mindless minions, and so Fetchigrol did."

"Carradoon is in chaos," the specter's voice said, though the dark humanoid's face gave no indication that it spoke. "As the fleeing humans are killed, they join our ranks."

Yharaskrik waved his hand to the side, to the four undead wizards he had lifted from their death, one even before the flames of a fireball had stopped crinkling its blackened skin. "And how easy it is!" the illithid said, the even cadence of its voice thrown aside for the first time in the conversation. "With this power alone, we are mighty."

"But we have more than this singular power," Hephaestus said.

Fetchigrol's spectral companion floated forward, willed by the Ghost King.

"The fodder of Shadowfell are ours for the calling," Solmé said. "The gate is not thick. The door is not locked. The crawlers hunger for the flesh of Toril."

"And as they kill, our ranks grow," Fetchigrol said.

Yharaskrik nodded and closed his dwarf eyes, pondering the possibilities. This curious twist of circumstance, this fortuitous blending of magic, intellect, and brute power, of Crenshinibon, Yharaskrik, and Hephaestus, had created seemingly unlimited possibilities.

But had it also created a common purpose?

To conquer, or to destroy? To meditate, to contemplate, to explore? What fruit had the tree of fate served? To what end?

Hephaestus's growl brought Yharaskrik from his contemplation, to see the dragon staring at him with suspicion.

"Where we eventually wander is not the immediate concern," the dragon warned, his voice thick with pent up rage. "I will have my revenge."

Yharaskrik heard the dragon's internal dialogue quite clearly, flashing with images of Spirit Soaring, the home of the priest who had aided in the demise of all three of the joined spirits. On that place, the dragon focused its hatred and wrath. They had flown over the building the night before, and even then, Yharaskrik and Crenshinibon had to overrule the reflexive anger of Hephaestus. Had it not been for those two mediating internal voices, the dragon would have swooped down upon the place in an explosive fit of sheer malevolence.

Yharaskrik did not openly disagree, and didn't even allow its mind to show any signal of contrary thought.

"Straightaway!" Hephaestus roared.

"No," the illithid then dared argue. "Magic is unwinding, arcane at least, and in some cases divine, but it has not fully unwound. It is not lost to the world, but merely undependable. This place, Spirit Soaring, is filled with mighty priests and wizards. To underestimate the assemblage of power there is fraught with peril. In the time of our choosing, it will fall, and they will fall. But no sooner."

Hephaestus growled again, long and low, but Yharaskrik feared no outburst from the beast, for he knew that Crenshinibon continually reinforced its reasoning within Hephaestus. The dragon wanted action, devastating and catastrophic, wanted to rain death upon all of those who had helped facilitate his downfall. Impulsive and explosive was Hephaestus's nature, was the way of dragonkind.

But the way of the illithid required patience and careful consideration, and no sentient creature in the world was more patient than Crenshinibon, who had seen the span of millennia.

They overruled Hephaestus and calmed the beast. Their promises of a smoldering ruin where Spirit Soaring stood were not without merit, intent, and honest expectation, and of course, Hephaestus knew that as surely as if the thought was his own.

The dracolich curled up with those fantasies. He, too, could be a creature of patience.

To a point.

* * * * *

"Hold that flank!" Rorick yelled to the men on the left-hand wall of the cave, scattered amidst a tumble of rocks. They stood in ankle-deep water and battled hard against a throng of skeletons and zombies. The center of the defensive line, bolstered by the three Bonaduce children and Pikel, held strong against the attacking undead. The water was nearly knee-deep there, its drag affecting the advancing monsters more than the defenders.

To the right, the contours and bends of the tunnel also favored the defenders. Before them, where the tunnel opened even wider, lay a deep pool. Skeletons and zombies alike that ventured there went completely underwater, and those that managed to claw back up were rained on by heavy clubs. That pool was the primary reason the defenders had chosen to make their stand there when at last the hordes had found them. Initially, it had seemed a prudent choice, but the relentlessness of their enemies was starting to make many, including Temberle and Hanaleisa, think that maybe they should have chosen a more narrow choke point than a thirty-foot expanse.

"They won't hold," Rorick said to his siblings even as Hanaleisa kicked the head off a skeleton and sent it flying far down the tunnel.

Hanaleisa didn't need clarification to know what he meant. Her gaze went immediately to the left, to the many rocks along that broken section of tunnel. They had believed those rocks to be an advantage, forcing the undead press of monsters to carve up their advancing line to get past the many obstacles. But since the monsters had engaged, those many scattered boulders were working against the defenders, who too often found themselves cut off from their allies.

Hanaleisa slapped Temberle on the shoulder and splashed away to the side. She had barely gone two steps, though, before Rorick cried out in pain. She spun back as Rorick fell, lifting his already injured leg, blood streaming anew. Temberle reached for him, but a splash sent Temberle tumbling. A skeletal fish broke the water and smacked him hard in the face.

All across the middle of the line, defenders began shifting and groaning as undead fish knifed through the water and found targets.

"Retreat!" one man cried. "Run away!"

"Nowhere to run!" shouted another.

"Back down the tunnel!" the first screamed back, and began splashing his way deeper into the cave with several others in his wake. The integrity of their center collapsed behind them.

Rorick and Temberle regained their footing at the same time. Rorick waved his brother away. Temberle, blood running freely from his broken nose, turned back fast and hoisted his heavy greatsword.

Hanaleisa glanced to the left flank just in time to see a man pulled down under a dozen rotting hands. Out of options, all of it crumbling before her eyes, she could only cry out, "Uncle Pikel!" as she had done so many times in her life, whenever confronted by a childhood crisis.

If Pikel was listening, it didn't show, for the green-bearded dwarf stood away from the front line, his eyes closed. He held his hand out before him, gripping his magical cudgel, and he waved his stump in slow circles. Hanaleisa started to call out to him again, but saw that he was already chanting.

The young monk glanced toward the left wall and back to the center. Realizing she had to trust her uncle, she bolted for the rocks, toward the group of skeletons pummeling and tearing the fallen defender. She leaped into their midst, fists and feet flailing with power and precision. She kicked one skeleton aside and crushed the chest of a zombie. She immediately went up on the ball of her foot, the other leg extended and pumping furiously as she turned a fast circle.

"Come to me!" she called to the fallen man's companions, many of whom seemed to be turning to flee, as had several of those from the center of the line.

Hanaleisa winced then as a skeletal hand clamped upon her shoulder, bony fingers digging a deep gash. She threw back an elbow that shattered the creature's face and sent it falling away.

Then she redoubled her kicking and punching, determined to fight to the bitter end.

The men and women deeper in the cave abandoned all thoughts of retreat and came on furiously. Hanaleisa had inspired them. Hanaleisa had shamed them.

The warrior monk took some satisfaction in that as the horde was beaten back and the fallen man was pulled from the undead grasp. She doubted it would matter in the end, but still, for some reason, it mattered to her. They would die with honor and courage, and that had to count for something.

She glanced at her brothers just as Pikel, on his fourth try, finally completed his spell. A shining white orb as big as Hanaleisa's fist popped from the dwarf's shillelagh and sailed over the heads of the lead defenders. The orb hit a skeleton and bounced off. Hanaleisa's mouth dropped open in surprise as the skeleton that had been hit locked up and iced over.

"What—?" she managed to say as the small orb splashed into the water. Then she and everyone else gasped in shock as the radius of the pond around the orb froze solid.

The fighters in front yelled out in surprise and pain as the icy grasp spread to them and knocked them backward or grabbed them and froze them in place. An unintended consequence, no doubt, but no matter, for the monstrous advance, including the insidious undead fish, was immediately halted.

Frigid trails spread from the center of the ice, moving to the sides and away from the defenders, following Pikel's will.

"Now!" Hanaleisa called to her fellows at the left wall, and they moved furiously to turn back the undead tide.

Those not caught in the ice chopped vigorously to free their companions. They moved with desperation when they saw newly arrived undead from behind the frozen area coming on undeterred, climbing up on the ice and using their stuck companions as handholds to help them navigate across the slippery surface.

But Pikel had bought the defenders enough time, and the battered and bruised group retreated down the tunnel, deeper under the mountains, until they crossed through a narrow corridor, a single-file passageway that finally opened—mercifully—into a wider chamber some hundred strides along. At the exit to that tunnel, they made their stand. Two warriors met the undead as they tried to come through.

And when those two grew weary or suffered injuries, two others took their place.

Meanwhile, behind them, Rorick organized a line of defenders who had found large rocks, and when he was certain he had enough, he called out for the defenders to stand aside. One by one, his line advanced and hurled rocks into the tunnel, driving back skeletons and zombies. As soon as each had let fly, they ran off to find another rock.

This went on for some time, until the rocks hit only other rocks, until the monsters were driven back and blocked behind a growing wall of stone. When it ended, the stubborn monsters still clawing on the back side of the barricade, Pikel stepped forward and began to gently rub the stone and dirt of the tunnel walls. He called to the plants, bidding them to come forth, and so they sent their vines and their roots, intertwining behind and among the stones, locking them ever so securely.

For the moment, at least, it seemed that the threat had ended. It had come with many cuts and bruises and even more serious wounds, and the man who had been pulled down amid the undead wouldn't be fighting any time soon, if he managed to survive his injuries. And the defenders were deep into the tunnels, in a place of darkness they did not know. How many other tunnels might they find under the foothills of the Snowflakes, and how many monsters might find those as well, and come against them yet again?

"So what are we to do?" a man asked as the enormity of their situation settled upon them.

"We hide, and we fight," said a determined Temberle, sniffling through his shattered nose.

"And we die," said another, an old, surly, gray-bearded fishing boat captain.

"Aye, then we get back up and fight for th'other side," another added.

Temberle, Hanaleisa, and Rorick all looked to each other, but had no rebuttal.

"Ooooh," said Pikel.

CHAPTER 11
LIVING NIGHTMARE

"I need to get you new mounts," Jarlaxle said with an exaggerated sigh.

"We done a thousand miles and more from Mithral Hall," Bruenor reminded. "And pushed them hard all the way. Even with the shoes. . . ." He shook his head. Indeed, the fine mules had reached their limit, for the time being at least, but had performed brilliantly. From dawn to dusk, they had pulled the wagon, every day. Aided by the magical shoes and the fine design and construction of their load, they had covered more ground each and every day than an average team might cross in a tenday.

"True enough," the drow admitted. "But they are weary indeed."

Drizzt and Bruenor looked at each other curiously as Pwent shouted, "I want one o' them!" and pointed at Athrogate's fire-spitting boar.

"Bwahaha!" Athrogate yelled back. "Be sure that I'm feeling big, ridin' into battle on me fiery pig! And when them orcs figure out me game, I squeeze him on the flanks and fart them into flame! Bwahaha!"

"Bwahaha!" Thibbledorf Pwent echoed.

"Can we just harness them two up to pull the damned wagon?" Bruenor asked, waving a hand at the other two dwarves. "I'll nail the magical shoes on their feet."

"You understand the pain I've known for the last decade," Jarlaxle said.

"Yet you keep him around," Drizzt pointed out.

"Because he is strong against my enemies and can hold back their charge," said Jarlaxle. "And I can outrun him should we need to retreat."

Jarlaxle handed the mule off to Drizzt, who slowly walked the weary beast around to the back of the wagon, where he had just tethered its partner. Their days of pulling the wagon were over, for a while at least.

The hells-born nightmare resisted Jarlaxle's tug as he tried to put it in the harness.

"He's not liking that," said Bruenor.

"He has no choice in the matter," Jarlaxle replied, and he managed at last to harness the beast. He clapped the dirt off his hands and moved to climb up beside Pwent and Bruenor on the jockey box. "Keep the pace strong and steady, good dwarf. You will find the demon horse more than up to the . . ." He paused, and in pulling himself up, encountered the skeptical expressions of both dwarves. "I give you my mount, and you would have me walk?" Jarlaxle asked as if wounded.

Pwent looked to Bruenor.

"Let him up," Bruenor decided.

"I'll protect ye, me king!" Pwent declared as Jarlaxle took his seat next to the battlerager, with Pwent between the mercenary and Bruenor.

"He'd kill you before you ever knew the fight had started," Drizzt remarked as he walked past.

Pwent's eyes went wide with alarm.

"Oh, it is true," Jarlaxle assured him.

Pwent started to stutter and stammer, but Bruenor nudged him hard.

"What, me king?" the battlerager asked.

"Just shut up," said Bruenor, and Jarlaxle laughed.

The dwarf king snapped the reins, but instead of moving ahead, the nightmare snorted fire and turned its head around in protest.

"Please, allow me," Jarlaxle said with obvious alarm as he grabbed at the reins, which Bruenor relinquished.

With no movement of the reins at all, Jarlaxle willed the nightmare forward. The demonic creature had no trouble pulling the wagon. The only thing that slowed the pace was the drow's deference to the two mules tied to the back, both exhausted from the long road.

And indeed it had been long, for they had covered most of the leagues by morning, and the Snowflake Mountains were in sight, though fully a day's travel away.

Jarlaxle assured them that his magical beast could continue after the sun had set, that it could even see in the dark, but out of continued deference to the mules, who had given the journey their all, Bruenor called for a halt that mid afternoon. They went about setting their camp in the foothills.

Jarlaxle dismissed his nightmare back to its home on a lower plane, and Athrogate did likewise with his demonic boar. Then Athrogate and Pwent went out to find logs and boulders to fashion some defenses for their camp. They had barely started moving, though, and Jarlaxle and Bruenor had just untied the mules when the beasts began shifting nervously and snorting in protest.

"What's that about?" Bruenor asked.

Jarlaxle tugged the reins of his mule straight down, hard, but the creature snorted in protest and pulled back.

"Wait," Drizzt said to them. He was in the wagon, standing beside the seated Catti-brie, and when the others looked to him for clarification, they went silent, seeing the ranger on his guard, his eyes locked on the trees across the road.

"What're ye seeing, elf?" Bruenor whispered, but Drizzt just shook his hand, which was outstretched toward the dwarf, bidding him to silence.

Jarlaxle quietly retied the mules to the wagon, his gaze darting between Drizzt and the trees.

Drizzt slid Taulmaril off his shoulder and strung it.

"Elf?" Bruenor whispered.

"What in the Nine Hells?" Thibbledorf Pwent howled then, from behind the trio.

Bruenor and Jarlaxle both looked back at him to see a long-armed, short-legged creature with bloated gray and black skin dragging itself over the boulders toward Pwent and Athrogate. Drizzt never turned his gaze from the trees, and soon enough saw another of the same monster crash out of the underbrush.

The drow froze—he knew those strange creatures all too well, those clawing, huddled, shadowy things. He had gone to their umbral home.

Catti-brie was there.

And Regis.

Had he gone there again? He lifted his bow and leveled it for a shot, but took a deep breath, thinking that he might again be in that state of mental confusion. Would he let fly only to put an arrow through Bruenor's heart?

"Shoot it, Drizzt," he heard Jarlaxle say in Deep Drow—a language Drizzt hadn't heard spoken in a long time. It was as if Jarlaxle had read his thoughts perfectly. *"You are not imagining this!"*

Drizzt pulled back and let fly, and the magical bow launched a searing line of energy, like lightning, at the fleshy beast, splattering its chest and throwing it back into the brush.

But where there was one, there were many, and a shout behind from the two dwarves clued Drizzt in to that fact even as more of them crashed out onto the road before him.

The ranger pumped his arms furiously, reaching into his magical quiver to draw forth arrow after arrow, nock it, and let it fly, tearing the darkness with sizzling lines of bright lightning. So thick were the beasts that almost every arrow hit a fleshy mass, some burning through to strike a second monster behind the first. The stench of burning flesh fouled the air, and a sickly bubbling and popping sound filled the dead calm between the thunderous blasts of Taulmaril.

Despite the devastation he rained on the crawlers, they came on. Many crossed the road and neared the wagon. Drizzt let fly another shot, then had to drop Taulmaril and draw out his blades to meet the onslaught.

Beside him, Bruenor leaped down from the wagon, banging his old, trusted shield, emblazoned with the foaming mug of Clan Battlehammer. He gripped his many-notched axe, a weapon he had carried for decades upon decades. As the dwarf leaped down, Jarlaxle sprang up onto the seat and drew out a pair of thin wands, including the one he had used earlier to restrain Drizzt.

"Fireball," he explained to Bruenor, who looked at him, about to ask why he wasn't on the ground with a weapon in his hand.

"Then light 'em up!"

But Jarlaxle considered for a moment, and shook his head, unsure of the casting. If his other wand malfunctioned, he might glue himself to the wagon, but if this one backfired, he'd light himself up, and Bruenor and Catti-brie, too.

To the dwarf's surprise, Jarlaxle shifted both wands to his left hand, then snapped his right wrist, bringing forth a blade from his magical bracer. A second snap of his wrist elongated that blade to a short sword. A third and final thrust made it a long sword.

Jarlaxle moved to put the fireball wand away, but changed his mind and slid the other one into his belt. If the situation deteriorated to where he needed to use a device, he decided, he'd have to take the chance.

* * * * *

Athrogate worked his morningstars magnificently, the heavy spiked balls humming at the ends of their chains, weaving out before him, to this side and that, and over his head.

"Get out yer weapon!" he yelled at Thibbledorf Pwent.

"I *am* me weapon, ye dolt!" the battlerager yelled back, and as the fleshy creature crawled nearer, just before Athrogate stepped forward to launch a barrage of flying morningstars, Pwent charged and dived upon the enemy, fists pumping, knees thumping. Locked in place with his fist spikes, the trapped creature flailing and biting at him, Pwent went into a wild and furious gyration, a violent convulsion, a seizure of sorts, it seemed.

The dwarf's ridged armor tore apart the beast's flesh, fast reducing the monster to a misshapen lump of pulped meat.

"Bwahaha!" Athrogate cheered, grinning, saluting and bellylaughing as he leaped past Pwent and went into an arm-rolling assault of morningstar over morningstar at the next beast coming in.

The blunt weapons weren't quite as lethal against the thick and malleable flesh, which gave way under the weight of their punishment. A typical fighter with a normal morningstar would have found himself in sorry shape against the shadowy crawlers, but Athrogate was no typical fighter. His strength was that of a giant, his skills honed over centuries of battle, and his morningstars, too, were far from the usual.

He worked the weapons expertly, maneuvering himself right in front of the battered creature before coming in with a mighty overhead chop that splattered the crawler across the stone before him.

He had no time to salute himself, and just enough time to tell Pwent to get up, before another three beasts came in hard at him, with many more following.

Black clawing hands reached at him repeatedly, but Athrogate kept his morningstars spinning, driving them back. Out of the corner of his eye, though, the dwarf saw another monster, on the branch of a tree not far away, and when that beast leaped at him, Athrogate had no manner of defense.

He did manage to close his eyes.

* * * * *

Bruenor reminded himself that Catti-brie lay helpless behind him in the wagon. With that thought in the dwarf's mind, the first crawler dragging itself at him got cut in half, head to crotch, by a mighty two-handed overhead chop. Ignoring a fountain of blood and gore, Bruenor kicked his way through the mess and took out a second with a sidelong cut, blocking the third's slashing claws with his heavy buckler.

He felt a fourth coming from the other way and instinctively cut across hard with his axe, not realizing until it was too late that it was a drow, not a fleshy beast.

But the nimble Jarlaxle leaped up and tucked in his legs. "Careful, friend," he said as he landed, though he slurred his words for the wand he carried in his teeth. He stepped in front of the surprised dwarf, stabbing forward with two swords, popping deep holes in the chest of the next approaching monster.

"Could've warned me," Bruenor grumbled, and went back to chopping and slashing. A screech behind him and to his right warned him that the beasts had reached the mules.

*****

Drizzt didn't even have a moment to take in the sight of Bruenor and Jarlaxle fighting side by side, something he never expected to see. He rushed in front of the duo, slashing with every stride, and into a fast spin, blades cutting hard and barely even slowing when they sliced through the meaty body of a crawler. A second spin followed, the mighty ranger moving along as he turned, and he came out of it with three running strides, stabbing repeatedly. He pulled up short and turned, then leaped and flipped sidelong over another of the creatures, managing to stab down twice as he went over. Drizzt landed lightly on the other side of it, immediately falling into another spin, his scimitars humming through the air and through gray-black flesh all around him.

The drow turned back toward the wagon then, and took heart in seeing Jarlaxle's nightmare punishing any crawlers that came too near, the hellish steed stomping its hooves and blasting out miniature fireballs.

Drizzt cut in behind it, his eyes going wide as he saw a beast coming over the opposite side rail. The drow hit the jockey box in full stride and leaped over the rail without slowing. He darted in front of Catti-brie at full speed, his scimitars cutting apart the beast as he passed.

How he wanted to stay with her! But he couldn't, not with the mules tugging and thrashing in terror.

He sprang down right between them, agilely avoiding their kicks and stomps, and deftly clearing away enemies with precision thrusts and stabs.

Just behind the mules, he stopped and veered again, thinking to re-run the route.

No need, he realized as soon as he took note of Jarlaxle and Bruenor, fighting together as if they had shared a mentor and a hundred battles. Jarlaxle's fighting style, favoring forward-rolling his blades and stabbing, compared to Drizzt's wide-armed slashes, complemented Bruenor's straight-ahead ferocity. In tandem, they worked in short, angled bursts for one to engage a creature, then hand it off to his partner for the killing blow.

With a surprised grin, Drizzt slipped behind them instead of in front of them, running a circuit of the wagon and taking care to give the furiously thrashing nightmare a wide berth.

* * * * *

Athrogate yelled out, thinking himself doomed, but a second form flew through the air, head down, helmet spike leveled. Thibbledorf Pwent hit the leaping crawler squarely, skewering it with his spiked helm and pushing it aside with him as he crashed to the rocky ground. He bounced up and began hopping about, the fleshy beast bouncing atop his head, fully stuck and dying fast.

"Oh, but that's great!" Athrogate cried. "That's just great!"

Too enraged to hear him, the fierce battlerager charged into a group of the beasts, thrashing and punching and kneeing and kicking, even biting when one clawed hand came too near his face.

Athrogate rushed up beside him, morningstars spinning furiously, splattering black flesh with every powerful swing. Side by side, the dwarves advanced, enemies flying all about, one still bobbing in its death throes atop the helmet spike of Thibbledorf Pwent.

Bruenor and Jarlaxle fought a more defensive battle, holding their ground with measured chops and stabs. As the ranks of monsters thinned and the wagon became secure, Drizzt hopped up on the bench, retrieved his bow, and began firing toward the tree line with flashing arrows, further thinning the horde coming at Bruenor and Jarlaxle.

Pwent and Athrogate, their rocky campsite cleared, joined the others, and Drizzt again dropped the bow and drew out his scimitars. With a communal nod and knowing grins, the five went out in a line of devastation, sweeping clear the grassy patch near the road and sweeping clear the road as well before turning and running as one back to the wagon.

With nothing left to hit, four of the group, the dwarves and Jarlaxle, each took up positions north, south, east, and west around the wagon. Drizzt scrambled into the wagon bed beside Catti-brie, Taulmaril the Heartseeker in hand, ready to support his comrades.

His attention was soon turned to his beloved cargo, though, and he looked down to see Catti-brie jerking spasmodically, standing upright though she was not trying to walk. She floated off the ground, her eyes rolling back in her head.

"Oh, no," Drizzt muttered, and he had to fall back. Most agonizing of all, he had to step away from his tortured wife.

CHAPTER 12
WHEN THE SHADOWS CAME TO THE LIGHT

Danica and Cadderly rushed through the hallways of Spirit Soaring to see what the commotion was all about. They had to push through a bevy of whispering wizards and priests to squeeze their way out the door, and the grand front porch of the structure was no less crowded.

"Stay up here!" a mage called to Danica as she squirmed through and jumped down the steps to the cobblestones. "Cadderly, don't let her . . ."

The man eased up on his protests as Cadderly lifted a hand to silence him. The priest trusted in Danica, and reminded the others to do the same. Still, Cadderly was more than a little perplexed by the sight before him. Deer, rabbits, squirrels, and all manner of animals charged across the lawn of Spirit Soaring, in full flight.

"There was a bear," an older priest explained.

"A bear is scaring them like this?" Cadderly asked with obvious skepticism.

"Bear was running just as fast, just as frightened," the priest clarified, and as Cadderly frowned in disbelief, several others nodded, confirming the wild tale.

"A bear?"

"Big bear. Has to be a fire."

But Cadderly looked to the south, from whence the animals came, and he saw no smoke darkening the late afternoon sky. He sniffed repeatedly, but found no scent of smoke in the air. He looked at Danica, who was making her way to the southern tree line. Somewhere beyond her came the roar of another bear, then one of a great cat.

Cadderly pushed his way to the front steps and cautiously descended. A deer bounded out of the trees, leaping frantically across the lawn. Cadderly clapped his hands, figuring to frighten the creature enough to make it veer to the side, but it never seemed to hear or even see him. It went leaping by, knocking him back as it passed.

"I told you!" the first mage cried at him. "There's no sensibility in them."

In the woods, the bear roared again, more powerfully, more insistently.

"Danica!" Cadderly called.

The bear was roaring out in protest and in pain, its threatening growls interspersed with higher-pitched squeals.

"Danica!" Cadderly cried again, more insistently, and he started toward the trees. He stopped abruptly as Danica burst out of the brush.

"Inside! Inside!" she yelled to them all.

Cadderly looked at her questioningly, then his eyes widened in surprise and horror as a horde of crawling beasts, long arms propelling them along at tremendous speed, charged out of the trees behind her.

The priest had studied the catalogs of Faerûn's many and varied animals and monsters, but he had never seen anything quite like these. In that instant of identification, Cadderly got the image of a legless man crawling on long, powerful arms, but that reflexive thought did not hold under closer scrutiny. Wide, hunched shoulders surmounted squat torsos, and the dark-skinned creatures used their arms to walk. They had something resembling feet at the end of their stubby legs, like a sea mammal's flippers. Their locomotion was half hop, half drag. Had they stood straight up, they would nearly match an average man, despite their vestigial feet and their compressed heads, a sort of half-sphere set on their shoulders.

Their faces were far from human in appearance, with no forehead to speak of, a flat nose, nostrils open forward, and shining yellow eyes—malignant eyes. But their mouths, all toothy and vicious, most alarmed Cadderly and everyone else staring at the beasts. They stretched almost the width of their elongated faces, with a hinged bottom jaw that protruded forward and seemed to project right from the top of the chest, snapping upward hungrily in an eager underbite.

Danica was ahead of the monstrosities, and a fast runner, but one of them closed fast on her, cutting an intercepting angle.

Cadderly started to call out to her with horror, but bit it off as she dropped her weight to her heels and skidded to a stop, threw herself around in a circle, and leaped into the air, tucking her legs up high as the creature came in under her. It too stopped fast, long arms reaching up, but Danica's legs were faster and they drove down hard against the monster's upturned face. She used the press as a springboard and leaped away. The monster bounced under the weight of the blow.

Danica put her head down and ran with all speed, sparing a heartbeat to wave Cadderly back into the cathedral, to remind him with her desperate expression that he, too, was in grave danger.

As the priest turned, he saw just how grave that danger was. Coming out of the woods were more of the crawling beasts, many more. That unseen but oft-heard bear lumbered out, too, thrashing and stumbling, covered with the shadowy creatures.

His heart pounding, Cadderly leaped to the stairs, but on the porch, the many wizards and priests were in a panic, crushing against the door with few actually getting inside. To both sides of the double doors, windows flew open, those inside beckoning their companions to dive in from the porch.

They weren't going to make it, Cadderly realized as he glanced back at Danica. How he wished he had his hand crossbow, or even his walking stick! But he had come down thinking that nothing was seriously out of sorts. Physically, he was unarmed.

But he still had Deneir.

Cadderly turned on the top step and closed his eyes, falling into prayer, praying for some solution. He began spellcasting before he even realized what he was attempting.

He opened his eyes and threw his arms wide. Danica hit the bottom step and sprang up past him, a host of creatures right behind her.

A blast of energy rolled out from Cadderly across the ground and through it in a great, rolling wave, lifting the cobblestones and grass, and many of the creatures.

More waves came forth, washing the beasts back in a series of rolling semicircles, like a ripple of waves from the shore of a still pond. The hungry beasts tried to fight past it, but inevitably lost ground, washing farther and farther backward.

"What is that?" a wizard asked in obvious awe, and despite his concentration, Cadderly heard the woman.

He had no answer.

None, that is, except that his spell had bought them the time they needed, and into Spirit Soaring they all went, Danica and Cadderly coming last, with Danica practically pulling her stunned husband in behind her.

* * * * *

Danica was relieved to hear other people calling out commands to guard the windows and doors, because Cadderly could do little at that moment, and he needed her. She looked around only briefly, suddenly realizing that someone was missing. Spirit Soaring was a huge place of many, many rooms, so she hadn't noticed the absence before. But in that moment of urgency and danger, she knew that the Spirit Soaring family was incomplete.

Where was Ivan Bouldershoulder?

Danica glanced around again, trying to recall when last she had seen the boisterous dwarf. But Cadderly's gasp brought her back to the situation at hand.

"What did you do out there?" Danica asked him. "I have never seen—"

"I know not at all," he admitted. "I went to Deneir, seeking spells, seeking a solution."

"And he answered!"

Cadderly looked at her with a blank expression for a moment before shaking his head with concern. "The *Metatext*, the Weave..." he whispered. "He is part of it now."

Danica stared at him, puzzled.

"As if the two—perhaps the three of them, Deneir, *Metatext*, and Weave—are no longer separate," Cadderly tried to explain.

"But save for Mystra, the gods were never a part of—"

"No, more than that," Cadderly said, shaking his head more forcefully. "He was writing to the Weave, patterning it with numbers, and now..."

The sound of breaking glass, followed by shouts, followed by screams, broke short the conversation.

"They come," said Danica, and she started off, pulling Cadderly behind her.

They found their first battle in the room only two doors down from the foyer, where a group of priests met the incursion of a pair of the beasts head on. Smashing away with their maces, and mostly armored, the priests had the situation well in hand.

Cadderly took the lead, running fast to the central stairwell and sprinting up three steps at a time to get up to the fourth floor and his private quarters. Just inside the doorway, he grabbed his belt, a wide leather girdle with a holster on either side for his hand crossbows. He looped a bandolier of specially crafted bolts around his neck and sprinted back to join Danica, loading the crossbows as he went.

They started for the stairs, but then discovered an unwelcome talent of the strange, crawling beasts: they were expert climbers. Down the hall a window shattered, and they heard thumps as one of the creatures pull itself through.

Danica moved in front of Cadderly as he dashed that way, but as they reached the room and kicked the door wide, he pushed her aside and lifted his arm, leveling the crossbow.

A beast was in the room, a second in the window frame, and both opened wide their mouths in vicious snarls.

Cadderly fired, the bolt flashing across the room to strike the chest of the beast in the window. The dart's side supports folded inward, collapsing on themselves and crushing the small vial they held. That concussion ignited magical oil in an explosive burst that blew a huge hole in the monster's black flesh. The force blew the crawler back out the window.

Cadderly aimed his second crossbow at the remaining creature, but turned his arm aside as Danica charged it. She stutter-stepped at the last moment, brought her left leg across to her right, and swept it back powerfully, deflecting both clawing arms aside. She expertly turned her hips as she went, gaining momentum, for as her left foot touched down, she snap-kicked with her right, driving the tip of her foot into the beast's left eye.

It howled and thrashed, arms swinging back furiously, predictably, and Danica easily stepped out of reach, then followed through with a forward step and front kick to the creature's chest that drove it back against the wall.

Again it reacted with fury, and again she easily leaped out of reach.

This was the way to fight the creatures, she decided then. Strike hard and back out, repeatedly, never staying close enough to engage those awful claws.

Cadderly was more than glad that she had the situation under control when they heard the window in the adjoining room shatter. He spun around the jamb, turning to kick open the next door, and swept into the room with his left arm upraised.

The beast huddled right before him, waiting to spring at him.

With a startled cry, Cadderly fired the hand crossbow, the bolt hitting the charging crawler barely two feet away, close enough that he felt the rush of concussive force as the dart exploded. Then the beast was gone, blown back across the room where it settled against the wall, its long arms out wide and trembling, a hole in its torso so large that Cadderly realized he could slide his fist into it with ease.

His breathing came in surprised gasps, but he heard a commotion just outside. He dropped the hand crossbow from his left hand—it bounced off his mid thigh, for it was securely tethered—and worked fast to reload the other weapon.

He nearly dropped the explosive dart when Danica rushed into the hall behind him, slamming the door of the first room.

"Too many!" she cried. "And they're coming in all around us. We've got to call up help from below."

"Go! Go!" Cadderly yelled back, fumbling with the dart as a shadowy form filled the window across the room.

Danica, hardly noticing the nearby enemy, ran for the stairwell. The fleshy beast hurled itself at Cadderly.

The crossbow string slipped from his grasp, and he was lucky to stop the dart from falling out of its grooved table. His eyes flashed from bow to beast and back again, and back, to see a filthy clawed hand slashing at his face.

* * * * *

The center stairs at Spirit Soaring ran down a flight, turned around a landing, then ran down another flight in the opposite direction, two flights for every story of the building. Danica didn't actually run down the steps. She went halfway down the first flight and hopped the railing, landing lightly halfway down the second flight. She didn't bounce right to the third set of stairs, but leaped down to the landing to reconnoiter the third floor.

As she had feared, she was met by the sound of breaking glass. She yelled down the stairs again and sprang halfway down the next stairway, then leaped to the fourth set of steps. She heard the commotion of many people running up the stairs.

"Break into patrols to secure each floor!" Danica yelled to them, her point accentuated when the lead group reached the landing to the second story and immediately encountered a pair of the beasts rushing down the hallway at them.

Waggling fingers sent bolts of magical force reaching out. Armored clerics crowded into the doorway to shield the unarmored wizards.

Few at Spirit Soaring were untested or unseasoned in battle, and so several broke off from the first group with precision and discipline, most continuing up the stairs.

Danica was already gone from the spot, sprinting back up three steps at a time. She had been away from Cadderly for longer than she had anticipated, and though she trusted in him—how could she not, when she had seen him face down a terrible dragon and a vampire, and when she had watched him, through sheer willpower and divine magic, create the magnificent library cathedral?—she knew that he was alone up there on the fourth floor.

Alone and with more than two dozen windows to defend in that wing alone.

* * * * *

He cried out in alarm and turned away from the blow, but not enough to avoid the long, vicious claws. He felt the skin under his left eye tear away, and the weight of the blow nearly knocked him senseless.

Cadderly wasn't even aware that he had pulled the trigger of his hand crossbow. The bolt wasn't set perfectly on the table, but it snapped out anyway, and good fortune alone had the weapon turned in the correct direction. The bolt stabbed into the monster's flesh, collapsed, and exploded, throwing the beast backward. It flew against the wall, shrieking in a ghastly squeal. Clawed hands grabbed at the blasted-open wound.

Cadderly heard the scream, but couldn't tell whether it was pain, defeat, or victory. Bent low, he stumbled out of the room, blood streaming down his face and dripping on the floor. The blow hadn't touched his eye, but it was already swollen so badly he could see only splashes of indistinguishable light.

Staggering and disoriented, he heard more creatures dragging themselves through other rooms. Load! Load! his thoughts silently screamed, and he fumbled to do just that, but quickly realized that he hadn't the time.

He closed his eyes and called out to Deneir.

All he found were numbers, patterns written on the Weave.

His confusion lasted until a creature burst into the hall before him. The numbers formed a pattern in his mind, and a spell issued from his lips.

A gleaming shield of divine energy enwrapped the priest as the creature rushed in, and though Cadderly instinctively recoiled from its bashing, clawing attacks, they did not, could not, seriously harm him.

They couldn't penetrate the magical barrier he had somehow enacted.

Another spell flowed into his thoughts, and he wasted no time in uttering the words, dropping his hand crossbows to hang by their tethers and throwing his hands high into the air. He felt the energy running through him, divine and wonderful and powerful, as if he pulled it out of the air. It tingled down his arms and through his torso, down his legs and into the floor, and there it rolled out in every direction, an orange-red glow spider-webbing through the floor planks.

The creature whacking at him immediately began to howl in pain, and Cadderly ambled down the hall, taking the consecrated ground with him. Too stupid to realize its error, the fleshy beast followed and continued to scream out, its lower torso sizzling under the burn of radiant energy.

More creatures came at him and tried to attack, but began howling as they entered the circle of power. The magic still moved with Cadderly as he turned toward the stairs.

There, the mighty priest saw Danica gawking at him.

The first creature died. Another one fell, then a third, consumed by the power of Deneir, the power of the unknown dweomer Cadderly had cast. He waved for Danica to run away, but she didn't, and went to join him instead.

As soon as she drew near, she too began to glisten under the light of his divine shield.

"What have you done?" she asked him.

"I have no idea," Cadderly replied. He wasn't about to stand there and question his good fortune.

"Let's clear the floor," Danica said, and together they moved down the hallway.

Danica led with a flurry of kicks and punches that finished off two of the beasts as they writhed in pain when the consecrated ground came under them.

One creature tried to scramble into a side room, and Danica turned toward it. But Cadderly cast forth a pointing finger and cried out another prayer. A shaft of light, a lance of divine energy, shot out and skewered the beast, which howled and crashed into the doorjamb as Danica neared.

The crawler survived the spearlike energy, but it sparkled and glowed, making it easy for the expert Danica to line up her blows and quickly dispatch it.

By the time five bloodied and battered priests arrived on the landing of the stairs to support the couple, one wing of the fourth floor had been swept clear of monsters. Cadderly still emanated the circle of power flowing around him, and discovered too that his wounds were magically mending.

The other priests looked at him with puzzlement and intrigue, but he had no answers for them. He had called to Deneir, and Deneir, or some other being of power, had answered his prayers with unknown dweomers.

There was no time to sit and contemplate, Cadderly knew, for Spirit Soaring was a gigantic structure full of windows, full of side rooms and alcoves, plus narrow back passages and a multilevel substructure.

They fought throughout the night and into the early dawn, until no more monsters came through the windows. Still they fought throughout the morning, weary and battered, and with several of their companions dead, painstakingly clearing the large spaces of Spirit Soaring.

Cadderly and Danica both knew that many rooms remained to be explored and cleared, but they were all exhausted. The task began to reinforce the windows with heavy boards, to tend the wounded, and to organize battle groups for the coming night and the next possible attack.

"Where is Ivan?" Danica asked Cadderly when they finally had a few moments alone.

"He went to Carradoon, I thought."

"No, just Pikel, with Rorey and . . ." the names caught in Danica's throat. All three of her children had gone to Carradoon, had traveled through the mountain forests from which those hideous creatures had come.

"Cadderly?" she whispered, her voice breaking. He, too, had to take a deep breath to stop himself from falling over in fear.

"We have to go to them," he said.

But Danica was shaking her head. "You have to stay here," she replied.

"You cannot—"

"I can move more quickly on my own."

"We have no idea what precipitated this," Cadderly complained. "We don't even know what power we're up against!"

"And who better than I to find out?" his wife asked, and she managed a little grin of confidence.

A very little grin of confidence.

CHAPTER 13
I AM NOT YOUR ENEMY

She wore a little knowing smile, a smile at odds with her eyes, which had rolled again to white. She was floating off the ground.

"Ye mean to kill him?" she asked, as if she were talking to someone standing before her. As she spoke, her eyes came back into focus.

"The accent," Jarlaxle remarked as Catti-brie's shoulders shifted back—as if she thought she was leaning back in a chair, perhaps.

"If ye be killing Entreri to free Regis and to stop him from hurting anyone else, then me heart says it's a good thing," the woman said, and leaned forward intently. "But if ye're meaning to kill him to prove yerself or to deny what he is, then me heart cries."

"Calimport," Drizzt whispered, vividly recalling the scene.

"Wha—?" Bruenor started to ask, but Catti-brie continued, cutting him short.

"Suren the world's not fair, me friend. Suren by the measure of hearts, ye been wronged. But are ye after the assassin for yer own anger? Will killing Entreri cure the wrong?

"Look in the mirror, Drizzt Do'Urden, without the mask. Killin' Entreri won't change the color of his skin—or the color of yer own."

"Elf?" Bruenor asked, but at that shocking moment, Drizzt couldn't even hear him.

The weight of that long-ago encounter with Catti-brie came cascading back to him. He was there again, in the moment, in that small room, receiving one of the most profound slaps of cold wisdom anyone had ever cared enough about him to deliver. It was the moment he realized that he loved Catti-brie, though it would be years before he dared act on those feelings.

He glanced at Bruenor and Jarlaxle, a bit embarrassed, too much overwhelmed, and turned again to his beloved, who continued that old conversation—word for word.

". . . if only ye'd learn to look," she said, her lips turned in that disarming, charming smile that she had so often flashed Drizzt's way, each time melting any resistance he might have to what she was saying.

"And if only ye'd ever learned to love. Suren ye've let things slip past, Drizzt Do'Urden."

She turned her head, as if some commotion had occurred nearby, and Drizzt remembered that Wulfgar had entered the room at that moment. Wulfgar was Catti-brie's lover at that time, though she'd just hinted that her heart was for Drizzt.

And it was, he knew, even then.

Drizzt began to shake as he remembered what was to come. Jarlaxle moved up behind him then, and reached around Drizzt's head. For an instant, Drizzt tensed, thinking the mercenary had a garrote. It was no garrote, however, but an eye patch, which Jarlaxle tied on securely before shoving Drizzt forward.

"Go to her!" he demanded.

Only a step away, Drizzt heard again the words that had, in retrospect, changed his life, the words that had freed him.

"Just for thoughts, me friend," Catti-brie said quietly, and Drizzt had to pause before continuing to her, had to let her finish. "Are ye more trapped by the way the world sees ye, or by the way ye see the world seein' ye?"

Tears streaming from his lavender eyes, Drizzt fell over her in a great hug, pulling down her outstretched arms. He didn't cross into that shadowed plane, protected as he was by Jarlaxle's eye patch. Drizzt pulled Catti-brie down to him and hugged her close, and kept on hugging her until she finally relaxed and slipped back to a sitting position.

At last, Drizzt looked at the others, at Jarlaxle in particular.

"I am not your enemy, Drizzt Do'Urden," he said.

"What'd ye do?" Bruenor demanded.

"The eye patch protects the mind from intrusion, magical or psionic," Jarlaxle explained. "Not fully, but enough so that a wary Drizzt would not be drawn again into that place where . . ."

"Where Regis's mind now dwells," said Drizzt.

"Be sure that I'm not knowin' a bit o' what ye're talking about," said Bruenor, planting his hands firmly on his hips. "What in the Nine Hells is going on, elf?"

Drizzt wore a confused expression and began to shake his head.

"It is as if two planes of existence, or two worlds from different planes, are crashing together," Jarlaxle said, and all of them looked at him as if he had grown an ettin's second head.

Jarlaxle took a deep breath and gave a little laugh. "It is no accident that I found you on the road," he said.

"Ye think we ever thinked it one, ye dolt?" asked Bruenor, drawing a helpless chuckle from the drow mercenary.

"And no accident that I sent Athrogate there—Stuttgard, if you will—into Mithral Hall to coax you on the road to Spirit Soaring."

"Yeah, the Crystal Shard," Bruenor muttered in a tone that showed obvious skepticism.

"All that I told you is true," Jarlaxle replied. "But yes, good dwarf, my tale was not complete."

"Me heart's skippin' to hear it."

"There is a dragon."

"There always is," said Bruenor.

"I and my friend here were being pursued," Jarlaxle explained.

"Nasty buggers," said Athrogate.

"Pursued by creatures who could raise the dead with ease," said Jarlaxle. "The architects of the Crystal Shard, I believe, who have somehow transcended the limitations of this plane."

"Yup, ye're losing me in the trees again," said Bruenor.

"Creatures of two worlds, like Catti-brie," Drizzt said.

"Maybe. I cannot know for certain. That they are of, or possess the ability to be of two dimensions, I am certain. From this hat, I can produce dimensional holes, and so I did, and threw one such item at the creature pursuing me."

"The one what kept melting before me morningstars could flatten it out," Athrogate explained.

"Plane shifting," Jarlaxle said. "And it did so as my dimensional hole fell over it, and the combination of two extra-dimensional magics tore a rift to the Astral Plane."

"Then the creature's gone," said Bruenor.

"Forever, I expect," Jarlaxle agreed.

"And ye're needin' us and needin' Cadderly why, then?"

"Because it was an emissary, not the source. And the source..."

"The dragon," said Drizzt.

"Always is," Bruenor said again.

Jarlaxle shrugged, unwilling to commit to that. "Whatever it is, it remains alive, and with the terrible power to send its thoughts across the world, and send its emissaries out as well. It's been calling forth minions from the realm of the dead with abandon, and perhaps"—he paused and looked back to the scene of the slaughtered beasts around them—"the power to call forth minions from this other place, this dark place."

"What're ye about, ye durned elf?" Bruenor demanded. "What did ye pull us along to?"

"Along the road that will find an answer for your dear daughter's plight, I hope," Jarlaxle replied without hesitation. "And yes, I put you beside Athrogate and I in our own quest, as well."

"Ye dropped us in the middle of it, ye mean!" Bruenor growled.

"I'm wantin' to punch yer skinny face!" Pwent shouted.

"We were already in the middle of it," Drizzt said, and when all turned to regard him as he knelt there hugging Catti-brie, it was hard for any to disagree. Drizzt looked at Jarlaxle and said, "The whole world is in the middle of it."

CHAPTER
SCOUTS' DISMAY
14

"We cannot just wait here for them to assail us again at twilight!" a young wizard cried, and many others took up that refrain.

"We do not even know if that will happen," reminded Ginance, an older woman, a priest of Cadderly's order who had been cataloging scrolls at Spirit Soaring since its earliest days. "We have never encountered such creatures as these . . . these lumps of ugly flesh! We know not if they have an aversion to sunlight, or if they broke off the attack at dawn for strategic reasons."

"They left when the dawn's light showed in the east," the first protested. "That tells me we've a good place to start in our counterattack, and counter we must—aggressively."

"Aye!" several others shouted.

The discussion in the nave of Spirit Soaring had been going on for some time, and thus far Cadderly had remained quiet, gauging the demeanor of the room. Several wizards and priests, all of them visitors to the library, had been killed in the brutal assault of the previous night. Cadderly was glad to see that the remaining group, some seventy-five men and women, most highly trained and skilled in the arcane or divine arts, had not given in to despair after that unexpected battle. Their fighting spirit was more than evident, and that, Cadderly knew, would be an important factor if they were to sort through their predicament.

He focused again on Ginance, his friend and one of the wisest and most knowledgeable members of his clergy.

"We don't even know if Spirit Soaring is cleared of the beasts," she said, quieting the exuberance.

"None are out biting at us, the vicious creatures!" the first mage argued. Ginance seemed at a loss to overcome the tidal wave of shouts that followed, all calling for action beyond the confines of the cathedral.

"You presume that they're mindless, or at least stupid," Cadderly finally put in, and though he hadn't shouted the words, as soon as he started talking, the room went silent and all eyes focused his way.

The priest took a deep breath at that reminder, yet again, of his importance and reputation. He had built Spirit Soaring, and that was no small thing. Still, he remained unnerved by the reverence shown him, particularly given that many of his guests were far more seasoned in the art of warfare than he. One group of priests from Sundabar had spent years traversing the lower planes, battling demons and devils. Yet even they stared at him, hanging on his every word.

"You assume they ran away because they didn't like the sunlight, rather than for tactical reasons," Cadderly explained, carefully choosing his words. He shook his foolish nervousness away by reminding himself of his missing children, and the missing Bouldershoulder brothers. "And now you assume that if there were any more of the beasts still inside Spirit Soaring, they would rush right out ravenously instead of hiding away to strike at more opportune moments."

"And what do you believe, good Cadderly?" asked the same young wizard who had been so fiery and obstinate with Ginance. "Do we sit and fortify, to prepare for the next onslaught, or do we go out and find our enemies?"

"Both," Cadderly replied, and many heads, particularly the older veterans, nodded in agreement. "Many of you did not come here alone, but with trusted friends and associates, so I will leave it up to you to decide on the sizes and dispositions of battle groups.

I would suggest both brawn and magic, and magic both divine and arcane. We don't know when this . . . plague will end, or whether or not it will get worse, so we must do our best to cover all contingencies."

"I would suggest groups of no less than seven," said one of the older wizards.

They began talking amongst themselves again, which Cadderly thought best. Those men and women didn't need his guidance on the details. Ginance came over to him then, still troubled about the notion that Spirit Soaring might be hosting some uninvited guests.

"Are all of our brethren available after last night?" Cadderly asked her.

"Most. We have two score or so brothers ready to scour Spirit Soaring—unless you would have some go out with the others."

"Just a few," Cadderly decided. "Offer our more worldly brothers—those who have spent the most time gathering herbs that might be used medicinally, who best know the terrain surrounding the library—to the various scouting teams sorted out by our many guests. But let us keep most of our own inside Spirit Soaring, as they know best the many catacombs, tunnels, and antechambers. That is your task, of course."

Ginance took that great compliment with a bow. "Lady Danica would be most helpful, as would Ivan . . ." She paused at the sour look Cadderly flashed her way.

"Danica will be out of Spirit Soaring within a short time," Cadderly explained. "Mostly in search of Ivan, who seems to be missing, and . . ."

"They're safely in Carradoon," Ginance assured him. "All three, and Pikel, too."

"Let us hope," was all Cadderly could reply.

* * * * *

A short while later, Cadderly sat on the balcony of his private room, looking southeast, toward Carradoon. So many thoughts fought for his attention as he worried about his children, about Danica who had gone out to look for them and for the missing Ivan Bouldershoulder. He feared for his home, Spirit Soaring, and the implications its downfall might have on his order and more personally, upon him. The horde of unknown monsters that had come against them so violently and determinedly had done little true damage to the cathedral's structure, but Cadderly had felt the shatter of every window upon his own body, as if someone had flicked a finger hard against his skin. He was intimately bound to the place, and in ways that even he didn't truly yet understand.

So many worries, and not least among them, Cadderly Bonaduce worried about his god and the state of the world. He had gone there, to the Weave, and had found Deneir, he was sure. He had been granted spells the likes of which he had never before known.

It was Deneir, but it was not Deneir, as if the god was changing before his very eyes, as if Deneir, his god, the rock of philosophical thought that Cadderly had used as the foundation of his very existence, was becoming part of something else, something different, perhaps bigger . . . and perhaps darker.

It seemed to Cadderly as if Deneir, in his attempt to unravel the mystery of the unraveling, was writing himself into the fabric of the Weave, or trying to write the Weave into the *Metatext* and taking himself with it in the process!

A flash of fire from a wooded valley to the east brought Cadderly back to the present. He stood up and walked to the railing, peering more intently into the distance. A few trees were on fire—one of the scouting wizards had enacted a fireball, or a priest had called down a column of flame, no doubt.

Which meant that they had encountered monsters.

Cadderly swept his gaze to the south, in line with distant Carradoon, off beyond the lower peaks. He could see the western bank of Impresk Lake on that clear day, and he tried to take some solace in the water's calm appearance.

He prayed that their near catastrophe was local to Spirit

Soaring, that his children and Pikel had gone to Carradoon oblivious to the deadly horde that had come into the mountains behind them.

"Find them, Danica," he whispered to the late morning breezes.

* * * * *

She had gone out from Spirit Soaring first that day. Going alone allowed Danica to move more swiftly. Trained in stealth and speed, the woman quickly put the library far behind her, moving southeast down the packed-dirt road to Carradoon. She stayed just to the side of the open trail, moving through the brush with ease and speed.

Her hopes began to climb as the sun rose behind her, with no sign of monsters or destruction.

But then the smell of burned flesh filled her nostrils.

Cautious, but still moving with great speed, Danica ran to the top of an embankment beside the road, overlooking the scene of a recent battle: a ruined wagon and charred ground.

The Baldurian wizards.

She descended the steep decline, noting the piles of melted flesh and having no difficulty recognizing them as the remains of the same type of monsters that had assaulted Spirit Soaring the night before.

After a quick inspection revealed no human remains, Danica glanced back to the northwest, toward Spirit Soaring. Ivan had been out gathering wood the night those four had left, she recalled, and typically, the dwarf did so to the sides of the eastern road—the very road upon which she stood.

Danica's hopes for her friend began to sink. Had he encountered a similar shadowy horde? Had he seen the Baldurian wizards' fight and come down to aid them?

Neither scenario boded well. Ivan was as tough a fighter as Danica had ever known, capable and smart, but was out alone, and the sheer numbers that had come against Spirit Soaring, and had obviously hit the four mighty wizards on the road, could surely overwhelm anyone.

The woman took a deep, steadying breath, forcing herself not to jump to pessimistic conclusions regarding the wizards, Ivan, or the implications for her own children.

They were all capable, she reminded herself again, supremely so.

And there were no human or dwarf bodies that she could identify.

She began to look around more carefully for clues. Where had the monsters come from, and where had they gone?

She found a trail, a swath of dead trees and brown grass leading northward.

With a glance to the east, toward Carradoon, and a quick prayer for her children, Danica went hunting.

* * * * *

The blood on Ginance's face told Cadderly that his concern that some beasts hid within Spirit Soaring had been prudent.

"The catacombs crawl with the creatures," the woman explained. "We're clearing them room by room, crypt by crypt."

"Methodically," Cadderly observed.

Ginance nodded. "We leave no openings behind us. We will not be flanked."

Cadderly was glad to hear the confirmation, the reminder that the priests who had come to the call of Spirit Soaring over the last years were intelligent and studious. They were disciples of Deneir and of Gond, after all, two gods who demanded intelligence and reason as the cornerstones of faith.

Ginance held up her light tube, a combination of magic and mechanics using an unending spell of light and a tube of coated material to create a perpetual bulls-eye lantern. Every priest at Spirit Soaring had one, and with implements such as those, they could chase the darkness out of the deepest recesses.

"Leave nothing behind you," Cadderly said, and with a nod, Ginance took her leave.

Cadderly paced his small room, angry at his own inactivity, at the responsibilities that held him there. He should be with

Danica, he told himself. But he shook that notion aside, knowing well that his wife could travel more swiftly, more stealthily, and more safely by herself. Then he thought he should be clearing the library with Ginance.

"No," he decided.

His place wasn't in the catacombs, but neither was it in his private quarters. He needed time to recuperate and mentally reset both his determination and his sense of calm before going back into the realm of the spiritual in his search to find Deneir.

No, not to find him, he realized, for he knew where his god had gone. Into the *Metatext*.

Perhaps for all time.

It fell on Cadderly to sort it out, and in doing so, to try to unravel the strange alterations of the divine spells that had come to him unbidden.

But not just then.

Cadderly strapped on his weapon belt and refilled his dart bandolier before looping it over his shoulder and across his chest. He considered his spindle-disks, a pair of hard, fist-sized semicircular plates bound by a small rod, around which were wrapped the finest of elven cords. Cadderly could send the disks spinning to the end of their three-foot length and back again at great speed, and could alter the angle easily to strike like a snake at any foe. He wasn't certain how much effect the weapon might have on the malleable flesh of the strange invaders, but he put the weapons in his belt pouch anyway.

He started toward the door, passing the wall mirror as he went, and there he paused and considered himself and his purpose, and the most important duty before him, that of leadership.

He looked fine in his white shirt and brown breeches, but he decided those weren't enough, especially since he looked very much like a young man, as young as his own children. With a smile, the not-so-young priest went to his wardrobe and took out his layered light blue traveling cloak and looped it over his shoulders. Then came his hat, also light blue, wide-brimmed and with a red band bearing the candle-over-eye emblem of

Deneir set in gold on the front. A smooth walking stick, its top carved into the likeness of a ram's head, completed the look, and Cadderly took a moment to pause before the mirror again, and to reflect.

He looked so much like the young man who had first discovered the truth of his faith.

What a journey it had been! What adventure! In constructing Spirit Soaring, Cadderly had been forced into a moment of ultimate sacrifice. The creation magic had aged him, swiftly, continually, and greatly, to the point where all around him, even his beloved Danica, had thought he would surely perish for the effort. At the completion of the magnificent structure, Cadderly was prepared to die, and seemed about to. But that had been no more than a trial by Deneir, and the same magic that had wearied him then reinvigorated him after, reversing his aging to the strange point where he appeared and felt like a man of twenty once again, full of the strength and energy of youth, but with the wisdom of a weathered veteran more than twice his apparent age.

And he was being called again to the struggle, but Cadderly feared the implications were greater to the wider world even than the advent of the chaos curse.

He looked at himself in the mirror carefully, at the Chosen of Deneir, ready for battle and ready to reason his way through chaos.

In Spirit Soaring, Cadderly gained confidence. His god would not desert him, and he was surrounded by loyal friends and mighty allies.

Danica would find their children.

Spirit Soaring would prevail and they would lead the way to whatever might come when the time of magical turbulence sorted out.

He had to believe that.

And he had to make sure that everyone around him knew that he believed it.

Cadderly went down to the main audience hall of the first floor and left the large double doors open wide, awaiting the return of the scouts.

He didn't have to wait for long. As Cadderly entered the hall under the arch from the stairwell, the first group of returning scouts stumbled into Spirit Soaring's front doors—half the group, at least. Four members had been left dead on the field.

Cadderly had barely taken his seat when a pair of his Deneirrath priests entered, flanking a young and burly visiting priest— surrounding and supporting him, with one trying to bandage the man's ripped and burned shield arm.

"They were everywhere," the scout explained to Cadderly. "We were attacked less than half a league from here. A wizard tried a fireball, but it blew up short and smoked my arm. A priest tried to heal me on the field, but his spell caused an injury instead—to himself. His whole chest burst open, and . . . bah, we can't depend on any magic now!"

Cadderly nodded grimly through the recounting. "I saw the fight from my balcony, I believe. To the east . . . ?"

"North," the priest scout corrected. "North and west."

Those words stung Cadderly, for the fireball he had witnessed was opposite that direction. The priest's claim that "they were everywhere" reverberated in Cadderly's thoughts, and he tried hard to tell himself that his children were safe in Carradoon.

"Without reliable magic, our struggle will be more difficult," Cadderly said.

"Worse than you think," said one of the Spirit Soaring escorts, and he looked to the scout to elaborate.

"Four of our nine were slain," the man said. "But they didn't stay dead."

"Resurrection?" Cadderly asked.

"Undead," the man explained. "They got back up and started fighting again—this time against the rest of us."

"There was a priest or a wizard among the monsters' ranks?"

The man shrugged. "They fell, they died, they got back up."

Cadderly started to respond but bit it short, his eyes going wide. In the fight at Spirit Soaring the night before, at least fifteen men and women had been killed, and had been laid in a side room on the first level of the catacombs.

Cadderly leaped from his chair, alarm evident on his face.

"What is it?" the priest scout asked.

"Come along, all three," he said, scrambling toward the back of the room. He veered to a side door to corridors that would allow him to navigate the maze of the great library more quickly.

* * * * *

Danica picked her way carefully but quickly along the trail, staying just to the side of the swath of devastation. It ran anywhere from five to ten long strides across, with broken trees and torn turf along its center, as if some great creature had ambled through. She saw only patches of deadness along the edges—not complete decay as she found in the middle of the trail, but spotty areas where sections of trees seemingly had simply died—along both sides.

The monk was loath to walk across that swath, or even enter the area of deepest decay, but when she saw a print on an open patch of ground, she knew that she had to learn more. She held her breath as she approached, for she recognized it as a footprint indeed, a giant footprint, four-toed and with great claws, the impression of a dragon's foot.

Danica knelt low and inspected the area, taking particular interest in the grass. Not all of it was dead on the trail, but the nearer to the footprints, the more profound the devastation. She stood up and looked around at the standing trees along the sides, and envisioned a dragon walking through, crushing down any trees or shrubs in its path, occasionally flexing its wings, perhaps, which would have put them in contact with the bordering trees.

She focused on the dead patches of those trees, so stark in contrast with the vibrancy of the forest itself. Had the mere touch of the beast's wings killed them?

She looked again at the footprint, and at the profound absence of life in the vegetation immediately surrounding it.

A dragon, but a dragon that killed so profoundly with a mere touch?

Danica swallowed hard, realizing that the hunched, fleshy crawlers might be the least of their problems.

CHAPTER

THE WEIGHT OF LEADERSHIP

15

"They're less likely to take comfort in his dwarf heritage if they think him an idiot," Hanaleisa explained to Temberle, who was more than a little upset at the whispers he was hearing among the ranks of the Carradden refugees.

Temberle had insisted that Pikel, the only dwarf in the group and the only one who seemed able to conjure magical light in the otherwise lightless tunnels, would lead them through the dark. Though a few had expressed incredulity at the notion of following the inarticulate, green-bearded dwarf, none had openly disagreed. How could they, after all, when Pikel had undeniably been the hero of the last fight, freezing the water and allowing a retreat from certain disaster?

But that was yesterday, and the march of the last few hours had been a series of starts and stops, of backtracking and the growing certainty that they were lost. They had encountered no walking dead, at least, but that seemed cold comfort in those dank and dirty caves, crawling through tunnels and openings that had even the children on all fours, and with crawly bugs scurrying all around them.

"They're scared," Temberle whispered back. "They'd be complaining no matter who took the lead."

"Because we're lost." As she spoke, Hanaleisa nodded her chin at Pikel, who stood up front, lighted shillelagh tucked under his stumped arm while he scratched at his thick green beard with his good hand. The strange-looking dwarf stared at a trio of tunnels branching out before him, obviously without a clue.

"How could we *not* be lost?" Temberle asked. "Has anyone been through here, ever?"

Hanaleisa conceded that point with a shrug, but pulled her brother along as she moved to join the dwarf and Rorick, who stood by Pikel's side, leaning on a staff someone had given him to aid his movement with his torn ankle.

"Do you know where we are, Uncle Pikel?" Hanaleisa asked as she approached.

The dwarf looked at her and shrugged.

"Do you know where Carradoon is? Which direction?"

Without even thinking about it, obviously sure of his answer, Pikel pointed back the way they had come, and to the right, what Hanaleisa took to be southeast.

"He's trying to get us higher into the mountains before finding a way out of the tunnels," Rorick explained.

"No," Temberle was quick to reply, and both Rorick and Pikel looked at him curiously.

"Eh?" said the dwarf.

"We have to get out of the tunnels," Temberle explained. "Now."

"Uh-uh," Pikel disagreed, and he grabbed up his cudgel and held both of his arms out before him, mimicking a zombie to accentuate his point.

"Certainly we're far enough from Carradoon to escape that madness," said Temberle.

"Uh-uh."

"We're not that far," Rorick explained. "The tunnels are winding back and forth. If we came out on a high bluff, Carradoon would still be in sight."

"I do not disagree," said Temberle.

"But we have to get out of the tunnels as soon as possible," Hanaleisa added. "Dragging a gravely wounded man through these narrow and dirty spaces is sure to be the end of him."

"And going above ground is likely to be the end of all of us," Rorick shot back.

Hanaleisa and Temberle exchanged knowing looks. Watching the dead rise and come against them had profoundly unnerved Rorick, and certainly, the older twins shared that disgust and terror.

Hanaleisa walked over and draped her arm across Pikel's shoulders. "Get us in sight of the open air, at least," she whispered to him. "These close quarters and the unending darkness is playing on the nerves of all."

Pikel reiterated his zombie posture.

"I know, I know," Hanaleisa said. "I don't want to go out and face those things again, either. But we're not dwarves, Uncle Pikel. We can't stay down here forever."

Pikel leaned on his cudgel and gave a great, heaving sigh. He tucked the club under his stump and stuck a finger in his mouth, slurping about for a moment before pulling it forth with a hollow popping sound. He closed his eyes and began to chant as he held the wet finger up before him, magically sensitizing himself to the current of air.

He pointed to the right-hand corridor.

"That will get us out?" Hanaleisa asked.

Pikel shrugged, apparently unwilling to make any promises. He took up his glowing cudgel and led the way.

*****

"We require the other four," decided Yharaskrik, still in the body of Ivan and speaking through the dwarf's mouth. "The lich First Grandfather Wu is lost to us, for now at least, but four others are missing and awaiting recall."

"They are busy," Hephaestus insisted.

"No matter is more important than the one before us."

The dracolich emitted a low, threatening growl. "I will have them," he said.

"The drow and the human?"

"You know who I mean."

"We already have lost First Grandfather Wu to the drow," Yharaskrik reminded. "It is possible that Jarlaxle was killed in that same conflict."

"We do not know what happened to First Grandfather Wu."

"We know that he is lost to us, that he is . . . gone. There is nothing more we need know. He found Jarlaxle and was defeated, and whether the drow was also killed—"

"Is something we would know if you cared to search!" Hephaestus said, and there it was, the true source of his simmering rage.

"Do not overreach," the illithid in the dwarf's body retorted. "We are great and mighty, and our power will only multiply as more minions are brought through the rift, and more undead are called to our service—perhaps we will soon learn how to raise the bodies of the crawlers, then our army will be unending. But mighty, too, are our enemies, and none more so than the one we have here, within our reach, at the place they call Spirit Soaring."

"Magic is failing."

"But it has not failed. It is unpredictable, of course, but potent still."

"Fetchigrol and Solmé have bottled this mighty enemy up in his hole," Hephaestus argued with dismissive sarcasm, his voice dripping as he referred to Cadderly as "mighty."

"They are out on the trails even now."

"Where many have been killed!"

"A few, no more," Yharaskrik said. "And many of our minions were consumed in the battle. They do not issue from an inexhaustible source, great Hephaestus."

"But the walking dead do—millions and millions will answer our call. And as they kill, their ranks increase," the dracolich proclaimed.

"The summoning is easy for those of this world who have fallen," Yharaskrik agreed. "But it is not without cost to the power of Crenshinibon—and who more likely than the powerful Cadderly to discover a countering magic?"

"I will have them!" Hephaestus roared. "The drow and his human companion—that Calishite. I will have them and I will devour them!"

The body of Ivan Bouldershoulder settled back on its heels. The illithid within was shaking the yellow-haired head with dismay and resignation. "A creature of centuries should know more of patience," Yharaskrik scolded quietly. "One enemy at a time. Let us destroy Cadderly and Spirit Soaring, then we can go hunting. We recall the four apparitions—"

"No!"

"We will need all of our power to—"

"No! Two in the north and two in the south. Two for the drow and two for the human. If First Grandfather Wu returns, then bring him back to our side, but the other four will hunt until they have found the drow and the human. I will have those treacherous fools. And fear not for Cadderly and his forces. We will peck at them until they are weak, then the catastrophe of Hephaestus will fall over them. I went out to Solmé this very day and the ground beneath me died at my passing, and the touch of my wings rotted the trees. I fear no mortal, not this Cadderly nor anyone else. I am Hephaestus, I am catastrophe. Look upon me and know doom!"

With a large part of his enormous consciousness still residing within the coil of the dragon, sharing that body with Hephaestus and Crenshinibon, Yharaskrik understood that it could not convince the dragon otherwise. The illithid also realized, to its dismay, that Hephaestus was gaining the upper hand in the competition for the alliance of Crenshinibon.

Perhaps the illithid had erred in abandoning that coil with so much of its consciousness. Perhaps it was time to return to the others within the life-force of Hephaestus, to better battle the stubborn dragon.

A smile creased the face of Ivan Bouldershoulder—an ironic one indeed, Yharaskrik thought, because he was at that moment concluding that sacrificing the dwarf to the rage of Hephaestus might placate the dragon for a while, long enough for Yharaskrik to regain some measure of dominance.

* * * * *

A chorus of weary cheers erupted when at last the beleaguered refugees of Carradoon saw a stream of daylight. Never had any imagined how deep and dark mountain tunnels could be—except for Pikel, of course, who had been raised in dwarven mines.

Even Rorick, who had warned against going outside, couldn't hide his relief at learning that there was indeed an ending to those lightless corridors. With great hopes, they turned a long and curving corner leading to daylight.

And arrived with a communal, profound, and disappointed sigh.

"Uh-oh," said Pikel, for they had not come to the end of the tunnel, but merely to a natural chimney, and a very long and narrow one at that.

"We're deeper than I believed," Temberle admitted, staring up the shaft, which extended upward for more than a hundred feet. Most of it could not be climbed, and was too narrow in many places for any attempt, even for nimble Hanaleisa or Rorick, who were the slimmest of the group.

"Did you know we were this far down?" Hanaleisa asked Pikel, and in reply the dwarf began drawing mountains in the air, then merely shrugged.

His reasoning was correct, Hanaleisa and the other onlookers knew, for their current depth was likely more dependent upon the contours of the mountainous land above than the relatively mild grade of the tunnels they had been traversing.

The high shaft confirmed, though, that they were indeed moving deeper into the Snowflakes.

"You have to get us out," Temberle said to Pikel.

"To battle hordes of undead?" Rorick reminded him, and Temberle shot his brother an irritated look.

"Or at least, you have to show us . . . show *them*"—he glanced back at the many Carradden moving into sight around the corner—"that there is a way out. Even if we don't go outside," he added, looking pointedly at his little brother, "it remains important that we know we *can* go outside again. We're not dwarves."

A cry sounded down the line. "They're fighting in the back!" a woman yelled. "Undead! Undead sailors again!"

"We know there's a way out," Hanaleisa said somberly, "because now we know there's a way in."

"Even if it's the way we already came," Temberle added, and he and Hanaleisa made their way along the line to take up arms once again, to battle bloodthirsty monsters in an unending nightmare.

By the time Hanaleisa and Temberle arrived at the scuffle, the small skirmish had ended, leaving a trio of waterlogged and rotted zombies crumpled in the corridor. But one of the Carradden, too, had fallen, caught by surprise. Her neck had been broken in the opening salvo.

"What are we to do with her?" a man asked, speaking above the wails of the woman's husband, a fellow sailor.

"Burn her, and be quick!" another shouted, which elicited many cries of protest and many more shouts of assent. Both sides in the debate became more insistent with each passing shout, and it seemed as if the whole argument would explode into more fighting then and there.

"We cannot burn her!" Hanaleisa yelled above it all, and whether by deference to one of Cadderly's children or simply because of the strength and surety in her voice, Hanaleisa's yell interrupted the cacophony of the brewing storm, at least for the moment.

"Ye'd have her stand up, then, to walk like one o' them?" an old seadog argued. "Better to burn her now and be sure."

"We haven't any fire, nor any tools for making fire," Hanaleisa shot back. "And even if we did, would you have us trudging through tunnels filled with such a smell and reminder as that?"

The dead woman's husband finally tore away from those trying to hold him back, and shoved his way through the crowd to kneel beside his wife. He took up her head, cradling it in his arms, his strong shoulders bobbing with sobs.

Hanaleisa and Temberle looked at each other, not knowing what to do.

"Cut off her head, then!" someone yelled from the back, and the dead woman's husband lifted a hateful and threatening gaze in the direction of the gruesome suggestion.

"No!" Hanaleisa yelled, again quieting the crowd. "No. Find some rocks. We'll bury her under a cairn, respectfully, as she deserves."

That seemed to mollify the distraught husband somewhat, but some in the crowd began to protest all the more loudly.

"And if she comes to a state of undeath like all the others, and charges at us?" a nearby dissenter remarked to Hanaleisa and Temberle. "Are you two going to have the will to cut her down, and in front of this poor man here? Are you sure you're not being cruel in thinking to be kind?"

Hanaleisa found it a hard point to argue, and the weight of responsibility for the calamity pressed down heavily on her young shoulders. She looked back at the husband, who obviously recognized her dilemma. He stared at her pleadingly.

"A few heavier rocks, then," Hanaleisa said. "If whatever abomination that is animating the dead reaches her, which I think unlikely," she added for the sake of the distraught man, "then she will not be able to rise against us, or anyone else."

"No, she'll be trapped flailing under our heavy stones, and what an eternity that's to be!" the old seadog said. More yelling ensued, and again the husband's expression fell as he hugged his dear dead wife more closely.

"Aye, so if we cut off her head and that happens, then she can tuck it under one arm, what, and walk about forever like that?" another man chided the first.

"I hate this," Temberle whispered to his sister.

"We've no choice," Hanaleisa reminded him. "If we don't lead, who will?"

In the end, they settled on Hanaleisa's suggestion, building a cairn of heavy rocks to securely inter the dead woman. At Hanaleisa's private suggestion, Pikel then performed a ceremony to consecrate the ground around the cairn, with Hanaleisa assuring all, particularly the husband, that such a ritual would make it very unlikely that any necromantic magic could disturb her rest.

That seemed to calm the bereaved husband somewhat, and mollify the protestors, though in fact, Pikel had no such real ceremony to offer and the impromptu dance and song he offered was no more than a show.

At that dark time, in that dark place, Hanaleisa thought a show was just as good.

She realized it was better than the alternatives, of which she could not think of even one.

CHAPTER 16
DARK HOLES

Danica saw the cave entrance far in the distance, long before she realized that the trail of death led to that spot. She knew instinctively that such a creature as had caused that withering and decay would not long bask in sunlight.

The trail meandered a bit, but soon bent toward the dark face of the distant mountain, where it ended abruptly. Likely, the dragon had taken flight.

When Danica at last arrived at the base of the mountain, she looked up at the black mouth of the cavern. It was indeed large enough to admit a great wyrm, a subtle crease high in the mountain wall, inaccessible to any unable to fly.

Or unable to climb with the skill of a master monk.

Danica closed her eyes and fell inside herself, connecting mind and body in complete harmony. She envisioned herself as lighter, as unbounded by the press of gravity. Slowly, the woman opened her eyes again, lifting her chin to scan a path among the stones. Few others would have seen much possibility there, but to Danica, a ridge no wider than a finger seemed as inviting as a ledge upon which five men could stand abreast.

She mentally lifted her body, then reached up to a narrow ledge and locked her fingers in place, counting out the cadence of the next few movements. She scrambled like a spider, seeming effortless, walking the wall on all fours, hands and feet reaching and stretching. Danica moved horizontally as well as vertically, shifting toward better ridges, more broken stones and better handholds.

The sun crossed its midpoint, and still Danica climbed. The wind howled around her, but she ignored its cold bite, and would not let it dislodge her. Of more concern to her was her timing. Her estimate in beginning her ascent was that the creature she sought was a beast of the darkness, and the last place she wanted to be when it emerged from its hole was splayed out on a cliff face, hundreds of feet above the ground.

With that unsettling thought in mind, Danica pushed on, her fingers and toes finding holds, however tentatively. She constantly shifted her weight to minimize the pull against any one limb or even one digit. As she neared the cave opening, the ascent became more broken and not so steep, with several stretches where she could pause and catch her breath. One long expanse was more a walk than a climb. Danica took her time along that trail and paid extra care to use any cover she could find among the many tumbled stones along the path that led to the stygian darkness of the waiting cave.

* * * * *

Numbers.

He was counting and adding, subtracting and counting some more. A compulsion dominated his every thought, to count and to add, to seek patterns in the many numbers that flitted though his thoughts.

Ivan Bouldershoulder had always been fond of numbers. Designing a new tool or implement, working through the proper ratios and calculating the necessary strength of each piece had been among the dwarf craftsman's greatest joys. As when Cadderly had come to him with a tapestry depicting dark elves and their legendary hand crossbows. Working from that image and his knowledge and intuition alone, Ivan had replicated those delicate weapons to near perfection.

Numbers. It was all about numbers. Everything was about numbers—at least, that's what Cadderly had always argued. Everything could be reduced to numbers and deconstructed at will from that point forward, if only the intelligence doing the reducing was great enough to understand the patterns involved.

That was the difference between the mortals and the gods, Cadderly had often remarked. The gods could reduce life itself to numbers.

Such thoughts had never found a home in the far less theorizing and far more pragmatic Ivan Bouldershoulder, but apparently, he realized, Cadderly's sermons had created a far bigger imprint on his brain than he had assumed.

He thought of the implication of numbers, and that memory of a long-ago conversation was the only thing that made the befuddled dwarf realize that the numbers constantly flashing before him just then were nothing more than a purposeful and malicious distraction.

Ivan felt as if he were waking up beside a babbling brook, that moment of recognition of the sound giving him a real space outside of his dreams, a piece of solidity and reality from which to bring his thoughts fully to the waking world.

The numbers continued to flash more insistently. The patterns flickered and disappeared.

Distraction.

Something was keeping him off balance and out of sorts, away from consciousness itself. He couldn't close his eyes against the intrusion, because his eyes were already closed.

No, not closed, he suddenly understood—whether they were closed or not was of no practical consequence, because he wasn't the one using them, or seeing through them. He was lost, wandering aimlessly within the swirl of his own thoughts.

And something had put him there.

And something had kept him there—some force, some creature, some intellect that was inside him.

The dwarf had broken the enchantment of distraction and

lashed out from the cocoon of numbers, though he flailed blindly.

A memory flashed quickly through his thoughts, of fighting on a rocky slope north of Mithral Hall, of a piece of shale spinning through the air and taking the arm from his brother.

As abruptly as Pikel's arm, the memory was gone, but Ivan kept running through the darkness of his own mind, seeking flashes and moments of his own identity.

He found another recollection, a time when he had flown on a dragon. It wasn't anything substantial, just a sensation of freedom, the wind blowing through his hair, dragging his beard out behind him.

A brief flicker of mountains' majesty unfolding before him.

It seemed a fitting metaphor to the dwarf. He felt the same way, but within himself. It was as if his mind had been lifted above the landscape of all that was Ivan Bouldershoulder, as if he were overlooking himself from afar, a spectator in his own thoughts.

But at least he knew. He had escaped the distraction and knew again who he was.

Ivan began to fight. He grabbed at every memory and held it fast, steeling his thoughts to ensure that what he remembered was true. He saw Pikel, he saw Cadderly, he saw Danica and the kids.

The kids.

He had watched them grow from drooling, helpless critters to adulthood, tall and straight and full of potential. He took pride in them as if they were his own children, and he would not let that notion go.

No creature in all the multiverse was more stubborn than a dwarf, after all. And few dwarves were as far-thinking as Ivan Bouldershoulder. He began immediately to use his recognition of the creature telepathically dominating him to begin a flow of information back the other way.

He knew his surroundings through the memory of that other being. He understood the threats around him, to some extent, and he felt keenly the power of the dracolich.

If he wanted to survive, if there was any way to survive, he knew, in that moment when he would at last find a way to reassert control of his mortal coil, that he couldn't allow himself to be confused and couldn't allow himself to be surprised.

*****

The face of Ivan Bouldershoulder, controlled solely by Yharaskrik the illithid, smiled.

The dwarf was waking up.

Because of the illithid's own uncertainty, Yharaskrik knew, for as it had begun to consider the wisdom of returning fully to consciousness within the draconic host of Crenshinibon, so it had also, unavoidably, lessened its grasp on the dwarf.

Yharaskrik understood well that once a possessed creature of strong intellect and determination—a dwarf perhaps more than any other race—had broken out of the initial mental invasion of psionic power, it was like a trickle of water through an earthen dam.

It couldn't be stopped, even if Yharaskrik had decided that it was critical to stop it. It could be temporarily plugged, perhaps, but never fully stopped, for all of the mental cobwebs Yharaskrik had enacted to keep the dwarf locked in a dark hole were beginning to erode.

The illithid amused itself with a notion of freeing the dwarf right before the waiting maw of fearsome Hephaestus. He thought of departing the dwarf's mind almost fully, but leaving just a bit of consciousness within Ivan so that it could feel the desperate terror and the last moments of the dwarf's life.

What, after all, could be more invasive and intrusive than being so intimate a part of another being's final moments?

And indeed, Yharaskrik had done that very thing many times before, as it pondered the truth of death. To the illithid's frustration, however, never had it been able to send its own consciousness over into the realm of death with that of its host.

It didn't matter, the illithid decided as it pushed away those past failures with a mental sigh. It still enjoyed those voyeur moments, of sharing those ultimate sensations and fears uninvited, of intruding upon the deepest privacy any sentient creature could ever know.

Through the eyes of Ivan Bouldershoulder, Yharaskrik looked upon Hephaestus. The dracolich lay curled at the back of the largest chamber in the mountain cavern, not asleep, for sleep was for the living, but in a state of deep meditation and plotting, and fantasizing of the victories to come.

No, the illithid decided as it sensed the dragon's continuing feelings of superiority. Yharaskrik would not give Hephaestus the satisfaction of that particular kill.

Methodically, the illithid in the dwarf's body walked over to retrieve Ivan's antlered helmet and his heavy axe, formulating the plan as it went. It wanted to feel the dwarf's extended terror, his fury and his fear. Yharaskrik moved out of the cave, signaling the four undead wizards to follow, and stepped out onto the rocky descent a short way, then paused, calling Fetchigrol to its side.

On Yharaskrik's command, the specter crossed the unseen threshold once more, past the realm of death and into the other world, the Shadowfell, that had been opened to them through the power of the falling Weave.

Yharaskrik paused only a moment longer, to taunt the thoughts of Ivan Bouldershoulder.

Then it let the dwarf have the control and sensibilities of his mortal coil back once more, surrounded by enemies and with nowhere to run, and no way to win.

* * * * *

Ivan knew where he was and what was coming against him—he had garnered that from the consciousness of his possessor. He felt no shock from the illithid departing, and so Ivan Bouldershoulder woke up swinging. His axe hummed through the air in great sweeping cuts. He smashed the burned wizard, sending up a cloud of flecks of blackened skin. His backhand opened wide the chest of a second zombie and sent the horrid creature tumbling away.

When another came in at him behind the arc of that cut, Ivan lowered his head and butted hard, the deer antlers on his helmet poking deep holes in the charging beast.

With a groan, the undead wizard fell backward off the helmet spikes, just in time to catch the dwarf's axe swing right in the side of its head. The axe blew through and dived into the fourth as it shuffled up to grasp at the dwarf.

By that time, Ivan's initial fury played out, more enemies swarmed toward him: huddled, fleshy beasts.

Ivan sprinted down the trail, away from the cave, though he knew from memory that the route was surely a dead end, a long drop. But the invading consciousness still hovered over him, he sensed, anticipating just such a run.

So Ivan turned and bulled his way through the close pursuit of a pair of crawling beasts, knocking them aside with sheer ferocity and strength. He ran all the faster, right for the cave mouth, and straight into it.

And there lay the moldering skeleton of a titanic dragon, itself imbued with the animate power of the undead. It was already moving when Ivan came upon it, leaping up onto its four legs with amazing dexterity.

The sight nearly knocked the breath out of Ivan. He knew that something big and terrible was in that cave before he'd fully awakened, but he couldn't have anticipated a catastrophe of such proportions.

A lesser dwarf, a lesser warrior, would have hesitated right there at the entrance, and the huddled beasts would have fallen over him from behind, and even had he somehow prevailed in that crush, the great monster before him would have had him.

But Ivan did not hesitate. He lifted his axe high and charged the dracolich, bellowing a war cry to his god, Moradin. He had no doubt he was going to die, but he would do so in a manner of his choosing, in the manner of a true warrior.

* * * * *

The first sounds of battle alerted Danica. She scrambled around a stone and her heart fell, for there she saw Ivan, fighting valiantly against overwhelming odds of crawling beasts and a few horribly maimed walking dead. Behind them, directing them, Danica sensed, was some spectral being, huddled and shadowy and shimmering like simultaneously thinning and thickening gray smoke. Danica's first instinct was to go to Ivan, or rush behind the pursuing throng and attack the leading creature, but even as she digested the awful scene, the dwarf turned and sprinted away, up the trail toward the great cave.

The monsters pursued. The specter rushed behind them.

Danica followed.

Into the cave went Ivan. Into the cave went the monsters and the zombies and the specter. To the edge of the entrance went Danica, and there she skidded to an abrupt stop, and there she saw Ivan's doom, saw her own doom, saw the doom of all the world.

Danica couldn't even catch her breath in the sight of the great dracolich, and enough of the dragon remained intact for her to recognize the red scales of the wyrm. Her gaze locked on the beast's face, half-rotted, white bone showing, eye sockets burned out horribly, and a peculiar, green-glowing horn protruding from the very middle of its forehead.

She felt the power emanating from that horn.

Awful power.

Ivan's battle cry broke her trance, and she looked down at the dwarf's charge, his axe up high over his head as if he meant to tear his way right through the beast. He charged at the dracolich's front leg, and the wyrm lifted its foot at the last moment.

Ivan dived, and so did a trio of huddled fleshy beasts and one of the undead—one of the wizards from Baldur's Gate, Danica recognized with a heavy heart.

The beast stamped with power that shook the whole of the mountain spur, sending cracks spiderwebbing across the stone floor.

The air around its foot was sprayed with blood and gore, a crimson mist of ultimate destruction, a stamp of pure finality.

Danica couldn't contain her gasp.

A few of the creatures that had not followed the dwarf to doom, falling back and stumbling every which way from the sheer concussion of the stomp, noted that faint noise.

Then Danica was running away from the cave, hungry beasts in close pursuit. She sprinted down the trail, trying to figure out how or where she might go, for the navigable angle of decline would not hold, not in any direction.

She glanced over her shoulder, turned back, and cut fast behind a stone outcropping, and cut the other way around another, trying to gain some distance so that she could get over a ledge and begin her descent down the cliff face.

But there were too many, and every turn did no more than put different monsters close on her tail.

She ran out of room and skidded to the edge of the cliff, perched at the point of the longest drop, for not only did it rise above the hundreds of feet of cliffs that had led Danica to that awful place, it went far deeper on one side, into a gorge low in the foothills of the Snowflakes.

Danica turned around, then fell flat as a beast leaped at her. It sailed over her, its hungry cry turning to a scream of terror, fast receding as it plummeted to oblivion.

Up hopped Danica, kicking out to knock back the next monster in line. The third, as if oblivious to the fate of the first, leaped into the air and tumbled at her. Again she ducked, though not as fully, and the creature brushed her as it went over. Danica fought hard and regained her balance just in time.

But the creature's flailing claw caught her shoulder and tugged her back.

All the fury and tumult of the moment seemed to stop suddenly and Danica's ears filled with the emptiness of a mournful wind.

And she was falling.

She twisted around, looking down a thousand feet and more to the tops of very tall trees.

She thought of Cadderly, of her children, of a life not yet complete.

PART 3

THE SUM OF THEIR PARTS

THE SUM OF THEIR PARTS

We live in a dangerous world, and one that seems more dangerous now that the way of magic is in transition, or perhaps even collapse. If Jarlaxle's guess is correct, we have witnessed the collision of worlds, or of planes, to the point where rifts will bring newer and perhaps greater challenges to us all.

It is, I suspect, a time for heroes.

I have come to terms with my own personal need for action. I am happiest when there are challenges to be met and overcome. I feel in those times of great crisis that I am part of something larger than myself—a communal responsibility, a generational duty—and to me, that is great comfort.

We will all be needed now, every blade and every brain, every scholar and every warrior, every wizard and every priest. The events in the Silver Marches, the worry I saw on Lady Alustriel's face, are not localized, but, I fear, resonate across the breadth of Toril. I can only imagine the chaos in Menzoberranzan with the decline of the wizards and priests; the entire matriarchal society might well be in jeopardy, and those greatest of Houses might find themselves besieged by legions of angry kobolds.

Our situation on the World Above is likely to be no less dire, and so it is the time for heroes. What does that mean, to be a hero? What is it that elevates some above the hordes of fighters and battle-mages? Certainly circumstance plays a role—extraordinary valor, or action, is more likely in moments of highest crisis.

And yet, in those moments of greatest crisis, the result is, more often than not, disaster. No hero emerges. No savior leads the charge across the battlefield, or slays the dragon, and the town is immersed in flames.

In our world, for good or for ill, the circumstances favorable to creating a hero have become all too common.

It is not, therefore, just circumstance, or just good fortune. Luck may play a part, and indeed some people—I count myself among them—are more lucky than others, but since I do not believe that there are blessed souls and cursed souls, or that this or that god is leaning over our shoulders and involving himself in our daily affairs, then I do know that there is one other necessary quality for those who find a way to step above the average.

If you set up a target thirty strides away and assemble the hundred best archers in any given area to shoot at it, they'd all hit the mark. Add in a bet of gold and a few would fall away, to the hoots of derision from their fellows.

But now replace the target with an assassin, and have that assassin holding at dagger-point the person each successive archer most loves in the world. The archer now has one shot. Just one. If he hits the mark—the assassin—his loved one will be saved. If he misses the assassin, it is certain doom for his beloved.

A hero will hit that mark. Few mere archers would.

That is the extra quality involved, the ability to hold poise and calm and rational thought no matter how devastating the consequences of failure, the ability to go to that place of pure concentration in times most emotionally and physically tumultuous. Not just once and not by luck. The hero makes that shot.

The hero lives for that shot. The hero trains for that shot, every day, for endless hours, with purest concentration.

Many fine warriors live in the world, wielding blade or lightning bolt, who serve well in their respective armies, who weather the elements and the enemies with quiet and laudable stoicism. Many are strong in their craft, and serve with distinction.

But when all teeters precariously on the precipice of disaster, when victory or defeat rests upon matters beyond simple strength and courage and valor, when all balances on that sword-edged line between victory or defeat, the hero finds a way—a way that seems impossible to those who do not truly understand the give and take of battle, the ebb and flow of sword play, the logical follow-up to counter an enemy's advantage.

For a warrior is one trained in the techniques of various weaponry, one who knows how to lift a shield or parry a thrust and properly counter, but a true warrior, a hero, extends beyond those skills. Every movement is instinctual, is engrained into every muscle to flow with perfect and easy coordination. Every block is based on clear thinking—so clear that it is as much anticipatory as reflexive. And every weakness in an opponent becomes apparent at first glance.

The true warrior fights from a place of calm, of controlled rage and quelled fear. Every situation comes to sharpened focus, every avenue of solution shines its path clearly. And the hero goes one step beyond that, finding a way, any way, to pave a path of victory when there is no apparent route.

The hero finds a way, and when that way is shown, however difficult the path, the hero makes the thrust or the block or the last frantic riposte, stealing his opponent's victory. As when Regis used his ruby pendant to paralyze a battle-mage in Luskan. As when Wulfgar threw himself at the yochlol to save Catti-brie. As when Catti-brie made that desperate shot in the sewers of Calimport to drive off Entreri, who had gained the advantage over me. As when Bruenor used his cunning, his strength, and his unshakable will to defeat Shimmergloom in the darkness of Mithral Hall.

Certain doom is a term not known in the vocabulary of the hero, for it is precisely at those times when doom seems most certain—when Bruenor rode the flaming shadow dragon down to the depths of Garumn's Gorge—that the warrior who would be hero elevates himself above the others. It is, instinctually, not about him or his life.

The hero makes the shot.

We are all to be tested now, I fear. In this time of confusion and danger, many will be pulled to the precipice of disaster, and most will fall over that dark ledge. But a few will step beyond that line, will find a way and will make that shot.

In those moments, however, it is important to recognize that reputation means nothing, and while past deeds might inspire confidence, they are no guarantee of present or future victory.

I hope that Taulmaril is steady in my hands when I stand upon that precipice, for I know that I walk into the shadows of doom, where black pits await, and I need only to think of broken Regis or look at my beloved Catti-brie to understand the stakes of this contest.

I hope that I am given that shot at this assassin, whomever or whatever it may be, who holds us all at dagger-point, for if so, I intend to hit the mark.

For that is the last point to make about the hero. In the aforementioned archery contest, the hero wants to be the one chosen to take that most critical shot. When the stakes are highest, the hero wants the outcome to be in his hands. It's not about hubris, but about necessity, and the confidence that the would-be hero has trained and prepared for exactly that one shot.

—Drizzt Do'Urden

CHAPTER 17
NOTHING BUT THE WIND

It all stopped. Everything. The battle, the fear, and the chase. It was over, replaced by only the sound of the wind and the grand view from on high. A sensation of emptiness and solitude washed over the monk. Of freedom. Of impending death.

A twist, a shift, and pure control had Danica upright immediately, and she turned around to face the cliff from which she had just tumbled. She reached out and lunged forward, her eyes scanning before her and below her, all in an instant, yielding a sudden recognition and complete sorting of the larger jags and angles. She slapped her palm against the stone, then the other one, then back and forth repeatedly. With each contact her muscles twitched against the momentum of the fall.

A jut of stone far below and to the left had her thrusting her left foot out that way, and as she slapped the stone with both hands together, she gave the slightest push, again and again, ten times in rapid succession as she descended, subtly shifting to the left.

Her toe touched a jag and she threw her weight to that foot, bending her leg to absorb the impact. She couldn't begin to stop the momentum of her descent with just that, but she managed to push back with some success, stealing some of her speed.

It was the way of the monk. Danica could run down the wall of a tall building and land without injury. She had done it on more than one occasion. But of course, a tall building was nowhere near the height of that cliff, and the grade was more difficult, sometimes sheer and straight, sometimes less than sheer, sometimes more than sheer. But she worked with all her concentration, her muscles answering her demands.

Another jag gave her the opportunity to break a bit more of her momentum, and a narrow ledge allowed her to plant both feet and work her leg muscles against the relentless pull of gravity.

After that, halfway to the ground, the woman looked more like a spider running frantically along a wall, her arms and legs pumping furiously.

A dark form fell past her, startling her and nearly stealing her concentration. One of the fleshy beasts, she recognized, but she didn't begin to speculate on how it might have fallen.

She had no time for that, no time for anything but absolute concentration on the task before her.

Nothing but the wind filled her senses, that and the contours of the cliff.

She was almost to the ground, still falling too quickly to survive. Danica couldn't hope to land and roll to absorb the tremendous impact. So she hooked her feet together against the stone and threw herself over backward, rolling over just in time to see the tall pines she had viewed from above.

Then she was crashing through the branches, needles flying, wood splintering. A broken branch hooked her and tore a fair slice of skin out of her side and ripped away half her shirt. A heavier branch not much farther below didn't break, but bent, and Danica rolled off it head over heels, tumbling and crashing, rebounding off the heaviest lower branches and breaking through amidst a spray of green needles, and still with thirty feet to fall.

Half blinded by pain, barely conscious, the monk still managed to sort herself out and spin to get her feet beneath her.

She bent and rolled sidelong as she landed. Over and over she went, three times, five times, seven times. She stopped with a gasp, explosions of pain rolling up from her legs, from her torn side, from a shoulder she knew to be dislocated.

Danica managed to turn over a bit, to see a lump of splattered black flesh.

At least she didn't look like that, she thought. But though she had avoided the mutilation suffered by the crawlers, she feared that the result would be the same and that she would not survive the fall.

Cold darkness closed in.

But Danica fought it, telling herself that the dracolich would come looking for her, reminding herself that she was not safe, that even if she somehow managed to not die from the battering she had taken in the fall, the beast would have her.

She rolled to her belly and pushed up on her elbows, or tried to, but her shoulder would not allow it and the waves of agony that rippled out overwhelmed her. She propped herself up on one arm, and there vomited, gasping. Tears filled her almond-shaped eyes as her retching, and the spasms in her ribs, elicited a whole new level of agony.

She had to move, she told herself.

But she had no more to give.

The cold darkness closed in again, and even mighty Danica could not resist.

* * * * *

Looking out the door of the side room in the darkened gorge, Catti-brie could barely make out the forms of her companions in the other chamber's flickering torchlight. They were all trapped at the apparent dead end, shadow hounds coming in swift pursuit, a dragon blocking the way before them. Drizzt was lost to them, and Wulfgar, beside Catti-brie, had taken the brunt of the dragon's breath, a horrid cloud of blackness and despair that had left him numb and nearly helpless.

She peered out the door, desperate for an answer, praying that her father would find a way to save them all. She didn't know what to make of it when Bruenor took off the gem-studded helmet and replaced it with his broken-horned old helm.

When he handed the crown to Regis and said, "Keep the helm safe. It's the crown of the King of Mithral Hall," his intent became all too clear.

The halfling protested, "Then it is yours," and the same gripping fear that coursed through Catti-brie was evident in Regis's voice.

"Nay, not by me right or me choice. Mithral Hall is no more, Rumble—Regis. Bruenor of Icewind Dale, I am, and have been for two hundred years, though me head's too thick to know it!"

Catti-brie barely heard the next words as she gasped and understood all too clearly what Bruenor was about to do. Regis asked him something she couldn't hear, but understood that it was the very same question whose awful answer screamed at her in her own thoughts.

Bruenor came into clear sight then, running out of the room and charging straight for the gorge. "Here's one from yer tricks, boy!" he yelled, looking at the small side chamber concealing Catti-brie and Wulfgar. "But when me mind's to jumping on the back of a worm, I ain't about to miss!"

There it was, spoken openly, a declaration of the ultimate sacrifice for the sake of the rest of them, trapped deep in the bowels of the caverns once known as Mithral Hall by a great dragon of shadow.

"Bruenor!" Catti-brie heard herself cry, though she was hardly conscious of speaking, so numbed was she by the realization that she was about to lose the dwarf, her beloved adoptive father, the great Bruenor who had served as the foundation of her entire life, the strength of Catti-brie Battlehammer.

The world moved in slow motion for the young woman at that terrible moment, as Bruenor sprinted across the floor to the gorge, reaching over his shoulder to set his cloak afire—and under it was a keg of oil!

The dwarf didn't waver and didn't slow as he reached the lip and went over, axe high, back aflame.

Compulsion and terror combined to drag Catti-brie over to that ledge, arriving at the same time as Regis, both gawking down at the burning dwarf, locked upon the back of the great shadow dragon.

Bruenor had not wavered, but his actions had taken all the strength from Catti-brie, to be sure! She could hardly hold herself upright as she watched her father die, giving his life so that she, Wulfgar, and Regis could cross the gorge and escape the darkness of Mithral Hall.

But she'd never find the strength to make it, she feared, and Bruenor would die in vain.

Wulfgar was beside her then, grimacing against the magical despair, fighting through it with the determination of a barbarian of Icewind Dale. Catti-brie could hardly comprehend his intent as he lifted his wondrous warhammer high and flung it down at the dragon.

"Are ye mad?" she cried, grabbing at him.

"Take up your bow," he told her, and he was Wulfgar again, freed of the dragon's insidious spell. "If a true friend of Bruenor's you be, then let him not fall in vain!"

A true friend? The words hit Catti-brie hard, reminding her poignantly that she was so much more than a friend to that dwarf, her father, the anchor of her life.

She knew that Wulfgar was right, and took up her bow in shaking hands, and sighted her target through tear-filled eyes.

She couldn't help Bruenor. She couldn't save him from the choice he had made—the choice that had possibly saved the three of them.

It was the toughest shot she had ever had to make, but she had to make it, for Bruenor's sake.

The silver-flashing arrow streaked away from Taulmaril, its lightning flash filling Catti-brie's wet eyes.

* * * * *

Someone grabbed her and pulled her arms down to her side. She heard the hiss of a distant whisper, but could make out no words, nor could she see the one whose touch she felt.

It was Drizzt, she knew from the tenderness and strength in those delicate hands.

But Drizzt was lost to her, to them all. It made no sense.

And Bruenor....

But the gorge was gone, the dragon was gone, her father was gone, all the world was gone, replaced by that land of brown mists and crawling, shadowy beasts, coming at her, clawing at her.

They could not reach her, they could not hurt her, but Catti-brie found little comfort in the emptiness. She felt nothing, was aware of nothing but the crawling, misshapen, ugly forms in a land she did not recognize.

In a place where she was completely alone.

And worse than that, worst of all, a line of division between two realities so narrow and blurry that the sheer incongruence of it all stole from Catti-brie something much more personal than her friends and familiar surroundings.

She tried to resist, tried to focus on the feeling of those strong arms around her—it had to be Drizzt!—but she realized that she couldn't even feel the grasp any longer, if it was there.

The huddled images began to blur. The two worlds competed with flashing scenes in her mind and a discordant cacophony of disconnected sounds, a clash of two realities from which there was no escape.

She fell within herself, trying to hold on to her memories, her reality, her individuality.

But there was nothing to hold onto, no grounding pole to remind her of anything, of Catti-brie, even.

She had no cogent thought and no clear memories, and no self-awareness.

She was so utterly lost that she didn't even know that she was utterly lost.

* * * * *

A speck of bright orange found its way past Danica's closed eyelid, knifing through the blackness that had taken her senses. Wearily, she managed to crack open that eye, to be greeted by the sunrise, the brilliant orb just showing its upper edge in the east, in the V-shaped crook between two mountains. It almost seemed to Danica as if those distant mountains were guiding the light directly to her, to her eyes, to awaken her.

The events of the previous day played out in her thoughts,

and she couldn't begin to sort out where dreams had ended and awful reality had begun.

Or had it all been a dream?

But then why was she lying in a canyon beside a great cliff?

Slowly the woman started to unwind it all, and the darkness receded.

She pulled herself up to her elbows, or tried to until waves of agony in her shoulder laid her low once more. Wincing against the pain, her eyes tightly closed, Danica recalled the fall, the tumble through the trees, then she backtracked from there to the scene atop the cliff in the lair of the undead dragon.

Ivan was dead.

The weight of that hit Danica hard. She heard again the stomp of the dracolich and saw once more the splattering flesh flying about the cavern. She thought of all the times she had seen Ivan with her kids, the doting uncle offering the wisdom wrought of tough lessons, unlike the doting Pikel, who was so much softer-edged than his brother.

"Pikel," she whispered into the grass, overwhelmed by the thought of telling him about Ivan.

The mention of Pikel brought Danica's thoughts careening back to her own children, who were out, somewhere, with the dwarf.

She opened her eyes—the lower rim of the sun was visible, the morning moving along.

Her children were in trouble. That notion seemed inescapable. They were either in trouble or the danger had already found them and taken them, and that, Danica would not allow herself to accept.

With a growl of defiance, the monk pulled up to one arm and tucked her legs under her, then threw herself up and back into a kneeling position, her left arm hanging limp, not quite at her side but a bit behind her. She couldn't turn her head against the pain to look at her shoulder, but she knew it was dislocated.

That wouldn't do.

Danica scanned the area behind her, the stone of the cliff wall. With a determined nod, she leaped to her feet, and before the pain could slow her, she rushed toward the wall, jumped into the air, and turned as she descended, slamming the back of her injured shoulder against the stone.

She heard a loud popping sound and knew it was a prelude to agony. Indeed, the waves that came at her had her doubled over and vomiting.

But she could see her shoulder, aligned once more, and the pain fast subsided. She could even move her arm again, though the slightest motion hurt badly.

She stood leaning against the stone wall for a long while, falling within herself to find a place of calm against the furious storm that roiled in her battered form.

When she at last opened her eyes, she first focused upon one of the fallen crawlers, flattened and splattered against the ground. She managed to look up behind her, up the cliff, thinking of the dracolich and what she had to do to warn those who might help her defeat the beast.

She looked south, guided by her mothering instincts, toward the road to Carradoon and her children, and there she desperately wanted to go. But she focused on an area not so far to the south, trying to get a sense of the valley in proportion to the direct north-south trail to Spirit Soaring.

Danica nodded, recognizing that she wouldn't have to cross the mountainous barrier to find that road. Fairly certain of her location—she was in a deep valley several miles from the cathedral—she started away on unsteady legs, her ankle threatening to roll under her with each step.

Soon after, she was leaning on a walking stick, fighting the pain and dreading the trail up to her home. The road was much steeper than the trail from Carradoon, and she toyed with the idea of continuing all the way around to the port city, then using the more passable pathways instead.

She couldn't help but laugh at herself for that feeble justification. She'd lose a day and more of travel time taking that route, a day and more Cadderly and the others didn't have to spare.

She came upon the north-south road some time after highsun,

her strength sapped, her clothes sticking to her with sweat. Again she looked southeast toward unseen Carradoon, and thought of her children. She closed her eyes and turned south, then looked upon the road home, the road she needed to take for all their sakes.

She recalled that the road continued fairly flat for about a quarter of a mile, then began an onerous climb up into the Snowflakes. She had to make that climb. It was not a choice, but a duty. Cadderly had to know.

And Danica meant to walk all through the night to tell him. She started off at a slow pace, practically dragging one foot and leaning heavily on the walking stick in her right hand, her left arm hanging loose at her side. Every step jolted that shoulder, and so Danica paused and tore off a piece of her already torn shirt, fashioning it into a makeshift sling.

With a sigh of determination, the woman started away again, a little more quickly, but with her strength fast waning.

She lost track of time, but knew the shadows were lengthening around her, then she heard something—a rider or a wagon— approaching from behind. Danica shuffled off the trail and threw herself down behind a bush and a rock, crawling into a place to watch the road behind her. She chewed hard on her bottom lip to keep from gasping out in pain, but even that notion and sensation were soon lost to her as her curious quarry came into view.

She saw the horse first, a skeletal black beast with fire around its hooves. It snorted smoke from its flared nostrils. A hell horse, a nightmare, and as Danica noted the wagon driver—or more particularly, the driver's great, wide-brimmed and plumed hat, and the ebon color of his skin—she remembered him.

"Jarlaxle?" she whispered, and more curious still, he sat with another dark elf Danica surely recognized.

The thought of that rogue Jarlaxle riding along with Drizzt Do'Urden knocked Danica even more emotionally off-balance. How could it be?

And what did it mean, for her and for Cadderly?

As the wagon neared, she made out a couple of heads above the rail of the backboard. Dwarves, obviously. A squeal from the side turned her attention to a third dwarf riding a pig that looked like it grazed on the lower planes right beside the nightmare pulling the wagon.

Danica told herself that it couldn't be Drizzt Do'Urden, and warned herself that it was not out of the realm of possibility that the fiendish Jarlaxle might be behind all of the trouble that had come to Erlkazar. She couldn't risk going to them, she told herself repeatedly as the wagon bounced along the trail, nearing her hiding place.

Despite those very real and grounded reservations, as the wagon rolled up barely ten feet from her, the nightmare snorting flames and pounding the road with its fiery hooves, the desperate woman, realizing instinctively that she was out of options, pulled herself up to her knees and called out for help.

"Lady Danica!" Jarlaxle cried, and Drizzt spoke her name at the same time.

Together the two drow leaped down from the wagon and ran to her, moving to opposite sides of her and falling on bended knee. Together they gently cradled and supported her, and glanced at each other with equal disbelief that anything could have so battered the magnificent warrior-monk.

"What'd ye know, elf?" one of the dwarves called, climbing from the back of the wagon. "That Cadderly's girl?"

"Lady Danica," Drizzt explained.

"You must . . ." the woman gasped. "You must get me to Cadderly. I must warn him . . ."

Her voice trailed off and she faltered, her consciousness slipping away.

"We will," Drizzt promised. "Rest easy."

* * * * *

Drizzt looked at Jarlaxle, grave concern evident on his face. He wasn't sure Danica could survive the journey.

"I have potions," Jarlaxle assured him, but with less confidence than Drizzt would have hoped for. Besides, who could be sure what effects his potions might produce in such a time of wild magic?

They made Danica as comfortable as they could in the back of the wagon, laying her beside Catti-brie, who sat against the backboard and still seemed totally unaware of her surroundings. Jarlaxle stayed beside the monk, spooning magical healing potions into her mouth, while Bruenor drove the wagon as fast as the nightmare could manage. Drizzt and Pwent ran near flank, fearing that whatever had hit Danica might not be far afield. On Jarlaxle's bidding, Athrogate and the hell boar stayed near, riding just in front of the nightmare.

"It's getting steeper," Bruenor warned a short time later. "Yer horse ain't for liking it."

"The mules are rested now," Jarlaxle replied. "Go as far as we can, then we'll put them back up front."

"Night'll be falling by then."

"Perhaps we should ride through."

Bruenor didn't want to agree, but he found himself nodding despite his reservations.

"Elf?" the dwarf asked, seeing Drizzt approach from some brush to the side of the trail.

"Nothing," Drizzt answered. "I have seen no sign of any monsters, and no trail to be found save Danica's own."

"Well, that's a good thing," Bruenor said. He reached over and grabbed at Drizzt's belt to help the drow hop up the side of the rolling wagon.

"Her breathing is steady," Drizzt noted of Danica, and Jarlaxle nodded.

"The potions have helped," said Jarlaxle. "There is a measure of predictable magic remaining."

"Bah, but she ain't said a word," said Bruenor.

"I've kept her in a stupor," Jarlaxle explained. "For her own sake. A simple enchantment," he added reassuringly when both Drizzt and Bruenor looked at him with suspicion. He pulled from his vest a pendant with a dangling ruby, remarkably like the one worn by Regis.

"Hey, now!" Bruenor protested and pulled hard on the reins, bringing the wagon up short.

"It's not Regis's," Jarlaxle assured him.

"You had his, in Luskan," Drizzt remembered.

"For a time, yes," said Jarlaxle. "Long enough to have my artisans replicate it." As Bruenor and Drizzt continued to stare at him hard, Jarlaxle just shrugged and explained, "It's what I do."

Drizzt and Bruenor looked at each other and sighed.

"I did not steal anything from him, and I could have, easily enough," Jarlaxle argued. "I did not kill him, or you, and I could have—"

"Easily enough," Drizzt had to agree.

"When can you free her of the trance?" Drizzt asked.

Jarlaxle glanced down at Danica, the monk seeming much more at ease, and he started to say, "Soon." Before the word got out of his mouth, Danica's hand shot up and grasped the dangling chain that held the ruby pendant. With a twist and turn that appeared so subtle and simple as she sat up from the wagon bed, she spun the startled Jarlaxle around and jerked the chain behind him, twisting it even more to hold the drow fast in a devastating chokehold.

"You were told never to return, Jarlaxle Baenre," Danica said, her mouth right beside the dark elf's ear.

"Your gratitude overwhelms me, Lady," the drow managed to gasp in reply.

He stiffened as Danica pulled and twisted. "Move your fingers a bit more into position to grasp a weapon, drow," she coaxed. "I can snap your neck as easily as a dry twig."

"A little help?" Jarlaxle whispered to Drizzt.

"Danica, let him go," Drizzt said. "He is not our enemy. Not now."

Danica loosened her grip, just a bit, and stared skeptically at the ranger, then looked to Bruenor.

Drizzt nudged the silent dwarf.

"Good to meet ye at last, Lady Danica," Bruenor said. "King Bruenor Battlehammer, at yer ser—"

Drizzt elbowed him again.

"Aye, let the rat go," Bruenor bade her. " 'Twas Jarlaxle that gived ye the potions that saved yer hide, and he's been a help with me daughter there."

Danica glanced from one to the other, then looked over at Catti-brie. "What's wrong with her?" she asked as she released Jarlaxle, who shifted forward to get away from her.

"I never thought I would see Jarlaxle caught so easily," Drizzt remarked.

"I share your surprise," the mercenary admitted.

Drizzt smiled, briefly enjoying the moment. He came over the rail of the wagon then, stepping past Jarlaxle to go to Danica, who leaned against the tailgate.

"I'll not underestimate that one again," Jarlaxle promised quietly.

"You must get me to Spirit Soaring," Danica said, and Drizzt nodded.

"That is where we were going," he explained. "Catti-brie was touched by the falling Weave—some kind of blue fire. She is trapped within her own mind, it seems, and in a dark place of huddled, crawling creatures."

Danica perked up at that description.

"You have seen them?" Jarlaxle remarked.

"Long-armed, short-legged—almost no-legged—gray-skinned beasts attacked Spirit Soaring in force last night," she explained. "I was out scouting..." Her voice trailed off as she gave a great sigh.

"Ivan Bouldershoulder is dead," she said. Bruenor cried out and Drizzt winced. From the side of the wagon, Thibbledorf Pwent wailed. "The dragon—a dracolich, an undead dragon... and something more..."

"A dracolich?" Jarlaxle said.

"Dead dragon walking—dead dragon talking, dead dragon furious, I'm thinking that curious!" Athrogate rhymed, and Thibbledorf Pwent nodded in appreciation, drawing a scowl from Bruenor.

A dumbfounded Danica stared at the bizarre Athrogate.

"You have to admit that one does not see a dracolich every day," Jarlaxle deadpanned.

Danica seemed even more at a loss.

"Something stranger still, you mentioned?" Jarlaxle prompted.

"Its touch is death," the monk explained. "I found it by following a trail of utter devastation, a complete withering of everything the beast had touched. Trees, grass, everything."

"Never heared o' such a thing," said Bruenor.

"When I saw the beast, gigantic and terrible, I knew my guess to be correct. Its mere touch is death. It is death incarnate, and something more—a horn in its head, glowing with power," Danica went on, her eyes closed as if she had to force herself to remember things she did not want to recall. "I think it was . . ."

"Crenshinibon, the Crystal Shard," said Jarlaxle, nodding with every word.

"Yes."

"That durned thing again," Bruenor grumbled. "So there ye go, elf. Ye didn't break it."

"I did," Jarlaxle corrected. "And that is part of the problem, I fear."

Bruenor just shook his hairy head.

Danica pointed to a tall peak not far behind them and to the north. "He controls them." She looked directly at Jarlaxle. "I believe the dragon is Hephaestus, the great red wyrm whose breath destroyed the artifact, or so we thought."

"It is indeed Hephaestus," Jarlaxle assured her.

"Ye think ye might be tellin' us what ye're about anytime soon?" Bruenor grumbled.

"I already told you my fears," Jarlaxle said. "The dragon and the liches, somehow freed of the prison artifact of their own creation—"

"The Crystal Shard," said Danica, and she tapped her forehead. "Here, on the dracolich."

"Joined by the magic of the collapsing Weave," said Jarlaxle, "merged by the collision of worlds."

Danica looked at him, incredulous.

"I know not either, Lady Danica," Jarlaxle explained. "It's all a guess. But this is all related, of that I am certain." He looked at Catti-brie, her eyes wide open but unseeing. "Her affliction, these beasts, the dragon risen from the dead . . . all of it . . . all part of the same catastrophe, the breadth of which we still do not know."

"And so we have come to find out," said Drizzt. "To bring Catti-brie to Cadderly in the hope that he might help her."

"And I'm thinking that ye'll be needin' our help, too," Bruenor said to Danica.

Danica could only sigh and nod in helpless agreement. She glanced at the distant cliff, the lair of the dracolich and the Crystal Shard, the grave of Ivan Bouldershoulder. She tried not to look past that point, but she couldn't help herself. She feared for her children.

CHAPTER 18
THE SEVERING

It was more than independent thought, Yharaskrik knew. It was independent desire.

Such a thing could not be tolerated. The seven liches that had created the Crystal Shard were represented by the singular power of Crenshinibon only. They had no say in the matter, and no opinions or wants that were pertinent.

But to the perceptive illithid, there was no missing the desire behind Fetchigrol's request. The creature wasn't acting purely on expediency or any compulsion to please its three masters joined as the Ghost King. Fetchigrol wanted something.

And Crenshinibon's addition to the internal debate brewing within the Ghost King was nothing but supportive of the lich-turned-specter.

Yharaskrik telepathically appealed to Hephaestus to deny the lich, and tried to imbue a sense of the depth of his trepidation, but he had to walk a fine line, not wanting the Crystal Shard to recognize that concern.

The illithid couldn't tell whether the dragon caught its subtle inflection of thought, or whether Hephaestus, still less than enamored with Yharaskrik, simply didn't care. The dragon's response came back in the form of eagerness, exactly as Fetchigrol had requested.

"How greatly might we tap the minions of the reformed Shadowfell before we cease to be their masters in this, our world?" Yharaskrik said aloud.

Hephaestus wrestled full control of the dracolich's mouth to respond. "You fear these huddled lumps of flesh?"

"There is more to the Shadowfell than the crawlers," Yharaskrik replied after a brief struggle to regain the use of the voice. "Better that we use the undead of our plane for our armies—their numbers are practically unlimited."

"And they are ineffective!" the dracolich roared, shaking the stone of the chamber. "Mindless . . ."

"But controllable," the illithid interrupted, the words twisting as both creatures fought for physical control.

"We are the Ghost King!" Hephaestus bellowed. "We are supreme."

Yharaskrik started to fight back, but paused as he considered Fetchigrol standing before him and nodding. He could feel the satisfaction coming from the shadowy creature, and he knew that Crenshinibon had sided with Hephaestus, that permission had been given to Fetchigrol to fly back to Carradoon and raise a great army of crawlers to catch and slaughter those people who had fled into the tunnels.

The satisfaction of that creature! Why could not Hephaestus understand the danger in any independent emotions emanating from one of the seven? They were to have no satisfaction, other than in serving, but Fetchigrol was acting on his own personal ego, not a compulsion to serve the greater host. He had been shown up by Solmé, who went to the Shadowfell to raise an army while Fetchigrol merely reanimated dead flesh to do his bidding. The escape of so many from Carradoon had added to that sense of failure in the specter, and so the creature was trying to rectify the situation.

But the specter should not have cared. Why could Hephaestus not understand that?

We are greater with competent generals, came a thought, and Yharaskrik knew it to be Crenshinibon, who would not speak aloud with the dragon's voice.

"They would not dare cross us," Hephaestus agreed.

Let us use their anger.

To what possible gain? Yharaskrik thought, but was careful to shield from the others. What gain would they garner by pursuing the fleeing Carradden? Why should any of them waste their moments concerned about the fate of refugees?

"Your caution grows wearying," the dracolich said as Fetchigrol exited the cavern, bound for Carradoon. Yharaskrik's initial recognition that it was Hephaestus speaking was given pause by the word choice and the timbre of the voice, reflecting more a reasoned remark than the bellow typical of Hephaestus. "Can we not simply destroy for the enjoyment of the act?"

The illithid had no physical body of its own, so it possessed no heels, but Yharaskrik surely fell back on its heels at that revealing moment. It had not adequately shielded its concerns from the other two. The mind flayer had no place to hide from . . .

From which?

The Ghost King, the mind of the dragon answered, reading every thought as if it were his own.

Yharaskrik understood at that moment that the bond between Hephaestus and Crenshinibon was tightening, that they were truly becoming one being, one mind.

The illithid couldn't even begin to hide its fear that the same fate awaited it. As a mind flayer, Yharaskrik was well-versed in the notion of a hive mind—in its Underdark homeland, hundreds of its kind would join together in a common receptacle of intelligence and philosophy and theory-craft. But those were other illithids, equal beings of equal intelligence.

"And the Ghost King is greater than your kin," the dracolich's voice answered. "Is that your fear?"

Its every thought was open to them!

"There is a place for you, Yharaskrik," the Ghost King promised. "Hephaestus is the instinct, the anger, and the physical power. Crenshinibon is the collection of near-eternal wisdom and the dispassion—hence judgment—of a true god. Yharaskrik is the freedom of far-reaching projection and the understanding of the surrealism of worlds joined."

One word, buried in the middle of that declaration of power, revealed to Yharaskrik the truth: judgment. Of the parts of the proposed whole, judgment sat atop the hierarchy, and so it was Crenshinibon that meant to hold its identity. The dragon would be the reactive, the illithid would serve as the informative, and Crenshinibon would control it all.

And so it was Crenshinibon, Yharaskrik realized in that awful moment, who was granting the liches a greater measure of autonomy, and only because the Crystal Shard knew with full confidence that they would ever remain slaves to it, their ultimate creation.

Yharaskrik's only chance would be to get through to Hephaestus, to convince the dragon that he would lose his own identity in that ultimately subservient role.

In response to that unhidden notion, the dracolich laughed, a horrid, scraping noise.

* * * * *

Solmé had bested Fetchigrol. Centuries before, they and five others had joined in common purpose, a complete unification into a singular artifact of great power and infinite duration. Fetchigrol wasn't supposed to care that Solmé had outdone him. Crenshinibon's explanation had been instructive, not a chastisement.

The apparition, an extension of something greater than Fetchigrol, a tool for the furthering of Crenshinibon and nothing more, wasn't supposed to care.

But he did. When Fetchigrol stood at the docks of ruined Carradoon later that same night and reached through the planes to the Shadowfell, he felt elation. His own, not Crenshinibon's.

And when his consciousness returned to Toril, rift in hand, and tore open the divide, he took great satisfaction—his own, not Crenshinibon's—in knowing that the next instructive lecture would be aimed at Solmé and not at himself.

Huddled crawlers poured through the rift. Fetchigrol didn't control them, but he guided them, showing them the little inlet just north of the docks, where the waters of Impresk Lake calmed and the tunnel complex began. The crawlers didn't fear the tunnels. They liked the dark recesses, and no creature in all the multiverse more enjoyed the hunt than the ravenous, fleshy beasts of the dark Shadowfell.

More came through as the rift swirled in on itself and started to mend, to return to the stasis of natural order.

Fetchigrol, Crenshinibon's blessing clear in his eager thoughts, tore it open wide again.

And he ripped it open again when it began to diminish sometime later, knowing all the while that each reopening weakened the fabric of separation between the two worlds. That fabric, that reality of what had always been, was the only real means of control. Gradually, the third tear began to mend.

Fetchigrol tore it wide yet again!

Fewer crawlers came through with each rift, for the shadowy gray region the apparitions had been inhabiting was nearly emptied of the things.

Fetchigrol, who would not lose to Solmé, reached deeper into the Shadowfell. He recklessly widened his call to the far edges of the gray plain, to regions he could not see.

He never saw or heard it coming, for the beast was a creature of shadow, and silent as such. A black cloud descended over the apparition, fully engulfing him.

In that terrible instant, he knew he had failed. It didn't matter the issue, for there was no anchor to the specific disaster.

Just failure. Utter, complete, and irrevocable. Fetchigrol felt it profoundly. It devoured any thoughts he might have for the situation at hand.

The shadow dragon couldn't get through the rift, but it managed to snake its head out far enough to snap its great jaws over the despairing apparition.

And Fetchigrol had no escape. To plane shift would merely place him more fully before the devouring dragon on the other side of the tear. Nor did he have any desire to escape, for the despair wrought by the shadow dragon's black cloud of breath made Fetchigrol understand that obliteration was preferable.

And so he was obliterated.

* * * * *

In the Shadowfell, the dragon receded, but marked the spot of the tear, expecting that soon it might widen enough for it to pass through. When it left, other beasts found their way to the opening.

Nightwings, giant black bats, opened wide their leathery wings and took flight above the ruins of Carradoon, eager to feast on the lighter flesh of the material world.

Fearsome dread wraiths, humanoid, emaciated, and cloaked in tattered dark rags, who could leach the life-force of a victim with a touch, crawled through in hunting packs.

And a nightwalker, a giant, hairless humanoid twenty feet tall, all sinewy and with the strength of a mountain giant, squeezed its way through the rift and onto the shores of Impresk Lake.

* * * * *

In the cave on the cliff, the Ghost King knew.

Fetchigrol was gone, his energy winked out, lost to them.

Yharaskrik was an illithid. Illithids were creature of callous logic and did not gloat, but dragons were creatures of emotion, and so when the illithid pointed out that it had been right in its condemnation of Fetchigrol's plan, a wall of rage came back at it.

From both Hephaestus and Crenshinibon.

For a moment, Yharaskrik didn't understand the Crystal Shard's agreement with the volatile beast. Crenshinibon, too, was an artifact of pragmatic and logical thinking. Unemotional, like the illithid.

But unlike Yharaskrik, Crenshinibon was also ambitious.

And so Yharaskrik knew at that moment that the bond would not hold, that the triumvirate in the dracolich's consciousness would not and could not remain tenable. It thought to find a host outside the dragon's body, but dismissed the notion immediately, realizing that nothing was as mighty as the dracolich, after all, and Hephaestus would not suffer the illithid to survive.

It had to fight.

Hephaestus was all anger and venom, that wall of rage, and the illithid went at him methodically, poking holes with logic and reasoning, reminding its opponent of the inarguable truths, for those truths alone—the recklessness of opening wide a gate to an unknown plane, and the needed caution in continuing against a foe as powerful as the combined might of Spirit Soaring—could serve as a premise on which to build its case.

By every measure of the principles of debate, Yharaskrik was far beyond its opponent. The simple truth and logic were on its side. The illithid poked its holes and appealed to reason over rage, repeatedly, thinking to turn the favor of Crenshinibon, who, he feared, would ultimately decide the outcome of their struggle.

The battle within became a wild assault without, as Hephaestus's dracolich form thrashed and clawed at the stone, breathed fire that melted stone and minion alike, and bull-rushed walls, shaking the entire mountain in great tremors.

Gradually, Hephaestus began to play out his rage, and the internal battle diminished as it became a session of dialogue and discourse. With Yharaskrik leading the way, the Ghost King began to sort how it might correct for the loss of Fetchigrol. The Ghost King began to accept the past and look to the next move in the wider, and more important struggle.

Yharaskrik took some small comfort in the victory, fully recognizing that it might be temporary in nature and fully expecting that it would battle Hephaestus many more times before things were finally settled.

The illithid turned its thoughts and arguments to the very real possibility that Fetchigrol's demise indicated that the apparition had reached too far into what had once been the Plane of Shadow. But for reasons still unknown to the Ghost King, the Plane of Shadow had become something more, something bigger and more dangerous. It also seemed to be somehow moving closer to the Prime Material Plane, and in that event, what consequences might result?

Crenshinibon seemed not to care, reasoning that out of chaos, the Ghost King could only grow stronger.

And if a dangerous and too-powerful organized force had come through the rift, the Ghost King could simply fly away. The Crystal Shard, Yharaskrik understood implicitly, was far more concerned about the loss of two of the seven.

For Hephaestus, there remained only unrelenting and simmering anger, and most of all, the dragon's consciousness growled at the thought of not being able to exact revenge on those who had so ruined the beast in life.

While Yharaskrik thought of times to come and how to shape the wider path, and Crenshinibon considered the remaining five and whether any repairs were called for, the dragon only pressed, incessantly, for an immediate assault on Spirit Soaring.

They were not one, but three, and to Yharaskrik, the walls separating the triumvirate that was the Ghost King seemed as impenetrably thick and daunting as ever. And from that came the illithid's inescapable conclusion that it must find a way to dominate, to force oneness under its own commanding will and intellect.

And it hoped it could hide that dangerous ambition from its too-intimate fellows.

CHAPTER 19
PRIESTS OF NOTHING

"We are nothing! There is nothing!" the priest screamed, storming about the audience hall in Spirit Soaring, accentuating every word with an angry stomp of his foot. His point was furthered by the blood matting his hair and caked about the side of his face and shoulder, a wound that looked worse than it was. Of the five who had been with him out and about the Snowflakes, he had been the most fortunate by far, for the only other survivor had lost a leg and the other seemed doomed to amputation—and only if the poor woman even survived.

"Sit down, Menlidus, you old fool!" one of his peers yelled. "Do you think this tirade helpful?"

Cadderly hoped Menlidus, a fellow priest of Deneir, would take that advice, but he doubted it, and since the man was more than a decade his senior—and looked at least three decades older than Cadderly—he hoped he wouldn't have to intervene to forcibly silence the angry man. Besides, Cadderly understood the frustration behind the priest's rant, and didn't wholly dismiss his despairing conclusions. Cadderly, too, had gone to Deneir and feared that his god had been lost to him forever, as if Deneir had somehow simply written himself into the numerical maze that was the *Metatext*.

"I am the fool?" Menlidus said, stopping his shouting and pacing, and tapping a finger to his chest as he painted a wry smile on his face. "I have called pillars of flame down upon those who are foes of our god. Or have you forgotten, Donrey?"

"Most surely, I have not," Donrey replied. "Nor have I forgotten the Time of Troubles, or any of the many desperate situations we have faced before, and have endured."

Cadderly appreciated those words, as apparently, he saw in looking around at the large gathering, did everyone else in the room.

Menlidus, though, began to laugh. "Not like this," he said.

"We cannot make that judgment until we know what this silence is truly all about."

"It is about the folly of our lives, friend," the defeated Menlidus said quietly. "All of us, and do look at us! Artists! Painters! Poets! Man and woman, dwarf and elf, who seek deeper meaning in art and in faith. Artists, I say, who evoke emotion and profundity with our paintings and our scribblings, who cleverly place words for the effect dramatic." His snicker cut deep. "Or are we illusionists, I wonder?"

"You do not believe that," said Donrey.

"Who believe our own illusions," Menlidus qualified. "Because we have to. Because the alternative, the idea that there is nothing more, that it is all a creation of imagination to maintain sanity, is too awful to contemplate, is it not? Because the truth that these gods we worship are not immortal beings, but tricksters promising us eternity to extract from us fealty, is ultimately jarring and inspiring despair, is it not?"

"I think we have heard enough, brother," said a woman, a renowned mage who also was possessed of significant clerical prowess.

"Have we?"

"Yes," she said, and there was no mistaking the edge to her voice, not quite threatening but certainly leading in that direction.

"We are priests, one and all," Menlidus said.

"Not so," several wizards pointed out, and again the bloody priest gave a little laugh.

"Yes, so," Menlidus argued. "What we call divine, you call arcane—our altars are not so different!"

Cadderly couldn't help but wince at that, for the notion that all magic emanated from one source brought him back to his younger days in the Edificant Library. Then he had been an agnostic priest, and he too had wondered if the arcane and the divine were no more than different labels for the same energy.

"Save that ours accepts the possibility of change, as it is not rooted in dogma!" one wizard cried, and the volume began to rise about the chamber, wizards and priests lining up against each other in verbal sparring.

"Then perhaps I speak not to you," Menlidus said after Cadderly locked him with a scowl. "But for us priests, are we not those, above all others, who claim to speak the truth? The divine truth?"

"Enough, brother, I beg," Cadderly said then, knowing where Menlidus was going despite the man's temporary calm, and not liking it at all.

He moved toward Menlidus slowly, wearing a carefully maintained expression of serenity. Having heard nothing from Danica or his missing children, Cadderly was anything but serene. His gut churned and his thoughts whirled.

"Do we not?" Menlidus shouted at him. "Cadderly of Deneir, above all others, who created Spirit Soaring on the good word and power of Deneir, should not doubt my claim!"

"It is more complex than that," said Cadderly.

"Does not your experience show that our precepts are not foolish dogma, but rather divine truth?" Menlidus argued. "If you were but a conduit for Deneir in the construction of this awe-inspiring cathedral, this library for all the world, do you not laugh in the face of such doubts as expressed by our secular friends?"

"We all have our moments of doubt," Cadderly said.

"We cannot!" Menlidus exclaimed, stamping his foot. That movement seemed to break him, though, a sudden weariness pulling his broad shoulders down in a profound slump. "And yet, we must, for we are shown the truth." He looked across the room at poor Dahlania, one leg gone, as she lay near death. "I begged for a blessing of healing," he mumbled. "Even a simple one—any spell at all to alleviate her pain. Deneir did not answer that plea."

"There is more to this sad tale," Cadderly said quietly. "You cannot blame—"

"All my life has been in service to him. And this one moment when I call upon him for my most desperate need, he ignores me."

Cadderly heaved a sigh and placed a comforting hand on Menlidus's shoulder, but the man grew agitated and shrugged that touch away.

"Because we are priests of *nothing!*" Menlidus shouted to the room. "We feign wisdom and insight, and deceive ourselves into seeing ultimate truth in the lines of a painting or the curves of a sculpture. We place meaning where there is none, I say, and if there truly are any gods left, they must surely derive great amusement from our pitiful delusions."

Cadderly didn't have to look around the room at the weary and beleaguered faces to understand the cancer that was spreading among them, a trial of will and faith that threatened to break them all. He thought to order Menlidus out of the room, to chastise the man loudly and forcefully, but he dismissed that idea. Menlidus wasn't creating the illness, but was merely shouting it to the rafters.

Cadderly couldn't find Deneir—his prayers, too, went unanswered. He feared that Deneir had left him forever, that the too-inquisitive god had written himself into the Weave or had become lost in its eternal tangle. Cadderly had found power, though, in the fight against the fleshy beasts of shadow, casting spells as mighty as any he might have asked from Deneir.

But those spells, he believed—he feared—hadn't come from the one he had known as Deneir. He didn't know what being, if any being, had bestowed within him the power to consecrate the ground beneath his feet with such blessed magic.

And that was most troubling of all.

For Menlidus's point was well taken: If the gods were not immortal, then was their place for their followers any more lasting?

For if the gods were not powerful and wise enough to defeat the calamity that had come to Faerûn, then what hope for men?

And worse, *what was the point of it all?* Cadderly dismissed that devastating thought almost as soon as it came to him, but it indeed fluttered through his mind, and through the minds of all those gathered there.

Menlidus spat his devastating litany one emphatic last time. "Priests of nothing."

* * * * *

"We are leaving," Menlidus said to Cadderly early the next morning, after an eerily quiet night. That respite had not set well with poor Cadderly, however, for Danica had not yet returned.

No word from his wife, no word of his missing children, and perhaps worst of all, Cadderly still found no answers to his desperate calls to Deneir.

"We?" he replied.

Menlidus motioned through the door, across the hall and into a side chamber, where a group of about a dozen men and women stood dressed for the road.

"You're all leaving?" Cadderly asked, incredulous. "Spirit Soaring is under a cloud of assault and you would desert—"

"Deneir deserted me. I did not desert him," Menlidus replied sharply, but with a calm surety. "As their gods deserted them, and as the Weave abandoned three of them, wizards all, who find their life's pursuit a sad joke, as is mine."

"It didn't take much of a test to shake your faith, Menlidus," Cadderly scolded him, though he wanted to take the words back as soon as he heard them escape his mouth. The poor priest had suffered a failing of magic at the very worst moment, after all, and had watched a friend die because of that failure. Cadderly knew that he was wrong to judge such despair, even if he didn't agree with the man's conclusion.

"Perhaps not, Cadderly, Chosen of Nothing," Menlidus replied. "I only know what I feel and believe—or no longer believe."

"Where are you going?"

"Carradoon first, then to Cormyr, I expect."

Cadderly perked up at that.

"Your children, of course," said Menlidus. "Fear not, my old friend, for though I no longer share your enthusiasm for our faith, I will not forget my friendship to Cadderly Bonaduce and his family. We will seek out your children, do not doubt, and make sure that they are safe."

Cadderly nodded, and wanted nothing more than that. Still, he felt compelled to point out the obvious problem. "Your road is a dangerous one. Perhaps you should remain here—and I'll not lie to you, we need you here. We barely repelled that last attack, and have no idea of what may come against us next. Our dark enemies are out there, in force, as many of our patrols painfully learned."

"We're strong enough to punch our way through them," Menlidus replied. "I would counsel you to convince everyone to come with us. Abandon Spirit Soaring—this is a library and a cathedral, not a fortress."

"This is the work of Deneir. I can no more abandon it than I can abandon that who I am."

"A priest of nothing?"

Cadderly sighed, and Menlidus patted him on the shoulder, a symbolic reversal of fortunes. "They should all leave with us, Cadderly, my old friend. For all our sakes, we should go down to Carradoon as one mighty group. Escape this place, I counsel, and raise an army to come back and—"

"No."

Menlidus looked at him hard, but there was no arguing against that tone of finality in Cadderly's voice.

"My place is Spirit Soaring," Cadderly said.

"To the bitter end?"

Cadderly didn't blink.

"You would condemn the others here to the same fate?" Menlidus asked.

"Their choices are their own to make. I do think we're safer here than out there on the open trails. How many patrol parties met with disaster, your own included? Here, we have a chance to defend. Out there, we're fighting on a battlefield of our enemy's choosing."

Menlidus considered Cadderly for just a moment longer, then snorted and waved his hand, motioning to the people across the hall. They hoisted bags, shields, and weapons and followed the man down the corridor.

"We're left with less than fifty to defend Spirit Soaring," Ginance remarked, coming to Cadderly as the angry fallen priest departed. "If the crawling beasts come at us with the ferocity of the first fight, we will be hard-pressed."

"We are more ready for an attack now," Cadderly replied. "Implements are more reliable than spells, it would seem."

"That is the consensus, yes," said Ginance. "Potions and wands did not fail in the field, even as spellcasting misfired or fell empty."

"We have many potions. We have wands and rods and staves, enchanted weapons and shields," said Cadderly. "Make certain that they are properly distributed as you sort our defenses. Power to every wall."

Ginance nodded and started away, but Cadderly stopped her by adding, "Catch up to Menlidus and offer him all that we can spare to take with him on his journey. I fear that his party will need all that we can give, and a fair measure of good luck, to get down the mountainside."

Ginance paused at the door, then smiled and nodded. "Simply because he abandons Deneir does not mean that Deneir should abandon him," she said.

Cadderly managed a weak smile at that, all the while fearing that Deneir, though perhaps inadvertently and through circumstances beyond his control, had already done exactly that, to all of them.

But Cadderly had no time to think about any of that, he reminded himself, no time to consider his absent wife and missing children. He had found some measure of powerful magic in his moment of need. For all their sakes, he had to learn the source of that magic.

He had barely begun his contemplation when shouts interrupted him.

Their enemies had not waited for sunset.

Cadderly rushed down the stairs, strapping on his weapons as he went, nearly running over Ginance at the bottom.

"Menlidus," she cried, pointing to the main doors, which stood open.

Cadderly ran there and fell back with a gasp. Menlidus and all the others of his band were returning, walking stiff-legged, arms hanging at their sides, vacant stares through dead eyes—for those who still had their eyes.

All around the zombies came the crawling beasts, dragging and hopping at full speed.

"Fight well!" Cadderly called out to his defenders. All about the first and second floors of Spirit Soaring, manning every wall, window, and doorway, priests and wizards lifted shields and weapons, wands and scrolls.

* * * * *

A couple of hundred yards ahead, a burst of flames erupted far above them—above the branches of distant trees on a high ridge on the mountain road. Drizzt, Jarlaxle, and Bruenor sat up straight on the wagon's jockey box, startled, and behind them, Danica stirred.

"That's Spirit Soaring," Drizzt remarked.

"What is?" Danica asked, scooting forward to the back of the seat and peering up between Drizzt and Bruenor.

A column of black smoke began to climb into the sky above the tree line.

"It is," Danica said breathlessly. "Drive them faster!"

Drizzt glanced at Danica and had to blink in amazement at how quickly the woman had healed. Her training and discipline, combined with Jarlaxle's potions and monk abilities, had restored the woman greatly.

Drizzt made a mental note to speak with Danica about her

training, but he ended the line of thought abruptly and nudged Bruenor. Understanding his intent, the dwarf nodded and jumped off the side of the wagon, with Drizzt fast following. Bruenor called for Pwent as they ran around the back, setting themselves against the tailgate.

"Push them hard!" Drizzt called to Jarlaxle when the three were set, and the drow snapped the reins and clicked at the mules, while the three in back put their shoulders to the wagon and shoved with all their strength, legs pumping furiously, helping the wagon up the steep incline.

Danica was out beside them in a heartbeat, and though she winced when she braced her injured shoulder against the wagon, she kept pushing.

As they crested a ridge, Jarlaxle shouted, "Jump!" and the four grabbed on tightly and lifted their legs as the wagon gained speed. It was a short-lived burst, though, for another steep incline lay before them. The mules strained, the foursome strained, too, and the wagon moved along slowly.

The huddled forms of crawlers crept out on the trail before them, but before Jarlaxle could yell out a warning, another form, a dwarf on a fiery hell boar, burst through the brush on the opposite side of the road, wisps of smoke rising from the branches behind him. Athrogate plowed into the crawlers, the demon boar hopping and stomping its hooves, sending out rings of fiery bursts. One crawler was gored and sent flying, another trampled under smoking hooves, but a third, near the other side of the road, had time to react and use its powerful arms to twist and leap up high above the snorting boar, right in the path of Athrogate.

"Bwahaha!" the dwarf howled, his morningstars already spinning in opposing circles.

The weapons swung around at the monster simultaneously, right low, left high, both connecting to send the crawling thing into an aerial sidelong spin. Athrogate expertly curled his right arm under his left in the follow-through, then reversed his momentum and snapped that weapon back in a fierce backhand that smacked the creature in its ugly face—and to add a finishing touch, the dwarf enacted the morningstar's magic after the first strike, its nubby spikes secreting explosive oil onto the weapon head.

A pop and a flash revealed the magic to the onlookers. Even without the explosion, they quickly knew that added power was behind the strike as the creature executed several complete rotations before it hit the ground.

Hardly slowing, Athrogate charged his mount right through the brush on the far side, morningstars spinning, boar snorting fire.

He emerged after the wagon had passed, chasing and battering a crawler with every step, and as the creature fell dead, Athrogate squeezed his legs and twisted the boar into line, running fast after his companions.

He caught up to them just as the wagon came over the last ridge, the road twisting through a narrow tree line onto the open grounds of the magnificent Spirit Soaring.

The lawn was crawling with fleshy beasts, as were Spirit Soaring's walls. The upper corner of the building was burning, belching black smoke from several windows.

Athrogate skidded his boar to a stop beside Bruenor and Pwent. "Come on, ye dwarfs, and kick yer heels! We'll give 'em a beatin' that'll make 'em squeal!"

Bruenor gave only a cursory glance at the nodding Drizzt before scrambling around the side of the wagon bed, leaping up, and retrieving his many-notched axe. Pwent already carried his weapons, and was first to Athrogate's side.

"Ye protect me king!" Pwent demanded of him, and Athrogate gave a hearty "Bwahaha!" in reply. That was good enough for Thibbledorf Pwent, whose idea of "defend" was to charge ahead so quickly and madly that the many enemies flanking him could never catch up.

"Ye keepin' the pig?" Bruenor asked as he rambled up.

"Aye, she's a good way to introduce meself!"

Athrogate spearheaded the three-dwarf wedge, trotting his boar at a pace that the two runners could easily match.

Behind them, Jarlaxle kept firm control of the mules and the wagon, and looked to Danica and Drizzt.

with its free hand, so too did Bruenor bring his axe across. The heavy axe and the powerful dwarf easily parried that strike, and worse for the crawler, Bruenor's swing was hardly slowed by the collision, his fine weapon opening wide the crawler's midsection.

Bruenor gave a second hoist and shoved with his shield to throw that beast away, then chopped back the other way with his axe, cracking it into the skull of another attacker. A sudden twist and reangled tug broke apart the skull and freed the axe. Bruenor waded along, flanked by his devastating team.

* * * * *

Twenty strides behind the ferocious dwarves, Drizzt and Jarlaxle didn't have the luxury of watching the devastating display of martial prowess, for they, too, were quickly hard-pressed.

Drizzt broke center and right, Jarlaxle center and left, each facing their respective foes with typical drow speed and sword play. With his straight blades, Jarlaxle quick-stepped front and back, rolling his hands only so much as to align his blade tips for more deadly stabs. Every step of Jarlaxle's dance was punctuated by forward-prodding sword blades. Those crawlers who ventured too near to Jarlaxle fell back full of small, precise holes.

For Drizzt, with his curving blades, the dance was more one of swinging swaths, each blade slicing across with such force, precision, and momentum that all before it, reaching limbs and pressing monsters, fell back or fell to the ground. While Jarlaxle rarely turned in his battle, Drizzt rarely faced the same direction for more than a heartbeat or two. Quickly realizing that his best attribute against the monsters was his agility, the drow ranger twirled and leaped, spun and dropped low as he came around.

Then up into the air he went again, once even quick-stepping atop the heads of two crawlers that futilely tried to keep pace with his movements.

Drizzt landed right behind them, with more monsters coming at him, but it was all a ruse, for he was up in the air once more, leaping backward and high, tucking his legs in a back flip over the pair of crawlers he had just trod upon. Because they turned in their efforts to keep up with him, he found himself once again behind them.

Down came his scimitars and down went the two crawlers, skulls creased.

More were there to take their places, the fearless and ravenous beasts coming on with abandon. Though both drow fought brilliantly, the pair made little headway toward Spirit Soaring.

And despite their best efforts, crawlers slipped in behind them, rushing for the wagon.

* * * * *

Bruenor saw them first. "Me girl!" he screamed, glancing back at a beast pulling itself up the side of the wagon.

"We're too far!" he scolded his companions, dwarf and drow. "Turn back!"

Pwent and Athrogate, covered in the gore of splattered creatures, immediately spun around. Bruenor pivoted the formation, the three beginning a second and even more ferocious charge back the way they'd come.

"Drizzt! Elf!" Bruenor yelled with every step, desperate for his friend to reach Catti-brie's side.

* * * * *

Drizzt, too, understood that the beasts had been cunning enough to get in behind them. He attempted the same kind of turn that Bruenor and his companions had taken.

But he was hard-pressed, as was Jarlaxle, each alone with crawlers intent on keeping them from retreating to the wagon. Drizzt could only fight on and hope to find a gap, and yell back warnings to Danica.

A crawler pulled itself over the rail of the wagon's side and Drizzt sucked in his breath.

"Jarlaxle!" he begged.

Five strides away from him, Jarlaxle nodded and threw down the feather. Immediately a gigantic flightless bird stood beside the mercenary.

"Go!" Jarlaxle yelled, maneuvering to Drizzt's side as the bird commanded the field.

Side by side they went, trying to find some rhythm, some compliment to their varied styles. But Drizzt knew that they could not reach the wagon in time.

And Bruenor, screaming from behind him, knew it too.

But all five, drow and dwarves alike, breathed easier when a form stood tall before the crawler on the wagon, for up popped Danica, her sling hanging empty, her fists balled before her chest. Up went one leg, straight above her head, and her amazing dexterity was matched by her strength as she drove her foot down atop the crawler's head.

With a sickening *crack,* that head flattened even more and the beast dropped from the side of the wagon as surely and swiftly as if a mountain had fallen atop it.

All five of the companions fighting to approach the wagon shouted out to Danica as a crawler leaped over the other side of the wagon at her back. But she needed no such warning, coming out of her devastating stomp with a perfect pivot to back-kick the second beast in its ugly face. It, too, bounced away.

A third creature clambered over the rail and a circle kick suddenly filled its grinning maw. Danica remained up on her right leg and went up to the ball of her foot to execute a complete spin and slam a fourth crawler.

Yet another beast climbing up the side was met with a flurry of fists, a rapid explosion of ten short punches that turned its face to mush. Before it could fall away, Danica hooked it under the armpit and turned powerfully, launching it across the wagon to bowl over and dislodge another of its companions.

The woman turned fast and fell into a defensive crouch, seeing a pair of monsters up front on the jockey box. One jerked weirdly and the other followed, then fine drow swords exploded out of their chests. Both crawlers were jerked off opposite sides of the wagon and the swords slipped free. Jarlaxle stood on the seat alone.

With a smile, the drow snapped his right wrist up, and his magical blade transformed from sword to dirk. With a wink, Jarlaxle launched the dagger toward Danica—right past her, to impale a crawler and knock it off the wagon's backside.

He tipped his hat, flicked another dagger from his wrist, and turned to rejoin Drizzt, who had defeated a quartet of crawlers as they had tried to attack the mules.

"You three, with the wagon," Drizzt told the dwarves as they arrived.

As Jarlaxle leaped down beside him and gave a nod to his fellow drow, Drizzt led the way forward toward the screeching, pecking, stomping diatryma.

"You lead, I secure," Jarlaxle said, the command ringing clearly to Drizzt Do'Urden.

In that short charge and retreat, in that moment of desperation to rescue the wagon, the two had found a level of confidence and complement that Drizzt had never thought possible. His beloved wife was in that wagon, helpless, and yet he had stopped to engage the first line of crawlers near the mules, fully confident that Jarlaxle would secure the jockey box and reinforce Danica's desperate defense of Catti-brie.

So on they went, fighting as one. Drizzt led the way with his leaps and slashing cuts while a series of daggers reached out behind him, flew out around him. Every time he lifted a scimitar, a dagger whistled under his arm. Every time he dived and rolled right, a dagger shot past his left—or a stream of daggers, for Jarlaxle's bracers gave him an inexhaustible and ready supply.

To their side, the crawling beasts finally pulled down the diatryma, but it didn't matter, for behind the drow, Bruenor tugged the mules and wagon along while Pwent and Athrogate flanked him, throwing themselves at any monsters venturing too near. Danica held the wagon bed, striking with devastating effect at any who dared try to climb aboard.

Finally they were rolling along, their enemies thinning before them. Drizzt darted left and right, taking great chances, diving into rolls and leaping into spins, confident every time that a dagger would fly his way in support if any monster found a hole in his defenses.

* * * * *

Inside Spirit Soaring, word of the allies' charge began to spread among the priests and wizards, and they began to call out their support and to cheer with great relief the unexpected reinforcements. And from more than one came a cry of relief at the return of Lady Danica!

All around the library, the calls went out and the defenders took heart, none more so than Cadderly. With his hand crossbows and devastating darts, he had methodically cleared most of the second story balconies of invaders, and had left a dozen dead before the front door for good measure, shooting down from on high.

But with his wife in sight, flanked by heroes of great renown, the priest was so overcome that he forgot how to breathe. He stared at the wagon, creeping across the courtyard toward Spirit Soaring, where Drizzt Do'Urden and Jarlaxle—Jarlaxle!—sprinted back and forth, working as if they were a single, four-armed warrior, Drizzt leaping and spinning, mowing down crawlers whose arms went up to grab at him always a heartbeat too late.

And Jarlaxle came behind like god-thrown lightning, stabbing the beasts with short, deadly strokes and nimbly dancing through them as they fell to the ground, mortally wounded.

There were dwarves, too, and Cadderly recognized King Bruenor from that legendary one-horned helm and the foaming mug shield, working his axe with deadly efficiency and tugging the mules along, while two other dwarf warriors flanked the team. Any beasts that ventured too near were crushed by a blur of spinning morningstars on one side, or torn apart by the multitude of spikes and ridges adorning the wild dwarf on the other.

There was Danica, and oh, but she had never looked more

beautiful to Cadderly than at that very moment. She had been battered, he could see, and that stung his heart, but her warrior spirit ignored her wounds, and she worked her dance magnificently about the wagon bed. Not a creature could get close to clearing the rails.

Below the balcony where he stood, Cadderly heard his fellow priests shouting to "Form up!" and he knew they meant to go out and meet the incoming band. When he took a moment to stop gawking at the magnificence of the six warriors in action, he realized that help would be sorely needed.

Many monsters became aware of fresh meat on the approaching wagon. The attack on the building had all but ceased. Every ravenous eye turned toward easy prey.

Cadderly realized the awful truth. For all the power of those six, they would never make it. A horde of monsters stood poised to wash over them like breaking waves on a low beach.

His beloved wife would never come home.

From the balcony, he turned into the cathedral, thinking to rush to the stairwell. He skidded to an abrupt stop, hearing a distant call—as he had in that previous moment of desperation when he had been caught alone on the upper floors with the attacking crawlers.

He turned, his eyes guided to a cloud in the sky above. He reached for that cloud and called to it, and a portion of it broke away. A chariot of cloud, pulled by a winged horse, raced down from on high. Cadderly climbed atop the balcony's rail and the speeding chariot swooped down before him. Hardly even thinking about his actions, for he was leaping onto a cloud, the priest jumped aboard. The winged horse followed his every mental command, sweeping down from the balcony right before the astonished eyes of the priests and wizards who were gathering to charge out the front door. As one, they gasped and fell back into the cathedral. Cadderly's chariot soared out above the frightened crawlers.

Some of the undead, Menlidus among them, turned to intercept the new foe, but Cadderly looked upon them and channeled the divinity flowing within him, releasing a mighty burst of radiance that knocked the undead monsters back and blasted them to ash.

He grimaced at the destruction of his dear friend, but Cadderly pushed away the sadness and continued on, fast nearing the wagon and the six warriors and the host of crawlers battling them. Again he cast a spell, though he knew not what it was, simply trusting the power he felt within. He looked at the largest mob of monsters and shouted a single word—not just any word, but a thunderous word, an explosion of vocal power aimed at enemies alone, for it did not affect the spiked-armored dwarf, who thrashed wildly in the middle of the throng.

But the wild dwarf was struck dumbfounded and confused when all the monsters clawing and biting at him were yanked away. Through the air they went, flailing helplessly against the weight of the priest's thunder. They landed hard some thirty steps distant, bouncing and tumbling, scrambling away, wanting no part of the godlike priest and his words of doom.

Cadderly paid them no more heed, bringing his chariot up beside the wagon and bidding his friends to climb aboard. He spoke another word of power and a great light ignited around him and the wagon. All of the crawlers caught within it began to thrash and burn, but the others, the drow, the dwarves, and the two women, felt no pain. Instead, they were washed with healing warmth, their many recent wounds mending in the brilliant yellow beams of magical light.

Bruenor yelled at Drizzt, who had told him to climb aboard the chariot. When the dwarf king hesitated, Athrogate and Pwent, running along beside him, hooked him under the arms and dragged him up.

Drizzt sprang aboard the wagon and into the bed, catching Danica's eye. "Watch those beasts for me," he said, trusting her fully. He sheathed his blades, went to his beloved, and scooped her into his arms. With Danica leading, they made the chariot easily.

Jarlaxle did not follow, but waved Cadderly away. He threw

daggers into the nearest thrashing crawler for good measure, then brought forth his nightmare, summoning it before the terrified team. The drow ran around the mules, conjuring another sword from his enchanted bracer as he went, while his nightmare pounded the ground with fiery hooves. A few clever slashes set the mules free, and Jarlaxle, reigns in hand, ran between and past them, and jumped upon his nightmare.

He kicked the steed into a charge, galloping along the path cleared by Cadderly's cloud chariot. He tugged the mules along and guided them up on the porch and through the open front doors before any of the crawlers could intercept him.

Priests slammed the doors closed behind the drow and his four-legged escorts. Jarlaxle immediately dismissed his nightmare and handed the mules off to astonished onlookers.

"It would not do to waste a perfectly good team," he explained. "And these two have taken us a long way." He finished with a laugh—which lasted only as long as it took him to turn and come face to face with Cadderly.

"I told you never to return to this place," the priest said, ignoring the many curious onlookers crowding around him, demanding to know what sort of magic he had found to conjure a chariot of cloud, to speak thunder, to glow with the radiance of a healing god, to reduce the undead to ashes with a single word. They, who could not reliably cast the simplest of dweomers any longer, had witnessed a display of power that the greatest priests and wizards of Faerûn could hardly imagine.

Jarlaxle bowed low in response, tipping his unfeathered hat. He didn't answer, though, other than to motion to Drizzt, who came fast to his side, as Danica was fast to Cadderly's.

"He is not our enemy," Danica assured her husband. "Not any more."

"I keep trying to tell you that," Jarlaxle agreed.

Cadderly looked to Drizzt, who nodded his agreement.

"Enough of that, and who truly cares?" a wizard yelled, bulling his way up to Cadderly. "Where did you find such power? What prayers were those? To throw a multitude of enemies aside with a mere word! A chariot of cloudstuff? Pray tell, good Cadderly. Is this Deneir, come to your call?"

Cadderly looked at the man hard, looked at them all, his face a mask of studious concentration. "I know not," he admitted. "I do not hear the voice of Deneir, yet I believe that he is involved somehow." He looked directly at Drizzt as he finished. "It is as if Deneir is giving this answer to me, one last gift . . ."

"Last?" Ginance called out with alarm, and many others mumbled and grumbled.

Cadderly looked at them and could only shrug, for he truly didn't know the answer to the riddle that was his newfound power. He shifted his gaze to Jarlaxle. "I trust my wife, and I trust Drizzt, and so you are welcome here in this time of mutual need."

"With information you will find valuable," Jarlaxle assured him, but the drow was cut short by a sharp cry from the back of the gathering. All eyes turned toward Catti-brie. Drizzt had set her down on a divan at the side of the foyer, but she was floating in the air, her arms out as if she were under water, her eyes rolled to white and her hair floating around her, again as if she were weightless.

She turned her head and spat, then snapped back the other way as if someone had slapped her across the face. Her eyes once more shone blue, though they were surely seeing something other than that which was before her.

"She is demon-possessed!" a priest cried.

Drizzt donned the eye patch Jarlaxle had given to him and rushed to his wife, grabbing her in a hug and gently pulling her down.

"Take care, for she is in a dark place that welcomes new victims," Jarlaxle said to Cadderly as he moved to join Drizzt. Cadderly looked at him curiously but went in anyway, taking Catti-brie's hand.

Cadderly's form jolted as if shocked by lightning. His eyes twitched and his entire form changed, a ghostly superimposition of an angelic body, complete with feathery wings, over his normal human form.

Catti-brie cried out then and so did Cadderly. Jarlaxle grabbed the priest and tugged him back. The ghostly lines of Cadderly's form disappeared, leaving him gawking at the woman.

"She is caught between worlds," Jarlaxle said.

Cadderly looked at him, licked his suddenly dry lips, and did not disagree.

CHAPTER 20
A DWARF'S STUBBORNNESS

He felt the sensation seeping into his consciousness, the willpower of another being trying to possess him. But Ivan Bouldershoulder was ready for it. He was no simpleton, and no novice to any kind of warfare. He had felt the dominating willpower of a vampire—right before he had utterly destroyed the thing—and he had studied the methods of wizards and illusionist, and even illithids, like any well-prepared dwarf warrior.

The creature had caught him by surprise with the first intrusion, true. Spirit Soaring and the Snowflakes had been a peaceful place for years, the one notable exception being the arrival of Artemis Entreri, Jarlaxle Baenre, and the Crystal Shard, but since Cadderly had completed the new library, Ivan and everyone else had come to think of the place as home, as peaceful, as safe.

Even with the turbulence of the wider world and the current problems with magic—the types of problems that had never really concerned the likes of Ivan Bouldershoulder, who trusted his muscle more than any waggling fingers—Ivan hadn't been ready for the onslaught of the Ghost King. And he'd certainly not been ready for the intrusion that had overwhelmed him and stolen from him his very body. But for nearly the entire time he had been possessed, Ivan had studied his possessor. Rather than flail against an opaque wall he could not penetrate, the dwarf had bided his time, gathering what information he could, trying to take from his possessor even as it continued to rob him.

Thus, when Yharaskrik had released him on that high mountain plateau, Ivan was ready for the fight—or more accurately, for the flight. And the illithid had inadvertently shown him the way: a crack in the floor beneath the dracolich that was more than a crack, that was indeed a shaft leading down into the mountains and, Ivan had hoped, into the catacomb of tunnels that wound through the lower stones.

With nowhere else to go, and doom certain if he stayed above, Ivan had scrambled straight for that route, counting on surprise to get him past the crushing claws of the great beast.

To his good fortune, when the dragon's foot had stomped, a host of the fleshy beasts had been right behind him, and the splatter and spray of flesh and gore and blood had provided wonderful cover for his desperate dive.

To his ultimate good fortune, the shaft had not run straight down for very far, gradually winding to the side and easing the impact as he connected with the dirt and stone. And it had widened, allowing him to twist in his descent and get his heavy boots out in front of him, digging them in against the slide. The last drop had hurt—twenty feet straight down with nothing but dark air around him as he broke through the roof of an underground chamber, but even there, the dwarf had found that extra bit of heroism, the one heroes only rarely discussed openly: good luck.

He had landed in water. It wasn't very deep and wasn't very clean, but it was enough to cushion his fall. He had lost his antlered helm up above but had retrieved his axe, and he was alive, and in a place where the monstrous dracolich couldn't follow.

Luck had given him a chance.

Soon after, though, Ivan Bouldershoulder figured that his luck had run out.

For the rest of the day, he had wandered in the darkness, splashing, for he could find no dry land in the chamber, and no exit. He had felt some movement around his legs in the thigh-deep murk, and figured there might be some fish or some other crawly things in the underground pool, so maybe he could catch them and figure out a way to survive for some time.

Either way, he believed that he would surely die alone and miserable in the dark.

So be it.

Then the illithid had come calling, whispering into his subconscious, trying to pry its way back into control.

Ivan put up a wall of anger and sheer dwarven stubbornness that held the creature at bay, and he knew with confidence that he could hold it indefinitely, that he would not be possessed again.

"Go away, ye silly beast," he said. He focused and concentrated on every word as he spoke. "What'd'ye want with me in here, where there's no way out?"

It seemed a logical enough refutation. Indeed, what did the illithid have to gain?

But still the creature seeped into his thoughts, demanding control.

"What, can ye make me fly, then, ye fool?" Ivan shouted into the darkness. "Fly me back up to yer dead dragon and the little beasties ye so love?"

He felt the anger then, and the revulsion, and understood that he had caught the mind flayer a bit off its guard, though just for a fleeting moment.

Ivan let his own guard slip, just a bit.

He felt the other being inside his mind clearly then, striving for dominance. A wave of utter disgust nearly buckled the dwarf's knees. But he held fast, and purposely lowered his guard just a bit more.

He was soon walking toward the northern end of the wide chamber. He could barely make out the boulders piled along that wall. Guided by Yharaskrik's will, counting on the illithid having a wider view of his surroundings than he, the dwarf climbed up onto the lower stones. He pulled one aside and felt the slightest breeze, and as his eyes adjusted to the more intense gloom beyond, he saw that a long, wide tunnel lay before him.

Done with ye! his thoughts screamed and Ivan Bouldershoulder began the fight of his life. He pushed back against the overwhelming intellect and willpower of the mind flayer with every measure of stubbornness and anger a dwarf could muster. He thought of his brother, of his clan, of King Bruenor, of Cadderly and Danica and the kids, of everything that made him who he was, that gave joy to his life and strength to his limbs.

He denied Yharaskrik. He screamed at Yharaskrik, aloud and in his every thought. He thrashed physically, hurling himself against the stones, tearing at the tunnel opening to widen it, ignoring the falling rocks that banged off his arms and shoulders. And he thrashed mentally as well, screaming at the wretched beast to be gone from his mind.

From *his* mind!

Such rage enveloped him that Ivan tore the rocks free with bloody fingers and felt no pain. Such strength accompanied that rage that he flung the stones, some half his weight, far behind him to splash into the murky pool. And still he ignored the bruises and cuts, and the strain on his corded muscles. He let the rage take him fully and hold him, a wall of denial, a demand that the illithid get out.

The hole was wide enough to crawl through—wide enough for two Ivans to crawl through side by side—and still the dwarf dug at the stones with his battered hands, using that physical sensation to give focus to his rage.

He had no idea how long he went on like that, a few heartbeats or a few thousand, but finally, an exhausted Ivan Bouldershoulder fell through the opening and rolled into the tunnel. He landed flat on his face and lay there, gasping, for a long while.

Despite the pain, a wry grin widened on his hairy face, for Ivan knew that he was truly alone.

The tentacle-faced beast had been denied.

He slept, then, right there in the mud, amidst the stones, keeping himself mentally ready to fend off another intrusion and hoping that no wandering creature of the Underdark would find him and devour him as he lay exhausted and battered in the darkness.

* * * * *

Rorick dived to the floor, just under the clawing feet of a huge black bat. "Uncle Pikel!" he screamed, beseeching the druid to do something.

Pikel balled up his fist, pumped his arms, and stamped his feet in frustration, for he had nothing, nothing at all, to offer. Magic was gone—even his natural affinity with animals had flown. He thought back to only a few days earlier, when he had coaxed the roots out of the walls to secure the barricades—a temporary thing, apparently, since pursuit came from that direction. The dwarf knew he couldn't reach that level of magic, perhaps not ever again, and his frustration played out, in that dark chamber deep beneath the Snowflakes.

"Ooooh!" he whined, and he stamped his sandaled feet harder. His whine became a growl as he saw the same bat that had sent Rorick diving for cover angle its wings and come around directly at him.

Pikel blamed the bat. It made no sense, of course, but none of it made a lot of sense to Pikel just then. So he blamed the bat. That bat. Only that bat. That one bat had caused the failure of magic, and had chased away his god.

He squatted and picked up his cudgel. It wasn't enchanted anymore, no longer a magical shillelagh, but it was still a solid club, as the bat found out.

The black leathery thing swooped at Pikel, and the dwarf leaped and spun, launching the most powerful strike he had ever managed with his strong arm, even from the days when he had the use of both. The hard wood crunched against bat skull, shattering the bone.

The nightwing fell as surely as if a huge boulder had fallen upon it from on high, crashing down atop Pikel, the two of them rolling away in a tumble of dwarf and black bat.

Pikel head-butted and kicked with abandon. He bit and poked with his stubby arm. He swung his cudgel with short but heavy strokes, battering the creature relentlessly.

Nearby, a man screamed as a nightwing swooped in and caught him by the shoulders in its huge clawed feet, but Pikel didn't hear it. Several others cried out, and a woman shrieked in horror when the bat flew straight for a wall and let loose its prey, hurling the poor man against the rocks, where his bones shattered with a sickening crackle.

Pikel didn't hear it. He was still swinging his club and kicking with fury, though the bat that enwrapped him with those great wings was already dead.

"Get up, Uncle Pikel!" Hanaleisa yelled at him as she leaped past.

"Huh?" the dwarf replied, and he pulled one wing down from in front of his face and followed the sound to see Hanaleisa sprinting toward Rorick, who was still flat on the ground. Standing above him, Temberle cut his greatsword back and forth in long sweeping arcs above his head, trying to cut at a stubborn nightwing that fluttered up and down above him as if to taunt him. He couldn't hit the agile bat.

But Hanaleisa did, leaping high into the air as she rushed past Temberle, somersaulting as she went to enhance the power of her kick. She kicked the bat solidly in the side, sending it several feet away as she tumbled over and landed, still in a run.

The nightwing turned its attention her way as it righted itself in the air, and swooped to give chase.

With that distraction, Temberle's sword at last caught up to it, slashing a leathery wing back to front. The nightwing flopped weirdly in the air and fluttered down, and Hanaleisa and Temberle were upon it before it managed to get the wounded wing out from under itself.

Hanaleisa was the first to break away, calling out orders, trying to establish some measure of order and supporting lines of defense. But the whole of the wide chamber was in a frenzy, with nightwings fluttering all around them, with wounded men and woman, backs torn wide, one scalped by a raking claw, screaming and running and diving for cover.

A group of more than a dozen grabbed up all of the precious

torches stored at the far end of the hall, at the mouth of a tunnel the group had planned to traverse after their rest stop, and went running away.

Others followed in the chaos.

Temberle knocked down another bat, and Hanaleisa matched him.

Other nightwings swept out of the chamber in pursuit down the tunnels.

When it finally ended, just over a score of refugees remained, with three of those badly wounded.

"It won't hold," Hanaleisa said to her brothers and uncle as they gathered together their scant supplies and few remaining torches. "We need to find a way out of here."

"Uh-uh!" Pikel emphatically disagreed.

"Then light your staff!" Hanaleisa yelled at him.

"Ooooh," said the dwarf.

"Hana!" Rorick scolded.

The monk held forth her hands and took a deep breath, composing herself. "I'm sorry. But we need to move along, and quickly."

"We cannot stay here," Temberle agreed. "We need to get as close to Spirit Soaring as we can manage, and we need to get out of these tunnels."

He looked at Pikel, but the dwarf just shrugged, hardly confident.

"We have no other option," Temberle assured him.

A commotion behind them turned them around, and Rorick said, "The scout returns!"

They rushed to the fisherman, Alagist, and even in the torchlight, they could see that he was thoroughly shaken. "We feared you dead," Hanaleisa said. "When the bats came in—"

"Forget the damned bats," the man replied, and the punctuation of his sentence came as a thump from the distant corridor, like a rumble of thunder.

"What—?" Temberle and Rorick said together.

"A footstep," Alagist said.

"Uh-oh," said Pikel.

"What magic?" Hanaleisa asked the dwarf.

"Uh-oh," he repeated.

"Gather up the wounded!" Temberle called to all still in the chamber. "Take everything we can carry! We must be gone from this place!"

"He can't be moved," a woman called from beside an unconscious man.

"We have no choice," Temberle said to her, rushing over to help.

The chamber shuddered under the reverberations of another heavy footstep.

The woman didn't argue as Temberle hoisted the wounded man over one shoulder.

Pikel, torch in hand, led the way out of the chamber.

* * * * *

"Come on, then!" Ivan yelled into the darkness. "Not with yer head, ye damned squid, but all o' ye! Come and play!" He didn't have his axe, but he hoisted a pair of rocks and banged them together with enthusiasm bordering on murderous glee.

That physical manifestation of anger echoed the dwarf's sheer rage, and once more, the intrusions of Yharaskrik faded to nothingness. If the illithid had come to him that time with any hope of possessing him again, Ivan believed with confidence, that delusion had come to an end.

But the dwarf was still alone, battered and bloody and lost in the dark, with no real expectation that there was a way out of those forever-twisting tunnels. He glanced over his shoulder to the watery cavern, and considered for a moment going back and trying to figure out a way in which he could survive on the fish, or whatever those swimming things might be. Could he somehow strain or heat the murky water enough to make it potable?

"Bah!" he snorted into the darkness, and decided that it was better to die trying than to simply exist in a dark and empty hole!

So off Ivan trudged, rocks in hands, a scowl on his face, and a wall of rage within him just looking for an outlet.

He walked for hours, often stumbling and tripping, for though his eyes adjusted quickly to the darkness, he still had to feel his way along. He found many side passages, some that led to dead ends, and others he took simply because they "felt" more promising. Even with his dwarf's senses, so at home underground, Ivan had little idea of where he actually was in relation to the World Above, and even in relation to where he had first dropped down into the murky underground pond. With every turn, Ivan held his breath, hoping he wasn't just going in circles.

At every turn, too, the dwarf tucked one of his stone weapons under his armpit, wetted his finger, and held it aloft in search of air currents.

Finally, he felt the slightest breeze on that upraised finger. Ivan held his breath and stared into the blackness. He knew it could be but a crack, a teasing, impassable chimney, a torturous wormhole he could never squeeze through.

He slammed his rocks together and stomped along, clinging to optimism and armoring himself with anger. An hour later, he was still in darkness, but the air felt lighter to him, and he felt a distinct sensation on that wetted finger whenever he lifted it.

Then he saw a light. A tiny spark, far away, rebounding off many turns and twists. But a light nonetheless. Along the walls, rocks took more definitive shape to the dwarf's fine underground vision. The darkness was surely less absolute.

Ivan rumbled along, thinking about how he could organize a counterstrike against the dracolich and the illithid and their huddled, shadowy minions. His fears went from his own dilemma to his friends up above, to Cadderly and Danica, the kids and his brother. His pace increased, for Ivan was always one who would fight like a badger for his own sake, but who would fight like a horde of hell-spawned badgers when his friends were involved.

Soon, though, he slowed again, for the light was not daylight, he came to realize, nor was it any of the glowing fungi so common in the Underdark. It was firelight—torchlight, likely.

Down there, that probably meant the light of an enemy.

Ready for a fight, Ivan crept ahead. Knuckles whitening on stones, Ivan gritted his teeth and imagined the sensation of crushing a few skulls.

A single voice stole that bellicose attitude and had him blinking in astonishment.

"Oo oi!"

CHAPTER 21
FACING THE TRUTH

Cadderly emerged from the room after spending more than half the morning with Catti-brie, his face ashen, his eyes showing profound weariness.

Drizzt, waiting in the anteroom, looked to him with hope, and Jarlaxle, who stood beside Drizzt, looked instead at his dark elf companion. The mercenary recognized the truth splayed on Cadderly's face even if Drizzt did not—or could not.

"You have found her?" Drizzt asked.

Cadderly sighed, just slightly, and handed the eye patch to him. "It is as we believed," he said, speaking to Jarlaxle more than Drizzt.

The drow mercenary nodded and Cadderly turned to face Drizzt. "Catti-brie is caught in a dark place between two worlds, our own and a place of shadow," the priest explained. "The touch of the falling Weave has had many ill effects upon wizards and priests across Faerûn, and no two maladies appear to be the same, from what little I have seen. For Argust of Memnon, the touch proved instantly fatal, turning him to ice—just empty ice, no substance, no flesh beneath it. The desert sun reduced him to a puddle in short order. Another priest carries with him a most awful disease, with open sores across his body, and is surely failing. Many stories . . ."

"I care not of them," Drizzt interrupted, and Jarlaxle, hearing the edge creeping into the ranger's voice, put a comforting hand on Drizzt's shoulder. "You have found Catti-brie, caught between the worlds, you say, though in truth I fear it is all a grand illusion masking a sinister design—perhaps the Red Wizards, or—"

"It is no illusion. The Weave itself has come undone, some of the gods have fled, died . . . we're not yet certain. And whether it is the cause of the falling Weave, or a result of it, a second world is falling all around ours, and that junction seems also to have increased the expanse of the Plane of Shadow, or perhaps even opened doorways into some other realm of shadows and darkness," said Cadderly.

"And you have found her—Catti-brie, I mean—trapped between this place and our own world. How do we retrieve her fully, and bring her back . . ." His voice trailed off as he stared into Cadderly's too-sympathetic face.

"There is a way!" Drizzt shouted, and he grabbed the priest by the front of his tunic. "Do not tell me that it is hopeless!"

"I would not," Cadderly replied. "All sorts of unexplained and unexpected events are occurring all around us, on a daily basis! I have found spells I did not know I possessed, and did not know Deneir could grant, and with all humility and honesty, I say that I am not certain it is even Deneir granting them to me! You ask me for answers, my friend, and I do not have them."

Drizzt let him go, the drow's shoulders sagging, along with his aching heart. He offered a slight nod of appreciation to Cadderly. "I will go and tell Bruenor."

"Let me," said Jarlaxle, and that brought a surprised look from Drizzt. "You go to your wife."

"My wife cannot feel my touch."

"You do not know that," Jarlaxle scolded. "Go and hold her, for both your sakes."

Drizzt looked from Jarlaxle to Cadderly, who nodded his agreement. The distraught drow put on the magical eye patch as he entered the adjacent chamber.

"She is lost to us," Jarlaxle said softly to Cadderly when they were alone.

"We do not know that."

Jarlaxle continued to stare at him, and Cadderly, grim-faced, could not disagree. "I see no way for us to retrieve her," the priest admitted. "And even if we could, I fear that the damage to her mind is already beyond repair. By any means I can fathom, Cattibrie is forever lost to us."

Jarlaxle swallowed hard, though he was not surprised by the prognosis. He wouldn't tell King Bruenor quite everything, he decided.

* * * * *

Another defeat, Yharaskrik pointed out.

We weakened them!

We barely scratched their walls, the illithid imparted. *And now they have new and powerful allies.*

More of my enemies in one place for me to throttle!

Cadderly and Jarlaxle and Drizzt Do'Urden. I know this Drizzt Do'Urden, and he is not to be taken lightly.

I know him as well. Crenshinibon unexpectedly joined the internal dialogue, and the illithid detected a simmering hatred behind the simple telepathic statement.

We should fly from this place, Yharaskrik dared to suggest. *The rift has brought uncontrollable beasts from the shadowy plane, and Cadderly has found unexpected allies . . .*

No cogent response came from the dragon, just a continuous, angry growl reverberating through the thoughts of the triumvirate that was the Ghost King, a wall of anger and resentment, and perhaps the most resounding "no" Yharaskrik had ever heard.

Through the far-reaching mental eyes of the illithid, its consciousness flying wide to scout the region, they had seen the rift in Carradoon. They had seen the giant nightwalkers and the nightwings and understood that a new force had come to the Prime Material Plane. And through the eyes of the illithid, they had witnessed the latest battle at Spirit Soaring, the coming of the dwarves and the drow, the power revealed by Cadderly—that unknown priestly magic had unnerved Yharaskrik most of all, for he had felt the magical thunder in Cadderly's ward and had retreated from the brilliance of the priest's beam of light. Yharaskrik, ancient and once part of a great communal mind flayer hive, thought it knew of every magical dweomer on Toril, but it had never seen anything like the power of the unpredictable priest that day.

The melted flesh of crawlers and the ash piles of the raised dead served as grim reminders to the mind flayer that Cadderly was not to be underestimated.

Thus, the dracolich's continuing growl of denial was not a welcome echo in Yharaskrik's expansive mind. The illithid waited for the sound to abate, but it did not. It listened for a third voice in the conversation, one of moderation, but heard nothing.

Then it knew. In a sudden insight, a revelation of a minuscule but all-important shift, the mind flayer realized that the Ghost King was no longer a triumvirate. The resonance of the growl deepened, more a chorus of two than the grumble of one. Two that had become one.

No words filtered out of that rumbling wall of anger, but Yharaskrik knew its warnings would go unheeded. They would not flee. They—the mind flayer and that dual being with whom it shared the host dragon corpse, for no longer could Yharaskrik count Hephaestus and Crenshinibon as separate entities!—would show no restraint. Not the rift, not Cadderly's unexplained new powers, not the arrival of powerful reinforcements for Spirit Soaring, would slow the determined vengeance of the Ghost King.

The growl continued, a maddening and incessant wall, a pervasive answer to the illithid's concerns that brooked no intelligent debate, or, the creature understood, no room for a change of plans, whatever new circumstances or new enemies might be revealed.

The Ghost King meant to attack Spirit Soaring.

Yharaskrik tried to send its thoughts around the growl, to find Crenshinibon, or what remained of the Crystal Shard as an independent sentience. It tried to construct logic to stop the dracolich's angry vibrations.

It found nothing, and every path led to one road only: eviction.

It was no longer a disagreement, no longer a debate about their course of action. It was a revolt, full and without resolution. Hephaestus-Crenshinibon was trying to evict Yharaskrik, as surely as had the dwarf in the tunnels below.

Unlike that occasion, however, the mind flayer had nowhere else to go.

The growl rolled on.

Yharaskrik threw wave after wave of mental energy at the dragon-shard mind. It gathered its psionic powers and released them in ways subtle and clever.

The growl rolled on.

The illithid assailed the Ghost King with a wall of discordant notions and emotions, a cacophony of twisted notes that would have driven a wise man mad.

The growl rolled on.

It attacked every fear buried within Hephaestus. It conjured images of the exploding Crystal Shard from those years before, when the light had burned the eyes from Hephaestus's head.

The growl rolled on. The mind flayer found no wedge between the dragon and the artifact. They were one, so completely united that even Yharaskrik couldn't fathom where one ended and the other began, or which was in control, or which even, to the illithid's great surprise and distress, was initiating the growl.

And it went on, unabated, unflinching, incessant and forevermore if necessary, the illithid understood.

Clever beast!

There was nothing left there for the mind flayer. It would have no control of the great dracolich limbs. It would find no conversation or debate. It would find nothing there but the growl, heartbeats and days and years and centuries. Just the growl, just the opaque wall of a singular note that would forevermore dull its own sensibilities, that would steal its curiosity, that would force it to stay within, confined to an endless battle.

Against Hephaestus alone, Yharaskrik knew it could prevail.

Against Crenshinibon alone, Yharaskrik held confidence that it would find a way to win.

Against both of them, there was only the growl. It all came clear to the illithid, then. The Crystal Shard, as arrogant as Yharaskrik itself, and as stubborn as the dragon, as patient as time, had chosen. To the illithid, that choice at first seemed illogical, for why would Crenshinibon side with the lesser intellect of the dragon?

Because the Crystal Shard was more possessed of ego than the illithid had recognized. More than logic drove Crenshinibon. By joining with Hephaestus, the Crystal Shard would dominate.

The growl rolled on.

Time itself lost meaning in the rumble. There was no yesterday and no tomorrow, no hope nor fear, no pleasure nor pain.

Just a wall, not thickening, not thinning, impenetrable and impassable.

Yharaskrik couldn't win. It couldn't hold. The Ghost King became a creature of two, not three, and those two became one, as Yharaskrik departed.

The disembodied intellect of the great mind flayer began to dissipate almost immediately, oblivion looming.

* * * * *

All the wizened and experienced minds remaining at Spirit Soaring gathered in lectures and seminars, sharing their observations and intuition about the crash of worlds and the advent of the dark place, a reformed Plane of Shadow they came to call the Shadowfell. All reservations were cast aside, priest and mage, human, dwarf, and drow.

They were all together, plotting and planning, seeking an answer. They were quick to agree that the fleshy beasts crawling over Spirit Soaring were likely of another plane, and no one argued the basic premise of some other world colliding, or at least interacting in dangerous ways, with their own world. But so many other questions remained.

"And the walking dead?" Danica asked.

"Crenshinibon's addition to the tumult," Jarlaxle explained with surprising confidence. "The Crystal Shard is an artifact of necromancy more than anything else."

"You claimed it destroyed—Cadderly's divination showed us the way to destroy it, and we met those conditions. How then . . . ?"

"The collision of worlds?" Jarlaxle asked more than stated. "The fall of the Weave? The simple chaos of the times? I do not believe that it has returned to us as it was—that former incarnation of Crenshinibon was indeed destroyed. But in its destruction, it is possible that the liches who created it have come free of it. I believe that I battled one, and that you encountered one as well."

"You make many presumptions," Danica remarked.

"A line of reasoning to begin our investigation. Nothing more."

"And you think these things, these liches, are the leaders?" asked Cadderly.

Before Jarlaxle could answer, Danica cut him short. "The leader is the dracolich."

"Joined with the remnants of Crenshinibon, and thus with the liches," said Jarlaxle.

"Well, whatever it is, something bad's going on, something badder than anything I e'er seen in me long years o' living," said Bruenor, and he looked toward the doorway to Catti-brie's room as he spoke. An uncomfortable silence ensued, and Bruenor harrumphed a great and profound frustration and took his leave to be with his wounded daughter.

To the surprise of all, especially Cadderly, the priest found himself beside Jarlaxle as the conversation resumed. The drow had surprising insights on the dual-world hypothesis. He had experience with the shadowy form they both understood to be one of the liches that had created Crenshinibon in that long-lost age. These ideas seemed to Cadderly the most informative of all.

Not Drizzt, nor Bruenor, not even Danica fathomed as clearly as Jarlaxle the trap into which Catti-brie had fallen, or the dire, likely irreparable implications of a new world imprinting on the old, or of a shattering of the wall between light and shadow. Not the other mages nor the priests quite grasped the permanence of the change that had found them all, of the loss of magic and of some, if not all the gods. But Jarlaxle understood.

Deneir was gone, Cadderly had come to accept, and the god was not coming back, at least not in the form Cadderly had come to know. The Weave, the source of Toril's magic, could not be rewound. It appeared as though Mystra herself—all of her domain—was simply there one moment, gone the next.

"Some magic will continue," Jarlaxle said as the discussion neared its end. It had become little more than a rehash of belabored points. "Your exploits prove that."

"Or they are the last gasps of magic dying," Cadderly replied. Jarlaxle shrugged and reluctantly nodded at the possibility of that theory.

"Is this world that is joining with ours a place of magic and gods?" Danica asked. "The beasts we have seen—"

"Have nothing to do with the new world, I think, which may be imbued, as is our own, with both magic and brute force," Jarlaxle interrupted without reservation. "The crawlers come from the Shadowfell." Cadderly nodded agreement with the drow.

"Then, is their magic dying?" Drizzt asked. "Has this collision you speak of destroyed their Weave, as well?"

"Or will the two intertwine in new ways, perhaps with this Plane of Shadow, this Shadowfell, between them?" Jarlaxle said.

"We cannot know," said Cadderly. "Not yet."

"What next?" asked Drizzt, and his voice took on an unusual timbre, one of distinct desperation—desperation wrought by his fears for Catti-brie, the others knew.

"We know what tools we have," Cadderly said, and he stood up and crossed his arms over his chest. "We will match strength with strength, and hope that some magic, at least, will find its way to our many spellcasters."

"You have shown as much already," said Jarlaxle.

"In a manner I cannot predict, much less control or summon."

"I have faith in you," Jarlaxle replied, and that statement gave all four of them pause, for it seemed so impossible that Jarlaxle would be saying that of Cadderly—or anyone!

"Should Cadderly extend similar confidence?" Danica said to the drow.

Jarlaxle burst into laughter, helpless and absurd laughter, and Cadderly joined him, and Danica joined them, too.

But Drizzt could not, his gaze sliding to the side of the room, to the door behind which Catti-brie sat in unending darkness.

Lost to him.

* * * * *

Desperation gripped the normally serene Yharaskrik as the reality of its situation closed in around it. Memories flew away and equations became muddled. It had known physical oblivion before, when Hephaestus had released his great fiery breath upon Crenshinibon, blasting the artifact. Only through an amazing bit of good fortune—the falling Weave touching the residual power of the artifact with the remnants of Yharaskrik nearby—had the illithid come to consciousness again.

But oblivion loomed once again, and with no hope of reprieve. The disembodied intellect flailed without focus for just a few precious moments before the desperate mind flayer reached out toward the nearest vessel.

But Ivan Bouldershoulder was ready, and the dwarf put up such a wall of denial and rage that Yharaskrik couldn't begin to make headway into his consciousness. So shut out was the illithid that Yharaskrik had no understanding of where it was, or that it was surrounded by lesser beings that might indeed prove susceptible to possession.

Yharaskrik didn't even fight back against that refusal, for it knew that possession would not solve its problem. It could not inhabit an unwilling host forever, and should it insert all of its consciousness into the physical form of a lesser being, should it fully possess a dwarf, a human, or even an elf, it would become limited by that being's physiology.

There was no real escape. But even as it rebounded away from Ivan Bouldershoulder, the mind flayer had another thought, and cast a wide net, its consciousness reaching out across the leagues of Faerûn. It needed another awakened intellect, another psionicist, a fellow thinker.

It knew of one. It reached for one as its homeless intellect began to flounder.

In a lavish chamber beneath the port city of Luskan, many miles to the northwest, Kimmuriel Oblodra, lieutenant of Bregan D'aerthe, second-in-command behind only Jarlaxle Baenre, felt a sensation, a calling.

A desperate plea.

CHAPTER
A WHISPER IN THE DARK
22

The night was quiet, the forest beyond the wide courtyard of Spirit Soaring dark and still.

Too quiet, Jarlaxle thought as he stared out from a second-story balcony, where he kept his assigned watch. He heard others in the hallways behind him expressing hope at the calm, but to Jarlaxle, the deceptive peace was just the opposite. The pause revealed to him that their enemies were not foolhardy. The last attack had become a massacre of fleshy crawling beasts—their burned and blasted lumps littered the lawn still.

But they weren't finished, to be sure. Given Danica's report, given Jarlaxle's understanding of the hatred toward him and toward Cadderly and Danica, he saw no possibility that Spirit Soaring would suddenly be left in peace.

This night was peaceful, though—undeniably so, paradoxically so, eerily so. And in that quiet, with not even the breath of wind accompanying it, Jarlaxle, and Jarlaxle alone, heard a call.

His eyes widened despite his near-perfect control over his emotions, and he reflexively glanced around. He knew how tentative his—and Athrogate's—welcome was at Spirit Soaring, and he could hardly believe his misfortune as another ally, one who would not likely be accepted by any at Spirit Soaring, demanded an audience.

He tried to push that quiet but insistent call away, but its urgency only heightened.

Jarlaxle looked to the forest and focused his thoughts on one large tree, just behind the foliage border. Then, with another glance around, the drow slipped over the balcony railing and nimbly climbed to the ground. He disappeared into the darkness, making his careful way across the wide courtyard.

* * * * *

"Bah, just as I told ye, elf," a sneering Bruenor Battlehammer said to Drizzt as they watched Jarlaxle slip down from his perch. "Ain't no friend to any other'n Jarlaxle, that one."

A profound sigh reflected Drizzt's deep disappointment.

"I'll go get Pwent and bottle up that damned annoying dwarf ol' big-hat there brung with him." Bruenor started to turn away, but Drizzt caught him by the shoulder.

"We don't know what this is about," he reminded them. "More scouting? Did Jarlaxle see something?"

"Bah!" Bruenor snorted, pulling away. "Go and see if ye got to see, but I'm already knowing."

"Await my return," Drizzt said.

Bruenor glared at him.

"Please, trust me in this," Drizzt begged. "There is too much at stake for all of us, for Catti-brie. If anyone can help us solve the riddle of her troubles, it is Jarlaxle."

"Thought it was Cadderly. Ain't that why we're here?"

"Him, too," said Drizzt, and as Bruenor visibly relaxed, he slipped out the window and moved after Jarlaxle. Not a wary creature stirred at his silent passing.

* * * * *

Ever do I find you in curious places, Kimmuriel Oblodra's fingers waggled to Jarlaxle, using the intricate hand language of the drow. *With Cadderly Bonaduce and his pathetic priests? Truly?*

In this time, we all share concerns, and profit from . . . accommodations of mutual benefit, Jarlaxle's fingers answered. *The situation here is desperate, even grave.*

I know more about it than you do, Kimmuriel assured him, and Jarlaxle wore a puzzled expression.

"About the failing of the Weave, perhaps . . . ?" he said quietly.

Kimmuriel shook his head and responded aloud. "About your predicament. About Hephaestus and Crenshinibon."

"And the illithid," Jarlaxle added.

"Because of the illithid," Kimmuriel corrected. "Yharaskrik, without form and dissipating, found me in Luskan. He is no more a part of this creature they call the Ghost King. He was cast out, to fade to nothingness."

"And he seeks revenge?"

"Revenge is not the way of illithids," Kimmuriel explained. "Though no doubt Yharaskrik enjoyed the bargain I offered."

Do tell, said Jarlaxle, with his fingers and his amused expression.

"Its only hope was to journey to the Astral Plane, a place of consciousness without corporeal restraint," Kimmuriel explained. "With the failure of conventional magic and divine magic, its best opportunity for such a journey was a fellow practitioner of psionics—me. Without its own body as anchor, the mind flayer could not facilitate the flight alone."

"You let it go?" Jarlaxle asked, raising his voice just a bit. He wasn't as angry as intrigued, however, revealed by the way he reached up to tug at the diatryma feather that was nearly fully regrown in his enchanted hat.

"To survive as the years pass, Yharaskrik must find a mind hive of illithids. We of psionic power are not unaffected by that which is occurring across the multiverse, and having such allies. . . ."

"They are wretched creatures."

Kimmuriel shrugged. "They are among the most brilliant of all the mortal beings. I know not what will happen to my powers, nor to magic, divine or arcane. I know only that the world is changing—has changed. Even shifting here through the dimensions proved a great risk, but one that I needed to take."

"To warn me."

"To warn and to instruct, for in return for passage, Yharaskrik revealed to me all it knows about the Ghost King, and about the remnants of the artifact, Crenshinibon."

"I am touched at your concern for me."

"You are necessary," said Kimmuriel, drawing a laugh from Jarlaxle.

"Do tell me, then," Jarlaxle said. "How might I, might we, defeat this Ghost King?"

Kimmuriel nodded and recounted it all in detail then, echoing Yharaskrik's lecture about the being that was both Hephaestus and Crenshinibon, about its powers and its limitations. He explained the minions and the gates that brought them to Faerûn. He talked of one such rift he had sensed, though had not yet inspected, still opened wide in the lakeside town to the southeast. He spoke of human and dwarf refugees hiding in tunnels.

"You trust this mind flayer?" Jarlaxle asked in the end.

"Illithids are trustworthy," Kimmuriel replied. "Loathsome, at times, fascinating always, but as long as their goals are understood, their logic is easily followed. In this case, Yharaskrik's goal was survival. Its plight was real and immediate, and caused by the Ghost King. Knowing that truth, as I did, I trust in its recounting."

Jarlaxle believed that he held some insight into the mindset of illithids as well, for he had been a companion of Kimmuriel Oblodra for a long, long time, and if someone had ever deigned to put a squishy octopoid head on that particular drow, it surely would have fit Kimmuriel well.

* * * * *

In the brush not far away, Drizzt Do'Urden listened to it all with interest, though much of it was no more than a confirmation of that which they had already surmised about their mighty enemy. Then he listened to Jarlaxle's reply and instructions, with wide-eyed disbelief, and truly he felt vindicated in trusting Jarlaxle.

"You cannot demand of me that I take such a risk with Bregan D'aerthe," he heard Kimmuriel argue.

"It is worth the potential gain," Jarlaxle replied. "And think of the opportunity here for you to discern so much more of the mystery that is occurring all around us!"

That last line apparently had the desired effect on Kimmuriel, for the drow bowed to Jarlaxle, turned to the side, and literally cut the air with an outstretched finger, leaving a sizzling vertical blue line in its wake. With a wave, Kimmuriel turned that two-dimensional blue line into a doorway and stepped through, disappearing from sight.

Jarlaxle stood for a bit, hands on hips, digesting it all. Then, with a shake of his head, one of disbelief, even bemusement, the mercenary headed back for Spirit Soaring.

By the time Drizzt arrived, only moments after Jarlaxle, the summons was already out for him and Bruenor to an audience with Cadderly.

And Jarlaxle, of course.

CHAPTER 23

GAUNTLET THROWN

The Ghost King emerged from its cave with a deafening roar and a stomp of clawed feet that sent fleshy crawlers flying. The magnificent creature stepped out without heed to the scrambling beasts. Its great tail, part skeletal and part rotting dragon flesh, swept aside any too near. Its torn leathery wings buffeted those to either side with a great wind.

No plotting guided the attack, no care for minions or any role they might play. Rage drove the Ghost King. Freed of the caution of Yharaskrik, the great beast followed its emotions. The Ghost King could not be defeated by mere mortals, whose magic was failing. The Ghost King need not plot and connive and tread with fearful caution.

Wings wide, the Ghost King leaped from the pinnacle and rode the updrafts to climb above the Snowflakes. With eyes magical, the Ghost King saw across the miles to the symbol of its enemies, the place on which it focused its rage.

Higher it climbed, above the few wispy clouds that dulled part of the starry night sky. And there it circled, gathering speed, gathering its hatred. And like a bolt from on high, the Ghost King folded its wings, tipped down its huge head, and plummeted for Spirit Soaring.

Though Hephaestus's lips were mostly withered away, any watching would have noted a wicked smile upon the dracolich's face.

*****

Twenty-one priests and wizards, almost half the contingent of residents and visitors remaining at Spirit Soaring, licked dry lips and clutched stones coated in explosive oil. The other half tried to sleep in the too-quiet night. They checked and rechecked their other implements, weapons and armor, magical rings and wands, scrolls and potion bottles, nervously awaiting the attack they knew would come.

It would be a greater beast, too, Cadderly had informed them after his meeting with the newcomers, the drow and the dwarves. A dragon, an undead dracolich, the master of the many minions they had slaughtered, would lead the next attack, so Cadderly had assured them with confidence.

More than a few of them had seen a dragon before, a handful had even witnessed the awful splendor of a dracolich. They were seasoned veterans, after all, travelers mostly, who had come to Spirit Soaring to try to make sense of a dangerous world gone mad.

Their mouths were dry, to a man and woman, for what sort of previous experiences could have offered them—could have offered anyone—solace at that desperate time?

They stood alert, spread over every vantage point of Spirit Soaring, their counterparts sleeping in small groups nearby, weapons at their sides. The attack would come soon, Cadderly had said. Perhaps that very night.

In the central chamber of the second floor, with easy access to corridors that would deliver them to any wall in short order, Cadderly, Danica, the two drow, and the three dwarves waited as well, none of them finding sleep. All of them expected, with each arrival of Ginance and her roving patrol group, to hear that the beast was upon them.

Spirit Soaring was alert, was ready.

But nothing could have truly prepared the fifty-four souls in the cathedral for the advent of the Ghost King. Some few sentries near the northeastern corner of the great building noted the movement from high above and pointed at the giant missile hurtling down at Spirit Soaring. A few managed to scream out a warning, and one lifted a shield in ridiculous defense.

With strength unimaginable, the Ghost King pulled up from its plummet just before it slammed the building, extending its great hind legs out before it and crashing in.

Not a person, not even King Bruenor, so strong on his feet, not even Athrogate, possessed of the low center of balance of a dwarf and the strength of a mountain giant, remained on his feet under the weight of that collision. Spirit Soaring shook to its foundation, glass shattering all over the structure under the sheer force of the impact and the twist of the magical building's indomitable frame. Doors popped open and corridors twisted. Bricks fell from every chimney.

The thunderous sound of a dragon's roar muted every scream, crash, and shatter.

The defenders pulled themselves up and did not shy from the fray. By the time Cadderly and his elite group arrived on the scene, where the wall had been torn away and the Ghost King stood, a dozen rocks had already been thrown, their magical oil exploding at they hit the flesh and bone of the beast.

The Ghost King swiveled its great head on a serpentine neck, fiery eyes selecting a group of annoying rock-throwers, but before the beast could bring its rage to bear on those men and woman, a wizard's fireball, thrown from a necklace of enchanted rubies, engulfed its face in biting flames.

Lightning blasts followed. A pillar of divine fire swept down from above to scorch the back of the dracolich's neck.

And the beast roared, and the beast thrashed, and the building shook, and again men and women, elf and drow and dwarf, tumbled. A swipe of the dracolich's mighty tail slapped the length of the building, shattering more glass, breaking stone facing and cracking thick timber supports.

The room lay broken open, the beast clearly visible to Cadderly's approaching group. The three dwarves spearheading did not hesitate in the face of that catastrophe, and could not slow. They had to be the focus of the battle, by the plans Cadderly had drawn.

As soon as he had felt the thunder of the initial impact, the wound to the place built of his magic, Cadderly had felt the assault on his own body. As the dracolich came into sight, Cadderly felt the magic building within him. Wrought of his desperation, his anger, his denial of the horror of it, the power of spells unknown began to stir.

Whether sensing that power or just recognizing Cadderly, the Ghost King locked its eyes on the approaching group and opened wide its jaws.

"Dive!" Bruenor yelled, and Thibbledorf Pwent dived into Bruenor and knocked him aside, the two of them falling atop the rolling Athrogate.

Flanking the dwarves, Drizzt, Jarlaxle, and Danica easily sidestepped from the direct line to the beast.

But Cadderly didn't move left or right. He thrust his hands forward, hand crossbow in one, walking stick in the other, and chanted in words he did not know.

Dragonfire poured forth from the beast, filling the room in front of them. While Spirit Soaring's magical structure diminished the effect on the walls and floor, the furniture, books, and bric-a-brac went up in bursts of flame, and the gout of immolation rushed across the floor at its living targets, jetting for the open doorway. And there it was stopped by Cadderly's ward.

As the conflagration lessened, the priest fired his hand crossbow, more an act of defiance and challenge than to inflict true damage to the mighty beast, though Cadderly did smile as the bolt exploded against the dracolich's face.

Into the burning room ran the seven, meeting the beast head on. Rocks flew in from left and right, smacking the dracolich and exploding with sudden bursts of magical flame. More magic roared in as well, a hornet's nest of stings, a hurricane of lightning, a god's wrath of fire.

Wings beat against Spirit Soaring in reply. The great tail slapped left and right, crushing stone and wood and throwing wizards and priests aside. But the beast did not turn its focus from that one room, from those seven puny heroes.

"And so we meet," the Ghost King said, its voice shaking the smoldering timbers.

Cadderly fired another dart into its ugly face.

Bruenor, Athrogate, and Pwent didn't pause, bursting through the doorway and charging across the room.

Dragonfire drove them back.

"In together!" Cadderly demanded, and the seven tightened ranks around the priest, with his fire ward and his protection from the dracolich's withering touch.

Spell after spell came forth from the priest, in words none of them understood, and each of the defenders felt hardened against the deadly touch of the beast. On they went, marching right into the blinding roil of the Ghost King's breath. Those fires parted around them and reformed behind them as the dracolich continued its long exhale, so that the group of seven was fully surrounded by opaque walls of streaming flames.

But they moved forward, and as soon as the Ghost King finished, Cadderly cried for a charge.

And charge they did, Bruenor lifting high his axe, Athrogate beside him and spinning his morningstars, and Thibbledorf Pwent darting right between them, leaping at the beast with abandon. The battlerager latched on to one of the dracolich's great hind legs, dug his leg spikes in for support, and began whacking away with both hands, shaving skin and bone with his ridged armor as he thrashed.

Drizzt and Danica moved right behind the dwarves— Drizzt started to, but Cadderly grabbed him by the arm, then cupped his hand over Drizzt's right fist as Drizzt held his scimitar.

"You are the agent of all that is good!" Cadderly charged the surprised drow. The priest spoke another few words that neither he nor Drizzt understood, and Icingdeath glowed more brightly with a divine white light, one that overwhelmed its normal bluish hue. "Vanquish the beast!" Cadderly demanded, except it wasn't truly Cadderly, or *only* Cadderly talking, Drizzt realized to his hope and his horror. It was as if someone else, some*thing* else, some god or angel, had possessed the priest and placed that power and responsibility upon the drow.

Drizzt blinked but didn't dare hesitate other than to call forth Guenhwyvar. He spun back with such fury that it left him stumbling at the dracolich. He moved beside Danica, who leaped and spun and kicked out wide, hitting the beast with rapid and heavy blows. The Ghost King bit down at her, but she was too quick to be caught like that, and she threw herself aside at the last moment.

The snapping jaws cracked in the empty air, and Drizzt rushed in, glowing weapon in hand. He stabbed with Twinkle, the fine blade knifing through some rotting skin to crack against bone, then he slashed with Icingdeath, with his scimitar Cadderly had somehow infused with the power of divine might.

The strike sounded like the drop of a gigantic boulder, a sudden and sharp retort that dwarfed the boom of a fireball and made Athrogate's oil-soaked strikes seem like the tapping of a bird. The Ghost King's head flew back, a great chunk of its cheekbone and upper jaw flying from its face to the courtyard below.

Flying, too, went Guenhwyvar, a great leap that brought the panther clawing at the beast's ugly face.

Everyone else, even wild Pwent, paused a moment to stare in disbelief.

"Impressive," Jarlaxle congratulated, standing beside the gawking Cadderly. The drow threw down his plume, bringing forth the giant diatryma bird. Then he lifted his arms, a wand in each hand. From one came thundering lightning, from the other a line of viscous globs of green goo that the drow aimed to splatter across the wyrm's face, hoping to blind it or hinder its snapping jaws.

What a force they were!

But what an enemy they had found.

The Ghost King did not lift away and flee, did not shy even from Drizzt and that awful weapon. It stomped its leg, crushing through the support beams and driving straight down through the ceiling of the structure's first floor. Poor Pwent was ground by the walls and fell away, all twisted, to the main level.

The Ghost King shook its head wildly and Guenhwyvar went flying away. Then the beast swung its head back with battering ram force at Drizzt, a blow that would have killed him had it hit him squarely. But no one ever hit Drizzt Do'Urden squarely. As the head swung in, Drizzt dived over sideways, just ahead of it. Still, the sheer weight of the glancing blow forced him to roll repeatedly in an attempt to absorb the force. He tumbled out of room, slamming hard into the wrecked chamber's side wall, a burst of embers flying up behind him.

Stung and a bit dazed but hardly down, Drizzt rushed back at the beast. He watched Athrogate sail up in the air before him, caught by a foreleg. The dwarf's oil-soaked morningstar crashed and exploded against the bone, splintering it, but still the Ghost King managed to throw the dwarf far.

"Me head to shake, me bones to break!" the indomitable Athrogate yelled out even as he flew across the room and crashed to the floor. "He flinged me, a flat stone across a still lake!" he finished as he skipped up from the floor and slammed the corner of the wall near the outer break—only the word "lake" came out "la-*aa-aa-aa*-ke" as he fell to the ground outside.

With the two dwarves and Guenhwyvar out of the fray, Danica and Bruenor were sorely pressed. Bruenor pushed back hits from under his shield, his legs bowing but not buckling, his axe ever ready to respond with a heavy chop. Danica leaped and spun, rolled and somersaulted through the air, always half a step ahead of claw or bite.

"We can't hold it!" Jarlaxle said through gritted teeth. Even when Drizzt got back into the fight, his divinely weighted scimitar driving hard against the beast, the mercenary's grim visage didn't soften.

Jarlaxle spoke the painful truth. For all their power and gallant efforts, they were inflicting only minor wounds on the beast, and attrition was already working against them. Then cries went out that crawlers were swarming from the forest, and many on the periphery of the fight had to turn their attention outward.

In that awful moment of honesty, it seemed that all would end for Spirit Soaring and her defenders.

Caddery reached up with his arms, and up further with his magic, and to all witnessing the event, it seemed as if the mighty priest had plucked a star or the sun itself from the sky and pulled it down over his own body.

Cadderly shone with such radiance that beams of his emanating light streamed through every crack in Spirit Soaring's planking. Beyond the broken wall, the courtyard and the forest shone as though lit by a clear midday.

The night was completely gone, and so too were the wounds of all those near the priest. Pain and fatigue were replaced by warmth and invigoration, the likes of which they had never known.

The opposite effect jarred the Ghost King, and the beast recoiled in shock and torturous pain.

Beyond the wall, the approaching crawlers fell back on their flat feet, long arms flailing to try, futilely, to block the heavenly light. Wisps of smoke rose from their black skins. Those that could roll backward scrambled for the shadows of the trees.

The Ghost King's roar shook the building to its foundation yet again. The beast did not fly away, but flailed all the more wildly, thumping Bruenor, who took every blow with a snarl and a swipe of retribution. The creature's foreleg cut nothing but air as it swiped at Danica, whose acrobatics defied gravity as she lifted and twisted and turned. The dracolich's great jaws snapped down on the diatryma and lifted the flailing bird into the air, where the massive head thrashed right and left and bit down, cutting the bird in half.

The creature tried to bite at the dodging woman, but there was Drizzt, rushing in, his blades rolling left and right and straight overhead, every swipe of the enchanted Icingdeath stabbing out a bit farther, slicing through dragon scale, melting dragon flesh, and exploding dragon bone.

The Ghost King slipped back from the ledge, its hind legs reaching to find footing on the ground. Barely had it stepped down before Thibbledorf Pwent hit it with a flying head butt, his helmet spike digging into the beast's calf and securing his hold. From the other side came Athrogate, one morningstar in hand, the other lost in the fall. He spun the heavy ball above his head in both hands, brought forth its oily might, and struck the Ghost King's other leg with such force that a red scale disintegrated beneath the blow and the beast's desiccated flesh splintered and dissolved all the way to the bone, which cracked loudly.

And above all the pain from those furious warriors, above the continuing sting of Jarlaxle's lightning bolts and the hindrance of the drow's viscous globs, there was the ever-intrusive agony of Cadderly's light. That awful light, divine spurs that permeated every inch of the Ghost King's being.

The beast breathed its fire into the room again, but Cadderly's ward remained to repel the effect, and his light healed his friends as soon as they were stung by the flames.

The effort cost the Ghost King dearly, for all the while it locked its great head in position to fill the room with its fires, Drizzt, who scrambled onto its leg and up to its neck, found the unhindered opportunity to pummel the dragon's skull. Again and again, Icingdeath came down with fury, bone and flesh and scales exploding under each thunderous strike.

The dragon's fiery breath ended abruptly with Drizzt's last strike. The Ghost King shuddered with such force that all, Drizzt and Athrogate included, were thrown aside. The creature leaped back, far out into the courtyard.

"Finish it!" Jarlaxle cried to all, and indeed, it seemed at that moment that the dracolich was in its last throes, that a concerted assault could actually bring the beast down.

And so they tried, but their weapons and spells and missiles passed through the Ghost King without consequence. For there was suddenly nothing tangible to the beast, just its shape outlined in blue light. Thibbledorf Pwent went charging out from the base of Spirit Soaring, roaring as only a battlerager could bellow, and leaped with abandon—right through the intangible beast to bounce down on the turf.

Even more significant to Drizzt, as he moved to follow Pwent, was the apparition of Guenhwyvar across the courtyard. The panther did not charge at the Ghost King. Ears flattened with uncharacteristic trepidation, Guenhwyvar, never afraid of anything, turned and fled.

Drizzt gawked in surprise. He looked to the beast on the field, to Pwent as he ran all around the glowing form, inside it even, thrashing to no effect.

Then suddenly, nothing at all remained to be seen of the Ghost King as the beast faded, just faded to nothingness. It was gone.

The defenders looked on with shock. Cadderly stared with amazement after the blue-white image and gasped at his memories of the Prophecies of Alaundo and of this year, 1385, the Year of Blue Fire. Coincidence, or fitting representation of their greater catastrophe? Before he could delve any deeper into his contemplations, from a room much farther inside Spirit Soaring, Catti-brie screamed in abject terror.

PART 4

SACRIFICE

SACRIFICE

The recognition of utter helplessness is more than humbling; it is devastating. On those occasions when it is made clear to someone, internally, that willpower or muscle or technique will not be enough to overcome the obstacles placed before him, that he is helpless before those obstacles, there follows a brutal mental anguish.

When Wulfgar was taken by Errtu in the Abyss, he was beaten and physically tortured, but on those few occasions I was able to coax my friend to speak of that time, those notes he sang most loudly in despair were those of his helplessness. The demon, for example, would make him believe that he was free and was living with the woman he loved, then would slaughter her and their illusionary children before Wulfgar's impotent gaze.

That torture created Wulfgar's most profound and lasting scars.

When I was a child in Menzoberranzan, I was taught a lesson universal to male drow. My sister Briza took me out to the edge of our cavern homeland where a gigantic earth elemental waited. The beast was harnessed and Briza handed me the end of the rein.

"Hold it back," she instructed.

I didn't quite understand, and when the elemental took a step away, the rope was pulled from my hand.

Briza struck me with her whip, of course, and no doubt, she enjoyed it.

"Hold it back," she said again.

I took the rope and braced myself. The elemental took a step and I went flying after it. It didn't even know that I existed, or that I was tugging with all my insignificant strength to try to hinder its movement.

Briza scowled as she informed me that I would try again.

This test must be a matter of cleverness, I decided, and instead of just bracing myself, I looped the rope around a nearby stalagmite, to Briza's approving nods, and dug in my heels.

The elemental, on command, took a step and whipped me around the stone as if I were no more than a bit of parchment in a furious gale. The monster didn't slow, didn't even notice.

In that moment, I was shown my limitations, without equivocation. I was shown my impotence.

Briza then held the elemental in place with an enchantment and dismissed it with a second one. The point she was trying to make was that the divine magic of Lolth overwhelmed both muscle and technique. This was no more than another subjugation tactic by the ruling matron mothers, to make the males of Menzoberranzan understand their lowly place, their inferiority, particularly to those more in Lolth's favor.

For me, and I suspect for many of my kin, the lesson was more personal and less societal, for that was my first real experience encountering a force supremely beyond my willpower, utterly beyond my control. It wasn't as if had I tried harder or been more clever I might have changed the outcome. The elemental would have stepped away unhindered and unbothered no matter my determination.

To say I was humbled would be an understatement. There, in that dark cavern, I learned the first truth of both mortality and mortal flesh.

And now I feel that terrible measure of impotence again. When I look at Catti-brie, I know that she is beyond my ability to help. We all dream about being the hero, about finding the solution, about winning the moment and saving the day. And we all harbor, to some degree, the notion that our will can overcome, that determination and strength of mind can push us to great ends—and indeed they can.

To a point.

Death is the ultimate barrier, and when faced with impending death, personally or for someone you love, a mortal being will encounter, most of all, ultimate humility.

We all believe that we can defeat that plague or that disease, should it befall us, through sheer willpower. It is a common mental defense against the inevitability we all know we share. I wonder, then, if the worst reality of a lingering death is the sense that your own body is beyond your ability to control.

In my case, the pain I feel in looking at Catti-brie is manifold, and not least among the variations is my own sense of helplessness. I deny the looks that Cadderly and Jarlaxle exchanged, expressions that revealed their hearts and minds. They cannot be right in their obvious belief that Catti-brie is beyond our help and surely doomed!

I demand that they are not right.

And yet I know that they are. Perhaps I only "know" because I fear beyond anything I have ever known that they are correct, and if they are, then I will know no closure. I cannot say good-bye to Catti-brie because I fear that I already have.

And thus, in moments of weakness, I lose faith and know that they are right. My love, my dearest friend, is lost to me forever—and there again lurches my stubbornness, for my first instinct was to write "likely forever." I cannot admit the truth even as I admit the truth!

So many times have I seen my friends return from the brink of death: Bruenor on the back of a dragon, Wulfgar from the Abyss, Catti-brie from the dark plane of Tarterus. So many times have the odds been beaten. In the end, we always prevail!

But that is not true. And perhaps the cruelest joke of all is the confidence, the surety, that our good fortune and grand exploits have instilled in my friends, the Companions of the Hall.

How much worse becomes the cruel reality when at last we are touched by inescapable tragedy.

I look at Catti-brie and I am reminded of my limitations. My fantasies of saving the moment and the day are dashed against jagged and immovable rocks. I want to save her and I cannot. I look at Catti-brie, wandering lost, and in those moments when I can accept that this state is forever, my hopes become less about victory and more about...

I can hardly think it. Have I truly been reduced to hoping that this woman I love will pass on quickly and peacefully?

And still the fight goes on around us, I am sure, in this world gone mad. And still will my scimitars be put to use in a struggle that has, I fear, only just begun. And still will I be needed to mediate between Bruenor and Jarlaxle, Cadderly and Jarlaxle. I cannot skulk away and be alone with my mounting grief and pain. I cannot abrogate my responsibilities to those around me.

But it all, so suddenly, seems less important to me. Without Catti-brie, what is the point of our fight? Why defeat the dracolich when the outcome will not change, since we are all doomed in the end? Is it not true that that which we deem important is, in the grand scheme of the millennia and the multiverse, utterly and completely irrelevant?

This is the demon of despair wrought of impotence. More profound than the helplessness created by Shimmergloom the shadow dragon's dark cloud of breath. More profound than the lesson of the drow matron mothers. For that question, "What is the point?" is the most insidious and destructive of all.

I must deny it. I cannot give in to it, for the sake of those around me and for the sake of myself, and yes, for the sake of Catti-brie, who would not allow me to surrender to such a concept.

Truly this inner turmoil tests me more than any demon, any dragon, any horde of ravaging orcs ever could.

For as this dark moment shows me the futility, so too it demands of me the faith—the faith that there is something beyond this mortal coil, that there is a place of greater understanding and universal community than this temporary existence.

Else it is all a sad joke.

—Drizzt Do'Urden

CHAPTER 24

WANDERING IN THE DARKNESS

"How can I be tellin' ye what I ain't for knowing?" Ivan grumbled, putting Temberle back on his heels.

"I thought... you might know..." the young man stammered.

"You are a dwarf," Hanaleisa added dryly.

"So's he!" Ivan fumed, poking a finger Pikel's way. His obstinate expression melted when he looked back to the Bonaduce siblings, both wearing skeptical expressions. "Yeah, I know," Ivan agreed with an exasperated sigh.

"Doo-dad," said Pikel, and with an imperious "harrumph" of his own, he walked away.

"He's durned good in the higher tunnels, though," Ivan said in his brother's defense. "When there's roots pokin' through. He talks to 'em, and the damned things talk back!"

"Our current plight?" Rorick reminded, walking over to join the discussion. "The folk are sick of tunnels and growing ever more agitated."

"They'd rather be out in Carradoon, would they?" Ivan retorted. It was sarcasm, of course, but to everyone's surprise, Rorick didn't blink.

"They're saying that very thing," he informed the others.

"They forget what chased us here in the first place," said Temberle, but Rorick shook his head with every word.

"They forget nothing—and we've been fighting those same monsters in the tunnels, anyway."

"From defensible positions, on ground of our choosing," said Hanaleisa, to which Rorick merely shrugged.

"Do ye think ye might be finding yer way back to the tunnels near to Carradoon?" Ivan asked Temberle and Hanaleisa.

"You cannot . . ." Temberle started, but Hanaleisa cut him short.

"We can," she said. "I've been marking the tunnels at various junctures. We can get back close to where we started, I'm sure."

"Might be our best option," said Ivan.

"No," said Temberle.

"We're not knowin' what's still there, boy," Ivan reminded. "And we know what's waiting for us in the mountains, and I know ye didn't see nothing the size o' that damned wyrm in Carradoon, else ye'd all be dead. I'd like to give ye a better choice—I'd like a better choice for meself!—but I'm not for knowing another way out o' these tunnels, and the one I came down can't be climbed, and I wouldn't be climbing back that way anyhow!"

Temberle and Hanaleisa exchanged concerned looks, and both glanced across the torchlit chamber to the haggard refugees. The weight of responsibility pressed down upon them, for their decisions would affect everyone in that chamber, perhaps fatally.

"Choice ain't for ye, anyway," Ivan blustered a few heartbeats later, as if reading their thoughts, certainly reading their expressions. "Ye done good in gettin' these folk from Carradoon, and I'll be sure to tell yer Ma and Da that when we get back to Spirit Soaring. But I'm here now, and last time I bothered to look, I've got a bit o' rank and experience on the both o' ye put together.

"We can't stay down here. Yer brother's right on that. If we were all kin dwarves, we'd just widen a few holes, put up a few walls, call the place home, and be done with it. But we ain't, and we got to get out, and I can't be getting us out unless we're going back the way ye came in."

"We'll be fighting there," Hanaleisa warned.

"More the reason to go, then!" Ivan declared with a toothy grin.

And they went, back the way they had come, and when they weren't sure of either left or right, because Hanaleisa's markings were neither complete nor always legible, they guessed and pressed on. And when they guessed wrong, they turned around and marched back, double-time, by the barking commands of Ivan Bouldershoulder.

Bark he did, but he added a much-needed enthusiasm, full of optimistic promise. His energy proved contagious and the group made great headway that first day. The second went along splendidly as well, except for one unusually long detour that nearly dropped Ivan, who insisted on leading the way, into a deep pit.

By the third day, their steps came smaller and the barks became mere words. Still they went along, for what choice did they have? When they heard the growls of monsters echoing along distant tunnels, though they all cringed at the notion of more fighting, they took hope that such sounds meant they were nearing the end of their Underdark torment. Hungry, as they had fed on nothing more than a few mushrooms and a few cave fish, thirsty, as most of the water they found was too fetid to drink, they took a deep breath and pushed forward.

Around a bend in the corridor, where the tunnel soon widened into a large chamber, they saw their enemies—not undead monsters, but the crawling fleshy beasts that Ivan knew so well—at the same time their enemies saw them. Driven by the knowledge that he had led those poor, beleaguered folks, including Cadderly's precious children, into danger, Ivan Bouldershoulder was fast to the charge. Fury drove his steps, and determination that he would not be the cause of disaster brought great strength to his limbs. The dwarf hit the advancing enemy line like a huge rock denying the tide. Crawlers flowed around him, but those nearest exploded under the weight of Ivan's mighty axe.

Flanking him left came Temberle and Hanaleisa, a great slash of the blade and a flurry of fists, and to the right came Pikel and Rorick. Rorick attempted only one spell, and when it utterly failed, he took up the dagger he carried on his belt and was glad that he, like his siblings, had been taught how to fight.

For Pikel, there was no magical glow to his club, no shillelagh enchantment to add weight to his blows. But like his brother, Pikel had gone to a deeper place of anger, a place where he was fighting not just for himself, but for others who could hardly defend against such enemies.

"Oo oi!" he yelled repeatedly, emphasizing each shout by cracking his cudgel across the head of a crawling beast. He could only swing with one arm, it was true, and swung a weapon absent its usual enchantment, but crawler after crawler was bowled back or fell straight to the ground, shuddering in its death throes, its skull battered to shards.

With that living prow of five skilled fighters, the embattled refugees pushed on and drove their enemies back. Any thought that they should slow and close ranks, or flee back the way they had come, was denied by Ivan—not with words, but because he would neither slow nor turn. He seemed as if he cared not if those flanking and supporting him kept up.

For Ivan, this wasn't about tactics, but about anger—anger at all of it: at the dragon and at the danger that threatened Cadderly's children; at the frustration of his brother, who felt abandoned by his god; at the loss of security in the place he called home. Left and right went his axe, with no thought of defense—not a blocking arm or a creature leaping at him deterred his cuts. He sliced a grasping arm off where his axe hit it, and more than one fleshy beast did leap upon him, only to get a head-butt or a jab in the face from the pommel of the axe. Then, as the foolish creature inevitably fell away, Ivan kicked and spat and ultimately split the thing's head wide with that double-bladed, monstrous weapon he carried.

He waded along, the floor slick with blood and gore, with brains and slabs of flesh.

He got too far ahead of the others, and creatures came at him from every side, even from behind.

And creatures died all around the frenzied dwarf.

They grabbed at him and clawed at him. Blood showed on every patch of Ivan that was not armored, and creatures died with strands of his yellow hair in their long fingers. But he didn't slow, and his blows rained down with even more strength and fury.

Soon enough, even the stupid crawlers understood to stay away from that one, and Ivan could have walked across the rest of the chamber unhindered. Only then did he turn back to support the line.

The fight went on and on, until every swing of a weapon came with aching arms, until the whole of the refugee band gasped for every breath as they struggled to continue the battle. But continue they did, and the crawlers died and died. When it was at last over, the remnants of the strange enemy finally fleeing down side corridors, the wide chamber full of blood and bodies, the ranks of the refugees had not significantly thinned.

But if there was an end to their battle, none of them could see it.

"To Carradoon," the indomitable Hanaleisa bade Ivan and Pikel, raising her voice so that all could hear, and hoping against hope that her feigned optimism would prove contagious.

The meager food, the constant fighting, the lack of daylight, the smell of death, and the grieving of so many for so many had depleted the band, she knew, as did everyone else. The reprieve that was Ivan, adding his bold, confident, and fearless voice, had proven a temporary uplift.

"We'll be fighting, every step!" complained one of the fishermen, sitting on a rock, his face streaked with blood—his own and that of a crawler—and with tears. "My stomach's growling for food and my arms are aching."

"And there's nothing back the way we came but dark death!" another shouted at him, and so yet another argument ensued.

"Get us out of here," Hanaleisa whispered to Ivan. "Now."

They didn't bury their dead under piles of heavy stones, and they made no formal plans for their wounded, just offered each a shoulder and dragged themselves along. They were moving again soon after the fight, but it seemed an inch at a time.

"If it comes to fightin' again, the two of ye will make us win or make us lose," Ivan informed Temberle and Hanaleisa. "We can't move along as fast, 'tis true, but we can't fight any slower or we die.

They'll be lookin' to you two. Ye find that deeper place and pull out the strength ye need."

The twins exchanged fearful glances, but those fast became expressions of determination.

* * * * *

In a quiet chamber not far from where the Bouldershoulders, the Bonaduce children, and the other refugees earned their hard-fought victory, the absolute darkness was interrupted by a blue-glowing dot, hovering more than six feet above the stone floor. As if some unseen hand was drawing with it, the dot moved along, cutting the blackness with a blue line.

It hung there, sizzling with magical power for a few moments, then seemed to expand, moving from two dimensions to three, forming a glowing doorway.

A young drow male stepped through that doorway, materializing from thin air, it seemed. Hand crossbow in one hand, sword in the other, the warrior slipped in silently, peering intently down the corridor, one way, then another. After a quick search of the area, he moved in front of the portal, stood up straight, and sheathed his sword.

On that signal, another dark elf stepped into the corridor. Fingers waggling in the silent language of the race, he ordered the first scout to move back behind the magical entry and take up a sentry position.

More drow stepped out, moving methodically and with precision and discipline, securing the area.

The portal sizzled, its glow increasing. More dark elves stepped through, including Kimmuriel Oblodra, who had created the psionic dimensional rift. A drow beside him began to signal with his fingers, but Kimmuriel, showing great confidence, grabbed his hand and bade him to whisper instead.

"You are certain of this?" the drow, Mariv by name, asked.

"He is following Jarlaxle's recommendation and request," answered the second drow who had come through the portal,

Valas Hune, a scout of great renown. "So, no, Mariv, our friend is not certain because he knows that Jarlaxle is not certain. That one is always acting as if he is sure of his course, but all of his life's been a gamble, hasn't it?"

"That is his charm, I fear," said Kimmuriel.

"And why we follow him," Mariv said with a shrug.

"You follow him because you agreed to follow him, and promised to follow him," Kimmuriel reminded, clearly uncomfortable with, or condescending toward, such a line of reasoning. Kimmuriel Oblodra, after all, was perhaps the only drow close enough to Jarlaxle to understand the truth of that one: the appearance of a great gamble might be Jarlaxle's charm, but Kimmuriel knew that the source of the charm was truly a farce. Jarlaxle seemed to gamble all the time, but his course was rarely one of uncertainty. That was why the logical and pragmatic, never-gambling Kimmuriel trusted Jarlaxle. It had nothing to do with charm, and everything to do with the realization of that which Jarlaxle promised.

"You may, of course, change your mind," he finished to Mariv, "but it would not be a course I would advise."

"Unless he'd prefer you dead," Valas Hune remarked to Mariv with a sly grin, and he moved away to make sure the perimeter was secure.

"I know you're uncomfortable with this mission," Kimmuriel said to Mariv, and such empathy was indeed rare, almost nonexistent, from the callous and logical drow psionicist. Mariv had been Kimmuriel's appointee, and had climbed the ranks of Bregan D'aerthe during Jarlaxle's absence, when the band had been fully under Kimmuriel's direction. The young wizard was in Kimmuriel's highest favor, one of three in the third tier of the mercenary band where Kimmuriel was undisputed second and Jarlaxle was undisputed leader. Even with the drawdown and current unpredictability of magic, the resourceful Mariv retained Kimmuriel's good graces, for he was possessed of many magical items of considerable power and was no novice with the blade as well. Well-versed with the sword, having graduated from

Melee-Magthere, the drow martial school, before his tenure at Sorcere, the academy for wizards, Mariv remained a potent force even in a time of the collapsing Weave.

Kimmuriel stood quiet then, and waved away all other conversation, waiting for the rest of his strike force to come through the gate, and for all the preparations around him to be completed. As soon as those things were done, all eyes turned his way.

"You know why we have come," Kimmuriel said quietly to those around him. "Your orders are without exception. Strike true and strike as instructed—and *only* as instructed."

The psionicist knew that more than a few of the Bregan D'aerthe warriors remained confused about their mission, and some were even repulsed by it. He didn't care. He trusted his underlings to perform as instructed, for to do otherwise was to face the wrath of not only the ultimately deadly Jarlaxle, but of Kimmuriel, and no one could exact exquisite torture more profoundly than a psionicist.

Two score of Bregan D'aerthe's force had entered the tunnels beneath the Snowflakes not far from the destroyed town of Carradoon. They moved out, silent, methodical, deadly.

CHAPTER 25
THE AWFUL TRUTH

It started hesitantly, one cheer of victory among a sea of doubting and skeptical expressions. For those outside of Spirit Soaring, the dwarves on the ground and the wizards and priests fighting from the balconies and rooftops, they saw only that single image of the great dracolich dematerializing before their astonished eyes, fading to seeming nothingness under the brilliant light of Cadderly's conjured sun.

It was gone, of that they were all certain, and the assault of its minions had also ended with the disappearance of the great wyrm. The wizards didn't even bother sending magical bolts out at the retreating hordes, so intent were they on the empty spot where the dracolich had been.

Then that one cheer became a chorus of absolute relief. Clapping, whistling, and shouting with joy, they moved toward the spot where the beast had departed the field as if pulled by gravity.

The cheers grew louder, shouts of joy and hope. Wizards proclaimed that the Weave itself would mend. Priests cried out in joy that they would once more be able to speak with their gods. Cheers for Cadderly rolled across the walls, some proclaiming him a god, a deity who could bring the sun itself to bear on his enemies.

"All fear Cadderly!"

But that was outside Spirit Soaring. That euphoria was for those who could not hear Catti-brie screaming.

With magical anklets speeding his strides, Drizzt outpaced Cadderly, Danica, and even Bruenor, desperate as the dwarf king was to reach his daughter. The drow scrambled through the corridors, leaped a banister to the fifth step of a rising staircase, and sprinted up to the third floor three steps at a time. He banged against walls so he didn't have to slow in his turns down the side corridors, and when he came to her door, Jarlaxle's eye patch in hand, along with his divinely weighted scimitar, he shouldered right through it.

Jarlaxle was waiting for him, though how the mercenary had beaten him to the room, Drizzt could not fathom and didn't have time to consider.

Catti-brie huddled against the back wall, screaming no more, but trembling with abject terror. She shielded her face with upraised arms, and between those intervening limbs, Drizzt could see that her white eyes were wide indeed.

He leaped toward her, but Jarlaxle caught him and tugged him back.

"The patch!" Jarlaxle warned.

Drizzt had enough of his senses remaining to pause for a moment and don the enchanted eye patch, dropping Icingdeath to the floor in the process. He went to his beloved and enveloped her, wrapping her in a great hug and trying to calm her.

Catti-brie seemed no less frightened when the other three arrived a few heartbeats later.

"What's it about?" Bruenor demanded of both Cadderly and Jarlaxle.

Jarlaxle had his suspicions and started to answer, but he bit his response off short and shook his head. In truth, he had no real evidence, nor did Cadderly, and they all looked to Drizzt, whose eye—the one not covered by the patch—like his wife's, had gone wide with horror.

* * * * *

They had not destroyed the Ghost King—that much was obvious to Drizzt as he hugged Catti-brie close and slipped into the pit of despair that had become her prison.

Her eyes looked into that alien world. He, briefly, resided in a gray shadow of the world around him, mountainous terrain to mimic the Snowflakes, in the Shadowfell.

The Ghost King was there.

On the plain before Catti-brie, the dracolich thrashed and roared in defiance and pain. Its bones shone whiter, its skin, where the scales had fallen away, showed an angry red mottled by great blisters. Seared by holy light, the beast seemed out of its mind with pain and rage, and though he had just faced it in battle, Drizzt could not imagine standing before it at that horrible time.

Cadderly had stung the beast profoundly, but Drizzt could easily recognize that the wounds would not prove mortal. Already the beast seemed on the mend, and that act of reconstitution was the most terrifying of all.

The beast reared up in all of its fiendish glory, and it began to turn, faster and faster, and from its spinning form emanated shadows, like demonic arms of darkness. They reached across the plain, grasping scrambling crawlers, who shrieked, but only once, then fell dead.

Drizzt had never witnessed anything like it, and he concentrated on only a small portion of the spectacle. For the sake of his own sanity, he had to keep his emotional and mental distance from the conduit that was Catti-brie.

The Ghost King was leaching the life energy out of anything it could reach, was stealing the life-force from the crawlers and using that energy to mend its considerable wounds.

Drizzt knew that the monster would recover fully, and soon. Then the Ghost King would return to Spirit Soaring.

With great effort and greater remorse, the drow pulled himself away from his beloved wife. He couldn't comfort her. She felt not at all his embrace, and heard not at all his gentle calls.

He had to return to his companions. He had to warn them. Finally, he managed to let go, then broke the mental link to

Catti-brie. The effort left him so drained that he collapsed on the floor of the room.

He felt strong hands grab him and hoist him upright, then guide him to sit on the edge of the small bed.

Drizzt opened his eyes, pulling back the eye patch.

"Bah, but another of her fits?" said Athrogate, who had just come to the door, Thibbledorf Pwent beside him.

"No," answered Cadderly, who stared at Drizzt. All eyes went to the priest, and many of them, Danica most of all, gasped in surprise at the sight of the man.

He wasn't young any more.

For years, it had taken first-time visitors to Spirit Soaring considerable effort to reconcile the appearance of Cadderly Bonaduce, the accomplished and venerable priest whose remarkable exploits stretched back two decades, for he appeared as young as his own children. But before the disbelieving stares of the three dwarves, two drow, and his wife, that youth had dissipated.

Cadderly looked at least middle-aged, and more. His skin sagged, his shoulders slumped a bit, and his muscles thinned even as the others stood gawking. He looked older than Danica, older than he was, nearer to sixty than to fifty.

"Cadderly," Danica gasped. He managed a smile back at her and held his hand up to keep her and the others at bay.

He seemed to stabilize, and he appeared as a man in his fifties, not much older than his actual age.

"Humans," Athrogate snorted.

"The magic of the cathedral," Jarlaxle said. "The wounded cathedral."

"What do you know?" Danica snapped at the drow mercenary.

"The truth," said Cadderly, and Danica turned to him, approached him, and he allowed her a hug. "My youth, my health—are wound within the walls of Spirit Soaring," he explained to them. "The beast wounded it—wounded us!" He gave a helpless little laugh. "And surely wounded me."

"We will fix it," Danica breathlessly promised.

310

But Cadderly shook his head. "It isn't a matter of wood and nails and stone," he said.

"Then Deneir will fix it with you," Jarlaxle said, drawing curious stares with his unexpected compassion.

Cadderly started to shake his head, then looked at the drow and nodded, for it was no time for any expression of pessimism.

"But first we must ready ourselves for the return of the Ghost King," Jarlaxle remarked, and he led everyone's gaze to Drizzt Do'Urden, who sat on the bed staring helplessly at Catti-brie.

"What's she seeing, elf?" Athrogate demanded. "What memory this time?"

"No memory," Drizzt whispered. He could hardly even find his voice. "She cowers before the raging Ghost King."

"In the Shadowfell," Cadderly reasoned, and Drizzt nodded.

"It is there, in all its fury, and there it heals its wounds," the drow said, looking so pitifully, so helplessly, at his lost and terrified wife. He couldn't reach her. He couldn't help her. He could only look on and pray that somehow Catti-brie would find her way out of darkness.

For a fleeting moment, it occurred to Drizzt Do'Urden that his wife might truly be better off dead, for it seemed that her torment might have no end. He thought back to that quiet morning on the road from Silverymoon when, despite the troubles with the ways of magic, all had seemed so right in his world, beside the woman he loved. It had been only a matter of tendays since that falling magical strand had descended upon Catti-brie and had taken her from Drizzt, but to him, sitting on that bed, so near and yet so distant from his wife, it truly seemed a lifetime ago.

All of that pain and confusion showed on his face, he realized, when he looked at his companions. Bruenor stood in the doorway, trembling with rage, tears streaking his hairy cheeks, his strong fists balled at his sides so tightly that his grip could have crushed stone. He studied Danica, so troubled by her own spouse's dilemma, still taking the time to alternate her gaze between Cadderly, whom she stood beside, and Drizzt, and with equal sympathy and fear showing for both.

Jarlaxle put a hand on Drizzt's shoulder. "If there's a way to get her back, we will find it," he promised, and Drizzt knew he meant every word. When Drizzt looked past him to Bruenor, he recognized that the dwarf understood Jarlaxle's sincerity.

But both also knew that it wouldn't do any good.

"It heals, and it will return," Cadderly said. "We must prepare, and quickly."

"To what end?" asked a voice from the hallway, and they all turned to see Ginance and the others standing there. The speaker, a wizard, held one arm in close, for his robe's sleeve had fallen to tatters and the arm underneath it had withered to dried skin and bone. One of the dracolich's tail swipes had touched him there.

"If we defeat it again, will it not simply retreat once more to this other world of which you speak?" Ginance asked. Cadderly winced at the devastating question from his normally optimistic assistant.

Everyone understood Cadderly's grimace, particularly Drizzt, for the simple truth of Ginance's remark could not be denied. How could they defeat a beast who could so readily retreat, and so easily heal, as Drizzt had witnessed when he had hugged Catti-brie?

"We will find a way," Cadderly promised. "Before Spirit Soaring, in the old structure that was the Edificant Library, we fought a vampire. That creature, too, could run from the field if the battle turned badly. But we found a way."

"Aye, yer dwarfs sucked the gassy thing into a bellows!" howled Thibbledorf Pwent, who had made Ivan Bouldershoulder tell him that story over and over again during the time Ivan and Pikel had spent at Mithral Hall. "And spat him out into a running stream under the sunshine!"

"What're ye saying?" Athrogate demanded, his eyes wide with intrigue and awe. "Are ye speaking true?"

"He is," Cadderly confirmed, and he tossed a wink at the rest of the crew, all of them glad for the light-hearted respite.

"Bwahaha!" roared Athrogate. "I'm thinking that we're needin' a song for that one!"

The faces around them, particularly those in the hallway,

didn't change much, however, as the weight of the situation quickly pressed the brief respite away.

"We need to prepare," Cadderly said again, when all had muted to an uncomfortable silence.

"Or we should leave this place, and quickly," said the wizard with the withered arm. "Run fast for Baldur's Gate, or some other great city where the beast daren't approach."

"Where an army of archers will greet it with doom too sudden for its clever retreat!" another voice chimed in from beyond the room's door.

Drizzt watched Cadderly through it all, as the chorus for retreat grew louder and more insistent, and Drizzt understood the priest's personal turmoil. Cadderly could not disagree with the logic of swift departure, of running far from that seemingly doomed place.

But Cadderly could not go. Damage to Spirit Soaring manifested in his personal being. And Cadderly and Danica could not go far, since their children were still missing and might be out there, or in Carradoon.

Drizzt looked to Bruenor for guidance.

"I ain't leaving," the dwarf king said without hesitation, commanding the gathering. "Let the beast come back, and we'll pound it into dust."

"That is foolish..." the wizard with the withered arm started to argue, but Bruenor's expression stopped the debate before it could begin, and made the man blanch almost as surely as had the sight of the dracolich.

"I ain't leaving," Bruenor said again. "Unless it's to go find Cadderly's kids, or to go and find me missing friend, Pikel, who stood beside me and me kin in our time o' trial. He's lost his brother, so Lady Danica tells me, but he's not to lose his friends from Mithral Hall."

"Then you'll be dead," someone in the hall dared to say.

"We're all to die," Bruenor retorted. "Some of us're already dead, though we're not knowin' it. For when ye're to run and leave yer friends behind, then ye're surely dead."

Someone started to reply with an argument, but Cadderly shouted, "Not now!" So rare was it that the priest raised his voice in such a way that all conversation in the room and without stopped. "Go and assess the damage," Cadderly instructed them all. "Count our wounds . . ."

"And our dead," the withered wizard added with a hiss.

"And our dead," Cadderly conceded. "Go and learn, go and think, and do so quickly." He looked at Drizzt and asked, "How long do we have?"

But the drow could only shrug.

"Quickly," Cadderly said again. "And for those who would leave, organize your wagons as fast as you can. It would not do you well to be caught on the road when the Ghost King returns."

*****

His giant hat in hand, Jarlaxle entered the private quarters of Cadderly and Danica, who sat around the priest's desk, staring at his every step.

"You surprise me," Cadderly greeted him.

"You surprise everyone around you with this new magic you've found," Jarlaxle replied, and he took the chair Danica indicated, beside her and opposite Cadderly.

"No," Cadderly replied. "I have not found any new magic. It has found me. I can't even begin to explain it, and so how can I claim ownership of it? I know not from where it comes, or if it will be there when I need it in the next crisis."

"Let us hope," said Jarlaxle.

Outside the room's south window came a commotion, horses whinnying and men calling out orders.

"They're all leaving," Jarlaxle said. "Even your friend Ginance."

"I told her to go," said Cadderly. "This is not her fight."

"You would flee, too, if you could," Jarlaxle gathered from his tone.

With a heavy sigh, Cadderly stood up and walked to the window to glance at the activity in the courtyard. "This battle has confirmed an old fear," he explained. "When I built Spirit Soaring, weaving the magic Deneir allowed to flow through this mere mortal coil, it aged me. As the cathedral neared completion, I became an old man."

"We had already said our farewells," Danica added.

"I thought I had reached the end of my life, and that was acceptable to me, for I had fulfilled my duty to my god." He paused and looked at Jarlaxle curiously. "Are you religious?" he asked.

"The only deity I grew up knowing was one I would have preferred not to know," the drow answered.

"You are more worldly than that," said Cadderly.

"No," Jarlaxle answered. "I follow no particular god. I thought to interview them first, to see what paradise they might offer when at last I have left this life."

Danica crinkled her face at that, but Cadderly managed a laugh. "Always a quip from Jarlaxle."

"Because I do not consider the question a serious one."

"No?" Cadderly asked with exaggerated surprise. "What could be more serious than discovering that which is in your heart?"

"I know what is in my heart. Perhaps I simply do not feel the need to find a name for it."

Cadderly laughed again. "I would be a liar if I told you I didn't understand."

"I would be a liar if I bothered to answer your ignorance. Or a fool."

"Jarlaxle is no fool," Danica cut in, "but of the former charge, I reserve judgment."

"You wound me to my heart, Lady Danica," said the drow, but his grin was wide, and Danica couldn't resist a smile.

"Why haven't you left?" Cadderly asked bluntly. It was that question, Jarlaxle knew, that was the reason he'd been asked to join the couple. "The road is clear and our situation seems near to hopeless, and yet you remain."

"Young man . . ."

"Not so young," Cadderly corrected.

"By my standards, you will be young when you have passed your one-hundredth birthday, and young still when you have spent another century rotting in the ground," said Jarlaxle. "But to the point, I have nowhere to run that this Ghost King cannot find me. It found me in the north, outside of Mirabar. And as it found me, I knew it would find you."

"And Artemis Entreri?" Danica asked, to which Jarlaxle shrugged.

"Years have passed since I last spoke with him."

"So you came here hoping that I would have an answer to your dilemma," said Cadderly.

Again the drow shrugged. "Or that we might work together to find a solution to our common problem," he answered. "And I did not come without powerful allies to our cause."

"And you feel no guilt in involving Drizzt, Bruenor, Catti-brie, and that Pwent creature in such a desperate struggle?" Danica asked. "You would march them to near-certain doom?"

"Apparently I have more faith in us than you do, Lady," Jarlaxle quipped, and turned to Cadderly. "I was not disingenuous when I proposed to Bruenor and Drizzt that they would do well in bringing Catti-brie to this place. I knew that many of the great minds of our time had no doubt come to Spirit Soaring in search of answers—and what could provide a greater clue to the reality that has descended upon us than the affliction of Catti-brie? Even regarding the Ghost King, I believe it is all connected—more so now that Drizzt has told us that she is watching the beast in that other world in which her mind is trapped."

"They are connected," Cadderly agreed, speaking before Danica could respond. "Both are manifestations of the same catastrophe."

"In one, we may find clues to the other," said Jarlaxle. "We already have! Thank your god that Catti-brie was here, that we could discern the truth of the Ghost King's defeat, and know that the beast would return."

"If I could find my god, I would thank him," Cadderly replied dryly. "But you are correct, of course. So now we know, Jarlaxle.

The beast will return, whole, angry, and wiser than in our first battle. Do you intend to remain to battle it again?"

"Such a course offers me the best chance to prevail, I expect, and so yes, good sir Cadderly, with your permission, I and my dwarf companion would like to stand beside you for that next battle."

"Granted," Danica said, cutting Cadderly short, and when she looked at him, he flashed her a smile of appreciation. "But do you have any ideas? They say you are a clever one."

"You have not witnessed enough of me to come to that conclusion on your own?" Jarlaxle said to her, and he patted his heart as if she had wounded him profoundly.

"Not really, no," she replied.

Jarlaxle burst out in laughter, but only briefly. "We must kill it quickly—that much is obvious," he said. "I see no way to hinder its ability to walk between the worlds, and so we must defeat it abruptly and completely."

"We struck at it with every magic I could manage," said Cadderly. "I merely hope to be able to replicate some of those spells—I hold no illusions that there are greater powers to access."

"There are other ways," Jarlaxle said, and he nodded his chin toward Cadderly's hand crossbow and bandolier.

"I shot it repeatedly," Cadderly reminded him.

"And a hundred bees might sting a man to little effect," the drow replied. "But I have been to a desert where the bees were the size of a man. Trust me when I tell you that you would not wish to feel the sting of but one of those."

"What do you mean?" asked Danica.

"My companion, Athrogate, is a clever one, and King Bruenor more so than he," Jarlaxle replied.

"Would that Ivan Bouldershoulder were still with us!" said Cadderly, his tone more full of hope than of lament.

"Siege weapons? A ballista?" Danica asked, and Jarlaxle shrugged again.

"Drizzt, Bruenor, and his battlerager will remain as well," Jarlaxle informed Cadderly, and the drow stood up from his chair. "Ginance and some others offered to take Catti-brie away, but Drizzt refused." He looked Cadderly directly in the eye as he added, "They don't intend to lose."

"Catti-brie should have been allowed to go," said Danica.

"No," Cadderly replied, and when both looked at him, they saw him staring out the window. Danica could see that he was suddenly deep in thought. "We need her," he said in a tone that revealed him to be certain of his claim, though not yet sure why.

* * * * *

"Copper for yer thoughts, elf," Bruenor said. He moved behind Drizzt, who stood on a balcony overlooking the courtyard of Spirit Soaring, staring out at the ruined forest where the dracolich had passed.

Drizzt glanced back at him and acknowledged him with a nod, but didn't otherwise reply—just gazed into the distance.

"Ah, me girl," Bruenor whispered, moving up beside him, for how could Drizzt be thinking of anything else? "Ye think she's lost to us."

Still Drizzt didn't reply.

"I should smack ye one for losing faith in her, elf," Bruenor said.

Drizzt looked at him again, and he withered under that honest gaze, the level of the dwarf's own confidence overwhelming his bluster.

"Then why're we stayin'?" Bruenor managed to ask, a last gasp of defiance to the drow's irresistible reasoning.

Drizzt wore a puzzled look.

"If not for bringing me girl back, then why're we staying here?" Bruenor clarified.

"You would leave a friend in need?"

"Why're we keepin' her here, then?" Bruenor went on. "Why not put her on one o' them wagons rolling away, bound for a safer place?"

"I don't believe half of them will make it out of the forest alive."

"Bah, that's not what ye're thinking!" Bruenor scolded. "Ye're thinking that we'll find a way. That as we kill this dragon thing, we'll also find a way to get me girl back. It's what ye're thinking, elf, and don't ye lie to me."

"It is what I'm hoping," Drizzt admitted, "not thinking. The two are not the same. Hoping against reason."

"Not so much, else ye wouldn't keep her here, where we're all likely to die."

"Is there a safe place in all the world?" Drizzt asked. "And something else. When the dracolich began to shift to the other plane, Guenhwyvar fled."

"Smart cat would've run off long before that," said Bruenor.

"Guenhwyvar fears no battle, but she understands the dilemma of dimensions joined. Remember when the crystal tower in Icewind Dale collapsed?"

"Aye," said Bruenor, his face brightening just a bit. "And Rumblebelly rode the damned cat to her home."

"Remember Pasha Pook's palace in Calimport?"

"Aye, a sea o' cats following yer Guenhwyvar from her home. What're ye thinking, elf? That yer cat might get you to me girl on the other plane, and might bring ye both back?"

"I don't know," Drizzt admitted.

"But ye're thinking there might be a way?" Bruenor asked in a tone as desperately hopeful as any the drow had ever heard from his dwarf friend.

He fixed Bruenor with a stare and a grin. "Isn't there always a way?"

Bruenor managed a nod at that, and as Drizzt turned his gaze outward from the balcony, he looked to the trees.

"What are they doing?" Drizzt asked a moment later, when Thibbledorf Pwent and Athrogate bobbed out of the forest, carrying a heavy log shoulder to shoulder.

"If we're meaning to stay and fight, then we're meaning to win," said Bruenor.

"But what are they doing, exactly?" Drizzt asked.

"I'm afraid to ask them two," Bruenor admitted, and he and Drizzt shared a much-needed chuckle.

"Ye going to bring in the damned cat again this fight?" Bruenor asked.

"I fear to. The seam between these worlds, between life and death as well, is too unpredictable. I would not lose Guen as I have lost . . ."

His voice trailed off, but he didn't need to finish the thought for Bruenor to understand.

"World's gone crazy," the dwarf said.

"Or maybe it always was."

"Nah, but don't ye start talking like that," Bruenor scolded. "We've put a lot o' good years and good work under our girdles, and ye know it."

"And we even made peace with orcs," said Drizzt, and Bruenor's face tightened and he let out a little growl.

"Ye're a warm fire on a cold winter night, elf," he muttered.

Drizzt smiled all the wider, stood up straight, and stretched his arms and back. "We're staying and we're fighting, my friend. And one more thing we're doing . . ."

"Winning," said Bruenor. "We might get me girl back and we might not, elf, but I'm meaning to stay mad for a bit."

He punched Drizzt in the shoulder.

"Ye ready to kill us a dragon, elf?"

Drizzt didn't answer, but the look he gave to Bruenor, his lavender eyes full of a fire the dwarf king had seen so many times before, made Bruenor almost pity the dracolich.

Down on the courtyard below, Pwent, who was leading the pair, stumbled and the two dwarves crashed down in a heap with their heavy cargo.

"If them two don't kill us all with their plannin', that wyrm ain't getting back to its hiding place," Bruenor declared. "Or if it does, then I'm meaning to find a way to chase it there and be done with it!"

Drizzt nodded, more than ready for the fight, but mixed with his expression of determination was a bit of intrigue at that last statement. His hand went to his belt pouch, to Guenhwyvar, and he wondered.

He had traveled the planes with the cat before, after all.

"What're ye thinking, elf?" Bruenor asked.

Drizzt flashed him those eyes again, so full of determination and simmering anger.

Bruenor nodded and smiled, no less determined and no less angry.

* * * * *

"Is there no way to learn?" Danica asked Cadderly.

Cadderly shook his head. "I've tried. I've asked, of Deneir or of any sentience I might find anywhere."

"I can't do this any more," Danica admitted. She slumped in her chair and put her hands over her face. Cadderly was at her side in a heartbeat, hugging her, but he had little to offer. He was no less tormented than she.

Their children were out there somewhere, maybe alive and maybe, very possibly, dead.

"I have to go back out," Danica said, straightening and taking a deep, steadying breath. "I have to go to Carradoon."

"You tried already, and it nearly killed you," Cadderly reminded. "The forest is no less—"

"I know!" Danica snapped at him. "I know and I don't care. I can't stay here and just wait and hope."

"I cannot go!" Cadderly shouted back at her.

"I know," Danica said softly, tenderly, and she reached up and ran her fingers across Cadderly's cheek. "You are bound here, tied to this place, I know. You cannot desert it, because if it falls, you fall, and our enemies win. But I have recovered from my wounds, and we have driven off the beast for now." Cadderly started to interrupt, but Danica silenced him by putting a finger over his lips. "I know, my love," she said. "The Ghost King will return and attack Spirit Soaring once more. I know. And it is a fight I welcome, for I will see that creature destroyed. But . . ."

"But our children are out there," Cadderly finished for her. "They're alive—I know they are! If any of them had fallen, Spirit Soaring would feel the loss."

Danica looked at him, curious.

"They are of me, as this place is of me," Cadderly tried to explain. "They are alive, I am sure."

Danica fell back a bit and stared at her husband. She understood his confidence, but knew, too, that it was based more on a need to believe that the children were alive and well than on anything substantive.

"You cannot stay here," Cadderly said, surprising her, and she sat up straight, her eyes wide.

"You are about to fight the most desperate battle of your life, and you would send me away?"

"If the Ghost King returns and is to be defeated . . ." Cadderly paused there, seeming almost embarrassed.

"It will be by the power of Cadderly, and not the fists of Danica," she reasoned.

Cadderly shrugged. "We are a powerful team, we seven, each armed in our own ways to do battle with such a beast as the Ghost King."

"But I least of all," the woman said. She held up her empty hands. "My weapons are less effective than Bruenor's axe, and I haven't the tricks of Jarlaxle."

"There is no one I would rather have fighting beside me than you," Cadderly said. "But truly, there is no one in all the world who might better elude the monsters in the forest and find our children. And if we don't have them, then . . ."

"Then what is the point?" Danica finished for him. She leaned in and kissed him passionately.

"They are alive," Cadderly said.

"And I will find them," Danica whispered back.

She was out of Spirit Soaring within the hour, moving among the trees alongside the road to Carradoon, invisible and silent in the dark night.

CHAPTER
D A W N
26

"Why aren't we fighting?" Temberle whispered to Ivan. Even his hushed tone seemed to echo in the too-quiet tunnels.

"Not for knowin'," Ivan replied to Temberle and to all the remaining refugees in the group, which numbered less than twenty. "Hoping it's your da's work."

"Boom," Pikel said hopefully, and loudly, drawing gasps from all the others. "Oops," the green-bearded dwarf apologized, slapping his hand over his mouth.

"Or they're setting a trap for us," Hanaleisa interjected. Ivan was nodding as she spoke, about to make the same observation. "Perhaps they've learned from the slaughter."

"So what are we to do?" asked Rorick, and when she looked at her younger brother, Hanaleisa saw real fear there, and put a comforting hand on his shoulder.

"We go on, for what choice do we got?" said Ivan, and he purposely lifted his voice. "If they be lying in wait for us, then we'll just kill 'em and walk on over their rottin' bodies."

Ivan slapped his bloodstained axe across his open hand and nodded with determination, then stomped away.

"Oo oi!" Pikel agreed, and adjusted his cooking pot helmet and scrambled to follow.

Not far from that site, the beleaguered band entered a room

that presented yet another puzzle, but a welcome one at first glance. The chamber floor was littered with dead crawlers and dead giant bats, and even a dead giant.

The group scanned for clues, mostly looking for the bodies of those who had fought the beasts. Was it another fleeing refugee group?

"Did they kill each other?" Temberle asked, voicing a question they were all asking themselves.

"Not unless they use tiny bows," one of the refugees answered. Temberle and the others moved to the man's position, bringing the meager torchlight to bear. They found him holding a small dart, like those Cadderly used with his hand crossbows.

"Father!" Rorick said hopefully.

"If it was, he was busy," said Hanaleisa as she moved around, finding the same darts littering the floor and the bodies. She shook her head with doubt. Only two such hand crossbows were kept at Spirit Soaring, but dozens, perhaps hundreds, of darts had been fired in that fight. She pulled one from the corpse of a crawler and held it up, shaking her head even more. None of the darts showed her father's added feature: the collapsible center where the tiny vials of explosive oil were stored.

"These ain't Cadderly's," Ivan confirmed a moment later. Since he had designed and built Cadderly's hand crossbows and its quarrels, his words carried undeniable truth.

"Then who?" asked Rorick.

"We weren't that far away," Temberle added. "And this battle's not so old. This happened fast, and it happened quietly." He looked with great alarm at his sister and his Uncle Ivan.

"Poison-tipped," said Hanaleisa.

More than a few eyes widened at that, for most folk knew the dire implications of poison-tipped hand crossbow darts.

"Has the whole world gone upside down, then?" asked Ivan, his tone more sober—even somber—than ever. "I'm thinking the sooner we get to the surface, the better we'll be."

"Uh-huh," Pikel agreed.

On they marched, swiftly, and with all feeling that the enemy of their enemy would most certainly not prove to be their friend.

* * * * *

The hairless, black-skinned giant lurched forward another step. *Click. Click. Click.*

The monster groaned as three more darts punctured its skin, adding to the drow sleep poison coursing its veins. Its next step came heavier, foot dragging.

Click. Click. Click.

The giant went down on one knee, barely conscious of the movement. Small, dodging forms came at it, left, right, and center, slender blades gleaming with magic. The nightwalker waved its arms, trying to deflect the approaching enemies, to block and to swat aside the dark elves as though they were gnats. But every swing, waved under the weight of a most profound weariness, was waved too slowly to catch the agile warriors. Every block failed to drive off the stabs and thrusts and slashes, and the giant nightwalker swatted nothing but the cavern's stagnant air.

They didn't maul the giant. Every strike landed precisely and efficiently in an area that would allow the smoothest and swiftest flow of blood. The behemoth didn't get hit a hundred times, not more than a score even, but as it settled to a prone position on the floor, overcome by poison and loss of blood, the nightwalker's wounds were surely mortal.

The last group, Valas Hune signaled to Kimmuriel. *The way is clear.*

Kimmuriel nodded and followed his lead team through the chamber. Another giant bat crashed down against the far wall, coaxed to sleep in mid flight. Many crawlers still thrashed on the floor, their movements uncoordinated and unfocused but defiant until one of the drow warriors found the time to finish the job with a sure stroke to the neck.

Out of that chamber, the Bregan D'aerthe force moved down a corridor to an area of tunnels and chambers puddled by lake water.

After only a few more twists and turns, every dark elf squinted against the brightness of the surface. Night had fallen long ago, but the moon was up, and sensitive drow eyes stung under the brilliance of Selûne's glow.

Can we not simply leave this place? more than one set of fingers dared flash Kimmuriel's way, but they were met one and all with a stern look that offered no compromise.

He had determined that they needed to go to the ruined town on the lakeshore before leaving the uncivilized reaches between Old Shanatar and Great Bhaerynden, and so to the place known as Carradoon they would go.

They exited the tunnels in the cove north of the city and easily scaled the cliffs to the bluff overlooking the ruined town. More than half the structures had burned to the ground, and less than a handful of those remaining had avoided the conflagration. The air hung thick with smoke and the stench of death, and skeletons of ship masts dotted the harbor, like markers for mass graves. The dark elves moved down in tight formation, even more cautious outside than in the more familiar environ of the tunnels. A giant nightwing occasionally flew overhead, but unless it ventured too near, the disciplined drow held their shots.

Led by Valas Hune, scouts broke left and right, flanking, leading, and ensuring that no pursuit was forthcoming.

What do you seek in this ruin? Valas's fingers asked of Kimmuriel soon after they had entered the city proper.

Kimmuriel indicated that he wasn't quite certain, but assured the scout that something there was worth investigating. He sensed it, felt it keenly.

A commotion to the side broke the discussion short as both drow contemplated the beginnings of a battle along a road parallel to their path. Another giant nightwalker had found the band and foolishly came on. The tumult increased briefly as the closest drow engaged and lured the behemoth to a narrow stretch between two buildings, a place where drow hand crossbows could not miss the huge target.

Kimmuriel and the bulk of his force continued along before the thing was even dead, confident in the discipline and tactics of the skilled and battle-proven company.

A scout returning from the quay delivered the report Kimmuriel had awaited, and he led swiftly to the spot.

"That bodes ill," Valas Hune remarked—the first words spoken since they had come out of the tunnels—when they came in sight of the rift. Every dark elf viewing the spectacle knew it immediately for what it was: a tear in the fabric of two separate worlds, a magical gate.

They stopped a respectful distance away, defenders sliding out like tentacles to secure the area as only Bregan D'aerthe could.

"Purposeful? Or an accident of misfiring magic?" Valas Hune asked.

"It matters not," answered Kimmuriel. "Though I expect that we will encounter many such rifts."

"A good thing, then, that drow never tire of killing."

Valas Hune fell silent when he realized that Kimmuriel, eyes closed, was no longer listening. He watched as the psionicist settled back, then lifted his hands toward the dimensional rift and popped wide his eyes, throwing forth his mental energy.

Nothing happened.

"Purposeful," Kimmuriel answered. "And foolish."

"You cannot close it?"

"An illithid hive could not close it. Sorcere on their strongest day could not close it," he said, referring to the great academy of the magical Art in Menzoberranzan.

"Then what?"

Kimmuriel looked to Mariv, who produced a thick wood-and-metallic rod the length of his forearm. Delicate runes of red and brown adorned the cylindrical item. Mariv handed it to Kimmuriel.

"The rod that cancels magical effects?" Valas Hune asked.

Kimmuriel looked to a young warrior, the same who had led the way through the gate in the tunnels, bidding him forth. He signaled the rod's command words with the fingers of his free hand as he passed the powerful item to the younger drow.

Licking dry lips, the drow moved toward the rift. His long white hair started to dance as he neared, as if tingling with energy, or struck, perhaps, by winds blowing on the other side of the dimensional gate.

He glanced at Kimmuriel, who nodded for him to proceed.

The young drow lifted the rod up to the rift, licked his lips again, and spoke the words of command. The magical implement flared with a brief burst of power that flowed its length and leaped out at the rift.

Back came a profound darkness, a gray mist that rolled through the conduit and surged into the hand of the drow warrior, who wasn't wise enough or quick enough to drop the rod in time.

He did drop it when his arm fell limp. He looked at Kimmuriel and the others, his face stretching into the most profound expression of terror any of them had ever witnessed as his life-force withered to shadowstuff and his empty husk fell dead to the ground.

No one went to aid him, or even to investigate.

"We cannot close it," Kimmuriel announced. "We are done here."

He led them away at a swift pace, Valas recalling his scouts as they went. As soon as he thought them far enough so that the rift's continuing fields wouldn't interfere, Kimmuriel enacted another of his dimensional doorways.

"Back to Luskan?" Mariv asked as the next least of the band was brought forward to ensure the integrity of the gate.

"For now, yes," answered Kimmuriel, who was thinking that perhaps their road would lead them much farther than Luskan, all the way back into the Underdark and Menzoberranzan, where they would become part of a drow defense comprised of twenty thousand warriors, priestesses, and wizards.

The young drow stepped through and signaled from the other side, from the subterranean home Kimmuriel's band had constructed under the distant port city on the Sword Coast.

The Bregan D'aerthe force departed the Barony of Impresk as swiftly and silently as they had come.

*****

The human refugees' eyes, too, stung as they came in sight of the surface world after several long and miserable days of wandering and fighting in the dark tunnels. Squinting against the sunrise reflecting across Impresk Lake, Ivan led the group to the edge of the cave at the back of the small cove.

The rest of the group crowded up beside him, eager to feel the sun on their faces, desperate to be out from under tons of rock and earth. Collectively, they took great comfort in the quiet of the morning, with no sounds other than the songs of birds and the lap of waves against the rocks.

Ivan brought them quickly into the open air. They had found more slaughtered nightwings, nightwalkers, and crawlers. Convinced that the tunnels were infested with dark elves, Ivan and the others were happy indeed to be out of them!

Getting out of the cove took longer than expected. They didn't dare venture out near the deeper water, having seen too much of the undead fish. Getting up the cliff face, for they had come down with magical help from Pikel, was no easy task for the weary humans or the short-legged dwarves. They tried several routes unsuccessfully and eventually crossed the cove and climbed the lower northern rise. The sun was high in the eastern sky when they at last managed to circle around and come in sight of Carradoon.

For a long, long while, they stood on the high bluff looking down at the ruins, saying not a word, making not a sound other than the occasional sob.

"We got no reason to go in there," Ivan asserted at length.

"We have friends—" a man started to protest.

"Ain't nothing alive in there," Ivan interrupted. "Nothing alive ye're wantin' to see, at least."

"Our homes!" a woman wailed.

"Are gone," Ivan replied.

"Then what are we to do?" the first man shouted at him.

"Ye get on the road and get out o' here," said Ivan. "Meself and me brother're for Spirit Soaring . . ."

"Me brudder!" Pikel cheered, and pumped his stump into the air.

"And Cadderly's kids with us," Ivan added.

"Shalane is no farther, and down a safer road," the man argued.

"Then take it," Ivan said to him. "And good luck to ye." It seemed as simple as that to the dwarf, and he started away to the west, a route to circumvent the destroyed Carradoon and pick up the trail that led into the mountains and back to Spirit Soaring.

"What is happening to the world, Uncle Ivan?" Hanaleisa whispered.

"Durned if I know, girl. Durned if I know."

CHAPTER 27

ELSEWHERE LUCIDITY

Cadderly tapped a finger against his lips as he studied the woman playing out the scene before him. She was talking to Guenhwyvar, he believed, and he couldn't help but feel like a voyeur as he studied her reenactment of a private moment.

"Oh, but she's so pretty and fancy, isn't she?" Catti-brie said, her hand brushing the air as if she were petting the great panther as it curled near her feet. "With her lace and finery, so tall and so straight, and not a silly word to pass those painted lips, no, no."

She was there, but she wasn't, Cadderly sensed. Her movements were too complete and too complex to be merely a normal memory. No, she was reliving the moment precisely as it had occurred. Catti-brie's mind was back in time while her physical form was trapped in the current time and space.

With his unique experience regarding physical aging and regression, Cadderly was struck by the woman's apparent madness. Was she really mad, he wondered, or was she, perhaps, trapped in a bona fide but unknown series of disjointed bubbles in the vast ocean of time? Cadderly had often pondered the past, had often wondered if each passing moment was a brief observance of an eternal play, or whether the past was truly lost as soon as the next moment was found.

Watching Catti-brie, it seemed to him that the former wasn't as unrealistic as logic implied.

Was there a way to travel in time? Was there a way to bring foresight to those unanticipated preludes to disaster?

"Do ye think her pretty, Guen?" Catti-brie asked, drawing him from his contemplation.

The door behind Cadderly opened, and he glanced to see Drizzt enter the room, the drow wincing as soon as he recognized that Catti-brie had entered another of her fits. Cadderly begged him to silence with a wave and a finger over pursed lips, and Drizzt, Catti-brie's dinner tray in hand, stood very still, staring at his beloved wife.

"Drizzt thinks her pretty," Catti-brie continued, oblivious to them. "He goes to Silverymoon whenever he can, and part o' that's because he's thinking Alustriel pretty." The woman paused and looked up, though surely not at Cadderly and Drizzt, and wore a smile that was both sweet and pained. "I hope he finds love, I do," she told the panther they could not see. "But not with her, or one o' her court, for then he's sure to leave us. I'm wantin' him happy, but that I could'no' take."

Cadderly looked at Drizzt questioningly.

"When first we retook Mithral Hall," he said.

"You and Lady Alustriel?" Cadderly asked.

"Friends," Drizzt replied, never taking his eyes off his wife. "She allowed me passage in Silverymoon, and there I knew I could make great strides toward finding some measure of acceptance in the World Above." He motioned to Catti-brie. "How long?"

"She has been in this different place for quite a while."

"And there she is my Catti," Drizzt lamented. "In this elsewhere of her mind, she finds herself."

The woman began to shake then, her hands twitching, her head going back, her eyes rolling up to white. The purple glow of faerie fire erupted around her once more and she rose a bit higher from the floor, arms going out wide, her auburn hair blowing in some unfelt wind.

Drizzt put the tray down and adjusted the eye patch. He

hesitated only a few moments, at Cadderly's insistence, as the priest moved closer to Catti-brie, even dared touch her during the dangerous time of transition. Cadderly closed his eyes and opened his mind to the possibilities swirling in the discordant spasms of the tortured woman.

He fell back, quickly replaced by Drizzt, who wrapped Catti-brie in a tight hug and eased her to the floor. The drow looked at Cadderly, his expression begging for an explanation, but he saw the priest even more perplexed, wide-eyed and staring at his hand.

Drizzt, too, took note of the hand that Cadderly had placed upon Catti-brie. What appeared as a blue translucence solidified and became flesh tone once more.

"What was that?" the drow asked as soon as Catti-brie settled.

"I do not know," Cadderly admitted.

"Words I hear too often in these times."

"Agreed."

"But you seem certain that my wife cannot be saved," said Drizzt, a sharper tone edging into his voice.

"I do not wish to give such an impression."

"I've seen the way you and Jarlaxle shake your heads when the conversation comes to her. You don't believe we can bring her back to us—not whole, at least. You have lost hope for her, but would you, I wonder, if it was Lady Danica here, in that state, and not Catti-brie?"

"My friend, surely you don't—"

"Am I to surrender my hope as well? Is that what you expect of me?"

"You're not the only one here clinging to desperate hope, my friend," Cadderly scolded.

Drizzt eased back a bit at that reminder. "Danica will find them," he offered, but how hollow his words sounded. He continued in a soft voice, "I feel as if there is no firmament beneath my feet."

Cadderly nodded in sympathy.

"Should I battle the dracolich with the hope that in its defeat, I will find again my wife?" Drizzt blurted, his voice rising again.

"Or should I battle the beast with rage because I will never again find her?"

"You ask of me . . . these are questions . . ." Cadderly blew a heavy sigh and lifted his hands, helpless. "I do not know, Drizzt Do'Urden. Nothing can be certain regarding Catti-brie."

"We know she's mad."

Cadderly started to reply, "Do we?" but he held it back, not wishing to involve Drizzt in his earlier ponderings.

Was Catti-brie truly insane, or was she reacting rationally to the reality that was presented to her? Was she re-living her life out of sequence or was she truly returning to those bubbles of time-space and experiencing those moments as reality?

The priest shook his head, for he had no time to travel the possibilities of such a line of reasoning, particularly since the scholars and sages, and the great wizards and great priests who had visited Spirit Soaring had thoroughly dismissed any such possibility of traveling freely through time.

"But madness can be a temporary thing," Drizzt remarked. "And yet, you and Jarlaxle think her lost forever. Why?"

"When the madness is tortured enough, the mind can be permanently wounded," Cadderly replied, his dour tone making it clear that such was an almost certain outcome and not a remote possibility. "And your wife's madness seems tortured, indeed. I fear—Jarlaxle and I fear—that even if the spell that is upon her is somehow ended, a terrible scar will remain."

"You fear, but you do not know."

Cadderly nodded, conceding the point. "And I have witnessed miracles before, my friend. In this very place. Do not surrender your hope."

That was all he could give, and all that Drizzt had hoped to hear, in the end. "Do you think the gods have any miracles left in them?" the dark elf quietly asked.

Cadderly gave a helpless laugh and shrugged. "I grabbed the sun itself and pulled it to me," he reminded the drow. "I know not how, and I didn't try to do it. I grabbed a cloud and made of it a chariot. I know not how, and didn't try to do it. My voice became thunder . . . truly, my friend, I wonder why anyone would bother asking me questions at this time. And I wonder more why anyone would believe any of my answers."

Drizzt had to smile at that, and so he did, with a nod of acceptance. He turned his gaze to Catti-brie and reached out to gently stroke her thick hair. "I cannot lose her."

"Let us destroy our enemy, then," Cadderly offered. "Then we will turn all of our attention, all of our thoughts, and all of our magic to Catti-brie, to find her in her . . . elsewhere lucidity . . . and bring her sense back to our time and space."

"Guenhwyvar," Drizzt said, and Cadderly blinked in surprise.

"She was petting the cat, yes."

"No, I mean in the next fight," Drizzt explained. "When the Ghost King began to leave the field, Guenhwyvar fled faster. She does not run from a fight. Not from a raging elemental or a monstrous demon, and not from a dragon or dracolich. But she fled, ears down, full speed away into the trees."

"Perhaps she was hunting one of the crawlers."

"She was running. Recall Jarlaxle's tale of his encounter with the specter he believes was once a lich of the Crystal Shard."

"Guenhwyvar is not of this plane, and she feared creating a rift as the Ghost King opened a dimensional portal," Cadderly reasoned.

"One that perhaps Guenhwyvar could navigate," Drizzt replied. "One that perhaps I could navigate with her, to that other place."

Cadderly couldn't help but smile at the reasoning, and Drizzt offered a curious expression. "There is an old saying that great minds follow similar paths to the same destination," he said.

"Guen?" Drizzt asked hopefully, patting his belt pouch. But Cadderly was shaking his head.

"The panther is of the Astral Plane," the priest explained. "She cannot, of her own will, go to where the Ghost King resides, unless someone there possessed a figurine akin to your own and summoned her."

"She fled the field."

"Because she feared a rift, a great tear that would consume all near to her, and the Ghost King, if their dangerous abilities came crashing together. Perhaps that rift would send our enemy to the Astral Plane, or to some other plane, but likely the creature is anchored enough both here and in the Shadowfell that it could return." He was still shaking his head. "But I have little faith in that course and fear a potential for greater disaster."

"Greater?" Drizzt asked, and he began a hollow laugh. "Greater?"

"Are we at the point where we reach blindly for the most desperate measures we can find?" Cadderly asked.

"Are we not?"

The priest shrugged again. "I don't know," he admitted, his gaze fixing on Catti-brie again. "Perhaps we will find another way."

"Perhaps Deneir will deliver a miracle?"

"We can hope."

"You mean pray."

"That, too."

* * * * *

He lifted the spoon to her lips and she did not resist, taking the food methodically. Drizzt dabbed a napkin into a small bowl of warm water and wiped a bit of the porridge from her lips.

She seemed not to notice, as she seemed not to notice the taste of the food he offered. Every time he put a spoonful into Catti-brie's mouth, every time she showed no expression at all, it pained Drizzt and reminded him of the futility of it all. He had flavored the porridge exactly as his wife liked, but he understood with each spoonful that he could have skipped the cinnamon and honey and used bitter spices instead. It wouldn't have mattered one bit to Catti-brie.

"I still remember that moment on Kelvin's Cairn," he said to her. "When you relived it before my eyes, it all came back into such clear focus, and I recalled your words before you spoke them. I remember the way you had your hair, with those bangs and the uneven length from side to side. Never trust a dwarf with scissors, right?"

He managed a little laugh that Catti-brie seemed not to hear.

"I did not love you then, of course. Not like this. But that moment remained so special to me, and so important. The look on your face, my love—the way you looked inside of me instead of at my skin. I knew I was home when I found you on Kelvin's Cairn. At long last, I was home.

"And even though I had no idea for many years that there could ever be more between us—not until that time in Calimport— you were ever special to me. And you still are, and I need you to come back to me, Catti. Nothing else matters. The world is a darker place. With the Ghost King and the falling Weave, and the implications of this catastrophe, I know that so many trials will fall before me, before all goodly folk. But I believe that I can meet those challenges, that we together will find a way. We always find a way!

"But only if you come back to me. To defeat a mighty foe, a warrior must *want* to defeat a mighty foe. What is the point, my love, if I am alone once more?"

He exhaled and sat there, staring at her, but she didn't blink, didn't react at all. She hadn't heard him. He might pretend differently for the sake of his own sanity, but Drizzt knew in his heart that Catti-brie wasn't lurking there, just beneath the damaged surface, taking it all in.

Drizzt wiped a tear from his lavender eyes, and as the moistness went away, it was replaced by that same look that had at once shaken and encouraged Bruenor, the promise of the Hunter, the determination, the simmering rage.

Drizzt leaned forward and kissed Catti-brie on the forehead and told himself that it had all been wrought by the Ghost King, that the dracolich was the source of all that had gone so very wrong in the world, not a result of some larger disaster.

No more tears for Drizzt Do'Urden. He meant to destroy the beast.

CHAPTER 28

DRIVEN BY HATRED

They knew their enemy would return, and they knew where they wanted to fight it, but when it happened, as expected as it was, sturdy Athrogate and Thibbledorf Pwent gasped more profoundly than they cried out.

The Ghost King came back to the material world of Toril in exactly the same place that it had departed, appearing first and briefly in its translucent blue-white glow. Quickly it was whole again, on the courtyard outside the cathedral, and even as Pwent and Athrogate shouted out, their bellows echoing through the deserted hallways, the great beast leaped into the air and took wing, flying high into the night sky.

"It's up there! It's up there, me king!" Pwent cried, hopping up and down and pointing skyward. Bruenor, Drizzt, and the others arrived in the room adjacent to the balcony from which the two dwarves had been keeping watch.

"The dracolich appeared in the same place?" Caddisly asked, clearly interpreting some importance in that fact.

"Just like ye guessed," Athrogate answered. "Glowin' and all, then it jumped away."

"It's up there, me king!" Pwent shouted again.

Drizzt, Caddisly, Bruenor, and Jarlaxle exchanged determined nods. "It doesn't get away from us this time," said Bruenor.

All eyes went to Cadderly at that proclamation, and the priest's nod was one of confidence.

"Inside," Cadderly ordered them all. "The beast will return with fury and fire. Spirit Soaring will protect us."

* * * * *

Danica took a deep breath and grabbed at a nearby tree trunk to steady herself when she heard the awful, otherworldly shriek of the dracolich taking flight. She couldn't help but glance back toward Spirit Soaring, already miles behind her, and she had to remind herself that Cadderly was surrounded by powerful allies, and that Deneir, or some other divine entity, miraculously heard his pleas.

"They will prevail," Danica said softly—very softly, for she knew that the forest about her was full of monsters. She had watched groups of crawlers scratch by on the road and had felt the thunderous steps of some gigantic black behemoth, the likes of which she had never before known.

She was halfway to Carradoon and had hoped to be there already, but the going had been slow and cautious. As much as she wanted a fight, Danica could ill afford one. Her focus was Carradoon and Carradoon alone, to find her children, while Cadderly and the others dealt with the Ghost King at Spirit Soaring.

That was the plan—they knew the undead dragon would return—and Danica had to steel herself against any second-guessing. She had to trust Cadderly. She couldn't turn back.

"My children," she whispered. "Temberle and Rorick, and Hana, my Hana . . . I will find you."

Behind her, high in the sky, the Ghost King's shriek split the night as profoundly as a bolt of lightning and the roar of thunder.

Danica ignored it and focused on the trees before her, picking her careful and swift way through the haunted woods.

"Kill him, Cadderly," she said under her breath, over and over again.

*****

Without the cautionary interference of Yharaskrik, the Ghost King reveled in its flight, knowing that its vulnerable target lay below, knowing that soon enough it would destroy Spirit Soaring and the fools who had remained within.

The sweet taste of impending revenge filled Hephaestus's dead throat, and the dragon wanted nothing more than to dive at the building at full speed and tear it to kindling. But surprisingly to both entities that made up the Ghost King, recklessness was tempered by the pain of their recent defeat. The Ghost King still felt the blinding sting of Cadderly's fires, and the weight of Drizzt's scimitar. Though confident that its second assault would be different, the Ghost King meant to take no unnecessary chances.

And so from on high, up among the clouds, the beast called upon its minions once more, summoning them from the forests around Spirit Soaring, compelling them to soften the ground.

"They will not kill Cadderly," the beast said into the high winds. "But they will reveal him!"

The Ghost King folded its wings and dived, then opened them wide and rode the momentum and the currents in a spiraling pattern above the building, its magically enhanced eyesight scouring the land below.

Already the forest was alive with movement as crawlers and nightwings, huddled wraiths, and even a giant nightwalker swarmed toward Spirit Soaring.

The Ghost King's laugh rumbled like distant thunder.

*****

They heard the break of glass, one of the few panes left intact from the previous assault, but the building did not shudder.

"By the gods," Cadderly cursed.

"Damned crawlers!" Bruenor agreed.

They were in the widest audience hall on the first story of the building, a windowless affair with only a few connecting corridors.

Pwent and Athrogate stood at the rail on the northern balcony with their tied-off logs, some twenty-five feet above the others. Bruenor, Cadderly, and the rest stood on the raised dais where Cadderly usually held audience, across from the double doors and the main corridor that led to the cathedral's foyer. Drizzt stood at the open doorway of a small, secure anteroom, where lay Catti-brie.

Drizzt bent low to tuck a blanket more tightly around his wife, and whispered, "He won't get you. On my life, my love, I will kill that beast. I will find a way back to you, or a way to lead you back to us."

Catti-brie didn't react, but lay staring into the distance.

Drizzt leaned in and kissed her on the cheek. "I promise," he whispered. "I love you."

Not far from them, Drizzt heard wood splintering. He stood up straight and moved out of the small anteroom, securing the door behind him.

Cadderly shivered as he felt the unclean beasts crawling into the broken windows of Spirit Soaring.

"Clear the place?" Athrogate yelled down.

"No, hold your positions!" Cadderly ordered, and even as he spoke, the door on the balcony nearest the two dwarves began to rattle and bang. Cadderly fell within himself, trying to join with the magic that strengthened Spirit Soaring, begging the cathedral, begging Deneir, to hold strong.

"Come on, then," Cadderly whispered to the Ghost King. "Lead the way."

"He learned from his loss," Jarlaxle remarked as Drizzt rejoined them. "He's sending in the fodder. He's not to be trapped alone as before."

Cadderly flashed an alarmed look at Drizzt and Bruenor.

"I'll bring him in," Drizzt promised, and he charged across the room to the double doors, the other three close behind.

Cadderly grabbed him before he could leave the room. As Drizzt turned, the priest gripped his right hand, in which he held Icingdeath, then reached for the hilt of Twinkle with his other hand. Cadderly closed his eyes and chanted, and Drizzt felt again an infusion of power into both his weapons.

"Bruenor, the door," Jarlaxle said, drawing out a pair of black metal wands. "And do duck aside."

Jarlaxle nodded to Drizzt, then to Bruenor, who flung wide the double doors. Beyond them, the corridor to the foyer teemed with crawlers, and nightwings fluttered above them.

A lightning bolt blasted from Jarlaxle's wand to sear the darkness. The second wand responded in kind, then the first took its turn, and the second fired again. Flesh smoldered, bats tumbled, a stench filled the holy place.

A fifth bolt followed, a sixth fast behind. Monsters scrambled to get out of the corridor, or melted where they stood. The seventh blast shook the walls of Spirit Soaring.

"Go!" Jarlaxle ordered Drizzt, and loosed yet another explosive line of sizzling energy.

And right behind it went Drizzt Do'Urden, running and leaping, spinning and slashing with seeming abandon. But every stroke was planned and timed perfectly, clearing the way and propelling Drizzt along. A nightwing dived at him, or fell at him—the beast was badly scored from the many lightning bolts. Drizzt hit it with a solid backhand and his divinely-weighted scimitar threw the giant bat aside, the blade tearing its flesh with brutal ease.

The drow leaped atop the heads of a pair of trembling, dying crawlers and sprang away onto a third, bowling it over, spinning as he went and cutting another beast in half as he twirled around. He reached the foyer doors, both hanging loose from the battering of the eight lightning bolts.

"Jarlaxle!" Drizzt cried, and he skidded down and kicked the doors open, revealing a foyer stuffed with enemies.

Lightning bolts streaked over the hunched drow, one, two, blasting, burning, blinding, and scattering the beasts. Then Drizzt was up behind them, his mighty scimitars battering the creatures aside.

Out the door Drizzt went, into the courtyard.

"Fight me, dragon!" he yelled. A foolish nightwing dived at Drizzt from on high and was met by a flashing scimitar that cleaved through flesh and bone and infused a web of searing divine light into the creature of darkness. The batlike beast went spinning backward, up into the air, dead long before it tumbled and flopped to the ground.

From all around, from the walls and broken windows of Spirit Soaring, everything seemed to pause for just a moment. Drizzt had drawn attention to himself, indeed, and the monsters swarmed his way, leaping from the trees across the courtyard and from the walls of Spirit Soaring.

A wicked grin creased the dark elf's face. "Come on, then," he whispered, and he gave a private nod to Catti-brie.

* * * * *

"We got to go to him!" cried Bruenor. Along with Cadderly and Jarlaxle, he had eased out of the audience chamber and crept nearer the foyer, gaining a view of the open courtyard beyond.

"Hold, dwarf," Jarlaxle replied. He was looking to Cadderly as he spoke and taking note of the priest's equal confidence in Drizzt.

Bruenor started to reply, but bit it short with a gasp as he saw the first wave of monsters swarm at Drizzt.

The drow ranger exploded into motion, leaping and spinning, stepping atop monstrous heads and backs, slashing with devastating speed and precision. One after another, crawlers crumbled to heaps of quivering flesh or went sailing back, launched by a swinging, divinely-weighted blade. Drizzt leaped from a beast's back and hit the ground in a fast run up atop another, where he double stabbed, spun to the side, and caught yet another crawler with a deadly backhand. The drow continued his spin and darted out of it past the first dying beast to stab a fourth, slash a fifth, and leap above a sixth, thrusting down to mortally wound that one as he passed overhead with Twinkle, slashing up high to take the legs from a swooping nightwing in the same movement.

"You've known him a long time . . ." Jarlaxle said to Bruenor.

"Ain't never seen that," the dumbfounded dwarf admitted.

Drizzt, whirling like a maelstrom, moved beyond their line of sight then, past the angle of the open double doors. But the erupting sounds and shrieks told the friends that his furious charge had not slowed. He veered back into view, sprinting the opposite way, cutting a swath of devastation with every stride, every thrust, and every swing. Crawlers flew and crumbled, nightwings tumbled dead from on high, but the divine glow on Drizzt's scimitars did not diminish, even seemed to flare with more purpose and anger.

A crash in the room behind them turned the three around to see a crawler thrashing in its death throes in the middle of the floor. A second dropped down from above, accompanied by the glee-filled cackle of Thibbledorf Pwent.

"Trust in Drizzt!" Caddlery commanded the other two, and the priest led the charge back into the audience hall, the battlefield of their choosing.

* * * * *

The sheer exuberance of Thibbledorf Pwent held the breach at the broken doorway. Thrashing and punching, the dwarf laughed all the harder with every bit of gore that splattered his ridged armor and with every sickening puncture of a knee-spike or a gauntlet.

"Get out o' the way!" Athrogate yelled at him repeatedly, the equally-wild dwarf wanting a chance to hit something.

"Bwahaha!" Thibbledorf Pwent responded, perfectly mimicking Athrogate's signature cry.

"Huh," Athrogate said, for that gave him pause. Only a brief pause, however, before he let out a hearty "Bwahaha!" of his own.

Thibbledorf Pwent dived out of the way and a pair of crawlers rushed onto the balcony to confront Athrogate, who promptly buried them under a barrage of his powerful morningstars, setting free another heartfelt howl of laughter.

Pwent, meanwhile, went right to the corridor exit, battering the next beasts in line. He hooked one with a glove spike and did a deft, swift turn and throw, launching the flailing thing over the balcony. Then the dwarf fell back, inviting more crawlers into the room, where he and Athrogate, side by side, destroyed them.

*****

He did not slow and did not tire. The image of his wounded wife stayed crystal clear in his thoughts and drove him on, and because he felt no fatigue, he began to wonder if the power Cadderly had infused into his weapons was somehow providing strength and stamina to him, as well.

It was a fleeting thought, for the present predicament crowded out all but his most intense warrior instincts. Drizzt gave himself no time to reflect, for every turn brought him face-on with enemies, and every leap became a series of contortions and tucks to avoid a host of reaching arms or raking claws.

But it mattered not how many of those claws and arms came at Drizzt Do'Urden. He stayed ahead of them, every one, and his blades, so full of fury and might, cleared the way, whichever way he chose to go. Carnage piled around him and a mist of monster blood filled the air. Every other step fell atop the fleshy corpse of a dead enemy.

"Fight me, dragon!" he yelled, and his voice rang with an almost mocking glee. "Come down from on high, coward!"

In the space of those two sentences, another four crawlers fell dead, and even the stupidly vicious beasts were beginning to shy from the mad drow warrior. The trend continued—instead of rushing to avoid enemies, Drizzt found himself chasing them. And all the while, he continued calling out his challenges to the Ghost King.

That challenge was answered, not by the dragon, but by another creature, a gigantic nightwalker, that stepped from the forest and thundered at the dancing drow.

Drizzt had fought one of those behemoths before, and knew well how formidable they were, their deceptively thin limbs tightly wound with layers of muscle that could crush the life from him with hardly a thought.

Drizzt smiled and charged.

*****

As they shied from Drizzt, many of the monsters charged in through the open double doors of Spirit Soaring and down the corridor leading to the audience hall. The leading crawler almost got through the door, but Bruenor was beside that entryway, his back to the wall, and he perfectly timed the mighty two-handed sweep of his axe, burying it in the crawler's chest and stopping the thing dead in its tracks.

A yank from the dwarf sent the thing rolling away, and as he did, he released his left hand, jerked his arm back to reposition his shield, and threw himself into the next beast scrambling through the door. Dwarf and crawler rolled aside, leaving the path open to Jarlaxle and his lightning bolts, one, two, flashing down the crowded hallway.

Behind those stepped Cadderly, right up to the doorway, and he threw his arms up high and pulled down magical power, releasing it through his feet and spreading it in a glowing circle right there in the archway. The priest fell back and the stubborn crawlers came on, and as they stepped upon Cadderly's consecrated ground, they were consumed by devastating radiance. They shrieked and they smoldered and they crumbled down, writhing in mortal agony.

Jarlaxle threw another pair of lightning bolts down the corridor.

Another crawler came flying over the balcony from above, but up there, as in the audience room, the situation was fast quieting.

"Come on, ye little beasties!" Athrogate yelled down the empty corridor above.

"Come on, dragon," Cadderly said in reply.

"Come on, Drizzt," Bruenor had to add.

* * * * *

With brutal speed and ferocity, the black-skinned behemoth snapped a punch out at the charging drow, and a lesser warrior than Drizzt would have been crushed by that blow. The ranger, though, with his speed multiplied by his anklets, and his razor-edged reflexes, stepped left as the giant began its swing. Anticipating that the behemoth would react to that movement, Drizzt fast-stepped back the other way so he ran unhindered as the creature's fist plowed through the air.

Drizzt didn't slow as he charged past the giant, but he did leap and spin to gain momentum as he slashed out with Icingdeath. He meant to strike the giant's kneecap, and to use that impact to reverse his momentum and his spin so he could scramble to the side, but to Drizzt's surprise, he felt no sense of impact.

Drizzt landed almost as if he had hit nothing solid at all, and despite his previous experiences with his divinely-infused weapons, he found himself almost stupefied by the reality that he had cut right through the behemoth's leg.

Improvising, Drizzt flipped diagonally to his left, lifting himself over and twisting around as he did to place himself directly behind the giant. A further twist stabbed Icingdeath up into the back of the giant's other thigh, and the howling creature had to rise up on its tiptoes even as it lurched to grab at its other severed leg.

Drizzt retracted Icingdeath, but only to make way for Twinkle as that blade slashed across, taking with it the giant's remaining leg.

Down crashed the massive beast, its screams reaching out to the Ghost King more than Drizzt's spoken challenges ever could.

Drizzt didn't bother finishing the giant—it would bleed out and die on its own—and instead positioned himself for a run to the cathedral. Everything fled before him, nightwings fluttering into the darkness and crawlers climbing all over each other to get away. He caught a few and killed each with a single, devastating stroke, and ran a more circuitous route to his planned position to further scatter the horde.

A cry from above rent the night, a scream painful in its intensity and sheer volume. Drizzt dived into a somersault and rolled to his feet, planting them firmly and facing that scream. He saw the dracolich's fire-filled eyes first, like shooting stars diving toward him, then saw the green glow of Crenshinibon, the beast's newest horn.

"Come on!" Drizzt shouted, and he slapped his scimitars together, sparks flying from the impact.

In a single movement, he sheathed them and pulled Taulmaril from his shoulder. Grinning wickedly, Drizzt let fly a silver-streaking arrow, then a second, then a line of them, reaching out and stinging the beast as it plummeted from on high.

CHAPTER 29

CHASING IT TO THE ENDS OF REALITY

"There!" Rorick cried, pointing at the sky high above the mountains.

They had heard the shriek of doom, and following Rorick's gaze, they saw the Ghost King as it glided across the starry canopy.

"Over our home," Hanaleisa said, and all five began to run. With every tenth step, though, Ivan called for a halt. Finally, the others slowed, gasping for breath.

"We stay together or we're suren dead," the yellow-bearded dwarf scolded. "I can'no' run with ye, girl!"

"And I cannot watch from afar as my home is attacked," Hanaleisa countered.

"And ye can'no' get there," said Ivan. "Half a day and more o' walking—hours of running. Ye mean to run for hours, do ye?"

"If I—" Hanaleisa started to retort, but she went quiet at Pikel's "Shh!" All eyes focused on the green-bearded dwarf as he hopped about, pointing into the dark forest.

A moment later, they heard the shuffling of many creatures moving swiftly through the underbrush. As one, the group braced for an attack, but they quickly realized that those creatures, minions of the Ghost King, they believed, were not coming for them but were running flat out to the west, up the hillsides toward Spirit Soaring. Their enemies swarmed to the distant battle.

"Quick, then, but not running," Ivan ordered. "And stay close, all o' ye!"

Hanaleisa spearheaded the charge, and at a swift pace. With her intensive training in stealth and stamina, and the graceful manner of her movements, she was sure that she could indeed run all the way home, as far as it was, even though the path was mostly uphill. But she couldn't abandon the others, surrounded by enemies, and particularly Rorick with his torn ankle, struggling with every step.

"Mother and Father are surrounded by a hundred capable mages and priests," Temberle tried to reassure her—and reassure himself, she sensed from the tone of his voice. "They will defeat this threat."

Soon after, with nearly a mile behind them, the group had to slow, both from exhaustion and because the forest around them teemed with shadowy creatures. On more than one occasion, Hanaleisa held up her hand to stop those behind her and fell low behind a tree trunk or a bush, expecting a fight. Every time, though, the noisy beasts scrambling ahead or to the sides seemed possessed of a singular purpose, and that purpose had nothing to do with the little band of Carradden refugees.

Gradually, Hanaleisa began to press on even when enemies sounded very near—a part of her hoped that some would come against them, she had to privately admit. Anything they killed out in the wilds would be one less attacker at the gates of Spirit Soaring.

But then Hanaleisa sensed something different, some movement that seemed intent upon them. She slid behind a broad tree and motioned for the others to stop, then held her breath as something approached very near, opposite her on the other side of the tree.

She jumped out as her opponent did the same, and launched a series of blows that would have leveled a skilled warrior.

But every strike was intercepted by an open hand that slapped her attacks aside. It took Hanaleisa only a moment to understand her defeat, only a heartbeat to recognize her opponent as the woman who had trained her all her life.

"Mother!" she cried, and Danica fell over her in the tightest hug she had ever known.

Rorick and Temberle echoed Hanaleisa's call and they, along with Ivan and Pikel, rushed up to embrace Danica.

Tears of profound relief and sheer joy filled Danica's eyes as she crushed each of her children close to her, and as she fell over Pikel. And those tears streaked a face full of confusion when she looked upon Ivan.

"I saw you die," she said. "I was on the cliff, outside the cave, when the dracolich crushed you."

"Crushed them what was chasing me, ye mean," Ivan corrected. "Dumb thing didn't even know it was standing above a hole—small for a dragon, but a tunnel for meself!"

"But . . ." Danica started. She just shook her head and kissed Ivan on his hairy cheek.

"You found a way," she said. "We'll find a way."

"Where's Father?" Hanaleisa asked.

"He remains at Spirit Soaring," Danica replied, and she glanced nervously up the mountains, "facing the Ghost King."

"He's surrounded by an army of wizards and warrior priests," Rorick insisted, but Danica shook her head.

"He's with a small group of powerful allies," Danica corrected, and she looked at Ivan and Pikel. "King Bruenor and one of his battleragers, and Drizzt Do'Urden."

"Bruenor," Ivan gasped. "Me king, come to us in our time o' need."

"Drizzit Dudden," Pikel added with a signature giggle.

"Lead on, Milady," Ivan bade Danica. "Might that we'll get there when there's still something to hit!"

* * * * *

The Ghost King didn't open wide its wings to break out of the stoop. Down it came, a missile from on high, wings folded, eyes burning, jaws wide. At the very last moment, right before it crashed, the Ghost King snapped its head up and flipped its wings out, altering nothing but its angle of descent. It hit the ground and plowed through the turf, digging a trench as it skidded at its prey. And if that alone were not enough to put a fast end to the fool who would challenge a god, the Ghost King breathed forth its flaming breath.

On and on it went, consuming all in its path, reaching to the very doorway of Spirit Soaring. The flesh of dead crawlers bubbled and burst and disintegrated beneath the conflagration, grass charred and obliterated.

"Drizzt!" Bruenor, Cadderly, and Jarlaxle yelled together from inside the cathedral, knowing their friend was surely consumed.

The gout of flames might have continued much longer, for it seemed an endless catastrophe, but a scimitar swung by a drow who should have been buried in that assault smashed hard against the side of the Ghost King's face.

Jolted, stunned that Drizzt had been quick enough to get out of the way, the Ghost King tried to turn its fury upon him.

But a second blow, so heavy with magical power, snapped the dracolich's head to the side yet again.

The Ghost King hopped up to its hind legs, towering over the drow even though it stood in a trench deeper than two tall men, a hollow torn by the weight of its cometlike impact.

Barely had it stood when the beast bit down at the drow, spearlike teeth snapping loudly, and in Spirit Soaring's doorway, Bruenor gasped, thinking his friend taken whole.

But again Drizzt moved ahead of his enemy, again the drow, so intent on the image of his wounded bride, so perfect in his focus and so adroit his reflexes, dived at precisely the right angle, forward and inside the reach of the Ghost King. As he came up, three lightning-fast steps brought him to the beast's right hind leg, where his scimitars bit deep.

Yet the power of Cadderly's magic and the fury of Drizzt Do'Urden could not do to that godlike being what he had done in dismembering the nightwalker, and for all of his rage and fury and focus, Drizzt never lost one simple truth: He could not beat the Ghost King alone.

And so he was moving again, and with all speed, even as he struck hard. Again the dragon snapped its killing fangs at him, and again he dodged and ran, at a full sprint away from the dracolich and toward Spirit Soaring.

Instinctively, Drizzt swerved out wide and dived again, and felt the heat at his back as the Ghost King breathed forth its murderous fires once more. Drizzt crossed that blackened line back the other way the moment it ended, again just ahead of the pursuing, biting monster.

He bolted through the double doors just ahead of the Ghost King and called out for Cadderly, for there was nowhere to turn.

And as he knew would happen, the Ghost King's fires followed him inside, rushing fast for his back and engulfing him fully, filling the passageway behind and in front with dragonfire.

* * * * *

Cadderly groaned in pain as roiling flames gnawed at Spirit Soaring, at the magic that sustained the priest and his creation. He held his radiant hands out before him, reaching for the corridor, reaching for Drizzt, praying he had reacted quickly enough.

Only when Drizzt scrambled into the room, out of the blast of dragonfire, did Cadderly allow himself to breathe. But his relief, the relief of them all, lasted only a moment before the whole of the great structure shuddered violently.

Cadderly fell back and grimaced, then again as another explosion rocked Spirit Soaring. Its walls, even for their magic, could not withstand the fury of the Ghost King, who crashed in, tearing with tooth and claw, battering aside walls, wood and stone alike, with its skull. Ripping, shredding, and battering its way along, the Ghost King moved into the structure, widening the passageway and crashing through the lower ceiling outside the audience chamber.

Inside that hall, the four companions fell back, step by step, trying to hold their calm and their confidence. A look at Cadderly did nothing to bolster their resolve. With every crash and tear against Spirit Soaring, the priest shuddered—and aged. Before their astonished eyes, Cadderly's hair went from gray to white, his face became creased and lined, his posture stooped.

The front wall of the audience chamber cracked, then blew apart as the monster slammed through. The Ghost King lifted its head and issued a deafening wail of pure hatred.

The building shook as the wyrm stomped into the room, then shook again with its next heavy step, which brought it within striking distance of its intended prey.

"For me king!" yelled Thibbledorf Pwent, who sat atop a tied-off log up on the high balcony. Right before him, standing on the rail, Athrogate cut free the lead log and gave it a heave to send it swinging down from on high.

The giant spear stabbed into the side of the Ghost King, hitting it squarely just under its shoulder, just under its wing, and indeed, the creature lurched, if only a bit, under the weight of that blow.

An inconsequential weight, though, against the godlike dracolich.

Except that Thibbledorf Pwent then cut loose the second log, the one on which he sat. "Wahoo!" he yelled as he swung past Athrogate, who gave a shove for good measure, and followed the same trajectory as the first beam.

More than the dwarf's added weight enhanced the blow as log hit log, end to end, for the front end of that second log had been hollowed out and filled with explosive oil. Like a gigantic version of Cadderly's hand crossbow bolts, the dwarven version collapsed in on itself and exploded with the force of a thunderbolt.

The front log blew forward, lifting the Ghost King and throwing it far and fast against the opposite wall. The back log blew to splinters, and the dwarf who had been sitting upon it flew forward, arms and legs flailing, and chased the dracolich through the air to the wall, catching it like a living grapnel even as the ceiling crumbled down atop the stunned Ghost King. Like a biting fly on the side of a horse, Thibbledorf Pwent scrambled and stabbed.

The Ghost King ignored him, though, for on came Drizzt, leading the charge, Bruenor behind. Still beside the shaken

Cadderly, Jarlaxle lifted his wands and began a barrage.

Taulmaril's stinging arrows led Drizzt's assault, flashing at the Ghost King's face to keep the creature occupied. As he neared, Drizzt threw the bow aside and reached for his blades.

He unsheathed only Icingdeath, however, his eyes sparking with sudden inspiration.

* * * * *

He felt his bones cracking like the beams of Spirit Soaring itself. His back twisted in a painful hunch, and his arms trembled from the effort of trying to hold them up before him.

But Cadderly knew that the moment of truth was at hand, the moment of Cadderly and Spirit Soaring and Deneir—somehow he sensed that it was the Scribe of Oghma's last moment, his god's final act.

He needed power then, and he found it, and as he had done in the previous battle with the Ghost King, the priest seemed to reach up and bring the sun itself down upon him. Allies drew strength and healing energy—so much so that Athrogate hardly groaned as he leaped down from the balcony, his twisted ankles untwisting before the pain even registered.

The Ghost King felt the brutal sting of Cadderly's light, and the priest advanced. The dracolich filled the room with dragonfire, but Cadderly's ward held strong and the sting did not stop the assault.

The Ghost King focused on Drizzt instead, determined to be rid of that wretched warrior, but again it could not bite quickly enough to catch the dancing elf, and as it tried to position its strikes to corner Drizzt against the rubble of the broken wall, it found itself cornered instead.

Drizzt leaped up against the dracolich and caught hold with his free hand on the monster's rib, exposed by the wide hole blown into it by the dwarven bolt, and before the Ghost King or anyone else could begin to analyze the drow's surprising move, Drizzt pulled himself right inside the beast, right into the lung, torn wide.

The Ghost King shuddered and thrashed with abandon, out of its mind with agony as the drow, both weapons drawn, began tearing it apart from the inside. So violent was its movements, so shattering its cries, so furious its breath that the other combatants staggered to a stop and pressed hands over their ears, and even Pwent fell off the creature.

But inside, Drizzt played out his fury, and Cadderly held forth his radiant light to bolster his allies and consume his enemy.

The Ghost King pushed away from the wall, stumbling and kicking, smashing a foot right through the floor to crash down into the catacombs below. It shrieked and breathed its fire, and the weakened magic of Spirit Soaring could not resist the bite of those flames. The smoke grew thick, dulling the blinding brilliance of Cadderly's light, but not weakening its effect.

"Kill it, and quickly!" Jarlaxle yelled as the beast shuddered and shook with agony. Bruenor raised his axe and charged, Athrogate set his morningstars to spinning, and Thibbledorf Pwent leaped onto a leg and thrashed as only a battlerager could.

A blue glow overwhelmed the yellow hue of Cadderly's radiance, and the three dwarves felt their weapons hitting only emptiness.

Drizzt fell through the insubstantial torso, landing lightly on the floor, but sliding and slipping on the blood and gore that covered him. Pwent tumbled face down with an "Oomph!"

"It flees!" Jarlaxle shouted, and behind him, in the small room, Catti-brie cried out. In the main hall, the Ghost King vanished.

Cadderly was first to the anteroom, though every step seemed to pain the old man. He pulled the latch and threw open the door, and from under his white shirt produced the ruby pendant Jarlaxle had loaned to him.

Before him, Catti-brie trembled and cried out. Behind him, Drizzt pulled out the onyx figurine. Cadderly looked at Drizzt and shook his head.

"Guenhwyvar will not get you there," said the priest.

"We cannot allow it to escape us again," Drizzt said. He moved inexorably toward Catti-brie, drawn to her in her pain.

"It will not," Cadderly promised. He gave a profound sigh. "Tell Danica that I love her, and promise me that you will find and protect my children."

"We will," Jarlaxle answered, and Drizzt, Bruenor, and Caddarly all looked at him in astonishment. Had not the weight of the situation been pressing so enormously upon all of them at that moment, all three would have burst out in laughter.

It was a fleeting moment of relief, though. Cadderly nodded his appreciation to Jarlaxle and turned back to Catti-brie, bringing the ruby pendant up before her. With his free hand he gently touched her face and he moved very near to her, falling into her thoughts and seeing through her eyes.

A collective gasp sounded from the two drow and the three dwarves, and Caddarly began to glow with the same bluish-white hue of the departing Ghost King. That gasp became a cry as the priest faded to nothingness.

Catti-brie cried out again, but more in surprise, it seemed, than in fear.

With a determined grunt, Drizzt again reached for Guenhwyvar, but Jarlaxle grabbed his wrist. "Don't," the mercenary bade him.

A crash behind them stole the moment, and all turned to see a giant support beam lying diagonally from the balcony to the floor, thick with flames.

"Out," Jarlaxle said, and Drizzt moved to Catti-brie and scooped her up in his arms.

*****

It was a shadow image of the world he had left, absent the fabricated structures, a land of dull resolution and often utter darkness, of huddled ugly beasts and terrifying monsters. But in those clouds of shadowstuff shone a singular brilliance, the light of Caddarly, and before him loomed the most profound darkness of all, the Ghost King.

And there the two did battle, light against darkness, the radiance of Deneir's last gift to his Chosen against the combined powers of perversion. For a long, long while, light seared through shadows, and the flowing shadows rolled back to cover the radiance. For a long, long while, neither seemed to gain an advantage, and the other creatures of the dark plane looked on in awe.

Then those creatures fell back, for the shadow could not grow against that radiance, that unrelenting warmth of Cadderly Bonaduce. Possessed of great draconic intelligence and the wisdom of centuries, the Ghost King knew the truth as well.

For the king had been usurped and the new Ghost King stood amidst the darkness, and in that final struggle, Cadderly could not be defeated.

With a cry of protest, the dracolich lifted away and fled, and Cadderly, too, did not remain. For it was not his place, and there, he cared not if the evil beast lived or died.

But he could not allow the creature to return to his homeland.

He knew the sacrifice before him. He knew that he could not cross back through the membrane between worlds, that he was trapped by duty to Deneir, to what was right, and to his family and friends.

With a smile of contentment, certain of a life well-lived, Cadderly left that world of darkness for a place almost, but not quite, his home.

CHAPTER 30
THE LAST MEMORIES OF CHANGING GODS

She did not lie limp in Drizzt's arms, but rather seemed to be watching an awe-inspiring spectacle, and from her twitches and gasps, Drizzt could only imagine the battle his friend Cadderly was waging with the Ghost King.

"Kill it," he found himself whispering as he stumbled out of the ruined cathedral, through the double doors and onto the wide porch. What he really meant was a private prayer to Cadderly to find a way to bring Catti-brie back to him. "Kill it," meant all of it, from the tangible and symbolic dracolich to the insanity that had gripped the world and had entrapped Catti-brie. It was his last chance, he believed. If Cadderly could not find a way to break the spell over his beloved wife, she would remain forever lost to him.

To the relief of them all, no monsters remained to confront them as they escaped the building. The courtyard was littered with dead, killed by Drizzt or by the ferocious assault of the Ghost King. The lawn, once so serene and beautiful, showed the blackened scar of dragonfire, great brown swaths of dead grass from the dracolich's touch, and the massive trench dug by the diving wyrm.

Jarlaxle and Bruenor led the way out of the structure, and when they looked back at the grand cathedral, at the life's work of Cadderly Bonaduce, they understood better why the assault had taken such a toll on the priest. Fires leaped from several places, most dramatically from the wing they had just departed. Where the initial assault of dragonfire had been muted by the power of the cathedral's magic, the protective spells had worn thin. The fire wouldn't consume the place entirely, but the damage was extensive.

"Put her down, friend," Jarlaxle said, taking Drizzt's arm.

Drizzt shook his head and pulled away, and at that moment, Catti-brie's eyes flickered, and for a moment, just a moment, Drizzt thought he saw clarity there, thought he saw, within her—she recognized him!

"Me girl!" Bruenor cried, obviously seeing the same.

But a fleeting thing it was, if anything at all, and Catti-brie settled almost immediately back into the same lethargic state that had dominated her days since the falling Weave had wounded her.

Drizzt called to her repeatedly and shook her gently. "Catti! Catti-brie! Wake up!"

But he received no response.

As the weight of her condition sank in, Athrogate gave a cry, and all eyes went to him, then followed his gaze to the cathedral's open doorway.

Out walked Cadderly. Not flesh and blood, but a translucent, ghostly form of the old priest, hunched but walking with a purpose. He approached them and walked right through them, and everyone shuddered with a profound sense of coldness as he neared and passed.

They called to him, but he could not hear, as if they didn't exist. And so, they knew, in Cadderly's new reality, they did not.

The old priest ambled to the tree line, the other six following, and against the backdrop of leaping orange flames, Cadderly began to walk and whisper, bending low, his hand just off the ground. Behind him, a line of blue-white light glowed softly along the grass, and they realized that Cadderly was laying that line as he went.

"A ward," Jarlaxle realized. He tentatively stepped over it, and showed relief indeed when it did not harm him.

"Like the barrier in Luskan," Drizzt agreed. "The magic that was put down to seal off the old city, where the undead walk."

Cadderly continued his circuit, indeed walking the perimeter of Spirit Soaring.

"If the Ghost King returns, it must be to this spot," Jarlaxle said, though he seemed less than confident of his assessment and his reasoning sounded more like a plea. "The undead will not be able to cross out of this place."

"But how long's he got to weave it?" Bruenor asked.

"He knew," Drizzt gasped. "His words for Danica . . ."

"Forever," Jarlaxle whispered.

It took a long while for the priest to complete his first circuit, and he began his second anew, for the magic ward where he had started was already fading. Barely after Cadderly commenced the second pass, a voice called out from the darkness of the forest. "Father!" cried Rorick Bonaduce. "He is old! Mother, why does he look so old?"

Out of the trees rushed Danica and her children, with Ivan and Pikel. Joyful greetings and reunions had to wait, though, dampened by the pain that lay evident on the faces of three young adults, and on the woman who had so loved Cadderly.

Drizzt felt Danica's pain profoundly as he stood holding Catti-brie.

"What happened?" Danica asked, hurrying to join them.

"We drove it off, and hurt it badly," said Jarlaxle.

"Cadderly chased it when it left," said Bruenor.

Danica looked past them to the burning Spirit Soaring. She knew why her ghostly husband seemed so old, of course. Spirit Soaring was ruined, its magic diminished to near nothingness, and that magic supported Cadderly as surely as it held strong the timbers, stone, and glass of Deneir's cathedral. The magic had made Cadderly young, and had kept him young.

The spell had been destroyed.

Her husband had been destroyed, too, or . . . what? She looked at him and did not know.

"His last thoughts were of you," Drizzt said to her. "He loved you. He loves you still, as he serves Deneir, as he serves us all."

"He will come back from this," Hanaleisa said with determination. "He will finish his task and return to us!"

No one contradicted her, for what was to be gained? But a look from Danica told Drizzt that she, too, sensed the truth. Cadderly had become the Ghost King. Cadderly, his service to Spirit Soaring and to the wider world, was eternal.

The ghostly priest was halfway through his third circuit when dawn broke over the eastern horizon, and the others, exhausted, continued to follow him.

His glow diminished with the rising sun until he was gone from sight entirely, to the gasps—hopeful and horrified—of his children.

"He's gone!" Temberle cried.

"He's coming back to us," Rorick declared.

"Not gone," Jarlaxle said a moment later, and he motioned the others over to him. The glowing line continued on its way, and near to its brightest point, its newest point, the air was much colder. Cadderly was still there, unseen in the daylight.

The fires had diminished greatly in Spirit Soaring, but the group did not go back inside the cathedral, instead setting a camp just outside the front door. Weariness alone brought them some sleep, in cautious shifts, and as dusk descended, the Ghost King, the apparition of Cadderly, returned to view, walking, forever walking, his lonely circuit.

Soon after, some crawlers returned, a small group seeming intent on again attacking Spirit Soaring. They broke out of the forest and shrieked as one as they neared Cadderly's glowing line. Off they ran, into the darkness.

"Cadderly's ward," Bruenor said. "A good one."

The group rested a little easier after that.

"We have to leave this place," Jarlaxle remarked to them all later that night, and that drew many looks, few appreciative. "We do," the drow insisted. "We have to tell the world what has happened here."

"You go and tell them, then," Hanaleisa growled at him, but Danica put her hand on her daughter's forearm to quiet her.

"The monsters have retreated, but they remain out there," Jarlaxle warned.

"Then we stay in here where they can't get at us," Rorick argued.

"The dracolich can return inside that ward," Jarlaxle warned. "We must lea—"

Drizzt stopped him with an upraised hand and turned to Danica. "In the morning, first light," he bade her.

"This is our home. Where will we go?"

"Mithral Hall, and Silverymoon from there," Drizzt answered. "If there is an answer to be found, look to Lady Alustriel."

Danica turned to her children, who frowned as one, but had no words to counter the obvious reality. The food they could salvage from inside the structure couldn't sustain them forever.

As a compromise, they waited another two nights, but by then, even Hanaleisa and Rorick had to admit that their father was not coming back to them.

And so it was a solemn caravan that made its way out of Spirit Soaring one bright morning. The wagon hadn't been badly damaged out in the courtyard, and with five skilled dwarves supplying the know-how, they managed to repair it completely. Even better news followed when they found the poor mules, frightened and hungry but very much alive, roaming a distant corridor of the cathedral's first floor, their magical shoes intact.

They set a slow pace down to empty, ruined Carradoon, then north to the road to Mithral Hall. They knew they would find enemies in the Snowflakes, and so they did, but with the combined strength of the five dwarves, the Bonaduce family, and the two drow, no sufficient number of crawlers, giant bats, or even nightwalkers could pose any real threat.

They set an easier pace than the fury that had brought them south, and two tendays later, they crossed the Surbrin and entered Mithral Hall.

* * * * *

Hunched and uncomplaining, the Ghost King Cadderly circled the ruins of Spirit Soaring that night.

And every night, forevermore.

*****

It was all a blur, all a swirl, an overriding grayness that defied lucidity. Flashes of images, most of them terrifying, stabbed at her sensibilities and jolted her from memory to memory, to senses of the life she had known.

It was all an ungraspable blur.

But then Catti-brie saw a dot within that sea of movement, a focal point, like the end of a rope reaching out to her through the fog. In her mind and with her hand she reached out for that point of clarity and to her surprise, she touched it. It was firm and smooth, the purest ivory.

The clouds swirled out, retreating from that point, and Catti-brie saw with her eyes clearly then, and in the present, for the first time in tendays. She looked to her lifeline, a single horn. She followed it.

A unicorn.

"Mielikki," she breathed.

Her heart pounded. She tried to fight through the confusion, to sort out all that had transpired.

The strand of the Weave! She remembered the strand of the Weave touching her and wounding her.

It was still there, inside of her. The gray clouds roiled at the edges of her focus.

"Mielikki," she said again, knowing beyond doubt that it was she, the goddess, who stood before her.

The unicorn bowed and went down on its front knees, inviting her.

Catti-brie's heart beat furiously; she thought it would jump out of her chest. Tears filled her eyes as she tried to deny what was coming next, and she silently begged to delay.

The unicorn looked at her, great sympathy in its large dark eyes. Then it stood once more and backed away a step.

"Give me this one night," Catti-brie whispered.

She rushed out of the room and padded on bare feet to the next door in Mithral Hall, the one she knew so well, the one she shared with Drizzt.

He lay on the bed in fitful sleep when she entered the room, and she released the bindings of her magical garment and let it drop to the floor as she slid in beside him.

He started, and turned, and Catti-brie met him with a passionate kiss. They fell together, overwhelmed, and made love until they collapsed into each other's arms.

Drizzt's sleep was more profound then, and when she heard the soft tap of the unicorn's horn on the closed door, Catti-brie understood that Mielikki was compelling him to slumber.

And calling her to her destiny.

She slid out from under Drizzt's arm, raised up on one elbow, and kissed him on the ear. "I will always love you, Drizzt Do'Urden," she said. "My life was full and without regret because I knew you and was completed by you. Sleep well, my love."

She slipped out of the bed and reached for her magical blouse. But she stopped and shook her head, moving instead to her dresser. There she found clothes Alustriel of Silverymoon had given to her: a white, layered gown full of pleats and folds, but sleeveless and low-cut, and with no even hemline. It was a wrap designed to flow with her every movement, and to enhance, not hide, her beauty of form.

She took a hooded black cloak and threw it over her shoulders, and gave a twirl to see it trailing.

She went out on bare feet. She didn't need shoes any more.

The unicorn was waiting, but offered no protest as Catti-brie quietly led it down the dim corridor, to a door not far away. Within lay Regis, tormented, emaciated, hanging on to life by a thread and by the near-continual efforts of the loyal priests of Mithral Hall, one of whom sat in a chair near the halfling's bed, deep in slumber.

Catti-brie didn't have to undo the bindings holding Regis's arms and legs, for there was much she would leave behind. Regis broke free of his fleshy coil then, and the woman, his guide and companion, gently lifted him into her arms. He started to groan, but she whispered to him softly, and with the magic of Mielikki filling her breath, the halfling calmed.

Out in the hall, the unicorn went down to its knees and Catti-brie sat sidesaddle upon its back. They started down the corridor.

*****

A cry from a familiar voice awakened Drizzt, its panic so at odds with the wonderful, lingering warmth of the previous night.

But if Bruenor's frantic call didn't fully break the sleepy spell, the image that came into focus, at the same time Drizzt became aware of the sensations of his touch, surely did.

Catti-brie was there with him, in his bed, her eyes closed and a look of serenity on her face, as if she was asleep.

But she wasn't asleep.

Drizzt sat bolt upright, gagging and choking, eyes wide, hands trembling.

"Catti," he cried. "Catti, no!" He fell over her, so cool and still, and lifted her unresponsive form to him. "No, no, come back to me."

"Elf!" Bruenor shrieked again—shrieked and not yelled. Never before had Drizzt heard such a keen from the stoic and level-headed dwarf. "Oh, by the gods, elf!"

Drizzt lowered Catti-brie to the bed. He didn't know whether to touch her, to kiss her, to try to breathe life into her. He didn't know what to do, but Bruenor's third cry had him rolling out of bed and stumbling through his door.

He burst out into the hall, naked and sweating, and nearly ran over Bruenor, who was shaking and stumbling down the corridor, and carrying in his arms the lifeless form of Regis.

"Oh, elf."

"Bruenor, Catti-brie. . . . " Drizzt stammered, but Bruenor interrupted him.

"She's on the damned horse with Rumblebelly!"

Drizzt looked at him dumbfounded, and Bruenor nodded his chin down the corridor and stumbled toward the nearest connecting hallway. Drizzt supported him and pulled him along, and together

THE GHOST KING

they turned the corner. There ahead of them, they saw the vision that had accounted for no small part of Bruenor's frantic cry.

A unicorn carried Catti-brie, riding sidesaddle and cradling Regis in her arms. Not the equine creature or the woman looked back, despite the commotion of pursuit and drow and dwarf calling out to them.

The corridor turned sharply again, but the unicorn did not.

It walked right into the stone and was gone.

Drizzt and Bruenor stumbled to a halt, gasping and stuttering over words that would not come.

Behind them came a commotion as other dwarves reacted to the cries of their king, and Jarlaxle, too, ran up to the horrified pair. Many cries went up for Regis, lying dead in Bruenor's arms, for the halfling who had served well as steward of Mithral Hall and as a close advisor to their greatest king.

Jarlaxle offered his cloak to Drizzt, but had to put it on the ranger, who was out of his mind with terror and pain. Finally, Drizzt focused on Jarlaxle, grabbing the mercenary by the folds of his shirt and running him up against a wall.

"Find her!" Drizzt begged, against all logic, for he knew where the woman lay, still and cold. "You must find her! I'll do anything you demand . . . all the riches in the world!"

"Mithral Hall and everything in it!" Bruenor yelled.

Jarlaxle tried to calm the ranger and Bruenor. He nodded and he patted Drizzt's shoulder, though of course he had no idea where to begin, or what precisely he would be looking for—Catti-brie's soul?

Their promises of fealty and riches rang strangely discordant to Jarlaxle at that moment. He would find her, or would try, at least. Of that, he had no doubt.

But to Jarlaxle's surprise, he had no intention of taking a copper for his efforts, and wanted no promise of fealty from Drizzt Do'Urden.

Maybe something else compelled him then.

EPILOGUE

She felt it like a heartbeat beneath her bare feet, the land alive, the rhythm of life itself, and it compelled her to dance. And though she had never been a dancer, her movements were fluid and graceful, a perfect expression of the springtime forest into which she had been placed. And though her hip had been wounded badly—forever wounded, they had all believed—she felt no pain when she lifted her leg high, or leaped and spun in an inspired pirouette.

She came upon Regis sitting in a small field of wildflowers, looking out at the ripples on a small pond. She offered a smile and a laugh, and danced around him.

"Are we dead?" he asked.

Catti-brie had no answer. There was the world out there, somewhere beyond the trees of the springtime forest, and there was . . . here. This existence. This pocket of paradise, an expression of what had been from the goddess Mielikki, a gift given to her and to Regis, and to all Toril.

"Why are we here?" the halfling, who was no longer tormented by shadowy, huddled monsters, asked.

Because they had lived a good life, Catti-brie knew. Because this was Mielikki's gift—to Drizzt as much as to them—an expression of wondrous memory from the goddess who knew that the world had changed forever.

Catti-brie danced away, singing, and though she had never been a singer, her voice sounded with perfect pitch and tone, another effect of the enchanted wood.

They remained on Toril, though they didn't know it, in a small pocket of an eternal springtime forest amidst a world growing dark and cold. They were of that place, as surely as, and even more so, than Cadderly had been of Spirit Soaring. To leave would be to invite the nightmares and the stupor of abject confusion.

For any others to enter would invite unto them variations of the same.

For the glen was the expression of Mielikki, a place of possibilities, of what could be and not of what was. There were no monsters there, though animals abounded. And the gift was a private one and not to be shared, a secret place, the goddess Mielikki's indelible mark, Mielikki's fitting monument, on a world that had moved in a new direction.

* * * * *

Two piles of rocks.

Two cairns, one holding Regis and one holding Catti-brie. Just over a month earlier, Drizzt and Catti-brie had been on the road to Silverymoon, and despite the trouble with the Weave, it had been a joyous journey. For more than eight years, Drizzt had felt complete, had felt as if all the joys had been doubled and all the pain halved as he danced through his life arm-in-arm with that wonderful woman who had never shown him anything less than honesty and compassion and love.

Then it was gone, stolen from him, and in a way he simply could not comprehend. He tried to take solace in telling himself that her pain had ended, that she was at peace—with Mielikki, obviously, given the vision of the unicorn. She had been suffering those last tendays, after all.

But it didn't work, and he could only shake his head and fight to hold back his tears, and hold back his desire to throw himself across that cold and hard cairn assembled in a decorated lower chamber of Mithral Hall.

He looked to the smaller stone pile and remembered his journey with Regis to Luskan, then thought back much farther, to their first days together in Icewind Dale.

The drow dropped his hand on Guenhwyvar, whom he had called for the ceremony. It was fitting that the panther was there, and if he had known any way to accomplish it, it would have been fitting to have Wulfgar there. Drizzt resolved then to go to Icewind Dale to inform his barbarian friend face-to-face.

Then it all broke. The notion of telling Wulfgar finally cracked the stoic posture of Drizzt Do'Urden. He began to sob, his shoulders bobbing, and he felt himself sinking toward the floor, as if the stones were rising up to bury him—and how he wished they would!

Bruenor grabbed him, and cried with him.

Drizzt shook himself out of it in short order, and stood tall with a cold grimace, and such a look it was that it chilled everyone in the room.

"It's goin' to be all right, elf," Bruenor whispered.

Drizzt only stared straight ahead with cold, hard, unfocused anger.

He knew he would never be the same; he knew that the inner growling would not diminish with the passing of days, of tendays, of months, or years, or decades perhaps. There was no shining and hopeful light at the end of that dark passage.

Not this time.

* * * * *

When Regis wanted to find something he could use as a fishing line, he found it. When he searched for a hook and pole, those, too, were readily discovered. And when he pulled his first knucklehead trout from the small pond, the halfling gasped in surprise and wondered if perhaps he was in Icewind Dale!

But no, he knew, for even if that strange forest was located in that land it was not of that land.

Scrimshaw tools were not far away, and Regis was not surprised to find them. He wanted them and they were there, and so he began to wonder if the place itself was a dream, a grand illusion.

Heaven or hell?

Would he wake up?

Did he want to?

He spent his days fishing and at his scrimshaw, and he was warm and happy. He ate meals more delicious than anything he had ever known, and went to sleep with his belly full and dreamed beautiful dreams. And the song of Catti-brie filled the forest air, though he saw her only in fleeting moments, far away, leaping onto sunbeams and moonbeams as if they were ladders to the heavens.

Dancing, always dancing. The forest was alive through her movements and her song, and the songs of birds accompanied her gaily in the sunshine, and with haunting beauty in the soft darkness of the night.

He was not unhappy and not frustrated, but many times, Regis, for the sake of his own curiosity, tried to walk in a straight line, to veer neither left nor right a single step in an attempt to find the end of the forest.

But every time, somehow, inexplicably, he found himself back where he had started, on the banks of a small pond.

He could only put his hands on his hips and laugh—and retrieve his fishing pole.

* * * * *

And so it went, and time became meaningless, the days and the seasons mattering not at all.

It snowed in the forest, but it was not cold, and the flowers did not stop blooming, and Catti-brie, the magical soul of Mielikki's expression, did not slow her dance nor quiet her song.

It was her place, her forest, and there, she knew happiness and serenity and peace of mind, and if challenges came against the forest, she would meet them. Regis knew all of that, too, and knew that he was a guest there, welcome forevermore, but not as intricately tied to the land as was his companion.

And so the halfling took it upon himself to become a caretaker of sorts. He cut a garden and tended it to perfection. He built himself a home within a hillside, with a round door and a cozy hearth, with shelves of wondrous scrimshaw he had sculpted and plates and cups of wood, and a table always set . . .

. . . for guests who never came.

DUNGEONS & DRAGONS

JAMES WYATT

THE GATES OF MADNESS

PART ONE

An exclusive five-part prequel to the worlds-spanning
DUNGEONS & DRAGONS® event

THE ABYSSAL PLAGUE

NERATH, BEFORE THE FALL.

The Chained God spoke, and the Progenitor whispered its reply.

"I will be free," the Chained God said, "and all will perish."

"Perish," the Progenitor whispered, an echo in the desolate infinity of the Chained God's prison.

The Chained God formed a hand of darkness and bone and stretched a finger toward the glowing liquid. Its light turned the darkness of his substance to blood.

"They will drown in blood," he said.

"Blood," whispered the Progenitor.

His finger touched the liquid surface and it sprang to life at his touch, coiling around the bone and joining with his shadow, hungry for his substance.

Once again the Chained God saw what it was and what it had been. He saw the world crumbling as it consumed everything, leaving behind only the void that was his prison.

"So it shall be," he said, his voice the only sound in the whole of the void.

"All will perish," the Progenitor whispered.

* * * * *

"The Fire Lord will consume the world!"

Nowhere watched a blast of flames roar from one of the cultist's outstretched hands and wash over his companions. Brendis raised his shield to block the brunt of the flames, and Nowhere saw a hint of the divine glow that indicated the paladin's magic at work, protecting himself and the eladrin wizard behind him from the searing heat. He allowed a hint of a smile to touch his lips as the echo of the blast faded in the strange vault beneath the capital. Brendis and Sherinna could take care of themselves—that was why he liked working with them. They didn't need him, and he didn't need them, except occasionally to distract their opponents long enough for him to get close. Like now.

"The might of the gods stands against you and your Fire Lord," Brendis said, raising his sword and striding toward the red-robed cultists.

Nowhere slid the wavy-bladed dagger from his belt in perfect silence and assessed the three cultists. The nearest one, shrinking back from Brendis's approach, was a portly man whose bald head bore tattoos in patterns of flame. The one who had shouted his defiance and blasted fire at Brendis and Sherinna was a small man with squinting eyes and a thin beard, clutching a staff and muttering invocations to the Fire Lord. The third cultist was a hulking brute with a huge iron sword that trailed fire as he swung it at the paladin.

With all three cultists glaring at Brendis, Nowhere stepped silently behind the portly one. Nowhere and his companions had been working to root out this cult of fire-worshipers for weeks, and he had more than one painful injury to repay, not even to speak of the buildings the cultists had burned to the ground, the wares and treasures consumed in flame. He lined up his attack in an instant and drove his dagger into his target's spine. A gurgling scream rose in the man's throat, cut short as Nowhere pulled the blade back and drew it quickly across the cultist's neck.

The muttering cultist turned in surprise, and his squinting eyes widened as he saw Nowhere's horns and the bony ridge of his jaw.

"A tiefling?" the cultist said. "Heir of fallen Bael Turath, why not cast your lot with us? What love can you bear this world?"

Nowhere shrugged. "I don't see any profit in your line of thinking. There's a great deal to like in this world."

"Our reward lies not in this world, but in what remains when it is gone." The cultist punctuated his words by thrusting his hand toward Nowhere, palm first. Another blast of flame sprang toward the spot where Nowhere had been standing, but the tiefling was already in motion, rolling away from the fire and coming to his feet right beside the startled cultist.

"You expect a reward from the primordial monster that burns the world to ash?" Nowhere stabbed with his blade, cutting a gash in the cultist's arm as the man tried to twist away. "I don't think the primordials work that way."

"You think the gods are any better?" The cultist had produced a dagger of his own, but he held it clumsily and seemed more interested in opening the distance between them than landing a solid blow.

"I never said that," Nowhere said, and his blade found a home in the cultist's neck.

"Nowhere!"

The tiefling spun at the paladin's shout, then dropped into a crouch below the third cultist's sword, which came swirling over him in a tempest of fire. The heat of the flames trailing from the iron sword still seared his skin, and he threw himself backward to find a safe distance.

The cultist's hood had fallen back from his face to reveal the monstrous visage of a hobgoblin, marked with scars in the fashion of the warlords of the Dragondown Coast, far to the east. Nowhere frowned. Brendis had been sure that this fire cult was a local problem, nothing more than a few malcontents stirring up trouble in the underbelly of the capital. But if it was drawing members or other support from the eastern warlords, it might be far more.

A bolt of crackling lightning shot from Sherinna's slender fingers to engulf the hobgoblin, searing his skin and sending a wave of convulsions through his body. Brendis took the opportunity of the hobgoblin's momentary paralysis to step forward and swing his sword cleanly through the hobgoblin's neck.

Sherinna rubbed her hands together, as though the lightning joining her fingers to the dead hobgoblin could have carried the cultist's corruption to her. "Are any of them still alive?" she asked, nodding toward the ones Nowhere had dispatched.

"No," the tiefling said, frowning. "I thought we'd question the big one."

Brendis scowled. "Sorry," he said. "I figured the one with the staff was the leader."

"Well, one of you should search them," Sherinna said, her lips curled in disgust. "See if there's anything that might identify other cult members."

"Nowhere?" Brendis said.

"With pleasure."

* * * * *

A buzzing fly brought Albric close to consciousness for a moment. He waved a hand uselessly near his head and sank back into dreaming.

He dreamed he was covered in flies, swarming around him, drinking at his eyes and mouth, laying their eggs in his ears and his open wounds. Then he was the flies, his consciousness fractured into thousands of tiny minds, all sharing a single purpose—to feast on flesh. Then he was a man once more, and the world was a fleshy body beneath him, and he joined with the swarm of all living things to consume the world.

As they ate and ate, gorging themselves on the flesh of the world, what was left in its place was fire and chaos, a swirling maelstrom of annihilation. He slipped from the carcass of the world and fell into the maelstrom. He looked down its yawning gullet, and there he saw the Eye.

It was a roiling mass of shadow, with numberless dark tendrils writhing out from it, reaching toward him as he fell. It bore no pupil, no colored ring of iris, nothing that made it resemble the eye of any living thing, but it saw—Albric was seen, and he was empty before it.

Its tentacles coiled around him and slowed his fall, and they whispered their secrets to him. He strained to hear and understand, but most of what they said was beyond understanding.

Another fly buzzed in his ear and Albric sat up, looking wildly around him.

"Bael Turath," he said, panting. "The Living Gate."

* * * * *

"What is this symbol?" Brendis said, putting the letter into Sherinna's outstretched hand.

The eladrin wizard studied the parchment, focusing her attention on the fiery eye traced at the bottom of the page. "The Elder Elemental Eye," she said. Fear tinged her voice, and Nowhere saw Brendis react to the name.

"Should I know what that means?" the tiefling asked.

"It means our problem isn't confined to this little cult of fire lovers," Brendis said.

Nowhere pointed at the corpse of the hobgoblin who had carried the letter. "I thought he made that pretty clear. If they were drawing members from the Dragondown Coast, it's obviously not a local problem. But what is the Elemental Eye?"

Sherinna's eyes were unfocused—an expression she adopted when deep in thought. It always gave Nowhere the impression that she was staring into a space between worlds, somehow, or perhaps peering into her home in the Feywild. When she didn't answer, Brendis shrugged.

"I'm not exactly sure," the paladin said. "It's some kind of primordial force. I think some of the more malign primordials are said to work with it or maybe even for it—including Imix, the Fire Lord these scum were so excited about." Brendis's eyes strayed to the idol the cultists had erected here in their makeshift temple, a vaguely humanoid shape roughly formed from clay. Nowhere guessed that the crude protrusions along the figure's shoulders and the top of its head were supposed to indicate that the figure was burning, or perhaps made of fire.

What the cultists lacked in artistic skill, Nowhere thought, they made up for in fanatic devotion. They were ready enough to die for their cause.

Nowhere scratched his bony chin. "The letter suggests they're trying to bring their master—the Elemental Eye, I presume—into the world. Terror and destruction follow in his wake, of course," he said. "It sounds like the same dire-sounding rhetoric these fire cultists were spewing. So why do you two look so worried?"

Brendis sighed and got to his feet, turning away from the others. "I was so sure that we were just facing a local cult of troublemakers expressing their discontent with the Empire's firm and steady hand by claiming the Fire Lord as their patron. I miscalculated and led us into conflict with a much larger threat."

"You don't like being wrong," Nowhere said. He'd known that about Brendis for years.

The paladin turned back to face him, his face grim. "Especially not when lives are at stake."

"We need to find whoever sent this letter," Sherinna said, emerging from her musing. "This 'Dreaming Prophet,' as he calls himself."

"Tomorrow," Nowhere said. "After we sell the brass candlesticks and the ruby on that one's finger, and celebrate our victory over the cult of the Fire Lord . . . Right?" He looked to Brendis for support, even though the paladin wasn't much for the kind of celebration Nowhere enjoyed. Brendis's eyes were fixed on the wizard.

"Now," Sherinna said, and there was an urgency in her voice that squelched the argument in Nowhere's throat.

* * * * *

A second city, with its own wards and laws and commerce, thrived in the storm sewers and ancient tunnels beneath Nerath's grand capital. Nowhere was as comfortable in the maze of its chambers and passages as he was in the equally labyrinthine streets on the surface—he'd spent most of his life moving between the surface world and the undercity. Brendis and Serinna were not so comfortable in the world of torchlight and refuse, but their long hunt for the arsonists and murderers that made up the Fire Lord's cult had forced even the two of them to learn the undercity's ways. Nowhere had made sure of that—he couldn't have them relying on him to guide them.

So even though he saw the trepidation in their eyes when he suggested that they split up, he knew they could handle themselves. Either of the two informants that had pointed them to the Fire Lord's temple might be able to lead them to the Dreaming Prophet. If the matter was as urgent as Sherinna suggested, it would be best to speak to both informants at the same time. Brendis and Sherinna would talk to the tavernkeeper who had observed some of the cult members' clandestine meetings, and Nowhere would pay a visit to the other.

The night hag.

Tavet the Heartless lived in a sprawling network of natural caverns in the deeper reaches of the undercity known, prosaically enough, as the Caves. Her fame as an information broker was exceeded only by her infamous cruelty. It was said that she stole secrets from the prominent figures of the undercity and even the city above by infiltrating their dreams. Nowhere approached her cavern home with every sense alert for danger in the deep shadows that surrounded him.

He stopped just outside the entrance to her cave and opened the sack he carried. The smell of blood assaulted his nostrils as he drew out the bundle he'd purchased from a butcher in the nearby Gloomside district. "Blood and flesh for Tavet the Heartless," he called. He opened the package, took the blood-drenched cow's heart in one hand and held it forward. He imagined he could feel a hint of resistance in the air as his hand crossed the threshold of her lair, but the blood parted the barrier. Suddenly the cavern beyond didn't seem quite so dark, and he saw the misshapen shadow of the night hag's body shambling toward him.

"Drop it." Her voice was the croak of a bullfrog and the howl of a wolf, all the unnerving sounds of night wrapped around two small words.

Nowhere let the heart fall on the ground and turned his back. He heard the hag shuffle forward and tried to stop listening, but he couldn't block the sounds of her bloody feast.

"Enter," she said when she was done.

Nowhere turned back to the cave mouth, and the night hag was lost in the darkness again. Steeling his nerves, he stepped across the threshold.

"You come alone this time?"

"I did not wish to try your patience again," Nowhere said. Tavet and Brendis had not gotten along well on their previous visit.

"Or perhaps you seek a bargain your friend would not condone." Her voice came from all around him and echoed in the small cave.

Nowhere peered into the shadows, trying to find a hint of the night hag's outline. Although he saw far more than Brendis's human eyes could have, he could not find a trace of her. "I need more information," he said.

"You found the head of your little fire cult and discovered that it was just the hand of a much larger cult. Now you seek another head."

"That's right," Nowhere said. She'd made a logical deduction based on the information they sought last time and what she knew about the situation, nothing more. And whether she meant to or not, she'd revealed that she had the information he wanted.

"When will it stop?" the night hag asked. "When you find out that the next head is just another hand, will you seek the next head? And the next?"

"My companions believe that the Fire Lord's cult was part of a larger cult serving something called the Elder Elemental Eye, and that cult seeks to unleash its master on the world."

"What do you believe?"

"I pulled a ruby ring off one of those cultists that could ransom the emperor's third son. As long as they want to keep hunting heads, I'll come along for the ride."

"And are you willing to continue paying the price I ask?"

"If you keep providing information we can use, I'll continue paying for it. We're looking for someone called the Dreaming Prophet. You're an expert on dreams, I've heard. So do you know where we can find this person?"

"I want Sherinna."

"What?" Nowhere's voice cracked around a lump that formed suddenly in his throat.

The night hag laughed, a barking croak that filled the cavern. "Not this time, tiefling. But eventually. No meat is as sweet to me as the flesh of a fair fey princess."

"No. I won't hand her over to you."

"We shall see. In the meantime, I can tell you where to find the Dreaming Prophet for a very reasonable price. But when you find this head and start looking for the next, and the next after that, consider carefully how much you are willing to pay."

* * * * *

"Flee. Now."

Albric awoke from his dream and leapt from the filthy pile of straw and fur he used as a bed. He started to gather his belongings, but as soon as his fingers touched the golden symbol of the Elder Elemental Eye, the voice from his dream resounded in his mind again: "Now!" He seized the medallion and bolted from the filth and squalor that had been his home and his temple for the past three years, into the stench and decay of the city sewers. Without a backward glance, he hurried away at the Dark God's bidding, intent on the task before him.

* * * * *

Brendis braced himself against the stench and kicked open the flimsy door.

"He's gone," Nowhere said. The tiefling moved into the tiny room, his eyes darting to every crevice. He stooped over the wretched bed and placed a hand gingerly on the furs. "It's still warm. We must have just missed him."

"We could wait for him," Brendis said. "He's sure to be back, with all this junk still here."

Sherinna knelt beside a pile of loose pages beside one wall and began leafing through the papers.

"How can anyone live like this?" Brendis wondered aloud.

"Most people don't have a choice," Nowhere said. "We weren't all born in the sunlight."

"No, but there must be other options," the paladin said. "Even the worst parts of the surface city are better than this."

"Not much better. And where is a lunatic cult leader going to find respectable lodging?"

"Fair point," Brendis said.

Sherinna stood up, still holding a large sheet of parchment. "Well," she said, "I don't think he's coming back here."

"Why not?" Nowhere asked.

The eladrin held up the parchment, and Nowhere and Brendis stepped closer to peer at the writing that covered every inch of it. Dense columns of cramped text sent Nowhere's mind reeling as he tried to absorb the ravings of the mad cultist, the Dreaming Prophet. Images of swarming flies and feasting maggots leaped from the text to assault his thoughts, and the proclamation of the world's doom ran like a steady drone beneath the maddening melody of the text. But five words appeared over and over, scrawled in the margins and written in a large hand across the page: "Bael Turath. The Living Gate."

Nowhere sighed. "I suppose we're going to Bael Turath."

VIE FOR GLORY
NEVERWINTER

GAUNTLGRYM
Neverwinter Saga, Book I
R.A. SALVATORE

NEVERWINTER
Neverwinter Saga, Book II
R.A. SALVATORE

BRIMSTONE ANGELS
Legends of Neverwinter
ERIN M. EVANS
November 2011

NEVERWINTER
RPG for PC
Coming in 2011

NEVERWINTER CAMPAIGN SETTING
For the D&D® Roleplaying Game
August 2011

THE LEGEND OF DRIZZT
Neverwinter Tales
Comic Books Written by R.A. Salvatore & Geno Salvatore
August 2011

THE LEGEND OF DRIZZT™
Cooperative Board Game
October 2011

Find these great products at your favorite bookseller or game shop.
DungeonsandDragons.com

Neverwinter, Dungeons & Dragons, D&D, Wizards of the Coast, their respective logos and The Legend of Drizzt are trademarks of Wizards of the Coast LLC in the U.S.A. and other countries. ©2011 Wizards.

"Now, when I hear FORGOTTEN REALMS, I think Paul S. Kemp."
— fantasy book spot.

FORGOTTEN REALMS

From *The New York Times* Best-Selling Author

PAUL S. KEMP

He never knew his father, a dark figure that history remembers only as the Shadowman. But as a young paladin, he'll have to confront the shadows within him, a birthright that leads all the way back to a lost and forgotten god.

CYCLE OF NIGHT

BOOK I
GODBORN
SUMMER 2012

BOOK II
GODBOUND
FALL 2012

BOOK III
GODSLAYER
SPRING 2013

"Paul S. Kemp has . . . barreled into dark fantasy with a quick wit, incomparable style, and an unabashed desire to portray the human psyche in all of its horrific and uplifting glory."
— Pat Ferrara, Mania.com

ALSO AVAILABLE AS E-BOOKS!

FORGOTTEN REALMS, DUNGEONS & DRAGONS, WIZARDS OF THE COAST, and their respective logos are trademarks of Wizards of the Coast LLC in the U.S.A. and other countries. Other trademarks are property of their respective owners. ©2010 Wizards.

THE ABYSSAL PLAGUE

From the molten core of a dead universe

Hunger
Spills a seed of evil

Fury
So pure, so concentrated, so infectious

Hate
Its corruption will span worlds

The Temple of Yellow Skulls
Don Bassingthwaite

Sword of the Gods
Bruce R. Cordell

Under the Crimson Sun
Keith R.A. DeCandido

Oath of Vigilance
James Wyatt

Shadowbane
Erik Scott de Bie

Find these novels at your favorite bookseller.
Also available as ebooks.

DungeonsandDragons.com

Dungeons & Dragons, D&D, Wizards of the Coast, and their respective logos are trademarks of Wizards of the Coast LLC in the U.S.A. and other countries. ©2011 Wizards.

EPIC STORIES
UNFORGETTABLE CHARACTERS
UNBEATABLE VALUE
OMNIBUS EDITIONS — THREE BOOKS IN ONE

FORGOTTEN REALMS

Empyrean Odyssey
Thomas M. Reid

The Last Mythal
Richard Baker
(Ebook Exclusive)

Ed Greenwood Presents Waterdeep I

Ed Greenwood Presents Waterdeep II
December 2011

DRAGONLANCE

Dragonlance Legends
Margaret Weis & Tracy Hickman
September 2011

EBERRON

Draconic Prophecies
James Wyatt
October 2011
(Ebook Exclusive)

Find these great books at your favorite bookseller.
DungeonsandDragons.com

Dungeons & Dragons, D&D, Forgotten Realms, Dragonlance, Eberron, Wizards of the Coast, and their respective logos are trademarks of Wizards of the Coast LLC in the U.S.A. and other countries. ©2011 Wizards.